By Diana Gabaldon

DIANA GABALDON

VOYAGER

A DELL BOOK

Published by
Bantam Dell
a division of
Random House, Inc.

LIBRARY OF CONGRESS CATALOG CARD NUMBER:
93-021907

ISBN: 978-0-440-21756-5

Reprinted by arrangement with Delacorte Press

MANUFACTURED IN THE UNITED STATES OF AMERICA

Published simultaneously in Canada

Dell mass market edition/November 1994
Dell reissue/September 2002

45 44 43 42 41 40 39
OPM

To my children,
Laura Juliet,
Samuel Gordon,
and Jennifer Rose,

Who gave me the heart, the blood, and the bones
of this book.

Acknowledgments

The author's deepest thanks to:

Jackie Cantor, as always, for being the rare and marvelous sort of editor who thinks it's all right if a book is long as long as it's good; my husband, Doug Watkins, for his literary eye, his marginal notes (e.g., "nipples *again*?"), and the jokes he insists I steal from him to give to Jamie Fraser; my elder daughter, Laura, who says, "If you come talk to my class about writing again, just talk about books and don't tell them about whale penises, okay?"; my son, Samuel, who walks up to total strangers in the park and says, "Have you read my mother's book?"; my younger daughter, Jenny, who says, "Why don't you wear makeup like on your book covers *all* the time, Mommy?"; Margaret J. Campbell, scholar; Barry Fodgen, English poet; and Pindens Cinola Oleroso Loventon Greenpeace Ludovic, dog, for generously allowing me to use their personae as the basis for the excesses of imagination (Mr. Fodgen wishes to note for the record that his dog Ludo has never actually tried to copulate with anyone's leg, wooden or not, but does understand the concept of artistic license); Perry Knowlton, who as well as being an excellent literary agent is also a fount of knowledge about bowlines, mainsails, and matters nautical, as well as the niceties of French grammar and the proper way to gut a deer; Robert Riffle, noted authority on what plants grow where, and what they look like while doing so; Kathryn (whose last name was either Boyle or Frye; all I remember is that it had to do with cooking), for the useful information on tropical diseases, particularly the picturesque habits of loa loa worms; Michael Lee West, for detailed descriptions of Jamaica, including regional dialect and folklore anecdotes; Dr. Mahlon West, for advice on typhoid fever; William Cross, Paul Block (and Paul's father), and Chrystine Wu (and Chrystine's parents), for invaluable assistance with Chinese vocabulary, history, and cultural attitudes; my father-in-law, Max Watkins, who, as always, provided useful comments on the appearance and habits of horses, including which way they face when the wind is blowing; Peggy Lynch, for wanting to know what Jamie would say if he saw a picture of his daughter in a bikini; Lizy Buchan, for telling me the story about her husband's ancestor who escaped Culloden; Dr. Gary Hoff, for medical detail; Fay Zachary, for lunch and critical comment; Sue Smiley, for critical reading and suggesting the blood vow; David Pijawka, for the materials on Jamaica and his most poetic description of what the air feels like after a Caribbean rainstorm; Iain MacKinnon Taylor, and his brother Hamish Taylor, for their most helpful suggestions and corrections of Gaelic spelling and usages; and as always, the various members of the CompuServe Literary Forum, including Janet McConnaughey, Marte Brengle, Akua Lezli Hope, John L. Myers, John E. Simpson, Jr., Sheryl Smith, Alit, Norman Shimmel, Walter Hawn, Karen Pershing, Margaret Ball, Paul Solyn, Diane Engel, David Chaifetz, and many others, for being interested, providing useful discussion, and laughing in the right places.

Prologue

When I was small, I never wanted to step in puddles. Not because of any fear of drowned worms or wet stockings; I was by and large a grubby child, with a blissful disregard for filth of any kind.

It was because I couldn't bring myself to believe that that perfect smooth expanse was no more than a thin film of water over solid earth. I believed it was an opening into some fathomless space. Sometimes, seeing the tiny ripples caused by my approach, I thought the puddle impossibly deep, a bottomless sea in which the lazy coil of tentacle and gleam of scale lay hidden, with the threat of huge bodies and sharp teeth adrift and silent in the far-down depths.

And then, looking down into reflection, I would see my own round face and frizzled hair against a featureless blue sweep, and think instead that the puddle was the entrance to another sky. If I stepped in there, I would drop at once, and keep on falling, on and on, into blue space.

The only time I would dare to walk through a puddle was at twilight, when the evening stars came out. If I looked in the water and saw one lighted pinprick there, I could splash through unafraid—for if I should fall into the puddle and on into space, I could grab hold of the star as I passed, and be safe.

Even now, when I see a puddle in my path, my mind half-halts—though my feet do not—then hurries on, with only the echo of the thought left behind.

What if, this time, you fall?

PART ONE

Battle, and the Loves of Men

1

The Corbies' Feast

Many a Highland chieftain fought,
Many a gallant man did fall.
Death itself were dearly bought,
All for Scotland's King and law.

—*"Will Ye No Come Back Again?"*

April 16, 1746

He was dead. However, his nose throbbed painfully, which he thought odd in the circumstances. While he placed considerable trust in the understanding and mercy of his Creator, he harbored that residue of elemental guilt that made all men fear the chance of hell. Still, all he had ever heard of hell made him think it unlikely that the torments reserved for its luckless inhabitants could be restricted to a sore nose.

On the other hand, this couldn't be heaven, on several counts. For one, he didn't deserve it. For another, it didn't look it. And for a third, he doubted that the rewards of the blessed included a broken nose, any more than those of the damned.

While he had always thought of Purgatory as a gray sort of place, the faint reddish light that hid everything around him seemed suitable. His mind was clearing a bit, and his power to reason was coming back, if slowly. Someone, he thought rather crossly, ought to see him and tell him just what the sentence was, until he should have suffered enough to be purified, and at last to enter the Kingdom of God. Whether he was expecting a demon or an angel was uncertain. He had no idea of the staffing requirements of Purgatory; it wasn't a matter the dominie had addressed in his schooldays.

While waiting, he began to take stock of whatever other torments he might be required to endure. There were numerous cuts, gashes, and bruises here and there, and he was fairly sure he'd broken the fourth finger of his right hand again—difficult to protect it, the way it stuck out so stiff, with the joint frozen. None of that was too bad, though. What else?

Claire. The name knifed across his heart with a pain that was more racking than anything his body had ever been called on to withstand.

If he had had an actual body anymore, he was sure it would have doubled up in agony. He had known it would be like this, when he sent her back to the stone circle. Spiritual anguish could be taken as a standard condition in Purgatory, and he had expected all along that the pain of separation would be his chief punishment—sufficient, he thought, to atone for anything he'd ever done: murder and betrayal included.

He did not know whether persons in Purgatory were allowed to pray or not, but tried anyway. *Lord,* he prayed, *that she may be safe. She and the child.* He was sure she would have made it to the circle itself; only two months gone with child, she was still light and fleet of foot—and the most stubbornly determined woman he had ever met. But whether she had managed the dangerous transition back to the place from which she had come—sliding precariously through whatever mysterious layers lay between then and now, powerless in the grip of the rock—that he could never know, and the thought of it was enough to make him forget even the throbbing in his nose.

He resumed his interrupted inventory of bodily ills, and became inordinately distressed at the discovery that his left leg appeared to be missing. Sensation stopped at the hip, with a sort of pins-and-needles tingling at the joint. Presumably he would get it back in due time, either when he finally arrived in Heaven, or at the least, at Judgment Day. And after all, his brother-in-law Ian managed very well on the wooden peg he wore to replace *his* missing leg.

Still, his vanity was troubled. Ah, that must be it; a punishment meant to cure him of the sin of vanity. He mentally set his teeth, determined to accept whatever came to him with fortitude, and such humility as he could manage. Still, he couldn't help reaching an exploratory hand (or whatever he was using for a hand) tentatively downward, to see just where the limb now ended.

The hand struck something hard, and the fingers tangled in wet, snarled hair. He sat up abruptly, and with some effort, cracked the layer of dried blood that had sealed his eyelids shut. Memory flooded back, and he groaned aloud. He had been mistaken. This *was* hell. But James Fraser was unfortunately not dead, after all.

The body of a man lay across his own. Its dead weight crushed his left leg, explaining the absence of feeling. The head, heavy as a spent cannonball, pressed facedown into his abdomen, the damp, matted hair a dark spill on the wet linen of his shirt. He jerked upward in sudden panic; the head rolled sideways into his lap and a half-open eye stared sightlessly up behind the sheltering strands of hair.

It was Jack Randall, his fine red captain's coat so dark with the wet it looked almost black. Jamie made a fumbling effort to push the body away, but found himself amazingly weak; his hand splayed feebly against Randall's shoulder, and the elbow of his other arm buckled suddenly as he tried to support himself. He found himself lying once more flat on his back, the sleeting sky pale gray and whirling dizzily overhead. Jack Randall's head moved obscenely up and down on his stomach with each gasping breath.

He pressed his hands flat against the boggy ground—the water rose up cold through his fingers and soaked the back of his shirt— and wriggled sideways. Some warmth was trapped between them; as the limp dead weight slid slowly free, the freezing rain struck his newly exposed flesh with a shock like a blow, and he shivered violently with sudden chill.

As he squirmed on the ground, struggling with the crumpled, mud-stained folds of his plaid, he could hear sounds above the keening of the April wind; far-off shouts and a moaning and wailing, like the calling of ghosts in the wind. And overall, the raucous calling of crows. Dozens of crows, from the sound.

That was strange, he thought dimly. Birds shouldn't fly in a storm like this. A final heave freed the plaid from under him, and he fumbled it over his body. As he reached to cover his legs, he saw that his kilt and left leg were soaked with blood. The sight didn't distress him; it seemed only vaguely interesting, the dark red smears a contrast to the grayish green of the moor plants around him. The echoes of battle faded from his ears, and he left Culloden Field to the calling of the crows.

He was wakened much later by the calling of his name.

"Fraser! Jamie Fraser! Are ye here?"

No, he thought groggily. I'm not. Wherever he had been while unconscious, it was a better place than this. He lay in a small declivity, half-filled with water. The sleeting rain had stopped, but the wind hadn't; it whined over the moor, piercing and chilling. The sky had darkened nearly to black; it must be near evening, then.

"I saw him go down here, I tell ye. Right near a big clump of gorse." The voice was at a distance, fading as it argued with someone.

There was a rustle near his ear, and he turned his head to see the crow. It stood on the grass a foot away, a blotch of wind-ruffled black feathers, regarding him with a bead-bright eye. Deciding that he posed no threat, it swiveled its neck with casual ease and jabbed its thick sharp bill into Jack Randall's eye.

Jamie jerked up with a cry of revulsion and a flurry of movement that sent the crow flapping off, squawking with alarm.

"Ay! Over there!"

There was a squelching through boggy ground, and a face before him, and the welcome feel of a hand on his shoulder.

"He's alive! Come on, MacDonald! D'ye lend a hand here; he'll no be walkin' on his own." There were four of them, and with a good deal of effort, they got him up, arms draped helpless about the shoulders of Ewan Cameron and Iain MacKinnon.

He wanted to tell them to leave him; his purpose had returned to him with the waking, and he remembered that he had meant to die. But the sweetness of their company was too much to resist. The rest had restored the feeling in his dead leg, and he knew the seriousness of the wound. He would die soon in any case; thank God that it need not be alone, in the dark.

"Water?" The edge of the cup pressed against his lip, and he roused himself long enough to drink, careful not to spill it. A hand pressed briefly against his forehead and dropped away without comment.

He was burning; he could feel the flames behind his eyes when

e closed them. His lips were cracked and sore from the heat, but
was better than the chills that came at intervals. At least when he
as fevered, he could lie still; the shaking of the chills woke the
eeping demons in his leg.

Murtagh. He had a terrible feeling about his godfather, but no
emory to give it shape. Murtagh was dead; he knew that must be
, but didn't know why or how he knew. A good half of the
ighland army was dead, slaughtered on the moor—so much he
ad gathered from the talk of the men in the farmhouse, but he had
o memory of the battle himself.

He had fought with armies before, and knew such loss of mem-
ry was not uncommon in soldiers; he had seen it, though never
efore suffered it himself. He knew the memories would come
ack, and hoped he would be dead before they did. He shifted at
e thought, and the movement sent a jolt of white-hot pain
rough his leg that made him groan.

"All right, Jamie?" Ewan rose on one elbow next to him,
orried face wan in the dawning light. A bloodstained bandage
ircled his head, and there were rusty stains on his collar, from the
calp wound left by a bullet's graze.

"Aye, I'll do." He reached up a hand and touched Ewan's
oulder in gratitude. Ewan patted it, and lay back down.

The crows were back. Black as night themselves, they had gone
 roost with the darkness, but with the dawn they were back—
irds of war, the corbies had come to feast on the flesh of the
llen. It could as well be his own eyes the cruel beaks picked out,
e thought. He could feel the shape of his eyeballs beneath his
ds, round and hot, tasty bits of jelly rolling restless to and fro,
oking vainly for oblivion, while the rising sun turned his lids a
ark and bloody red.

Four of the men were gathered near the single window of the
rmhouse, talking quietly together.

"Make a run for it?" one said, with a nod outside. "Christ,
an, the best of us can barely stagger—and there's six at least
anna walk at all."

"If ye can go, be going," said a man from the floor. He gri-
aced toward his own leg, wrapped in the remains of a tattered
uilt. "Dinna linger on our account."

Duncan MacDonald turned from the window with a grim smile,

shaking his head. The window's light shone off the rough plan
of his face, deepening the lines of fatigue.

"Nay, we'll bide," he said. "For one thing, the English a
thick as lice on the ground; ye can see them swarm from tl
window. There's no man would get away whole from Drumoss
now."

"Even those that fled the field yesterday will no get far,
MacKinnon put in softly. "Did ye no hear the English troo
passing in the night at the quick-march? D'ye think it will be ha
for them to hunt down our ragtag lot?"

There was no response to this; all of them knew the answer tc
well. Many of the Highlanders had been barely able to stand on tl
field before the battle, weakened as they were by cold, fatigue, an
hunger.

Jamie turned his face to the wall, praying that his men ha
started early enough. Lallybroch was remote; if they could get fa
enough from Culloden, it was unlikely they would be caught. Ar
yet Claire had told him that Cumberland's troops would ravage th
Highlands, ranging far afield in their thirst for revenge.

The thought of her this time caused only a wave of terribl
longing. God, to have her here, to lay her hands on him, to tend hi
wounds and cradle his head in her lap. But she was gone—gon
away two hundred years from him—and thank the Lord that sh
was! Tears trickled slowly from under his closed lids, and he rolle
painfully onto his side, to hide them from the others.

Lord, that she might be safe, he prayed. *She and the child.*

Toward midafternoon, the smell of burning came suddenly o
the air, wafting through the glassless window. It was thicker tha
the smell of black-powder smoke, pungent, with an underlyin
odor that was faintly horrible in its reminiscent smell of roastin
meat.

"They are burning the dead," said MacDonald. He ha
scarcely moved from his seat by the window in all the time the
had been in the cottage. He looked like a death's-head himsel
hair coal-black and matted with dirt, scraped back from a face i
which every bone showed.

Here and there, a small, flat crack sounded on the moor. Gun
shots. The coups de grace, administered by those English officer

ith a sense of compassion, before a tartan-clad wretch should be
acked on the pyre with his luckier fellows. When Jamie looked
p, Duncan MacDonald still sat by the window, but his eyes were
osed.

Next to him, Ewan Cameron crossed himself. "May we find as
uch mercy," he whispered.

They did. It was just past noon on the second day when booted
et at last approached the farmhouse, and the door swung open on
lent leather hinges.

"Christ." It was a muttered exclamation at the sight within the
armhouse. The draft from the door stirred the fetid air over
rimed, bedraggled, bloodstained bodies that lay or sat huddled on
he packed-dirt floor.

There had been no discussion of the possibility of armed resis-
ance; they had no heart and there was no point. The Jacobites
imply sat, waiting the pleasure of their visitor.

He was a major, all fresh and new in an uncreased uniform,
ith polished boots. After a moment's hesitation to survey the
habitants, he stepped inside, his lieutenant close behind.

"I am Lord Melton," he said, glancing around as though seek-
ng the leader of these men, to whom his remarks might most
roperly be addressed.

Duncan MacDonald, after a glance of his own, stood slowly,
nd inclined his head. "Duncan MacDonald, of Glen Richie," he
aid. "And others"—he waved a hand—"late of the forces of His
Majesty, King James."

"So I surmised," the Englishman said dryly. He was young, in
is early thirties, but he carried himself with a seasoned soldier's
onfidence. He looked deliberately from man to man, then reached
nto his coat and produced a folded sheet of paper.

"I have here an order from His Grace, the Duke of Cumber-
and," he said. "Authorizing the immediate execution of any man
ound to have engaged in the treasonous rebellion just past." He
lanced around the confines of the cottage once more. "Is there
ny man here who claims innocence of treason?"

There was the faintest breath of laughter from the Scots. Inno-
ence, with the smoke of battle still black on their faces, here on
he edge of the slaughter-field?

"No, my lord," said MacDonald, the faintest of smiles on h lips. "Traitors all. Shall we be hanged, then?"

Melton's face twitched in a small grimace of distaste, the settled back into impassivity. He was a slight man, with small, fi bones, but carried his authority well, nonetheless.

"You will be shot," he said. "You have an hour, in which prepare yourselves." He hesitated, shooting a glance at his lieu tenant, as though afraid to sound overgenerous before his subord nate, but continued. "If any of you wish writing materials— compose a letter, perhaps—the clerk of my company will atten you." He nodded briefly to MacDonald, turned on his heel, an left.

It was a grim hour. A few men availed themselves of the offer pen and ink, and scribbled doggedly, paper held against the slanted wooden chimney for lack of another firm writing surfac Others prayed quietly, or simply sat, waiting.

MacDonald had begged mercy for Giles McMartin and Frede ick Murray, arguing that they were barely seventeen, and shou not be held to the same account as their elders. This request wa denied, and the boys sat together, white-faced against the wall holding each other's hands.

For them, Jamie felt a piercing sorrow—and for the others her loyal friends and gallant soldiers. For himself, he felt only relie No more to worry, nothing more to do. He had done all he coul for his men, his wife, his unborn child. Now let this bodily miser be ended, and he would go grateful for the peace of it.

More for form's sake than because he felt the need of it, h closed his eyes and began the Act of Contrition, in French, as h always said it. *Mon Dieu, je regrette* . . . And yet he didn't; was much too late for any sort of regret.

Would he find Claire at once when he died? he wondered. C perhaps, as he expected, be condemned to separation for a time In any case, he would see her again; he clung to the convictio much more firmly than he embraced the tenets of the Church. Go had given her to him; He would restore her.

Forgetting to pray, he instead began to conjure her face behin his eyelids, the curve of cheek and temple, a broad fair brow th always moved him to kiss it, just there, in that small smooth sp between her eyebrows, just at the top of her nose, between clea amber eyes. He fixed his attention on the shape of her mouth arefully imagining the full, sweet curve of it, and the taste and the eel and the joy of it. The sounds of praying, the pen-scratching nd the small, choked sobs of Giles McMartin faded from his ears.

It was midafternoon when Melton returned, this time with six oldiers in attendance, as well as the Lieutenant and the clerk. again, he paused in the doorway, but MacDonald rose before he ould speak.

"I'll go first," he said, and walked steadily across the cottage. s he bent his head to go through the door, though, Lord Melton aid a hand on his sleeve.

"Will you give your full name, sir? My clerk will make note of ."

MacDonald glanced at the clerk, a small bitter smile tugging at ne corner of his mouth.

"A trophy list, is it? Aye, well." He shrugged and drew himself pright. "Duncan William MacLeod MacDonald, of Glen Richie." He bowed politely to Lord Melton. "At your service— ir." He passed through the door, and shortly there came the ound of a single pistol-shot from near at hand.

The boys were allowed to go together, hands still clutched ightly as they passed through the door. The rest were taken one by ne, each asked for his name, that the clerk might make a record f it. The clerk sat on a stool by the door, head bent to the papers n his lap, not looking up as the men passed by.

When it came Ewan's turn, Jamie struggled to prop himself on is elbows, and grasped his friend's hand, as hard as he could.

"I shall see ye soon again," he whispered.

Ewan's hand shook in his, but the Cameron only smiled. Then e leaned across simply and kissed Jamie's mouth, and rose to go.

They left the six who could not walk to the last.

"James Alexander Malcolm MacKenzie Fraser," he said, peaking slowly to allow the clerk time to get it down right. 'Laird of Broch Tuarach." Patiently, he spelled it, then glanced p at Melton.

"I must ask your courtesy, my lord, to give me help to stand."

Melton didn't answer him, but stared down at him, his expres- ion of remote distaste altering to one of mingled astonishment nd something like dawning horror.

"Fraser?" he said. "Of Broch Tuarach?"

"I am," Jamie said patiently. Would the man not hurry a bit?

Being resigned to being shot was one thing, but listening to yo
friends being killed in your hearing was another, and not ju
calculated to settle the nerves. His arms were trembling with tl
strain of propping him, and his bowels, not sharing the resignati
of his higher faculties, were twitching with a gurgling dread.

"Bloody hell," the Englishman muttered. He bent and peere
at Jamie where he lay in the shadow of the wall, then turned a
beckoned to his lieutenant.

"Help me get him into the light," he ordered. They werer
gentle about it, and Jamie grunted as the movement sent a bolt
pain from his leg right up through the top of his head. It made hi
dizzy for a moment, and he missed what Melton was saying
him.

"Are you the Jacobite they call 'Red Jamie'?" he asked agai
impatiently.

A streak of fear went through Jamie at that; let them know I
was the notorious Red Jamie, and they wouldn't shoot hir
They'd take him in chains to London to be tried—a prize of wa
And after that, it would be the hangman's rope, and lying ha
strangled on the gallows platform while they slit his belly a
ripped out his bowels. His bowels gave another long, rumblir
gurgle; they didn't think much of the notion either.

"No," he said, with as much firmness as he could manag
"Just get on wi' it, eh?"

Ignoring this, Melton dropped to his knees, and ripped open tl
throat of Jamie's shirt. He gripped Jamie's hair and jerked bac
his head.

"Damn!" Melton said. Melton's finger prodded him in tl
throat, just above the collarbone. There was a small triangular sc
there, and this appeared to be what was causing his interrogator
concern.

"James Fraser of Broch Tuarach; red hair and a three-corner
scar on his throat." Melton let go of the hair and sat back on b
heels, rubbing his chin in a distracted sort of way. Then he pulle
himself together and turned to the Lieutenant, gesturing at the fi
men remaining in the farm cottage.

"Take the rest," he ordered. His fair brows were knitted to
gether in a deep frown. He stood over Jamie, scowling, while tl
other Scottish prisoners were removed.

"I have to think," he muttered. "Damme, I must think!"

"Do that," said Jamie, "if you're able. I must lie down, my-self." They had propped him sitting against the far wall, his leg stretched out in front of him, but sitting upright after two days of lying flat was more than he could manage; the room was tilting drunkenly, and small flashing lights kept coming before his eyes. He leaned to one side, and eased himself down, hugging the dirt floor, eyes closed as he waited for the dizziness to pass.

Melton was muttering under his breath, but Jamie couldn't make out the words; didn't care greatly in any case. Sitting up in the sunlight, he had seen his leg clearly for the first time, and he was fairly sure that he wouldn't live long enough to be hanged.

The deep angry red of inflammation spread from midthigh up-ward, much brighter than the remaining smears of dried blood. The wound itself was purulent; with the stench of the other men lessening, he could smell the faint sweet-foul odor of the dis-charge. Still, a quick bullet through the head seemed much prefer-able to the pain and delirium of death by infection. Did you hear the bang? he wondered, and drifted off, the cool pounded dirt smooth and comforting as a mother's breast under his hot cheek.

He wasn't really asleep, only drifting in a feverish doze, but Melton's voice in his ear jerked him to alertness.

"Grey," the voice was saying, "John William Grey! Do you know that name?"

"No," he said, mazy with sleep and fever. "Look, man, either shoot me or go away, aye? I'm ill."

"Near Carryarrick." Melton's voice was prodding, impatient. "A boy, a fair-haired boy, about sixteen. You met him in the wood."

Jamie squinted up at his tormentor. The fever distorted his vision, but there seemed something vaguely familiar about the fine-boned face above him, with those large, almost girlish eyes.

"Oh," he said, catching a single face from the flood of images that swirled erratically through his brain. "The wee laddie that tried to kill me. Aye, I mind him." He closed his eyes again. In the odd way of fever, one sensation seemed to blend into another. He had broken John William Grey's arm; the memory of the boy's fine bone beneath his hand became the bone of Claire's forearm as he tore her from the grip of the stones. The cool misty breeze stroked his face with Claire's fingers.

"Wake up, damn you!" His head snapped on his neck as Mel ton shook him impatiently. "Listen to me!"

Jamie opened his eyes wearily. "Aye?"

"John William Grey is my brother," Melton said. "He told m of his meeting with you. You spared his life, and he made you promise—is that true?"

With great effort, he cast his mind back. He had met the bo two days before the first battle of the rebellion; the Scottish victor at Prestonpans. The six months between then and now seemed vast chasm; so much had happened in between.

"Aye, I recall. He promised to kill me. I dinna mind if you do for him, though." His eyelids were drooping again. Did he have t be awake in order to be shot?

"He said he owed you a debt of honor, and he does." Melto stood up, dusting the knees of his breeches, and turned to hi lieutenant, who had been watching the questioning with consider able bewilderment.

"It's the deuce of a situation, Wallace. This . . . this Jacobit scut is famous. You've heard of Red Jamie? The one on the broad sheets?" The Lieutenant nodded, looking curiously down at th bedraggled form in the dirt at his feet. Melton smiled bitterly.

"No, he doesn't look so dangerous now, does he? But he's sti Red Jamie Fraser, and His Grace would be more than pleased t hear of such an illustrious prisoner. They haven't yet foun Charles Stuart, but a few well-known Jacobites would please th crowds at Tower Hill nearly as much."

"Shall I send a message to His Grace?" The Lieutenan reached for his message box.

"No!" Melton wheeled to glare down at his prisoner. "That' the difficulty! Besides being prime gallows bait, this filthy wretc is also the man who captured my youngest brother near Presto and rather than shooting the brat, which is what he deserved spared his life and returned him to his companions. Thus," he sai through his teeth, "incurring a bloody great debt of honor upo my family!"

"Dear me," said the Lieutenant. "So you can't give him to Hi Grace, after all."

"No, blast it! I can't even shoot the bastard, without dishonor ing my brother's sworn word!"

The prisoner opened one eye. "I willna tell anyone if you on't," he suggested, and promptly closed it again.

"Shut up!" Losing his temper entirely, Melton kicked the pris-her, who grunted at the impact, but said nothing more.

"Perhaps we could shoot him under an assumed name," the ieutenant suggested helpfully.

Lord Melton gave his aide a look of withering scorn, then oked out the window to judge the time.

"It will be dark in three hours. I'll oversee the burial of the her executed prisoners. Find a small wagon, and have it filled ith hay. Find a driver—pick someone discreet, Wallace, that eans bribable, Wallace—and have them here as soon as it's ark."

"Yes, sir. Er, sir? What about the prisoner?" The Lieutenant estured diffidently toward the body on the floor.

"What about him?" Melton said brusquely. "He's too weak to awl, let alone walk. He isn't going anywhere—at least not until e wagon gets here."

"Wagon?" The prisoner was showing signs of life. In fact, nder the stimulus of agitation, he had managed to raise himself nto one arm. Bloodshot blue eyes gleamed wide with alarm, nder the spikes of matted red hair. "Where are ye sending me?" urning from the door, Melton cast him a glance of intense dis-ke.

"You're the laird of Broch Tuarach, aren't you? Well, that's here I'm sending you."

"I dinna want to go home! I want to be shot!"

The Englishmen exchanged a look.

"Raving," the Lieutenant said significantly, and Melton nod-ed.

"I doubt he'll live through the journey—but his death won't be n my head, at least."

The door shut firmly behind the Englishmen, leaving Jamie raser quite alone—and still alive.

2

The Hunt Begins

"Of course he's dead!" Claire's voice was sharp with agitation; it rang loudly in the half-empty study, echoing among the rifled bookshelves. She stood against the cork-lined wall like a prisoner awaiting a firing squad, staring from her daughter to Roger Wakefield and back again.

"I don't think so." Roger felt terribly tired. He rubbed a hand over his face, then picked up the folder from the desk; the one containing all the research he'd done since Claire and her daughter had first come to him, three weeks before, and asked his help.

He opened the folder and thumbed slowly through the contents. The Jacobites of Culloden. The Rising of the '45. The gallant Scots who had rallied to the banner of Bonnie Prince Charlie, and cut through Scotland like a blazing sword—only to come to ruin and defeat against the Duke of Cumberland on the gray moor of Culloden.

"Here," he said, plucking out several sheets clipped together. The archaic writing looked odd, rendered in the black crispness of a photocopy. "This is the muster roll of the Master of Lovat's regiment."

He thrust the thin sheaf of papers at Claire, but it was her daughter, Brianna, who took the sheets from him and began to turn the pages, a slight frown between her reddish brows.

"Read the top sheet," Roger said. "Where it says 'Officers.'"

"All right. 'Officers,'" she read aloud, " 'Simon, Master of Lovat' . . ."

"The Young Fox," Roger interrupted. "Lovat's son. And five
ore names, right?"

Brianna cocked one brow at him, but went on reading.

" 'William Chisholm Fraser, Lieutenant; George D'Amerd Fra-
:r Shaw, Captain; Duncan Joseph Fraser, Lieutenant; Bayard
Iurray Fraser, Major,' " she paused, swallowing, before reading
e last name, " '. . . James Alexander Malcolm MacKenzie
raser, Captain.' " She lowered the papers, looking a little pale.
My father."

Claire moved quickly to her daughter's side, squeezing the
irl's arm. She was pale, too.

"Yes," she said to Roger. "I know he went to Culloden. When
e left me . . . there at the stone circle . . . he meant to go
ack to Culloden Field, to rescue his men who were with Charles
tuart. And we know he did"—she nodded at the folder on the
esk, its manila surface blank and innocent in the lamplight—
you found their names. But . . . but . . . Jamie . . ." Speak-
g the name aloud seemed to rattle her, and she clamped her lips
ght.

Now it was Brianna's turn to support her mother.

"He meant to go back, you said." Her eyes, dark blue and
ncouraging, were intent on her mother's face. "He meant to take
is men away from the field, and then go back to the battle."

Claire nodded, recovering herself slightly.

"He knew he hadn't much chance of getting away; if the En-
lish caught him . . . he said he'd rather die in battle. That's
hat he meant to do." She turned to Roger, her gaze an unsettling
mber. Her eyes always reminded him of hawk's eyes, as though
he could see a good deal farther than most people. "I can't
elieve he didn't die there—so many men did, and *he* meant to!"

Almost half the Highland army had died at Culloden, cut down
a a blast of cannonfire and searing musketry. But not Jamie Fra-
er.

"No," Roger said doggedly. "That bit I read you from Link-
ater's book—" He reached to pick it up, a white volume, entitled
he Prince in the Heather.

" *'Following the battle,' "* he read, " *'eighteen wounded Jaco-
ite officers took refuge in the farmhouse near the moor. Here they
ay in pain, their wounds untended, for two days. At the end of that
ime, they were taken out and shot. One man, a Fraser of the*

Master of Lovat's regiment, escaped the slaughter. The rest a
buried at the edge of the domestic park.'

"See?" he said, laying the book down and looking earnestly
the two women over its pages. "An officer, of the Master
Lovat's regiment." He grabbed up the sheets of the muster rol

"And here they are! Just six of them. Now, we know the man
the farmhouse can't have been Young Simon; he's a well-knov
historical figure, and we know very well what happened to hi
He retreated from the field—unwounded, mind you—with a grov
of his men, and fought his way north, eventually making it back
Beaufort Castle, near here." He waved vaguely at the full-leng
window, through which the nighttime lights of Inverness twinkl
faintly.

"Nor was the man who escaped Leanach farmhouse any of th
other four officers—William, George, Duncan, or Bayard," Rog
said. "Why?" He snatched another paper out of the folder a
brandished it, almost triumphantly. "Because they all *did* die
Culloden! All four of them were killed on the field—I found the
names listed on a plaque in the church at Beauly."

Claire let out a long breath, then eased herself down into the o
leather swivel chair behind the desk.

"Jesus H. Christ," she said. She closed her eyes and leane
forward, elbows on the desk, and her head against her hands, th
thick, curly brown hair spilling forward to hide her face. Brian
laid a hand on Claire's back, face troubled as she bent over h
mother. She was a tall girl, with large, fine bones, and her long re
hair glowed in the warm light of the desk lamp.

"If he didn't die . . ." she began tentatively.

Claire's head snapped up. "But he *is* dead!" she said. Her fa
was strained, and small lines were visible around her eyes. "F
God's sake, it's two hundred years; whether he died at Culloden
not, he's dead now!"

Brianna stepped back from her mother's vehemence, and lov
ered her head, so the red hair—her father's red hair—swung dov
beside her cheek.

"I guess so," she whispered. Roger could see she was fightin
back tears. And no wonder, he thought. To find out in short ord
that first, the man you had loved and called "Father" all your li
really *wasn't* your father, secondly, that your real father was
Highland Scot who had lived two hundred years ago, and thirdl

realize that he had likely perished in some horrid fashion, unthinkably far from the wife and child he had sacrificed himself to save . . . enough to rattle one, Roger thought.

He crossed to Brianna and touched her arm. She gave him a brief, distracted glance, and tried to smile. He put his arms around her, even in his pity for her distress thinking how marvelous she felt, all warm and soft and springy at once.

Claire still sat at the desk, motionless. The yellow hawk's eyes had gone a softer color now, remote with memory. They rested sightlessly on the east wall of the study, still covered from floor to ceiling with the notes and memorabilia left by the Reverend Wakefield, Roger's late adoptive father.

Looking at the wall himself, Roger saw the annual meeting notice sent by the Society of the White Rose—those enthusiastic, eccentric souls who still championed the cause of Scottish independence, meeting in nostalgic tribute to Charles Stuart, and the Highland heroes who had followed him.

Roger cleared his throat slightly.

"Er . . . if Jamie Fraser didn't die at Culloden . . ." he said.

"Then he likely died soon afterward." Claire's eyes met Roger's, straight on, the cool look back in the yellow-brown depths. "You have no idea how it was," she said. "There was a famine in the Highlands—none of the men had eaten for days before the battle. He was wounded—we know that. Even if he escaped, there would have been . . . no one to care for him." Her voice caught slightly at that; she was a doctor now, had been a healer even then, twenty years before, when she had stepped through a circle of standing stones, and met destiny with James Alexander Malcolm MacKenzie Fraser.

Roger was conscious of them both; the tall, shaking girl he held in his arms, and the woman at the desk, so still, so poised. She had traveled through the stones, through time; been suspected as a spy, arrested as a witch, snatched by an unimaginable quirk of circumstance from the arms of her first husband, Frank Randall. And three years later, her second husband, James Fraser, had sent her back through the stones, pregnant, in a desperate effort to save her and the unborn child from the onrushing disaster that would soon engulf him.

Surely, he thought to himself, she's been through enough? But Roger was a historian. He had a scholar's insatiable, amoral curi-

osity, too powerful to be constrained by simple compassion. Mo
than that, he was oddly conscious of the third figure in the fami
tragedy in which he found himself involved—Jamie Fraser.

"If he didn't die at Culloden," he began again, more firml
"then perhaps I can find out what did happen to him. Do you wa
me to try?" He waited, breathless, feeling Brianna's warm brea
through his shirt.

Jamie Fraser had had a life, and a death. Roger felt obscure
that it was his duty to find out all the truth; that Jamie Fraser
women deserved to know all they could of him. For Brianna, suc
knowledge was all she would ever have of the father she had nev
known. And for Claire—behind the question he had asked was th
thought that had plainly not yet struck her, stunned with shock a
she was: she had crossed the barrier of time twice before. Sl
could, just possibly, do it again. And if Jamie Fraser had not die
at Culloden . . .

He saw awareness flicker in the clouded amber of her eyes, a
the thought came to her. She was normally pale; now her fac
blanched white as the ivory handle of the letter opener before h
on the desk. Her fingers closed around it, clenching so the knuc
les stood out in knobs of bone.

She didn't speak for a long time. Her gaze fixed on Brianna ar
lingered there for a moment, then returned to Roger's face.

"Yes," she said, in a whisper so soft he could barely hear he
"Yes. Find out for me. Please. Find out."

3

Frank and Full Disclosure

The foot traffic was heavy on the bridge over the River Ness, with folk streaming home to their teas. Roger moved in front of me, his wide shoulders protecting me from the buffets of the crowd around us.

I could feel my heart beating heavily against the stiff cover of the book I was clutching to my chest. It did that whenever I paused to think what we were truly doing. I wasn't sure which of the two possible alternatives was worse; to find that Jamie had died at Culloden, or to find that he hadn't.

The boards of the bridge echoed hollowly underfoot, as we trudged back toward the manse. My arms ached from the weight of the books I carried, and I shifted the load from one side to the other.

"Watch your bloody wheel, man!" Roger shouted, nudging me adroitly to the side, as a workingman on a bicycle plowed head-downward through the bridge traffic, nearly running me against the railing.

"Sorry!" came back the apologetic shout, and the rider gave a wave of the hand over his shoulder, as the bike wove its way between two groups of schoolchildren, coming home for their teas. I glanced back across the bridge, in case Brianna should be visible behind us, but there was no sign of her.

Roger and I had spent the afternoon at the Society for the Preservation of Antiquities. Brianna had gone down to the Highland Clans office, there to collect photocopies of a list of documents Roger had compiled.

"It's very kind of you to take all this trouble, Roger," I said, raising my voice to be heard above the echoing bridge and the river's rush.

"It's all right," he said, a little awkwardly, pausing for me to catch him up. "I'm curious," he added, smiling a little. "You know historians—can't leave a puzzle alone." He shook his head, trying to brush the windblown dark hair out of his eyes without using his hands.

I did know historians. I'd lived with one for twenty years. Frank hadn't wanted to leave this particular puzzle alone, either. But neither had he been willing to solve it. Frank had been dead for two years, though, and now it was my turn—mine and Brianna's.

"Have you heard yet from Dr. Linklater?" I asked, as we came down the arch of the bridge. Late in the afternoon as it was, the sun was still high, so far north as we were. Caught among the leaves of the lime trees on the riverbank, it glowed pink on the granite cenotaph that stood below the bridge.

Roger shook his head, squinting against the wind. "No, but it's been only a week since I wrote. If I don't hear by the Monday, I'll try telephoning. Don't worry"—he smiled sideways at me—"I was very circumspect. I just told him that for purposes of a study I was making, I needed a list—if one existed—of the Jacobite officers who were in Leanach farmhouse after Culloden, and if any information exists as to the survivor of that execution, could he refer me to the original sources?"

"Do you know Linklater?" I asked, easing my left arm by tilting the books sideways against my hip.

"No, but I wrote my request on the Balliol College letterhead, and made tactful reference to Mr. Cheesewright, my old tutor, who *does* know Linklater." Roger winked reassuringly, and I laughed.

His eyes were a brilliant, lucent green, bright against his olive skin. Curiosity might be his stated reason for helping us to find out Jamie's history, but I was well aware that his interest went a good bit deeper—in the direction of Brianna. I also knew that the interest was returned. What I didn't know was whether Roger realized that as well.

Back in the late Reverend Wakefield's study, I dropped my armload of books on the table in relief, and collapsed into the wing chair by the hearth, while Roger went to fetch a glass of lemonade from the manse's kitchen.

My breathing slowed as I sipped the tart sweetness, but my pulse stayed erratic, as I looked over the imposing stack of books we had brought back. Was Jamie in there somewhere? And if he was . . . my hands grew wet on the cold glass, and I choked the thought off. Don't look too far ahead, I cautioned myself. Much better to wait, and see what we might find.

Roger was scanning the shelves in the study, in search of other possibilities. The Reverend Wakefield, Roger's late adoptive father, had been both a good amateur historian, and a terrible pack rat; letters, journals, pamphlets and broadsheets, antique and contemporary volumes—all were crammed cheek by jowl together on the shelves.

Roger hesitated, then his hand fell on a stack of books sitting on the nearby table. They were Frank's books—an impressive achievement, so far as I could tell by reading the encomiums printed on the dust jackets.

"Have you ever read this?" he asked, picking up the volume entitled *The Jacobites*.

"No," I said. I took a restorative gulp of lemonade, and coughed. "No," I said again. "I couldn't." After my return, I had resolutely refused to look at any material dealing with Scotland's past, even though the eighteenth century had been one of Frank's areas of specialty. Knowing Jamie dead, and faced with the necessity of living without him, I avoided anything that might bring him to mind. A useless avoidance—there was no way of keeping him out of my mind, with Brianna's existence a daily reminder of him —but still, I could not read books about the Bonnie Prince—that terrible, futile young man—or his followers.

"I see. I just thought you might know whether there might be something useful in here." Roger paused, the flush deepening over his cheekbones. "Did—er, did your husband—Frank, I mean," he added hastily. "Did you tell him . . . um . . . about . . ." His voice trailed off, choked with embarrassment.

"Well, of course I did!" I said, a little sharply. "What did you think—I'd just stroll back into his office after being gone for three years and say, 'Oh, hullo there, darling, and what would you like for supper tonight?' "

"No, of course not," Roger muttered. He turned away, eyes fixed on the bookshelves. The back of his neck was deep red with embarrassment.

"I'm sorry," I said, taking a deep breath. "It's a fair question to ask. It's only that it's—a bit raw, yet." A good deal more than a bit. I was both surprised and appalled to find just how raw the wound still was. I set the glass down on the table at my elbow. If we were going on with this, I was going to need something stronger than lemonade.

"Yes," I said. "I told him. All about the stones—about Jamie. Everything."

Roger didn't reply for a moment. Then he turned, halfway, so that only the strong, sharp lines of his profile were visible. He didn't look at me, but down at the stack of Frank's books, at the back-cover photo of Frank, leanly dark and handsome, smiling for posterity.

"Did he believe you?" Roger asked quietly.

My lips felt sticky from the lemonade, and I licked them before answering.

"No," I said. "Not at first. He thought I was mad; even had me vetted by a psychiatrist." I laughed, shortly, but the memory made me clench my fists with remembered fury.

"Later, then?" Roger turned to face me. The flush had faded from his skin, leaving only an echo of curiosity in his eyes. "What did he think?"

I took a deep breath and closed my eyes. "I don't know."

The tiny hospital in Inverness smelled unfamiliar, like carbolic disinfectant and starch.

I couldn't think, and tried not to feel. The return was much more terrifying than my venture into the past had been, for there, I had been shrouded by a protective layer of doubt and disbelief about where I was and what was happening, and had lived in constant hope of escape. Now I knew only too well where I was, and I knew that there was no escape. Jamie was dead.

The doctors and nurses tried to speak kindly to me, to feed me and bring me things to drink, but there was no room in me for anything but grief and terror. I had told them my name when they asked, but wouldn't speak further.

I lay in the clean white bed, fingers clamped tight together over my vulnerable belly, and kept my eyes shut. I visualized over and over the last things I had seen before I stepped through the stones—the rainy moor and Jamie's face—knowing that if I looked too long at my new surroundings, these sights would fade, replaced by mundane things like the nurses and the vase of flowers by my bed. I pressed one thumb secretly against the base of the other, taking an obscure comfort in the tiny wound there, a small cut in the shape of a J. Jamie had made it, at my demand—the last of his touch on my flesh.

I must have stayed that way for some time; I slept sometimes, dreaming of the last few days of the Jacobite Rising—I saw again the dead man in the wood, asleep beneath a coverlet of bright blue fungus, and Dougal MacKenzie dying on the floor of an attic in Culloden House; the ragged men of the Highland army, asleep in the muddy ditches; their last sleep before the slaughter.

I would wake screaming or moaning, to the scent of disinfectant and the sound of soothing words, incomprehensible against the echoes of Gaelic shouting in my dreams, and fall asleep again, my hurt clutched tight in the palm of my hand.

And then I opened my eyes and Frank was there. He stood in the door, smoothing back his dark hair with one hand, looking uncertain—and no wonder, poor man.

I lay back on the pillows, just watching him, not speaking. He had the look of his ancestors, Jack and Alex Randall; fine, clear, aristocratic features and a well-shaped head, under a spill of straight dark hair. His face had some indefinable difference from theirs, though, beyond the small differences of feature. There was no mark of fear or ruthlessness on him; neither the spirituality of Alex nor the icy arrogance of Jack. His lean face looked intelligent, kind, and slightly tired, unshaven and with smudges beneath his eyes. I knew without being told that he had driven all night to get here.

"Claire?" He came over to the bed, and spoke tentatively, as though not sure that I really was Claire.

I wasn't sure either, but I nodded and said, "Hullo, Frank." My voice was scratchy and rough, unaccustomed to speech.

He took one of my hands, and I let him have it.

"Are you . . . all right?" he said, after a minute. He was frowning slightly as he looked at me.

"I'm pregnant." That seemed the important point, to my disordered mind. I had not thought of what I would say to Frank, if I ever saw him again, but the moment I saw him standing in the door, it seemed to come clear in my mind. I would tell him I was pregnant, he would leave, and I would be alone with my last sight of Jamie's face, and the burning touch of him on my hand.

His face tightened a bit, but he didn't let go of my other hand. *"I know. They told me."* He took a deep breath and let it out. *"Claire—can you tell me what happened to you?"*

I felt quite blank for a moment, but then shrugged.

"I suppose so," I said. I mustered my thoughts wearily; I didn't want to be talking about it, but I had some feeling of obligation to this man. Not guilt, not yet; but obligation none-theless. I had been married to him.

"Well," I said, *"I fell in love with someone else, and I married him. I'm sorry,"* I added, in response to the look of shock that crossed his face, *"I couldn't help it."*

He hadn't been expecting that. His mouth opened and closed for a bit and he gripped my hand, hard enough to make me wince and jerk it out of his grasp.

"What do you mean?" he said, his voice sharp. *"Where have you been, Claire?"* He stood up suddenly, looming over the bed.

"Do you remember that when I last saw you, I was going up to the stone circle on Craigh na Dun?"

"Yes?" He was staring down at me with an expression somewhere between anger and suspicion.

"Well"—I licked my lips, which had gone quite dry—*"the fact is, I walked through a cleft stone in that circle, and ended up in 1743."*

"Don't be facetious, Claire!"

"You think I'm being funny?" The thought was so absurd that I actually began to laugh, though I felt a good long way from real humor.

"Stop that!"

I quit laughing. Two nurses appeared at the door as though

*by magic; they must have been lurking in the hall nearby.
Frank leaned over and grabbed my arm.*

"Listen to me," he said through his teeth. "You are going
to tell me where you've been and what you've been doing!"

"I am telling you! Let go!" I sat up in bed and yanked at
my arm, pulling it out of his grasp. "I told you; I walked
through a stone and ended up two hundred years ago. And I
met your bloody ancestor, Jack Randall, there!"

Frank blinked, entirely taken aback. "Who?"

"Black Jack Randall, and a bloody, filthy, nasty pervert he
was, too!"

Frank's mouth hung open, and so did the nurses'. I could
hear feet coming down the corridor behind them, and hurried
voices.

"I had to marry Jamie Fraser to get away from Jack Randall, but then—Jamie—I couldn't help it, Frank, I loved him
and I would have stayed with him if I could, but he sent me
back because of Culloden, and the baby, and—" I broke off,
as a man in a doctor's uniform pushed past the nurses by the
door.

"Frank," I said tiredly, "I'm sorry. I didn't mean it to
happen, and I tried all I could to come back—really, I did—
but I couldn't. And now it's too late."

Despite myself, tears began to well up in my eyes and roll
down my cheeks. Mostly for Jamie, and myself, and the child I
carried, but a few for Frank as well. I sniffed hard and swallowed, trying to stop, and pushed myself upright in the bed.

"Look," I said, "I know you won't want to have anything
more to do with me, and I don't blame you at all. Just—just
go away, will you?"

His face had changed. He didn't look angry anymore, but
distressed, and slightly puzzled. He sat down by the bed,
ignoring the doctor who had come in and was groping for my
pulse.

"I'm not going anywhere," he said, quite gently. He took
my hand again, though I tried to pull it away. "This—Jamie.
Who was he?"

I took a deep, ragged breath. The doctor had hold of my
other hand, still trying to take my pulse, and I felt absurdly

panicked, as though I were being held captive between them. I fought down the feeling, though, and tried to speak steadily.

"James Alexander Malcolm MacKenzie Fraser," I said, spacing the words, formally, the way Jamie had spoken them to me when he first told me his full name—on the day of our wedding. The thought made another tear overflow, and I blotted it against my shoulder, my hands being restrained.

"He was a Highlander. He was k-killed at Culloden." It was no use, I was weeping again, the tears no anodyne to the grief that ripped through me, but the only response I had to unendurable pain. I bent forward slightly, trying to encapsulate it, wrapping myself around the tiny, imperceptible life in my belly, the only remnant left to me of Jamie Fraser.

Frank and the doctor exchanged a glance of which I was only half-conscious. Of course, to them, Culloden was part of the distant past. To me, it had happened only two days before.

"Perhaps we should let Mrs. Randall rest for a bit," the doctor suggested. "She seems a wee bit upset just now."

Frank looked uncertainly from the doctor to me. "Well, she certainly does seem upset. But I really want to find out . . . what's this, Claire?" Stroking my hand, he had encountered the silver ring on my fourth finger, and now bent to examine it. It was the ring Jamie had given me for our marriage; a wide silver band in the Highland interlace pattern, the links engraved with tiny, stylized thistle blooms.

"No!" I exclaimed, panicked, as Frank tried to twist it off my finger. I jerked my hand away and cradled it, fisted, beneath my bosom, cupped in my left hand, which still wore Frank's gold wedding band. "No, you can't take it, I won't let you! That's my wedding ring!"

"Now, see here, Claire—" Frank's words were interrupted by the doctor, who had crossed to Frank's side of the bed, and was now bending down to murmur in his ear. I caught a few words—"not trouble your wife just now. The shock"— and then Frank was on his feet once more, being firmly urged away by the doctor, who gave a nod to one of the nurses in passing.

I barely felt the sting of the hypodermic needle, too engulfed in the fresh wave of grief to take notice of anything. I dimly heard Frank's parting words, "All right—but Claire, I

will know!" And then the blessed darkness came down, and I
slept without dreaming, for a long, long time.

Roger tilted the decanter, bringing the level of the spirit in the
glass up to the halfway point. He handed it to Claire with a half-
smile.

"Fiona's grannie always said whisky is good for what ails ye."

"I've seen worse remedies." Claire took the glass and gave him
back the half-smile in exchange.

Roger poured out a drink for himself, then sat down beside her,
sipping quietly.

"I tried to send him away, you know," she said suddenly,
lowering her glass. "Frank. I told him I knew he couldn't feel the
same for me, no matter what he believed had happened. I said I
would give him a divorce; he must go away and forget about me—
take up the life he'd begun building without me."

"He wouldn't do it, though," Roger said. It was growing chilly
in the study as the sun went down, and he bent and switched on the
ancient electric fire. "Because you were pregnant?" he guessed.

She shot him a sudden sharp look, then smiled, a little wryly.

"Yes, that was it. He said no one but a cad would dream of
abandoning a pregnant woman with virtually no resources. Particularly one whose grip on reality seemed a trifle tenuous," she
added ironically. "I wasn't quite without resources—I had a bit of
money from my uncle Lamb—but Frank wasn't a cad, either."
Her glance shifted to the bookshelves. Her husband's historical
works stood there, side by side, spines gleaming in the light of the
desklamp.

"He was a very decent man," she said softly. She took another
sip of her drink, closing her eyes as the alcoholic fumes rose up.

"And then—he knew, or suspected, that he couldn't have children himself. Rather a blow, for a man so involved in history and
genealogies. All those dynastic considerations, you see."

"Yes, I can see that," Roger said slowly. "But wouldn't he feel
—I mean, another man's child?"

"He might have." The amber eyes were looking at him again,
their clearness slightly softened by whisky and reminiscence.
"But as it was, since he didn't—*couldn't*—believe anything I said
about Jamie, the baby's father was essentially unknown. If he

didn't know who the man was—and convinced himself that I didn't really know either, but had just made up these delusions out of traumatic shock—well, then, there was no one ever to say that the child *wasn't* his. Certainly not me,'' she added, with just a tinge of bitterness.

She took a large swallow of whisky that made her eyes water slightly, and took a moment to wipe them.

''But to make sure, he took me clean away. To Boston,'' she went on. ''He'd been offered a good position at Harvard, and no one knew us there. That's where Brianna was born.''

The fretful crying jarred me awake yet again. I had gone back to bed at 6:30, after getting up five times during the night with the baby. A bleary-eyed look at the clock showed the time now as 7:00. A cheerful singing came from the bathroom, Frank's voice raised in "Rule, Britannia," over the noise of rushing water.

I lay in bed, heavy-limbed with exhaustion, wondering whether I had the strength to endure the crying until Frank got out of the shower and could bring Brianna to me. As though the baby knew what I was thinking, the crying rose two or three tones and escalated to a sort of periodic shriek, punctuated by frightening gulps for air. I flung back the covers and was on my feet, propelled by the same sort of panic with which I had greeted air raids during the War.

I lumbered down the chilly hall and into the nursery, to find Brianna, aged three months, lying on her back, yelling her small red head off. I was so groggy from lack of sleep that it took a moment for me to realize that I had left her on her stomach.

''Darling! You turned over! All by yourself!'' Terrorized by her audacious act, Brianna waved her little pink fists and squalled louder, eyes squeezed shut.

I snatched her up, patting her back and murmuring to the top of her red-fuzzed head.

''Oh, you precious darling! What a clever girl you are!''

''What's that? What's happened?'' Frank emerged from the bathroom, toweling his head, a second towel wrapped about his loins. ''Is something the matter with Brianna?''

He came toward us, looking worried. As the birth grew closer, we had both been edgy; Frank irritable and myself terrified, having no idea what might happen between us, with the appearance of Jamie Fraser's child. But when the nurse had taken Brianna from her bassinet and handed her to Frank, with the words "Here's Daddy's little girl," his face had grown blank, and then—looking down at the tiny face, perfect as a rosebud—gone soft with wonder. Within a week, he had been hers, body and soul.

I turned to him, smiling. "She turned over! All by herself!"

"Really?" His scrubbed face beamed with delight. "Isn't it early for her to do that?"

"Yes, it is. Dr. Spock says she oughtn't to be able to do it for another month, at least!"

"Well, what does Dr. Spock know? Come here, little beauty; give Daddy a kiss for being so precocious." He lifted the soft little body, encased in its snug pink sleep-suit, and kissed her button of a nose. Brianna sneezed, and we both laughed.

I stopped then, suddenly aware that it was the first time I had laughed in nearly a year. Still more, that it was the first time I had laughed with Frank.

He realized it too; his eyes met mine over the top of Brianna's head. They were a soft hazel, and at the moment, filled with tenderness. I smiled at him, a little tremulous, and suddenly very much aware that he was all but naked, with water droplets sliding down his lean shoulders and shining on the smooth brown skin of his chest.

The smell of burning reached us simultaneously, jarring us from this scene of domestic bliss.

"The coffee!" Thrusting Bree unceremoniously into my arms, Frank bolted for the kitchen, leaving both towels in a heap at my feet. Smiling at the sight of his bare buttocks, gleaming an incongruous white as he sprinted into the kitchen, I followed him more slowly, holding Bree against my shoulder.

He was standing at the sink, naked, amid a cloud of malodorous steam rising from the scorched coffeepot.

"Tea, maybe?" I asked, adroitly anchoring Brianna on my

hip with one arm while I rummaged in the cupboard. "None of the orange pekoe leaf left, I'm afraid; just Lipton's teabags."

Frank made a face; an Englishman to the bone, he would rather lap water out of the toilet than drink tea made from teabags. The Lipton's had been left by Mrs. Grossman, the weekly cleaning woman, who thought tea made from loose leaves messy and disgusting.

"No, I'll get a cup of coffee on my way to the university. Oh, speaking of which, you recall that we're having the Dean and his wife to dinner tonight? Mrs. Hinchcliffe is bringing a present for Brianna."

"Oh, right," I said, without enthusiasm. I had met the Hinchcliffes before, and wasn't all that keen to repeat the experience. Still, the effort had to be made. With a mental sigh, I shifted the baby to the other side and groped in the drawer for a pencil to make a grocery list.

Brianna burrowed into the front of my red chenille dressing gown, making small voracious grunting noises.

"You can't be hungry again," I said to the top of her head. "I fed you not two hours ago." My breasts were beginning to leak in response to her rooting, though, and I was already sitting down and loosening the front of my gown.

"Mrs. Hinchcliffe said that a baby shouldn't be fed every time it cries," Frank observed. "They get spoilt if they aren't kept to a schedule."

It wasn't the first time I had heard Mrs. Hinchcliffe's opinions on child-rearing.

"Then she'll be spoilt, won't she?" I said coldly, not looking at him. The small pink mouth clamped down fiercely, and Brianna began to suck with mindless appetite. I was aware that Mrs. Hinchcliffe also thought breast-feeding both vulgar and insanitary. I, who had seen any number of eighteenth-century babies nursing contentedly at their mothers' breasts, didn't.

Frank sighed, but didn't say anything further. After a moment, he put down the pot holder and sidled toward the door.

"Well," he said awkwardly. "I'll see you around six then, shall I? Ought I to bring home anything—save you going out?"

I gave him a brief smile, and said, "No, I'll manage."

"Oh, good." He hesitated a moment, as I settled Bree more comfortably on my lap, head resting on the crook of my arm, the round of her head echoing the curve of my breast. I looked up from the baby, and found him watching me intently, eyes fixed on the swell of my half-exposed bosom.

My own eyes flicked downward over his body. I saw the beginnings of his arousal, and bent my head over the baby, to hide my flushing face.

"Goodbye," I muttered, to the top of her head.

He stood still a moment, then leaned forward and kissed me briefly on the cheek, the warmth of his bare body unsettlingly near.

"Goodbye, Claire," he said softly. *"I'll see you tonight."*

He didn't come into the kitchen again before leaving, so I had a chance to finish feeding Brianna and bring my own feelings into some semblance of normality.

I hadn't seen Frank naked since my return; he had always dressed in bathroom or closet. Neither had he tried to kiss me before this morning's cautious peck. The pregnancy had been what the obstetrician called "high-risk," and there had been no question of Frank's sharing my bed, even had I been so disposed—which I wasn't.

I should have seen this coming, but I hadn't. Absorbed first in sheer misery, and then in the physical torpor of oncoming motherhood, I had pushed away all considerations beyond my bulging belly. After Brianna's birth, I had lived from feeding to feeding, seeking small moments of mindless peace, when I could hold her oblivious body close and find relief from thought and memory in the pure sensual pleasure of touching and holding her.

Frank, too, cuddled the baby and played with her, falling asleep in his big chair with her stretched out atop his lanky form, rosy cheek pressed flat against his chest, as they snored together in peaceful companionship. He and I did not touch each other, though, nor did we truly talk about anything beyond our basic domestic arrangements—except Brianna.

The baby was our shared focus; a point through which we could at once reach each other, and keep each other at arm's length. It looked as though arm's length was no longer close enough for Frank.

I could do it—physically, at least. I had seen the doctor for a checkup the week before, and he had—with an avuncular wink and a pat on the bottom—assured me that I could resume "relations" with my husband at any time.

I knew Frank hadn't been celibate since my disappearance. In his late forties, he was still lean and muscular, dark and sleek, a very handsome man. Women clustered about him at cocktail parties like bees round a honeypot, emitting small hums of sexual excitement.

There had been one girl with brown hair whom I had noticed particularly at the departmental party; she stood in the corner and stared at Frank mournfully over her drink. Later she became tearfully and incoherently drunk, and was escorted home by two female friends, who took turns casting evil looks at Frank and at me, standing by his side, silently bulging in my flowered maternity dress.

He'd been discreet, though. He was always home at night, and took pains not to have lipstick on his collar. So, now he meant to come home all the way. I supposed he had some right to expect it; was that not a wifely duty, and I once more his wife?

There was only one small problem. It wasn't Frank I reached for, deep in the night, waking out of sleep. It wasn't his smooth, lithe body that walked my dreams and roused me, so that I came awake moist and gasping, my heart pounding from the half-remembered touch. But I would never touch that man again.

"Jamie," I whispered, "Oh, Jamie." My tears sparkled in the morning light, adorning Brianna's soft red fuzz like scattered pearls and diamonds.

It wasn't a good day. Brianna had a bad diaper rash, which made her cross and irritable, needing to be picked up every few minutes. She nursed and fussed alternately, pausing to spit up at intervals, making clammy wet patches on whatever I wore. I changed my blouse three times before eleven o'clock.

The heavy nursing bra I wore chafed under the arms, and

my nipples felt cold and chapped. Midway through my laborious tidying-up of the house, there was a whooshing clank from under the floorboards, and the hot-air registers died with a feeble sigh.

"No, next week won't do," I said over the telephone to the furnace-repair shop. I looked at the window, where the cold February fog was threatening to seep under the sill and engulf us. "It's forty-two degrees in here, and I have a three-month-old baby!" The baby in question was sitting in her baby seat, swaddled in all her blankets, squalling like a scalded cat. Ignoring the quacking of the person on the other end, I held the receiver next to Brianna's wide open mouth for several seconds.

"See?" I demanded, lifting the phone to my ear again.

"Awright, lady," said a resigned voice on the other end of the line. "I'll come out this afternoon, sometime between noon and six."

"Noon and six? Can't you narrow it down a little more than that? I have to get out to the market," I protested.

"You ain't the only dead furnace in town, lady," the voice said with finality, and hung up. I glanced at the clock; eleven-thirty. I'd never be able to get the marketing done and get back in half an hour. Marketing with a small baby was more like a ninety-minute expedition into Darkest Borneo, requiring massive amounts of equipment and tremendous expenditures of energy.

Gritting my teeth, I called the expensive market that delivered, ordered the necessities for dinner, and picked up the baby, who was by now the shade of an eggplant, and markedly smelly.

"That looks ouchy, darling. You'll feel much better if we get it off, won't you?" I said, trying to talk soothingly as I wiped the brownish slime off Brianna's bright-red bottom. She arched her back, trying to escape the clammy washcloth, and shrieked some more. A layer of Vaseline and the tenth clean diaper of the day; the diaper service truck wasn't due 'til tomorrow, and the house reeked of ammonia.

"All right, sweetheart, there, there." I hoisted her up on my shoulder, patting her, but the screeching went on and on. Not that I could blame her; her poor bottom was nearly raw.

Ideally, she should be let to lie about on a towel with nothing on, but with no heat in the house, that wasn't feasible. She and I were both wearing sweaters and heavy winter coats, which made the frequent feedings even more of a nuisance than usual; excavating a breast could take several minutes, while the baby screamed.

Brianna couldn't sleep for more than ten minutes at a time. Consequently, neither could I. When we did drift off together at four o'clock, we were roused within a quarter of an hour by the crashing arrival of the furnace man, who pounded on the door, not bothering to set down the large wrench he was holding.

Jiggling the baby against my shoulder with one hand, I began cooking the dinner with the other, to the accompaniment of screeches in my ear and the sounds of violence from the cellar below.

"I ain't promising nothin', lady, but you got heat for now." The furnace man appeared abruptly, wiping a smear of grease from his creased forehead. He leaned forward to inspect Brianna, who was lying more or less peacefully across my shoulder, loudly sucking her thumb.

"How's that thumb taste, sweetie?" he inquired. "They say you shouldn't oughta let 'em suck their thumbs, you know," he informed me, straightening up. "Gives 'em crooked teeth and they'll need braces."

"Is that so?" I said through my own teeth. "How much do I owe you?"

Half an hour later, the chicken lay in its pan, stuffed and basted, surrounded by crushed garlic, sprigs of rosemary, and curls of lemon peel. A quick squeeze of lemon juice over the buttery skin, and I could stick it in the oven and go get myself and Brianna dressed. The kitchen looked like the result of an incompetent burglary, with cupboards hanging open and cooking paraphernalia strewn on every horizontal surface. I banged shut a couple of cupboard doors, and then the kitchen door itself, trusting that that would keep Mrs. Hinchcliffe out, even if good manners wouldn't.

Frank had brought a new pink dress for Brianna to wear. It was a beautiful thing, but I eyed the layers of lace around the neck dubiously. They looked not only scratchy, but delicate.

"Well, we'll give it a try," I told her. *"Daddy will like you to look pretty. Let's try not to spit up in it, hm?"*

Brianna responded by shutting her eyes, stiffening, and grunting as she extruded more slime.

"Oh, well done!" I said, sincerely. It meant changing the crib sheet, but at least it wouldn't make the diaper rash worse. The mess attended to and a fresh diaper in place, I shook out the pink dress, and paused to carefully wipe the snot and drool from her face before popping the garment over her head. She blinked at me and gurgled enticingly, windmilling her fists.

I obligingly lowered my head and went *"Pfffft!"* into her navel, which made her squirm and gurgle with joy. We did it a few more times, then began the painstaking job of getting into the pink dress.

Brianna didn't like it; she started to complain as I put it over her head, and as I crammed her chubby little arms into the puffed sleeves, put back her head and let out a piercing cry.

"What is it?" I demanded, startled. I knew all her cries by now and mostly, what she meant by them, but this was a new one, full of fright and pain. *"What's the matter, darling?"*

She was screaming furiously now, tears rolling down her face. I turned her frantically over and patted her back, thinking she might have had a sudden attack of colic, but she wasn't doubled up. She was struggling violently, though, and as I turned her back over to pick her up, I saw the long red line running up the tender inside of her waving arm. A pin had been left in the dress, and had scored her flesh as I forced the sleeve up her arm.

"Oh, baby! Oh, I'm so sorry! Mummy's so sorry!" Tears were running down my own face as I eased the stabbing pin free and removed it. I clutched her to my shoulder, patting and soothing, trying to calm my own feelings of panicked guilt. Of course I hadn't meant to hurt her, but she wouldn't know that.

"Oh, darling," I murmured. *"It's all right now. Yes, Mummy loves you, it's all right."* Why hadn't I thought to check for pins? For that matter, what sort of maniac would package a baby's clothes using straight pins? Torn between

fury and distress, I eased Brianna into the dress, wiped her chin, and carried her into the bedroom, where I laid her on my twin bed while I hastily changed to a decent skirt and a fresh blouse.

The doorbell rang as I was pulling on my stockings. There was a hole in one heel, but no time to do anything about it now. I stuck my feet into the pinching alligator pumps, snatched up Brianna, and went to answer the door.

It was Frank, too laden with packages to use his key. One-handed, I took most of them from him and parked them on the hall table.

"Dinner all ready, dear? I've brought a new tablecloth and napkins—thought ours were a bit shabby. And the wine, of course." He lifted the bottle in his hand, smiling, then leaned forward to peer at me, and stopped smiling. He looked disapprovingly from my disheveled hair to my blouse, freshly stained with spit-up milk.

"Christ, Claire," he said. "Couldn't you fix yourself up a bit? I mean, it's not as though you have anything else to do, at home all day—couldn't you take a few minutes for a—"

"No," I said, quite loudly. I pushed Brianna, who was wailing again with fretful exhaustion, into his arms.

"No," I said again, and took the wine bottle from his unresisting hand.

"NO!" I shrieked, stamping my foot. I swung the bottle widely, and he dodged, but it was the doorjamb I struck, and purplish splatters of Beaujolais flew across the stoop, leaving glass shards glittering in the light from the entryway.

I flung the shattered bottle into the azaleas and ran coatless down the walk and into the freezing fog. At the foot of the walk, I passed the startled Hinchcliffes, who were arriving half an hour early, presumably in hopes of catching me in some domestic deficiency. I hoped they'd enjoy their dinner.

I drove aimlessly through the fog, the car's heater blasting on my feet, until I began to get low on gas. I wasn't going home; not yet. An all-night cafe? Then I realized that it was Friday night, and getting on for twelve o'clock. I had a place to go, after all. I turned back toward the suburb where we lived, and the Church of St. Finbar.

At this hour, the chapel was locked to prevent vandalism and burglary. For the late adorers, there was a push-button lock set just below the door handle. Five buttons, numbered one to five. By pushing three of them, in the proper combination, the latch could be sprung to allow lawful entry.

I moved quietly along the back of the chapel, to the logbook that sat at the feet of St. Finbar, to record my arrival.

"St. Finbar?" Frank had said incredulously. "There isn't such a saint. There can't possibly be."

"There is," I said, with a trace of smugness. "An Irish bishop, from the twelfth century."

"Oh, Irish," said Frank dismissively. "That explains it. But what I can't understand," he said, careful to be tactful, "is, er, well . . . why?"

"Why what?"

"Why go in for this Perpetual Adoration business? You've never been the least devout, no more than I have. And you don't go to Mass or anything; Father Beggs asks me every week where you are."

I shook my head. "I can't really say, Frank. It's just something . . . I need to do." I looked at him, helpless to explain adequately. "It's . . . peaceful there," I said, finally.

He opened his mouth as though to speak further, then turned away, shaking his head.

It *was* peaceful. The car park at the church was deserted, save for the single car of the adorer on duty at this hour, gleaming an anonymous black under the arc lights. Inside, I signed my name to the log and walked forward, coughing tactfully to alert the eleven o'clock adorer to my presence without the rudeness of direct speech. I knelt behind him, a heavyset man in a yellow windcheater. After a moment, he rose, genuflected before the altar, turned and walked to the door, nodding briefly as he passed me.

The door hissed shut and I was alone, save for the Sacrament displayed on the altar, in the great golden sunburst of the monstrance. There were two candles on the altar, big ones. Smooth and white, they burned steadily in the still air, without a flicker. I closed my eyes for a moment, just listening to the silence.

Everything that had happened during the day whirled

through my mind in a disjointed welter of thoughts and feelings. Coatless, I was shaking with cold from the short walk through the parking lot, but slowly I grew warm again, and my clenched hands relaxed in my lap.

At last, as usually happened here, I ceased to think. Whether it was the stoppage of time in the presence of eternity, or only the overtaking of a bone-deep fatigue, I didn't know. But the guilt over Frank eased, the wrenching grief for Jamie lessened, and even the constant tug of motherhood upon my emotions receded to the level of background noise, no louder than the slow beating of my own heart, regular and comforting in the dark peace of the chapel.

"O Lord," I whispered, "I commend to Your mercy the soul of Your servant James." And mine, I added silently. And mine.

I sat there without moving, watching the flickering glow of the candle flames in the gold surface of the monstrance, until the soft footsteps of the next adorer came down the aisle behind me, ending in the heavy creak of genuflection. They came once each hour, day and night. The Blessed Sacrament was never left alone.

I stayed for a few minutes more, then slid out of the pew, with my own nod toward the altar. As I walked toward the back of the chapel, I saw a figure in the back row, under the shadow of the statue of St. Anthony. It stirred as I approached, then the man rose to his feet and made his way to the aisle to meet me.

"What are you doing here?" I whispered.

Frank nodded toward the form of the new adorer, already kneeling in contemplation, and took my elbow to guide me out.

I waited until the chapel door had closed behind us before pulling away and whirling to confront him.

"What is this?" I said angrily. "Why did you come after me?"

"I was worried about you." He gestured toward the empty car park, where his large Buick nestled protectively next to my small Ford. "It's dangerous, a lone woman walking about in the very late night in this part of town. I came to see you home. That's all."

He didn't mention the Hinchcliffes, or the dinner party. My annoyance ebbed a bit.

"Oh," I said. "What did you do with Brianna?"

"Asked old Mrs. Munsing from next door to keep an ear out in case she cried. But she seemed dead asleep; I didn't think there was much chance. Come along now, it's cold out."

It was; the freezing air off the bay was coiling in white tendrils around the posts of the arc lights, and I shivered in my thin blouse.

"I'll meet you at home, then," I said.

The warmth of the nursery reached out to embrace me as I went in to check Brianna. She was still asleep, but restless, turning her russet head from side to side, the groping little mouth opening and closing like the breathing of a fish.

"She's getting hungry," I whispered to Frank, who had come in behind me and was hovering over my shoulder, peering fondly at the baby. "I'd better feed her before I come to bed; then she'll sleep later in the morning."

"I'll get you a hot drink," and he vanished through the door to the kitchen as I picked up the sleepy, warm bundle.

She had only drained one side, but she was full. The slack mouth pulled slowly away from the nipple, rimmed with milk, and the fuzzy head fell heavily back on my arm. No amount of gentle shaking or calling would rouse her to nurse on the other side, so at last I gave up and tucked her back in her crib, patting her back softly until a faint, contented belch wafted up from the pillow, succeeded by the heavy breathing of absolute satiation.

"Down for the night, is she?" Frank drew the baby blanket, decorated with yellow bunnies, up over her.

"Yes." I sat back in my rocking chair, mentally and physically too exhausted to get up again. Frank came to stand behind me; his hand rested lightly on my shoulder.

"He's dead, then?" he asked gently.

I told you so, I started to say. Then I stopped, closed my mouth and only nodded, rocking slowly, staring at the dark crib and its tiny occupant.

My right breast was still painfully swollen with milk. No

matter how tired I was, I couldn't sleep until I took care of it. With a sigh of resignation, I reached for the breast pump, an ungainly and ridiculous-looking rubber contraption. Using it was undignified and uncomfortable, but better than waking up in an hour in bursting pain, sopping wet from overflowing milk.

I waved a hand at Frank, dismissing him.

"Go ahead. It will only take a few minutes, but I have to . . ."

Instead of leaving or answering, he took the pump from my hand and laid it down on the table. As though it moved of its own will, without direction from him, his hand rose slowly through the warm, dark air of the nursery and cupped itself gently around the swollen curve of my breast.

His head bowed and his lips fastened softly on my nipple. I groaned, feeling the half-painful prickle of the milk rushing through the tiny ducts. I put a hand behind his head, and pressed him slightly closer.

"Harder," I whispered. His mouth was soft, gentle in its pressure, nothing like the relentless grasp of a baby's hard, toothless gums, that fasten on like grim death, demanding and draining, releasing the bounteous fountain at once in response to their greed.

Frank knelt before me, his mouth a supplicant. Was this how God felt, I wondered, seeing the adorers before Him— was He, too, filled with tenderness and pity? The haze of fatigue made me feel as though everything happened in slow motion, as though we were under water. Frank's hands moved slowly as sea fronds, swaying in the current, moving over my flesh with a touch as gentle as the brush of kelp leaves, lifting me with the strength of a wave, and laying me down on the shore of the nursery rug. I closed my eyes, and let the tide carry me away.

———

The front door of the old manse opened with a screech of rust hinges, announcing the return of Brianna Randall. Roger was o his feet and into the hall at once, drawn by the sound of girl voices.

"A pound of best butter—that's what you told me to ask fo

d I did, but I kept wondering whether there was such a thing as
cond-best butter, or worst butter—'' Brianna was handing over
rapped packages to Fiona, laughing and talking at once.

"Well, and if ye got it from that auld rascal Wicklow, worst is
hat it's likely to be, no matter what he says," Fiona interrupted.
Oh, and ye've got the cinnamon, that's grand! I'll make cinna-
on scones, then; d'ye want to come and watch me do it?''

"Yes, but first I want supper. I'm starved!" Brianna stood on
ptoe, sniffing hopefully in the direction of the kitchen. "What are
e having—haggis?''

"Haggis! Gracious, ye silly Sassenach—ye dinna have haggis
the spring! Ye have it in the autumn when the sheep are killed.''

"Am I a Sassenach?" Brianna seemed delighted at the name.

"Of course ye are, gowk. But I like ye fine, anyway.''

Fiona laughed up at Brianna, who towered over the small Scot-
sh girl by nearly a foot. Fiona was nineteen, prettily charming
d slightly plump; next to her, Brianna looked like a medieval
rving, strong-boned and severe. With her long, straight nose and
e long hair glowing red-gold beneath the glass bowl of the
iling fixture, she might have walked out of an illuminated manu-
ript, vivid enough to endure a thousand years unchanged.

Roger was suddenly conscious of Claire Randall, standing near
s elbow. She was looking at her daughter, with an expression in
hich love, pride, and something else were mingled—memory,
rhaps? He realized, with a slight shock, that Jamie Fraser too
ust have had not only the striking height and Viking red hair he
d bequeathed to his daughter, but likely the same sheer physical
esence.

It was quite remarkable, he thought. She didn't do or say any-
ing so out of the ordinary, and yet Brianna undeniably drew
:ople. There was some attraction about her, almost magnetic,
at drew everyone near into the glow of her orbit.

It drew him; Brianna turned and smiled at him, and without
nsciousness of having moved, he found himself near enough to
e the faint freckles high on her cheekbones, and smell the whiff
pipe tobacco that lingered in her hair from her expeditions to
e shops.

"Hullo," he said, smiling. "Any luck with the Clans office, or
ve you been too busy playing dogsbody for Fiona?''

"Dogsbody?" Brianna's eyes slanted into blue triangles of

amusement. *"Dogsbody?* First I'm a Sassenach, and now I'm dogsbody. What do you Scots call people when you're trying to *nice?"*

"Darrrrlin'," he said, rolling his *r*'s exaggeratedly, and maki both girls laugh.

"You sound like an Aberdeen terrier in a bad mood," Cla observed. "Did you find anything at the Highland Clans libra Bree?"

"Lots of stuff," Brianna replied, rummaging through the sta of photocopies she had set down on the hall table. "I managed read most of it while they were making the copies—this one v the most interesting." She pulled a sheet from the stack a handed it to Roger.

It was an extract from a book of Highland legends; an en headed "Leap O' the Cask."

"Legends?" said Claire, peering over his shoulder. "Is t what we want?"

"Could be." Roger was perusing the sheet, and spoke absent his attention divided. "So far as the Scottish Highlands go, m of the history is oral, up to the mid-nineteenth century or so. T means there wasn't a great distinction made between stories abc real people, stories of historical figures, and the stories abc mythical things like water horses and ghosts and the doings of Auld Folk. Scholars who wrote the stories down often didn't kn for sure which they were dealing with, either—sometimes it wa combination of fact and myth, and sometimes you could tell tha was a real historical occurrence being described.

"This one, for instance"—he passed the paper to Claire "sounds like a real one. It's describing the story behind the na of a particular rock formation in the Highlands."

Claire brushed the hair behind her ear and bent her head to re squinting in the dim light of the ceiling fixture. Fiona, too acc tomed to musty papers and boring bits of history to be interest disappeared back into her kitchen to see to the dinner.

" 'Leap O' the Cask,' " Claire read. " *'This unusual form tion, located some distance above a burn, is named after the st of a Jacobite laird and his servant. The laird, one of the fortunates to escape the disaster of Culloden, made his way w difficulty to his home, but was compelled to lie hidden in a cave his lands for nearly seven years, while the English hunted*

Highlands for the fugitive supporters of Charles Stuart. The laird's tenants loyally kept his presence a secret, and brought food and supplies to the laird in his hiding place. They were careful always to refer to the hidden man only as the "Dunbonnet," in order to avoid any chance of giving him away to the English patrols who frequently crossed the district.

" 'One day, a boy bringing a cask of ale up the trail to the laird's cave met a group of English dragoons. Bravely refusing either to answer the soldiers' questions, or to give up his burden, the boy was attacked by one of the dragoons, and dropped the cask, which bounded down the steep hill, and into the burn below.' "

She looked up from the paper, raising her eyebrows at her daughter.

"Why this one? We know—or we think we know," she corrected, with a wry nod toward Roger, "that Jamie escaped from Culloden, but so did a lot of other people. What makes you think this laird might have been Jamie?"

"Because of the Dunbonnet bit, of course," Brianna answered, as though surprised that she should ask.

"What?" Roger looked at her, puzzled. "What about the Dunbonnet?"

In answer, Brianna picked up a hank of her thick red hair and waggled it under his nose.

"Dunbonnet!" she said impatiently. "A dull brown bonnet, right? He wore a hat all the time, because he had hair that could be recognized! Didn't you say the English called him 'Red Jamie'? They knew he had red hair—he had to hide it!"

Roger stared at her, speechless. The hair floated loose on her shoulders, alive with fiery light.

"You could be right," Claire said. Excitement made her eyes bright as she looked at her daughter. "It was like yours—Jamie's hair was just like yours, Bree." She reached up and softly stroked Brianna's hair. The girl's face softened as she looked down at her mother.

"I know," she said. "I was thinking about that while I was reading—trying to see him, you know?" She stopped and cleared her throat, as though something might be caught in it. "I could see him, out in the heather, hiding, and the sun shining off his hair. You said he'd been an outlaw; I just—I just thought he must have

known pretty well . . . how to hide. If people were trying to ki
him," she finished softly.

"Right." Roger spoke briskly, to dispel the shadow in Br
anna's eyes. "That's a marvelous job of guesswork, but maybe w
can tell for sure, with a little more work. If we can find Leap C
the Cask on a map—"

"What kind of dummy do you think I am?" Brianna said scor
fully. "I thought of that." The shadow disappeared, replaced b
an expression of smugness. "That's why I was so late; I made th
clerk drag out every map of the Highlands they had." She with
drew another photocopied sheet from the stack and poked a fing
triumphantly near the upper edge.

"See? It's so tiny, it doesn't show up on most maps, but th
one had it. Right there; there's the village of Broch Mordha, whic
Mama says is near the Lallybroch estate, and there"—her fing
moved a quarter-inch, pointing to a line of microscopic prin
"See?" she repeated. "He went back to his estate—Lallybroch–
and that's where he hid."

"Not having a magnifying glass to hand, I'll take your word f
it that that says 'Leap O' the Cask,'" Roger said, straightenin
up. He grinned at Brianna. "Congratulations, then," he said. '
think you've found him—that far, at least."

Brianna smiled, her eyes suspiciously bright. "Yeah," she sai
softly. She touched the two sheets of paper with a gentle finge
"My father."

Claire squeezed her daughter's hand. "If you have your father
hair, it's nice to see you have your mother's brains," she sai
smiling. "Let's go and celebrate your discovery with Fiona's di
ner."

"Good job," Roger said to Brianna, as they followed Clai
toward the dining room. His hand rested lightly on her waist. "Yo
should be proud of yourself."

"Thanks," she said, with a brief smile, but the pensive expre
sion returned almost at once to the curve of her mouth.

"What is it?" Roger asked softly, stopping in the hall. "'
something the matter?"

"No, not really." She turned to face him, a small line visibl
between the ruddy brows. "It's only—I was just thinking, tryin

o imagine—what do you think it was like for him? Living in a
:ave for seven years? And what happened to him then?''

Moved by an impulse, Roger leaned forward and kissed her
ightly between the brows.

''I don't know, darlin','' he said. ''But maybe we'll find out.''

PART TWO

Lallybroch

4

The Dunbonnet

Lallybroch
November 1752

He came down to the house once a month to shave, when one of the boys brought him word it was safe. Always at night, moving soft-footed as a fox through the dark. It seemed necessary, somehow, a small gesture toward the concept of civilization.

He would slip like a shadow through the kitchen door, to be met with Ian's smile or his sister's kiss, and would feel the transformation begin. The basin of hot water, the freshly stropped razor would be laid ready for him on the table, with whatever there was for shaving soap. Now and then it was real soap, if Cousin Jared had sent some from France; more often just half-rendered tallow, eye-stinging with lye.

He could feel the change begin with the first scent of the kitchen—so strong and rich, after the wind-thin smells of loch and moor and wood—but it wasn't until he had finished the ritual of shaving that he felt himself altogether human once more.

They had learned not to expect him to talk until he had shaved; words came hard after a month's solitude. Not that he could think of nothing to say; it was more that the words inside formed a logjam in his throat, battling each other to get out in the short time he had. He needed those few minutes of careful grooming to pick and choose, what he would say first and to whom.

There was news to hear and to ask about—of English patrols in the district, of politics, of arrests and trials in London and Edinburgh. That he could wait for. Better to talk to Ian about the estate, to Jenny about the children. If it seemed safe, the children would

be brought down to say hello to their uncle, to give him slee
hugs and damp kisses before stumbling back to their beds.

"He'll be getting a man soon" had been his first choice
conversation when he came in September, with a nod towa
Jenny's eldest child, his namesake. The ten-year-old sat at t
table with a certain constraint, immensely conscious of the dign
of his temporary position as man of the house.

"Aye, all I need's another of the creatures to worry over," I
sister replied tartly, but she touched her son's shoulder in passin
with a pride that belied her words.

"Have ye word from Ian, then?" His brother-in-law had be
arrested—for the fourth time—three weeks before, and taken
Inverness under suspicion of being a Jacobite sympathizer.

Jenny shook her head, bringing a covered dish to set before hi
The thick warm smell of partridge pie drifted up from the prick
crust, and made his mouth water so heavily, he had to swalle
before he could speak.

"It's naught to fret for," Jenny said, spooning out the pie o
his plate. Her voice was calm, but the small vertical line betwe
her brows deepened. "I've sent Fergus to show them the deed
sasine, and Ian's discharge from his regiment. They'll send h
home again, so soon as they realize he isna the laird of Lallybroo
and there's naught to be gained by deviling him." With a glance
her son, she reached for the ale jug. "Precious chance they have
provin' a wee bairn to be a traitor."

Her voice was grim, but held a note of satisfaction at t
thought of the English court's confusion. The rain-spattered de
of sasine that proved transfer of the title of Lallybroch from t
elder James to the younger had made its appearance in co
before, each time foiling the Crown's attempt to seize the estate
the property of a Jacobite traitor.

He would feel it begin to slip away when he left—that th
veneer of humanity—more of it gone with each step away fr
the farmhouse. Sometimes he would keep the illusion of warm
and family all the way to the cave where he hid; other times
would disappear almost at once, torn away by a chill wind, ra
and acrid with the scent of burning.

The English had burned three crofts, beyond the high fie
Pulled Hugh Kirby and Geoff Murray from their firesides and sh
them by their own doorsteps, with no question or word of form

accusation. Young Joe Fraser had escaped, warned by his wife, who had seen the English coming, and had lived three weeks with Jamie in the cave, until the soldiers were well away from the district—and Ian with them.

In October, it had been the older lads he spoke to; Fergus, the French boy he had taken from a Paris brothel, and Rabbie MacNab, the kitchenmaid's son, Fergus's best friend.

He had drawn the razor slowly down one cheek and round the angle of his jaw, then wiped the lathered blade against the edge of the basin. From the corner of one eye, he caught a faint glimpse of fascinated envy on the face of Rabbie MacNab. Turning slightly, he saw that the three boys—Rabbie, Fergus, and Young Jamie—were all watching him intently, mouths slightly open.

"Have ye no seen a man shave before?" he asked, cocking one brow.

Rabbie and Fergus glanced at each other, but left it to Young Jamie, as titular owner of the estate, to answer.

"Oh, well . . . aye, Uncle," he said, blushing. "But . . . I m-mean"—he stammered slightly and blushed even harder—"with my da gone, and even when he's home, we dinna see him shave himself always, and well, you've just such a lot of *hair* on your face, Uncle, after a whole month, and it's only we're so glad to see you again, and . . ."

It dawned on Jamie quite suddenly that to the boys he must seem a most romantic figure. Living alone in a cave, emerging at dark to hunt, coming down out of the mist in the night, filthy and wild-haired, beard all in a fierce red sprout—yes, at their age, it likely seemed a glamorous adventure to be an outlaw and live hidden in the heather, in a dank, cramped cave. At fifteen and sixteen and ten, they had no notion of guilt or bitter loneliness, of the weight of a responsibility that could not be relieved by action.

They might understand fear, of a sort. Fear of capture, fear of death. Not the fear of solitude, of his own nature, fear of madness. Not the constant, chronic fear of what his presence might do to them—if they thought about that risk at all, they dismissed it, with the casual assumption of immortality that was the right of boys.

"Aye, well," he had said, turning casually back to the looking glass as Young Jamie stuttered to a halt. "Man is born to sorrow and whiskers. One of the plagues of Adam."

"Of Adam?" Fergus looked openly puzzled, while the other tried to pretend they had the slightest idea what Jamie was talkin about. Fergus, as a Frenchie, was not expected to know everything

"Oh, aye." Jamie pulled his upper lip down over his teeth an scraped delicately beneath his nose. "In the beginning, when Go made man, Adam's chin was as hairless as Eve's. And their bodie both smooth as a newborn child's," he added, seeing Young Ja mie's eyes dart toward Rabbie's crotch. Beardless Rabbie stil was, but the faint dark down on his upper lip bespoke new sprout ings elsewhere.

"But when the angel wi' the flaming sword drove them out o Eden, no sooner had they passed the gate of the garden, when th hair began to sprout and itch on Adam's chin, and ever since, ma has been cursed with shaving." He finished his own chin with final flourish, and bowed theatrically to his audience.

"But what about the other hair?" Rabbie demanded. "Ye dinn shave *there*!" Young Jamie giggled at the thought, going re again.

"And a damn good thing, too," his elder namesake observed "Ye'd need the devil of a steady hand. No need of a looking glass though," he added, to a chorus of giggles.

"What about the ladies?" Fergus said. His voice broke on th word "ladies," in a bullfrog croak that made the other two laug harder. "Certainly *les filles* have hair there, too, but they do nc shave it—usually not, anyway," he added, clearly thinking o some of the sights of his early life in the brothel.

Jamie heard his sister's footsteps coming down the hall.

"Oh, well, that's no a curse," he told his rapt audience, pickin up the basin and tossing the contents neatly through the ope window. "God gave that as a consolation to man. If ye've ever th privilege of seeing a woman in her skin, gentlemen," he saic looking over his shoulder toward the door and lowering his voic confidentially, "ye'll observe that the hair there grows in th shape of an arrow—pointing the way, ye ken, so as a poor ignorar man can find his way safe home."

He turned grandly away from the guffawing and sniggers be hind him, to be struck suddenly with shame as he saw his siste coming down the hall with the slow, waddling stride of advance pregnancy. She was holding the tray with his supper on top of he

welling stomach. How could he have demeaned her so, for a
rude jest and the sake of a moment's camaraderie with the boys?

"Be still!" he had snapped at the boys, who stopped giggling
abruptly and stared at him in puzzlement. He hastened forward to
take the tray from Jenny and set it on the table.

It was a savoury made of goat's meat and bacon, and he saw
Fergus's prominent Adam's apple bob in the slender throat at the
smell of it. He knew they saved the best of the food for him; it
didn't take much looking at the pinched faces across the table.
When he came, he brought what meat he could, snared rabbits or
grouse, sometimes a nest of plover's eggs—but it was never
enough, for a house where hospitality must stretch to cover the
needs of not only family and servants, but the families of the
murdered Kirby and Murray. At least until spring, the widows and
children of his tenants must bide here, and he must do his best to
feed them.

"Sit down by me," he said to Jenny, taking her arm and gently
guiding her to a seat on the bench beside him. She looked surprised—it was her habit to wait on him when he came—but sat
down gladly enough. It was late, and she was tired; he could see
the dark smudges beneath her eyes.

With great firmness, he cut a large slab of the savoury and set
the plate before her.

"But that's all for you!" Jenny protested. "I've eaten."

"Not enough," he said. "Ye need more—for the babe," he
added, with inspiration. If she would not eat for herself, she would
for the child. She hesitated a moment longer, but then smiled at
him, picked up her spoon, and began to eat.

Now it was November, and the chill struck through the thin shirt
and breeches he wore. He hardly noticed, intent on his tracking. It
was cloudy, but with a thin-layered mackerel sky, through which
the full moon shed plenty of light.

Thank God it wasn't raining; impossible to hear through the
pattering of raindrops, and the pungent scent of wet plants masked
the smell of animals. His nose had grown almost painfully acute
through the long months of living outdoors; the smells of the
house sometimes nearly knocked him down when he stepped inside.

He wasn't quite close enough to smell the musky scent of the

stag, but he heard the telltale rustle of its brief start when
scented *him*. Now it would be frozen, one of the shadows th
rippled across the hillside around him, under the racing clouds

He turned as slowly as he possibly could toward the spot whe
his ears had told him the stag stood. His bow was in his hand,
arrow ready to the string. He would have one shot—maybe—wh
the stag bolted.

Yes, there! His heart sprang into his throat as he saw the antle
pricking sharp and black above the surrounding gorse. He steadi
himself, took a deep breath, and then the one step forward.

The crash of a deer's flight was always startlingly loud,
frighten back a stalker. This stalker was prepared, though. I
neither startled nor pursued, but stood his ground, sighting alo
the shaft of the arrow, following with his eye the track of t
springing deer, judging the moment, holding fire, and then t
bowstring slapped his wrist with stinging force.

It was a clean shot, just behind the shoulder, and a good thi
too; he doubted he had the strength to run down a full-grown sta
It had fallen in a clear spot behind a clump of gorse, legs stu
out, stiff as sticks, in the oddly helpless way of dying ungulat
The hunter's moon lit its glazing eye, so the soft dark stare w
hidden, the mystery of its dying shielded by blank silver.

He pulled the dirk from his belt and knelt by the deer, hast
saying the words of the gralloch prayer. Old John Murray, Ia
father, had taught him. His own father's mouth had twist
slightly, hearing it, from which he gathered that this prayer w
perhaps not addressed to the same God they spoke to in church
Sunday. But his father had said nothing, and he had mumbled t
words himself, scarcely noticing what he said, in the nervo
excitement of feeling old John's hand, steady on his own, for t
first time pressing down the knife blade into hairy hide and stea
ing flesh.

Now, with the sureness of practice, he thrust up the stic
muzzle in one hand, and with the other, slit the deer's throat.

The blood spurted hot over knife and hand, pumping two
three times, the jet dying away to a steady stream as the carca
drained, the great vessels of the throat cut through. Had he paus
to think, he might not have done it, but hunger and dizziness a
the cold fresh intoxication of the night had taken him far past t

oint of thinking. He cupped his hands beneath the running stream
nd brought them steaming to his mouth.

The moon shone black on his cupped, spilling hands, and it was
s though he absorbed the deer's substance, rather than drank it.
he taste of the blood was salt and silver, and the heat of it was his
wn. There was no startlement of hot or cold as he swallowed,
nly the taste of it, rich in his mouth, and the head-swimming, hot-
etal smell, and the sudden clench and rumble of his belly at the
earness of food.

He closed his eyes and breathed, and the cold damp air came
ack, between the hot reek of the carcass and his senses. He
wallowed once, then wiped the back of his hand across his face,
leaned his hands on the grass, and set about the business at hand.

There was the sudden effort of moving the limp, heavy carcass,
nd then the gralloch, the long stroke of mingled strength and
elicacy that slit the hide between the legs, but did not penetrate
e sac that held the entrails. He forced his hands into the carcass,
hot wet intimacy, and again there was an effortful tug that
rought out the sac, slick and moon-shining in his hands. A slash
bove and another below, and the mass slid free, the transforma-
on of black magic that changed a deer to meat.

It was a small stag, although it had points to its antlers. With
ick, he could carry it alone, rather than leave it to the mercy of
xes and badgers until he could bring help to move it. He ducked
shoulder under one leg, and slowly rose, grunting with effort as
e shifted the burden to a solid resting place across his back.

The moon cast his shadow on a rock, humped and fantastic, as
e made his slow, ungainly way down the hill. The deer's antlers
obbed above his shoulder, giving him in shadowed profile the
emblance of a horned man. He shivered slightly at the thought,
emembering tales of witches' sabbats, where the Horned One
ame, to drink the sacrifice of goat's or rooster's blood.

He felt a little queasy, and more than a little light-headed. More
nd more, he felt the disorientation, the fragmenting of himself
etween day and night. By day, he was a creature of the mind
lone, as he escaped his damp immobility by a stubborn, disci-
lined retreat into the avenues of thought and meditation, seeking
efuge in the pages of books. But with the rising of the moon, all
ense fled, succumbing at once to sensation, as he emerged into
e fresh air like a beast from its lair, to run the dark hills beneath

the stars, and hunt, driven by hunger, drunk with blood and moo
light.

He stared at the ground as he walked, night-sight keen enoug
to keep his footing, despite the heavy burden. The deer was lim
and cooling, its stiff, soft hair scratching against the back of h
neck, and his own sweat cooling in the breeze, as though he shar
his prey's fate.

It was only as the lights of Lallybroch manor came into vie
that he felt at last the mantle of humanity fall upon him, and mir
and body joined as one again as he prepared himself to greet h
family.

5

To Us a Child Is Given

Three weeks later, there was still no word of Ian's return. No word of any kind, in fact. Fergus had not come to the cave in several days, leaving Jamie in a fret of worry over ow things might be at the house. If nothing else, the deer he had not would have gone long since, with all the extra mouths to feed, nd there would be precious little from the kailyard at this time of ear.

He was sufficiently worried to risk an early visit, checking his ares and coming down from the hills just before sunset. Just in ase, he was careful to pull on the woolen bonnet, knitted of rough un yarn, that would hide his hair from any telltale fingering of te sunbeams. His size alone might provoke suspicion, but not rtainty, and he had full confidence in the strength of his legs to rry him out of harm's way should he have the ill luck to meet ith an English patrol. Hares in the heather were little match for mie Fraser, given warning.

The house was strangely quiet as he approached. There was ne of the usual racket made by children: Jenny's five, and the x bairns belonging to the tenants, to say nothing of Fergus and bbie MacNab, who were a long way from being too old to chase ch other round the stables, screeching like fiends.

The house felt strangely empty round him, as he paused just side the kitchen door. He was standing in the back hall, the ntry to one side, the scullery to the other, and the main kitchen st beyond. He stood stock-still, reaching out with all his senses, tening as he inhaled the overpowering smells of the house. No,

there was someone here; the faint sound of a scrape, followed by
soft, regular clinking came from behind the cloth-padded door th
kept the heat of the kitchen from seeping out into the chilly ba
pantry.

It was a reassuringly domestic sound, so he pushed open t
door cautiously, but without undue fear. His sister, Jenny, alo
and vastly pregnant, was standing at the table, stirring somethi
in a yellow bowl.

"What are you doing in here? Where's Mrs. Coker?"

His sister dropped the spoon with a startled shriek.

"Jamie!" Pale-faced, she pressed a hand to her breast a
closed her eyes. "Christ! Ye scairt the bowels out of me." Sl
opened her eyes, dark blue like his own, and fixed him with
penetrating stare. "And what in the name of the Holy Mother a
ye doing here now? I wasna expecting ye for a week at least."

"Fergus hasna come up the hill lately; I got worried," he sa
simply.

"Ye're a sweet man, Jamie." The color was coming back in
her face. She smiled at her brother and came close to hug him.
was an awkward business, with the impending baby in the wa
but pleasant, nonetheless. He rested his cheek for a moment on t
sleek darkness of her head, breathing in her complex aroma
candle wax and cinnamon, tallow-soap and wool. There was
unusual element to her scent this evening; he thought she w
beginning to smell of milk.

"Where is everyone?" he asked, releasing her reluctantly.

"Well, Mrs. Coker's dead," she answered, the faint crease b
tween her brows deepening.

"Aye?" he said softly, and crossed himself. "I'm sorry for it
Mrs. Coker had been first housemaid and then housekeeper for t
family, since the marriage of his own parents, forty-odd yea
before. "When?"

"Yesterday forenoon. 'Twasn't unexpected, poor soul, and
was peaceful. She died in her own bed, like she wanted, and Fath
McMurtry prayin' over her."

Jamie glanced reflexively toward the door that led to the se
vants' rooms, off the kitchen. "Is she still here?"

His sister shook her head. "No. I told her son they should ha
the wake here at the house, but the Cokers thought, everythi
being like it is"—her small moue encompassed Ian's absen

rking Redcoats, refugee tenants, the dearth of food, and his own
nconvenient presence in the cave—"they thought better to have it
t Broch Mordha, at her sister's place. So that's where everyone's
one. I told them I didna feel well enough to go," she added, then
miled, raising an impish brow. "But it was really that I wanted a
w hours' peace and quiet, wi' the lot of them gone."

"And here I've come, breakin' in on your peace," Jamie said
uefully. "Shall I go?"

"No, clot-heid," his sister said affably. "Sit ye down, and I'll
et on wi' the supper."

"What's to eat, then?" he asked, sniffing hopefully.

"Depends on what ye've brought," his sister replied. She
oved heavily about the kitchen, taking things from cupboard and
utch, pausing to stir the large kettle hung over the fire, from
vhich a thin steam was rising.

"If ye've brought meat, we'll have it. If not, it's brose and
ough."

He made a face at this; the thought of boiled barley and shin-
eef, the last remnants of the salted beef carcass they'd bought
wo months before, was unappealing.

"Just as well I had luck, then," he said. He upended his game
ag and let the three rabbits fall onto the table in a limp tumble of
ray fur and crumpled ears. "And blackthorn berries," he added,
pping out the contents of the dun bonnet, now stained inside with
ne rich red juice.

Jenny's eyes brightened at the sight. "Hare pie," she declared.
"There's no currants, but the berries will do even better, and
nere's enough butter, thank God." Catching a tiny blink of move-
nent among the gray fur, she slapped her hand down on the table,
eatly obliterating the minuscule intruder.

"Take them out and skin 'em, Jamie, or the kitchen will be
opping wi' fleas."

Returning with the skinned carcasses, he found the piecrust
ell advanced, and Jenny with smears of flour on her dress.

"Cut them into collops and break the bones for me, will ye,
amie?" she said, frowning at *Mrs. McClintock's Receipts for
ookery and Pastry-Work,* laid open on the table beside the pie
an.

"Surely ye can make hare pie without looking in the wee
ook?" he said, obligingly taking the big bone-crushing wooden

mallet from the top of the hutch where it was kept. He grimaced a he took it into his hand, feeling the weight of it. It was very lik the one that had broken his right hand several years before, in a English prison, and he had a sudden vivid memory of the shattere bones in a hare pie, splintered and cracked, leaking salty bloo and marrow-sweetness into the meat.

"Aye, I can," his sister answered abstractedly, thumbin through the pages. "It's only that when ye havena got half th things ye need to make a dish, sometimes there's something els you'll come across in here, that ye can use instead." She frowne at the page before her. "Ordinarily, I'd use claret in the sauce, b we've none in the house, save one of Jared's casks in the prie hole, and I dinna want to broach that yet—we might need it."

He didn't need telling what she might use it for. A cask of clare might grease the skids for Ian's release—or at least pay for new of his welfare. He stole a sidewise glance at the great round (Jenny's belly. It wasn't for a man to say, but to his not inexper enced eyes, she looked damn near her time. Absently, he reache over the kettle and swished the blade of his dirk to and fro in th scalding liquid, then pulled it out and wiped it clean.

"Whyever did ye do that, Jamie?" He turned to find Jenn staring at him. The black curls were coming undone from the ribbon, and it gave him a pang to see the glimmer of a single whi hair among the ebony.

"Oh," he said, too obviously offhand as he picked up or carcass, "Claire—she told me ye ought to wash off a blade boiling water before ye touched food with it."

He felt rather than saw Jenny's eyebrows rise. She had aske him about Claire only once, when he had come home from Cull den, half-conscious and mostly dead with fever.

"She is gone," he had said, and turned his face away. "Dinr speak her name to me again." Loyal as always, Jenny had not, ar neither had he. He could not have said what made him say it toda unless perhaps it was the dreams.

He had them often, in varying forms, and it always unsettl him the day after, as though for a moment Claire had really bee near enough to touch, and then had drawn away again. He cou swear that sometimes he woke with the smell of her on hir musky and rich, pricked with the sharp, fresh scents of leaves a green herbs. He had spilled his seed in his sleep more than on

hile dreaming, an occurrence that left him faintly shamed and
neasy in mind. To distract both of them, he nodded at Jenny's
omach.

"How close is it?" he asked, frowning at her swollen midsec-
on. "Ye look like a puffball mushroom—one touch, and poof!"
e flicked his fingers wide in illustration.

"Oh, aye? Well, and I could wish it was as easy as poof." She
rched her back, rubbing at the small of it, and making her belly
rotrude in an alarming fashion. He pressed back against the wall,
 give it room. "As for when, anytime, I expect. No telling for
ure." She picked up the cup and measured out the flour; precious
ttle left in the bag, he noted with some grimness.

"Send up to the cave when it starts," he said suddenly. "I'll
ome down, Redcoats or no."

Jenny stopped stirring and stared at him.

"You? Why?"

"Well, Ian's not here," he pointed out, picking up one skinned
arcass. With the expertise of long practice, he neatly disjointed a
igh and cut it free from the backbone. Three quick smacks with
e boning mallet and the pale flesh lay flattened and ready for the
ie.

"And a great lot of help he'd be if he was," Jenny said. "He
ook care of his part o' the business nine months ago." She wrin-
led her nose at her brother and reached for the plate of butter.

"Mmphm." He sat down to continue his work, which brought
er belly close to his eye-level. The contents, awake and active,
as shifting to and fro in a restless manner, making her apron
witch and bulge as she stirred. He couldn't resist reaching out to
ut a light hand against the monstrous curve, to feel the surprising
rong thrusts and kicks of the inhabitant, impatient of its cramped
onfinement.

"Send Fergus for me when it's time," he said again.

She looked down at him in exasperation and batted his hand
way with the spoon. "Have I no just been telling ye, I dinna need
e? For God's sake, man, have I not enough to worry me, wi' the
ouse full of people, and scarce enough to feed them, Ian in gaol
 Inverness, and Redcoats crawling in at the windows every time I
ok round? Should I have to worry that ye'll be taken up, as
ell?"

"Ye needna be worrit for me; I'll take care." He didn't look at

her, but focused his attention on the forejoint he was slici
through.

"Well, then, have a care and stay put on the hill." She look
down her long, straight nose, peering at him over the rim of t
bowl. "I've had six bairns already, aye? Ye dinna think I c
manage by now?"

"No arguing wi' you, is there?" he demanded.

"No," she said promptly. "So you'll stay."

"I'll come."

Jenny narrowed her eyes and gave him a long, level look.

"Ye're maybe the most stubborn gomerel between here a
Aberdeen, no?"

A smile spread across her brother's face as he looked up at h

"Maybe so," he said. He reached across and patted her heavi
belly. "And maybe no. But I'm coming. Send Fergus when i
time."

It was near dawn three days later that Fergus came panting
the slope to the cave, missing the trail in the dark, and maki
such a crashing through the gorse bushes that Jamie heard h
coming long before he reached the opening.

"Milord . . ." he began breathlessly as he emerged by t
head of the trail, but Jamie was already past the boy, pulling
cloak around his shoulders as he hurried down toward the hou

"But, milord . . ." Fergus's voice came behind him, panti
and frightened. "Milord, the soldiers . . ."

"Soldiers?" He stopped suddenly and turned, waiting imp
tiently for the French lad to make his way down the slope. "W
soldiers?" he demanded, as Fergus slithered the last few feet.

"English dragoons, milord. Milady sent me to tell you—on
account are you to leave the cave. One of the men saw the soldi
yesterday, camped near Dunmaglas."

"Damn."

"Yes, milord." Fergus sat down on a rock and fanned hims
narrow chest heaving as he caught his breath.

Jamie hesitated, irresolute. Every instinct fought against goi
back into the cave. His blood was heated by the surge of exci
ment caused by Fergus's appearance, and he rebelled at t

ought of meekly crawling back into hiding, like a grub seeking
efuge beneath its rock.

"Mmphm," he said. He glanced down at Fergus. The changing
ght was beginning to outline the boy's slender form against the
lackness of the gorse, but his face was still a pale smudge,
marked with a pair of darker smudges that were his eyes. A certain
uspicion was stirring in Jamie. Why had his sister sent Fergus at
nis odd hour?

If it had been necessary urgently to warn him about the
ragoons, it would have been safer to send the boy up during the
ight. If the need was not urgent, why not wait until the next
ight? The answer to that was obvious—because Jenny thought
he might not be able to send him word the next night.

"How is it with my sister?" he asked Fergus.

"Oh, well, milord, quite well!" The hearty tone of this assur-
nce confirmed all Jamie's suspicions.

"She's having the child, no?" he demanded.

"No, milord! Certainly not!"

Jamie reached down and clamped a hand on Fergus's shoulder.
'he bones felt small and fragile beneath his fingers, reminding
im uncomfortably of the rabbits he had broken for Jenny. None-
heless, he forced his grip to tighten. Fergus squirmed, trying to
ase away.

"Tell me the truth, man," Jamie said.

"No, milord! Truly!"

The grip tightened inexorably. "Did she tell you not to tell
ne?"

Jenny's prohibition must have been a literal one, for Fergus
nswered this question with evident relief.

"Yes, milord!"

"Ah." He relaxed his grip and Fergus sprang to his feet, now
alking volubly as he rubbed his scrawny shoulder.

"She said I must not tell you anything except about the soldiers,
nilord, for if I did, she would cut off my cods and boil them like
urnips and sausage!"

Jamie could not repress a smile at this threat.

"Short of food we may be," he assured his protégé, "but not
hat short." He glanced at the horizon, where a thin line of pink
howed pure and vivid behind the black pines' silhouette. "Come
long, then; it'll be full light in half an hour."

There was no hint of silent emptiness about the house th
dawn. Anyone with half an eye could see that things were not
usual at Lallybroch; the wash kettle sat on its plinth in the yar
with the fire gone out under it, full of cold water and sodd
clothes. Moaning cries from the barn—like someone being stra
gled—indicated that the sole remaining cow urgently requir
milking. An irritable blatting from the goat shed let him know th
the female inhabitants would like some similar attention as wel

As he came into the yard, three chickens ran past in a feathe
squawk, with Jehu the rat terrier in close pursuit. With a qui
dart, he leapt forward and booted the dog, catching it just und
the ribs. It flew into the air with a look of intense surprise on i
face, then, landing with a yip, picked itself up and made off.

He found the children, the older boys, Mary MacNab, and th
other housemaid, Sukie, all crammed into the parlor, under th
watchful eye of Mrs. Kirby, a stern and rock-ribbed widow, wh
was reading to them from the Bible.

" 'And Adam was not deceived, but the woman being deceiv
was in the transgression,' " read Mrs. Kirby. There was a lou
rolling scream from upstairs, which seemed to go on and on. Mr
Kirby paused for a moment, to allow everyone to appreciate
before resuming the reading. Her eyes, pale gray and wet as ra
oysters, flickered toward the ceiling, then rested with satisfactic
on the row of strained faces before her.

" 'Notwithstanding, she shall be saved in childbearing, if sh
continue in faith and charity and holiness with sobriety,' " sh
read. Kitty burst into hysterical sobbing and buried her head in h
sister's shoulder. Maggie Ellen was growing bright red benea
her freckles, while her elder brother had gone dead-white at th
scream.

"Mrs. Kirby," said Jamie. "Be still, if ye please."

The words were civil enough, but the look in his eyes must hav
been the one that Jehu saw just before his boot-assisted flight, fc
Mrs. Kirby gasped and dropped the Bible, which landed on th
floor with a papery thump.

Jamie bent and picked it up, then showed Mrs. Kirby his teet
The expression evidently was not successful as a smile, but ha
some effect nonetheless. Mrs. Kirby went quite pale, and put
hand to her ample bosom.

"Perhaps ye'd go to the kitchen and make yourself useful," l

id, with a jerk of his head that sent Sukie the kitchenmaid
uttling out like a windblown leaf. With considerably more dig-
ty, but no hesitation, Mrs. Kirby rose and followed her.

Heartened by this small victory, Jamie disposed of the parlor's
her occupants in short order, sending the widow Murray and her
ughters out to deal with the wash kettle, the smaller children out
catch chickens under the supervision of Mary MacNab. The
der lads departed, with obvious relief, to tend the stock.

The room empty at last, he stood for a moment, hesitating as to
hat to do next. He felt obscurely that he should stay in the house,
a guard, though he was acutely aware that he could—as Jenny
d said—do nothing to help, whatever happened. There was an
familiar mule hobbled in the dooryard; presumably the midwife
as upstairs with Jenny.

Unable to sit, he prowled restlessly around the parlor, the Bible
his hand, touching things. Jenny's bookshelf, battered and
arred from the last incursion of Redcoats, three months ago. The
g silver epergne. That was slightly dented, but had been too
avy to fit into a soldier's knapsack, and so had escaped the
fering of smaller objects. Not that the English had got so much;
e few truly valuable items, along with the tiny store of gold they
d left, were safely tucked away in the priest hole with Jared's
ine.

Hearing a prolonged moan from above, he glanced down invol-
tarily at the Bible in his hand. Not really wanting to, still he let
e book fall open, showing the page at the front where the mar-
ges, births, and deaths of the family were recorded.

The entries began with his parents' marriage. Brian Fraser and
len MacKenzie. The names and the date were written in his
other's fine round hand, with underneath, a brief notation in his
ther's firmer, blacker scrawl. *Marrit for love,* it said—a pointed
servation, in view of the next entry, which showed Willie's
rth, which had occurred scarcely two months past the date of the
arriage.

Jamie smiled, as always, at sight of the words, and glanced up at
e painting of himself, aged two, standing with Willie and Bran,
e huge deerhound. All that was left of Willie, who had died of
e smallpox at eleven. The painting had a slash through the can-
s—the work of a bayonet, he supposed, taking out its owner's
istration.

"And if ye hadna died," he said softly to the picture, "th
what?"

Then what, indeed. As he closed the book, his eye caught
last entry—*Caitlin Maisri Murray, born December 3, 1749, d*
December 3, 1749. Aye, if. If the Redcoats had not come
December 2, would Jenny have borne the child too early? If th
had had enough food, so that she, like the rest of them, would
more than skin and bones and the bulge of her belly, would t
have helped?

"No telling, is there?" he said to the painting. Willie's paint
hand rested on his shoulder; he had always felt safe, with Wil
standing behind him.

Another scream came from upstairs, and a spasm of fe
clenched his hands on the book.

"Pray for us, Brother," he whispered, and crossing himse
laid down the Bible and went out to the barn to help with
stock.

There was little to do here; Rabbie and Fergus between the
were more than able to take care of the few animals that remain
and Young Jamie, at ten, was big enough to be a substantial he
Looking about for something to do, Jamie gathered up an arm
of scattered hay and took it down the slope to the midwife's mu
When the hay was gone, the cow would have to be slaughter
unlike the goats, it couldn't get enough forage on the winter hi
to sustain it, even with the picked grass and weeds the sm
children brought in. With luck, the salted carcass would last the
through 'til spring.

As he came back into the barn, Fergus looked up from
manure fork.

"This is a proper midwife, of good repute?" Fergus demand
He thrust out a long chin aggressively. "Madame should not
entrusted to the care of a peasant, surely!"

"How should I know?" Jamie said testily. "D'ye think I h
anything to do wi' engaging midwives?" Mrs. Martin, the c
midwife who had delivered all previous Murray children, had di
—like so many others—during the famine in the year follow
Culloden. Mrs. Innes, the new midwife, was much younger;
hoped she had sufficient experience to know what she was doi

Rabbie seemed inclined to join the argument as well. He
owled blackly at Fergus. "Aye, and what d'ye mean 'peasant'?
're a peasant, too, or have ye not noticed?"

Fergus stared down his nose at Rabbie with some dignity, de-
ite the fact that he was forced to tilt his head backward in order
do so, he being several inches shorter than his friend.

"Whether I am a peasant or not is of no consequence," he said
ftily. "I am not a midwife, am I?"

"No, ye're a fiddle-ma-fyke!" Rabbie gave his friend a rough
ish, and with a sudden whoop of surprise, Fergus fell backward,
land heavily on the stable floor. In a flash, he was up. He lunged
Rabbie, who sat laughing on the edge of the manger, but Ja-
ie's hand snatched him by the collar and pulled him back.

"None of that," said his employer. "I willna have ye spoilin'
nat little hay's left." He set Fergus back on his feet, and to
stract him, asked, "And what d'ye ken of midwives anyway?"

"A great deal, milord." Fergus dusted himself off with elegant
stures. "Many of the ladies at Madame Elise's were brought to
·d while I was there—"

"I daresay they were," Jamie interjected dryly. "Or is it child-
·d ye mean?"

"Childbed, certainly. Why, I was born there myself!" The
ench boy puffed his narrow chest importantly.

"Indeed." Jamie's mouth quirked slightly. "Well, and I trust ye
ade careful observations at the time, so as to say how such
atters should be arranged?"

Fergus ignored this piece of sarcasm.

"Well, of course," he said, matter-of-factly, "the midwife will
turally have put a knife beneath the bed, to cut the pain."

"I'm none so sure she did that," Rabbie muttered. "At least it
esna sound much like it." Most of the screaming was inaudible
om the barn, but not all of it.

"And an egg should be blessed with holy water and put at the
ot of the bed, so that the woman shall bring forth the child
sily," Fergus continued, oblivious. He frowned.

"I gave the woman an egg myself, but she did not appear to
ow what to do with it. And I had been keeping it especially for
e last month, too," he added plaintively, "since the hens
arcely lay anymore. I wanted to be sure of having one when it
is needed.

"Now, following the birth," he went on, losing his doubts the enthusiasm of his lecture, "the midwife must brew a tea of th placenta, and give it to the woman to drink, so that her milk w flow strongly."

Rabbie made a faint retching sound. "Of the *afterbirth*, mean?" he said disbelievingly. "God!"

Jamie felt a bit queasy at this exhibition of modern medic knowledge himself.

"Aye, well," he said to Rabbie, striving for casualness, "the eat frogs, ye know. And snails. I suppose maybe afterbirth isna strange, considering." Privately, he wondered whether it mig not be long before they were all eating frogs and snails, b thought that a speculation better kept to himself.

Rabbie made mock puking noises. "Christ, who'd be Frenchie!"

Fergus, standing close to Rabbie, whirled and shot out a ligh ning fist. Fergus was small and slender for his age, but strong f all that, and with a deadly aim for a man's weak points, knowled acquired as a juvenile pickpocket on the streets of Paris. The blo caught Rabbie squarely in the wind, and he doubled over with sound like a stepped-on pig's bladder.

"Speak with respect of your betters, if you please," Fergus sa haughtily. Rabbie's face turned several shades of red and h mouth opened and closed like a fish's, as he struggled to get h breath back. His eyes bulged with a look of intense surprise, an he looked so ridiculous that it was a struggle for Jamie not laugh, despite his worry over Jenny and his irritation at the boy squabbling.

"Will ye wee doiters no keep your paws off—" he began, whe he was interrupted by a cry from Young Jamie, who had until no been silent, fascinated by the conversation.

"What?" Jamie whirled, hand going automatically to the pist he carried whenever he left the cave, but there was not, as he ha half-expected, an English patrol in the stableyard.

"What the hell is it?" he demanded. Then, following Youn Jamie's pointing finger, he saw them. Three small black speck drifting across the brown crumple of dead vines in the potato fiel

"Ravens," he said softly, and felt the hair rise on the back his neck. For those birds of war and slaughter to come to a hou

uring a birth was the worst sort of ill luck. One of the filthy beasts as actually settling on the rooftree, as he watched.

With no conscious thought, he took the pistol from his belt and raced the muzzle across his forearm, sighting carefully. It was a ong shot, from the door of the stable to the rooftree, and sighted pward, too. Still . . .

The pistol jerked in his hand and the raven exploded in a cloud f black feathers. Its two companions shot into the air as though own there by the explosion, and flapped madly away, their parse cries fading quickly on the winter air.

"Mon Dieu!" Fergus exclaimed. *"C'est bien, ça!"*

"Aye, bonny shooting, sir." Rabbie, still red-faced and a little reathless, had recovered himself in time to see the shot. Now he odded toward the house, pointing with his chin. "Look, sir, is at the midwife?"

It was. Mrs. Innes poked her head out of the second-story win- ow, fair hair flying loose as she leaned out to peer into the yard elow. Perhaps she had been drawn by the sound of the shot, aring some trouble. Jamie stepped into the stableyard and waved the window to reassure her.

"It's all right," he shouted. "Only an accident." He didn't ean to mention the ravens, lest the midwife tell Jenny.

"Come up!" she shouted, ignoring this. "The bairn's born, and our sister wants ye!"

Jenny opened one eye, blue and slightly slanted like his own. "So ye came, aye?"

"I thought someone should be here—if only to pray for ye," he id gruffly.

She closed the eye and a small smile curved her lips. She oked, he thought, very like a painting he had seen in France—an d one by some Italian fellow, but a good picture, nonetheless.

"Ye're a silly fool—and I'm glad of it," she said softly. She ened her eyes and glanced down at the swaddled bundle she ld in the crook of her arm.

"D'ye want to see him?"

"Oh, a him, is it?" With hands experienced by years of un- ehood, he lifted the tiny package and cuddled it against himself, shing back the flap of blanket that shaded its face.

Its eyes were closed tight shut, the lashes not visible in the dee crease of the eyelids. The eyelids themselves lay at a sharp ang above the flushed smooth rounds of the cheeks, giving promi that it might—in this one recognizable feature, at least—resemb its mother.

The head was oddly lumpy, with a lopsided appearance th made Jamie think uncomfortably of a kicked-in melon, but t small fat mouth was relaxed and peaceful, the moist pink underl quivering faintly with the snore attendant on the exhaustion being born.

"Hard work, was it?" he said, speaking to the child, but it w the mother who answered him.

"Aye, it was," Jenny said. "There's whisky in the armoire— will ye fetch me a glass?" Her voice was hoarse and she had clear her throat before finishing the request.

"Whisky? Should ye not be having ale wi' eggs beaten up it?" he asked, repressing with some difficulty a mental vision Fergus's suggestion of appropriate sustenance for newly deliver mothers.

"Whisky," his sister said definitely. "When ye were lyi downstairs crippled and your leg killin' ye, did I give ye ale w eggs beaten up in it?"

"Ye fed me stuff a damn sight worse than that," her broth said, with a grin, "but ye're right, ye gave me whisky, too." I laid the sleeping child carefully on the coverlet, and turned to g the whisky.

"Has he a name, yet?" he asked, nodding toward the baby as I poured out a generous cup of the amber liquid.

"I'll call him Ian, for his da." Jenny's hand rested gently for moment on the rounded skull, lightly furred with a gold-brow fuzz. A pulse beat visibly in the soft spot on top; it seemed hi eously fragile to Jamie, but the midwife had assured him the bal was a fine, lusty lad, and he supposed he must take her word for Moved by an obscure impulse to protect that nakedly exposed so spot, he picked up the baby once more, pulling the blanket up ov its head.

"Mary MacNab told me about you and Mrs. Kirby," Jen remarked, sipping. "Pity I didna see it—she said the wretch auld besom nearly swallowed her tongue when ye spoke to her.

Jamie smiled in return, gently patting the baby's back as it la against his shoulder. Dead asleep, the little body lay inert as a boneless ham, a soft comforting weight.

"Too bad she didn't. How can ye stand the woman, living in the same house wi' ye? I'd strangle her, were I here every day."

His sister snorted and closed her eyes, tilting her head back to let the whisky slide down her throat.

"Ah, folk fash ye as much as ye let them; I dinna let her, much. Still," she added, opening her eyes, "I canna say as I'll be sorry to be rid of her. I have it in my mind to palm her off on auld Kettrick, down at Broch Mordha. His wife and his daughter both died last year, and he'll be wanting someone to do for him."

"Aye, but if I were Samuel Kettrick, I'd take the widow Murray," Jamie observed, "not the widow Kirby."

"Peggy Murray's already provided for," his sister assured him. "She'll wed Duncan Gibbons in the spring."

"That's fast work for Duncan," he said, a little surprised. Then a thought occurred to him, and he grinned at her. "Does either o' them know it yet?"

"No," she said, grinning back. Then the smile faded into a speculative look.

"Unless you were thinking of Peggy yourself, that is?"

"Me?" Jamie was as startled as if she had suddenly suggested he might wish to jump out of the second-story window.

"She's only five and twenty," Jenny pursued. "Young enough for more bairns, and a good mother."

"How much of that whisky have ye had?" Her brother bent forward and pretended to examine the level of the decanter, cupping the baby's head in one palm to prevent it wobbling. He straightened up and gave his sister a look of mild exasperation.

"I'm living like an animal in a cave, and ye wish me to take a wife?" He felt suddenly hollow inside. To prevent her seeing that the suggestion had upset him, he rose and walked up and down the room, making unnecessary small humming noises to the bundle in his arms.

"How long is it since ye've lain wi' a woman, Jamie?" his sister asked conversationally behind him. Shocked, he turned on his heel to stare at her.

"What the hell sort of question is that to ask a man?"

"You've not gone wi' any of the unwed lasses between Lallybroch and Broch Mordha," she went on, paying no attention.

"Or I'd have heard of it. None of the widows, either, I dinn
think?" She paused delicately.

"Ye know damn well I haven't," he said shortly. He could fee
his cheeks flushing with annoyance.

"Why not?" his sister asked bluntly.

"Why *not*?" He stared at her, his mouth slightly open. "Hav
ye lost your senses? What d'ye think, I'm the sort of man woul
slink about from house to house, bedding any woman who didn
drive me out wi' a girdle in her hand?"

"As if they would. No, you're a good man, Jamie." Jenn
smiled, half sadly. "Ye wouldna take advantage of any woman
Ye'd marry first, no?"

"No!" he said violently. The baby twitched and made a sleep
sound, and he transferred it automatically to his other shoulder
patting, as he glared at his sister. "I dinna mean to marry again, s
ye just abandon all thought of matchmaking, Jenny Murray!
willna have it, d'ye hear?"

"Oh, I hear," she said, unperturbed. She pushed herself highe
on the pillow, so as to look him in the eye.

"Ye mean to live a monk to the end of your days?" she aske
"Go to your grave wi' no son to bury you or bless your name?"

"Mind your own business, damn ye!" Heart pounding, h
turned his back on her and strode to the window, where he stoo
staring sightlessly out over the stableyard.

"I ken ye mourn Claire." His sister's voice came softly fror
behind him. "D'ye think I could forget Ian, if he doesna com
back? But it's time ye went on, Jamie. Ye dinna think Claire wou
mean ye to live alone all your life, with no one to comfort ye o
bear your children?"

He didn't answer for a long time, just stood, feeling the so
heat of the small fuzzy head pressed against the side of his nec
He could see himself dimly in the misted glass, a tall dirty gang
of a man, the round white bundle incongruous beneath his ow
grim face.

"She was with child," he said softly at last, speaking to th
reflection. "When she—when I lost her." How else could he p
it? There was no way to tell his sister where Claire was—where h
hoped she was. That he could not think of another woman, hopin
that Claire still lived, even knowing her truly lost to him for goo

There was a long silence from the bed. Then Jenny said quietly, "Is that why ye came today?"

He sighed and turned sideways toward her, leaning his head against the cool glass. His sister was lying back, her dark hair loose on the pillow, eyes gone soft as she looked at him.

"Aye, maybe," he said. "I couldna help my wife; I suppose I thought I might help you. Not that I could," he added, with some bitterness. "I am as useless to you as I was to her."

Jenny stretched out a hand to him, face filled with distress. "Jamie, _mo chridhe_," she said, but then stopped, eyes widening in sudden alarm as a splintering crash and the sound of screams came from the house below.

"Holy Mary!" she said, growing even whiter. "It's the English!"

"Christ." It was as much a prayer as an exclamation of surprise. He glanced quickly from the bed to the window, judging the possibilities of hiding versus those of escape. The sounds of booted feet were already on the stair.

"The cupboard, Jamie!" Jenny whispered urgently, pointing. Without hesitation, he stepped into the armoire, and pulled the door to behind him.

The door of the chamber sprang open with a crash a moment later, to be filled with a red-coated figure in a cocked hat, holding a drawn sword before him. The Captain of dragoons paused, and darted his eyes all round the chamber, finally settling on the small figure in the bed.

"Mrs. Murray?" he said.

Jenny struggled to pull herself upright.

"I am. And what in flaming hell are ye doing in my house?" she demanded. Her face was pale and shiny with sweat, and her arms trembled, but she held her chin up and glared at the man. "Get out!"

Disregarding her, the man moved into the room and over to the window; Jamie could see his indistinct form disappear past the edge of the wardrobe, then reappear, back turned as he spoke to Jenny.

"One of my scouts reported hearing a shot from the vicinity of this house, not long since. Where are your men?"

"I have none." Her trembling arms would not support her longer, and Jamie saw his sister ease herself back, collapsing on the pillows. "You've taken my husband already—my eldest son no more than ten." She did not mention Rabbie or Fergus; boys their age were old enough to be treated—or mistreated—as men should the Captain take the notion. With luck, they would have taken to their heels at the first sight of the English.

The Captain was a hard-bitten man of middle age, and no overly given to credulity.

"The keeping of weapons in the Highlands is a serious of fense," he said, and turned to the soldier who had come into the room behind him. "Search the house, Jenkins."

He had to raise his voice in the giving of the order, for there was a rising commotion in the stairwell. As Jenkins turned to leave the room, Mrs. Innes, the midwife, burst past the soldier who tried to bar her way.

"Leave the poor lady alone!" she cried, facing the Captain with fists clenched at her sides. The midwife's voice shook and her hair was coming down from its snood, but she stood her ground. "Get out, ye wretches! Leave her be!"

"I am not mistreating your mistress," the Captain said, with some irritation, evidently mistaking Mrs. Innes for one of the maids. "I am merely—"

"And her not delivered but an hour since! It isna decent eve for ye to lay eyes on her, so much as—"

"Delivered?" The Captain's voice sharpened, and he glance from the midwife to the bed in sudden interest. "You have borne child, Mrs. Murray? Where is the infant?"

The infant in question stirred inside its wrappings, disturbed the tightened grip of its horror-stricken uncle.

From the depths of the wardrobe, he could see his sister's fac white to the lips and set like stone.

"The child is dead," she said.

The midwife's mouth dropped open in shock, but luckily the Captain's attention was riveted on Jenny.

"Oh?" he said slowly. "Was it—"

"Mama!" The cry of anguish came from the doorway as Young Jamie broke free of a soldier's grip and hurled himself at h mother. "Mama, the baby's dead? No, no!" Sobbing, he flur himself on his knees and buried his head in the bedclothes.

As though to refute his brother's statement, baby Ian gave ev dence of his living state by kicking his legs with considerab vigor against his uncle's ribs and emitting a series of small snuf-fling grunts, which fortunately went unheard in the commotion outside.

Jenny was trying to comfort Young Jamie, Mrs. Innes was fu-tilely attempting to raise the boy, who kept a death grip on his mother's sleeve, the Captain was vainly trying to make himself heard above Young Jamie's grief-stricken wails, and over all, the muted sound of boots and shouting vibrated through the house.

Jamie rather thought the Captain was inquiring as to the loca-tion of the infant's body. He clutched the body in question closer, joggling it in an attempt to prevent any disposition on its part to cry. His other hand went to the hilt of his dirk, but it was a vain gesture; it was doubtful that even cutting his own throat would be of help, if the wardrobe was opened.

Baby Ian made an irascible noise, suggesting that he disliked being joggled. With visions of the house in flames and the inhabit-ants slaughtered, the noise sounded as loud to Jamie as his elder nephew's anguished howls.

"You did it!" Young Jamie had gotten to his feet, face wet and swollen with tears and rage, and was advancing on the Captain, curly black head lowered like a small ram's. "You killed my brother, ye English prick!"

The Captain was somewhat taken aback by this sudden attack, and actually took a step back, blinking at the boy. "No, boy, you're quite mistaken. Why, I only—"

"Prick! Cod! *A mhic an diabhoil!*" Entirely beside himself, Young Jamie was stalking the Captain, yelling every obscenity he had ever heard used, in Gaelic or English.

"Enh," said baby Ian in the elder Jamie's ear. "Enh, enh!" This sounded very much like the preliminary to a full-fledged screech, and in a panic, Jamie let go of his dirk and thrust his thumb into the soft, moist opening from which the sounds were issuing. The baby's toothless gums clamped on to his thumb with a ferocity that nearly made him exclaim aloud.

"Get out! Get out! Get out or I'll kill ye!" Young Jamie was screaming at the Captain, face contorted with rage. The Redcoat looked helplessly at the bed, as though to ask Jenny to call off this implacable small foe, but she lay as though dead with her eyes closed.

"I shall wait for my men downstairs," the Captain said, with

what dignity he could, and withdrew, shutting the door hasti
behind him. Deprived of his enemy, Young Jamie fell to the floo
and collapsed into helpless weeping.

Through the crack in the door, Jamie saw Mrs. Innes look
Jenny, mouth opening to ask a question. Jenny shot up from th
bedclothes like Lazarus, scowling ferociously, finger pressed
her lips to enjoin silence. Baby Ian champed viciously at th
thumb, growling at its failure to yield any sustenance.

Jenny swung herself to the side of the bed and sat there, waitin
The sounds of the soldiers below throbbed and eddied through th
house. Jenny was shaking with weakness, but she reached out
hand toward the armoire where her men lay hidden.

Jamie drew a deep breath and braced himself. It would have t
be risked; his hand and wrist were wet with saliva, and the baby
growls of frustration were growing louder.

He stumbled from the wardrobe, drenched with sweat, an
thrust the infant at Jenny. Baring her breast with a single wrencl
she pressed the small head to her nipple, and bent over the tin
bundle, as though to protect it. The beginnings of a squawk disap
peared into the muffled sounds of vigorous sucking, and Jamie s
down on the floor quite suddenly, feeling as though someone ha
run a sword behind his knees.

Young Jamie had sat up at the sudden opening of the wardrob
and now sat spraddled against the door, his face blank with bewi
dered shock as he looked from his mother to his uncle and bac
again. Mrs. Innes knelt beside him, whispering urgently in his ea
but no sign of comprehension showed on the small, tear-streake
face.

By the time shouts and the creaking of harness outside bet
kened the soldiers' departure, Young Ian lay replete and snoring i
his mother's arms. Jamie stood by the window, just out of sigh
watching them go.

The room was silent, save for the liquid noise of Mrs. Inne
drinking whisky. Young Jamie sat close against his mother, chee
pressed to her shoulder. She had not looked up once since takin
the baby, and still sat, head lowered over the child in her lap, he
black hair hiding her face.

Jamie stepped forward and touched her shoulder. The warmt
of her seemed shocking, as though cold dread were his natur

ate and the touch of another person somehow foreign and unnat-
ral.

"I'll go to the priest hole," he said softly, "and to the cave
hen it's dark."

Jenny nodded, but without looking up at him. There were sev-
al white hairs among the black, he saw, glinting silver by the
arting down the center of her head.

"I think . . . I should not come down again," he said at last.
For a time."

Jenny said nothing, but nodded once more.

6

Being Now Justifie
by His Bloo

As it was, he did come down to the house once more. For tw
months, he stayed close hidden in the cave, scarcely darir
to come out at night to hunt, for the English soldiers we
still in the district, quartered at Comar. The troops went out by da
in small patrols of eight or ten, combing the countryside, lootir
what little there was to steal, destroying what they could not us
And all with the blessing of the English Crown.

A path led close by the base of the hill where his cavern w
concealed. No more than a rude track, it had begun as a deer pat
and still largely served that use, though it was a foolish stag th
would venture within smelling distance of the cave. Still, som
times when the wind was right, he would see a small group of th
red deer on the path, or find fresh spoor in the exposed mud of th
track next day.

It was helpful as well for such people as had business on th
mountainside—few enough as those were. The wind had bee
blowing downwind from the cave, and he had no expectation
seeing deer. He had been lying on the ground just within the ca
entrance, where enough light filtered through the overhangir
screen of gorse and rowan for him to read on fine days. There we
not a great many books, but Jared managed still to smuggle a fe
with his gifts from France.

This violent rain forced me to a new work, viz., to cut a hole
through my new fortification, like a sink, to let the water go
out, which would else have drowned my cave. After I had

*been in my cave some time, and found still no more shocks of
the earthquake follow, I began to be more composed; and
now, to support my spirits, which indeed wanted it very much,
I went to my little store and took a small sup of rum, which
however, I did then and always very sparingly, knowing I
could have no more when that was gone.*

*It continued raining all that night, and great part of the
next day, so that I could not stir abroad; but my mind being
more composed, I began to think . . .*

The shadows across the page moved as the bushes above him
stirred. Instincts attuned, he caught the shift of the wind at once—
and on it, the sound of voices.

He sprang to his feet, hand on the dirk that never left his side.
Barely pausing to put the book carefully on its ledge, he grasped
the knob of granite that he used as a handhold and pulled himself
up into the steep narrow crevice that formed the cave's entrance.

The bright flash of red and metal on the path below hit him with
a blow of shock and annoyance. Damn. He had little fear that any
of the soldiers would leave the path—they were poorly equipped
for making their way even through the normal stretches of open,
spongy peat and heather, let alone an overgrown, brambly slope
like this—but having them so close meant he could not risk leaving the cave before dark, even to get water or relieve himself. He
cast a quick glance at his water jug, knowing as he did so that it
was nearly empty.

A shout pulled his attention back to the track below, and he
nearly lost his grip on the rock. The soldiers had bunched themselves around a small figure, humped under the weight of a small
cask it bore on its shoulder. Fergus, on his way up with a cask of
fresh-brewed ale. Damn, and damn again. He could have done
with that ale; it had been months since he'd had any.

The wind had changed again, so he caught only small snatches
of words, but the small figure seemed to be arguing with the
soldier in front of him, gesticulating violently with its free hand.

"Idiot!" said Jamie, under his breath. "Give it to them and
begone, ye wee clot!"

One soldier made a two-handed grab at the cask, and missed as
the small dark-haired figure jumped nimbly back. Jamie smacked
himself on the forehead with exasperation. Fergus could never

resist insolence when confronted with authority—especially English authority.

The small figure now was skipping backward, shouting something at his pursuers.

"Fool!" Jamie said violently. "Drop it and run!"

Instead of either dropping the cask or running, Fergus, apparently sure of his own speed, turned his back on the soldiers and waggled his rump insultingly at them. Sufficiently incensed to risk their footing in the soggy vegetation, several of the Redcoats jumped the path to follow.

Jamie saw their leader raise an arm and shout in warning. It had evidently dawned on him that Fergus might be a decoy, trying to lead them into ambush. But Fergus too was shouting, and evidently the soldiers knew enough gutter French to interpret what he was saying, for while several of the men halted at their leader's shout, four of the soldiers hurled themselves at the dancing boy.

There was a scuffle and more shouting as Fergus dodged, twisting like an eel between the soldiers. In all the commotion and above the whining wind, Jamie could not have heard the rush of the saber being drawn from its scabbard, but ever after felt as though he had, as though the faint swish and ring of drawn metal had been the first inkling of disaster. It seemed to ring in his ear whenever he remembered the scene—and he remembered it for a very long time.

Perhaps it was something in the attitudes of the soldiers, an irritableness of mood that communicated itself to him in the cave. Perhaps only the sense of doom that had clung to him since Culloden, as though everything in his vicinity were tainted; at risk by virtue only of being near him. Whether he had heard the sound of the saber or not, his body had tensed itself to spring before he saw the silver arc of the blade swing through the air.

It moved almost lazily, slowly enough for his brain to have tracked its arc, deduced its target, and shouted, wordless, *no!* Surely it moved slowly enough that he could have darted down into the midst of the swarming men, seized the wrist that wielded the sword and twisted the deadly length of metal free, to tumble harmless to the ground.

The conscious part of his brain told him this was nonsense, even as it froze his hands around the granite knob, anchoring him gainst the overwhelming impulse to heave himself out of the arth and run forward.

You can't, it said to him, a thready whisper under the fury and he horror that filled him. *He has done this for you; you cannot take it senseless. You can't,* it said, cold as death beneath the earing rush of futility that drowned him. *You can do nothing.*

And he did nothing, nothing but watch, as the blade completed ts lazy swing, crashed home with a small, almost inconsequential hunk! and the disputed cask tumbled end over end over end down he slope of the burn, its final splash lost in the merry gurgle of rown water far below.

The shouting ceased abruptly in shocked silence. He scarcely eard when it resumed; it sounded so much like the roaring in his ars. His knees gave way, and he realized dimly that he was about o faint. His vision darkened into reddish black, shot with stars and treaks of light—but not even the encroaching dark would blot out he final sight of Fergus's hand, that small and deft and clever ickpocket's hand, lying still in the mud of the track, palm turned pward in supplication.

He waited for forty-eight long, dragging hours before Rabbie MacNab came to whistle on the path below the cave.

"How is he?" he said without preliminary.

"Mrs. Jenny says he'll be all right," Rabbie answered. His oung face was pale and drawn; plainly he had not yet recovered rom the shock of his friend's accident. "She says he's not fevered, and there's no trace of rot yet in the"—he swallowed audibly—"in the . . . stump."

"The soldiers took him down to the house, then?" Not waiting or an answer, he was already making his way down the hillside.

"Aye, they were all amoil wi' it. I think"—Rabbie paused to distentangle his shirt from a clinging brier, and had to hurry to atch up with his employer—"I think they were sorry about it. he Captain said so, at least. And he gave Mrs. Jenny a gold overeign—for Fergus."

"Oh, aye?" Jamie said. "Verra generous." And did not speak gain, until they reached the house.

* * *

Fergus was lying in state in the nursery, ensconced in a bed ▐
the window. His eyes were closed when Jamie entered the roo▐
long lashes lying softly against thin cheeks. Seen without its cu▐
tomary animation, his usual array of grimaces and poses, his fa▐
looked quite different. The slightly beaked nose above the lon▐
mobile mouth gave him a faintly aristocratic air, and the bon▐
hardening beneath the skin gave some promise that his face mig▐
one day pass from boyish charm to outright handsomeness.

Jamie moved toward the bed, and the dark lashes lifted at on▐

"Milord," Fergus said, and a weak smile restored his face ▐
once to its familiar contours. "You are safe here?"

"God, laddie, I'm sorry." Jamie sank to his knees by the be▐
He could scarcely bear to look at the slender forearm that l▐
across the quilt, its frail bandaged wrist ending in nothing, b▐
forced himself to grip Fergus's shoulder in greeting, and rub▐
palm gently over the shock of dark hair.

"Does it hurt much?" he asked.

"No, milord," Fergus said. Then a sudden belying twinge ▐
pain crossed his features, and he grinned shamefacedly. "We▐
not so much. And Madame has been most generous with t▐
whisky."

There was a tumbler full of it on the sidetable, but no more th▐
a thimbleful had been drunk. Fergus, weaned on French wine, d▐
not really like the taste of whisky.

"I'm sorry," Jamie said again. There was nothing else to sa▐
Nothing he *could* say, for the tightening in his throat. He look▐
hastily down, knowing that it would upset Fergus to see him wee▐

"Ah, milord, do not trouble yourself." There was a note of t▐
old mischief in Fergus's voice. "Me, I have been fortunate."

Jamie swallowed hard before replying.

"Aye, you're alive—and thank God for it!"

"Oh, beyond that, milord!" He glanced up to see Fergus sm▐
ing, though still very pale. "Do you not recall our agreeme▐
milord?"

"Agreement?"

"Yes, when you took me into your service in Paris. You told ▐
then that should I be arrested and executed, you would ha▐
Masses said for my soul for the space of a year." The remaini▐
hand fluttered toward the battered greenish medal that hung ab▐

his neck—St. Dismas, patron saint of thieves. "But if I should lose an ear or a hand while doing your service—"

"I would support you for the rest of your life." Jamie was unsure whether to laugh or cry, and contented himself with patting the hand that now lay quiet on the quilt. "Aye, I remember. You may trust me to keep the bargain."

"Oh, I have always trusted you, milord," Fergus assured him. Clearly he was growing tired; the pale cheeks were even whiter than they had been, and the shock of black hair fell back against the pillow. "So I am fortunate," he murmured, still smiling. "For in one stroke, I am become a gentleman of leisure, *non*?"

Jenny was waiting for him when he left Fergus's room.

"Come down to the priest hole wi' me," he said, taking her by the elbow. "I need to talk wi' ye a bit, and I shouldna stay in the open longer."

She followed him without comment, down to the stone-floored back hall that separated kitchen and pantry. Set into the flags of the floor was a large wooden panel, perforated with drilled holes, apparently mortared into the floorstones. Theoretically, this gave air to the root cellar below, and in fact—should any suspicious person choose to investigate, the root cellar, reached by a sunken door outside the house, did have just such a panel set into its ceiling.

What was not apparent was that the panel also gave light and air to a small priest hole that had been built just behind the root cellar, which could be reached by pulling up the panel, mortared frame and all, to reveal a short ladder leading down into the tiny room.

It was no more than five feet square, equipped with nothing in the way of furniture beyond a rude bench, a blanket, and a chamber pot. A large jug of water and a small box of hard biscuit completed the chamber's accoutrements. It had in fact been added to the house only within the last few years, and therefore was not really a priest hole, as no priest had occupied it or was likely to. A hole it definitely was, though.

Two people could occupy the hole only by sitting side by side on the bench, and Jamie sat down beside his sister as soon as he had replaced the panel overhead and descended the ladder. He sat still for a moment, then took a breath and started.

"I canna bear it anymore," he said. He spoke so softly that Jenny was forced to bend her head close to hear him, like a priest receiving some penitent's confession. "I can't. I must go."

They sat so close together that he could feel the rise and fall of her breast as she breathed. Then she reached out and took hold of his hand, her small firm fingers tight on his.

"Will ye try France again, then?" He had tried to escape to France twice before, thwarted each time by the tight watch the English placed on all ports. No disguise was sufficient for a man of his remarkable height and coloring.

He shook his head. "No. I shall let myself be captured."

"Jamie!" In her agitation, Jenny allowed her voice to rise momentarily, then lowered it again in response to the warning squeeze of his hand.

"Jamie, ye canna do that!" she said, lower. "Christ, man, ye'll be hangit!"

He kept his head bent as though in thought, but shook it, not hesitating.

"I think not." He glanced at his sister, then quickly away. "Claire—she had the Sight." As good an explanation as any, he thought, if not quite the truth. "She saw what would happen at Culloden—she knew. And she told me what would come after."

"Ah," said Jenny softly. "I wondered. So that was why she bade me plant potatoes—and build this place."

"Aye." He gave his sister's hand a small squeeze, then let go and turned slightly on the narrow seat to face her. "She told me that the Crown would go on hunting Jacobite traitors for some time—and they have," he added wryly. "But that after the first few years, they would no longer execute the men that were captured—only imprison them."

"Only!" his sister echoed. "If ye mun go, Jamie, take to the heather then, but to give yourself up to an English prison, whether they'll hang ye or no—"

"Wait." His hand on her arm stopped her. "I havena told it all to ye yet. I dinna mean just to walk up to the English and surrender. There's a goodly price on my head, no? Be a shame to let that go to waste, d'ye not think?" He tried to force a smile in his voice; she heard it and glanced sharply up at him.

"Holy Mother," she whispered. "So ye mean to have someone betray ye?"

"Seemingly, aye." He had decided upon the plan, alone in the cave, but it had not seemed quite real until now. "I thought perhaps Joe Fraser would be best for it."

Jenny rubbed her fist hard against her lips. She was quick; he knew she had grasped the plan at once—and all its implications.

"But Jamie," she whispered. "Even if they dinna hang ye outright—and that's the hell of a risk to take—Jamie, ye could be killed when they take ye!"

His shoulders slumped suddenly, under the weight of misery and exhaustion.

"God, Jenny," he said, "d'ye think I care?"

There was a long silence before she answered.

"No, I don't," she said. "And I canna say as I blame ye, either." She paused a moment, to steady her voice. "But *I* still care." Her fingers gently touched the back of his head, stroking his hair. "So ye'll mind yourself, won't ye, clot-heid?"

The ventilation panel overhead darkened momentarily, and there was the tapping sound of light footsteps. One of the kitchenmaids, on her way to the pantry, perhaps. Then the dim light came back, and he could see Jenny's face once more.

"Aye," he whispered at last. "I'll mind."

It took more than two months to complete the arrangements. When at last word came, it was full spring.

He sat on his favorite rock, near the cave's entrance, watching the evening stars come out. Even in the worst of the year after Culloden, he had always been able to find a moment of peace at this time of the day. As the daylight faded, it was as though objects became faintly lit from within, so they stood outlined against sky or ground, perfect and sharp in every detail. He could see the shape of a moth, invisible in the light, now limned in the dusk with a triangle of deeper shadow that made it stand out from the trunk it sat upon. In a moment, it would take wing.

He looked out across the valley, trying to stretch his eyes as far as the black pines that edged the distant cliffside. Then up, among the stars. Orion there, striding stately over the horizon. And the Pleiades, barely visible in the darkening sky. It might be his last sight of the sky for some time, and he meant to enjoy it. He thought of prison, of bars and locks and solid walls, and remem-

bered Fort William. Wentworth Prison. The Bastille. Walls o
stone, four feet thick, that blocked all air and light. Filth, stenc
hunger, entombment . . .

He shrugged such thoughts away. He had chosen his way, an
was satisfied with it. Still, he searched the sky, looking for Tauru
Not the prettiest of constellations, but his own. Born under th
sign of the bull, stubborn and strong. Strong enough, he hoped,
do what he intended.

Among the growing night sounds, there was a sharp, high whi
tle. It might have been the homing song of a curlew on the loc
but he recognized the signal. Someone was coming up the path—
friend.

It was Mary MacNab, who had become kitchenmaid at La
lybroch, after the death of her husband. Usually it was her so
Rabbie, or Fergus, who brought him food and news, but she ha
come a few times before.

She had brought a basket, unusually well supplied, with a col
roast partridge, fresh bread, several young green onions, a bunc
of early cherries, and a flask of ale. Jamie examined the bount
then looked up with a wry smile.

"My farewell feast, eh?"

She nodded, silent. She was a small woman, dark hair heavi
streaked with gray, and her face lined by the difficulties of lif
Still, her eyes were soft and brown, and her lips still full and gent
curved.

He realized that he was staring at her mouth, and hastily turne
again to the basket.

"Lord, I'll be so full I'll not be able to move. Even a cake, nov
However did ye ladies manage that?"

She shrugged—she wasn't a great chatterer, Mary MacNab—
and taking the basket from him, proceeded to lay the meal on th
wooden tabletop, balanced on stones. She laid places for both
them. This was nothing out of the ordinary; she had supped wi
him before, to give him the gossip of the district while they at
Still, if this was his last meal before leaving Lallybroch, he wa
surprised that neither his sister nor the boys had come to share
Perhaps the farmhouse had visitors that would make it difficult f
them to leave undetected.

He gestured politely for her to sit first, before taking his ow
place, cross-legged on the hard dirt floor.

"Ye've spoken wi' Joe Fraser? Where is it to be, then?" he asked, taking a bite of cold partridge.

She told him the details of the plan; a horse would be brought before dawn, and he would ride out of the narrow valley by way of the pass. Then turn, cross the rocky foothills and come down, back into the valley by Feesyhant's Burn, as though he were coming home. The English would meet him somewhere between Struy and Eskadale, most likely at Midmains; it was a good place for an ambush, for the glen rose steeply there on both sides, but with a wooded patch by the stream where several men could conceal themselves.

After the meal, she packed the basket tidily, leaving out enough food for a small breakfast before his dawn leaving. He expected her to go then, but she did not. She rummaged in the crevice where he kept his bedding, spread it neatly upon the floor, turned back the blankets and knelt beside the pallet, hands folded on her lap.

He leaned back against the wall of the cave, arms folded. He looked down at the crown of her bowed head in exasperation.

"Oh, like that, is it?" he demanded. "And whose idea was this? Yours, or my sister's?"

"Does it matter?" She was composed, her hands perfectly still on her lap, her dark hair smooth in its snood.

He shook his head and bent down to pull her to her feet.

"No, it doesna matter, because it's no going to happen. I appreciate your meaning, but—"

His speech was interrupted by her kiss. Her lips *were* as soft as they looked. He grasped her firmly by both wrists and pushed her away from him.

"No!" he said. "It isna necessary, and I dinna want to do it." He was uncomfortably aware that his body did not agree at all with his assessments of necessity, and still more uncomfortable at the knowledge that his breeches, too small and worn thin, made the magnitude of the disagreement obvious to anyone who cared to look. The slight smile curving those full, sweet lips suggested that she was looking.

He turned her toward the entrance and gave her a light push, to which she responded by stepping aside and reaching behind her for the fastenings to her skirt.

"Don't do that!" he exclaimed.

"How d'ye mean to stop me?" she asked, stepping out of the

garment and folding it tidily over the single stool. Her slender
fingers went to the laces of her bodice.

"If ye won't leave, then I'll have to," he replied with decision.
He whirled on his heel and headed for the cave entrance, when he
heard her voice behind him.

"My lord!" she said.

He stopped, but did not turn around. "It isna suitable to call me
that," he said.

"Lallybroch is yours," she said. "And will be so long as ye
live. If ye're its laird, I'll call ye so."

"It isna mine. The estate belongs to Young Jamie."

"It isna Young Jamie that's doing what you are," she answered
with decision. "And it isna your sister that's asked me to do what
I'm doin'. Turn round."

He turned, reluctantly. She stood barefoot in her shift, her hair
loose over her shoulders. She was thin, as they all were these days,
but her breasts were larger than he had thought, and the nipples
showed prominently through the thin fabric. The shift was as worn
as her other garments, frayed at the hem and shoulders, almost
transparent in spots. He closed his eyes.

He felt a light touch on his arm, and willed himself to stand
still.

"I ken weel enough what ye're thinkin'," she said. "For I saw
your lady, and I know how it was between the two of ye. I never
had that," she added, in a softer voice, "not wi' either of the two
men I wed. But I know the look of a true love, and it's not in my
mind to make ye feel ye've betrayed it."

The touch, feather-light, moved to his cheek, and a work-worn
thumb traced the groove that ran from nose to mouth.

"What I want," she said quietly, "is to give ye something
different. Something less, mayhap, but something ye can use,
something to keep ye whole. Your sister and the bairns canna give
ye that—but I can." He heard her draw breath, and the touch on
his face lifted away.

"Ye've given me my home, my life, and my son. Will ye no let
me gi'e ye this small thing in return?"

He felt tears sting his eyelids. The weightless touch moved
across his face, wiping the moisture from his eyes, smoothing the
roughness of his hair. He lifted his arms, slowly, and reached out

he stepped inside his embrace, as neatly and simply as she had
id the table and the bed.

"I . . . havena done this in a long time," he said, suddenly
hy.

"Neither have I," she said, with a tiny smile. "But we'll re-
1ember how 'tis."

PART THREE

When I Am Thy Captive

7

A Faith in Documents

T he envelope from Linklater arrived in the morning post.
"Look how fat it is!" Brianna exclaimed. "He's sent
something!" The tip of her nose was pink with excitement.

"Looks like it," said Roger. He was outwardly calm, but I
could see the pulse beating in the hollow of his throat. He picked
up the thick manila envelope and held it for a moment, weighing
it. Then he ripped the flap recklessly with his thumb, and yanked
out a sheaf of photocopied pages.

The cover letter, on heavy university stationery, fluttered out. I
snatched it from the floor and read it aloud, my voice shaking a
little.

" 'Dear Dr. Wakefield,' " I read. " 'This is in reply to your
inquiry regarding the execution of Jacobite officers by the Duke of
Cumberland's troops following the Battle of Culloden. The main
source of the quote in my book to which you refer, was the private
journal of one Lord Melton, in command of an infantry regiment
under Cumberland at the time of Culloden. I have enclosed photocopies of the relevant pages of the journal; as you will see, the
story of the survivor, one James Fraser, is an odd and touching
one. Fraser is not an important historical character, and not in
line with the thrust of my own work, but I have often thought of
investigating further, in hopes of determining his eventual fate.
Should you find that he did survive the journey to his own estate, I
should be happy if you would inform me. I have always rather
hoped that he did, though his situation as described by Melton

makes the possibility seem unlikely. Sincerely yours, Eric Lin
later.' ''

The paper rattled in my hand, and I set it down, very carefull
on the desk.

''Unlikely, huh?'' Brianna said, standing on tiptoe to see ov
Roger's shoulder. ''Ha! He *did* make it back, we know he did

''We think he did,'' Roger corrected, but it was only scholar
caution; his grin was as broad as Brianna's.

''Will ye be havin' tea or cocoa to your elevenses?'' Fiona
curly dark head poked through the study doorway, interrupting t
excitement. ''There's fresh ginger-nut biscuits, just baked.'' T
scent of warm ginger came into the study with her, wafting enti
ingly from her apron.

''Tea, please,'' said Roger, just as Brianna said, ''Oh, coc
sounds great!'' Fiona, wearing a smug expression, pushed in t
tea cart, sporting both tea cozy and pot of cocoa, as well as a pla
of fresh ginger-nut biscuits.

I accepted a cup of tea myself, and sat down in the wing cha
with the pages of Melton's journal. The flowing eighteenth-ce
tury handwriting was surprisingly clear, in spite of the archa
spelling, and within minutes, I was in the confines of Leana
farmhouse, imagining the sound of buzzing flies, the stir of clos
packed bodies, and the harsh smell of blood soaking into t
packed-dirt floor.

''. . . *in satisfaction of my brother's debt of honor, I could n*
do otherwise than to spare Fraser's life. I therefore omitted I
name from the list of traitors executed at the farmhouse, and ha
made arrangement for his transport to his own estate. I cannot fe
myself either altogether merciful toward Fraser in the taking
this action, nor yet altogether culpable with respect to my servi
toward the Duke, as Fraser's situation, with a great wound in I
leg festering and pustulent, makes it unlikely that he will survi
the journey to his home. Still, honor prevents my acting otherwi
and I will confess that my spirit was lightened to see the m
removed, still living, from the field, as I turned my own attentio
to the melancholy task of disposing of the bodies of his comrad
So much killing as I have seen these last two days oppresses me
the entry ended simply.

I laid the pages down on my knee, swallowing heavily. ''*A gre*
wound . . . festering and pustulent . . .'' I knew, as Roger a

Brianna could not, just how serious such a wound would have been, with no antibiotics, nothing in the way of proper medical treatment; not even the crude herbal poultices available to a Highland charmer at the time. How long would it have taken, jolting from Culloden to Broch Tuarach in a wagon? Two days? Three? How could he have lived, in such a state, and neglected for so long?

"He did, though." Brianna's voice broke in upon my thoughts, answering what seemed to be a similar thought expressed by Roger. She spoke with simple assurance, as though she had seen all the events described in Melton's journal, and were sure of their outcome. "He did get back. He was the Dunbonnet, I know it."

"The Dunbonnet?" Fiona, tut-tutting over my cold cup of undrunk tea, looked over her shoulder in surprise. "Heard of the Dunbonnet, have ye?"

"Have *you*?" Roger looked at the young housekeeper in astonishment.

She nodded, casually dumping my tea into the aspidistra that stood by the hearth and refilling my cup with fresh steaming brew.

"Oh, aye. My grannie tellt me that tale, often and often."

"Tell us!" Brianna leaned forward, intent, her cocoa cupped between her palms. "Please, Fiona! What's the story?"

Fiona seemed mildly surprised to find herself suddenly the center of so much attention, but shrugged good-naturedly.

"Och, it's just the story of one o' the followers o' the Bonnie Prince. When there was the great defeat at Culloden, and sae many were killed, a few escaped. Why, one man fled the field and swam the river to get away, but the Redcoats were after him, nonetheless. He came to a kirk along his way, and a service going on inside, and he dashing in, prayed mercy from the minister. The minister and the people took pity on him, and he put on the minister's robe, so when the Redcoats burst in moments later, there he was, standing at the pulpit, preachin' the sermon, and the water from his beard and clothes puddled up about his feet. The Redcoats thought they were mistaken, and went on down the road, and so he escaped—and everyone in the kirk said 'twas the best sermon they ever heard!" Fiona laughed heartily, while Brianna frowned, and Roger looked puzzled.

"That was the Dunbonnet?" he said. "But I thought—"

"Och, no!" she assured him. "That was no the Dunbonnet—

only the Dunbonnet was another o' the men who got away fro
Culloden. He came back to his own estate, but because the Sa
senachs were hunting men all across the Highlands, he lay hidd
there in a cave for seven years.''

Hearing this, Brianna slumped back in her chair with a sigh
relief. ''And his tenants called him the Dunbonnet so as not
speak his name and betray him,'' she murmured.

''Ye ken the story?'' Fiona asked, astonished. ''Aye, that
right.''

''And did your grannie say what happened to him after that?
Roger prompted.

''Oh, aye!'' Fiona's eyes were round as butterscotch drop
''That's the best part o' the story. See, there was a great fami
after Culloden; folk were starvin' in the glens, turned out of the
houses in winter, the men shot and the cots set afire. The Dunbo
net's tenants managed better than most, but even so, there came
day when the food ran out, and their bellies garbeled from daw
'til dark—no game in the forest, nay grain in the field, and tl
weans dyin' in their mothers' arms for lack o' milk to feed them

A cold chill swept over me at her words. I saw the faces of tl
Lallybroch inhabitants—the people I had known and loved-
pinched with cold and starvation. Not only horror filled me; the
was guilt, too. I had been safe, warm, and well fed, instead
sharing their fate—because I had done as Jamie wanted, and le
them. I looked at Brianna, smooth red head bent in absorption, an
the tight feeling in my chest eased a bit. She too had been safe f
these past years, warm, well fed, and loved—because I had do
as Jamie wanted.

''So he made a bold plan, the Dunbonnet did,'' Fiona wa
continuing. Her round face was alight with the drama of her tal
''He arranged that one of his tenants should go to the English, an
offer to betray him. There was a good price on his head, for he
been a great warrior for the Prince. The tenant would take the go
o' the reward—to use for the folk on the estate, o' course—an
tell the English where the Dunbonnet might be taken.''

My hand clenched so convulsively at this that the delicate ha
dle of my teacup snapped clean off.

''Taken?'' I croaked, my voice hoarse with shock. ''Did th
hang him?''

Fiona blinked at me in surprise. ''Why, no,'' she said. ''Th anted to, my grannie said, and took him to trial for treason, but the end, they shut him up in a prison instead—but the gold went his tenants, and so they lived through the famine,'' she ended eerfully, obviously regarding this as the happy ending.

"Jesus Christ,'' Roger breathed. He set his cup down carefully, d sat staring into space, transfixed. "Prison."

"You sound like that's *good*,'' Brianna protested. The corners her mouth were tight with distress, and her eyes slightly shiny.

"It is,'' Roger said, not noticing her distress. "There weren't at many prisons where the English imprisoned Jacobite traitors, d they all kept official records. Don't you see?'' he demanded, oking from Fiona's bewilderment to Brianna's scowl, then set- ng on me in hope of finding understanding. "If he went to ison, I can find him." He turned then, to look up at the towering elves of books that lined three walls of the study, holding the te Reverend Wakefield's collection of Jacobite arcana.

"He's in there,'' Roger said softly. "On a prison roll. In a cument—real evidence! Don't you see?'' he demanded again, rning back to me. "Going to prison made him a part of written story again! And somewhere in there, we'll find him!''

"And what happened to him then,'' Brianna breathed. "When : was released.''

Roger's lips pressed tight together, to cut off the alternative that rang to his mind, as it had to mine—"or died.''

"Yes, that's right,'' he said, taking Brianna's hand. His eyes et mine, deep green and unfathomable. "When he was re- ased.''

A week later, Roger's faith in documents remained unshaken. ie same could not be said for the eighteenth-century table in the te Reverend Wakefield's study, whose spindly legs wobbled and eaked alarmingly beneath their unaccustomed burden.

This table normally was asked to accommodate no more than a all lamp, and a collection of the Reverend's smaller artifacts; it as pressed into service now only because every other horizontal rface in the study already overflowed with papers, journals, oks, and bulging manila envelopes from antiquarian societies, iversities, and research libraries across England, Scotland, and eland.

"If you set one more page on that thing, it's going to collapse"
Claire observed, as Roger carelessly reached out, meaning to dr
the folder he was carrying on the little inlaid table.

"Ah? Oh, right." He switched direction in midair, look
vainly for another place to put the folder, and finally settled
placing it on the floor at his feet.

"I've just about finished with Wentworth," Claire said. S
indicated a precarious stack on the floor with her toe. "Have
got in the records for Berwick yet?"

"Yes, just this morning. Where did I put them, though?" Ro
stared vaguely about the room, which strongly resembled the sa
ing of the library at Alexandria, just before the first torch was
He rubbed his forehead, trying to concentrate. After a week
spending ten-hour days thumbing the handwritten registers
British prisons, and the letters, journals, and diaries of their gov
nors, searching for any official trace of Jamie Fraser, Roger w
beginning to feel as though his eyes had been sandpapered.

"It was blue," he said at last. "I distinctly remember it w
blue. I got those from McAllister, the History Lecturer at Trin
at Cambridge, and Trinity College uses those big envelopes in p
blue, with the college's coat of arms on the front. Maybe Fion
seen it. Fiona!"

He stepped to the study door and called down the hall towa
the kitchen. Despite the lateness of the hour, the light was still
and the heartening scent of cocoa and freshly baked almond ca
lingered in the air. Fiona would never abandon her post wh
there was the faintest possibility that someone in her vicin
might require nourishment.

"Och, aye?" Fiona's curly brown head poked out of
kitchen. "There'll be cocoa ready directly," she assured hi
"I'm only waiting for the cake to be out of the oven."

Roger smiled at her with deep affection. Fiona had not
slightest use herself for history—never read anything beyond
Weekly magazine—but she never questioned his activities, tra
quilly dusting the heaps of books and papers daily, without both
ing about their contents.

"Thanks, Fiona," he said. "I was only wondering, thou
have you seen a big blue envelope—a fat one, about so?"
measured with his hands. "It came in the morning post, but I
misplaced it."

"Ye left it in the upstairs bath," she said promptly. "There's at great thick book wi' the gold writing and the picture of the onnie Prince on the front up there, and three letters ye'd just ened, and there's the gas bill, too, which ye dinna want to be rgetting, it's due on the fourteenth o' the month. I've put it all on e top of the geyser, so as to be out of the way." A tiny, sharp ng! from the oven timer made her withdraw her head abruptly ith a smothered exclamation.

Roger turned and went up the stairs two at a time, smiling. ven other inclinations, Fiona's memory might have made her a holar. As it was, she was no mean research assistant. So long as particular document or book could be described on the basis of s appearance, rather than its title or contents, Fiona was bound to ow exactly where it was.

"Och, it's nothing," she had assured Roger airily, when he had ed to apologize earlier for the mess he was making of the house. Ye'd think the Reverend was still alive, wi' such a moil of papers rewn everywhere. It's just like old times, no?"

Coming down more slowly, with the blue envelope in his hands, wondered what his late adoptive father might have thought of is present quest.

"In it up to the eyebrows, I shouldn't wonder," he murmured to mself. He had a vivid memory of the Reverend, bald head eaming under the old-fashioned bowl lamps that hung from the ll ceiling, as he pottered from his study to the kitchen, where old rs. Graham, Fiona's grandmother, would have been manning the ove, supplying the old man's bodily needs during bouts of late-ght scholarship, just as Fiona was now doing for him.

It made one wonder, he thought, as he went into the study. In e old days, when a man's son usually followed his father's ofession, was that only a matter of convenience—wanting to ep the business in the family—or was there some sort of family edisposition for some kinds of work? Were some people actually rn to be smiths, or merchants, or cooks—born to an inclination d an aptitude, as well as to the opportunity?

Clearly it didn't apply to everyone; there were always the people ho left their homes, went a-wandering, tried things hitherto un-own in their family circles. If that weren't so, probably there uld be no inventors, no explorers; still, there seemed to be a certain affinity for some careers in some families, even in the restless modern times of widespread education and easy travel

What he was really wondering about, he thought to himself, w Brianna. He watched Claire, her curly gold-shot head bent over t desk, and found himself wondering how much Brianna would like her, and how much like the shadowy Scot—warrior, farm courtier, laird—who had been her father?

His thoughts were still running on such lines a quarter-hc later, when Claire closed the last folder on her stack and sat bac sighing.

"Penny for your thoughts?" she asked, reaching for her drir

"Not worth that much," Roger replied with a smile, coming c of his reverie. "I was only wondering how people come to be wl they are. How did you come to be a doctor, for instance?"

"How did I come to be a doctor?" Claire inhaled the stea from her cup of cocoa, decided it was too hot to drink, and set back on the desk, among the litter of books and journals a pencil-scribbled sheets of paper. She gave Roger a half-smile a rubbed her hands together, dispersing the warmth of the cup.

"How did you come to be a historian?"

"More or less honestly," he answered, leaning back in t Reverend's chair and waving at the accumulation of papers a trivia all around them. He patted a small gilt traveling clock tl sat on the desk, an elegant bit of eighteenth-century workmansh with miniature chimes that struck the hour, the quarter, and t half.

"I grew up in the midst of it all; I was ferreting round t Highlands in search of artifacts with my father from the time could read. I suppose it just seemed natural to keep doing it. F you?"

She nodded and stretched, easing her shoulders from the lo hours of stooping over the desk. Brianna, unable to stay awal had given up and gone to bed an hour before, but Claire and Rog had gone on with their search through the administrative recor of British prisons.

"Well, it was something like that for me," she said. "It was so much that I suddenly decided I must become a doctor—it w just that I suddenly realized one day that I'd *been* one for a lo time—and then I wasn't, and I missed it."

She spread her hands out on the desk and flexed her fingers, long and supple, the nails buffed into neat, shiny ovals.

"There used to be an old song from the First World War," she said reflectively. "I used to hear it sometimes when some of Uncle Lamb's old army friends would come round and stay up late and get drunk. It went, 'How You Gonna Keep 'em Down on the Farm, After They've Seen Paree?' " She sang the first line, then broke off with a wry smile.

"I'd seen Paree," she said softly. She looked up from her hands, alert and present, but with the traces of memory in her eyes, fixed on Roger with the clarity of a second sight. "And a lot of other things besides. Caen and Amiens, Preston, and Falkirk, the Hôpital des Anges and the so-called surgery at Leoch. I'd *been* a doctor, in every way there is—I'd delivered babies, set bones, stitched wounds, treated fevers . . ." She trailed off, and shrugged. "There was a terrible lot I didn't know, of course. I knew how much I could learn—and that's why I went to medical school. But it didn't really make a difference, you know." She dipped a finger into the whipped cream floating on her cocoa, and licked it off. "I have a diploma with an M.D. on it—but I was a doctor long before I set foot in medical school."

"It can't possibly have been as easy as you make it sound." Roger blew on his own cocoa, studying Claire with open interest. "There weren't many women in medicine then—there aren't that many women doctors *now,* come to that—and you had a family, besides."

"No, I can't say it was easy at all." Claire looked at him quizzically. "I waited until Brianna was in school, of course, and we had enough money to afford someone to come in to cook and clean—but . . ." She shrugged and smiled ironically. "I stopped sleeping for several years, there. That helped a bit. And oddly enough, Frank helped, too."

Roger tested his own cup and found it almost cool enough to drink. He held it between his hands, enjoying the heat of the thick white porcelain seeping into his palms. Early June it might be, but the nights were cool enough to make the electric fire still a necessity.

"Really?" he said curiously. "Only from the things you've said about him, I shouldn't have thought he'd have liked your wanting to go to medical school or be a doctor."

"He didn't." Her lips pressed tight together; the motion tol
Roger more than words might, recalling arguments, conversation
half-finished and abandoned, an opposition of stubbornness an
devious obstruction rather than of open disapproval.

What a remarkably expressive face she had, he thought, watch
ing her. He wondered quite suddenly whether his own was a
easily readable. The thought was so unsettling that he dipped hi
face into his mug, gulping the cocoa, although it was still a bit to
hot.

He emerged from the cup to find Claire watching him, slight
sardonic.

"Why?" he asked quickly, to distract her. "What made hi
change his mind?"

"Bree," she said, and her face softened as it always did at th
mention of her daughter. "Bree was the only thing really impo
tant to Frank."

———

*I had, as I'd said, waited until Brianna began school be-
fore beginning medical school myself. But even so, there was
a large gap between her hours and my own, which we filled
haphazardly with a series of more or less competent house-
keepers and baby-sitters; some more, most of them less.*

*My mind went back to the frightful day when I had gotten a
call at the hospital, telling me that Brianna was hurt. I had
dashed out of the place, not pausing to change out of the
green linen scrub-suit I was wearing, and raced for home,
ignoring all speed limits, to find a police car and an ambulance lighting the night with bloodred pulses, and a knot of
interested neighbors clustered on the street outside.*

*As we pieced the story together later, what had happened
was that the latest temporary sitter, annoyed at my being late
yet again, had simply put on her coat at quitting time and left,
abandoning seven-year-old Brianna with instructions to
"wait for Mommy." This she had obediently done, for an
hour or so. But as it began to get dark, she had become
frightened in the house alone, and determined to go out and
find me. Making her way across one of the busy streets near
our house, she had been struck by a car turning into the
street.*

She wasn't—thank God!—hurt badly; the car had been moving slowly, and she had only been shaken and bruised by the experience. Not nearly as shaken as I was, for that matter. Nor as bruised, when I came into the living room to find her lying on the sofa, and she looked at me, tears welling afresh on her stained cheeks and said, "Mommy! Where were *you? I couldn't find you!"*

It had taken just about all my reserves of professional composure to comfort her, to check her over, re-tend her cuts and scrapes, thank her rescuers—who, to my fevered mind, all glared accusingly at me—and put her to bed with her teddy bear clutched securely in her arms. Then I sat down at the kitchen table and cried myself.

Frank patted me awkwardly, murmuring, but then gave it up, and with more practicality, went to make tea.

"I've decided," I said, when he set the steaming cup in front of me. I spoke dully, my head feeling thick and clogged. "I'll resign. I'll do it tomorrow."

"Resign?" Frank's voice was sharp with astonishment. "From the school? What for?"

"I can't stand it anymore." I never took cream or sugar in my tea. Now I added both, stirring and watching the milky tendrils swirl through the cup. "I can't stand leaving Bree, and not knowing if she's well cared for—and knowing she isn't happy. You know she doesn't really like any of the sitters we've tried."

"I know that, yes." He sat opposite me, stirring his own tea. After a long moment, he said, "But I don't think you should resign."

It was the last thing I had expected; I had thought he would greet my decision with relieved applause. I stared at him in astonishment, then blew my nose yet again on the wadded tissue from my pocket.

"You don't?"

"Ah, Claire." He spoke impatiently, but with a tinge of affection nonetheless. "You've known forever who you are. Do you realize at all how unusual it is to know that?"

"No." I wiped my nose with the shredding tissue, dabbing carefully to keep it in one piece.

Frank leaned back in his chair, shaking his head as he looked at me.

"No, I suppose not," he said. He was quiet for a minute, looking down at his folded hands. They were long-fingered, narrow; smooth and hairless as a girl's. Elegant hands, made for casual gestures and the emphasis of speech.

He stretched them out on the table and looked at them as though he'd never seen them before.

"I haven't got that," he said quietly at last. "I'm good, all right. At what I do—the teaching, the writing. Bloody splendid sometimes, in fact. And I like it a good bit, enjoy what I do. But the thing is—" He hesitated, then looked at me straight on, hazel-eyed and earnest. "I could do something else, and be as good. Care as much, or as little. I haven't got that absolute conviction that there's something in life I'm meant to do—and you have."

"Is that good?" The edges of my nostrils were sore, and my eyes puffed from crying.

He laughed shortly. "It's damned inconvenient, Claire. To you and me and Bree, all three. But my God, I do envy you sometimes."

He reached out for my hand, and after a moment's hesitation, I let him have it.

"To have that passion for anything"—a small twitch tugged the corner of his mouth—"or anyone. That's quite splendid, Claire, and quite terribly rare." He squeezed my hand gently and let it go, turning to reach behind him for one of the books on the shelf beside the table.

It was one of his references, Woodhill's Patriots, *a series of profiles of the American Founding Fathers.*

He laid his hand on the cover of the book, gently, as though reluctant to disturb the rest of the sleeping lives interred there.

"These were people like that. The ones who cared so terribly much—enough to risk everything, enough to change and do things. Most people aren't like that, you know. It isn't that they don't care, but that they don't care so greatly." He took my hand again, this time turning it over. One finger traced the lines that webbed my palm, tickling as it went.

"Is it there, I wonder?" he said, smiling a little. "Are

some people destined for a great fate, or to do great things? Or is it only that they're born somehow with that great passion—and if they find themselves in the right circumstances, then things happen? It's the sort of thing you wonder, studying history . . . but there's no way of telling, really. All we know is what they accomplished.

"But Claire—" His eyes held a definite note of warning, as he tapped the cover of his book. "They paid for it," he said.

"I know." I felt very remote now, as though I were watching us from a distance; I could see it quite clearly in my mind's eye; Frank, handsome, lean, and a little tired, going beautifully gray at the temples. Me, grubby in my surgical scrubs, my hair coming down, the front of my shirt crumpled and stained with Brianna's tears.

We sat in silence for some time, my hand still resting in Frank's. I could see the mysterious lines and valleys, clear as a road map—but a road to what unknown destination?

I had had my palm read once years before, by an old Scottish lady named Graham—Fiona's grandmother, in fact. "The lines in your hand change as you change," she had said. "It's no so much what you're born with, as what ye make of yourself."

And what had I made of myself, what was I making? A mess, that was what. Neither a good mother, nor a good wife, nor a good doctor. A mess. Once I had thought I was whole— had seemed to be able to love a man, to bear a child, to heal the sick—and know that all these things were natural parts of me, not the difficult, troubled fragments into which my life had now disintegrated. But that had been in the past, the man I had loved was Jamie, and for a time, I had been part of something greater than myself.

"I'll take Bree."

I was so deep in miserable thought that for a moment Frank's words didn't register, and I stared at him stupidly.

"What did you say?"

"I said," he repeated patiently, "that I'll take Bree. She can come from her school to the university, and play at my office until I'm ready to come home."

I rubbed my nose. "I thought you didn't think it appropri-

ate for staff to bring their children to work." He had been quite critical of Mrs. Clancy, one of the secretaries, who had brought her grandson to work for a month when his mother was sick.

He shrugged, looking uncomfortable.

"Well, circumstances alter cases. And Brianna's not likely to be running up and down the halls shrieking and spilling ink like Bart Clancy."

"I wouldn't bet my life on it," I said wryly. "But you'd do that?" A small feeling was growing in the pit of my clenched stomach; a cautious, unbelieving feeling of relief. I might not trust Frank to be faithful to me—I knew quite well he wasn't —but I did trust him unequivocally to care for Bree.

Suddenly the worry was removed. I needn't hurry home from the hospital, filled with dread because I was late, hating the thought of finding Brianna crouched in her room sulking because she didn't like the current sitter. She loved Frank; I knew she would be ecstatic at the thought of going to his office every day.

"Why?" I asked bluntly. "It isn't that you're dead keen on my being a doctor; I know that."

"No," he said thoughtfully. "It isn't that. But I do think there isn't any way to stop you—perhaps the best I can do is to help, so that there will be less damage to Brianna." His features hardened slightly then, and he turned away.

"So far as he ever felt he had a destiny—something he w really meant to do—he felt that Brianna was it," Claire said. S stirred her cocoa meditatively.

"Why do you care, Roger?" she asked him suddenly. "W are you asking me?"

He took a moment to answer, slowly sipping his cocoa. It w rich and dark, made with new cream and a sprinkle of brov sugar. Fiona, always a realist, had taken one look at Brianna at given up her attempts to lure Roger into matrimony via his stoi ach, but Fiona was a cook the same way Claire was a doctor; bo to skill, and unable not to use it.

"Because I'm a historian, I suppose," he answered finally. I watched her over the rim of his cup. "I need to know. What people really did, and why they did it."

"And you think I can tell you that?" She glanced sharply at him. "Or that I know?"

He nodded, sipping. "You know, better than most people. Most of a historian's sources haven't your"—he paused and gave her a grin—"your unique perspective, shall we say?"

There was a sudden lessening of tension. She laughed and picked up her own cup. "We shall say that," she agreed.

"The other thing," he went on, watching her closely, "is that you're honest. I don't think you *could* lie, even if you wanted to."

She glanced at him sharply, and gave a short, dry laugh.

"Everyone can lie, young Roger, given cause enough. Even me. It's only that it's harder for those of us who live in glass faces; we have to think up our lies ahead of time."

She bent her head and shuffled through the papers before her, turning the pages over slowly, one by one. They were lists of names, these sheets, lists of prisoners, copied from the ledger books of British prisons. The task was complicated by the fact that not all prisons had been well run.

Some governors kept no official lists of their inmates, or listed them haphazardly in their journals, in among the notations of daily expenditure and maintenance, making no great distinction between the death of a prisoner and the slaughter of two bullocks, salted for meat.

Roger thought Claire had abandoned the conversation, but a moment later she looked up again.

"You're quite right, though," she said. "I'm honest—from default, more than anything. It isn't easy for me *not* to say what I'm thinking. I imagine you see it because you're the same way."

"Am I?" Roger felt absurdly pleased, as though someone had given him an unexpected present.

Claire nodded, a small smile on her lips as she watched him.

"Oh, yes. It's unmistakable, you know. There aren't many people like that—who will tell you the truth about themselves and anything else right out. I've only met three people like that, I think —four now," she said, her smile widening to warm him.

"There was Jamie, of course." Her long fingers rested lightly on the stack of papers, almost caressing in their touch. "Master

Raymond, the apothecary I knew in Paris. And a friend I met
medical school—Joe Abernathy. Now you. I think.''

She tilted her cup and swallowed the last of the rich brow
liquid. She set it down and looked directly at Roger.

"Frank was right, in a way, though. It isn't necessarily easier
you know what it is you're meant to do—but at least you do
waste time in questioning or doubting. If you're honest—well, th
isn't necessarily easier, either. Though I suppose if you're hone
with yourself and know what you are, at least you're less likely
feel that you've wasted your life, doing the wrong thing.''

She set aside the stack of papers and drew up another—a set
folders with the characteristic logo of the British Museum on t
covers.

"Jamie had that,'' she said softly, as though to herself. "I
wasn't a man to turn away from anything he thought his jo
Dangerous or not. And I think he won't have felt himself wasted
no matter what happened to him.''

She lapsed into silence, then, absorbed in the spidery tracings
some long-dead writer, looking for the entry that might tell h
what Jamie Fraser had done and been, and whether his life ha
been wasted in a prison cell, or ended in a lonely dungeon.

The clock on the desk struck midnight, its chimes surprising
deep and melodious for such a small instrument. The quarter-ho
struck, and then the half, punctuating the monotonous rustle
pages. Roger put down the sheaf of flimsy papers he had bee
thumbing through, and yawned deeply, not troubling to cover h
mouth.

"I'm so tired I'm seeing double,'' he said. "Shall we go
with it in the morning?''

Claire didn't answer for a moment; she was looking into th
glowing bars of the electric fire, a look of unutterable distance
her face. Roger repeated his question, and slowly she came ba
from wherever she was.

"No,'' she said. She reached for another folder, and smiled
Roger, the look of distance lingering in her eyes. "You go o
Roger,'' she said. "I'll—just look a little longer.''

When I finally found it, I nearly flipped right past it. I had n
been reading the names carefully, but only skimming the pages f

e letter "J." "John, Joseph, Jacques, James." There were James
dward, James Alan, James Walter, ad infinitum. Then it was
ere, the writing small and precise across the page: "Jms. Mac-
enzie Fraser, of Brock Turac."

I put the page down carefully on the table, shut my eyes for a
oment to clear them, then looked again. It was still there.

"Jamie," I said aloud. My heart was beating heavily in my
hest. "Jamie," I said again, more quietly.

It was nearly three o'clock in the morning. Everyone was
sleep, but the house, in the manner of old houses, was still awake
round me, creaking and sighing, keeping me company. Strangely
nough, I had no desire to leap up and wake Brianna or Roger, to
ll them the news. I wanted to keep it to myself for a bit, as
ough I were alone here in the lamp-lit room with Jamie himself.

My finger traced the line of ink. The person who had written
at line had seen Jamie—perhaps had written this with Jamie
anding in front of him. The date at the top of the page was May
6, 1753. It had been close to this time of year, then. I could
nagine how the air had been, chilly and fresh, with the rare spring
un across his shoulders, lighting sparks in his hair.

How had he worn his hair then—short, or long? He had pre-
rred to wear it long, plaited or tailed behind. I remembered the
asual gesture with which he would lift the weight of it off his
eck to cool himself in the heat of exercise.

He would not have worn his kilt—the wearing of all tartans had
een outlawed after Culloden. Breeks, then, likely, and a linen
irt. I had made such sarks for him; I could feel the softness of
e fabric in memory, the billowing length of the three full yards it
ok to make one, the long tails and full sleeves that let the High-
nd men drop their plaids and sleep or fight with a sark their only
arment. I could imagine his shoulders broad beneath the rough-
oven cloth, his skin warm through it, hands touched with the
ill of the Scottish spring.

He had been imprisoned before. How would he have looked,
cing an English prison clerk, knowing all too well what waited
r him? Grim as hell, I thought, staring down that long, straight
ose with his eyes a cold, dark blue—dark and forbidding as the
aters of Loch Ness.

I opened my own eyes, realizing only then that I was sitting on
e edge of my chair, the folder of photocopied pages clasped tight

to my chest, so caught up in my conjuration that I had not ev
paid attention to which prison these registers had come from.

There were several large prisons that the English had used reg
larly in the eighteenth century, and a number of minor ones.
turned the folder over, slowly. Would it be Berwick, near t
border? The notorious Tolbooth of Edinburgh? Or one of t
southern prisons, Leeds Castle or even the Tower of London?

"Ardsmuir," said the notecard neatly stapled to the front of t
folder.

"Ardsmuir?" I said blankly. "Where the hell is *that*?"

8

Honor's Prisoner

A rdsmuir is the carbuncle on God's bum," Colonel Harry Quarry said. He raised his glass sardonically to the young man by the window. "I've been here a twelve-month, and that's eleven months and twenty-nine days too long. Give you joy of your new posting, my lord."

Major John William Grey turned from the window over the courtyard, where he had been surveying his new domain.

"It does appear a trifle incommodious," he agreed dryly, picking up his own glass. "Does it rain *all* the time?"

"Of course. It's Scotland—and the backside of bloody Scotland, at that." Quarry took a deep pull at his whisky, coughed, and exhaled noisily as he set down the empty glass.

"The drink is the only compensation," he said, a trifle hoarsely. "Call on the local booze-merchants in your best uniform, and they'll make you a decent price. It's astounding cheap, without the tariff. I've left you a note of the best stills." He nodded toward the massive oaken desk at the side of the room, planted four-square on its island of carpet like a small fortress confronting the barren room. The illusion of fortifications was enhanced by the banners of regiment and nation that hung from the stone wall behind it.

"The guards' roster is here," Quarry said, rising and groping in the top desk drawer. He slapped a battered leather folder on the desktop, and added another on top of that. "And the prisoners' roll. You have one hundred and ninety-six at the moment; two hundred is the usual count, give or take a few deaths from sickness or the odd poacher taken up in the countryside."

"Two hundred," Grey said. "And how many in the guard barracks?"

"Eighty-two, by number. In use, about half that." Quarr reached into the drawer again and withdrew a brown glass bott with a cork. He shook it, heard it slosh, and smiled sardonicall "The commander isn't the only one to find consolation in drin Half the sots are usually incapable at roll call. I'll leave this fe you, shall I? You'll need it." He put the bottle back and pulled o the lower drawer.

"Requisitions and copies here; the paperwork's the worst of th post. Not a great deal to do, really, if you've a decent clerk. Yo haven't, at the moment; I had a corporal who wrote a fairish han but he died two weeks ago. Train up another, and you'll hav nothing to do save to hunt for grouse and the Frenchman's Gold. He laughed at his own joke; rumors of the gold that Louis France had supposedly sent to his cousin Charles Stuart were ri in this end of Scotland.

"The prisoners are not difficult?" Grey asked. "I had unde stood them to be mostly Jacobite Highlanders."

"They are. But they're docile enough." Quarry paused, look ing out of the window. A small line of ragged men was issuin from a door in the forbidding stone wall opposite. "No heart them after Culloden," he said matter-of-factly. "Butcher Bill saw to that. And we work them hard enough that they've no vigo left for troublemaking."

Grey nodded. Ardsmuir fortress was undergoing renovatio rather ironically using the labor of the Scots incarcerated therei He rose and came to join Quarry at the window.

"There's a work crew going out now, for peat-cutting." Quarr nodded at the group below. A dozen bearded men, ragged a scarecrows, formed an awkward line before a red-coated soldie who walked up and down, inspecting them. Evidently satisfied, l shouted an order and jerked a hand toward the outer gate.

The prisoners' crew was accompanied by six armed soldier who fell in before and behind, muskets held in marching orde their smart appearance a marked contrast to the ragged Highland ers. The prisoners walked slowly, oblivious to the rain that soake their rags. A mule-drawn wagon creaked behind, a bundle of pe knives gleaming dully in its bed.

Quarry frowned, counting them. "Some must be ill; a wo

crew is eighteen men—three prisoners to a guard, because of the knives. Though surprisingly few of them try to run,'' he added, turning away from the window. ''Nowhere to go, I suppose.'' He left the desk, kicking aside a large woven basket that sat on the hearth, filled with crude chunks of a rough dark-brown substance.

''Leave the window open, even when it's raining,'' he advised. ''The peat smoke will choke you, otherwise.'' He took a deep breath in illustration and let it out explosively. ''God, I'll be glad to get back to London!''

''Not much in the way of local society, I collect?'' Grey asked dryly. Quarry laughed, his broad red face creasing in amusement at the notion.

''Society? My dear fellow! Bar one or two passable blowzabellas down in the village, 'society' will consist solely of conversation with your officers—there are four of them, one of whom is capable of speaking without the use of profanity—your orderly, and one prisoner.''

''A prisoner?'' Grey looked up from the ledgers he had been perusing, one fair brow lifted in inquiry.

''Oh, yes.'' Quarry was prowling the office restlessly, eager to be off. His carriage was waiting; he had stayed only to brief his replacement and make the formal handover of command. Now he paused, glancing at Grey. One corner of his mouth curled up, enjoying a secret joke.

''You've heard of Red Jamie Fraser, I expect?''

Grey stiffened slightly, but kept his face as unmoved as possible.

''I should imagine most people have,'' he said coldly. ''The man was notorious during the Rising.'' Quarry had heard the story, damn him! All of it, or only the first part?

Quarry's mouth twitched slightly, but he merely nodded.

''Quite. Well, we have him. He's the only senior Jacobite officer here; the Highlander prisoners treat him as their chief. Consequently, if any matters arise involving the prisoners—and they will, I assure you—he acts as their spokesman.'' Quarry was in his stocking feet; now he sat and tugged on long cavalry boots, in preparation for the mud outside.

''*Seumas, mac an fhear dhuibh,* they call him, *or just Mac Dubh.* Speak Gaelic, do you? Neither do I—Grissom does, though; he says it means 'James, son of the Black One.' Half the guards are afraid of him—those that fought with Cope at Prestoн pans. Say he's the Devil himself. Poor devil, now!'' Quarry gave brief snort, forcing his foot into the boot. He stamped once, settle it, and stood up.

''The prisoners obey him without question; but give orde without his putting his seal to them, and you might as well talking to the stones in the courtyard. Ever had much to do wiн Scots? Oh, of course; you fought at Culloden with your brother regiment, didn't you?'' Quarry struck his brow at his pretende forgetfulness. Damn the man! He *had* heard it all.

''You'll have an idea, then. Stubborn does not begin to descriн it.'' He flapped a hand in the air as though to dismiss an entiн contingent of recalcitrant Scots.

''Which means,'' Quarry paused, enjoying it, ''you'll need Fr. ser's goodwill—or at least his cooperation. I had him take supp with me once a week, to talk things over, and found it answere very well. You might try the same arrangement.''

''I suppose I might.'' Grey's tone was cool, but his hands weн clenched tight at his sides. When icicles grew in hell, he migн take supper with James Fraser!

''He's an educated man,'' Quarry continued, eyes bright wiн malice, fixed on Grey's face. ''A great deal more interesting talk to than the officers. Plays chess. You have a game now an then, do you not?''

''Now and then.'' The muscles of his abdomen were clencheн so tightly that he had trouble drawing breath. Would this bulleн headed fool not stop talking and leave?

''Ah, well, I'll leave you to it.'' As though divining Grey wish, Quarry settled his wig more firmly, then took his cloak froн the hook by the door and swirled it rakishly about his shoulder He turned toward the door, hat in hand, then turned back.

''Oh, one thing. If you do dine with Fraser alone—don't turн your back on him.'' The offensive jocularity had left Quarry face; Grey scowled at him, but could see no evidence that tн warning was meant as a joke.

''I mean it,'' Quarry said, suddenly serious. ''He's in irons, bн it's easy to choke a man with the chain. And he's a very larн fellow, Fraser.''

''I know.'' To his fury, Grey could feel the blood rising in hн cheeks. To hide it, he swung about, letting the cold air from tн alf-open window play on his countenance. "Surely," he said, to he rain-slick gray stones below, "if he is the intelligent man you ay, he would not be so foolish as to attack me in my own quarters, n the midst of the prison? What would be the purpose in it?"

Quarry didn't answer. After a moment, Grey turned around, to ind the other staring at him thoughtfully, all trace of humor gone rom the broad, ruddy face.

"There's intelligence," Quarry said slowly. "And then there re other things. But perhaps you're too young to have seen hate nd despair at close range. There's been a deal of it in Scotland, hese last ten years." He tilted his head, surveying the new commander of Ardsmuir from his vantage point of fifteen years' seiority.

Major Grey *was* young, no more than twenty-six, and with a air-complexioned face and girlish lashes that made him look still ounger than his years. To compound the problem, he was an inch r two shorter than the average, and fine-boned, as well. He drew imself up straight.

"I am aware of such things, Colonel," he said evenly. Quarry vas a younger son of good family, like himself, but still his supe-ior in rank; he must keep his temper.

Quarry's bright hazel gaze rested on him in speculation.

"I daresay."

With a sudden motion, he clapped his hat on his' head. He ouched his cheek, where the darker line of a scar sliced across the uddy skin; a memento of the scandalous duel that had sent him nto exile at Ardsmuir.

"God knows what you did to be sent here, Grey," he said, haking his head. "But for your own sake, I hope you deserved it! uck to you!" And with a swirl of blue cloak, he was gone.

"Better the Devil ye ken than the Devil ye don't," Murdo indsay said, shaking his head lugubriously. "Handsome Harry vas nain sae bad."

"No, he wasna, then," agreed Kenny Lesley. "But ye'll ha' een here when he came, no? He was a deal better than that shite-ace Bogle, aye?"

"Aye," said Murdo, looking blank. "What's your meaning, nan?"

"So if Handsome was better than Bogle," Lesley explaine patiently, "then Handsome was the Devil we didna ken, and Bog the one that we did—but Handsome was better, in spite of that, s you're wrong, man."

"I am?" Murdo, hopelessly confused by this bit of reasonin glowered at Lesley. "No, I'm not!"

"Ye are, then," Lesley said, losing patience. "Ye're alway wrong, Murdo! Why d'ye argue, when ye're never in the right c it?"

"I'm no arguin'!" Murdo protested indignantly. "Ye're taki exception to *me,* not t'other way aboot."

"Only because ye're wrong, man!" Lesley said. "If ye we right, I'd have said not a word."

"I'm not wrong! At least I dinna think so," Murdo mutter unable to recall precisely what he had said. He turned, appealin to the large figure seated in the corner. "Mac Dubh, was wrong?"

The tall man stretched himself, the chain of his irons chimin faintly as he moved, and laughed.

"No, Murdo, ye're no wrong. But we canna say if ye're rig yet awhile. Not 'til we see what the new Devil's like, aye?" Seein Lesley's brows draw down in preparation for further dispute, h raised his voice, speaking to the room at large. "Has anyone see the new Governor yet? Johnson? MacTavish?"

"I have," Hayes said, pushing gladly forward to warm h hands at the fire. There was only one hearth in the large cell, an room for no more than six men before it at a time. The other fort were left in bitter chill, huddling together in small groups fc warmth.

Consequently, the agreement was that whoever had a tale to te or a song to sing might have a place by the hearth, for as long as h spoke. Mac Dubh had said this was a bard-right, that when th bards came to the old castles, they would be given a warm plac and plenty to eat and drink, to the honor of the laird's hospitality There was never food or drink to spare here, but the warm plac was certain.

Hayes relaxed, eyes closed and a beatific smile on his face as h spread his hands to the warmth. Warned by restive movement either side, though, he hastily opened his eyes and began to spea

"I saw him when he came in from his carriage, and then agai

en I brought up a platter o' sweeties from the kitchens, whilst
and Handsome Harry were nattering to ain another." Hayes
wned in concentration.

"He's fair-haired, wi' long yellow locks tied up wi' blue rib-
n. And big eyes and long lashes, too, like a lassie's." Hayes
red at his listeners, batting his own stubby lashes in mock
tation.

Encouraged by the laughter, he went on to describe the new
vernor's clothes—"fine as a laird's"—his equipage and ser-
nt—"one of they Sassenachs as talks like he's burnt his
gue"—and as much as had been overheard of the new man's
ech.

"He talks sharp and quick, like he'll know what's what,"
yes said, shaking his head dubiously. "But he's verra young,
bye—he looks scarce more than a wean, though I'd reckon he's
der than his looks."

"Aye, he's a bittie fellow, smaller than wee Angus," Baird
imed in, with a jerk of the head at Angus MacKenzie, who
ked down at himself in startlement. Angus had been twelve
en he fought beside his father at Culloden. He had spent nearly
f his life in Ardsmuir, and in consequence of the poor fare of
ison, had never grown much bigger.

"Aye," Hayes agreed, "but he carries himself well; shoulders
uare and a ramrod up his arse."

This gave rise to a burst of laughter and ribald comment, and
yes gave way to Ogilvie, who knew a long and scurrilous story
out the laird of Donibristle and the hogman's daughter. Hayes
t the hearth without resentment, and went—as was the custom
to sit beside Mac Dubh.

Mac Dubh never took his place on the hearth, even when he told
em the long stories from the books that he'd read—*The Adven-
res of Roderick Random, The History of Tom Jones, a Foundling,*
everyone's favorite, *Robinson Crusoe.* Claiming that he needed
e room to accommodate his long legs, Mac Dubh sat always in
s same spot in the corner, where everyone might hear him. But
e men who left the fire would come, one by one, and sit down on
e bench beside him, to give him the warmth that lingered in their
othes.

"Shall ye speak to the new Governor tomorrow, d'ye think,
ac Dubh?" Hayes asked as he sat. "I met Billy Malcolm, com-

ing in from the peat-cutting, and he shouted to me as the rats w
grown uncommon bold in their cell just now. Six men bitten t
sennight as they slept, and two of them festering.''

Mac Dubh shook his head, and scratched at his chin. He h
been allowed a razor before his weekly audiences with Ha
Quarry, but it had been five days since the last of these, and
chin was thick with red stubble.

"I canna say, Gavin," he said. "Quarry did say as he'd tell
new fellow of our arrangement, but the new man might have
own ways, aye? If I'm called to see him, though, I shall be sure
say about the rats. Did Malcolm ask for Morrison to come and
to the festering, though?" The prison had no doctor; Morris
who had a touch for healing, was permitted by the guards t
from cell to cell to tend the sick or injured, at Mac Dubh's reque

Hayes shook his head. "He hadna time to say more—they w
marching past, aye?"

"Best I send Morrison," Mac Dubh decided. "He can ask Bi
is there aught else amiss there." There were four main cells wh
the prisoners were kept in large groups; word passed among the
by means of Morrison's visits and the mingling of men on t
work crews that went out daily to haul stone or cut peats on t
nearby moor.

Morrison came at once when summoned, pocketing four of t
carved rats' skulls with which the prisoners improvised games
chess. Mac Dubh groped under the bench where he sat, draw
out the cloth bag he carried when he went to the moor.

"Och, not more o' the damn thistles," Morrison protest
seeing Mac Dubh's grimace as he groped in the bag. "I can
make them eat those things; they all say, do I think them kine,
maybe pigs?"

Mac Dubh gingerly set down a fistful of wilted stalks, a
sucked his pricked fingers.

"They're stubborn as pigs, to be sure," he remarked. "It's o
milk thistle. How often must I tell ye, Morrison? Take the this
heads off, and mash the leaves and stems fine, and if they're
prickly to eat spread on a bannock, then make a tea of them a
have them drink it. I've yet to see pigs drink tea, tell them."

Morrison's lined face cracked in a grin. An elderly man,
knew well enough how to handle recalcitrant patients; he o
liked to complain for the fun of it.

"Aye, well, I'll say have they ever seen a toothless cow?" he ‍d, resigned, as he tucked the limp greens carefully into his own ‍ck. "But you'll be sure to bare your teeth at Joel McCulloch, ‍xt time ye see him. He's the worst o' them, for not believin' as ‍e greens do help wi' the scurvy."

"Say as I'll bite him in the arse," Mac Dubh promised, with a ‍sh of his excellent teeth, "if I hear he hasna eaten his thistles."

Morrison made the small amused noise that passed for a belly ‍igh with him, and went to gather up the bits of ointment and the ‍w herbs he had for medicines.

Mac Dubh relaxed for the moment, glancing about the room to ‍sure no trouble brewed. There were feuds at the moment; he'd ‍ttled Bobby Sinclair and Edwin Murray's trouble a week back, ‍d while they were not friends, they were keeping their distance ‍om one another.

He closed his eyes. He was tired; he had been hauling stone all ‍y. Supper would be along in a few minutes—a tub of parritch ‍d some bread to be shared out, a bit of brose too if they were ‍cky—and likely most of the men would go to sleep soon after, ‍aving him a few minutes of peace and semiprivacy, when he ‍ed not listen to anyone or feel he must do anything.

He had had no time as yet even to wonder about the new Gover-‍r, important as the man would be to all their lives. Young, Hayes ‍d said. That might be good, or might be bad.

Older men who had fought in the Rising were often prejudiced ‍ainst Highlanders—Bogle, who had put him in irons, had fought ‍th Cope. A scared young soldier, though, trying to keep abreast ‍ an unfamiliar job, could be more rigid and tyrannical than the ‍ustiest of old colonels. Aye, well, and nothing to be done but ‍ait to see.

He sighed and shifted his posture, incommoded—for the ten-‍ousandth time—by the manacles he wore. He shifted irritably, ‍nging one wrist against the edge of the bench. He was large ‍ough that the weight of the irons didn't trouble him overmuch, ‍t they chafed badly with the work. Worse was the inability to ‍read his arms more than eighteen inches apart; this gave him ‍amp and a clawing feeling, deep in the muscle of chest and back, ‍t left him only when he slept.

"Mac Dubh," said a soft voice beside him. "A word in your ‍r, if I might?" He opened his eyes to see Ronnie Sutherland

perched alongside, pointed face intent and foxlike in the fa
glow from the fire.

''Aye, Ronnie, of course.'' He pushed himself upright, and j
both his irons and the thought of the new Governor firmly from
mind.

Dearest Mother, John Grey wrote, later that night.

*I am arrived safely at my new post, and find it comfortable.
Colonel Quarry, my predecessor—he is the Duke of Clarence's nephew, you recall?—made me welcome and acquainted with my charge. I am provided with a most excellent servant, and while I am bound to find many things
about Scotland strange at first, I am sure I will find the
experience interesting. I was served an object for my supper that the steward told me was called a "haggis." Upon
inquiry, this proved to be the interior organ of a sheep,
filled with a mixture of ground oats and a quantity of
unidentifiable cooked flesh. Though I am assured the inhabitants of Scotland esteem this dish a particular delicacy, I sent it to the kitchens and requested a plain boiled
saddle of mutton in its place. Having thus made my first—
humble!—meal here, and being somewhat fatigued by the
long journey—of whose details I shall inform you in a subsequent missive—I believe I shall now retire, leaving further descriptions of my surroundings—with which I am imperfectly acquainted at present, as it is dark—for a future
communication.*

He paused, tapping the quill on the blotter. The point left sm
dots of ink, and he abstractedly drew lines connecting these, ma
ing the outlines of a jagged object.

Dared he ask about George? Not a direct inquiry, that would
do, but a reference to the family, asking whether his mother h
happened to encounter Lady Everett lately, and might he ask to
remembered to her son?

He sighed and drew another point on his object. No. His wi
owed mother was ignorant of the situation, but Lady Everet
husband moved in military circles. His brother's influence wou

ep the gossip to a minimum, but Lord Everett might catch a
hiff of it, nonetheless, and be quick enough to put two and two
gether. Let him drop an injudicious word to his wife about
eorge, and the word pass on from Lady Everett to his mother
. . the Dowager Countess Melton was not a fool.

She knew quite well that he was in disgrace; promising young
ficers in the good graces of their superiors were not sent to the
se-end of Scotland to oversee the renovation of small and unim-
rtant prison-fortresses. But his brother Harold had told her that
e trouble was an unfortunate affair of the heart, implying suffi-
ent indelicacy to stop her questioning him about it. She likely
ought he had been caught with his colonel's wife, or keeping a
hore in his quarters.

An unfortunate affair of the heart! He smiled grimly, dipping
s pen. Perhaps Hal had a greater sensitivity than he'd thought, in
describing it. But then, all his affairs had been unfortunate,
ce Hector's death at Culloden.

With the thought of Culloden, the thought of Fraser came back
him; something he had been avoiding all day. He looked from
e blotter to the folder which held the prisoners' roll, biting his
. He was tempted to open it, and look to see the name, but what
int was there in that? There might be scores of men in the
ghlands named James Fraser, but only one known also as Red
mie.

He felt himself flush as waves of heat rolled over him, but it was
t nearness to the fire. In spite of that, he rose and went to the
ndow, drawing in great lungfuls of air as though the cold draft
uld cleanse him of memory.

"Pardon, sir, but will ye be wantin' yer bed warmed now?" The
ottish speech behind him startled him, and he whirled round to
d the tousled head of the prisoner assigned to tend his quarters
king through the door that led to his private rooms.

"Oh! Er, yes. Thank you . . . MacDonell?" he said doubt-
lly.

"MacKay, my lord," the man corrected, without apparent re-
ntment, and the head vanished.

Grey sighed. There was nothing that could be done tonight. He
me back to the desk and gathered up the folders, to put them
ay. The jagged object he had drawn on the blotter looked like
e of those spiked maces, with which ancient knights had

crushed the heads of their foes. He felt as though he had sw[a]-
lowed one, though perhaps this was no more than indigesti[on]
occasioned by half-cooked mutton.

He shook his head, pulled the letter to him and signed it hasti[ly]
With all affection, your obt. son, John Wm. Grey. He sho[ok]
sand over the signature, sealed the missive with his ring and se[t]
aside to be posted in the morning.

He rose and stood hesitating, surveying the shadowy reaches [of]
the office. It was a great, cold, barren room, with little in it bar t[he]
huge desk and a couple of chairs. He shivered; the sullen glow [of]
the peat bricks on the hearth did little to warm its vast space[,]
particularly with the freezing wet air coming in at the window[.]

He glanced once more at the prisoners' roll. Then he be[nt,]
opened the lower drawer of the desk, and drew out the brown gl[ass]
bottle. He pinched out the candle, and made his way toward [his]
bed by the dull glow of the hearth.

The mingled effects of exhaustion and whisky should have se[nt]
him to sleep at once, but sleep kept its distance, hovering over [his]
bed like a bat, but never lighting. Every time he felt hims[elf]
sinking into dreams, a vision of the wood at Carryarrick ca[me]
before his eyes, and he found himself lying once more wide-awa[ke]
and sweating, his heart thundering in his ears.

He had been sixteen then, excited beyond bearing by his fi[rst]
campaign. He had not got his commission then, but his broth[er]
Hal had taken him along with the regiment, so that he might ge[t a]
taste of soldiering.

Camped at night near a dark Scottish wood, on their way to j[oin]
General Cope at Prestonpans, John had found himself too nervo[us]
to sleep. What would the battle be like? Cope was a great gener[al,]
all Hal's friends said so, but the men around the fires told fright[ful]
stories of the fierce Highlanders and their bloody broadswor[ds.]
Would he have the courage to face the dreadful Highland charg[e?]

He couldn't bring himself to mention his fears even to Hect[or.]
Hector loved him, but Hector was twenty, tall and muscular a[nd]
fearless, with a lieutenant's commission and dashing stories [of]
battles fought in France.

He didn't know, even now, whether it had been an urge [to]
emulate Hector, or merely to impress him, that had led him to [the]

In either case, when he saw the Highlander in the wood, and
recognized him from the broadsheets as the notorious Red Jamie
Fraser, he had determined to kill or capture him.

The notion of returning to camp for help *had* occurred to him,
but the man was alone—at least John had thought he was alone—
and evidently unawares, seated quietly upon a log, eating a bit of
bread.

And so he had drawn his knife from his belt and crept quietly
through the wood toward that shining red head, the haft slippery in
his grasp, his mind filled with visions of glory and Hector's praise.
Instead, there had been a glancing blow as his knife flashed
down, his arm locked tight round the Scot's neck to choke him,
and then—

Lord John Grey flung himself over in his bed, hot with remem-
brance. They had fallen back, rolling together in the crackling
oak-leaf dark, grappling for the knife, thrashing and fighting—for
his life, he had thought.

First the Scot had been under him, then twisting, somehow over.
He had touched a great snake once, a python that a friend of his
uncle's had brought from the Indies, and that was what it had been
like, Fraser's touch, lithe and smooth and horribly powerful, moving like the muscular coils, never where you expected it to be.

He had been flung ignominiously on his face in the leaves, his
wrist twisted painfully behind his back. In a frenzy of terror,
convinced he was about to be slain, he had wrenched with all his
strength at his trapped arm, and the bone had snapped, with a red-
black burst of pain that rendered him momentarily senseless.

He had come to himself moments later, slumped against a tree,
facing a circle of ferocious-looking Highlanders, all in their
plaids. In the midst of them stood Red Jamie Fraser—and the
woman.

Grey clenched his teeth. Curse that woman! If it hadn't been for
her—well, God knew what might have happened. What *had* happened was that she had spoken. She was English, a lady by her
speech, and he—idiot that he was!—had leapt at once to the conclusion that she was a hostage of the vicious Highlanders, no
doubt kidnapped for the purpose of ravishment. Everyone said that
Highlanders indulged in rapine at every opportunity, and took
delight in dishonoring Englishwomen; how should he have known
otherwise!

And Lord John William Grey, aged sixteen and filled to t
brim with regimental notions of gallantry and noble purpo
bruised, shaken, and fighting the pain of his broken arm, had tri
to bargain, to save her from her fate. Fraser, tall and mocking, h
played him like a salmon, stripping the woman half-naked befo
him to force from him information about the position and streng
of his brother's regiment. And then, when he had told all he cou
Fraser had laughingly revealed that the woman was his wi
They'd all laughed; he could hear the ribald Scottish voices no
hilarious in memory.

Grey rolled over, shifting his weight irritably on the unacce
tomed mattress. And to make it all worse, Fraser had not even h
the decency to kill him, but instead had tied him to a tree, whe
he would be found by his friends in the morning. By which tir
Fraser's men had visited the camp and—with the information
had given them!—had immobilized the cannon they were bringi
to Cope.

Everyone had found out, of course, and while excuses we
made because of his age and his noncommissioned status, he h
been a pariah and an object of scorn. No one would speak to hi
save his brother—and Hector. Loyal Hector.

He sighed, rubbing his cheek against the pillow. He could s
Hector still, in his mind's eye. Dark-haired and blue-eyed, tend
mouthed, always smiling. It had been ten years since Hector h
died at Culloden, hacked to pieces by a Highland broadsword, a
still John woke in the dawn sometimes, body arched in clutchi
spasm, feeling Hector's touch.

And now this. He had dreaded this posting, being surround
by Scots, by their grating voices, overwhelmed with the memo
of what they had done to Hector. But never, in the most disr
moments of anticipation, had he thought he would ever me
James Fraser again.

The peat fire on the hearth died gradually to hot ash, then co
and the window paled from deep black to the sullen gray of a rai
Scottish dawn. And still John Grey lay sleepless, burning ey
fixed on the smoke-blackened beams above him.

Grey rose in the morning unrested, but with his mind made u
He was here. Fraser was here. And neither could leave, for t

ɔreseeable future. So. He must see the man now and again—he
ɾould be speaking to the assembled prisoners in an hour, and must
ɪspect them regularly thereafter—but he would not see him pri-
ately. If he kept the man himself at a distance, perhaps he could
lso keep at bay the memories he stirred. And the feelings.

For while it was the memory of his past rage and humiliation
ɪat had kept him awake to begin with, it was the other side of the
resent situation that had left him still wakeful at dawn. The
owly dawning realization that Fraser was now *his* prisoner; no
ɔnger his tormentor, but a prisoner, like the others, entirely at his
ɪercy.

He rang the bell for his servant and padded to the window to see
ow the weather kept, wincing at the chill of the stone under his
are feet.

It was, not surprisingly, raining. In the courtyard below, the
risoners were already being formed up in work crews, wet to the
cin. Shivering in his shirt, Grey pulled in his head and shut the
indow halfway; a nice compromise between death from suffoca-
on and death from the ague.

It had been visions of revenge that kept him tossing in his bed
; the window lightened and the rain pattered on the sill; thoughts
f Fraser confined to a tiny cell of freezing stone, kept naked
rough the winter nights, fed on slops, stripped and flogged in the
ɔurtyard of the prison. All that arrogant power humbled, reduced
• groveling misery, dependent solely on his word for a moment's
•lief.

Yes, he thought all those things, imagined them in vivid detail,
veled in them. He heard Fraser beg for mercy, imagined himself
sdaining, haughty. He thought these things, and the spiked ob-
ct turned over in his guts, piercing him with self-disgust.

Whatever he might once have been to Grey, Fraser now was a
:aten foe; a prisoner of war, and the charge of the Crown. He was
ʲrey's charge, in fact; a responsibility, and his welfare the duty of
ɔnor.

His servant had brought hot water for shaving. He splashed his
ɪeeks, feeling the warmth soothe him, laying to rest the tor-
ɪented fancies of the night. That was all they were, he realized—
ɪncies, and the realization brought him a certain relief.

He might have met Fraser in battle and taken a real and savage
easure in killing or maiming him. But the inescapable fact was

that so long as Fraser was his prisoner, he could not in honor har
the man. By the time he had shaved and his servant had dresse
him, he was recovered enough to find a certain grim humor in tl
situation.

His foolish behavior at Carryarrick had saved Fraser's life
Culloden. Now, that debt discharged, and Fraser in his powe
Fraser's sheer helplessness as a prisoner made him complete
safe. For whether foolish or wise, naive or experienced, all tl
Greys were men of honor.

Feeling somewhat better, he met his gaze in the looking glas
set his wig to rights, and went to eat breakfast before giving h
first address to the prisoners.

"Will you have your supper served in the sitting room, sir, or
here?" MacKay's head, uncombed as ever, poked into the offic

"Um?" Grey murmured, absorbed in the papers spread out (
the desk. "Oh," he said, looking up. "In here, if you please." I
waved vaguely at the corner of the huge desk and returned to h
work, scarcely looking up when the tray with his food arriv(
sometime later.

Quarry had not been joking about the paperwork. The she
quantity of food alone required endless orders and requisitions-
all orders to be submitted in duplicate to London, *if* he pleased!-
let alone the hundreds of other necessities required by the priso
ers, the guards, and the men and women from the village wl
came in by the day to clean the barracks and work in the kitchen
He had done nothing all day but write and sign requisitions. I
must find a clerk soon, or die of sheer ennui.

Two hundred lb. wheat flowr, he wrote, *for prisoners' use. S
hogsheads ale, for use of barracks.* His normally elegant handwr
ing had quickly degenerated into a utilitarian scrawl, his styli:
signature become a curt *J. Grey.*

He laid down his pen with a sigh and closed his eyes, massagi
the ache between his brows. The sun had not bothered to show i
face once since his arrival, and working all day in a smoky roo
by candlelight left his eyes burning like lumps of coal. His boo
had arrived the day before, but he had not even unpacked the
too exhausted by nightfall to do more than bathe his aching eyes
cold water and go to sleep.

He heard a small, stealthy sound, and sat up abruptly, his eyes popping open. A large brown rat sat on the corner of his desk, a morsel of plum cake held in its front paws. It didn't move, but merely looked at him speculatively, whiskers twitching.

"Well, God damn my eyes!" Grey exclaimed in amazement. "Here, you bugger! That's *my* supper!"

The rat nibbled pensively at the plum cake, bright beady eyes fixed on the Major.

"Get out of it!" Enraged, Grey snatched up the nearest object and let fly at the rat. The ink bottle exploded on the stone floor in a spray of black, and the startled rat leapt off the desk and fled precipitously, galloping between the legs of the even more startled MacKay, who appeared at the door to see what the noise was.

"Has the prison got a cat?" Grey demanded, dumping the contents of his supper tray into the waste can by his desk.

"Aye, sir, there's cats in the storerooms," MacKay offered, crawling backward on hands and knees to wipe up the small black footprints the rat had left in its precipitous flight through the ink puddle.

"Well, fetch one up here, if you please, MacKay," Grey ordered. "At once." He grunted at the memory of that obscenely naked tail draped nonchalantly over his plate. He had encountered rats often enough in the field, of course, but there was something about having his own personal supper molested before his eyes that seemed particularly infuriating.

He strode to the window and stood there, trying to clear his head with fresh air, as MacKay finished his mopping-up. Dusk was drawing down, filling the courtyard with purple shadows. The stones of the cell wing opposite looked even colder and more dreary than usual.

The turnkeys were coming through the rain from the kitchen wing; a procession of small carts laden with the prisoners' food; huge pots of steaming oatmeal and baskets of bread, covered with cloths against the rain. At least the poor devils had hot food after their wet day's work in the stone quarry.

A thought struck him as he turned from the window.

"Are there many rats in the cells?" he asked MacKay.

"Aye, sir, a great many," the prisoner replied, with a final wipe to the threshold. "I'll tell the cook to make ye up a fresh tray, shall I, sir?"

"If you please," Grey said. "And then if you will, Mr. Ma Kay, please see that each cell is provided with its own cat."

MacKay looked slightly dubious at this. Grey paused in the of retrieving his scattered papers.

"Is there something wrong, MacKay?"

"No, sir," MacKay replied slowly. "Only the wee brown bea ties do keep down the cockchafers. And with respect, sir, I din think the men would care to have a cat takin' all their rats."

Grey stared at the man, feeling mildly queasy.

"The prisoners eat the rats?" he asked, with a vivid memory sharp yellow teeth nibbling at his plum cake.

"Only when they're lucky enough to catch one, sir," MacK said. "Perhaps the cats would be a help wi' that, after all. Will t be all for tonight, sir?"

9

The Wanderer

rey's resolve concerning James Fraser lasted for two
weeks. Then the messenger arrived from the village of
Ardsmuir, with news that changed everything.

"Does he still live?" he asked the man sharply. The messenger,
e of the inhabitants of Ardsmuir village who worked for the
son, nodded.

"I saw him mysel', sir, when they brought him in. He's at the
me Tree now, being cared for—but I didna think he looked as
ugh care would be enough, sir, if ye take my meaning." He
sed one brow significantly.

"I take it," Grey answered shortly. "Thank you, Mr.—"

"Allison, sir, Rufus Allison. Your servant, sir." The man ac-
pted the shilling offered him, bowed with his hat under his arm,
d took his leave.

Grey sat at his desk, staring out at the leaden sky. The sun had
arcely shone for a day since his arrival. He tapped the end of the
ill with which he had been writing on the desk, oblivious to the
mage he was inflicting on the sharpened tip.

The mention of gold was enough to prick up any man's ears, but
pecially his.

A man had been found this morning, wandering in the mist on
e moor near the village. His clothes were soaked not only with
e damp, but with seawater, and he was out of his mind with
ver.

He had talked unceasingly since he was found, babbling for the
ost part, but his rescuers were unable to make much sense of his

ravings. The man appeared to be Scottish, and yet he spoke in
incoherent mixture of French and Gaelic, with here and there
odd word of English thrown in. And one of those words had be
"gold."

The combination of Scots, gold, and the French tongue, me
tioned in this area of the country, could bring only one thought
the mind of anyone who had fought through the last days of
Jacobite rising. The Frenchman's Gold. The fortune in gold b
lion that Louis of France had—according to rumor—sent secre
to the aid of his cousin, Charles Stuart. But sent far too late.

Some stories said that the French gold had been hidden by t
Highland army during the last headlong retreat to the North,
fore the final disaster at Culloden. Others held that the gold h
never reached Charles Stuart, but had been left for safekeeping
a cave near the place where it had come ashore on the northwe
ern coast.

Some said that the secret of the hiding place had been lost,
guardian killed at Culloden. Others said that the hiding place w
still known, but a close-kept secret, held among the members o
single Highland family. Whatever the truth, the gold had ne
been found. Not yet.

French and Gaelic. Grey spoke passable French, the result
several years fighting abroad, but neither he nor any of his office
spoke the barbarous Gaelic, save a few words Sergeant Grisse
had learned as a child from a Scottish nursemaid.

He could not trust a man from the village; not if there w
anything to this tale. The Frenchman's Gold! Beyond its value
treasure—which would belong to the Crown in any case—the go
had a considerable and personal value to John William Grey. T
finding of that half-mythical hoard would be his passport out
Ardsmuir—back to London and civilization. The blackest di
grace would be instantly obscured by the dazzle of gold.

He bit the end of the blunted quill, feeling the cylinder cra
between his teeth.

Damn. No, it couldn't be a villager, nor one of his officers.
prisoner, then. Yes, he could use a prisoner without risk, for
prisoner would be unable to make use of the information for
own ends.

Damn again. All of the prisoners spoke Gaelic, many had son

lish as well—but only one spoke French besides. *He is an*
cated man, Quarry's voice echoed in his memory.

"Damn, damn, *damn!*" Grey muttered. It couldn't be helped.
son had said the wanderer was very ill; there was no time to
k for alternatives. He spat out a shred of quill.

"Brame!" he shouted. The startled corporal poked his head in.
"Yes, sir?"

"Bring me a prisoner named James Fraser. At once."

he Governor stood behind his desk, leaning on it as though the
e slab of oak were in fact the bulwark it looked. His hands
e damp on the smooth wood, and the white stock of his uni-
m felt tight around his neck.

lis heart leapt violently as the door opened. The Scot came in,
irons chinking slightly, and stood before the desk. The candles
e all lit, and the office nearly as bright as day, though it was
rly full dark outside.

le had seen Fraser several times, of course, standing in the
rtyard with the other prisoners, red head and shoulders above
st of the other men, but never close enough to see his face
arly.

le looked different. That was both shock and relief; for so long,
had seen a clean-shaven face in memory, dark with threat or
ght with mocking laughter. This man was short-bearded, his
e calm and wary, and while the deep blue eyes were the same,
y gave no sign of recognition. The man stood quietly before the
k, waiting.

irey cleared his throat. His heart was still beating too fast, but
east he could speak calmly.

"Mr. Fraser," he said. "I thank you for coming."

he Scot bent his head courteously, but did not answer that he
had no choice in the matter; his eyes said that.

"Doubtless you wonder why I have sent for you," Grey said.
sounded insufferably pompous to his own ears, but was unable
emedy it. "I find that a situation has arisen in which I require
r assistance."

"What is that, Major?" The voice was the same—deep and
cise, marked with a soft Highland burr.

le took a deep breath, bracing himself on the desk. He would

rather have done anything but ask help of this particular man, l
there was no bloody choice. Fraser was the only possibility.

"A man has been found wandering the moor near the coas
he said carefully. "He appears to be seriously ill, and his speecl
deranged. However, certain . . . matters to which he refers ;
pear to be of . . . substantial interest to the Crown. I require
talk with him, and discover as much as I can of his identity, ;
the matters of which he speaks."

He paused, but Fraser merely stood there, waiting.

"Unfortunately," Grey said, taking another breath, "the mar
question has been heard to speak in a mixture of Gaelic ;
French, with no more than a word or two of English."

One of the Scot's ruddy eyebrows stirred. His face did
change in any appreciable way, but it was evident that he l
grasped the implications of the situation.

"I see, Major." The Scot's soft voice was full of irony. "A
you would like my assistance to interpret for ye what this n
might have to say."

Grey couldn't trust himself to speak, but merely jerked his he
in a short nod.

"I fear I must decline, Major." Fraser spoke respectfully,
with a glint in his eye that was anything but respectful. Gre
hand curled tight around the brass letter-opener on his blotter.

"You decline?" he said. He tightened his grasp on the lett
opener in order to keep his voice steady. "Might I inquire w
Mr. Fraser?"

"I am a prisoner, Major," the Scot said politely. "Not
interpreter."

"Your assistance would be—appreciated," Grey said, trying
infuse the word with significance without offering outright br
ery. "Conversely"—his tone hardened—"a failure to render
gitimate assistance—"

"It is not legitimate for ye either to extort my services or
threaten me, Major." Fraser's voice was a good deal harder th
Grey's.

"I did not threaten you!" The edge of the letter-opener v
cutting into his hand; he was forced to loosen his grip.

"Did ye no? Well, and I'm pleased to hear it." Fraser turi
toward the door. "In that case, Major, I shall bid ye good nigh

Grey would have given a great deal simply to have let him go. ﬀortunately, duty called.

"Mr. Fraser!" The Scot stopped, a few feet from the door, but dn't turn.

Grey took a deep breath, steeling himself to it.

"If you do what I ask, I will have your irons struck off," he id.

Fraser stood quite still. Young and inexperienced Grey might , but he was not unobservant. Neither was he a poor judge of en. Grey watched the rise of his prisoner's head, the increased nsion of his shoulders, and felt a small relaxation of the anxiety at had gripped him since the news of the wanderer had come.

"Mr. Fraser?" he said.

Very slowly, the Scot turned around. His face was quite expres- ꞓnless.

"You have a bargain, Major," he said softly.

It was well past midnight when they arrived in the village of ꞏdsmuir. No lights showed in the cottages they passed, and Grey und himself wondering what the inhabitants thought, as the und of hooves and the jingle of arms passed by their windows ꞏe at night, a faint echo of the English troops who had swept ꞏough the Highlands ten years before.

The wanderer had been taken to the Lime Tree, an inn so called cause for many years, it had boasted a huge lime tree in the rd; the only tree of any size for thirty miles. There was nothing ft now but a broad stump—the tree, like so many other things, d perished in the aftermath of Culloden, burned for firewood by ꞏmberland's troops—but the name remained.

At the door, Grey paused and turned to Fraser.

"You will recall the terms of our agreement?"

"I will," Fraser answered shortly, and brushed past him.

In return for having the irons removed, Grey had required three ꞏngs: firstly, that Fraser would not attempt to escape during the ꞏrney to or from the village. Secondly, Fraser would undertake give a full and true account of all that the vagrant should say. ꞏd thirdly, Fraser would give his word as a gentleman to speak to ꞏone but Grey of what he learned.

There was a murmur of Gaelic voices inside; a sound of sur-

prise as the innkeeper saw Fraser, and deference at the sight of tl
Redcoat behind him. The goodwife stood on the stair, an oil-dip
her hand making the shadows dance around her.

Grey laid a hand on the innkeeper's arm, startled.

"Who is that?" There was another figure on the stairs, a
apparition, clothed all in black.

"That is the priest," Fraser said quietly, beside him. "The ma
will be dying, then."

Grey took a deep breath, trying to steady himself for wh
might come.

"Then there is little time to waste," he said firmly, setting
booted foot on the stair. "Let us proceed."

The man died just before dawn, Fraser holding one of his hand
the priest the other. As the priest leaned over the bed, mumbling
Gaelic and Latin, making Popish signs over the body, Fraser s
back on his stool, eyes closed, still holding the small, frail hand
his own.

The big Scot had sat by the man's side all night, listenin
encouraging, comforting. Grey had stood by the door, not wishi
to frighten the man by the sight of his uniform, both surprised a
oddly touched at Fraser's gentleness.

Now Fraser laid the thin weathered hand gently across the st
chest, and made the same sign as the priest had, touching for
head, heart, and both shoulders in turn, in the sign of a cross. I
opened his eyes, and rose to his feet, his head nearly brushing tl
low rafters. He nodded briefly to Grey, and preceded him dov
the narrow stair.

"In here." Grey motioned to the door of the taproom, empty
this hour. A sleepy-eyed barmaid laid the fire for them a
brought bread and ale, then went out, leaving them alone.

He waited for Fraser to refresh himself before asking.

"Well, Mr. Fraser?"

The Scot set down his pewter mug and wiped a hand across ł
mouth. Already bearded, with his long hair neatly plaited, ł
didn't look disheveled by the long night watch, but there were da
smudges of tiredness under his eyes.

"All right," he said. "It doesna make a great deal of sens
Major," he added warningly, "but this is all he said." And

oke carefully, pausing now and then to recall a word, stopping
ain to explain some Gaelic reference. Grey sat listening in deep-
ing disappointment; Fraser had been correct—it didn't make
uch sense.

"The white witch?" Grey interrupted. "He spoke of a white
itch? And seals?" It scarcely seemed more farfetched than the
st of it, but still he spoke disbelievingly.

"Aye, he did."

"Say it to me again," Grey commanded. "As best you remem-
r. If you please," he added.

He felt oddly comfortable with the man, he realized, with a
eling of surprise. Part of it was sheer fatigue, of course; all his
ual reactions and feelings were numbed by the long night and
e strain of watching a man die by inches.

The entire night had seemed unreal to Grey; not least was this
ld conclusion, wherein he found himself sitting in the dim dawn
ght of a country tavern, sharing a pitcher of ale with Red Jamie
aser.

Fraser obeyed, speaking slowly, stopping now and then to re-
ll. With the difference of a word here or there, it was identical to
e first account—and those parts of it that Grey himself had been
le to understand were faithfully translated.

He shook his head, discouraged. Gibberish. The man's ravings
d been precisely that—ravings. If the man had ever seen any
ld—and it did sound as though he had, at one time—there was
 telling where or when from this hodgepodge of delusion and
verish delirium.

"You are quite positive that is all he said?" Grey grasped at the
m hope that Fraser might have omitted some small phrase, some
atement that would yield a clue to the lost gold.

Fraser's sleeve fell back as he lifted his cup; Grey could see the
ep band of raw flesh about his wrist, dark in the gray early light
 the taproom. Fraser saw him looking at it, and set down the cup,
 frail illusion of companionship shattered.

"I keep my bargains, Major," Fraser said, with cold formality.
 rose to his feet. "Shall we be going back now?"

They rode in silence for some time. Fraser was lost in his own
oughts, Grey sunk in fatigue and disappointment. They stopped
 a spring to refresh themselves, just as the sun topped the small
ls to the north.

Grey drank cold water, then splashed it on his face, feeling t
shock of it revive him momentarily. He had been awake for mo
than twenty-four hours, and was feeling slow and stupid.

Fraser had been awake for the same twenty-four hours, but ga
no sign of being troubled by the fact. He was crawling busi
around the spring on his hands and knees, evidently plucki
some sort of weed from the water.

"What are you doing, Mr. Fraser?" Grey asked, in some bew
derment.

Fraser looked up, mildly surprised, but not embarrassed in t
slightest.

"I am picking watercress, Major."

"I see that," Grey said testily. "What for?"

"To eat, Major," Fraser replied evenly. He took the stain
cloth bag from his belt and dropped the dripping green mass in
it.

"Indeed? Are you not fed sufficiently?" Grey asked blankly.
have never heard of people eating watercress."

"It's green, Major."

In his fatigued state, the Major had suspicions that he was bei
practiced upon.

"What in damnation other color ought a weed to be?" he d
manded.

Fraser's mouth twitched slightly, and he seemed to be debati
something with himself. At last he shrugged slightly, wiping I
wet hands on the sides of his breeks.

"I only meant, Major, that eating green plants will stop
getting scurvy and loose teeth. My men eat such greens as I ta
them, and cress is better-tasting than most things I can pick on t
moor."

Grey felt his brows shoot up.

"Green plants stop scurvy?" he blurted. "Wherever did y
get that notion?"

"From my wife!" Fraser snapped. He turned away abrupt
and stood, tying the neck of his sack with hard, quick movemen

Grey could not prevent himself asking.

"Your wife, sir—where is she?"

The answer was a sudden blaze of dark blue that seared him
the backbone, so shocking was its intensity.

Perhaps you are too young to know the power of hate a

spair. Quarry's voice spoke in Grey's memory. He was not; he ́cognized them at once in the depths of Fraser's eyes.

Only for a moment, though; then the man's normal veil of cool ́liteness was back in place.

"My wife is gone," Fraser said, and turned away again, so ́ruptly that the movement verged on rudeness.

Grey felt himself shaken by an unexpected feeling. In part it ́as relief. The woman who had been both cause of and party to ̇s humiliation was dead. In part, it was regret.

Neither of them spoke again on the journey back to Ardsmuir.

Three days later, Jamie Fraser escaped. It had never been a ́fficult matter for prisoners to escape from Ardsmuir; no one ever ́d, simply because there was no place for a man to go. Three ́iles from the prison, the coast of Scotland dropped into the ́ean in a spill of crumbled granite. On the other three sides, ́thing but empty moorland stretched for miles.

Once, a man might take to the heather, depending on clan and ́nsmen for support and protection. But the clans were crushed, ́e kin dead, the Scottish prisoners removed far away from their ́wn clan lands. Starving on the bleak moor was little improvement ́a prison cell. Escape was not worth it—to anyone but Jamie ́aser, who evidently had a reason.

The dragoons' horses kept to the road; while the surrounding ́oor looked smooth as a velvet counterpane, the purpling heather ́as a thin layer, deceptively spread over a foot or more of wet, ́ongy peat moss. Even the red deer didn't walk at random in that ́ggy mass—Grey could see four of the animals now, stick fig- ́es a mile away, the line of their track through the heather seem- ́g no wider than a thread.

Fraser, of course, was not mounted. That meant that the escaped ́isoner might be anywhere on the moor, free to follow the red ́er's paths.

It was John Grey's duty to pursue his prisoner and attempt his ́capture. It was something more than duty that had made him ́rip the garrison for his search party, and urge them on with only ́e briefest of stops for rest and food. Duty, yes, and an urgent

desire to find the French gold and win approval from his maste
—and reprieve from this desolate Scottish exile. But there wa
anger, too, and an odd sense of personal betrayal.

Grey wasn't sure whether he was more angry at Fraser fo
breaking his word, or at himself, for having been fool enough
believe that a Highlander—gentleman or not—held a sense
honor equal to his own. But angry he was, and determined
search every deer path on this moor if necessary, in order to la
James Fraser by the heels.

They reached the coast the next night, well after dark, after
laborious day of combing the moor. The fog had thinned awa
over the rocks, swept out by the offshore wind, and the sea sprea
out before them, cradled by cliffs and strewn with tiny barr
islets.

John Grey stood beside his horse on the clifftops, looking dow
at the wild black sea. It was a clear night on the coast, thank Go
and the moon was at the half; its gleam painted the spray-w
rocks, making them stand out hard and shining as silver ingo
against black velvet shadows.

It was the most desolate place he had ever seen, though it had
sort of terrible beauty about it that made the blood run cold in h
veins. There was no sign of James Fraser. No sign of life at al

One of the men with him gave a sudden exclamation of su
prise, and drew his pistol.

"There!" he said. "On the rocks!"

"Hold your fire, fool," said another of the soldiers, grabbi
his companion's arm. He made no effort to disguise his contem
"Have you ne'er seen seals?"

"Ah . . . no," said the first man, rather sheepishly. He lo
ered his pistol, staring out at the small dark forms on the roc
below.

Grey had never seen seals, either, and he watched them wi
fascination. They looked like black slugs from this distance, t
moonlight gleaming wetly on their coats as they raised restle
heads, seeming to roll and weave unsteadily as they made th
awkward way on land.

His mother had had a cloak made of sealskin, when he was
boy. He had been allowed to touch it once, marveling at the feel
it, dark and warm as a moonless summer night. Amazing that su
thick, soft fur came from these slick, wet creatures.

"The Scots call them silkies," said the soldier who had recog-
ed them. He nodded at the seals with the proprietary air of
cial knowledge.

"Silkies?" Grey's attention was caught; he stared at the man
th interest. "What else do you know about them, Sykes?"

The soldier shrugged, enjoying his momentary importance.
Not a great deal, sir. The folk hereabout have stories about them,
ugh; they say sometimes one of them will come ashore and
ve off its skin, and inside is a beautiful woman. If a man should
d the skin, and hide it, so she can't go back, why then—she'll
forced to stay and be his wife. They make good wives, sir, or so
n told."

"At least they'd always be wet," murmured the first soldier,
d the men erupted in guffaws that echoed among the cliffs,
cous as seabirds.

"That's enough!" Grey had to raise his voice, to be heard
ve the rash of laughter and crude suggestions.

"Spread out!" Grey ordered. "I want the cliffs searched in both
ections—and keep an eye out for boats below; God knows
re's room enough to hide a sloop behind some of those is-
ds."

Abashed, the men went without comment. They returned an
ur later, wet from spray and disheveled with climbing, but with
sign of Jamie Fraser—or the Frenchman's Gold.

At dawn, as the light stained the slippery rocks red and gold,
all parties of dragoons were sent off to search the cliffs in both
ections, making their way carefully down the rocky clefts and
mbled piles of stone.

Nothing was found. Grey stood by a fire on the clifftop, keeping
eye on the search. He was swathed in his greatcoat against the
ing wind, and fortified periodically by hot coffee, supplied by
servant.

The man at the Lime Tree had come from the sea, his clothes
aked in saltwater. Whether Fraser had learned something from
man's words that he had not told, or had decided only to take
chance of looking for himself, surely he also would have gone
the sea. And yet there was no sign of James Fraser, anywhere
ng this stretch of coast. Worse yet, there was no sign of the
d.

"If he went in anywhere along this stretch, Major, you'll have

seen the last of him, I'm thinking.'' It was Sergeant Grisso
standing beside him, gazing down at the crash and whirl of wa
through the jagged rocks below. He nodded at the furious wat

''They call this spot the Devil's Cauldron, because of the way
boils all the time. Fishermen drowned off this coast are seld
found; there are wicked currents to blame for it, of course, but f
say the Devil seizes them and pulls them below.''

''Do they?'' Grey said bleakly. He stared down into the sma
and spume forty feet below. ''I wouldn't doubt it, Sergeant.''

He turned back toward the campfire.

''Give orders to search until nightfall, Sergeant. If nothing
found, we'll start back in the morning.''

Grey lifted his gaze from his horse's neck, squinting throu
the dim early light. His eyes felt swollen from peat smoke and la
of sleep, and his bones ached from several nights spent lying
damp ground.

The ride back to Ardsmuir would take no more than a day. T
thought of a soft bed and a hot supper was delightful—but then
would have to write the official dispatch to London, confessi
Fraser's escape—the reason for it—and his own shameful fail
to recapture the man.

The feeling of bleakness at this prospect was reinforced by
deep griping in the major's lower abdomen. He raised a han
signaling a halt, and slid wearily to the ground.

''Wait here,'' he said to his men. There was a small hilloc
few hundred feet away; it would afford him sufficient privacy
the relief he sorely needed; his bowels, unaccustomed to Scott
parritch and oatcake, had rebelled altogether at the exigencies o
field diet.

The birds were singing in the heather. Away from the noise
hooves and harness, he could hear all the tiny sounds of the wa
ing moor. The wind had changed with the dawn, and the scent
the sea came inland now, whispering through the grass. So
small animal made a rustling noise on the other side of a go
bush. It was all very peaceful.

Straightening up from what too late struck him as a most und
nified posture, Grey raised his head and looked straight into
face of James Fraser.

He was no more than six feet away. He stood still as one of the
deer, the moor wind brushing over him, with the rising sun
gled in his hair.

They stood frozen, staring at each other. The smell of the sea
ne faintly on the wind. There was no sound but the sea wind
d the singing of meadowlarks for a moment. Then Grey drew
nself up, swallowing to bring his heart down from his throat.

"I fear you take me at a disadvantage, Mr. Fraser," he said
lly, fastening his breeches with as much self-possession as he
ild muster.

The Scot's eyes were the only part of him to move, down over
ey and slowly back up. Looked over his shoulder, to where six
ned soldiers stood, pointing their muskets. Dark blue eyes met
, straight on. At last, the edge of Fraser's mouth twitched, and
said, "I think ye take me at the same, Major."

amie Fraser sat shivering on the stone floor of the empty sto[ne]
room, clutching his knees and trying to get warm. He thoug[ht]
he likely would never be warm again. The chill of the sea h[ad]
seeped into his bones, and he could still feel the churn of [the]
crashing breakers, deep in his belly.

He wished for the presence of the other prisoners—Morris[on,]
Hayes, Sinclair, Sutherland. Not only for company, but for t[he]
heat of their bodies. On bitter nights, the men would huddle clo[se]
together for warmth, breathing each other's stale breath, tolerat[ing]
the bump and knock of close quarters for the sake of warmth.

He was alone, though. Likely they would not return him to t[he]
large cell with the other men until after they had done whatev[er]
they meant to do to him as punishment for escaping. He lean[ed]
back against the wall with a sigh, morbidly aware of the bones [of]
his spine pressing against the stone, and the fragility of the fle[sh]
covering them.

He was very much afraid of being flogged, and yet he hop[ed]
that would be his punishment. It would be horrible, but it would [be]
soon over—and infinitely more bearable than being put back [in]
irons. He could feel in his flesh the crash of the smith's hamm[er]
echoing through the bones of his arm as the smith pounded [the]
fetters firmly into place, holding his wrist steady on the anvil.

His fingers sought the rosary around his neck. His sister h[ad]
given it to him when he left Lallybroch; the English had let h[im]
keep it, as the string of beechwood beads had no value.

"Hail Mary, full of grace," he muttered, "blessed art thou
ongst women."

He hadn't much hope. That wee yellow-haired fiend of a major
d seen, damn his soul—he knew just how terrible the fetters had
en.

"Blessed is the fruit of thy womb, Jesus. Holy Mary, Mother of
d, pray for us sinners . . ."

The wee Major had made him a bargain, and he had kept it. The
jor would not be thinking so, though.

He had kept his oath, had done as he promised. Had relayed the
rds spoken to him, one by one, just as he had heard them from
wandering man. It was no part of his bargain to tell the En-
shman that he knew the man—or what conclusions he had
wn from the muttered words.

He had recognized Duncan Kerr at once, changed though he
s by time and mortal illness. Before Culloden, he had been a
ksman of Colum MacKenzie, Jamie's uncle. After, he had es-
ed to France, to eke out what living might be made there.

"Be still, *a charaid; bi sàmhach,*" he had said softly in Gaelic,
pping to his knees by the bed where the sick man lay. Duncan
s an elderly man, his worn face wasted by illness and fatigue,
d his eyes were bright with fever. At first he had thought
ncan too far gone to know him, but the wasted hand had
pped his with surprising strength, and the man had repeated
ough his rasping breath *"mo charaid."* My kinsman.

The innkeeper was watching, from his place near the door,
ering over Major Grey's shoulder. Jamie had bent his head and
ispered in Duncan's ear, "All you say will be told to the En-
sh. Speak wary." The landlord's eyes narrowed, but the dis-
ce between them was too far; Jamie was sure he hadn't heard.
en the Major had turned and ordered the innkeeper out, and he
s safe.

He couldn't tell whether it was the effect of his warning, or only
derangement of fever, but Duncan's speech wandered with his
nd, often incoherent, images of the past overlapping with those
the present. Sometimes he had called Jamie "Dougal," the
ne of Colum's brother, Jamie's other uncle. Sometimes he
pped into poetry, sometimes he simply raved. And within the
ings and the scattered words, sometimes there was a grain of
se—or more than sense.

"It is cursed," Duncan whispered. "The gold is cursed. Do
be warned, lad. It was given by the white witch, given for
King's son. But the Cause is lost, and the King's son fled, and
will not let the gold be given to a coward."

"Who is she?" Jamie asked. His heart had sprung up a
choked him at Duncan's words, and it beat madly as he ask
"The white witch—who is she?"

"She seeks a brave man. A MacKenzie, it is for Himself. M
Kenzie. It is theirs, she says it, for the sake of him who is dea

"Who is the witch?" Jamie asked again. The word Dunc
used was *ban-druidh*—a witch, a wisewoman, a white lady. Th
had called his wife that, once. Claire—his own white lady.
squeezed Duncan's hand tight in his own, willing him to keep
senses.

"Who?" he said again. "Who is the witch?"

"The witch," Duncan muttered, his eyes closing. "The wit
She is a soul-eater. She is death. He is dead, the MacKenzie, h
dead."

"Who is dead? Colum MacKenzie?"

"All of them, all of them. All dead. All dead!" cried the s
man, clutching tight to his hand. "Colum, and Dougal, and Ell
too."

Suddenly his eyes opened, and fixed on Jamie's. The fever h
dilated his pupils, so his gaze seemed a pool of drowning blac

"Folk do say," he said, with surprising clarity, "as how El
MacKenzie did leave her brothers and her home, and go to w
with a silkie from the sea. She heard them, aye?" Duncan smi
dreamily, the black stare swimming with distant vision. "S
heard the silkies singing, there upon the rocks, one, and two, a
three of them, and she saw from her tower, one and two, and th
of them, and so she came down, and went to the sea, and so un
it, to live wi' the silkies. Aye? Did she no?"

"So folk say," Jamie had answered, mouth gone dry. Ellen h
been his mother's name. And that was what folk had said, wh
she had left her home, to elope with Brian Dubh Fraser, a m
with the shining black hair of a silkie. The man for whose sake
was himself now called Mac Dubh—Black Brian's son.

Major Grey stood close, on the other side of the bed, br
furrowed as he watched Duncan's face. The Englishman had
Gaelic, but Jamie would have been willing to wager that he kn

e word for gold. He caught the Major's eye, and nodded, bend-
g again to speak to the sick man.

"The gold, man," he said, in French, loud enough for Grey to
ar. "Where is the gold?" He squeezed Duncan's hand as hard
he could, hoping to convey some warning.

Duncan's eyes closed, and he rolled his head restlessly, to and
o upon the pillow. He muttered something, but the words were
o faint to catch.

"What did he say?" the Major demanded sharply. "What?"

"I don't know." Jamie patted Duncan's hand to rouse him.
Speak to me, man, tell me again."

There was no response save more muttering. Duncan's eyes had
lled back in his head, so that only a thin line of gleaming white
owed beneath the wrinkled lids. Impatient, the Major leaned
rward and shook him by one shoulder.

"Wake up!" he said. "Speak to us!"

At once Duncan Kerr's eyes flew open. He stared up, up, past
e two faces bending over him, seeing something far beyond
em.

"She will tell you," he said, in Gaelic. "She will come for
u." For a split second, his attention seemed to return to the inn
om where he lay, and his eyes focused on the men with him.
For both of you," he said distinctly.

Then he closed his eyes, and spoke no more, but clung ever
ghter to Jamie's hand. Then after a time, his grip relaxed, his
nd slid free, and it was over. The guardianship of the gold had
ssed.

And so, Jamie Fraser had kept his word to the Englishman—
d his obligation to his countrymen. He had told the Major all
at Duncan had said, and the devil of a help to him that had been!
nd when the opportunity of escape offered, he had taken it—
ne to the heather and sought the sea, and done what he could
ith Duncan Kerr's legacy. And now he must pay the price of his
tions, whatever that turned out to be.

There were footsteps coming down the corridor outside. He
utched his knees harder, trying to quell the shivering. At least it
uld be decided now, either way.

". . . pray for us sinners now, and at the hour of our death,
nen."

The door swung open, letting in a shaft of light that made him

blink. It was dark in the corridor, but the guard standing over hi
held a torch.

"On your feet." The man reached down and pulled him
against the stiffness of his joints. He was pushed toward the do
stumbling. "You're wanted upstairs."

"Upstairs? Where?" He was startled at that—the smith's for
was downstairs from where he was, off the courtyard. And th
wouldn't flog him so late in the evening.

The man's face twisted, fierce and ruddy in the torchlight. "'
the Major's quarters," the guard said, grinning. "And may G
have mercy on your soul, Mac Dubh."

"No, sir, I will not say where I have been." He repeated
firmly, trying not to let his teeth chatter. He had been brought n
to the office, but to Grey's private sitting room. There was a fire
the hearth, but Grey was standing in front of it, blocking most
the warmth.

"Nor why you chose to escape?" Grey's voice was cool a
formal.

Jamie's face tightened. He had been placed near the bookshe
where the light of a triple-branched candlestick fell on his fac
Grey himself was no more than a silhouette, black against t
fire's glow.

"That is my private affair," he said.

"Private affair?" Grey echoed incredulously. "Did you s
your private affair?"

."I did."

The Governor inhaled strongly through his nose.

"That is possibly the most outrageous thing I have heard in n
life!"

"Your life has been rather brief, then, Major," Fraser said. '
you will pardon my saying so." There was no point in dragging
out or trying to placate the man. Better to provoke a decision
once and get it over with.

He had certainly provoked something; Grey's fists clench
tight at his sides, and he took a step toward him, away from t
fire.

"Have you any notion what I could do to you for this?" Gr
inquired, his voice low and very much controlled.

"Aye, I have. Major." More than a notion. He knew from perience what they might do to him, and he wasn't looking rward to it. It wasn't as though he'd a choice about it, though.

Grey breathed heavily for a moment, then jerked his head.

"Come here, Mr. Fraser," he ordered. Jamie stared at him, zzled.

"Here!" he said peremptorily, pointing to a spot directly before m on the hearthrug. "Stand here, sir!"

"I am not a dog, Major!" Jamie snapped. "Ye'll do as ye like i' me, but I'll no come when ye call me to heel!"

Taken by surprise, Grey uttered a short, involuntary laugh.

"My apologies, Mr. Fraser," he said dryly. "I meant no of-nse by the address. I merely wish you to approach nearer. If you ill?" He stepped aside and bowed elaborately, gesturing to the earth.

Jamie hesitated, but then stepped warily onto the patterned rug. rey stepped close to him, nostrils flared. So close, the fine bones d fair skin of his face made him look almost girlish. The Major t a hand on his sleeve, and the long-lashed eyes sprang wide in 1ock.

"You're wet!"

"Yes, I am wet," Jamie said, with elaborate patience. He was so freezing. A fine, continuous shiver ran through him, even this ose to the fire.

"Why?"

"Why?" Jamie echoed, astonished. "Did you not order the 1ards to douse me wi' water before leaving me in a freezing 11?"

"I did not, no." It was clear enough that the Major was telling e truth; his face was pale under the ruddy flush of the firelight, d he looked angry. His lips thinned to a fine line.

"I apologize for this, Mr. Fraser."

"Accepted, Major." Small wisps of steam were beginning to se from his clothes, but the warmth was seeping through the mp cloth. His muscles ached from the shivering, and he wished could lie down on the hearthrug, dog or not.

"Did your escape have anything to do with the matter of which u learned at the Lime Tree Inn?"

Jamie stood silent. The ends of his hair were drying, and small isps floated across his face.

"Will you swear to me that your escape had *nothing* to do wi⟩ that matter?"

Jamie stood silent. There seemed no point in saying anythir⟩ now.

The little Major was pacing up and down the hearth before hi⟩ hands locked behind his back. Now and then, the Major glanc⟩ up at him, and then resumed his pacing.

Finally he stopped in front of Jamie.

"Mr. Fraser," he said formally. "I will ask you once more⟩ why did you escape from the prison?"

Jamie sighed. He wouldn't get to stand by the fire much long⟩

"I cannot tell you, Major."

"Cannot or will not?" Grey asked sharply.

"It doesna seem a useful distinction, Major, as ye willna he⟩ anything, either way." He closed his eyes and waited, trying⟩ soak up as much heat as possible before they took him away.

Grey found himself at a loss, both for words and action. *Stu⟩ born does not begin to describe it,* Quarry had said. It didn't.

He took a deep breath, wondering what to do. He found hims⟩ embarrassed by the petty cruelty of the guards' revenge; the mo⟩ so because it was just such an action he had first contemplat⟩ upon hearing that Fraser was his prisoner.

He would be perfectly within his rights now to order the m⟩ flogged, or put back in irons. Condemned to solitary confineme⟩ put on short rations—he could in justice inflict any of a doz⟩ different punishments. And if he did, the odds of his ever findi⟩ the Frenchman's Gold became vanishingly small.

The gold *did* exist. Or at least there was a good probability th⟩ it did. Only a belief in that gold would have stirred Fraser to act⟩ he had.

He eyed the man. Fraser's eyes were closed, his lips set firm⟩ He had a wide, strong mouth, whose grim expression was som⟩ what belied by the sensitive lips, set soft and exposed in their cu⟩ nest of red beard.

Grey paused, trying to think of some way to break past t⟩ man's wall of bland defiance. To use force would be worse th⟩ useless—and after the guards' actions, he would be ashamed⟩ order it, even had he the stomach for brutality.

The clock on the mantelpiece struck ten. It was late; there w⟩

o sound in the fortress, save the occasional footsteps of the sol-
ier on sentry in the courtyard outside the window.

Clearly neither force nor threat would work in gaining the truth.
Reluctantly, he realized that there was only one course open to
im, if he still wished to pursue the gold. He must put aside his
eelings about the man and take Quarry's suggestion. He must
ursue an acquaintance, in the course of which he might worm out
f the man some clue that would lead him to the hidden treasure.

If it existed, he reminded himself, turning to his prisoner. He
ook a deep breath.

"Mr. Fraser," he said formally, "will you do me the honor to
ake supper tomorrow in my quarters?"

He had the momentary satisfaction of having startled the Scot-
ish bastard, at least. The blue eyes opened wide, and then Fraser
egained the mastery of his face. He paused for a moment, and
hen bowed with a flourish, as though he wore a kilt and swinging
laid, and not damp prison rags.

"It will be my pleasure to attend ye, Major," he said.

March 7, 1755

Fraser was delivered by the guard and left to wait in the sitting
oom, where a table was laid. When Grey came through the door
rom his bedroom a few moments later, he found his guest stand-
ng by the bookshelf, apparently absorbed in a copy of *La Nou-
elle Héloïse*.

"You are interested in French novels?" he blurted, not realizing
ntil too late how incredulous the question sounded.

Fraser glanced up, startled, and snapped the book shut. Very
eliberately, he returned it to its shelf.

"I *can* read, Major," he said. He had shaved; a slight flush
urned high on his cheekbones.

"I—yes, of course I did not mean—I merely—" Grey's own
heeks were more flushed than Fraser's. The fact was that he *had*
ubconsciously assumed that the other did not read, his evident
ducation notwithstanding, merely because of his Highland accent
nd shabby dress.

While his coat might be shabby, Fraser's manners were not. He
gnored Grey's flustered apology, and turned to the bookshelf.

''I have been telling the men the story, but it has been som time since I read it; I thought I would refresh my memory as to th sequence of the ending.''

''I see.'' Just in time, Grey stopped himself from saying ''The understand it?''

Fraser evidently read the unspoken question in his face, for h said dryly, ''All Scottish children are taught their letters, Major Still, we have a great tradition of storytelling in the Highlands.'

''Ah. Yes. I see.''

The entry of his servant with dinner saved him from furthe awkwardness, and the supper passed uneventfully, though ther was little conversation, and that little, limited to the affairs of th prison.

The next time, he had had the chess table set up before the fire and invited Fraser to join him in a game before the supper wa served. There had been a brief flash of surprise from the slante blue eyes, and then a nod of acquiescence.

That had been a small stroke of genius, Grey thought in retro spect. Relieved of the need for conversation or social courtesie they had slowly become accustomed to each other as they sat ove the inlaid board of ivory and ebony-wood, gauging each othe silently by the movements of the chessmen.

When they had at length sat down to dine, they were no longe quite strangers, and the conversation, while still wary and forma was at least true conversation, and not the awkward affair of start and stops it had been before. They discussed matters of the priso had a little conversation of books, and parted formally, but o good terms. Grey did not mention gold.

And so the weekly custom was established. Grey sought to pu his guest at ease, in the hopes that Fraser might let drop some clu to the fate of the Frenchman's Gold. It had not come so fa despite careful probing. Any hint of inquiry as to what had tran spired during the three days of Fraser's absence from Ardsmu met with silence.

Over the mutton and boiled potatoes, he did his best to draw h odd guest into a discussion of France and its politics, by way o iscovering whether there might exist any links between Fraser nd a possible source of gold from the French Court.

Much to his surprise, he was informed that Fraser had in fact pent two years living in France, employed in the wine business, rior to the Stuart rebellion.

A certain cool humor in Fraser's eyes indicated that the man vas well aware of the motives behind this questioning. At the ame time, he acquiesced gracefully enough in the conversation, 1ough taking some care always to lead questions away from his ersonal life, and instead toward more general matters of art and ociety.

Grey had spent some time in Paris, and despite his attempts at robing Fraser's French connections, found himself becoming in- erested in the conversation for its own sake.

"Tell me, Mr. Fraser, during your time in Paris, did you chance o encounter the dramatic works of Monsieur Voltaire?"

Fraser smiled. "Oh, aye, Major. In fact, I was privileged to ntertain Monsieur Arouet—Voltaire being his nom de plume, ye?—at my table, on more than one occasion."

"Really?" Grey cocked a brow in interest. "And is he as great wit in person as with the pen?"

"I couldna really say," Fraser replied, tidily forking up a slice f mutton. "He seldom said anything at all, let alone much spar- ling with wit. He only sat hunched over in his chair, watching veryone, wi' his eyes rolling about from one to another. I 1ouldna be at all surprised to hear that things said at my dinner ble later appeared on the stage, though fortunately I never en- ountered a parody of myself in his work." He closed his eyes in lomentary concentration, chewing his mutton.

"Is the meat to your taste, Mr. Fraser?" Grey inquired politely. was gristled, tough, and seemed barely edible to him. But then, e might well think differently, had he been eating oatmeal, eeds, and the occasional rat.

"Aye, it is, Major, I thank ye." Fraser dabbed up a bit of wine auce and brought the last bite to his lips, making no demur when rey signaled MacKay to bring back the platter.

"Monsieur Arouet wouldna appreciate such an excellent meal, m afraid," Fraser said, shaking his head as he helped himself to ore mutton.

"I should expect a man so feted in French society to have

somewhat more exacting tastes,'' Grey answered dryly. Half h own meal remained on his plate, destined for the supper of the c Augustus.

Fraser laughed. ''Scarcely that, Major,'' he assured Grey. ' have never seen Monsieur Arouet consume anything beyond glass of water and a dry biscuit, no matter how lavish the occasio He's a wizened wee scrap of a man, ye ken, and a martyr to th indigestion.''

''Indeed?'' Grey was fascinated. ''Perhaps that explains th cynicism of some of the sentiments I have seen expressed in h plays. Or do you not think that the character of an author shows the construction of his work?''

''Given some of the characters that I have seen appear in play and novels, Major, I should think the author a bit depraved wh drew them entirely from himself, no?''

''I suppose that is so,'' Grey answered, smiling at the thought some of the more extreme fictional characters with whom he wa acquainted. ''Though if an author constructs these colorful pe sonages from life, rather than from the depths of imaginatio surely he must boast a most varied acquaintance!''

Fraser nodded, brushing crumbs from his lap with the line napkin.

''It was not Monsieur Arouet, but a colleague of his—a la novelist—who remarked to me once that writing novels was cannibal's art, in which one often mixed small portions of one friends and one's enemies together, seasoned them with imagin tion, and allowed the whole to stew together into a savory conco tion.''

Grey laughed at the description, and beckoned to MacKay take away the plates and bring in the decanters of port and sherr

''A delightful description, indeed! Speaking of cannibal though, have you chanced to be acquainted with Mr. Defoe *Robinson Crusoe*? It has been a favorite of mine since boyhood

The conversation turned then to romances, and the exciteme of the tropics. It was very late indeed when Fraser returned to h cell, leaving Major Grey entertained, but no wiser concerni either the source or the disposition of the Frenchman's Gold.

April 2, 1755

John Grey opened the packet of quills his mother had sent from London. Swan's quills, both finer and stronger than common goose-quills. He smiled faintly at the sight of them; an unsubtle reminder that his correspondence was in arrears.

His mother would have to wait until tomorrow, though. He took out the small monogrammed penknife he always carried, and slowly trimmed a quill to his liking, composing in his mind what he meant to say. By the time he dipped his quill into the ink, the words were clear in his mind, and he wrote quickly, seldom pausing.

2 April, 1755
To Harold, Lord Melton, Earl of Moray

My dear Hal, he wrote, *I write to inform you of a recent occurrence that has much engaged my attention. It may amount in the end to nothing, but if there be any substance in the matter, is of great import.* The details of the wandering man's appearance, and the report of his ravings followed swiftly, but Grey found himself slowing as he told of Fraser's escape and recapture.

The fact that Fraser vanished from the precincts of the prison so soon following these events suggests strongly to me that there was in truth some substance in the vagrant's words.

If this was the case, however, I find myself at a loss to account for Fraser's subsequent actions. He was recaptured within three days of his escape, at a point no more than a mile from the coast. The countryside beyond the prison is deserted for a great many miles beyond the village of Ardsmuir, and there is little likelihood of his meeting with a confederate to whom he might pass word of the treasure. Every house in the village has been searched, as was Fraser himself, with no trace discovered of any gold. It is a remote district, and I am reasonably sure that he communicated with no one outside the prison prior to his escape—I am positive that he has not done so since, for he is closely watched.

Grey stopped, seeing once more the windswept figure of Jame
Fraser, wild as the red stags and as much at home on the moor a
one of them.

He had not the slightest doubt that Fraser could have eluded th
dragoons easily, had he so chosen, but he had not. He had delibei
ately allowed himself to be recaptured. Why? He resumed writing
more slowly.

*It may be, of course, that Fraser failed to find the trea-
sure, or that such a treasure does not exist. I find myself
somewhat inclined to this belief, for if he were in possession of a great sum, surely he would have departed from
the district at once. He is a strong man, well accustomed
to rough living, and entirely capable, I believe, of making
his way overland to some point on the coast from which
he might make an escape by sea.*

Grey bit the end of the quill gently, tasting ink. He made a fac
at the bitterness, rose, and spat out the window. He stood there fc
a minute, looking out into the cold spring night, absently wipin
his mouth.

It had finally occurred to him to ask; not the question he ha
been asking all along, but the more important one. He had done
at the conclusion of a game of chess, which Fraser had won. Th
guard was standing at the door, ready to escort Fraser back to hi
cell; as the prisoner had risen from his seat, Grey had stood uj
too.

''I shall not ask you again why you left the prison,'' he had sai
calmly conversational. ''But I will ask you—why did you com
back?''

Fraser had frozen briefly, startled. He turned back and me
Grey's eyes directly. For a moment he said nothing. Then hi
mouth curled up in a smile.

''I suppose I must value the company, Major; I can tell ye, it
not the food.''

Grey snorted slightly, remembering. Unable to think of a sui
able response, he had allowed Fraser to leave. It was only later tha
night that he had laboriously arrived at an answer, at last havin

ad the wit to ask questions of himself rather than of Fraser. What ould he, Grey, have done, had Fraser *not* returned?

The answer was that his next step would have been an inquiry to Fraser's family connections, in case the man had sought refge or help from them.

And that, he was fairly sure, was the answer. Grey had not taken art in the subjugation of the Highlands—he had been posted to aly and France—but he had heard more than enough of that articular campaign. He had seen the blackened stones of too any charred cottages, rising like cairns amid the ruined fields, as e traveled north to Ardsmuir.

The fierce loyalties of the Scottish Highlanders were legendary. Highlander who had seen those cots in flames might well hoose to suffer prison, irons, or even flogging, to save his family visitation from English soldiers.

Grey sat and took up his quill, dipping it afresh.

You will know, I think, the mettle of the Scots, he wrote. That ne in particular, he thought wryly.

It is unlikely that any force or threat I can exert will induce Fraser to reveal the whereabouts of the gold—should it exist, and if it does not, I can still less expect any threat to be effective! I have instead chosen to begin a formal acquaintance with Fraser, in his capacity as chief of the Scottish prisoners, in hopes of surprising some clue from his conversation. So far, I have gained nothing from this process. One further avenue of approach suggests itself, however.

For obvious reasons, he went on, writing slowly as he formed e thought, *I do not wish to make this matter known officially.* o call attention to a hoard that might well prove to be chimerical as dangerous; the chance of disappointment was too great. Time hough, if the gold was found, to inform his superiors and collect s deserved reward—escape from Ardsmuir; a posting back to vilization.

Therefore I approach you, dear brother, and ask your help in discovering what particulars may obtain regarding the family of James Fraser. I pray you, do not let anyone

*be alarmed by your inquiries; if such family connections
exist, I would have them ignorant of my interest for the
present. My deepest thanks for any efforts you may be
able to exert on my behalf, and believe me always,*

He dipped the pen once more and signed with a small flourish

Your humble servant and most affectionate brother,
                                John William Grey

May 15, 175

"The men sick of *la grippe*," Grey inquired, "how do the
fare?" Dinner was over, and with it their conversation of book
Now it was time for business.

Fraser frowned over the single glass of sherry that was all h
would accept in the way of drink. He still had not tasted it, thoug
dinner had been over for some time.

"None so well. I have more than sixty men ill, fifteen of the
verra badly off." He hesitated. "Might I ask . . ."

"I can promise nothing, Mr. Fraser, but you may ask," Gre
answered formally. He had barely sipped his own sherry, nor mo
than tasted his dinner; his stomach had been knotted with anticipa
tion all day.

Jamie paused a moment longer, calculating his chances. H
wouldn't get everything; he must try for what was most importan
but leave Grey room to reject some requests.

"We have need of more blankets, Major, more fires, and mo
food. And medicines."

Grey swirled the sherry in his cup, watching the light from th
fire play in the vortex. Ordinary business first, he reminded hin
self. Time enough for the other, later.

"We have no more than twenty spare blankets in store," h
answered, "but you may have those for the use of the very sick.
fear I cannot augment the ration of food; the rat-spoilage has bee
considerable, and we lost a great quantity of meal in the collaps
of the storeroom two months ago. We have limited resource
and—"

"It is not so much a question of more," Fraser put in quickl

'But rather of the type of food. Those who are most ill cannot readily digest the bread and parritch. Perhaps a substitution of some sort might be arranged?'' Each man was given, by law, a quart of oatmeal parritch and a small wheaten loaf each day. Thin barley brose supplemented this twice each week, with a quart of meat stew added on Sunday, to sustain the needs of men working at manual labor for twelve to sixteen hours per day.

Grey raised one eyebrow. ''What are you suggesting, Mr. Fraser?''

''I assume that the prison does have some allowance for the purchase of salt beef, turnips and onions, for the Sunday stew?''

''Yes, but that allowance must provide for the next quarter's supplies.''

''Then what I suggest, Major, is that you might use that money now to provide broth and stew for those who are sick. Those of us who are hale will willingly forgo our share of meat for the quarter.''

Grey frowned. ''But will the prisoners not be weakened, with no meat at all? Will they not be unable to work?''

''Those who die of the grippe will assuredly not work,'' Fraser pointed out acerbically.

Grey snorted briefly. ''True. But those of you who remain healthy will not be healthy long, if you give up your rations for so long a time.'' He shook his head. ''No, Mr. Fraser, I think not. It is better to let the sick take their chances than to risk many more falling ill.''

Fraser was a stubborn man. He lowered his head for a moment, then looked up to try again.

''Then I would ask your leave to hunt for ourselves, Major, if the Crown cannot supply us with adequate food.''

''Hunt?'' Grey's fair brows rose in astonishment. ''Give you weapons and allow you to wander the moors? God's teeth, Mr. Fraser!''

''I think God doesna suffer much from the scurvy, Major,'' Jamie said dryly. ''*His* teeth are in no danger.'' He saw the twitch of Grey's mouth and relaxed slightly. Grey always tried to suppress his sense of humor, no doubt feeling that put him at a disadvantage. In his dealings with Jamie Fraser, it did.

Emboldened by that telltale twitch, Jamie pressed on.

''Not weapons, Major. And not wandering. Will ye give us

leave to set snares upon the moor when we cut peats, though? And to keep such meat as we take?'' A prisoner would now and then contrive a snare as it was, but as often as not, the catch would b taken from him by the guards.

Grey drew a deep breath and blew it out slowly, considering.

''Snares? Would you not require materials for the constructio of these snares, Mr. Fraser?''

''Only a bit of string, Major,'' Jamie assured him. ''A dozen balls, no more, of any sort of twine or string, and ye may leave th rest to us.''

Grey rubbed slowly at his cheek in contemplation, then nodded

''Very well.'' The Major turned to the small secretary, plucked the quill out of its inkwell and made a note. ''I shall give orders to that effect tomorrow. Now, as to the rest of your requests . . .''

A quarter-hour later, it was settled. Jamie sat back at last, sigh ing, and finally took a sip of his sherry. He considered that he had earned it.

He had permission not only for the snares, but for the peat cutters to work an extra half-hour per day, the extra peats to provide for an additional small fire in each cell. No medicine were to be had, but he had leave for Sutherland to send a messag to a cousin in Ullapool, whose husband was an apothecary. If th cousin's husband was willing to send medicines, the prisoner could have them.

A decent evening's work, Jamie thought. He took another sip c sherry and closed his eyes, enjoying the warmth of the fire agains his cheek.

Grey watched his guest beneath lowered lids, seeing the broa shoulders slump a little, tension eased now that their business wa finished. Or so Fraser thought. Very good, Grey thought to him self. Yes, drink your sherry and relax. I want you thoroughly of guard.

He leaned forward to pick up the decanter, and felt the crackl of Hal's letter in his breast pocket. His heart began to beat faster

''Will you not take a drop more, Mr. Fraser? And tell me—how does your sister fare these days?''

He saw Fraser's eyes spring open, and his face whiten with shock.

''How are matters there at—Lallybroch, they call it, do the

ot?'' Grey pushed aside the decanter, keeping his eyes fixed on is guest.

"I could not say, Major." Fraser's voice was even, but his eyes vere narrowed to slits.

"No? But I daresay they do very well these days, what with the old you have provided them."

The broad shoulders tightened suddenly, bunched under the habby coat. Grey carelessly picked up one of the chessmen from he nearby board, tossing it casually from one hand to the other.

"I suppose Ian—your brother-in-law is named Ian, I think?— vill know how to make good use of it."

Fraser had himself under control again. The dark blue eyes met rey's directly.

"Since you are so well informed as to my connections, Major," e said evenly, "I must suppose that you also are aware that my ome lies well over a hundred miles from Ardsmuir. Perhaps you vill explain how I might have traveled that distance twice within he space of three days?"

Grey's eyes stayed on the chess piece, rolling idly from hand to and. It was a pawn, a cone-headed little warrior with a fierce ace, carved from a cylinder of walrus ivory.

"You might have met someone upon the moor who would have orne word of the gold—or borne the gold itself—to your fam-y."

Fraser snorted briefly.

"On Ardsmuir? How likely is it, Major, that I should by hap-enstance encounter a person known to me on that moor? Much ess that it should be a person whom I would trust to convey a nessage such as you suggest?" He set down his glass with final-y. "I met no one on the moor, Major."

"And should I trust *your* word to that effect, Mr. Fraser?" Grey llowed considerable skepticism to show in his voice. He glanced p, brows raised.

Fraser's high cheekbones flushed slightly.

"No one has ever had cause to doubt my word, Major," he said iffly.

"Have they not, indeed?" Grey was not altogether feigning his nger. "I believe you gave *me* your word, upon the occasion of my rdering your irons stricken off!"

"And I kept it!"

"Did you?" The two men sat upright, glaring at each other ov‹ the table.

"You asked three things of me, Major, and I have kept th‹ bargain in every particular!"

Grey gave a contemptuous snort.

"Indeed, Mr. Fraser? And if that is so, pray what was it caus‹ you suddenly to despise the company of your fellows and se‹ congress with the coneys on the moor? Since you assure me th‹ you met no one else—you give me *your word* that it is so." Th‹ last was spoken with an audible sneer that brought the color sur‹ ing into Fraser's face.

One of the big hands curled slowly into a fist.‹

"Aye, Major," he said softly. "I give ye *my word* that that ‹ so." He seemed to realize at this point that his fist was clenche‹ very slowly, he unfolded it, laying his hand flat on the table.

"And as to your escape?"

"And as to my escape, Major, I have told you that I will sa‹ nothing." Fraser exhaled slowly and sat back in his chair, ey‹ fixed on Grey under thick, ruddy brows.

Grey paused for a moment, then sat back himself, setting th‹ chess piece on the table.

"Let me speak plainly, Mr. Fraser. I do you the honor of assum‹ ing you to be a sensible man."

"I am deeply sensible of the honor, Major, I do assure you.‹

Grey heard the irony, but did not respond; he held the upp‹ hand now.

"The fact is, Mr. Fraser, that it is of no consequence wheth‹ you did in fact communicate with your family regarding the matt‹ of the gold. You might have done so. That possibility alone ‹ sufficient to warrant my sending a party of dragoons to search th‹ premises of Lallybroch—thoroughly—and to arrest and interr‹ gate the members of your family."

He reached into his breast pocket and withdrew a piece ‹ paper. Unfolding it, he read the list of names.

"Ian Murray—your brother-in-law, I collect? His wife, Jan‹ That would be your sister, of course. Their children, James— named for his uncle, perhaps?''—he glanced up briefly, lon‹ enough to catch a glimpse of Fraser's face, than returned to h‹ list—"Margaret, Katherine, Janet, Michael, and Ian. Quite ‹ brood," he said, in a tone of dismissal that equated the s‹

ounger Murrays with a litter of piglets. He laid the list on the
ble beside the chess piece.

"The three eldest children are old enough to be arrested and
terrogated with their parents, you know. Such interrogations are
equently ungentle, Mr. Fraser."

In this, he spoke no less than the truth, and Fraser knew it. All
lor had faded from the prisoner's face, leaving the strong bones
ark under the skin. He closed his eyes briefly, then opened them.

Grey had a brief memory of Quarry's voice, saying *"If you dine
 one with the man, don't turn your back on him."* The hair rose
iefly on the back of his neck, but he controlled himself, re-
rning Fraser's blue stare.

"What do you want of me?" The voice was low, and hoarse
ith fury, but the Scot sat motionless, a figure carved in cinnabar,
ded by the flame.

Grey took a deep breath.

"I want the truth," he said softly.

There was no sound in the chamber save the pop and hiss of the
ats in the grate. There was a flicker of movement from Fraser,
more than the twitch of his fingers against his leg, and then
thing. The Scot sat, head turned, staring into the fire as though
sought an answer there.

Grey sat quietly, waiting. He could afford to wait. At last, Fraser
rned back to face him.

"The truth, then." He took a deep breath; Grey could see the
east of his linen shirt swell with it—he had no waistcoat.

"I kept my word, Major. I told ye faithfully all that the man said
me that night. What I didna tell ye was that some of what he
id had meaning to me."

"Indeed." Grey held himself still, scarcely daring to move.
And what meaning was that?"

Fraser's wide mouth compressed to a thin line.

"I—spoke to you of my wife," he said, forcing the words out
though they hurt him.

"Yes, you said that she was dead."

"I said that she was *gone,* Major," Fraser corrected softly. His
es were fixed on the pawn. "It is likely she is dead, but—" He
opped and swallowed, then went on more firmly.

"My wife was a healer. What they call in the Highlands a
armer, but more than that. She was a white lady—a wise-

woman.'' He glanced up briefly. ''The word in Gaelic is *ba druidh;* it also means witch.''

''The white witch.'' Grey also spoke softly, but excitement w thrumming through his blood. ''So the man's words referred your wife?''

''I thought they might. And if so—'' The wide shoulders stirr in a slight shrug. ''I had to go,'' he said simply. ''To see.''

''How did you know where to go? Was that also something yo gleaned from the vagrant's words?'' Grey leaned forward slight curious. Fraser nodded, eyes still fixed on the ivory chess piec

''There is a spot I knew of, not too far distant from this plac where there is a shrine to St. Bride. St. Bride was also called 't white lady,' '' he explained, looking up. ''Though the shrine h been there a verra long time—since long before St. Bride came Scotland.''

''I see. And so you assumed that the man's words referred this spot, as well as to your wife?''

Again the shrug.

''I did not know,'' Fraser repeated. ''I couldna say whether meant anything to do with my wife, or whether 'the white witc only meant St. Bride—was only meant to direct me to the place or perhaps neither. But I felt I must go.''

He described the place in question, and at Grey's proddin gave directions for reaching it.

''The shrine itself is a small stone in the shape of an ancie cross, so weathered that the markings scarce show on it. It stan above a small pool, half-buried in the heather. Ye can find sm white stones in the pool, tangled among the roots of the heath that grows on the bank. The stones are thought to have gre powers, Major,'' he explained, seeing the other's blank look. ''B only when used by a white lady.''

''I see. And your wife . . . ?'' Grey paused delicately.

Fraser shook his head briefly.

''There was nothing there to do with her,'' he said softly. ''S is truly gone.'' His voice was low and controlled, but Grey cou hear the undertone of desolation.

Fraser's face was normally calm and unreadable; he did n change expression now, but the marks of grief were clear, etch in the lines beside mouth and eyes, thrown into darkness by t

:kering fire. It seemed an intrusion to break in upon such a
pth of feeling, unstated though it was, but Grey had his duty.

"And the gold, Mr. Fraser?" he asked quietly. "What of that?"

Fraser heaved a deep sigh.

"It was there," he said flatly.

"What!" Grey sat bolt upright in his chair, staring at the Scot.
You found it?"

Fraser glanced up at him then, and his mouth twisted wryly.

"I found it."

"Was it indeed the French gold that Louis sent for Charles
.uart?" Excitement was racing through Grey's bloodstream, with
ions of himself delivering great chests of gold louis d'or to his
periors in London.

"Louis never sent gold to the Stuarts," Fraser said, with cer-
nty. "No, Major, what I found at the saint's pool was gold, but
t French coin."

What he had found was a small box, containing a few gold and
ver coins, and a small leather pouch, filled with jewels.

"Jewels?" Grey blurted. "Where the devil did they come
m?"

Fraser cast him a glance of mild exasperation.

"I havena the slightest notion, Major," he said. "How should I
ow?"

"No, of course not," Grey said, coughing to cover his confu-
n. "Certainly. But this treasure—where is it now?"

"I threw it into the sea."

Grey stared blankly at him.

"You—what?"

"I threw it into the sea," Fraser repeated patiently. The slanted
e eyes met Grey's steadily. "Ye'll maybe have heard of a place
led the Devil's Cauldron, Major? It's no more than half a mile
m the saint's pool."

"Why? Why would you have done such a thing?" Grey de-
nded. "It isn't sense, man!"

"I wasna much concerned with sense at the time, Major,"
.ser said softly. "I had gone there hoping—and with that hope
ie, the treasure seemed no more to me than a wee box of stones
i bits of tarnished metal. I had no use for it." He looked up, one
w slightly raised in irony. "But I didna see the 'sense' in
ing it to King Geordie, either. So I flung it into the sea."

Grey sat back in his chair and mechanically poured out anoth[er] cup of sherry, hardly noticing what he was doing. His though[ts] were in turmoil.

Fraser sat, head turned away and chin propped on his fist, gaz[ing] ing into the fire, his face gone back to its usual impassivity. Th[e] light glowed behind him, lighting the long, straight line of his no[se] and the soft curve of his lip, shadowing jaw and brow with ster[n]ness.

Grey took a good-sized swallow of his drink and steadied him[self.

"It is a moving story, Mr. Fraser," he said levelly. "M[ost] dramatic. And yet there is no evidence that it is the truth."

Fraser stirred, turning his head to look at Grey. Jamie's slant[ed] eyes narrowed, in what might have been amusement.

"Aye, there is, Major," he said. He reached under the wais[t]band of his ragged breeches, fumbled for a moment, and held o[ut] his hand above the tabletop, waiting.

Grey extended his own hand in reflex, and a small obje[ct] dropped into his open palm.

It was a sapphire, dark blue as Fraser's own eyes, and a go[od] size, too.

Grey opened his mouth, but said nothing, choked with astonis[h]ment.

"There is your evidence that the treasure existed, Major." Fra[ser nodded toward the stone in Grey's hand. His eyes met Grey[']s across the tabletop. "And as for the rest—I am sorry to sa[y], Major, that ye must take my word for it."

"But—but—you said—"

"I did." Fraser was as calm as though they had been discussi[ng] the rain outside. "I kept that one wee stone, thinking that it mig[ht be some use, if I were ever to be freed, or that I might find so[me] chance of sending it to my family. For ye'll appreciate, Major"—light glinted derisively in Jamie's blue eyes—"that my fam[ily] couldna make use of a treasure of that sort, without attracting [a] deal of unwelcome attention. One stone, perhaps, but not a gr[eat] many of them."

Grey could scarcely think. What Fraser said was true; a High[land farmer like his brother-in-law would have no way of turni[ng] such a treasure into money without causing talk that would bri[ng] down the King's men on Lallybroch in short order. And Fras[er himself might well be imprisoned for the rest of his life. But still, to toss away a fortune so lightly! And yet, looking at the Scot, he could well believe it. If ever there was a man whose judgment would not be distorted by greed, James Fraser was it. Still—

"How did you keep this by you?" Grey demanded abruptly. "You were searched to the skin when you were brought back."

The wide mouth curved slightly in the first genuine smile Grey had seen.

"I swallowed it," Fraser said.

Grey's hand closed convulsively on the sapphire. He opened his hand and rather gingerly set the gleaming blue thing on the table by the chess piece.

"I see," he said.

"I'm sure ye do, Major," said Fraser, with a gravity that merely made the glint of amusement in his eyes more pronounced. "A diet of rough parritch has its advantages, now and again."

Grey quelled the sudden urge to laugh, rubbing a finger hard over his lip.

"I'm sure it does, Mr. Fraser." He sat for a moment, contemplating the blue stone. Then he looked up abruptly.

"You are a Papist, Mr. Fraser?" He knew the answer already; there were few adherents of the Catholic Stuarts who were not. Without waiting for a reply, he rose and went to the bookshelf in the corner. It took a moment to find; a gift from his mother, it was not part of his usual reading.

He laid the calf-bound Bible on the table, next to the stone.

"I am myself inclined to accept your word as a gentleman, Mr. Fraser," he said. "But you will understand that I have my duty to consider."

Fraser gazed at the book for a long moment, then looked up at Grey, his expression unreadable.

"Aye, I ken that fine, Major," he said quietly. Without hesitation, he laid a broad hand on the Bible.

"I swear in the name of Almighty God and by His Holy Word," he said firmly. "The treasure is as I told you." His eyes glowed in the firelight, dark and unfathomable. "And I swear on my hope of heaven," he added softly, "that it rests now in the sea."

11

The Torremolinos Gambit

With the question of the French gold thus settled, the returned to what had become their routine; a brief period of formal negotiation over the affairs of the prisoners, followed by informal conversation and sometimes a game of chess. This evening, they had come from the dinner table, still discussing Samuel Richardson's immense novel *Pamela*.

"Do you think that the size of the book is justified by the complexity of the story?" Grey asked, leaning forward to light a cheroot from the candle on the sideboard. "It must after all be a great expense to the publisher, as well as requiring a substantial effort from the reader, a book of that length."

Fraser smiled. He did not smoke himself, but had chosen to drink port this evening, claiming that to be the only drink whose taste would be unaffected by the stink of tobacco.

"What is it—twelve hundred pages? Aye, I think so. After all, is difficult to sum up the complications of a life in a short space with any hope of constructing an accurate account."

"True. I have heard the point made, though, that the novelist' skill lies in the artful selection of detail. Do you not suppose that volume of such length may indicate a lack of discipline in such selection, and hence a lack of skill?"

Fraser considered, sipping the ruby liquid slowly.

"I have seen books where that is the case, to be sure," he said "An author seeks by sheer inundation of detail to overwhelm the reader into belief. In this case, however, I think it isna so. Each character is most carefully considered, and all the incidents chosen eem necessary to the story. No, I think it is true that some stories simply require a greater space in which to be told.'' He took another sip and laughed.

"Of course, I admit to some prejudice in that regard, Major. Given the circumstances under which I read *Pamela,* I should have been delighted had the book been twice as long as it was.''

"And what circumstances were those?'' Grey pursed his lips and blew a careful smoke ring that floated toward the ceiling.

"I lived in a cave in the Highlands for several years, Major,'' Fraser said wryly. "I seldom had more than three books with me, and those must last me for months at a time. Aye, I'm partial to lengthy tomes, but I must admit that it is not a universal preference.''

"That's certainly true,'' Grey agreed. He squinted, following the track of the first smoke ring, and blew another. Just off target, it drifted to the side.

"I remember,'' he continued, sucking fiercely on his cheroot, encouraging it to draw, "a friend of my mother's—saw the book —in Mother's drawing room—'' He drew deeply, and blew once more, giving a small grunt of satisfaction as the new ring struck the old, dispersing it into a tiny cloud.

"Lady Hensley, it was. She picked up the book, looked at it in that helpless way so many females affect and said, 'Oh, Countess! You are so *courageous* to attack a novel of such stupendous size. I fear I should never dare to start so lengthy a book myself.' '' Grey cleared his throat and lowered his voice from the falsetto he had affected for Lady Hensley.

"To which Mother replied,'' he went on in his normal voice, 'Don't worry about it for a moment, my dear; you wouldn't understand it anyway.' ''

Fraser laughed, then coughed, waving away the remnants of another smoke ring.

Grey quickly snuffed out the cheroot, and rose from his seat.

"Come along, then; we've just time for a quick game.''

They were not evenly matched; Fraser was much the better player, but Grey could now and then contrive to rescue a match through sheer bravado of play.

Tonight, he tried the Torremolinos Gambit. It was a risky opening, a queen's knight opening. Successfully launched, it paved the way for an unusual combination of rook and bishop, depending for

its success upon a piece of misdirection by the king's knight an
king bishop's pawn. Grey used it seldom, for it was a trick tha
would not work on a mediocre player, one not sharp enough t
detect the knight's threat, or its possibilities. It was a gambit fo
use against a shrewd and subtle mind, and after nearly thre
months of weekly games, Grey knew quite well what sort of min
he was facing across the tinted ivory squares.

He forced himself not to hold his breath as he made the next-to
final move of the combination. He felt Fraser's eyes rest on hin
briefly, but didn't meet them, for fear of betraying his excitemen
Instead, he reached to the sideboard for the decanter, and refille
both glasses with the sweet dark port, keeping his eyes carefull
on the rising liquid.

Would it be the pawn, or the knight? Fraser's head was ben
over the board in contemplation, small reddish lights winking i
his hair as he moved slightly. The knight, and all was well;
would be too late. The pawn, and all was likely lost.

Grey could feel his heart beating heavily behind his breastbon
as he waited. Fraser's hand hovered over the board, then suddenl
decided, swooped down and touched the piece. The knight.

He must have let his breath out too noisily, for Fraser glance
sharply up at him, but it was too late. Careful to keep any ove
expression of triumph off his face, Grey castled.

Fraser frowned at the board for a long moment, eyes flickin
among the pieces, assessing. Then he jerked slightly, seeing it, an
looked up, eyes wide.

"Why ye cunning wee bastard!" he said, in a tone of surprise
respect. "Where in the bloody hell did ye learn *that* trick?"

"My elder brother taught it to me," Grey answered, losing h
customary wariness in a rush of delight at his success. He no
mally beat Fraser no more than three times in ten, and victory wa
sweet.

Fraser uttered a short laugh, and reaching out a long inde
finger, delicately tipped his king over.

"I should have expected something like that from a man lik
my Lord Melton," he observed casually.

Grey stiffened in his seat. Fraser saw the movement, and arche
one brow quizzically.

"It is Lord Melton ye mean, is it not?" he said. "Or perhap
you have another brother?"

"No," Grey said. His lips felt slightly numb, though that might nly be the cheroot. "No, I have only one brother." His heart had egun to pound again, but this time with a heavy, dull beat. Had ie Scottish bastard remembered all the time who he was?

"Our meeting was necessarily rather brief," the Scot said ryly. "But memorable." He picked up his glass and took a drink, vatching Grey across the crystal rim. "Perhaps ye didna know iat that I had met Lord Melton, on Culloden Field?"

"I knew. I fought at Culloden." All Grey's pleasure in his ictory had evaporated. He felt slightly nauseated from the smoke. 'I didn't know that you would recall Hal, though—or know of the elationship between us."

"As I have that meeting to thank for my life, I am not likely to orget it," Fraser said dryly.

Grey looked up. "I understand that you were not so thankful vhen Hal met you at Culloden."

The line of Fraser's mouth tightened, then relaxed.

"No," he said softly. He smiled without humor. "Your brother erra stubbornly refused to shoot me. I wasna inclined to be grate- ıl for the favor at the time."

"You wished to be shot?" Grey's eyebrows rose.

The Scot's eyes were remote, fixed on the chessboard, but learly seeing something else.

"I thought I had reason," he said softly. "At the time."

"What reason?" Grey asked. He caught a gimlet glance and dded hastily, "I mean no impertinence in asking. It is only—at iat time, I—I felt similarly. From what you have said of the tuarts, I cannot think that the loss of their cause would have led ou to such despair."

There was a faint flicker near Fraser's mouth, much too faint to e called a smile. He inclined his head briefly, in acknowledg- ient.

"There were those who fought for love of Charles Stuart—or om loyalty to his father's right of kingship. But you are right; I asna one of those."

He didn't explain further. Grey took a deep breath, keeping his yes fixed on the board.

"I said that I felt much as you did, at the time. I—lost a articular friend at Culloden," he said. With half his mind he ondered why he should speak of Hector to this man, of all men; a

Scottish warrior who had slashed his way across that deadly field
whose sword might well have been the one . . . At the same
time, he could not help but speak; there was no one to whom he
could speak of Hector, save this man, this prisoner who could
speak to no one else, whose words could do him no damage.

"He made me go and look at the body—Hal did, my brother,"
Grey blurted. He looked down at his hand, where the deep blue of
Hector's sapphire burned against his skin, a smaller version of the
one Fraser had reluctantly given him.

"He said that I must; that unless I saw him dead, I should never
really believe it. That unless I knew Hector—my friend—was
really gone, I would grieve forever. If I saw, and knew, I would
grieve, but then I should heal—and forget." He looked up, with a
painful attempt at a smile. "Hal is generally right, but not always."

Perhaps he had healed, but he would never forget. Certainly he
would not forget his last sight of Hector, lying wax-faced and still
in the early morning light, long dark lashes resting delicately on
his cheeks as they did when he slept. And the gaping wound that
had half-severed his head from his body, leaving the windpipe and
large vessels of the neck exposed in butchery.

They sat silent for a moment. Fraser said nothing, but picked up
his glass and drained it. Without asking, Grey refilled both glasses
for the third time.

He leaned back in his chair, looking curiously at his guest.

"Do you find your life greatly burdensome, Mr. Fraser?"

The Scot looked up then, and met his eyes with a long, level
gaze. Evidently, Fraser found nothing in his own face save curiosity, for the broad shoulders across the board relaxed their tension
somewhat, and the wide mouth softened its grim line. The Scot
leaned back, and flexed his right hand slowly, opening and closing
it to stretch the muscles. Grey saw that the hand had been damaged at one time; small scars were visible in the firelight, and two
of the fingers were set stiffly.

"Perhaps not greatly so," the Scot replied slowly. He met
Grey's eyes with dispassion. "I think perhaps the greatest burden
lies in caring for those we cannot help."

"Not in having no one for whom to care?"

Fraser paused before answering; he might have been weighing
the position of the pieces on the table.

"That is emptiness," he said at last, softly. "But no great burden."

It was late; there was no sound from the fortress around them ave the occasional step of the soldier on sentry in the courtyard elow.

"Your wife—she was a healer, you said?"

"She was. She . . . her name was Claire." Fraser swallowed, nen lifted his cup and drank, as though trying to dislodge some- ning stuck in his throat.

"You cared very much for her, I think?" Grey said softly.

He recognized in the Scot the same compulsion he had had a ew moments earlier—the need to speak a name kept hidden, to ring back for a moment the ghost of a love.

"I had meant to thank you sometime, Major," the Scot said oftly.

Grey was startled.

"Thank me? For what?"

The Scot looked up, eyes dark over the finished game.

"For that night at Carryarrick where we first met." His eyes ere steady on Grey's. "For what ye did for my wife."

"You remembered," Grey said hoarsely.

"I hadna forgotten," Fraser said simply. Grey steeled himself ₒ look across the table, but when he did so, he found no hint of ughter in the slanted blue eyes.

Fraser nodded at him, gravely formal. "Ye were a worthy foe, ᴵajor; I wouldna forget you."

John Grey laughed bitterly. Oddly enough, he felt less upset ᴀan he had thought he would, at having the shameful memory so ᴋplicitly recalled.

"If you found a sixteen-year-old shitting himself with fear a orthy foe, Mr. Fraser, then it is little wonder that the Highland my was defeated!"

Fraser smiled faintly.

"A man that doesna shit himself with a pistol held to his head, ᴵajor, has either no bowels, or no brains."

Despite himself, Grey laughed. One edge of Fraser's mouth ᵣned slightly up.

"Ye wouldna speak to save your own life, but ye would do it to ᵥe a lady's honor. The honor of my own lady," Fraser said ₒftly. "That doesna seem like cowardice to me."

The ring of truth was too evident in the Scot's voice to mistak⟩ or ignore.

"I did nothing for your wife," Grey said, rather bitterly. "Sh⟩ was in no danger, after all!"

"Ye didna ken that, aye?" Fraser pointed out. "Ye thought ⟩ save her life and virtue, at the risk of your own. Ye did her hon⟨ by the notion—and I have thought of it now and again, since I⟩ since I lost her." The hesitation in Fraser's voice was slight; onl⟩ the tightening of the muscles in his throat betrayed his emotion⟩

"I see." Grey breathed deep, and let it out slowly. "I am sor⟩ for your loss," he added formally.

They were both quiet for a moment, alone with their ghost⟩ Then Fraser looked up and drew in his breath.

"Your brother was right, Major," he said. "I thank ye, and I⟩ bid ye good e'en." He rose, set down his cup and left the roor⟩

It reminded him in some ways of his years in the cave, with h⟩ visits to the house, those oases of life and warmth in the desert ⟨ solitude. Here, it was the reverse, going from the crowded, co⟩ squalor of the cells up to the Major's glowing suite, able for a fe⟩ hours to stretch both mind and body, to relax in warmth ar⟩ conversation and the abundance of food.

It gave him the same odd sense of dislocation, though; th⟩ sense of losing some valuable part of himself that could not su⟩ vive the passage back to daily life. Each time, the passage becan⟩ more difficult.

He stood in the drafty passageway, waiting for the turnkey ⟩ unlock the cell door. The sounds of sleeping men buzzed in h⟩ ears and the smell of them wafted out as the door opened, punge⟩ as a fart.

He filled his lungs with a quick deep breath, and ducked h⟩ head to enter.

There was a stir among the bodies on the floor as he stepp⟩ into the room, his shadow falling black across the prone a⟩ bundled shapes. The door swung closed behind him, leaving t⟩ cell in darkness, but there was a ripple of awareness through t⟩ room, as men stirred awake to his coming.

"You're back late, Mac Dubh," said Murdo Lindsay, vo⟩ rusty with sleep. "Ye'll be sair tuckered tomorrow."

"I'll manage, Murdo," he whispered, stepping over bodies. He pulled off his coat and laid it carefully over the bench, then took up the rough blanket and sought his space on the floor, his long shadow flickering across the moon-barred window.

Ronnie Sinclair turned over as Mac Dubh lay down beside him. He blinked sleepily, sandy lashes nearly invisible in the moonlight.

"Did Wee Goldie feed ye decent, Mac Dubh?"

"He did, Ronnie, thank ye." He shifted on the stones, seeking a comfortable position.

"Ye'll tell us about it tomorrow?" The prisoners took an odd pleasure in hearing what he had been served for dinner, taking it as an honor that their chief should be well fed.

"Aye, I will, Ronnie," Mac Dubh promised. "But I must sleep now, aye?"

"Sleep well, Mac Dubh," came a whisper from the corner where Hayes was rolled up, curled like a set of teaspoons with MacLeod, Innes, and Keith, who all liked to sleep warm.

"Sweet dreams, Gavin," Mac Dubh whispered back, and little by little, the cell settled back into silence.

He dreamed of Claire that night. She lay in his arms, heavy-limbed and fragrant. She was with child; her belly round and smooth as a muskmelon, her breasts rich and full, the nipples dark as wine, urging him to taste them.

Her hand cupped itself between his legs, and he reached to return the favor, the small, fat softness of her filling his hand, pressing against him as she moved. She rose over him, smiling, her hair falling down around her face, and threw her leg across him.

"Give me your mouth," he whispered, not knowing whether he meant to kiss her or to have her take him between her lips, only knowing he must have her somehow.

"Give me yours," she said. She laughed and leaned down to him, hands on his shoulders, her hair brushing his face with the scent of moss and sunlight, and he felt the prickle of dry leaves against his back and knew they lay in the glen near Lallybroch, and her the color of the copper beeches all around; beech leaves and beechwood, gold eyes and a smooth white skin, skimmed with shadows.

Then her breast pressed against his mouth, and he took it eagerly, drawing her body tight against him as he suckled her. Her milk was hot and sweet, with a faint taste of silver, like a deer's blood.

"Harder," she whispered to him, and put her hand behind his head, gripping the back of his neck, pressing him to her. "Harder."

She lay at her length upon him, his hands holding for dear life to the sweet flesh of her buttocks, feeling the small solid weight of the child upon his own belly, as though they shared it now, protecting the small round thing between their bodies.

He flung his arms about her, tight, and she held him tight as he jerked and shuddered, her hair in his face, her hands in his hair, and the child between them, not knowing where any of the three of them began or ended.

He came awake suddenly, panting and sweating, half-curled on his side beneath one of the benches in the cell. It was not yet quite light, but he could see the shapes of the men who lay near him, and hoped he had not cried out. He closed his eyes at once, but the dream was gone. He lay quite still, his heart slowing, and waited for the dawn.

June 18, 1755

John Grey had dressed carefully this evening, with fresh linen and silk stockings. He wore his own hair, simply plaited, rinsed with a tonic of lemon-verbena. He had hesitated for a moment over Hector's ring, but at last had put it on, too. The dinner had been good; a pheasant he had shot himself, and a salad of greens in deference to Fraser's odd tastes for such things. Now they sat over the chessboard, lighter topics of conversation set aside in the concentration of the midgame.

"Will you have sherry?" He set down his bishop, and leaned back, stretching.

Fraser nodded, absorbed in the new position.

"I thank ye."

Grey rose and crossed the room, leaving Fraser by the fire. He reached into the cupboard for the bottle, and felt a thin trickle of

weat run down his ribs as he did so. Not from the fire, crackling
across the room; from sheer nervousness.

He brought the bottle back to the table, holding the goblets in
his other hand; the Waterford crystal his mother had sent. The
liquid purled into the glasses, shimmering amber and rose in the
firelight. Fraser's eyes were fixed on the cup, watching the rising
sherry, but with an abstraction that showed he was deep in his
thoughts. The dark blue eyes were hooded. Grey wondered what
he was thinking; not about the game—the outcome of that was
certain.

Grey reached out and moved his queen's bishop. It was no more
than a delaying move, he knew; still, it put Fraser's queen in
danger, and might force the exchange of a rook.

Grey got up to put a brick of peat on the fire. Rising, he
stretched himself, and strolled behind his opponent to view the
situation from this angle.

The firelight shimmered as the big Scot leaned forward to study
the board, picking up the deep red tones of James Fraser's hair,
echoing the glow of the light in the crystalline sherry.

Fraser had bound his hair back with a thin black cord, tied in a
bow. It would take no more than a slight tug to loosen it. John
Grey could imagine running his hand up under that thick, glossy
mass, to touch the smooth, warm nape beneath. To touch . . .

His palm closed abruptly, imagining sensation.

"It is your move, Major." The soft Scots voice brought him to
himself again, and he took his seat, viewing the chessboard
through sightless eyes.

Without really looking, he was intensely aware of the other's
movements, his presence. There was a disturbance of the air
round Fraser; it was impossible not to look at him. To cover his
glance, he picked up his sherry glass and sipped, barely noticing
the liquid gold taste of it.

Fraser sat still as a statue of cinnabar, only the deep blue eyes
live in his face as he studied the board. The fire had burned down,
and the lines of his body were limned with shadow. His hand, all
gold and black with the light of the fire on it, rested on the table,
still and exquisite as the captured pawn beside it.

The blue stone in John Grey's ring glinted as he reached for his
queen's bishop. *Is it wrong, Hector?* he thought. *That I should*

love a man who might have killed you? Or was it a way at last t put things right; to heal the wounds of Culloden for them both?

The bishop made a soft thump as he set the felted base dow with precision. Without stopping, his hand rose, as though moved without his volition. The hand traveled the short distanc through the air, looking as though it knew precisely what wanted, and set itself on Fraser's, palm tingling, curved finger gently imploring.

The hand under his was warm—so warm—but hard, and mo tionless as marble. Nothing moved on the table but the shimmer o the flame in the heart of the sherry. He lifted his eyes then, to mee Fraser's.

"Take your hand off me," Fraser said, very, very softly. "Or will kill you."

The hand under Grey's did not move, nor did the face abov but he could feel the shiver of revulsion, a spasm of hatred an disgust that rose from the man's core, radiating through his flesl

Quite suddenly, he heard once more the memory of Quarry' warning, as clearly as though the man spoke in his ear this mo ment.

If you dine with him alone—don't turn your back on him.

There was no chance of that; he could not turn away. Could no even look away or blink, to break the dark blue gaze that held hir frozen. Moving as slowly as though he stood atop an unexplode mine, he drew back his hand.

There was a moment's silence, broken only by the rain's patte and the hissing of the peat fire, when neither of them seemed t breathe. Then Fraser rose without a sound, and left the room.

12
Sacrifice

The rain of late November pattered down on the stones of the courtyard, and on the sullen rows of men, standing huddled under the downpour. The Redcoats who stood on guard over them didn't look much happier than the sodden prisoners.

Major Grey stood under the overhang of the roof, waiting. It wasn't the best weather for conducting a search and cleaning of the prisoners' cells, but at this time of year, it was futile to wait for good weather. And with more than two hundred prisoners in Ardsmuir, it was necessary to swab the cells at least monthly in order to prevent major outbreaks of illness.

The doors to the main cell block swung back, and a small file of prisoners emerged; the trusties who did the actual cleaning, closely watched by the guards. At the end of the line, Corporal Dunstable came out, his hands full of the small bits of contraband a search of this sort usually turned up.

"The usual rubbish, sir," he reported, dumping the collection of pitiful relics and anonymous junk onto the top of a cask that stood near the Major's elbow. "Just this, you might take notice of."

"This" was a small strip of cloth, perhaps six inches by four, in green tartan check. Dunstable glanced quickly at the lines of standing prisoners, as if intending to catch someone in a telltale action.

Grey sighed, then straightened his shoulders. "Yes, I suppose so." The possession of any Scottish tartan was strictly forbidden

by the Diskilting Act that had likewise disarmed the Highlander
and prevented the wearing of their native dress. He stepped i
front of the rows of men, as Corporal Dunstable gave a shar
shout to attract their attention.

"Whose is this?" The corporal raised the scrap high, and raise
his voice as well. Grey glanced from the scrap of bright cloth t
the row of prisoners, mentally ticking off the names, trying t
match them to his imperfect knowledge of tartans. Even within
single clan, the patterns varied so wildly that a given patter
couldn't be assigned with any certainty, but there were genera
patterns of color and design.

MacAlester, Hayes, Innes, Graham, MacMurtry, MacKenzie
MacDonald . . . stop. MacKenzie. That one. It was more an of
ficer's knowledge of men than any identification of the plaid wit
a particular clan that made him sure. MacKenzie was a youn
prisoner, and his face was a shade too controlled, too expressior
less.

"It's yours, MacKenzie. Isn't it?" Grey demanded. H
snatched the scrap of cloth from the corporal and thrust it unde
the young man's nose. The prisoner was white-faced under th
blotches of dirt. His jaw was clamped hard, and he was breathin
hard through his nose with a faint whistling sound.

Grey fixed the young man with a hard, triumphant stare. Th
young Scot had that core of implacable hate that they all had, b
he hadn't managed to build the wall of stoic indifference that hel
it in. Grey could feel the fear building in the lad; another secon
and he would break.

"It's mine." The voice was calm, almost bored, and spoke wit
such flat indifference that neither MacKenzie nor Grey registere
it at once. They stood locked in each other's eyes, until a larg
hand reached over Angus MacKenzie's shoulder and gentl
plucked the scrap of cloth from the officer's hand.

John Grey stepped back, feeling the words like a blow in the p
of his stomach. MacKenzie forgotten, he lifted his eyes the sever
inches necessary to look Jamie Fraser in the face.

"It isn't a Fraser tartan," he said, feeling the words force the
way past wooden lips. His whole face felt numb, a fact for whic
he was dimly grateful; at least his expression couldn't betray hir
before the ranks of the watching prisoners.

Fraser's mouth widened slightly. Grey kept his gaze fastened on , afraid to meet the dark blue eyes above.

"No, it isn't," Fraser agreed. "It's MacKenzie. My mother's lan."

In some far-off corner of his mind, Grey stored away another ny scrap of information with the small hoard of facts kept in the :weled coffer labeled "Jamie"—his mother was a MacKenzie. le knew that was true, just as he knew that the tartan didn't elong to Fraser.

He heard his voice, cool and steady, saying "Possession of clan irtans is illegal. You know the penalty, of course?"

The wide mouth curled in a one-sided smile.

"I do."

There was a shifting and a muttering among the ranks of the risoners; there was little actual movement, but Grey could feel ie alignment changing, as though they were in fact drawing)ward Fraser, circling him, embracing him. The circle had broken nd re-formed, and he was alone outside it. Jamie Fraser had gone ack to his own.

With an effort of will, Grey forced his gaze away from the soft, mooth lips, slightly chapped from exposure to sun and wind. The)ok in the eyes above them was what he had been afraid of; either fear nor anger—but indifference.

He motioned to a guard.

"Take him."

Major John William Grey bent his head over the work on his esk, signing requisitions without reading them. He seldom /orked so late at night, but there had not been time during the day, nd the paperwork was piling up. The requisitions must be sent to ondon this week.

"Two hundred pound wheat flowr," he wrote, trying to concen- ate on the neatness of the black squiggles under his quill. The ouble with such routine paperwork was that it occupied his atten- on but not his mind, allowing memories of the day to creep in nawares.

"Six hogsheds ale, for use of barracks." He set down the quill nd rubbed his hands briskly together. He could still feel the chill iat had settled in his bones in the courtyard that morning. There

was a hot fire, but it didn't seem to be helping. He didn't g
nearer; he had tried that once, and stood mesmerized, seeing th
images of the afternoon in the flames, roused only when the clot
of his breeches began to scorch.

He picked up the quill and tried again to banish the sights of th
courtyard from his mind.

It was better not to delay execution of sentences of this kind; th
prisoners became restless and nervy in anticipation and there wa
considerable difficulty in controlling them. Executed at once
though, such discipline often had a salutary effect, showing th
prisoners that retribution would be swift and dire, enhancing thei
respect for those who held their guardianship. Somehow Joh
Grey suspected that this particular occasion had not much en
hanced his prisoners' respect—for him, at least.

Feeling little more than the trickle of ice water through hi
veins, he had given his orders, swift and composed, and they ha
been obeyed with equal competence.

The prisoners had been drawn up in ranks around the four side
of the courtyard square, with shorter lines of guards arrange
facing them, bayonets fixed to the ready, to prevent any unseeml
outbreak.

But there had been no outbreak, seemly or otherwise. The pris
oners had waited in a chill silence in the light rain that misted th
stones of the courtyard, with little sound other than the norma
coughs and throat-clearings of any assemblage of men. It was th
beginning of winter, and catarrh was almost as common a scourg
in the barracks as it was in the damp cells.

He had stood watching impassively, hands folded behind hi
back, as the prisoner was led to the platform. Watched, feeling th
rain seep into the shoulders of his coat and run in tiny rivulet
down the neck of his shirt, as Jamie Fraser stood on the platform
yard away and stripped to the waist, moving without haste o
hesitation, as though this were something he had done before, a
accustomed task, of no importance in itself.

He had nodded to the two privates, who seized the prisoner'
unresisting hands and raised them, binding them to the arms of th
whipping post. They gagged him, and Fraser stood upright, th
rain running down his raised arms, and down the deep seam of hi
backbone, to soak the thin cloth of his breeches.

Another nod, to the sergeant who held the charge sheet, and

all surge of annoyance as the gesture caused a cascade of col-
ted rain from one side of his hat. He straightened his hat and
iden wig, and resumed his stance of authority in time to hear
: charge and sentence read.

". . . in contravention of the Diskilting Act, passed by His
ijesty's Parliament, for which crime the sentence of sixty lashes
ill be inflicted.''

Grey glanced with professional detachment at the sergeant-
rier designated to give the punishment; this was not the first
ie for any of them. He didn't nod this time; the rain was still
ling. A half-closing of the eyes instead, as he spoke the usual
·rds:

''Mr. Fraser, you will take your punishment.''

And he stood, eyes front and steady, watching, and hearing the
id of the landing flails and the grunt of the prisoner's breath,
·ced past the gag by the blow.

The man's muscles tightened in resistance to the pain. Again
d again, until each separate muscle stood hard under the skin.
·s own muscles ached with tension, and he shifted inconspicu-
·sly from one leg to another, as the brutal tedium continued.
in streams of red ran down the prisoner's spine, blood mixed
th water, staining the cloth of his breeches.

Grey could feel the men behind him, soldiers and prisoners
th, all eyes fixed on the platform and its central figure. Even the
ighing was silenced.

And over it all like a sticky coat of varnish sealing off Grey's
lings was a thin layer of self-disgust, as he realized that his eyes
·re fixed on the scene not out of duty, but from sheer inability to
·k away from the sheen of mingled rain and blood that gleamed
muscle, tightened in anguish to a curve of wrenching beauty.

The sergeant-farrier paused only briefly between blows. He was
·rrying it slightly; everyone wanted to get it over and get out of
·rain. Grissom counted each stroke in a loud voice, noting it on
sheet as he did so. The farrier checked the lash, running the
ands with their hard-waxed knots between his fingers to free
m of blood and bits of flesh, then raised the cat once more,
·ung it slowly twice round his head, and struck again. ''Thirty!''
d the sergeant.

Major Grey pulled out the lowest drawer of his desk, and was
·tly sick, all over a stack of requisitions.

*His fingers were dug hard into his palms, but the shaking
wouldn't stop. It was deep in his bones, like the winter cold.*

"Put a blanket over him; I'll tend him in a moment."

*The English surgeon's voice seemed to come from a long
way off; he felt no connection between the voice and the
hands that gripped him firmly by both arms. He cried out as
they shifted him, the torsion splitting the barely clotted
wounds on his back. The trickle of warm blood across his ribs
made the shaking worse, despite the rough blanket they laid
over his shoulders.*

*He gripped the edges of the bench on which he lay, cheek
pressed against the wood, eyes closed, struggling against the
shaking. There was a stir and a shuffle somewhere in the
room, but he couldn't take notice, couldn't take his attention
from the clenching of his teeth and the tightness of his joints.*

*The door closed, and the room grew quiet. Had they left
him alone?*

*No, there were footsteps near his head, and the blanket
over him lifted, folded back to his waist.*

"Mm. Made a mess of you, didn't he, boy?"

*He didn't answer; no answer seemed expected, in any
case. The surgeon turned away for a moment; then he felt a
hand beneath his cheek, lifting his head. A towel slid beneath
his face, cushioning it from the rough wood.*

*"I'm going to cleanse the wounds now," the voice said. It
was impersonal, but not unfriendly.*

*He drew in his breath through his teeth as a hand touched
his back. There was an odd whimpering noise. He realized he
had made it, and was ashamed.*

"How old are you, boy?"

*"Nineteen." He barely got the word out, before biting
down hard on a moan.*

*The doctor touched his back gently here and there, then
stood up. He heard the sound of the bolt being shot to, then
the doctor's steps returning.*

*"No one will come in now," the voice said kindly. "Go
ahead and cry."*

"Hey!" the voice was saying. "Wake up, man!"

He came slowly to consciousness; the roughness of wood beneath his cheek brought dream and waking together for a moment, and he couldn't remember where he was. A hand came out of the darkness, touching him tentatively on the cheek.

"Ye were greetin' in your sleep, man," the voice whispered. "Does it pain ye much?"

"A bit." He realized the other link between dreaming and waking as he tried to raise himself and the pain crackled over his back like sheet lightning. He let out his breath in an involuntary grunt and dropped back on the bench.

He had been lucky; he had drawn Dawes, a stout middle-aged soldier who didn't really like flogging prisoners, and did it only because it was part of his job. Still, sixty lashes did damage, even applied without enthusiasm.

"Nah, then, that's too hot by half. Want to scald him, do ye?" It was Morrison's voice, scolding. It would be Morrison, of course. Odd, he thought dimly. How whenever you had a group of men, they seemed to find their proper jobs, no matter whether it was a thing they'd done before. Morrison had been a cottar, like most of them. Likely a good hand with his beasts, but not thinking much about it. Now he was the natural healer for the men, the one they turned to with a griping belly or a broken thumb. Morrison knew little more than the rest, but the men turned to him when they were hurt, as they turned to Seumus Mac Dubh for reassurance and protection. And for justice.

The steaming cloth was laid across his back and he grunted with the sting of it, pressing his lips tight to keep from crying out. He could feel the shape of Morrison's small hand, lightly laid in the center of his back.

"Bide ye, man, 'til the heat passes."

As the nightmare faded, he blinked for a moment, adjusting himself to the nearby voices and the perception of company. He was in the large cell, in the shadowy nook by the chimney breast. Steam rose from the fire; there must be a cauldron boiling. He saw Walter MacLeod lower a fresh armful of rags into its depths, the steam touching MacLeod's dark beard and brows with red. Then, as the heated rags on his back cooled to a soothing warmth, he closed his eyes and sank back into a half-doze, lulled by the soft conversation of the men nearby.

It was familiar, this state of dreamy detachment. He had f
much the same ever since the moment when he had reached ov
young Angus's shoulder and closed his fist on the scrap of tart
cloth. As though with that choice, some curtain had come do
between him and the men around him; as though he were alone,
some quiet place of infinite remoteness.

He had followed the guard who took him, stripped hims
when told, but all without feeling as though he had truly wak
Taken his place on the platform and heard the words of crime a
sentence pronounced, without really listening. Not even the rou
bite of the rope on his wrists or the cold rain on his naked ba
had roused him. These seemed all things that had happened b
fore; nothing he said or did could change a thing; it was all fate

As for the flogging, he had borne it. There was no room then f
thought or regret, or for anything beyond the stubborn, despera
struggle such bodily insult required.

"Still, now, still." Morrison's hand rested on his neck, to p
vent his moving as the sodden rags were taken off and a fresh, h
poultice applied, momentarily rousing all the dormant nerves
fresh startlement.

One consequence of his odd state of mind was that all sen
tions seemed of equal intensity. He could, if he tried, feel ea
separate stripe across his back, see each one in his mind's eye a
vivid streak of color across the dark of imagination. But the pa
of the gash that ran from ribs to shoulder was of no more weight
consequence than the almost pleasant feeling of heaviness in h
legs, the soreness in his arms, or the soft tickling brush of his h
across his cheek.

His pulse beat slow and regular in his ears; the sigh of his brea
was a thing apart from the heave of his chest as he breathed.
existed only as a collection of fragments, each small piece with
own sensations, and none of them of any particular concern to t
central intelligence.

"Here, Mac Dubh," said Morrison's voice, next to his e
"Lift your head, and drink this."

The sharp scent of whisky struck him, and he tried to turn h
head away.

"I don't need it," he said.

"That ye do," Morrison said, with that firm matter-of-factn
that all healers seemed to have, as though they always knew bet

an you did what you felt like or what you required. Lacking
rength or will to argue, he opened his mouth and sipped the
hisky, feeling his neck muscles quiver under the strain of hold-
g his head up.

The whisky added its own bit to the chorus of sensations that
led him. A burn in throat and belly, sharp tingle up the back of
e nose, and a sort of whirling in his head that told him he had
unk too much, too fast.

"A bit more, now, aye, that's it," Morrison said, coaxing.
Good lad. Aye, that'll be better, won't it?" Morrison's thick
dy moved, so his vision of the darkened room was obscured. A
aft blew from the high window, but there seemed more stir about
m than was accounted for by the wind.

"Now, how's the back? Ye'll be stiff as a cornstook by the
orrow, but I think it's maybe no so bad as it might be. Here,
an, ye'll have a sup more." The rim of the horn cup pressed
sistently against his mouth.

Morrison was still talking, rather loudly, of nothing in particu-
r. There was something wrong about that. Morrison was not a
lkative man. Something was happening, but he couldn't see. He
ted his head, searching for what was wrong, but Morrison
essed it down again.

"Dinna trouble yourself, Mac Dubh," he said softly. "Ye canna
op it, anyway."

Surreptitious sounds were coming from the far corner of the
ll, the sounds Morrison had tried to keep him from hearing.
craping noises, brief mutters, a thud. Then the muffled sound of
ows, slow and regular, and a heavy gasping of fright and pain,
nctuated with a small whimpering sound of indrawn breath.

They were beating young Angus MacKenzie. He braced his
nds beneath his chest, but the effort made his back blaze and his
ad swim. Morrison's hand was back, forcing him down.

"Be still, Mac Dubh," he said. His tone was a mixture of
thority and resignation.

A wave of dizziness washed through him, and his hands slipped
f the bench. Morrison was right in any case, he realized. He
uldn't stop them.

He lay still then under Morrison's hand, eyes closed, and waited
r the sounds to stop. Despite himself, he wondered who it was,
at administrator of blind justice in the dark. Sinclair. His mind

supplied the answer without hesitation. And Hayes and Linds
helping, no doubt.

They could no more help themselves than he could, or Mor
son. Men did as they were born to. One man a healer, another
bully.

The sounds had stopped, except for a muffled, sobbing gas
His shoulders relaxed, and he didn't move as Morrison took aw
the last wet poultice and gently blotted him dry, the draft from tl
window making him shiver in sudden chill. He pressed his li
tight, to make no noise. They had gagged him this afternoon, a
he was glad of it; the first time he had been flogged, years ago, I
had bitten his lower lip nearly in two.

The cup of whisky pressed against his mouth, but he turned I
head aside, and it disappeared without comment to some pla
where it would find a more cordial reception. Milligan, likely, t
Irishman.

One man with the weakness for drink, another with a hatred
it. One man a lover of women, and another . . .

He sighed and shifted slightly on the hard plank bed. Morris
had covered him with a blanket and gone away. He felt drain
and empty, still in fragments, but with his mind quite cle
perched at some far remove from the rest of him.

Morrison had taken away the candle as well; it burned at the 1
end of the cell, where the men sat hunched companionably 1
gether, the light making black shapes of them, one indistinguis
able from another, rimmed in gold light like the pictures of fac
less saints in old missals.

He wondered where they came from, these gifts that shaped
man's nature. From God?

Was it like the descent of the Paraclete, and the tongues of f
that came to rest on the apostles? He remembered the picture
the Bible in his mother's parlor, the apostles all crowned with fi
and looking fair daft with the shock of it, standing about like
crowd of beeswax candles, lit for a party.

He smiled to himself at the memory, and closed his eyes. T
candle shadows wavered red on his lids.

Claire, his own Claire—who knew what had sent her to hi
had thrust her into a life she had surely not been born to? And I
she had known what to do, what she was meant to be, despite th
Not everyone was so fortunate as to know their gift.

There was a cautious shuffling in the darkness beside him. He opened his eyes and saw no more than a shape, but knew nonetheless who it was.

"How are ye, Angus?" he said softly in Gaelic.

The youngster knelt awkwardly by him, and took his hand.

"I am . . . all right. But you—sir, I mean . . . I—I'm sorry . . ."

Was it experience or instinct that made him tighten his own hand in reassurance?

"I am all right, too," he said. "Lay ye down, wee Angus, and take your rest."

The shape bent its head in an oddly formal gesture, and pressed a kiss on the back of his hand.

"I—may I stay by ye, sir?"

His hand weighed a ton, but he lifted it nonetheless and laid it on the young man's head. Then it slipped away, but he felt Angus's tension relax, as the comfort flowed from his touch.

He had been born a leader, then bent and shaped further to fit such a destiny. But what of a man who had not been born to the role he was required to fill? John Grey, for one. Charles Stuart for another.

For the first time in ten years, from this strange distance, he could find it in himself to forgive that feeble man who had once been his friend. Having so often paid the price exacted by his own gift, he could at last see the more terrible doom of having been born a king, without the gift of kingship.

Angus MacKenzie sat slumped against the wall next to him, head bowed upon his knees, his blanket over his shoulders. A small, gurgling snore came from the huddled form. He could feel sleep coming for him, fitting back the shattered, scattered parts of himself as it came, and knew he would wake whole—if very sore —in the morning.

He felt relieved at once of many things. Of the weight of immediate responsibility, of the necessity for decision. Temptation was gone, along with the possibility of it. More important, the burden of anger had lifted; perhaps it was gone for good.

So, he thought, through the gathering fog, John Grey had given him back his destiny.

Almost, he could be grateful.

I t was Roger who found her in the morning, curled up on t
study sofa under the hearthrug, papers scattered carelessly ov
the floor where they had spilled from one of the folders.

The light from the floor-length windows streamed in, floodi
the study, but the high back of the sofa had shaded Claire's fa
and prevented the dawn from waking her. The light was just n
pouring over the curve of dusty velvet to flicker among the stran
of her hair.

A glass face in more ways than one, Roger thought, looking
her. Her skin was so fair that the blue veins showed through
temple and throat, and the sharp, clear bones were so close b
neath that she might have been carved of ivory.

The rug had slipped half off, exposing her shoulders. One ar
lay relaxed across her chest, trapping a single, crumpled sheet
paper against her body. Roger lifted her arm carefully, to pull t
paper loose without waking her. She was limp with sleep, her fle
surprisingly warm and smooth in his grasp.

His eyes found the name at once; he had known she must ha
found it.

"James MacKenzie Fraser," he murmured. He looked up fro
the paper to the sleeping woman on the sofa. The light had ju
touched the curve of her ear; she stirred briefly and turned h
head, then her face lapsed back into somnolence.

"I don't know who you were, mate," he whispered to the u
seen Scot, "but you must have been something, to deserve her

Very gently, he replaced the rug over Claire's shoulders, a

vered the blind of the window behind her. Then he squatted and
thered up the scattered papers from the Ardsmuir folder. Ards-
ir. That was all he needed for now; even if Jamie Fraser's
entual fate was not recorded in the pages in his hands, it would
somewhere in the history of Ardsmuir prison. It might take
other foray into the Highland archives, or even a trip to London,
t the next step in the link had been forged; the path was clear.

Brianna was coming down the stairs as he pulled the door of the
dy closed, moving with exaggerated caution. She arched a brow
question and he lifted the folder, smiling.

"Got him," he whispered.

She didn't speak, but an answering smile spread across her face,
ght as the rising sun outside.

PART FOUR

The Lake District

14

Geneva

I think," Grey said carefully, "that you might consider changing your name."

He didn't expect an answer; in four days of travel, Fraser [ha]d not spoken a single word to him, managing even the awkward [bu]siness of sharing an inn room without direct communication. [Th]ey had shrugged and taken the bed, while Fraser, without ges[tu]re or glance, had wrapped himself in his threadbare cloak and [lai]n down before the hearth. Scratching an assortment of bites [fr]om fleas and bedbugs, Grey thought that Fraser might well have [ha]d the better end of the sleeping arrangements.

"Your new host is not well disposed toward Charles Stuart and [hi]s adherents, having lost his only son at Prestonpans," he went [on], addressing the iron-set profile visible next to him. Gordon [Du]nsany had been only a few years older than himself, a young [ca]ptain in Bolton's regiment. They might easily have died together [on] that field—if not for that meeting in the wood near Carryarrick.

"You can scarcely hope to conceal the fact that you are a Scot, [an]d a Highlander at that. If you will condescend to consider a [pi]ece of well-meant advice, it might be judicious not to use a name [wh]ich would be as easily recognized as your own."

Fraser's stony expression didn't alter in the slightest particular. [H]e nudged his horse with a heel and guided it ahead of Grey's [da]y, seeking the remains of the track, washed out by a recent [flo]od.

It was late afternoon when they crossed the arch of Ashness [br]idge and started down the slope toward Watendlath Tarn. The

Lake District of England was nothing like Scotland, Grey
flected, but at least there were mountains here. Round-flanked,
and dreamy mountains, not sternly forbidding like the Highla
crags, but mountains nonetheless.

Watendlath Tarn was dark and ruffled in the early autumn wir
its edges thick with sedge and marsh grass. The summer rains h
been more generous even than usual in this damp place, and t
tips of drowned shrubs poked limp and tattered above water th
had run over its banks.

At the crest of the next hill, the track split, going off in tv
directions. Fraser, some distance ahead, pulled his horse to a st
and waited for direction, the wind ruffling his hair. He had r
plaited it that morning, and it blew free, the flaming strands lifti
wild about his head.

Squelching his way up the slope, John William Grey looked
at the man above him, still as a bronze statue on his mount, sa
for that rippling mane. The breath dried in his throat, and he lick
his lips.

"O Lucifer, thou son of the morning," he murmured to hir
self, but forbore to add the rest of the quotation.

For Jamie, the four-day ride to Helwater had been torture. T
sudden illusion of freedom, combined with the certainty of
immediate loss, gave him a dreadful anticipation of his unknov
destination.

This, with the anger and sorrow of his parting from his m
fresh in memory—the wrenching loss of leaving the Highland
with the knowledge that the parting might well be permanent
and his waking moments suffused with the physical pain of lon
unused saddle muscles, were together enough to have kept him
torment for the whole of the journey. Only the fact that he h
given his parole kept him from pulling Major John William Gr
off his horse and throttling him in some peaceful lane.

Grey's words echoed in his ears, half-obliterated by the thru
ming beat of his angry blood.

"As the renovation of the fortress has largely been completed
with the able assistance of yourself and your men"—Grey h
allowed a tinge of irony to show in his voice—"the prisoners a

be removed to other accommodation, and the fortress of Ards-
ir garrisoned by troops of His Majesty's Twelfth Dragoons.

"The Scottish prisoners of war are to be transported to the
nerican Colonies," he continued. "They will be sold under
nd of indenture, for a term of seven years."

Jamie had kept himself carefully expressionless, but at that
ws, had felt his face and hands go numb with shock.

"Indenture? That is no better than slavery," he said, but did not
y much attention to his own words. America! A land of wilder-
ss and savages—and one to be reached across three thousand
les of empty, roiling sea! Indenture in America was a sentence
tamount to permanent exile from Scotland.

"A term of indenture is not slavery," Grey had assured him,
t the Major knew as well as he that the difference was merely a
ality, and true only insofar as indentured servants would—if
y survived—regain their freedom upon some predetermined
te. An indentured servant *was* to most other intents and pur-
ses the slave of his or her master—to be misused, whipped or
nded at will, forbidden by law to leave the master's premises
thout permission.

As James Fraser was now to be forbidden.

"You are not to be sent with the others." Grey had not looked
him while speaking. "You are not merely a prisoner of war, you
a convicted traitor. As such, you are imprisoned at the pleasure
His Majesty; your sentence cannot be commuted to transporta-
n without royal approval. And His Majesty has not seen fit to
e that approval."

Jamie was conscious of a remarkable array of emotions; be-
ath his immediate rage was fear and sorrow for the fate of his
n, mingled with a small flicker of ignominious relief that, what-
r his own fate was to be, it would not involve entrusting himself
the sea. Shamed by the realization, he turned a cold eye on
ey.

"The gold," he said flatly. "That's it, aye?" So long as there
nained the slightest chance of his revealing what he knew about
t half-mythical hoard, the English Crown would take no chance
having him lost to the sea demons or the savages of the Colo-
s.

The Major still would not look at him, but gave a small shrug,
good as assent.

"Where am I to go, then?" His own voice had sounded rusty
his ears, slightly hoarse as he began to recover from the shock
the news.

Grey had busied himself putting away his records. It was ea
September, and a warm breeze blew through the half-open w
dow, fluttering the papers.

"It's called Helwater. In the Lake District of England. You w
be quartered with Lord Dunsany, to serve in whatever men
capacity he may require." Grey did look up then, the expression
his light blue eyes unreadable. "I shall visit you there once ea
quarter—to ensure your welfare."

He eyed the Major's red-coated back now, as they rode sing
file through the narrow lanes, seeking refuge from his miseries
a satisfying vision of those wide blue eyes, bloodshot and popp
in amazement as Jamie's hands tightened on that slender thro
thumbs digging into the sun-reddened flesh until the Majo
small, muscular body should go limp as a killed rabbit in
grasp.

His Majesty's pleasure, was it? He was not deceived. This h
been Grey's doing; the gold only an excuse. He was to be sold a
servant, and kept in a place where Grey could see it, and glo
This was the Major's revenge.

He had lain before the inn hearth each night, aching in eve
limb, acutely aware of every twitch and rustle and breath of
man in the bed behind him, and deeply resentful of that awarene
By the pale gray of dawn, he was keyed to fury once more, lo
ing for the man to rise from his bed and make some disgrace
gesture toward him, so that he might release his fury in the passi
of murder. But Grey had only snored.

Over Helvellyn Bridge and past another of the strange gra
tarns, the red and yellow leaves of maple and larch whirling do
in showers past the lightly sweated quarters of his horse, strik
his face and sliding past him with a papery, whispering cares

Grey had stopped just ahead, and turned in the saddle, waiti
They had arrived, then. The land sloped steeply down into a v
ley, where the manor house lay half-concealed in a welter
autumn-bright trees.

Helwater lay before him, and with it, the prospect of a life

meful servitude. He stiffened his back and kicked his horse,
der than he intended.

Grey was received in the main drawing room, Lord Dunsany
ng cordially dismissive of his disheveled clothes and filthy
ots, and Lady Dunsany, a small round woman with faded fair
r, fulsomely hospitable.

'A drink, Johnny, you must have a drink! And Louisa, my dear,
haps you should fetch the girls down to greet our guest.''

As Lady Dunsany turned to give orders to a footman, his Lord-
p leaned close over the glass to murmur to him. ''The Scottish
soner—you've brought him with you?''

'Yes,'' Grey said. Lady Dunsany, now in animated conversa-
n with the butler about the altered dispositions for dinner, was
ikely to overhear, but he thought it best to keep his own voice
. ''I left him in the front hall—I wasn't sure quite what you
ant to do with him.''

'You said the fellow's good with horses, eh? Best make him a
om then, as you suggested.'' Lord Dunsany glanced at his
e, and carefully turned so that his lean back was to her, further
rding their conversation. ''I haven't told Louisa who he is,''
baronet muttered. ''All that scare about the Highlanders dur-
the Rising—country was quite paralyzed with fear, you know?
d she's never got over Gordon's death.''

'I quite see.'' Grey patted the old man's arm reassuringly. He
n't think Dunsany himself had got over the death of his son,
ugh he had rallied himself gamely for the sake of his wife and
ghters.

'I'll just tell her the man's a servant you've recommended to
Er . . . he's safe, of course? I mean . . . well, the
s . . .'' Lord Dunsany cast an uneasy eye toward his wife.

'Quite safe,'' Grey assured his host. ''He's an honorable man,
he's given his parole. He'll neither enter the house nor leave
boundaries of your property, save with your express permis-
.'' Helwater covered more than six hundred acres, he knew. It
a long way from freedom, and from Scotland as well, but
haps something better than either the narrow stones of Ards-
r or the distant hardships of the Colonies.

A sound from the doorway swung Dunsany around, restored
beaming joviality by the appearance of his two daughters.

"You'll remember Geneva, Johnny?" he asked, urging
guest forward. "Isobel was still in the nursery last time you ca
—how time does fly, does it not?" And he shook his head in m
dismay.

Isobel was fourteen, small and round and bubbly and blond, l
her mother. Grey didn't, in fact, remember Geneva—or rather
did, but the scrawny schoolgirl of years past bore little rese
blance to the graceful seventeen-year-old who now offered h
her hand. If Isobel resembled their mother, Geneva rather t
after her father, at least in the matter of height and leanness. L
Dunsany's grizzled hair might once have been that shining che
nut, and the girl had Dunsany's clear gray eyes.

The girls greeted the visitor with politeness, but were clea
more interested in something else.

"Daddy," said Isobel, tugging on her father's sleeve. "Ther
a *huge* man in the hall! He watched us all the time we w
coming down the stairs! He's scary-looking!"

"Who is he, Daddy?" Geneva asked. She was more reser
than her sister, but clearly also interested.

"Er . . . why, that must be the new groom John's brou
us," Lord Dunsany said, obviously flustered. "I'll have one of
footmen take him—" The baronet was interrupted by the sud
appearance of a footman in the doorway.

"Sir," he said, looking shocked at the news he bore, "there
Scotchman in the hall!" Lest this outrageous statement not
believed, he turned and gestured widely at the tall, silent fig
standing cloaked behind him.

At this cue, the stranger took a step forward, and spotting L
Dunsany, politely inclined his head.

"My name is Alex MacKenzie," he said, in a soft Highl
accent. He bowed toward Lord Dunsany, with no hint of mock
in his manner. "Your servant, my lord."

For one accustomed to the strenuous life of a Highland farm
a labor prison, the work of a groom on a Lake District stud f
was no great strain. For a man who had been mewed up in a
for two months—since the others had left for the Colonies—it

hell of a sweat. For the first week, while his muscles reaccus-
ned themselves to the sudden demands of constant movement,
nie Fraser fell into his hayloft pallet each evening too tired even
dream.

He had arrived at Helwater in such a state of exhaustion and
ntal turmoil that he had at first seen it only as another prison—
d one among strangers, far away from the Highlands. Now that
was ensconced here, imprisoned as securely by his word as by
rs, he found both body and mind growing easier, as the days
ssed by. His body toughened, his feelings calmed in the quiet
npany of horses, and gradually he found it possible to think
ionally again.

If he had no true freedom, he did at least have air, and light,
ce to stretch his limbs, and the sight of mountains and the
ely horses that Dunsany bred. The other grooms and servants
re understandably suspicious of him, but inclined to leave him
ne, out of respect for his size and forbidding countenance. It
s a lonely life—but he had long since accepted the fact that, for
n, life was unlikely ever to be otherwise.

The soft snows came down upon Helwater, and even Major
ey's official visit at Christmas—a tense, awkward occasion—
ssed without disturbing his growing feelings of content.

Very quietly, he made such arrangements as could be managed,
communicate with Jenny and Ian in the Highlands. Aside from
infrequent letters that reached him by indirect means, which he
d and then destroyed for safety's sake, his only reminder of
ne was the beechwood rosary he wore about his neck, con-
led beneath his shirt.

A dozen times a day he touched the small cross that lay over his
irt, conjuring each time the face of a loved one, with a brief
rd of prayer—for his sister, Jenny; for Ian and the children—his
nesake, Young Jamie, Maggie, and Katherine Mary, for the
ns Michael and Janet, and for Baby Ian. For the tenants of
llybroch; the men of Ardsmuir. And always, the first prayer at
rning, the last at night—and many between—for Claire. *Lord,*
t she may be safe. She and the child.

As the snow passed and the year brightened into spring, Jamie
iser was aware of only one fly in the ointment of his daily
stence—the presence of the Lady Geneva Dunsany.

Pretty, spoilt, and autocratic, the Lady Geneva was accustomed

to get what she wanted when she wanted it, and damn the con‑
nience of anyone standing in her way. She was a good hor
woman—Jamie would give her that—but so sharp-tongued a
whim-ridden that the grooms were given to drawing straws
determine who would have the misfortune of accompanying
on her daily ride.

Of late, though, the Lady Geneva had been making her o
choice of companion—Alex MacKenzie.

"Nonsense," she said, when he pleaded first discretion, a
then temporary indisposition, to avoid accompanying her into
secluded mist of the foothills above Helwater; a place she v
forbidden to ride, because of the treacherous footing and dang
ous fogs. "Don't be silly. Nobody's going to see us. Come or
And kicking her mare brutally in the ribs, was off before he co
stop her, laughing back over her shoulder at him.

Her infatuation with him was sufficiently obvious as to ma
the other grooms grin sidelong and make low-voiced remarks
each other when she entered the stable. He had a strong ur
when in her company, to boot her swiftly where it would do m
good, but so far had settled for maintaining a strict silence wher
her company, replying to all overtures with a mumpish grunt.

He trusted that she would get tired of this taciturn treatm
sooner or later, and transfer her annoying attentions to another
the grooms. Or—pray God—she would soon be married, and w
away from both Helwater and him.

It was a rare sunny day for the Lake Country, where the diff
ence between the clouds and the ground is often imperceptible
terms of damp. Still, on this May afternoon it was warm, wa
enough for Jamie to have found it comfortable to remove his sh
It was safe enough up here in the high field, with no likelihood
company beyond Bess and Blossom, the two stolid drayhor
pulling the roller.

It was a big field, and the horses old and well-trained to the ta
which they liked; all he need do was twitch the reins occasiona
to keep their noses heading straight. The roller was made of wo
rather than the older kind of stone or metal, and constructed wi
narrow slit between each board, so that the interior could be fi

th well-rotted manure, which dribbled out in a steady stream as
e roller turned, lightening the heavy contrivance as it drained.

Jamie thoroughly approved this innovation. He must tell Ian
out it; draw a diagram. The Gypsies would be coming soon; the
chenmaids and grooms were all talking of it. He would maybe
ve time to add another installment to the ongoing letter he kept,
nding the current crop of pages whenever a band of roving
kers or Gypsies came onto the farm. Delivery might be delayed
r a month, or three, or six, but eventually the packet would make
way into the Highlands, passed from hand to hand, and on to
s sister at Lallybroch, who would pay a generous fee for its
ception.

Replies from Lallybroch came by the same anonymous route—
r as a prisoner of the Crown, anything he sent or received by the
ails must be inspected by Lord Dunsany. He felt a moment's
citement at the thought of a letter, but tried to damp it down;
ere might be nothing.

"Gee!" he shouted, more as a matter of form than anything.
ss and Blossom could see the approaching stone fence as well
he could, and were perfectly well aware that this was the spot to
gin the ponderous turnabout. Bess waggled one ear and snorted,
d he grinned.

"Aye, I know," he said to her, with a light twitch of the rein.
But they pay me to say it."

Then they were settled in the new track, and there was nothing
ore to do until they reached the wagon standing at the foot of the
ld, piled high with manure for refilling the roller. The sun was
his face now, and he closed his eyes, reveling in the feel of
armth on his bare chest and shoulders.

The sound of a horse's high whinny stirred him from somno-
nce a quarter-hour later. Opening his eyes, he could see the rider
ming up the lane from the lower paddock, neatly framed be-
een Blossom's ears. Hastily, he sat up and pulled the shirt back
er his head.

"You needn't be modest on my account, MacKenzie." Geneva
insany's voice was high and slightly breathless as she pulled her
are to a walk beside the moving roller.

"Mmphm." She was dressed in her best habit, he saw, with a
irngorm brooch at her throat, and her color was higher than the
mperature of the day warranted.

"What are you doing?" she asked, after they had rolled a paced in silence for some moments.

"I am spreading shit, my lady," he answered precisely, looking at her.

"Oh." She rode on for the space of half a track, before venting further into conversation.

"Did you know I am to be married?"

He did; all the servants had known it for a month, Richards butler having been in the library, serving, when the solicitor ca from Derwentwater to draw up the wedding contract. The La Geneva had been informed two days ago. According to her ma Betty, the news had not been well received.

He contented himself with a noncommittal grunt.

"To Ellesmere," she said. The color rose higher in her chee and her lips pressed together.

"I wish ye every happiness, my lady." Jamie pulled briefly the reins as they came to the end of the field. He was out of seat before Bess had set her hooves; he had no wish at all to ling in conversation with the Lady Geneva, whose mood seemed th oughly dangerous.

"Happiness!" she cried. Her big gray eyes flashed and s slapped the thigh of her habit. "Happiness! Married to a man enough to be my own grandsire?"

Jamie refrained from saying that he suspected the Earl of Ell mere's prospects for happiness were somewhat more limited th her own. Instead, he murmured, "Your pardon, my lady," a went behind to unfasten the roller.

She dismounted and followed him. "It's a filthy bargain tween my father and Ellesmere! He's selling me, that's what it My father cares not the slightest trifle for me, or he'd never ha made such a match! Do you not think I am badly used?"

On the contrary, Jamie thought that Lord Dunsany, a m devoted father, had probably made the best match possible for spoilt elder daughter. The Earl of Ellesmere *was* an old m There was every prospect that within a few years, Geneva wo be left as an extremely wealthy young widow, and a countess, boot. On the other hand, such considerations might well not wei heavily with a headstrong miss—a stubborn, spoilt bitch, he c rected, seeing the petulant set of her mouth and eyes—of sev teen.

"I am sure your father acts always in your best interests, my ~~la~~dy," he answered woodenly. Would the little fiend not go away? She wouldn't. Assuming a more winsome expression, she came ~~an~~d stood close to his side, interfering with his opening the load-~~in~~g hatch of the roller.

"But a match with such a dried-up old man?" she said. "Surely ~~it~~ is heartless of Father to give me to such a creature." She stood ~~on~~ tiptoe, peering at Jamie. "How old are *you,* MacKenzie?"

His heart stopped beating for an instant.

"A verra great deal older than you, my lady," he said firmly. ~~"~~Your pardon, my lady." He slid past her as well as he might ~~wi~~thout touching her, and leapt up onto the manure wagon, ~~w~~hence he was reasonably sure she wouldn't follow him.

"But not ready for the boneyard yet, are you, MacKenzie?" ~~N~~ow she was in front of him, shading her eyes with her hand as ~~sh~~e peered upward. A breeze had come up, and wisps of her ~~ch~~estnut hair floated about her face. "Have you ever been married, ~~M~~acKenzie?"

He gritted his teeth, overcome with the urge to drop a shovelful ~~of~~ manure over her chestnut head, but mastered it and dug the ~~sh~~ovel into the pile, merely saying "I have," in a tone that ~~br~~ooked no further inquiries.

The Lady Geneva was not interested in other people's sensitivi-~~tie~~s. "Good," she said, satisfied. "You'll know what to do, then."

"To do?" He stopped short in the act of digging, one foot ~~pl~~aced on the shovel.

"In bed," she said calmly. "I want you to come to bed with ~~m~~e."

In the shock of the moment, all he could think of was the ~~lu~~dicrous vision of the elegant Lady Geneva, skirts thrown up over ~~he~~r face, asprawl in the rich crumble of the manure wagon.

He dropped the shovel. "*Here?*" he croaked.

"No, silly," she said impatiently. "In bed, in a proper bed. In ~~m~~y bedroom."

"You have lost your mind," Jamie said coldly, the shock reced-~~in~~g slightly. "Or I should think you had, if ye had one to lose."

Her face flamed and her eyes narrowed. "How dare you speak ~~th~~at way to me!"

"How dare ye speak so to *me*?" Jamie replied hotly. "A wee ~~la~~ssie of breeding to be makin' indecent proposals to a man twice

her age? And a groom in her father's house?'' he added, rec
lecting who he was. He choked back further remarks, recollect
also that this dreadful girl *was* the Lady Geneva, and he *was*
father's groom.

''I beg your pardon, my lady,'' he said, mastering his cho
with some effort. ''The sun is verra hot today, and no doubt it
addled your wits a bit. I expect ye should go back to the house
once and ask your maid to put cold cloths on your head.''

The Lady Geneva stamped her morocco-booted foot. ''My w
are not addled in the slightest!''

She glared up at him, chin set. Her chin was little and point
so were her teeth, and with that particular expression of deter
nation on her face, he thought she looked a great deal like
bloody-minded vixen she was.

''Listen to me,'' she said. ''I cannot prevent this abomina
marriage. But I am''—she hesitated, then continued firmly—
am *damned* if I will suffer my maidenhood to be given to a
gusting, depraved old monster like Ellesmere!''

Jamie rubbed a hand across his mouth. Despite himself, he
some sympathy for her. But *he* would be damned if he allowed
skirted maniac to involve him in her troubles.

''I am fully sensible of the honor, my lady,'' he said at last, w
a heavy irony, ''but I really cannot—''

''Yes, you can.'' Her eyes rested frankly on the front of
filthy breeches. ''Betty says so.''

He struggled for speech, emerging at first with little more th
incoherent sputterings. Finally he drew a deep breath and sa
with all the firmness he could muster, ''Betty has not the sligh
basis for drawing conclusions as to my capacity. I havena lai
hand on the lass!''

Geneva laughed delightedly. ''So you didn't take her to be
She said you wouldn't, but I thought perhaps she was only try
to avoid a beating. That's good; I couldn't possibly share a m
with my maid.''

He breathed heavily. Smashing her on the head with the sho
or throttling her were unfortunately out of the question. His
flamed temper slowly calmed. Outrageous she might be, but
sentially powerless. She could scarcely force him to go to her b

''Good day to ye, my lady,'' he said, as politely as possible.

ned his back on her and began to shovel manure into the hollow
ler.

'If you don't,'' she said sweetly, ''I'll tell my father you made
proper advances to me. He'll have the skin flayed off your
k.''

His shoulders hunched involuntarily. She couldn't possibly
ow. He had been careful never to take his shirt off in front of
one since he came here.

He turned carefully and stared down at her. The light of triumph
s in her eye.

'Your father may not be so well acquent' with me,'' he said,
ut he's kent *you* since ye were born. Tell him, and be damned to

She puffed up like a game cock, her face growing bright red
h temper. ''Is that so?'' she cried. ''Well, look at this, then, and
damned to *you*!'' She reached into the bosom of her habit and
led out a thick letter, which she waved under his nose. His
er's firm black hand was so familiar that a glimpse was
ugh.

'Give me that!'' He was down off the wagon and after her in a
h, but she was too fast. She was up in the saddle before he
ld grab her, backing with the reins in one hand, waving the
er mockingly in the other.

'Want it, do you?''

'Yes, I want it! Give it to me!'' He was so furious, he could
ily have done her violence, could he get his hands on her.
fortunately, her bay mare sensed his mood, and backed away,
rting and pawing uneasily.

'I don't think so.'' She eyed him coquettishly, the red of ill
per fading from her face. ''After all, it's really my duty to give
s to my father, isn't it? He ought really to know that his servants
carrying on clandestine correspondences, shouldn't he? Is
ny your sweetheart?''

'You've read my letter? Ye filthy wee bitch!''

'Such language,'' she said, wagging the letter reprovingly.
's my duty to help my parents, by letting them know what sorts
dreadful things the servants are up to, isn't it? And I am a
iful daughter, am I not, submitting to this marriage without a
eak?'' She leaned forward on her pommel, smiling mockingly,

and with a fresh spurt of rage, he realized that she was enjoy
this very much indeed.

"I expect Papa will find it very interesting reading," she sa
"Especially the bit about the gold to be sent to Lochiel in Fran
Isn't it still considered treason to be giving comfort to the Kin
enemies? *Tsk,*" she said, clicking her tongue roguishly. "H
wicked."

He thought he might be sick on the spot, from sheer terror. I
she have the faintest idea how many lives lay in that manicu
white hand? His sister, Ian, their six children, all the tenants a
families of Lallybroch—perhaps even the lives of the agents v
carried messages and money between Scotland and France, ma
taining the precarious existence of the Jacobite exiles there.

He swallowed, once, and then again, before he spoke.

"All right," he said. A more natural smile broke out on
face, and he realized how very young she was. Aye, well, an
wee adder's bite was as venomous as an auld one's.

"I won't tell," she assured him, looking earnest. "I'll give
your letter back afterward, and I won't ever say what was in i
promise."

"Thank you." He tried to gather his wits enough to mak
sensible plan. Sensible? Going into his master's house to rav
his daughter's maidenhood—at her request? He had never he
of a less sensible prospect.

"All right," he said again. "We must be careful." Wit
feeling of dull horror, he felt himself being drawn into the role
conspirator with her.

"Yes. Don't worry, I can arrange for my maid to be sent aw
and the footman drinks; he's always asleep before ten o'clock

"Arrange it, then," he said, his stomach curdling. "Mind
choose a safe day, though."

"A safe day?" She looked blank.

"Sometime in the week after ye've finished your courses,"
said bluntly. "You're less likely to get wi' child then."

"Oh." She blushed rosily at that, but looked at him with a r
interest.

They looked at each other in silence for a long moment, s
denly linked by the prospect of the future.

"I'll send you word," she said at last, and wheeling her h

ut, galloped away across the field, the mare's hooves kicking
spurts of the freshly spread manure.

Cursing fluently and silently, he crept beneath the row of
ches. There wasn't much moon, which was a blessing. Six yards
open lawn to cross in a dash, and he was knee-deep in the
umbine and germander of the flowerbed.

He looked up the side of the house, its bulk looming dark and
bidding above him. Yes, there was the candle in the window, as
'd said. Still, he counted the windows carefully, to verify it.
aven help him if he chose the wrong room. Heaven help him if
vas the right one, too, he thought grimly, and took a firm hold
the trunk of the huge gray creeper that covered this side of the
ise.

The leaves rustled like a hurricane and the stems, stout as they
re, creaked and bent alarmingly under his weight. There was
hing for it but to climb as swiftly as possible, and be ready to
l himself off into the night if any of the windows should sud-
ly be raised.

He arrived at the small balcony panting, heart racing, and
nched in sweat, despite the chilliness of the night. He paused a
ment, alone beneath the faint spring stars, to draw breath. He
d it to damn Geneva Dunsany once more, and then pushed
n her door.

She had been waiting, and had plainly heard his approach up the
. She rose from the chaise where she had been sitting and came
ard him, chin up, chestnut hair loose over her shoulders.

She was wearing a white nightgown of some sheer material, tied
he throat with a silk bow. The garment didn't look like the
htwear of a modest young lady, and he realized with a shock
t she was wearing her bridal-night apparel.

'So you came.'' He heard the note of triumph in her voice, but
o the faint quaver. So she hadn't been sure of him?

'I hadn't much choice,'' he said shortly, and turned to close the
nch doors behind him.

'Will you have some wine?'' Striving for graciousness, she
ved to the table, where a decanter stood with two glasses. How
d she managed that? he wondered. Still, a glass of something

wouldn't come amiss in the present circumstances. He node
and took the full glass from her hand.

He looked at her covertly as he sipped it. The nightdress
little to conceal her body, and as his heart gradually slowed fr
the panic of his ascent, he found his first fear—that he wouldn'
able to keep his half of the bargain—allayed without consci
effort. She was built narrowly, slim-hipped and small-breas'
but most definitely a woman.

Finished, he set down the glass. No point in delay, he thou,
"The letter?" he said abruptly.

"Afterward," she said, tightening her mouth.

"Now, or I leave." And he turned toward the window,
though about to execute the threat.

"Wait!" He turned back, but eyed her with ill-disguised im
tience.

"Don't you trust me?" she said, trying to sound winsome
charming.

"No," he said bluntly.

She looked angry at that, and thrust out a petulant lower lip,
he merely looked stonily over his shoulder at her, still facing
window.

"Oh, all right, then," she said at last, with a shrug. Digg
under the layers of embroidery in a sewing box, she unearthed
letter and tossed it onto the washing stand beside him.

He snatched it up and unfolded the sheets, to be sure of it.
felt a surge of mingled fury and relief at the sight of the viola
seal, and Jenny's familiar hand within, neat and strong.

"Well?" Geneva's voice broke in upon his reading, impati
"Put that down and come here, Jamie. I'm ready." She sat on
bed, arms curled around her knees.

He stiffened, and turned a very cold blue look on her, over
pages in his hands.

"You'll not use that name to me," he said. She lifted
pointed chin a trifle more and raised her plucked brows.

"Why not? It's yours. Your sister calls you so."

He hesitated for a moment, then deliberately laid the le
aside, and bent his head to the laces of his breeches.

"I'll serve ye properly," he said, looking down at his work
fingers, "for the sake of my own honor as a man, and yours a
woman. But"—he raised his head and the narrowed blue e

red into hers—"having brought me to your bed by means of
eats against my family, I'll not have ye call me by the name
y give me." He stood motionless, eyes fixed on hers. At last
e gave a very small nod, and her eyes dropped to the quilt.
She traced the pattern with a finger.

"What must I call you, then?" she asked at last, in a small
ice. "I *can't* call you MacKenzie!"

The corners of his mouth lifted slightly as he looked at her. She
ked quite small, huddled into herself with her arms locked
und her knees and her head bowed. He sighed.

"Call me Alex, then. It's my own name, as well."

She nodded without speaking. Her hair fell forward in wings
out her face, but he could see the brief shine of her eyes as she
eped out from behind its cover.

"It's all right," he said gruffly. "You can watch me." He
shed the loose breeches down, rolling the stockings off with
m. He shook them out and folded them neatly over a chair
fore beginning to unfasten his shirt, conscious of her gaze, still
, but now direct. Out of some idea of thoughtfulness, he turned
face her before removing the shirt, to spare her for a moment
e sight of his back.

"Oh!" The exclamation was soft, but enough to stop him.

"Is something wrong?" he asked.

"Oh, no . . . I mean, it's only that I didn't expect . . ." The
ir swung forward again, but not before he had seen the telltale
dening of her cheeks.

"You've not seen a man naked before?" he guessed. The shiny
wn head swayed back and forth.

"Noo," she said doubtfully, "I have, only . . . it
sn't . . ."

"Well, it usually isn't," he said matter-of-factly, sitting down
the bed beside her. "But if one is going to make love, it has to
, ye see."

"I see," she said, but still sounded doubtful. He tried to smile,
reassure her.

"Don't worry. It doesna get any bigger. And it wilna do any-
ng strange, if ye want to touch it." At least he hoped it
uldn't. Being naked, in such close proximity to a half-clad girl,
s doing terrible things to his powers of self-control. His traitor-
s, deprived anatomy didn't care a whit that she was a selfish,

blackmailing little bitch. Perhaps fortunately, she declined his
fer, shrinking back a little toward the wall, though her eyes stay
on him. He rubbed his chin dubiously.

"How much do you . . . I mean, have ye any idea how
done?"

Her gaze was clear and guileless, though her cheeks flamed

"Well, like the horses, I suppose?" He nodded, but felt a pa
recalling his wedding night, when he too had expected it to be l
horses.

"Something like that," he said, clearing his throat. "Slow
though. More gentle," he added, seeing her apprehensive look

"Oh. That's good. Nurse and the maids used to tell stor
about . . . men, and, er, getting married, and all . . . it sound
rather frightening." She swallowed hard. "W-will it hurt much
She raised her head suddenly and looked him in the eye.

"I don't mind if it does," she said bravely, "it's only that
like to know what to expect." He felt an unexpected small lik
for her. She might be spoilt, selfish, and reckless, but there w
some character to her, at least. Courage, to him, was no sm
virtue.

"I think not," he said. "If I take my time to ready you" (if
could take his time, amended his brain), "I think it will be
much worse than a pinch." He reached out and nipped a fold
skin on her upper arm. She jumped and rubbed the spot, l
smiled.

"I can stand that."

"It's only the first time it's like that," he assured her. "1
next time it will be better."

She nodded, then after a moment's hesitation, edged tow
him, reaching out a tentative finger.

"May I touch you?" This time he really did laugh, though
choked the sound off quickly.

"I think you'll have to, my lady, if I'm to do what you asked
me."

She ran her hand slowly down his arm, so softly that the tou
tickled, and his skin shivered in response. Gaining confidence,
let her hand circle his forearm, feeling the girth of it.

"You're quite . . . big." He smiled, but stayed motionle
letting her explore his body, at as much length as she might wi
He felt the muscles of his belly tighten as she stroked the length

ne thigh, and ventured tentatively around the curve of one but-
ock. Her fingers approached the twisting, knotted line of the scar
hat ran the length of his left thigh, but stopped short.

"It's all right," he assured her. "It doesna hurt me anymore."
he didn't reply, but drew two fingers slowly along the length of
he scar, exerting no pressure.

The questing hands, growing bolder, slid up over the rounded
urves of his broad shoulders, slid down his back—and stopped
ead. He closed his eyes and waited, following her movements by
he shifting of weight on the mattress. She moved behind him, and
as silent. Then there was a quivering sigh, and the hands touched
im again, soft on his ruined back.

"And you weren't afraid, when I said I'd have you flogged?"
er voice was queerly hoarse, but he kept still, eyes closed.

"No," he said. "I am not much afraid of things, anymore." In
ct, he was beginning to be afraid that he wouldn't be able to keep
is hands off her, or to handle her with the necessary gentleness,
hen the time came. His balls ached with need, and he could feel
is heartbeat, pounding in his temples.

She got off the bed, and stood in front of him. He rose suddenly,
artling her so that she stepped back a pace, but he reached out
d rested his hands on her shoulders.

"May I touch *you,* my lady?" The words were teasing, but the
uch was not. She nodded, too breathless to speak, and his arms
me around her.

He held her against his chest, not moving until her breathing
owed. He was conscious of an extraordinary mixture of feelings.
e had never in his life taken a woman in his arms without some
eling of love, but there was nothing of love in this encounter, nor
uld there be, for her own sake. There was some tenderness for
er youth, and pity at her situation. Rage at her manipulation of
m, and fear at the magnitude of the crime he was about to
mmit. But overall there was a terrible lust, a need that clawed at
s vitals and made him ashamed of his own manhood, even as he
knowledged its power. Hating himself, he lowered his head and
pped her face between his hands.

He kissed her softly, briefly, then a bit longer. She was trem-
ing against him as his hands undid the tie of her gown and slid it
ck off her shoulders. He lifted her and laid her on the bed.

He lay beside her, cradling her in one arm as the other hand

caressed her breasts, one and then the other, cupping each so s
felt the weight and the warmth of them, even as he did.

"A man should pay tribute to your body," he said softly, ra
ing each nipple with small, circling touches. "For you are beau
ful, and that is your right."

She let out her breath in a small gasp, then relaxed under I
touch. He took his time, moving as slowly as he could ma
himself do it, stroking and kissing, touching her lightly all ov
He didn't like the girl, didn't want to be here, didn't want to
doing this, but—it had been more than three years since he
touched a woman's body.

He tried to gauge when she might be readiest, but how in h
could he tell? She was flushed and panting, but she simply I
there, like a piece of porcelain on display. Curse the girl, could s
not even give him a clue?

He rubbed a trembling hand through his hair, trying to quell t
surge of confused emotion that pulsed through him with ea
heartbeat. He was angry, scared, and most mightily roused, mo
of which feelings were of no great use to him now. He closed I
eyes and breathed deeply, striving for calm, seeking for gentl
ness.

No, of course she couldn't show him. She'd never touched
man before. Having forced him here, she was, with a damnab
unwanted, unwarrantable trust, leaving the conduct of the who
affair up to him!

He touched the girl, gently, stroking her between the thighs. S
didn't part them for him, but didn't resist. She was faintly mo
there. Perhaps it would be all right now?

"All right," he murmured to her. "Be still, *mo chridhe*." Mu
muring what he hoped sounded like reassurances, he eased hi
self on top of her, and used his knee to spread her legs. He felt I
slight start at the heat of his body covering her, at the touch of I
cock, and he wrapped his hands in her hair to steady her, st
muttering things in soft Gaelic.

He thought dimly that it was a good thing he was speaki
Gaelic, as he was no longer paying any attention at all to what
was saying. Her small, hard breasts poked against his chest.

"Mo nighean," he murmured.

"Wait a minute," said Geneva. "I think perhaps . . ."

The effort of control made him dizzy, but he did it slowly, only easing himself the barest inch within.

"Ooh!" said Geneva. Her eyes flew wide.

"Uh," he said, and pushed a bit farther.

"Stop it! It's too big! Take it out!" Panicked, Geneva thrashed beneath him. Pressed beneath his chest, her breasts wobbled and rubbed, so that his own nipples leapt erect in pinpoints of abrupt sensation.

Her struggles were accomplishing by force what he had tried to do with gentleness. Half-dazed, he fought to keep her under him, while groping madly for something to say to calm her.

"But—" he said.

"Stop it!"

"I—"

"Take it *out*!" she screamed.

He clapped one hand over her mouth and said the only coherent thing he could think of.

"No," he said definitely, and shoved.

What might have been a scream emerged through his fingers as a strangled "Eep!" Geneva's eyes were huge and round, but dry.

In for a penny, in for a pound. The saying drifted absurdly through his head, leaving nothing in its wake but a jumble of incoherent alarms and a marked feeling of terrible urgency down between them. There was precisely one thing he was capable of doing at this point, and he did it, his body ruthlessly usurping control as it moved into the rhythm of its inexorable pagan joy.

It took no more than a few thrusts before the wave came down upon him, churning down the length of his spine and erupting like a breaker striking rocks, sweeping away the last shreds of conscious thought that clung, barnacle-like, to the remnants of his mind.

He came to himself a moment later, lying on his side with the sound of his own heartbeat loud and slow in his ears. He cracked one eyelid, and saw the shimmer of pink skin in lamplight. He must see if he'd hurt her much, but God, not just this minute. He shut his eye again and merely breathed.

"What . . . what are you thinking?" The voice sounded hesitant, and a little shaken, but not hysterical.

Too shaken himself to notice the absurdity of the question, he answered it with the truth.

"I was wondering why in God's name men want to bed vi gins."

There was a long moment of silence, and then a tremulou intake of breath.

"I'm sorry," she said in a small voice. "I didn't know it woul hurt you too."

His eyes popped open in astonishment, and he raised himself c one elbow to find her looking at him like a startled fawn. Her fac was pale, and she licked dry lips.

"Hurt me?" he said, in blank astonishment. "It didna hu *me.*"

"But"—she frowned as her eyes traveled slowly down th length of his body—"I thought it must. You made the most terr ble face, as though it hurt awfully, and you . . . you *groaned* lil a—"

"Aye, well," he interrupted hastily, before she could reveal ar more unflattering observations of his behavior. "I didna mea . . . I mean . . . that's just how men act, when they . . . c that," he ended lamely.

Her shock was fading into curiosity. "Do all men act like th when they're . . . doing that?"

"How should I—?" he began irritably, then stopped himse with a shudder, realizing that he did in fact know the answer that.

"Aye, they do," he said shortly. He pushed himself up to sitting position, and brushed the hair back from his forehea "Men are disgusting horrible beasts, just as your nurse told yo Have I hurt ye badly?"

"I don't think so," she said doubtfully. She moved her leg experimentally. "It did hurt, just for a moment, like you said would, but it isn't so bad now."

He breathed a sigh of relief as he saw that while she had ble the stain on the towel was slight, and she seemed not to be in pai She reached tentatively between her thighs and made a face disgust.

"Ooh!" she said. "It's all nasty and sticky!"

The blood rose to his face in mingled outrage and embarras ment.

"Here," he muttered, and reached for a washcloth from th stand. She didn't take it, but opened her legs and arched her bac

lightly, obviously expecting him to attend to the mess. He had a
strong urge to stuff the rag down her throat instead, but a glance at
the stand where his letter lay stopped him. It was a bargain, after
all, and she'd kept her part.

Grimly, he wet the cloth and began to sponge her, but he found
the trust with which she presented herself to him oddly moving.
He carried out his ministrations quite gently, and found himself, at
the end, planting a light kiss on the smooth slope of her belly.

"There."

"Thank you," she said. She moved her hips tentatively, and
reached out a hand to touch him. He didn't move, letting her
fingers trail down his chest and toy with the deep indentation of
his navel. The light touch hesitantly descended.

"You said . . . it would be better next time," she whispered.

He closed his eyes and took a deep breath. It was a long time
until the dawn.

"I expect it will," he said, and stretched himself once more
beside her.

"Ja—er, Alex?"

He felt as though he had been drugged, and it was an effort to
answer her. "My lady?"

Her arms came around his neck and she nestled her head in the
curve of his shoulder, breath warm against his chest.

"I love you, Alex."

With difficulty, he roused himself enough to put her away from
him, holding her by the shoulders and looking down into the gray
eyes, soft as a doe's.

"No," he said, but gently, shaking his head. "That's the third
rule. You may have no more than the one night. You may not call
me by my first name. And you may not love me."

The gray eyes moistened a bit. "But if I can't help it?"

"It isna love you feel now." He hoped he was right, for his sake
as well as her own. "It's only the feeling I've roused in your body.
It's strong, and it's good, but it isna the same thing as love."

"What's the difference?"

He rubbed his hands hard over his face. She *would* be a philosopher, he thought wryly. He took a deep breath and blew it out
before answering her.

''Well, love's for only one person. This, what you feel from n̶
—ye can have that with any man, it's not particular.''

Only one person. He pushed the thought of Claire firmly awa̶
and wearily bent again to his work.

He landed heavily in the earth of the flowerbed, not caring th̶
he crushed several small and tender plants. He shivered. This ho̶
before dawn was not only the darkest, but the coldest, as well, a̶
his body strongly protested being required to rise from a war̶
soft nest and venture into the chilly blackness, shielded from t̶
icy air by no more than a thin shirt and breeks.

He remembered the heated, rosy curve of the cheek he had be̶
to kiss before leaving. The shapes of her lingered, warm in h̶
hands, curving his fingers in memory, even as he groped in t̶
dark for the darker line of the stableyard's stone wall. Drained ̶
he was, it was a dreadful effort to haul himself up and climb ov̶
but he couldn't risk the creak of the gate awakening Hughes, t̶
head groom.

He felt his way across the inner yard, crowded with wagons a̶
packed bales, ready for the journey of the Lady Geneva to t̶
home of her new lord, following the wedding on Thursday next. ̶
last he pushed open the stable door and found his way up t̶
ladder to his loft. He lay down in the icy straw and pulled t̶
single blanket over him, feeling empty of everything.

15

By Misadventure

Appropriately enough, the weather was dark and stormy when the news reached Helwater. The afternoon exercise had been canceled, owing to the heavy downpour, and the horses were snug in their stalls below. The homely, peaceful sounds of munching and blowing rose up to the loft above, where Jamie Fraser reclined in a comfortable, hay-lined nest, an open book propped on his chest.

It was one of several he had borrowed from the estate's factor, Mr. Grieves, and he was finding it absorbing, despite the difficulty of reading by the poor light from the owl-slits beneath the eaves.

> *My lips, which I threw in his way, so as that he could not escape kissing them, fix'd, fir'd and embolden'd him: and now, glancing my eyes towards that part of his dress which cover'd the essential object of enjoyment, I plainly discover'd the swell and commotion there; and as I was now too far advanc'd to stop in so fair a way, and was indeed no longer able to contain myself, or wait the slower progress of his maiden bashfulness, I stole my hand upon his thighs, down one of which I could both see and feel a stiff hard body, confin'd by his breeches, that my fingers could discover no end to.*

"Oh, aye?" Jamie muttered skeptically. He raised his eyebrows and shifted himself on the hay. He had been aware that books like this existed, of course, but—with Jenny ordering the reading matter at Lallybroch—had not encountered one personally before. The type of mental engagement demanded was somewhat different from that required for the works of Messieurs Defoe and Fielding but he was not averse to variety.

> *Its prodigious size made me shrink again; yet I could not, without pleasure, behold, and even ventur'd to feel, such a length, such a breadth of animated ivory! perfectly well turn'd and fashion'd, the proud stiffness of which distended its skin, whose smooth polish and velvet softness might vie with that of the most delicate of our sex, and whose exquisite whiteness was not a little set off by a sprout of black curling hair round the root; then the broad and blueish casted incarnate of the head, and blue serpentines of its veins, altogether compos'd the most striking assemblage of figures and colors in nature. In short, it stood an object of terror and delight!*

Jamie glanced at his own crotch and snorted briefly at this, but flipped the page, the crash of thunder outside meriting no more than a twinge of his attention. He was so absorbed that at first he failed to hear the noises down below, the sound of voices drowned in the heavy rush and beat of the rain on the planks a few feet above his head.

"MacKenzie!" The repeated stentorian bellow finally penetrated his awareness, and he rolled hastily to his feet, quickly straightening his clothes as he went toward the ladder.

"Aye?" He thrust his head over the edge of the loft to see Hughes, just opening his mouth for another bellow.

"Oh, there 'ee are." Hughes shut his mouth, and beckoned with one gnarled hand, wincing as he did so. Hughes suffered mightily from rheumatics in damp weather; he had been riding out the storm snug in the small chamber beside the tack room, where he kept a bed and a jug of crudely distilled spirits. The aroma was perceptible from the loft, and grew substantially stronger as Jamie descended the ladder.

"You're to help ready the coach to drive Lord Dunsany and Lady Isobel to Ellesmere," Hughes told him, the moment his foot touched the flags of the stable floor. The old man swayed alarmingly, hiccuping softly to himself.

"Now? Are ye daft, man? Or just drunk?" He glanced at th

open half-door behind Hughes, which seemed a solid sheet of streaming water. Even as he looked, the sky beyond lit up with a sudden flare of lightning that threw the mountain beyond into sudden sharp relief. Just as suddenly, it disappeared, leaving its afterimage printed on his retina. He shook his head to clear the image, and saw Jeffries, the coachman, making his way across the yard, head bowed against the force of wind and water, cloak clutched tight about him. So it wasn't only a drunken fancy of Hughes's.

"Jeffries needs help wi' the horses!" Hughes was forced to lean close and shout to be heard over the noise of the storm. The smell of rough alcohol was staggering at close distance.

"Aye, but why? Why must Lord Dunsany—ah, feckit!" The head groom's eyes were red-rimmed and bleary; clearly there was no sense to be got out of him. Disgusted, Jamie pushed past the man and mounted the ladder two rungs at a time.

A moment to wrap his own worn cloak about him, a moment more to thrust the book he had been reading under the hay—stable lads were no respecters of property—and he was slithering down the ladder again, and out into the roar of the storm.

It was a hellish journey. The wind screamed through the pass, striking the bulky coach and threatening to overturn it at any moment. Perched aloft beside Jeffries, a cloak was little protection against the driving rain; still less was it a help when he was forced to dismount—as he did every few minutes, it seemed—and put his shoulder to the wheel to free the miserable contrivance from the clinging grip of a mudhole.

Still, he scarcely noticed the physical inconvenience of the journey, preoccupied as he was with the possible reasons for it. There couldn't be many matters of such urgency as to force an old man like Lord Dunsany outside on a day like this, let alone over the rutted road to Ellesmere. Some word had come from Ellesmere, and it could only concern the Lady Geneva or her child.

Hearing through the servants' gossip that Lady Geneva was due to be deliverd in January, he had counted quickly backward, cursed Geneva Dunsany once more, and then said a hasty prayer for her safe delivery. Since then, he had done his best not to think about it. He had been with her only three days before her wedding, he couldn't be sure.

A week before, Lady Dunsany had gone to Ellesmere to be with her daughter. Since then, she had sent daily messengers home, to fetch the dozen things she had forgotten to take and must have at once, and each of them, upon arrival at Helwater, had reported "No news yet." Now there was news, and it was plainly bad.

Passing back toward the front of the coach, after the latest battle with the mud, he saw the Lady Isobel's face peering out from beneath the isinglass sheet that covered the window.

"Oh, MacKenzie!" she said, her face contorted in fear and distress. "Please, is it much farther?"

He leaned close to shout in her ear, over the gurgle and rush of the gullies running down both sides of the road.

"Jeffries says it's four mile yet, milady! Two hours, maybe." If the damned and hell-bent coach didn't tip itself and its hapless passengers off the Ashness Bridge into Watendlath Tarn, he added silently to himself.

Isobel nodded her thanks, and lowered the window, but not before he had seen that the wetness upon her cheeks was due as much to tears as to the rain. The snake of anxiety wrapped round his heart slithered lower, to twist in his guts.

It was closer to three hours by the time the coach rolled at last into the courtyard at Ellesmere. Without hesitation, Lord Dunsany scrambled down and, scarcely pausing to give his younger daughter an arm, hurried into the house.

It took nearly another hour to unharness the team, rub down the horses, wash the caked-on mud from the coach's wheels, and put everything away in Ellesmere's stables. Numb with cold, fatigue, and hunger, he and Jeffries sought refuge and sustenance in Ellesmere's kitchens.

"Poor fellows, you're gone right blue wi' the cold," the cook observed. "Sit ye down 'ere, and I'll soon 'ave yer a hot bite." A sharp-faced, spare-framed woman, her figure belied her skill, for within minutes, a huge, savoury omelet was laid before them, garnished with liberal amounts of bread and butter, and a small pot of jam.

"Fair, quite fair," Jeffries pronounced, casting an appreciative eye on the spread. He winked at the cook. "Not as it wouldn' go down easier wi' a drop o' something to pave the way, eh? You look

he sort would have mercy on a pair o' poor half-frozen chaps,
vouldn't ye, darlin'?''

Whether it was this piece of Irish persuasion or the sight of their
Iripping, steaming clothes, the argument had its effect, and a
ottle of cooking brandy made its appearance next to the pep-
ermill. Jeffries poured a large tot and drank it off without hesita-
ion, smacking his lips.

"Ah, that's more like! Here, boyo." He passed the bottle to
amie, then settled himself comfortably to a hot meal and gossip
vith the female servants. "Well, then, what's to do here? Is the
abe born yet?"

"Oh, yes, last night!" the kitchen maid said eagerly. "We were
p all night, with the doctor comin', and fresh sheets and towels
alled for, and the house all topsle-turvy. But the babe's the least
f it!"

"Now, then," the cook broke in, frowning censoriously.
There's too much work to be standin' about gossiping. Get yer
n, Mary Ann—up to the study, and see if his Lordship'll be
vantin' anything else served now."

Jamie, wiping his plate with a slice of bread, observed that the
aid, far from being abashed at this rebuke, departed with alac-
ity, causing him to deduce that something of considerable interest
vas likely transpiring in the study.

The undivided attention of her audience thus obtained, the cook
llowed herself to be persuaded into imparting the gossip with no
nore than a token demur.

"Well, it started some months ago, when the Lady Geneva
tarted to show, poor thing. His Lordship'd been nicer than pie to
er, ever since they was married couldn't do enough for 'er, any-
ning she wanted ordered from Lunnon, always askin' was she
varm enough, 'ad she what she wanted to eat—fair dotin', 'is
ordship was. But then, when 'e found she was with child!" The
ook paused, to screw up her face portentously.

Jamie wanted desperately to know about the child; what was it,
nd how did it fare? There seemed no way to hurry the woman,
ough, so he composed his face to look as interested as possible,
aning forward encouragingly.

"Why, the shouting, and the carrryings-on!" the cook said,
rowing up her hands in dismayed illustration, " 'im shoutin',
nd 'er cryin', and the both of 'em stampin' up and down and

slammin' doors, and 'im callin' 'er names as isn't fit to be used i
a stableyard—and so I told Mary Ann, when she told me . . .'

"Was his Lordship not pleased about the child, then?" Jam
interrupted. The omelet was settling into a hard lump somewher
under his breastbone. He took another gulp of brandy, in hopes c
dislodging it.

The cook turned a bright, birdlike eye on him, eyebrow cocke
in appreciation at his intelligence. "Well, you'd think as 'e woul
be, wouldn't yer? But no indeed! Far from it," she added wit
emphasis.

"Why not?" said Jeffries, only mildly interested.

" 'E said," the cook said, dropping her voice in awe at th
scandalousness of the information, "as the child wasn't 'is!"

Jeffries, well along with his second glass, snorted in contempt
ous amusement. "Old goat with a young gel? I should think it lik
enough, but how on earth would his Lordship know for sure whos
the spawn was? Could be his as much as anyone's, couldn't i
with only her Ladyship's word to go by, eh?"

The cook's thin mouth stretched in a bright, malicious smil
"Oh, I don't say as 'e'd know whose it *was,* now—but there's on
sure way 'e'd know it wasn't *'is,* now isn't there?"

Jeffries stared at the cook, tilting back on his chair. "What?
he said. "You mean to tell me his Lordship's incapable?" A broa
grin at this juicy thought split his weatherbeaten face. Jamie fe
the omelet rising, and hastily gulped more brandy.

"Well, *I* couldn't say, I'm sure." The cook's mouth assumed
prim line, then split asunder to add, "though the chambermaid d
say as the sheets she took off the weddin' bed was as white :
when they'd gone on, to be sure."

It was too much. Interrupting Jeffries's delighted cackle, Jam
set down his glass with a thump, and bluntly said, "Did the chi
live?"

The cook and Jeffries both stared in astonishment, but the coo
after a moment's startlement, nodded in answer.

"Oh, yes, to be sure. Fine 'ealthy little lad, 'e is, too, or so
'ear. I thought you knew a'ready. It's 'is mother that's dead."

That blunt statement struck the kitchen with silence. Even Je
fries was still for a moment, sobered by death. Then he cross
himself quickly, muttered "God rest her soul," and swallowed t
rest of his brandy.

Jamie could feel his own throat burning, whether with brandy or tears, he could not say. Shock and grief choked him like a ball of yarn wedged in his gullet; he could barely manage to croak "When?"

"This morning," the cook said, wagging her head mournfully. "Just afore noon, poor girl. They thought for a time as she'd be all right, after the babe was born; Mary Ann said she was sittin' up, holdin' the wee thing and laughin'." She sighed heavily at the thought. "But then near dawn, she started to bleed again bad. They called back the doctor, and he came fast as could be, but—"

The door slamming open interrupted her. It was Mary Ann, eyes wide under her cap, gasping with excitement and exertion.

"Your master wants you!" she blurted out, eyes flicking between Jamie and the coachman. "The both of ye, at once, and oh, sir"—she gulped, nodding at Jeffries—"he says for God's sake, to bring your pistols!"

The coachman exchanged a glance of consternation with Jamie, then leapt to his feet and dashed out, in the direction of the stables. Like most coachmen, he carried a pair of loaded pistols beneath his seat, against the possibility of highwaymen.

It would take Jeffries a few minutes to find the arms, and longer if he waited to check that the priming had not been harmed by the wet weather. Jamie rose to his feet and gripped the dithering maidservant by the arm.

"Show me to the study," he said. "Now!"

The sound of raised voices would have led him there, once he had reached the head of the stair. Pushing past Mary Ann without ceremony, he paused for a moment outside the door, uncertain whether he should enter at once, or wait for Jeffries.

"That you can have the sheer heartless effrontery to make such accusations!" Dunsany was saying, his old man's voice shaking with rage and distress. "And my poor lamb not cold in her bed! You blackguard, you poltroon! I will not suffer the child to stay a single night under your roof!"

"The little bastard stays here!" Ellesmere's voice rasped hoarsely. It would have been apparent to a far less experienced observer that his Lordship was well the worse for drink. "Bastard that he is, he's my heir, and he stays with me! He's bought and paid for, and if his dam was a whore, at least she gave me a boy."

"Damn you!" Dunsany's voice had reached such a pitch of

shrillness that it was scarcely more than a squeak, but the outrag
in it was clear nonetheless. "Bought? You—you—you dare
suggest . . ."

"I don't suggest." Ellesmere's voice was still hoarse, but und
better control. "You sold me your daughter—and under false pre
tenses, I might add," the hoarse voice said sarcastically. "I pai
thirty thousand pound for a virgin of good name. The first cond
tion wasn't met, and I take leave to doubt the second." The soun
of liquid being poured came through the door, followed by th
scrape of a glass across a wooden tabletop.

"I would suggest that your burden of spirits is already exce
sive, sir," Dunsany said. His voice shook with an obvious attemp
at mastery of his emotions. "I can only attribute the disgustin
slurs you have cast upon my daughter's purity to your apparer
intoxication. That being so, I shall take my grandson, and go."

"Oh, your *grand*son, is it?" Ellesmere's voice was slurred an
sneering. "You seem damned sure of your daughter's 'purity
Sure the brat isn't yours? She said—"

He broke off with a cry of astonishment, accompanied by
crash. Not daring to wait longer, Jamie plunged through the doo
to find Ellesmere and Lord Dunsany entangled on the hearthru,
rolling to and fro in a welter of coats and limbs, both heedless
the fire behind them.

He took a moment to appraise the situation, then, seizing
fortuitous opening, reached into the fray and snatched his em
ployer upright.

"Be still, my lord," he muttered in Dunsany's ear, draggin
him back from Ellesmere's gasping form. Then, "Give over, y
auld fool!" he demanded, as Dunsany went on mindlessly strug
gling to reach his opponent. Ellesmere was almost as old as Dun
sany, but more strongly built and clearly in better health, despi
his drunkenness.

The Earl staggered to his feet, sparse hair disheveled and bloo
shot eyes glaring fixedly at Dunsany. He wiped his spittle-flecke
mouth with the back of his hand, fat shoulders heaving.

"Filth," he said, almost conversationally. "Lay hands . . . o
me, would you?" Still gasping for breath, he lurched toward th
bell rope.

It was by no means certain that Lord Dunsany would stay on h

eet, but there was no time to worry about that. Jamie let go of his
mployer, and lunged for Ellesmere's groping hand.

"No, my lord," he said, as respectfully as possible. Holding
llesmere in a crude bear-leading embrace, he forced the heavyset
arl back across the room. "I think it would be . . . unwise
. . to involve your . . . servants." Grunting, he pushed Elles-
ere into a chair.

"Best stay there, my lord." Jeffries, a drawn pistol in each
and, advanced warily into the room, his darting glance divided
etween Ellesmere, struggling to rise from the depths of the arm-
hair, and Lord Dunsany, who clung precariously to a table edge,
is aged face white as paper.

Jeffries glanced at Dunsany for instructions, and seeing none
orthcoming, instinctively looked to Jamie. Jamie was conscious
f a monstrous irritation; why should he be expected to deal with
is imbroglio? Still, it was important that the Helwater party
emove themselves from the premises with all haste. He stepped
orward and took Dunsany by the arm.

"Let us go now, my lord," he said. Detaching the wilting
unsany from the table, he tried to edge the tall old nobleman
oward the door. Just at this moment of escape, though, the door
as blocked.

"William?" Lady Dunsany's round face, splotched with the
arks of recent grief, showed a sort of dull bewilderment at the
ene in the study. In her arms was what looked like a large,
ntidy bundle of washing. She lifted this in a movement of vague
quiry. "The maid said you wanted me to bring the baby.
hat—" A roar from Ellesmere interrupted her. Heedless of the
ointing pistols, the Earl sprang from his chair and shoved the
awking Jeffries out of the way.

"He's mine!" Knocking Lady Dunsany roughly against the
aneling, Ellesmere snatched the bundle from her arms. Clutching
to his bosom, the Earl retreated toward the window. He glared at
unsany, panting like a cornered beast.

"Mine, d'ye hear?"

The bundle emitted a loud shriek, as if in protest at this asse ver-
ion, and Dunsany, roused from his shock by the sight of his
randson in Ellesmere's arms, started forward, his features con-
rted in fury.

"Give him to me!"

"Go to hell, you codless scut!" With an unforeseen agility Ellesmere dodged away from Dunsany. He flung back the draperies and cranked the window open with one hand, clutching the wailing child with the other.

"Get—out—of—my—house!" he panted, gasping with each revolution that edged the casement wider. "Go! Now, or I'll drop the little bastard, I swear I will!" To mark his threat, he thrust the yelling bundle toward the sill, and the empty dark where the wet stones of the courtyard waited, thirty feet below.

Past all conscious thought or any fear of consequence, James Fraser acted on the instinct that had seen him through a dozen battles. He snatched one pistol from the transfixed Jeffries, turned on his heel, and fired in the same motion.

The roar of the shot struck everyone silent. Even the child ceased to scream. Ellesmere's face went quite blank, thick eyebrows raised in question. Then he staggered, and Jamie leapt forward, noting with a sort of detached clarity the small round hole the baby's trailing drapery, where the pistol ball had passed through it.

He stood then rooted on the hearthrug, heedless of the fire scorching the backs of his legs; of the still-heaving body of Ellesmere at his feet; of the regular, hysterical shrieks of Lady Dunsany, piercing as a peacock's. He stood, eyes tight closed, shaking like a leaf, unable either to move or to think, arms wrapped tight about the shapeless, squirming, squawking bundle that contained his son.

"I wish to speak to MacKenzie. Alone."

Lady Dunsany looked distinctly out of place in the stable. Small, plump, and impeccable in black linen, she looked like a china ornament, removed from its spot of cherished safety on the mantelpiece, and in imminent and constant peril of breakage, here in this world of rough animals and unshaven men.

Hughes, with a glance of complete astonishment at his mistress, bowed and tugged at his forelock before retreating to his den behind the tack room, leaving MacKenzie face-to-face with her.

Close to, the impression of fragility was heightened by the paleness of her face, touched faintly with pink at the corners of nose and eyes. She looked like a very small and dignified rabbit.

ressed in mourning. Jamie felt that he should ask her to sit down, but there was no place for her to sit, save on a pile of hay or an upturned barrow.

"The coroner's court met this morning, MacKenzie," she said.

"Aye, milady." He had known that—they all had, and the other grooms had kept their distance from him all morning. Not out of respect; out of the dread for one who suffers from a deadly disease. Jeffries knew what had happened in the drawing room at Ellesmere, and that meant all the servants knew. But no one spoke of it.

"The verdict of the court was that the Earl óf Ellesmere met his death by misadventure. The coroner's theory is that his Lordship was—distraught"—she made a faint moue of distaste—"over my daughter's death." Her voice quivered faintly, but did not break. The fragile Lady Dunsany had borne up much better beneath the tragedy than had her husband; the servants' rumor had it that his Lordship had not risen from his bed since his return from Ellesmere.

"Aye, milady?" Jeffries had been called to give evidence. MacKenzie had not. So far as the coroner's court was concerned, the groom MacKenzie had never set foot on Ellesmere.

Lady Dunsany's eyes met his, straight on. They were a pale bluish-green, like her daughter Isobel's, but the blond hair that glowed on Isobel was faded on her mother, touched with white strands that shone silver in the sun from the open door of the stable.

"We are grateful to you, MacKenzie," she said quietly.

"Thank ye, milady."

"Very grateful," she repeated, still gazing at him intently. "MacKenzie isn't your real name, is it?" she said suddenly.

"No, milady." A sliver of ice ran down his spine, despite the warmth of the afternoon sun on his shoulders. How much had the Lady Geneva told her mother before her death?

She seemed to feel his stiffening, for the edge of her mouth lifted in what he thought was meant as a smile of reassurance.

"I think I need not ask what it is, just yet," she said. "But I do have a question for you. MacKenzie—do you want to go home?"

"Home?" He repeated the word blankly.

"To Scotland." She was watching him intently. "I know who

you are,'' she said. ''Not your name, but that you're one of John
Jacobite prisoners. My husband told me.''

Jamie watched her warily, but she didn't seem upset; no mo
so than would be natural in a woman who has just lost a daught
and gained a grandson, at least.

''I hope you will forgive the deception, milady,'' he said. ''H
Lordship—''

''Wished to save me distress,'' Lady Dunsany finished for hir
''Yes, I know. William worries too much.'' Still, the deep lir
between her brows relaxed a bit at the thought of her husband
concern. The sight, with its underlying echo of marital devotio
gave him a faint and unexpected pang.

''We are not rich—you will have gathered that from Elle
mere's remarks,'' Lady Dunsany went on. ''Helwater is rath
heavily in debt. My grandson, however, is now the possessor
one of the largest fortunes in the county.''

There seemed nothing to say to this but ''Aye, milady?'' thoug
it made him feel rather like the parrot who lived in the main salo
He had seen it as he crept stealthily through the flowerbeds
sunset the day before, taking the chance of approaching the hou
while the family were dressing for dinner, in an attempt to catch
glimpse through a window of the new Earl of Ellesmere.

''We are very retired here,'' she went on. ''We seldom vis
London, and my husband has little influence in high circle
But—''

''Aye, milady?'' He had some inkling by now of where h
Ladyship was heading with this roundabout conversation, and
feeling of sudden excitement hollowed the space beneath his rib

''John—Lord John Grey, that is—comes from a family wi
considerable influence. His stepfather is—well, that's of no cons
quence.'' She shrugged, the small black-linen shoulders di
missing the details.

''The point is that it might be possible to exert sufficient infl
ence on your behalf to have you released from the conditions
your parole, so that you might return to Scotland. So I have con
to ask you—do you want to go home, MacKenzie?''

He felt quite breathless, as though someone had punched hi
very hard in the stomach.

Scotland. To go away from this damp, spongy atmosphere, s
foot on that forbidden road and walk it with a free, long stride,

nto the crags and along the deer trails, to feel the air clearing and
harpening with the scent of gorse and heather. To go home!

To be a stranger no longer. To go away from hostility and
oneliness, come down into Lallybroch, and see his sister's face
ght with joy at the sight of him, feel her arms around his waist,
an's hug about his shoulders and the pummeling, grasping clutch
f the children's hands, tugging at his clothes.

To go away, and never to see or hear of his own child again. He
tared at Lady Dunsany, his face quite blank, so that she should
ot guess at the turmoil her offer had caused within him.

He had, at last, found the baby yesterday, lying asleep in a
asket near the nursery window on the second floor. Perched pre-
ariously on the branch of a huge Norway spruce, he had strained
is eyes to see through the screen of needles that hid him.

The child's face had been visible only in profile, one fat cheek
esting on its ruffled shoulder. Its cap had slipped awry, so he
ould see the smooth, arching curve of the tiny skull, lightly
usted with a pale gold fuzz.

"Thank God it isn't red," had been his first thought, and he had
rossed himself in reflexive thanksgiving.

"God, he's so small!" had been his second, coupled with an
verwhelming urge to step through the window and pick the boy
p. The smooth, beautifully shaped head would just fit, resting in
e palm of his hand, and he could feel in memory the small
quirming body that he had held so briefly to his heart.

"You're a strong laddie," he had whispered. "Strong and braw
nd bonny. But my God, you are so small!"

Lady Dunsany was waiting patiently. He bowed his head re-
pectfully to her, not knowing whether he was making a terrible
istake, but unable to do otherwise.

"I thank ye, milady, but—I think I shall not go . . . just yet."

One pale eyebrow quivered slightly, but she inclined her head to
m with equal grace.

"As you wish, MacKenzie. You have only to ask."

She turned like a tiny clockwork figure and left, going back to
e world of Helwater, a thousand times more his prison now than
had ever been.

To his extreme surprise, the next few years were in man ways among the happiest of Jamie Fraser's life, aside fro the years of his marriage.

Relieved of responsibility for tenants, followers, or anyone at a beyond himself and the horses in his charge, life was relative simple. While the coroner's court had taken no notice of hir Jeffries had let slip enough about the death of Ellesmere that th other servants treated him with distant respect, but did not pr sume on his company.

He had enough to eat, sufficient clothes to keep warm an decent, and the occasional discreet letter from the Highlands rea sured him that similar conditions obtained there.

One unexpected benefit of the quiet life at Helwater was that h had somehow resumed his odd half-friendship with Lord Joh Grey. The Major had, as promised, appeared once each quarte staying each time for a few days to visit with the Dunsanys. H had made no attempt to gloat, though, or even to speak with Jami beyond the barest formal inquiry.

Very slowly, Jamie had realized all that Lady Dunsany ha implied, in her offer to have him released. "John—Lord Joh Grey, that is—comes from a family with considerable influenc His stepfather is—well, that's of no consequence," she had sai It was of consequence, though. It had not been His Majesty pleasure that had brought him here, rather than condemning hi to the perilous ocean crossing and near-slavery in America; it ha been John Grey's influence.

And he had not done it for revenge or from indecent motives, or he never gloated, made no advances; never said anything beyond the most commonplace civilities. No, he had brought Jamie here because it was the best he could do; unable simply to release him at the time, Grey had done his best to ease the conditions of captivity—by giving him air, and light, and horses.

It took some effort, but he did it. When Grey next appeared in the stableyard on his quarterly visit, Jamie had waited until the Major was alone, admiring the conformation of a big sorrel gelding. He had come to stand beside Grey, leaning on the fence. They watched the horse in silence for several minutes.

"King's pawn to king four," Jamie said quietly at last, not looking at the man beside him.

He felt the other's start of surprise, and felt Grey's eyes on him, but didn't turn his head. Then he felt the creak of the wood beneath his forearm as Grey turned back, leaning on the fence again.

"Queen's knight to queen bishop three," Grey replied, his voice a little huskier than usual.

Since then, Grey had come to the stables during each visit, to spend an evening perched on Jamie's crude stool, talking. They had no chessboard and seldom played verbally, but the late-night conversations continued—Jamie's only connection with the world beyond Helwater, and a small pleasure to which both of them looked forward once each quarter.

Above everything else, he had Willie. Helwater was dedicated to horses; even before the boy could stand solidly on his feet, his grandfather had him propped on a pony to be led round the paddock. By the time Willie was three, he was riding by himself—under the watchful eye of MacKenzie, the groom.

Willie was a strong, courageous, bonny little lad. He had a blinding smile, and could charm birds from the trees if he liked. He was also remarkably spoilt. As the ninth Earl of Ellesmere and the only heir to both Ellesmere and Helwater, with neither mother or father to keep him under control, he ran roughshod over his doting grandparents, his young aunt, and every servant in the place—except MacKenzie.

And that was a near thing. So far, threats of not allowing the boy to help him with the horses had sufficed to quash Willie's worst excesses in the stables, but sooner or later, threats alone

were not going to be sufficient, and MacKenzie the groom foun
himself wondering just what was going to happen when he finall
lost his own control and clouted the wee fiend.

As a lad, he would himself have been beaten senseless by th
nearest male relative within earshot, had he ever dared to address
woman the way he had heard Willie speak to his aunt and th
maidservants, and the impulse to haul Willie into a deserted bo
stall and attempt to correct his manners was increasingly frequen

Still, for the most part, he had nothing but joy in Willie. The bo
adored MacKenzie, and as he grew older would spend hours in hi
company, riding on the huge draft horses as they pulled the heav
roller through the high fields, and perched precariously on the ha
wagons as they came down from the upper pastures in summer.

There was a threat to this peaceful existence, though, whic
grew greater with each passing month. Ironically, the threat cam
from Willie himself, and was one he could not help.

"What a handsome little lad he is, to be sure! And such a lovel
little rider!" It was Lady Grozier who spoke, standing on th
veranda with Lady Dunsany to admire Willie's peregrinations o
his pony around the edge of the lawn.

Willie's grandmother laughed, eyeing the boy fondly. "Oh, ye
He loves his pony. We have a terrible time getting him even
come indoors for meals. And he's even more fond of his groom
We joke sometimes that he spends so much time with MacKenz
that he's even starting to *look* like MacKenzie!"

Lady Grozier, who had of course paid no attention to a groor
now glanced in MacKenzie's direction.

"Why, you're right!" she exclaimed, much amused. "Ju
look; Willie's got just that same cock to his head, and the same s
to his shoulders! How funny!"

Jamie bowed respectfully to the ladies, but felt cold sweat po
out on his face.

He had seen this coming, but hadn't wanted to believe th
resemblance was sufficiently pronounced as to be visible to an
one but himself. Willie as a baby had been fat and pudding-face
and resembled no one at all. As he had grown, though, the pudg
ness had vanished from cheeks and chin, and while his nose w
still the soft snub of childhood, the hint of high, broad cheekbon
was apparent, and the slaty-blue eyes of babyhood had grown da

lue and clear, thickly fringed with sooty lashes, and slightly lanted in appearance.

Once the ladies had gone into the house, and he could be sure o one was watching, Jamie passed a hand furtively over his own eatures. Was the resemblance truly that great? Willie's hair was a oft middle brown, with just a tinge of his mother's chestnut leam. And those large, translucent ears—surely his own didn't tick out like that?

The trouble was that Jamie Fraser had not actually seen himself learly for several years. Grooms did not have looking glasses, and e had sedulously avoided the company of the maids, who might ave provided him with one.

Moving to the watering trough, he bent over it, casually, as hough inspecting one of the water striders that skated over its urface. Beneath the wavering surface, flecked with floating bits of ay and crisscrossed by the dimpling striders, his own face stared p at him.

He swallowed, and saw the reflection's throat move. It was by o means a complete resemblance, but it was definitely there. Iore in the set and shape of the head and shoulders, as Lady rozier had observed—but most definitely the eyes as well. Fraser yes; his father, Brian, had had them, and his sister, Jenny, as well. et the boy's bones go on pressing through his skin; let the child-ub nose grow long and straight, and the cheekbones still broader -and anyone would be able to see it.

The reflection in the trough vanished as he straightened up, and ood, staring blindly at the stable that had been home for the last veral years. It was July and the sun was hot, but it made no npression on the chill that numbed his fingers and sent a shiver p his back.

It was time to speak to Lady Dunsany.

By the middle of September, everything had been arranged. The ardon had been procured; John Grey had brought it the day efore. Jamie had a small amount of money saved, enough for aveling expenses, and Lady Dunsany had given him a decent orse. The only thing that remained was to bid farewell to his quaintances at Helwater—and Willie.

"I shall be leaving tomorrow." Jamie spoke matter-of-factly, not taking his eyes off the bay mare's fetlock. The horny grow' he was filing flaked away, leaving a dust of coarse black shaving on the stable floor.

"Where are you going? To Derwentwater? Can I come wi you?" William, Viscount Dunsany, ninth Earl of Ellesmer hopped down from the edge of the box stall, landing with a thun that made the bay mare start and snort.

"Don't do that," Jamie said automatically. "Have I not told · to move quiet near Milly? She's skittish."

"Why?"

"You'd be skittish, too, if I squeezed your knee." One big han darted out and pinched the muscle just above the boy's kne Willie squeaked and jerked back, giggling.

"Can I ride Millyflower when you're done, Mac?"

"No," Jamie answered patiently, for the dozenth time that da "I've told ye a thousand times, she's too big for ye yet."

"But I *want* to ride her!"

Jamie sighed but didn't answer, instead moving around to t other side of Mille Fleurs and picking up the left hoof.

"I *said* I want to ride Milly!"

"I heard ye."

"Then saddle her for me! Right now!"

The ninth Earl of Ellesmere had his chin thrust out as far as would go, but the defiant look in his eye was tempered with certain doubt as he intercepted Jamie's cold blue gaze. Jamie s the horse's hoof down slowly, just as slowly stood up, and drawi himself to his full height of six feet four, put his hands on his hi looked down at the Earl, three feet six, and said, very soft "No."

"Yes!" Willie stamped his foot on the hay-strewn floor. "Y *have* to do what I tell you!"

"No, I don't."

"Yes, you do!"

"No, I . . ." Shaking his head hard enough to make the r hair fly about his ears, Jamie pressed his lips tight together, th squatted down in front of the boy.

"See here," he said, "I havena got to do what ye say, for I no longer going to be groom here. I told ye, I shall be leavi tomorrow."

Willie's face went quite blank with shock, and the freckles on his nose stood out dark against the fair skin.

"You can't!" he said. "You can't leave."

"I have to."

"No!" The small Earl clenched his jaw, which gave him a truly startling resemblance to his paternal great-grandfather. Jamie thanked his stars that no one at Helwater had likely ever seen Simon Fraser, Lord Lovat. "I won't *let* you go!"

"For once, my lord, ye have nothing to say about it," Jamie replied firmly, his distress at leaving tempered somewhat by finally being allowed to speak his mind to the boy.

"If you leave . . ." Willie looked around helplessly for a threat, and spotted one easily to hand. "If you leave," he repeated more confidently, "I'll scream and shout and scare all the horses, so there!"

"Make a peep, ye little fiend, and I'll smack ye a good one!" Freed from his usual reserve, and alarmed at the thought of this spoiled brat upsetting the high-strung and valuable horses, Jamie glared at the boy.

The Earl's eyes bulged with rage, and his face went red. He took a deep breath, then whirled and ran down the length of the stable, shrieking and waving his arms.

Mille Fleurs, already on edge from having her hoofs fiddled with, reared and plunged, neighing loudly. Her distress was echoed by kicks and high-pitched whinnying from the box stalls nearby, where Willie was roaring out all the bad words he knew—no small store—and kicking frenziedly at the doors of the stalls.

Jamie succeeded in catching Mille Fleurs's lead-rope and with considerable effort, managed to get the mare outside without damage to himself or the horse. He tied her to the paddock fence, and then strode back into the stable to deal with Willie.

"Damn, damn, *damn*!" the Earl was shrieking. "Sluire! Quim! Shit! Swive!"

Without a word, Jamie grabbed the boy by the collar, lifted him off his feet and carried him, kicking and squirming, to the farrier's stool he had been using. Here he sat down, flipped the Earl over his knee, and smacked his buttocks five or six times, hard. Then he jerked the boy up and set him on his feet.

"I *hate* you!" The Earl's tear-smudged face was bright red and his fists trembled with rage.

"Well, I'm no verra fond of you either, ye little bastard!" Jam
snapped.

Willie drew himself up, fists clenched, purple in the face.

"I'm not a bastard!" he shrieked. "I'm not, I'm not! Take
back! Nobody can say that to me! Take it *back*, I said!"

Jamie stared at the boy in shock. There *had* been talk, then, a
Willie had heard it. He had delayed his going too long.

He drew a deep breath, and then another, and hoped that h
voice would not tremble.

"I take it back," he said softly. "I shouldna have used t
word, my lord."

He wanted to kneel and embrace the boy, or pick him up a
comfort him against his shoulder—but that was not a gesture
groom might make to an earl, even a young one. The palm of h
left hand stung, and he curled his fingers tight over the only f
therly caress he was ever likely to give his son.

Willie knew how an earl should behave; he was making a ma
terful effort to subdue his tears, sniffing ferociously and swiping
his face with a sleeve.

"Allow me, my lord." Jamie did kneel then, and wiped t
little boy's face gently with his own coarse handkerchief. Willie
eyes looked at him over the cotton folds, red-rimmed and woef

"Have you really got to go, Mac?" he asked, in a very sm
voice.

"Aye, I have." He looked into the dark blue eyes, so hea
breakingly like his own, and suddenly didn't give a damn wh
was right or who saw. He pulled the boy roughly to him, huggi
him tight against his heart, holding the boy's face close to h
shoulder, that Willie might not see the quick tears that fell into h
thick, soft hair.

Willie's arms went around his neck and clung tight. He cou
feel the small, sturdy body shake against him with the force
suppressed sobbing. He patted the flat little back, and smooth
Willie's hair, and murmured things in Gaelic that he hoped t
boy would not understand.

At length, he took the boy's arms from his neck and put h
gently away.

"Come wi' me to my room, Willie; I shall give ye something
keep."

He had long since moved from the hayloft, taking ov

ughes's snuggery beside the tack room when the elderly head room retired. It was a small room, and very plainly furnished, but had the twin virtues of warmth and privacy.

Besides the bed, the stool, and a chamber pot, there was a small ble, on which stood the few books that he owned, a large candle a pottery candlestick, and a smaller candle, thick and squat, that ood to one side before a small statue of the Virgin. It was a cheap ooden carving that Jenny had sent him, but it had been made in rance, and was not without artistry.

"What's that little candle for?" Willie asked. "Grannie says ly stinking Papists burn candles in front of heathen images."

"Well, I am a stinking Papist," Jamie said, with a wry twist of s mouth. "It's no a heathen image, though; it's a statue of the lessed Mother."

"You are?" Clearly this revelation only added to the boy's scination. "Why do Papists burn candles before statues, then?"

Jamie rubbed a hand through his hair. "Aye, well. It's . . . aybe a way of praying—and remembering. Ye light the candle, d say a prayer and think of people ye care for. And while it irns, the flame remembers them for ye."

"Who do you remember?" Willie glanced up at him. His hair as standing on end, rumpled by his earlier distress, but his blue es were clear with interest.

"Oh, a good many people. My family in the Highlands—my ster and her family. Friends. My wife." And sometimes the ndle burned in memory of a young and reckless girl named eneva, but he did not say that.

Willie frowned. "You haven't got a wife."

"No. Not anymore. But I remember her always."

Willie put out a stubby forefinger and cautiously touched the tle statue. The woman's hands were spread in welcome, a tender aternity engraved on the lovely face.

"I want to be a stinking Papist, too," Willie said firmly.

"Ye canna do that!" Jamie exclaimed, half-amused, half-uched at the notion. "Your grandmama and your auntie would mad."

"Would they froth at the mouth, like that mad fox you killed?" illie brightened.

"I shouldna wonder," Jamie said dryly.

"I want to do it!" The small, clear features were set in determi-

nation. "I won't tell Grannie or Auntie Isobel; I won't tell an
body. Please, Mac! Please let me! I want to be like you!"

Jamie hesitated, both touched by the boy's earnestness, an
suddenly wanting to leave his son with something more than th
carved wooden horse he had made to leave as a farewell presen
He tried to remember what Father McMurtry had taught them
the schoolroom about baptism. It was all right for a lay person
do it, he thought, provided that the situation was an emergenc
and no priest was to hand.

It might be stretching a point to call the present situation a
emergency, but . . . a sudden impulse made him reach down th
jug of water that he kept on the sill.

The eyes that were like his watched, wide and solemn, as h
carefully brushed the soft brown hair back from the high brow. H
dipped three fingers into the water and carefully traced a cross o
the lad's forehead.

"I baptize thee William James," he said softly, "in the name
the Father, the Son, and the Holy Ghost. Amen."

Willie blinked, crossing his eyes as a drop of water rolled dow
his nose. He stuck out his tongue to catch it, and Jamie laughe
despite himself.

"Why did you call me William James?" Willie asked cu
ously. "My other names are Clarence Henry George." He made
face; Clarence wasn't his idea of a good name.

Jamie hid a smile. "Ye get a new name when you're baptize
James is your special Papist name. It's mine, too."

"It is?" Willie was delighted. "I'm a stinking Papist now, li
you?"

"Aye, as much as I can manage, at least." He smiled down
Willie, then, struck by another impulse, reached into the neck
his shirt.

"Here. Keep this, too, to remember me by." He laid the beec
wood rosary gently over Willie's head. "Ye canna let anyone s
that, though," he warned. "And for God's sake, dinna tell anyo
you're a Papist."

"I won't," Willie promised. "Not a soul." He tucked the r
sary into his shirt, patting carefully to be sure that it was hidde

"Good." Jamie reached out and ruffled Willie's hair in d
missal. "It's almost time for your tea; ye'd best go on up to t
house now."

Willie started for the door, but stopped halfway, suddenly distressed again, with a hand pressed flat to his chest.

"You said to keep this to remember you. But I haven't got anything for you to remember me by!"

Jamie smiled slightly. His heart was squeezed so tight, he thought he could not draw breath to speak, but he forced the words out.

"Dinna fret yourself," he said. "I'll remember ye."

17

Monsters Risin

B rianna blinked, brushing back a bright web of hair caught the wind. "I'd almost forgotten what the sun looks like. she said, squinting at the object in question, shining wi unaccustomed ferocity on the dark waters of Loch Ness.

Her mother stretched luxuriously, enjoying the light wind. " say nothing of what fresh air is like. I feel like a toadstool that been growing in the dark for weeks—all pale and squashy."

"Fine scholars the two of you would make," Roger said, b grinned. All three of them were in high spirits. After the arduo slog through the prison records to narrow the search to Ardsmu they had had a run of luck. The records for Ardsmuir were co plete, in one spot, and—in comparison to most others—remar ably clear. Ardsmuir had been a prison for only fifteen yea following its renovation by Jacobite prison-labor, it had been co verted into a small permanent garrison, and the prison populati dispersed—mostly transported to the American Colonies.

"I still can't imagine why Fraser wasn't sent along to Ameri with the rest," Roger said. He had had a moment's panic the going over and over the list of transported convicts from Ard muir, searching the names one by one, nearly letter by letter, a still finding no Frasers. He had been certain that Jamie Fraser h died in prison, and had been in a cold sweat of fear over t thought of telling the Randall women—until the flip of a page h showed him Fraser's parole to a place named Helwater.

"I don't know," Claire said, "but it's a bloody good thing wasn't. He's—he *was*—" she caught herself quickly, but r quickly enough to stop Roger noticing the slip—"terribly, terribly seasick." She gestured at the surface of the loch before them, dancing with tiny waves. "Even going out on something like that would turn him green in minutes."

Roger glanced at Brianna with interest. "Are you seasick?"

She shook her head, bright hair lifting in the wind. "Nah." She patted her bare midriff smugly. "Cast-iron."

Roger laughed. "Want to go out, then? It's your holiday, after all."

"Really? Could we? Can you fish in there?" Brianna shaded her eyes, looking eagerly out over the dark water.

"Certainly. I've caught salmon and eels many a time in Loch Ness," Roger assured her. "Come along; we'll rent a wee boat at the dock in Drumnadrochit."

The drive to Drumnadrochit was a delight. The day was one of those clear, bright summer days that cause tourists from the South to stampede into Scotland in droves during August and September. With one of Fiona's larger breakfasts inside him, one of her lunches stowed in a basket in the trunk, and Brianna Randall, long hair blowing in the wind, seated beside him, Roger was strongly disposed to consider that all was right with the world.

He allowed himself to dwell with satisfaction on the results of their researches. It had meant taking additional leave from his college for the summer term, but it had been worth it.

After finding the record of James Fraser's parole, it had taken another two weeks of slog and inquiry—even a quick weekend trip by Roger and Bree to the Lake District, another by all three of them to London—and then the sight that had made Brianna whoop out loud in the middle of the British Museum's sacrosanct Reading Room, causing their hasty departure amid waves of icy disapproval. The sight of the Royal Warrant of Pardon, stamped with the seal of George III, *Rex Angleterre,* dated 1764, bearing the name of "James Alex*dr* M'Kensie Frazier."

"We're getting close," Roger had said, gloating over the photocopy of the Warrant of Pardon. "Bloody close!"

"Close?" Brianna had said, but then had been distracted by the sight of their bus approaching, and had not pursued the matter.

Roger had caught Claire's eye on him, though; she knew very we
what he meant.

She would, of course, have been thinking of it; he wondere
whether Brianna had. Claire had disappeared into the past in 194?
vanishing through the circle of standing stones on Craigh na Du
and reappearing in 1743. She had lived with Jamie Fraser fc
nearly three years, then returned through the stones. And she ha
come back nearly three years past the time of her original disap
pearance, in April of 1948.

All of which meant—just possibly—that if she were disposed t
try the trip back through the stones once more, she would likel
arrive twenty years past the time she had left—in 1766. And 176
was only two years past the latest known date at which Jami
Fraser had been located, alive and well. If he had survived anothe
two years, and if Roger could find him . . .

"There it is!" Brianna said suddenly. " 'Boats for Rent.' " Sh
pointed at the sign in the window of the dockside pub, and Roge
nosed the car into a parking slot outside, with no further thoug
of Jamie Fraser.

"I wonder why short men are so often enamored of very ta
women." Claire's voice behind him echoed Roger's thoughts wi
an uncanny accuracy—and not for the first time.

"Moth and flame syndrome, perhaps?" Roger suggeste
frowning at the diminutive barman's evident fascination with Br
anna. He and Claire were standing before the counter for rental
waiting for the clerk to write up the receipt while Brianna boug
bottles of Coca-Cola and brown ale to augment their lunch.

The young barman, who came up approximately to Brianna
armpit, was hopping to and fro, offering pickled eggs and slices
smoked tongue, eyes worshipfully upturned to the yellow-haltere
goddess before him. From her laughter, Brianna appeared to thi
the man "cute."

"I always told Bree not to get involved with short men," Clai
observed, watching this.

"Did you?" Roger said dryly. "Somehow I didn't envision yc
being all that much in the motherly advice line."

She laughed, disregarding his momentary sourness. "Well, I'

not, all that much. When you notice an important principle like that, though, it seems one's motherly duty to pass it along.''

"Something wrong with short men, is there?" Roger inquired.

"They tend to turn mean if they don't get their way," Claire answered. "Like small yapping dogs. Cute and fluffy, but cross them and you're likely to get a nasty nip in the ankle."

Roger laughed. "This observation is the result of years of experience, I take it?"

"Oh, yes." She nodded, glancing up at him. "I've never met an orchestra conductor over five feet tall. Vicious specimens, practically all of them. But tall men"—her lips curved slightly as she surveyed his six-feet-three-inch frame—"tall men are almost always very sweet and gentle."

"Sweet, eh?" said Roger, with a cynical glance at the barman, who was cutting up a jellied eel for Brianna. Her face expressed a wary distaste, but she leaned forward, wrinkling her nose as she took the bite offered on a fork.

"With women," Claire amplified. "I've always thought it's because they realize that they don't have anything to prove; when it's perfectly obvious that they can do anything they like whether you want them to or not, they don't need to try to prove it."

"While a short man—" Roger prompted.

"While a short one knows he can't do anything unless you let him, and the knowledge drives him mad, so he's always trying something on, just to prove he can."

"Mmphm." Roger made a Scottish noise in the back of his throat, meant to convey both appreciation of Claire's acuity, and general suspicion of what the barman might be wanting to prove to Brianna.

"Thanks," he said to the clerk, who shoved the receipt across the counter to him. "Ready, Bree?" he asked.

The loch was calm and the fishing slow, but it was pleasant on the water, with the August sun warm on their backs and the scent of raspberry canes and sun-warmed pine trees wafting from the nearby shore. Full of lunch, they all grew drowsy, and before long, Brianna was curled up in the bow, asleep with her head pillowed on Roger's jacket. Claire sat in the stern, blinking, but still awake.

"What about short and tall women?" Roger asked, resuming

their earlier conversation as he sculled slowly across the loch. H glanced over his shoulder at the amazing length of Brianna's legs awkwardly curled under her. "Same thing? The little one nasty?"

Claire shook her head meditatively, the curls beginning to wor their way loose from her hairclip. "No, I don't think so. It doesn seem to have anything to do with size. I think it's more a matter c whether they see men as The Enemy, or just see them as men, an on the whole, rather like them for it."

"Oh, to do with women's liberation, is it?"

"No, not at all," Claire said. "I saw just the same kinds c behavior between men and women in 1743 that you see now Some differences, of course, in how they each behave, but not s much in how they behave to each other."

She looked out over the dark waters of the loch, shading he eyes with her hand. She might have been keeping an eye out fo otters and floating logs, but Roger thought that far-seeing gaze wa looking a bit farther than the cliffs of the opposite shore.

"You like men, don't you?" he said quietly. "Tall men."

She smiled briefly, not looking at him.

"One," she said softly.

"Will you go, then—if I can find him?" He rested his oa momentarily, watching her.

She drew a deep breath before answering. The wind flushed he cheeks with pink and molded the fabric of the white shirt to he figure, showing off a high bosom and a slender waist. Too you to be a widow, he thought, too lovely to be wasted.

"I don't know," she said, a little shakily. "The thought of it— or rather, the *thoughts* of it! On the one hand, to find Jamie—an then, on the other, to . . . go through again." A shudder we through her, closing her eyes.

"It's indescribable, you know," she said, eyes still closed though she saw inside them the ring of stones on Craigh na Du "Horrible, but horrible in a way that isn't like other horrib things, so you can't say." She opened her eyes and smiled wry at him.

"A bit like trying to tell a man what having a baby is like; can more or less grasp the idea that it's painful, but he is equipped actually to understand what it feels like."

Roger grunted with amusement. "Oh, aye? Well, there's son

fference, you know. I've actually heard those bloody stones."
e shivered himself, involuntarily. The memory of the night, three
onths ago, when Gillian Edgars had gone through the stones,
as not one he willingly called to mind; it had come back to him
 nightmares several times, though. He heaved strongly on the
rs, trying to erase it.

"Like being torn apart, isn't it?" he said, his eyes intent on
rs. "There's something pulling at you, ripping, dragging, and
t just outside—inside you as well, so you feel your skull will fly
 pieces any moment. And the filthy noise." He shuddered again.
aire's face had gone slightly pale.

"I didn't know you could hear them," she said. "You didn't tell
e."

"It didn't seem important." He studied her a moment, as he
lled, then added quietly, "Bree heard them as well."

"I see." She turned to look back over the loch, where the wake
 the tiny boat spread its V-shaped wings. Far behind, the waves
om the passage of a larger boat reflected back from the cliffs and
ined again in the center of the loch, making a long, humped
rm of glistening water—a standing wave, a phenomenon of the
ch that had often been mistaken for a sighting of the monster.

"It's there, you know," she said suddenly, nodding down into
e black, peat-laden water.

He opened his mouth to ask what she meant, but then realized
at he *did* know. He had lived near Loch Ness for most of his life,
hed for eels and salmon in its waters, and heard—and laughed at
 every story of the "fearsome beastie" that had ever been told in
 pubs of Drumnadrochit and Fort Augustus.

Perhaps it was the unlikeliness of the situation—sitting here,
lmly discussing whether the woman with him should or should
t take the unimaginable risk of catapulting herself into an un-
own past. Whatever the cause of his certainty, it seemed sud-
nly not only possible, but sure, that the dark water of the loch
d unknown but fleshly mystery.

"What do you think it is?" he asked, as much to give his
sturbed feelings time to settle, as out of curiosity.

Claire leaned over the side, watching intently as a log drifted
to view.

"The one I saw was probably a plesiosaur," she said at last. She
in't look at Roger, but kept her gaze astern. "Though I didn't

take notes at the time.'' Her mouth twisted in something not qu
a smile.

"How many stone circles are there?" she asked abruptly. ''
Britain, in Europe. Do you know?''

"Not exactly. Several hundred, though,'' he answered ca
tiously. "Do you think they're all—"

"How should I know?" she interrupted impatiently. ''The po
is, they may be. They were set up to mark something, whi
means there may be the hell of a lot of places where that son
thing has happened." She tilted her head to one side, wiping t
windblown hair out of her face, and gave him a lopsided smil

"That would explain it, you know."

"Explain what?" Roger felt fogged by the rapid shifts of l
conversation.

"The monster." She gestured out over the water. "What
there's another of those—places—under the loch?"

"A time corridor—passage—whatever?" Roger looked
over the purling wake, staggered by the idea.

"It would explain a lot." There was a smile hiding at the corr
of her mouth, behind the veil of blowing hair. He couldn't t
whether she was serious or not. "The best candidates for mons
are all things that have been extinct for hundreds of thousands
years. If there's a time passage under the loch, that would ta
care of that little problem."

"It would also explain why the reports are sometimes diff
ent," Roger said, becoming intrigued by the idea. "If it's differ
creatures who come through."

"And it would explain why the creature—or creatures—have
been caught, and aren't seen all that often. Maybe they go back
other way, too, so they aren't in the loch all the time."

"What a marvelous idea!" Roger said. He and Claire grinn
at each other.

"You know what?" she said. "I'll bet that isn't going to ma
it on the list of popular theories."

Roger laughed, catching a crab, and droplets of water spra
over Brianna. She snorted, sat up abruptly, blinking, then s
back down, face flushed with sleep, and was breathing hea
within seconds.

"She was up late last night, helping me box up the last se

cords to go back to the University of Leeds," Roger said, defen-
ve on her behalf.

Claire nodded abstractedly, watching her daughter.

"Jamie could do that," she said softly. "Lie down and sleep
ywhere."

She fell silent. Roger rowed steadily on, toward the point of the
ch where the grim bulk of the ruins of Castle Urquhart stood
nid its pines.

"The thing is," Claire said at last, "it gets harder. Going
rough the first time was the most terrible thing I'd ever had
appen to me. Coming back was a thousand times worse." Her
es were fixed on the looming castle.

"I don't know whether it was because I didn't come back on the
ght day—it was Beltane when I went, and two weeks before,
hen I came back."

"Geilie—Gillian, I mean—she went on Beltane, too." In spite
the heat of the day, Roger felt slightly cold, seeing again the
gure of the woman who had been both his ancestor and his
ntemporary, standing in the light of a blazing bonfire, fixed for a
oment in the light, before disappearing forever into the cleft of
e standing stones.

"That's what her notebook said—that the door is open on the
n Feasts and the Fire Feasts. Perhaps it's only partly open as you
ar those times. Or perhaps she was wrong altogether; after all,
e thought you had to have a human sacrifice to make it work."

Claire swallowed heavily. The petrol-soaked remains of Greg
dgars, Gillian's husband, had been recovered from the stone
rcle by the police, on May Day. The record concluded of his
fe only, "Fled, whereabouts unknown."

Claire leaned over the side, trailing a hand in the water. A small
oud drifted over the sun, turning the loch a sudden gray, with
zens of small waves rising on the surface as the light wind
creased. Directly below, in the wake of the boat, the water was
rkly impenetrable. Seven hundred feet deep is Loch Ness, and
tter cold. What can live in a place like that?

"Would you go down there, Roger?" she asked softly. "Jump
erboard, dive in, go on down through that dark until your lungs
re bursting, not knowing whether there are things with teeth and
eat heavy bodies waiting?"

Roger felt the hair on his arms rise, and not only because ̶ sudden wind was chilly.

"But that's not all the question," she continued, still stari̶ into the blank, mysterious water. "Would you go, if Brianna w̶ down there?" She straightened up and turned to face him.

"Would you go?" The amber eyes were intent on his, unblir̶ ing as a hawk's.

He licked his lips, chapped and dried by the wind, and cas̶ quick look over his shoulder at Brianna, sleeping. He turned ba̶ to face Claire.

"Yes. I think I would."

She looked at him for a long moment, and then nodded, unsm̶ ing.

"So would I."

PART FIVE

You Can't Go Home Again

18

Roots

September 1968

The woman next to me probably weighed three hundred pounds. She wheezed in her sleep, lungs laboring to lift the burden of her massive bosom for the two-hundred-ousandth time. Her hip and thigh and pudgy arm pressed against ine, unpleasantly warm and damp.

There was no escape; I was pinned on the other side by the steel rve of the plane's fuselage. I eased one arm upward and flicked the overhead light in order to see my watch. Ten-thirty, by ondon time; at least another six hours before the landing in New ork promised escape.

The plane was filled with the collective sighs and snorts of ssengers dozing as best they might. Sleep for me was out of the estion. With a sigh of resignation, I dug into the pocket in front me for the half-finished romance novel I had stashed there. The le was by one of my favorite authors, but I found my attention ipping from the book—either back to Roger and Brianna, whom had left in Edinburgh, there to continue the hunt, or forward, to hat awaited me in Boston.

I wasn't sure just what *did* await me, which was part of the oblem. I had been obliged to come back, if only temporarily; I d long since exhausted my vacation, plus several extensions. here were matters to be ·dealt with at the hospital, bills to be llected and paid at home, the maintenance of the house and yard be attended to—I shuddered to think what heights the lawn in e backyard must have attained by now—friends to be called . . .

One friend in particular. Joseph Abernathy had been my closest

friend, from medical school on. Before I made any final—ar
likely irrevocable—decisions, I wanted to talk to him. I closed tl
book in my lap and sat tracing the extravagant loops of the tit
with one finger, smiling a little. Among other things, I owed
taste for romance novels to Joe.

I had known Joe since the beginning of my medical training. I
stood out among the other interns at Boston General, just as I di
I was the only woman among the budding doctors; Joe was tl
only black intern.

Our shared singularity gave us each a special awareness for tl
other; both of us sensed it clearly, though neither mentioned it. V
worked together very well, but both of us were wary—for goc
reason—of exposing ourselves, and the tenuous bond between u
much too nebulous to be called friendship, remained unacknow
edged until near the end of our internship.

I had done my first unassisted surgery that day—an uncompl
cated appendectomy, done on a teenage boy in good health. It ha
gone well, and there was no reason to think there would be posto
erative complications. Still, I felt an odd kind of possessivene
about the boy, and didn't want to go home until he was awake a
out of Recovery, even though my shift had ended. I change
clothes and went to the doctors' lounge on the third floor to wa

The lounge wasn't empty. Joseph Abernathy sat in one of tl
rump-sprung stuffed chairs, apparently absorbed in a copy of *U.
News & World Report*. He looked up as I entered, and nodde
briefly to me before returning to his reading.

The lounge was equipped with stacks of magazines—salvag
from the waiting rooms—and a number of tattered paperback
abandoned by departing patients. Seeking distraction, I thumb
past a six-month-old copy of *Studies in Gastroenterology,* a ra
ged copy of *Time* magazine, and a neat stack of *Watchtower* trac
Finally picking up one of the books, I sat down with it.

It had no cover, but the title page read *The Impetuous Pira.
*"A sensuous, compelling love story, boundless as the Spani
Main!"* said the line beneath the title. The Spanish Main, eh?
escape was what I wanted, I couldn't do much better, I thoug
and opened the book at random. It fell open automatically
page 42.

Tipping up her nose scornfully, Tessa tossed her lush blond tresses back, oblivious to the fact that this caused her voluptuous breasts to become even more prominent in the low-necked dress. Valdez's eyes widened at the sight, but he gave no outward sign of the effect such wanton beauty had on him.

"I thought that we might become better acquainted, Señorita," he suggested, in a low, sultry voice that made little shivers of anticipation run up and down Tessa's back.

"I have no interest in becoming acquainted with a . . . a . . . filthy, despicable, underhanded pirate!" she said.

Valdez's teeth gleamed as he smiled at her, his hand stroking the handle of the dagger at his belt. He was impressed by her fearlessness; so bold, so impetuous . . . and so beautiful.

I raised an eyebrow, but went on reading, fascinated.

With an air of imperious possession, Valdez swooped an arm about Tessa's waist.

"You forget, Señorita," he murmured, the words tickling her sensitive earlobe, "you are a prize of war; and the Captain of a pirate ship has first choice of the booty!"

Tessa struggled in his powerful arms as he bore her to the berth and tossed her lightly onto the jeweled coverlet. She struggled to catch her breath, watching in terror as he undressed, laying aside his azure-blue velvet coat and then the fine ruffled white linen shirt. His chest was magnificent, a smooth expanse of gleaming bronze. Her fingertips ached to touch it, even though her heart pounded deafeningly in her ears as he reached for the waistband of his breeches.

"But no," he said, pausing. "It is unfair of me to neglect you, Señorita. Allow me." With an irresistible smile, he bent and gently cupped Tessa's breasts in the heated palms of his callused hands, enjoying the voluptuous weight of them through the thin silken fabric. With a small scream, Tessa shrank away from his probing touch, pressing back against the lace-embroidered feather pillow.

"You resist? What a pity to spoil such fine clothing, Señorita . . ." He took a firm grasp on her jade-silk bodice and

yanked, causing Tessa's fine white breasts to leap out of their concealment like a pair of plump partridges taking wing.

I made a sound, causing Dr. Abernathy to look sharply over t top of his *U.S. News & World Report.* Hastily rearranging my fa into a semblance of dignified absorption, I turned the page.

Valdez's thick black curls swept her chest as he fastened his hot lips on Tessa's rose-pink nipples, making waves of anguished desire wash through her being. Weakened by the unaccustomed feelings that his ardor aroused in her, she was unable to move as his hand stealthily sought the hem of her gown and his blazing touch traced tendrils of sensation up the length of her slender thigh.

"Ah, mi amor," he groaned. "So lovely, so pure. You drive me mad with desire, mi amor. I have wanted you since I first saw you, so proud and cold on the deck of your father's ship. But not so cold now, my dear, eh?"

In fact, Valdez's kisses were wreaking havoc on Tessa's feelings. How, how could she be feeling such things for this man, who had cold-bloodedly sunk her father's ship, and murdered a hundred men with his own hands? She should be recoiling in horror, but instead she found herself gasping for breath, opening her mouth to receive his burning kisses, arching her body in involuntary abandon beneath the demanding pressure of his burgeoning manhood.

"Ah, mi amor," he gasped. "I cannot wait. But . . . I do not wish to hurt you. Gently, mi amor, gently."

Tessa gasped as she felt the increasing pressure of his desire making its presence known between her legs.

"Oh!" she said. "Oh, please! You can't! I don't want you to!" [Fine time to start making protests, I thought.]

"Don't worry, mi amor. Trust me."

Gradually, little by little, she relaxed under the touch of his hypnotic caresses, feeling the warmth in her stomach grow and spread. His lips brushed her breast, and his hot breath, murmuring reassurances, took away all her resistance. As she relaxed, her thighs opened without her willing it. Moving with infinite slowness, his engorged shaft teased aside the membrane of her innocence . . .

I let out a whoop and lost my grasp on the book, which slid off
y lap and fell on the floor with a plop near Dr. Abernathy's feet.

"Excuse me," I murmured, and bent to retrieve it, my face
ıming. As I came up with *The Impetuous Pirate* in my sweaty
asp, though, I saw that far from preserving his usual austere
ien, Dr. Abernathy was grinning widely.

"Let me guess," he said. "Valdez just teased aside the mem-
ane of her innocence?"

"Yes," I said, breaking out into helpless giggling again. "How
d you know?"

"Well, you weren't too far into it," he said, taking the book
om my hand. His short, blunt fingers flicked the pages expertly.
t had to be that one, or maybe the one on page 73, where he
ves her pink mounds with his hungry tongue."

"He *what*?"

"See for yourself." He thrust the book back into my hands,
inting to a spot halfway down the page.

Sure enough, "*. . . lifting aside the coverlet, he bent his coal-
ack head and laved her pink mounds with his hungry tongue.
ssa moaned and . . .*" I gave an unhinged shriek.

"You've actually *read* this?" I demanded, tearing my eyes away
om Tessa and Valdez.

"Oh, yeah," he said, the grin widening. He had a gold tooth,
r back on the right side. "Two or three times. It's not the best
ıe, but it isn't bad."

"The best one? There are *more* like this?"

"Sure. Let's see . . ." He rose and began digging through the
le of tattered paperbacks on the table. "You want to look for the
ıes with no covers," he explained. "Those are the best."

"And here I thought you never read anything but *Lancet* and
e *Journal of the AMA*," I said.

"What, I spend thirty-six hours up to my elbows in people's
ıts, and I want to come up here and read 'Advances in Gallblad-
r Resection'? Hell, no—I'd rather sail the Spanish Main with
aldez." He eyed me with some interest, the grin still not quite
ıne. "I didn't think you read anything but *The New England
urnal of Medicine,* either, Lady Jane," he said. "Appearances
e deceiving, huh?"

"Must be," I said dryly. "What's this 'Lady Jane'?"

"Oh, Hoechstein started that one," he said, leaning back with his fingers linked around one knee. "It's the voice, that accent t sounds like you just drank tea with the Queen. That's what you got, keeps the guys from bein' worse than they are. See, you sou like Winston Churchill—if Winston Churchill was a lady, tha —and that scares them a little. You've got somethin' el though"—he viewed me thoughtfully, rocking back in his ch "You have a way of talking like you expect to get your way, an you don't, you'll know the reason why. Where'd you learn tha

"In the war," I said, smiling at his description.

His eyebrows went up. "Korea?"

"No, I was a combat nurse during the Second World War France. I saw a lot of Head Matrons who could turn interns orderlies to jelly with a glance." And later, I had had a good d of practice, where that air of inviolate authority—assumed thou it might be—had stood me in good stead against people wit great deal more power than the nursing staff and interns of Bos General Hospital.

He nodded, absorbed in my explanation. "Yeah, that ma sense. I used Walter Cronkite, myself."

"Walter *Cron*kite?" I goggled at him.

He grinned again, showing his gold tooth. "You can think somebody better? Besides, I got to hear him for free on the ra or the TV every night. I used to entertain my mama—she wan me to be a preacher." He smiled, half ruefully. "If I talked l Walter Cronkite where we lived in those days, I wouldn't ha *lived* to go to med school."

I was liking Joe Abernathy more by the second. "I hope y mother wasn't disappointed that you became a doctor intstead c preacher."

"Tell you the truth, I'm not sure," he said, still grinni "When I told her, she stared at me for a minute, then heaved a sigh and said, 'Well, at least you can get my rheumatism medic for me cheap.' "

I laughed wryly. "I didn't get *that* much enthusiasm when I t my husband I was going to be a doctor. He stared at me, finally said if I was bored, why didn't I volunteer to write lett for the inmates of the nursing home."

Joe's eyes were a soft golden brown, like toffee drops. Th was a glint of humor in them as they fixed on me.

"Yeah, folks still think it's fine to say to your face that you ca

doing what you're doing. 'Why are you here, little lady, and not
me minding your man and child?' '' he mimicked.

He grinned wryly, and patted my hand. "Don't worry, they'll
ve it up sooner or later. They mostly don't ask me to my face
ymore why I ain't cleanin' the toilets, like God made me to."

Then the nurse had come with word that my appendix was
vake, and I had left, but the friendship begun on page 42 had
urished, and Joe Abernathy had become one of my best friends;
ssibly the only person close to me who truly understood what I
d, and why.

I smiled a little, feeling the slickness of the embossing on the
ver. Then I leaned forward and put the book back into the seat
cket. Perhaps I didn't want to escape just now.

Outside, a floor of moonlit cloud cut us off from the earth
low. Up here, everything was silent, beautiful and serene, in
arked contrast to the turmoil of life below.

I had the odd feeling of being suspended, motionless, cocooned
solitude, even the heavy breathing of the woman next to me
ly a part of the white noise that makes up silence, one with the
pid rush of the air-conditioning and the shuffle of the steward-
ses' shoes along the carpet. At the same time, I knew we were
shing on inexorably through the air, propelled at hundreds of
les per hour to some end—as for it being a safe one, we could
ly hope.

I closed my eyes, in suspended animation. Back in Scotland,
oger and Bree were hunting Jamie. Ahead, in Boston, my job—
d Joe—were waiting. And Jamie himself? I tried to push the
ought away, determined not to think of him until the decision
as made.

I felt a slight ruffling of my hair, and one lock brushed against
y cheek, light as a lover's touch. But surely it was no more than
e rush of air from the vent overhead, and my imagination that the
ale smells of perfume and cigarettes were suddenly underlaid by
e scents of wool and heather.

19

To Lay a Ghos

H ome at last, to the house on Furey Street, where I had liv with Frank and Brianna for nearly twenty years. The az leas by the door were not quite dead, but their leaves hu in limp, shabby clusters, a thick layer of fallen leaves curling the dry-baked bed underneath. It was a hot summer—there was any other kind in Boston—and the August rains hadn't come, ev though it was mid-September by now.

I set my bags by the front door and went to turn on the hose. had been lying in the sun; the green rubber snake was hot enou to burn my hand, and I shifted it uneasily from palm to palm un the rumble of water brought it suddenly alive and cooled it with burst of spray.

I didn't like azaleas all that much to start with. I would ha pulled them out long since, but I had been reluctant to alter a detail of the house after Frank's death, for Brianna's sake. Enou of a shock, I thought, to begin university and have your father in one year, without more changes. I had been ignoring the hou for a long time; I could go on doing so.

"All right!" I said crossly to the azaleas, as I turned off t hose. "I hope you're happy, because that's all you get. I want go have a drink myself. And a bath," I added, seeing their mu spattered leaves.

I sat on the edge of the big sunken tub in my dressing gov watching the water thunder in, churning the bubble bath i

ouds of perfumed sea-foam. Steam rose from the boiling sur-
ce; the water would be almost too hot.

I turned it off—one quick, neat twist of the tap—and sat for a
oment, the house around me still save for the crackle of popping
th bubbles, faint as the sounds of a far-off battle. I realized
rfectly well what I was doing. I had been doing it ever since I
epped aboard the Flying Scotsman in Inverness, and felt the
rum of the track come alive beneath my feet. I was testing
yself.

I had been taking careful note of the machines—all the contriv-
ces of modern daily life—and more important, of my own re-
onse to them. The train to Edinburgh, the plane to Boston, the
xicab from the airport, and all the dozens of tiny mechanical
ourishes attending—vending machines, streetlights, the plane's
ile-high lavatory, with its swirl of nasty blue-green disinfectant,
nisking waste and germs away with the push of a button. Restau-
nts, with their tidy certificates from the Department of Health,
aranteeing at least a better than even chance of escaping food
oisoning when eating therein. Inside my own house, the omni-
esent buttons that supplied light and heat and water and cooked
od.

The question was—did I care? I dipped a hand into the steam-
g bathwater and swirled it to and fro, watching the shadows of
e vortex dancing in the marble depths. Could I live without all
e "conveniences," large and small, to which I was accustomed?
I had been asking myself that with each touch of a button, each
mble of a motor, and was quite sure that the answer was "yes."
me didn't make all the difference, after all; I could walk across
e city and find people who lived without many of these conve-
ences—farther abroad and there were entire countries where
ople lived in reasonable content and complete ignorance of elec-
city.

For myself, I had never cared a lot. I had lived with my uncle
mb, an eminent archaeologist, since my own parents' death
en I was five. Consequently, I had grown up in conditions that
uld conservatively be called "primitive," as I accompanied him
all his field expeditions. Yes, hot baths and light bulbs were
e, but I had lived without them during several periods of my life
during the war, for instance—and never found the lack of them
te.

The water had cooled enough to be tolerable. I dropped th
dressing gown on the floor and stepped in, feeling a pleasa
shiver as the heat at my feet made my shoulders prickle in co
contrast.

I subsided into the tub and relaxed, stretching my legs. Eig
teenth-century hip baths were barely more than large barrels; o
normally bathed in segments, immersing the center of the boo
first, with the legs hanging outside, then stood up and rinsed th
upper torso while soaking the feet. More frequently, one bathe
from a pitcher and basin, with the aid of a cloth.

No, conveniences and comforts were merely that. Nothing e
sential, nothing I couldn't do without.

Not that conveniences were the only issue, by a long chalk. Th
past was a dangerous country. But even the advances of so-calle
civilization were no guarantee of safety. I had lived through tw
major "modern" wars—actually served on the battlefields of on
of them—and could see another taking shape on the telly eve
evening.

"Civilized" warfare was, if anything, more horrifying than
older versions. Daily life might be safer, but only if one cho
one's walk in it with care. Parts of Roxbury now were as dange
ous as any alley I had walked in the Paris of two hundred yea
past.

I sighed and pulled up the plug with my toes. No use specula
ing about impersonal things like bathtubs, bombs, and rapis
Indoor plumbing was no more than a minor distraction. The re
issue was the people involved, and always had been. Me, a
Brianna, and Jamie.

The last of the water gurgled away. I stood up, feeling sligh
light-headed, and wiped away the last of the bubbles. The b
mirror was misted with steam, but clear enough to show me m
self from the knees upward, pink as a boiled shrimp.

Dropping the towel, I looked myself over. Flexed my arm
raised them overhead, checking for bagginess. None; biceps a
triceps all nicely defined, deltoids neatly rounded and sloping i
the high curve of the pectoralis major. I turned slightly to one si
tensing and relaxing my abdominals—obliques in decent tone, t
rectus abdominis flattening almost to concavity.

"Good thing the family doesn't run to fat," I murmured. Un
Lamb had remained trim and taut to the day of his death at s

ty-five. I supposed my father—Uncle Lamb's brother—had
en constructed similarly, and wondered suddenly what my
other's backside had looked like. Women, after all, had a certain
ount of excess adipose tissue to contend with.

I turned all the way round and peered back over my shoulder at
e mirror. The long columnar muscles of my back gleamed wetly
I twisted; I still had a waist, and a good narrow one, too.

As for my own backside—"Well, no dimples, anyway," I said
ud. I turned around and stared at my reflection.

"It could be a lot worse," I said to it.

Feeling somewhat heartened, I put on my nightgown and went
out the business of putting the house to bed. No cats to put out,
dogs to feed—Bozo, the last of our dogs, had died of old age
e year before, and I had not wanted to get another, with Brianna
at school and my own hours at the hospital long and irregular.
Adjust the thermostat, check the locks of windows and doors,
e that the burners of the stove were off. That was all there was to
For eighteen years, the nightly route had included a stop in
ianna's room, but not since she had left for university.

Moved by a mixture of habit and compulsion, I pushed open the
or to her room and clicked on the light. Some people have the
ack of objects, and others haven't. Bree had it; scarcely an inch
wall space showed between the posters, photographs, dried
wers, scraps of tie-dyed fabric, framed certificates and other
pedimenta on the walls.

Some people have a way of arranging everything about them, so
e objects take on not only their own meaning, and a relation to
e other things displayed with them, but something more besides—
an indefinable aura that belongs as much to their invisible owner
to the objects themselves. *I am here because Brianna placed me
re,* the things in the room seemed to say. *I am here because she
who she is.*

It was odd that she should have that, really, I thought. Frank had
d it; when I had gone to empty his university office after his
ath, I had thought it like the fossilized cast of some extinct
imal; books and papers and bits of rubbish holding exactly the
ape and texture and vanished weight of the mind that had inhab-
d the space.

For some of Brianna's objects, the relation to her was obvio
—pictures of me, of Frank, of Bozo, of friends. The scraps
fabric were ones she had made, her chosen patterns, the colors s
liked—a brilliant turquoise, deep indigo, magenta, and clear y
low. But other things—why should the scatter of dried freshwa
snail shells on the bureau say to me "Brianna"? Why that o
lump of rounded pumice, taken from the beach at Truro, indist
guishable from a hundred thousand others—except for the fa
that she had taken it?

I didn't have a way with objects. I had no impulse either
acquire or to decorate—Frank had often complained of the Spa
tan furnishings at home, until Brianna grew old enough to take
hand. Whether it was the fault of my nomadic upbringing, or o
the way I was, I lived mostly inside my skin, with no impulse
alter my surroundings to reflect me.

Jamie was the same. He had had the few small objects, alwa
carried in his sporran for utility or as talismans, and beyond th
had neither owned nor cared for things. Even during the sh
period when we had lived luxuriously in Paris, and the longer ti
of tranquillity at Lallybroch, he had never shown any dispositi
to acquire objects.

For him as well, it might have been the circumstances of
early manhood, when he had lived like a hunted animal, nev
owning anything beyond the weapons he depended on for surviv
But perhaps it was natural to him also, this isolation from
world of things, this sense of self-sufficiency—one of the thir
that had made us seek completion in each other.

Odd all the same, that Brianna should have so much resembl
both her fathers, in their very different ways. I said a silent go
night to the ghost of my absent daughter, and put out the light

The thought of Frank went with me into the bedroom. The si
of the big double bed, smooth and untroubled under its dark bl
satin spread, brought him suddenly and vividly to mind, in a wa
had not thought of him in many months.

I supposed it was the possibility of impending departure th
made me think of him now. This room—this bed, in fact—w
where I had said goodbye to him for the last time.

"Can't you come to bed, Claire? It's past midnight." Frank ooked up at me over the edge of his book. He was already in bed imself, reading with the book propped upon his knees. The soft ool of light from the lamp made him look as though he were oating in a warm bubble, serenely isolated from the dark chilli-ss of the rest of the room. It was early January, and despite the rnace's best efforts, the only truly warm place at night was bed, der heavy blankets.

I smiled at him, and rose from my chair, dropping the heavy ool dressing gown from my shoulders.

"Am I keeping you up? Sorry. Just reliving this morning's rgery."

"Yes, I know," he said dryly. "I can tell by looking at you. Your es glaze over and your mouth hangs open."

"Sorry," I said again, matching his tone. "I can't be responsi-e for what my face is doing when I'm thinking."

"But what good does thinking do?" he asked, sticking a book-ark in his book. "You've done whatever you could—worrying out it now won't change . . . ah, well." He shrugged irritably d closed the book. "I've said it all before."

"You have," I said shortly.

I got into bed, shivering slightly, and tucked my gown down und my legs. Frank scooted automatically in my direction, and I d down under the sheets beside him, huddling together to pool r warmth against the cold.

"Oh, wait; I've got to move the phone." I flung back the covers d scrambled out again, to move the phone from Frank's side of e bed to mine. He liked to sit in bed in the early evening, chatting ith students and colleagues while I read or made surgical notes side him, but he resented being wakened by the late calls that me from the hospital for me. Resented it enough that I had ranged for the hospital to call only for absolute emergencies, or en I left instructions to keep me informed of a specific patient's ogress. Tonight I had left instructions; it was a tricky bowel section. If things went wrong, I might have to go back in in a irry.

Frank grunted as I turned out the light and slipped into bed ain, but after a moment, he rolled toward me, throwing an arm ross my middle. I rolled onto my side and curled against him, adually relaxing as my chilled toes thawed.

I mentally replayed the details of the operation, feeling aga
the chill at my feet from the refrigeration in the operating roo
and the initial, unsettling feeling of the warmth in the patien
belly as my gloved fingers slid inside. The diseased bowel itse
coiled like a viper, patterned with the purple splotches of ecch
mosis and the slow leakage of bright blood from tiny ruptures.

"I'd been thinking." Frank's voice came out of the darkne
behind me, excessively casual.

"Mm?" I was still absorbed in the vision of the surgery, b
struggled to pull myself back to the present. "About what?"

"My sabbatical." His leave from the university was due to sta
in a month. He had planned to make a series of short trips throu;
the northeastern United States, gathering material, then go
England for six months, returning to Boston to spend the last thr
months of the sabbatical writing.

"I'd thought of going to England straight off," he said car
fully.

"Well, why not? The weather will be dreadful, but if you
going to spend most of the time in libraries . . ."

"I want to take Brianna with me."

I stopped dead, the cold in the room suddenly coalescing into
small lump of suspicion in the pit of my stomach.

"She can't go now; she's only a semester from graduatio
Surely you can wait until we can join you in the summer? I've p
in for a long vacation then, and perhaps . . ."

"I'm going now. For good. Without you."

I pulled away and sat up, turning on the light. Frank lay blin
ing up at me, dark hair disheveled. It had gone gray at the templ
giving him a distinguished air that seemed to have alarming
fects on the more susceptible of his female students. I felt qu
astonishingly composed.

"Why now, all of a sudden? The latest one putting pressure
you, is she?"

The look of alarm that flashed into his eyes was so pronounc
as to be comical. I laughed, with a noticeable lack of humor.

"You actually thought I didn't know? God, Frank! You are
most . . . oblivious man!"

He sat up in bed, jaw tight.

"I thought I had been most discreet."

"You may have been at that," I said sardonically. "I count

x over the last ten years—if there were really a dozen or so, then
ou were quite the model of discretion.''

His face seldom showed great emotion, but a whitening beside
is mouth told me that he was very angry indeed.

''This one must be something special,'' I said, folding my arms
nd leaning back against the headboard in assumed casualness.
But still—why the rush to go to England now, and why take
ree?''

''She can go to boarding school for her last term,'' he said
iortly. ''Be a new experience for her.''

''Not one I expect she wants,'' I said. ''She won't want to leave
r friends, especially not just before graduation. And certainly
ot to go to an English boarding school!'' I shuddered at the
iought. I had come within inches of being immured in just such a
:hool as a child; the scent of the hospital cafeteria sometimes
voked memories of it, complete with the waves of terrified help-
ssness I had felt when Uncle Lamb had taken me to visit the
Iace.

''A little discipline never hurt anyone,'' Frank said. He had
covered his temper, but the lines of his face were still tight.
Might have done you some good.'' He waved a hand, dismissing
ie topic. ''Let that be. Still, I've decided to go back to England
irmanently. I've a good position offered at Cambridge, and I
ean to take it up. You won't leave the hospital, of course. But I
in't mean to leave my daughter behind.''

''Your daughter?'' I felt momentarily incapable of speech. So
e had a new job all set, and a new mistress to go along. He'd
een planning this for some time, then. A whole new life—but not
ith Brianna.

''My daughter,'' he said calmly. ''You can come to visit when-
er you like, of course . . .''

''You . . . bloody . . . bastard!'' I said.

''Do be reasonable, Claire.'' He looked down his nose, giving
e Treatment A, long-suffering patience, reserved for students
ppealing failing grades. ''You're scarcely ever home. If I'm gone,
ere will be no one to look after Bree properly.''

''You talk as though she's eight, not almost eighteen! For
eaven's sake, she's nearly grown.''

''All the more reason she needs care and supervision,'' he

snapped. "If you'd seen what I'd seen at the university—t
drinking, the drugging, the . . ."

"I do see it," I said through my teeth. "At fairly close range
the emergency room. Bree is not likely to—"

"She damn well is! Girls have no sense at that age—she'll
off with the first fellow who—"

"Don't be idiotic! Bree's very sensible. Besides, all young pe
ple experiment, that's how they learn. You can't keep her swa
dled in cotton wool all her life."

"Better swaddled than fucking a black man!" he shot back.
mottled red showed faintly over his cheekbones. "Like moth
like daughter, eh? But that's not how it's going to be, damn it, r
if I've anything to say about it!"

I heaved out of bed and stood up, glaring down at him.

"You," I said, "have not got one bloody, filthy, stinking thing
say, about Bree or anything else!" I was trembling with rage, a
had to press my fists into the sides of my legs to keep from strik
him. "You have the absolute, unmitigated gall to tell me that y
are leaving me to live with the latest of a succession of mistress
and then imply that I have been having an affair with Joe Ab
nathy? That is what you mean, isn't it?"

He had the grace to lower his eyes slightly.

"Everyone thinks you have," he muttered. "You spend all yc
time with the man. It's the same thing, so far as Bree is concern
Dragging her into . . . situations, where she's exposed to da
ger, and . . . and to those sorts of people . . ."

"Black people, I suppose you mean?"

"I damn well do," he said, looking up at me with eyes flashi
"It's bad enough to have the Abernathys to parties all the tin
though at least he's educated. But that obese person I met at th
house with the tribal tattoos and the mud in his hair? That rep
sive lounge lizard with the oily voice? And young Abernath
taken to hanging round Bree day and night, taking her to marc
and rallies and orgies in low dives . . ."

"I shouldn't think there are any high dives," I said, repress
an inappropriate urge to laugh at Frank's unkind but accura
assessment of two of Leonard Abernathy's more outré frien
"Did you know Lenny's taken to calling himself Muhammad I
mael Shabazz now?"

"Yes, he told me," he said shortly, "and I am taking no risk of ~~h~~aving my daughter become Mrs. Shabazz."

"I don't think Bree feels that way about Lenny," I assured him, ~~s~~truggling to suppress my irritation.

"She isn't going to, either. She's going to England with me."

"Not if she doesn't want to," I said, with great finality.

No doubt feeling that his position put him at a disadvantage, ~~F~~rank climbed out of bed and began groping for his slippers.

"I don't need your permission to take my daughter to En~~g~~land," he said. "And Bree's still a minor; she'll go where I say. ~~I'~~d appreciate it if you'd find her medical records; the new school ~~w~~ill need them."

"Your daughter?" I said again. I vaguely noticed the chill in ~~th~~e room, but was so angry that I felt hot all over. "Bree's my ~~d~~aughter, and you'll take her bloody nowhere!"

"You can't stop me," he pointed out, with aggravating calm~~n~~ess, picking up his dressing gown from the foot of the bed.

"The hell I can't," I said. "You want to divorce me? Fine. Use ~~a~~ny grounds you like—with the exception of adultery, which you ~~c~~an't prove, because it doesn't exist. But if you try to take Bree ~~a~~way with you, I'll have a thing or two to say about adultery. Do ~~y~~ou want to know how many of your discarded mistresses have ~~c~~ome to see me, to ask me to give you up?"

His mouth hung open in shock.

"I told them all that I'd give you up in a minute," I said, "if ~~y~~ou asked." I folded my arms, tucking my hands into my armpits. I ~~w~~as beginning to feel the chilliness again. "I did wonder why you ~~n~~ever asked—but I supposed it was because of Brianna."

His face had gone quite bloodless now, and showed white as a ~~s~~kull in the dimness on the other side of the bed.

"Well," he said, with a poor attempt at his usual self-posses~~si~~on, "I shouldn't have thought you minded. It's not as though you ~~e~~ver made a move to stop me."

I stared at him, completely taken aback.

"Stop you?" I said. "What should I have done? Steamed open ~~y~~our mail and waved the letters under your nose? Made a scene at ~~th~~e faculty Christmas party? Complained to the Dean?"

His lips pressed tight together for a moment, then relaxed.

"You might have behaved as though it mattered to you," he ~~s~~aid quietly.

"It mattered." My voice sounded strangled.

He shook his head, still staring at me, his eyes dark in t
lamplight.

"Not enough." He paused, face floating pale in the air abo
his dark dressing gown, then came round the bed to stand by m

"Sometimes I wondered if I could rightfully blame you,"
said, almost thoughtfully. "He looked like Bree, didn't he?
was like her?"

"Yes."

He breathed heavily, almost a snort.

"I could see it in your face—when you'd look at her, I could s
you thinking of him. Damn you, Claire Beauchamp," he said, ve
softly. "Damn you and your face that can't hide a thing you thi
or feel."

There was a silence after this, of the sort that makes you he
all the tiny unhearable noises of creaking wood and breathi
houses—only in an effort to pretend you haven't heard what w
just said.

"I did love you," I said softly, at last. "Once."

"Once," he echoed. "Should I be grateful for that?"

The feeling was beginning to come back to my numb lips.

"I did tell you," I said. "And then, when you wouldn't go .
Frank, I did try."

Whatever he heard in my voice stopped him for a moment.

"I did," I said, very softly.

He turned away and moved toward my dressing table, where
touched things restlessly, picking them up and putting them do
at random.

"I couldn't leave you at the first—pregnant, alone. Only a c
would have done that. And then . . . Bree." He stared sig
lessly at the lipstick he held in one hand, then set it gently back
the glassy tabletop. "I couldn't give her up," he said softly.
turned to look at me, eyes dark holes in a shadowed face.

"Did you know I couldn't sire a child? I . . . had myse
tested, a few years ago. I'm sterile. Did you know?"

I shook my head, not trusting myself to speak.

"Bree is mine, my daughter," he said, as though to himse
"The only child I'll ever have. I couldn't give her up." He gav
short laugh. "I couldn't give her up, but you couldn't see h

thout thinking of him, could you? Without that constant mem-
y, I wonder—would you have forgotten him, in time?''

''No.'' The whispered word seemed to go through him like an
ectric shock. He stood frozen for a moment, then whirled to the
oset and began to jerk on his clothes over his pajamas. I stood,
ms wrapped around my body, watching as he pulled on his
ercoat and stamped out of the room, not looking at me. The
llar of his blue silk pajamas stuck up over the astrakhan trim of
s coat.

A moment later, I heard the closing of the front door—he had
fficient presence of mind not to slam it—and then the sound of a
ld motor turning reluctantly over. The headlights swept across
e bedroom ceiling as the car backed down the drive, and then
re gone, leaving me shaking by the rumpled bed.

———➤

Frank didn't come back. I tried to sleep, but found myself lying
gid in the cold bed, mentally reliving the argument, listening for
e crunch of his tires in the drive. At last, I got up and dressed,
't a note for Bree, and went out myself.

The hospital hadn't called, but I might as well go and have a
ok at my patient; it was better than tossing and turning all night.
d, to be honest, I would not have minded had Frank come home
find me gone.

The streets were slick as butter, black ice gleaming in the street-
hts. The yellow phosphor glow lit whorls of falling snow; within
hour, the ice that lined the streets would be concealed beneath
sh powder, and twice as perilous to travel. The only consolation
s that there was no one on the streets at 4:00 A.M. to be imper-
d. No one but me, that is.

Inside the hospital, the usual warm, stuffy institutional smell
apped itself round me like a blanket of familiarity, shutting out
e snow-filled black night outside.

''He's okay,'' the nurse said to me softly, as though a raised
ice might disturb the sleeping man. ''All the vitals are stable,
d the count's okay. No bleeding.'' I could see that it was true;
e patient's face was pale, but with a faint undertone of pink, like
e veining in a white rose petal, and the pulse in the hollow of his
roat was strong and regular.

I let out the deep breath I hadn't realized I was holding.

"That's good," I said. *"Very good."* The nurse smiled warmly
me, and I had to resist the impulse to lean against him and di
solve. The hospital surroundings suddenly seemed like my on
refuge.

There was no point in going home. I checked briefly on r
remaining patients, and went down to the cafeteria. It still smell
like a boarding school, but I sat down with a cup of coffee ar
sipped it slowly, wondering what I would tell Bree.

It might have been a half-hour later when one of the ER nurs
hurried through the swinging doors and stopped dead at the sig
of me. Then she came on, quite slowly.

I knew at once; I had seen doctors and nurses deliver the nev
of death too often to mistake the signs. Very calmly, feeling not
ing whatever, I set down the almost full cup, realizing as I did
that for the rest of my life, I would remember that there was a ch
in the rim, and that the *"B"* of the gold lettering on the side w
almost worn away.

*". . . said you were here. Identification in his wallet . . . p
lice said . . . snow on black ice, a skid . . . DOA . . ."* T
nurse was talking, babbling, as I strode through the bright wh
halls, not looking at her, seeing the faces of the nurses at r
station turn toward me in slow motion, not knowing, but seei
from a glance at me that something final had happened.

He was on a gurney in one of the emergency room cubicles;
spare, anonymous space. There was an ambulance parked outsi
—perhaps the one that had brought him here. The double doors
the end of the corridor were open to the icy dawn. The amb
lance's red light was pulsing like an artery, bathing the corrid
in blood.

I touched him briefly. His flesh had the inert, plastic feel of t
recently dead, so at odds with the lifelike appearance. There w
no wound visible; any damage was hidden beneath the blank
that covered him. His throat was smooth and brown; no pu
moved in its hollow.

I stood there, my hand on the motionless curve of his che
looking at him, as I had not looked for some time. A strong a
delicate profile, sensitive lips, and a chiseled nose and jaw.
handsome man, despite the lines that cut deep beside his mou
lines of disappointment and unspoken anger, lines that even t
relaxation of death could not wipe away.

I stood quite still, listening. I could hear the wail of a new ambulance approaching, voices in the corridor. The squeak of gurney wheels, the crackle of a police radio, and the soft hum of a fluorescent light somewhere. I realized with a start that I was listening for Frank, expecting . . . what? That his ghost would be hovering still nearby, anxious to complete our unfinished business?

I closed my eyes, to shut out the disturbing sight of that motionless profile, going red and white and red in turn as the light throbbed through the open doors.

"Frank," I said softly, to the unsettled, icy air, "if you're still close enough to hear me—I did love you. Once. I did."

Then Joe was there, pushing through the crowded corridor, face anxious over his green scrub suit. He had come straight from surgery; there was a small spray of blood across the lenses of his glasses, a smear of it on his chest.

"Claire," he said, "God, Claire!" and then I started to shake. In ten years, he had never called me anything but "Jane" or "L.J." If he was using my name, it must be real. My hand showed startlingly white in Joe's dark grasp, then red in the pulsing light, and then I had turned to him, solid as a tree trunk, rested my head on his shoulder, and—for the first time—wept for Frank.

I leaned my face against the bedroom window of the house on Furey Street. It was hot and humid on this blue September evening, filled with the sound of crickets and lawn sprinklers. What I saw, though, was the uncompromising black and white of that winter's night two years before—black ice and the white of hospital linen, and then the blurring of all judgments in the pale gray dawn.

My eyes blurred now, remembering the anonymous bustle in the corridor and the pulsing red light of the ambulance that had washed the silent cubicle in bloody light, as I wept for Frank. Now I wept for him for the last time, knowing even as the tears slid down my cheeks that we had parted, once and for all, twenty-odd years before, on the crest of a green Scottish hill.

My weeping done, I rose and laid a hand on the smooth blue coverlet, gently rounded over the pillow on the left—Frank's side.

''Goodbye, my dear,'' I whispered, and went out to sleep dow[n] stairs, away from the ghosts.

It was the doorbell that woke me in the morning, from [my] makeshift bed on the sofa.

''Telegram, ma'am,'' the messenger said, trying not to stare [at] my nightgown.

Those small yellow envelopes have probably been responsi[ble] for more heart attacks than anything besides fatty bacon for brea[k] fast. My own heart squeezed like a fist, then went on beating i[n a] heavy, uncomfortable manner.

I tipped the messenger and carried the telegram down the h[all.] It seemed important not to open it until I had reached the relat[ive] safety of the bathroom, as though it were an explosive device th[at] must be defused under water.

My fingers shook and fumbled as I opened it, sitting on the ed[ge] of the tub, my back pressed against the tiled wall for reinfor[ce] ment.

It was a brief message—of course, a Scot would be thrifty w[ith] words, I thought absurdly.

HAVE FOUND HIM STOP, it read. WILL YOU COME BACK QUERY ROG[ER]

I folded the telegram neatly and put it back into its envelope[. I] sat there and stared at it for quite a long time. Then I stood up a[nd] went to dress.

20

Diagnosis

Joe Abernathy was seated at his desk, frowning at a small rectangle of pale cardboard he held in both hands.

"What's that?" I said, sitting on the edge of his desk without ceremony.

"A business card." He handed the card to me, looking at once amused and irritated.

It was a pale gray laid-finish card; expensive stock, fastidiously printed in an elegant serif type. *Muhammad Ishmael Shabazz III,* the center line read, with address and phone number below.

"Lenny?" I asked, laughing. "Muhammad Ishmael Shabazz *the Third*?"

"Uh-huh." Amusement seemed to be getting the upper hand. The gold tooth flashed briefly as he took the card back. "He says he's not going to take a white man's name, no slave name. He's going to reclaim his African heritage," he said sardonically. "All right, I say; I ask him, you gonna go round with a bone through your nose next thing? It's not enough he's got his hair out to *here*"—he gestured, fluffing his hands on either side of his own close-cropped head—"and he's going round in a thing down to his knees, looks like his sister made it in Home Ec class. No, Lenny—excuse me, Muhammad—he's got to be *African* all the way."

Joe waved a hand out the window, at his privileged vista over the park. "I tell him, look around, man, you see any lions? This look like Africa to you?" He leaned back in his padded chair, stretching out his legs. He shook his head in resignation. ''There no talkin' to a boy that age.''

''True,'' I said. ''But what's this 'Third' about?''

A reluctant gleam of gold answered me. ''Well, he was talkin all about his 'lost tradition' and his 'missing history' and all. H says, 'How am I going to hold my head up, face-to-face with a these guys I meet at Yale named Cadwallader IV and Sewe Lodge, Jr., and I don't even know my own grandaddy's name, don't know where I come from?' ''

Joe snorted. ''I told him, you want to know where you com from, kid, look in the mirror. Wasn't the *Mayflower,* huh?''

He picked up the card again, a reluctant grin on his face.

''So he says, if he's taking back his heritage, why not take back all the way? If his grandaddy wouldn't give him a name, he' give his grandaddy one. And the only trouble with *that,*'' he sai looking up at me under a cocked brow, ''is that it kind of leav me man in the middle. Now I have to be Muhammad Ishma Shabazz, *Junior,* so Lenny can be a 'proud African American.' He thrust himself back from the desk, chin on his chest, starin balefully at the pale gray card.

''You're lucky, L.J.,'' he said. ''At least Bree isn't giving yo grief about who her granddaddy was. All you have to worry abo is will she be doing dope and getting pregnant by some dra dodger who takes off for Canada.''

I laughed, with more than a touch of irony. ''That's what y think,'' I told him.

''Yeah?'' He cocked an interested eyebrow at me, then took o his gold-rimmed glasses and wiped them on the end of his tie. ''S how was Scotland?'' he asked, eyeing me. ''Bree like it?''

''She's still there,'' I said. ''Looking for *her* history.''

Joe was opening his mouth to say something when a tentati knock on the door interrupted him.

''Dr. Abernathy?'' A plump young man in a polo shirt peer doubtfully into the office, leaning over the top of a large cardboa box he held clutched to his substantial abdomen.

''Call me Ishmael,'' Joe said genially.

''What?'' The young man's mouth hung slightly open, and h glanced at me in bewilderment, mingled with hope. ''Are *you* D Abernathy?''

''No,'' I said, ''he is, when he puts his mind to it.'' I rose fro

he desk, brushing down my skirts. "I'll leave you to your ap-
ointment, Joe, but if you have time later—"

"No, stay a minute, L.J.," he interrupted, rising. He took the
ox from the young man, then shook his hand formally. "You'd
e Mr. Thompson? John Wicklow called to tell me you'd be
oming. Pleased to meet you."

"Horace Thompson, yes," the young man said, blinking
lightly. "I brought, er, a specimen . . ." He waved vaguely at
he cardboard box.

"Yes, that's right. I'd be happy to look at it for you, but I think
Dr. Randall here might be of assistance, too." He glanced at me,
he glint of mischief in his eyes. "I just want to see can you do it
o a dead person, L.J."

"Do *what* to a dead—" I began, when he reached into the
pened box and carefully lifted out a skull.

"Oh, pretty," he said in delight, turning the object gently to
nd fro.

"Pretty" was not the first adjective that struck me; the skull
vas stained and greatly discolored, the bone gone a deep streaky
rown. Joe carried it to the window and held it in the light, his
humbs gently stroking the small bony ridges over the eye sockets.

"Pretty lady," he said softly, talking as much to the skull as to
ne or Horace Thompson. "Full-grown, mature. Maybe late for-
es, middle fifties. Do you have the legs?" he asked, turning
bruptly to the plump young man.

"Yeah, right here," Horace Thompson assured him, reaching
nto the box. "We have the whole body, in fact."

Horace Thompson was probably someone from the coroner's
ffice, I thought. Sometimes they brought bodies to Joe that had
een found in the countryside, badly deteriorated, for an expert
pinion as to the cause of death. This one looked considerably
eteriorated.

"Here, Dr. Randall." Joe leaned over and carefully placed the
kull in my hands. "Tell me whether this lady was in good health,
hile I check her legs."

"Me? I'm not a forensic scientist." Still, I glanced automati-
ally down. It was either an old specimen, or had been weathered
xtensively; the bone was smooth, with a gloss that fresh speci-
nens never had, stained and discolored by the leaching of pig-
nents from the earth.

"Oh, all right." I turned the skull slowly in my hands, watching the bones, naming them each in my mind as I saw them. The smooth arch of the parietals, fused to the declivity of the tempora with the small ridge where the jaw muscle originated, the jutting projection that meshed itself with the maxillary into the graceful curve of the squamosal arch. She had had lovely cheekbones, high and broad. The upper jaw had most of its teeth—straight and white.

Deep eyes. The scooped bone at the back of the orbits was dark with shadow; even by tilting the skull to the side, I couldn't get light to illuminate the whole cavity. The skull felt light in m hands, the bone fragile. I stroked her brow and my hand ra upward, and down behind the occiput, my fingers seeking the dark hole at the base, the foramen magnum, where all the messages of the nervous system pass to and from the busy brain.

Then I held it close against my stomach, eyes closed, and felt the shifting sadness, filling the cavity of the skull like running water. And an odd faint sense—of surprise?

"Someone killed her," I said. "She didn't want to die." I opened my eyes to find Horace Thompson staring at me, his own eyes wide in his round, pale face. I handed him the skull, very gingerly. "Where did you find her?" I asked.

Mr. Thompson exchanged glances with Joe, then looked back me, both eyebrows still high.

"She's from a cave in the Caribbean," he said. "There were lot of artifacts with her. We think she's maybe between a hundre fifty and two hundred years old."

"She's *what*?"

Joe was grinning broadly, enjoying his joke.

"Our friend Mr. Thompson here is from the anthropology d partment at Harvard," he said. "His friend Wicklow knows m asked me would I have a look at this skeleton, to tell them what could about it."

"The nerve of you!" I said indignantly. "I thought she w some unidentified body the coroner's office dragged in."

"Well, she's unidentified," Joe pointed out. "And certainl liable to stay that way." He rooted about in the cardboard box lik a terrier. The end flap said PICT-SWEET CORN.

"Now what have we got here?" he said, and very careful drew out a plastic sack containing a jumble of vertebrae.

"She was in pieces when we got her," Horace explained.

"Oh, de headbone connected to de . . . neckbone," Joe sang softly, laying out the vertebrae along the edge of the desk. His tubby fingers darted skillfully among the bones, nudging them into alignment. "De neckbone connected to de . . . backbone . . ."

"Don't pay any attention to him," I told Horace. "You'll just encourage him."

"Now hear . . . de word . . . of de Lawd!" he finished triumphantly. "Jesus Christ, L.J., you're somethin' else! Look here." Horace Thompson and I bent obediently over the line of spiky vertebral bones. The wide body of the axis had a deep gouge; the posterior zygapophysis had broken clean off, and the fracture plane went completely through the centrum of the bone.

"A broken neck?" Thompson asked, peering interestedly.

"Yeah, but more than that, I think." Joe's finger moved over the line of the fracture plane. "See here? The bone's not just cracked, it's *gone* right there. Somebody tried to cut this lady's head clean off. With a dull blade," he concluded with relish.

Horace Thompson was looking at me queerly. "How did you know she'd been killed, Dr. Randall?" he asked.

I could feel the blood rising in my face. "I don't know," I said. "I—she—*felt* like it, that's all."

"Really?" He blinked a few times, but didn't press me further. "How odd."

"She does it all the time," Joe informed him, squinting at the femur he was measuring with a pair of calipers. "Mostly on live people, though. Best diagnostician I ever saw." He set down the calipers and picked up a small plastic ruler. "A *cave,* you said?"

"We think it was a . . . er, secret slave burial," Mr. Thompson explained, blushing, and I suddenly realized why he had seemed so abashed when he realized which of us was the Dr. Abernathy he had been sent to see. Joe shot him a sudden sharp glance, but then bent back to his work. He kept humming "Dem Dry Bones" faintly to himself as he measured the pelvic inlet, then went back to the legs, this time concentrating on the tibia. Finally he straightened up, shaking his head.

"Not a slave," he said.

Horace blinked. "But she must have been," he said. "The things we found with her . . . a clear African influence . . ."

"No," Joe said flatly. He tapped the long femur, where it reste on his desk. His fingernail clicked on the dry bone. "She wasn black."

"You can tell that? From bones?" Horace Thompson was vis bly agitated. "But I thought—that paper by Jensen, I mean— theories about racial physical differences—largely exploded— He blushed scarlet, unable to finish.

"Oh, they're there," said Joe, very dryly indeed. "If you wa to think blacks and whites are equal under the skin, be my gues but it ain't scientifically so." He turned and pulled a book fro the shelf behind him. *Tables of Skeletal Variance,* the title read

"Take a look at this," Joe invited. "You can see the differenc in a lot of bones, but especially in the leg bones. Blacks have completely different femur-to-tibia ratio than whites do. And th lady"—he pointed to the skeleton on his desk—"was white. Ca casian. No question about it."

"Oh," Horace Thompson murmured. "Well. I'll have to thi —I mean—it was very kind of you to look at her for me. Er, than you," he added, with an awkward little bow. We silently watche him bundle his bones back into the PICT-SWEET box, and then I was gone, pausing at the door to give us both another brief bob the head.

Joe gave a short laugh as the door closed behind him. "Want bet he takes her down to Rutgers for a second opinion?"

"Academics don't give up theories easily," I said, shruggin "I lived with one long enough to know that."

Joe snorted again. "So you did. Well, now that we've got M Thompson and his dead white lady sorted out, what can I do f *you,* L.J.?"

I took a deep breath and turned to face him.

"I need an honest opinion, from somebody I can depend on be objective. No," I amended, "I take that back. I need an opinio and then—depending on the opinion—maybe a favor."

"No problem," Joe assured me. "Especially the opinion. M specialty, opinions." He rocked back in his chair, unfolded h gold-rimmed glasses and set them firmly atop his broad nos Then he folded his hands across his chest, fingers steepled, an nodded at me. "Shoot."

"Am I sexually attractive?" I demanded. His eyes always r

ninded me of toffee drops, with their warm golden-brown color.
Now they went completely round, enhancing the resemblance.

Then they narrowed, but he didn't answer immediately. He
looked me over carefully, head to toe.

"It's a trick question, right?" he said. "I give you an answer
and one of those women's libbers jumps out from behind the door,
yells 'Sexist pig!' and hits me over the head with a sign that says
'Castrate Male Chauvinists.' Huh?"

"No," I assured him. "A sexist male chauvinist answer is
basically what I want."

"Oh, okay. As long as we're straight, then." He resumed his
perusal, squinting closely as I stood up straight.

"Skinny white broad with too much hair, but a great ass," he
said at last. "Nice tits, too," he added, with a cordial nod. "That
what you want to know?"

"Yes," I said, relaxing my rigid posture. "That's exactly what I
wanted to know. It isn't the sort of question you can ask just
anybody."

He pursed his lips in a silent whistle, then threw back his head
and roared with delight.

"Lady Jane! You've got you a *man*!"

I felt the blood rising in my cheeks, but tried to keep my dignity.
"I don't know. Maybe. Just maybe."

"Maybe, hell! Jesus Christ on a piece of toast, L.J., it's about
me!"

"Kindly quit cackling," I said, lowering myself into his visitor's chair. "It doesn't become a man of your years and station."

"My years? O*ho*," he said, peering shrewdly at me through the
glasses. "He's younger than you? That's what you're worried
about?"

"Not a lot," I said, the blush beginning to recede. "But I
haven't seen him in twenty years. You're the only person I know
who's known me for a long time; have I changed terribly since we
met?" I looked at him straight on, demanding honesty.

He looked at me, took off his glasses and squinted, then replaced them.

"No," he said. "You wouldn't, though, unless you got fat."

"I wouldn't?"

"Nah. Ever been to your high school reunion?"

"I didn't go to a high school."

His sketchy brows flicked upward. "No? Well, I have. And I te
you what, L.J.; you see all these people you haven't seen f
twenty years, and there's this split second when you meet som
body you used to know, when you think, 'My *God,* he
changed!,' and then all of a sudden, he hasn't—it's just like t
twenty years weren't there. I mean"—he rubbed his head vigo
ously, struggling for meaning—"you see they've got some gra
and some lines, and maybe they aren't just the same as they wen
but two minutes past that shock, and you don't see it anymor
They're just the same people they always were, and you have
make yourself stand back a ways to see that they aren't eightee
anymore.

"Now, if people get fat," he said meditatively, "*they* chang
some. It's harder to see who they were, because the faces chang
But you"—he squinted at me again—"you're never going to k
fat; you don't have the genes for it."

"I suppose not," I said. I looked down at my hands, claspe
together in my lap. Slender wristbones; at least I wasn't fat ye
My rings gleamed in the autumn sun from the window.

"Is it Bree's daddy?" he asked softly.

I jerked my head up and stared at him. "How the hell did yo
know that?" I said.

He smiled slightly. "I've known Bree how long? Ten years,
least." He shook his head. "She's got a lot of you in her, L.J., b
I've never seen anything of Frank. Daddy's got red hair, huh?" I
asked. "And he's one big son of a bitch, or everything I learned
Genetics 101 was a damn lie."

"Yes," I said, and felt a kind of delirious excitement at th
simple admission. Until I had told Bree herself and Roger abo
Jamie, I had said nothing about him for twenty years. The joy
suddenly being able to talk freely about him was intoxicating.

"Yes, he's big and red-haired, and he's Scottish," I said, ma
ing Joe's eyes go round once more.

"And Bree's in Scotland now?"

I nodded. "Bree is where the favor comes in."

Two hours later, I left the hospital for the last time, leavin
behind me a letter of resignation, addressed to the Hospital Boar
all the necessary documents for the handling of my property un

Brianna should be of age, and another one, to be executed at that time, turning everything over to her. As I drove out of the parking lot, I experienced a feeling of mingled panic, regret, and elation. I was on my way.

21

Q.E.D

"I found the deed of sasine." Roger's face was flushed wit[h] excitement. He had hardly been able to contain himself, wait[-]ing with open impatience at the train station in Invernes[s] while Brianna hugged me and my bags were retrieved. He ha[d] barely got us stuffed into his tiny Morris and the car's igniti[on] started before blurting out his news.

"What, for Lallybroch?" I leaned over the seat back betwee[n] him and Brianna, in order to hear him over the noise of the moto[r.]

"Yes, the one Jamie—your Jamie—wrote, deeding the propert[y] to his nephew, the younger Jamie."

"It's at the manse," Brianna put in, twisting to look at m[e.] "We were afraid to bring it with us; Roger had to sign his name i[n] blood to get it out of the SPA collection." Her fair skin wa[s] pinkened by excitement and the chilly day, raindrops in her rudd[y] hair. It was always a shock to me to see her again after an absenc[e] —mothers always think their children beautiful, but Bree real[ly] was.

I smiled at her, glowing with affection tinged with panic. Coul[d] I really be thinking of leaving her? Mistaking the smile for one o[f] pleasure in the news, she went on, gripping the back of the seat i[n] excitement.

"And you'll never guess what else we found!"

"What *you* found," Roger corrected, squeezing her knee wit[h] one hand as he negotiated the tiny orange car through a roun[d]about. She gave him a quick glance and a reciprocal touch with a

ir of intimacy about it that set off my maternal alarm bells on the
pot. Like that already, was it?

I seemed to feel Frank's shade glaring accusingly over my
houlder. Well, at least Roger wasn't black. I coughed and said,
"Really? What is it?"

They exchanged a glance and grinned widely at each other.

"Wait and see, Mama," said Bree, with irritating smugness.

"See?" she said, twenty minutes later, as I bent over the desk in
he manse's study. On the battered surface of the late Reverend
Wakefield's desk lay a sheaf of yellowed papers, foxed and
rowned at the edges. They were carefully enclosed in protective
lastic covers now, but obviously had been carelessly used at one
me; the edges were tattered, one sheet was torn roughly in half,
nd all the sheets had notes and annotations scribbled in the mar-
ins and inserted in the text. This was obviously someone's rough
raft—of something.

"It's the text of an article," Roger told me, shuffling through a
ile of huge folio volumes that lay on the sofa. "It was published
1 a sort of journal called *Forrester's,* put out by a printer called
lexander Malcolm, in Edinburgh, in 1765."

I swallowed, my shirtwaist dress feeling suddenly too tight un-
er the arms; 1765 was almost twenty years past the time when I
ad left Jamie.

I stared at the scrawling letters, browned with age. They were
vritten by someone of difficult penmanship, here cramped and
here sprawling, with exaggerated loops on "g" and "y." Perhaps
he writing of a left-handed man, who wrote most painfully with
is right hand.

"See, here's the published version." Roger brought the opened
olio to the desk and laid it before me, pointing. "See the date?
's 1765, and it matches this handwritten manuscript almost ex-
ctly; only a few of the marginal notes aren't included."

"Yes," I said. "And the deed of sasine . . ."

"Here it is." Brianna fumbled hastily in the top drawer and
ulled out a much crumpled paper, likewise encased in protective
lastic. Protection here was even more after the fact than with the
anuscript; the paper was rain-spattered, filthy and torn, many of

the words blurred beyond recognition. But the three signatures a the bottom still showed plainly.

By my hand, read the difficult writing, here executed with suc care that only the exaggerated loop of the ''y'' showed its kinshi with the careless manuscript, *James Alexander Malcolm MacKen zie Fraser.* And below, the two lines where the witnesses ha signed. In a thin, fine script, *Murtagh FitzGibbons Fraser,* and below that, in my own large, round hand, *Claire Beauchamp Fra ser.*

I sat down quite suddenly, putting my hand over the documen instinctively, as though to deny its reality.

''That's it, isn't it?'' said Roger quietly. His outward compo sure was belied by his hands, trembling slightly as he lifted th stack of manuscript pages to set them next to the deed. ''Yo signed it. Proof positive—if we needed it,'' he added, with a quic glance at Bree.

She shook her head, letting her hair fall down to hide her fac They didn't need it, either of them. The vanishing of Geili Duncan through the stones five months before had been all th evidence anyone could need as to the truth of my story.

Still, having it all laid out in black and white was rather stagger ing. I took my hand away and looked again at the deed, and then a the handwritten manuscript.

''Is it the same, Mama?'' Bree bent anxiously over the page her hair brushing softly against my hand. ''The article wasn signed—or it was, but with a pseudonym.'' She smiled briefl ''The author signed himself 'Q.E.D.' It looked the same to us, b we aren't either of us handwriting experts and we didn't want t give these to an expert until you'd seen them.''

''I think so.'' I felt breathless, but quite certain at the sam time, with an upwelling of incredulous joy. ''Yes, I'm almost sur Jamie wrote this.'' Q.E.D., indeed! I had an absurd urge to tear th manuscript pages out of their plastic shrouds and clutch them i my hands, to feel the ink and paper he had touched; the certai evidence that he had survived.

''There's more. Internal evidence.'' Roger's voice betrayed h pride. ''See there? It's an article against the Excise Act of 176 advocating the repeal of the restrictions on export of liquor fro the Scottish Highlands to England. Here it is''—his racing finge stopped suddenly on a phrase—'' 'for as has been known for ag

ast, "Freedom and Whisky gang tegither." ' See how he's put
at Scottish dialect phrase in quotes? He got it from somewhere
lse."

"He got it from me," I said softly. "I told him that—when he
as setting out to steal Prince Charles's port."

"I remembered." Roger nodded, eyes shining with excitement.
'But it's a quote from Burns," I said, frowning suddenly. "Per-
aps the writer got it there—wasn't Burns alive then?"

"He was," said Bree smugly, forestalling Roger. "But Robert
urns was six years old in 1765."

"And Jamie would be forty-four." Suddenly, it all seemed real.
Ie was alive—had been alive, I corrected myself, trying to keep
y emotions in check. I laid my fingers flat against the manuscript
ages, trembling.

"And if—" I said, and had to stop to swallow again.

"And if time goes on in parallel, as we think it does—" Roger
topped, too, looking at me. Then his eyes shifted to Brianna.

She had gone quite pale, but both lips and eyes were steady, and
er fingers were warm when she touched my hand.

"Then you can go back, Mama," she said softly. "You can find
im."

The plastic hangers rattled against the steel tubing of the dress
ack as I thumbed my way slowly through the available selection.

"Can I be helpin' ye at all, miss?" The salesgirl peered up at
e like a helpful Pekingese, blue-ringed eyes barely visible
rough bangs that brushed the top of her nose.

"Have you got any more of these old-fashioned sorts of
resses?" I gestured at the rack before me, thick with examples of
e current craze—laced-bodiced, long-skirted dresses in gingham
otton and velveteen.

The salesgirl's mouth was caked so thickly that I expected the
vhite lipstick to crack when she smiled, but it didn't.

"Oh, aye," she said. "Got a new lot o' the Jessica Gutenburgs
just today. Aren't they the grooviest, these old-style gowns?"
he ran an admiring finger over a brown velvet sleeve, then
hirled on her ballet flats and pointed toward the center of the
ore. "Just there, aye? Where it says, on the sign."

The sign, stuck on the top of a circular rack, said CAPTURE THE

CHARM OF THE EIGHTEENTH CENTURY in large white letters across t
top. Just below, in curlicue script, was the signature, *Jessi*
Gutenburg.

Reflecting on the basic improbability of anyone actually bei
named Jessica Gutenburg, I waded through the contents of t
rack, pausing at a truly stunning number in cream velvet, wi
satin inserts and a good deal of lace.

"Look lovely on, that would." The Pekingese was back, p
nose sniffing hopefully for a sale.

"Maybe so," I said, "but not very practical. You'd get filt
just walking out of the store." I pushed the white dress away wi
some regret, proceeding to the next size ten.

"Oh, I just love the red ones!" The girl clasped her hands
ecstasy at the brilliant garnet fabric.

"So do I," I murmured, "but we don't want to look too garis
Wouldn't do to be taken for a prostitute, would it?" The Peke ga
me a startled look through the thickets, then decided I was jokin
and giggled appreciatively.

"Now, that one," she said decisively, reaching past me, "tha
perfect, that is. That's your color, here."

Actually, it *was* almost perfect. Floor-length, with three-quart
sleeves edged with lace. A deep, tawny gold, with shimmers
brown and amber and sherry in the heavy silk.

I lifted it carefully off the rack and held it up to examine it.
trifle fancy, but it might do. The construction seemed halfwa
decent; no loose threads or unraveling seams. The machine-ma
lace on the bodice was just tacked on, but that would be ea
enough to reinforce.

"Want to try it on? The dressing rooms are just over there
The Peke was frisking about near my elbow, encouraged by n
interest. Taking a quick look at the price tag, I could see why; sl
must work on commission. I took a deep breath at the figur
which would cover a month's rent on a London flat, but th
shrugged. After all, what did I need money for?

Still, I hesitated.

"I don't know . . ." I said doubtfully, "it is lovely. But . .

"Oh, don't worry a bit about it's being too young for you," tl
Pekingese reassured me earnestly. "You don't look a day ov
twenty-five! Well . . . maybe thirty," she concluded lamely, a
ter a quick glance at my face.

"Thanks," I said dryly. "I wasn't worried about that, though. I don't suppose you have any without zippers, do you?"

"Zippers?" Her small round face went quite blank beneath the makeup. "Erm . . . no. Don't think we do."

"Well, not to worry," I said, taking the dress over my arm and turning toward the dressing room. "If I go through with this, zippers will be the least of it."

22

All Hallows' Ev

"Two golden guineas, six sovereigns, twenty-three shillings, eighteen florins ninepence, ten halfpence, an . . . twelve farthings." Roger dropped the last coin o the tinkling pile, then dug into his shirt pocket, lean face absorbed as he searched. "Oh, here." He brought out a small plastic b and carefully poured a handful of tiny copper coins into a pi alongside the other money.

"Doits," he explained. "The smallest denomination of Scotti coinage of the time. I got as many as I could, because that's like what you'd use most of the time. You wouldn't use the large coin unless you had to buy a horse or something."

"I know." I picked up a couple of sovereigns and tilted them my hand, letting them clink together. They were heavy—go coins, nearly an inch in diameter. It had taken Roger and Bree fo days in London, going from one rare-coin dealer to the next, assemble the small fortune gleaming in the lamplight before m

"You know, it's funny; these coins are worth a lot more no than their face value," I said, picking up a golden guinea, "but terms of what they'll buy, they were worth then just about as mu as now. This is six months' income for a small farmer."

"I was forgetting," Roger said, "that you know all this alread what things were worth and how they were sold."

"It's easy to forget," I said, eyes still on the money. From th corner of my vision, I saw Bree draw suddenly close to Roger, a his hand go out to her automatically.

I took a deep breath and looked up from the tiny heaps of gold nd silver. "Well, that's that. Shall we go and have some dinner?"

Dinner—at one of the pubs on River Street—was a largely lent affair. Claire and Brianna sat side by side on the banquette, ith Roger opposite. They barely looked at each other while they e, but Roger could see the frequent small touches, the tiny dges of shoulder and hip, the brushing of fingers that went on.

How would he manage, he wondered to himself. If it were his oice, or his parent? Separation came to all families, but most ten it was death that intervened, to sever the ties between parent d child. It was the element of choice here that made it so diffi- lt—not that it could ever be easy, he thought, forking in a outhful of hot shepherd's pie.

As they rose to leave after supper, he laid a hand on Claire's m.

"Just for the sake of nothing," he said, "will you try something r me?"

"I expect so," she said, smiling. "What is it?"

He nodded at the door. "Close your eyes and step out of the or. When you're outside, open them. Then come in and tell me hat's the first thing you saw."

Her mouth twitched with amusement. "All right. We'll hope e first thing I see isn't a policeman, or you'll have to come bail e out of jail for being drunk and disorderly."

"So long as it isn't a duck."

Claire gave him a queer look, but obediently turned toward the or of the pub and closed her eyes. Brianna watched her mother sappear through the door, hand extended to the paneling of the try to keep her bearings. She turned to Roger, copper eyebrows ised.

"What are you up to, Roger? *Ducks*?"

"Nothing," he said, eyes still fixed on the empty entrance. t's just an old custom. Samhain—Hallowe'en, you know?— at's one of the feasts when it was customary to try to divine the ture. And one of the ways of divination was to walk to the end of e house, and then step outside with your eyes closed. The first ing you see when you open them is an omen for the near fu- e."

"Ducks are bad omens?"

"Depends what they're doing," he said absently, still watchin the entry. "If they have their heads under their wings, that's deat What's keeping her?"

"Maybe we'd better go see," Brianna said nervously. "I don expect there are a lot of sleeping ducks in downtown Inverness but with the river so close . . ."

Just as they reached the door, though, its stained-glass windo darkened and it swung open to reveal Claire, looking mildly flu tered.

"You'll never believe what's the first thing I saw," she sai laughing as she saw them.

"Not a duck with its head under its wing?" asked Briann anxiously.

"No," her mother said, giving her a puzzled look. "A polic man. I turned to the right and ran smack into him."

"He was coming toward you, then?" Roger felt inexplicab relieved.

"Well, he was until I ran into him," she said. "Then w waltzed round the pavement a bit, clutching each other." Sh laughed, looking flushed and pretty, with her brown-sherry ey sparkling in the amber pub lights. "Why?"

"That's good luck," Roger said, smiling. "To see a man con ing toward you on Samhain means you'll find what you seek."

"Does it?" Her eyes rested on his, quizzical, then her face with a sudden smile. "Wonderful! Let's go home and celebrat shall we?"

The anxious constraint that had lain on them over dinn seemed suddenly to have vanished, to be replaced with a sort manic excitement, and they laughed and joked on the trip back the manse, where they drank toasts to past and future—Loch Mi neaig Scotch for Claire and Roger, Coca-Cola for Brianna—a talked excitedly about the plans for the next day. Brianna ha insisted on carving a pumpkin into a jack-o'-lantern, which sat o the sideboard, grinning benevolently on the proceedings.

"You've got the money, now," Roger said, for the tenth tim

"And your cloak," Brianna chimed in.

"Yes, yes, yes," Claire said impatiently. "Everything I need or everything I can manage, at least," she amended. She pause

en impulsively reached out and took both Bree and Roger by the
and.

"Thank you both," she said, squeezing their hands. Her eyes
one moist, and her voice was suddenly husky. "Thank you. I
n't say what I feel. I can't. But—oh, my dears, I will miss you!"

Then she and Bree were in each other's arms, Claire's head
cked into her daughter's neck, both of them hugged tight, as
ough simple force could somehow express the depth of feeling
tween them.

Then they broke apart, eyes wet, and Claire laid a hand on her
ughter's cheek. "I'd better go up now," she whispered. "There
e things to do, still. I'll see you in the morning, baby." She rose
tiptoe to plant a kiss on her daughter's nose, then turned and
rried from the room.

After her mother's exit, Brianna sat down again with her glass
Coke, and heaved a deep sigh. She didn't speak, but sat looking
to the fire, turning the glass slowly between her hands.

Roger busied himself, setting the room to rights for the night,
osing the windows, tidying the desk, putting away the reference
oks he had used to help Claire prepare for her journey. He
used by the jack-o'-lantern, but it looked so jolly, with the
ndlelight streaming from its slanted eyes and jagged mouth, that
couldn't bring himself to blow it out.

"I shouldn't think it's likely to set anything on fire," he re-
arked. "Shall we leave it?"

There was no answer. When he glanced at Brianna, he found
r sitting still as stone, eyes fixed on the hearth. She hadn't heard
m. He sat down beside her and took her hand.

"She might be able to come back," he said gently. "We don't
ow."

Brianna shook her head slowly, not taking her eyes from the
aping flames.

"I don't think so," she said softly. "She told you what it was
ke. She may not even make it through." Long fingers drummed
stlessly on a denimed thigh.

Roger glanced at the door, to be sure that Claire was safely
stairs, then sat down on the sofa next to Brianna.

"She belongs with him, Bree," he said. "Can ye not see it?
hen she speaks of him?"

"I see it. I know she needs him." The full lower lip trembled slightly. "But . . . I need *her*!" Brianna's hands clenched suddenly tight on her knees, and she bent forward, as though trying contain some sudden pain.

Roger stroked her hair, marveling at the softness of the glowin strands that slid through his fingers. He wanted to take her into h arms, as much for the feel of her as to offer comfort, but she wa rigid and unresponsive.

"You're grown, Bree," he said softly. "You live on your ow now, don't you? You may love her, but you don't need her an more—not the way you did when you were small. Has she no rig to her own joy?"

"Yes. But . . . Roger, you don't understand!" she burst ou She pressed her lips tight together and swallowed hard, then turne to him, eyes dark with distress.

"She's all that's left, Roger! The only one who really *kno* me. She and Daddy—Frank"—she corrected herself—"they we the ones who knew me from the beginning, the ones who saw m learn to walk and were proud of me when I did something good school, and who—" She broke off, and the tears overflowed, lea ing gleaming tracks in the firelight.

"This sounds really *dumb*," she said with sudden violenc "Really, really *dumb*! But it's—" she groped, helpless, th sprang to her feet, unable to stay still.

"It's like—there are all these things I don't even know!" s said, pacing with quick, angry steps. "Do you think I rememb what I looked like, learning to walk, or what the first word I sa was? No, but Mama does! And that's so *stupid,* because wh difference does it make, it doesn't make any difference at all, b it's important, it matters because *she* thought it was, and . . . o Roger, if she's gone, there won't be a soul left in the world w cares what I'm like, or thinks I'm special not because of anythir but just because I'm me! She's the only person in the world w really, really cares I was born, and if she's gone . . ." She sto still on the hearthrug, hands clenched at her sides, and mou twisted with the effort to control herself, tears wet on her cheel Then her shoulders slumped and the tension went out of her t figure.

"And that's just really dumb and selfish," she said, in a quie reasonable tone. "And you don't understand, and you think I awful."

"No," Roger said quietly. "I think maybe not." He stood and came behind her, putting his arms around her waist, urging her to lean back against him. She resisted at first, stiff in his arms, but then yielded to the need for physical comfort and relaxed, his chin dropped on her shoulder, head tilted to touch her own.

"I never realized," he said. "Not 'til now. D'ye remember all those boxes in the garage?"

"Which ones?" she said, with a sniffling attempt at a laugh. "There are hundreds."

"The ones that say 'Roger' on them." He gave her a slight squeeze and brought his arms up, crisscrossed on her chest, holding her snug against himself.

"They're full of my parents' old clobber," he said. "Pictures and letters and baby clothes and books and old bits of rubbish. The Reverend packed them up when he took me to live with him. Treated them just like his most precious historical documents—double-boxing, and mothproofing and all that."

He rocked slowly back and forth, swaying from side to side, carrying her with him as he watched the fire over her shoulder.

"I asked him once why he bothered to keep them—I didn't want any of it, didn't care. But he said we'd keep it just the same; it was my history, he said—and everyone needs a history."

Brianna sighed, and her body seemed to relax still further, joining him in his rhythmic, half-unconscious sway.

"Did you ever look inside them?"

He shook his head. "It isn't important what's in them," he said. "Only that they're there."

He let go of her then, and stepped back so that she turned to face him. Her face was blotched and her long, elegant nose a little swollen.

"You're wrong, you know," he said softly, and held out his hand to her. "It isn't only your mother who cares."

Brianna had gone to bed long since, but Roger sat on in the study, watching the flames die down in the hearth. Hallowe'en had always seemed to him a restless night, alive with waking spirits. Tonight was even more so, with the knowledge of what would happen in the morning. The jack-o'-lantern on the desk grinned in anticipation, filling the room with the homely scent of baking pies.

The sound of a footfall on the stair roused him from hi
thoughts. He had thought it might be Brianna, unable to sleep, bu
the visitor was Claire.

"I thought you might still be awake," she said. She was in he
nightdress, a pale glimmer of white satin against the dark hallway

He smiled and stretched out a hand, inviting her in. "No.
never could sleep on All Hallows'. Not after all the stories m
father told me; I always thought I could hear ghosts talking outsid
my window."

She smiled, coming into the firelight. "And what did the
say?"

" 'See'st thou this great gray head, with jaws which have n
meat?' " Roger quoted. "You know the story? The little tail
who spent the night in a haunted church, and met the hungr
ghost?"

"I do. I think if I'd heard *that* outside my window, I'd hav
spent the rest of the night hiding under the bedclothes."

"Oh, I usually did," Roger assured her. "Though once, when
was seven or so, I got up my nerve, stood up on the bed and pee
on the windowsill—the Reverend had just told me that pissing o
the doorposts is supposed to keep a ghost from coming in th
house."

Claire laughed delightedly, the firelight dancing in her eye
"Did it work?"

"Well, it would have worked better had the window bee
open," Roger said, "but the ghosts didn't come in, no."

They laughed together, and then one of the small awkwar
silences that had punctuated the evening fell between them, th
sudden realization of enormity gaping beneath the tightrope (
conversation. Claire sat beside him, watching the fire, her hand
moving restlessly among the folds of her gown. The light winke
from her wedding rings, silver and gold, in sparks of fire.

"I'll take care of her, you know," Roger said quietly, at las
"You do know that, don't you?"

Claire nodded, not looking at him.

"I know," she said softly. He could see the tears, caught trem
bling at the edge of her lashes, glowing with firelight. She fumble
in the pocket of her gown, and drew out a long white envelope

"You'll think me a dreadful coward," she said, "and I am. B
I . . . I honestly don't think I can do it—say goodbye to Bree,

ean.'' She stopped, to bring her voice under control, and then
eld out the envelope to him.

"I wrote it all down for her—everything I could. Will
ou . . . ?''

Roger took the envelope. It was warm from resting next to her
ody. From some obscure feeling that it must not be allowed to
row cold before it reached her daughter, he thrust it into his own
reast pocket, feeling the crackle of paper as the envelope bent.

"Yes,'' he said, hearing his own voice thicken. "Then you'll
o . . .''

"Early,'' she said, taking a deep breath. "Before dawn. I've
rranged for a car to pick me up.'' Her hands twisted together in
er lap. "If I—'' She bit her lip, then looked at Roger pleadingly.
I don't know, you see,'' she said. "I don't know whether I can
o it. I'm very much afraid. Afraid to go. Afraid not to go. Just—
fraid.''

"I would be, too.'' He held out his hand and she took it. He
eld it for a long time, feeling the pulse in her wrist, light and fast
gainst his fingers.

After a long time, she squeezed his hand gently and let go.

"Thank you, Roger,'' she said. "For everything.'' She leaned
ver and kissed him lightly on the lips. Then she rose and went
ut, a white ghost in the darkness of the hall, borne on the Hal-
we'en wind.

Roger sat on for some time alone, feeling her touch still warm
n his skin. The jack-o'-lantern was nearly burned out. The smell
f candle wax rose strongly in the restless air, and the pagan gods
oked out for the last time, through eyes of guttering flame.

The early morning air was cold and misty, and I was glad ⟨of⟩ the cloak. It had been twenty years since I'd worn one, b⟨ut⟩ with the sorts of things people wore nowadays, the Inver⟨⟩ness tailor who'd made it for me had not found an order for ⟨a⟩ woolen cloak with a hood at all odd.

I kept my eyes on the path. The crest of the hill had bee⟨n⟩ invisible, wreathed in mist, when the car had left me on the roa⟨d⟩ below.

"Here?" the driver had said, peering dubiously out of his win⟨⟩dow at the deserted countryside. "Sure, mum?"

"Yes," I'd said, half-choked with terror. "This is the place.⟨"⟩

"Aye?" He looked dubious, in spite of the large note I put ⟨in⟩ his hand. "D'ye want me to wait, mum? Or to come later, to fetc⟨h⟩ ye back?"

I was sorely tempted to say yes. After all, what if I lost m⟨y⟩ nerve? At the moment, my grip on that slippery substance seeme⟨d⟩ remarkably feeble.

"No," I said, swallowing. "No, that won't be necessary." If ⟨I⟩ couldn't do it, I would just have to walk back to Inverness, th⟨at⟩ was all. Or perhaps Roger and Brianna would come; I thought th⟨at⟩ would be worse, to be ignominiously retrieved. Or would it be ⟨a⟩ relief?

The granite pebbles rolled beneath my feet and a clod of dirt fe⟨ll⟩ in a small rushing shower, dislodged by my passage. I couldn⟨'t⟩ possibly really be doing this, I thought. The weight of the mone⟨y⟩

1 my reinforced pocket swung against my thigh, the heavy cer-
inty of gold and silver a reminder of reality. I *was* doing it.

I couldn't. Thoughts of Bree as I had seen her late last night,
eacefully asleep in her bed, assaulted me. The tendrils of remem-
ered horror reached out from the hilltop above, as I began to
ense the nearness of the stones. Screaming, chaos, the feeling of
eing torn in pieces. I couldn't.

I couldn't, but I kept on climbing, palms sweating, my feet
oving as though no longer under my control.

It was full dawn by the time I reached the top of the hill. The
ist lay below, and the stones stood clear and dark against a
rystal sky. The sight of them left me wet-palmed with apprehen-
on, but I walked forward, and passed into the circle.

They were standing on the grass in front of the cleft stone,
cing each other. Brianna heard my footsteps and whirled around
face me.

I stared at her, speechless with astonishment. She was wearing a
ssica Gutenburg dress, very much like the one I had on, except
at hers was a vivid lime green, with plastic jewels stitched across
e bosom.

"That's a perfectly horrible color for you," I said.

"It's the only one they had in my size," she answered calmly.

"What in the name of goodness are you doing here?" I de-
anded, recovering some remnant of coherence.

"We came to see you off," she said, and a hint of a smile
ickered on her lips. I looked at Roger, who shrugged slightly and
ave me a lopsided smile of his own.

"Oh. Yes. Well," I said. The stone stood behind Brianna, twice
e height of a man. I could look through the foot-wide crack, and
e the faint morning sun shining on the grass outside the circle.

"You're going," she said firmly, "or I am."

"You! Are you out of your mind?"

"No." She glanced at the cleft stone and swallowed. It might
ve been the lime-green dress that made her face look chalk-
hite. "I can do it—go through, I mean. I know I can. When
eilie Duncan went through the stones, I heard them. Roger did
o." She glanced at him as though for reassurance, then fixed her
ize firmly on me.

"I don't know whether I could find Jamie Fraser or not; maybe
ly you can. But if you won't try, then I will."

My mouth opened, but I couldn't find anything to say.

"Don't you see, Mama? He has to know—has to know he (it, he did what he meant to for us." Her lips quivered, and s pressed them together for a minute.

"We owe it to him, Mama," she said softly. "Somebody has find him, and tell him." Her hand touched my face, briefly. "T him I was born."

"Oh, Bree," I said, my voice so choked I could barely spea "Oh, Bree!"

She was holding my hands tight between her own, squeezi hard.

"He gave you to me," she said, so low I could hardly hear h "Now I have to give you back to him, Mama."

The eyes that were so like Jamie's looked down at me, blurr by tears.

"If you find him," she whispered, "when you find my father give him this." She bent and kissed me, fiercely, gently, th straightened and turned me toward the stone.

"Go, Mama," she said, breathless. "I love you. Go!"

From the corner of my eye, I saw Roger move toward her. I to one step, and then another. I heard a sound, a faint roaring. I to the last step, and the world disappeared.

PART SIX

Edinburgh

24

A. Malcolm, Printer

My first coherent thought was "It's raining. This must be Scotland." My second thought was that this observation was no great improvement over the random images jumbling around inside my head, banging into each other and setting off small synaptic explosions of irrelevance.

I opened one eye, with some difficulty. The lid was stuck shut, and my entire face felt cold and puffy, like a submerged corpse's. I shuddered faintly at the thought, the slight movement making me aware of the sodden fabric all around me.

It was certainly raining—a soft, steady drum of rain that raised a faint mist of droplets above the green moor. I sat up, feeling like a hippopotamus emerging from a bog, and promptly fell over backward.

I blinked and closed my eyes against the downpour. Some small sense of who I was—and where I was—was beginning to come back to me. *Bree*. Her face emerged suddenly into memory, with a jolt that made me gasp as though I'd been punched in the stomach. Jagged images of loss and the rip of separation pulled at me, a faint echo of the chaos in the stone passage.

Jamie. There it was; the anchor point to which I had clung, my single hold on sanity. I breathed slow and deep, hands folded over my pounding heart, summoning Jamie's face. For a moment, I thought I had lost him, and then it came, clear and bold in my mind's eye.

Once again, I struggled upright, and this time stayed, propped my outstretched hands. Yes, certainly it was Scotland. It could

hardly by anything else, of course, but it was also the Scotland
the past. At least, I *hoped* it was the past. It wasn't the Scotland
left, at any rate. The trees and bushes grew in different patter
there was a patch of maple saplings just below me that hadn't be
there when I'd climbed the hill—when? That morning? Two da
ago?

I had no idea how much time had passed since I had entered t
standing stones, or how long I had lain unconscious on the hillsi
below the circle. Quite a while, judging from the sogginess of i
clothing; I was soaked through to the skin, and small chilly riv
lets ran down my sides under my gown.

One numbed cheek was beginning to tingle; putting my hand
it, I could feel a pattern of incised bumps. I looked down and sa
a layer of fallen rowan berries, gleaming red and black among t
grass. Very appropriate, I thought, vaguely amused. I had fall
down under a rowan—the Highland protection against witchcr
and enchantment.

I grasped the smooth trunk of the rowan tree, and laborious
hauled myself to my feet. Still holding on to the tree for suppor
looked to the northeast. The rain had faded the horizon to a gr
invisibility, but I knew that Inverness lay in that direction. N
more than an hour's trip by car, along modern roads.

The road existed; I could see the outline of a rough track th
led along the base of the hill, a dark, silvery line in the gleami
green wetness of the moor plants. However, forty-odd miles
foot was a far cry from the journey by car that had brought n
here.

I was beginning to feel somewhat better, standing up. T
weakness in my limbs was fading, along with the feeling of cha
and disruption in my mind. It had been as bad as I'd feared, th
passage; perhaps worse. I could feel the terrible presence of t
stones above me, and shuddered, my skin prickling with cold.

I was alive, though. Alive, and with a small feeling of certaint
like a tiny glowing sun beneath my ribs. *He was here.* I knew
now, though I hadn't known it when I threw myself between t
stones; that had been a leap of faith. But I had cast out my thoug
of Jamie like a lifeline tossed into a raging torrent—and the li
had tightened in my grasp, and pulled me free.

I was wet, cold, and felt battered, as though I had been washi
about in the surf against a rocky shore. But I was here. At

mewhere in this strange country of the past was the man I had me to find. The memories of grief and terror were receding, as I alized that my die was cast. I could not go back; a return trip ould almost surely be fatal. As I realized that I was likely here to ay, all hesitations and terrors were superseded by a strange calm, most exultant. I could not go back. There was nothing to do but forward—to find him.

Cursing my carelessness in not having thought to tell the tailor make my cloak with a waterproof layer between fabric and ning, I pulled the water-soaked garment closer. Even wet, the ool held some warmth. If I began to move, I would grow warmer. quick pat reassured me that my bundle of sandwiches had made e trip with me. That was good; the thought of walking forty iles on an empty stomach was a daunting one.

With luck, I wouldn't have to. I might find a village or a house at had a horse I could buy. But if not, I was prepared. My plan as to go to Inverness—by whatever means offered itself—and ere take a public coach to Edinburgh.

There was no telling where Jamie was at the moment. He might e in Edinburgh, where his article had been published, but he ight easily be somewhere else. If I could not find him there, I uld go to Lallybroch, his home. Surely his family would know here he was—if any of them were left. The sudden thought illed me, and I shivered.

I thought of a small bookstore that I passed every morning on y way from the parking lot to the hospital. They had been having sale on posters; I had seen the display of psychedelic examples hen I left Joe's office for the last time.

"Today is the first day of the rest of your life," said one poster, ove an illustration of a foolish-looking chick, absurdly poking s head out of an eggshell. In the other window, another poster owed a caterpillar, inching its way up a flower stalk. Above the alk soared a brilliantly colored butterfly, and below was the otto "A journey of a thousand miles begins with a single step."

The most irritating thing about clichés, I decided, was how equently they were true. I let go of the rowan tree, and started wn the hill toward my future.

It was a long, jolting ride from Inverness to Edinburg
crammed cheek by jowl into a large coach with two other ladi
the small and whiny son of one of the ladies, and four gentlem
of varying sizes and dispositions.

Mr. Graham, a small and vivacious gentleman of advanc
years who was seated next to me, was wearing a bag of camph
and asafoetida about his neck, to the eyewatering discomfort of t
rest of the coach.

"Capital for dispelling the evil humors of influenza," he e
plained to me, waving the bag gently under my nose like a cens
"I have worn this daily through the autumn and winter month
and haven't been sick a day in nearly thirty years!"

"Amazing!" I said politely, trying to hold my breath. I did
doubt it; the fumes probably kept everyone at such a distance th
germs couldn't reach him.

The effects on the little boy didn't seem nearly so benefici
After a number of loud and injudicious remarks about the smell
the coach, Master Georgie had been muffled in his mother's b
som, from which he now peeped, looking rather green. I kept
close eye on him, as well as on the chamber pot beneath the se
opposite, in case quick action involving a conjunction of the tw
should be called for.

I gathered that the chamber pot was for use in incleme
weather or other emergency, as normally the ladies' modesty r
quired stops every hour or so, at which point the passengers wou
scatter into the roadside vegetation like a covey of quail, ev
those who did not require relief of bladder or bowels seeking sor
relief from the stench of Mr. Graham's asafoetida bag.

After one or two changes, Mr. Graham found his place besi
me superseded by Mr. Wallace, a plump young lawyer, returni
to Edinburgh after seeing to the disposition of the estate of
elderly relative in Inverness, as he explained to me.

I didn't find the details of his legal practice nearly as fascinati
as he did, but under the circumstances, his evident attraction to n
was mildly reassuring, and I passed several hours in playing wi
him upon a small chess set that he produced from a pocket an
laid upon his knee.

My attention was distracted both from the discomforts of t
journey and the intricacies of chess by anticipation of what I mig
find in Edinburgh. A. Malcolm. The name kept running throu

y mind like an anthem of hope. A. Malcolm. It had to be Jamie,
simply had to! James Alexander Malcolm MacKenzie Fraser.

"Considering the way the Highland rebels were treated after
Culloden, it would be very reasonable for him to use an assumed
ame in a place like Edinburgh," Roger Wakefield had explained
o me. "Particularly him—he was a convicted traitor, after all.
Made rather a habit of it, too, it looks like," he had added criti-
ally, looking over the scrawled manuscript of the antitax diatribe.
For the times, this is bloody near sedition."

"Yes, that sounds like Jamie," I had said dryly, but my heart
ad leapt at the sight of that distinctively untidy scrawl, with its
oldly worded sentiments. My Jamie. I touched the small hard
ectangle in my skirt pocket, wondering how long it would be,
efore we reached Edinburgh.

The weather kept unseasonably fine, with no more than the
ccasional drizzle to hinder our passage, and we completed the
ourney in less than two days, stopping four times to change
orses and refresh ourselves at posthouse taverns.

The coach debouched into a yard at the back of Boyd's
Whitehorse tavern, near the foot of the Royal Mile in Edinburgh.
he passengers emerged into the watery sunshine like newly
atched chrysalids, rumpled of wing and jerky in movement, un-
customed to mobility. After the dimness of the coach, even the
oudy gray light of Edinburgh seemed blinding.

I had pins and needles in my feet from so long sitting, but
urried nonetheless, hoping to escape from the courtyard while
y erstwhile companions were busy with the retrieval of their
elongings. No such luck; Mr. Wallace caught up with me near the
reet.

"Mrs. Fraser!" he said. "Might I beg the pleasure of accompa-
ying you to your destination? You will surely require some assis-
nce in the removal of your luggage." He looked over his shoul-
er toward the coach, where the ostlers were heaving the bags and
ortmanteaux apparently at random into the crowd, to the accom-
animent of incoherent grunts and shouts.

"Er . . ." I said. "Thank you, but I . . . er, I'm leaving my
ggage in charge of the landlord. My . . . my . . ." I groped
antically. "My husband's servant will come fetch it later."

His plump face fell slightly at the word "husband," but he
llied gallantly, taking my hand and bowing low over it.

"I quite see. May I express my profound appreciation for t
pleasure of your company on our journey, then, Mrs. Fraser? A
perhaps we shall meet again." He straightened up, surveying t
crowd that eddied past us. "Is your husband meeting you?
should be delighted to make his acquaintance."

While Mr. Wallace's interest in me had been rather flattering.
was rapidly becoming a nuisance.

"No, I shall be joining him later," I said. "So nice to have m
you, Mr. Wallace; I'll hope to see you again sometime." I sho
Mr. Wallace's hand enthusiastically, which disconcerted hi
enough for me to slither off through the throng of passenge
ostlers, and food sellers.

I didn't dare pause near the coachyard for fear he would cor
out after me. I turned and darted up the slope of the Royal Mi
moving as quickly as my voluminous skirts would allow, jostli
and bumping my way through the crowd. I had had the luck
pick a market day for my arrival, and I was soon lost to sight fro
the coachyard among the luckenbooths and oyster sellers wh
lined the street.

Panting like an escaped pickpocket, I stopped for breath ha
way up the hill. There was a public fountain here, and I sat dov
on the rim to catch my breath.

I was here. Really here. Edinburgh sloped up behind me, to tl
glowering heights of Edinburgh Castle, and down before me,
the gracious majesty of Holyrood Palace at the foot of the city

The last time I had stood by this fountain, Bonnie Prince Cha
lie had been addressing the gathered citizenry of Edinburgh, i
spiring them with the sight of his royal presence. He had bound
exuberantly from the rim to the carved center finial of the fou
tain, one foot in the basin, clinging to one of the spouting hea
for support, shouting "On to England!" The crowd had roare
pleased at this show of youthful high spirits and athletic prowess
would myself have been more impressed had I not noticed that tl
water in the fountain had been turned off in anticipation of tl
gesture.

I wondered where Charlie was now. He had gone back to Ita
after Culloden, I supposed, there to live whatever life was possib
for royalty in permanent exile. What he was doing, I neither kne
nor cared. He had passed from the pages of history, and from n

fe as well, leaving wreck and ruin in his wake. It remained to be en what might be salvaged now.

I was very hungry; I had had nothing to eat since a hasty reakfast of rough parritch and boiled mutton, made soon after awn at a posthouse in Dundaff. I had one last sandwich remain-g in my pocket, but had been reluctant to eat it in the coach, nder the curious gaze of my fellow travelers.

I pulled it out and carefully unwrapped it. Peanut butter and lly on white bread, it was considerably the worse for wear, with e purple stains of the jelly seeping through the limp bread, and e whole thing mashed into a flattened wodge. It was delicious.

I ate it carefully, savoring the rich, oily taste of the peanut utter. How many mornings had I slathered peanut butter on read, making sandwiches for Brianna's school lunches? Firmly appressing the thought, I examined the passersby for distraction. hey did look somewhat different from their modern equivalents; oth men and women tended to be shorter, and the signs of poor utrition were evident. Still, there was an overwhelming familiar-y to them—these were people I knew, Scots and English for the ost part, and hearing the rich burring babble of voices in the reet, after so many years of the flat nasal tones of Boston, I had uite an extraordinary feeling of coming home.

I swallowed the last rich, sweet bite of my old life, and crum-led the wrapper in my hand. I glanced around, but no one was oking in my direction. I opened my hand, and let the bit of lastic film fall surreptitiously to the ground. Wadded up, it rolled few inches on the cobbles, crinkling and unfolding itself as tough alive. The light wind caught it, and the small transparent teet took sudden wing, scudding over the gray stones like a leaf.

The draft of a set of passing wheels sucked it under a drayman's art; it winked once with reflected light, and was gone, disappear-g without notice from the passersby. I wondered whether my wn anachronistic presence would cause as little harm.

"You are dithering, Beauchamp," I said to myself. "Time to et on." I took a deep breath and stood up.

"Excuse me," I said, catching the sleeve of a passing baker's oy. "I'm looking for a printer—a Mr. Malcolm. Alexander Mal-olm." A feeling of mingled dread and excitement gurgled rough my middle. What if there was no printshop run by Alexan-er Malcolm in Edinburgh?

There was, though; the boy's face screwed up in thought ar then relaxed.

"Oh, aye, mum—just down the way and to your left. Carf: Close." And hitching his loaves up under his arm with a nod, I plunged back into the crowded street.

Carfax Close. I edged my way back into the crowd, pressi close to the buildings, to avoid the occasional shower of slops th splattered into the street from the windows high above. There we several thousand people in Edinburgh, and the sewage from all them was running down the gutters of the cobbled street, depen ing on gravity and the frequent rain to keep the city habitable.

The low, dark opening to Carfax Close yawned just ahea across the expanse of the Royal Mile. I stopped dead, looking at my heart beating hard enough to be heard a yard away, had anyo been listening.

It wasn't raining, but was just about to, and the dampness in tl air made my hair curl. I pushed it off my forehead, tidying it best I could without a mirror. Then I caught sight of a large plat glass window up ahead, and hurried forward.

The glass was misty with condensation, but provided a di reflection, in which my face looked flushed and wide-eyed, b otherwise presentable. My hair, however, had seized the opport nity to curl madly in all directions, and was writhing out of i hairpins in excellent imitation of Medusa's locks. I yanked tl pins out impatiently, and began to twist up my curls.

There was a woman inside the shop, leaning across the counte There were three small children with her, and I watched with ha an eye as she turned from her business to address them imp tiently, swatting with her reticule at the middle one, a boy who w fiddling with several stalks of fresh anise that stood in a pail water on the floor.

It was an apothecary's shop; glancing up, I saw the nam "Haugh" above the door, and felt a thrill of recognition. I h bought herbs here, during the brief time I had lived in Edinburg The decor of the window had been augmented sometime since I the addition of a large jar of colored water, in which floated som thing vaguely humanoid. A fetal pig, or perhaps an infant baboo it had leering, flattened features that pressed against the round side of the jar in a disconcerting fashion.

"Well, at least I look better than *you*!" I muttered, shoving in a
alcitrant pin.

I looked better than the woman inside, too, I thought. Her busi-
ss concluded, she was stuffing her purchase into the bag she
ried, her thin face frowning as she did so. She had the rather
ty look of a city dweller, and her skin was deeply lined, with
rp creases running from nose to mouth, and a furrowed fore-
d.

"De'il tak' ye, ye wee ratten," she was saying crossly to the
le boy as they all clattered out of the shop together. "Have I no
d ye time and again to keep yer paws in yer pockets?"

"Excuse me." I stepped forward, interrupting, impelled by a
den irresistible curiosity.

"Aye?" Distracted from maternal remonstration, she looked
nkly at me. Up close, she looked even more harried. The cor-
s of her mouth were pinched, and her lips folded in—no doubt
ause of missing teeth.

"I couldn't help admiring your children," I said, with as much
tense of admiration as I could manage on short notice. I
med kindly at them. "Such pretty babies! Tell me, how old are
y?"

Her jaw dropped, confirming the absence of several teeth. She
ked at me, then said, "Oh! Well, that's maist kind o' ye, mum.
. . . Maisri here is ten," she said, nodding at the eldest girl,
o was in the act of wiping her nose on her sleeve, "Joey's eight
ak' yer finger out o' yer nose, ye clattie imp!" she scolded,
n turned and proudly patted her youngest on the head. "And
Polly's just turned six this May."

"Really!" I gazed at the woman, affecting astonishment. "You
rcely look old enough to have children of that age. You must
e married very young."

he preened slightly, smirking.

"Och, no! Not so young as all that; why, I was all o' nineteen
en Maisri was born."

"Amazing," I said, meaning it. I dug in my pocket and offered
children each a penny, which they took with shy bobs of
nks. "Good day to you—and congratulations on your lovely
ily," I said to the woman, and walked away with a smile and a
e.

Nineteen when the eldest was born, and Maisri was ten now.

She was twenty-nine. And I, blessed by good nutrition, hygie
and dentistry, not worn down by multiple pregnancies and h
physical labor, looked a good deal younger than she. I took a d
breath, pushed back my hair, and marched into the shadows
Carfax Close.

It was a longish, winding close, and the printshop was at
foot. There were thriving businesses and tenements on either s
but I had no attention to spare for anything beyond the neat w
sign that hung by the door.

A. MALCOLM

PRINTER AND BOOKSELLER

it said, and beneath this, *Books, calling cards, pamphlets, br*
sheets, letters, etc.

I stretched out my hand and touched the black letters of
name. A. Malcolm. Alexander Malcolm. James Alexander M
colm MacKenzie Fraser. Perhaps.

Another minute, and I would lose my nerve. I shoved open
door and walked in.

There was a broad counter across the front of the room, wit
open flap in it, and a rack to one side that held several tray
type. Posters and notices of all sorts were tacked up on the o
site wall; samples, no doubt.

The door into the back room was open, showing the b
angular frame of a printing press. Bent over it, his back turne
me, was Jamie.

"Is that you, Geordie?" he asked, not turning around. He
dressed in shirt and breeches, and had a small tool of some kir
his hand, with which he was doing something to the innards o
press. "Took ye long enough. Did ye get the—"

"It isn't Geordie," I said. My voice was higher than u
"It's me," I said. "Claire."

He straightened up very slowly. He wore his hair long; a t
tail of a deep, rich auburn sparked with copper. I had time to
that the neat ribbon that tied it back was green, and then he tu
around.

He stared at me without speaking. A tremor ran down the mus-
lar throat as he swallowed, but still he didn't say anything.

It was the same broad, good-humored face, dark blue eyes
lant the high, flat cheekbones of a Viking, long mouth curling at
ends as though always on the verge of smiling. The lines
rrounding eyes and mouth were deeper, of course. The nose had
anged just a bit. The knife-edge bridge was slightly thickened
ar the base by the ridge of an old, healed fracture. It made him
ok fiercer, I thought, but lessened that air of aloof reserve, and
t his appearance a new rough charm.

I walked through the flap in the counter, seeing nothing but that
blinking stare. I cleared my throat.

"When did you break your nose?"

The corners of the wide mouth lifted slightly.

"About three minutes after I last saw ye—Sassenach."

There was a hesitation, almost a question in the name. There
s no more than a foot between us. I reached out tentatively and
ched the tiny line of the break, where the bone pressed white
ainst the bronze of his skin.

He flinched backward as though an electric spark had arced
tween us, and the calm expression shattered.

"You're real," he whispered. I had thought him pale already.
w all vestiges of color drained from his face. His eyes rolled up
d he slumped to the floor in a shower of papers and oddments
t had been sitting on the press—he fell rather gracefully for
ch a large man, I thought abstractedly.

It was only a faint; his eyelids were beginning to flutter by the
e I knelt beside him and loosened the stock at his throat. I had
doubts at all by now, but still I looked automatically as I pulled
heavy linen away. It was there, of course, the small triangular
r just above the collarbone, left by the knife of Captain Jona-
n Randall, Esquire, of His Majesty's Eighth Dragoons.

His normal healthy color was returning. I sat cross-legged on
floor and hoisted his head onto my thigh. His hair felt thick
d soft in my hand. His eyes opened.

"That bad, is it?" I said, smiling down at him with the same
rds he had used to me on the day of our wedding, holding my
d in his lap, twenty-odd years before.

"That bad, and worse, Sassenach," he answered, mouth twitch-

ing with something almost a smile. He sat up abruptly, staring
me.

"God in heaven, you *are* real!"

"So are you." I lifted my chin to look up at him. "I th-thoug
you were dead." I had meant to speak lightly, but my voice b
trayed me. The tears spilled down my cheeks, only to soak into t
rough cloth of his shirt as he pulled me hard against him.

I shook so that it was some time before I realized that he w
shaking, too, and for the same reason. I don't know how long
sat there on the dusty floor, crying in each other's arms with t
longing of twenty years spilling down our faces.

His fingers twined hard in my hair, pulling it loose so that
tumbled down my neck. The dislodged pins cascaded over r
shoulders and pinged on the floor like pellets of hail. My ov
fingers were clasped around his forearm, digging into the linen
though I were afraid he would disappear unless physically
strained.

As though gripped by the same fear, he suddenly grasped me
the shoulders and held me away from him, staring desperately i
my face. He put his hand to my cheek, and traced the bones o
and over again, oblivious to my tears and to my abundantly r
ning nose.

I sniffed loudly, which seemed to bring him to his senses, for
let go and groped hastily in his sleeve for a handkerchief, which
used clumsily to swab first my face, then his own.

"Give me that." I grabbed the erratically waving swatch
cloth and blew my nose firmly. "Now you." I handed him
cloth and watched as he blew his nose with a noise like a strang
goose. I giggled, undone with emotion.

He smiled too, knuckling the tears away from his eyes, unable
stop staring at me.

Suddenly I couldn't bear not to be touching him. I lunged
him, and he got his arms up just in time to catch me. I squee
until I could hear his ribs crack, and felt his hands roughly care
ing my back as he said my name over and over.

At last I could let go, and sat back a little. He glanced down
the floor between his legs, frowning.

"Did you lose something?" I asked, surprised.

He looked up and smiled, a little shyly.

"I was afraid I'd lost hold altogether and pissed myself, but it's right. I've just sat on the alepot."

Sure enough, a pool of aromatic brown liquid was spreading ·wly beneath him. With a squeak of alarm, I scrambled to my ·t and helped him up. After trying vainly to assess the damage hind, he shrugged and unfastened his breeches. He pushed the ht fabric down over his haunches, then stopped and looked at ·, blushing slightly.

"It's all right," I said, feeling a rich blush stain my own cheeks. Ve're married." I cast my eyes down, nonetheless, feeling a ·le breathless. "At least, I suppose we are."

He stared at me for a long moment, then a smile curved his ·de, soft mouth.

"Aye, we are," he said. Kicking free of the stained breeches, he ·pped toward me.

I stretched out a hand toward him, as much to stop as to wel-·me him. I wanted more than anything to touch him again, but ·s unaccountably shy. After so long, how were we to start again? He felt the constraint of mingled shyness and intimacy as well. ·pping a few inches from me, he took my hand. He hesitated for ·noment, then bent his head over it, his lips barely brushing my ·uckles. His fingers touched the silver ring and stopped there, ·ding the metal lightly between thumb and forefinger.

"I never took it off," I blurted. It seemed important he should ·ow that. He squeezed my hand lightly, but didn't let go.

"I want—" He stopped and swallowed, still holding my hand. ·s fingers found and touched the silver ring once more. "I want ·ra much to kiss you," he said softly. "May I do that?"

The tears were barely dammed. Two more welled up and over-·wed; I felt them, full and round, roll down my cheeks.

"Yes," I whispered.

He drew me slowly close to him, holding our linked hands just ·der his breast.

"I havena done this for a verra long time," he said. I saw the ·pe and the fear dark in the blue of his eyes. I took the gift and ·e it back to him.

"Neither have I," I said softly.

His hands cupped my face with exquisite gentleness, and he set ·mouth on mine.

· didn't know quite what I had been expecting. A reprise of the

pounding fury that had accompanied our final parting? I had
membered that so often, lived it over in memory, helpless
change the outcome. The half-rough, timeless hours of mut
possession in the darkness of our marriage bed? I had longed
that, wakened often sweating and trembling from the memory
it.

But we were strangers now, barely touching, each seeking
way toward joining, slowly, tentatively, seeking and giving uns
ken permission with our silent lips. My eyes were closed, an
knew without looking that Jamie's were, as well. We were, qu
simply, afraid to look at each other.

Without raising his head, he began to stroke me lightly, feel
my bones through my clothes, familiarizing himself again with
terrain of my body. At last his hand traveled down my arm a
caught my right hand. His fingers traced my hand until they fou
the ring again, and circled it, feeling the interlaced silver of
Highland pattern, polished with long wear, but still distinct.

His lips moved from mine, across my cheeks and eyes. I ger
stroked his back, feeling through his shirt the marks I couldn't s
the remnants of old scars, like my ring, worn but still distinct

"I've seen ye so many times," he said, his voice whisper
warm in my ear. "You've come to me so often. When I dream
sometimes. When I lay in fever. When I was so afraid and
lonely I knew I must die. When I needed you, I would always
ye, smiling, with your hair curling up about your face. But
never spoke. And ye never touched me."

"I can touch you now." I reached up and drew my hand ger
down his temple, his ear, the cheek and jaw that I could see. I
hand went to the nape of his neck, under the clubbed bronze h
and he raised his head at last, and cupped my face between
hands, love glowing strong in the dark blue eyes.

"Dinna be afraid," he said softly. "There's the two of
now."

We might have gone on standing there gazing at each ot
indefinitely, had the shop bell over the door not rung. I let go
Jamie and looked around sharply, to see a small, wiry man w
coarse dark hair standing in the door, mouth agape, holdin
small parcel in one hand.

"Oh, there ye are, Geordie! What's kept ye?" Jamie said.

Geordie said nothing, but his eyes traveled dubiously over his mployer, standing bare-legged in his shirt in the middle of the op, his breeches, shoes, and stockings discarded on the floor, d me in his arms, with my gown all crumpled and my hair ming down. Geordie's narrow face creased into a censorious own.

"I quit," he said, in the rich tones of the West Highlands. "The nting's one thing—I'm wi' ye there, and ye'll no think other-se—but I'm Free Church and my daddy before me and my andsire before him. Workin' for a Papist is one thing—the pe's coin's as good as any, aye?—but workin' for an immoral pist is another. Do as ye like wi' your own soul, man, but if it's me to orgies in the shop, it's come too far, that's what I say. I it!"

He placed the package precisely in the center of the counter, un on his heel and stalked toward the door. Outside, the Town ock on the Tolbooth began to strike. Geordie turned in the orway to glare accusingly at us.

"And it not even noon yet!" he said. The shop door slammed hind him.

Jamie stared after him for a moment, then sank slowly down to the floor again, laughing so hard, the tears came to his eyes. "And it's not even noon yet!" he repeated, wiping the tears off cheeks. "Oh, God, Geordie!" He rocked back and forth, asping his knees with both hands.

I couldn't help laughing myself, though I was rather worried. "I didn't mean to cause you trouble," I said. "Will he come ck, do you think?"

He sniffed and wiped his face carelessly on the tail of his shirt. "Oh, aye. He lives just across the way, in Wickham Wynd. I'll and see him in a bit, and . . . and explain," he said. He ked at me, realization dawning, and added, "God knows w!" It looked for a minute as though he might start laughing ain, but he mastered the impulse and stood up.

"Have you got another pair of breeches?" I asked, picking up discarded ones and draping them across the counter to dry.

"Aye, I have—upstairs. Wait a bit, though." He snaked a long n into the cupboard beneath the counter, and came out with a

neatly lettered notice that said GONE OUT. Attaching this to ʼ
outside of the door, and firmly bolting the inside, he turned to r

"Will ye step upstairs wiʼ me?" he said. He crooked an aʼ
invitingly, eyes sparkling. "If ye dinna think it immoral?"

"Why not?" I said. The impulse to explode in laughter was jʼ
below the surface, sparkling in my blood like champagne. "Weʼ
married, arenʼt we?"

The upstairs was divided into two rooms, one on either side
the landing, and a small privy closet just off the landing itself. ʼ
back room was plainly devoted to storage for the printing buʼ
ness; the door was propped open, and I could see wooden craʼ
filled with books, towering bundles of pamphlets neatly tied wʼ
twine, barrels of alcohol and powdered ink, and a jumble of odʼ
looking hardware that I assumed must be spare parts for a printʼ
press.

The front room was spare as a monkʼs cell. There was a chesʼ
drawers with a pottery candlestick on it, a washstand, a stool, ʼ
a narrow cot, little more than a camp bed. I let out my breath whʼ
I saw it, only then realizing that I had been holding it. He slʼ
alone.

A quick glance around confirmed that there was no sign oʼ
feminine presence in the room, and my heart began to beat witʼ
normal rhythm again. Plainly no one lived here but Jamie; he ʼ
pushed aside the curtain that blocked off a corner of the room, ʼ
the row of pegs revealed there supported no more than a coupleʼ
shirts, a coat and long waistcoat in sober gray, a gray wool cloʼ
and the spare pair of breeches he had come to fetch.

He had his back turned to me as he tucked in his shirt ʼ
fastened the new breeches, but I could see the self-consciousnʼ
in the tense line of his shoulders. I could feel a similar tensionʼ
the back of my own neck. Given a moment to recover from ʼ
shock of seeing each other, we were both stricken now with sʼ
ness. I saw his shoulders straighten and then he turned aroundʼ
face me. The hysterical laughter had left us, and the tears, thouʼ
his face still showed the marks of so much sudden feeling, anʼ
knew mine did, too.

"Itʼs verra fine to see ye, Claire," he said softly. "I thougʼ
never . . . well." He shrugged slightly, as though to ease ʼ
tightness of the linen shirt across his shoulders. He swallowʼ
then met my eyes directly.

"The child?" he said. Everything he felt was evident on his face; urgent hope, desperate fear, and the struggle to contain both. I smiled at him, and put out my hand. "Come here."

I had thought long and hard about what I might bring with me, should my journey through the stones succeed. Given my previous brush with accusations of witchcraft, I had been very careful. But there was one thing I had had to bring, no matter what the consequences might be if anyone saw them.

I pulled him down to sit beside me on the cot, and pulled out of my pocket the small rectangular package I had done up with such care in Boston. I undid its waterproof wrapping, and thrust its contents into his hands. "There," I said.

He took them from me, gingerly, like one handling an unknown and possibly dangerous substance. His big hands framed the photographs for a moment, holding them confined. Brianna's round newborn face was oblivious between his fingers, tiny fists curled in her blanket, slanted eyes closed in the new exhaustion of existence, her small mouth slightly open in sleep.

I looked up at his face; it was absolutely blank with shock. He held the pictures close to his chest, unmoving, wide-eyed and staring as though he had just been transfixed by a crossbow bolt through the heart—as I supposed he had.

"Your daughter sent you this," I said. I turned his blank face toward me and gently kissed him on the mouth. That broke the trance; he blinked and his face came to life again.

"My . . . she . . ." His voice was hoarse with shock. "Daughter. My daughter. She . . . knows?"

"She does. Look at the rest." I slid the first picture from his grasp, revealing the snapshot of Brianna, uproariously festooned with the icing of her first birthday cake, a four-toothed smile of fiendish triumph on her face as she waved a new plush rabbit overhead.

Jamie made a small inarticulate sound, and his fingers loosened. I took the small stack of photographs from him and gave them back, one at a time.

Brianna at two, stubby in her snowsuit, cheeks round and flushed as apples, feathery hair wisping from under her hood.

Bree at four, hair a smooth bell-shaped gleam as she sat, one ankle propped on the opposite knee as she smiled for the photographer, proper and poised in a white pinafore.

At five, in proud possession of her first lunchbox, waiting
board the school bus to kindergarten.

"She wouldn't let me go with her; she wanted to go alo
She's very b-brave, not afraid of anything . . ." I felt ha
choked as I explained, displayed, pointed to the changing ima?
that fell from his hands and slid down to the floor as he began
snatch each new picture.

"Oh, God!" he said, at the picture of Bree at ten, sitting on
kitchen floor with her arms around Smoky, the big Newfoundla
That one was in color; her hair a brilliant shimmer against
dog's shiny black coat.

His hands were shaking so badly that he couldn't hold
pictures anymore; I had to show him the last few—Bree fu
grown, laughing at a string of fish she'd caught; standing a
window in secretive contemplation; red-faced and tousled, lean
on the handle of the ax she had been using to split kindling. Th
showed her face in all the moods I could capture, always that fa
long-nosed and wide-mouthed, with those high, broad, flat Vik
cheekbones and slanted eyes—a finer-boned, more delicate v
sion of her father's, of the man who sat on the cot beside r
mouth working wordlessly, and the tears running soundless do
his own cheeks.

He splayed a hand out over the photographs, trembling fing
not quite touching the shiny surfaces, and then he turned
leaned toward me, slowly, with the improbable grace of a tall t
falling. He buried his face in my shoulder and went very quie
and thoroughly to pieces.

I held him to my breast, arms tight around the broad, shak
shoulders, and my own tears fell on his hair, making small d
patches in the ruddy waves. I pressed my cheek against the top
his head, and murmured small incoherent things to him as tho
he were Brianna. I thought to myself that perhaps it was I
surgery—even when an operation is done to repair existing da
age, the healing still is painful.

"Her name?" He raised his face at last, wiping his nose on
back of his hand. He picked up the pictures again, gently,
though they might disintegrate at his touch. "What did ye na
her?"

"Brianna," I said proudly.

"Brianna?" he said, frowning at the pictures. "What an awful ame for a wee lassie!"

I started back as though struck. "It is not awful!" I snapped. It's a beautiful name, and besides you *told* me to name her that! Vhat do you mean, it's an awful name?"

"*I* told ye to name her that?" He blinked.

"You most certainly did! When we—when we—the last time I w you." I pressed my lips tightly together so I wouldn't cry gain. After a moment, I had mastered my feelings enough to add, You told me to name the baby for your father. His name was rian, wasn't it?"

"Aye, it was." A smile seemed to be struggling for dominance the other emotions on his face. "Aye," he said. "Aye, you're ght, I did. It's only—well, I thought it would be a boy, is all."

"And you're sorry she wasn't?" I glared at him, and began atching up the scattered photographs. His hands on my arms opped me.

"No," he said. "No, I'm not sorry. Of course not!" His mouth itched slightly. "But I willna deny she's the hell of a shock, ssenach. So are you."

I sat still for a moment, looking at him. I had had months to epare myself for this, and still my knees felt weak and my omach was clenched in knots. He had been taken completely aawares by my appearance; little wonder if he was reeling a bit der the impact.

"I expect I am. Are you sorry I came?" I asked. I swallowed. Do—do you want me to go?"

His hands clamped my arms so tightly that I let out a small yelp. ealizing that he was hurting me, he loosened his grip, but kept a m hold nonetheless. His face had gone quite pale at the sugges- on. He took a deep breath and let it out.

"No," he said, with an approximation of calmness. "I don't. –" He broke off abruptly, jaw clamped. "No," he said again, ry definitely.

His hand slid down to take hold of mine, and with the other he ached down to pick up the photographs. He laid them on his ee, looking at them with head bent, so I couldn't see his face.

"Brianna," he said softly. "Ye say it wrong, Sassenach. Her me is Brianna." He said it with an odd Highland lilt, so that the

first syllable was accented, the second barely pronounced. *Bre*
anah.

.''*Bree*anah?'' I said, amused. He nodded, eyes still fixed on t
pictures.

"Brianna," he said. "It's a beautiful name."

"Glad you like it," I said.

He glanced up then, and met my eyes, with a smile hidden in t
corner of his long mouth.

"Tell me about her." One forefinger traced the pudgy featu
of the baby in the snowsuit. "What was she like as a wee lassi
What did she first say, when she learned to speak?"

His hand drew me closer, and I nestled close to him. He w
big, and solid, and smelled of clean linen and ink, with a wa
male scent that was as exciting to me as it was familiar.

" 'Dog,' " I said. "That was her first word. The second o
was 'No!' "

The smile widened across his face. "Aye, they all learn that o
fast. She'll like dogs, then?" He fanned the pictures out like car
searching out the one with Smoky. "That's a lovely dog with H
there. What sort is that?"

"A Newfoundland." I bent forward to thumb through the p
tures. "There's another one here with a puppy a friend of mi
gave her . . ."

The dim gray daylight had begun to fade, and the rain had be
pattering on the roof for some time, before our talk was int
rupted by a fierce subterranean growl emanating from below t
lace-trimmed bodice of my Jessica Gutenburg. It had been a lo
time since the peanut butter sandwich.

"Hungry, Sassenach?" Jamie asked, rather unnecessarily
thought.

"Well, yes, now that you mention it. Do you still keep food
the top drawer?" When we were first married, I had developed t
habit of keeping small bits of food on hand, to supply his consta
appetite, and the top drawer of any chest of drawers where
lived generally provided a selection of rolls, small cakes, or bits
cheese.

He laughed and stretched. "Aye, I do. There's no much the
just now, though, but a couple of stale bannocks. Better I take
down to the tavern, and—" The look of happiness engendered
perusing the photographs of Brianna faded, to be replaced by

ok of alarm. He glanced quickly at the window, where a soft
rplish color was beginning to replace the pale gray, and the look
alarm deepened.

"The tavern! Christ! I've forgotten Mr. Willoughby!" He was
his feet and groping in the chest for fresh stockings before I
uld say anything. Coming out with the stockings in one hand
d two bannocks in the other, he tossed the latter into my lap and
down on the stool, hastily yanking on the former.

"Who's Mr. Willoughby?" I bit into a bannock, scattering
umbs.

"Damn," he said, more to himself than me, "I said I'd come
him at noon, but it went out o' my head entirely! It must be
ir o'clock by now!"

"It is; I heard the clock strike a little while ago."

"Damn!" he repeated. Thrusting his feet into a pair of pewter-
ckled shoes, he rose, snatched his coat from the peg, and then
used at the door.

"You'll come wi' me?" he asked anxiously.

I licked my fingers and rose, pulling my cloak around me.

"Wild horses couldn't stop me," I assured him.

25

House of Jo

"Who is Mr. Willoughby?" I inquired, as we paus
under the arch of Carfax Close to peer out at
cobbled street.

"Er . . . he's an associate of mine," Jamie replied, with
wary glance at me. "Best put up your hood, it's pouring."

It was in fact raining quite hard; sheets of water fell from
arch overhead and gurgled down the gutters, cleansing the stre
of sewage and rubbish. I took a deep breath of the damp, clean
feeling exhilarated by the wildness of the evening and the clo
ness of Jamie, tall and powerful by my side. I had found him. I h
found him, and whatever unknowns life now held, they did
seem to matter. I felt reckless and indestructible.

I took his hand and squeezed it; he looked down and smiled
me, squeezing back.

"Where are we going?"

"To The World's End." The roar of the water made conver
tion difficult. Without further speech, Jamie took me by the elb
to help me across the cobbles, and we plunged down the st
incline of the Royal Mile.

Luckily, the tavern called The World's End was no more tha
hundred yards away; hard as the rain was, the shoulders of
cloak were scarcely more than dampened when we ducked
neath the low lintel and into the narrow entry-hall.

The main room was crowded, warm and smoky, a snug ref
from the storm outside. There were a few women seated on
benches that ran along the walls, but most of the patrons w

n. Here and there was a man in the well-kept dress of a mer-
nt, but most men with homes to go to were in them at this hour;
 tavern hosted a mix of soldiers, wharf rats, laborers and ap-
ntices, with here and there the odd drunkard for variety.

Heads looked up at our appearance, and there were shouts of
eting, and a general shuffling and pushing, to make room at one
the long tables. Clearly Jamie was well-known in The World's
d. A few curious glances came my way, but no one said any-
ng. I kept my cloak pulled close around me, and followed Jamie
ough the crush of the tavern.

'Nay, mistress, we'll no be stayin','' he said to the young
 maid who bustled forward with an eager smile. "I've only
ne for himself."

The girl rolled her eyes. "Oh, aye, and no before time, either!
ther's put him doon the stair."

'Aye, I'm late," Jamie said apologetically. "I had . . . busi-
s that kept me."

The girl looked curiously at me, but then shrugged and dimpled
 Jamie.

'Och, it's no trouble, sir. Harry took him doon a stoup of
ndy, and we've heard little more of him since."

'Brandy, eh?'' Jamie sounded resigned. "Still awake, is he?''
 reached into the pocket of his coat and brought out a small
ther pouch, from which he extracted several coins, which he
pped into the girl's outstretched hand.

'I expect so," she said cheerfully, pocketing the money. "I
rd him singin' a whiles since. Thankee, sir!''

With a nod, Jamie ducked under the lintel at the back of the
m, motioning me to follow. A tiny, barrel-ceilinged kitchen lay
ind the main taproom, with a huge kettle of what looked like
ter stew simmering in the hearth. It smelled delicious, and I
ld feel my mouth starting to water at the rich aroma. I hoped
could do our business with Mr. Willoughby over supper.

A fat woman in a grimy bodice and skirt knelt by the hearth,
fing billets of wood into the fire. She glanced up at Jamie and
ded, but made no move to get up.

Ie lifted a hand in response, and headed for a small wooden
r in the corner. He lifted the bolt and swung the door open to
al a dark stairway leading down, apparently into the bowels of

the earth. A light flickered somewhere far below, as though el
were mining diamonds beneath the tavern.

Jamie's shoulders filled the narrow stairwell, obstructing
view of whatever lay below us. When he stepped out into the op
space below, I could see heavy oak rafters, and a row of hu
casks standing on a long plank set on hurdles against the sto
wall.

Only a single torch burned at the foot of the stair. The cel
was shadowy, and its cavelike depths seemed quite deserted
listened, but didn't hear anything but the muffled racket of
tavern upstairs. Certainly no singing.

"Are you sure he's down here?" I bent to peer beneath the r
of casks, wondering whether perhaps the bibulous Mr. Willough
had been overcome with an excess of brandy and sought so
secluded spot to sleep it off.

"Oh, aye." Jamie sounded grim, but resigned. "The wee b
ger's hiding, I expect. He knows I dinna like it when he drinks
public houses."

I raised an eyebrow at this, but he merely strode into the sh
ows, muttering under his breath. The cellar stretched some w
and I could hear him, shuffling cautiously in the dark, long aft
lost sight of him. Left in the circle of torchlight near the stair
looked around with interest.

Besides the row of casks, there were a number of wooden cra
stacked near the center of the room, against an odd little chunk
wall that stood by itself, rising some five feet out of the ce
floor, running back into the darkness.

I had heard of this feature of the tavern when we had stayed
Edinburgh twenty years before with His Highness Prince Char
but what with one thing and another, I had never actually see
before. It was the remnant of a wall constructed by the city fath
of Edinburgh, following the disastrous Battle of Flodden Fiel
1513. Concluding—with some justice—that no good was likely
come of association with the English to the south, they had bui
wall defining both the city limits and the limit of the civili
world of Scotland. Hence "The World's End," and the name
stuck through several versions of the tavern that had eventu
been built upon the remnants of the old Scots' wishful thinki

"Damned little bugger." Jamie emerged from the shadow

obweb stuck in his hair, and a frown on his face. "He must be
ack of the wall."

Turning, he put his hands to his mouth and shouted something.
t sounded like incomprehensible gibberish—not even like Gaelic.
dug a finger dubiously into one ear, wondering whether the trip
hrough the stones had deranged my hearing.

A sudden movement caught the corner of my eye, causing me to
ook up, just in time to see a ball of brilliant blue fly off the top of
he ancient wall and smack Jamie squarely between the shoulder-
lades.

He hit the cellar floor with a frightful thump, and I dashed
oward his fallen body.

"Jamie! Are you all right?"

The prone figure made a number of coarse remarks in Gaelic
nd sat up slowly, rubbing his forehead, which had struck the
one floor a glancing blow. The blue ball, meanwhile, had re-
olved itself into the figure of a very small Chinese, who was
iggling in unhinged delight, sallow round face shining with glee
nd brandy.

"Mr. Willoughby, I presume?" I said to this apparition, keep-
g a wary eye out for further tricks.

He appeared to recognize his name, for he grinned and nodded
adly at me, his eyes creased to gleaming slits. He pointed to
imself, said something in Chinese, and then sprang into the air
nd executed several backflips in rapid succession, bobbing up on
is feet in beaming triumph at the end.

"Bloody flea." Jamie got up, wiping the skinned palms of his
ands gingerly on his coat. With a quick snatch, he caught hold of
he Chinaman's collar and jerked him off his feet.

"Come on," he said, parking the little man on the stairway and
rodding him firmly in the back. "We need to be going, and quick
ow." In response, the little blue-clad figure promptly sagged into
mpness, looking like a bag of laundry resting on the step.

"He's all right when he's sober," Jamie explained apologeti-
lly to me, as he hoisted the Chinese over one shoulder. "But he
ally shouldna drink brandy. He's a terrible sot."

"So I see. Where on earth did you get him?" Fascinated, I
llowed Jamie up the stairs, watching Mr. Willoughby's pigtail
ving back and forth like a metronome across the felted gray wool
Jamie's cloak.

"On the docks." But before he could explain further, the doo above opened, and we were back in the tavern's kitchen. The stou proprietor saw us emerge, and came toward us, her fat cheek puffed with disapproval.

"Now, Mr. Malcolm," she began, frowning, "ye ken verr weel as you're welcome here, and ye'll ken as weel that I'm no fussy woman, such not bein' a convenient attitude whe maintainin' a public hoose. But I've telt ye before, yon wee yellow mannie is no—"

"Aye, ye've mentioned it, Mrs. Patterson," Jamie interrupted He dug in his pocket and came up with a coin, which he handed t the stout publican with a bow. "And your forbearance is muc appreciated. It willna happen again. I hope," he added under hi breath. He placed his hat on his head, bowed again to Mrs. Patterson, and ducked under the low lintel into the main tavern.

Our reentry caused another stir, but a negative one this time People fell silent, or muttered half-heard curses under their breath I gathered that Mr. Willoughby was perhaps not this local's mo popular patron.

Jamie edged his way through the crowd, which gave way relu tantly. I followed as best I could, trying not to meet anyone's eye and trying not to breathe. Unused as I was to the unhygieni miasma of the eighteenth century, the stench of so many u washed bodies in a small space was nearly overwhelming.

Near the door, though, we met trouble, in the person of a buxo young woman whose dress was a notch above the sober drab of th landlady and her daughter. Her neckline was a notch lower, and hadn't much trouble in guessing her principal occupation. Al sorbed in flirtatious conversation with a couple of apprentice la when we emerged from the kitchen, she looked up as we passe and sprang to her feet with a piercing scream, knocking over a cu of ale in the process.

"It's him!" she screeched, pointing a wavering finger at Jami "The foul fiend!" Her eyes seemed to have trouble focusing; gathered that the spilled ale wasn't her first of the evening, early it was.

Her companions stared at Jamie with interest, the more so whe the young lady advanced, stabbing her finger in the air like o leading a chorus. "Him! The wee poolie I telt ye of—him that d the disgustin' thing to me!"

I joined the rest of the crowd in looking at Jamie with interest, but quickly realized, as did they, that the young woman was not talking to him, but rather to his burden.

"Ye neffit qurd!" she yelled, addressing her remarks to the seat of Mr. Willoughby's blue-silk trousers. "Hiddie-pyke! Slug!"

This spectacle of maidenly distress was rousing her companions; one, a tall, burly lad, stood up, fists clenched, and leaned on the table, eyes gleaming with ale and aggro.

"S'him, aye? Shall I knivvle him for ye, Maggie?"

"Dinna try, laddie," Jamie advised him shortly, shifting his burden for better balance. "Drink your drink, and we'll be gone."

"Oh, aye? And you're the little ked's pimpmaster, are ye?" The lad sneered unbecomingly, his flushed face turning in my direction. "At least your other whore's no yellow—le's ha' a look at er." He flung out a paw and grabbed the edge of my cloak, revealing the low bodice of the Jessica Gutenburg.

"Looks pink enough to me," said his friend, with obvious approval. "Is she like it all over?" Before I could move, he snatched at the bodice, catching the edge of the lace. Not designed for the rigors of eighteenth-century life, the flimsy fabric ripped halfway down the side, exposing quite a lot of pink.

"Leave off, ye whoreson!" Jamie swung about, eyes blazing, ee fist doubled in threat.

"Who ye miscallin', ye skrae-shankit skoot?" The first youth, unable to get out from behind the table, leapt on top of it, and launched himself at Jamie, who neatly sidestepped the lad, allowing him to crash face-first into the wall.

Jamie took one giant step toward the table, brought his fist down hard on top of the other apprentice's head, making the lad's jaw go back, then grabbed me by the hand and dragged me out the door.

"Come on!" he said, grunting as he shifted the Chinaman's slippery form for a better grip. "They'll be after us any moment!"

They were; I could hear the shouting as the more boisterous elements poured out of the tavern into the street behind us. Jamie took the first opening off the Royal Mile, into a narrow, dark wynd, and we splashed through mud and unidentifiable slops, ducked through an archway, and down another twisting alleyway that seemed to lead through the bowels of Edinburgh. Dark walls flashed past, and splintered wooden doors, and then we were round a corner, in a small courtyard, where we paused for breath.

"What . . . on earth . . . did he do?" I gasped. I couldn
imagine what the little Chinese could have done to a strappi
young wench like the recent Maggie. From all appearances, sl
could have squashed him like a fly.

"Well, it's the feet, ye ken," Jamie explained, with a glance
resigned irritation at Mr. Willoughby.

"Feet?" I glanced involuntarily at the tiny Chinese man's fee
neat miniatures shod in felt-soled black satin.

"Not his," Jamie said, catching my glance. "The women's.

"What women?" I asked.

"Well, so far it's only been whores," he said, glancing throug
the archway in search of pursuit, "but ye canna tell what he ma
try. No judgment," he explained briefly. "He's a heathen."

"I see," I said, though so far, I didn't. "What—"

"There they are!" A shout at the far end of the alley interrupte
my question.

"Damn, I thought they'd give it up. Come on, this way!"

We were off once more, down an alley, back onto the Roy
Mile, a few steps down the hill, and back into a close. I could he
shouts and cries behind us on the main street, but Jamie graspe
my arm and jerked me after him through an open doorway, into
yard full of casks, bundles, and crates. He looked frantical
about, then heaved Mr. Willoughby's limp body into a large barr
filled with rubbish. Pausing only long enough to drop a piece
canvas on the Chinese's head for concealment, he dragged n
behind a wagon loaded with crates, and pulled me down besi
him.

I was gasping from the unaccustomed exertion, and my hea
was racing from the adrenaline of fear. Jamie's face was flushe
with cold and exercise, and his hair was sticking up in sever
directions, but he was scarcely breathing hard.

"Do you do this sort of thing all the time?" I asked, pressing
hand to my bosom in a vain effort to make my heart slow dow

"Not exactly," he said, peering warily over the top of th
wagon in search of pursuit.

The echo of pounding feet came faintly, then disappeared, a
everything was quiet, save for the patter of rain on the boxes abo
us.

"They've gone past. We'd best stay here a bit, to make sur
though." He lifted down a crate for me to sit on, procured anoth

or himself, and sat down sighing, pushing the loose hair out of his ace with one hand.

He gave me a lopsided smile. "I'm sorry, Sassenach. I didna aink it would be quite so . . ."

"Eventful?" I finished for him. I smiled back and pulled out a andkerchief to wipe a drop of moisture from the end of my nose. "It's all right." I glanced at the large barrel, where stirrings and ustlings indicated that Mr. Willoughby was returning to a more or ess conscious state. "Er . . . how do you know about the feet?"

"He told me; he's a taste for the drink, ye ken," he explained, vith a glance at the barrel where his colleague lay concealed. "And when he's taken a drop too much, he starts talkin' about vomen's feet, and all the horrible things he wants to do wi' aem."

"What sort of horrible things can you do with a foot?" I was ascinated. "Surely the possibilities are limited."

"No, they aren't," Jamie said grimly. "But it isna something I vant to be talking about in the public street."

A faint singsong came from the depths of the barrel behind us. t was hard to tell, amid the natural inflections of the language, but thought Mr. Willoughby was asking a question of some sort.

"Shut up, ye wee poutworm," Jamie said rudely. "Another vord, and I'll walk on your damn face myself; see how ye like aat." There was a high-pitched giggle, and the barrel fell silent.

"He wants someone to walk on his face?" I asked.

"Aye. You," Jamie said briefly. He shrugged apologetically, nd his cheeks flushed a deeper red. "I hadna time to tell him who e were."

"Does he speak English?"

"Oh, aye, in a way, but not many people understand him when e does. I mostly talk to him in Chinee."

I stared at him. "You speak Chinese?"

He shrugged, tilting his head with a faint smile. "Well, I speak Chinee about as well as Mr. Willoughby speaks English, but then, e hasna got all that much choice in who he talks to, so he puts up vi' me."

My heart showed signs of returning to normal, and I leaned ack against the wagon bed, my hood farther forward against the rizzle.

"Where on earth did he get a name like Willoughby?" I asked.

While I was curious about the Chinese, I was even more curiou
about what a respectable Edinburgh printer was doing with one
but I felt a certain hesitance in prying into Jamie's life. Freshl
returned from the supposed dead—or its equivalent—I coul
hardly demand to know all the details of his life on the spot.

Jamie rubbed a hand across his nose. "Aye, well. It's only tha
his real name's Yi Tien Cho. He says it means 'Leans agains
heaven.' "

"Too hard for the local Scots to pronounce?" Knowing th
insular nature of most Scots, I wasn't surprised that they wer
disinclined to venture into strange linguistic waters. Jamie, wit
his gift for tongues, was a genetic anomaly.

He smiled, teeth a white gleam in the gathering darknes
"Well, it's no that, so much. It's only, if ye say his name just
wee bit off, like, it sounds verra much like a coarse word in Gaeli
I thought Willoughby would maybe do better."

"I see." I thought perhaps under the circumstances, I shouldn
ask just what the indelicate Gaelic word was. I glanced over m
shoulder, but the coast seemed clear.

Jamie caught the gesture and rose, nodding. "Aye, we can g
now; the lads will ha' gone back to the tavern by now."

"Won't we have to pass by The World's End on the way back
the printshop?" I asked dubiously. "Or is there a back way?"
was full dark by now, and the thought of stumbling through th
middens and muddy back passages of Edinburgh was unappea
ing.

"Ah . . . no. We willna be going to the printshop." I couldn
see his face, but there seemed a certain reserve in his manne
Perhaps he had a residence somewhere else in the city? I felt
certain hollowness at the prospect; the room above the printsho
was very clearly a monk's cell; but perhaps he had an entire hou
somewhere else—with a family in it? There had been no time f
any but the most essential exchange of information at the prin
shop. I had no way of knowing what he had done over the la
twenty years, or what he might now be doing.

Still, he had plainly been glad—to say the least—to see me, an
the air of frowning consideration he now bore might well have
do with his inebriated associate, rather than with me.

He bent over the barrel, saying something in Scots-accente
Chinese. This was one of the odder sounds I had ever heard; rath

ke the squeaks of a bagpipe tuning up, I thought, vastly enter-
ained by the performance.

Whatever he'd said, Mr. Willoughby replied to it volubly, inter-
upting himself with giggles and snorts. At last, the little Chinese
limbed out of the barrel, his diminutive figure silhouetted by the
ght of a distant lantern in the alleyway. He sprang down with fair
gility and promptly prostrated himself on the ground before me.

Bearing in mind what Jamie had told me about the feet, I took a
uick step back, but Jamie laid a reassuring hand on my arm.

"Nay, it's all right, Sassenach," he said. "He's only makin'
mends for his disrespect to ye earlier."

"Oh. Well." I looked dubiously at Mr. Willoughby, who was
abbling something to the ground under his face. At a loss for the
roper etiquette, I stooped down and patted him on the head.
vidently that was all right, for he leapt to his feet and bowed to
ie several times, until Jamie told him impatiently to stop, and we
nade our way back to the Royal Mile.

The building Jamie led us to was discreetly hidden down a
mall close just above the Kirk of the Canongate, perhaps a quar-
r-mile above Holyrood Palace. I saw the lanterns mounted by the
ates of the palace below, and shivered slightly at the sight. We
ad lived with Charles Stuart in the palace for nearly five weeks,
 the early, victorious phase of his short career. Jamie's uncle,
'olum MacKenzie, had died there.

The door opened to Jamie's knock, and all thoughts of the past
anished. The woman who stood peering out at us, candle in hand,
as petite, dark-haired, and elegant. Seeing Jamie, she drew him
 with a glad cry, and kissed his cheek in greeting. My insides
ueezed tight as a fist, but then relaxed again, as I heard him
reet her as "Madame Jeanne." Not what one would call a wife—
or yet, I hoped, a mistress.

Still, there was something about the woman that made me un-
asy. She was clearly French, though she spoke English well—not
 odd; Edinburgh was a seaport, and a fairly cosmopolitan city.
he was dressed soberly, but richly, in heavy silk cut with a flair,
ut she wore a good deal more rouge and powder than the average
cotswoman. What disturbed me was the way she was looking at
e—frowning, with a palpable air of distaste.

"Monsieur Fraser," she said, touching Jamie on the shoulder

with a possessive air that I didn't like at all, "if I might have word in private with you?"

Jamie, handing his cloak to the maid who came to fetch it, too a quick look at me, and read the situation at once.

"Of course, Madame Jeanne," he said courteously, reachir out a hand to draw me forward. "But first—allow me to introdu my wife, Madame Fraser."

My heart stopped beating for a moment, then resumed, with force that I was sure was audible to everyone in the small ent hall. Jamie's eyes met mine, and he smiled, the grip of his finge tightening on my arm.

"Your . . . wife?" I couldn't tell whether astonishment horror was more pronounced on Madame Jeanne's face. "B Monsieur Fraser . . . you bring her *here*? I thought . . . woman . . . well enough, but to insult our own *jeunes filles* is n good . . . but then . . . a *wife* . . ." Her mouth hung open u becomingly, displaying several decayed molars. Then she shoc herself suddenly back into an attitude of flustered poise, and i clined her head to me with an attempt at graciousness. *"Bonsc . . .* Madame."

"Likewise, I'm sure," I said politely.

"Is my room ready, Madame?" Jamie said. Without waiting f an answer, he turned toward the stair, taking me with him. "V shall be spending the night."

He glanced back at Mr. Willoughby, who had come in with u He had sat down at once on the floor, where he sat dripping rain, dreamy expression on his small, flat face.

"Er . . . ?" Jamie made a small questioning motion towa Mr. Willoughby, his eyebrows raised at Madame Jeanne. S stared at the little Chinese for a moment as though wonderir where he had come from, then, returned to herself, clapped b hands briskly for the maid.

"See if Mademoiselle Josie is at liberty, if you please, Pa line," she said. "And then fetch up hot water and fresh towels f Monsieur Fraser and his . . . wife." She spoke the word with sort of stunned amazement, as though she still didn't quite belie it.

"Oh, and one more thing, if you would be so kind, Madame? Jamie leaned over the banister, smiling down at her. "My wi will require a fresh gown; she has had an unfortunate accident

er wardrobe. If you could provide something suitable by morn-
ng? Thank you, Madame Jeanne. *Bonsoir*!''

I didn't speak, as I followed him up four flights of winding
tairs to the top of the house. I was much too busy thinking, my
nind in a whirl. "Pimpmaster," the lad in the pub had called him.
But surely that was only an epithet—such a thing was absolutely
npossible. For the Jamie Fraser I had known, it was impossible, I
orrected myself, looking up at the broad shoulders under the dark
ray serge coat. But for this man?

I didn't know quite what I had been expecting, but the room was
uite ordinary, small and clean—though that was extraordinary,
ome to think of it—furnished with a stool, a simple bed and chest
f drawers, upon which stood a basin and ewer and a clay candle-
tick with a beeswax candle, which Jamie lighted from the taper
e had carried up.

He shucked off his wet coat and draped it carelessly on the
:ool, then sat down on the bed to remove his wet shoes.

"God," he said, "I'm starving. I hope the cook's not gone to
ed yet."

"Jamie . . ." I said.

"Take off your cloak, Sassenach," he said, noticing me still
anding against the door. "You're soaked."

"Yes. Well . . . yes." I swallowed, then went on. "There's
ıst . . . er . . . Jamie, why have you got a regular room in a
rothel?" I burst out.

He rubbed his chin, looking mildly embarrassed. "I'm sorry,
assenach," he said. "I know it wasna right to bring ye here, but
was the only place I could think of where we might get your
:ess mended at short notice, besides finding a hot supper. And
en I had to put Mr. Willoughby where he wouldna get in more
ouble, and as we had to come here anyway . . . well"—he
anced at the bed—"it's a good deal more comfortable than my
ıt at the printshop. But perhaps it was a poor idea. We can leave,
ye feel it's not—"

"I don't mind about that," I interrupted. "The question is—
hy have you got a room in a brothel? Are you such a good
ıstomer that—"

"A customer?" He stared up at me, eyebrows raised. "Here?
od, Sassenach, what d'ye think I am?"

"Damned if I know," I said. "That's why I'm asking. Are yo
going to answer my question?"

He stared at his stocking feet for a moment, wiggling his toe
on the floorboard. At last he looked up at me, and answere
calmly, "I suppose so. I'm not a customer of Jeanne's, but she's
customer of mine—and a good one. She keeps a room for m
because I'm often abroad late on business, and I'd as soon have
place I can come to where I can have food and a bed at any hou
and privacy. The room is part of my arrangement with her."

I had been holding my breath. Now I let out about half of i
"All right," I said. "Then I suppose the next question is, wha
business has the owner of a brothel got with a printer?" Th
absurd thought that perhaps he printed advertising circulars fo
Madame Jeanne flitted through my brain, to be instantly dis
missed.

"Well," he said slowly. "No. I dinna think that's the ques
tion."

"It's not?"

"No." With one fluid move, he was off the bed and standing i
front of me, close enough for me to have to look up into his face.
had a sudden urge to take a step backward, but didn't, largel
because there wasn't room.

"The question is, Sassenach, why have ye come back?" he sai
softly.

"That's a hell of a question to ask me!" My palms pressed fl
against the rough wood of the door. "Why do you *think* I cam
back, damn you?"

"I dinna ken." The soft Scottish voice was cool, but even in th
dim light, I could see the pulse throbbing in the open throat of h
shirt.

"Did ye come to be my wife again? Or only to bring me wor
of my daughter?" As though he sensed that his nearness unnerve
me, he turned away suddenly, moving toward the window, whe
the shutters creaked in the wind.

"You are the mother of my child—for that alone, I owe ye m
soul—for the knowledge that my life hasna been in vain—that m
child is safe." He turned again to face me, blue eyes intent.

"But it has been a time, Sassenach, since you and I were on
You'll have had your life—then—and I have had mine here. You'

now nothing of what I've done, or been. Did ye come now because ye wanted to—or because ye felt ye must?''

My throat felt tight, but I met his eyes.

"I came now because before . . . I thought you were dead. I
thought you'd died at Culloden.''

His eyes dropped to the windowsill, where he picked at a splinter.

"Aye, I see," he said softly. "Well . . . I meant to be dead.''
He smiled, without humor, eyes intent on the splinter. "I tried
hard enough." He looked up at me again.

"How did ye find out I hadna died? Or where I was, come to
that?''

"I had help. A young historian named Roger Wakefield found
the records; he tracked you to Edinburgh. And when I saw 'A.
Malcolm,' I knew . . . I thought . . . it might be you," I ended
lamely. Time enough for the details later.

"Aye, I see. And then ye came. But still . . . why?''

I stared at him without speaking for a moment. As though he
felt the need of air, or perhaps only for something to do, he
fumbled with the latch of the shutters and thrust them halfway
open, flooding the room with the sound of rushing water, and the
cold, fresh smell of rain.

"Are you trying to tell me you don't want me to stay?" I said,
finally. "Because if so . . . I mean, I know you'll have a life now
. . . maybe you have . . . other ties . . .'' With unnaturally
acute senses, I could hear the small sounds of activity throughout
the house below, even above the rush of the storm, and the pounding of my own heart. My palms were damp, and I wiped them
surreptitiously against my skirt.

He turned from the window to stare at me.

"Christ!" he said. "Not want ye?" His face was pale now, and
his eyes unnaturally bright.

"I have burned for you for twenty years, Sassenach," he said
softly. "Do ye not know that? Jesus!" The breeze stirred the loose
wisps of hair around his face, and he brushed them back impatiently.

"But I'm no the man ye knew, twenty years past, am I?" He
turned away, with a gesture of frustration. "We know each other
now less than we did when we wed.''

"Do you want me to go?" The blood was pounding thickly i
my ears.

"No!" He swung quickly toward me, and gripped my should
tightly, making me pull back involuntarily. "No," he said, mo
quietly. "I dinna want ye to go. I told ye so, and I meant it. B
. . . I must know." He bent his head toward me, his face aliv
with troubled question.

"Do ye want me?" he whispered. "Sassenach, will ye take m
—and risk the man that I am, for the sake of the man ye knew?

I felt a great wave of relief, mingled with fear. It ran from h
hand on my shoulder to the tips of my toes, weakening my joint

"It's a lot too late to ask that," I said, and reached to touch h
cheek, where the rough beard was starting to show. It was so
under my fingers, like stiff plush. "Because I've already risk
everything I had. But whoever you are now, Jamie Fraser—ye
Yes, I do want you."

The light of the candle flame glowed blue in his eyes, as he he
out his hands to me, and I stepped wordless into his embrace.
rested my face against his chest, marveling at the feel of him in n
arms; so big, so solid and warm. Real, after the years of longi
for a ghost I could not touch.

Disentangling himself after a moment, he looked down at m
and touched my cheek, very gently. He smiled slightly.

"You've the devil's own courage, aye? But then, ye alwa
did."

I tried to smile at him, but my lips trembled.

"What about you? How do you know what *I'm* like? You dor
know what I've been doing for the last twenty years, either.
might be a horrible person, for all you know!"

The smile on his lips moved into his eyes, lighting them wi
humor. "I suppose ye might, at that. But, d'ye know, Sassenach-
I dinna think I care?"

I stood looking at him for another minute, then heaved a dee
sigh that popped a few more stitches in my gown.

"Neither do I."

It seemed absurd to be shy with him, but shy I was. The adve
tures of the evening, and his words to me, had opened up t
chasm of reality—those twenty unshared years that gaped betwee
us, and the unknown future that lay beyond. Now we had come
the place where we would begin to know each other again, a

discover whether we were in fact the same two who had once existed as one flesh—and whether we might be one again.

A knock at the door broke the tension. It was a small servingmaid, with a tray of supper. She bobbed shyly to me, smiled at Jamie, and laid both supper—cold meat, hot broth, and warm oatbread with butter—and the fire with a quick and practiced hand, then left us with a murmured "Good e'en to ye."

We ate slowly, talking carefully only of neutral things; I told him how I had made my way from Craigh na Dun to Inverness, and made him laugh with stories of Mr. Graham and Master Georgie. He in turn told me about Mr. Willoughby; how he had found the little Chinese, half-starved and dead drunk, lying behind a row of casks on the docks at Burntisland, one of the shipping ports near Edinburgh.

We said nothing much of ourselves, but as we ate, I became increasingly conscious of his body, watching his fine, long hands as he poured wine and cut meat, seeing the twist of his powerful torso under his shirt, and the graceful line of neck and shoulder as he stooped to retrieve a fallen napkin. Once or twice, I thought I saw his gaze linger on me in the same way—a sort of hesitant avidity—but he quickly glanced away each time, hooding his eyes so that I could not tell what he saw or felt.

As the supper concluded, the same thought was uppermost in both our minds. It could scarcely be otherwise, considering the place in which we found ourselves. A tremor of mingled fear and anticipation shot through me.

At last, he drained his wineglass, set it down, and met my eyes directly.

"Will ye . . ." He stopped, the flush deepening on his features, but met my eyes, swallowed once, and went on. "Will ye come to bed wi' me, then? I mean," he hurried on, "it's cold, and we're both damp, and—"

"And there aren't any chairs," I finished for him. "All right." I pulled my hand loose from his, and turned toward the bed, feeling a queer mix of excitement and hesitance that made my breath come short.

He pulled off his breeches and stockings quickly, then glanced at me.

"I'm sorry, Sassenach; I should have thought ye'd need help wi' your laces."

So he didn't undress women often, I thought, before I coul
stop myself, and my lips curved in a smile at the thought.

"Well, it's not laces," I murmured, "but if you'd give a hand i
the back there . . ." I laid aside my cloak, and turned my back t
him, lifting my hair to expose the neck of the dress.

There was a puzzled silence. Then I felt a finger sliding slow
down the groove of my backbone.

"What's that?" he said, sounding startled.

"It's called a zipper," I said, smiling, though he couldn't s
me. "See the little tab at the top? Just take hold of that, and pull
straight down."

The zipper teeth parted with a muted ripping noise, and th
remnants of Jessica Gutenburg sagged free. I pulled my arms o
of the sleeves and let the dress drop heavily around my fee
turning to face Jamie before I lost my nerve.

He jerked back, startled by this sudden chrysalis-sheddin
Then he blinked, and stared at me.

I stood in front of him in nothing but my shoes and garter
rose-silk stockings. I had an overwhelming urge to snatch th
dress back up, but I resisted it. I stiffened my spine, raised m
chin, and waited.

He didn't say a word. His eyes gleamed in the candlelight as h
moved his head slightly, but he still had that trick of hiding all h
thoughts behind an inscrutable mask.

"Will you bloody say something?" I demanded at last, in
voice that shook only a little.

His mouth opened, but no words came out. He shook his hea
slowly from side to side.

"Jesus," he whispered at last. "Claire . . . you are the mo
beautiful woman I have ever seen."

"You," I said with conviction, "are losing your eyesight. It
probably glaucoma; you're too young for cataracts."

He laughed at that, a little unsteadily, and then I saw that he w
in fact blinded—his eyes shone with moisture, even as he smile
He blinked hard, and held out his hand.

"I," he said, with equal conviction, "ha' got eyes like a haw
and always did. Come here to me."

A little reluctantly, I took his hand, and stepped out of t
inadequate shelter of the remains of my dress. He drew me gen
in, to stand between his knees as he sat on the bed. Then he kiss

me softly, once on each breast, and laid his head between them, his breath coming warm on my bare skin.

"Your breast is like ivory," he said softly, the word almost "breest" in the Highland Scots that always grew broad when he was truly moved. His hand rose to cup one breast, his fingers tanned into darkness against my own pale glow.

"Only to see them, sae full and sae round—Christ, I could lay my head here forever. But to touch ye, my Sassenach . . . you wi' your skin like white velvet, and the sweet long lines of your body . . ." He paused, and I could feel the working of his throat muscles as he swallowed, his hand moving slowly down the curving slope of waist and hip, the swell and taper of buttock and thigh.

"Dear God," he said, still softly. "I couldna look at ye, Sassenach, and keep my hands from you, nor have ye near me, and not want ye." He lifted his head then, and planted a kiss over my heart, then let his hand float down the gentle curve of my belly, lightly tracing the small marks left there by Brianna's birth.

"You . . . really don't mind?" I said hesitantly, brushing my own fingers over my stomach.

He smiled up at me with something half-rueful in his expression. He hesitated for a moment, then drew up the hem of his shirt.

"Do you?" he asked.

The scar ran from midthigh nearly to his groin, an eight-inch length of twisted, whitish tissue. I couldn't repress a gasp at its appearance, and dropped to my knees beside him.

I laid my cheek on his thigh, holding tight to his leg, as though I would keep him now—as I had not been able to keep him then. I could feel the slow, deep pulse of the blood through his femoral artery under my fingers—a bare inch away from the ugly gully of that twisting scar.

"It doesna fright ye, nor sicken ye, Sassenach?" he asked, laying a hand on my hair. I lifted my head and stared up at him.

"Of course not!"

"Aye, well." He reached to touch my stomach, his eyes holding mine. "And if ye bear the scars of your own battles, Sassenach," he said softly, "they dinna trouble me, either."

He lifted me to the bed beside him then, and leaned to kiss me. I kicked off my shoes, and curled my legs up, feeling the warmth of him through his shirt. My hands found the button at the throat fumbling to open it.

"I want to see you."

"Well, it's no much to see, Sassenach," he said, with an uncer tain laugh. "But whatever it is, it's yours—if ye want it."

He pulled the shirt over his head and tossed it on the floor, then leaned back on the palms of his hands, displaying his body.

I didn't know quite what I had been expecting. In fact, the sigh of his naked body took my breath away. He was still tall, o course, and beautifully made, the long bones of his body slee with muscle, elegant with strength. He glowed in the candleligh as though the light came from within him.

He had changed, of course, but the change was subtle; a though he had been put into an oven and baked to a hard finish. H looked as though both muscle and skin had drawn in just a bi grown closer to the bone, so he was more tightly knit; he had neve seemed gawky, but the last hint of boyish looseness had vanished

His skin had darkened slightly, to a pale gold, burned to bronz on face and throat, paling down the length of his body to a pur white, tinged with blue veins, in the hollow of his thighs. Hi pubic hair stood out in a ferocious auburn bush, and it was qui obvious that he had not been lying; he did want me, and ver badly.

My eyes met his, and his mouth quirked suddenly.

"I did say once I would be honest with ye, Sassenach."

I laughed, feeling tears sting my eyes at the same time, a rush o confused emotion surging up in me.

"So did I." I reached toward him, hesitant, and he took m hand. The strength and warmth of it were startling, and I jerke slightly. Then I tightened my grasp, and he rose to his feet, facin me.

We stood still then, awkwardly hesitating. We were intensel aware of each other—how could we not be? It was quite a sma room, and the available atmosphere was completely filled with charge like static electricity, almost strong enough to be visible. had a feeling of empty-bellied terror, like the sort you get at th top of a roller coaster.

"Are you as scared as I am?" I finally said, sounding hoarse my own ears.

He looked me over carefully, and raised one eyebrow.

"I dinna think I can be," he said. "You're covered wi' goose-flesh. Are ye scairt, Sassenach, or only cold?"

"Both," I said, and he laughed.

"Get in, then," he said. He released my hand and bent to turn back the quilt.

I didn't stop shaking when he slid under the quilt beside me, though the heat of his body was a physical shock.

"God, you're not cold!" I blurted. I turned toward him, and the warmth of him shimmered against my skin from head to toes. Instinctively drawn, I pressed close against him, shivering. I could feel my nipples tight and hard against his chest, and the sudden shock of his naked skin against my own.

He laughed a little uncertainly. "No, I'm not. I suppose I must be afraid, aye?" His arms came around me, gently, and I touched his chest, feeling hundreds of tiny goose bumps spring up under my fingertips, among the ruddy curling hairs.

"When we were afraid of each other before," I whispered, "on our wedding night—you held my hands. You said it would be easier if we touched."

He made a small sound as my fingertip found his nipple.

"Aye, I did," he said, sounding breathless. "Lord, touch me like that again." His hands tightened suddenly, holding me against him.

"Touch me," he said again softly, "and let me touch you, my Sassenach." His hand cupped me, stroking, touching, and my breast lay taut and heavy in his palm. I went on trembling, but now he was doing it, too.

"When we wed," he whispered, his breath warm against my cheek, "and I saw ye there, so bonny in your white dress—I couldna think of anything but when we'd be alone, and I could undo your laces and have ye naked, next to me in the bed."

"Do you want me now?" I whispered, and kissed the sun-burned flesh in the hollow above his collarbone. His skin was faintly salty to the taste, and his hair smelled of woodsmoke and pungent maleness.

He didn't answer, but moved abruptly, so I felt the hardness of him, stiff against my belly.

It was terror as much as desire that pressed me close against him. I wanted him, all right; my breasts ached and my belly was tight with it, the unaccustomed rush of arousal slippery between my legs, opening me for him. But as strong as lust, was the desire simply to be taken, to have him master me, quell my doubts in moment of rough usage, take me hard and swiftly enough to make me forget myself.

I could feel the urge to do it tremble in the hands that cupped my buttocks, in the involuntary jerk of his hips, brought up short as he stopped himself.

Do it, I thought, in an agony of apprehension. For God's sake do it now and don't be gentle!

I couldn't say it. I saw the need of it on his face, but he couldn't say it, either; it was both too soon and too late for such words between us.

But we had shared another language, and my body still recalled it. I pressed my hips against him sharply, grasping his, the curve of his buttocks clenched hard under my hands. I turned my face upward, urgent to be kissed, at the same moment that he bent abruptly to kiss me.

My nose hit his forehead with a sickening crunch. My eyes watered profusely as I rolled away from him, clutching my face.

"Ow!"

"Christ, have I hurt ye, Claire?" Blinking away the tears, could see his face, hovering anxiously over me.

"No," I said stupidly. "My nose is broken, though, I think."

"No, it isn't," he said, gently feeling the bridge of my nose. "When ye break your nose, it makes a nasty crunching sound, and ye bleed like a pig. It's all right."

I felt gingerly beneath my nostrils, but he was right; I wasn't bleeding. The pain had receded quickly, too. As I realized that, also realized that he was lying on me, my legs sprawled wide beneath him, his cock just touching me, no more than a hair breadth from the moment of decision.

I saw the realization dawn in his eyes as well. Neither of moved, barely breathing. Then his chest swelled as he took a deep breath, reached and took both my wrists in one hand. He pulled them up, over my head, and held me there, my body arched taut and helpless under him.

"Give me your mouth, Sassenach," he said softly, and bent me. His head blotted out the candlelight, and I saw nothing but dim glow and the darkness of his flesh as his mouth touched mine.

iently, brushing, then pressing, warm, and I opened to him with a
ttle gasp, his tongue seeking mine.

I bit his lip, and he drew back a little, startled.

"Jamie," I said against his lips, my own breath warm between
s. "Jamie!" That was all I could say, but my hips jerked against
im, and jerked again, urging violence. I turned my head and
astened my teeth in the flesh of his shoulder.

He made a small sound deep in his throat and came into me
ard. I was tight as any virgin and cried out, arching under him.

"Don't stop!" I said. "For God's sake, don't stop!"

His body heard me and answered in the same language, his
rasp of my wrists tightening as he plunged hard into me, the
orce of it reaching my womb with each stroke.

Then he let go of my wrists and half-fell on me, the weight of
im pinning me to the bed as he reached under, holding my hips
ard, keeping me immobile.

I whimpered and writhed against him, and he bit my neck.

"Be still," he said in my ear. I was still, only because I couldn't
ove. We lay pressed tight together, shuddering. I could feel the
ounding against my ribs, but didn't know whether it was my
eart, or his.

Then he moved in me, very slightly, a question of the flesh. It
as enough; I convulsed in answer, held helpless under him, and
lt the spasms of my release stroke him, stroke him, seize and
lease him, urging him to join me.

He reared up on both hands, back arched and head thrown back,
es closed and breathing hard. Then very slowly, he bent his head
rward and opened his eyes. He looked down at me with unutter-
le tenderness, and the candlelight gleamed briefly on the wet-
ss on his cheek, maybe sweat or maybe tears.

"Oh, Claire," he whispered. "Oh, God, Claire."

And his release began, deep inside me, without his moving,
ivering through his body so that his arms trembled, the ruddy
irs quivering in the dim light, and he dropped his head with a
und like a sob, his hair hiding his face as he spilled himself,
ch jerk and pulse of his flesh between my legs rousing an echo
my own.

When it was over, he held himself over me, still as stone for a
ng moment. Then, very gently, he lowered himself, pressed his
ad against mine, and lay as if dead.

I stirred at last from a deep, contented stupor, lifting my hand lay it over the spot where his pulse beat slow and strong, just at tl base of his breastbone.

"It's like bicycle riding, I expect," I said. My head reste peacefully in the curve of his shoulder, my hand idly playing wi the red-gold curls that sprang up in thickets across his chest. "D you know you've got lots more hairs on your chest than you use to?"

"No," he said drowsily, "I dinna usually count them. Hav bye-sickles got lots of hair, then?"

It caught me by surprise, and I laughed.

"No," I said. "I just meant that we seemed to recall what to c all right."

Jamie opened one eye and looked down at me consideringl "It would take a real daftie to forget *that,* Sassenach," he said. " may be lacking practice, but I havena lost all my faculties yet."

We were still for a long time, aware of each other's breathin sensitive to each small twitch and shifting of position. We fitte well together, my head curled into the hollow of his shoulder, tl territory of his body warm under my hand, both strange and fami iar, awaiting rediscovery.

The building was a solid one, and the sound of the storm ou side drowned most noises from within, but now and then tl sounds of feet or voices were dimly audible below us; a lo masculine laugh, or the higher voice of a woman, raised in profe sional flirtation.

Hearing it, Jamie stirred a little uncomfortably.

"I should maybe have taken ye to a tavern," he said. "It only—"

"It's all right," I assured him. "Though I must say, of all tl places I'd imagined being with you again, I somehow nev thought of a brothel." I hesitated, not wanting to pry, but curios got the best of me. "You . . . er . . . don't *own* this place, you, Jamie?"

He pulled back a little, staring down at me.

"Me? God in heaven, Sassenach, what d'ye think I am?"

"Well, I don't know, do I?" I pointed out, with some asperit "The first thing you do when I find you is faint, and as soon ve got you back on your feet, you get me assaulted in a pub and ased through Edinburgh in company with a deviant Chinese, ding up in a brothel—whose madam seems to be on awfully miliar terms with you, I might add.'' The tips of his ears had one pink, and he seemed to be struggling between laughter and dignation.

''You then take off your clothes, announce that you're a terrible rson with a depraved past, and take me to bed. What did you pect me to think?''

Laughter won out.

''Well, I'm no a saint, Sassenach,'' he said. ''But I'm no a mp, either.''

''Glad to hear it,'' I said. There was a momentary pause, and en I said, ''Do you mean to tell me what you *are,* or shall I go on nning down the disreputable possibilities until I come close?''

''Oh, aye?'' he said, entertained by this suggestion. ''What's ur best guess?''

I looked him over carefully. He lay at ease amid the tumbled eets, one arm behind his head, grinning at me.

''Well, I'd bet my shift you're not a printer,'' I said.

The grin widened.

''Why not?''

I poked him rudely in the ribs. ''You're much too fit. Most men their forties have begun to go soft round the middle, and you ven't a spare ounce on you.''

''That's mostly because I havena got anyone to cook for me,'' said ruefully. ''If you ate in taverns all the time, ye wouldna be t, either. Luckily, it looks as though ye eat regularly.'' He patted y bottom familiarly, and then ducked, laughing, as I slapped at s hand.

''Don't try to distract me,'' I said, resuming my dignity. ''At y rate, you didn't get muscles like that slaving over a printing ess.''

''Ever tried to work one, Sassenach?'' He raised a derisive ebrow.

''No.'' I furrowed my brow in thought. ''I don't suppose you've ken up highway robbery?''

''No,'' he said, the grin widening. ''Guess again.''

''Embezzlement.''

''No.''

"Well, likely not kidnapping for ransom," I said, and began tick other possibilities off on my fingers. "Petty thievery? N Piracy? No, you couldn't possibly, unless you've got over bei seasick. Usury? Hardly." I dropped my hand and stared at hin

"You were a traitor when I last knew you, but that scarce seems a good way of making a living."

"Oh, I'm still a traitor," he assured me. "I just havena be convicted lately."

"Lately?"

"I spent several years in prison for treason, Sassenach," said, rather grimly. "For the Rising. But that was some tin back."

"Yes, I knew that."

His eyes widened. "Ye knew that?"

"That and a bit more," I said. "I'll tell you later. But puttin that all aside for the present and returning to the point at issue what *do* you do for a living these days?"

"I'm a printer," he said, grinning widely.

"*And* a traitor?"

"And a traitor," he confirmed, nodding. "I've been arrest for sedition six times in the last two years, and had my premis seized twice, but the court wasna able to prove anything."

"And what happens to you if they *do* prove it, one of the times?"

"Oh," he said airily, waving his free hand in the air, "tl pillory. Ear-nailing. Flogging. Imprisonment. Transportation. Th sort of thing. Likely not hanging."

"What a relief," I said dryly. I felt a trifle hollow. I hadn't ev tried to imagine what his life might be like, if I found him. No that I had, I was a little taken aback.

"I did warn ye," he said. The teasing was gone now, and tl dark blue eyes were serious and watchful.

"You did," I said, and took a deep breath.

"Do ye want to leave now?" He spoke casually enough, bu saw his fingers clench and tighten on a fold of the quilt, so that tl knuckles stood out white against the sun-bronzed skin.

"No," I said. I smiled at him, as best I could manage. "I did come back just to make love with you once. I came to be with y —if you'll have me," I ended, a little hesitantly.

"If I'll have you!" He let out the breath he had been holdin

nd sat up to face me, cross-legged on the bed. He reached out and
ook my hands, engulfing them between his own.

"I—canna even say what I felt when I touched you today,
assenach, and knew ye to be real," he said. His eyes traveled
ver me, and I felt the heat of him, yearning, and my own heat,
elting toward him. "To find you again—and then to lose
e . . ." He stopped, throat working as he swallowed.

I touched his face, tracing the fine, clean line of cheekbone and
w.

"You won't lose me," I said. "Not ever again." I smiled,
moothing back the thick ruff of ruddy hair behind his ear. "Not
ven if I find out you've been committing bigamy and public
unkenness."

He jerked sharply at that, and I dropped my hand, startled.

"What is it?"

"Well—" he said, and stopped. He pursed his lips and glanced
me quickly. "It's just—"

"Just what? Is there something else you haven't told me?"

"Well, printing seditious pamphlets isna all that profitable," he
id, in explanation.

"I don't suppose so," I said, my heart starting to speed up
gain at the prospect of further revelations. "What else have you
en doing?"

"Well, it's just that I do a wee bit of smuggling," he said
pologetically. "On the side, like."

"A *smuggler*?" I stared. "Smuggling what?"

"Well, whisky mostly, but rum now and then, and a fair bit of
ench wine and cambric."

"So that's it!" I said. The pieces of the puzzle all settled into
ace—Mr. Willoughby, the Edinburgh docks, and the riddle of
ir present surroundings. "That's what your connection is with
is place—what you meant by saying Madame Jeanne is a cus-
mer?"

"That's it." He nodded. "It works verra well; we store the
quor in one of the cellars below when it comes in from France.
me of it we sell directly to Jeanne; some she keeps for us until
 can ship it on."

"Um. And as part of the arrangements . . ." I said delicately,
ou, er . . ."

The blue eyes narrowed at me.

"The answer to what you're thinking, Sassenach, is no," h said very firmly.

"Oh, is it?" I said, feeling extremely pleased. "Mind reade are you? And what am I thinking?"

"You were wondering do I take out my price in trade some times, aye?" He lifted one brow at me.

"Well, I was," I admitted. "Not that it's any of my business.

"Oh, isn't it, then?" He raised both ruddy brows and took m by both shoulders, leaning toward me.

"Is it?" he said, a moment later. He sounded a little breathles

"Yes," I said, sounding equally breathless. "And you don't—

"I don't. Come here."

He wrapped his arms around me, and pulled me close. Th body's memory is different from the mind's. When I thought, an wondered, and worried, I was clumsy and awkward, fumbling m way. Without the interference of conscious thought, my bo knew him, and answered him at once in tune, as though his touc had left me moments before, and not years.

"I was more afraid this time than on our wedding night," murmured, my eyes fixed on the slow, strong pulsebeat in th hollow of his throat.

"Were ye, then?" His arm shifted and tightened round m "Do I frighten ye, Sassenach?"

"No." I put my fingers on the tiny pulse, breathing the dee musk of his effort. "It's only . . . the first time . . . I didn think it would be forever. I meant to go, then."

He snorted faintly, the sweat gleaming lightly in the small ho low in the center of his chest.

"And ye did go, and came again," he said. "You're her there's no more that matters, than that."

I raised myself slightly to look at him. His eyes were close slanted and catlike, his lashes that striking color I remembered well because I had seen it so often; deep auburn at the tips, fadi to a red so pale as nearly to be blond at the roots.

"What did you think, the first time we lay together?" I aske The dark blue eyes opened slowly, and rested on me.

"It has always been forever, for me, Sassenach," he said si ply.

Sometime later, we fell asleep entwined, with the sound of t

ain falling soft against the shutters, mingling with the muffled
ounds of commerce below.

It was a restless night. Too tired to stay awake a moment longer,
was too happy to fall soundly asleep. Perhaps I was afraid he
vould vanish if I slept. Perhaps he felt the same. We lay close
ogether, not awake, but too aware of each other to sleep deeply. I
elt every small twitch of his muscles, every movement of his
reathing, and knew he was likewise aware of me.

Half-dozing, we turned and moved together, always touching, in
sleepy, slow-motion ballet, learning again in silence the lan-
uage of our bodies. Somewhere in the deep, quiet hours of the
ight, he turned to me without a word, and I to him, and we made
ve to each other in a slow, unspeaking tenderness that left us
ying still at last, in possession of each other's secrets.

Soft as a moth flying in the dark, my hand skimmed his leg, and
ound the thin deep runnel of the scar. My fingers traced its invisi-
le length and paused, with the barest of touches at its end, word-
ssly asking, "How?"

His breathing changed with a sigh, and his hand lay over mine.

"Culloden," he said, the whispered word an evocation of trag-
dy. Death. Futility. And the terrible parting that had taken me
om him.

"I'll never leave you," I whispered. "Not again."

His head turned on the pillow, his features lost in darkness, and
is lips brushed mine, light as the touch of an insect's wing. He
rned onto his back, shifting me next to him, his hand resting
eavy on the curve of my thigh, keeping me close.

Sometime later, I felt him shift again, and turn the bedclothes
ack a little way. A cool draft played across my forearm; the tiny
airs prickled upright, and then flattened beneath the warmth of
is touch. I opened my eyes, to find him turned on his side,
bsorbed in the sight of my hand. It lay still on the quilt, a carved
hite thing, all the bones and tendons chalked in gray as the room
egan its imperceptible shift from night to day.

"Draw her for me," he whispered, head bent as he gently
aced the shapes of my fingers, long and ghostly beneath the
arkness of his own touch.

"What has she of you, of me? Can ye tell me? Are her hands

like yours, Claire, or mine? Draw her for me, let me see her.'' H
laid his own hand down beside my own. It was his good hand, t
fingers straight and flat-jointed, the nails clipped short, square a
clean.

''Like mine,'' I said. My voice was low and hoarse with wa
ing, barely loud enough to register above the drumming of the ra
outside. The house beneath was silent. I raised the fingers of m
immobile hand an inch in illustration.

''She has long, slim hands like mine—but bigger than min
broad across the backs, and a deep curve at the outside, near t
wrist—like that. Like yours; she has a pulse just there, where yo
do.'' I touched the spot where a vein crossed the curve of h
radius, just where the wrist joins the hand. He was so still I cou
feel his heartbeat under my fingertip.

''Her nails are like yours; square, not oval like mine. But sh
has the crooked little finger on her right hand that I have,'' I sai
lifting it. ''My mother had it, too; Uncle Lambert told me.'' N
own mother had died when I was five. I had no clear memory
her, but thought of her whenever I saw my own hand unexpec
edly, caught in a moment of grace like this one. I laid the han
with the crooked finger on his, then lifted it to his face.

''She has this line,'' I said softly, tracing the bold sweep fro
temple to cheek. ''Your eyes, exactly, and those lashes and brow
A Fraser nose. Her mouth is more like mine, with a full botto
lip, but it's wide, like yours. A pointed chin, like mine, b
stronger. She's a big girl—nearly six feet tall.'' I felt his start
astonishment, and nudged him gently, knee to knee. ''She h
long legs, like yours, but very feminine.''

''And has she that small blue vein just there?'' His han
touched my own face, thumb tender in the hollow of my templ
''And ears like tiny wings, Sassenach?''

''She always complained about her ears—said they stuck out
I said, feeling the tears sting my eyes as Brianna came suddenly
life between us.

''They're pierced. You don't mind, do you?'' I said, talking fa
to keep the tears at bay. ''Frank did; he said it looked cheap, a
she shouldn't, but she wanted to do it, and I let her, when she w
sixteen. Mine were; it didn't seem right to say she couldn't whe
did, and her friends all did, and I didn't—didn't want—''

''Ye were right,'' he said, interrupting the flow of half-hyste

al words. "Ye did fine," he repeated, softly but firmly, holding
e close. "Ye were a wonderful mother, I know it."

I was crying again, quite soundlessly, shaking against him. He
eld me gently, stroking my back and murmuring. "Ye did well,"
e kept saying. "Ye did right." And after a little while, I stopped
rying.

"Ye gave me a child, *mo nighean donn*," he said softly, into the
loud of my hair. "We are together for always. She is safe; and we
ill live forever now, you and I." He kissed me, very lightly, and
id his head upon the pillow next to me. "Brianna," he whis-
ered, in that odd Highland way that made her name his own. He
ghed deeply, and in an instant, was asleep. In another, I fell
sleep myself, my last sight his wide, sweet mouth, relaxed in
eep, half-smiling.

26

Whore's Brunc.

From years of answering the twin calls of motherhood an medicine, I had developed the ability to wake from even t soundest sleep at once and completely. I woke so now, in mediately aware of the worn linen sheets around me, the drippi of the eaves outside, and the warm scent of Jamie's body minglin with the cold, sweet air that breathed through the crack of t shutters above me.

Jamie himself was not in bed; without reaching out or openin my eyes, I knew that the space beside me was empty. He was clo by, though. There was a sound of stealthy movement, and a fai scraping noise nearby. I turned my head on the pillow and open my eyes.

The room was filled with a gray light that washed the color fro everything, but left the pale lines of his body clear in the dimne: He stood out against the darkness of the room, solid as ivory, viv as though he were etched upon the air. He was naked, his ba turned to me as he stood in front of the chamber pot he had ju pulled from its resting place beneath the washstand.

I admired the squared roundness of his buttocks, the sm muscular hollow that dented each one, and their pale vulnerabilit The groove of his backbone, springing in a deep, smooth cur from hips to shoulders. As he moved slightly, the light caught t faint silver shine of the scars on his back, and the breath caught my throat.

He turned around then, face calm and faintly abstracted. He sa me watching him, and looked slightly startled.

I smiled but stayed silent, unable to think of anything to say. I
pt looking at him, though, and he at me, the same smile upon his
s. Without speaking, he moved toward me and sat on the bed,
e mattress shifting under his weight. He laid his hand open on
e quilt, and I put my own into it without hesitation.

"Sleep well?" I asked idiotically.

A grin broadened across his face. "No," he said. "Did you?"

"No." I could feel the heat of him, even at this distance, in
ite of the chilly room. "Aren't you cold?"

"No."

We fell quiet again, but could not take our eyes away from each
her. I looked him over carefully in the strengthening light, com-
ring memory to reality. A narrow blade of early sun knifed
ough the shutters' crack, lighting a lock of hair like polished
onze, gilding the curve of his shoulder, the smooth flat slope of
; belly. He seemed slightly larger than I had remembered, and
e hell of a lot more immediate.

"You're bigger than I remembered," I ventured. He tilted his
ad, looking down at me in amusement.

"You're a wee bit smaller, I think."

His hand engulfed mine, fingers delicately circling the bones of
wrist. My mouth was dry; I swallowed and licked my lips.

"A long time ago, you asked me if I knew what it was between
" I said.

His eyes rested on mine, so dark a blue as to be nearly black in a
ht like this.

"I remember," he said softly. His fingers tightened briefly on
ne. "What it is—when I touch you; when ye lie wi' me."

"I said I didn't know."

"I didna ken either." The smile had faded a bit, but was still
re, lurking in the corners of his mouth.

"I still don't," I said. "But—" and stopped to clear my throat.

"But it's still there," he finished for me, and the smile moved
m his lips, lighting his eyes. "Aye?"

t was. I was still as aware of him as I might have been of a
hted stick of dynamite in my immediate vicinity, but the feeling
ween us had changed. We had fallen asleep as one flesh, linked
the love of the child we had made, and had waked as two people
bound by something different.

"Yes. Is it—I mean, it's not just because of Brianna, do y
think?"

The pressure on my fingers increased.

"Do I want ye because you're the mother of my child?" I
raised one ruddy eyebrow in incredulity. "Well, no. Not that I'
no grateful," he added hastily. "But—no." He bent his head
look down at me intently, and the sun lit the narrow bridge of I
nose and sparked in his lashes.

"No," he said. "I think I could watch ye for hours, Sassena
to see how you have changed, or how ye're the same. Just to se
wee thing, like the curve of your chin"—he touched my j.
gently, letting his hand slide up to cup my head, thumb stroki
my earlobe—"or your ears, and the bittie holes for your earbo
Those are all the same, just as they were. Your hair—I called
mo nighean donn, d'ye recall? My brown one." His voice w
little more than a whisper, his fingers threading my curls betwe
them.

"I expect that's changed a bit," I said. I hadn't gone gray, I
there were paler streaks where my normal light brown had faded
a softer gold, and here and there, the glint of a single silver stra

"Like beechwood in the rain," he said, smiling and smoothi
a lock with one forefinger, "and the drops coming down from
leaves across the bark."

I reached out and stroked his thigh, touching the long scar t
ran down it.

"I wish I could have been there to take care of you," I s
softly. "It was the most horrible thing I ever did—leaving y
knowing . . . that you meant to be killed." I could hardly bear
speak the word.

"Well, I tried hard enough," he said, with a wry grimace t
made me laugh, in spite of my emotion. "It wasna my fault I di
succeed." He glanced dispassionately at the long, thick scar t
ran down his thigh. "Not the fault of the Sassenach wi' the ba
net, either."

I heaved myself up on one elbow, squinting at the scar. "
bayonet did that?"

"Aye, well. It festered, ye see," he explained.

"I know; we found the journal of the Lord Melton who sent y
home from the battlefield. He didn't think you'd make it." I

nd tightened on his knee, as though to reassure myself that he
s in fact here before me, alive.

He snorted. "Well, I damn nearly didn't. I was all but dead
en they pulled me out of the wagon at Lallybroch." His face
kened with memory.

"God, sometimes I wake up in the night, dreaming of that
gon. It was two days' journey, and I was fevered or chilled, or
h together. I was covered wi' hay, and the ends of it sticking in
eyes and my ears and through my shirt, and fleas hopping all
ough it and eating me alive, and my leg killing me at every jolt
he road. It was a verra bumpy road, too," he added broodingly.

"It sounds horrible," I said, feeling the word quite inadequate.

snorted briefly.

"Aye. I only stood it by imagining what I'd do to Melton if I
r met him again, to get back at him for not shooting me."

laughed again, and he glanced down at me, a wry smile on his
s.

"I'm not laughing because it's funny," I said, gulping a little.
m laughing because otherwise I'll cry, and I don't want to—
now, when it's over."

"Aye, I know." He squeezed my hand.

took a deep breath. "I—I didn't look back. I didn't think I
ld stand to find out—what happened." I bit my lip; the admis-
n seemed a betrayal. "It wasn't that I tried—that I wanted—to
get," I said, groping clumsily for words. "I couldn't forget
; you shouldn't think that. Not ever. But I—"

"Dinna fash yourself, Sassenach," he interrupted. He patted
hand gently. "I ken what ye mean. I try not to look back
self, come to that."

"But if I had," I said, staring down at the smooth grain of the
en, "if I had—I might have found you sooner."

The words hung in the air between us like an accusation, a
inder of the bitter years of loss and separation. Finally he
hed, deeply, and put a finger under my chin, lifting my face to

"And if ye had?" he said. "Would ye have left the lassie there
hout her mother? Or come to me in the time after Culloden,
en I couldna care for ye, but only watch ye suffer wi' the rest,
feel the guilt of bringing ye to such a fate? Maybe see ye die

of the hunger and sickness, and know I'd killed ye?'' He rais
one eyebrow in question, then shook his head.

''No. I told ye to go, and I told ye to forget. Shall I blame ye
doing as I said, Sassenach? No.''

''But we might have had more time!'' I said. ''We mi,
have—'' He stopped me by the simple expedient of bending a
putting his mouth on mine. It was warm and very soft, and
stubble of his face was faintly scratchy on my skin.

After a moment he released me. The light was growing, putt
color in his face. His skin glowed bronze, sparked with the cop
of his beard. He took a deep breath.

''Aye, we might. But to think of that—we cannot.'' His e
met mine steadily, searching. ''I canna look back, Sassenach, a
live,'' he said simply. ''If we have no more than last night, and t
moment, it is enough.''

''Not for me, it isn't!'' I said, and he laughed.

''Greedy wee thing, are ye no?''

''Yes,'' I said. The tension broken, I returned my attention
the scar on his leg, to keep away for the moment from the pain
contemplation of lost time and opportunity.

''You were telling me how you got that.''

''So I was.'' He rocked back a little, squinting down at the t
white line down the top of his thigh.

''Well, it was Jenny—my sister, ye ken?'' I did indeed reme
ber Jenny; half her brother's size, and dark as he was blazing fa
but a match and more for him in stubbornness.

''She said she wasna going to let me die,'' he said, with a rue
smile. ''And she didn't. My opinion didna seem to have anyth
to do wi' the matter, so she didna bother to ask me.''

''That sounds like Jenny.'' I felt a small glow of comfort at
thought of my sister-in-law. Jamie hadn't been alone as I fear
then; Jenny Murray would have fought the Devil himself to s,
her brother—and evidently had.

''She dosed me for the fever, and put poultices on my leg
draw the poison, but nothing worked, and it only got worse
swelled and stank, and then began to go black and rotten, so t
thought they must take the leg off, if I was to live.''

He recounted this quite matter-of-factly, but I felt a little fain
the thought.

''Obviously they didn't,'' I said. ''Why not?''

Jamie scratched his nose and rubbed a hand back through his hair, wiping the wild spill of it out of his eyes. "Well, that was Ian," he said. "He wouldna let her do it. He said he kent well enough what it was like to live wi' one leg, and while he didna mind it so much himself, he thought I wouldna like to—all things considered," he added, with a wave of the hand and a glance at me that encompassed everything—the loss of the battle, of the war, of me, of home and livelihood—of all the things of his normal life. I thought Ian might well have been right.

"So instead Jenny made three of the tenants come to sit on me and hold me still, and then she slit my leg to the bone wi' a kitchen knife and washed the wound wi' boiling water," he said casually.

"Jesus H. Christ!" I blurted, shocked into horror.

He smiled faintly at my expression. "Aye, well, it worked."

I swallowed heavily, tasting bile. "Jesus. I'd think you'd have been a cripple for life!"

"Well, she cleansed it as best she could, and stitched it up. She said she wasna going to let me die, and she wasna going to have me be a cripple, and she wasna going to have me lie about all the day feelin' sorry for myself, and—" He shrugged, resigned. "By the time she finished tellin' me all the things she wouldna let me do, it seemed the only thing left to me was to get well."

I echoed his laugh, and his smile broadened at the memory. "Once I could get up, she made Ian take me outside after dark and make me walk. Lord, we must ha' been a sight, Ian wi' his wooden leg, and me wi' my stick, limping up and down the road like a pair of lame cranes!"

I laughed again, but had to blink back tears; I could see all too well the two tall, limping figures, struggling stubbornly against darkness and pain, leaning on each other for support.

"You lived in a cave for a time, didn't you? We found the story of it."

His eyebrows went up in surprise. "A story about it? About me, ye mean?"

"You're a famous Highland legend," I told him dryly, "or you will be, at least."

"For living in a cave?" He looked half-pleased, half-embarassed. "Well, that's a foolish thing to make a story about, aye?"

"Arranging to have yourself betrayed to the English for the

price on your head was maybe a little more dramatic,'' I said, still more dryly. ''Taking rather a risk there, weren't you?''

The end of his nose was pink, and he looked somewhat abashed.

''Well,'' he said awkwardly, ''I didna think prison would be verra dreadful, and everything considered. . . .''

I spoke as calmly as I could, but I wanted to shake him, suddenly and ridiculously furious with him in retrospect.

''Prison, my arse! You knew perfectly well you might have been hanged, didn't you? And you bloody did it anyway!''

''I had to do something,'' he said, shrugging. ''And if the English were fool enough to pay good money for my lousy carcass —well, there's nay law against takin' advantage of fools, is there?'' One corner of his mouth quirked up, and I was torn between the urge to kiss him and the urge to slap him.

I did neither, but sat up in bed and began combing the tangles out of my hair with my fingers.

''I'd say it's open to question who the fool was,'' I said, not looking at him, ''but even so, you should know that your daughter's very proud of you.''

''She is?'' He sounded thunderstruck, and I looked up at him, laughing despite my irritation.

''Well, of course she is. You're a bloody hero, aren't you?''

He went quite red in the face at this, and stood up, looking thoroughly disconcerted.

''Me? No!'' He rubbed a hand through his hair, his habit when thinking or disturbed in his mind.

''No. I mean,'' he said slowly, ''I wasna heroic at all about it. I was only . . . I couldna bear it any longer. To see them all starving, I mean, and not be able to care for them—Jenny, and Ian and the children; all the tenants and their families.'' He looked helplessly down at me. ''I really didna care if the English hanged me or not,'' he said. ''I didna think they would, because of what ye'd told me, but even if I'd known for sure it meant that—I would ha' done it, Sassenach, and not minded. But it wasna bravery—not at all.'' He threw up his hands in frustration, turning away. ''There was nothing else I could do!''

''I see,'' I said softly, after a moment. ''I understand.'' He was standing by the chiffonier, still naked, and at this, he turned half-round to face me.

''Do ye, then?'' His face was serious.

"I know you, Jamie Fraser." I spoke with more certainty than I had felt at any time since the moment I stepped through the rock.

"Do ye, then?" he asked again, but a faint smile shadowed his mouth.

"I think so."

The smile on his lips widened, and he opened his mouth to reply. Before he could speak, though, there was a knock upon the chamber door.

I started as though I had touched a hot stove. Jamie laughed, and bent to pat my hip as he went to the door.

"I expect it's the chambermaid with our breakfast, Sassenach, not the constable. And we *are* marrit, aye?" One eyebrow rose quizzically.

"Even so, shouldn't you put something on?" I asked, as he reached for the doorknob.

He glanced down at himself.

"I shouldna think it's likely to come as a shock to anyone in this house, Sassenach. But to honor your sensibilities——" He grinned at me, and taking a linen towel from the washstand, wrapped it casually about his loins before pulling open the door.

I caught sight of a tall male figure standing in the hall, and promptly pulled the bedclothes over my head. This was a reaction of pure panic, for if it had been the Edinburgh constable or one of his minions, I could scarcely expect much protection from a couple of quilts. But then the visitor spoke, and I was glad that I was safely out of sight for the moment.

"Jamie?" The voice sounded rather startled. Despite the fact that I had not heard it in twenty years, I recognized it at once. Rolling over, I surreptitiously lifted a corner of the quilt and peeked out beneath it.

"Well, of course it's me," Jamie was saying, rather testily. "Have ye no got eyes, man?" He pulled his brother-in-law, Ian, into the room and shut the door.

"I see well enough it's you," Ian said, with a note of sharpness. "I just didna ken whether to believe my eyes!" His smooth brown hair showed threads of gray, and his face bore the lines of a good many years' hard work. But Joe Abernathy had been right; with his first words, the new vision merged with the old, and this was the Ian Murray I had known before.

"I came here because the lad at the printshop said ye'd no been there last night, and this was the address Jenny sends your letters to," he was saying. He looked round the room with wide, suspicious eyes, as though expecting something to leap out from behind the armoire. Then his gaze flicked back to his brother-in-law, who was making a perfunctory effort to secure his makeshift loincloth.

"I never thought to find ye in a kittle-hoosie, Jamie!" he said. "I wasna sure, when the . . . the lady answered the door downstairs, but then—"

"It's no what ye think, Ian," Jamie said shortly.

"Oh, it's not, aye? And Jenny worrying that ye'd make yourself ill, living without a woman so long!" Ian snorted. "I'll tell her she needna concern herself wi' your welfare. And where's my son then, down the hall with another o' the harlots?"

"Your son?" Jamie's surprise was evident. "Which one?"

Ian stared at Jamie, the anger on his long, half-homely face fading into alarm.

"Ye havena got him? Wee Ian's not here?"

"Young Ian? Christ, man, d'ye think I'd bring a fourteen-year old lad into a brothel?"

Ian opened his mouth, then shut it, and sat down on the stool.

"Tell ye the truth, Jamie, I canna say what ye'd do anymore," he said levelly. He looked up at his brother-in-law, jaw set. "Once I could. But not now."

"And what the hell d'ye mean by that?" I could see the angry flush rising in Jamie's face.

Ian glanced at the bed, and away again. The red flush didn' recede from Jamie's face, but I saw a small quiver at the corner o his mouth. He bowed elaborately to his brother-in-law.

"Your pardon, Ian, I was forgettin' my manners. Allow me to introduce ye to my companion." He stepped to the side of the bed and pulled back the quilts.

"No!" Ian cried, jumping to his feet and looking frantically a the floor, the wardrobe, anywhere but at the bed.

"What, will ye no give your regards to my wife, Ian?" Jami said.

"Wife?" Forgetting to look away, Ian goggled at Jamie in hor ror. "Ye've marrit a whore?" he croaked.

"I wouldn't call it that, exactly," I said. Hearing my voice, Ia jerked his head in my direction.

"Hullo," I said, waving cheerily at him from my nest of bedclothes. "Been a long time, hasn't it?"

I'd always thought the descriptions of what people did when
seeing ghosts rather exaggerated, but had been forced to revise my
opinions in light of the responses I had been getting since my
return to the past. Jamie had fainted dead away, and if Ian's hair
was not literally standing on end, he assuredly looked as though he
had been scared out of his wits.

Eyes bugging out, he opened and closed his mouth, making a
small gobbling noise that seemed to entertain Jamie quite a lot.

"That'll teach ye to go about thinkin' the worst of my character," he said, with apparent satisfaction. Taking pity on his quivering brother-in-law, Jamie poured out a tot of brandy and handed
him the glass. "Judge not, and ye'll no be judged, eh?"

I thought Ian was going to spill the drink on his breeches, but he
managed to get the glass to his mouth and swallow.

"What—?" He wheezed, eyes watering as he stared at me.
"How—?"

"It's a long story," I said, with a glance at Jamie. He nodded
briefly. We had had other things to think about in the last twenty-
four hours besides how to explain me to people, and under the
circumstances, I rather thought explanations could wait.

"I don't believe I know Young Ian. Is he missing?" I asked
politely.

Ian nodded mechanically, not taking his eyes off me.

"He stole away from home last Friday week," he said, sounding rather dazed. "Left a note that he'd gone to his uncle." He
took another swig of brandy, coughed and blinked several times,
then wiped his eyes and sat up straighter, looking at me.

"It'll no be the first time, ye see," he said to me. He seemed to
be regaining his self-confidence, seeing that I appeared to be flesh
and blood, and showed no signs either of getting out of bed or of
putting my head under my arm and strolling round without it, in
the accepted fashion of Highland ghosts.

Jamie sat down on the bed next to me, taking my hand in his.

"I've not seen Young Ian since I sent him home wi' Fergus six
months ago," he said. He was beginning to look as worried as Ian.
"You're sure he said he was coming to me?"

"Well, he hasna got any other uncles that I know of," Ian said,

rather acerbically. He tossed back the rest of the brandy and set th
cup down.

"Fergus?" I interrupted. "Is Fergus all right, then?" I felt
surge of joy at the mention of the French orphan whom Jamie ha
once hired in Paris as a pickpocket, and brought back to Scotlan
as a servant lad.

Distracted from his thoughts, Jamie looked down at me.

"Oh, aye, Fergus is a bonny man now. A bit changed, «
course." A shadow seemed to cross his face, but it cleared as h
smiled, pressing my hand. "He'll be fair daft at seein' you onc
more, Sassenach."

Uninterested in Fergus, Ian had risen and was pacing back an
forth across the polished plank floor.

"He didna take a horse," he muttered. "So he'd have nothin
anyone would rob him for." He swung round to Jamie. "How d
ye come, last time ye brought the lad here? By the land round th
Firth, or did ye cross by boat?"

Jamie rubbed his chin, frowning as he thought. "I didna com
to Lallybroch for him. He and Fergus crossed through the Carrya
rick Pass and met me just above Loch Laggan. Then we cam
down through Struan and Weem and . . . aye, now I remembe
We didna want to cross the Campbell lands, so we came to th
east, and crossed the Forth at Donibristle."

"D'ye think he'd do that again?" Ian asked. "If it's the on
way he knows?"

Jamie shook his head doubtfully. "He might. But he kens th
coast is dangerous."

Ian resumed his pacing, hands clasped behind his back. "I be
him 'til he could barely stand, let alone sit, the last time he ra
off," Ian said, shaking his head. His lips were tight, and I gather
that Young Ian was perhaps rather a trial to his father. "Ye'd thi
the wee fool would think better o' such tricks, aye?"

Jamie snorted, but not without sympathy.

"Did a thrashing ever stop you from doing anything you'd s
your mind on?"

Ian stopped his pacing and sat down on the stool again, sighin

"No," he said frankly, "but I expect it was some relief to m
father." His face cracked into a reluctant smile, as Jamie laughe

"He'll be all right," Jamie declared confidently. He stood u
and let the towel drop to the floor as he reached for his breeche

"I'll go and put about the word for him. If he's in Edinburgh, we'll hear of it by nightfall.''

Ian cast a glance at me in the bed, and stood up hastily.

"I'll go wi' ye.''

I thought I saw a shadow of doubt flicker across Jamie's face, but then he nodded and pulled the shirt over his head.

"All right,'' he said, as his head popped through the slit. He frowned at me.

"I'm afraid ye'll have to stay here, Sassenach,'' he said.

"I suppose I will,'' I said dryly. "Seeing that I haven't any clothes.'' The maid who brought our supper had removed my dress, and no replacement had as yet appeared.

Ian's feathery brows shot up to his hairline, but Jamie merely nodded.

"I'll tell Jeanne on the way out,'' he said. He frowned slightly, thinking. "It may be some time, Sassenach. There are things— well, I've business to take care of.'' He squeezed my hand, his expression softening as he looked at me.

"I dinna want to leave ye,'' he said softly. "But I must. You'll stay here until I come again?''

"Don't worry,'' I assured him, waving a hand at the linen towel he had just discarded. "I'm not likely to go anywhere in that.''

The thud of their feet retreated down the hall and faded into the sounds of the stirring house. The brothel was rising, late and languid by the stern Scottish standards of Edinburgh. Below me I could hear the occasional slow muffled thump, the clatter of shutters thrust open nearby, a cry of "Gardyloo!" and a second later, the splash of slops flung out to land on the street far below.

Voices somewhere far down the hall, a brief inaudible exchange, and the closing of a door. The building itself seemed to stretch and sigh, with a creaking of timbers and a squeaking of stairs, and a sudden puff of coal-smelling warm air came out from the back of the cold hearth, the exhalation of a fire lit on some lower floor, sharing my chimney.

I relaxed into the pillows, feeling drowsy and heavily content. I was slightly and pleasantly sore in several unaccustomed places, and while I had been reluctant to see Jamie go, there was no denying that it was nice to be alone for a bit to mull things over.

* * *

I felt much like one who has been handed a sealed cask containing a long-lost treasure. I could feel the satisfying weig and the shape of it, and know the great joy of its possession, b still did not know exactly what was contained therein.

I was dying to know everything he had done and said a thought and been, through all the days between us. I had of cour known that if he had survived Culloden, he would have a life—a knowing what I did of Jamie Fraser, it was unlikely to be a simp one. But knowing that, and being confronted with the reality of were two different things.

He had been fixed in my memory for so long, glowing b static, like an insect frozen in amber. And then had come Roger brief historical sightings, like peeks through a keyhole; separa pictures like punctuations, alterations; adjustments of memor each showing the dragonfly's wings raised or lowered at a diffe ent angle, like the single frames of a motion picture. Now time h begun to run again for us, and the dragonfly was in flight befo me, flickering from place to place, so I saw little more yet than t glitter of its wings.

There were so many questions neither of us had had a chance ask yet—what of his family at Lallybroch, his sister Jenny and h children? Obviously Ian was alive, and well, wooden leg notwit standing—but had the rest of the family and the tenants of t estate survived the destruction of the Highlands? If they had, w was Jamie here in Edinburgh?

And if they were alive—what would we tell them about n sudden reappearance? I bit my lip, wondering whether there w *any* explanation—short of the truth—which might make sense. might depend on what Jamie had told them when I disappear after Culloden; there had seemed no need to concoct a reason f my vanishing at the time; it would simply be assumed that I ha perished in the aftermath of the Rising, one more of the namele corpses lying starved on the rocks or slaughtered in a leafless gle

Well, we'd manage that when we came to it, I supposed. I w more curious just now about the extent and the danger of Jamie less legitimate activities. Smuggling and sedition, was it? I w aware that smuggling was nearly as honorable a profession in t Scottish Highlands as cattle-stealing had been twenty years befo and might be conducted with relatively little risk. Sedition w omething else, and seemed like an occupation of dubious safety or a convicted ex-Jacobite traitor.

That, I supposed, was the reason for his assumed name—or one eason, at any rate. Disturbed and excited as I had been when we rrived at the brothel the night before, I had noticed that Madame eanne referred to him by his own name. So presumably he smug-led under his own identity, but carried out his publishing activi-ies—legal and illegal—as Alex Malcolm.

I had seen, heard and felt enough, during the all too brief hours f the night, to be fairly sure that the Jamie Fraser I had known till existed. How many other men he might be now remained to e seen.

There was a tentative rap at the door, interrupting my thoughts. Breakfast, I thought, and not before time. I was ravenous.

"Come in," I called, and sat up in bed, pulling up the pillows to ean against.

The door opened very slowly, and after quite a long pause, a ead poked its way through the opening, much in the manner of a nail emerging from its shell after a hailstorm.

It was topped with an ill-cut shag of dark brown hair so thick hat the cropped edges stuck out like a shelf above a pair of large ars. The face beneath was long and bony; rather pleasantly omely, save for a pair of beautiful brown eyes, soft and huge as a eer's, that rested on me with a mingled expression of interest and esitancy.

The head and I regarded each other for a moment.

"Are you Mr. Malcolm's . . . woman?" it asked.

"I suppose you could say so," I replied cautiously. This was bviously not the chambermaid with my breakfast. Neither was it kely to be one of the other employees of the establishment, being vidently male, though very young. He seemed vaguely familiar, nough I was sure I hadn't seen him before. I pulled the sheet a bit igher over my breasts. "And who are you?" I inquired.

The head thought this over for some time, and finally answered, vith equal caution, "Ian Murray."

"Ian Murray?" I shot up straight, rescuing the sheet at the last noment. "Come in here," I said peremptorily. "If you're who I nink you are, why aren't you where you're supposed to be, and vhat are you doing here?" The face looked rather alarmed, and howed signs of withdrawal.

"Stop!" I called, and put a leg out of bed to pursue him. The big brown eyes widened at the sight of my bare limb, and he froze. "Come in, I said."

Slowly, I withdrew the leg beneath the quilts, and equally slowly, he followed it into the room.

He was tall and gangly as a fledgling stork, with perhaps nine stone spread sparsely over a six-foot frame. Now that I knew who he was, the resemblance to his father was clear. He had his mother's pale skin, though, which blushed furiously red as it occurred to him suddenly that he was standing next to a bed containing a naked woman.

"I . . . er . . . was looking for my . . . for Mr. Malcolm, I mean," he murmured, staring fixedly at the floorboards by his feet.

"If you mean your uncle Jamie, he's not here," I said.

"No. No, I suppose not." He seemed unable to think of anything to add to this, but remained staring at the floor, one foot twisted awkwardly to the side, as though he were about to draw it up under him, like the wading bird he so much resembled.

"Do ye ken where . . ." he began, lifting his eyes, then, as he caught a glimpse of me, lowered them, blushed again and fell silent.

"He's looking for you," I said. "With your father," I added. "They left here not half an hour ago."

His head snapped up on its skinny neck, goggling.

"My father?" he gasped. "My father was here? Ye know him?"

"Why, yes," I said, without thinking. "I've known Ian for quite a long time."

He might be Jamie's nephew, but he hadn't Jamie's trick of inscrutability. Everything he thought showed on his face, and I could easily trace the progression of his expressions. Raw shock at learning of his father's presence in Edinburgh, then a sort of awestruck horror at the revelation of his father's long-standing acquaintance with what appeared to be a woman of a certain occupation, and finally the beginnings of angry absorption, as the young man began an immediate revision of his opinions of his father's character.

"Er—" I said, mildly alarmed. "It isn't what you think. I mean, your father and I—it's really your uncle and I, I mean—"

vas trying to figure out how to explain the situation to him without etting into even deeper waters, when he whirled on his heel and tarted for the door.

"Wait a minute," I said. He stopped, but didn't turn around. Iis well-scrubbed ears stood out like tiny wings, the morning light luminating their delicate pinkness. "How old are you?" I asked.

He turned around to face me, with a certain painful dignity. "I'll be fifteen in three weeks," he said. The red was creeping up is cheeks again. "Dinna worry, I'm old enough to know—what ort of place this is, I mean." He jerked his head toward me in an ttempt at a courtly bow.

"Meaning no offense to ye, mistress. If Uncle Jamie—I mean, —" He groped for suitable words, failed to find any, and finally lurted, "Verra pleased to meet ye, mum!" turned and bolted hrough the door, which shut hard enough to rattle in its frame.

I fell back against the pillows, torn between amusement and larm. I did wonder what the elder Ian was going to say to his son when they met—and vice versa. As long as I was wondering, I vondered what had brought the younger Ian here in search of amie. Evidently, he knew where his uncle was likely to be found; et judging from his diffident attitude, he had never before ven-ured into the brothel.

Had he extracted the information from Geordie at the print-hop? That seemed unlikely. And yet, if he hadn't—then that neant he had learned of his uncle's connection with this place rom some other source. And the most likely source was Jamie imself.

But in that case, I reasoned, Jamie likely already knew that his nephew was in Edinburgh, so why pretend he hadn't seen the boy? an was Jamie's oldest friend; they had grown up together. If vhatever Jamie was up to was worth the cost of deceiving his rother-in-law, it was something serious.

I had got no further with my musings, when there came another nock on the door.

"Come in," I said, smoothing out the quilts in anticipation of he breakfast tray to be placed thereon.

When the door opened, I had directed my attention at a spot bout five feet above the floor, where I expected the chamber-naid's head to materialize. Upon the last opening of the door, I had had to adjust my vision upward a foot, to accommodate th appearance of Young Ian. This time, I was obliged to drop it.

"What in the bloody hell are you doing here?" I demanded a the diminutive figure of Mr. Willoughby entered on hands an knees. I sat up and hastily tucked my feet underneath me, pullin, not only sheet but quilts well up around my shoulders.

In answer, the Chinese advanced to within a foot of the bec then let his head fall to the floor with a loud clunk. He raised it an repeated the process with great deliberation, making a horri sound like a melon being cleaved with an ax.

"Stop that!" I exclaimed, as he prepared to do it a third time

"Thousand apology," he explained, sitting up on his heels an blinking at me. He was quite a bit the worse for wear, and the dar red mark where his forehead had smacked the floor didn't ad anything to his appearance. I trusted he didn't mean he'd bee going to hit his head on the floor a thousand times, but I wasn sure. He obviously had the hell of a hangover; for him to hav attempted it even once was impressive.

"That's quite all right," I said, edging cautiously back again: the wall. "There's nothing to apologize for."

"Yes, apology," he insisted. "Tsei-mi saying wife. Lady bein most honorable First Wife, not stinking whore."

"Thanks a lot," I said. "Tsei-mi? You mean Jamie? Jami Fraser?"

The little man nodded, to the obvious detriment of his head. H clutched it with both hands and closed his eyes, which prompti disappeared into the creases of his cheeks.

"Tsei-mi," he affirmed, eyes still closed. "Tsei-mi sayin apology to most honored First Wife. Yi Tien Cho most humbl servant." He bowed deeply, still holding on to his head. "Yi Tie Cho," he added, opening his eyes and tapping his chest to indicat that that was his name, in case I should be confusing him with an other humble servants in the vicinity.

"That's quite all right," I said. "Er, pleased to meet you."

Evidently heartened by this, he slid bonelessly onto his fac prostrating himself before me.

"Yi Tien Cho lady's servant," he said. "First Wife please t walk on humble servant, if like."

"Ha," I said coldly. "I've heard about you. Walk on you, eh Not bloody likely!"

A slit of gleaming black eye showed, and he giggled, so irrepressibly that I couldn't help laughing myself. He sat up again, smoothing down the spikes of dirt-stiffened black hair that sprang, porcupine-like, from his skull.

"I wash First Wife's feet?" he offered, grinning widely.

"Certainly not," I said. "If you really want to do something helpful, go and tell someone to bring me breakfast. No, wait a minute," I said, changing my mind. "First, tell me where you met Jamie. If you don't mind," I added, to be polite.

He sat back on his heels, head bobbing slightly. "Docks," he said. "Two year ago. I come China, long way, no food. Hiding barrel," he explained, reaching his arms in a circle, to demonstrate his means of transportation.

"A stowaway?"

"Trade ship," he nodded. "On docks here, stealing food. Stealing brandy one night, getting stinking drunk. Very cold to sleep; die soon, but Tsei-mi find." He jabbed a thumb at his chest once more. "Tsei-mi's humble servant. Humble servant First Wife." He bowed to me, swaying alarmingly in the process, but came upright again without mishap.

"Brandy seems to be your downfall," I observed. "I'm sorry I haven't anything to give you for your head; I don't have any medicines with me at the moment."

"Oh, not worry," he assured me. "I having healthy balls."

"How nice for you," I said, trying to decide whether he was gearing up for another attempt on my feet, or merely still too drunk to distinguish basic anatomy. Or perhaps there was some connection, in Chinese philosophy, between the well-being of head and testicles? Just in case, I looked round for something that might be used as a weapon, in case he showed a disposition to begin burrowing under the bedclothes.

Instead, he reached into the depths of one baggy blue-silk sleeve and with the air of a conjuror, drew out a small white silk bag. He upended this, and two balls dropped out into his palm. They were larger than marbles and smaller than baseballs; about the size, in fact, of the average testicle. A good deal harder, though, being apparently made of some kind of polished stone, greenish in color.

"Healthy balls," Mr. Willoughby explained, rolling them together in his palm. They made a pleasant clicking noise.

"Streaked jade, from Canton," he said. "Best kind of healthy balls."

"Really?" I said, fascinated. "And they're medicinal—good for you, that's what you're saying?"

He nodded vigorously, then stopped abruptly with a faint moan. After a pause, he spread out his hand, and rolled the balls to and fro, keeping them in movement with a dextrous circling of his fingers.

"All body one part; hand all parts," he said. He poked a finger toward his open palm, touching delicately here and there between the smooth green spheres. "Head there, stomach there, liver there," he said. "Balls make all good."

"Well, I suppose they're as portable as Alka-Seltzer," I said. Possibly it was the reference to stomach that caused my own to emit a loud growl at this point.

"First Wife wanting food," Mr. Willoughby observed shrewdly.

"Very astute of you," I said. "Yes, I do want food. Do you suppose you could go and tell someone?"

He dumped the healthy balls back into their bag at once, and springing to his feet, bowed deeply.

"Humble servant go now," he said, and went, crashing rather heavily into the door post on his way out.

This was becoming ridiculous, I thought. I harbored substantial doubt as to whether Mr. Willoughby's visit would result in food; he'd be lucky to make it to the bottom of the stair without falling on his head, if I was any judge of his condition.

Rather than go on sitting here in the nude, receiving random deputations from the outside world, I thought it time to take steps. Rising and carefully wrapping a quilt around my body, I took a few, out into the corridor.

The upper floor seemed deserted. Aside from the room I had left, there were only two other doors up here. Glancing up, I could see unadorned rafters overhead. We were in the attic, then; chances were that the other rooms here were occupied by servants who were presumably now employed downstairs.

I could hear faint noises drifting up the stairwell. Something else drifted up, as well—the scent of frying sausage. A loud gustaory rumble informed me that my stomach hadn't missed this, and furthermore, that my innards considered the consumption of one peanut butter sandwich and one bowl of soup in one twenty-four-hour period a wholly inadequate level of nutrition.

I tucked the ends of the quilt in, sarong-fashion, just above my breasts, and picking up my trailing skirts, followed the scent of food downstairs.

The smell—and the clinking, clattering, sloshing noises of a number of people eating—were coming from a closed door on the first floor above ground level. I pushed it open, and found myself at the end of a long room equipped as a refectory.

The table was surrounded by twenty-odd women, a few gowned for day, but most of them in a state of dishabille that made my quilt modest by comparison. A woman near the end of the table caught sight of me hovering in the doorway, and beckoned, companionably sliding over to make room for me on the end of the long bench.

"You'll be the new lass, aye?" she said, looking me over with interest. "You're a wee bit older than Madame usually takes on—he likes 'em no more than five and twenty. You're no bad at all, though," she assured me hastily. "I'm sure you'll do fine."

"Good skin and a pretty face," observed the dark-haired lady across from us, sizing me up with the detached air of one appraising horseflesh. "And nice bubbies, what I can see." She lifted her chin slightly, peering across the table at what could be seen of my cleavage.

"Madame doesna like us to take the kivvers off the beds," my original acquaintance said reprovingly. "Ye should wear your shift, if ye havena something pretty to show yourself in yet."

"Aye, be careful with the quilt," advised the dark-haired girl, still scrutinizing me. "Madame'll dock your wages, an' ye get spots on the bedclothes."

"What's your name, my dearie?" A short, rather plump girl with a round, friendly face leaned past the dark girl's elbow to smile at me. "Here we're all chatterin' at ye, and not welcomed ye proper at all. I'm Dorcas, this is Peggy"—she jerked a thumb at the dark-haired girl, then pointed across the table to the fair-haired woman beside me—"and that's Mollie."

"My name is Claire," I said, smiling and hitching the quilt a bit higher in self-consciousness. I wasn't sure how to correct their impression that I was Madame Jeanne's newest recruit; for the moment, that seemed less important than getting some breakfast.

Apparently divining my need, the friendly Dorcas reached to the sideboard behind her, passed me a wooden plate, and shoved a large dish of sausages in my direction.

The food was well cooked and would have been good in any case; starved as I was, it was ambrosial. A hell of a lot better than the hospital cafeteria's breakfasts, I observed to myself, taking another ladle of fried potatoes.

"Had a rough one for your first, aye?" Millie, next to me, nodded at my bosom. Glancing down, I was mortified to see a large red patch peeking above the edge of my quilt. I couldn't see my neck, but the direction of Millie's interested gaze made it clear that the small tingling sensations there were evidence of further bite-marks.

"Your nose is a wee bit puffed, too," Peggy said, frowning at me critically. She reached across the table to touch it, disregarding the fact that the gesture caused her flimsy wrap to fall open to the waist. "Slap ye, did he? If they get too rough, ye should call out, ye know; Madame doesna allow the customers to mistreat us—give a good screech and Bruno will be in there in a moment."

"Bruno?" I said, a little faintly.

"The porter," Dorcas explained, busily spooning eggs into her mouth. "Big as a bear—that's why we call him Bruno. What's his name really?" she asked the table at large, "Horace?"

"Theobald," corrected Millie. She turned to call to a servingmaid at the end of the room, "Janie, will ye fetch in more ale? The new lassie's had none yet!"

"Aye, Peggy's right," she said, turning back to me. She wasn't at all pretty, but had a nicely shaped mouth and a pleasant expression. "If ye get a man likes to play a bit rough, that's one thing—and don't sic Bruno on a good customer, or there'll be hell to pay and you'll do the paying. But if ye think ye might really be damaged, then just give a good skelloch. Bruno's never far away during the night. Oh, here's the ale," she added, taking a big pewter mug from the servingmaid and plonking it in front of me.

"She's no damaged," Dorcas said, having completed her survey of the visible aspects of my person. "A bit sore between the legs, though, aye?" she said shrewdly, grinning at me.

"Ooh, look, she's *blushing*," said Mollie, giggling with de-
ht. "Ooh, you *are* a fresh one, aren't ye?"

I took a deep gulp of the ale. It was dark, rich, and extremely
elcome, as much for the width of the cup rim that hid my face as
r its taste.

"Never mind." Mollie patted my arm kindly. "After breakfast,
I show ye where the tubs are. Ye can soak your parts in warm
ter, and they'll be good as new by tonight."

"Be sure to show her where the jars are, too," put in Dorcas.
Sweet herbs," she explained to me. "Put them in the water
fore ye sit in it. Madame likes us to smell sweet."

"Eef ze men want to lie wiz a feesh, zey would go to ze docks;
ees more cheap," Peggy intoned, in what was patently meant
be an imitation of Madame Jeanne. The table erupted in giggles,
ich were rapidly quelled by the sudden appearance of Madame
rself, who entered through a door at the end of the room.

Madame Jeanne was frowning in a worried fashion, and seemed
preoccupied to notice the smothered hilarity.

"*Tsk!*" murmured Mollie, seeing the proprietor. "An early
stomer. I hate it when they come in the middle o' breakfast,"
e grumbled. "Stop ye digesting your food proper, it does."

"Ye needn't worry, Mollie; it's Claire'll have to take him,"
ggy said, tossing her dark plait out of the way. "Newest lass
es the ones no one wants," she informed me.

"Stick your finger up his bum," Dorcas advised me. "That
ngs 'em off faster than anything. I'll save ye a bannock for
er, if ye like."

"Er . . . thanks," I said. Just then, Madame Jeanne's eye lit
on me, and her mouth dropped open in a horrified "O."

"What are *you* doing here?" she asked, rushing up to grab me
the arm.

"Eating," I said, in no mood to be snatched at. I detached my
m from her grasp and picked up my ale cup.

"*Merde!*" she said. "Did no one bring you food this morn-
?"

"No," I said. "Nor yet clothes." I gestured at the quilt, which
s in imminent danger of falling off.

"*Nez de Cléopatre!*" she said violently. She stood up and
nced around the room, eyes flashing daggers. "I will have the

worthless scum of a maid flayed for this! A thousand apolog
Madame!''

"That's quite all right," I said graciously, aware of the looks
astonishment on the faces of my breakfast companions. "I've
a wonderful meal. Nice to have met you all, ladies," I said, ris
and doing my best to bow graciously while clutching my qu
"Now, Madame . . . about my gown?"

Amid Madame Jeanne's agitated protestations of apology, a
reiterated hopes that I would not find it necessary to tell Monsi
Fraser that I had been exposed to an undesirable intimacy with
working members of the establishment, I made my clumsy way
two more flights of stairs, and into a small room draped w
hanging garments in various stages of completion, with bolts
cloth stacked here and there in the corners of the chamber.

"A moment, please," Madame Jeanne said, and with a d
bow, left me to the company of a dressmaker's dummy, wit
large number of pins protruding from its stuffed bosom.

Apparently this was where the costuming of the inmates to
place. I walked around the room, quilt trailing, and observed s
eral flimsy silk wrappers under construction, together with a c
ple of elaborate gowns with very low necks, and a number
rather imaginative variations on the basic shift and camisol
removed one shift from its hook, and put it on.

It was made of fine cotton, with a low, gathered neck, a
embroidery in the form of multiple hands that curled enticin
under the bosom and down the sides of the waist, spreading
into a rakish caress atop the hips. It hadn't been hemmed, but
otherwise complete, and gave me a great deal more freedom
movement than had the quilt.

I could hear voices in the next room, where Madame was app
ently haranguing Bruno—or so I deduced the identity of the m
rumble.

"I do not care *what* the miserable girl's sister has done,"
was saying, "do you not realize that the wife of Monsieur Ja
was left naked and starving—"

"Are you sure she's his wife?" the deep male voice asked.
had heard—"

"So had I. But if he says this woman is his wife, I am

sposed to argue, *n'est-ce pas?*'' Madame sounded impatient.
Now, as to this wretched Madeleine—''

''It's not her fault, Madame,'' Bruno broke in. ''Have you not
ard the news this morning—about the Fiend?''

Madame gave a small gasp. ''No! Not another?''

''Yes, Madame.'' Bruno's voice was grim. ''No more than a
w doors away—above the Green Owl tavern. The girl was Made-
ne's sister; the priest brought the news just before breakfast. So
u can see—''

''Yes, I see.'' Madame sounded a little breathless. ''Yes, of
urse. Of course. Was it—the same?'' Her voice quivered with
staste.

''Yes, Madame. A hatchet or a big knife of some sort.'' He
wered his voice, as people do when recounting horrid things.
The priest told me that her head had been completely severed.
r body was near the door of her room, and her head''—his
ice dropped even lower, almost to a whisper—''her head was
ting on the mantelpiece, looking into the room. The landlord
ooned when he found her.''

A heavy thud from the next room suggested that Madame
anne had done likewise. Gooseflesh rippled up my arms, and my
n knees felt a trifle watery. I was beginning to agree with
mie's fear that his installing me in a house of prostitution had
en injudicious.

At any rate, I was now clad, if not entirely dressed, and I went
o the room next door, to find Madame Jeanne in semi-recline on
e sofa of a small parlor, with a burly, unhappy-looking man
ting on the hassock near her feet.

Madame started up at the sight of me. ''Madame Fraser! Oh, I
so sorry! I did not mean to leave you waiting, but I have
d . . .'' she hesitated, looking for some delicate expression
. . some distressing news.''

''I'd say so,'' I said. ''What's this about a Fiend?''

''You heard?'' She was already pale, now her complexion went
ew shades whiter, and she wrung her hands. ''What will he say?
 will be furious!'' she moaned.

''Who?'' I asked. ''Jamie, or the Fiend?''

''Your husband,'' she said. She looked about the parlor, dis-
cted. ''When he hears that his wife has been so shamefully
glected, mistaken for a *fille de joie* and exposed to—to—''

"I really don't think he'll mind,"· I said. "But I would like hear about the Fiend."

"You would?" Bruno's heavy eyebrows rose. He was a k man, with sloping shoulders and long arms that made him lo rather like a gorilla; a resemblance enhanced by a low brow and receding chin. He looked eminently suited to the role of bound in a brothel.

"Well." He hesitated, glancing at Madame Jeanne for gu ance, but the proprietor caught sight of the small enameled clo on the mantelpiece and jumped to her feet with an exclamation shock.

"Crottin!" she exclaimed. "I must go!" And with no mc than a perfunctory wave in my direction, she sped from the roo leaving Bruno and me looking after her in surprise.

"Oh," he said, recovering himself. "That's right, it was co ing at ten o'clock." It was a quarter-past ten, by the enamel clo Whatever "it" was, I hoped it would wait.

"Fiend," I prompted.

Like most people, Bruno was only too willing to reveal all t gory details, once past a pro forma demur for the sake of soc delicacy.

The Edinburgh Fiend was—as I had deduced from the conv sation thus far—a murderer. Like an early-day Jack the Ripper, specialized in women of easy virtue, whom he killed with blo from a heavy-bladed instrument. In some cases, the bodies h been dismembered or otherwise "interfered with," as Bruno sa in lowered voice.

The killings—eight in all—had occurred at intervals over t last two years. With one exception, the women had been killed their own rooms; most lived alone—two had been killed in bro els. Hence Madame's agitation, I supposed.

"What was the exception?" I asked.

Bruno crossed himself. "A nun," he whispered, the words e dently still a shock to him. "A French Sister of Mercy."

The Sister, coming ashore at Edinburgh with a group of n bound for London, had been abducted from the docks, without a of her companions noticing her absence in the confusion. By time she was discovered in one of Edinburgh's wynds, after nig fall, it was far too late.

"Raped?" I asked, with clinical interest.

Bruno eyed me with considerable suspicion.

"I do not know," he said formally. He rose heavily to his feet, s simian shoulders drooping with fatigue. I supposed he had en on duty all night; it must be his bedtime now. "If you will cuse me, Madame," he said, with remote formality, and went t.

I sat back on the small velvet sofa, feeling mildly dazed. Some-w I hadn't realized that quite so much went on in brothels in the ytime.

There was a sudden loud hammering at the door. It didn't sound e knocking, but as though someone really were using a metal-aded hammer to demand admittance. I got to my feet to answer e summons, but without further warning, the door burst open, d a slender imperious figure strode into the room, speaking ench in an accent so pronounced and an attitude so furious that I uld not follow it all.

"Are you looking for Madame Jeanne?" I managed to put in, izing a small pause when he stopped to draw breath for more vective. The visitor was a young man of about thirty, slightly ilt and strikingly handsome, with thick black hair and brows. He ared at me under these, and as he got a good look at me, an traordinary change went across his face. The brows rose, his ack eyes grew huge, and his face went white.

"Milady!" he exclaimed, and flung himself on his knees, em-acing me about the thighs as he pressed his face into the cotton ift at crotch level.

"Let go!" I exclaimed, shoving at his shoulders to detach him. don't work here. Let go, I say!"

"Milady!" he was repeating in tones of rapture. "Milady! You ve come back! A miracle! God has restored you!"

He looked up at me, smiling as tears streamed down his face. had large white perfect teeth. Suddenly memory stirred and ifted, showing me the outlines of an urchin's face beneath the an's bold visage.

"Fergus!" I said. "Fergus, is that really you? Get up, for God's e—let me see you!"

He rose to his feet, but didn't pause to let me inspect him. He thered me into a rib-cracking hug, and I clutched him in return, unding his back in the excitement of seeing him again. He had

been ten or so when I last saw him, just before Culloden. Now
was a man, and the stubble of his beard rasped against my chee

"I thought I was seeing a ghost!" he exclaimed. "It is rea
you, then?"

"Yes, it's me," I assured him.

"You have seen milord?" he asked excitedly. "He knows y
are here?"

"Yes."

"Oh!" He blinked and stepped back half a pace, as somethi
occurred to him. "But—but what about—" He paused, clea
confused.

"What about what?"

"There ye are! What in the name of God are ye doing up he
Fergus?" Jamie's tall figure loomed suddenly in the doorway. I
eyes widened at the sight of me in my embroidered shift. "Wh
are your clothes?" he asked. "Never mind," he said then, wavi
his hand impatiently as I opened my mouth to answer. "I have
time just now. Come along, Fergus, there's eighteen ankers
brandy in the alleyway, and the excisemen on my heels!"

And with a thunder of boots on the wooden staircase, they we
gone, leaving me alone once more.

◆━━▶

I wasn't sure whether I should join the party downstairs or n
but curiosity got the better of discretion. After a quick visit to
sewing room in search of more extensive covering, I made my w
down, a large shawl half-embroidered with hollyhocks flung rou
my shoulders.

I had gathered only a vague impression of the layout of
house the night before, but the street noises that filtered throu
the windows made it clear which side of the building faced
High Street. I assumed the alleyway to which Jamie had refer
must be on the other side, but wasn't sure. The houses of Ed
burgh were frequently constructed with odd little wings and tw
ing walls, to take advantage of every inch of space.

I paused on the large landing at the foot of the stairs, listen
for the sound of rolling casks as a guide. As I stood there, I fe
sudden draft on my bare feet, and turned to see a man standing
the open doorway from the kitchen.

He seemed as surprised as I, but after blinking at me, he smiled ..d stepped forward to grip me by the elbow.

"And a good morning to you, my dear. I didn't expect to find .y of you ladies up and about so early in the morning."

"Well, you know what they say about early to bed and early to ..e," I said, trying to extricate my elbow.

He laughed, showing rather badly stained teeth in a narrow jaw. No, what do they say about it?"

"Well, it's something they say in America, come to think of it," ..eplied, suddenly realizing that Benjamin Franklin, even if cur- ..ntly publishing, probably didn't have a wide readership in Edin- ..rgh.

"Got a wit about you, chuckie," he said, with a slight smile. ..end you down as a decoy, did she?"

"No. Who?" I said.

"The madam," he said, glancing around. "Where is she?"

"I have no idea," I said. "Let go!"

Instead, he tightened his grip, so that his fingers dug uncomfort- .ly into the muscles of my upper arm. He leaned closer, whisper- ..g in my ear with a gust of stale tobacco fumes.

"There's a reward, you know," he murmured confidentially. A percentage of the value of the seized contraband. No one ..uld need to know but you and me." He flicked one finger ..ntly under my breast, making the nipple stand up under the thin ..tton. "What d'ye say, chuck?"

I stared at him. "The excisemen are on my heels," Jamie had ..id. This must be one, then; an officer of the Crown, charged with .e prevention of smuggling and the apprehension of smugglers. ..hat had Jamie said? "The pillory, transportation, flogging, im- ..isonment, ear-nailing," waving an airy hand as though such ..nalties were the equivalent of a traffic ticket.

"Whatever are you talking about?" I said, trying to sound ..zzled. "And for the last time, let go of me!" He couldn't be ..ne, I thought. How many others were there around the build- ..g?

"Yes, please let go," said a voice behind me. I saw the excise- ..an's eyes widen as he glanced over my shoulder.

Mr. Willoughby stood on the second stair in rumpled blue silk, .arge pistol gripped in both hands. He bobbed his head politely .. the excise officer.

"Not stinking whore," he explained, blinking owlishly. "Hc orable wife."

The exciseman, clearly startled by the unexpected appearan of a Chinese, gawked from me to Mr. Willoughby and back aga

"Wife?" he said disbelievingly. "You say she's your *wife?*"

Mr. Willoughby, clearly catching only the salient word, nodd pleasantly.

"Wife," he said again. "Please letting go." His eyes were mc bloodshot slits, and it was apparent to me, if not to the excisema that his blood was still approximately 80 proof.

The exciseman pulled me toward himself and scowled at N Willoughby. "Now, listen here—" he began. He got no furth for Mr. Willoughby, evidently assuming that he had given fa warning, raised the pistol and pulled the trigger.

There was a loud crack, an even louder shriek, which must ha been mine, and the landing was filled with a cloud of gray powd smoke. The exciseman staggered back against the paneling, a lo of intense surprise on his face, and a spreading rosette of blood the breast of his coat.

Moving by reflex, I leapt forward and grasped the man unc the arms, easing him gently down to the floorboards of the lar ing. There was a flurry of noise from above, as the inhabitants the house crowded, chattering and exclaiming, onto the upp landing, attracted by the shot. Bounding footsteps came up t lower stairs two at a time.

Fergus burst through what must be the cellar door, a pistol in I hand.

"Milady," he gasped, catching sight of me sitting in the corr with the exciseman's body sprawled across my lap. "What ha you done?"

"Me?" I said indignantly. "*I* haven't done anything; it's . mie's pet Chinaman." I nodded briefly toward the stair, where N Willoughby, the pistol dropped unregarded by his feet, had s down on the step and was now regarding the scene below with benign and bloodshot eye.

Fergus said something in French that was too colloquial translate, but sounded highly uncomplimentary to Mr. W loughby. He strode across the landing, and reached out a hand grasp the little Chinaman's shoulder—or so I assumed, until I sa

at the arm he extended did not end in a hand, but in a hook of
eaming dark metal.

"Fergus!" I was so shocked at the sight that I stopped my
tempts to stanch the exciseman's wound with my shawl. "What
-what—" I said incoherently.

"What?" he said, glancing at me. Then, following the direction
my gaze, said, "Oh, that," and shrugged. "The English. Don't
orry about it, milady, we haven't time. You, *canaille,* get down-
airs!" He jerked Mr. Willoughby off the stairs, dragged him to
e cellar door and shoved him through it, with a callous disregard
r safety. I could hear a series of bumps, suggesting that the
hinese was rolling downstairs, his acrobatic skills having tempo-
ily deserted him, but had no time to worry about it.

Fergus squatted next to me, and lifted the exciseman's head by
e hair. "How many companions are with you?" he demanded.
Tell me quickly, *cochon,* or I slit your throat!"

From the evident signs, this was a superfluous threat. The man's
es were already glazing over. With considerable effort, the cor-
rs of his mouth drew back in a smile.

"I'll see . . . you . . . burn . . . in . . . hell," he whis-
red, and with a last convulsion that fixed the smile in a hideous
tus upon his face, he coughed up a startling quantity of bright
d foamy blood, and died in my lap.

More feet were coming up the stairs at a high rate of speed.
mie charged through the cellar door and barely stopped himself
fore stepping on the excise officer's trailing legs. His eyes trav-
ed up the body's length and rested on my face with horrified
mazement.

"What have ye done, Sassenach?" he demanded.

"Not her—the yellow pox," Fergus put in, saving me the trou-
e. He thrust the pistol into his belt and offered me his real hand.
Come, milady, you must get downstairs!"

Jamie forestalled him, bending over me as he jerked his head in
e direction of the front hall.

"I'll manage here," he said. "Guard the front, Fergus. The
ual signal, and keep your pistol hidden unless there's need."

Fergus nodded and vanished at once through the door to the
ll.

Jamie had succeeded in bundling the corpse awkwardly in the
awl; he lifted it off me, and I scrambled to my feet, greatly

relieved to be rid of it, in spite of the blood and other objectional
substances soaking the front of my shift.

"Ooh! I think he's *dead*!" An awestruck voice floated do
from above, and I looked up to see a dozen prostitutes peeri
down like cherubim from on high.

"Get back to your rooms!" Jamie barked. There was a chor
of frightened squeals, and they scattered like pigeons.

Jamie glanced around the landing for traces of the incident, I
luckily there were none—the shawl and I had caught everythi

"Come on," he said.

The stairs were dim and the cellar at the foot pitch-black
stopped at the bottom, waiting for Jamie. The exciseman had n
been lightly built, and Jamie was breathing hard when he reach
me.

"Across to the far side," he said, gasping. "A false wall. Ho
my arm."

With the door above shut, I couldn't see a thing; luckily Jan
seemed able to steer by radar. He led me unerringly past· lan
objects that I bumped in passing, and finally came to a halt. I co
smell damp stone, and putting out a hand, felt a rough wall befo
me.

Jamie said something loudly in Gaelic. Apparently it was t
Celtic equivalent of "open sesame," for there was a short silen
then a grating noise, and a faint glowing line appeared in t
darkness before me. The line widened into a slit, and a section
the wall swung out, revealing a small doorway, made of a wooc
framework, upon which cut stones were mounted so as to look l
part of the wall.

The concealed cellar was a large room, at least thirty feet lo
Several figures were moving about, and the air was ripely suffoc
ing with the smell of brandy. Jamie dumped the body unceremo
ously in a corner, then turned to me.

"God, Sassenach, are ye all right?" The cellar seemed to
lighted with candles, dotted here and there in the dimness. I co
just see his face, skin drawn tight across his cheekbones.

"I'm a little cold," I said, trying not to let my teeth chatt
"My shift is soaked with blood. Otherwise I'm all right. I think

"Jeanne!" He turned and called toward the far end of the cell
and one of the figures came toward us, resolving itself into a ve
worried-looking madam. He explained the situation in a f

ords, causing the worried expression to grow considerably
orse.

"Horreur!" she said. "Killed? On my premises? With *wit-
esses?"*

"Aye, I'm afraid so." Jamie sounded calm. "I'll manage about
. But in the meantime, ye must go up. He might not have been
lone. You'll know what to do."

His voice held a tone of calm assurance, and he squeezed her
rm. The touch seemed to calm her—I hoped that was why he had
one it—and she turned to leave.

"Oh, and Jeanne," Jamie called after her. "When ye come
ack, can ye bring down some clothes for my wife? If her gown's
ot ready, I think Daphne is maybe the right size."

"Clothes?" Madame Jeanne squinted into the shadows where I
ood. I helpfully stepped out into the light, displaying the results
f my encounter with the exciseman.

Madame Jeanne blinked once or twice, crossed herself, and
rned without a word, to disappear through the concealed door-
ay, which swung to behind her with a muffled thud.

I was beginning to shake, as much with reaction as with the
old. Accustomed as I was to emergency, blood, and even sudden
eath, the events of the morning had been more than a little har-
wing. It was like a bad Saturday night in the emergency room.

"Come along, Sassenach," Jamie said, putting a hand gently on
e small of my back. "We'll get ye washed." His touch worked
n me as well as it had on Madame Jeanne; I felt instantly better, if
ill apprehensive.

"Washed? In what? Brandy?"

He gave a slight laugh at that. "No, water. I can offer ye a
athtub, but I'm afraid it will be cold."

It was extremely cold.

"Wh-wh-where did this water come from?" I asked, shivering.
Off a glacier?" The water gushed out of a pipe set in the wall,
ormally kept plugged with an insanitary-looking wad of rags,
rapped to form a rough seal around the chunk of wood that
rved as a plug.

I pulled my hand out of the chilly stream and wiped it on the
ift, which was too far gone for anything to make much differ-
ace. Jamie shook his head as he maneuvered the big wooden tub
oser to the spout.

"Off the roof," he answered. "There's a rainwater cistern there. The guttering pipe runs down the side of the building, a the cistern pipe is hidden inside it." He looked absurdly proud himself, and I laughed.

"Quite an arrangement," I said. "What do you use the wa for?"

"To cut the liquor," he explained. He gestured at the far side the room, where the shadowy figures were working with nota! industry among a large array of casks and tubs. "It comes in hundred and eighty degrees above proof. We mix it here wi' p water, and recask it for sale to the taverns."

He shoved the rough plug back into the pipe, and bent to p the big tub across the stone floor. "Here, we'll take it out of way; they'll be needing the water." One of the men was in fi standing by with a small cask clasped in his arms; with no m than a curious glance at me, he nodded to Jamie and thrust cask beneath the stream of water.

Behind a hastily arranged screen of empty barrels, I peer dubiously down into the depths of my makeshift tub. A sin candle burned in a puddle of wax nearby, glimmering off surface of the water and making it look black and bottomless stripped off, shivering violently, thinking that the comforts of water and modern plumbing had seemed a hell of a lot easier renounce when they were close at hand.

Jamie groped in his sleeve and pulled out a large handkerchi at which he squinted dubiously.

"Aye, well, it's maybe cleaner than your shift," he said, shru ging. He handed it to me, then excused himself to oversee ope tions at the other end of the room.

The water was freezing and so was the cellar, and as I ginge sponged myself, the icy trickles running down my stomach a thighs brought on small fits of shivering.

Thoughts of what might be happening overhead did little to ea my feelings of chilly apprehension. Presumably, we were sa enough for the moment, so long as the false cellar wall deceiv any searching excisemen.

But if the wall failed to hide us, our position was all but ho less. There appeared to be no way out of this room but by the d in the false wall—and if that wall was breached, we would only be caught red-handed in possession of quite a lot of cont

⟩d brandy, but also in custody of the body of a murdered King's ⟩fficer.

And surely the disappearance of that officer would provoke an ⟩ensive search? I had visions of excisemen combing the brothel, ⟩estioning and threatening the women, emerging with complete ⟩scriptions of myself, Jamie, and Mr. Willoughby, as well as ⟩eral eyewitness accounts of the murder. Involuntarily, I glanced ⟩he far corner, where the dead man lay beneath his bloodstained ⟩oud, covered with pink and yellow hollyhocks. The Chinaman ⟩s nowhere to be seen, having apparently passed out behind the ⟩cers of brandy.

⟩'Here, Sassenach. Drink this; your teeth are chattering so, ⟩u're like to bite through your tongue.'' Jamie had reappeared by ⟩ seal hole like a St. Bernard dog, bearing a firkin of brandy.

⟩'Th-thanks.'' I had to drop the washcloth and use both hands to ⟩ady the wooden cup so it wouldn't clack against my teeth, but ⟩ brandy helped; it dropped like a flaming coal into the pit of my ⟩mach and sent small curling tendrils of warmth through my ⟩gid extremities as I sipped.

⟩'Oh, God, that's better,'' I said, stopping long enough to gasp ⟩ breath. ''Is this the uncut version?''

⟩'No, that would likely kill ye. This is maybe a little stronger ⟩n what we sell, though. Finish up and put something on; then ye ⟩ have a bit more.'' Jamie took the cup from my hand and gave ⟩ back the handkerchief washcloth. As I hurriedly finished my ⟩dly ablutions, I watched him from the corner of my eye. He was ⟩wning as he gazed at me, clearly deep in thought. I had imag-⟩d that his life was complicated; it hadn't escaped me that my ⟩sence was undoubtedly complicating it a good bit more. I ⟩uld have given a lot to know what he was thinking.

⟩'What are you thinking about, Jamie?'' I said, watching him ⟩elong as I swabbed the last of the smudges from my thighs. The ⟩ter swirled around my calves, disturbed by my movements, and ⟩ candlelight lit the waves with sparks, as though the dark blood ⟩ad washed from my body now glowed once more live and red in ⟩ water.

The frown vanished momentarily as his eyes cleared and fixed ⟩ my face.

'I am thinking that you're verra beautiful, Sassenach,'' he said ⟩tly.

"Maybe if one has a taste for gooseflesh on a large scale," said tartly, stepping out of the tub and reaching for the cup.

He grinned suddenly at me, teeth flashing white in the dimn of the cellar.

"Oh, aye," he said. "Well, you're speaking to the only man Scotland who has a terrible cockstand at sight of a pluck chicken."

I spluttered in my brandy and choked, half-hysterical from te sion and terror.

Jamie quickly shrugged out of his coat and wrapped the g ment around me, hugging me close against him as I shivered a coughed and gasped.

"Makes it hard to pass a poulterer's stall and stay decent," murmured in my ear, briskly rubbing my back through the fabr "Hush, Sassenach, hush now. It'll be fine."

I clung to him, shaking. "I'm sorry," I said. "I'm all right. I my fault, though. Mr. Willoughby shot the exciseman because thought he was making indecent advances to me."

Jamie snorted. "That doesna make it your fault, Sassenach," said dryly. "And for what it's worth, it's no the first time Chinaman's done something foolish, either. When he's dri taken, he'll do anything, and never mind how mad it is."

Suddenly Jamie's expression changed as he realized what I h said. He stared down at me, eyes wide. "Did ye say 'excisema Sassenach?"

"Yes, why?"

He didn't answer, but let go my shoulders and whirled on heel, snatching the candle off the cask in passing. Rather than left in the dark, I followed him to the corner where the corpse under its shawl.

"Hold this." Jamie thrust the candle unceremoniously into hand and knelt by the shrouded figure, pulling back the stain fabric that covered the face.

I had seen quite a few dead bodies; the sight was no shock, it still wasn't pleasant. The eyes had rolled up beneath half-clos lids, which did nothing to help the generally ghastly effect. Jan frowned at the dead face, drop-jawed and waxy in the candlelig and muttered something under his breath.

"What's wrong?" I asked. I had thought I would never warm again, but Jamie's coat was not only thick and well-made

d the remnants of his own considerable body heat. I was still
d, but the shivering had eased.

"This isna an exciseman," Jamie said, still frowning. "I know
the Riding Officers in the district, and the Superintending Of-
ers, too. But I've no seen this fellow before." With some dis-
te, he turned back the sodden flap of the coat and groped inside.
He felt about gingerly but thoroughly inside the man's clothing,
erging at last with a small penknife, and a small booklet bound
red paper.

" 'New Testament,' " I read, with some astonishment.

amie nodded, looking up at me with one brow raised. "Excise-
n or no, it seems a peculiar thing to bring with ye to a kittle-
osie." He wiped the little booklet on the shawl, then drew the
ds of fabric quite gently back over the face, and rose to his feet,
king his head.

'That's the only thing in his pockets. Any Customs inspector or
ciseman must carry his warrant upon his person at all times, for
erwise he's no authority to carry out a search of premises or
ze goods." He glanced up, eyebrows raised. "Why did ye think
was an exciseman?"

hugged the folds of Jamie's coat around myself, trying to
member what the man had said to me on the landing. "He asked
whether I was a decoy, and where the madam was. Then he
d that there was a reward—a percentage of seized contraband,
t's what he said—and that no one would know but him and me.
d you'd said there were excisemen after you," I added. "So
urally I thought he was one. Then Mr. Willoughby turned up
things rather went to pot."

amie nodded, still looking puzzled. "Aye, well. I havena got
idea who he is, but it's a good thing that he isna an exciseman.
ought at first something had come verra badly unstuck, but it's
ely all right."

'Unstuck?"

He smiled briefly. "I've an arrangement with the Superintend-
Customs Officer for the district, Sassenach."

gaped at him. "Arrangement?"

He shrugged. "Well, bribery then, if ye like to be straight out
ut it." He sounded faintly irritated.

'No doubt that's standard business procedure?" I said, trying
sound tactful. One corner of his mouth twitched slightly.

"Aye, it is. Well, in any case, there's an understanding, as might say, between Sir Percival Turner and myself, and to find h sending excise officers into this place would worry me consid ably."

"All right," I said slowly, mentally juggling all the half-und stood events of the morning, and trying to make a pattern of the "But in that case, what did you mean by telling Fergus the cisemen were on your heels? And why has everyone been raci round like chickens with their heads off?"

"Oh, that." He smiled briefly, and took my arm, turning away from the corpse at our feet. "Well, it's an arrangement, a said. And part of it is that Sir Percival must satisfy his own mast in London, by seizing sufficient amounts of contraband now a again. So we see to it that he's given the opportunity. Wally a the lads brought down two wagonloads from the coast; one of best brandy, and the other filled with spiled casks and the punk wine, topped off with a few ankers of cheap swill, just to give it flavor.

"I met them just outside the city this morning, as we plann and then we drove the wagons in, takin' care to attract the atte tion of the Riding Officer, who just happened to be passing wit small number of dragoons. They came along and we led them canty chase through the alleyways, until the time for me and good tubs to part company wi' Wally and his load of swill. Wa jumped off his wagon then, and made awa', and I drove like h down here, wi' two or three dragoons following, just for sho like. Looks good in a report, ye ken." He grinned at me, quoti *" 'The smugglers escaped in spite of industrious pursuit, but Majesty's valiant soldiers succeeded in capturing an en wagonload of spirits, valued at sixty pounds, ten shillings.'* You know the sort of thing?"

"I expect so," I said. "Then it was you and the good liquor t was arriving at ten? Madame Jeanne said—"

"Aye," he said, frowning. "She was meant to have the ce door open and the ramp in place at ten sharp—we havena got lo to get everything unloaded. She was bloody late this mornin had to circle round twice to keep from bringing the drago straight to the door."

"She was a bit distracted," I said, remembering suddenly ab

ie Fiend. I told Jamie about the murder at the Green Owl, and he
rimaced, crossing himself.

"Poor lass," he said.

I shuddered briefly at the memory of Bruno's description, and
1oved closer to Jamie, who put an arm about my shoulders. He
issed me absently on the forehead, glancing again at the shawl-
)vered shape on the ground.

"Well, whoever he was, if he wasna an exciseman, there are
kely no more of them upstairs. We should be able to get out of
ere soon."

"That's good." Jamie's coat covered me to the knees, but I felt
ie covert glances cast from the far end of the room at my bare
ilves, and was all too uncomfortably aware that I was naked
ider it. "Will we be going back to the printshop?" What with
ie thing and another, I didn't think I wanted to take advantage of
[adame Jeanne's hospitality any longer than necessary.

"Maybe for a bit. I'll have to think." Jamie's tone was ab-
racted, and I could see that his brow was furrowed in thought.
'ith a brief hug, he released me, and began to walk about the
:llar, staring meditatively at the stones underfoot.

"Er . . . what did you do with Ian?"

He glanced up, looking blank; then his face cleared.

"Oh, Ian. I left him making inquiries at the taverns above the
[arket Cross. I'll need to remember to meet him, later," he mut-
red, as though making a note to himself.

"I met Young Ian, by the way," I said conversationally.

Jamie looked startled. "He came here?"

"He did. Looking for you—about a quarter of an hour after you
ft, in fact."

"Thank God for small mercies!" He rubbed a hand through his
iir, looking simultaneously amused and worried. "I'd have had
e devil of a time explaining to Ian what his son was doing here."

"You *know* what he was doing here?" I asked curiously.

"No, I don't! He was supposed to be—ah, well, let it be. I
nna be worrit about it just now." He relapsed into thought,
nerging momentarily to ask, "Did Young Ian say where he was
•ing, when he left ye?"

I shook my head, gathering the coat around myself, and he
dded, sighed, and took up his slow pacing once more.

I sat down on an upturned tub and watched him. In spite of the general atmosphere of discomfort and danger, I felt absurd happy simply to be near him. Feeling that there was little I cou do to help the situation at present, I settled myself with the co wrapped round me, and abandoned myself to the momentary plea sure of looking at him—something I had had no chance to do, i the tumult of events.

In spite of his preoccupation, he moved with the surefoot grace of a swordsman, a man so aware of his body as to be able forget it entirely. The men by the casks worked by torchlight; gleamed on his hair as he turned, lighting it like a tiger's fur, wi stripes of gold and dark.

I caught the faint twitch as two fingers of his right hand flic ered together against the fabric of his breeches, and felt a strang little lurch of recognition in the gesture. I had seen him do that thousand times as he was thinking, and seeing it now again, felt a though all the time that had passed in our separation was no mo than the rising and setting of a single sun.

As though catching my thought, he paused in his strolling ar smiled at me.

"You'll be warm enough, Sassenach?" he asked.

"No, but it doesn't matter." I got off my tub and went to jo him in his peregrinations, slipping a hand through his arm. "Ma ing any progress with the thinking?"

He laughed ruefully. "No. I'm thinking of maybe half a doze things together, and half of them things I canna do anything abou Like whether Young Ian's where he should be."

I stared up at him. "Where he should be? Where do you thir he should be?"

"He *should* be at the printshop," Jamie said, with some emph sis. "But he *should* ha' been with Wally this morning, and I wasn't."

"With Wally? You mean you knew he wasn't at home, when h father came looking for him this morning?"

He rubbed his nose with a finger, looking at once irritated ar amused. "Oh, aye. I'd promised Young Ian I wouldna say an thing to his da, though, until he'd a chance to explain himself. N that an explanation is likely to save his arse," he added.

Young Ian had, as his father said, come to join his uncle Edinburgh without the preliminary bother of asking his parent leave. Jamie had discovered this dereliction fairly quickly, but ha

ot wanted to send his nephew alone back to Lallybroch, and had
ot yet had time to escort him personally.

"It's not that he canna look out for himself," Jamie explained,
musement winning in the struggle of expressions on his face.
'He's a nice capable lad. It's just—well, ye ken how things just
appen around some folk, without them seeming to have anything
much to do wi' it?"

"Now that you mention it, yes," I said wryly. "I'm one of
hem."

He laughed out loud at that. "God, you're right, Sassenach!
Maybe that's why I like Young Ian so well; he 'minds me of you."

"He reminded me a bit of *you*," I said.

Jamie snorted briefly. "God, Jenny will maim me, and she
ears her baby son's been loitering about a house of ill repute. I
ope the wee bugger has the sense to keep his mouth shut, once
e's home."

"I hope he *gets* home," I said, thinking of the gawky almost-
fteen-year-old I had seen that morning, adrift in an Edinburgh
lled with prostitutes, excisemen, smugglers, and hatchet-wield-
g Fiends. "At least he isn't a girl," I added, thinking of this last
em. "The Fiend doesn't seem to have a taste for young boys."

"Aye, well, there are plenty of others who have," Jamie said
ourly. "Between Young Ian and you, Sassenach, I shall be lucky
my hair's not gone white by the time we get out of this stinking
ellar."

"Me?" I said in surprise. "You don't need to worry about
e."

"I don't?" He dropped my arm and rounded on me, glaring. "I
inna need to worry about ye? Is that what ye said? Christ! I leave
e safely in bed waiting for your breakfast, and not an hour later, I
nd ye downstairs in your shift, clutching a corpse to your bosom!
nd now you're standing in front of me bare as an egg, with
fteen men over there wondering who in hell ye are—and how
'ye think I'm going to explain ye to them, Sassenach? Tell me
at, eh?" He shoved a hand through his hair in exasperation.

"Sweet bleeding Jesus! And I've to go up the coast in two days
ithout fail, but I canna leave ye in Edinburgh, not wi' Fiends
eepin' about with hatchets, and half the people who've seen ye
inking you're a prostitute, and . . . and . . ." The lacing
round his pigtail broke abruptly under the pressure, and his hair

fluffed out round his head like a lion's mane. I laughed. He glare
for a moment longer, but then a reluctant grin made its way slow
through the frown.

"Aye, well," he said, resigned. "I suppose I'll manage."

"I suppose you will," I said, and stood on tiptoe to brush hi
hair back behind his ears. Working on the same principle tha
causes magnets of opposing polarities to snap together whe
placed in close proximitry, he bent his head and kissed me.

"I had forgotten," he said, a moment later.

"Forgotten what?" His back was warm through the thin shir

"Everything." He spoke very softly, mouth against my hai
"Joy. Fear. Fear, most of all." His hand came up and smoothe
my curls away from his nose.

"I havena been afraid for a verra long time, Sassenach," h
whispered. "But now I think I am. For there is something to b
lost, now."

I drew back a little, to look up at him. His arms were locke
tight around my waist, his eyes dark as bottomless water in th
dimness. Then his face changed and he kissed me quickly on th
forehead.

"Come along, Sassenach," he said, taking me by the arm. "I'
tell the men you're my wife. The rest of it will just have to bide.

27

Up in Flames

The dress was a trifle lower cut than necessary, and a bit tight in the bosom, but on the whole, not a bad fit.

"And how did you know Daphne would be the right size?" I asked, spooning up my soup.

"I said I didna bed wi' the lasses," Jamie replied circumspectly. "I never said I didna look at them." He blinked at me like a large red owl—some congenital tic made him incapable of closing one eye in a wink—and I laughed.

"That gown becomes ye a good deal more than it did Daphne, though." He cast a glance of general approval at my bosom and waved at a servingmaid carrying a platter of fresh bannocks.

Moubray's tavern was doing a thriving dinner business. Several cuts above the snug, smoky atmosphere to be found in The World's End and similar serious drinking establishments, Moubray's was a large and elegant place, with an outside stair that ran up to the second floor, where a commodious dining room accommodated the appetites of Edinburgh's prosperous tradesmen and public officials.

"Who are you at the moment?" I asked. "I heard Madame Jeanne call you 'Monsieur Fraser'—are you Fraser in public, though?"

He shook his head and broke a bannock into his soup bowl. "No, at the moment, I'm Sawney Malcolm, Printer and Publisher."

"Sawney? That's a nickname for Alexander, is it? I should have thought 'Sandy' was more like it, especially considering your

hair.'' Not that his hair was sandy-colored in the least, I reflecte
looking at it. It was like Bree's hair—very thick, with a slig
wave to it, and all the colors of red and gold mixed; copper ar
cinnamon, auburn and amber, red and roan and rufous, all mi
gled together.

I felt a sudden wave of longing for Bree; at the same time,
longed to untie Jamie's hair from its formal plait and run n
hands up under it, to feel the solid curve of his skull, and the so
strands tangled in my fingers. I could still recall the tickle of
spilling loose and rich across my breasts in the morning light.

My breath coming a little short, I bent my head to my oyst
stew.

Jamie appeared not to have noticed; he added a large pat
butter to his bowl, shaking his head as he did so.

''Sawney's what they say in the Highlands,'' he informed m
''And in the Isles, too. Sandy's more what ye'd hear in the Lo
lands—or from an ignorant Sassenach.'' He lifted one eyebrow
me, smiling, and raised a spoonful of the rich, fragrant stew to h
mouth.

''All right,'' I said. ''I suppose more to the point, though—wh
am *I*?''

He had noticed, after all. I felt one large foot nudge mine, ar
he smiled at me over the rim of his cup.

''You're my wife, Sassenach,'' he said gruffly. ''Always. N
matter who I may be—you're my wife.''

I could feel the flush of pleasure rise in my face, and see tl
memories of the night before reflected in his own. The tips of h
ears were faintly pink.

''You don't suppose there's too much pepper in this stew?''
asked, swallowing another spoonful. ''Are you sure, Jamie?''

''Aye,'' he said. ''Aye, I'm sure,'' he amended, ''and no, tl
pepper's fine. I like a wee bit of pepper.'' The foot moved slight
against mine, the toe of his shoe barely brushing my ankle.

''So I'm Mrs. Malcolm,'' I said, trying out the name on n
tongue. The mere fact of saying ''Mrs.'' gave me an absurd litt
thrill, like a new bride. Involuntarily, I glanced down at the silv
ring on my right fourth finger.

Jamie caught the glance, and raised his cup to me.

''To Mrs. Malcolm,'' he said softly, and the breathless feelir
came back.

He set down the cup and took my hand; his own was big and so warm that a general feeling of glowing heat spread rapidly through my fingers. I could feel the silver ring, separate from my flesh, its metal heated by his touch.

"To have and to hold," he said, smiling.

"From this day forward," I said, not caring in the least that we were attracting interested glances from the other diners.

Jamie bent his head and pressed his lips against the back of my hand, an action that turned the interested glances into frank stares. A clergyman was seated across the room; he glared at us and said something to his companions, who turned round to stare. One was a small, elderly man; the other, I was surprised to see, was Mr. Wallace, my companion from the Inverness coach.

"There are private rooms upstairs," Jamie murmured, blue eyes dancing over my knuckles, and I lost interest in Mr. Wallace.

"How interesting," I said. "You haven't finished your stew."

"Damn the stew."

"Here comes the servingmaid with the ale."

"Devil take her." Sharp white teeth closed gently on my knuckle, making me jerk slightly in my seat.

"People are watching you."

"Let them, and I trust they've a fine day for it."

His tongue flicked gently between my fingers.

"There's a man in a green coat coming this way."

"To hell—" Jamie began, when the shadow of the visitor fell upon the table.

"A good day to you, Mr. Malcolm," said the visitor, bowing politely. "I trust I do not intrude?"

"You do," said Jamie, straightening up but keeping his grip on my hand. He turned a cool gaze on the newcomer. "I think I do not know ye, sir?"

The gentleman, an Englishman of maybe thirty-five, quietly dressed, bowed again, not intimidated by this marked lack of hospitality.

"I have not had the pleasure of your acquaintance as yet, sir," he said deferentially. "My master, however, bade me greet you, and inquire whether you—and your companion—might be so agreeable as to take a little wine with him."

The tiny pause before the word "companion" was barely discernible, but Jamie caught it. His eyes narrowed.

"My wife and I," he said, with precisely the same sort of pau
before "wife," "are otherwise engaged at the moment. Shou
your master wish to speak wi' me—"

"It is Sir Percival Turner who sends to ask, sir," the secretary
for so he must be—put in quickly. Well-bred as he was, I
couldn't resist a tiny flick of one eyebrow, as one who uses a nan
he expects to conjure with.

"Indeed," said Jamie dryly. "Well, with all respect to Sir Pe
cival, I am preoccupied at present. If you will convey him n
regrets?" He bowed, with a politeness so pointed as to con
within a hair of rudeness, and turned his back on the secretar
That gentleman stood for a moment, his mouth slightly open, the
pivoted smartly on his heel and made his way through the scatt
of tables to a door on the far side of the dining room.

"Where was I?" Jamie demanded. "Oh, aye—to hell wi' ge
tlemen in green coats. Now, about these private rooms—"

"How are you going to explain me to people?" I asked.

He raised one eyebrow.

"Explain what?" He looked me up and down. "Why must
make excuses for ye? You're no missing any limbs; you're n
poxed, hunchbacked, toothless or lame—"

"You know what I mean," I said, kicking him lightly under th
table. The lady sitting near the wall nudged her companion a
widened her eyes disapprovingly at us. I smiled nonchalantly
them.

"Aye, I do," he said, grinning. "However, what wi' Mr. W
loughby's activities this morning, and one thing and another,
havena had much chance to think about the matter. Perhaps I
just say—"

"My dear fellow, so you are married! Capital news! Simp
capital! My deepest congratulations, and may I be—dare I hope
be?—the first to extend my felicitations and best wishes to yo
lady?"

A small, elderly gentleman in a tidy wig leaned heavily on
gold-knobbed stick, beaming genially at us both. It was the litt
gentleman who had been sitting with Mr. Wallace and the clerg
man.

"You will pardon the minor discourtesy of my sending Johns
to fetch you earlier, I am sure," he said deprecatingly. "It is on
that my wretched infirmity prevents rapid movement, as you see.

Jamie had risen to his feet at the appearance of the visitor, and ith a polite gesture, now drew out a chair.

"You'll join us, Sir Percival?" he said.

"Oh, no, no indeed! Shouldn't dream of intruding on your new ppiness, my dear sir. Truly, I had no idea—" Still protesting acefully, he sank down into the proffered chair, wincing as he tended his foot beneath the table.

"I am a martyr to gout, my dear," he confided, leaning close ough for me to smell his foul old-man's breath beneath the intergreen that spiced his linen.

He didn't look corrupt, I thought—breath notwithstanding—but en appearances could be deceiving; it was only about four hours ice I had been mistaken for a prostitute.

Making the best of it, Jamie called for wine, and accepted Sir rcival's continued effusions with some grace.

"It is rather fortunate that I should have encountered you here, y dear fellow," the elderly gentleman said, breaking off his wery compliments at last. He laid a small, manicured hand on mie's sleeve. "I had something particular to say to you. In fact, I d sent a note to the printshop, but my messenger failed to find u there."

"Ah?" Jamie cocked an eyebrow in question.

"Yes," Sir Percival went on. "I believe you had spoken to me some weeks ago, I scarce recall the occasion—of your intention travel north on business. A matter of a new press, or something the sort?" Sir Percival had quite a sweet face, I thought, hand-mely patrician despite his years, with large, guileless blue eyes.

"Aye, that's so," Jamie agreed courteously. "I am invited by r. McLeod of Perth, to see a new style of letterpress he's re-ntly put in use."

"Quite." Sir Percival paused to remove a snuffbox from his cket, a pretty thing enameled in green and gold, with cherubs on e lid.

"I really should not advise a trip to the north just now," he id, opening the box and concentrating on its contents. "Really I ould not. The weather is like to be inclement at this season; I am re it would not suit Mrs. Malcolm." Smiling at me like an derly angel, he inhaled a large pinch of snuff and paused, linen ndkerchief at the ready.

Jamie sipped at his wine, his face blandly composed.

"I am grateful for your advice, Sir Percival," he said. "You perhaps have received word from your agents of recent storms the north?"

Sir Percival sneezed, a small, neat sound, like a mouse with cold. He was rather like a white mouse altogether, I thought seeing him dab daintily at his pointed pink nose.

"Quite," he said again, putting away the kerchief and blinking benevolently at Jamie. "No, I would—as a particular friend wi your welfare at heart—most strongly advise that you remain Edinburgh. After all," he added, turning the beam of his benevolence on me, "you surely have an inducement to remain comfortably at home now, do you not? And now, my dear young people. am afraid I must take my leave; I must not detain you any long from what must be your wedding breakfast."

With a little assistance from the hovering Johnson, Sir Percival got up and tottered off, his gold-knobbed stick tap-tapping on the floor.

"He seems a nice old gent," I remarked, when I was sure he was far enough away not to hear me.

Jamie snorted. "Rotten as a worm-riddled board," he said. He picked up his glass and drained it. "Ye'd think otherwise," he said meditatively, putting it down and staring after the wizened figure now cautiously negotiating the head of the stairs. "A man as close as Sir Percival is to Judgment Day, I mean. Ye'd think fear o' the Devil would prevent him, but not a bit."

"I suppose he's like everyone else," I said cynically. "Most people think they're going to live forever."

Jamie laughed, his exuberant spirits returning with a rush.

"Aye, that's true," he said. He pushed my wineglass toward me. "And now you're here, Sassenach, I'm convinced of it. Drink up, *mo nighean donn,* and we'll go upstairs."

"Post coitum omne animalium triste est," I remarked, with my eyes closed.

There was no response from the warm, heavy weight on my chest, save the gentle sigh of his breathing. After a moment though, I felt a sort of subterranean vibration, which I interpreted as amusement.

"That's a verra peculiar sentiment, Sassenach," Jamie said, his voice blurred with drowsiness. "Not your own, I hope?"

"No." I stroked the damp bright hair back from his forehead, and he turned his face into the curve of my shoulder, with a small contented snuffle.

The private rooms at Moubray's left a bit to be desired in the way of amorous accommodation. Still, the sofa at least offered a padded horizontal surface, which, if you came right down to it, was all that was necessary. While I had decided that I was not past wanting to commit passionate acts after all, I was still too old to want to commit them on the bare floorboards.

"I don't know who said it—some ancient philosopher or other. It was quoted in one of my medical textbooks; in the chapter on the human reproductive system."

The vibration made itself audible as a small chuckle.

"Ye'd seem to have applied yourself to your lessons to good purpose, Sassenach," he said. His hand passed down my side and wormed its way slowly underneath to cup my bottom. He sighed with contentment, squeezing slightly.

"I canna think when I have felt less *triste*," he said.

"Me either," I said, tracing the whorl of the small cowlick that lifted the hair from the center of his forehead. "That's what made me think of it—I rather wondered what led the ancient philosopher to that conclusion."

"I suppose it depends on the sorts of *animaliae* he'd been fornicating with," Jamie observed. "Maybe it was just that none of them took to him, but he must ha' tried a fair number, to make such a sweeping statement."

He held tighter to his anchor as the tide of my laughter bounced him gently up and down.

"Mind ye, dogs sometimes do look a trifle sheepish when they've done wi' mating," he said.

"Mm. And how do sheep look, then?"

"Aye, well, female sheep just go on lookin' like sheep—not havin' a great deal of choice in the matter, ye ken."

"Oh? And what do the male sheep look like?"

"Oh, they look fair depraved. Let their tongues hang out, drool-ing, and their eyes roll back, while they make disgusting noises. Like most male animals, aye?" I could feel the curve of his grin

against my shoulder. He squeezed again, and I pulled gently on th
ear closest to hand.

"I didn't notice your tongue hanging out."

"Ye werena noticing; your eyes were closed."

"I didn't hear any disgusting noises, either."

"Well, I couldna just think of any on the spur of the moment
he admitted. "Perhaps I'll do better next time."

We laughed softly together, and then were quiet, listening
each other breathe.

"Jamie," I said softly at last, smoothing the back of his hea
"I don't think I've ever been so happy."

He rolled to one side, shifting his weight carefully so as not
squash me, and lifted himself to lie face-to-face with me.

"Nor me, my Sassenach," he said, and kissed me, very light
but lingering, so that I had time just to close my lips in a tiny bi
on the fullness of his lower lip.

"It's no just the bedding, ye ken," he said, drawing back a lit
at last. His eyes looked down at me, a soft deep blue like the war
tropic sea.

"No," I said, touching his cheek. "It isn't."

"To have ye with me again—to talk wi' you—to know I can s
anything, not guard my words or hide my thoughts—God, Sass
nach," he said, "the Lord knows I am lust-crazed as a lad, and
canna keep my hands from you—or anything else—" he adde
wryly, "but I would count that all well lost, had I no more than t
pleasure of havin' ye by me, and to tell ye all my heart."

"It was lonely without you," I whispered. "So lonely."

"And me," he said. He looked down, long lashes hiding h
eyes, and hesitated for a moment.

"I willna say that I have lived a monk," he said quietly. "Wh
I had to—when I felt that I must or go mad—"

I laid my fingers against his lips, to stop him.

"Neither did I," I said. "Frank—"

His own hand pressed gently against my mouth. Both dumb,
looked at each other, and I could feel the smile growing behind
hand, and my own under his, to match it. I took my hand away

"It doesna signify," he said. He took his hand off my mout

"No," I said. "It doesn't matter." I traced the line of his li
with my finger.

"So tell me all your heart," I said. "If there's time."

He glanced at the window to gauge the light—we were to meet an at the printshop at five o'clock, to check the progress of the earch for Young Ian—and then rolled carefully off me.

"There's two hours, at least, before we must go. Sit up and put our clothes on, and I'll have them bring some wine and biscuits."

This sounded wonderful. I seemed to have been starving ever ince I found him. I sat up and began to rummage through the pile f discarded clothes on the floor, looking for the set of stays the ow-necked gown required.

"I'm no ways sad, but I do maybe feel a bit ashamed," Jamie bserved, wriggling long, slender toes into a silk stocking. "Or I hould, at least."

"Why is that?"

"Well, here I am, in paradise, so to speak, wi' you and wine and iscuits, while Ian's out tramping the pavements and worrying for is son."

"Are you worried about Young Ian?" I asked, concentrating on ly laces.

He frowned slightly, pulling on the other stocking.

"Not so much worried for him as afraid he may not turn up efore tomorrow."

"What happens tomorrow?" I asked, and then belatedly re- alled the encounter with Sir Percival Turner. "Oh, your trip to the orth—that was supposed to be tomorrow?"

He nodded. "Aye, there's a rendezvous set at Mullin's Cove, omorrow being the dark of the moon. A lugger from France, wi' a ›ad of wine and cambric."

"And Sir Percival was warning you not to make that rendez- ›us?"

"So it seems. What's happened, I canna say, though I expect ll find out. Could be as there's a visiting Customs Officer in the istrict, or he's had word of some activity on the coast there that as nothing to do wi' us, but could interfere." He shrugged and nished his last garter.

He spread out his hands upon his knees then, palm up, and owly curled the fingers inward. The left curled at once into a fist, ›mpact and neat, a blunt instrument ready for battle. The fingers f his right hand curled more slowly; the middle finger was ˉooked, and would not lie along the second. The fourth finger

would not curl at all, but stuck out straight, holding the little finge
at an awkward angle beside it.

He looked from his hands to me, smiling.

"D'ye remember the night when ye set my hand?"

"Sometimes, in my more horrible moments." That night wa
one to remember—only because it couldn't be forgotten. Agains
all odds, I had rescued him from Wentworth Prison and a deat
sentence—but not in time to prevent his being cruelly tortured an
abused by Black Jack Randall.

I picked up his right hand and transferred it to my own knee. H
let it lie there, warm, heavy and inert, and didn't object as I fe
each finger, pulling gently to stretch the tendons and twisting t
see the range of motion in the joints.

"My first orthopedic surgery, that was," I said wryly.

"Have ye done a great many things like that since?" he aske
curiously, looking down at me.

"Yes, a few. I'm a surgeon—but it doesn't mean then what
means now," I added hastily. "Surgeons in my time don't pu
teeth and let blood. They're more like what's meant now by th
word 'physician'—a doctor with training in all the fields of med
cine, but with a specialty."

"Special, are ye? Well, ye've always been that," he said, gri
ning. The crippled fingers slid into my palm and his thumb stroke
my knuckles. "What is it a surgeon does that's special, then?"

I frowned, trying to think of the right phrasing. "Well, as best
can put it—a surgeon tries to effect healing . . . by means of
knife."

His long mouth curled upward at the notion.

"A nice contradiction, that; but it suits ye, Sassenach."

"It does?" I said, startled.

He nodded, never taking his eyes off my face. I could see hi
studying me closely, and wondered self-consciously what I mu
look like, flushed from lovemaking, with my hair in wild disorde

"Ye havena been lovelier, Sassenach," he said, smile growi
wider as I reached up to smooth my hair. He caught my hand, a
kissed it gently. "Leave your curls be.

"No," he said, holding my hands trapped while he looked m
over, "no, a knife is verra much what you are, now I think of it.
clever-worked scabbard, and most gorgeous to see, Sassenach"-
he traced the line of my lips with a finger, provoking a smile-

'but tempered steel for a core . . . and a wicked sharp edge, I do think.''

"Wicked?" I said, surprised.

"Not heartless, I don't mean," he assured me. His eyes rested on my face, intent and curious. A smile touched his lips. "No, never that. But you can be ruthless strong, Sassenach, when the need is on ye."

I smiled, a little wryly. "I can," I said.

"I have seen that in ye before, aye?" His voice grew softer and his grasp on my hand tightened. "But now I think ye have it much more than when ye were younger. You'll have needed it often since, no?"

I realized quite suddenly why he saw so clearly what Frank had never seen at all.

"You have it too," I said. "And you've needed it. Often." Unconsciously, my fingers touched the jagged scar that crossed his middle finger, twisting the distal joints.

He nodded.

"I have wondered," he said, so low I could scarcely hear him. "Wondered often, if I could call that edge to my service, and sheathe it safe again. For I have seen a great many men grow hard in that calling, and their steel decay to dull iron. And I have wondered often, was I master in my soul, or did I become the slave of my own blade?

"I have thought again and again," he went on, looking down at our linked hands . . . "that I had drawn my blade too often, and spent so long in the service of strife that I wasna fit any longer for human intercourse."

My lips twitched with the urge to make a remark, but I bit them instead. He saw it, and smiled, a little wryly.

"I didna think I should ever laugh again in a woman's bed, Sassenach," he said. "Or even come to a woman, save as a brute, blind with need." A note of bitterness came into his voice.

I lifted his hand, and kissed the small scar on the back of it.

"I can't see you as a brute," I said. I meant it lightly, but his face softened as he looked at me, and he answered seriously.

"I know that, Sassenach. And it is that ye canna see me so that gives me hope. For I am—and know it—and yet perhaps . . ." He trailed off, watching me intently.

"You have that—the strength. Ye have it, and your soul as wel So perhaps my own may be saved."

I had no notion what to say to this, and said nothing for a whil but only held his hand, caressing the twisted fingers and the larg hard knuckles. It was a warrior's hand—but he was not a warrio now.

I turned the hand over and smoothed it on my knee, palm up Slowly, I traced the deep lines and rising hillocks, and the tin letter "C" at the base of his thumb; the brand that marked hin mine.

"I knew an old lady in the Highlands once, who said the lines i your hand don't predict your life; they reflect it."

"Is that so, then?" His fingers twitched slightly, but his palm lay still and open.

"I don't know. She said you're born with the lines of your han —with a life—but then the lines change, with the things you do and the person you are." I knew nothing about palmistry, but could see one deep line that ran from wrist to midpalm, forkin several times.

"I think that might be the one they call a life-line," I said. "Se all the forks? I suppose that would mean you'd changed your life lot, made a lot of choices."

He snorted briefly, but with amusement rather than derision.

"Oh, aye? Well, that's safe enough to say." He peered into h palm, leaning over my knee. "I suppose the first fork would l when I met Jack Randall, and the second when I wed you—se they're close together, there."

"So they are." I ran my finger slowly along the line, making h fingers twitch slightly as it tickled. "And Culloden maybe wou be another?"

"Perhaps." But he did not wish to talk of Culloden. His ow finger moved on. "And when I went to prison, and came bac again, and came to Edinburgh."

"And became a printer." I stopped and looked up at hin brows raised. "How on earth *did* you come to be a printer? It's th last thing I would have thought of."

"Oh, that." His mouth widened in a smile. "Well—it was accident, aye?"

To start with he had only been looking for a business that would help to conceal and facilitate the smuggling. Possessed of a sizable sum from a recent profitable venture, he had determined to purchase a business whose normal operations involved a large wagon and team of horses, and some discreet premises that could be used for the temporary storage of goods in transit.

Carting suggested itself, but was rejected precisely because the operations of that business made its practitioners subject to more or less constant scrutiny from the Customs. Likewise, the ownership of a tavern or inn, while superficially desirable because of the large quantities of supplies brought in, was too vulnerable in its legitimate operation to hide an illegitimate one; tax collectors and Customs agents hung about taverns like fleas on a fat dog.

"I thought of printing, when I went to a place to have some notices made up," he explained. "As I was waiting to put in my order, I saw the wagon come rumbling up, all loaded wi' boxes of paper and casks of alcohol for the ink powder, and I thought, by God, that's it! For excisemen would never be troubling a place like that."

It was only after purchasing the shop in Carfax Close, hiring Geordie to run the press, and actually beginning to fill orders for posters, pamphlets, folios, and books, that the other possibilities of his new business had occurred to him.

"It was a man named Tom Gage," he explained. He loosed his hand from my grasp, growing eager in the telling, gesturing and rubbing his hands through his hair as he talked, disheveling himself with enthusiasm.

"He brought in small orders for this or that—innocent stuff, all of it—but often, and stayed to talk over it, taking trouble to talk to me as well as to Geordie, though he must have seen I knew less about the business than he did himself."

He smiled at me wryly.

"I didna ken much about printing, Sassenach, but I do ken men."

It was obvious that Gage was exploring the sympathies of Alexander Malcolm; hearing the faint sibilance of Jamie's Highland speech, he had prodded delicately, mentioning this acquaintance and that whose Jacobite sympathies had led them into trouble after the Rising, picking up the threads of mutual acquaintance, skillfully directing the conversation, stalking his prey. Until at last, the amused prey had bluntly told him to bring what he wanted mad no King's man would hear of it.

"And he trusted you." It wasn't a question; the only man wh had ever trusted Jamie Fraser in error was Charles Stuart—and that case, the error was Jamie's.

"He did." And so an association was begun, strictly business the beginning, but deepening into friendship as time went o Jamie had printed all the materials generated by Gage's sma group of radical political writers—from publicly acknowledge articles to anonymous broadsheets and pamphlets filled with mat rial incriminating enough to get the authors summarily jailed hanged.

"We'd go to the tavern down the street and talk, after th printing was done. I met a few of Tom's friends, and finally To said I should write a small piece myself. I laughed and told hi that, with my hand, by the time I'd penned anything that could read, we'd all be dead—of old age, not hanging.

"I was standing by the press as we were talking, setting the typ wi' my left hand, not even thinking. He just stared at me, and the he started to laugh. He pointed at the tray, and at my hand, ar went on laughing, 'til he had to sit down on the floor to stop.'

He stretched out his arms in front of him, flexing his hands ar studying them dispassionately. He curled one hand into a fist ar bent it slowly up toward his face, making the muscles of his ar ripple and swell under the linen.

"I'm hale enough," he said. "And with luck, may be so for good many years yet—but not forever, Sassenach. I ha' fought w sword and dirk many times, but to every warrior comes the da when his strength will fail him." He shook his head and stretche out a hand toward his coat, which lay on the floor.

"I took these, that day wi' Tom Gage, to remind me of it," said.

He took my hand and put into it the things he had taken from h pocket. They were cool, and hard to the touch, small heav oblongs of lead. I didn't need to feel the incised ends to kno what the letters on the type slugs were.

"Q.E.D.," I said.

"The English took my sword and dirk away," he said softl His finger touched the slugs that lay in my palm. "But Tom Ga

ut a weapon into my hands again, and I think I shall not lay it
own.''

We walked arm in arm down the cobbled slope of the Royal
Mile at a quarter to five, suffused with a glow engendered by
everal bowls of well-peppered oyster stew and a bottle of wine,
hared at intervals during our ''private communications.''

The city glowed all around us, as though sharing our happiness.
Edinburgh lay under a haze that would soon thicken to rain again,
ut for now, the light of the setting sun hung gold and pink and red
n the clouds, and shone in the wet patina of the cobbled street, so
nat the gray stones of the buildings softened and streamed with
eflected light, echoing the glow that warmed my cheeks and
hone in Jamie's eyes when he looked at me.

I drifted down the street in this state of soft-headed self-absorp-
on, it was several minutes before I noticed anything amiss. A
nan, impatient of our meandering progress, stepped briskly
round us, and then came to a dead stop just in front of me,
naking me trip on the wet stones and throw a shoe.

He flung up his head and stared skyward for a moment, then
urried off down the street, not running, but walking as fast as he
ould go.

''What's the matter with him?'' I said, stooping to retrieve my
hoe. Suddenly I noticed that all around us, folk were stopping,
taring up, and then starting to rush down the street.

''What do you think—?'' I began, but when I turned to Jamie,
e too was staring intently upward. I looked up, too, and it took
nly a moment to see that the red glow in the clouds above was a
ood deal deeper than the general color of the sunset sky, and
eemed to flicker in an uneasy fashion most uncharacteristic of
unsets.

''Fire,'' he said. ''God, I think it's in Leith Wynd!''

At the same moment, someone farther down the street raised
ne cry of ''Fire!'' and as though this official diagnosis had given
nem leave to run at last, the hurrying figures below broke loose
nd cascaded down the street like a herd of lemmings, anxious to
ing themselves into the pyre.

A few saner souls ran upward, past us, also shouting ''Fire!''

but presumably with the intent of alerting whatever passed for fire department.

Jamie was already in motion, tugging me along as I hopp awkwardly on one foot. Rather than stop, I kicked the other sh off, and followed him, slipping and stubbing my toes on the co wet cobbles as I ran.

The fire was not in Leith Wynd, but next door, in Carfax Clos The mouth of the close was choked with excited onlookers, sho ing and craning in an effort to see, shouting incoherent questio at one another. The smell of smoke struck hot and punge through the damp evening air, and waves of crackling heat be against my face as I ducked into the close.

Jamie didn't hesitate, but plunged into the crowd, making a pa by main force. I pressed close behind him before the human wav could close again, and elbowed my way through, unable to s anything but Jamie's broad back ahead of me.

Then we popped out in the front of the crowd, and I could s all too well. Dense clouds of gray smoke rolled out of both t printshop's lower windows, and I could hear a whispering, crac ling noise that rose above the noise of the spectators as though t fire were talking to itself.

"My press!" With a cry of anguish, Jamie darted up the fro step and kicked in the door. A cloud of smoke rolled out of t open doorway and engulfed him like a hungry beast. I caught brief glimpse of him, staggering from the impact of the smok then he dropped to his knees and crawled into the building.

Inspired by this example, several men from the crowd ran up t steps of the printshop, and likewise disappeared into the smok filled interior. The heat was so intense that I felt my skirts blo against my legs with the wind of it, and wondered how the m could stand it, there inside.

A fresh outbreak of shouting in the crowd behind me a nounced the arrival of the Town Guard, armed with buckets. Obv ously accustomed to this task, the men flung off their wine-r uniform coats and began at once to attack the fire, smashing t windows and flinging pails of water through them with a fier abandon. Meanwhile, the crowd swelled, its noise augmented by constant cascade of pattering feet down the many staircases of t close, as families on the upper floors of the surrounding buildin hastily ushered hordes of excited children down to safety.

I couldn't think that the efforts of the bucket brigade, valiant as they were, would have much effect on what was obviously a fire well under way. I was edging back and forth on the pavement, trying vainly to see anything moving within, when the lead man in the bucket line uttered a startled cry and leapt back, just in time to avoid being crowned by a tray of lead type that whizzed through the broken window and landed on the cobbles with a crash, scattering slugs in all directions.

Two or three urchins wriggled through the crowd and snatched at the slugs, only to be cuffed and driven off by indignant neighbors. One plump lady in a kertch and apron darted forward, risking life and limb, and took custody of the heavy type-tray, dragging it back to the curb, where she crouched protectively over it like a hen on a nest.

Before her companions could scoop up the fallen type, though, they were driven back by a hail of objects that rained from both windows: more type trays, roller bars, inking pads, and bottles of ink, which broke on the pavement, leaving big spidery blotches that ran into the puddles spilled by the fire fighters.

Encouraged by the draft from the open door and windows, the voice of the fire had grown from a whisper into a self-satisfied, chuckling roar. Prevented from flinging water through the windows by the rain of objects being thrown out of them, the leader of the Town Guard shouted to his men, and holding a soaked handkerchief over his nose, ducked and ran into the building, followed by a half-dozen of his fellows.

The line quickly re-formed, full buckets coming hand to hand round the corner from the nearest pump and up the stoop, excited lads snatching the empty buckets that bounced down the step, to race back with them to the pump for refilling. Edinburgh is a stone city, but with so many buildings crammed cheek by jowl, all equipped with multiple hearths and chimneys, fire must be still a frequent occurrence.

Evidently so, for a fresh commotion behind me betokened the belated arrival of the fire engine. The waves of people parted like the Red Sea, to allow passage of the engine, drawn by a team of men rather than horses, which could not have negotiated the tight quarters of the wynds.

The engine was a marvel of brass, glowing like a coal itself in the reflected flames. The heat was becoming more intense; I could

feel my lungs dry and labor with each gulp of hot air, and wa
terrified for Jamie. How long could he breathe, in that hellish fo
of smoke and heat, let alone the danger of the flames themselves

"Jesus, Mary, and Joseph!" Ian, forcing his way through th
crowd despite his wooden leg, had appeared suddenly by my e
bow. He grabbed my arm to keep his balance as another rain
objects forced the people around us back again.

"Where's Jamie?" he shouted in my ear.

"In there!" I bellowed back, pointing.

There was a sudden bustle and commotion at the door of th
printshop, with a confused shouting that rose even over the sour
of the fire. Several sets of legs appeared, shuffling to and fr
beneath the emergent plume of smoke that billowed from the doo
Six men emerged, Jamie among them, staggering under the weigh
of a huge piece of bulky machinery—Jamie's precious printir
press. They eased it down the step and pushed it well into th
crowd, then turned back to the printshop.

Too late for any more rescue maneuvers; there was a crash fro
inside, a fresh blast of heat that sent the crowd scuttling backwar
and suddenly the windows of the upper story were lit with dancir
flames inside. A small stream of men issued from the buildin
coughing and choking, some of them crawling, blackened wi
soot and dampened with the sweat of their efforts. The engir
crew pumped madly, but the thick stream of water from their ho
made not the slightest impression on the fire.

Ian's hand clamped down on my arm like the jaws of a trap.

"Ian!" he shrieked, loud enough to be heard above the nois
of crowd and fire alike.

I looked up in the direction of his gaze, and saw a wraithli
shape at the second-story window. It seemed to struggle brief
with the sash, and then to fall back or be enveloped in the smok

My heart leapt into my mouth. There was no telling whether th
shape was indeed Young Ian, but it was certainly a human forr
Ian had lost no time in gaping, but was stumping toward the do
of the printshop with all the speed his leg would allow.

"Wait!" I shouted, running after him.

Jamie was leaning on the printing press, chest heaving as h
tried to catch his breath and thank his assistants at the same tim

"Jamie!" I snatched at his sleeve, ruthlessly jerking him awa
from a red-faced barber, who kept excitedly wiping sooty han

n his apron, leaving long black streaks among the smears of dried
ɔap and the spots of blood.

''Up there!'' I shouted, pointing. ''Young Ian's upstairs!''

Jamie stepped back, swiping a sleeve across his blackened face,
nd stared wildly at the upper windows. Nothing was to be seen
ut the roiling shimmer of the fire against the panes.

Ian was struggling in the hands of several neighbors who sought
• prevent his entering the shop.

''No, man, ye canna go in!'' the Guard captain cried, trying to
rasp Ian's flailing hands. ''The staircase has fallen, and the roof
'ill go next!''

Despite his stringy build and the handicap of his leg, Ian was
ll and vigorous, and the feeble grasp of his well-meaning Town
uard captors—mostly retired pensioners from the Highland regi-
ents—was no match for his mountain-hardened strength, rein-
ɔrced as it was by parental desperation. Slowly but surely, the
hole confused mass jerked by inches up the steps of the print-
ɪop as Ian dragged his would-be rescuers with him toward the
ames.

I felt Jamie draw breath, gulping air as deep as he could with his
:ared lungs, and then he was up the steps as well, and had Ian
und the waist, dragging him back.

''Come down, man!'' he shouted hoarsely. ''Ye'll no manage—
e stair is gone!'' He glanced round, saw me, and thrust Ian
ɔdily backward, off-balance and staggering, into my arms.
Hold him,'' he shouted, over the roar of the flames. ''I'll fetch
ɔwn the lad!''

With that, he turned and dashed up the steps of the adjoining
ɪilding, pushing his way through the patrons of the ground-floor
ɪocolate shop, who had emerged onto the pavement to gawk at
e excitement, pewter cups still clutched in their hands.

Following Jamie's example, I locked my arms tight around
n's waist and didn't let go. He made an abortive attempt to
llow Jamie, but then stopped and stood rigid in my arms, his
:art beating wildly just under my cheek.

''Don't worry,'' I said, pointlessly. ''He'll do it; he'll get him
ıt. He will. I know he will.''

Ian didn't answer—might not have heard—but stood still and
ıff as a statue in my grasp, breath coming harshly with a sound
:e a sob. When I released my hold on his waist, he didn't move

or turn, but when I stood beside him, he snatched my hand an
held it hard. My bones would have ground together, had I not bee
squeezing back just as hard.

It was no more than a minute before the window above th
chocolate shop opened and Jamie's head and shoulders appeared
red hair glowing like a stray tongue of flame escaped from th
main fire. He climbed out onto the sill, and cautiously turne
squatting, until he faced the building.

Rising to his stocking feet, he grasped the gutter of the roo
overhead and pulled, slowly raising himself by the strength of h
arms, long toes scrabbling for a grip in the crevices between th
mortared stones of the housefront. With a grunt audible even ove
the sound of fire and crowd, he eeled over the edge of the roof an
disappeared behind the gable.

A shorter man could not have managed. Neither could Ian, wit
his wooden leg. I heard Ian say something under his breath;
prayer I thought, but when I glanced at him, his jaw was clenche
face set in lines of fear.

"What in hell is he going to do up there?" I thought, and wa
unaware that I had spoken aloud until the barber, shading his eye
next to me, replied.

"There's a trapdoor built in the roof o' the printshop, ma'an
Nay doubt Mr. Malcolm means to gain access to the upper stor
so. Is it his 'prentice up there, d'ye know?"

"No!" Ian snapped, hearing this. "It's my son!"

The barber shrank back before Ian's glare, murmuring "O
aye, just so, sir, just so!" and crossing himself. A shout from th
crowd grew into a roar as two figures appeared on the roof of th
chocolate shop, and Ian dropped my hand, springing forward.

Jamie had his arm round Young Ian, who was bent and reelin
from the smoke he had swallowed. It was reasonably obvious th
neither of them was going to be able to negotiate a return throug
the adjoining building in his present condition.

Just then, Jamie spotted Ian below. Cupping his hand around h
mouth, he bellowed "Rope!"

Rope there was; the Town Guard had come equipped. Ia
snatched the coil from an approaching Guardsman, leaving th
worthy blinking in indignation, and turned to face the house.

I caught the gleam of Jamie's teeth as he grinned down at h
brother-in-law, and the look of answering wryness on Ian's fac

low many times had they thrown a rope between them, to raise
ıay to the barn loft, or bind a load to the wagon for carrying?

The crowd fell back from the whirl of Ian's arm, and the heavy
coil flew up in a smooth parabola, unwinding as it went, landing
n Jamie's outstretched arm with the precision of a bumblebee
ighting on a flower. Jamie hauled in the dangling tail, and disap-
·eared momentarily, to anchor the rope about the base of the
uilding's chimney.

A few precarious moments' work, and the two smoke-black-
ned figures had come to a safe landing on the pavement below.
'oung Ian, rope slung under his arms and round his chest, stood
pright for a moment, then, as the tension of the rope slackened,
is knees buckled and he slid into a gangling heap on the cobbles.

'"Are ye all right? *A bhalaich,* speak to me!'' Ian fell to his
nees beside his son, anxiously trying to unknot the rope round
'oung Ian's chest, while simultaneously trying to lift up the lad's
olling head.

Jamie was leaning against the railing of the chocolate shop,
lack in the face and coughing his lungs out, but otherwise appar-
ntly unharmed. I sat down on the boy's other side, and took his
ead on my lap.

I wasn't sure whether to laugh or cry at the sight of him. When I
ad seen him in the morning, he had been an appealing-looking
d, if no great beauty, with something of his father's homely,
ood-natured looks. Now, at evening, the thick hair over one side
f his forehead had been singed to a bleached red stubble, and his
yebrows and lashes had been burned off entirely. The skin be-
eath was the soot-smeared bright pink of a suckling pig just off
ıe spit.

I felt for a pulse in the spindly neck and found it, reassuringly
rong. His breathing was hoarse and irregular, and no wonder; I
oped the lining of his lungs had not been burned. He coughed,
·ng and rackingly, and the thin body convulsed on my lap.

"Is he all right?" Ian's hands instinctively grabbed his son
·neath the armpits and sat him up. His head wobbled to and fro,
·d he pitched forward into my arms.

"I think so; I can't tell for sure." The boy was still coughing,
ıt not fully conscious; I held him against my shoulder like an
ıormous baby, patting his back futilely as he retched and gagged.

"Is he all right?" This time it was Jamie, squatting breathless alongside me. His voice was so hoarse I wouldn't have recognizit, roughened as it was by smoke.

"I think so. What about you? You look like Malcolm X,"
said, peering at him over Young Ian's heaving shoulder.

"I do?" He put a hand to his face, looking startled, the
grinned reassuringly. "Nay, I canna say how I look, but I'm no a
ex-Malcolm yet; only a wee bit singed round the edges."

"Get back, get back!" The Guard captain was at my side, gra
beard bristling with anxiety, plucking at my sleeve. "Move you
self, ma'am, the roof's going!"

Sure enough, as we scrambled to safety, the roof of the prin
shop fell in, and an awed sound rose from the watching crowd a
an enormous fountain of sparks whirled skyward, brilliant again
the darkening sky.

As though heaven resented this intrusion, the spume of fiery a
was answered by the first pattering of raindrops, plopping heavi
on the cobbles all around us. The Edinburghians, who surely oug
to have been accustomed to rain by now, made noises of conste
nation and began to scuttle back into the surrounding buildin
like a herd of cockroaches, leaving nature to complete the fi
engine's work.

A moment later, Ian and I were alone with Young Ian. Jami
having dispensed money liberally to the Guard and other assi
tants, and having arranged for his press and its fittings to I
housed in the barber's storeroom, trudged wearily toward us.

"How's the lad?" he asked, wiping a hand down his face. Th
rain had begun to come down more heavily, and the effect on h
soot-blackened countenance was picturesque in the extreme. I
looked at him, and for the first time, the anger, worry, and fe
faded somewhat from his countenance. He gave Jamie a lopsid
smile.

"He doesna look a great deal better than ye do yourself, man
but I think he'll do now. Give us a hand, aye?"

Murmuring small Gaelic endearments suitable for babies, I
bent over his son, who was by this time sitting up groggily on t
curbstone, swaying to and fro like a heron in a high wind.

By the time we reached Madame Jeanne's establishment, Youn
Ian could walk, though still supported on either side by his fath
and uncle. Bruno, who opened the door, blinked incredulously

he sight, and then swung the door open, laughing so hard he could
arely close it after us.

I had to admit that we were nothing much to look at, wet
hrough and streaming with rain. Jamie and I were both barefoot,
nd Jamie's clothes were in rags, singed and torn and covered with
treaks of soot. Ian's dark hair straggled in his eyes, making him
ook like a drowned rat with a wooden leg.

Young Ian, though, was the focus of attention, as multiple heads
ame popping out of the drawing room in response to the noise
runo was making. With his singed hair, swollen red face, beaky
ose, and lashless, blinking eyes, he strongly resembled the
edgling young of some exotic bird species—a newly hatched
amingo, perhaps. His face could scarcely grow redder, but the
ack of his neck flamed crimson, as the sound of feminine giggles
ollowed us up the stairs.

Safely ensconced in the small upstairs sitting room, with the
oor closed, Ian turned to face his hapless offspring.

"Going to live, are ye, ye wee bugger?" he demanded.

"Aye, sir," Young Ian replied in a dismal croak, looking rather
s though he wished the answer were "No."

"Good," his father said grimly. "D'ye want to explain your-
elf, or shall I just belt hell out of ye now and save us both time?"

"Ye canna thrash someone who's just had his eyebrows burnt
ff, Ian," Jamie protested hoarsely, pouring out a glass of porter
om the decanter on the table. "It wouldna be humane." He
rinned at his nephew and handed him the glass, which the boy
lutched with alacrity.

"Aye, well. Perhaps not," Ian agreed, surveying his son. One
orner of his mouth twitched. Young Ian was a pitiable sight; he
as also an extremely funny one. "That doesna mean ye aren't
oing to get your arse blistered later, mind," he warned the boy,
and that's besides whatever your mother means to do to ye when
e sees ye again. But for now, lad, take your ease."

Not noticeably reassured by the magnanimous tone of this last
atement, Young Ian didn't answer, but sought refuge in the
epths of his glass of porter.

I took my own glass with a good deal of pleasure. I had realized
elatedly just why the citizens of Edinburgh reacted to rain with
uch repugnance; once one was wet through, it was the devil to get

dry again in the damp confines of a stone house, with no change
clothes and no heat available but a small hearthfire.

I plucked the damp bodice away from my breasts, caught You
Ian's interested glance, and decided regretfully that I rea
couldn't take it off with the boy in the room. Jamie seemed to ha
been corrupting the lad to quite a sufficient extent already.
gulped the porter instead, feeling the rich flavor purl warming
through my innards.

"D'ye feel well enough to talk a bit, lad?" Jamie sat do
opposite his nephew, next to Ian on the hassock.

"Aye . . . I think so," Young Ian croaked cautiously. I
cleared his throat like a bullfrog and repeated more firmly, "Aye
can."

"Good. Well, then. First, how did ye come to be in the pri
shop, and then, how did it come to be on fire?"

Young Ian pondered that one for a minute, then took anoth
gulp of his porter for courage and said, "I set it."

Jamie and Ian both sat up straight at that. I could see Jam
revising his opinion as to the advisability of thrashing peop
without eyebrows, but he mastered his temper with an obvio
effort, and said merely, "Why?"

The boy took another gulp of porter, coughed, and drank aga
apparently trying to decide what to say.

"Well," he began uncertainly, "there was a man," and came
a dead stop.

"A man," Jamie prompted patiently when his nephew show
signs of having become suddenly deaf and dumb. "What man?

Young Ian clutched his glass in both hands, looking deep
unhappy.

"Answer your uncle this minute, clot," Ian said sharply. "(
I'll take ye across my knee and tan ye right here."

With a mixture of similar threats and promptings, the two m
managed to extract a more or less coherent story from the boy

Young Ian had been at the tavern at Kerse that morning, whe
he had been told to meet Wally, who would come down from t
rendezvous with the wagons of brandy, there to load the punk
casks and spoiled wine to be used as subterfuge.

"Told?" Ian asked sharply. "Who told ye?"

"I did," Jamie said, before Young Ian could speak. He wave
hand at his brother-in-law, urging silence. "Aye, I kent he w

re. We'll talk about it later, Ian, if ye please. It's important we
ow what happened today.''

Ian glared at Jamie and opened his mouth to disagree, then shut
with a snap. He nodded to his son to go on.

''I was hungry, ye see,'' Young Ian said.

''When are ye not?'' his father and uncle said together, in
rfect unison. They looked at each other, snorted with sudden
ighter, and the strained atmosphere in the room eased slightly.

''So ye went into the tavern to have a bite,'' Jamie said. ''That's
right, lad, no harm done. And what happened while ye were
re?''

That, it transpired, was where he had seen the man. A small,
ty-looking fellow, with a seaman's pigtail, and a blind eye,
king to the landlord.

''He was askin' for you, Uncle Jamie,'' Young Ian said, grow-
g easier in his speech with repeated applications of porter. ''By
ur own name.''

Jamie started, looking surprised. ''Jamie Fraser, ye mean?''
ung Ian nodded, sipping. ''Aye. But he knew your other name
well—Jamie Roy, I mean.''

''Jamie Roy?'' Ian turned a puzzled glance on his brother-in-
v, who shrugged impatiently.

''It's how I'm known on the docks. Christ, Ian, ye know what I
''

''Aye, I do, but I didna ken the wee laddie was helpin' ye to do
' Ian's thin lips pressed tight together, and he turned his atten-
n back to his son. ''Go on, lad. I willna interrupt ye again.''

The seaman had asked the tavernkeeper how best an old seadog,
wn on his luck and looking for employment, might find one
nie Fraser, who was known to have a use for able men. The
idlord pleading ignorance of that name, the seaman had leaned
)ser, pushed a coin across the table, and in a lowered voice asked
iether the name ''Jamie Roy'' was more familiar.

The landlord remaining deaf as an adder, the seaman had soon
t the tavern, with Young Ian right behind him.

''I thought as how maybe it would be good to know who he was,
d what he meant,'' the lad explained, blinking.

''Ye might have thought to leave word wi' the publican for
illy,'' Jamie said. ''Still, that's neither here nor there. Where
l he go?''

Down the road at a brisk walk, but not so brisk that a healt‍
boy could not follow at a careful distance. An accomplish‍
walker, the seaman had made his way into Edinburgh, a distar‍
of some five miles, in less than an hour, and arrived at last at t‍
Green Owl tavern, followed by Young Ian, near wilted with thi‍
from the walk.

I started at the name, but didn't say anything, not wanting ‍
interrupt the story.

"It was terrible crowded," the lad reported. "Something ha‍
pened in the morning, and everyone was talking of it—but th‍
shut up whenever they saw me. Anyway, it was the same there‍
He paused to cough and clear his throat. "The seaman order‍
drink—brandy—then asked the landlord was he acquainted wi‍
supplier of brandy named Jamie Roy or Jamie Fraser."

"Did he, then?" Jamie murmured. His gaze was intent on ‍
nephew, but I could see the thoughts working behind his hi‍
forehead, making a small crease between his thick brows.

The man had gone methodically from tavern to tavern, dogg‍
by his faithful shadow, and in each establishment had order‍
brandy and repeated his question.

"He must have a rare head, to be drinkin' that much brandy‍
Ian remarked.

Young Ian shook his head. "He didna drink it. He only sm‍
it."

His father clicked his tongue at such a scandalous waste of go‍
spirit, but Jamie's red brows climbed still higher.

"Did he taste any of it?" he asked sharply.

"Aye. At the Dog and Gun, and again at the Blue Boar. He h‍
nay more than a wee taste, though, and then left the glass ‍
touched. He didna drink at all at the other places, and we went ‍
five o' them, before . . ." He trailed off, and took another dri‍

Jamie's face underwent an astonishing transformation. From ‍
expression of frowning puzzlement, his face went complet‍
blank, and then resolved itself into an expression of revelation‍

"Is that so, now," he said softly to himself. "Indeed." ‍
attention came back to his nephew. "And then what happen‍
lad?"

Young Ian was beginning to look unhappy again. He gulped, ‍
tremor visible all the way down his skinny neck.

"Well, it was a terrible long way from Kerse to Edinburgh," he
gan, "and a terrible dry walk, too . . ."

His father and uncle exchanged jaundiced glances.

"Ye drank too much," Jamie said, resigned.

"Well, I didna ken he was going to so many taverns, now, did
?" Young Ian cried in self-defense, going pink in the ears.

"No, of course not, lad," Jamie said kindly, smothering the
ginning of Ian's more censorious remarks. "How long did ye
t?"

Until midway down the Royal Mile, it turned out, where Young
n, overcome by the cumulation of early rising, a five-mile walk,
d the effects of something like two quarts of ale, had dozed off
a corner, waking an hour later to find his quarry long gone.

"So I came here," he explained. "I thought as how Uncle
mie should know about it. But he wasna here." The boy glanced
me, and his ears grew still pinker.

"And just why did ye think he *should* be here?" Ian favored his
spring with a gimlet eye, which then swiveled to his brother-in-
. The simmering anger Ian had been holding in check since the
rning suddenly erupted. "The filthy gall of ye, Jamie Fraser,
in' my son to a bawdy house!"

"A fine one you are to talk, Da!" Young Ian was on his feet,
aying a bit, but with his big, bony hands clenched at his sides.

"Me? And what d'ye mean by that, ye wee gomerel?" Ian
ed, his eyes going wide with outrage.

"I mean you're a damned hypocrite!" his son shouted hoarsely.
reachin' to me and Michael about purity and keepin' to one
man, and all the time ye're slinkin' about the city, sniffin' after
ores!"

"What?" Ian's face had gone entirely purple. I looked in some
rm to Jamie, who appeared to be finding something funny in the
sent situation.

"You're a . . . a . . . goddamned whited sepulchre!" Young
came up with the simile triumphantly, then paused as though
ing to think of another to equal it. His mouth opened, though
thing emerged but a soft belch.

"That boy is rather drunk," I said to Jamie.

He picked up the decanter of porter, eyed the level within, and
it down.

"You're right," he said. "I should ha' noticed sooner, but i
hard to tell, scorched as he is."

The elder Ian wasn't drunk, but his expression strongly resel
bled his offspring's, what with the suffused countenance, poppi
eyes, and straining neck cords.

"What the bloody, stinking hell d'ye mean by that, ye whelp'
he shouted. He moved menacingly toward Young Ian, who took
involuntary step backward and sat down quite suddenly as l
calves met the edge of the sofa.

"Her," he said, startled into monosyllables. He pointed at n
to make it clear. "Her! You deceivin' my mam wi' this filt
whore, that's what I mean!"

Ian fetched his son a clout over the ear that knocked him sprav
ing on the sofa.

"Ye great clot!" he said, scandalized. "A fine way to speak
your auntie Claire, to say nothing o' me and your mam!"

"Aunt?" Young Ian gawped at me from the cushions, looki
so like a nestling begging for food that I burst out laughing despi
myself.

"You left before I could introduce myself this morning," I sa

"But you're dead," he said stupidly.

"Not yet," I assured him. "Unless I've caught pneumonia fro
sitting here in a damp dress."

His eyes had grown perfectly round as he stared at me. Now
fugitive gleam of excitement came into them.

"Some o' the auld women at Lallybroch say ye were a wis
woman—a white lady, or maybe even a fairy. When Uncle Jan
came home from Culloden without ye, they said as how ye
maybe gone back to the fairies, where ye maybe came from. Is t
true? D'ye live in a dun?"

I exchanged a glance with Jamie, who rolled his eyes toward t
ceiling.

"No," I said. "I . . . er, I . . ."

"She escaped to France after Culloden," Ian broke in sudden
with great firmness. "She thought your uncle Jamie was killed
the battle, so she went to her kin in France. She'd been one
Prince *Tearlach*'s particular friends—she couldna come back
Scotland after the war without puttin' herself in sore danger. I
then she heard of your uncle, and as soon as she kent that l

husband wasna deid after all, she took ship at once and came to find him."

Young Ian's mouth hung open slightly. So did mine.

"Er, yes," I said, closing it. "That's what happened."

The lad turned large, shining eyes from me to his uncle.

"So ye've come back to him," he said happily. "God, that's romantic!"

The tension of the moment was broken. Ian hesitated, but his eyes softened as he looked from Jamie to me.

"Aye," he said, and smiled reluctantly. "Aye, I suppose it is."

"I didna expect to be doing this for him for a good two or three years yet," Jamie remarked, holding his nephew's head with an expert hand as Young Ian retched painfully into the spittoon I was holding.

"Aye, well, he's always been forward," Ian answered resignedly. "Learnt to walk before he could stand, and was forever tumblin' into the fire or the washpot or the pigpen or the cowbyre." He patted the skinny, heaving back. "There, lad, let it come."

A little more, and the lad was deposited in a wilted heap on the sofa, there to recover from the effects of smoke, emotion, and too much porter under the censoriously mingled gaze of uncle and father.

"Where's that damn tea I sent for?" Jamie reached impatiently for the bell, but I stopped him. The brothel's domestic arrangements were evidently still disarranged from the excitements of the morning.

"Don't bother," I said. "I'll go down and fetch it." I scooped up the spittoon and carried it out with me at arm's length, hearing Ian say behind me, in a reasonable tone of voice, "Look, fool—"

I found my way to the kitchen with no difficulty, and obtained the necessary supplies. I hoped Jamie and Ian would give the boy a few minutes' respite; not only for his own sake, but so that I would miss nothing of his story.

I had clearly missed *something;* when I returned to the small sitting room, an air of constraint hung over the room like a cloud, and Young Ian glanced up and then quickly away to avoid my eye. Jamie was his usual imperturbable self, but the elder Ian looked almost as flushed and uneasy as his son. He hurried forward to take the tray from me, murmuring thanks, but would not meet my eye.

I raised one eyebrow at Jamie, who gave me a slight smile and a shrug. I shrugged back and picked up one of the bowls on the tray.

"Bread and milk," I said, handing it to Young Ian, who at once looked happier.

"Hot tea," I said, handing the pot to his father.

"Whisky," I said, handing the bottle to Jamie, "and cold tea for the burns." I whisked the lid off the last bowl, in which a number of napkins were soaking in cold tea.

"Cold tea?" Jamie's ruddy brows lifted. "Did the cook have no butter?"

"You don't put butter on burns," I told him. "Aloe juice, or the juice of a plantain or plantago, but the cook didn't have any of that. Cold tea is the best we could manage."

I poulticed Young Ian's blistered hands and forearms and blotted his scarlet face gently with the tea-soaked napkins while Jamie and Ian did the honors with teapot and whisky bottle, after which we all sat down, somewhat restored, to hear the rest of Ian's story.

"Well," he began, "I walked about the city for a bit, tryin' to think what best to do. And finally my head cleared a bit, and I reasoned that if the man I'd been followin' was goin' from tavern to tavern down the High Street, if I went to the other end and started *up* the street, I could maybe find him that way."

"That was a bright thought," Jamie said, and Ian nodded approvingly, the frown lifting a bit from his face. "Did ye find him?"

Young Ian nodded, slurping a bit. "I did, then."

Running down the Royal Mile nearly to the Palace of Holyrood at the foot, he had toiled his way painstakingly up the street, stopping at each tavern to inquire for the man with the pigtail and one eye. There was no word of his quarry anywhere below the Canongate, and he was beginning to despair of his idea, when suddenly he had seen the man himself, sitting in the taproom of the Holyrood Brewery.

Presumably this stop was for respite, rather than information, for the seaman was sitting at his ease, drinking beer. Young Ian had darted behind a hogshead in the yard, and remained there watching, until at length the man rose, paid his score, and made his leisurely way outside.

"He didna go to any more taverns," the boy reported, wiping a stray drop of milk off his chin. "He went straight to Carfax Close, to the printshop."

Jamie said something in Gaelic under his breath. "Did he? And what then?"

"Well, he found the shop shut up, of course. When he saw the door was locked, he looked careful like, up at the windows, as though he was maybe thinking of breaking in. But then I saw him look about, at all the folk coming and going—it was a busy time of day, wi' all the folk coming to the chocolate shop. So he stood on the stoop a moment, thinking, and then he set off back up the close—I had to duck into the tailor's shop on the corner so as not to be seen."

The man had paused at the entrance of the close, then, making up his mind, had turned to the right, gone down a few paces, and disappeared into a small alley.

"I kent as how the alley led up to the court at the back of the close," Young Ian explained. "So I saw at once what he meant to be doing."

"There's a wee court at the back of the close," Jamie explained, seeing my puzzled look. "It's for rubbish and deliveries and such—but there's a back door out of the printshop opens onto it."

Young Ian nodded, putting down his empty bowl. "Aye. I thought it must be that he meant to get into the place. And I thought of the new pamphlets."

"Jesus," Jamie said. He looked a little pale.

"Pamphlets?" Ian raised his brows at Jamie. "What kind of pamphlets?"

"The new printing for Mr. Gage," Young Ian explained.

Ian still looked as blank as I felt.

"Politics," Jamie said bluntly. "An argument for repeal of the last Stamp Act—with an exhortation to civil opposition—by violence, if necessary. Five thousand of them, fresh-printed, stacked in the back room. Gage was to come round and get them in the morning, tomorrow."

"Jesus," Ian said. He had gone even paler than Jamie, at whom he stared in a sort of mingled horror and awe. "Have ye gone

straight out o' your mind?'' he inquired. ''You, wi' not an inch o
your back unscarred? Wi' the ink scarce dry on your pardon fo
treason? You're mixed up wi' Tom Gage and his seditious society
and got my son involved as well?''

His voice had been rising throughout, and now he sprang to hi
feet, fists clenched.

''How could ye do such a thing, Jamie—how? Have we no
suffered enough for your actions, Jenny and me? All through th
war and after—Christ, I'd think you'd have your fill of prisons an
blood and violence!''

''I have,'' Jamie said shortly. ''I'm no part of Gage's group
But my business is printing, aye? He paid for those pamphlets.'

Ian threw up his hands in a gesture of vast irritation. ''Oh, aye
And that will mean a great deal when the Crown's agents arrest y
and take ye to London to be hangit! If those things were to b
found on your premises—'' Struck by a sudden thought, h
stopped and turned to his son.

''Oh, that was it?'' he asked. ''Ye kent what those pamphlet
were—that's why ye set them on fire?''

Young Ian nodded, solemn as a young owl.

''I couldna move them in time,'' he said. ''Not five thousand
The man—the seaman—he'd broke out the back window, and h
was reachin' in for the doorlatch.''

Ian whirled back to face Jamie.

''Damn you!'' he said violently. ''Damn ye for a reckless
harebrained fool, Jamie Fraser! First the Jacobites, and now this!'

Jamie had flushed up at once at Ian's words, and his face gre
darker at this.

''Am I to blame for Charles Stuart?'' he said. His eyes flashe
angrily and he set his teacup down with a thump that sloshed te
and whisky over the polished tabletop. ''Did I not try all I could t
stop the wee fool? Did I not give up everything in that fight—
everything, Ian! My land, my freedom, my wife—to try to save u
all?'' He glanced at me briefly as he spoke, and I caught one ver
small quick glimpse of just what the last twenty years had cos
him.

He turned back to Ian, his brows lowering as he went on, voic
growing hard.

''And as for what I've cost your family—what have ye profite

an? Lallybroch belongs to wee James now, no? To *your* son, not
nine!''

Ian flinched at that. ''I never asked—'' he began.

''No, ye didn't. I'm no accusing ye, for God's sake! But the
act's there—Lallybroch's no mine anymore, is it? My father left
t to me, and I cared for it as best I could—took care o' the land
nd the tenants—and ye helped me, Ian.'' His voice softened a bit.
'I couldna have managed without you and Jenny. I dinna begrudge deeding it to Young Jamie—it had to be done. But
till . . .'' He turned away for a moment, head bowed, broad
houlders knotted tight beneath the linen of his shirt.

I was afraid to move or speak, but I caught Young Ian's eye,
illed with infinite distress. I put a hand on his skinny shoulder for
mutual reassurance, and felt the steady pounding of the pulse in
he tender flesh above his collarbone. He set his big, bony paw on
ny hand and held on tight.

Jamie turned back to his brother-in-law, struggling to keep his
oice and temper under control. ''I swear to ye, Ian, I didna let the
ad be put in danger. I kept him out of the way so much as I
ossibly could—didna let the shoremen see him, or let him go out
n the boats wi' Fergus, hard as he begged me.'' He glanced at
'oung Ian and his expression changed, to an odd mixture of affec-
ion and irritation.

''I didna ask him to come to me, Ian, and I told him he must go
ome again.''

''Ye didna *make* him go, though, did you?'' The angry color
vas fading from Ian's face, but his soft brown eyes were still
arrow and bright with fury. ''And ye didna send word, either. For
iod's sake, Jamie, Jenny hasna slept at night anytime this
nonth!''

Jamie's lips pressed tight. ''No,'' he said, letting the words
scape one at a time. ''No. I didn't. I—'' He glanced at the boy
gain, and shrugged uncomfortably, as though his shirt had grown
uddenly too tight.

''No,'' he said again. ''I meant to take him home myself.''

''He's old enough to travel by himself,'' Ian said shortly. ''He
ot here alone, no?''

''Aye. It wasna that.'' Jamie turned aside restlessly, picking up
teacup and rolling it to and fro between his palms. ''No, I meant

to take him, so that I could ask your permission—yours an
Jenny's—for the lad to come live wi' me for a time.''

Ian uttered a short, sarcastic laugh. ''Oh, aye! Give our permi-
sion for him to be hangit or transported alongside you, eh?''

The anger flashed across Jamie's features again as he looked u
from the cup in his hands.

''Ye know I wouldna let any harm come to him,'' he said. ''F(
Christ's sake, Ian, I care for the lad as though he were my ow
son, and well ye ken it, too!''

Ian's breath was coming fast; I could hear it from my plac
behind the sofa. ''Oh, I ken it well enough,'' he said, staring har
into Jamie's face. ''But he's not your son, aye? He's mine.''

Jamie stared back for a long moment, then reached out an
gently set the teacup back on the table. ''Aye,'' he said quietl
''He is.''

Ian stood for a moment, breathing hard, then wiped a han
carelessly across his forehead, pushing back the thick dark hair

''Well, then,'' he said. He took one or two deep breaths, an
turned to his son.

''Come along, then,'' he said. ''I've a room at Halliday's.''

Young Ian's bony fingers tightened on mine. His throat worke(
but he didn't move to rise from his seat.

''No, Da,'' he said. His voice quivered, and he blinked hard, n(
to cry. ''I'm no going wi' ye.''

Ian's face went quite pale, with a deep red patch over the ang(
lar cheekbones, as though someone had slapped him hard on bo
cheeks.

''Is that so?'' he said.

Young Ian nodded, swallowing. ''I—I'll go wi' ye in the mor
ing, Da; I'll go home wi' ye. But not now.''

Ian looked at his son for a long moment without speaking. The
his shoulders slumped, and all the tension went out of his body

''I see,'' he said quietly. ''Well, then. Well.''

Without another word, he turned and left, closing the door ve
carefully behind him. I could hear the awkward thump of h
wooden leg on each step, as he made his way down the stair. The
was a brief sound of shuffling as he reached the bottom, the
Bruno's voice in farewell, and the thud of the main door shuttin
And then there was no sound in the room but the hiss of t
hearthfire behind me.

The boy's shoulder was shaking under my hand, and he was holding tighter than ever to my fingers, crying without making a sound.

Jamie came slowly to sit beside him, his face full of troubled helplessness.

"Ian, oh, wee Ian," he said. "Christ, laddie, ye shouldna have done that."

"I had to." Ian gasped and gave a sudden snuffle, and I realized that he had been holding his breath. He turned a scorched countenance on his uncle, raw features contorted in anguish.

"I didna want to hurt Da," he said. "I didn't!"

Jamie patted his knee absently. "I know, laddie," he said, "but to say such a thing to him—"

"I couldna tell him, though, and I had to tell you, Uncle Jamie!"

Jamie glanced up, suddenly alert at his nephew's tone.

"Tell me? Tell me what?"

"The man. The man wi' the pigtail."

"What about him?"

Young Ian licked his lips, steeling himself.

"I think I kilt him," he whispered.

Startled, Jamie glanced at me, then back at Young Ian.

"How?" he asked.

"Well . . . I lied a bit," Ian began, voice trembling. The tears were still welling in his eyes, but he brushed them aside. "When I went into the printshop—I had the key ye gave me—the man was already inside."

The seaman had been in the backmost room of the shop, where the stacks of newly printed orders were kept, along with the stocks of fresh ink, the blotting papers used to clean the press, and the small forge where worn slugs were melted down and recast into fresh type.

"He was taking some o' the pamphlets from the stack, and putting them inside his jacket," Ian said, gulping. "When I saw him, I screeched at him to put them back, and he whirled round at me wi' a pistol in his hand."

The pistol had discharged, scaring Young Ian badly, but the ball had gone wild. Little daunted, the seaman had rushed at the boy, raising the pistol to club him instead.

"There was no time to run, or to think," he said. He had let go my hand by now, and his fingers twisted together upon his kne

"I reached out for the first thing to hand and threw it."

The first thing to hand had been the lead-dipper, the lon;
handled copper ladle used to pour molten lead from the meltir
pot into the casting molds. The forge had been still alight, thoug
well banked, and while the melting pot held no more than a sma
puddle, the scalding drops of lead had flown from the dipper in
the seaman's face.

"God, how he screamed!" A strong shudder ran through Youn
Ian's slender frame, and I came round the end of the sofa to s
next to him and take both his hands.

The seaman had reeled backward, clawing at his face, and ups
the small forge, knocking live coals everywhere.

"That was what started the fire," the boy said. "I tried to beat
out, but it caught the edge of the fresh paper, and all of a sudde
something went *whoosh!* in my face, and it was as though tl
whole room was alight."

"The barrels of ink, I suppose," Jamie said, as though to hir
self. "The powder's dissolved in alcohol."

The sliding piles of flaming paper fell between Young Ian ai
the back door, a wall of flame that billowed black smoke ar
threatened to collapse upon him. The seaman, blinded and screan
ing like a banshee, had been on his hands and knees between tl
boy and the door into the front room of the printshop and safet

"I—I couldna bear to touch him, to push him out o' the way
he said, shuddering again.

Losing his head completely, he had run up the stairs instead, b
then found himself trapped as the flames, racing through the ba
room and drawing up the stair like a chimney, rapidly filled tl
upper room with blinding smoke.

"Did ye not think to climb out the trapdoor onto the roof?
Jamie asked.

Young Ian shook his head miserably. "I didna ken it w
there."

"Why *was* it there?" I asked curiously.

Jamie gave me the flicker of a smile. "In case of need. It's
foolish fox has but one exit to his bolthole. Though I must say,
wasna fire I was thinking of when I had it made." He shook l
head, ridding himself of the distraction.

"But ye think the man didna escape the fire?" he asked.

"I dinna see how he could," Young Ian answered, beginning to sniffle again. "And if he's dead, then I killed him. I couldna tell Da I was a m-mur—-mur—" He was crying again, too hard to get the word out.

"You're no a murderer, Ian," Jamie said firmly. He patted his nephew's shaking shoulder. "Stop now, it's all right—ye havena done wrong, laddie. Ye haven't, d'ye hear?"

The boy gulped and nodded, but couldn't stop crying or shaking. At last I put my arms around him, turned him and pulled his head down onto my shoulder, patting his back and making the sort of small soothing noises one makes to little children.

He felt very odd in my arms; nearly as big as a full-grown man, but with fine, light bones, and so little flesh on them that it was like holding a skeleton. He was talking into the depths of my bosom, his voice so disjointed by emotion and muffled by fabric that it was difficult to make out the words.

". . . mortal sin . . ." he seemed to be saying, ". . . damned to hell . . . couldna tell Da . . . afraid . . . canna go home ever . . ."

Jamie raised his brows at me, but I only shrugged helplessly, smoothing the thick, bushy hair on the back of the boy's head. At last Jamie leaned forward, took him firmly by the shoulders and sat him up.

"Look ye, Ian," he said. "No, look—look at me!"

By dint of supreme effort, the boy straightened his drooping neck and fixed brimming, red-rimmed eyes on his uncle's face.

"Now, then." Jamie took hold of his nephew's hands and squeezed them lightly. "First—it's no a sin to kill a man that's trying to kill you. The Church allows ye to kill if ye must, in defense of yourself, your family, or your country. So ye havena committed mortal sin, and you're no damned."

"I'm not?" Young Ian sniffed mightily, and mopped at his face with a sleeve.

"No, you're not." Jamie let the hint of a smile show in his eyes. "We'll go together and call on Father Hayes in the morning, and ye'll make your confession and be absolved then, but he'll tell ye the same as I have."

"Oh." The syllable held profound relief, and Young Ian's scrawny shoulders rose perceptibly, as though a burden had rolled off them.

Jamie patted his nephew's knee again. "For the second thing ye needna fear telling your father."

"No?" Young Ian had accepted Jamie's word on the state of his soul without hesitation, but sounded profoundly dubious about this secular opinion.

"Well, I'll not say he'll no be upset," Jamie added fairly. "In fact, I expect it will turn the rest of his hair white on the spot. But he'll understand. He isna going to cast ye out or disown ye, that's what you're scairt of."

"You think he'll understand?" Young Ian looked at Jamie with eyes in which hope battled with doubt. "I—I didna think he . . . has my da ever killed a man?" he asked suddenly.

Jamie blinked, taken aback by the question. "Well," he said slowly, "I suppose—I mean, he's fought in battle, but I—to tell ye the truth, Ian, I dinna ken." He looked a little helplessly at his nephew.

"It's no the sort of thing men talk much about, aye? Except sometimes soldiers, when they're deep in drink."

Young Ian nodded, absorbing this, and sniffed again, with a horrid gurgling noise. Jamie, groping hastily in his sleeve for a handkerchief, looked up suddenly, struck by a thought.

"That's why ye said ye must tell me, but not your da? Because ye knew I've killed men before?"

His nephew nodded, searching Jamie's face with troubled, trusting eyes. "Aye. I thought . . . I thought ye'd know what to do."

"Ah." Jamie drew a deep breath, and exchanged a glance with me. "Well . . ." His shoulders braced and broadened, and I could see him accept the burden Young Ian had laid down. He sighed.

"What ye do," he said, "is first to ask yourself if ye had a choice. You didn't, so put your mind at ease. Then ye go to confession, if ye can; if not, say a good Act of Contrition—that's good enough, when it's no a mortal sin. Ye harbor no fault in mind," he said earnestly, "but the contrition is because ye greatly regret the necessity that fell on ye. It does sometimes, and there's no preventing it.

"And then say a prayer for the soul of the one you've killed," he went on, "that he may find rest, and not haunt ye. Ye ken the prayer called Soul Peace? Use that one, if ye have leisure to think

f it. In a battle, when there is no time, use Soul Leading—'Be
his soul on Thine arm, O Christ, Thou King of the City of
Heaven, Amen.' "

"Be this soul on Thine arm, O Christ, Thou King of the City of
Heaven, Amen," Young Ian repeated under his breath. He nodded
lowly. "Aye, all right. And then?"

Jamie reached out and touched his nephew's cheek with great
gentleness. "Then ye live with it, laddie," he said softly. "That's
ll."

28

Virtue's Guardian

"**Y**ou think the man Young Ian followed has something to do with Sir Percival's warning?" I lifted a cover on the supper tray that had just been delivered and sniffed appreciatively; it seemed a very long time since Moubray's stew.

Jamie nodded, picking up a sort of hot stuffed roll.

"I should be surprised if he had not," he said dryly. "While there's likely more than one man willing to do me harm, I canna think it likely that gangs o' them are roaming about Edinburgh." He took a bite and chewed industriously, shaking his head.

"Nay, that's clear enough, and nothing to be greatly worrit over."

"It's not?" I took a small bite of my own roll, then a bigger one. "This is delicious. What is it?"

Jamie lowered the roll he had been about to take a bite of, and squinted at it. "Pigeon minced wi' truffles," he said, and stuffed it into his mouth whole.

"No," he said, and paused to swallow. "No," he said again, more clearly. "That's likely just a matter of a rival smuggler. There are two gangs that I've had a wee bit of difficulty with now and then." He waved a hand, scattering crumbs, and reached for another roll.

"The way the man behaved—smellin' the brandy, but seldom tasting it—he may be a *dégustateur de vin*; someone that can tell from a sniff where a wine was made, and from a taste, which year it was bottled. A verra valuable fellow," he added thoughtfully, "and a choice hound to set on my trail."

Wine had come along with the supper. I poured out a glass and passed it under my own nose.

"He could track you—you, personally—through the brandy?" asked curiously.

"More or less. You'll remember my cousin Jared?"

"Of course I do. You mean he's still alive?" After the slaughter of Culloden and the erosions of its aftermath, it was wonderfully heartening to hear that Jared, a wealthy Scottish émigré with a prosperous wine business in Paris, was still among the quick, and not the dead.

"I expect they'll have to head him up in a cask and toss him into the Seine to get rid of him," Jamie said, teeth gleaming white in his soot-stained countenance. "Aye, he's not only alive, but njoying it. Where d'ye think I get the French brandy I bring into Scotland?"

The obvious answer was "France," but I refrained from saying o. "Jared, I suppose?" I said instead.

Jamie nodded, mouth full of another roll. "Hey!" He leaned orward and snatched the plate out from under the tentative reach of Young Ian's skinny fingers. "You're no supposed to be eating uch stuff like that when your wame's curdled," he said, frowning nd chewing. He swallowed and licked his lips. "I'll call for more bread and milk for ye."

"But Uncle," said Young Ian, looking longingly at the savory olls. "I'm awfully hungry." Purged by confession, the boy had recovered his spirits considerably, and evidently, his appetite as well.

Jamie looked at his nephew and sighed. "Aye, well. Ye swear ou're no going to vomit on me?"

"No, Uncle," Young Ian said meekly.

"All right, then." Jamie shoved the plate in the boy's direction, nd returned to his explanation.

"Jared sends me mostly the second-quality bottling from his wn vineyards in the Moselle, keepin' the first quality for sale in rance, where they can tell the difference."

"So the stuff you bring into Scotland is identifiable?"

He shrugged, reaching for the wine. "Only to a *nez,* a *dégus-uteur,* that is. But the fact is, that wee Ian here saw the man taste he wine at the Dog and Gun and at the Blue Boar, and those are

the two taverns on the High Street that buy brandy from m⟨
exclusively. Several others buy from me, but from others as well⟨

"In any case, as I say, I'm none so concerned at havin' some
one look for Jamie Roy at a tavern." He lifted his wineglass an⟨
passed it under his own nose by reflex, made a slight, unconsciou⟨
face, and drank. "No," he said, lowering the glass, "what worrie⟨
me is that the man should have found his way to the printshop. Fo⟨
I've taken particular pains to make sure that the folk who se⟨
Jamie Roy on the docks at Burntisland are not the same ones wh⟨
pass the time o' day in the High Street with Mr. Alec Malcolm, th⟨
printer."

I knitted my brows, trying to work it out.

"But Sir Percival called you Malcolm, and he knows you're ⟨
smuggler," I protested.

Jamie nodded patiently. "Half the men in the ports near Edin⟨
burgh are smugglers, Sassenach," he said. "Aye, Sir Percival ken⟨
fine I'm a smuggler, but he doesna ken I'm Jamie Roy—let alon⟨
James Fraser. He thinks I bring in bolts of undeclared silk an⟨
velvet from Holland—because that's what I pay him in." H⟨
smiled wryly. "I trade brandy for them, to the tailor on the corne⟨
Sir Percival's an eye for fine cloth, and his lady even more. But h⟨
doesna ken I've to do wi' the liquor—let alone how much—⟨
he'd be wanting a great deal more than the odd bit of lace an⟨
yardage, I'll tell ye."

"Could one of the tavern owners have told the seaman abou⟨
you? Surely they've seen you."

He ruffled a hand through his hair, as he did when thinkin⟨
making a few short hairs on the crown stand up in a whorl of tin⟨
spikes.

"Aye, they've seen me," he said slowly, "but only as a cu⟨
tomer. Fergus handles the business dealings wi' the taverns—an⟨
Fergus is careful never to go near the printshop. He always mee⟨
me here, in private." He gave me a crooked grin. "No one que⟨
tions a man's reasons for visiting a brothel, aye?"

"Could that be it?" I asked, struck by a sudden thought. "A⟨
man can come here without question. Could the seaman Young Ia⟨
followed have seen you here—you and Fergus? Or heard you⟨
description from one of the girls? After all, you're not the mo⟨
inconspicuous man I've ever seen." He wasn't, either. While the⟨
might be any number of redheaded men in Edinburgh, few of the⟨

towered to Jamie's height, and fewer still strode the streets with
the unconscious arrogance of a disarmed warrior.

"That's a verra useful thought, Sassenach," he said, giving me
a nod. "It will be easy enough to find out whether a pigtailed
seaman with one eye has been here recently; I'll have Jeanne ask
among her lassies."

He stood up, and stretched rackingly, his hands nearly touching
the wooden rafters.

"And then, Sassenach, perhaps we'll go to bed, aye?" He lowered his arms and blinked at me with a smile. "What wi' one thing
and another, it's been the bloody hell of a day, no?"

"It has, rather," I said, smiling back.

Jeanne, summoned for instructions, arrived together with Fergus, who opened the door for the madam with the easy familiarity
of a brother or cousin. Little wonder if he felt at home, I supposed;
he had been born in a Paris brothel, and spent the first ten years of
his life there, sleeping in a cupboard beneath the stairs, when not
making a living by picking pockets on the street.

"The brandy is gone," he reported to Jamie. "I have sold it to
MacAlpine—at a small sacrifice in price, I regret, milord. I
thought a quick sale the best."

"Better to have it off the premises," Jamie said, nodding.
"What have ye done wi' the body?"

Fergus smiled briefly, his lean face and dark forelock lending
him a distinctly piratical air.

"Our intruder also has gone to MacAlpine's tavern, milord—
suitably disguised."

"As what?" I demanded.

The pirate's grin turned on me; Fergus had turned out a very
handsome man, the disfigurement of his hook notwithstanding.

"As a cask of crème de menthe, milady," he said.

"I do not suppose anyone has drunk crème de menthe in Edinburgh anytime in the last hundred years," observed Madame
Jeanne. "The heathen Scots are not accustomed to the use of
civilized liqueurs; I have never seen a customer here take anything
beyond whisky, beer, or brandywine."

"Exactly, Madame," Fergus said, nodding. "We do not want
Mr. MacAlpine's tapmen broaching the cask, do we?"

"Surely somebody's going to look in that cask sooner or later,"
said. "Not to be indelicate, but—"

"Exactly, milady," Fergus said, with a respectful bow to me
"Though crème de menthe has a very high content of alcohol. The
tavern's cellar is but a temporary resting place on our unknown
friend's journey to his eternal rest. He goes to the docks tomorrow, and thence to somewhere quite far away. It is only that I did
not want him cluttering up Madame Jeanne's premises in the
meantime."

Jeanne addressed a remark in French to St. Agnes that I didn't
quite catch, but then shrugged and turned to go.

"I will make inquiries of *les filles* concerning this seaman to
morrow, Monsieur, when they are at leisure. For now—"

"For now, speaking of leisure," Fergus interrupted, "might
Mademoiselle Sophie find herself unemployed this evening?"

The madam favored him with a look of ironic amusement
"Since she saw you come in, *mon petit saucisson,* I expect that
she has kept herself available." She glanced at Young Ian
slouched against the cushions like a scarecrow from which all the
straw stuffing has been removed. "And will I find a place for the
young gentleman to sleep?"

"Oh, aye." Jamie looked consideringly at his nephew. "I sup
pose ye can lay a pallet in my room."

"Oh, no!" Young Ian blurted. "You'll want to be alone wi
your wife, will ye not, Uncle?"

"What?" Jamie stared at him uncomprehendingly.

"Well, I mean . . ." Young Ian hesitated, glancing at me, and
then hastily away. "I mean, nay doubt you'll be wanting to . .
er . . . mmphm?" A Highlander born, he managed to infuse the
last noise with an amazing wealth of implied indelicacy.

Jamie rubbed his knuckles hard across his upper lip.

"Well, that's verra thoughtful of ye, Ian," he said. His voice
quivered slightly with the effort of not laughing. "And I'm flat
tered that ye have such a high opinion of my virility as to think I'm
capable of anything but sleeping in bed after a day like this. But
think perhaps I can forgo the satisfaction of my carnal desires for
one night—fond as I am of your auntie," he added, giving me
faint grin.

"But Bruno tells me the establishment is not busy tonight,"
Fergus put in, glancing round in some bewilderment. "Why does
the boy not—"

"Because he's no but fourteen, for God's sake!" Jamie said,
ndalized.

"Almost fifteen!" Young Ian corrected, sitting up and looking
erested.

"Well, that is certainly sufficient," Fergus said, with a glance at
adame Jeanne for confirmation. "Your brothers were no older
en I first brought them here, and they acquitted themselves
norably."

"You *what*?" Jamie goggled at his protégé.

"Well, someone had to," Fergus said, with slight impatience.
Normally, a boy's father—but of course, le Monsieur is not—
aning no disrespect to your esteemed father, of course," he
ded, with a nod to Young Ian, who nodded back like a mechani-
toy, "but it is a matter for experienced judgment, you under-
nd?

"Now"—he turned to Madame Jeanne, with the air of a gour-
nd consulting the wine steward—"Dorcas, do you think, or
elope?"

"No, no," she said, shaking her head decidedly, "it should be
second Mary, absolutely. The small one."

"Oh, with the yellow hair? Yes, I think you are right," Fergus
d approvingly. "Fetch her, then."

Jeanne was off before Jamie could manage more than a stran-
d croak in protest.

"But—but—the lad canna—" he began.

"Yes, I can," Young Ian said. "At least, I think I can." It
sn't possible for his face to grow any redder, but his ears were
nson with excitement, the traumatic events of the day com-
tely forgotten.

"But it's—that is to say—I canna be letting ye—" Jamie broke
and stood glaring at his nephew for a long moment. Finally, he
ew his hands up in the air in exasperated defeat.

"And what am I to say to your mother?" he demanded, as the
or opened behind him.

Framed in the door stood a very short young girl, plump and
t as a partridge in her blue silk chemise, her round sweet face
ming beneath a loose cloud of yellow hair. At the sight of her,
ung Ian froze, scarcely breathing.

When at last he must draw breath or die, he drew it, and turned
Jamie. With a smile of surpassing sweetness, he said, "Well,

Uncle Jamie, if I were you''—his voice soared up in a sud
alarming soprano, and he stopped, clearing his throat before
suming in a respectable baritone—''I wouldna tell her. Good ni
to ye, Auntie,'' he said, and walked purposefully forward.

''I canna decide whether I must kill Fergus or thank hir
Jamie was sitting on the bed in our attic room, slowly unbutton
his shirt.

I laid the damp dress over the stool and knelt down in fron
him to unbuckle the knee buckles of his breeches.

''I suppose he was trying to do his best for Young Ian.''

''Aye—in his bloody immoral French way.'' Jamie reac
back to untie the lace that held his hair back. He had not plaite
again when we left Moubray's, and it fell soft and loose on
shoulders, framing the broad cheekbones and long straight n
so that he looked like one of the fiercer Italian angels of
Renaissance.

''Was it the Archangel Michael who drove Adam and Eve
of the Garden of Eden?'' I asked, stripping off his stockings.

He gave a slight chuckle. ''Do I strike ye so—as the guardia
virtue? And Fergus as the wicked serpent?'' His hands came
der my elbows as he bent to lift me up. ''Get up, Sassenach
shouldna be on your knees, serving me.''

''You've had rather a time of it today yourself,'' I answe
making him stand up with me. ''Even if you didn't have to
anyone.'' There were large blisters on his hands, and while he
wiped away most of the soot, there was still a streak down the s
of his jaw.

''Mm.'' My hands went around his waist to help with the wa
band of his breeches, but he held them there, resting his cheek
a moment against the top of my head.

''I wasna quite honest wi' the lad, ye ken,'' he said.

''No? I thought you did wonderfully with him. He felt be
after he talked to you, at least.''

''Aye, I hope so. And maybe the prayers and such will hel
they canna hurt him, at least. But I didna tell him everything.

''What else is there?'' I tilted up my face to his, touching
lips softly with my own. He smelled of smoke and sweat.

''What a man most often does, when he's soul-sick wi' kill

to find a woman, Sassenach,'' he answered softly. "His own, if
 can; another, if he must. For she can do what he cannot—and
al him.''

My fingers found the lacing of his fly; it came loose with a tug.
"That's why you let him go with the second Mary?"

He shrugged, and stepping back a pace, pushed the breeches
wn and off. "I couldna stop him. And I think perhaps I was
ght to let him, young as he is." He smiled crookedly at me. "At
st he'll not be fashing and fretting himself over that seaman
night.''

"I don't imagine so. And what about you?" I pulled the che-
se off over my head.

"Me?" He stared down at me, eyebrows raised, the grimy linen
irt hanging loose upon his shoulders.

I glanced behind him at the bed.

"Yes. You haven't killed anyone, but do you want to . . .
mphm?" I met his gaze, raising my own brows in question.

The smile broadened across his face, and any resemblance to
ichael, stern guardian of virtue, vanished. He lifted one shoul-
r, then the other, and let them fall, and the shirt slid down his
ms to the floor.

"I expect I do," he said. "But you'll be gentle wi' me, aye?"

I n the morning, I saw Jamie and Ian off on their pious erra.
and then set off myself, stopping to purchase a large wic
basket from a vendor in the street. It was time I began to eq
myself again, with whatever I could find in the way of medi
supplies. After the events of the preceding day, I was beginning
fear I would have need of them before long.

Haugh's apothecary shop hadn't changed at all, through l
glish occupation, Scottish Rising, and the Stuarts' fall, and
heart rose in delight as I stepped through the door into the ri
familiar smells of hartshorn, peppermint, almond oil, and anis

The man behind the counter was Haugh, but a much youn,
Haugh than the middle-aged man I had dealt with twenty ye
before, when I had patronized this shop for tidbits of milit
intelligence, as well as for nostrums and herbs.

The younger Haugh did not know me, of course, but w
courteously about the business of finding the herbs I want
among the neatly ranged jars on his shelves. A good many w
common—rosemary, tansy, marigold—but a few on my list ma
the young Haugh's ginger eyebrows rise, and his lips purse
thoughtfulness as he looked over the jars.

There was another customer in the shop, hovering near
counter, where tonics were dispensed and compounds ground
order. He strode back and forth, hands clasped behind his ba
obviously impatient. After a moment, he came up to the count

"How long?" he snapped at Mr. Haugh's back.

"I canna just say, Reverend." The apothecary's voice was apologetic. "Louisa did say as 'twould need to be boiled."

The only reply to this was a snort, and the man, tall and narrow-shouldered in black, resumed his pacing, glancing from time to time at the doorway to the back room, where the invisible Louisa was presumably at work. The man looked slightly familiar, but I had no time to think where I had seen him before.

Mr. Haugh was squinting dubiously at the list I had given him. "Aconite, now," he muttered. "Aconite. And what might that be, I wonder?"

"Well, it's a poison, for one thing," I said. Mr. Haugh's mouth dropped open momentarily.

"It's a medicine, too," I assured him. "But you have to be careful in the use of it. Externally, it's good for rheumatism, but a very tiny amount taken by mouth will lower the rate of the pulse. Good for some kinds of heart trouble."

"Really," Mr. Haugh said, blinking. He turned to his shelves, looking rather helpless. "Er, do ye ken what it smells like, maybe?"

Taking this for invitation, I came round the counter and began to sort through the jars. They were all carefully labeled, but the labels of some were clearly old, the ink faded, and the paper peeling at the edges.

"I'm afraid I'm none so canny wi' the medicines as my da t," young Mr. Haugh was saying at my elbow. "He'd taught me good bit, but then he passed on a year ago, and there's things re as I dinna ken the use of, I'm afraid."

"Well, that one's good for cough," I said, taking down a jar of ecampane with a glance at the impatient Reverend, who had ken out a handkerchief and was wheezing asthmatically into it. Particularly sticky-sounding coughs."

I frowned at the crowded shelves. Everything was dusted and immaculate, but evidently not filed according either to alphabeti-l or botanical order. Had old Mr. Haugh merely remembered here things were, or had he a system of some kind? I closed my es and tried to remember the last time I had been in the shop.

To my surprise, the image came back easily. I had come for xglove then, to make the infusions for Alex Randall, younger other of Black Jack Randall—and Frank's six-times great-andfather. Poor boy, he had been dead now twenty years, though

he had lived long enough to sire a son. I felt a twinge of curios
at the thought of that son, and of his mother, who had been
friend, but I forced my mind away from them, back to the image
Mr. Haugh, standing on tiptoe to reach up to his shelves, over n
the right-hand side . . .

"There." Sure enough, my hand rested near the jar labe
FOXGLOVE. To one side of it was a jar labeled HORSETAIL, to
other, LILY OF THE VALLEY ROOT. I hesitated, looking at them, r
ning over in my mind the possible uses of those herbs. Card
herbs, all of them. If aconite was to be found, it would be close
then.

It was. I found it quickly, in a jar labeled AULD WIVES HUID.

"Be careful with it." I handed the jar gingerly to Mr. Hau,
"Even a bit of it will make your skin go numb. Perhaps I'd bet
have a glass bottle for it." Most of the herbs I'd bought had be
wrapped up in squares of gauze or twisted in screws of paper,
the young Mr. Haugh nodded and carried the jar of aconite i
the back room, held at arm's length, as though he expected it
explode in his face.

"Ye'd seem to know a good deal more about the medicines th
the lad," said a deep, hoarse voice behind me.

"Well, I've somewhat more experience than he has, likely."
turned to find the minister leaning on the counter, watching
under thick brows with pale blue eyes. I realized with a start wh
I had seen him; in Moubray's, the day before. He gave no sign
recognizing me; perhaps because my cloak covered Daphn
dress. I had noticed that many men took relatively little notice
the face of a woman *en décolletage,* though it seemed a regrettal
habit in a clergyman. He cleared his throat.

"Mmphm. And d'ye ken what to do for a nervous compla
then?"

"What sort of nervous complaint?"

He pursed his lips and frowned, as though unsure whether
trust me. The upper lip came to a slight point, like an owl's be
but the lower was thick and pendulous.

"Well . . . 'tis a complicated case. But to speak genera
now"—he eyed me carefully—"what would ye give for a sort
. . . fit?"

"Epileptic seizure? Where the person falls down a
twitches?"

He shook his head, showing a reddened band about his neck,
here the high white stock had chafed it.

"No, a different kind of fit. Screaming and staring."

"Screaming *and* staring?"

"Not at once, ye ken," he added hastily. "First the one, and
en the other—or rather, roundabout. First she'll do naught but
are for days on end, not speaking, and then of a sudden, she'll
cream fit to wake the deid."

"That sounds very trying." It did; if he had a wife so afflicted,
could easily explain the deep lines of strain that bracketed his
outh and eyes, and the blue circles of exhaustion beneath his
yes.

I tapped a finger on the counter, considering. "I don't know; I'd
ave to see the patient."

The minister's tongue touched his lower lip. "Perhaps . . .
ould ye be willing maybe, to come and see her? It isn't far," he
ded, rather stiffly. Pleading didn't come naturally to him, but the
rgency of his request communicated itself despite the stiffness of
s figure.

"I can't, just now," I told him. "I have to meet my husband.
ut perhaps this afternoon—"

"Two o'clock," he said promptly. "Henderson's, in Carrub-
r's Close. Campbell is the name, the Reverend Archibald Camp-
ell."

Before I could say yes or no, the curtain between the front room
d the back twitched aside, and Mr. Haugh appeared with two
ottles, one of which he handed to each of us.

The Reverend eyed his with suspicion, as he groped in his
ocket for a coin.

"Weel, and there's your price," he said ungraciously, slapping
on the counter. "And we'll hope as you've given me the right
ne, and no the lady's poison."

The curtain rustled again and a woman looked out after the
eparting form of the minister.

"Good riddance," she remarked. "Happence for an hour's
ork, and insult on the top of it! The Lord might ha' chosen
etter, is all I can say!"

"Do you know him?" I asked, curious whether Louisa might
ave any helpful information about the afflicted wife.

"Not to say I ken him weel, no," Louisa said, staring at me in frank curiosity. "He's one o' they Free Church meenisters, as i always rantin' on the corner by the Market Cross, tellin' folk a their behavior's of nay consequence at all, and all that's needfu for salvation is that they shall 'come to grips wi' Jesus'—like as Our Lord was to be a fair-day wrestler!" She sniffed disdainfull at this heretical viewpoint, crossing herself against contaminatio

"I'm surprised the likes of the Reverend Campbell shoul come in our shop, hearin' what he thinks o' Papists by and large. Her eyes sharpened at me.

"But you'll maybe be Free Church yoursel', ma'am; meanin no offense to ye, if so."

"No, I'm a Catholic—er, a Papist, too," I assured her. "I wa only wondering whether you knew anything about the Reverend wife, and her condition."

Louisa shook her head, turning to deal with a new customer.

"Nay, I've ne'er seen the lady. But whatever's the matter wi her," she added, frowning after the departed Reverend, "I'm su that livin' wi' *him* doesna improve it any!"

The weather was chill but clear, and only a faint hint of smok lingered in the Rectory garden as a reminder of the fire. Jamie an I sat on a bench against the wall, absorbing the pale winter sun shine as we waited for Young Ian to finish his confession.

"Did you tell Ian that load of rubbish he gave Young Ian yeste day? About where I'd been all this time?"

"Oh, aye," he said. "Ian's a good deal too canny to believe i but it's a likely enough story, and he's too good a friend to insi on the truth."

"I suppose it will do, for general consumption," I agreed. "B shouldn't you have told it to Sir Percival, instead of letting hi think we were newlyweds?"

He shook his head decidedly. "Och, no. For the one thing, S Percival has no notion of my real name, though I'll lay a year takings he knows it isna Malcolm. I dinna want him to be thinkin of me and Culloden together, by any means. And for another, story like the one I gave Ian would cause the devil of a lot mo talk than the news that the printer's taken a wife."

" 'Oh, what a tangled web we weave,' " I intoned, " 'whe first we practice to deceive.' "

He gave me a quick blue glance, and the corner of his mouth
ted slightly.

"It gets a bit easier with practice, Sassenach," he said. "Try
ving wi' me for a time, and ye'll find yourself spinning silk out
your arse easy as sh—, er, easy as kiss-my-hand."

I burst out laughing.

"I want to see you do that," I said.

"You already have." He stood up and craned his neck, trying to
e over the wall into the Rectory garden.

"Young Ian's being the devil of a time," he remarked, sitting
wn again. "How can a lad not yet fifteen have that much to
nfess?"

"After the day and night he had yesterday? I suppose it depends
w much detail Father Hayes wants to hear," I said, with a vivid
collection of my breakfast with the prostitutes. "Has he been in
ere all this time?"

"Er, no." The tips of Jamie's ears grew slightly pinker in the
orning light. "I, er, I had to go first. As an example, ye ken."

"No wonder it took some time," I said, teasing. "How long has
been since you've been to confession?"

"I told Father Hayes it was six months."

"And was it?"

"No, but I supposed if he was going to shrive me for thieving,
sault, and profane language, he might as well shrive me for
ing, too."

"What, no fornication or impure thoughts?"

"Certainly not," he said austerely. "Ye can think any manner
horrible things without sin, and it's to do wi' your wife. It's
ly if you're thinking it about other ladies, it's impure."

"I had no idea I was coming back to save your soul," I said
imly, "but it's nice to be useful."

He laughed, bent and kissed me thoroughly.

"I wonder if that counts as an indulgence," he said, pausing for
eath. "It ought to, no? It does a great deal more to keep a man
om the fires of hell than saying the rosary does. Speaking of
nich," he added, digging into his pocket and coming out with a
ther chewed-looking wooden rosary, "remind me that I must say
y penance sometime today. I was about to start on it, when ye
me up."

"How many Hail Marys are you supposed to say?" I asked,

fingering the beads. The chewed appearance wasn't illusion; the were definite small toothmarks on most of the beads.

"I met a Jew last year," he said, ignoring the question. ' natural philosopher, who'd sailed round the world six times. I told me that in both the Musselman faith and the Jewish teaching it was considered an act of virtue for a man and his wife to lie each other.

"I wonder if that has anything to do wi' both Jews and M selmen being circumcised?" he added thoughtfully. "I nev thought to ask him that—though perhaps he would ha' found indelicate to say."

"I shouldn't think a foreskin more or less would impair virtue," I assured him.

"Oh, good," he said, and kissed me once more.

"What happened to your rosary?" I asked, picking up string where it had fallen on the grass. "It looks like the rats ha been at it."

"Not rats," he said. "Bairns."

"What bairns?"

"Oh, any that might be about." He shrugged, tucking the bea back in his pocket. "Young Jamie has three now, and Maggie a Kitty two each. Wee Michael's just married, but his wife's bree ing." The sun was behind him, darkening his face, so that teeth flashed suddenly white when he smiled. "Ye didna ken were a great-aunt seven times over, aye?"

"A great-aunt?" I said, staggered.

"Well, I'm a great-uncle," he said cheerfully, "and I have found it a terrible trial, except for having my beads gnawed wh the weans are cutting teeth—that, and bein' expected to answer 'Nunkie' a lot."

Sometimes twenty years seemed like an instant, and sometim it seemed like a very long time indeed.

"Er . . . there isn't a feminine equivalent of 'Nunkie,' hope?"

"Oh, no," he assured me. "They'll all call ye Great-Aur Claire, and treat ye wi' the utmost respect."

"Thanks a lot," I muttered, with visions of the hospital's ge atric wing fresh in my mind.

Jamie laughed, and with a lightness of heart no doubt enge

ered by being newly freed from sin, grasped me around the waist
nd lifted me onto his lap.

"I've never before seen a great-auntie wi' a lovely plump arse
ke that," he said with approval, bouncing me slightly on his
nees. His breath tickled the back of my neck as he leaned for-
ard. I let out a small shriek as his teeth closed lightly on my ear.

"Are ye all right, Auntie?" said Young Ian's voice just behind
s, full of concern.

Jamie started convulsively, nearly unshipping me from his lap,
en tightened his hold on my waist.

"Oh, aye," he said. "It's just your auntie saw a spider."

"Where?" said Young Ian, peering interestedly over the bench.

"Up there." Jamie rose, standing me on my feet, and pointed to
e lime tree, where—sure enough—the web of an orb weaver
retched across the crook of two branches, sparkling with damp.
he weaver herself sat in the center, round as a cherry, wearing a
audy pattern of green and yellow on her back.

"I was telling your auntie," Jamie said, as Young Ian examined
e web in lashless fascination, "about a Jew I met, a natural
ilosopher. He'd made a study of spiders, it seems; in fact, he
as in Edinburgh to deliver a learned paper to the Royal Society,
spite of being a Jew."

"Really? Did he tell ye a lot about spiders?" Young Ian asked
gerly.

"A lot more than I cared to know," Jamie informed his
ephew. "There are times and places for talkin' of spiders that lay
gs in caterpillars so the young hatch out and devour the poor
ast while it's still alive, but during supper isna one of them. He
d say one thing I thought verra interesting, though," he added,
quinting at the web. He blew gently on it, and the spider scuttled
iskly into hiding.

"He said that spiders spin two kinds of silk, and if ye have a
ns—and can make the spider sit still for it, I suppose—ye can
e the two places where the silk comes out; spinnerets, he called
em. In any case, the one kind of silk is sticky, and if a wee bug
uches it, he's done for. But the other kind is dry silk, like the
rt ye'd embroider with, but finer."

The orb weaver was advancing cautiously toward the center of
r web again.

"See where she walks?" Jamie pointed to the web, anchored by a number of spokes, supporting the intricate netlike whorl. "T spokes there, those are spun of the dry silk, so the spider can wa over it herself wi' no trouble. But the rest o' the web is the stic kind of silk—or mostly so—and if ye watch a spider careful quite a long time, you'll see that she goes only on the dry stran for if she walked on the sticky stuff, she'd be stuck herself."

"Is that so?" Ian breathed reverently on the web, watchin intently as the spider moved away along her nonskid road safety.

"I suppose there's a moral there for web weavers," Jamie o served to me, sotto voce. "Be sure ye know which of your stran are sticky."

"I suppose it helps even more if you have the kind of luck th will conjure up a handy spider when you need one," I said dry

He laughed and took my arm.

"That's not luck, Sassenach," he told me. "It's watchfulne Ian, are ye coming?"

"Oh, aye." Young Ian abandoned the web with obvious relu tance and followed us to the kirkyard gate.

"Oh, Uncle Jamie, I meant to ask, can I borrow your rosary" he said, as we emerged onto the cobbles of the Royal Mile. "T priest told me I must say five decades for my penance, and tha too many to keep count of on my fingers."

"Surely." Jamie stopped and fished in his pocket for the rosar "Be sure to give it back, though."

Young Ian grinned. "Aye, I reckon you'll be needing it yourse Uncle Jamie. The priest told me he was verra wicked," Young I confided to me, with a lashless wink, "and told me not to be li him."

"Mmphm." Jamie glanced up and down the road, gauging t speed of an approaching handcart, edging its way down the ste incline. Freshly shaved that morning, his cheeks had a rosy glo about them.

"How many decades of the rosary are you supposed to say penance?" I asked curiously.

"Eighty-five," he muttered. The rosiness of his freshly shav cheeks deepened.

Young Ian's mouth dropped open in awe.

"How long has it been since ye went to confession, Uncle?" he
ked.

"A long time," Jamie said tersely. "Come on!"

Jamie had an appointment after dinner to meet with a Mr. Har-
ng, representative of the Hand in Hand Assurance Society,
ich had insured the premises of the printshop, to inspect the
hy remains with him and verify the loss.

"I willna need ye, laddie," he said reassuringly to Young Ian,
o looked less than enthusiastic about the notion of revisiting the
ene of his adventures. "You go wi' your auntie to see this
adwoman."

"I canna tell how ye do it," he added to me, raising one brow.
You're in the city less than two days, and all the afflicted folk for
les about are clutching at your hems."

"Hardly all of them," I said dryly. "It's only one woman, after
, and I haven't even seen her yet."

"Aye, well. At least madness isna catching—I hope." He
ssed me briefly, then turned to go, clapping Young Ian compan-
nably on the shoulder. "Look after your auntie, Ian."

Young Ian paused for a moment, looking after the tall form of
s departing uncle.

"Do you want to go with him, Ian?" I asked. "I can manage
ne, if you—"

"Oh, no, Auntie!" He turned back to me, looking rather
ashed. "I dinna want to go, at all. It's only—I was wondering—
ll, what if they . . . find anything? In the ashes?"

"A body, you mean," I said bluntly. I had realized, of course,
at the distinct possibility that Jamie and Mr. Harding *would* find
e body of the one-eyed seaman was the reason Jamie had told
n to accompany me.

The boy nodded, looking ill at ease. His skin had faded to a sort
rosy tan, but was still too dark to show any paleness due to
otion.

"I don't know," I said. "If the fire was a very hot one, there
ay be nothing much left to find. But don't worry about it." I
uched his arm in reassurance. "Your uncle will know what to
."

"Aye, that's so." His face brightened, full of faith in his uncle's

ability to handle any situation whatever. I smiled when I saw
expression, then realized with a small start of surprise that I h
that faith, too. Be it drunken Chinese, corrupt Customs agents,
Mr. Harding of the Hand in Hand Assurance Society, I hadn't a
doubt that Jamie would manage.

"Come on, then," I said, as the bell in the Canongate K
began to ring. "It's just on two now."

Despite his visit to Father Hayes, Ian had retained a certain
of dreamy bliss, which returned to him now, and there was lit
conversation as we made our way up the slope of the Royal Mile
Henderson's lodging house, in Carrubber's Close.

It was a quiet hotel, but luxurious by Edinburgh standards, w
a patterned carpet on the stairs and colored glass in the str
window. It seemed rather rich surroundings for a Free Chur
minister, but then I knew little about Free Churchmen; perha
they took no vow of poverty as the Catholic clergy did.

Showed up to the third floor by a young boy, we found the d
opened to us at once by a heavyset woman wearing an apron an
worried expression. I thought she might be in her mid-twenti
though she had already lost several of her front teeth.

"You'll be the lady as the Reverend said would call?" s
asked. Her expression lightened a bit at my nod, and she swu
the door wider.

"Mr. Campbell's had to go oot the noo," she said in a bro
Lowland accent, "but he said as how he'd be most obliged to h
yer advice regardin' his sister, mum."

Sister, not wife. "Well, I'll do my best," I said. "May I s
Miss Campbell?"

Leaving Ian to his memories in the sitting room, I accompani
the woman, who introduced herself as Nellie Cowden, to the ba
bedroom.

Miss Campbell was, as advertised, staring. Her pale blue ey
were wide open, but didn't seem to be looking at anything
certainly not at me.

She sat in the sort of wide, low chair called a nursing chair, w
her back to the fire. The room was dim, and the backlighting ma
her features indistinct, except for the unblinking eyes. Seen clo
to, her features were still indistinct; she had a soft, round fa
undistinguished by any apparent bone structure, and baby-fi
brown hair, neatly brushed. Her nose was small and snub, her ch

uble, and her mouth hung pinkly open, so slack as to obscure its
tural lines.

"Miss Campbell?" I said cautiously. There was no response
om the plump figure in the chair. Her eyes did blink, I saw,
ough much less frequently than normal.

"She'll nae answer ye, whilst she's in this state," Nellie Cow-
n said behind me. She shook her head, wiping her hands upon
r apron. "Nay, not a word."

"How long has she been like this?" I picked up a limp, pudgy
nd and felt for the pulse. It was there, slow and quite strong.

"Oh, for twa days so far, this time." Becoming interested, Miss
owden leaned forward, peering into her charge's face. "Usually
e stays like that for a week or more—thirteen days is the longest
e's done it."

Moving slowly—though Miss Campbell seemed unlikely to be
armed—I began to examine the unresisting figure, meanwhile
king questions of her attendant. Miss Margaret Campbell was
rty-seven, Miss Cowden told me, the only relative of the Rever-
d Archibald Campbell, with whom she had lived for the past
enty years, since the death of their parents.

"What starts her doing this? Do you know?"

Miss Cowden shook her head. "No tellin', mum. Nothin' seems
start it. One minute she'll be lookin' aboot, talkin' and laughin',
tin' her dinner like the sweet child she is, and the next—
eesht!" She snapped her fingers, then, for effect, leaned for-
rd and snapped them again, deliberately, just under Miss Camp-
ll's nose.

"See?" she said. "I could hae six men wi' trumpets pass
rough the room, and she'd pay it nay more mind."

I was reasonably sure that Miss Campbell's trouble was mental,
t physical, but I made a complete examination, anyway—or as
mplete as could be managed without undressing that clumsy,
ert form.

"It's when she comes oot of it that's the worst, though," Miss
wden assured me, squatting next to me as I knelt on the floor to
eck Miss Campbell's plantar reflexes. Her feet, loosed from
es and stockings, were damp and smelled musty.

I drew a fingernail firmly down the sole of each foot in turn,
ecking for a Babinski reflex that might indicate the presence of

a brain lesion. Nothing, though; her toes curled under, in norm
startlement.

"What happens then? Is that the screaming the Reverend me
tioned?" I rose to my feet. "Will you bring me a lighted cand
please?"

"Oh, aye, the screamin'." Miss Cowden hastened to oblig
lighting a wax taper from the fire. "She do shriek somethin' aw
then, on and on 'til she's worn herself oot. Then she'll fall asle
—sleep the clock around, she will—and wake as though nothi
had happened."

"And she's quite all right when she wakes?" I asked. I mov
the candle flame slowly back and forth, a few inches before t
patient's eyes. The pupils shrank in automatic response to t
light, but the irises stayed fixed, not following the flame. My ha
itched for the solid handle of an ophthalmoscope, to examine t
retinas, but no such luck.

"Well, not to say all right," Miss Cowden said slowly. I turn
from the patient to look at her and she shrugged, massive shou
ders powerful under the linen of her blouse.

"She's saft in the heid, puir dear," she said, matter-of-fact
"Has been for nigh on twenty year."

"You haven't been taking care of her all that time, surely?"

"Oh, no! Mr. Campbell had a woman as cared for her whe
they lived, in Burntisland, but the woman was none so young, a
didna wish to leave her home. So when the Reverend made up l
mind to take up the Missionary Society's offer, and to take l
sister wi' him to the West Indies—why, he advertised for a stro
woman o' good character who wouldna mind travel to be an a
gail for her . . . and here I am." Miss Cowden gave me a ga
toothed smile in testimony to her own virtues.

"The West Indies? He's planning to take Miss Campbell on
ship to the West Indies?" I was staggered; I knew just enough
sailing conditions to think that any such trip would be a maj
ordeal to a woman in good health. This woman—but then I reco
sidered. All things concerned, Margaret Campbell might endu
such a trip better than a normal woman—at least if she remain
in her trance.

"He thought as the change of climate might be good for her
Miss Cowden was explaining. "Get her away from Scotland, a

the dreadful memories. Ought to ha' done it long since, is what
ay.''

''What sort of dreadful memories?'' I asked. I could see by the
:am in Miss Cowden's eye that she was only too ready to tell
:. I had finished the examination by this time, and concluded
it there was little physically wrong with Miss Campbell save
ictivity and poor diet, but there was the chance that something
her history might suggest some treatment.

''Weel,'' she began, sidling toward the table, where a decanter
l several glasses stood on a tray, ''it's only what Tilly Lawson
d me, her as looked after Miss Campbell for sae long, but she
l swear it was the truth, and her a godly woman. If ye'd care to
e a drop of cordial, mum, for the sake o' the Reverend's hospi-
ty?''

The chair Miss Campbell sat on was the only one in the room,
Miss Cowden and I perched inelegantly on the bed, side by
e, and watched the silent figure before us, as we sipped our
ckberry cordial, and she told me Margaret Campbell's story.

Margaret Campbell had been born in Burntisland, no more than
e miles from Edinburgh, across the Firth of Forth. At the time
the '45, when Charles Stuart had marched into Edinburgh to
laim his father's throne, she had been seventeen.

''Her father was a Royalist, o' course, and her brother in a
vernment regiment, marching north to put down the wicked
els,'' said Miss Cowden, taking a tiny sip of the cordial to
ke it last. ''But not Miss Margaret. Nay, she was for the Bonnie
nce, and the Hielan' men that followed him.''

One, in particular, though Miss Cowden did not know his name.
t a fine man he must have been, for Miss Margaret stole away
m her home to meet him, and told him all the bits of informa-
n that she gleaned from listening to her father and his friends,
l from her brother's letters home.

But then had come Falkirk; a victory, but a costly one, followed
retreat. Rumor had attended the flight of the Prince's army to
north, and not a soul doubted but that their flight led to de-
iction. Miss Margaret, desperate at the rumors, left her home at
d of night in the cold March spring, and went to find the man
loved.

Now here the account had been uncertain—whether it was that
had found the man and he had spurned her, or that she had not

found him in time, and been forced to turn back from Cullod
Moor—but in any case, turn back she did, and the day after
battle, she had fallen into the hands of a band of English soldie

"Dreadful, what they did to her," Miss Cowden said, loweri
her voice as though the figure in the chair could hear. "Drea
ful!" The English soldiers, blind with the lust of the hunt and
kill, pursuing the fugitives of Culloden, had not stopped to ask
name or the sympathies of her family. They had known by
speech that she was a Scot, and that knowledge had been enou

They had left her for dead in a ditch half full of freezing wat
and only the fortuitous presence of a family of tinkers, hiding
the nearby brambles for fear of the soldiers, had saved her.

"I canna help but think it a pity they did save her, un-Christ
thing it is to say," Miss Cowden whispered. "If not, the puir la
might ha' slippit her earthly bonds and gone happy to God. But
it is—" She gestured clumsily at the silent figure, and drank do
the last drops of her cordial.

Margaret had lived, but did not speak. Somewhat recovered,
silent, she traveled with the tinkers, moving south with them
avoid the pillaging of the Highlands that took place in the wake
Culloden. And then one day, sitting in the yard of a pothou
holding the tin to collect coppers as the tinkers busked and sa
she had been found by her brother, who had stopped with
Campbell regiment to refresh themselves on the way back to th
quarters at Edinburgh.

"She kent him, and him her, and the shock o' their meeti
gave her back her voice, but not her mind, puir thing. He took
home, o' course, but she was always as though she was in the p
—sometime before she met the Hielan' man. Her father was de
then, from the influenza, and Tilly Lawson said as the shock
seeing her like that kilt her mother, but could be as that were
influenza, too, for there was a great deal of it about that year.

The whole affair had left Archibald Campbell deeply emb
tered against both Highland Scots and the English army, and
had resigned his commission. With his parents dead, he fou
himself middling well-to-do, but the sole support of his damag
sister.

"He couldna marry," Miss Cowden explained, "for w
woman would have him, and she"—with a nod toward the fire
"was thrown into the bargain?"

In his difficulties, he had turned to God, and become a minister. nable to leave his sister, or to bear the confinement of the family use at Burntisland with her, he had purchased a coach, hired a oman to look after Margaret, and begun to make brief journeys to the surrounding countryside to preach, often taking her with m.

In his preaching he had found success, and this year had been ked by the Society of Presbyterian Missionaries if he would dertake his longest journey yet, to the West Indies, there to ganize churches and appoint elders on the colonies of Barbados d Jamaica. Prayer had given him his answer, and he had sold the mily property in Burntisland and moved his sister to Edinburgh ile he made preparations for the journey.

I glanced once more at the figure by the fire. The heated air m the hearth stirred the skirts about her feet, but beyond that all movement, she might have been a statue.

"Well," I said with a sigh, "there's not a great deal I can do for r, I'm afraid. But I'll give you some prescriptions—receipts, I ean—to have made up at the apothecary's before you go."

If they didn't help, they couldn't hurt, I reflected, as I copied wn the short lists of ingredients. Chamomile, hops, rue, tansy, d verbena, with a strong pinch of peppermint, for a soothing nic. Tea of rose hips, to help correct the slight nutritional defi- ncy I had noted—spongy, bleeding gums, and a pale, bloated ok about the face.

"Once you reach the Indies," I said, handing Miss Cowden the per, "you must see that she eats a great deal of fruit—oranges, apefruit, and lemons, particularly. You should do the same," I ded, causing a look of profound suspicion to flit across the aid's wide face. I doubted she ate any vegetable matter beyond e occasional onion or potato, save her daily parritch.

The Reverend Campbell had not returned, and I saw no real ason to wait for him. Bidding Miss Campbell adieu, I pulled en the door of the bedroom, to find Young Ian standing on the er side of it.

"Oh!" he said, startled. "I was just comin' to find ye, Auntie. s nearly half-past three, and Uncle Jamie said—"

"Jamie?" The voice came from behind me, from the chair side the fire.

Miss Cowden and I whirled to find Miss Campbell sitting bolt upright, eyes still wide but focused now. They were focused on t doorway, and as Young Ian stepped inside, Miss Campbell beg to scream.

Rather unsettled by the encounter with Miss Campbell, You Ian and I made our way thankfully back to the refuge of t brothel, where we were greeted matter-of-factly by Bruno a taken to the rear parlor. There we found Jamie and Fergus deep conversation.

"True, we do not trust Sir Percival," Fergus was saying, "but this case, what point is there to his telling you of an ambush, sa that such an ambush is in fact to occur?"

"Damned if I ken why," Jamie said frankly, leaning back a stretching in his chair. "And that being so, we do, as ye sa conclude that there's meant to be an ambush by the exciseme Two days, he said. That would be Mullen's Cove." Then, catchi sight of me and Ian, he half-rose, motioning us to take seats.

"Will it be the rocks below Balcarres, then?" Fergus asked

Jamie frowned in thought, the two stiff fingers of his right ha drumming slowly on the tabletop.

"No," he said at last. "Let it be Arbroath; the wee cove und the abbey there. Just to be sure, aye?"

"All right." Fergus pushed back the half-empty plate of o cakes from which he had been refreshing himself, and rose. shall spread the word, milord. Arbroath, in four days." With a m to me, he swirled his cloak about his shoulders and went out.

"Is it the smuggling, Uncle?" Young Ian asked eagerly. ' there a French lugger coming?" He picked up an oatcake and into it, scattering crumbs over the table.

Jamie's eyes were still abstracted, thinking, but they cleared he glanced sharply at his nephew. "Aye, it is. And *you,* Young I are having nothing to do with it."

"But I could help!" the boy protested. "You'll need somec to hold the mules, at least!"

"After all your da said to you and me yesterday, wee Ian Jamie raised his brows. "Christ, ye've a short memory, lad!"

Ian looked mildly abashed at this, and took another oatcake cover his confusion. Seeing him momentarily silent, I took opportunity to ask my own questions.

"You're going to Arbroath to meet a French ship that's bringing a smuggled liquor?" I asked. "You don't think that's dangerous, after Sir Percival's warning?"

Jamie glanced at me with one brow still raised, but answered patiently enough.

"No. Sir Percival was warning me that the rendezvous in two days' time is known. That was to take place at Mullen's Cove. I've an arrangement wi' Jared and his captains, though. If a rendezvous canna be kept for some reason, the lugger will stand offshore and come in again the next night—but to a different place. And there's a third fallback as well, should the second meeting not come off."

"But if Sir Percival knows the first rendezvous, won't he know the others, too?" I persisted.

Jamie shook his head and poured out a cup of wine. He quirked a brow at me to ask whether I wanted any, and upon my shaking my head, sipped it himself.

"No," he said. "The rendezvous points are arranged in sets of three, between me and Jared, sent by sealed letter inside a packet addressed to Jeanne, here. Once I've read the letter, I burn it. The men who'll help meet the lugger will all know the first point, of course—I suppose one o' them will have let something slip," he added, frowning into his cup. "But no one—not even Fergus—kens the other two points unless we need to make use of one. And then we do, all the men ken well enough to guard their tongues."

"But then it's bound to be safe, Uncle!" Young Ian burst out. "Please let me come! I'll keep well back out o' the way," he promised.

Jamie gave his nephew a slightly jaundiced look.

"Aye, ye will," he said. "You'll come wi' me to Arbroath, but you and your auntie will stay at the inn on the road above the abbey until we've finished. I've got to take the laddie home to Lallybroch, Claire," he explained, turning to me. "And mend things as best I can with his parents." The elder Ian had left Halliday's that morning before Jamie and Young Ian arrived, leaving no message, but presumably bound for home. "Ye willna mind the journey? I wouldna ask it, and you just over your travel from Inverness"—his eyes met mine with a small, conspiratorial smile—"but I must take him back as soon as may be."

"I don't mind at all," I assured him. "It will be good to see Jenny and the rest of your family again."

"But Uncle—" Young Ian blurted. "What about—"

"Be still!" Jamie snapped. "That will be all from you, ladd
Not another word, aye?"

Young Ian looked wounded, but took another oatcake and i
serted it into his mouth in a marked manner, signifying his inte
tion to remain completely silent.

Jamie relaxed then, and smiled at me.

"Well, and how was your visit to the madwoman?"

"Very interesting," I said. "Jamie, do you know any peop
named Campbell?"

"Not above three or four hundred of them," he said, a sm
twitching his long mouth. "Had ye a particular Campbell
mind?"

"A couple of them." I told him the story of Archibald Cam
bell and his sister, Margaret, as related to me by Nellie Cowde

He shook his head at the tale, and sighed. For the first time,
looked truly older, his face tightened and lined by memory.

"It's no the worst tale I've heard, of the things that happen
after Culloden," he said. "But I dinna think—wait." He stoppe
and looked at me, eyes narrowed in thought. "Margaret Campbe
Margaret. Would she be a bonny wee lass—perhaps the size o' t
second Mary? And wi' soft brown hair like a wren's feather, an
verra sweet face?"

"She probably was, twenty years ago," I said, thinking of th
still, plump figure sitting by the fire. "Why, do you know her af
all?"

"Aye, I think I do." His brow was furrowed in thought, and
looked down at the table, drawing a random line through t
spilled crumbs. "Aye, if I'm right, she was Ewan Cameron
sweetheart. You'll mind Ewan?"

"Of course." Ewan had been a tall, handsome joker of a ma
who had worked with Jamie at Holyrood, gathering bits of intel
gence that filtered through from England. "What's become
Ewan? Or should I not ask?" I said, seeing the shadow come ov
Jamie's face.

"The English shot him," he said quietly. "Two days after Cu
loden." He closed his eyes for a moment, then opened them a
smiled tiredly at me.

"Well, then, may God bless the Reverend Archie Campbell. I
heard of him, a time or two, during the Rising. He was a bo

ɔldier, folk said, and a brave one—and I suppose he'll need to be ɔw, poor man." He sat a moment longer, then stood up with ecision.

"Aye, well, there's a great deal to be done before we leave dinburgh. Ian, you'll find the list of the printshop customers ɔstairs on the table; fetch it down to me and I'll mark off for ye e ones with orders outstanding. Ye must go to see each one and ffer back their money. Unless they choose to wait until I've ɔund new premises and laid in new stock—that might take as uch as two months, though, tell them."

He patted his coat, where something made a small jingling ɔund.

"Luckily the assurance money will pay back the customers, and ave a bit left over. Speaking of which"—he turned and smiled at e—"your job, Sassenach, is to find a dressmaker who will man- ge ye a decent gown in two days' time. For I expect Daphne ɔould like her dress back, and I canna take ye home to Lallybroch aked."

The chief entertainment of the ride north to Arbroath w watching the conflict of wills between Jamie and You Ian. I knew from long experience that stubbornness w one of the major components of a Fraser's character. Ian seem not unduly handicapped in that respect, though only half a Fras either the Murrays were no slouches with regard to stubbornne or the Fraser genes were strong ones.

Having had the opportunity to observe Brianna at close ran for many years, I had my own opinion about that, but kept qui merely enjoying the spectacle of Jamie having for once met I match. By the time we passed Balfour, he was wearing a distinc hunted look.

This contest between immovable object and irresistible fo continued until early evening of the fourth day, when we reach Arbroath to find that the inn where Jamie had intended to leave I and myself no longer existed. No more than a tumbled-down sto wall and one or two charred roof-beams remained to mark t spot; otherwise, the road was deserted for miles in either directi

Jamie looked at the heap of stones in silence for some time. was reasonably obvious that he could not just leave us in t middle of a desolate, muddy road. Ian, wise enough not to pr the advantage, kept also silent, though his skinny frame fai vibrated with eagerness.

"All right, then," Jamie said at last, resigned. "Ye'll come. I only so far as the cliff's edge, Ian—d'ye hear? You'll take care your auntie."

"I hear, Uncle Jamie," Young Ian replied, with deceptive ᵉekness. I caught Jamie's wry glance, though, and understood t if Ian was to take care of auntie, auntie was also to take care of ᵃ. I hid a smile, nodding obediently.

The rest of the men were timely, arriving at the rendezvous ᵢnt on the cliffside just after dark. A couple of the men seemed ᵍuely familiar, but most were just muffled shapes; it was two ᵛs past the dark of the moon, but the tiny sliver rising over the ᵗizon made conditions here little more illuminating than those ᵗaining in the brothel's cellars. No introductions were made, the ᵐn greeting Jamie with unintelligible mutters and grunts.

There was one unmistakable figure, though. A large mule-ᵂwn wagon appeared, rattling its way down the road, driven by ᵍgus and a diminutive object that could only be Mr. Willoughby, ᵒm I had not seen since he had shot the mysterious man on the ᵗirs of the brothel.

'He hasn't a pistol with him tonight, I hope," I murmured to ᵐie.

'Who?" he said, squinting into the gathering gloom. "Oh, the ᵗinee? No, none of them have." Before I could ask why not, he ᵈ gone forward, to help back the wagon around, ready to make a ᵗaway toward Edinburgh, so soon as the contraband should be ᵈded. Young Ian pressed his way forward, and I, mindful of my ᵉ as custodian, followed him.

Mr. Willoughby stood on tiptoe to reach into the back of the ᵍon, emerging with an odd-looking lantern, fitted with a ᵗrced metal top and sliding metal sides.

'Is that a dark lantern?" I asked, fascinated.

'Aye, it is," said Young Ian, importantly. "Ye keep the slides ᵗt until we see the signal out at sea." He reached for the lantern. ᵉere, give it me; I'll take it—I ken the signal."

Mr. Willoughby merely shook his head, pulling the lantern out ᵒ Young Ian's grasp. "Too tall, too young," he said. "Tsei-mi ᵉso," he added, as though that settled the matter once and for

'What?" Young Ian was indignant. "What d'ye mean too tall ᵈ too young, ye wee—"

'He means," said a level voice behind us, "that whoever's ᵗding the lantern is a bonny target, should we have visitors. Mr. ᵂloughby kindly takes the risk of it, because he's the smallest

man among us. You're tall enough to see against the sky, wee I▮
and young enough to have nay sense yet. Stay out o' the w▮
aye?''

Jamie gave his nephew a light cuff over the ear, and passed by▮
kneel on the rocks by Mr. Willoughby. He said something lo▮
voiced in Chinese, and there was the ghost of a laugh from ▮
Chinaman. Mr. Willoughby opened the side of the lantern, holdi▮
it conveniently to Jamie's cupped hands. A sharp click, repea▮
twice, and I caught the flicker of sparks struck from a flint.

It was a wild piece of coast—not surprising, most of Scotlan▮
coast was wild and rocky—and I wondered how and where ▮
French ship would anchor. There was no natural bay, only a cu▮
ing of the coastline behind a jutting cliff that sheltered this s▮
from observation from the road.

Dark as it was, I could see the white lines of the surf purling
across the small half-moon beach. No smooth tourist beach this ▮
small pockets of sand lay ruffled and churned between heaps ▮
seaweed and pebbles and juts of rock. Not an easy footing for m▮
carrying casks, but convenient to the crevices in the surroundi▮
rocks, where the casks could be hidden.

Another black figure loomed up suddenly beside me.

''Everyone's settled, sir,'' it said softly. ''Up in the rocks.''

''Good, Joey.'' A sudden flare lit Jamie's profile, intent on ▮
newly caught wick. He held his breath as the flame steadied a▮
grew, taking up oil from the lantern's reservoir, then let it out w▮
a sigh as he gently closed the metal slide.

''Fine, then,'' he said, standing up. He glanced up at the clif▮
the south, observing the stars over it, and said, ''Nearly n▮
o'clock. They'll be in soon. Mind ye, Joey—no one's to move ▮
I call out, aye?''

''Aye, sir.'' The casual tone of the answer made it apparent t▮
this was a customary exchange, and Joey was plainly surpri▮
when Jamie gripped his arm.

''Be sure of it,'' Jamie said. ''Tell them all again—no ▮
moves 'til I give the word.''

''Aye, sir,'' Joey said again, but this time with more respect. ▮
faded back into the night, making no sound on the rocks.

''Is something wrong?'' I asked, pitching my voice barely l▮
enough to be heard over the breakers. Though the beach and cl▮

:re evidently deserted, the dark setting and the secretive conduct my companions compelled caution.

Jamie shook his head briefly; he'd been right about Young Ian, I ɔught—his own dark silhouette was clear against the paler black the sky behind him.

"I dinna ken." He hesitated for a moment, then said, "Tell me, ssenach—d'ye smell anything?"

Surprised, I obligingly took a deep sniff, held it for a moment, d let it out. I smelled any number of things, including rotted aweed, the thick smell of burning oil from the dark lantern, and ∋ pungent body odor of Young Ian, standing close beside me, eating with a mix of excitement and fear.

"Nothing odd, I don't think," I said. "Do you?"

The silhouette's shoulders rose and dropped in a shrug. "Not w. A moment ago, I could ha' sworn I smelt gunpowder."

"I dinna smell anything," Young Ian said. His voice broke from citement, and he hastily cleared his throat, embarrassed. "Willie acLeod and Alec Hays searched the rocks. They didna find any ιn of excisemen."

"Aye, well." Jamie's voice sounded uneasy. He turned to ung Ian, grasping him by the shoulder.

"Ian, you're to take charge of your auntie, now. The two of ye t back of the gorse bushes there. Keep well away from the ιgon. If anything should happen—"

The beginnings of Young Ian's protest were cut off, apparently a tightening of Jamie's hand, for the boy jerked back with a all grunt, rubbing his shoulder.

"*If* anything should happen," Jamie continued, with emphasis, ou're to take your auntie and go straight home to Lallybroch. nna linger."

"But—" I said.

"Uncle!" Young Ian said.

"Do it," said Jamie, in tones of steel, and turned aside, the cussion concluded.

Young Ian was grim on the trip up the cliff trail, but did as he s told, dutifully escorting me some distance past the gorse shes and finding a small promontory where we might see out ιe way over the water.

"We can see from here," he whispered unnecessarily.

We could indeed. The rocks fell away in a shallow bowl beneath

us, a broken cup filled with darkness, the light of the water spilli
from the broken edge where the sea hissed in. Once I caught a ti
movement, as a metal buckle caught the faint light, but for t
most part, the ten men below were completely invisible.

I squinted, trying to pick out the location of Mr. Willough
with his lantern, but saw no sign of light, and concluded that
must be standing behind the lantern, shielding it from sight fro
the cliff.

Young Ian stiffened suddenly next to me.

"Someone's coming!" he whispered. "Quick, get behind me
Stepping courageously out in front of me, he plunged a hand und
his shirt, into the band of his breeches, and withdrew a pistol; da
as it was, I could see the faint gleam of starlight along the barr

He braced himself, peering into the dark, slightly hunched ov
the gun with both hands clamped on the weapon.

"Don't shoot, for God's sake!" I hissed in his ear. I didn't d
grab his arm for fear of setting off the pistol, but was terrified l
he make any noise that might attract attention to the men bele

"I'd be obliged if ye'd heed your auntie, Ian," came Jami
soft, ironic tones from the blackness below the cliff edge. "I'd
soon not have ye blow my head off, aye?"

Ian lowered the pistol, shoulders slumping with what mig
have been a sigh either of relief or disappointment. The go
bushes quivered, and then Jamie was before us, brushing go
prickles from the sleeve of his coat.

"Did no one tell ye not to come armed?" Jamie's voice w
mild, with no more than a note of academic interest. "It's
hanging offense to draw a weapon against an officer of the Kin
Customs," he explained, turning to me. "None o' the men a
armed, even wi' so much as a fish knife, in case they're taker

"Aye, well, Fergus said they wouldna hang me, because i
beard's not grown yet," Ian said awkwardly. "I'd only be tra
ported, he said."

There was a soft hiss as Jamie drew in his breath through
teeth in exasperation.

"Oh, aye, and I'm sure your mother will be verra pleased
hear ye've been shipped off to the Colonies, even if Fergus w
right!" He put out his hand. "Give me that, fool.

"Where did ye get it, anyway?" he asked, turning the pis
over in his hand. "Already primed, too. I knew I smelt gunpo

er. Lucky ye didna blow your cock off, carrying it in your
reeches.''

Before Young Ian could answer, I interrupted, pointing out to
ea.

"Look!''

The French ship was little more than a blot on the face of the
ea, but its sails shone pale in the glimmer of starlight. A two-
asted ketch, it glided slowly past the cliff and stood off, silent as
ne of the scattered clouds behind it.

Jamie was not watching the ship, but looking downward, toward
point where the rock face broke in a tumble of boulders, just
oove the sand. Looking where he was looking, I could just make
ut a tiny prickle of light. Mr. Willoughby, with the lantern.

There was a brief flash of light that glistened across the wet
cks and was gone. Young Ian's hand was tense on my arm. We
aited, breaths held, to the count of thirty. Ian's hand squeezed
y arm, just as another flash lit the foam on the sand.

"What was that?'' I said.

"What?'' Jamie wasn't looking at me, but out at the ship.

"On the shore; when the light flashed, I thought I saw some-
ing half-buried in the sand. It looked like—''

The third flash came, and a moment later, an answering light
one from the ship—a blue lantern, an eerie dot that hung from
e mast, doubling itself in reflection in the dark water below.

I forgot the glimpse of what appeared to be a rumpled heap of
othing, carelessly buried in the sand, in the excitement of watch-
g the ship. Some movement was evident now, and a faint splash
ached our ears as something was thrown over the side.

"The tide's coming in,'' Jamie muttered in my ear. "The
akers float; the current will carry them ashore in a few minutes.''

That solved the problem of the ship's anchorage—it didn't need
e. But how then was the payment made? I was about to ask
hen there was a sudden shout, and all hell broke loose below.

Jamie thrust his way at once through the gorse bushes, followed
short order by me and Young Ian. Little could be seen distinctly,
ut there was a considerable turmoil taking place on the sandy
each. Dark shapes were stumbling and rolling over the sand, to
e accompaniment of shouting. I caught the words "Halt, in the
ing's name!'' and my blood froze.

"Excisemen!'' Young Ian had caught it, too.

Jamie said something crude in Gaelic, then threw back his hea[d]
and shouted himself, his voice carrying easily across the beac[h]
below.

"Eirich 'illean!" he bellowed. *"Suas am bearrach is teich!"*

Then he turned to Young Ian and me. "Go!" he said.

The noise suddenly increased as the clatter of falling roc[k]
joined the shouting. Suddenly a dark figure shot out of the gor[se]
by my feet and made off through the dark at high speed. Anoth[er]
followed, a few feet away.

A high-pitched scream came from the dark below, high enoug[h]
to be heard over the other noises.

"That's Willoughby!" Young Ian exclaimed. "They've g[ot]
him!"

Ignoring Jamie's order to go, we both crowded forward to pe[er]
through the screen of gorse. The dark-lantern had fallen atilt a[nd]
the slide had come open, shooting a beam of light like a spotlig[ht]
over the beach, where the shallow graves in which the Custom[s]
men had buried themselves gaped in the sand. Black figur[es]
swayed and struggled and shouted through the wet heaps of se[a-]
weed. A dim glow of light around the lantern was sufficient [to]
show two figures clasped together, the smaller kicking wildly as [it]
was lifted off its feet.

"I'll get him!" Young Ian sprang forward, only to be pulled [up]
with a jerk as Jamie caught him by the collar.

"Do as you're told and see my wife safe!"

Gasping for breath, Young Ian turned to me, but I wasn't goi[ng]
anywhere, and set my feet firmly in the dirt, resisting his tug [on]
my arm.

Ignoring us both, Jamie turned and ran along the clifftop, sto[p-]
ping several yards away. I could see him clearly in silhoue[tte]
against the sky, as he dropped to one knee and readied the pist[ol]
bracing it on his forearm to sight downward.

The sound of the shot was no more than a small cracking nois[e,]
lost amid the tumult. The result of it, though, was spectacular. T[he]
lantern exploded in a shower of burning oil, abruptly darkeni[ng]
the beach and silencing the shouting.

The silence was broken within seconds by a howl of mingl[ed]
pain and indignation. My eyes, momentarily blinded by the fla[sh]
of the lantern, adapted quickly, and I saw another glow—the li[ght]
of several small flames, which seemed to be moving erratically [a-]

and down. As my night vision cleared, I saw that the flames rose
from the coat sleeve of a man, who was dancing up and down as
he howled, beating ineffectually at the fire started by the burning
oil that had splashed him.

The gorse bushes quivered violently as Jamie plunged over the
cliffside and was lost to view below.

"Jamie!"

Roused by my cry, Young Ian yanked harder, pulling me half
off my feet and forcibly dragging me away from the cliff.

"Come on, Auntie! They'll be up here, next thing!"

This was undeniably true; I could hear the shouts on the beach
coming closer, as the men swarmed up the rocks. I picked up my
skirts and went, following the boy as fast as we could go through
the rough marrow-grass of the clifftop.

I didn't know where we were going, but Young Ian seemed to.
He had taken off his coat and the white of his shirt was easily
visible before me, floating like a ghost through the thickets of
alder and birch that grew farther inland.

"Where are we?" I panted, coming up alongside him when he
slowed at the bank of a tiny stream.

"The road to Arbroath's just ahead," he said. He was breathing
heavily, and a dark smudge of mud showed down the side of his
shirt. "It'll be easier going in a moment. Are ye all right, Auntie?
Shall I carry ye across?"

I politely declined this gallant offer, privately noting that I undoubtedly weighed as much as he did. I took off my shoes and
stockings, and splashed my way knee-deep across the streamlet,
feeling icy mud well up between my toes.

I was shivering violently when I emerged, and did accept Ian's
offer of his coat—excited as he was, and heated by the exercise, he
was clearly in no need of it. I was chilled not only by the water and
the cold November wind, but by fear of what might be happening
behind us.

We emerged panting onto the road, the wind blowing cold in
our faces. My nose and lips were numb in no time, and my hair
blew loose behind me, heavy on my neck. It's an ill wind that
blows nobody good, though; it carried the sound of voices to us,
moments before we would have walked into them.

"Any signal from the cliff?" a deep male voice asked. Ian
stopped so abruptly in his tracks that I bumped into him.

"Not yet," came the reply. "I thought I heard a bit of shoutin' that way, but then the wind turned."

"Well, get up that tree again then, heavy-arse," the first voice said impatiently. "If any o' the whoresons get past the beach we'll nibble 'em here. Better us get the headmoney than the buggers on the beach."

"It's cold," grumbled the second voice. "Out in the open where the wind gnaws your bones. Wish we'd drawn the watch at the abbey—at least it would be warm there."

Young Ian's hand was clutching my upper arm tight enough to leave bruises. I pulled, trying to loosen his grip, but he paid no attention.

"Aye, but less chance o' catching the big fish," the first voice said. "Ah, and what I might do with fifty pound!"

"Awright," said the second voice, resigned. "Though how we're to see red hair in the dark, I've no notion."

"Just lay 'em by the heels, Oakie; we'll look at their heads later."

Young Ian was finally roused from his trance by my tugging, and stumbled after me off the road and into the bushes.

"What do they mean, by the watch at the abbey?" I demanded, as soon as I thought we were out of earshot of the watchers on the road. "Do you know?"

Young Ian's dark thatch bobbed up and down. "I think so, Auntie. It must be Arbroath abbey. That's the meeting point, aye?"

"Meeting point?"

"If something should go wrong," he explained. "Then it's every man for himself, all to meet at the abbey as soon as they can."

"Well, it couldn't go more wrong," I observed. "What was your uncle shouted when the Customs men popped up?"

Young Ian had half-turned to listen for pursuit from the road; now the pale oval of his face turned back to me. "Oh—he said 'Up, lads! Over the cliff and run!'"

"Sound advice," I said dryly. "So if they followed it, most of the men may have gotten away."

"Except Uncle Jamie and Mr. Willoughby." Young Ian was running one hand nervously through his hair; it reminded me forcibly of Jamie, and I wished he would stop.

"Yes." I took a deep breath. "Well, there's nothing we can do bout them just now. The other men, though—if they're headed or the abbey—"

"Aye," he broke in, "that's what I was tryin' to decide; ought I o as Uncle Jamie said, and take ye to Lallybroch, or had I best try o get to the abbey quick and warn the others as they come?"

"Get to the abbey," I said, "as fast as you can."

"Well, but—I shouldna like to leave ye out here by yourself, untie, and Uncle Jamie said—"

"There's a time to follow orders, Young Ian, and a time to think or yourself," I said firmly, tactfully ignoring the fact that I was in act doing the thinking for him. "Does this road lead to the ab- ey?"

"Aye, it does. No more than a mile and a quarter." Already he vas shifting to and fro on the balls of his feet, eager to be gone.

"Good. You cut round the road and head for the abbey. I'll waik traight along the road, and see if I can distract the excisemen until ou're safely past. I'll meet you at the abbey. Oh, wait—you'd est take your coat."

I surrendered the coat reluctantly; besides being loath to part vith its warmth, it felt like giving up my last link with a friendly uman presence. Once Young Ian was away, I would be com- letely alone in the cold dark of the Scottish night.

"Ian?" I held his arm, to keep him a moment longer.

"Aye?"

"Be careful, won't you?" On impulse, I stood on tiptoe and issed his cold cheek. I was near enough to see his brows arch in urprise. He smiled, and then he was gone, an alder branch snap- ing back into place behind him.

It was very cold. The only sounds were the *whish* of the wind hrough the bushes and the distant murmur of the surf. I pulled the voolen shawl tightly round my shoulders, shivering, and headed ack toward the road.

Ought I to make a noise? I wondered. If not, I might be attacked vithout warning, since the waiting men might hear my footsteps ut couldn't see that I wasn't an escaping smuggler. On the other and, if I strolled through singing a jaunty tune to indicate that I vas a harmless woman, they might just lie hidden in silence, not wanting to give away their presence—and giving away their presence was exactly what I had in mind. I bent and picked up a rock from the side of the road. Then, feeling even colder than before, I stepped out onto the road and walked straight on, without a word

31

Smugglers' Moon

The wind was high enough to keep the trees and bushes in a constant stir, masking the sound of my footsteps on the road—and those of anyone who might be stalking me, too. Less than a fortnight past the feast of Samhain, it was the sort of wild night that made one easily believe that spirits and evil might well be abroad.

It wasn't a spirit that grabbed me suddenly from behind, hand clamped tight across my mouth. Had I not been prepared for just such an eventuality, I would have been startled senseless. As it was, my heart gave a great leap and I jerked convulsively in my captor's grasp.

He had grabbed me from the left, pinning my left arm tight against my side, his right hand over my mouth. *My* right arm was free, though. I drove the heel of my shoe into his kneecap, bucking his leg, and then, taking advantage of his momentary stagger, leaned forward and smashed backward at his head with the rock in my hand.

It was of necessity a glancing blow, but it struck hard enough that he grunted with surprise, and his grip loosened. I kicked and squirmed, and as his hand slipped across my mouth, I got my teeth into a finger and bit down as hard as I could.

"The maxillary muscles run from the sagittal crest at the top of the skull to an insertion on the mandible," I thought, dimly recalling the description from *Grey's Anatomy.* "This gives the jaw and teeth considerable crushing power; in fact, the average human jaw is capable of exerting over three hundred pounds of force."

I didn't know whether I was bettering the average, but I wa
undeniably having an effect. My assailant was thrashing franticall
to and fro in a futile effort to dislodge the death grip I had on hi
finger.

His hold on my arm had loosened in the struggle, and he wa
forced to lower me. As soon as my feet touched the dirt onc
more, I let go of his hand, whirled about, and gave him as hearty
root in the stones with my knee as I could manage, given m
skirts.

Kicking men in the testicles is vastly overrated as a means c
defense. That is to say, it does work—and spectacularly well—bu
it's a more difficult maneuver to carry out than one might think
particularly when one is wearing heavy skirts. Men are extremel
careful of those particular appendages, and thoroughly wary o
any attempt on them.

In this case, though, my attacker was off guard, his legs wid
apart to keep his balance, and I caught him fairly. He made
hideous wheezing noise like a strangled rabbit and doubled up i
the roadway.

"Is that you, Sassenach?" The words were hissed out of th
darkness to my left. I leapt like a startled gazelle, and uttered a
involuntary scream.

For the second time within as many minutes, a hand clappe
itself over my mouth.

"For God's sake, Sassenach!" Jamie muttered in my ear. "It'
me."

I didn't bite him, though I was strongly tempted to.

"I know," I said, through my teeth, when he released m
"Who's the other fellow that grabbed me, though?"

"Fergus, I expect." The amorphous dark shape moved away
few feet and seemed to be prodding another shape that lay on th
road, moaning faintly. "Is it you, Fergus?" he whispered. Receiv
ing a sort of choked noise in response, he bent and hauled th
second shape to its feet.

"Don't talk!" I urged them in a whisper. "There are exciseme
just ahead!"

"Is that so?" said Jamie, in a normal voice. "They're no ver
curious about the noise we're making, are they?"

He paused, as though waiting for an answer, but no sound cam but the low keening of the wind through the alders. He laid a hand on my arm and shouted into the night.

"MacLeod! Raeburn!"

"Aye, Roy," said a mildly testy voice in the shrubbery. "We're here. Innes, too, and Meldrum, is it?"

"Aye, it's me."

Shuffling and talking in low voices, more shapes emerged from the bushes and trees.

". . . four, five, six," Jamie counted. "Where are Hays and the Gordons?"

"I saw Hays go intae the water," one of the shapes volunteered. "He'll ha' gone awa' round the point. Likely the Gordons and Kennedy did, too. I didna hear anything as though they'd been taken."

"Well enough," Jamie said. "Now, then, Sassenach. What's this about excisemen?"

Given the nonappearance of Oakie and his companion, I was beginning to feel rather foolish, but I recounted what Ian and I had heard.

"Aye?" Jamie sounded interested. "Can ye stand yet, Fergus? Ye can? Good lad. Well, then, perhaps we'll have a look. Meldrum, have ye a flint about ye?"

A few moments later, a small torch struggling to stay alight in his hand, he strode down the road, and around the bend. The smugglers and I waited in tense silence, ready either to run or to rush to his assistance, but there were no noises of ambush. After what seemed like an eternity, Jamie's voice floated back along the road.

"Come along, then," he said, sounding calm and collected.

He was standing in the middle of the road, near a large alder. The torchlight fell round him in a flickering circle, and at first I saw nothing but Jamie. Then there was a gasp from the man beside me, and a choked sound of horror from another.

Another face appeared, dimly lit, hanging in the air just behind Jamie's left shoulder. A horrible, congested face, black in the torchlight that robbed everything of color, with bulging eyes and tongue protruding. The hair, fair as dry straw, rose stirring in the wind. I felt a fresh scream rise in my throat, and choked it off.

"Ye were right, Sassenach," Jamie said. "There *was* an exciseman." He tossed something to the ground, where it landed with a small plop! "A warrant," he said, nodding toward the object "His name was Thomas Oakie. Will any of ye ken him?"

"Not like he is now," a voice muttered behind me. "Christ, hi mither wouldna ken him!" There was a general mutter of nega tion, with a nervous shuffling of feet. Clearly, everyone was a anxious to get away from the place as I was.

"All right, then." Jamie stopped the retreat with a jerk of hi head. "The cargo's lost, so there'll be no shares, aye? Will anyon need money for the present?" He reached for his pocket. "I ca provide enough to live on for a bit—for I doubt we'll be workin the coast for a time."

One or two of the men reluctantly advanced within clear sigh of the thing hanging from the tree to receive their money, but th rest of the smugglers melted quietly away into the night. Within few minutes, only Fergus—still white, but standing on his own— Jamie, and I were left.

"Jesu!" Fergus whispered, looking up at the hanged man "Who will have done it?"

"I did—or so I expect the tale will be told, aye?" Jamie gaze upward, his face harsh in the sputtering torchlight. "We'll no tarr longer, shall we?"

"What about Ian?" I said, suddenly remembering the boy. "H went to the abbey, to warn you!"

"He did?" Jamie's voice sharpened. "I came from that direc tion, and didna meet him. Which way did he go, Sassenach?"

"That way," I said, pointing.

Fergus made a small sound that might have been laughter.

"The abbey's the other way," Jamie said, sounding amused "Come on, then; we'll catch him up when he realizes his mistak and comes back."

"Wait," said Fergus, holding up a hand. There was a cautiou rustling in the shrubbery, and Young Ian's voice said, "Uncl Jamie?"

"Aye, Ian," his uncle said dryly. "It's me."

The boy emerged from the bushes, leaves stuck in his hair, eye wide with excitement.

"I saw the light, and thought I must come back to see tha Auntie Claire was all right," he explained. "Uncle Jamie, y mustna linger about wi' a torch—there are excisemen about!"

Jamie put an arm about his nephew's shoulders and turned him, before he should notice the thing hanging from the alder tree.

"Dinna trouble yourself, Ian," he said evenly. "They've gone."

Swinging the torch through the wet shrubbery, he extinguished it with a hiss.

"Let's go," he said, his voice calm in the dark. "Mr. Willoughby's down the road wi' the horses; we'll be in the Highlands by dawn."

PART SEVEN

Home Again

32

The Prodigal's Return

It was a four-day journey on horseback to Lallybroch from Arbroath, and there was little conversation for most of it. Both Young Ian and Jamie were preoccupied, presumably for different reasons. For myself, I was kept busy wondering, not only about the recent past, but about the immediate future.

Ian must have told Jamie's sister, Jenny, about me. How would she take my reappearance?

Jenny Murray had been the nearest thing I had ever had to a sister, and by far the closest woman friend of my life. Owing to circumstance, most of my close friends in the last fifteen years had been men; there were no other female doctors, and the natural gulf between nursing staff and medical staff prevented more than casual acquaintance with other women working at the hospital. As for the women in Frank's circle, the departmental secretaries and university wives . . .

More than any of that, though, was the knowledge that of all the people in the world, Jenny was the one who might love Jamie Fraser as much—if not more—than I did. I was eager to see Jenny again, but could not help wondering how she would take the story of my supposed escape to France, and my apparent desertion of her brother.

The horses had to follow each other in single file down the narrow track. My own bay slowed obligingly as Jamie's chestnut paused, then turned aside at his urging into a clearing, half-hidden by an overhang of alder branches.

A gray stone cliff rose up at the edge of the clearing, its cracks

and bumps and ridges so furred with moss and lichen that
looked like the face of an ancient man, all spotted with whisker
and freckled with warts. Young Ian slid down from his pony with
sigh of relief; we had been in the saddle since dawn.

"Oof!" he said, frankly rubbing his backside. "I've gone a
numb."

"So have I," I said, doing the same. "I suppose it's better tha
being saddlesore, though." Unaccustomed to riding for lon
stretches, both Young Ian and I had suffered considerably durin
the first two days of the journey; in fact, too stiff to dismount b
myself the first night, I had had to be ignominiously hoisted off m
horse and carried into the inn by Jamie, much to his amusemen

"How does Uncle Jamie do it?" Ian asked me. "His arse mus
be made of leather."

"Not to look at," I replied absently. "Where's he gon
though?" The chestnut, already hobbled, was nibbling at the gras
under an oak to one side of the clearing, but of Jamie himsel
there was no sign.

Young Ian and I looked blankly at each other; I shrugged, an
went over to the cliff face, where a trickle of water ran down th
rock. I cupped my hands beneath it and drank, grateful for the co
liquid sliding down my dry throat, in spite of the autumn air th
reddened my cheeks and numbed my nose.

This tiny glen clearing, invisible from the road, was characteri
tic of most of the Highland scenery, I thought. Deceptively barre
and severe, the crags and moors were full of secrets. If you didn
know where you were going, you could walk within inches of
deer, a grouse, or a hiding man, and never know it. Small wond
that many of those who had taken to the heather after Cullode
had managed to escape, their knowledge of the hidden plac
making them invisible to the blind eyes and clumsy feet of th
pursuing English.

Thirst slaked, I turned from the cliff face and nearly ran int
Jamie, who had appeared as though sprung out of the earth I
magic. He was putting his tinderbox back into the pocket of h
coat, and the faint smell of smoke clung to his coat. He dropped
small burnt stick to the grass and ground it to dust with his foo

"Where did you come from?" I said, blinking at this appari
tion. "And where have you been?"

"There's a wee cave just there," he explained, jerking a thumb behind him. "I only wanted to see whether anyone's been in it."

"Have they?" Looking closely, I could see the edge of the outcrop that concealed the cave's entrance. Blending as it did with the other deep cracks in the rock face, it wouldn't be visible unless you were deliberately looking for it.

"Aye, they have," he said. His brows were slightly furrowed, not in worry, but as though he were thinking about something. "There's charcoal mixed wi' the earth; someone's had a fire here."

"Who do you think it was?" I asked. I stuck my head around the outcrop, but saw nothing but a narrow bar of darkness, a small rift in the face of the mountain. It looked thoroughly uninviting. I wondered whether any of his smuggling connections might have traced him all the way from the coast to Lallybroch. Was he worried about pursuit, or an ambush? Despite myself, I looked over my shoulder, but saw nothing but the alders, dry leaves rustling in the autumn breeze.

"I dinna ken," he said absently. "A hunter, I suppose; there are grouse bones scattered about, too."

Jamie didn't seem perturbed by the unknown person's possible identity, and I relaxed, the feeling of security engendered by the Highlands wrapping itself about me once more. Both Edinburgh and the smugglers' cove seemed a long way away.

Young Ian, fascinated by the revelation of the invisible cave, had disappeared through the crevice. Now he reappeared, brushing a cobweb out of his hair.

"Is this like Cluny's Cage, Uncle?" he asked, eyes bright.

"None so big, Ian," Jamie answered with a smile. "Poor Cluny could scarce fit through the entrance o' this one; he was a stout big fellow, forbye, near twice my girth." He touched his chest ruefully, where a button had been torn loose by squeezing through the narrow entrance.

"What's Cluny's Cage?" I asked, shaking the last drops of icy water from my hands and thrusting them under my armpits to thaw out.

"Oh—that's Cluny MacPherson," Jamie replied. He bent his head, and splashed the chilly water up into his face. Lifting his head, he blinked the sparkling drops from his lashes and smiled at me. "A verra ingenious man, Cluny. The English burnt his house,

and pulled down the foundation, but Cluny himself escaped. H
built himself a wee snuggery in a nearby cavern, and sealed ove
the entrance wi' willow branches all woven together and chinke
wi' mud. Folk said ye could stand three feet away, and no notio
that the cave was there, save the smell of the smoke from Cluny'
pipe.''

"Prince Charles stayed there too, for a bit, when he was hunte
by the English," Young Ian informed me. "Cluny hid him fo
days. The English bastards hunted high and low, but never foun
His Highness—or Cluny, either!" he concluded, with consider
able satisfaction.

"Come here and wash yourself, Ian," Jamie said, with a hint (
sharpness that made Young Ian blink. "Ye canna face your paren
covered wi' filth."

Ian sighed, but obediently bent his head over the trickle (
water, sputtering and gasping as he splashed his face, which whil
not strictly speaking filthy, undeniably bore one or two sma
stains of travel.

I turned to Jamie, who stood watching his nephew's ablutior
with an air of abstraction. Did he look ahead, I wondered, to wh.
promised to be an awkward meeting at Lallybroch, or back t
Edinburgh, with the smoldering remains of his printshop and th
dead man in the basement of the brothel? Or back further still, t
Charles Edward Stuart, and the days of the Rising?

"What do you tell your nieces and nephews about him?"
asked quietly, under the noise of Ian's snorting. "Abou
Charles?"

Jamie's gaze sharpened and focused on me; I had been righ
then. His eyes warmed slightly, and the hint of a smile acknow
edged the success of my mind-reading, but then both warmth ar
smile disappeared.

"I never speak of him," he said, just as quietly, and turne
away to catch the horses.

Three hours later, we came through the last of the windswe
passes, and out onto the final slope that led down to Lallybroc
Jamie, in the lead, drew up his horse and waited for me and Youn
Ian to come up beside him.

"There it is," he said. He glanced at me, smiling, one eyebrow raised. "Much changed, is it?"

I shook my head, rapt. From this distance, the house seemed completely unchanged. Built of white harled stone, its three stories gleamed immaculately amid its cluster of shabby outbuildings and the spread of stone-dyked brown fields. On the small rise behind the house stood the remains of the ancient broch, the circular stone tower that gave the place its name.

On closer inspection, I could see that the outbuildings had changed a bit; Jamie had told me that the English soldiery had burned the dovecote and the chapel the year after Culloden, and I could see the gaps where they had been. A space where the wall of the kailyard had been broken through had been repaired with stone of a different color, and a new shed built of stone and scrap lumber was evidently serving as a dovecote, judging from the row of plump feathered bodies lined up on the rooftree, enjoying the late autumn sun.

The rose brier planted by Jamie's mother, Ellen, had grown up into a great, sprawling tangle latticed to the wall of the house, only now losing the last of its leaves.

A plume of smoke rose from the western chimney, carrying away toward the south on a wind from the sea. I had a sudden vision of the fire in the hearth of the sitting room, its light rosy on Jenny's clear-cut face in the evening as she sat in her chair, reading aloud from a novel or book of poems while Jamie and Ian sat absorbed in a game of chess, listening with half an ear. How many evenings had we spent that way, the children upstairs in their beds, and me sitting at the rosewood secretary, writing down receipts for medicines or doing some of the interminable domestic mending?

"Will we live here again, do you think?" I asked Jamie, careful to keep any trace of longing from my voice. More than any other place, the house at Lallybroch had been home to me, but that had been a long time ago—and any number of things had changed since then.

He paused for a long minute, considering. Finally he shook his head, gathering up the reins in his hand. "I canna say, Sassenach," he said. "It would be pleasant, but—I dinna ken how things may be, aye?" There was a small frown on his face, as he looked down at the house.

"It's all right. If we live in Edinburgh—or even in France—it's all right, Jamie.'' I looked up into his face and touched his hand i reassurance. ''As long as we're together.''

The faint look of worry lifted momentarily, lightening his fea tures. He took my hand, raised it to his lips, and kissed it gently

''I dinna mind much else myself, Sassenach, so long as ye' stay by me.''

We sat gazing into each other's eyes, until a loud, self-con scious cough from behind alerted us to Young Ian's presence Scrupulously careful of our privacy, he had been embarrassingl circumspect on the trip from Edinburgh, crashing off through th heather to a great distance when we camped, and taking remark able pains so as not inadvertently to surprise us in an indiscree embrace.

Jamie grinned and squeezed my hand before letting it go an turning to his nephew.

''Almost there, Ian,'' he said, as the boy negotiated his pony u beside us. ''We'll be there well before supper if it doesna rain,'' h added, squinting under his hand to gauge the possibilities of th clouds drifting slowly over the Monadhliath Mountains.

''Mmphm.'' Young Ian didn't sound thrilled at the prospec and I glanced at him sympathetically.

'' 'Home is the place where, when you have to go there, the have to take you in,' '' I quoted.

Young Ian gave me a wry look. ''Aye, that's what I'm afraid o Auntie.''

Jamie, hearing this exchange, glanced back at Young Ian, an blinked solemnly—his own version of an encouraging wink.

''Dinna be downhearted, Ian. Remember the story o' the Prod gal Son, aye? Your mam will be glad to see ye safe back.''

Young Ian cast him a glance of profound disillusion.

''If ye expect it's the fatted calf that's like to be kilt, Unc Jamie, ye dinna ken my mother so well as ye think.''

The lad sat gnawing his lower lip for a moment, then dre himself up in the saddle with a deep breath.

''Best get it over, aye?'' he said.

''Will his parents really be hard on him?'' I asked, watchir Young Ian pick his way carefully down the rocky slope.

Jamie shrugged.

''Well, they'll forgive him, of course, but he's like to get a ra ballocking and his backside tanned before that. I'll be lucky to g ff wi' the same," he added wryly. "Jenny and Ian are no going to e verra pleased wi' me, either, I'm afraid." He kicked up his nount, and started down the slope.

"Come along, Sassenach. Best get it over, aye?"

I wasn't sure what to expect in terms of a reception at Lalvbroch, but in the event, it was reassuring. As on all previous rrivals, our presence was heralded by the barking of a miscellaneus swarm of dogs, who galloped out of hedge and field and ailyard, yapping first with alarm, and then with joy.

Young Ian dropped his reins and slid down into the furry sea of velcome, dropping into a crouch to greet the dogs who leapt on im and licked his face. He stood up smiling with a half-grown uppy in his arms, which he brought over to show me.

"This is Jocky," he said, holding up the squirming brown and vhite body. "He's mine; Da gave him to me."

"Nice doggie," I told Jocky, scratching his floppy ears. The og barked and squirmed ecstatically, trying to lick me and Ian imultaneously.

"You're getting covered wi' dog hairs, Ian," said a clear, high oice, in tones of marked disapproval. Looking up from the dog, I aw a tall, slim girl of seventeen or so, rising from her seat by the ide of the road.

"Well, you're covered wi' foxtails, so there!" Young Ian reorted, swinging about to address the speaker.

The girl tossed a headful of dark brown curls and bent to brush t her skirt, which did indeed sport a number of the bushy grasseads, stuck to the homespun fabric.

"Da says ye dinna deserve to have a dog," she remarked. Running off and leaving him like ye did."

Young Ian's face tightened defensively. "I did think o' taking im," he said, voice cracking slightly. "But I didna think he'd be afe in the city." He hugged the dog tighter, chin resting between e furry ears. "He's grown a bit; I suppose he's been eating all ght?"

"Come to greet us, have ye, wee Janet? That's kind." Jamie's oice spoke pleasantly from behind me, but with a cynical note at made the girl glance up sharply and blush at the sight of him.

"Uncle Jamie! Oh, and . . ." Her gaze shifted to me, and she ducked her head, blushing more furiously.

"Aye, this is your auntie Claire." Jamie's hand was firm under my elbow as he nodded toward the girl. "Wee Janet wasna born yet, last ye were here, Sassenach. Your mother will be to home, expect?" he said, addressing Janet.

The girl nodded, wide-eyed, not taking her fascinated gaze from my face. I leaned down from my horse and extended a hand, smiling.

"I'm pleased to meet you," I said.

She stared for a long moment, then suddenly remembered her manners, and dropped into a curtsy. She rose and took my hand gingerly, as though afraid it might come off in her grasp. squeezed hers, and she looked faintly reassured at finding m merely flesh and blood.

"I'm . . . pleased, mum," she murmured.

"Are Mam and Da verra angry, Jen?" Young Ian gently put the puppy on the ground near her feet, breaking her trance. She glanced at her younger brother, her expression of impatience tinged with some sympathy.

"Well, and why wouldn't they be, clot-heid?" she said. "Mam thought ye'd maybe met a boar in the wood, or been taken b Gypsies. She scarcely slept until they found out where ye' gone," she added, frowning at her brother.

Ian pressed his lips tight together, looking down at the ground but didn't answer.

She moved closer, and picked disapprovingly at the damp ye low leaves adhering to the sleeves of his coat. Tall as she was, h topped her by a good six inches, gangly and rawboned next to he trim competence, the resemblance between them limited to th rich darkness of their hair and a fugitive similarity of expression

"You're a sight, Ian. Have ye been sleepin' in your clothes?"

"Well, of course I have," he said impatiently. "What d'y think, I ran away wi' a nightshirt and changed into it every nig on the moor?"

She gave a brief snort of laughter at this picture, and his expres sion of annoyance faded a bit.

"Oh, come on, then, gowk," she said, taking pity on him "Come into the scullery wi' me, and we'll get ye brushed an combed before Mam and Da see ye."

He glared at her, then turned to look up at me, with an expression of mingled bewilderment and annoyance. "Why in the name o' heaven," he demanded, his voice cracking with strain, "does everyone think bein' *clean* will help?"

Jamie grinned at him, and dismounting, clapped him on the shoulder, raising a small cloud of dust.

"It canna hurt anything, Ian. Go along wi' ye; I think perhaps it's as well if your parents havena got so many things to deal with all at once—and they'll be wanting to see your auntie first of all."

"Mmphm." With a morose nod of assent, Young Ian moved reluctantly off toward the back of the house, towed by his determined sister.

"What have ye been eating?" I heard her say, squinting up at him as they went. "You've a great smudge of filth all round your mouth."

"It isna filth, it's whiskers!" he hissed furiously under his breath, with a quick backward glance to see whether Jamie and I had heard this exchange. His sister stopped dead, peering up at him.

"Whiskers?" she said loudly and incredulously. *"You?"*

"Come on!" Grabbing her by the elbow, he hustled her off through the kailyard gate, his shoulders hunched in self-conciousness.

Jamie lowered his head against my thigh, face buried in my skirts. To the casual observer, he might have been occupied in loosening the saddlebags, but the casual observer couldn't have seen his shoulders shaking or felt the vibration of his soundless laughter.

"It's all right, they're gone," I said, a moment later, gasping for breath myself from the strain of silent mirth.

Jamie raised his face, red and breathless, from my skirts, and used a fold of the cloth to dab his eyes.

"Whiskers? *You?*" he croaked in imitation of his niece, setting us both off again. He shook his head, gulping for air. "Christ, he's like her mother! That's just what Jenny said to me, in just that voice, when she caught me shavin' for the first time. I nearly cut my throat." He wiped his eyes again on the back of his hand, and rubbed a palm tenderly across the thick, soft stubble that coated his own jaws and throat with an auburn haze.

"Do you want to go and shave yourself before we meet Jenny and Ian?" I asked, but he shook his head.

"No," he said, smoothing back the hair that had escaped from its lacing. "Young Ian's right; bein' clean won't help."

They must have heard the dogs outside; both Ian and Jenny were in the sitting room when we came in, she on the sofa knitting woolen stockings, while he stood before the fire in plain brown coat and breeks, warming the backs of his legs. A tray of small cakes with a bottle of home-brewed ale was set out, plainly in readiness for our arrival.

It was a very cozy, welcoming scene, and I felt the tiredness of the journey drop away as we entered the room. Ian turned at once as we came in, self-conscious but smiling, but it was Jenny that I looked for.

She was looking for me, too. She sat still on the couch, her eyes wide, turned to the door. My first impression was that she was quite different, the second, that she had not changed at all. The black curls were still there, thick and lively, but blanched and streaked with a deep, rich silver. The bones, too, were the same— the broad, high cheekbones, strong jaw, and long nose that she shared with Jamie. It was the flickering firelight and the shadow of the gathering afternoon that gave the strange impression of change, one moment deepening the lines beside her eyes and mouth 'til she looked like a crone; the next erasing them with the ruddy glow of girlhood, like a 3-D picture in a box of Cracker Jack.

On our first meeting in the brothel, Ian had acted as if I were a ghost. Jenny did much the same now, blinking slightly, her mouth slightly open, but not otherwise changing expression as I crossed the room toward her.

Jamie was just behind me, his hand at my elbow. He squeezed lightly as we reached the sofa, then let go. I felt rather as though I were being presented at Court, and resisted the impulse to curtsy.

"We're home, Jenny," he said. His hand rested reassuringly on my back.

She glanced quickly at her brother, then stared at me again.

"It's you, then, Claire?" Her voice was soft and tentative, familiar, but not the strong voice of the woman I remembered.

"Yes, it's me," I said. I smiled and reached out my hands to her. "It's good to see you, Jenny."

She took my hands, lightly. Then her grip strengthened and she rose to her feet. "Christ, it *is* you!" she said, a little breathless, and suddenly the woman I had known was back, dark blue eyes alive and dancing, searching my face with curiosity.

"Well, of course it is," Jamie said gruffly. "Surely Ian told ye; did ye think he was lying?"

"You'll scarce have changed," she said, ignoring her brother as she touched my face wonderingly. "Your hair's a bit lighter, but my God, ye look the same!" Her fingers were cool; her hands smelled of herbs and red-currant jam, and the faint hint of ammonia and lanolin from the dyed wool she was knitting.

The long-forgotten smell of the wool brought everything back at once—so many memories of the place, and the happiness of the time I had lived here—and my eyes blurred with tears.

She saw it, and hugged me hard, her hair smooth and soft against my face. She was much shorter than I, fine-boned and delicate to look at, but still I had the feeling of being enveloped, warmly supported and strongly held, as though by someone larger than myself.

She released me after a moment, and stood back, half-laughing. "God, ye even smell the same!" she exclaimed, and I burst out laughing, too.

Ian had come up; he leaned down and embraced me gently, brushing his lips against my cheek. He smelled faintly of dried hay and cabbage leaves, with the ghost of peat smoke laid over his own deep, musky scent.

"It's good to see ye back again, Claire," he said. His soft brown eyes smiled at me, and the sense of homecoming deepened. He stood back a little awkwardly, smiling. "Will ye eat something, maybe?" He gestured toward the tray on the table.

I hesitated a moment, but Jamie moved toward it with alacrity.

"A drop wouldna come amiss, Ian, thank ye kindly," he said. "You'll have some, Claire?"

Glasses were filled, the biscuits passed, and small spoken pleasantries murmured through mouthfuls as we sat down around the fire. Despite the outward cordiality, I was strongly aware of an underlying tension, not all of it to do with my sudden reappearance.

Jamie, seated beside me on the oak settle, took no more than sip of his ale, and the oatcake sat untasted on his knee. I knew hadn't accepted the refreshments out of hunger, but in order mask the fact that neither his sister nor his brother-in-law ha offered him a welcoming embrace.

I caught a quick glance passing between Ian and Jenny; and longer stare, unreadable, exchanged between Jenny and Jamie. stranger here in more ways than one, I kept my own eyes ca down, observing under the shelter of my lashes. Jamie sat to n left; I could feel the tiny movement between us as the two sti fingers of his right hand drummed their small tattoo against h thigh.

The conversation, what there was of it, petered out, and t room fell into an uncomfortable silence. Through the faint hissi of the peat fire, I could hear a few distant thumps in the directi of the kitchen, but nothing like the sounds I remembered in th house, of constant activity and bustling movement, feet alwa pounding on the stair, and the shouts of children and squalling babies splitting the air in the nursery overhead.

"How are all of your children?" I asked Jenny, to break t silence. She started, and I realized that I had inadvertently ask the wrong question.

"Oh, they're well enough," she replied hesitantly. "All ver bonny. And the grandchildren, too," she added, breaking into sudden smile at the thought of them.

"They've mostly gone to Young Jamie's house," Ian put answering my real question. "His wife's had a new babe just t week past, so the three girls have gone to help a bit. And M chael's up in Inverness just now, to fetch down some things con in from France."

Another glance flicked across the room, this one between Ia and Jamie. I felt the small tilt of Jamie's head, and saw Ian's nc quite-nod in response. And what in hell was *that* about? I wo dered. There were so many invisible cross-currents of emotion the room that I had a sudden impulse to stand up and call t meeting to order, just to break the tension.

Apparently Jamie felt the same. He cleared his throat, looki directly at Ian, and addressed the main point on the agenda, sa ing, "We've brought the lad home with us."

Ian took a deep breath, his long, homely face hardening slight

"Have ye, then?" The thin layer of pleasantry spread over the occasion vanished suddenly, like morning dew.

I could feel Jamie beside me, tensing slightly as he prepared to defend his nephew as best he might.

"He's a good lad, Ian," he said.

"Is he, so?" It was Jenny who answered, her fine black brows drawn down in a frown. "Ye couldna tell, the way he acts at home. But perhaps he's different wi' you, Jamie." There was a strong note of accusation in her words, and I felt Jamie tense at my side.

"It's kind of ye to speak up for the lad, Jamie," Ian put in, with a cool nod in his brother-in-law's direction. "But I think we'd best hear from Young Ian himself, if ye please. Will he be upstairs?"

A muscle near Jamie's mouth twitched, but he answered noncommittally. "In the scullery, I expect; he wanted to tidy himself a bit before seein' ye." His right hand slid down and pressed against my leg in warning. He hadn't mentioned meeting Janet, and I understood; she had been sent away with her siblings, so that Jenny and Ian could deal with the matters of my appearance and their prodigal son in some privacy, but had crept back unbeknownst to her parents, wanting either to catch a glimpse of her notorious aunt Claire, or to offer succor to her brother.

I lowered my eyelids, indicating that I understood. No point in mentioning the girl's presence, in a situation already so fraught with tension.

The sound of feet and the regular thump of Ian's wooden leg sounded in the uncarpeted passage. Ian had left the room in the direction of the scullery; now he returned, grimly ushering Young Ian before him.

The prodigal was as presentable as soap, water, and razor could make him. His bony jaws were reddened with scraping and the hair on his neck was clotted in wet spikes, most of the dust beaten from his coat, and the round neck of his shirt neatly buttoned to the collarbone. There was little to be done about the singed half of his head, but the other side was neatly combed. He had no stock, and there was a large rip in the leg of his breeks, but all things considered, he looked as well as someone could who expects momentarily to be shot.

"Mam," he said, ducking his head awkwardly in his mother's direction.

"Ian," she said softly, and he looked up at her, clearly startled

at the gentleness of her tone. A slight smile curved her lips as sh
saw his face. "I'm glad you're safe home, *mo chridhe*," she saic

The boy's face cleared abruptly, as though he had just heard th
reprieve read to the firing squad. Then he caught a glimpse of hi
father's face, and stiffened. He swallowed hard, and bent his hea
again, staring hard at the floorboards.

"Mmphm," Ian said. He sounded sternly Scotch; much mor
like the Reverend Campbell than the easygoing man I had know
before. "Now then, I want to hear what ye've got to say fc
yourself, laddie."

"Oh. Well . . . I . . ." Young Ian trailed off miserably, the
cleared his throat and had another try. "Well . . . nothing
really, Father," he murmured.

"Look at me!" Ian said sharply. His son reluctantly raised hi
head and looked at his father, but his gaze kept flicking away, a
though afraid to rest very long on the stern countenance befor
him.

"D'ye ken what ye did to your mother?" Ian demanded. "Di
appeared and left her thinkin' ye dead or hurt? Gone off without
word, and not a smell of ye for three days, until Joe Fraser broug
down the letter ye left? Can ye even think what those three day
were like for her?"

Either Ian's expression or his words seemed to have a stron
effect on his errant offspring; Young Ian bowed his head agai
eyes fixed on the floor.

"Aye, well, I thought Joe would bring the letter sooner," H
muttered.

"Aye, that letter!" Ian's face was growing more flushed as H
talked. " 'Gone to Edinburgh,' it said, cool as dammit." H
slapped a hand flat on the table, with a smack that made everyor
jump. "Gone to Edinburgh! Not a 'by your leave,' not an 'I'll ser
word,' not a thing but 'Dear Mother, I have gone to Edinburg
Ian'!"

Young Ian's head snapped up, eyes bright with anger.

"That's not true! I said 'Don't worry for me,' and I said 'Lo
Ian'! I did! Did I no, Mother?" For the first time, he looked
Jenny, appealing.

She had been still as a stone since her husband began to tal
her face smooth and blank. Now her eyes softened, and the hint (
a curve touched her wide, full mouth again.

"Ye did, Ian," she said softly. "It was kind to say—but I did worry, aye?"

His eyes fell, and I could see the oversized Adam's apple bobble in his lean throat as he swallowed.

"I'm sorry, Mam," he said, so low I could scarcely hear him. I—I didna mean . . ." His words trailed off, ending in a small shrug.

Jenny made an impulsive movement, as though to extend a hand to him, but Ian caught her eye, and she let the hand fall to her lap.

"The thing is," Ian said, speaking slowly and precisely, "it's no the first time, is it, Ian?"

The boy didn't answer, but made a small twitching movement that might have been assent. Ian took a step closer to his son. Close as they were in height, the differences between them were obvious. Ian was tall and lanky, but firmly muscled for all that, and a powerful man, wooden leg or no. By comparison, his son seemed almost frail, fledgling-boned and gawky.

"No, it's not as though ye had no idea what ye were doing; not like we'd never told ye the dangers, not like we'd no forbidden ye to go past Broch Mordha—not like ye didna ken we'd worry, aye? Ye kent all that—and ye did it anyway."

This merciless analysis of his behavior caused a sort of indefinite quiver, like an internal squirm, to go through Young Ian, but he kept up a stubborn silence.

"Look at me, laddie, when I'm speakin' to ye!" The boy's head rose slowly. He looked sullen now, but resigned; evidently he had been through scenes like this before, and knew where they were heading.

"I'm not even going to ask your uncle what ye've been doing," Ian said. "I can only hope ye weren't such a fool in Edinburgh as ye've been here. But ye've disobeyed me outright, and broken your mother's heart, whatever else ye've done."

Jenny moved again, as though to speak, but a brusque movement of Ian's hand stopped her.

"And what did I tell ye the last time, wee Ian? What did I say when I gave ye your whipping? You tell me that, Ian!"

The bones in Young Ian's face stood out, but he kept his mouth shut, sealed in a stubborn line.

"Tell me!" Ian roared, slamming his hand on the table again. Young Ian blinked in reflex, and his shoulder blades drew to-

gether, then apart, as though he were trying to alter his size, an
unsure whether to grow larger or try to be smaller. He swallowe
hard, and blinked once more.

''Ye said—ye said ye'd skin me. Next time.'' His voice broke
a ridiculous squeak on the last word, and he clamped his mou
hard shut on it.

Ian shook his head in heavy disapproval. ''Aye. And I thoug
ye'd have enough sense to see there was no next time, but I w
wrong about that, hm?'' He breathed in heavily and let it out wi
a snort.

''I'm fair disgusted wi' ye, Ian, and that's the truth.'' He jerke
his head toward the doorway. ''Go outside. I'll see ye by the gat
presently.''

There was a tense silence in the sitting room, as the sound of tl
miscreant's dragging footsteps disappeared down the passage.
kept my own eyes carefully on my hands, folded in my lap. Besi
me, Jamie drew a slow, deep breath and sat up straighter, steeli
himself.

''Ian.'' Jamie spoke mildly to his brother-in-law. ''I wish y
wouldna do that.''

''What?'' Ian's brow was still furrowed with anger as he turne
toward Jamie. ''Thrash the lad? And what have you to say about
aye?''

Jamie's jaw tensed, but his voice stayed calm.

''I've nothing to say about it, Ian—he's your son; you'll do
ye like. But maybe you'll let me speak for the way he's acted?

''How he's acted?'' Jenny cried, starting suddenly to life. Sl
might leave dealing with her son to Ian, but when it came to h
brother, no one was likely to speak for her. ''Sneakin' away in tl
night like a thief, ye mean? Or perhaps ye'll mean consorting w
criminals, and risking his neck for a cask of brandy!''

Ian silenced her with a quick gesture. He hesitated, still frow
ing, but then nodded abruptly at Jamie, giving permission.

''Consorting wi' criminals like me?'' Jamie asked his sister,
definite edge to his voice. His eyes met hers straight on, matchi
slits of blue.

''D'ye ken where the money comes from, Jenny, that keeps ye
and your bairns and everyone here in food, and the roof fro

allin' in over your head? It's not from me printing up copies o' he Psalms in Edinburgh!''

"And did I think it was?" she flared at him. "Did I ask ye what e did?"

"No, ye didn't," he flashed back. "I think ye'd rather not know —but ye do know, don't you?"

"And will ye blame me for what ye do? It's *my* fault that I've hildren, and that they must eat?" She didn't flush red like Jamie lid; when Jenny lost her temper, she went dead white with fury.

I could see him struggling to keep his own temper. "Blame ye? No, of course I dinna blame ye—but is it right for you to blame ne, that Ian and I canna keep ye all just working the land?"

Jenny too was making an effort to subdue her rising temper. 'No,'' she said. "Ye do what ye must, Jamie. Ye ken verra well I lidna mean you when I said 'criminals,' but—"

"So ye mean the men who work for me? I do the same things, enny. If they're criminals, what am I, then?" He glared at her, yes hot with resentment.

"You're my brother," she said shortly, "little pleased as I am o say so, sometimes. Damn your eyes, Jamie Fraser! Ye ken quite vell I dinna mean to quarrel wi' whatever ye see fit to do! If ye obbed folk on the highway, or kept a whorehouse in Edinburgh, twould be because there was no help for it. That doesna mean I vant ye takin' my son to be part of it!"

Jamie's eyes tightened slightly at the corners at the mention of vhorehouses in Edinburgh, and he darted a quick glance of accu-ation at Ian, who shook his head. He looked mildly stunned at his vife's ferocity.

"I've said not a word," he said briefly. "Ye ken how she is."

Jamie took a deep breath and turned back to Jenny, obviously etermined to be reasonable.

"Aye, I see that. But ye canna think I would take Young Ian into anger—God, Jenny, I care for him as though he were my own on!''

"Aye?" Her skepticism was pronounced. "So that's why ye ncouraged him to run off from his home, and kept him with ye, 'i' no word to ease our minds about where he was?"

Jamie had the grace to look abashed at this.

"Aye, well, I'm sorry for that," he muttered. "I meant to—" le broke off with an impatient gesture. "Well, it doesna matter

what I meant; I should have sent word, and I didna. But as fo
encouraging him to run off—''

''No, I dinna suppose ye did,'' Ian interrupted. ''Not directly
anyway.'' The anger had faded from his long face. He looked tire
now, and a little sad. The bones in his face were more pronounced
leaving him hollow-cheeked in the waning afternoon light.

''It's only that the lad loves ye, Jamie,'' he said quietly. ''I se
him listen when ye visit, and talk of what ye do; I can see his face
He thinks it's all excitement and adventure, how ye live, and
good long way from shoveling goat-shit for his mother's garden.
He smiled briefly, despite himself.

Jamie gave his brother-in-law a quick smile in return, and
lifted shoulder. ''Well, but it's usual for a lad of that age to want
bit of adventure, no? You and I were the same.''

''Whether he wants it or no, he shouldna be having the sort c
adventures he'll get with you,'' Jenny interrupted sharply. Sh
shook her head, the line between her brows growing deeper as sh
looked disapprovingly at her brother. ''The good Lord kens a
there's a charm on your life, Jamie, or ye'd ha' been dead a doze
times.''

''Aye, well. I suppose He had something in mind to preserve m
for.'' Jamie glanced at me with a brief smile, and his hand soug
mine. Jenny darted a glance at me, too, her face unreadable, the
returned to the subject at hand.

''Well, that's as may be,'' she said. ''But I canna say as th
same's true for Young Ian.'' Her expression softened slightly a
she looked at Jamie.

''I dinna ken everything about the way ye live, Jamie—but I ke
you well enough to say it's likely not the way a wee laddie shou
live.''

''Mmphm.'' Jamie rubbed a hand over his stubbled jaw, an
tried again. ''Aye, well, that's what I mean about Young Ian. He
carried himself like a man this last week. I dinna think it right f
ye to thrash him like a wee laddie, Ian.''

Jenny's eyebrows rose, graceful wings of scorn.

''A man, now, is he? Why, he's but a baby, Jamie—he's not b
fourteen!''

Despite his annoyance, one side of Jamie's mouth curl
slightly.

''I was a man at fourteen, Jenny,'' he said softly.

She snorted, but a film of moisture shone suddenly over her eyes.

"Ye thought ye were." She stood and turned away abruptly, blinking. "Aye, I mind ye then," she said, face turned to the bookshelf. She reached out a hand as though to support herself, grasping the edge.

"Ye were a bonny lad, Jamie, riding off wi' Dougal to your first raid, and your dirk all bright on your thigh. I was sixteen, and I thought I'd never seen a sight so fair as you on your pony, so straight and tall. And I mind ye coming back, too, all covered in mud, and a scratch down the side of your face from falling in brambles, and Dougal boasting to Da how brawly ye'd done—driven off six kine by yourself, and had a dunt on the head from the flat of a broadsword, and not made a squeak about it." Her face once more under control, she turned back from her contemplation of the books to face her brother. "That's what a man is, aye?"

A hint of humor stole back into Jamie's face as he met her gaze.

"Aye, well, there's maybe a bit more to it than that," he said.

"Is there," she said, more dryly still. "And what will that be? To be able to bed a girl? Or to kill a man?"

I had always thought Janet Fraser had something of the Sight, particularly where her brother was concerned. Evidently the talent extended to her son, as well. The flush over Jamie's cheekbones deepened, but his expression didn't change.

She shook her head slowly, looking steadily at her brother. "Nay, Young Ian's not a man yet—but you are, Jamie; and ye ken the difference verra well."

Ian, who had been watching the fireworks between the two Frasers with the same fascination as I had, now coughed briefly.

"Be that as it may," he said dryly. "Young Ian's been waiting for his whipping for the last quarter-hour. Whether or not it's suitable to beat him, to make him wait any longer for it is a bit cruel, aye?"

"Have ye really got to do it, Ian?" Jamie made one last effort, turning to appeal to his brother-in-law.

"Well," said Ian slowly, "as I've told the lad he's going to be thrashed, and he kens verra well he's earned it, I canna just go back on my word. But as for me doing it—no, I dinna think I will." A faint gleam of humor showed in the soft brown eyes. He reached into a drawer of the sideboard, drew out a thick leather strap, and thrust it into Jamie's hand. "You do it."

"Me?" Jamie was horror-struck. He made a futile attempt to shove the strap back into Ian's hand, but his brother-in-law ignored it. "I canna thrash the lad!"

"Oh, I think ye can," Ian said calmly, folding his arms. "Ye've said often enough ye care for him as though he were your son." He tilted his head to one side, and while his expression stayed mild, the brown eyes were implacable. "Well, I'll tell ye, Jamie— it's no that easy to be his da; best ye go and find that out now, aye?"

Jamie stared at Ian for a long moment, then looked to his sister. She raised one eyebrow, staring him down.

"You deserve it as much as he does, Jamie. Get ye gone."

Jamie's lips pressed tight together and his nostrils flared white. Then he whirled on his heel and was gone without speaking. Rapid steps sounded on the boards, and a muffled slam came from the far end of the passage.

Jenny cast a quick glance at Ian, a quicker one at me, and then turned to the window. Ian and I, both a good deal taller, came to stand behind her. The light outside was failing rapidly, but there was still enough to see the wilting figure of Young Ian, leaning dispiritedly against a wooden gate, some twenty yards from the house.

Looking around in trepidation at the sound of footsteps, he saw his uncle approaching and straightened up in surprise.

"Uncle Jamie!" His eye fell on the strap then, and he straightened a bit more. "Are . . . are *you* goin' to whip me?"

It was a still evening, and I could hear the sharp hiss of air through Jamie's teeth.

"I suppose I'll have to," he said frankly. "But first I must apologize to ye, Ian."

"To me?" Young Ian sounded mildly dazed. Clearly he wasn't used to having his elders think they owed him an apology, especially before beating him. "Ye dinna need to do that, Uncle Jamie."

The taller figure leaned against the gate, facing the smaller one, head bent.

"Aye, I do. It was wrong of me, Ian, to let ye stay in Edinburgh, and it was maybe wrong, too, to tell ye stories and make ye think of running away to start with. I took ye to places I shouldna, and might have put ye in danger, and I've caused more of a moil wi' your parents than maybe ye should be in by yourself. I'm sorry for it, Ian, and I'll ask ye to forgive me.''

"Oh.'' The smaller figure rubbed a hand through his hair, plainly at a loss for words. "Well . . . aye. Of course I do, Uncle.''

"Thank ye, Ian.''

They stood in silence for a moment, then Young Ian heaved a sigh and straightened his drooping shoulders.

"I suppose we'd best do it, then?''

"I expect so.'' Jamie sounded at least as reluctant as his nephew, and I heard Ian, next to me, snort slightly, whether with indignation or amusement, I couldn't tell.

Resigned, Young Ian turned and faced the gate without hesitation. Jamie followed more slowly. The light was nearly gone and we could see no more than the outlines of figures at this distance, but we could hear clearly from our position at the window. Jamie was standing behind his nephew, shifting uncertainly, as though unsure what to do next.

"Mmphm. Ah, what does your father . . .''

"It's usually ten, Uncle.'' Young Ian had shed his coat, and tugged at his waist now, speaking over his shoulder. "Twelve if it's pretty bad, and fifteen if it's really awful.''

"Was this only bad, would ye say, or pretty bad?''

There was a brief, unwilling laugh from the boy.

"If Father's makin' *you* do it, Uncle Jamie, it's really awful, but I'll settle for pretty bad. Ye'd better give me twelve.''

There was another snort from Ian at my elbow. This time, it was definitely amusement. "Honest lad,'' he murmured.

"All right, then.'' Jamie drew in his breath and pulled his arm back, but was interrupted by Young Ian.

"Wait, Uncle, I'm no quite ready.''

"Och, ye've got to do that?'' Jamie's voice sounded a bit strangled.

"Aye. Father says only girls are whipped wi' their skirts down,'' Young Ian explained. "Men must take it bare-arsed.''

"He's damn well right about *that* one,'' Jamie muttered, his quarrel with Jenny obviously still rankling. "Ready now?''

The necessary adjustments made, the larger figure stepped back and swung. There was a loud crack, and Jenny winced in sympathy with her son. Beyond a sudden intake of breath, though, the lad was silent, and stayed so through the rest of the ordeal, though I blanched a bit myself.

Finally Jamie dropped his arm, and wiped his brow. He held out a hand to Ian, slumped over the fence. "All right, lad?" Young Ian straightened up, with a little difficulty this time, and pulled up his breeks. "Aye, Uncle. Thank ye." The boy's voice was a little thick, but calm and steady. He took Jamie's outstretched hand. To my surprise, though, instead of leading the boy back to the house, Jamie thrust the strap into Ian's other hand.

"Your turn," he announced, striding over to the gate and bending over.

Young Ian was as shocked as those of us in the house.

"What!" he said, stunned.

"I said it's your turn," his uncle said in a firm voice. "I punished you; now you've got to punish me."

"I canna do that, Uncle!" Young Ian was as scandalized as though his uncle had suggested he commit some public indecency.

"Aye, ye can," said Jamie, straightening up to look his nephew in the eye. "Ye heard what I said when I apologized to ye, did ye no?" Ian nodded in a dazed fashion. "Weel, then. I've done wrong just as much as you, and I've to pay for it, too. I didna like whipping you, and ye're no goin' to like whipping me, but we're both goin' through wi' it. Understand?"

"A-aye, Uncle," the boy stammered.

"All right, then." Jamie tugged down his breeches, tucked up his shirttail, and bent over once more, clutching the top rail. He waited a second, then spoke again, as Ian stood paralyzed, strap dangling from his nerveless hand.

"Go on." His voice was steel; the one he used with the whisky smugglers; not to obey was unthinkable. Ian moved timidly to do as he was ordered. Standing back, he took a halfhearted swing. There was a dull thwacking sound.

"That one didna count," Jamie said firmly. "Look, man, it was just as hard for me to do it to you. Make a proper job of it, now."

The thin figure squared its shoulders with sudden determination, and the leather whistled through the air. It landed with a crack like lightning. There was a startled yelp from the figure on the fence, and a suppressed giggle, at least half shock, from Jenny.

Jamie cleared his throat. "Aye, that'll do. Finish it, then."

We could hear Young Ian counting carefully to himself under
 breath between strokes of the leather, but aside from a smoth-
d "Christ!" at number nine, there was no further sound from
 uncle.

With a general sigh of relief from inside the house, Jamie rose
 the fence after the last stroke, and tucked his shirt into his
eeks. He inclined his head formally to his nephew. "Thank ye,
.." Dropping the formality, he then rubbed his backside, saying
 a tone of rueful admiration, "Christ, man, ye've an arm on ye!"

"So've you, Uncle," said Ian, matching his uncle's wry tones.
e two figures, barely visible now, stood laughing and rubbing
mselves for a moment. Jamie flung an arm about his nephew's
oulders and turned him toward the house. "If it's all the same to
u, Ian, I dinna want to have to do that again, aye?" he said,
nfidentially.

"It's a bargain, Uncle Jamie."

A moment later, the door opened at the end of the passage, and
th a look at each other, Jenny and Ian turned as one to greet the
urning prodigals.

"**Y**ou look rather like a baboon," I observed.

"Oh, aye? And what's one of those?" In spite of t⟩ freezing November air pouring in through the half-op⟩ window, Jamie showed no signs of discomfort as he dropped ⟩ shirt onto the small pile of clothing.

He stretched luxuriously, completely naked. His joints ma⟩ little popping noises as he arched his back and stretched upwa⟩ fists resting easily on the smoke-dark beams overhead.

"Oh, God, it feels good not to be on a horse!"

"Mm. To say nothing of having a real bed to sleep in, instead ⟩ wet heather." I rolled over, luxuriating in the warmth of the hea⟩ quilts, and the relaxation of sore muscles into the ineffable so⟩ ness of the goose-down mattress.

"D'ye mean to tell me what's a baboon, then?" Jamie inquire⟩ "Or are ye just makin' observations for the pleasure of it?" ⟩ turned to pick up a frayed willow twig from the washstand, a⟩ began to clean his teeth. I smiled at the sight; if I had had no oth⟩ impact during my earlier sojourn in the past, I had at least be⟩ instrumental in seeing that virtually all of the Frasers and Murra⟩ of Lallybroch retained their teeth, unlike most Highlanders—⟩ like most Englishmen, for that matter.

"A baboon," I said, enjoying the sight of his muscular ba⟩ flexing as he scrubbed, "is a sort of very large monkey with a r⟩ behind."

He snorted with laughter and choked on the willow tw⟩ "Well," he said, removing it from his mouth, "I canna fault y⟩

servations, Sassenach." He grinned at me, showing brilliant ⸺ite teeth, and tossed the twig aside. "It's been thirty years since ⸺yone took a tawse to me," he added, passing his hands tenderly ⸺r the still-glowing surfaces of his rear. "I'd forgot how much it ⸺ngs."

"And here Young Ian was speculating that your arse was tough ⸺ saddle leather," I said, amused. "Was it worth it, do you ⸺nk?"

"Oh, aye," he said, matter-of-factly, sliding into bed beside ⸺. His body was hard and cold as marble, and I squeaked but ⸺n't protest as he gathered me firmly against his chest. "Christ, ⸺'re warm," he murmured. "Come closer, hm?" His legs in⸺uated themselves between mine, and he cupped my bottom, ⸺wing me in.

⸺e gave a sigh of pure content, and I relaxed against him, ⸺ling our temperatures start to equalize through the thin cotton ⸺the nightdress Jenny had lent me. The peat fire in the hearth had ⸺n lit, but hadn't been able to do much yet toward dispelling the ⸺ll. Body heat was much more effective.

"Oh, aye, it was worth it," he said. "I could have beaten Young ⸺ half-senseless—his father has, once or twice—and it would ⸺ done nothing but make him more determined to run off, once ⸺ got the chance. But he'll walk through hot coals before he risks ⸺in' to do something like that again."

⸺e spoke with certainty, and I thought he was undoubtedly ⸺ht. Young Ian, looking bemused, had received absolution from ⸺ parents, in the form of a kiss from his mother and a swift hug ⸺m his father, and then retired to his bed with a handful of cakes, ⸺re no doubt to ponder the curious consequences of disobedi⸺⸺.

⸺Jamie too had been absolved with kisses, and I suspected that ⸺s was more important to him than the effects of his performance ⸺ Young Ian.

"At least Jenny and Ian aren't angry with you any longer," I ⸺d.

"No. It's no really that they were angry so much, I think; it's ⸺y that they dinna ken what to do wi' the lad," he explained. ⸺hey've raised two sons already, and Young Jamie and Michael ⸺ fine lads both; but both of them are more like Ian—soft-spoke,

and easy in their manner. Young Ian's quiet enough, but he's
great deal more like his mother—and me.''

"Frasers are stubborn, eh?" I said, smiling. This bit of cl
doctrine was one of the first things I had learned when I n
Jamie, and nothing in my subsequent experience had sugges
that it might be in error.

He chuckled, soft and deep in his chest.

"Aye, that's so. Young Ian may look like a Murray, but he's
Fraser born, all right. And it's no use to shout at a stubborn m
or beat him, either; it only makes him more set on having
way."

"I'll bear that in mind," I said dryly. One hand was strok
my thigh, gradually inching the cotton nightdress upward. Jami
internal furnace had resumed its operations, and his bare legs w
warm and hard against mine. One knee nudged gently, seeking
entrance between my thighs. I cupped his buttocks and squeez
gently.

"Dorcas told me that a number of gentlemen pay very well
the privilege of being smacked at the brothel. She says they find
. . . arousing."

Jamie snorted briefly, tensing his buttocks, then relaxing a
stroked them lightly.

"Do they, then? I suppose it's true, if Dorcas says so, bu
canna see it, myself. There are a great many more pleasant ways
get a cockstand, if ye ask me. On the other hand," he added fair
"perhaps it makes a difference if it's a bonny wee lassie in
shift on the other end o' the strap, and not your father—or yo
nephew, come to that."

"Perhaps it does. Shall I try sometime?" The hollow of
throat lay just by my face, sunburned and delicate, showing
faint white triangle of a scar just above the wide arch of
collarbone. I set my lips on the pulsebeat there, and he shiver
though neither of us was cold any longer.

"No," he said, a little breathless. His hand fumbled at the ne
of my shift, pulling loose the ribbons. He rolled onto his ba
then, lifting me suddenly above him as though I weighed nothi
at all. A flick of his finger brought the loosened chemise do
over my shoulders, and my nipples rose at once as the cold
struck them.

His eyes were more slanted than usual as he smiled up at m

lf-lidded as a drowsing cat, and the warmth of his palms encir-
d both breasts.

"I said I could think of more pleasant ways, aye?"

The candle had guttered and gone out, the fire on the hearth
rned low, and a pale November starlight shone through the
sted window. Dim as it was, my eyes were so adapted to the
k that I could pick out all the details of the room; the thick
ite porcelain jug and basin, its blue band black in the starlight,
small embroidered sampler on the wall, and the rumpled heap
Jamie's clothes on the stool by the bed.

Jamie was clearly visible, too; covers thrown back, chest gleam-
; faintly from exertion. I admired the long slope of his belly,
ere small whorls of dark auburn hair spiraled up across the
e, fresh skin. I couldn't keep my fingers from touching him,
cing the lines of the powerfully sprung ribs that shaped his
so.

"It's so good," I said dreamily. "So good to have a man's body
touch."

"D'ye like it still, then?" He sounded half-shy, half-pleased, as
ondled him. His own arm came around my shoulder, stroking
hair.

"Mm-hm." It wasn't a thing I had consciously missed, but
ring it now reminded me of the joy of it; that drowsy intimacy in
ich a man's body is as accessible to you as your own, the
ange shapes and textures of it like a sudden extension of your
n limbs.

I ran my hand down the flat slope of his belly, over the smooth
of hipbone and the swell of muscled thigh. The remnants of
light caught the red-gold fuzz on arms and legs, and glowed in
auburn thicket nested between his thighs.

"God, you are a wonderful hairy creature," I said. "Even
re." I slid my hand down the smooth crease of his thigh and he
ead his legs obligingly, letting me touch the thick, springy curls
the crease of his buttocks.

"Aye, well, no one's hunted me yet for my pelt," he said
nfortably. His hand cupped my own rear firmly, and a large
mb passed gently over the rounded surface. He propped one
1 behind his head, and looked lazily down the length of my
ly.

"You're even less worth the skinning than I am, Sassenach."

"I should hope so." I moved slightly to accommodate his tou as he extended his explorations, enjoying the warmth of his han on my naked back.

"Ever seen a smooth branch that's been in still water a lon time?" he asked. A finger passed lightly up my spine, raising ripple of gooseflesh in its wake. "There are tiny wee bubbles on hundreds and thousands and millions of them, so it looks though it's furred all about wi' a silver frost." His fingers brush my ribs, my arms, my back, and the tiny down-hairs rose even where in the wake of his touch, tingling.

"That's what ye look like, my Sassenach," he said, almo whispering. "All smooth and naked, dipped in silver."

Then we lay quiet for a time, listening to the drip of rain ou side. A cold autumn air drifted through the room, mingling wi the fire's smoky warmth. He rolled onto his side, facing away fro me, and drew the quilts up to cover us.

I curled up behind him, knees fitting neatly behind his own. T firelight shone dully from behind me now, gleaming over t smooth round of his shoulder and dimly illuminating his back could see the faint lines of the scars that webbed his shoulde thin streaks of silver on his flesh. At one time, I had known tho scars so intimately, I could have traced them with my finge blindfolded. Now there was a thin half-moon curve I didn't kno a diagonal slash that hadn't been there before, the remnants o violent past I hadn't shared.

I touched the half-moon, tracing its length.

"No one's hunted you for your pelt," I said softly, "b they've hunted you, haven't they?"

His shoulder moved slightly, not quite a shrug. "Now a then," he said.

"Now?" I asked.

He breathed slowly for a moment or two before answering.

"Aye," he said. "I think so."

My fingers moved down to the diagonal slash. It had been deep cut; old and well healed as the damage was, the line w sharp and clear beneath my fingertips.

"Do you know who?"

"No." He was quiet for a moment; then his hand closed ov my own, where it lay across his stomach. "But I maybe ken why

The house was very quiet. With most of the children and grandchildren gone, there were only the far-off servants in their quarters
behind the kitchen, Ian and Jenny in their room at the far end of
the hall, and Young Ian somewhere upstairs—all asleep. We could
have been alone at the end of the world; both Edinburgh and the
smugglers' cove seemed very far away.

"Do ye recall, after the fall of Stirling, not so long before
Culloden, when all of a sudden there was gossip from everywhere,
about gold being sent from France?"

"From Louis? Yes—but he never sent it." Jamie's words sum-
med up those brief frantic days of Charles Stuart's reckless rise
and precipitous fall, when rumor had been the common currency
of conversation. "There was always gossip—about gold from
France, ships from Spain, weapons from Holland—but nothing
came of most of it."

"Oh, something came—though not from Louis—but no one
kent it, then."

He told me then of his meeting with the dying Duncan Kerr,
and the wanderer's whispered words, heard in the inn's attic under
the watchful eye of an English officer.

"He was fevered, Duncan, but not crazed wi' it. He kent he was
dying, and he kent me, too. It was his only chance to tell someone
he thought he could trust—so he told me."

"White witches and seals?" I repeated. "I must say, it sounds
like gibberish. But you understood it?"

"Well, not all of it," Jamie admitted. He rolled over to face me,
frowning slightly. "I've no notion who the white witch might be. At
the first, I thought he meant you, Sassenach, and my heart
nearly stopped when he said it." He smiled ruefully, and his hand
tightened on mine, clasped between us.

"I thought all at once that perhaps something had gone wrong—
maybe ye'd not been able to go back to Frank and the place ye
came from—maybe ye'd somehow ended in France, maybe ye
were there right then—all kinds o' fancies went through my
head."

"I wish it had been true," I whispered.

He gave me a lopsided smile, but shook his head.

"And me in prison? And Brianna would be what—just ten or
eleven? No, dinna waste your time in regretting, Sassenach. You're

here now, and ye'll never leave me again.'' He kissed me gen
on the forehead, then resumed his tale.

''I didna have any idea where the gold had come from, bu
kent his telling me where it was, and why it was there. It w
Prince *Tearlach*'s, sent for him. And the bit about the silkies—
He raised his head a little and nodded toward the window, whe
the rose brier cast its shadows on the glass.

''Folk said when my mother ran away from Leoch that she
gone to live wi' the silkies; only because the maid that saw r
father when he took her said as he looked like a great silkie who
shed his skin and come to walk on the land like a man. And
did.'' Jamie smiled and passed a hand through his own thick ha
remembering. ''He had hair thick as mine, but a black like jet.
would shine in some lights, as though it was wet, and he mov
quick and sleekit, like a seal through the water.'' He shrugg
suddenly, shaking off the recollection of his father.

''Well, so. When Duncan Kerr said the name Ellen, I kent it w
my mother he meant—as a sign that he knew my name and n
family, kent who I was; that he wasna raving, no matter how
sounded. And knowin' that—'' He shrugged again. ''The Engli
man had told me where they found Duncan, near the coast. The
are hundreds of bittie isles and rocks all down that coast, but on
one place where the silkies live, at the ends of the MacKen
lands, off Coigach.''

''So you went there?''

''Aye, I did.'' He sighed deeply, his free hand drifting to t
hollow of my waist. ''I wouldna have done it—left the prison
mean—had I not still thought it maybe had something to do v
you, Sassenach.''

Escape had been an enterprise of no great difficulty; prison
were often taken outside in small gangs, to cut the peats t
burned on the prison's hearths, or to cut and haul stone for t
ongoing work of repairing the walls.

For a man to whom the heather was home, disappearing h
been easy. He had risen from his work and turned aside by
hummock of grass, unfastening his breeches as though to reli
himself. The guard had looked politely away, and looking back
moment later, beheld nothing but an empty moor, holding no tra
of Jamie Fraser.

''See, it was little trouble to slip off, but men seldom did,''

xplained. "None of us were from near Ardsmuir—and had we
een, there was little left for most o' the men to gang to."

The Duke of Cumberland's men had done their work well. As
ne contemporary had put it, evaluating the Duke's achievement
ter, "He created a desert and called it peace." This modern
pproach to diplomacy had left some parts of the Highlands all but
eserted; the men killed, imprisoned, or transported, crops and
ouses burned, the women and children turned out to starve or
ek refuge elsewhere as best they might. No, a prisoner escaping
om Ardsmuir would have been truly alone, without kin or clan to
rn to for succor.

Jamie had known there would be little time before the English
ommander realized where he must be heading and organized a
arty of pursuit. On the other hand, there were no real roads in this
mote part of the kingdom, and a man who knew the country was
a greater advantage on foot than were the pursuing outlanders
n horseback.

He had made his escape in midafternoon. Taking his bearings
y the stars, he had walked through the night, arriving at the coast
ar dawn the next day.

"See, I kent the silkies' place; it's well known amongst the
IacKenzies, and I'd been there once before, wi' Dougal."

The tide had been high, and the seals mostly out in the water,
unting crabs and fish among the fronds of floating kelp, but the
ark streaks of their droppings and the indolent forms of a few
llers marked the seals' three islands, ranged in a line just inside
e lip of a small bay, guarded by a clifflike headland.

By Jamie's interpretation of Duncan's instructions, the treasure
y on the third island, the farthest away from the shore. It was
early a mile out, a long swim even for a strong man, and his own
rength was sapped from the hard prison labor and the long walk
ithout food. He had stood on the clifftop, wondering whether this
as a wild-goose chase, and whether the treasure—if there was
e—was worth the risk of his life.

"The rock was all split and broken there; when I came too close
the edge, chunks would fall awa' from my feet and plummet
wn the cliff. I didna see how I'd ever reach the water, let alone
e seals' isle. But then I was minded what Duncan said about
llen's tower," Jamie said. His eyes were open, fixed not on me,

but on that distant shore where the crash of falling rock was lost
the smashing of the waves.

The "tower" was there; a small spike of granite that stuck
no more than five feet from the tip of the headland. But below th
spike, hidden by the rocks, was a narrow crack, a small chimn
that ran from top to bottom of the eighty-foot cliff, providing
possible passage, if not an easy one, for a determined man.

From the base of Ellen's tower to the third island was still over
quarter-mile of heaving green water. Undressing, he had cross
himself, and commending his soul to the keeping of his mother,
had dived naked into the waves.

He made his way slowly out from the cliff, floundering a
choking as the waves broke over his head. No place in Scotland
that far from the sea, but Jamie had been raised inland, his expe
ence of swimming limited to the placid depths of lochs and t
pools of trout streams.

Blinded by salt and deafened by the roaring surf, he had foug
the waves for what seemed hours, then thrust his head and sho
ders free, gasping for breath, only to see the headland looming-
not behind, as he had thought, but to his right.

"The tide was goin' out, and I was goin' with it," he sa
wryly. "I thought, well, that's it, then, I'm gone, for I knew
could never make my way back. I hadna eaten anything in tv
days, and hadn't much strength left."

He ceased swimming then, and simply spread himself on h
back, giving himself to the embrace of the sea. Light-headed fro
hunger and effort, he had closed his eyes against the light a
searched his mind for the words of the old Celtic prayer again
drowning.

He paused for a moment then, and was quiet for so long tha
wondered whether something was wrong. But at last he dre
breath and said shyly, "I expect ye'll think I'm daft, Sassenach
havena told anyone about it—not even Jenny. But—I heard n
mother call me, then, right in the middle of praying." I
shrugged, uncomfortable.

"It was maybe only that I'd been thinking of her when I left t
shore," he said. "And yet—" He fell silent, until I touched h
face.

"What did she say?" I asked quietly.

"She said, 'Come here to me, Jamie—come to me, laddie!'

e drew a deep breath and let it out slowly. "I could hear her
lain as day, but I couldna see anything; there was no one there,
ot even a silkie. I thought perhaps she was callin' me from
leaven—and I was so tired I really would not ha' minded dying
len, but I rolled myself over and struck out toward where I'd
eard her voice. I thought I would swim ten strokes and then stop
gain to rest—or to sink."

But on the eighth stroke, the current had taken him.

"It was just as though someone had picked me up," he said,
ounding still surprised at the memory of it. "I could feel it under
ne and all around; the water was a bit warmer than it had been,
nd it carried me with it. I didna have to do anything but paddle a
it, to keep my head above water."

A strong, curling current, eddying between headland and is-
nds, it had taken him to the edge of the third islet, where no more
nan a few strokes brought him within reach of its rocks.

It was a small lump of granite, fissured and creviced like all the
ncient rocks of Scotland, and slimed with seaweed and seal drop-
ings to boot, but he crawled on shore with all the thankfulness of
shipwrecked sailor for a land of palm trees and white-sand
eaches. He fell down upon his face on the rocky shelf and lay
ere, grateful for breath, half-dozing with exhaustion.

"Then I felt something looming over me, and there was a terri-
le stink o' dead fish," he said. "I got up onto my knees at once,
nd there he was—a great bull seal, all sleek and wet, and his
lack eyes starin' at me, no more than a yard away."

Neither fisher nor seaman himself, Jamie had heard enough
tories to know that bull seals were dangerous, particularly when
reatened by intrusions upon their territory. Looking at the open
louth, with its fine display of sharp, peglike teeth, and the burly
lls of hard fat that girdled the enormous body, he was not dis-
osed to doubt it.

"He weighed more than twenty stone, Sassenach," he said. "If
e wasna inclined to rip the flesh off my bones, still he could ha'
nocked me into the sea wi' one swipe, or dragged me under to
rown."

"Obviously he didn't, though," I said dryly. "What hap-
ened?"

He laughed. "I think I was too mazed from tiredness to do

anything sensible,'' he said. ''I just looked at him for a moment and then I said, 'It's all right; it's only me.' ''

''And what did the seal do?''

Jamie shrugged slightly. ''He looked me over for a bit longer— silkies dinna blink much, did ye know that? It's verra unnerving to have one look at ye for long—then he gave a sort of a grunt and slid off the rock into the water.''

Left in sole possession of the tiny islet, Jamie had sat blankly for a time, recovering his strength, and then at last began a methodical search of the crevices. Small as the area was, it took little time to find a deep split in the rock that led down to a wide hollow space, a foot below the rocky surface. Floored with dry sand and located in the center of the island, the hollow would be safe from flooding in all but the worst storms.

''Well, don't keep me in suspense,'' I said, poking him in the stomach. ''Was the French gold there?''

''Well, it was and it wasn't, Sassenach,'' he answered, neatly sucking in his stomach. ''I'd been expecting gold bullion; that's what the rumor said that Louis would send. And thirty thousand pounds' worth of gold bullion would make a good-sized hoard. But all there was in the hollow was a box, less than a foot long, and a small leather pouch. The box did have gold in it, though— and silver, too.''

Gold and silver indeed. The wooden box had contained two hundred and five coins, gold ones and silver ones, some as sharply cut as though new-minted, some with their markings worn nearly to blankness.

''Ancient coins, Sassenach.''

''Ancient? What, you mean very old—''

''Greek, Sassenach, and Roman. Verra old indeed.''

We lay staring at each other in the dim light for a moment, not speaking.

''That's incredible,'' I said at last. ''It's treasure, all right, but not—''

''Not what Louis would send, to help feed an army, no,'' he finished for me. ''No, whoever put this treasure there, it wasn't Louis or any of his ministers.''

''What about the bag?'' I said, suddenly remembering. ''What was in the pouch you found?''

''Stones, Sassenach. Gemstones. Diamonds and pearls and

meralds and sapphires. Not many, but nicely cut and big nough." He smiled, a little grimly. "Aye, big enough."

He had sat on a rock under the dim gray sky, turning the coins nd the jewels over and over between his fingers, stunned into ewilderment. At last, roused by a sensation of being watched, he ad looked up to find himself surrounded by a circle of curious eals. The tide was out, the females had come back from their shing, and twenty pairs of round black eyes surveyed him cauously.

The huge black male, emboldened by the presence of his harem, ad come back too. He barked loudly, darting his head threatengly from side to side, and advanced on Jamie, sliding his threeundred-pound bulk a few feet closer with each booming exclaation, propelling himself with his flippers across the slick rock.

"I thought I'd best leave, then," he said. "I'd found what I ame to find, after all. So I put the box and the pouch back where 'd found them—I couldna carry them ashore, after all, and if I did —what then? So I put them back, and crawled down into the vater, half-frozen wi' cold."

A few strokes from the island had taken him again into the urrent heading landward; it was a circular current, like most ddies, and the gyre had carried him to the foot of the headland vithin half an hour, where he crawled ashore, dressed, and fell sleep in a nest of marrow-grass.

He paused then, and I could see that while his eyes were open nd fixed on me, it wasn't me they saw.

"I woke at dawn," he said softly. "I have seen a great many awns, Sassenach, but never one like that one.

"I could feel the earth turn beneath me, and my own breath oming wi' the breathing of the wind. It was as though I had no kin nor bone, but only the light of the rising sun inside me."

His eyes softened, as he left the moor and came back to me.

"So then the sun came up higher," he said, matter-of-factly. "And when it warmed me enough to stand, I got up and went nland toward the road, to meet the English."

"But why did you go back?" I demanded. "You were free! You ad money! And—"

"And where would I spend such money as that, Sassenach?" he sked. "Walk into a cottar's hearth and offer him a gold denarius, or a wee emerald?'' He smiled at my indignation and shook his head.

"Nay," he said gently, "I had to go back. Aye, I could ha' lived on the moor for a time—half-starved and naked, but I might have managed. But they were hunting me, Sassenach, and hunting hard for thinking that I might know where the gold was hid. No cot near Ardsmuir would be safe from the English, so long as I was free and might be thought to seek refuge there.

"I've seen the English hunting, ye ken," he added, a harder note creeping into his voice. "Ye'll have seen the panel in the entry hall?"

I had; one panel of the glowing oak that lined the hall below had been smashed in, perhaps by a heavy boot, and the crisscross scars of saber slashes marred the paneling from door to stairs.

"We keep it so to remember," he said. "To show to the weans and tell them when they ask—this is what the English are."

The suppressed hate in his voice struck me low in the pit of the stomach. Knowing what I knew of what the English army had done in the Highlands, there was bloody little I could say in argument. I said nothing, and he continued after a moment.

"I wouldna expose the folk near Ardsmuir to that kind of attention, Sassenach." At the word "Sassenach," his hand squeezed mine and a small smile curved the corner of his mouth. Sassenach I might be to him, but not English.

"For that matter," he went on, "were I not taken, the hunt would likely come here again—to Lallybroch. If I would risk the folk near Ardsmuir, I would not risk my own. And even without that—" He stopped, seeming to struggle to find words.

"I had to go back," he said slowly. "For the sake of the men there, if for nothing else."

"The men in the prison?" I said, surprised. "Were some of the Lallybroch men arrested with you?"

He shook his head. The small vertical line that appeared between his brows when he thought hard was visible, even by starlight.

"No. There were men there from all over the Highlands—from every clan, almost. Only a few men from each clan—remnants and ragtag. But the more in need of a chief, for all that."

"And that's what you were to them?" I spoke gently, restraining the urge to smooth the line away with my fingers.

"For lack of any better," he said, with the flicker of a smile.

He had come from the bosom of family and tenants, from a strength that had sustained him for seven years, to find a lack of hope and a loneliness that would kill a man faster than the damp and the filth and the quaking ague of the prison.

And so, quite simply, he had taken the ragtag and remnants, the castoff survivors of the field of Culloden, and made them his own, that they and he might survive the stones of Ardsmuir as well. Reasoning, charming, and cajoling where he could, fighting where he must, he had forced them to band together, to face their captors as one, to put aside ancient clan rivalries and allegiances, and take him as their chieftain.

"They were mine," he said softly. "And the having of them kept me alive." But then they had been taken from him and from each other—wrenched apart and sent into indenture in a foreign land. And he had not been able to save them.

"You did your best for them. But it's over now," I said softly.

We lay in each other's arms in silence for a long time, letting the small noises of the house wash over us. Different from the comfortable commercial bustle of the brothel, the tiny creaks and sighing spoke of quiet, and home, and safety. For the first time, we were truly alone together, removed from danger and distraction.

There was time, now. Time to hear the rest of the story of the gold, to hear what he had done with it, to find out what had happened to the men of Ardsmuir, to speculate about the burning of the printshop, Young Ian's one-eyed seaman, the encounter with His Majesty's Customs on the shore by Arbroath, to decide what to do next. And since there was time, there was no need to speak of any of that, now.

The last peat broke and fell apart on the hearth, its glowing interior hissing red in the cold. I snuggled closer to Jamie, burying my face in the side of his neck. He tasted faintly of grass and sweat, with a whiff of brandy.

He shifted his body in response, bringing us together all down our naked lengths.

"What, again?" I murmured, amused. "Men your age aren't supposed to do it again so soon."

His teeth nibbled gently on my earlobe. "Well, you're doing it too, Sassenach," he pointed out. "And you're older than I am."

"That's different," I said, gasping a little as he moved suddenly over me, his shoulders blotting out the starlit window. "I'm woman."

"And if ye weren't a woman, Sassenach," he assured me, set tling to his work, "I wouldna be doing it either. Hush, now."

I woke just past dawn to the scratching of the rose brier agains the window, and the muffled thump and clang of breakfast fixin in the kitchen below. Peering over Jamie's sleeping form, I saw that the fire was dead out. I slid out of bed, quietly so as not t wake him. The floorboards were icy under my feet and I reached shivering, for the first available garment.

Swathed in the folds of Jamie's shirt, I knelt on the hearth an went about the laborious business of rekindling the fire, thinkin rather wistfully that I might have included a box of safety matche in the short list of items I had thought worthwhile to bring. Strik ing sparks from a flint to catch kindling does work, but not usuall on the first try. Or the second. Or . . .

Somewhere around the dozenth attempt, I was rewarded by tiny black spot on the twist of tow I was using for kindling. It grev at once and blossomed into a tiny flame. I thrust it hastily bu carefully beneath the little tent of twigs I had prepared, to shelte the blooming flame from the cold breeze.

I had left the window ajar the night before, to ensure not bein, suffocated by the smoke—peat fires burned hot, but dully, with lot of smoke, as the blackened beams overhead attested. Just now though, I thought we could dispense with fresh air—at least until got the fire thoroughly under way.

The pane was rimed at the bottom with a light frost; winter wa not far off. The air was so crisp and fresh that I paused befor shutting the window, breathing in great gulps of dead leaf, drie apples, cold earth, and damp, sweet grass. The scene outside wa perfect in its still clarity, stone walls and dark pines drawn shar as black quillstrokes against the gray overcast of the morning.

A movement drew my eye to the top of the hill, where the roug track led to the village of Broch Mordha, ten miles distant. One b one, three small Highland ponies came up over the rise, an started down the hill toward the farmhouse.

They were too far away for me to make out the faces, but could see by the billowing skirts that all three riders were women

Perhaps it was the girls—Maggie, Kitty, and Janet—coming back from Young Jamie's house. My own Jamie would be glad to see them.

I pulled the shirt, redolent of Jamie, around me against the chill, deciding to take advantage of what privacy might remain to us this morning by thawing out in bed. I shut the window, and paused to lift several of the light peat bricks from the basket by the hearth and feed them carefully to my fledgling fire, before shedding the shirt and crawling under the covers, numb toes tingling with delight at the luxurious warmth.

Jamie felt the chill of my return, and rolled instinctively toward me, gathering me neatly in and curling round me spoon-fashion. He sleepily rubbed his face against my shoulder.

"Sleep well, Sassenach?" he muttered.

"Never better," I assured him, snuggling my cold bottom into the warm hollow of his thighs. "You?"

"Mmmmm." He responded with a blissful groan, wrapping his arms about me. "Dreamed like a fiend."

"What about?"

"Naked women, mostly," he said, and set his teeth gently in the flesh of my shoulder. "That, and food." His stomach rumbled softly. The scent of biscuits and fried bacon in the air was faint but unmistakable.

"So long as you don't confuse the two," I said, twitching my shoulder out of his reach.

"I can tell a hawk from a handsaw, when the wind sets north by nor'west," he assured me, "and a sweet, plump lassie from a salt-cured ham, too, appearances notwithstanding." He grabbed my buttocks with both hands and squeezed, making me yelp and kick him in the shins.

"Beast!"

"Oh, a beast, is it?" he said, laughing. "Well, then . . ." Growling deep in his throat, he dived under the quilt and proceeded to nip and nibble his way up the insides of my thighs, blithely ignoring my squeaks and the hail of kicks on his back and shoulders. Dislodged by our struggles, the quilt slid off onto the floor, revealing the tousled mass of his hair, flying wild over my thighs.

"Perhaps there's less difference than I thought," he said, his head popping up between my legs as he paused for breath. He pressed my thighs flat against the mattress and grinned up at me, spikes of red hair standing on end like a porcupine's quills. "Ye do taste a bit salty, come to try it. What do ye—"

He was interrupted by a sudden bang as the door flew open and rebounded from the wall. Startled, we turned to look. In the doorway stood a young girl I had never seen before. She was perhaps fifteen or sixteen, with long flaxen hair and big blue eyes. The eyes were somewhat bigger than normal, and filled with an expression of horrified shock as she stared at me. Her gaze moved slowly from my tangled hair to my bare breasts, and down the slopes of my naked body, until it encountered Jamie, lying prone between my thighs, white-faced with a shock equal to hers.

"Daddy!" she said, in tones of total outrage. "*Who* is that woman?"

"D addy?" I said blankly. *"Daddy?"*

Jamie had turned to stone when the door opened. Now he shot bolt upright, snatching at the fallen quilt. He shoved the disheveled hair out of his face, and glared at the girl.

"What in the name of bloody hell are you doing here?" he demanded. Red-bearded, naked, and hoarse with fury, he was a formidable sight, and the girl took a step backward, looking uncertain. Then her chin firmed and she glared back at him.

"I came with Mother!"

The effect on Jamie could not have been greater had she shot him through the heart. He jerked violently, and all the color went out of his face.

It came flooding back, as the sound of rapid footsteps sounded on the wooden staircase. He leapt out of bed, tossing the quilt hastily in my direction, and grabbed his breeks.

He had barely pulled them on when another female figure burst into the room, skidded to a halt, and stood staring, bug-eyed, at the bed.

"It's true!" She whirled toward Jamie, fists clenched against the cloak she still wore. "It's true! It's the Sassenach witch! How could ye do such a thing to me, Jamie Fraser?"

"Be still, Laoghaire!" he snapped. "I've done nothing to ye!"

I sat up against the wall, clutching the quilt to my bosom and staring. It was only when he spoke her name that I recognized her. Twenty-odd years ago, Laoghaire MacKenzie had been a slender sixteen-year-old, with rose-petal skin, moonbeam hair, and a violent—and unrequited—passion for Jamie Fraser. Evidently, a few things had changed.

She was nearing forty and no longer slender, having thickened considerably. The skin was still fair, but weathered, and stretched plumply over cheeks flushed with anger. Strands of ashy hair straggled out from under her respectable white kertch. The pale blue eyes were the same, though—they turned on me again, with the same expression of hatred I had seen in them long ago.

"He's mine!" she hissed. She stamped her foot. "Get ye back to the hell that ye came from, and leave him to me! Go, I say!"

As I made no move to obey, she glanced wildly about in search of a weapon. Catching sight of the blue-banded ewer, she seized it and drew back her arm to fling it at me. Jamie plucked it neatly from her hand, set it back on the bureau, and grasped her by the upper arm, hard enough to make her squeal.

He turned her and shoved her roughly toward the door. "Get ye downstairs," he ordered. "I'll speak wi' ye presently, Laoghaire."

"You'll speak wi' me? Speak wi' me, is it!" she cried. Face contorted, she swung her free hand at him, raking his face from eye to chin with her nails.

He grunted, grabbed her other wrist, and dragging her to the door, pushed her out into the passage and slammed the door to and turned the key.

By the time he turned around again, I was sitting on the edge of the bed, fumbling with shaking hands as I tried to pull my stockings on.

"I can explain it to ye, Claire," he said.

"I d-don't think so," I said. My lips were numb, along with the rest of me, and it was hard to form words. I kept my eyes fixed on my feet as I tried—and failed—to tie my garters.

"Listen to me!" he said violently, bringing his fist down on the table with a crash that made me jump. I jerked my head up, and caught a glimpse of him towering over me. With his red hair tumbled loose about his shoulders, his face unshaven, bare-chested, and the raw marks of Laoghaire's nails down his cheek, he looked like a Viking raider, bent on mayhem. I turned away to look for my shift.

It was lost in the bedclothes; I scrabbled about among the sheets. A considerable pounding had started up on the other side of the door, accompanied by shouts and shrieks, as the commotion attracted the other inhabitants of the house.

"You'd best go and explain things to your daughter," I said, pulling the crumpled cotton over my head.

"She's not my daughter!"

"No?" My head popped out of the neck of the shift, and I lifted my chin to stare up at him. "And I suppose you aren't married to Laoghaire, either?"

"I'm married to you, damn it!" he bellowed, striking his fist on the table again.

"I don't think so." I felt very cold. My stiff fingers couldn't manage the lacing of the stays; I threw them aside, and stood up to look for my gown, which was somewhere on the other side of the room—behind Jamie.

"I need my dress."

"You're no going anywhere, Sassenach. Not until—"

"Don't call me that!" I shrieked it, surprising both of us. He stared at me for a moment, then nodded.

"All right," he said quietly. He glanced at the door, now reverberating under the force of the pounding. He drew a deep breath and straightened, squaring his shoulders.

"I'll go and settle things. Then we'll talk, the two of us. Stay here, Sass—Claire." He picked up his shirt and yanked it over his head. Unlocking the door, he stepped out into the suddenly silent corridor and closed it behind him.

I managed to pick up the dress, then collapsed on the bed and sat shaking all over, the green wool crumpled across my knees.

I couldn't think in a straight line. My mind spun in small circles around the central fact; he was married. Married to Laoghaire! And he had a family. And yet he had wept for Brianna.

"Oh, Bree!" I said aloud. "Oh, God, Bree!" and began to cry —partly from shock, partly at the thought of Brianna. It wasn't logical, but this discovery seemed a betrayal of her, as much as of me—or of Laoghaire.

The thought of Laoghaire turned shock and sorrow to rage in a moment. I rubbed a fold of green wool savagely across my face, leaving the skin red and prickly.

Damn him! How dare he? If he had married again, thinking me

dead, that was one thing. I had half-expected, half-feared it. But to marry that woman—that spiteful, sneaking little bitch who had tried to murder me at Castle Leoch . . . but he likely didn't know that, a small voice of reason in my head pointed out.

"Well, he *should* have known!" I said. "Damn him to hell, how could he take her, anyway?" The tears were rolling heedlessly down my face, hot spurts of loss and fury, and my nose was running. I groped for a handkerchief, found none, and in desperation, blew my nose at last on a corner of the sheet.

It smelled of Jamie. Worse, it smelled of the two of us, and the faint, musky lingerings of our pleasure. There was a small tingling spot on the inside of my thigh, where Jamie had nipped me, a few minutes before. I brought the flat of my hand down hard on the spot in a vicious slap, to kill the feeling.

"Liar!" I screamed. I grabbed the pitcher Laoghaire had tried to throw at me, and hurled it myself. It crashed against the door in an explosion of splinters.

I stood in the middle of the room, listening. It was quiet. There was no sound from below; no one was coming to see what had made the crash. I imagined they were all much too concerned with soothing Laoghaire to worry about me.

Did they live here, at Lallybroch? I recalled Jamie, taking Fergus aside, sending him ahead, ostensibly to tell Ian and Jenny we were coming. And, presumably, to warn them about me, and get Laoghaire out of the way before I arrived.

What in the name of God did Jenny and Ian think about this? Clearly they must know about Laoghaire—and yet they had received me last night, with no sign of it on their faces. But if Laoghaire had been sent away—why did she come back? Even trying to think about it made my temples throb.

The act of violence had drained enough rage for me to be able once more to control my shaking fingers. I kicked the stays into a corner and pulled the green gown over my head.

I had to get out of there. That was the only half-coherent thought in my head, and I clung to it. I had to leave. I couldn't stay, not with Laoghaire and her daughters in the house. They belonged there—I didn't.

I managed to tie up the garters this time, do up the laces of the dress, fasten the multiple hooks of the overskirt, and find my shoes. One was under the washstand, the other by the massive oak armoire, where I had kicked them the night before, dropping my clothes carelessly anywhere in my eagerness to crawl into the welcoming bed and nestle warmly in Jamie's arms.

I shivered. The fire had gone out again, and there was an icy draft from the window. I felt chilled to the bone, despite my clothes.

I wasted some time in searching for my cloak before realizing that it was downstairs; I had left it in the parlor the day before. I pushed my fingers through my hair, but was too upset to look for a comb. The strands crackled with electricity from having the woolen dress pulled over my head, and I slapped irritably at the floating hairs that stuck to my face.

Ready. Ready as I'd be, at least. I paused for one last look around, then heard footsteps coming up the stair.

Not fast and light, like the last ones. These were heavier, and slow, deliberate. I knew without seeing him that it was Jamie coming—and that he wasn't anxious to see me.

Fine. I didn't want to see him, either. Better just to leave at once, without speaking. What was there to say?

I backed away as the door opened, unaware that I was moving, until my legs hit the edge of the bed. I lost my balance and sat down. Jamie paused in the doorway, looking down at me.

He had shaved. That was the first thing I noticed. In echo of Young Ian the day before, he had hastily shaved, brushed his hair back and tidied himself before facing trouble. He seemed to know what I was thinking; the ghost of a smile passed over his face, as he rubbed his freshly scraped chin.

"D'ye think it will help?" he asked.

I swallowed, and licked dry lips, but didn't answer. He sighed, and answered himself.

"No, I suppose not." He stepped into the room and closed the door. He stood awkwardly for a moment, then moved toward the bed, one hand extended toward me. "Claire—"

"Don't touch me!" I leapt to my feet and backed away, circling toward the door. His hand fell to his side, but he stepped in front of me, blocking the way.

"Will ye no let me explain, Claire?"

"It seems to be a little late for that," I said, in what I meant to be a cold, disdainful tone. Unfortunately, my voice shook.

. He pushed the door shut behind him.

"Ye never used to be unreasonable," he said quietly.

"And don't tell me what I used to be!" The tears were much too near the surface, and I bit my lip to hold them back.

"All right." His face was very pale; the scratches Laoghaire had given him showed as three red lines, livid down his cheek.

"I dinna live with her," he said. "She and the girls live a Balriggan, over near Broch Mordha." He watched me closely, but I said nothing. He shrugged a little, settling the shirt on his shoulders, and went on.

"It was a great mistake—the marriage between us."

"With two children? Took you a while to realize, didn't it?" burst out.

His lips pressed tight together.

"The lassies aren't mine; Laoghaire was a widow wi' the two bairns when I wed her."

"Oh." It didn't make any real difference, but still, I felt a small wave of something like relief, on Brianna's behalf. She was the sole child of Jamie's heart, at least, even if I—

"I've not lived wi' them for some time; I live in Edinburgh, and send money to them, but—"

"You don't need to tell me," I interrupted. "It doesn't make any difference. Let me by, please—I'm going."

The thick, ruddy brows drew sharply together.

"Going where?"

"Back. Away. I don't know—let me by!"

"You aren't going anywhere," he said definitely.

"You can't stop me!"

He reached out and grabbed me by both arms.

"Aye, I can," he said. He could; I jerked furiously, but couldn't budge the iron grip on my biceps.

"Let go of me this minute!"

"No, I won't!" He glared at me, eyes narrowed, and I suddenly realized that calm as he might seem outwardly, he was very nearly as upset as I was. I saw the muscles of his throat move as he swallowed, controlling himself enough to speak again.

"I willna let ye go until I've explained to ye, why . . ."

"What is there to explain?" I demanded furiously. "You married again! What else is there?"

The color was rising in his face; the tips of his ears were already ed, a sure sign of impending fury.

"And have you lived a nun for twenty years?" he demanded, haking me slightly. "Have ye?"

"No!" I flung the word at his face, and he flinched slightly. No, I bloody haven't! And I don't think you've been a monk, ither—I never did!"

"Then—" he began, but I was much too furious to listen any- ore.

"You lied to me, damn you!"

"I never did!" The skin was stretched tight over his cheek- ones, as it was when he was very angry indeed.

"You did, you bastard! You know you did! Let go!" I kicked m sharply in the shin, hard enough to numb my toes. He ex- aimed in pain, but didn't let go. Instead, he squeezed harder, aking me yelp.

"I never said a thing to ye—"

"No, you didn't! But you lied, anyway! You let me think you eren't married, that there wasn't anyone, that you—that you—" was half-sobbing with rage, gasping between words. "You ould have told me, the minute I came! Why in hell didn't you ll me?" His grip on my arms slackened, and I managed to rench myself free. He took a step toward me, eyes glittering with ry. I wasn't afraid of him; I drew back my fist and hit him in the est.

"Why?" I shrieked, hitting him again and again and again, the und of the blows thudding against his chest. "Why, why, *why*!"

"Because I was afraid!" He got hold of my wrists and threw e backward, so I fell across the bed. He stood over me, fists enched, breathing hard.

"I am a coward, damn you! I couldna tell ye, for fear ye would ave me, and unmanly thing that I am, I thought I couldna bear at!"

"Unmanly? With two wives? Ha!"

I really thought he would slap me; he raised his arm, but then s open palm clenched into a fist.

"Am I a man? To want you so badly that nothing else matters? see you, and know I would sacrifice honor or family or life elf to lie wi' you, even though ye'd left me?"

"You have the filthy, unmitigated, bleeding gall to say such a

thing to me?'' My voice was so high, it came out as a thin an
vicious whisper. ''You'll blame *me*?''

He stopped then, chest heaving as he caught his breath.

''No. No, I canna blame you.'' He turned aside, blindly. ''How
could it have been your fault? Ye wanted to stay wi' me, to die
with me.''

''I did, the more fool I,'' I said. ''*You* sent me back, you made
me go! And now you want to blame me for going?''

He turned back to me, eyes dark with desperation.

''I had to send ye away! I had to, for the bairn's sake!'' His eyes
went involuntarily to the hook where his coat hung, the pictures of
Brianna in its pocket. He took one deep, quivering breath, and
calmed himself with a visible effort.

''No,'' he said, much more quietly. ''I canna regret that, what
ever the cost. I would have given my life, for her and for you. If
took my heart and soul, too . . .''

He drew a long, quivering breath, mastering the passion that
shook him.

''I canna blame ye for going.''

''You blame me for coming back, though.''

He shook his head as though to clear it.

''No, God no!''

He grabbed my hands tight between his own, the strength of his
grip grinding the bones together.

''Do ye know what it is to live twenty years without a heart? To
live half a man, and accustom yourself to living in the bit that
left, filling in the cracks wi' what mortar comes handy?''

''Do I know?'' I echoed. I struggled to loose myself, to little
effect. ''Yes, you bloody bastard, I know that! What did you think
I'd gone straight back to Frank and lived happy ever after?'' I
kicked at him as hard as I could. He flinched, but didn't let go.

''Sometimes I hoped ye did,'' he said, speaking through
clenched teeth. ''And then sometimes I could see it—him with
you, day and night, lyin' with ye, taking your body, holding my
child! And God, I could kill ye for it!''

Suddenly, he dropped my hands, whirled, and smashed his fist
through the side of the oak armoire. It was an impressive blow; the
armoire was a sturdy piece of furniture. It must have bruised his
knuckles considerably, but without hesitation, he drove the other

ist into the oak boards as well, as though the shining wood were rank's face—or mine.

"Feel like that about it, do you?" I said coldly, as he stepped back, panting. "I don't even have to imagine you with Laoghaire —I've bloody *seen* her!"

"I dinna care a fig for Laoghaire, and never have!"

"Bastard!" I said again. "You'd marry a woman without wanting her, and then throw her aside the minute—"

"Shut up!" he roared. "Hold your tongue, ye wicked wee itch!" He slammed a fist down on the washstand, glaring at me. "I'm damned the one way or the other, no? If I felt anything for er, I'm a faithless womanizer, and if I didn't, I'm a heartless east."

"You should have told me!"

"And if I had?" He grabbed my hand and jerked me to my feet, olding me eye to eye with him. "You'd have turned on your heel nd gone without a word. And having seen ye again—I tell ye, I ould ha' done far worse than lie to keep you!"

He pressed me tight against his body and kissed me, long and ard. My knees turned to water, and I fought to keep my feet, uttressed by the vision of Laoghaire's angry eyes, and her voice, choing shrill in my ears. *He's mine!*

"This is senseless," I said, pulling away. Fury had its own ntoxication, but the hangover was setting in fast, a black dizzy ortex. My head swam so that I could hardly keep my balance. "I an't think straight. I'm leaving."

I lurched toward the door, but he caught me by the waist, yanking me back.

He whirled me toward himself and kissed me again, hard nough to leave a quicksilver taste of blood in my mouth. It was either affection nor desire, but a blind passion, a determination to ossess me. He was through talking.

So was I. I pulled my mouth away and slapped him hard across e face, fingers curved to rake his flesh.

He jerked back, cheek scraped raw, then twisted his fingers tight my hair, bent and took my mouth again, deliberate and savage, gnoring the kicks and blows I rained on him.

He bit my lower lip, hard, and when I opened my lips, gasping, rust his tongue into my mouth, stealing breath and words together.

He threw me bodily onto the bed where we had lain laughing an hour before, and pinned me there at once with the weight of his body.

He was most mightily roused.

So was I.

Mine, he said, without uttering a word. *Mine!*

I fought him with boundless fury and no little skill, and *Yours,* my body echoed back. *Yours, and may you be damned for it!*

I didn't feel him rip my gown, but I felt the heat of his body on my bare breasts, through the thin linen of his shirt, the long, hard muscle of his thigh straining against my own. He took his hand off my arm to tear at his breeches, and I clawed him from ear to breast, striping his skin with pale red.

We were doing our level best to kill each other, fueled by the rage of years apart—mine for his sending me away, his for my going, mine for Laoghaire, his for Frank.

"Bitch!" he panted. "Whore!"

"Damn you!" I got a hand in his own long hair, and yanked, pulling his face down to me again. We rolled off the bed and landed on the floor in a tangled heap, rolling to and fro in a welter of half-uttered curses and broken words.

I didn't hear the door open. I didn't hear anything, though she must have called out, more than once. Blind and deaf, I knew nothing but Jamie until the shower of cold water struck us, sudden as an electric shock. Jamie froze. All the color left his face, leaving the bones jutting stark beneath the skin.

I lay dazed, drops of water dripping from the ends of his hair onto my breasts. Just behind him, I could see Jenny, her face as white as his, holding an empty pan in her hands.

"Stop it!" she said. Her eyes were slanted with a horrified anger. "How could ye, Jamie? Rutting like a wild beast, and no carin' if all the house hears ye!"

He moved off me, slowly, clumsy as a bear. Jenny snatched quilt from the bed and flung it over my body.

On all fours, he shook his head like a dog, sending droplets of water flying. Then, very slowly, he got to his feet, and pulled his ripped breeches back into place.

"Are ye no ashamed?" she cried, scandalized.

Jamie stood looking down at her as though he had never seen

any creature quite like her, and was making up his mind what she might be. The wet ends of his hair dripped over his bare chest.

"Yes," he said at last, quite mildly. "I am."

He seemed dazed. He closed his eyes and a brief, deep shudder went over him. Without a word, he turned and went out.

35

Flight from Eden

Jenny helped me to the bed, making small clucking noises, whether of shock or concern, I couldn't tell. I was vaguely conscious of hovering figures in the doorway—servants, I supposed—but wasn't disposed to pay much attention.

"I'll find ye something to put on," she murmured, fluffing a pillow and pushing me back onto it. "And perhaps a bit of a drink. You're all right?"

"Where's Jamie?"

She glanced at me quickly, sympathy mixed with a gleam of curiosity.

"Dinna be afraid; I'll no let him at ye again." She spoke firmly, then pressed her lips tight together, frowning as she tucked the quilt around me. "How he could do such a thing!"

"It wasn't his fault—not this." I ran a hand through my tangled hair, indicating my general dishevelment. "I mean—I did it, as much as he did. It was both of us. He—I—" I let my hand fall, helpless to explain. I was bruised and shaken, and my lips were swollen.

"I see," was all Jenny said, but she gave me a long, assessing look, and I thought it quite possible that she did see.

I didn't want to talk about the recent happenings, and she seemed to sense this, for she kept quiet for a bit, giving a soft-voiced order to someone in the hall, then moving about the room, straightening furniture and tidying things. I saw her pause for a moment as she saw the holes in the armoire, then she stooped to pick up the larger pieces of the shattered ewer.

As she dumped them into the basin, there was a faint thud from the house below; the slam of the big main door. She stepped to the window and pushed the curtain aside.

"It's Jamie," she said. She glanced at me, and let the curtain fall. "He'll be going up to the hill; he goes there, if he's troubled. That, or he gets drunk wi' Ian. The hill's better."

I gave a small snort.

"Yes, I expect he's troubled, all right."

There was a light step in the hallway, and the younger Janet appeared, carefully balancing a tray of biscuits, whisky, and water. She looked pale and scared.

"Are ye . . . well, Aunt?" she asked tentatively, setting down the tray.

"I'm fine," I assured her, pushing myself upright and reaching for the whisky decanter.

A sharp glance having assured Jenny of the same, she patted her daughter's arm and turned toward the door.

"Stay wi' your auntie," she ordered. "I'll go and find a dress." Janet nodded obediently, and sat down by the bed on a stool, watching me as I ate and drank.

I began to feel physically much stronger with a little food inside me. Internally, I felt quite numb; the recent events seemed at once dreamlike and yet completely clear in my mind. I could recall the smallest details; the blue calico bows on the dress of Laoghaire's daughter, the tiny broken veins in Laoghaire's cheeks, a rough-torn fingernail on Jamie's fourth finger.

"Do you know where Laoghaire is?" I asked Janet. The girl had her head down, apparently studying her own hands. At my question, she jerked upright, blinking.

"Oh!" she said. "Oh. Aye, she and Marsali and Joan went back to Balriggan, where they live. Uncle Jamie made them go."

"Did he," I said flatly.

Janet bit her lip, twisting her hands in her apron. Suddenly she looked up at me.

"Aunt—I'm so awfully sorry!" Her eyes were a warm brown, like her father's, but swimming now with tears.

"It's all right," I said, having no idea what she meant, but trying to be soothing.

"But it was me!" she burst out. She looked thoroughly miserable, but determined to confess. "I—I told Laoghaire ye were here. That's why she came."

"Oh." 'Well, that explained that, I supposed. I finished the whisky and set the glass carefully back on the tray.

"I didna think—I mean, I didna have it in mind to cause a kebbie-lebbie, truly not. I didna ken that you—that she—"

"It's all right," I said again. "One of us would have found out sooner or later." It made no difference, but I glanced at her with some curiosity. "Why did you tell her, though?"

The girl glanced cautiously over her shoulder, hearing steps start up from below. She leaned close to me.

"Mother told me to," she whispered. And with that, she rose and hastily left the room, brushing past her mother in the doorway.

I didn't ask. Jenny had found a dress for me—one of the elder girls'—and there was no conversation beyond the necessary as she helped me into it.

When I was dressed and shod, my hair combed and put up, I turned to her.

"I want to go," I said. "Now."

She didn't argue, but only looked me over, to see that I was strong enough. She nodded then, dark lashes covering the slanted blue eyes so like her brother's.

"I think that's best," she said quietly.

It was late morning when I left Lallybroch for what I knew would be the last time. I had a dagger at my waist, for protection, though it was unlikely I would need it. My horse's saddlebags held food and several bottles of ale; enough to see me back to the stone circle. I had thought of taking back the pictures of Brianna from Jamie's coat, but after a moment's hesitation, had left them. She belonged to him forever, even if I didn't.

It was a cold autumn day, the morning's gray promise fulfilled with a mourning drizzle. No one was in sight near the house, as Jenny led the horse out of the stable, and held the bridle for me to mount.

I pulled the hood of my cloak farther forward, and nodded to her. Last time, we had parted with tears and embraces, as sisters. She let go the reins, and stood back, as I turned the horse's head toward the road.

"Godspeed!" I heard her call behind me. I didn't answer, nor did I look back.

I rode most of the day, without really noticing where I was going; taking heed only for the general direction, and letting the gelding pick his own way through the mountain passes.

I stopped when the light began to go; hobbled the horse to graze, lay down wrapped in my cloak, and dropped straight asleep, unwilling to stay awake for fear I might think, and remember. Numbness was my only refuge. I knew it would go, but I clung to its gray comfort so long as I might.

It was hunger that brought me unwillingly back to life the next day. I had not paused to eat through all the day before, nor when rising in the morning, but by noon my stomach had begun to register loud protests, and I stopped in a small glen beside a sparkling burn, and unwrapped the food that Jenny had slipped into my saddlebag.

There were oatcakes and ale, and several small loaves of fresh-baked bread, slit down the middle, stuffed with sheepmilk cheese and homemade pickle. Highland sandwiches, the hearty fare of shepherds and warriors, as characteristic of Lallybroch as peanut butter had been of Boston. Very suitable, that my quest should end with one of these.

I ate a sandwich, drank one of the stone bottles of ale, and swung back into the saddle, turning the horse's head to the north-east once more. Unfortunately, while the food had brought fresh strength to my body, it had given fresh life to my feelings as well. As we climbed higher and higher into the clouds, my spirits fell lower—and they hadn't been high to begin with.

The horse was willing enough, but I wasn't. Near midafternoon, I felt that I simply couldn't go on. Leading the horse far enough into a small thicket that it wouldn't be noticeable from the road, I hobbled it loosely, and walked farther under the trees myself, 'til I came to the trunk of a fallen aspen, smooth-skinned, stained green with moss.

I sat slumped over, elbows on my knees and head on my hands. I ached in every joint. Not really from the encounter of the day before, or from the rigors of riding; from grief.

Constraint and judgment had been a great deal of my life. I had learned at some pains the art of healing; to give and to care, but always stopping short of that danger point where too much was given to make me effective. I had learned detachment and disengagement, to my cost.

With Frank, too, I had learned the balancing act of civility; kindness and respect that did not pass those unseen boundaries into passion. And Brianna? Love for a child cannot be free; from the first signs of movement in the womb, a devotion springs up as powerful as it is mindless, irresistible as the process of birth itself. But powerful as it is, it is a love always of control; one is in charge, the protector, the watcher, the guardian—there is great passion in it, to be sure, but never abandon.

Always, always, I had had to balance compassion with wisdom, love with judgment, humanity with ruthlessness.

Only with Jamie had I given everything I had, risked it all. I had thrown away caution and judgment and wisdom, along with the comforts and constraints of a hard-won career. I had brought him nothing but myself, been nothing but myself with him, given him soul as well as body, let him see me naked, trusted him to see me whole and cherish my frailties—because he once had.

I had feared he couldn't, again. Or wouldn't. And then had known those few days of perfect joy, thinking that what had once been true was true once more; I was free to love him, with everything I had and was, and be loved with an honesty that matched my own.

The tears slid hot and wet between my fingers. I mourned for Jamie, and for what I had been, with him.

Do you know, his voice said, whispering, *what it means, to say again "I love you," and to mean it?*

I knew. And with my head in my hands beneath the pine trees, I knew I would never mean it again.

Sunk as I was in miserable contemplation, I didn't hear the footsteps until he was nearly upon me. Startled by the crack of a branch nearby, I rocketed off the fallen tree like a rising pheasant and whirled to face the attacker, heart in my mouth and dagger in hand.

"Christ!" My stalker shied back from the open blade, clearly as startled as I was.

"What the hell are you doing here?" I demanded. I pressed my free hand to my chest. My heart was pounding like a kettledrum and I was sure I was as white as he was.

"Jesus, Auntie Claire! Where'd ye learn to pull a knife like that? Ye scairt hell out of me." Young Ian passed a hand over his brow, Adam's apple bobbing as he swallowed.

"The feeling is mutual," I assured him. I tried to sheathe the dagger, but my hand was shaking too much with reaction to manage it. Knees wobbling, I sank back on the aspen trunk and laid the knife on my thigh.

"I repeat," I said, trying to gain mastery of myself, "what are you doing here?" I had a bloody good idea what he was doing here, and I wasn't having any. On the other hand, I needed a moment's recovery from the fright before I could reliably stand up.

Young Ian bit his lip, glanced around, and at my nod of permission, sat down awkwardly on the trunk beside me.

"Uncle Jamie sent me—" he began. I didn't pause to hear more, but got up at once, knees or no knees, thrusting the dagger into my belt as I turned away.

"Wait, Aunt! Please!" He grabbed at my arm, but I jerked loose, pulling away from him.

"I'm not interested," I said, kicking the fronds of bracken aside. "Go home, wee Ian. I've places to go." I hoped I had, at least.

"But it isn't what you think!" Unable to stop me leaving the clearing, he was following me, arguing as he ducked low branches. "He needs you, Aunt, really he does! Ye must come back wi' me!"

I didn't answer him; I had reached my horse, and bent to undo the hobbles.

"Auntie Claire! Will ye no listen to me?" He loomed up on the other side of the horse, gawky height peering at me over the saddle. He looked very much like his father, his good-natured, half-homely face creased with anxiety.

"No," I said briefly. I stuffed the hobbles into the saddlebag, and put my foot into the stirrup, swinging up with a satisfyingly majestic swish of skirts and petticoats. My dignified departure was hampered at this point by the fact that Young Ian had the horse's reins in a death grip.

"Let go," I said peremptorily.

"Not until ye hear me out," he said. He glared up at me, jaw clenched with stubbornness, soft brown eyes ablaze. I glared back at him. Gangling as he was, he had Ian's skinny muscularity, unless I was prepared to ride him down, there seemed little choice but to listen to him.

All right, I decided. Fat lot of good it would do, to him or his double-dealing uncle, but I'd listen.

"Talk," I said, mustering what patience I could.

He drew a deep breath, eyeing me warily to see whether I meant it. Deciding that I did, he blew his breath out, making the soft brown hair over his brow flutter, and squared his shoulders to begin.

"Well," he started, seeming suddenly unsure. "It . . . I . . he . . ."

I made a low sound of exasperation in my throat. "Start at the beginning," I said. "But don't make a song and dance of it, hm?"

He nodded, teeth set in his upper lip as he concentrated.

"Well, there was the hell of a stramash broke out at the house after ye left, when Uncle Jamie came back," he began.

"I'll just bet there was," I said. Despite myself, I was conscious of a small stirring of curiosity, but fought it down, assuming an expression of complete indifference.

"I've never seen Uncle Jamie sae furious," he said, watching my face carefully. "Nor Mother, either. They went at it hammer and tongs, the two o' them. Father tried to quiet them, but it was like they didna even hear him. Uncle Jamie called Mother a meddling besom, and a *lang-nebbit* . . . and . . . and a lot of worse names," he added, flushing.

"He shouldn't have been angry with Jenny," I said. "She was only trying to help—I think." I felt sick with the knowledge that I had caused this rift, too. Jenny had been Jamie's mainstay since the death of their mother when both were children. Was there no end to the damage I had caused by coming back?

To my surprise, Jenny's son smiled briefly. "Well, it wasna all one-sided," he said dryly. "My mother's no the person to be taking abuse lying down, ye ken. Uncle Jamie had a few tooth marks on him before the end of it." He swallowed, remembering.

"In fact, I thought they'd damage each other, surely; Mother went for Uncle Jamie wi' an iron girdle, and he snatched it from

er and threw it through the kitchen window. Scairt the chickens
ut o' the yard,'' he added, with a feeble grin.

"Less about chickens, Young Ian," I said, looking down at him
oldly. "Get on with it; I want to leave."

"Well, then Uncle Jamie knocked over the bookshelf in the
arlor—I dinna think he did it on purpose,'' the lad added hastily,
he was just too fashed to see straight—and went out the door.
ather stuck his head out the window and shouted at him where
as he going, and he said he was going to find you.''

"Then why are you here, and not him?" I was leaning forward
ightly, watching his hand on the reins; if his fingers showed signs
f relaxation, perhaps I could twitch the rein out of his grasp.

Young Ian sighed. "Well, just as Uncle Jamie was setting out on
is horse, Aunt . . . er . . . I mean his wi—" He blushed mis-
ably. "Laoghaire. She . . . she came down the hill and into the
ooryard.''

At this point, I gave up pretending indifference.

"And what happened then?"

He frowned. "There was an awful collieshangie, but I couldna
ear much. Auntie . . . I mean Laoghaire—she doesna seem to
now how to fight properly, like my mam and Uncle Jamie. She
st weeps and wails a lot. Mam says she snivels," he added.

"Mmphm," I said. "And so?"

Laoghaire had slid off her own mount, clutched Jamie by the
g, and more or less dragged him off as well, according to Young
n. She had then subsided into a puddle in the dooryard, clutch-
g Jamie about the knees, weeping and wailing as was her usual
bit.

Unable to escape, Jamie had at last hauled Laoghaire to her feet,
ung her bodily over his shoulder, and carried her into the house
d up the stairs, ignoring the fascinated gazes of his family and
rvants.

"Right," I said. I realized that I had been clenching my jaw,
d consciously unclenched it. "So he sent you after me because
was too occupied with his *wife*. Bastard! The gall of him! He
inks he can just send someone to fetch me back, like a hired girl,
cause it doesn't suit his convenience to come himself? He
inks he can have his cake and eat it, does he? Bloody arrogant,
lfish, overbearing . . . Scot!'' Distracted as I was by the pic-

ture of Jamie carrying Laoghaire upstairs, "Scot" was the worst epithet I could come up with on short notice.

My knuckles were white where my hand clutched the edge of the saddle. Not caring about subtlety anymore, I leaned down, snatching for the reins.

"Let go!"

"But Auntie Claire, it's not that!"

"What's not that?" Caught by his tone of desperation, I glanced up. His long, narrow face was tight with the anguished need to make me understand.

"Uncle Jamie didna stay to tend Laoghaire!"

"Then why did he send you?"

He took a deep breath, renewing his grip on my reins.

"She shot him. He sent me to find ye, because he's dying."

"If you're lying to me, Ian Murray," I said, for the dozenth time, "you'll regret it to the end of your life—which will be short!"

I had to raise my voice to be heard. The rising wind came whooshing past me, lifting my hair in streamers off my shoulders, whipping my skirts tight around my legs. The weather was suitably dramatic; great black clouds choked the mountain passes, boiling over the crags like seafoam, with a faint distant rumble of thunder like far-off surf on packed sand.

Lacking breath, Young Ian merely shook his bowed head as he leaned into the wind. He was afoot, leading both ponies across a treacherously boggy stretch of ground near the edge of a tiny loch. I glanced instinctively at my wrist, missing my Rolex.

It was difficult to tell where the sun was, with the in-rolling storm filling half the western sky, but the upper edge of the dark-tinged clouds glowed a brilliant white that was almost gold. I had lost the knack of telling time by sun and sky, but thought it was no more than midafternoon.

Lallybroch lay several hours ahead; I doubted we would reach by dark. Meaching my way reluctantly toward Craigh na Dun, had taken nearly two days to reach the small wood where Young Ian had caught up with me. He had, he said, spent only one day in the pursuit; he had known roughly where I was headed, and he himself had shod the pony I rode; my tracks had been plain to him where they showed in the mud-patches among the heather on the open moor.

Two days since I had left, and one—or more—on the journey back. Three days, then, since Jamie had been shot.

I could get few useful details from Young Ian; having succeeded in his mission, he wanted only to return to Lallybroch as fast as possible, and saw no point in further conversation. Jamie's gunshot wound was in the left arm, he said. That was good, so far as it went. The ball had penetrated into Jamie's side, as well. That wasn't good. Jamie was conscious when last seen—that was good—but was starting a fever. Not good at all. As to the possible effects of shock, the type or severity of the fever, or what treatment had so far been administered, Young Ian merely shrugged.

So perhaps Jamie was dying; perhaps he wasn't. It wasn't a chance I could take, as Jamie himself would know perfectly well. I wondered momentarily whether he might conceivably have shot himself, as a means of forcing me to return. Our last interview would have left him in little doubt as to my response had he come after me, or used force to make me return.

It was beginning to rain, in soft spatters that caught in my hair and lashes, blurring my sight like tears. Past the boggy spot, Young Ian had mounted again, leading the way upward to the final pass that led to Lallybroch.

Jamie was devious enough to have thought of such a plan, all right, and certainly courageous enough to have carried it out. On the other hand, I had never known him to be reckless. He had taken plenty of bold risks—marrying me being one of them, I thought ruefully—but never without an estimation of the cost, and a willingness to pay it. Would he have thought drawing me back to Lallybroch worth the chance of actually dying? That hardly seemed logical, and Jamie Fraser was a very logical man.

I pulled the hood of my cloak further over my head, to keep the increasing downpour out of my face. Young Ian's shoulders and thighs were dark with wet, and the rain dripped from the brim of his slouch hat, but he sat straight in the saddle, ignoring the weather with the stoic nonchalance of a trueborn Scot.

Very well. Given that Jamie likely hadn't shot himself, was he shot at all? He might have made up the story, and sent his nephew to tell it. On consideration, though, I thought it highly unlikely that

Young Ian could have delivered the news so convincingly, were it false.

I shrugged, the movement sending a cold rivulet down inside the front of my cloak, and set myself to wait with what patience I could for the journey to be ended. Years in the practice of medicine had taught me not to anticipate; the reality of each case was bound to be unique, and so must be my response to it. My emotions, however, were much harder to control than my professional reactions.

Each time I had left Lallybroch, I had thought I would never return. Now here I was, going back once more. Twice now, I had left Jamie, knowing with certainty that I would never see him again. And yet here I was, going back to him like a bloody homing pigeon to its loft.

"I'll tell you one thing, Jamie Fraser," I muttered under my breath. "If you aren't at death's door when I get there, you'll live to regret it!"

36

Practical and Applied Witchcraft

t was several hours past dark when we arrived at last, soaked to the skin. The house was silent, and dark, save for two dimly lighted windows downstairs in the parlor. There was a single arning bark from one of the dogs, but Young Ian shushed the imal, and after a quick, curious nosing at my stirrup, the black-d-white shape faded back into the darkness of the dooryard.

The warning had been enough to alert someone; as Young Ian d me into the hall, the door to the parlor opened. Jenny poked r head out, her face drawn with worry.

At the sight of Young Ian, she popped out into the hallway, her pression transformed to one of joyous relief, at once superseded the righteous anger of a mother confronted by an errant off-ring.

"Ian, ye wee wretch!" she said. "Where have ye been all this ne? Your da and I ha' been worrit sick for ye!" She paused long ough to look him over anxiously. "You're all right?"

At his nod, her lips grew tight again. "Aye, well. You're for it w, laddie, I'll tell ye! And just where the devil *have* ye been, yway?"

Gangling, knob-jointed, and dripping wet, Young Ian looked e nothing so much as a drowned scarecrow, but he was still ge enough to block me from his mother's view. He didn't an-er Jenny's scolding, but shrugged awkwardly and stepped aside, posing me to his mother's startled gaze.

If my resurrection from the dead had disconcerted her, this :ond reappearance stunned her. Her deep blue eyes, normally as

slanted as her brother's, opened so wide, they looked round. She
stared at me for a long moment, without saying anything, then her
gaze swiveled once more to her son.

"A cuckoo," she said, almost conversationally. "That's what
ye are, laddie—a great cuckoo in the nest. God knows whose son
ye were meant to be; it wasna mine."

Young Ian flushed hotly, dropping his eyes as the red burned in
his cheeks. He pushed the feathery damp hair out of his eyes with
the back of one hand.

"I—well, I just . . ." he began, eyes on his boots, "I couldna
just . . ."

"Oh, never mind about it now!" his mother snapped. "Get ye
upstairs to your bed; your da will deal wi' ye in the morning."

Ian glanced helplessly at the parlor door, then at me. He
shrugged once more, looked at the sodden hat in his hands as
though wondering how it had got there, and shuffled slowly down
the hall.

Jenny stood quite still, eyes fixed on me, until the padded door
at the end of the hallway closed with a soft thump behind Young
Ian. Her face showed lines of strain, and the shadows of sleeplessness smudged her eyes. Still fine-boned and erect, for once she
looked her age, and more.

"So you're back," she said flatly.

Seeing no point in answering the obvious, I nodded briefly. The
house was quiet around us, and full of shadows, the hallway
lighted only by a three-pronged candlestick set on the table.

"Never mind about it now," I said, softly, so as not to disturb
the house's slumber. There was, after all, only one thing of importance at the moment. "Where's Jamie?"

After a small hesitation, she nodded as well, accepting my presence for the moment. "In there," she said, waving toward the
parlor door.

I started toward the door, then paused. There was the one thing
more. "Where's Laoghaire?" I asked.

"Gone," she said. Her eyes were flat and dark in the candlelight, unreadable.

I nodded in response, and stepped through the door, closing
gently but firmly behind me.

Too long to be laid on the sofa, Jamie lay on a camp bed set up before the fire. Asleep or unconscious, his profile rose dark and sharp-edged against the light of the glowing coals, unmoving.

Whatever he was, he wasn't dead—at least not yet. My eyes growing accustomed to the dim light of the fire, I could see the slow rise and fall of his chest beneath nightshirt and quilt. A flask of water and a brandy bottle sat on the small table by the bed. The added chair by the fire had a shawl thrown over its back; Jenny had been sitting there, watching over her brother.

There seemed no need now for haste. I untied the strings at the neck of my cloak, and spread the soggy garment over the chairback, taking the shawl in substitute. My hands were cold; I put them under my arms, hugging myself, to bring them to something like a normal temperature before I touched him.

When I did venture to place a thawed hand on his forehead, I nearly jerked it back. He was hot as a just-fired pistol, and he twitched and moaned at my touch. Fever, indeed. I stood looking down at him for a moment, then carefully moved to the side of the bed and sat down in Jenny's chair. I didn't think he would sleep long, with a temperature like that, and it seemed a shame to wake him needlessly soon, merely to examine him.

The cloak behind me dripped water on the floor, a slow, arrhythmic patting. It reminded me unpleasantly of an old Highland superstition—the "death-drop." Just before a death occurs, the story goes, the sound of water dripping is heard in the house, by those sensitive to such things.

I wasn't, thank heaven, subject to noticing supernatural phenomena of that sort. No, I thought wryly, it takes something like a crack through time to get *your* attention. The thought made me smile, if only briefly, and dispelled the frisson I had felt at the thought of the death-drop.

As the rain chill left me, though, I still felt uneasy, and for obvious reasons. It wasn't that long ago that I had stood by another makeshift bed, deep in the night-watches, and contemplated death, and the waste of a marriage. The thoughts I had begun in the wood hadn't stopped on the hasty journey back to Lallybroch, and they continued now, without my conscious volition.

Honor had led Frank to his decision—to keep me as his wife, and raise Brianna as his own. Honor, and an unwillingness to decline a responsibility he felt was his. Well, here before me lay another honorable man.

Laoghaire and her daughters, Jenny and her family, the Scots prisoners, the smugglers, Mr. Willoughby and Geordie, Fergus and the tenants—how many other responsibilities had Jamie shouldered, through our years apart?

Frank's death had absolved me of one of my own obligations Brianna herself of another. The Hospital Board, in their eternal wisdom, had severed the single great remaining tie that bound me to that life. I had had time, with Joe Abernathy's help, to relieve myself of the smaller responsibilities, to depute and delegate divest and resolve.

Jamie had had neither warning nor choice about my reappearance in his life; no time to make decisions or resolve conflicts And he was not one to abandon his responsibilities, even for the sake of love.

Yes, he'd lied to me. Hadn't trusted me to recognize his responsibilities, to stand by him—or to leave him—as his circumstances demanded. He'd been afraid. So had I; afraid that he wouldn' choose me, confronted with the struggle between a twenty-year old love and a present-day family. So I'd run away.

"Who you jiving, L.J.?" I heard Joe Abernathy's voice say derisive and affectionate. I had fled toward Craigh na Dun with al the speed and decision of a condemned felon approaching the steps of the gallows. Nothing had slowed my journey but the hope that Jamie would come after me.

True, the pangs of conscience and wounded pride had spurred me on, but the one moment when Young Ian had said, "He' dying," had shown those up for the flimsy things they were.

My marriage to Jamie had been for me like the turning of a great key, each small turn setting in play the intricate fall of tumblers within me. Bree had been able to turn that key as well edging closer to the unlocking of the door of myself. But the fina turn of the lock was frozen—until I had walked into the printshop in Edinburgh, and the mechanism had sprung free with a final decisive click. The door now was ajar, the light of an unknown future shining through its crack. But it would take more strength than I had alone to push it open.

I watched the rise and fall of his breath, and the play of light and shadow on the strong, clean lines of his face, and knew that nothing truly mattered between us but the fact that we both still lived

o here I was. Again. And whatever the cost of it might be to him
r me, here I stayed.

I didn't realize that his eyes had opened until he spoke.

"Ye came back, then," he said softly. "I knew ye would."

I opened my mouth to reply, but he was still talking, eyes fixed
n my face, pupils dilated to pools of darkness.

"My love," he said, almost whispering. "God, ye do look so
vely, wi' your great eyes all gold, and your hair so soft round
ur face." He brushed his tongue across dry lips. "I knew ye
ust forgive me, Sassenach, once ye knew."

Once I knew? My brows shot up, but I didn't speak; he had
ore to say.

"I was so afraid to lose ye again, *mo chridhe*," he murmured.
So afraid. I havena loved anyone but you, my Sassenach, never
nce the day I saw ye—but I couldna . . . I couldna bear . . ."
s voice drifted off in an unintelligible mumble, and his eyes
osed again, lashes lying dark against the high curve of his cheek.

I sat still, wondering what I should do. As I watched, his eyes
ened suddenly once again. Heavy and drowsy with fever, they
ught my face.

"It willna be long, Sassenach," he said, as though reassuring
e. One corner of his mouth twitched in an attempt at a smile.
Not long. Then I shall touch ye once more. I do long to touch
u."

"Oh, Jamie," I said. Moved by tenderness, I reached out and
d my hand along his burning cheek.

His eyes snapped wide with shock, and he jerked bolt upright in
d, letting out a bloodcurdling yell of anguish as the movement
red his wounded arm.

"Oh God, oh Christ, oh Jesus Lord God Almighty!" he said,
nt half-breathless and clutching at his left arm. "You're real!
oody stinking filthy pig-swiving hell! Oh, Christ!"

"Are you all right?" I said, rather inanely. I could hear startled
clamations from the floor above, muffled by the thick planks,
d the thump of feet as one after another of Lallybroch's inhabit-
ts leapt from their beds to investigate the uproar.

Jenny's head, eyes even wider than before, poked through the
rlor door. Jamie saw her, and somehow found sufficient breath
roar "Get *out*!" before doubling up again with an agonized
an.

"Je-sus," he said between clenched teeth. "What in God's ho
name are ye doing here, Sassenach?"

"What do you mean, what am I doing here?" I said. "You se
for me. And what do you mean, I'm real?"

He unclenched his jaw and tentatively loosened his grip on h
left arm. The resultant sensation proving unsatisfactory, h
promptly grabbed it again and said several things in French in
volving the reproductive organs of assorted saints and animals.

"For God's sake, lie down!" I said. I took him by the shoulde
and eased him back onto the pillows, noting with some alarm ho
close his bones were to the surface of his heated skin.

"I thought ye were a fever dream, 'til you touched me," h
said, gasping. "What the hell d'ye mean, popping up by my be
and scarin' me to death?" He grimaced in pain. "Christ, it fee
like my damn arm's come off at the shoulder. Och, bugger it!" H
exclaimed, as I firmly detached the fingers of his right hand fro
his left arm.

"Didn't you send Young Ian to tell me you were dying?" I sai
deftly rolling back the sleeve of his nightshirt. The arm was wour
in a huge bandage above the elbow, and I groped for the end of th
linen strip.

"Me? No! Ow, that hurts!"

"It'll hurt worse before I'm through with you," I said, carefull
unwrapping. "You mean the little bastard came after me on h
own? You didn't *want* me to come back?"

"Want ye back? No! Want ye to come back to me for nothi
but pity, the same as ye might show for a dog in a ditch? Bloo
hell! No! I forbade the little bugger to go after ye!" He scowl
furiously at me, ruddy brows knitting together.

"I'm a doctor," I said coldly, "not a veterinarian. And if y
didn't want me back, what was all that you were saying before y
realized I was real, hm? Bite the blanket or something; the end
stuck, and I'm going to pull it loose."

He bit his lip instead, and made no noise but a swift intake of a
through his nose. It was impossible to judge his color in th
firelight, but his eyes closed briefly, and small beads of swe
popped out on his forehead.

I turned away for a moment, groping in the drawer of Jenny
desk where the extra candles were kept. I needed more light befo
I did anything.

"I suppose Young Ian told me you were dying just to get me
ack here. He must have thought I wouldn't come otherwise."
he candles were there; fine beeswax, from the Lallybroch hives.

"For what it's worth, I am dying." His voice came from behind
ae, dry and blunt, despite his breathlessness.

I turned back to him in some surprise. His eyes rested on my
ace quite calmly, now that the pain in his arm had lessened a bit,
ut his breath was still coming unevenly, and his eyes were heavy
nd bright with fever. I didn't respond at once, but lit the candles I
ad found, placing them in the big candelabra that usually deco-
ited the sideboard, unused save for great occasions. The flames
f five additional candles brightened the room as though in prepa-
ition for a party. I bent over the bed, noncommital.

"Let's have a look at it."

The wound itself was a ragged dark hole, scabbed at the edges
ad faintly blue-tinged. I pressed the flesh on either side of the
ound; it was red and angry-looking, and there was a considerable
epage of pus. Jamie stirred uneasily as I drew my fingertips
:ntly but firmly down the length of the muscle.

"You have the makings of a very fine little infection there, my
d," I said. "Young Ian said it went into your side; a second shot,
  did it go through your arm?"

"It went through. Jenny dug the ball out of my side. That wasna
• bad, though. Just an inch or so in." He spoke in brief spurts,
as tightening involuntarily between sentences.

"Let me see where it went through."

Moving very slowly, he turned his hand to the outside, letting
e arm fall away from his side. I could see that even that small
ovement was intensely painful. The exit wound was just above
e elbow joint, on the inside of the upper arm. Not directly oppo-
te the entrance wound, though; the ball had been deflected in its
issage.

"Hit the bone," I said, trying not to imagine what that must
ive felt like. "Do you know if the bone's broken? I don't want to
•ke you more than I need to."

"Thanks for small mercies," he said, with an attempt at a
aile. The muscles of his face trembled, though, and went slack
th exhaustion.

"No, I think it's not broken," he said. "I've broken my collarbone and my hand before, and it's no like that, though it hurts a bit."

"I expect it does." I felt my way carefully up the swell of his biceps, testing for tenderness. "How far up does the pain go?"

He glanced at his wounded arm, almost casually. "Feels like I've a hot poker in my arm, not a bone. But it's no just the arm pains me now; my whole side's gone stiff and sore." He swallowed, licking his lips again. "Will ye give me a taste of the brandy?" he asked. "It hurts to feel my heart beating," he added apologetically.

Without comment, I poured a cup of water from the flask on the table, and held it to his lips. He raised one brow, but drank thirstily, then let his head fall back against the pillow. He breathed deeply for a moment, eyes closed, then opened them and looked directly at me.

"I've had two fevers in my life that near killed me," he said. "I think this one likely will. I wouldna send for ye, but . . . I'm glad you're here." He swallowed once, then went on. "I . . . wanted to say to ye that I'm sorry. And to bid ye a proper farewell. I wouldna ask ye to stay 'til the end, but . . . would ye . . . would ye stay wi' me—just for a bit?"

His right hand was pressed flat against the mattress, steadying him. I could see that he was fighting hard to keep any note of pleading from his voice or eyes, to make it a simple request, one that could be refused.

I sat down on the bed beside him, careful not to jar him. The firelight glowed on one side of his face, sparking the red-gold stubble of his beard, picking up the small flickers of silver here and there, leaving the other side masked in shadow. He met my eyes, not blinking. I hoped the yearning that showed in his face was not quite so apparent on my own.

I reached out and ran a hand gently down the side of his face, feeling the soft scratchiness of beard stubble.

"I'll stay for a bit," I said. "But you're not going to die."

He raised one eyebrow. "You brought me through one bad fever, using what I still think was witchcraft. And Jenny got me through the next, wi' naught but plain stubbornness. I suppose wi' the both of ye here, ye might just manage it, but I'm no at all sure I want to go through such an ordeal again. I think I'd rather just die and ha' done with it, if it's all the same to you."

"Ingrate," I said. "Coward." Torn between exasperation and tenderness, I patted his cheek and stood up, groping in the deep pocket of my skirt. There was one item I had carried on my person at all times, not trusting it to the vagaries of travel.

I laid the small, flat case on the table and flipped the latch. "I'm not going to let you die this time either," I informed him, "greatly as I may be tempted." I carefully extracted the roll of gray flannel and laid it on the table with a soft clinking noise. I unrolled the flannel, displaying the gleaming row of syringes, and rummaged in the box for the small bottle of penicillin tablets.

"What in God's name are those?" Jamie asked, eyeing the syringes with interest. "They look wicked sharp."

I didn't answer, occupied in dissolving the penicillin tablets in a vial of sterile water. I selected a glass barrel, fitted a needle, and pressed the tip through the rubber covering the mouth of the bottle. Holding it up to the light, I pulled back slowly on the plunger, watching the thick white liquid fill the barrel, checking for bubbles. Then pulling the needle free, I depressed the plunger tightly until a drop of liquid pearled from the point and rolled slowly down the length of the spike.

"Roll onto your good side," I said, turning to Jamie, "and pull up your shirt."

He eyed the needle in my hand with keen suspicion, but reluctantly obeyed. I surveyed the terrain with approval.

"Your bottom hasn't changed a bit in twenty years," I remarked, admiring the muscular curves.

"Neither has yours," he replied courteously, "but I'm no inviting you expose it. Are ye suffering a sudden attack of lustfulness?"

"Not just at present," I said evenly, swabbing a patch of skin with a cloth soaked in brandy.

"That's a verra nice make of brandy," he said, peering back over his shoulder, "but I'm more accustomed to apply it at the other end."

"It's also the best source of alcohol available. Hold still now, relax." I jabbed deftly and pressed the plunger slowly in.

"Ouch!" Jamie rubbed his posterior resentfully.

"It'll stop stinging in a minute." I poured an inch of brandy into the cup. "Now you can have a bit to drink—a very little bit."

He drained the cup without comment, watching me roll up the

collection of syringes. Finally he said, "I thought ye stuck pins ill-wish dolls when ye meant to witch someone; not in the peop themselves."

"It's not a pin, it's a hypodermic syringe."

"I dinna care what ye call it; it felt like a bloody horseshoe na Would ye care to tell me why jabbing pins in my arse is going help my arm?"

I took a deep breath. "Well, do you remember my once tellin you about germs?"

He looked quite blank.

"Little beasts too small to see," I elaborated. "They can g into your body through bad food or water, or through op wounds, and if they do, they can make you ill."

He stared at his arm with interest. "I've germs in my arm, ha I?"

"You very definitely have." I tapped a finger on the small fl box. "The medicine I just shot into your backside kills germ though. You get another shot every four hours 'til this time tomo row, and then we'll see how you're doing."

I paused. Jamie was staring at me, shaking his head.

"Do you understand?" I asked. He nodded slowly.

"Aye, I do. I should ha' let them burn ye, twenty years ago

After giving him a shot and settling him comfortably, I sat
watching until he fell asleep again, allowing him to hold
my hand until his own grip relaxed in sleep and the big
and dropped slack by his side.

I sat by his bed for the rest of the night, dozing sometimes, and
using myself by means of the internal clock all doctors have,
ared to the rhythms of a hospital's shift changes. Two more
ots, the last at daybreak, and by then the fever had loosed its
ld perceptibly. He was still very warm to the touch, but his flesh
 longer burned, and he rested easier, falling asleep after the last
ot with no more than a few grumbles and a faint moan as his
m twinged.

"Bloody eighteenth-century germs are no match for penicil-
," I told his sleeping form. "No resistance. Even if you had
philis, I'd have it cleaned up in no time."

And what then? I wondered, as I staggered off to the kitchen in
arch of hot tea and food. A strange woman, presumably the cook
 the housemaid, was firing up the brick oven, ready to receive
 daily loaves that lay rising in their pans on the table. She didn't
em surprised to see me, but cleared away a small space for me to
 down, and brought me tea and fresh girdle-cakes with no more
an a quick "Good mornin' to ye, mum" before returning to her
rk.

Evidently, Jenny had informed the household of my presence.
d that mean she accepted it herself? I doubted it. Clearly, she
 wanted me to go, and wasn't best pleased to have me back. If I

was going to stay, there was plainly going to be a certain amoun of explanation about Laoghaire, from both Jenny and Jamie. And was going to stay.

"Thank you," I said politely to the cook, and taking a fresh cur of tea with me, went back to the parlor to wait until Jamie saw fr to wake up again.

People passed by the door during the morning, pausing now and then to peep through, but always went on hurriedly when I looked up. At last, Jamie showed signs of waking, just before noon; he stirred, sighed, groaned as the movement jarred his arm, and sub sided once more.

I gave him a few moments to realize that I was there, but hi eyes stayed shut. He wasn't asleep, though; the lines of his body were slightly tensed, not relaxed in slumber. I had watched hin sleep all night; I knew the difference.

"All right," I said. I leaned back in the chair, settling mysel comfortably, well out of his reach. "Let's hear it, then."

A small slit of blue showed under the long auburn lashes, the disappeared again.

"Mmmm?" he said, pretending to wake slowly. The lashe fluttered against his cheeks.

"Don't stall," I said crisply. "I know perfectly well you'r awake. Open your eyes and tell me about Laoghaire."

The blue eyes opened and rested on me with an expression c some disfavor.

"You're no afraid of giving me a relapse?" he inquired. "I'v always heard sick folk shouldna be troubled owermuch. It se them back."

"You have a doctor right here," I assured him. "If you pass o from the strain, I'll know what to do about it."

"That's what I'm afraid of." His narrowed gaze flicked to th little case of drugs and hypodermics on the table, then back to m "My arse feels like I've sat in a gorse bush wi' no breeks on.'

"Good," I said pleasantly. "You'll get another one in an hou Right now, you're going to talk."

His lips pressed tight together, but then relaxed as he sighed. I pushed himself laboriously upright against the pillows, on handed. I didn't help him.

"All right," he said at last. He didn't look at me, but down the quilt, where his finger traced the edge of the starred design

"Well, it was when I'd come back from England."

He had come up from the Lake District and over the Carter's ‍ar, that great ridge of high ground that divides England from ‍cotland, on whose broad back the ancient courts and markets of ‍e Borders had been held.

"There's a stone there to mark the border, maybe you'll know; ‍ looks the sort of stone to last awhile." He glanced at me, ‍ ‍estioning, and I nodded. I did know it; a huge menhir, some ten ‍et tall. In my time, someone had carved on its one face ENGLAND, ‍ ‍d on the other, SCOTLAND.

There he stopped to rest, as thousands of travelers had stopped ‍er the years, his exiled past behind him, the future—and home ‍below and beyond, past the hazy green hollows of the Low- ‍nds, up into the gray crags of the Highlands, hidden by fog.

His good hand ran back and forth through his hair, as it always ‍d when he thought, leaving the cowlicks on top standing up in ‍all, bright whorls.

"You'll not know how it is, to live among strangers for so ‍ng."

"Won't I?" I said, with some sharpness. He glanced up at me, ‍artled, then smiled faintly, looking down at the coverlet.

"Aye, maybe ye will," he said. "Ye change, no? Much as ye ‍ant to keep the memories of home, and who ye are—you're ‍anged. Not one of the strangers; ye could never be that, even if ‍ wanted to. But different from who ye were, too."

I thought of myself, standing silent beside Frank, a bit of flot- ‍m in the eddies of university parties, pushing a pram through the ‍lly parks of Boston, playing bridge and talking with other wives ‍d mothers, speaking the foreign language of middle-class do- ‍sticity. Strangers indeed.

"Yes," I said. "I know. Get on."

He sighed, rubbing his nose with a forefinger. "So I came ‍ck," he said. He looked up, a smile hidden in the corner of his ‍uth. "What is it ye told wee Ian? 'Home is the place where, ‍en ye have to go there, they have to take ye in'?"

"That's it," I said. "It's a quotation from a poet called Frost. ‍t what do you mean? Surely your family was glad to see you!"

He frowned, fingering the quilt. "Aye, they were," he said ‍wly. "It's not that—I dinna mean they made me feel unwel- ‍me, not at all. But I had been away so long—Michael and wee

Janet and Ian didna even remember me.'' He smiled ruefully
''They'd heard about me, though. When I came into the kitchen
they'd squash back against the walls and stare at me, wi' their eye
gone round.''

He leaned forward a little, intent on making me understand.

''See, it was different, when I hid in the cave. I wasna in the
house, and they seldom saw me, but I was always *here,* I wa
always part of them. I hunted for them; I kent when they were
hungry, or cold, or when the goats were ill or the kail crop poor, o
a new draft under the kitchen door.

''Then I went to prison,'' he said abruptly. ''And to England.
wrote to them—and they to me—but it canna be the same, to see a
few black words on the paper, telling things that happened month
before.

''And when I came back—'' He shrugged, wincing as the
movement jarred his arm. ''It was different. Ian would ask me
what I thought of fencing in auld Kirby's pasture, but I'd know
he'd already set Young Jamie to do it. I'd walk through the fields
and folk would squint at me, suspicious, thinking me a stranger
Then their eyes would go big as they'd seen a ghost, when they
knew me.''

He stopped, looking out at the window, where the brambles o
his mother's rose beat against the glass as the wind changed. ''
was a ghost, I think.'' He glanced at me shyly. ''If ye ken what
mean.''

''Maybe,'' I said. Rain was streaking the glass, with drops th
same gray as the sky outside.

''You feel like your ties to the earth are broken,'' I said softly
''Floating through rooms without feeling your footsteps. Hearing
people speak to you, and not making sense of it. I remember tha
—before Bree was born.'' But I had had one tie then; I had her, t
anchor me to life.

He nodded, not looking at me, and then was quiet for a minute
The peat fire hissed on the hearth behind me, smelling of th
Highlands, and the rich scent of cock-a-leekie and baking brea
spread through the house, warm and comforting as a blanket.

''I was here,'' he said softly, ''but not home.''

I could feel the pull of it around me—the house, the family, th
place itself. I, who couldn't remember a childhood home, felt th
urge to sit down here and stay forever, enmeshed in the thousan

ands of daily life, bound securely to this bit of earth. What
uld it have meant to him, who had lived all his life in the
ength of that bond, endured his exile in the hope of coming
ck to it, and then arrived to find himself still rootless?

"And I suppose I was lonely," he said quietly. He lay still on
: pillow, eyes closed.

"I suppose you were," I said, careful to let no tone either of
mpathy or condemnation show. I knew something of loneliness,
.

He opened his eyes then, and met my gaze with a naked hon-
y. "Aye, there was that too," he said. "Not the main thing, no
but aye, that too."

Jenny had tried, with varying degrees of gentleness and insis-
ice, to persuade him to marry again. She had tried intermittently
ce the days after Culloden, presenting first one and then another
·sonable young widow, this and that sweet-tempered virgin, all
no avail. Now, bereft of the feelings that had sustained him so
, desperately seeking some sense of connection—he had lis-
ed.

"Laoghaire was married to Hugh MacKenzie, one of Colum's
ksmen," he said, eyes closed once more. "Hugh was ki..ed at
lloden, though, and two years later, Laoghaire married Simon
cKimmie of clan Fraser. The two lassies—Marsali and Joan—
y're his. The English arrested him a few years later, and took
n to prison in Edinburgh." He opened his eyes, looking up at
: dark ceiling beams overhead. "He had a good house, and
·perty worth seizing. That was enough to make a Highland man
·aitor, then, whether he'd fought for the Stuarts openly or not."
s voice was growing hoarse, and he stopped to clear his throat.

"Simon wasn't as lucky as I was. He died in prison, before they
ild bring him to trial. The Crown tried for some time to take the
ate, but Ned Gowan went to Edinburgh, and spoke for
oghaire, and he managed to save the main house and a little
ney, claiming it was her dower right."

'Ned Gowan?" I spoke with mingled surprise and pleasure.
[e can't still be alive, surely?" It was Ned Gowan, a small and
erly solicitor who advised the MacKenzie clan on legal matters,
o had saved me from being burned as a witch, twenty years
·ore. I had thought him quite ancient then.

Jamie smiled, seeing my pleasure. ''Oh, aye. I expect they'
have to knock him on the head wi' an ax to kill him. He looks ju
the same as he always did, though he must be past seventy now.

''Does he still live at Castle Leoch?''

He nodded, reaching to the table for the tumbler of water. H
drank awkwardly, right-handed, and set it back.

''What's left of it. Aye, though he's traveled a great deal thes
last years, appealing treason cases and filing lawsuits to recove
property.'' Jamie's smile had a bitter edge. ''There's a sayin
aye? 'After a war, first come the corbies to eat the flesh; and the
the lawyers, to pick the bones.' ''

His right hand went to his left shoulder, massaging it uncon
sciously.

''No, he's a good man, is Ned, in spite of his profession. H
goes back and forth to Inverness, to Edinburgh—sometimes eve
to London or Paris. And he stops here from time to time, to brea
his journey.''

It was Ned Gowan who had mentioned Laoghaire to Jenn
returning from Balriggan to Edinburgh. Pricking up her ear
Jenny had inquired for further details, and finding these satisfa
tory, had at once sent an invitation to Balriggan, for Laoghaire ar
her two daughters to come to Lallybroch for Hogmanay, whi
was near.

*The house was bright that night, with candles lit in the
windows, and bunches of holly and ivy fixed to the staircase
and the doorposts. There were not so many pipers in the
Highlands as there had been before Culloden, but one had
been found, and a fiddler as well, and music floated up the
stairwell, mixed with the heady scent of rum punch, plum
cake, almond squirts, and Savoy biscuits.*

*Jamie had come down late and hesitant. Many people here
he had not seen in nearly ten years, and he was not eager to
see them now, feeling changed and distant as he did. But
Jenny had made him a new shirt, brushed and mended his
coat, and combed his hair smooth and plaited it for him
before going downstairs to see to the cooking. He had no
excuse to linger, and at last had come down, into the noise
and swirl of the gathering.*

"Mister Fraser!" Peggy Gibbons was the first to see him; she hurried across the room, face glowing, and threw her arms about him, quite unabashed. Taken by surprise, he hugged her back, and within moments was surrounded by a small crowd of women, exclaiming over him, holding up small children born since his departure, kissing his cheeks and patting his hands.

The men were shyer, greeting him with a gruff word of welcome or a slap on the back as he made his way slowly through the rooms, until, qu:te overwhelmed, he had escaped temporarily into the laird's study.

Once his father's room, and then his own, it now belonged to his brother-in-law, who had run Lallybroch through the years of his absence. The ledgers and stockbooks and accounts were all lined up neatly on the edge of the battered desk; he ran a finger along the leather spines, feeling a sense of comfort at the touch. It was all in here; the planting and the harvests, the careful purchases and acquisitions, the slow accumulations and dispersals that were the rhythm of life to the tenants of Lallybroch.

On the small bookshelf, he found his wooden snake. Along with everything else of value, he had left it behind when he went to prison. A small icon carved of cherrywood, it had been the gift of his elder brother, dead in childhood. He was sitting in the chair behind the desk, stroking the snake's well-worn curves, when the door of the study opened.

"Jamie?" she had said, hanging shyly back. He had not bothered to light a lamp in the study; she was silhouetted by the candles burning in the hall. She wore her pale hair loose, like a maid, and the light shone through it, haloing her unseen face.

"You'll remember me, maybe?" she had said, tentative, reluctant to come into the room without invitation.

"Aye," he said, after a pause. *"Aye, of course I do."*

"The music's starting," she said. It was; he could hear the whine of the fiddle and the stamp of feet from the front parlor, along with an occasional shout of merriment. It showed signs of being a good party already; most of the guests would be asleep on the floor come morning.

"Your sister says you're a bonny dancer," she said, still shy, but determined.

"It will ha' been some time since I tried," he said, feeling shy himself, and painfully awkward, though the fiddle music ached in his bones and his feet twitched at the sound of it.

"It's 'Tha mo Leabaidh 'san Fhraoch'—'In the Heather's my Bed'—you'll ken that one. Will ye come and try wi' me?" She had held out a hand to him, small and graceful in the half-dark. And he had risen, clasped her outstretched hand in his own, and taken his first steps in pursuit of himself.

"It was in here," he said, waving his good hand at the room where we sat. "Jenny had had the furniture cleared away, all but one table wi' the food and the whisky, and the fiddler stood by the window there, wi' a new moon over his shoulder." He nodded at the window, where the rose vine trembled. Something of the light of that Hogmanay feast lingered on his face, and I felt a small pang, seeing it.

"We danced all that night, sometimes wi' others, but mostly with each other. And at the dawn, when those still awake went to the end o' the house to see what omens the New Year might bring, the two of us went, too. The single women took it in turns to spin about, and walk through the door wi' their eyes closed, then spin again and open their eyes to see what the first thing they might see would be—for that tells them about the man they'll marry, ye ken."

There had been a lot of laughter, as the guests, heated by whisky and dancing, pushed and shoved at the door. Laoghaire had held back, flushed and laughing, saying it was a game for young girls and not for a matron of thirty-four, but the others had insisted, and try she had. Spun three times clockwise and opened the door, stepped out into the cold dawnlight and spun again. And when she opened her eyes, they had rested on Jamie's face, wide with expectation.

"So . . . there she was, a widow wi' two bairns. She needed a man, that was plain enough. I needed . . . something." He gazed into the fire, where the low flame glimmered through the red mass of the peat; heat without much light. "I supposed that we might help each other."

They had married quietly at Balriggan, and he had moved his

v possessions there. Less than a year later, he had moved out
ain, and gone to Edinburgh.

"What on earth happened?" I asked, more than curious.

He looked up at me, helpless.

"I canna say. It wasna that anything was wrong, exactly—only
t nothing was right." He rubbed a hand tiredly between his
ws. "It was me, I think; my fault. I always disappointed her
nehow. We'd sit down to supper and all of a sudden the tears
uld well up in her eyes, and she'd leave the table sobbing, and
 sitting there wi' not a notion what I'd done or said wrong."

His fist clenched on the coverlet, then relaxed. "God, I *never*
ew what to do for her, or what to say! Anything I said just made
worse, and there would be days—nay, weeks!—when she'd not
ak to me, but only turn away when I came near her, and stand
ring out the window until I went away again."

His fingers went to the parallel scratches down the side of his
ck. They were nearly healed now, but the marks of my nails still
owed on his fair skin. He looked at me wryly.

"You never did that to me, Sassenach."

"Not my style," I agreed, smiling faintly. "If I'm mad at you,
u'll bloody know why, at least."

He snorted briefly and lay back on his pillows. Neither of us
ke for a bit. Then he said, staring up at the ceiling, "I thought I
na want to hear anything about what it was like—wi' Frank, I
an. I was maybe wrong about that."

"I'll tell you anything you want to know," I said. "But not just
w. It's still your turn."

He sighed and closed his eyes.

"She was afraid of me," he said softly, a minute later. "I tried
be gentle wi' her—God, I tried again and again, everything I
ew to please a woman. But it was no use."

His head turned restlessly, making a hollow in the feather pil-
.

"Maybe it was Hugh, or maybe Simon. I kent them both, and
y were good men, but there's no telling what goes on in a
rriage bed. Maybe it was bearing the children; not all women
 stand it. But something hurt her, sometime, and I couldna heal
or all my trying. She shrank away when I touched her, and I
ld see the sickness and the fear in her eyes." There were lines

of sorrow around his own closed eyes, and I reached impulsive
for his hand.

He squeezed it gently and opened his eyes. "That's why I le
finally," he said softly. "I couldna bear it anymore."

I didn't say anything, but went on holding his hand, putting
finger on his pulse to check it. His heartbeat was reassuringly sl
and steady.

He shifted slightly in the bed, moving his shoulders and maki
a grimace of discomfort as he did so.

"Arm hurt a lot?" I asked.

"A bit."

I bent over him, feeling his brow. He was very warm, but r
feverish. There was a line between the thick ruddy brows, and
smoothed it with a knuckle.

"Head ache?"

"Yes."

"I'll go and make you some willow-bark tea." I made to ri
but his hand on my arm stopped me.

"I dinna need tea," he said. "It would ease me, though,
maybe I could lay my head in your lap, and have ye rub
temples a bit?" Blue eyes looked up at me, limpid as a spring sl

"You don't fool me a bit, Jamie Fraser," I said. "I'm not goi
to forget about your next shot." Nonetheless, I was already mo
ing the chair out of the way, and sitting down beside him on
bed.

He made a small grunting sound of content as I moved his he
into my lap and began to stroke it, rubbing his temples, smoothi
back the thick wavy mass of his hair. The back of his neck w
damp; I lifted the hair away and blew softly on it, seeing
smooth fair skin prickle into gooseflesh at the nape of his nec

"Oh, that feels good," he murmured. Despite my resolve not
touch him beyond the demands of caretaking until everythi
between us was resolved, I found my hands molding themselves
the clean, bold lines of his neck and shoulders, seeking the ha
knobs of his vertebrae and the broad, flat planes of his shoul
blades.

He was firm and solid under my hands, his breath a warm care
on my thigh, and it was with some reluctance that I at last eas
him back onto the pillow and reached for the ampule of penicill

"All right," I said, turning back the sheet and reaching for t

m of his shirt. "A quick stick, and you'll—" My hand brushed
er the front of his nightshirt, and I broke off, startled.

"Jamie!" I said, amused. "You can't possibly!"

"I dinna suppose I can," he agreed comfortably. He curled up
his side like a shrimp, his lashes dark against his cheek. "But a
n can dream, no?"

I didn't go upstairs to bed that night, either. We didn't talk
ıch, just lay close together in the narrow bed, scarcely moving,
as not to jar his injured arm. The rest of the house was quiet,
eryone safely in bed, and there was no sound but the hissing of
e fire, the sigh of the wind, and the scratch of Ellen's rosebush at
e window, insistent as the demands of love.

"Do ye know?" he said softly, somewhere in the black, small
ırs of the night. "Do ye know what it's like to be with someone
ıt way? To try all ye can, and seem never to have the secret of
m?"

"Yes," I said, thinking of Frank. "Yes, I do know."

"I thought perhaps ye did." He was quiet for a moment, and
en his hand touched my hair lightly, a shadowy blur in the
elight.

"And then . . ." he whispered, "then to have it back again,
ıt knowing. To be free in all ye say or do, and know that it is
ht."

"To say 'I love you,' and mean it with all your heart," I said
tly to the dark.

"Aye," he answered, barely audible. "To say that."

His hand rested on my hair, and without knowing quite how it
ppened, I found myself curled against him, my head just fitting
the hollow of his shoulder.

"For so many years," he said, "for so long, I have been so
ny things, so many different men." I felt him swallow, and he
fted slightly, the linen of his nightshirt rustling with starch.

"I was 'Uncle' to Jenny's children, and 'Brother' to her and
. 'Milord' to Fergus, and 'Sir' to my tenants. 'Mac Dubh' to the
n of Ardsmuir and 'MacKenzie' to the other servants at
lwater. 'Malcolm the printer,' then, and 'Jamie Roy' at the
cks." The hand stroked my hair, slowly, with a whispering
ınd like the wind outside. "But here," he said, so softly I could

barely hear him, "here in the dark, with you . . . I have n
name."

I lifted my face toward his, and took the warm breath of hi
between my own lips.

"I love you," I said, and did not need to tell him how I meant i

38

I Meet a Lawyer

A s I had predicted, eighteenth-century germs were no match
for a modern antibiotic. Jamie's fever had virtually disappeared within twenty-four hours, and within the next two
ys the inflammation in his arm began to subside as well, leaving
 more than a reddening about the wound itself and a very slight
 zing of pus when pressed.

On the fourth day, after satisfying myself that he was mending
cely, I dressed the wound lightly with coneflower salve, banged it again, and left to dress and make my own toilet upstairs.
Ian, Janet, Young Ian, and the servants had all put their heads in
intervals over the last few days, to see how Jamie progressed.
nny had been conspicuously absent from these inquiries, but I
ew that she was still entirely aware of everything that happened
her house. I hadn't announced my intention of coming upstairs,
t when I opened the door to my bedroom, there was a large
cher of hot water standing by the ewer, gently steaming, and a
sh cake of soap laid alongside it.

I picked it up and sniffed. Fine-milled French soap, perfumed
th lily of the valley, it was a delicate comment on my status in
 household—honored guest, to be sure; but not one of the
nily, who would all make do as a matter of course with the
ual coarse soap made of tallow and lye.

"Right," I muttered. "Well, we'll see, won't we?" and lathered
 cloth for washing.

As I was arranging my hair in the glass a half-hour later, I heard
 sounds below of someone arriving. Several someones, in fact,

from the sounds of it. I came down the stairs to find a small mob of children in residence, streaming in and out of the kitchen and front parlor, with here and there a strange adult visible in the midst of them, who stared curiously at me as I came down the stairs.

Entering the parlor, I found the camp bed put away and Jamie shaved and in a fresh nightshirt, neatly propped up on the sofa under a quilt with his left arm in a sling, surrounded by four or five children. These were shepherded by Janet, Young Ian, and a smiling young man who was a Fraser of sorts by the shape of his nose but otherwise bore only the faintest resemblances to the tiny boy I had seen last at Lallybroch twenty years before.

"There she is!" Jamie exclaimed with pleasure at my appearance, and the entire roomful of people turned to look at me, with expressions ranging from pleasant greeting to gape-mouthed awe.

"You'll remember Young Jamie?" the elder Jamie said, nodding to the tall, broad-shouldered young man with curly black hair and a squirming bundle in his arms.

"I remember the curls," I said, smiling. "The rest has changed a bit."

Young Jamie grinned down at me. "I remember ye well, Auntie," he said, in a deep-brown voice like well-aged ale. "Ye held me on your knee and played Ten Wee Piggies wi' my toes."

"I can't possibly have," I said, looking up at him in some dismay. While it seemed to be true that people really didn't change markedly in appearance between their twenties and their forties, they most assuredly did so between four and twenty-four.

"Perhaps ye can have a go wi' wee Benjamin here," Young Jamie suggested with a smile. "Maybe the knack of it will come back to ye." He bent and carefully laid his bundle in my arms.

A very round face looked up at me with that air of befuddlement so common to new babies. Benjamin appeared mildly confused at having me suddenly exchanged for his father, but didn't object. Instead, he opened his small pink mouth very wide, inserted his fist and began to gnaw on it in a thoughtful manner.

A small blond boy in homespun breeks leaned on Jamie's knee, staring up at me in wonder. "Who's that, Nunkie?" he asked in loud whisper.

"That's your great-auntie Claire," Jamie said gravely. "Ye have heard about her, I expect?"

"Oh, aye," the little boy said, nodding madly. "Is she as old as rannie?"

"Even older," Jamie said, nodding back solemnly. The lad wked up at me for a moment, then turned back to Jamie, face rewed up in scorn.

"Get on wi' ye, Nunkie! She doesna look anything like as old Grannie! Why, there's scarce a bit o' silver in her hair!"

"Thank you, child," I said, beaming at him.

"Are ye sure that's our great-auntie Claire?" the boy went on, oking doubtfully at me. "Mam says Great-Auntie Claire was aybe a witch, but this lady doesna look much like it. She hasna t a single wart on her nose that *I* can see!"

"Thanks," I said again, a little more dryly. "And what's your me?"

He turned suddenly shy at being thus directly addressed, and ried his head in Jamie's sleeve, refusing to speak.

"This is Angus Walter Edwin Murray Carmichael," Jamie anered for him, ruffling the silky blond hair. "Maggie's eldest n, and most commonly known as Wally."

"We call him Snot-rag," a small red-haired girl standing by my ee informed me. " 'Cause his neb is always clotted wi' gook."

Angus Walter jerked his face out of his uncle's shirt and glared his female relation, his features beet-red with fury.

"Is *not*!" he shouted. "Take it back!" Not waiting to see ether she would or not, he flung himself at her, fists clenched, t was jerked off his feet by his great-uncle's hand, attached to collar.

"Ye dinna hit girls," Jamie informed him firmly. "It's not nly."

"But she said I was snotty!" Angus Walter wailed. "I *must* hit r!"

"And it's no verra civil to pass remarks about someone's pernal appearance, Mistress Abigail," Jamie said severely to the le girl. "Ye should apologize to your cousin."

"Well, but he *is* . . ." Abigail persisted, but then caught Jae's stern eyes and dropped her own, flushing scarlet. "Sorry, lly," she murmured.

Wally seemed at first indisposed to consider this adequate comnsation for the insult he had suffered, but was at last prevailed upon to cease trying to hit his cousin by his uncle promising him a story.

"Tell the one about the kelpie and the horseman!" my red haired acquaintance exclaimed, pushing forward to be in on it.

"No, the one about the Devil's chess game!" chimed in one of the other children. Jamie seemed to be a sort of magnet for them; two boys were plucking at his coverlet, while a tiny brown-haired girl had climbed up onto the sofa back by his head, and begun intently plaiting strands of his hair.

"Pretty, Nunkie," she murmured, taking no part in the hail of suggestions.

"It's Wally's story," Jamie said firmly, quelling the incipient riot with a gesture. "He can choose as he likes." He drew a clean handkerchief out from under the pillow and held it to Wally's nose, which was in fact rather unsightly.

"Blow," he said in an undertone, and then, louder, "and then tell me which you'll have, Wally."

Wally snuffled obligingly, then said, "St. Bride and the geese, please, Nunkie."

Jamie's eyes sought me, resting on my face with a thoughtful expression.

"All right," he said, after a pause. "Well, then. Ye'll ken that the greylag mate for life? If ye kill a grown goose, hunting, ye must always wait, for the mate will come to mourn. Then ye must try to kill the second, too, for otherwise it will grieve itself to death, calling through the skies for the lost one."

Little Benjamin shifted in his wrappings, squirming in my arm. Jamie smiled and shifted his attention back to Wally, hanging open-mouthed on his great-uncle's knee.

"So," he said, "it was a time, more hundreds of years past than you could ken or dream of, that Bride first set foot on the stone of the Highlands, along with Michael the Blessed . . ."

Benjamin let out a small squawk at this point, and began to rootle at the front of my dress. Young Jamie and his siblings seemed to have disappeared, and after a moment's patting and joggling had proved vain, I left the room in search of Benjamin's mother, leaving the story in progress behind me.

I found the lady in question in the kitchen, embedded in a large company of girls and women, and after turning Benjamin over

er, spent some time in introductions, greeting, and the sort of
tual by which women appraise each other, openly and otherwise.

The women were all very friendly; evidently everyone knew or
ad been told who I was, for while they introduced me from one to
nother, there was no apparent surprise at the return of Jamie's
rst wife—either from the dead or from France, depending on
hat they'd been told.

Still, there were very odd undercurrents passing through the
athering. They scrupulously avoided asking me questions; in an-
ther place, this might be mere politeness, but not in the High-
nds, where any stranger's life history was customarily extracted
the course of a casual visit.

And while they treated me with great courtesy and kindness,
ere were small looks from the corner of the eye, the passing of
ances exchanged behind my back, and casual remarks made
ietly in Gaelic.

But strangest of all was Jenny's absence. She was the hearthfire
Lallybroch; I had never been in the house when it was not
ffused with her presence, all the inhabitants in orbit about her
ke planets about the sun. I could think of nothing less like her
an that she should leave her kitchen with such a mob of com-
ny in the house.

Her presence was as strong now as the perfume of the fresh pine
ughs that lay in a large pile in the back pantry, their presence
ginning to scent the house; but of Jenny herself, not a hair was
be seen.

She had avoided me since the night of my return with Young Ian
natural enough, I supposed, under the circumstances. Neither
d I sought an interview with her. Both of us knew there was a
ckoning to be made, but neither of us would seek it then.

It was warm and cozy in the kitchen—too warm. The intermin-
ed scents of drying cloth, hot starch, wet diapers, sweating bod-
s, oatcake frying in lard, and bread baking were becoming a bit
o heady, and when Katherine mentioned the need of a pitcher of
eam for the scones, I seized the opportunity to escape, volun-
ering to fetch it down from the dairy shed.

After the press of heated bodies in the kitchen, the cold, damp
outside was so refreshing that I stood still for a minute, shaking

the kitchen smells out of my petticoats and hair before making my
way to the dairy shed. This shed was some distance away from the
main house, convenient to the milking shed, which in turn was
built to adjoin the two small paddocks in which sheep and goats
were kept. Cattle were kept in the Highlands, but normally for
beef, rather than milk, cow's milk being thought suitable only for
invalids.

To my surprise, as I came out of the dairy shed, I saw Fergus
leaning on the paddock fence, staring moodily at the mass of
milling wooly backs below. I had not expected to see him here,
and wondered whether Jamie knew he had returned.

Jenny's prized Merino sheep—imported, hand-fed and a great
deal more spoilt than any of her grandchildren—spotted me as I
passed, and rushed en masse for the side of their pen, blatting
frenziedly in hope of tidbits. Fergus looked up, startled at the
racket, then waved halfheartedly. He called something, but it was
impossible to hear him over the uproar.

There was a large bin of frost-blasted cabbage heads near the
pen; I pulled out a large, limp green head, and doled out leaves to
a dozen or so pairs of eagerly grasping lips, in hopes of shutting
them up.

The ram, a huge wooly creature named Hughie, with testicles
that hung nearly to the ground like wool-covered footballs, shouldered his massive way into the front rank with a loud and autocratic *Bahh!* Fergus, who had reached my side by this time, picked
up a whole cabbage and hurled it at Hughie with considerable
force and fair accuracy.

"Tais-toi!" he said irritably.

Hughie shied and let out an astonished, high-pitched *Beh!* as the
cabbage bounced off his padded back. Then, shaking himself back
into some semblance of dignity, he trotted off, testes swinging
with offended majesty. His flock, sheeplike, trailed after him, uttering a low chorus of discontented *bahs* in his wake.

Fergus glowered malevolently after them.

"Useless, noisy, smelly beasts," he said. Rather ungratefully, I
thought, given that the scarf and stockings he was wearing had
almost certainly been woven from their wool.

"Nice to see you again, Fergus," I said, ignoring his mood.
"Does Jamie know you're back yet?" I wondered just how much
Fergus knew of recent events, if he had just arrived at Lallybroch

"No," he said, rather listlessly. "I suppose I should tell him I m here." In spite of this, he made no move toward the house, but ntinued staring into the churned mud of the paddock. Some-ing was obviously eating at him; I hoped nothing had gone rong with his errand.

"Did you find Mr. Gage all right?" I asked.

He looked blank for a moment, then a spark of animation came ck into his lean face.

"Oh, yes. Milord was right; I went with Gage to warn the other embers of the Society, and then we went together to the tavern here they were to meet. Sure enough, there was a nest of Cus-ms men there waiting, disguised. And may they be waiting as ng as their fellow in the cask, ha ha!"

The gleam of savage amusement died out of his eyes then, and e sighed.

"We cannot expect to be paid for the pamphlets, of course. And en though the press was saved, God knows how long it may be til milord's business is reestablished."

He spoke with such mournfulness that I was surprised.

"You don't help with the printing business, do you?" I asked.

He raised one shoulder and let it fall. "Not to say help, milady. ut milord was kind enough to allow me to invest a part of my are of the profits from the brandy in the printing business. In ne, I should have become a full partner."

"I see," I said sympathetically. "Do you need money? Perhaps can—"

He shot me a glance of surprise, and then a smile that displayed s perfect, square white teeth.

"Thank you, milady, but no. I myself need very little, and I ve enough." He patted the side pocket of his coat, which jingled assuringly.

He paused, frowning, and thrust both wrists deep into the pock-s of his coat.

"Noo . . ." he said slowly. "It is only—well, the printing siness is most respectable, milady."

"I suppose so," I said, slightly puzzled. He caught my tone and iled, rather grimly.

"The difficulty, milady, is that while a smuggler may be in ssession of an income more than sufficient for the support of a

wife, smuggling as a sole profession is not likely to appeal to th
parents of a respectable young lady.''

''Oho,'' I said, everything becoming clear. ''You want to ge
married? To a respectable young lady?''

He nodded, a little shyly.

''Yes, madame. But her mother does not favor me.''

I couldn't say I blamed the young lady's mother, all thing
considered. While Fergus was possessed of dark good looks and
dashing manner that might well win a young girl's heart, he lacke
a few of the things that might appeal somewhat more to conserva
tive Scottish parents, such as property, income, a left hand, and
last name.

Likewise, while smuggling, cattle-lifting, and other forms c
practical communism had a long and illustrious history in th
Highlands, the French did not. And no matter how long Fergu
himself had lived at Lallybroch, he remained as French as Notr
Dame. He would, like me, always be an outlander.

''If I were a partner in a profitable printing firm, you see, pe
haps the good lady might be induced to consider my suit,'' h
explained. ''But as it is . . .'' He shook his head disconsolatel

I patted his arm sympathetically. ''Don't worry about it,''
said. ''We'll think of something. Does Jamie know about this gir
I'm sure he'd be willing to speak to her mother for you.''

To my surprise, he looked quite alarmed.

''Oh, no, milady! Please, say nothing to him—he has a gre
many things of more importance to think of just now.''

On the whole, I thought this was probably true, but I was su
prised at his vehemence. Still, I agreed to say nothing to Jami
My feet were growing chilly from standing in the frozen mud, an
I suggested that we go inside.

''Perhaps a little later, milady,'' he said. ''For now, I believe
am not suitable company even for sheep.'' With a heavy sigh, I
turned and trudged off toward the dovecote, shoulders slumped

To my surprise, Jenny was in the parlor with Jamie. She ha
been outside; her cheeks and the end of her long, straight no
were pink with the cold, and the scent of winter mist lingered
her clothes.

''I've sent Young Ian to saddle Donas,'' she said. She frown

her brother. "Can ye stand to walk to the barn, Jamie, or had he
˙st bring the beast round for ye?"

Jamie stared up at her, one eyebrow raised.

"I can walk wherever it's needful to go, but I'm no going
ʌywhere just now."

"Did I not tell ye he'd be coming?" Jenny said impatiently.
Amyas Kettrick stopped by here late last night, and said he'd just
▸me from Kinwallis. Hobart's meaning to come today, he said."
ˑe glanced at the pretty enameled clock on the mantel. "If he left
ˑter breakfast, he'll be here within the hour."

Jamie frowned at his sister, tilting his head back against the
fa.

"I told ye, Jenny, I'm no afraid of Hobart MacKenzie," he said
ortly. "Damned if I'll run from him!"

Jenny's brows rose as she looked coldly at her brother.

"Oh, aye?" she said. "Ye weren't afraid of Laoghaire, either,
d look where that got ye!" She jerked her head at the sling on
s arm.

Despite himself, Jamie's mouth curled up on one side.

"Aye, well, it's a point," he said. "On the other hand, Jenny, ye
n guns are scarcer than hen's teeth in the Highlands. I dinna
ınk Hobart's going to come and ask to borrow my own pistol to
ʌoot me with."

"I shouldna think he'd bother; he'll just walk in and spit ye
ʀough the gizzard like the silly gander ye are!" she snapped.

Jamie laughed, and she glared at him. I seized the moment to
ˑerrupt.

"Who," I inquired, "is Hobart MacKenzie, and why exactly
ˑes he want to spit you like a gander?"

Jamie turned his head to me, the light of amusement still in his
ˑes.

"Hobart is Laoghaire's brother, Sassenach," he explained. "As
ˑr spitting me or otherwise—"

"Laoghaire's sent for him from Kinwallis, where he lives,"
ˑnny interrupted, "and told him about . . . all this." A slight,
˙patient gesture encompassed me, Jamie, and the awkward situa-
ˑn in general.

"The notion being that Hobart's meant to come round and
˙punge the slight upon his sister's honor by expunging me,"

Jamie explained. He seemed to find the idea entertaining. I wasn'
so sure about it, and neither was Jenny.

"You're not worried about this Hobart?" I asked.

"Of course not," he said, a little irritably. He turned to hi
sister. "For God's sake, Jenny, ye ken Hobart MacKenzie! Th
man couldna stick a pig without cutting off his own foot!"

She looked him up and down, evidently gauging his ability t
defend himself against an incompetent pigsticker, and reluctantl
concluding that he might manage, even one-handed.

"Mmphm," she said. "Well, and what if he comes for ye an
ye kill him, aye? What then?"

"Then he'll be dead, I expect," Jamie said dryly.

"And ye'll be hangit for murder," she shot back, "or on th
run, wi' all the rest of Laoghaire's kin after ye. Want to start
blood feud, do ye?"

Jamie narrowed his eyes at his sister, emphasizing the alread
marked resemblance between them.

"What I want," he said, with exaggerated patience, "is m
breakfast. D'ye mean to feed me, or d'ye mean to wait until I fair
from hunger, and then hide me in the priest hole 'til Hoba
leaves?"

Annoyance struggled with humor on Jenny's fine-boned face a
she glared at her brother. As usual with both Frasers, humor wo
out.

"It's a thought," she said, teeth flashing in a brief, reluctar
smile. "If I could drag your stubborn carcass that far, I'd club y
myself." She shook her head and sighed.

"All right, Jamie, ye'll have it your way. But ye'll try not t
make a mess on my good Turkey carpet, aye?"

He looked up at her, long mouth curling up on one side.

"It's a promise, Jenny," he said. "Nay bloodshed in the pa
lor."

She snorted. "Clot," she said, but without rancor. "I'll sen
Janet wi' your parritch." And she was gone, in a swirl of skir
and petticoats.

"Did she say Donas?" I asked, looking after her in bemus
ment. "Surely it isn't the same horse you took from Leoch!"

"Och, no." Jamie tilted his head back, smiling up at me. "Th
is Donas's grandson—or one of them. We give the name to th
sorrel colts in his honor."

[leaned over the back of the sofa, gently feeling down the
gth of the injured arm from the shoulder.

''Sore?'' I asked, seeing him wince as I pressed a few inches
)ve the wound. It was better; the day before, the area of soreness
[started higher.

'Not bad,'' he said. He removed the sling and tried gingerly
ending the arm, grimacing. ''I dinna think I'll turn handsprings
hile yet, though.''

[laughed.

'No, I don't suppose so.'' I hesitated. ''Jamie—this Hobart.
u really don't think—''

'I don't,'' he said firmly. ''And if I did, I'd still want my
akfast first. I dinna mean to be killed on an empty stomach.''

. laughed again, somewhat reassured.

'I'll go and get it for you,'' I promised.

As I stepped out into the hall, though, I caught sight of a flutter
)ugh one of the windows, and stopped to look. It was Jenny,
aked and hooded against the cold, headed up the slope to the
n. Seized by a sudden impulse, I snatched a cloak from the hall
: and darted out after her. I had things to say to Jenny Murray,
I this might be the best chance of catching her alone.

caught up with her just outside the barn; she heard my step
ind her and turned, startled. She glanced about quickly, but
′ we were alone. Realizing that there was no way of putting off
onfrontation, she squared her shoulders under the woolen cloak
[lifted her head, meeting my eyes straight on.

'I thought I'd best tell Young Ian to unsaddle the horse,'' she
l. ''Then I'm going to the root cellar to fetch up some onions
a tart. Will ye come with me?''

'I will.'' Pulling my cloak tight around me against the winter
id, I followed her into the barn.

t was warm inside, at least by contrast with the chill outdoors,
k, and filled with the pleasant scent of horses, hay, and manure.
aused a moment to let my eyes adapt to the dimness, but Jenny
ked directly down the central aisle, footsteps light on the stone
)r.

′oung Ian was sprawled at length on a pile of fresh straw; he sat
blinking at the sound.

Jenny glanced from her son to the stall, where a soft-eyed sorre was peacefully munching hay from its manger, unburdened b saddle or bridle.

"Did I not tell ye to ready Donas?" she asked the boy, he voice sharp.

Young Ian scratched his head, looking a little sheepish, an stood up.

"Aye, mam, ye did," he said. "But I didna think it worth th time to saddle him, only to have to unsaddle him again."

Jenny stared up at him.

"Oh, aye?" she said. "And what made ye so certain h wouldna be needed?"

Young Ian shrugged, and smiled down at her.

"Mam, ye ken as well as I do that Uncle Jamie wouldna ru away from anything, let alone Uncle Hobart. Don't ye?" he adde gently.

Jenny looked up at her son and sighed. Then a reluctant smi lighted her face and she reached up, smoothing the thick, untie hair away from his face.

"Aye, wee Ian. I do." Her hand lingered along his ruddy chee then dropped away.

"Go along to the house, then, and have second breakfast w your uncle," she said. "Your auntie and I are goin' to the ro cellar. But ye come and fetch me smartly, if Mr. Hobart MacKen zie should come, aye?"

"Right away, Mam," he promised, and shot for the hous impelled by the thought of food.

Jenny watched him go, moving with the clumsy grace of young whooping crane, and shook her head, the smile still on h lips.

"Sweet laddie," she murmured. Then, recalled to the prese circumstances, she turned to me with decision.

"Come along, then," she said. "I expect ye want to talk to m aye?"

Neither of us said anything until we reached the quiet sanctua of the root cellar. It was a small room dug under the hous pungent with the scent of the long braided strings of onions an garlic that hung from the rafters, the sweet, spicy scent of dri pples, and the moist, earthy smell of potatoes, spread in lumpy rown blankets over the shelves that lined the cellar.

"D'ye remember telling me to plant potatoes?" Jenny asked, assing a hand lightly over the clustered tubers. "That was a lucky ning; 'twas the potato crop kept us alive, more than one winter fter Culloden."

I remembered, all right. I had told her as we stood together on a old autumn night, about to part—she to return to a newborn baby, to hunt for Jamie, an outlaw in the Highlands, under sentence of eath. I had found him, and saved him—and Lallybroch, evi- ently. And she had tried to give them both to Laoghaire.

"Why?" I said softly, at last. I spoke to the top of her head, ent over her task. Her hand went out with the regularity of clock- ork, pulling an onion from the long hanging braid, breaking the ugh, withered stems from the plait and tossing it into the basket ne carried.

"Why did you do it?" I said. I broke off an onion from another raid, but instead of putting it in the basket, held it in my hands, olling it back and forth like a baseball, hearing the papery skin istle between my palms.

"Why did I do what?" Her voice was perfectly controlled gain; only someone who knew her well could have heard the note f strain in it. I knew her well—or had, at one time.

"Why did I make the match between my brother and Laoghaire, ye mean?" She glanced up quickly, smooth black brows raised a question, but then bent back to the braid of onions. "You're ght; he wouldna have done it, without I made him."

"So you did make him do it," I said. The wind rattled the door f the root cellar, sending a small sifting of dirt down upon the at-stone steps.

"He was lonely," she said, softly. "So lonely. I couldna bear to :e him so. He was wretched for so long, ye ken, mourning for ›u."

"I thought he was dead," I said quietly, answering the unspo- ∴n accusation.

"He might as well have been," she said, sharply, then raised ∴r head and sighed, pushing back a lock of dark hair.

"Aye, maybe ye truly didna ken he'd lived; there were a great any who didn't, after Culloden—and it's sure he thought *you* ere dead and gone then. But he was sair wounded, and not only

his leg. And when he came home from England—" She shook he
head, and reached for another onion. "He was whole enough t
look at, but not—" She gave me a look, straight on, with thos
slanted blue eyes, so disturbingly like her brother's. "He's no th
sort of man should sleep alone, aye?"

"Granted," I said shortly. "But we did live, the both of us
Why did you send for Laoghaire when we came back with Young
Ian?"

Jenny didn't answer at first, but only went on reaching fo
onions, breaking, reaching, breaking, reaching.

"I liked you," she said at last, so low I could barely hear he
"Loved ye, maybe, when ye lived here with Jamie, before."

"I liked you, too," I said, just as softly. "Then why?"

Her hands stilled at last and she looked up at me, fists balled a
her sides.

"When Ian told me ye'd come back," she said slowly, eye
fastened on the onions, "ye could have knocked me flat wi'
down-feather. At first, I was excited, wanting to see ye—wantin
to know where ye'd been—" she added, arching her brow
slightly in inquiry. I didn't answer, and she went on.

"But then I was afraid," she said softly. Her eyes slid away
shadowed by their thick fringe of black lashes.

"I saw ye, ye ken," she said, still looking off into some unsee
able distance. "When he wed Laoghaire, and them standing by th
altar—ye were there wi' them, standing at his left hand, betwix
him and Laoghaire. And I kent that meant ye would take hir
back."

The hair prickled slightly on the nape of my neck. She shoo
her head slowly, and I saw she had gone pale with the memory
She sat down on a barrel, the cloak spreading out around her like
flower.

"I'm not one of those born wi' the Sight, nor one who has
regular. I've never had it before, and hope never to have it agai
But I saw ye there, as clear as I see ye now, and it scairt me so tha
I had to leave the room, right in the midst o' the vows." Sh
swallowed, looking at me directly.

"I dinna ken who ye are," she said softly. "Or . . . or . .
what. We didna ken your people, or your place. I never asked ye
did I? Jamie chose ye, that was enough. But then ye were gone

nd after so long—I thought he might have forgot ye enough to
ved again, and be happy.''

"He wasn't, though," I said, hoping for confirmation from
enny.

She gave it, shaking her head.

"No," she said quietly. "But Jamie's a faithful man, aye? No
natter how it was between the two of them, him and Laoghaire, if
e'd sworn to be her man, he wouldna leave her altogether. It
idna matter that he spent most of his time in Edinburgh; I kent
e'd always come back here—he'd be bound here, to the High-
ands. But then you came back."

Her hands lay still in her lap, a rare sight. They were still finely
haped, long-fingered and deft, but the knuckles were red and
ough with years of work, and the veins stood out blue beneath the
in white skin.

"D'ye ken," she said, looking into her lap, "I have never been
irther than ten miles from Lallybroch, in all my life?"

"No," I said, slightly startled. She shook her head slowly, then
ooked up at me.

"You have, though," she said. "You've traveled a great deal, I
xpect." Her gaze searched my face, looking for clues.

"I have."

She nodded, as though thinking to herself.

"You'll go again," she said, nearly whispering. "I kent ye
ould go again. You're not bound here, not like Laoghaire—not
ke me. And he would go with ye. And I should never see him
gain." She closed her eyes briefly, then opened them, looking at
e under her fine dark brows.

"That's why," she said. "I thought if ye kent about Laoghaire,
e'd go again at once—you did—" she added, with a faint gri-
ace, "and Jamie would stay. But ye came back." Her shoulders
se in a faint, helpless shrug. "And I see it's no good; he's bound
ye, for good or ill. It's you that's his wife. And if ye leave again,
e will go with ye."

I searched helplessly for words to reassure her. "But I won't. I
on't go again. I only want to stay here with him—always."

I laid a hand on her arm and she stiffened slightly. After a
oment, she laid her own hand over mine. It was chilled, and the
of her long, straight nose was red with cold.

"Folk say different things of the Sight, aye?" she said after a moment. ''Some say it's doomed; whatever ye see that way must come to pass. But others say nay, it's no but a warning; take heed and ye can change things. What d'ye think, yourself?'' She looked sideways at me, curiously.

I took a deep breath, the smell of onions stinging the back of my nose. This was hitting home in no uncertain terms.

''I don't know,'' I said, and my voice shook slightly. ''I'd always thought that of course you could change things if you knew about them. But now . . . I don't know,'' I ended softly, thinking of Culloden.

Jenny watched me, her eyes so deep a blue as almost to be black in the dim light. I wondered again just how much Jamie had told her—and how much she knew without the telling.

''But ye must try, even so,'' she said, with certainty. ''Ye couldna just leave it, could ye?''

I didn't know whether she meant this personally, but I shook my head.

''No,'' I said. ''You couldn't. You're right; you have to try.''

We smiled at each other, a little shyly.

''You'll take good care of him?'' Jenny said suddenly. ''Even if ye go? Ye will, aye?''

I squeezed her cold fingers, feeling the bones of her hand light and fragile-seeming in my grasp.

''I will,'' I said.

''Then that's all right,'' she said softly, and squeezed back.

We sat for a moment, holding each other's hands, until the door of the root cellar swung open, admitting a blast of rain and wind down the stairs.

''Mam?'' Young Ian's head poked in, eyes bright with excitement. ''Hobart MacKenzie's come! Da says to come quick!''

Jenny sprang to her feet, barely remembering to snatch up the basket of onions.

''Has he come armed, then?'' she asked anxiously. ''Has he brought a pistol or a sword?''

Ian shook his head, his dark hair lifting wildly in the wind.

''Oh, no, Mam!'' he said. ''It's worse. He's brought a lawyer!''

Anything less resembling vengeance incarnate than Hobart MacKenzie could scarcely be imagined. A small, light-boned man

about thirty, he had pale blue, pale-lashed eyes with a tendency
water, and indeterminate features that began with a receding
airline and dwindled down into a similarly receding chin that
emed to be trying to escape into the folds of his stock.

He was smoothing his hair at the mirror in the hall when we
me in the front door, a neatly curled bob wig sitting on the table
side him. He blinked at us in alarm, then snatched up the wig
d crammed it on his head, bowing in the same motion.

"Mrs. Jenny," he said. His small, rabbity eyes flicked in my
rection, away, then back again, as though he hoped I really
asn't there, but was very much afraid I was.

Jenny glanced from him to me, sighed deeply, and took the bull
the horns.

"Mr. MacKenzie," she said, dropping him a formal curtsy.
Might I present my good-sister, Claire? Claire, Mr. Hobart Mac-
nzie of Kinwallis."

His mouth dropped open and he simply gawked at me. I started
extend a hand to him, but thought better of it. I would have liked
know what Emily Post had to recommend in a situation like
s, but as Miss Post wasn't present, I was forced to improvise.

"How nice to meet you," I said, smiling as cordially as possi-
.

"Ah . . ." he said. He bobbed his head tentatively at me.
Jm . . . your . . . servant, ma'am."

Fortunately, at this point in the proceedings, the door to the
rlor opened. I looked at the small, neat figure framed in the
orway, and let out a cry of delighted recognition.

"Ned! Ned Gowan!"

It was indeed Ned Gowan, the elderly Edinburgh lawyer who
d once saved me from burning as a witch. He was noticeably
re elderly now, shrunken with age and so heavily wrinkled as to
k like one of the dried apples I had seen in the root cellar.

The bright black eyes were the same, though, and they fastened
me at once with an expression of joy.

"My dear!" he exclaimed, hastening forward at a rapid hobble.
seized my hand, beaming, and pressed it to his withered lips in
vent gallantry.

'I had heard that you—"

'How did you come to be—"

'—so delightful to see you!"

"—so happy to see you again, but—"

A cough from Hobart MacKenzie interrupted this rapturou exchange, and Mr. Gowan looked up, startled, then nodded.

"Oh, aye, of course. Business first, my dear," he said, with gallant bow to me, "and then if ye will, I should be most charme to hear the tale of your adventures."

"Ah . . . I'll do my best," I said, wondering just how muc he would insist on hearing.

"Splendid, splendid." He glanced about the hall, bright littl eyes taking in Hobart and Jenny, who had hung up her cloak an was smoothing her hair. "Mr. Fraser and Mr. Murray are alread in the parlor. Mr. MacKenzie, if you and the ladies would conser to join us, perhaps we can settle your affairs expeditiously, an proceed to more congenial matters. If you will allow me, m dear?" He crooked a bony arm to me invitingly.

Jamie was still on the sofa where I had left him, and in approx mately the same condition—that is, alive. The children were gon with the exception of one chubby youngster who was curled up o Jamie's lap, fast asleep. Jamie's hair now sported several sma plaits on either side, with silk ribbons woven gaily through ther which gave him an incongruously festive air.

"You look like the Cowardly Lion of Oz," I told him in a undertone, sitting down on a hassock behind his sofa. I didn think it likely that Hobart MacKenzie intended any outright mi chief, but if anything happened, I meant to be in close reach Jamie.

He looked startled, and put a hand to his head.

"I do?"

"Shh," I said, "I'll tell you later."

The other participants had now arranged themselves around t parlor, Jenny sitting down by Ian on the other love seat, a Hobart and Mr. Gowan taking two velvet chairs.

"We are assembled?" Mr. Gowan inquired, glancing arou the room. "All interested parties are present? Excellent. Well, begin with, I must declare my own interest. I am here in t capacity of solicitor to Mr. Hobart MacKenzie, representing t interests of Mrs. James Fraser"—he saw me start, and added, w recision—"that is, the *second* Mrs. James Fraser, née Laoghaire MacKenzie. That is understood?"

He glanced inquiringly at Jamie, who nodded.

"It is."

"Good." Mr. Gowan picked up a glass from the table next to im and took a tiny sip. "My clients, the MacKenzies, have accepted my proposal to seek a legal solution to the imbroglio, which I understand has resulted from the sudden and unexpected —though of course altogether happy and fortuitous—" he added, with a bow to me, "return of the first Mrs. Fraser."

He shook his head reprovingly at Jamie.

"You, my dear young man, have contrived to entangle yourself 1 considerable legal difficulties, I am sorry to say."

Jamie raised one eyebrow and looked at his sister.

"Aye, well, I had help," he said dryly. "Just what difficulties re we speakin' of?"

"Well, to begin with," Ned Gowan said cheerily, his sparkling lack eyes sinking into nets of wrinkles as he smiled at me, "the rst Mrs. Fraser would be well within her rights to bring a civil uit against ye for adultery, and criminal fornication, forbye. Penlties for which include—"

Jamie glanced back at me, with a quick blue gleam.

"I think I'm no so worrit by that possibility," he told the lwyer. "What else?"

Ned Gowan nodded obligingly and held up one withered hand, olding down the fingers as he ticked off his points.

"With respect to the second Mrs. Fraser—née Laoghaire MacLenzie—ye could, of course, be charged wi' bigamous misconuct, intent to defraud, actual fraud committed—whether wi' atent or no, which is a separate question—felonious misrepresenttion"—he happily folded down his fourth finger and drew reath for more—"and . . ."

Jamie had been listening patiently to this catalogue. Now he iterrupted, leaning forward.

"Ned," he said gently, "what the hell does the bloody woman ant?"

The small lawyer blinked behind his spectacles, lowered his and, and cast up his eyes to the beams overhead.

"Weel, the lady's chief desire as stated," he said circumspectly, "is to see ye castrated and disemboweled in the market square at Broch Mordha, and your head mounted on a stake over her gate."

Jamie's shoulders vibrated briefly, and he winced as the movement jarred his arm.

"I see," he said, his mouth twitching.

A smile gathered up the wrinkles by Ned's ancient mouth.

"I was obliged to inform Mrs.—that is, the lady—" he amended, with a glance at me and a slight cough, "that her remedies under the law were somewhat more limited than would accommodate her desires."

"Quite," Jamie said dryly. "But I assume the general idea is that she doesna particularly want me back as a husband?"

"No," Hobart put in unexpectedly. "Crow's bait, maybe, but not a husband."

Ned cast a cold glance at his client.

"Ye willna compromise your case by admitting things in advance of settlement, aye?" he said reprovingly. "Or what are ye payin' me for?" He turned back to Jamie, professional dignity unimpaired.

"While Miss MacKenzie does not wish to resume a marital position wi' regard to you—an action which would be impossible in any case," he added fairly, "unless ye should wish to divorce the present Mrs. Fraser, and remarry—"

"No, I dinna want to do that," Jamie assured him hurriedly, with another glance at me.

"Well, in such case," Ned went on, unruffled, "I should advise my clients that it is more desirable where possible to avoid the cost —and the publicity—" he added, cocking an invisible eyebrow in admonition to Hobart, who nodded hastily, "of a suit at law, with a public trial and its consequent exposure of facts. That being the case—"

"How much?" Jamie interrupted.

"Mr. Fraser!" Ned Gowan looked shocked. "I havena mentioned anything in the nature of a pecuniary settlement as yet—"

"Only because ye're too busy enjoying yourself, ye wicked auld rascal," Jamie said. He was irritated—a red patch burned over each cheekbone—but amused, too. "Get to it, aye?"

Ned Gowan inclined his head ceremoniously.

"Weel, ye must understand," he began, "that a successful suit brought under the charges as described might result in Miss Mac

Kenzie and her brother mulcting ye in substantial damages—verra substantial indeed," he added, with a faint lawyerly gloating at the prospect.

"After all, Miss MacKenzie has not only been subject to public humiliation and ridicule leading to acute distress of mind, but is also threatened with loss of her chief means of support—"

"She isna threatened wi' any such thing," Jamie interrupted heatedly. "I told her I should go on supporting her and the two lassies! What does she think I am?"

Ned exchanged a glance with Hobart, who shook his head.

"Ye dinna want to know what she thinks ye are," Hobart assured Jamie. "I wouldna have thought she kent such words, myself. But ye do mean to pay?"

Jamie nodded impatiently, rubbing his good hand through his hair.

"Aye, I will."

"Only until she's marrit again, though." Everyone's head turned in surprise toward Jenny, who nodded firmly to Ned Gowan.

"If Jamie's married to Claire, the marriage between him and Laoghaire wasna valid, aye?"

The lawyer bowed.

"That is true, Mrs. Murray."

"Well, then," Jenny said, in a decided manner. "She's free to marry again at once, is she no? And once she does, my brother shouldna be providing for her household."

"An excellent point, Mrs. Murray." Ned Gowan took up his quill and scratched industriously. "Well, we make progress," he declared, laying it down again and beaming at the company. "Now, the next point to be covered . . ."

An hour later, the decanter of whisky was empty, the sheets of foolscap on the table were filled with Ned Gowan's chicken-scratchings, and everyone lay limp and exhausted—except Ned himself, spry and bright-eyed as ever.

"Excellent, excellent," he declared again, gathering up the sheets and tapping them neatly into order. "So—the main provisions of the settlement are as follows: Mr. Fraser agrees to pay to Miss MacKenzie the sum of five hundred pounds in compensation for distress, inconvenience, and the loss of his conjugal services"—Jamie snorted slightly at this, but Ned affected not to hear him, continuing his synopsis—"and in addition, agrees to maintain her household at the rate of one hundred pounds per annum, until such time as the aforesaid Miss MacKenzie may marry again, at which time such payment shall cease. Mr. Fraser agrees also to provide a bride-portion for each of Miss MacKenzie's daughters, of an additional three hundred pounds, and as a final provision, agrees not to pursue a prosecution against Miss MacKenzie for assault with intent to commit murder. In return, Miss MacKenzie acquits Mr. Fraser of any and all other claims. This is in accordance with your understanding and consent, Mr. Fraser?" He quirked a brow at Jamie.

"Aye, it is," Jamie said. He was pale from sitting up too long, and there was a fine dew of sweat at his hairline, but he sat straight and tall, the child still asleep in his lap, thumb firmly embedded in her mouth.

"Excellent," Ned said again. He rose, beaming, and bowed to the company. "As our friend Dr. John Arbuthnot says, 'Law is a bottomless pit.' But not more so at the moment than my stomach. Is that delectable aroma indicative of a saddle of mutton in our vicinity, Mrs. Jenny?"

At table, I sat to one side of Jamie, Hobart MacKenzie to the other, now looking pink and relaxed. Mary MacNab brought in the joint, and by ancient custom, set it down in front of Jamie. Her gaze lingered on him a moment too long. He picked up the long wicked carving knife with his good hand and offered it politely to Hobart.

"Will ye have a go at it, Hobart?" he said.

"Och, no," Hobart said, waving it away. "Better let your wife carve it. I'm no hand wi' a knife—likely cut my finger off instead. You know me, Jamie," he said comfortably.

Jamie gave his erstwhile brother-in-law a long look over the saltcellar.

"Once I would ha' thought, so, Hobart," he said. "Pass me the whisky, aye?"

"The thing to do is to get her married at once," Jenny declared. The children and grandchildren had all retired, and Ned and Hobart had departed for Kinwallis, leaving the four of us to take stock over brandy and cream cakes in the laird's study.

Jamie turned to his sister. "The matchmaking's more in your ne, aye?" he said, with a noticeable edge to his voice. "I expect ou can think of a suitable man or two for the job, if ye put your ind to it?"

"I expect I can," she said, matching his edge with one of her wn. She was embroidering; the needle stabbed through the linen bric, flashing in the lamplight. It had begun to sleet heavily utside, but the study was cozy, with a small fire on the hearth and e pool of lamplight spilling warmth over the battered desk and s burden of books and ledgers.

"There's the one thing about it," she said, eyes on her work. Where d'ye mean to get twelve hundred pounds, Jamie?"

I had been wondering that myself. The insurance settlement on e printshop had fallen far short of that amount, and I doubted at Jamie's share of the smuggling proceeds amounted to any-ing near that magnitude. Certainly Lallybroch itself could not pply the money; survival in the Highlands was a chancy busi-ss, and even several good years in a row would provide only the rest surplus.

"Well, there's only the one place, isn't there?" Ian looked from s sister to his brother-in-law and back. After a short silence, mie nodded.

"I suppose so," he said reluctantly. He glanced at the window, here the rain was slashing across the glass in slanting streaks. A vicious time of year for it, though."

Ian shrugged, and sat forward a bit in his chair. "The spring le will be in a week."

Jamie frowned, looking troubled.

"Aye, that's so, but . . ."

"There's no one has a better right to it, Jamie," Ian said. He ached out and squeezed his friend's good arm, smiling. "It was eant for Prince Charles's followers, aye? And ye were one of ose, whether ye wanted to be or no."

Jamie gave him back a rueful half-smile.

"Aye, I suppose that's true." He sighed. "In any case, it's the ly thing I can see to do." He glanced back and forth between n and Jenny, evidently debating whether to add something else. is sister knew him even better than I did. She lifted her head om her work and looked at him sharply.

"What is it, Jamie?" she said.

He took a deep breath.

"I want to take Young Ian," he said.

"No," she said instantly. The needle had stopped, stuck half-way through a brilliant red bud in the pattern, the color of blood against the white smock.

"He's old enough, Jenny," Jamie said quietly.

"He's not!" she objected. "He's but barely fifteen; Michael and Jamie were both sixteen at least, and better grown."

"Aye, but wee Ian's a better swimmer than either of his brothers," Ian said judiciously. His forehead was furrowed with thought. "It will have to be one of the lads, after all," he pointed out to Jenny. He jerked his head toward Jamie, cradling his arm in its sling. "Jamie canna very well be swimming himself, in his present condition. Or Claire, for that matter," he added, with a smile at me.

"Swim?" I said, utterly bewildered. "Swim *where*?"

Ian looked taken aback for a moment; then he glanced at Jamie, brows lifted.

"Oh. Ye hadna told her?"

Jamie shook his head. "I had, but not all of it." He turned to me. "It's the treasure, Sassenach—the seals' gold."

Unable to take the treasure with him, he had concealed it in its place and returned to Ardsmuir.

"I didna ken what best to do about it," he explained. "Duncan Kerr gave the care of it to me, but I had no notion who it belonged to, or who put it there, or what I was to do with it. 'The white witch' was all Duncan said, and that meant nothing to me but you, Sassenach."

Reluctant to make use of the treasure himself, and yet feeling that someone should know about it, lest he die in prison, he had sent a carefully coded letter to Jenny and Ian at Lallybroch, giving the location of the cache, and the use for which it had—presumably—been meant.

Times had been hard for Jacobites then, sometimes even more so for those who had escaped to France—leaving lands and fortunes behind—than for those who remained to face English persecution in the Highlands. At about the same time, Lallybroch had experienced two bad crops in a row, and letters had reached them from France, asking for any help possible to succor erstwhile companions there, in danger of starvation.

"We had nothing to send; in fact, we were damn close to starv-
g here," Ian explained. "I sent word to Jamie, and he said as he
ought perhaps it wouldna be wrong to use a small bit of the
:asure to help feed Prince *Tearlach*'s followers."

"It seemed likely it was put there by one of the Stuarts' sup-
•rters," Jamie chimed in. He cocked a ruddy brow at me, and his
outh quirked up at one corner. "I thought I wouldna send it to
ince Charles, though."

"Good thinking," I said dryly. Any money given to Charles
uart would have been wasted, squandered within weeks, and
yone who had known Charles intimately, as Jamie had, would
ow that very well.

Ian had taken his eldest son, Jamie, and made his way across
otland to the seals' cove near Coigach. Fearful of any word of
e treasure getting out, they had not sought a fisherman's boat,
it instead Young Jamie had swum to the seals' rock as his uncle
d several years before. He had found the treasure in its place,
stracted two gold coins and three of the smaller gemstones, and
creting these in a bag tied securely round his neck, had replaced
e rest of the treasure and made his way back through the surf,
riving exhausted.

They had made their way to Inverness then, and taken ship to
ance, where their cousin Jared Fraser, a successful expatriate
ne merchant, had helped them to change the coins and jewels
scretely into cash, and taken the responsibility of distributing it
1ong the Jacobites in need.

Three times since, Ian had made the laborious trip to the coast
th one of his sons, each time to abstract a small part of the
dden fortune to supply a need. Twice the money had gone to
ends in need in France; once it had been needed to purchase
sh planting-stock for Lallybroch and provide the food to see its
1ants through a long winter when the potato crop failed.

Only Jenny, Ian, and the two elder boys, Jamie and Michael,
ew of the treasure. Ian's wooden leg prevented his swimming to
seals' island, so one of his sons must always make the trip with
n. I gathered that it had been something of a rite of passage for
th Young Jamie and Michael, entrusted with such a great secret.
w it might be Young Ian's turn.

"No," Jenny said again, but I thought her heart wasn't in it. Ian
is already nodding thoughtfully.

"Would ye take him with ye to France, too, Jamie?"

Jamie nodded.

"Aye, that's the thing. I shall have to leave Lallybroch, and sta away for a good bit, for Laoghaire's sake—I canna be living her with you, under her nose," he said apologetically to me, "at leas not until she's suitably wed to someone else." He switched hi attention back to Ian.

"I havena told ye everything that's happened in Edinburgh, Iar but all things considered, I think it likely best I stay away fror there for a time, too."

I sat quiet, trying to digest this news. I hadn't realized tha Jamie meant to leave Lallybroch—leave Scotland altogether, sounded like.

"So what d'ye mean to do, Jamie?" Jenny had given up an pretense of sewing, and sat with her hands in her lap.

He rubbed his nose, looking tired. This was the first day he ha been up; I privately thought he should have been back in bed hou ago, but he had insisted upon staying up to preside over dinner an visit with everyone.

"Well," he said slowly, "Jared's offered more than once t take me into his firm. Perhaps I shall stay in France, at least for year. I was thinking Young Ian could go with us, and be schoole in Paris."

Jenny and Ian exchanged a long look, one of those in whic long-married couples are capable of carrying out complete co versations in the space of a few heartbeats. At last, Jenny tilted h head a bit to one side. Ian smiled and took her hand.

"It'll be all right, *mo nighean dubh,*" he said to her in a lov tender voice. Then he turned to Jamie.

"Aye, take him. It'll be a great chance for the lad."

"You're sure?" Jamie hesitated, speaking to his sister, rath than Ian. Jenny nodded. Her blue eyes glistened in the lampligh and the end of her nose was slightly red.

"I suppose it's best we give him his freedom while he sti thinks it's ours to give," she said. She looked at Jamie, then at m straight and steady. "But you'll take good care of him, aye?"

39

Lost, and by the Wind Grieved

This part of Scotland was as unlike the leafy glens and lochs near Lallybroch as the North Yorkshire moors. Here there were virtually no trees; only long sweeps of rock-strewn heather, rising into crags that touched the lowering sky and disappeared abruptly into curtains of mist.

As we got nearer to the seacoast, the mist became heavier, setting in earlier in the afternoon, lingering longer in the morning, so that only for a couple of hours in the middle of the day did we have anything like clear riding. The going was consequently slow, but none of us minded greatly, except Young Ian, who was beside himself with excitement, impatient to arrive.

"How far is it from the shore to the seals' island?" he asked Jamie for the tenth time.

"A quarter mile, I make it," his uncle replied.

"I can swim that far," Young Ian repeated, for the tenth time. His hands were clenched tightly on the reins, and his bony jaw set with determination.

"Aye, I know ye can," Jamie assured him patiently. He glanced at me, the hint of a smile hidden in the corner of his mouth. "Ye willna need to, though; just swim straight for the island, and the current will carry ye."

The boy nodded, and lapsed into silence, but his eyes were bright with anticipation.

The headland above the cove was mist-shrouded and deserted. Our voices echoed oddly in the fog, and we soon stopped talking, out of an abiding sense of eeriness. I could hear the seals barking far below, the sound wavering and mixing with the crash of the surf, so that now and then it sounded like sailors hallooing to one another over the sound of the sea.

Jamie pointed out the rock chimney of Ellen's tower to Young Ian, and taking a coil of rope from his saddle, picked his way over the broken rock of the headland to the entrance.

"Keep your shirt on 'til you're down," he told the lad, shouting to be heard above the wave. "Else the rock will tear your back to shreds."

Ian nodded understanding, then, the rope tied securely round his middle, gave me a nervous grin, took two jerky steps, and disappeared into the earth.

Jamie had the other end of the rope wrapped round his own waist, paying out the length of it carefully with his sound hand as the boy descended. Crawling on hands and knees, I made my way over the short turf and pebbles to the crumbling edge of the cliff, where I could look over to the half-moon beach below.

It seemed a very long time, but finally I saw Ian emerge from the bottom of the chimney, a small, antlike figure. He untied his rope, peered around, spotted us at the top of the cliff, and waved enthusiastically. I waved back, but Jamie merely muttered, "All right, get on, then," under his breath.

I could feel him tense beside me as the boy stripped off to his breeks and scrambled down the rocks to the water, and I felt his flinch as the small figure dived headlong into the gray-blue waves.

"Brrr!" I said, watching. "The water must be freezing!"

"It is," Jamie said with feeling. "Ian's right; it's a vicious time of year to be swimming."

His face was pale and set. I didn't think it was the result of discomfort from his wounded arm, though the long ride and the exercise with the rope couldn't have done it any good. While he had shown nothing but encouraging confidence while Ian was making his descent, he wasn't making any effort to hide his worry now. The fact was that there was no way for us to reach Ian should anything go wrong.

"Maybe we should have waited for the mist to lift," I said more to distract him than because I thought so.

"If we had 'til next Easter, we might," he agreed ironically. "Though I'll grant ye, I've seen it clearer than this," he added, squinting into the swirling murk below.

The three islands were only intermittently visible from the cliff
s the fog swept across them. I had been able to see the bobbing
lot of Ian's head for the first twenty yards as he left the shore, but
ιow he had disappeared into the mist.

"Do you think he's all right?" Jamie bent to help me scramble
pright. The cloth of his coat was damp and rough under my
ingers, soaked with mist and the fine droplets of ocean spray.

"Aye, he'll do. He's a bonny swimmer; and it's none so diffi-
ult a swim, either, once he's into the current." Still, he stared
ιto the mist as though sheer effort could pierce its veils.

On Jamie's advice, Young Ian had timed his descent to begin
/hen the tide began to go out, so as to have as much assistance as
ossible from the tide-race. Looking over the edge, I could see a
oating mass of bladder wrack, half-stranded on the widening
trip of beach.

"Perhaps two hours before he comes back." Jamie answered
ιy unspoken question. He turned reluctantly from his vain perusal
f the mist-hidden cove. "Damn, I wish I'd gone myself, arm or
o arm."

"Both Young Jamie and Michael have done it," I reminded
im. He gave me a rueful smile.

"Oh, aye. Ian will do fine. It's only that it's a good deal easier
o do something that's a bit dangerous than it is to wait and worry
'hile someone else does it."

"Ha," I told him. "So now you know what it's like being
ιarried to *you*."

He laughed.

"Oh, aye, I suppose so. Besides, it would be a shame to cheat
ung Ian of his adventure. Come on, then, let's get out of the
ind."

We moved inland a bit, away from the crumbling edge of the
iff, and sat down to wait, using the horses' bodies as shelter.
ough, shaggy Highland ponies, they appeared unmoved by the
ιpleasant weather, merely standing together, heads down, tails
rned against the wind.

The wind was too high for easy conversation. We sat quietly,
aning together like the horses, with our backs to the windy
ιore.

"What's that?" Jamie raised his head, listening.

"What?"

"I thought I heard shouting."

"I expect it's the seals," I said, but before the words were out of my mouth, he was up and striding toward the cliff's edge.

The cove was still full of curling mist, but the wind had uncovered the seals' island, and it was clearly visible, at least for the moment. There were no seals on it now, though.

A small boat was drawn up on a sloping rock shelf at one side of the island. Not a fisherman's boat; this one was longer and more pointed at the prow, with one set of oars.

As I stared, a man appeared from the center of the island. He carried something under one arm, the size and shape of the box Jamie had described. I didn't have long to speculate as to the nature of this object, though, for just then a second man came up the far slope of the island and into sight.

This one was carrying Young Ian. He had the boy's half-naked body slung carelessly over one shoulder. It swung head down, arms dangling with a limpness that made it clear the boy was unconscious or dead.

"Ian!" Jamie's hand clamped over my mouth before I could shout again.

"Hush!" He dragged me to my knees to keep me out of sight. We watched, helpless, as the second man heaved Ian carelessly into the boat, then took hold of the gunwales to run it back into the water. There wasn't a chance of making the descent down the chimney and the swim to the island before they succeeded in making their escape. But escape to where?

"Where did they come from?" I gasped. Nothing else stirred in the cove below, save the mist and the shifting kelp-beds, turning in the tide.

"A ship. It's a ship's boat." Jamie added something low and heartfelt in Gaelic, and then was gone. I turned to see him fling himself on one of the horses and wrench its head around. Then he was off, riding hell-for-leather across the headland, away from the cove.

Rough as the footing across the headland was, the horses were shod for it better than I was. I hastily mounted and followed Jamie, a high-pitched whinny of protest from Ian's hobbled mount ringing in my ears.

It was less than a quarter of a mile to the ocean side of the headland, but it seemed to take forever to reach it. I saw Jamie ahead of me, his hair flying loose in the wind, and beyond him, the ship, lying to offshore.

The ground broke away in a tumble of rock that fell down to the ocean, not so steep as the cliffs of the cove, but much too rough to take a horse down. By the time I had reined up, Jamie was off his horse, and picking his way down the rubble toward the water.

To the left, I could see the longboat from the island, pulling round the curve of the headland. Someone on the ship must have been looking out for them, for I heard a faint hail from the direction of the ship, and saw small figures suddenly appear in the rigging.

One of these must also have seen us, for there was a sudden agitation aboard, with heads popping up above the rail and more yelling. The ship was blue, with a broad black band painted all round it. There was a line of gunports set in this band, and as I watched, the forward one opened, and the round black eye of the gun peeked out.

"Jamie!" I shrieked, as loudly as I could. He looked up from the rocks at his feet, saw where I was pointing, and hurled himself flat in the rubble as the gun went off.

The report wasn't terribly loud, but there was a sort of whistling noise past my head that made me duck instinctively. Several of the rocks around me exploded in puffs of flying rock chips, and it occurred to me, rather belatedly, that the horses and I were a great deal more visible there at the top of the headland than Jamie was on the cliff below.

The horses, having grasped this essential fact long before I did, were on their way back to where we had left their hobbled fellow well before the dust had settled. I flung myself bodily over the edge of the headland, slid several feet in a shower of gravel, and wedged myself into a deep crevice in the cliff.

There was another explosion somewhere above my head, and I pressed myself even closer into the rock. Evidently the people on board the ship were satisfied with the effect of their last shot, for relative silence now descended.

My heart was hammering against my ribs, and the air around my face was full of a fine gray dust that gave me an irresistible urge to cough. I risked a look over my shoulder, and was in time to see the longboat being hoisted aboard ship. Of Ian and his two captors, there was no sign.

The gunport closed silently as I watched, and the rope that hel< the anchor slithered up, streaming water. The ship turned slowly seeking wind. The air was light and the sails barely puffed, bu even that was enough. Slowly, then faster, she was moving towar< the open sea. By the time Jamie had reached my roosting place the ship had all but vanished in the thick cloudbank that obscure< the horizon.

"Jesus" was all he said when he reached me, but he clutche< me hard for a moment. "Jesus."

He let go then, and turned to look out over the sea. Nothin< moved save a few tendrils of slow-floating mist. The whole worl< seemed stricken with silence; even the occasional cries of th< murres and shearwaters had been cut off by the cannon's boom.

The gray rock near my foot showed a fresh patch of lighter gray where shot had struck off a wide flake of stone. It was no mor< than three feet above the crevice where I had taken refuge.

"What shall we do?" I felt numbed, both by the shock of th< afternoon, and by the sheer enormity of what had happened. Im< possible to believe that in less than an hour, Ian had disappeare< from us as completely as though he had been wiped off the face o the earth. The fogbank loomed thick and impenetrable, a little wa off the coast before us, a barrier as impassible as the curtai between earth and the underworld.

My mind kept replaying images: the mist, drifting over th outlines of the silkies' island, the sudden appearance of the boa the men coming over the rocks, Ian's lanky, teenage body, white skinned as the mist, skinny limbs dangling like a disjointed doll' I had seen everything with that clarity that attends tragedy; ever detail fixed in my mind's eye, to be shown again and again, alway with that half-conscious feeling that, this time, I should be able t alter it.

Jamie's face was set in rigid lines, the furrows cut deep fror nose to mouth.

"I don't know," he said. "Damn me to hell, I don't *know* wha to do!" His hands flexed suddenly into fists at his sides. He shu his eyes, breathing heavily.

I felt even more frightened at this admission. In the brief time had been back with him, I had grown once more accustomed t having Jamie always know what to do, even in the direst circum<

tances. This confession seemed more upsetting than anything that had yet happened.

A sense of helplessness swirled round me like the mist. Every nerve cried out to do *something*. But what?

I saw the streak of blood on his cuff then; he had gashed his hand, climbing down the rocks. That, I could help, and I felt a sense of thankfulness that there was, after all, one thing I could do, however small.

"You've cut yourself," I said. I touched his injured hand. "Let me see; I'll wrap it for you."

"No," he said. He turned away, face strained, still looking desperately out into the fog. When I reached for him again, he jerked away.

"No, I said! Leave it be!"

I swallowed hard and wrapped my arms about myself under my cloak. There was little wind now, even on the headland, but it was cold and clammy nonetheless.

He rubbed his hand carelessly against the front of his coat, leaving a rusty smear. He was still staring out to sea, toward the spot where the ship had vanished. He closed his eyes, and pressed his lips tight together. Then he opened them, made a small gesture of apology toward me, and turned toward the headland.

"I suppose we must catch the horses," he said quietly. "Come on."

We walked back across the thick, short turf and strewn rocks without speaking, silent with shock and grief. I could see the horses, small stick-legged figures in the distance, clustered together with their hobbled companion. It seemed to have taken hours to run from the headland to the outer shore; going back seemed much longer.

"I don't think he was dead," I said, after what seemed like a year. I laid a hand tentatively on Jamie's arm, meaning to be comforting, but he wouldn't have noticed if I had struck him with a blackjack. He walked on slowly, head down.

"No," he said, and I saw him swallow hard. "No, he wasn't dead, or they'd not have taken him."

"*Did* they take him aboard the ship?" I pressed. "Did you see them?" I thought it might be better for him if he would talk.

He nodded. "Aye, they passed him aboard; I saw it clear. I suppose that's some hope," he muttered, as though to himself. "If

they didna knock him on the head at once, maybe they won't.'
Suddenly remembering that I was there, he turned and looked at
me, eyes searching my face.

''You're all right, Sassenach?''

I was scraped raw in several places, covered with filth, and
shaky-kneed with fright, but basically sound.

''I'm fine.'' I put my hand on his arm again. This time he let it
stay.

''That's good,'' he said softly, after a moment. He tucked my
hand into the crook of his elbow, and we went on.

''Have you any idea who they were?'' I had to raise my voice
slightly to be heard above the wash of the surf behind us, but I
wanted to keep him talking if I could.

He shook his head, frowning. The effort of talking seemed to be
bringing him slowly out of his own shock.

''I heard one of the sailors shout to the men in the boat, and he
spoke in French. But that proves nothing—sailors come from everywhere. Still, I have seen enough of ships at the docks to think
that this one didna have quite the look of a merchant—nor the
look of an English ship at all,'' he added, ''though I couldna say
why, exactly. The way the sails were rigged, maybe.''

''It was blue, with a black line painted round it,'' I said. ''That
was all I had time to see, before the guns started firing.''

Was it possible to trace a ship? The germ of the idea gave me
hope; perhaps the situation was not so hopeless as I had first
thought. If Ian was not dead, and we could find out where the ship
was going . . .

''Did you see a name on it?'' I asked.

''A name?'' He looked faintly surprised at the notion. ''What
on the ship?''

''Do ships not usually have their names painted on the sides?'' I
asked.

''No, what for?'' He sounded honestly puzzled.

''So you could bloody tell who they are!'' I said, exasperated.
Taken by surprise by my tone, he actually smiled a little.

''Aye, well, I should expect that perhaps they dinna much want
anyone telling who they are, given their business,'' he said dryly.

We paced on together for a few moments, thinking. Then I said
curiously, ''Well, but how do legitimate ships tell who each other
is, if they haven't got names painted on?''

He glanced at me, one eyebrow raised.

"I should know you from another woman," he pointed out, "and ye havena got your name stitched upon your bosom."

"Not so much as a letter 'A,'" I said, flippantly, but seeing his blank look, added, "You mean ships look different enough—and there are few enough of them—that you can tell one from another just by looking?"

"Not me," he said honestly. "I know a few; ships where I ken the captain, and have been aboard to do business, or a few like the packet boats, that go back and forth so often that I've seen them in port dozens of times. But a sailing man would ken a great deal more."

"Then it *might* be possible to find out what the ship that took Ian is called?"

He nodded, looking at me curiously. "Aye, I think so. I have been trying to call to mind everything about it as we walked, so as to tell Jared. He'll know a great many ships, and a great many more captains—and perhaps one of them will know a blue ship, wide in the beam, with three masts, twelve guns, and a scowling figurehead."

My heart bounded upward. "So you *do* have a plan!"

"I wouldna call it so much as a plan," he said. "It's only I canna think of anything else to do." He shrugged, and wiped a hand over his face. Tiny droplets of moisture were condensing on us as we walked, glistening in the ruddy hairs of his eyebrows and coating his cheeks with a wetness like tears. He sighed.

"The passage is arranged from Inverness. The best I can see to do is to go; Jared will be expecting us in Le Havre. When we see him, perhaps he can help us to find out what the blue ship is called, and maybe where it's bound. Aye," he said dryly, anticipating my question, "ships have home ports, and if they dinna belong to the Navy, they have runs they commonly make, and papers for the harbormaster, too, showing where they're bound."

I began to feel better than I had since Ian had descended Ellen's tower.

"If they're not pirates or privateers, that is," he added, with a warning look which put an immediate damper on my rising spirits.

"And if they are?"

"Then God knows, but I don't," he said briefly, and would not say any more until we reached the horses.

They were grazing on the headland near the tower where we ha
left Ian's mount, behaving as though nothing had happened, pre
tending to find the tough sea grass delicious.

"Tcha!" Jamie viewed them disapprovingly. "Silly beasts."
He grabbed the coil of rope and wrapped it twice round a project
ing stone. Handing me the end, with a terse instruction to hold i
he dropped the free end down the chimney, shed his coat an
shoes, and disappeared down the rope himself without furthe
remark.

Sometime later, he came back up, sweating profusely, with
small bundle tucked under his arm. Young Ian's shirt, coat, shoe
and stockings, with his knife and the small leather pouch in whic
the lad kept such valuables as he had.

"Do you mean to take them home to Jenny?" I asked. I tried t
imagine what Jenny might think, say, or do at the news, an
succeeded all too well. I felt a little sick, knowing that the hollow
aching sense of loss I felt was as nothing to what hers would b

Jamie's face was flushed from the climb, but at my words, th
blood drained from his cheeks. His hands tightened on the bundl

"Oh, aye," he said, very softly, with great bitterness. "Aye,
shall go home and tell my sister that I have lost her youngest son
She didna want him to come wi' me, but I insisted. I'll take care c
him, I said. And now he is hurt and maybe dead—but here are h
clothes, to remember him by?" His jaw clenched, and he swa
lowed convulsively.

"I'd rather be dead myself," he said.

He knelt on the ground then, shaking out the articles of cloth
ing, folding them carefully, and laying them together in a pile. H
folded the coat carefully around the other things, stood up, an
stuffed the bundle into his saddlebag.

"Ian will be needing them, I expect, when we find him," I sai
trying to sound convinced.

Jamie looked at me, but after a moment, he nodded.

"Aye," he said softly. "I expect he will."

It was too late in the day to begin the ride to Inverness. The su
was setting, announcing the fact with a dull reddish glow th
barely penetrated the gathering mist. Without speaking, we beg;
to make camp. There was cold food in the saddlebags, but neith
of us had the heart to eat. Instead, we rolled ourselves up in cloa

nd blankets and lay down to sleep, cradled in small hollows that
amie had scooped in the earth.

I couldn't sleep. The ground was hard and stony beneath my
ips and shoulders, and the thunder of the surf below would have
een sufficient to keep me awake, even had my mind not been
lled with thoughts of Ian.

Was he badly hurt? The limpness of his body had bespoken
ome damage, but I had seen no blood. Presumably, he had merely
een hit on the head. If so, what would he feel when he woke, to
nd himself abducted, and being carried farther from home and
amily with each passing minute?

And how were we ever to find him? When Jamie had first
entioned Jared, I had felt hopeful, but the more I thought of it,
e slimmer seemed the prospects of actually finding a single ship,
hich might now be sailing in any direction at all, to anyplace in
e world. And would his captors bother to keep Ian, or would
ey, on second thoughts, conclude that he was a dangerous nui-
nce, and pitch him overboard?

I didn't think I slept, but I must have dozed, my dreams full of
ouble. I woke shivering with cold, and edged out a hand, reach-
g for Jamie. He wasn't there. When I sat up, I found that he had
read his blanket over me while I dozed, but it was a poor substi-
te for the heat of his body.

He was sitting some distance away, with his back to me. The
fshore wind had risen with the setting of the sun, and blown
me of the mist away; a half-moon shed enough light through the
ouds to show me his hunched figure clearly.

I got up and walked over to him, folding my cloak tight about
e against the chill. My steps made a light crunching sound on the
umbled granite, but the sound was drowned in the sighing rum-
e of the sea below. Still, he must have heard me; he didn't turn
ound, but gave no sign of surprise when I sank down beside him.

He sat with his chin in his hands, his elbows on his knees, eyes
ide and sightless as he gazed out into the dark water of the cove.
the seals were awake, they were quiet tonight.

"Are you all right?" I said quietly. "It's beastly cold." He was
earing nothing but his coat, and in the small, chilled hours of the
ght, in the wet, cold air above the sea, that was far from enough.
:ould feel the tiny, constant shiver that ran through him when I
t my hand on his arm.

"Aye, I'm fine," he said, with a marked lack of conviction.

I merely snorted at this piece of prevarication, and sat down next to him on another chunk of granite.

"It wasn't your fault," I said, after we had sat in silence for some time, listening to the sea.

"Ye should go and sleep, Sassenach." His voice was even, but with an undertone of hopelessness that made me move closer to him, trying to embrace him. He was clearly reluctant to touch me, but I was shivering very obviously myself by this time.

"I'm not going anywhere."

He sighed deeply and pulled me closer, settling me upon his knee, so that his arms came inside my cloak, holding tight. Little by little, the shivering eased.

"What are you doing out here?" I asked at last.

"Praying," he said softly. "Or trying to."

"I shouldn't have interrupted you." I made as though to move away, but his hold on me tightened.

"No, stay," he said. We stayed clasped close; I could feel the warmth of his breathing in my ear. He drew in his breath as though about to speak, but then let it out without saying anything. I turned and touched his face.

"What is it, Jamie?"

"Is it wrong for me to have ye?" he whispered. His face was bone-white, his eyes no more than dark pits in the dim light. "I keep thinking—is it my fault? Have I sinned so greatly, wanting you so much, needing ye more than life itself?"

"Do you?" I took his face between my hands, feeling the wide bones cold under my palms. "And if you do—how can that be wrong? I'm your wife." In spite of everything, the simple word "wife" made my heart lighten.

He turned his face slightly, so his lips lay against my palm, and his hand came up, groping for mine. His fingers were cold, too, and hard as driftwood soaked in seawater.

"I tell myself so. God has given ye to me; how can I not love you? And yet—I keep thinking, and canna stop."

He looked down at me then, brow furrowed with trouble.

"The treasure—it was all right to use it when there was need, feed the hungry, or to rescue folk from prison. But to try to buy my freedom from guilt—to use it only so that I might live free

allybroch with you, and not trouble myself over Laoghaire—I think maybe that was wrong to do.''

I drew his hand down around my waist, and pulled him close. He came, eager for comfort, and laid his head on my shoulder.

"Hush," I said to him, though he hadn't spoken again. "Be still. Jamie, have you ever done something for yourself alone—not with any thought of anyone else?"

His hand rested gently on my back, tracing the seam of my bodice, and his breathing held the hint of a smile.

"Oh, many and many a time," he whispered. "When I saw you. When I took ye, not caring did ye want me or no, did ye have somewhere else to be, someone else to love."

"Bloody man," I whispered in his ear, rocking him as best I could. "You're an awful fool, Jamie Fraser. And what about Brianna? That wasn't wrong, was it?"

"No." He swallowed; I could hear the sound of it clearly, and feel the pulse beat in his neck where I held him. "But now I have taken ye back from her, as well. I love you—and I love Ian, like he was my own. And I am thinking maybe I cannot have ye both."

"Jamie Fraser," I said again, with as much conviction as I could put into my voice, "you're a terrible fool." I smoothed the hair back from his forehead and twisted my fist in the thick tail at his nape, pulling his head back to make him look at me.

I thought my face must look to him as his did to me; the bleached bones of a skull, with the lips and eyes dark as blood.

"You didn't force me to come to you, or snatch me away from Brianna. I came, because I wanted to—because I wanted *you,* as much as you did me—and my being here has nothing to do with what's happened. We're *married,* blast you, by any standard you are to name—before God, man, Neptune, or what-have-you."

"Neptune?" he said, sounding a little stunned.

"Be quiet," I said. "We're married, I say, and it isn't wicked for you to want me, or to have me, and no God worth his salt would take your nephew away from you because you wanted to be happy. So there!

"Besides," I added, pulling back and looking up at him a moment later, "I'm not bloody going back, so what could you do about it, anyway?"

The small vibration in his chest this time was laughter, not cold.

"Take ye and be damned for it, I expect," he said. He kissed my forehead gently. "Loving you has put me through hell more than once, Sassenach; I'll risk it again, if need be."

"Bah," I said. "And you think loving *you*'s been a bed of roses, do you?"

This time he laughed out loud.

"No," he said, "but you'll maybe keep doing it?"

"Maybe I will, at that."

"You're a verra stubborn woman," he said, the smile clear in his voice.

"It bloody takes one to know one," I said, and then we were both quiet for quite some time.

It was very late—perhaps four o'clock in the morning. The half-moon was low in the sky, seen only now and then through the moving clouds. The clouds themselves were moving faster; the wind was shifting and the mist breaking up, in the turning hour between dark and dawn. Somewhere below, one of the seals barked loudly, once.

"Do ye think perhaps ye could stand to go now?" Jamie said suddenly. "Not wait for the daylight? Once off the headland, the going's none so bad that the horses canna manage in the dark."

My whole body ached from weariness, and I was starving, but stood up at once, and brushed the hair out of my face.

"Let's go," I said.

PART EIGHT

On the Water

40

I Shall Go Down to the Sea

"It will have to be the *Artemis*." Jared flipped shut the cover of his portable writing desk and rubbed his brow, frowning. Jamie's cousin had been in his fifties when I knew him before, and was now well past seventy, but the snub-nosed hatchet face, the spare, narrow frame, and the tireless capacity for work were just the same. Only his hair marked his age, gone from lank darkness to a scanty, pure and gleaming white, jauntily tied with a red silk ribbon.

"She's no more than a midsized sloop, with a crew of forty or so," he remarked. "But it's late in the season, and we'll not likely do better—all of the Indiamen will have gone a month since. *Artemis* would have gone with the convoy to Jamaica, was she not laid up for repair."

"I'd sooner have a ship of yours—and one of your captains," Jamie assured him. "The size doesna matter."

Jared cocked a skeptical eyebrow at his cousin. "Oh? Well, and we may find it matters more than ye think, out at sea. It's like to be squally, this late in the season, and a sloop will be bobbin' like a cork. Might I ask how ye weathered the Channel crossing in the packet boat, cousin?"

Jamie's face, already drawn and grim, grew somewhat grimmer at this question. The completest of landlubbers, he was not just prone to seasickness, but prostrated by it. He had been violently ill all the way from Inverness to Le Havre, though sea and weather had been quite calm. Now, some six hours later, safe ashore in

Jared's warehouse by the quay, there was still a pale tinge to his lips and dark circles beneath his eyes.

"I'll manage," he said shortly.

Jared eyed him dubiously, well aware of his response to seagoing craft of any kind. Jamie could scarcely set foot on a ship at anchor without going green; the prospect of his crossing the Atlantic, sealed inescapably in a small and constantly tossing ship for two or three months, was enough to boggle the stoutest mind. It had been troubling mine for some time.

"Well, I suppose there's no help for it," Jared said with a sigh, echoing my thought. "And at least you'll have a physician to hand," he added, with a smile at me. "That is, I suppose you intend accompanying him, my dear?"

"Yes indeed," I assured him. "How long will it be before the ship is ready? I'd like to find a good apothecary's, to stock my medicine chest before the voyage."

Jared pursed his lips in concentration. "A week, God willing," he said. "*Artemis* is in Bilbao at the moment; she's to carry a cargo of tanned Spanish hides, with a load of copper from Italy—she'll ship that here, once she arrives, which should be day after tomorrow, with a fair wind. I've no captain signed on for the voyage yet, but a good man in mind; I may have to go to Paris to fetch him, though, and that will be two days there and two back. Add a day to complete stores, fill the water casks, add all the bits and pieces, and she should be ready to leave at dawn tomorrow week."

"How long to the West Indies?" Jamie asked. The tension in him showed in the lines of his body, little affected either by our journey or by the brief rest. He was strung taut as a bow, and likely to remain so until we had found Young Ian.

"Two months, in the season," Jared replied, the small frown still lining his forehead. "But you're a month past the season now; hit the winter gales and it could be three. Or more."

Or never, but Jared, ex-seaman that he was, was too superstitious—or too tactful—to voice this possibility. Still, I saw him touch the wood of his desk surreptitiously for luck.

Neither would he voice the other thought that occupied my mind; we had no positive proof that the blue ship was headed for the West Indies. We had only the records Jared had obtained for us from the Le Havre harbormaster, showing two visits by the ship—

ptly named *Bruja*—within the last five years, each time giving her ome port as Bridgetown, on the island of Barbados.

"Tell me about her again—the ship that took Young Ian," Jared aid. "How did she ride? High in the water, or sunk low, as if she vere loaded heavy for a voyage?"

Jamie closed his eyes for a moment, concentrating, then opened hem with a nod. "Heavy-laden, I could swear it. Her gunports vere no more than six feet from the water."

Jared nodded, satisfied. "Then she was leaving port, not com- ng in. I've messengers out to all the major ports in France, Portu- al, and Spain. With luck, they'll find the port she shipped from, nd then we'll know her destination for sure from her papers." His hin lips quirked suddenly downward. "Unless she's turned pirate, nd sailing under false papers, that is."

The old wine merchant carefully set aside the lap desk, its arved mahogany richly darkened by years of use, and rose to his eet, moving stiffly.

"Well, that's the most that can be done for the moment. Let's o to the house, now; Mathilde will have supper waiting. Tomor- ow I'll take ye over the manifests and orders, and your wife can nd her bits of herbs."

It was nearly five o'clock, and full dark at this time of year, but ared had two linksmen waiting to escort us the short distance to is house, equipped with torches to light the way and armed with tout clubs. Le Havre was a thriving port city, and the quay district vas no place to walk alone after dark, particularly if one was nown as a prosperous wine merchant.

Despite the exhaustion of the Channel crossing, the oppressive lamminess and pervasive fish-smell of Le Havre, and a gnawing unger, I felt my spirits rise as we followed the torches through the ark, narrow streets. Thanks to Jared, we had at least a chance of nding Young Ian.

Jared had concurred with Jamie's opinion that if the pirates of e *Bruja*—for so I thought of them—had not killed Young Ian on e spot, they were likely to keep him unharmed. A healthy young ale of any race could be sold as a slave or indentured servant in e West Indies for upward of two hundred pounds; a respectable um by current standards.

If they did intend so to dispose of Young Ian profitably, *and* if e knew the port to which they were sailing, it should be a reason-

ably easy matter to find and recover the boy. A gust of wind and a
few chilly drops from the hovering clouds dampened my optimism
slightly, reminding me that while it might be no great matter to
find Ian once we had reached the West Indies, both the *Bruja* and
the *Artemis* had to reach the islands first. And the winter storms
were beginning.

The rain increased through the night, drumming insistently on
the slate roof above our heads. I would normally have found the
sound soothing and soporific; under the circumstances, the low
thrum seemed threatening, not peaceful.

Despite Jared's substantial dinner and the excellent wines that
accompanied it, I found myself unable to sleep, my mind summoning images of rain-soaked canvas and the swell of heavy seas.
At least my morbid imaginings were keeping only myself awake;
Jamie had not come up with me but had stayed to talk with Jared
about the arrangements for the upcoming voyage.

Jared was willing to risk a ship and a captain to help in the
search. In return, Jamie would sail as supercargo.

"As *what*?" I had said, hearing this proposal.

"The supercargo," Jared had explained patiently. "That's the
man whose duty it is to oversee the loading, the unloading, and the
sale and disposition of the cargo. The captain and the crew merely
sail the ship; someone's got to look after the contents. In a case
where the welfare of the cargo will be affected, the supercargo's
orders may override even the captain's authority."

And so it was arranged. While Jared was more than willing to
go to some risk in order to help a kinsman, he saw no reason not to
profit from the arrangement. He had therefore made quick provision for a miscellaneous cargo to be loaded from Bilbao and Le
Havre; we would sail to Jamaica to unload the bulk of it, and
would arrange for the reloading of the *Artemis* with rum produced
by the sugarcane plantation of Fraser et Cie on Jamaica, for the
return trip.

The return trip, however, would not occur until good sailing
weather returned, in late April or early May. For the time between
arrival on Jamaica in February and return to Scotland in May,
Jamie would have disposal of the *Artemis* and her crew, to travel to

Barbados—or other places—in search of Young Ian. Three months. I hoped it would be enough.

It was a generous arrangement. Still, Jared, who had been an expatriate wine-seller for many years in France, was wealthy enough that the loss of a ship, while distressing, would not cripple him. The fact did not escape me that while Jared was risking a small portion of his fortune, we were risking our lives.

The wind seemed to be dying; it no longer howled down the chimney with quite such force. Sleep proving still elusive, I got out of bed, and with a quilt wrapped round my shoulders for warmth, went to the window.

The sky was a deep, mottled gray, the scudding rain clouds edged with brilliant light from the moon that hid behind them, and the glass was streaked with rain. Still, enough light seeped through the clouds for me to make out the masts of the ships moored at the quay, less than a quarter of a mile away. They swayed to and fro, their sails furled tight against the storm, rising and falling in uneasy rhythm as the waves rocked the boats at anchor. In a week's time, I would be on one.

I had not dared to think what life might be like once I had found Jamie, lest I not find him after all. Then I *had* found him, and in quick succession, had contemplated life as a printer's wife among the political and literary worlds of Edinburgh, a dangerous and fugitive existence as a smuggler's lady, and finally, the busy, settled life of a Highland farm, which I had known before and loved.

Now, in equally quick succession, all these possibilities had been jerked away, and I faced an unknown future once more.

Oddly enough, I was not so much distressed by this as excited by it. I had been settled for twenty years, rooted as a barnacle by my attachments to Brianna, to Frank, to my patients. Now fate—and my own actions—had ripped me loose from all those things, and I felt as though I were tumbling free in the surf, at the mercy of forces a great deal stronger than myself.

My breath had misted the glass. I traced a small heart in the cloudiness, as I had used to do for Brianna on cold mornings. Then, I would put her initials inside the heart—B.E.R., for Brianna Ellen Randall. Would she still call herself Randall? I wondered, or Fraser, now? I hesitated, then drew two letters inside the outline of the heart—a "J" and a "C."

I was still standing before the window when the door opened and Jamie came in.

"Are ye awake still?" he asked, rather unnecessarily.

"The rain kept me from sleeping." I went and embraced him, glad of his warm solidness to dispel the cold gloom of the night.

He hugged me, resting his cheek against my hair. He smelt faintly of seasickness, much more strongly of candlewax and ink.

"Have you been writing?" I asked.

He looked down at me in astonishment. "I have, but how did ye know that?"

"You smell of ink."

He smiled slightly, stepping back and running his hand through his hair. "You've a nose as keen as a truffle pig's, Sassenach."

"Why, thank you, what a graceful compliment," I said. "What were you writing?"

The smile disappeared from his face, leaving him looking strained and tired.

"A letter to Jenny," he said. He went to the table, where he shed his coat and began to unfasten his stock and jabot. "I didna want to write her until we'd seen Jared, and I could tell her what plans we had, and what the prospects were for bringing Ian home safe." He grimaced, and pulled the shirt over his head. "God knows what she'll do when she gets it—and thank God, I'll be at sea when she does," he added wryly, emerging from the folds of linen.

It couldn't have been an easy piece of composition, but I thought he seemed easier for the writing of it. He sat down to take off his shoes and stockings, and I came behind him to undo the clubbed queue of his hair.

"I'm glad the writing's over, at least," he said, echoing my thought. "I'd been dreading telling her, more than anything else."

"You told her the truth?"

He shrugged. "I always have."

Except about me. I didn't voice the thought, though, but began to rub his shoulders, kneading the knotted muscles.

"What did Jared do with Mr. Willoughby?" I asked, massaging, bringing the Chinese to mind. He had accompanied us on the Channel crossing, sticking to Jamie like a small blue-silk shadow. Jared, used to seeing everything on the docks, had taken Mr. Willoughby in stride, bowing gravely to him and addressing him with a few words of Mandarin, but his housekeeper had viewed his unusual guest with considerably more suspicion.

"I believe he's gone to sleep in the stable." Jamie yawned, and stretched himself luxuriously. "Mathilde said she wasna accustomed to have heathens in the house and didna mean to start now. She was sprinkling the kitchen wi' holy water after he ate supper here." Glancing up, he caught sight of the heart I had traced on the windowpane, black against the misted glass, and smiled.

"What's that?"

"Just silliness," I said.

He reached up and took my right hand, the ball of his thumb caressing the small scar at the base of my own thumb, the letter "J" he had made with the point of his knife, just before I left him, before Culloden.

"I didna ask," he said, "whether ye wished to come with me. I could leave ye here; Jared would have ye stay wi' him and welcome, here or in Paris. Or ye could go back to Lallybroch, if ye wished."

"No, you didn't ask," I said. "Because you knew bloody well what the answer would be."

We looked at each other and smiled. The lines of heartsickness and weariness had lifted from his face. The candlelight glowed softly on the burnished crown of his head as he bent and gently kissed the palm of my hand.

The wind still whistled in the chimney, and the rain ran down the glass like tears outside, but it no longer mattered. Now I could sleep.

The sky had cleared by morning. A brisk, cold breeze rattled the windowpanes of Jared's study, but couldn't penetrate to the cozy room inside. The house at Le Havre was much smaller than his lavish Paris residence, but still boasted three stories of solid half-timbered comfort.

I pushed my feet farther toward the crackling fire, and dipped my quill into the inkwell. I was making up a list of all the things I thought might be needed in the medical way for a two-month voyage. Distilled alcohol was both the most important and the easiest to obtain; Jared had promised to get me a cask in Paris.

"We'd best label it something else, though," he'd told me. "O
the sailors will have drunk it before you've left port."

Purified lard, I wrote slowly, *St.-John's-wort; garlic, te
pounds; yarrow.* I wrote *borage,* then shook my head and crosse
it out, replacing it with the older name by which it was more likel
known now, *bugloss.*

It was slow work. At one time, I had known the medicinal use
of all the common herbs, and not a few uncommon ones. I had ha
to; they were all that was available.

At that, many of them were surprisingly effective. Despite th
skepticism—and outspoken horror—of my supervisors and col
leagues at the hospital in Boston, I had used them occasionally o
my modern patients to good effect. ("Did you *see* what Dr. Ran
dall did?" a shocked intern's cry echoed in memory, making m
smile as I wrote. "She fed the stomach in 134B *boiled flowers!*"

The fact remained that one wouldn't use yarrow and comfrey o
a wound if iodine were available, nor treat a systemic infectio
with bladderwort in preference to penicillin.

I had forgotten a lot, but as I wrote the names of the herbs, th
look and the smell of each one began to come back to me—th
dark, bituminous look and pleasant light smell of birch oil, th
sharp tang of the mint family, the dusty sweet smell of chamomil
and the astringency of bistort.

Across the table, Jamie was struggling with his own lists. A
poor penman, he wrote laboriously with his crippled right han
pausing now and then to rub the healing wound above his le
elbow and mutter curses under his breath.

"Have ye lime juice on your list, Sassenach?" he inquire
looking up.

"No. Ought I to have?"

He brushed a strand of hair out of his face and frowned at th
sheet of paper in front of him.

"It depends. Customarily, it would be the ship's surgeon wh
provides the lime juice, but in a ship the size of the *Artemis,* ther
generally isn't a surgeon, and the provision of foodstuffs falls t
the purser. But there isn't a purser, either; there's no time to find
dependable man, so I shall fill that office, too."

"Well, if you'll be purser and supercargo, I expect I'll be th
closest thing to a ship's surgeon," I said, smiling slightly. "I'll g
the lime juice."

"All right." We returned to a companionable scratching, unbroken until the entrance of Josephine, the parlormaid, to announce the arrival of a person. Her long nose wrinkled in unconscious disapproval at the information.

"He waits upon the doorstep. The butler tried to send him away, but he insists that he has an appointment with you, Monsieur James?" The questioning tone of this last implied that nothing could seem more unlikely, but duty compelled her to relay the improbable suggestion.

Jamie's eyebrows rose. "A person? What sort of person?" Josephine's lips primmed together as though she really could not bring herself to say. I was becoming curious to see this person, and ventured over to the window. Sticking my head far out, I could see the top of a very dusty black slouch hat on the doorstep, and not much more.

"He looks like a peddler; he's got a bundle of some kind on his back," I reported, craning out still farther, hands on the sill. Jamie clutched me by the waist and drew me back, thrusting his own head out in turn.

"Och, it's the coin dealer Jared mentioned!" he exclaimed. "Bring him up, then."

With an eloquent expression on her narrow face, Josephine departed, returning in short order with a tall, gangling youth of perhaps twenty, dressed in a badly outmoded style of coat, wide unbuckled breeches that flapped limply about his skinny shanks, drooping stockings and the cheapest of wooden sabots.

The filthy black hat, courteously removed indoors, revealed a thin face with an intelligent expression, adorned with a vigorous, if scanty, brown beard. Since virtually no one in Le Havre other than a few seamen wore a beard, it hardly needed the small shiny black skullcap on the newcomer's head to tell me he was a Jew.

The boy bowed awkwardly to me, then to Jamie, struggling with the straps of his peddler's pack.

"Madame," he said, with a bob that made his curly sidelocks dance, "Monsieur. It is most good of you to receive me." He spoke French oddly, with a singsong intonation that made him hard to follow.

While I entirely understood Josephine's reservations about this . . . person, still, he had wide, guileless blue eyes that made me smile at him despite his generally unprepossessing appearance.

"It's we who should be grateful to you," Jamie was saying. "I had not expected you to come so promptly. My cousin tells me your name is Mayer?"

The coin dealer nodded, a shy smile breaking out amid the sprigs of his youthful beard.

"Yes, Mayer. It is no trouble; I was in the city already."

"Yet you come from Frankfort, no? A long way," Jamie said politely. He smiled as he looked over Mayer's costume, which looked as though he had retrieved it from a rubbish tip. "And a dusty one, too, I expect," he added. "Will you take wine?"

Mayer looked flustered at this offer, but after opening and closing his mouth a few times, finally settled on a silent nod of acceptance.

His shyness vanished, though, once the pack was opened. Though from the outside the shapeless bundle looked as though it might contain, at best, a change of ragged linen and Mayer's midday meal, once opened it revealed several small wooden racks, cleverly fitted into a framework inside the pack, each rack packed carefully with tiny leather bags, cuddling together like eggs in a nest.

Mayer removed a folded square of fabric from beneath the racks, whipped it open, and spread it with something of a flourish on Jamie's desk. Then one by one, Mayer opened the bags and drew out the contents, placing each gleaming round reverently on the deep blue velvet of the cloth.

"An Aquilia Severa aureus," he said, touching one small coin that glowed with the deep mellowness of ancient gold from the velvet. "And here, a Sestercius of the Calpurnia family." His voice was soft and his hands sure, stroking the edge of a silver coin only slightly worn, or cradling one in his palm to demonstrate the weight of it.

He looked up from the coins, eyes bright with the reflections of the precious metal.

"Monsieur Fraser tells me that you desire to inspect as many of the Greek and Roman rarities as possible. I have not my whole stock with me, of course, but I have quite a few—and I could send to Frankfort for others, if you desire."

Jamie smiled, shaking his head. "I'm afraid we haven't time, Mr. Mayer. We—"

"Just Mayer, Monsieur Fraser," the young man interrupted, perfectly polite, but with a slight edge in his voice.

"Indeed." Jamie bowed slightly. "I hope my cousin shall not have misled you. I shall be most happy to pay the cost of your journey, and something for your time, but I am not wishful to purchase any of your stock myself . . . Mayer."

The young man's eyebrows rose in inquiry, along with one shoulder.

"What I wish," Jamie said slowly, leaning forward to look closely at the coins on display, "is to compare your stock with my recollection of several ancient coins I have seen, and then—should I see any that are similar—to inquire whether you—or your family, I should say, for I expect you are too young yourself—should be familiar with anyone who might have purchased such coins twenty years ago."

He glanced up at the young Jew, who was looking justifiably astonished, and smiled.

"That may be asking a bit much of you, I know. But my cousin tells me that your family is one of the few who deals in such matters, and is by far the most knowledgeable. If you can acquaint me likewise with any persons in the West Indies with interests in this area, I should be deeply obliged to you."

Mayer sat looking at him for a moment, then inclined his head, the sunlight winking from the border of small jet beads that adorned his skullcap. It was plain that he was intensely curious, but he merely touched his pack and said, "My father or my uncle would have sold such coins, not me; but I have here the catalogue and record of every coin that has passed through our hands in thirty years. I will tell you what I can."

He drew the velvet cloth toward Jamie and sat back.

"Do you see anything here like the coins you remember?"

Jamie studied the rows of coins with close attention, then gently nudged a silver piece, about the size of an American quarter. Three leaping porpoises circled its edge, surrounding a charioteer at the center.

"This one," he said. "There were several like it—small differences, but several with these porpoises." He looked again, picked out a worn gold disc with an indistinct profile, then a silver one, somewhat larger and in better condition, with a man's head shown both full-face and in profile.

"These," he said. "Fourteen of the gold ones, and ten of the ones with two heads."

"Ten!" Mayer's bright eyes popped wide with astonishment. "I should not have thought there were so many in Europe."

Jamie nodded. "I'm quite certain—I saw them closely; handled them, even."

"These are the twin heads of Alexander," Mayer said, touching the coin with reverence. "Very rare indeed. It is a tetradrachm struck to commemorate the battle fought at Amphipolos, and the founding of a city on the site of the battlefield."

Jamie listened with attention, a slight smile on his lips. While he had no great interest in ancient money himself, he did have a great appreciation for a man with a passion.

A quarter of an hour more, another consultation of the catalogue, and the business was complete. Four Greek drachmas of type Jamie recognized had been added to the collection, several small gold and silver coins, and a thing called a quintinarius, Roman coin in heavy gold.

Mayer bent and reached into his pack once more, this time pulling out a sheaf of foolscap pages furled into a roll and tied with ribbon. Untied, they showed row upon row of what looked from a distance like bird tracks; on closer inspection, they proved to be Hebraic writing, inked small and precise.

He thumbed slowly through the pages, stopping here and there with a murmured "Um," then passing on. At last he laid the pages on his shabby knee and looked up at Jamie, head cocked to one side.

"Our transactions are naturally carried out in confidence, Monsieur," he said, "and so while I could tell you, for example, that certainly we had sold such and such a coin, in such and such year, I should not be able to tell you the name of the purchaser." He paused, evidently thinking, then went on.

"We did in fact sell coins of your description—three drachmas, two each of the heads of Egalabalus and the double head of Alexander, and no fewer than six of the gold Calpurnian aurei in the year 1745." He hesitated.

"Normally, that is all I could tell you. However . . . in this case, Monsieur, I happen to know that the original buyer of these coins is dead—has been dead for some years, in fact. Really,

nnot see that under the circumstances . . ." He shrugged, mak-
g up his mind.

"The purchaser was an Englishman, Monsieur. His name was
larence Marylebone, Duke of Sandringham."

"Sandringham!" I exclaimed, startled into speech.

Mayer looked curiously at me, then at Jamie, whose face be-
ayed nothing beyond polite interest.

"Yes, Madame," he said. "I know that the Duke is dead, for he
ossessed an extensive collection of ancient coins, which my uncle
ought from his heirs in 1746—the transaction is listed here." He
ised the catalogue slightly, and let it fall.

I knew the Duke of Sandringham was dead, too, and by more
amediate experience. Jamie's godfather, Murtagh, had killed
m, on a dark night in March 1746, soon before the battle of
alloden brought an end to the Jacobite rebellion. I swallowed
iefly, recalling my last sight of the Duke's face, its blueberry
es fixed in an expression of intense surprise.

Mayer's eyes went back and forth between us, then he added
sitantly, "I can tell you also this; when my uncle purchased the
ike's collection after his death, there were no tetradrachms in

"No," Jamie murmured, to himself. "There wouldn't have
en." Then, recollecting himself, he stood and reached for the
canter that stood on the sideboard.

"I thank you, Mayer," he said formally. "And now, let us drink
you and your wee book, there."

A few minutes later, Mayer was kneeling on the floor, doing up
e fastenings of his ragged pack. The small pouch filled with
ver livres that Jamie had given him in payment was in his
cket. He rose and bowed in turn to Jamie and to me before
aightening and putting on his disreputable hat.

"I bid you goodbye, Madame," he said.

"Goodbye to you, too, Mayer," I replied. Then I asked, some-
at hesitantly, "Is 'Mayer' really your only name?"

Something flickered in the wide blue eyes, but he answered
litely, heaving the heavy sack onto his back, "Yes, Madame.
e Jews of Frankfort are not allowed to use family names." He
ked up and smiled lopsidedly. "For the sake of convenience,
e neighbors call us after an old red shield that was painted on the

front of our house, many years ago. But beyond that . . . no Madame. We have no name.''

Josephine came then to conduct our visitor to the kitchen, taking care to walk several paces in front of him, her nostrils pinched white as though smelling something foul. Mayer stumbled after her, his clumsy sabots clattering on the polished floor.

Jamie relaxed in his chair, eyes abstracted in deep thought.

I heard the door close downstairs a few minutes later, with what was almost a slam, and the click of sabots on the stone step below. Jamie heard it too, and turned toward the window.

''Well, Godspeed to ye, Mayer Red-Shield,'' he said, smiling.

''Jamie,'' I said, suddenly thinking of something, ''do you speak German?''

''Eh? Oh, aye,'' he said vaguely, his attention still fixed on the window and the noises outside.

''What is 'red shield' in German?'' I asked.

He looked blank for a moment, then his eyes cleared as his brain made the proper connection.

''*Rothschild,* Sassenach,'' he said. ''Why?''

''Just a thought,'' I said. I looked toward the window, where the clatter of wooden shoes was long since lost in the noises of the street. ''I suppose everyone has to start somewhere.''

''Fifteen men on a dead man's chest,'' I observed. ''Yo-ho-ho and a bottle of rum.''

Jamie gave me a look.

''Oh, aye?'' he said.

''The Duke being the dead man,'' I explained. ''Do you think the seals' treasure was really his?''

''I couldna say for sure, but it seems at least likely.'' Jamie's two stiff fingers tapped briefly on the table in a meditative rhythm. ''When Jared mentioned Mayer the coin dealer to me, I thought worth inquiring—for surely the most likely person to have sent the *Bruja* to retrieve the treasure was the person who put it there.''

''Good reasoning,'' I said, ''but evidently it wasn't the same person, if it was the Duke who put it there. Do you think the whole treasure amounted to fifty thousand pounds?''

Jamie squinted at his reflection in the rounded side of the

inter, considering. Then he picked it up and refilled his glass, to ssist thought.

"Not as metal, no. But did ye notice the prices that some of ose coins in Mayer's catalogue have sold for?"

"I did."

"As much as a thousand pound—sterling!—for a moldy bit of etal!" he said, marveling.

"I don't think metal molds," I said, "but I take your point. nyway," I said, dismissing the question with a wave of my hand, the point here is this: Do you suppose the seals' treasure could ve been the fifty thousand pounds that the Duke had promised to e Stuarts?"

In the early days of 1744, when Charles Stuart had been in ance, trying to persuade his royal cousin Louis to grant him me sort of support, he had received a ciphered offer from the uke of Sandringham, of fifty thousand pounds—enough to hire a nall army—on condition that he enter England to retake the rone of his ancestors.

Whether it had been this offer that finally convinced the vacil- ting Prince Charles to undertake his doomed excursion, we uld never know. It might as easily have been a challenge from meone he was drinking with, or a slight—real or imagined—by s mistress, that had sent him to Scotland with nothing more than ́ companions, two thousand Dutch broadswords, and several sks of brandywine with which to charm the Highland chieftains.

In any case, the fifty thousand pounds had never been received, cause the Duke had died before Charles reached England. An- her of the speculations that troubled me on sleepless nights was e question of whether that money would have made a difference. Charles Stuart had received it, would he have taken his ragged ghland army all the way to London, retaken the throne and gained his father's crown?

If he had—well, if he had, the Jacobite rebellion might have cceeded, Culloden might not have happened, I should never ve gone back through the circle of stone . . . and I and Bri- na would likely both have died in childbed and been dust these ny years past. Surely twenty years should have been enough to ch me the futility of "if."

Jamie had been considering, meditatively rubbing the bridge of ̣ nose.

"It might have been," he said at last. "Given a proper mark‹ for the coins and gems—ye ken such things take time to sell; if must dispose of them quickly, you'll get but a fraction of the pric But given long enough to search out good buyers—aye, it mig reach fifty thousand."

"Duncan Kerr was a Jacobite, wasn't he?"

Jamie frowned, nodding. "He was. Aye, it could be—thou God knows it's an awkward kind of fortune to be handing to t‹ commander of an army to pay his troops!"

"Yes, but it's also small, portable, and easy to hide," I point‹ out. "And if you were the Duke, and busy committing treason ‹ dealing with the Stuarts, that might be important to you. Sendi‹ fifty thousand pounds in sterling, with strongboxes and carriag and guards, would attract the hell of a lot more attention th‹ sending one man secretly across the Channel with a small wood‹ box."

Jamie nodded again. "Likewise, if ye had a collection of su‹ rarities already, it would attract no attention to be acquiring mo‹ and no one would likely notice what coins ye had. It would be simple matter to take out the most valuable, replace them w‹ cheap ones, and no one the wiser. No banker who might talk, we ye to shift money or land." He shook his head admiringly.

"It's a clever scheme, aye, whoever made it." He looked inquiringly at me.

"But then, why did Duncan Kerr come, nearly ten years aft Culloden? And what happened to him? Did he come to leave t‹ fortune on the silkies' isle then, or to take it away?"

"And who sent the *Bruja* now?" I finished for him. I shook r‹ head, too.

"Damned if I know. Perhaps the Duke had a confederate some sort? But if he did, we don't know who it was."

Jamie sighed, and impatient with sitting for so long, stood and stretched. He glanced out the window, estimating the heig of the sun, his usual method of telling time, whether a clock w‹ handy or not.

"Aye, well, we'll have time for speculation once we're at s‹ It's near on noon, now, and the Paris coach leaves at th‹ o'clock."

The apothecary's shop in the Rue de Varennes was gone. In its place were a thriving tavern, a pawnbroker's, and a small goldsmith's shop, crammed companionably cheek by jowl.

"Master Raymond?" The pawnbroker knitted grizzled brows. "I have heard of him, Madame"—he darted a wary glance at me, suggesting that whatever he had heard had not been very admirable—"but he has been gone for several years. If you are requiring a good apothecary, though, Krasner in the Place d'Aloes, or perhaps Madame Verrue, near the Tuileries . . ." He stared with interest at Mr. Willoughby, who accompanied me, then leaned over the counter to address me confidentially.

"Might you be interested in selling your Chinaman, Madame? I have a client with a marked taste for the Orient. I could get you a very good price—with no more than the usual commission, I assure you."

Mr. Willoughby, who did not speak French, was peering with marked contempt at a porcelain jar painted with pheasants, done in an Oriental style.

"Thank you," I said, "but I think not. I'll try Krasner."

Mr. Willoughby had attracted relatively little attention in Le Havre, a port city teeming with foreigners of every description. On the streets of Paris, wearing a padded jacket over his blue-silk pajamas, and with his queue wrapped several times around his head for convenience, he caused considerable comment. He did, however, prove surprisingly knowledgeable about herbs and medicinal substances.

"Bai jei ai," he told me, picking up a pinch of mustard seed from an open box in Krasner's emporium. "Good for *shen-yen*—kidneys."

"Yes, it is," I said, surprised. "How did you know?"

He allowed his head to roll slightly from side to side, as I had learned was his habit when pleased at being able to astonish someone.

"I know healers one time," was all he said, though, before turning to point at a basket containing what looked like balls of dried mud.

"Shan-yü," he said authoritatively. "Good—*very* good—cleanse blood, liver he work good, no dry skin, help see. You try."

I stepped closer to examine the objects in question and found them to be a particularly homely sort of dried eel, rolled into balls and liberally coated with mud. The price was quite reasonable though, so to please him, I added two of the nasty things to the basket over my arm.

The weather was mild for early December, and we walked back toward Jared's house in the Rue Tremoulins. The streets were bright with winter sunshine, and lively with vendors, beggars, prostitutes, shopgirls, and the other denizens of the poorer part of Paris, all taking advantage of the temporary thaw.

At the corner of the Rue du Nord and the Allée des Canards though, I saw something quite out of the ordinary; a tall, slope-shouldered figure in black frock coat and a round black hat.

"Reverend Campbell!" I exclaimed.

He whirled about at being so addressed; then, recognizing me bowed and removed his hat.

"Mistress Malcolm!" he said. "How most agreeable to see you again." His eye fell on Mr. Willoughby, and he blinked, features hardening in a stare of disapproval.

"Er . . . this is Mr. Willoughby," I introduced him. "He's a . . . associate of my husband's. Mr. Willoughby, the Reverend Archibald Campbell."

"Indeed." The Reverend Campbell normally looked quite austere, but contrived now to look as though he had breakfasted on barbed wire, and found it untasty.

"I thought that you were sailing from Edinburgh to the West Indies," I said, in hopes of taking his gelid eye off the Chinaman It worked; his gaze shifted to me, and thawed slightly.

"I thank you for your kind inquiries, Madame," he said. "I still harbor such intentions. However, I had urgent business to transact first in France. I shall be departing from Edinburgh on Thursday week."

"And how is your sister?" I asked. He glanced at Mr. Willoughby with dislike, then taking a step to one side so as to be out of the Chinaman's direct sight, lowered his voice.

"She is somewhat improved, I thank you. The draughts you prescribed have been most helpful. She is much calmer, and sleeps quite regularly now. I must thank you again for your kind attentions."

"That's quite all right," I said. "I hope the voyage will agree with her." We parted with the usual expressions of good will, and

Mr. Willoughby and I walked down the Rue du Nord, back toward Jared's house.

"Reverend meaning most holy fella, not true?" Mr. Willoughby said, after a short silence. He had the usual Oriental difficulty in pronouncing the letter "r," which made the word "Reverend" more than slightly picturesque, but I gathered his meaning well enough.

"True," I said, glancing down at him curiously. He pursed his lips and pushed them in and out, then grunted in a distinctly amused manner.

"Not so holy, *that* Reverend fella," he said.

"What makes you say so?"

He gave me a bright-eyed glance, full of shrewdness.

"I see him one time, Madame Jeanne's. Not loud talking then. Very quiet then, Reverend fella."

"Oh, really?" I turned to look back, but the Reverend's tall figure had disappeared into the crowd.

"Stinking whores," Mr. Willoughby amplified, making an extremely rude gesture in the vicinity of his crotch in illustration.

"Yes, I gathered," I said. "Well, I suppose the flesh is weak now and then, even for Scottish Free Church ministers."

At dinner that night, I mentioned seeing the Reverend, though without adding Mr. Willoughby's remarks about the Reverend's extracurricular activities.

"I ought to have asked him where in the West Indies he was going," I said. "Not that he's a particularly scintillating companion, but it might be useful to know someone there."

Jared, who was consuming veal patties in a businesslike way, paused to swallow, then said, "Dinna trouble yourself about that, my dear. I've made up a list for you of useful acquaintances. I've written letters for ye to carry to several friends there, who will certainly lend ye assistance."

He cut another sizable chunk of veal, wiped it through a puddle of wine sauce, and chewed it, while looking thoughtfully at Jamie.

Having evidently come to a decision of some kind, he swallowed, took a sip of wine, and said in a conversational voice, "We met on the level, Cousin."

I stared at him in bewilderment, but Jamie, after a moment's pause, replied, "And we parted on the square."

Jared's narrow face broke into a wide smile.

"Ah, that's a help!" he said. "I wasna just sure, aye? but I thought it worth the trial. Where were ye made?"

"In prison," Jamie replied briefly. "It will be the Inverness lodge, though."

Jared nodded in satisfaction. "Aye, well enough. There are lodges on Jamaica and Barbados—I'll have letters for ye to the Masters there. But the largest lodge is on Trinidad—better than two thousand members there. If ye should need great help in finding the lad, that's where ye must ask. Word of everything that happens in the islands comes through that lodge, sooner or later."

"Would you care to tell me what you're talking about?" interrupted.

Jamie glanced at me and smiled.

"Freemasons, Sassenach."

"You're a Mason?" I blurted. "You didn't tell me that!"

"He's not meant to," Jared said, a bit sharply. "The rites of Freemasonry are secret, known only to the members. I wouldna have been able to give Jamie an introduction to the Trinidad lodge had he not been one of us already."

The conversation became general again, as Jamie and Jared fell to discussing the provisioning of the *Artemis,* but I was quiet, concentrating on my own veal. The incident, small as it was, had reminded me of all the things I didn't know about Jamie. At one time, I should have said I knew him as well as one person can know another.

Now, there would be moments, talking intimately together, falling asleep in the curve of his shoulder, holding him close in the act of love, when I felt I knew him still, his mind and heart as clear to me as the lead crystal of the wineglasses on Jared's table.

And others, like now, when I would stumble suddenly over some unsuspected bit of his past, or see him standing still, eyes shrouded with recollections I didn't share. I felt suddenly unsure and alone, hesitating on the brink of the gap between us.

Jamie's foot pressed against mine under the table, and he looked across at me with a smile hidden in his eyes. He raised his glass a little, in a silent toast, and I smiled back, feeling obscurely comforted. The gesture brought back a sudden memory of our wedding night, when we had sat beside each other sipping wine, strangers frightened of each other, with nothing between us but a marriage contract—and the promise of honesty.

There are things ye maybe canna tell me, he had said. *I willna
[a]sk ye, or force ye. But when ye do tell me something, let it be the
[tr]uth. There is nothing between us now but respect, and respect
[ha]s room for secrets, I think—but not for lies.*

I drank deeply from my own glass, feeling the strong bouquet of
[th]e wine billow up inside my head, and a warm flush heat my
[ch]eeks. Jamie's eyes were still fixed on me, ignoring Jared's solil-
[o]quy about ship's biscuit and candles. His foot nudged mine in
[si]lent inquiry, and I pressed back in answer.

"Aye, I'll see to it in the morning," he said, in reply to a
[qu]estion from Jared. "But for now, Cousin, I think I shall retire.
[It]'s been a long day." He pushed back his chair, stood up, and
[he]ld out his arm to me.

"Will ye join me, Claire?"

I stood up, the wine rushing through my limbs, making me feel
[w]arm all over and slightly giddy. Our eyes met with a perfect
[un]derstanding. There was more than respect between us now, and
[ro]om for all our secrets to be known, in good time.

In the morning, Jamie and Mr. Willoughby went with Jared, to
[co]mplete their errands. I had another errand of my own—one that
[I] preferred to do alone. Twenty years ago, there had been two
[pe]ople in Paris whom I cared for deeply. Master Raymond was
[o]ne; dead or disappeared. The chances that the other might still
[be] living were slim, but still, I had to see, before I left Europe for
[w]hat might be the last time. With my heart beating erratically, I
[st]epped into Jared's coach, and told the coachman to drive to the
[H]ôpital des Anges.

The grave was set in the small cemetery reserved for the con-
[ve]nt, under the buttresses of the nearby cathedral. Even though the
[ai]r from the Seine was damp and cold, and the day cloudy, the
[w]alled cemetery held a soft light, reflected from the blocks of pale
[li]mestone that sheltered the small plot from wind. In the winter,
[th]ere were no shrubs or flowers growing, but leafless aspens and
[bi]rches spread a delicate tracery against the sky, and a deep green
[m]oss cradled the stones, thriving despite the cold.

It was a small stone, made of a soft white marble. A pair of

cherub's wings spread out across the top, sheltering the singl
word that was the stone's only other decoration. "Faith," it rea

I stood looking down at it until my vision blurred. I had broug
a flower; a pink tulip—not the easiest thing to find in Paris i
December, but Jared kept a conservatory. I knelt down and laid
on the stone, stroking the soft curve of the petal with a finger, a
though it were a baby's cheek.

"I thought I wouldn't cry," I said a little later.

I felt the weight of Mother Hildegarde's hand on my head.

"Le Bon Dieu orders things as He thinks best," she said softl
"But He seldom tells us why."

I took a deep breath and wiped my cheeks with a corner of m
cloak. "It was a long time ago, though." I rose slowly to my fe
and turned to find Mother Hildegarde watching me with an expre
sion of deep sympathy and interest.

"I have noticed," she said slowly, "that time does not real
exist for mothers, with regard to their children. It does not matt
greatly how old the child is—in the blink of an eye, the mother ca
see the child again as it was when it was born, when it learned
walk, as it was at any age—at any time, even when the child
fully grown and a parent itself."

"Especially when they're asleep," I said, looking down aga
at the little white stone. "You can always see the baby then."

"Ah." Mother nodded, satisfied. "I thought you had had mo
children; you have the look, somehow."

"One more." I glanced at her. "And how do you know
much about mothers and children?"

The small black eyes shone shrewdly under heavy brow ridg
whose sparse hairs had gone quite white.

"The old require very little sleep," she said, with a deprecato
shrug. "I walk the wards at night, sometimes. The patients talk
me."

She had shrunk somewhat with advancing age, and the wi
shoulders were slightly bowed, thin as a wire hanger beneath th
black serge of her habit. Even so, she was still taller than I, a
towered over most of the nuns, more scarecrow-like, but imposi
as ever. She carried a walking stick but strode erect, firm of tre
and with the same piercing eye, using the stick more frequently
prod idlers or direct underlings than to lean on.

I blew my nose and we turned back along the path to the co

ent. As we walked slowly back, I noticed other small stones set
ere and there among the larger ones.

"Are those all children?" I asked, a little surprised.

"The children of the nuns," she said matter-of-factly. I gaped
her in astonishment, and she shrugged, elegant and wry as
ways.

"It happens," she said. She walked a few steps farther, then
dded, "Not often, of course." She gestured with her stick around
e confines of the cemetery.

"This place is reserved for the sisters, a few benefactors of the
ôpital—and those they love."

"The sisters or the benefactors?"

"The sisters. Here, you lump!"

Mother Hildegarde paused in her progress, spotting an orderly
aning idly against the church wall, smoking a pipe. As she be-
ted him in the elegantly vicious Court French of her girlhood, I
ood back, looking around the tiny cemetery.

Against the far wall, but still in consecrated ground, was a row
small stone tablets, each with a single name, "Bouton." Below
ch name was a Roman numeral, I through XV. Mother Hilde-
rde's beloved dogs. I glanced at her current companion, the
xteenth holder of that name. This one was coal-black, and curly
a Persian lamb. He sat bolt upright at her feet, round eyes fixed
the delinquent orderly, a silent echo of Mother Hildegarde's
tspoken disapproval.

The sisters, and those they love.

Mother Hildegarde came back, her fierce expression altering at
ce to the smile that transformed her strong gargoyle features
o beauty.

"I am so pleased that you have come again, *ma chère,*" she
d. "Come inside; I shall find things that may be useful to you
your journey." Tucking the stick in the crook of her arm, she
tead took my forearm for support, grasping it with a warm bony
nd whose skin had grown paper-thin. I had the odd feeling that
was not I who supported her, but the other way around.

As we turned into the small yew alley that led to the entrance to
Hôpital, I glanced up at her.

"I hope you won't think me rude, Mother," I said hesitantly,
ut there is one question I wanted to ask you . . ."

"Eighty-three," she replied promptly. She grinned broadly,

showing her long yellow horse's teeth. "Everyone wants
know," she said complacently. She looked back over her should
toward the tiny graveyard, and lifted one shoulder in a dismissi
Gallic shrug.

"Not yet," she said confidently. "*Le Bon Dieu* knows ho
much work there is still to do."

41

We Set Sail

It was a cold, gray day—there is no other kind in Scotland in December—when the *Artemis* touched at Cape Wrath, on the northwest coast.

I peered out of the tavern window into a solid gray murk that [hi]d the cliffs along the shore. The place was depressingly reminis[c]ent of the landscape near the silkies' isle, with the smell of dead [se]aweed strong in the air, and the crashing of waves so loud as to [pro]hibit conversation, even inside the small pothouse by the wharf. [Yo]ung Ian had been taken nearly a month before. Now it was past [C]hristmas, and here we were, still in Scotland, no more than a few [m]iles from the seals' island.

Jamie was striding up and down the dock outside, in spite of the [co]ld rain, too restless to stay indoors by the fire. The sea journey [fr]om France back to Scotland had been no better for him than the [la]st Channel crossing, and I knew the prospect of two or three [m]onths aboard the *Artemis* filled him with dread. At the same [ti]me, his impatience to be in pursuit of the kidnappers was so [ac]ute that any delay filled him with frustration. More than once I [ha]d awakened in the middle of the night to find him gone, walking [th]e streets of Le Havre alone.

Ironically, this final delay was of his own making. We had [to]uched at Cape Wrath to retrieve Fergus, and with him, the small [gr]oup of smugglers whom Jamie had sent him to fetch, before [le]aving ourselves for Le Havre.

"There's no telling what we shall find in the Indies, Sasse[na]ch," Jamie had explained to me. "I dinna mean to go up against

a shipload of pirates single-handed, nor yet to fight wi' men
dinna ken alongside me.'' The smugglers were all men of th
shore, accustomed to boats and the ocean, if not to ships; the
would be hired on as part of the *Artemis*'s crew, shorthanded i
consequence of the late season in which we sailed.

Cape Wrath was a small port, with little traffic at this time
year. Besides the *Artemis,* only a few fishing boats and a ketc
were tied up at the wooden wharf. There was a small pothous
though, in which the crew of the *Artemis* cheerfully passed the
time while waiting, the men who would not fit inside the hou
crouching under the eaves, swilling pots of ale passed through th
windows by their comrades indoors. Jamie walked on the shor
coming in only for meals, when he would sit before the fire, th
wisps of steam rising from his soggy garments symptomatic of h
increasing aggravation of soul.

Fergus was late. No one seemed to mind the wait but Jamie an
Jared's captain. Captain Raines, a small, plump, elderly ma
spent most of his time on the deck of his ship, keeping on
weather eye on the overcast sky, and the other on his baromete

"That's verra strong-smelling stuff, Sassenach," Jamie o
served, during one of his brief visits to the taproom. "What is it?"

"Fresh ginger," I answered, holding up the remains of the ro
I was grating. "It's the thing most of my herbals say is best f
nausea.''

"Oh, aye?" He picked up the bowl, sniffed at the contents, an
sneezed explosively, to the vast amusement of the onlookers.
snatched back the bowl before he could spill it.

"You don't take it like snuff," I said. "You drink it in tea. An
I hope to heaven it works, because if it doesn't, we'll be scoopi
you out of the bilges, if bilges are what I think they are.''

"Oh, not to worry, missus," one of the older hands assured m
overhearing. "Lots o' green hands feel a bit queerlike the first d
or two. But usually they comes round soon enough; by the thi
day, they've got used to the pitch and roll, and they're up in t
rigging, happy as larks.''

I glanced at Jamie, who was markedly unlarklike at the momer
Still, this comment seemed to give him some hope, for he brigh
ened a bit, and waved to the harassed servingmaid for a glass
ale.

"It may be so," he said. "Jared said the same; that seasickne

)esna generally last more than a few days, provided the seas
en't too heavy.'' He took a small sip of his ale, and then, with
owing confidence, a deeper swallow. ''I can stand three days of
I suppose.''

Late in the afternoon of the second day, six men appeared,
inding their way along the stony shore on shaggy Highland po-
es.

''There's Raeburn in the lead,'' Jamie said, shading his eyes
d squinting to distinguish the identities of the six small dots.
Kennedy after him, then Innes—he's missing the left arm, see?
and Meldrum, and that'll be MacLeod with him, they always
le together like that. Is the last man Gordon, then, or Fergus?''

''It must be Gordon,'' I said, peering over his shoulder at the
proaching men, ''because it's much too fat to be Fergus.''

''Where the devil is Fergus, then?'' Jamie asked Raeburn, once
e smugglers had been greeted, introduced to their new ship-
ates, and sat down to a hot supper and a cheerful glass.

Raeburn bobbed his head in response, hastily swallowing the
mains of his pasty.

''Weel, he said to me as how he'd some business to see to, and
uld I see to the hiring of the horses, and speak to Meldrum and
acLeod about coming, for they were out wi' their own boat at
e time, and not expected back for a day or twa more, and . . .''

''What business?'' Jamie said sharply, but got no more than a
rug in reply. Jamie muttered something under his breath in
aelic, but returned to his own supper without further comment.

The crew being now complete—save Fergus—preparations be-
n in the morning for getting under way. The deck was a scene of
ganized confusion, with bodies darting to and fro, popping up
rough hatchways, and dropping suddenly out of the rigging like
ad flies. Jamie stood near the wheel, keeping out of the way, but
nding a hand whenever a matter requiring muscle rather than
ill arose. For the most part, though, he simply stood, eyes fixed
the road along the shore.

''We shall have to sail by midafternoon, or miss the tide.''
ptain Raines spoke kindly, but firmly. ''We'll have surly
eather within twenty-four hours; the glass is falling, and I feel it in
y neck.'' The Captain tenderly massaged the part in question,

and nodded at the sky, which had gone from pewter to lead-gr₃ since early morning. "I'll not set sail in a storm if I can help and if we mean to make the Indies as soon as possible—"

"Aye, I understand, Captain," Jamie interrupted him. "course; ye must do as seems best." He stood back to let a bustli₃ seaman go past, and the Captain disappeared, issuing orders as ₃ went.

As the day wore on, Jamie seemed composed as usual, but noticed that the stiff fingers fluttered against his thigh more a₃ more often, the only outward sign of worry. And worried he wa₃ Fergus had been with him since the day twenty years before, wh₃ Jamie had found him in a Paris brothel, and hired him to ste Charles Stuart's letters.

More than that; Fergus had lived at Lallybroch since befo Young Ian was born. The boy had been a younger brother Fergus, and Jamie the closest thing to a father that Fergus had ev known. I could not imagine any business so urgent that it wou have kept him from Jamie's side. Neither could Jamie, and h fingers beat a silent tattoo on the wood of the rail.

Then it was time, and Jamie turned reluctantly away, tearing h eyes from the empty shore. The hatches were battened, the lin coiled, and several seamen leapt ashore to cast free the moori₃ hawsers; there were six of them, each a rope as thick around as ₃ wrist.

I put a hand on Jamie's arm in silent sympathy.

"You'd better come down below," I said. "I've got a spi lamp. I'll brew you some hot ginger tea, and then you—"

The sound of a galloping horse echoed along the shore, t scrunch of hoofbeats on gravel echoing from the cliffside well advance of its appearance.

"There he is, the wee fool," Jamie said, his relief evident voice and body. He turned to Captain Raines, one brow raised question. "There's enough of the tide left? Aye, then, let's go.

"Cast off!" the Captain bellowed, and the waiting han sprang into action. The last of the lines tethering us to the pili₃ was slipped free and neatly coiled, and all around us, lines tig₃ ened and sails snapped overhead, as the bosun ran up and do₃ the deck, bawling orders in a voice like rusty iron.

"She moves! She stirs! 'She seems to feel / the thrill of li along her keel!' " I declaimed, delighted to feel the deck qui₃

eneath my feet as the ship came alive, the energy of all the crew
poured into its inanimate hulk, transmuted by the power of the
wind-catching sails.

"Oh, God," said Jamie hollowly, feeling the same thing. He
grasped the rail, closed his eyes, and swallowed.

"Mr. Willoughby says he has a cure for seasickness," I said,
watching him sympathetically.

"Ha," he said, opening his eyes. "I ken what he means, and if
he thinks I'll let him—what the bloody hell!"

I whirled to look, and saw what had caused him to break off.
Fergus was on deck, reaching up to help down a girl perched
awkwardly above him on the railing, her long blond hair whipping
in the wind. Laoghaire's daughter—Marsali MacKimmie.

Before I could speak, Jamie was past me and striding toward the
pair.

"What in the name of holy God d'ye mean by this, ye wee
oofs?" he was demanding, by the time I made my way into
earshot through the obstacle course of lines and seamen. He
loomed menacingly over the pair, a foot taller than either of them.

"We are married," Fergus said, bravely moving in front of
Marsali. He looked both scared and excited, his face pale beneath
the shock of black hair.

"Married!" Jamie's hands clenched at his sides, and Fergus
took an involuntary step backward, nearly treading on Marsali's
toes. "What d'ye mean, 'married'?"

I assumed this was a rhetorical question, but it wasn't; Jamie's
appreciation of the situation had, as usual, outstripped mine by
yards and seized at once upon the salient point.

"Have ye bedded her?" he demanded bluntly. Standing behind
him, I couldn't see his face, but I knew what it must look like, if
only because I could see the effect of his expression on Fergus.
The Frenchman turned a couple of shades paler and licked his lips.

"Er . . . no, milord," he said, just as Marsali, eyes blazing,
thrust her chin up and said defiantly, "Yes, he has!"

Jamie glanced briefly back and forth between the two of them,
snorted loudly, and turned away.

"Mr. Warren!" he called down the deck to the ship's sailing
master. "Put back to the shore, if ye please!"

Mr. Warren stopped, openmouthed, in the middle of an order
addressed to the rigging, and stared, first at Jamie, then—quite

elaborately—at the receding shoreline. In the few moments sinc
the appearance of the putative newlyweds, the *Artemis* had move
more than a thousand yards from the shore, and the rocks of th
cliffs were slipping by with increasing speed.

"I don't believe he can," I said. "I think we're already in th
tide-race."

No sailor himself, Jamie had spent sufficient time in the com
pany of seamen at least to understand the notion that time and tic
wait for no one. He breathed through his teeth for a moment, the
jerked his head toward the ladder that led belowdecks.

"Come down, then, the both of ye."

Fergus and Marsali sat together in the tiny cabin, huddled c
one berth, hands clutched tight. Jamie waved me to a seat on th
other berth, then turned to the pair, hands on his hips.

"Now, then," he said. "What's this nonsense of bein' ma
ried?"

"It is true, milord," Fergus said. He was quite pale, but his da
eyes were bright with excitement. His one hand tightened on Ma
sali's, his hook resting across his thigh.

"Aye?" Jamie said, with the maximum of skepticism. "An
who married ye?"

The two glanced at each other, and Fergus licked his lips brief
before replying.

"We—we are handfast."

"Before witnesses," Marsali put in. In contrast to Fergus
paleness, a high color burned in her cheeks. She had her mother
roseleaf skin, but the stubborn set of her jaw had likely come fro
somewhere else. She put a hand to her bosom, where somethi
crackled under the fabric. "I ha' the contract, and the signature
here."

Jamie made a low growling noise in his throat. By the laws
Scotland, two people could in fact be legally married by claspi
hands before witnesses—handfasting—and declaring themselv
to be man and wife.

"Aye, well," he said. "But ye're no bedded, yet, and a co
tract's not enough, in the eyes o' the Church." He glanced out
the stern casement, where the cliffs were just visible through t
ragged mist, then nodded with decision.

"We'll stop at Lewes for the last provisions. Marsali will
ashore there; I'll send two seamen to see her home to her mother

"Ye'll do no such thing!" Marsali cried. She sat up straight, ring at her stepfather. "I'm going wi' Fergus!"

"Oh, no, you're not, my lassie!" Jamie snapped. "D'ye have feeling for your mother? To run off, wi' no word, and leave her be worrit—"

"I left word." Marsali's square chin was high. "I sent a letter m Inverness, saying I'd married Fergus and was off to sail wi' u."

"Sweet bleeding Jesus! She'll think I kent all about it!" Jamie ked horror-stricken.

"We—I—did ask the lady Laoghaire for the honor of her ughter's hand, milord," Fergus put in. "Last month, when I me to Lallybroch."

"Aye. Well, ye needna tell me what she said," Jamie said dryly, ing the sudden flush on Fergus's cheeks. "Since I gather the neral answer was no."

"She said he was a bastard!" Marsali burst out indignantly. And a criminal, and—and—"

"He is a bastard and a criminal," Jamie pointed out. "And a pple wi' no property, either, as I'm sure your mother noticed."

"I dinna care!" Marsali gripped Fergus's hand and looked at n with fierce affection. "I want him."

Taken aback, Jamie rubbed a finger across his lips. Then he k a deep breath and returned to the attack.

"Be that as it may," he said, "ye're too young to be married."

"I'm fifteen; that's plenty old enough!"

"Aye, and he's thirty!" Jamie snapped. He shook his head, Nay, lassie, I'm sorry about it, but I canna let ye do it. If it were thing else, the voyage is too dangerous—"

"You're taking *her*!" Marsali's chin jerked contemptuously in direction.

"You'll leave Claire out of this," Jamie said evenly. "She's ne of your concern, and—"

"Oh, she's not? You leave my mother for this English whore, d make her a laughingstock for the whole countryside, and it's my concern, is it?" Marsali leapt up and stamped her foot on deck. "And you ha' the hellish nerve to tell me what *I* shall ?"

"I have," Jamie said, keeping hold of his temper with some ficulty. "My private affairs are not your concern—"

"And mine aren't any of yours!"

Fergus, looking alarmed, was on his feet, trying to calm the gi

"Marsali, *ma chère,* you must not speak to milord in such way. He is only—"

"I'll speak to him any way I want!"

"No, you will not!" Surprised at the sudden harshness in Fergus's tone, Marsali blinked. Only an inch or two taller than h new wife, the Frenchman had a certain wiry authority that ma him seem much bigger than he was.

"No," he said more softly. "Sit down, *ma p'tite.*" He press her back down on the berth, and stood before her.

"Milord has been to me more than a father," he said gently the girl. "I owe him my life a thousand times. He is also yo stepfather. However your mother may regard him, he has witho doubt supported and sheltered her and you and your sister. Y owe him respect, at the least."

Marsali bit her lip, her eyes bright. Finally she ducked her he awkwardly at Jamie.

"I'm sorry," she murmured, and the air of tension in the cab lessened slightly.

"It's all right, lassie," Jamie said gruffly. He looked at her a sighed. "But still, Marsali, we must send ye back to yo mother."

"I won't go." The girl was calmer now, but the set of h pointed chin was the same. She glanced at Fergus, then at Jami "He says we havena bedded together, but we have. Or at any ra I shall say we have. If ye send me home, I'll tell everyone that he had me; so ye see—I shall either be married or ruined." Her to was reasonable and determined. Jamie closed his eyes.

"May the Lord deliver me from women," he said between h teeth. He opened his eyes and glared at her.

"All right!" he said. "You're married. But you'll do it rig before a priest. We'll find one in the Indies, when we land. A until ye've been blessed, Fergus doesna touch you. Aye?" I turned a ferocious gaze on both of them.

"Yes, milord," said Fergus, his features suffused with jo *"Merci beaucoup!"* Marsali narrowed her eyes at Jamie, but se ing that he wasn't to be moved, she bowed her head demurel with a sidelong glance at me.

"Yes, Daddy," she said.

The question of Fergus's elopement had at least distracted Janie's mind temporarily from the motion of the ship, but the palliative effect didn't last. He held on grimly nevertheless, turning greener by the moment, but refusing to leave the deck and go below, so long as the shore of Scotland was in sight.

"I may never see it again," he said gloomily, when I tried to persuade him to go below and lie down. He leaned heavily on the rail he had just been vomiting over, eyes resting longingly on the unprepossessingly bleak coast behind us.

"No, you'll see it," I said, with an unthinking surety. "You're coming back. I don't know when, but I know you'll come back."

He turned his head to look up at me, puzzled. Then the ghost of smile crossed his face.

"You've seen my grave," he said softly. "Haven't ye?"

I hesitated, but he didn't seem upset, and I nodded.

"It's all right," he said. He closed his eyes, breathing heavily. "Don't . . . don't tell me when, though, if ye dinna mind."

"I can't," I said. "There weren't any dates on it. Just your name—and mine."

"Yours?" His eyes popped open.

I nodded again, feeling my throat tighten at the memory of that granite slab. It had been what they call a "marriage stone," a quarter-circle carved to fit with another in a complete arch. I had, of course, seen only the one half.

"It had all your names on it. That's how I knew it was you. And underneath, it said 'Beloved husband of Claire.' At the time, I didn't see how—but now, of course, I do."

He nodded slowly, absorbing it. "Aye, I see. Aye, well, I suppose if I shall be in Scotland, and still married to you—then maybe 'when' doesna matter so much." He gave me a shadow of his usual grin, and added wryly, "It also means we'll find Young Ian safe, for I'll tell ye, Sassenach, I willna set foot in Scotland again without him."

"We'll find him," I said, with an assurance I didn't altogether feel. I put a hand on his shoulder and stood beside him, watching Scotland slowly recede in the distance.

By the time evening set in, the rocks of Scotland had disap peared in the sea mists, and Jamie, chilled to the bone and pale a a sheet, suffered himself to be led below and put to bed. At thi point, the unforeseen consequences of his ultimatum to Fergu became apparent.

There were only two small private cabins, besides the Captain' if Fergus and Marsali were forbidden to share one until their unio was formally blessed, then clearly Jamie and Fergus would have t take one, and Marsali and I the other. It seemed destined to be rough voyage, in more ways than one.

I had hoped that the sickness might ease, if Jamie couldn't se the slow heave and fall of the horizon, but no such luck.

"Again?" said Fergus, sleepily rousing on one elbow in hi berth, in the middle of the night. "How can he? He has eate nothing all day!"

"Tell *him* that," I said, trying to breathe through my mouth as sidled toward the door, a basin in my hands, making my way wit difficulty through the tiny, cramped quarters. The deck rose an fell beneath my unaccustomed feet, making it hard to keep m balance.

"Here, milady, allow me." Fergus swung bare feet out of be and stood up beside me, staggering and nearly bumping into me a he reached for the basin.

"You should go and sleep now, milady," he said, taking it fro my hands. "I will see to him, be assured."

"Well . . ." The thought of my berth was undeniably temp ing. It had been a long day.

"Go, Sassenach," Jamie said. His face was a ghastly whit sheened with sweat in the dim light of the small oil light tha burned on the wall. "I'll be all right."

This was patently untrue; at the same time, it was unlikely th my presence would help particularly. Fergus could do the little th could be done; there was no known cure for seasickness, after al One could only hope that Jared was right, and that it would ease itself as the *Artemis* made its way out into the longer swells of t Atlantic.

"All right," I said, giving in. "Perhaps you'll feel better in tł morning."

Jamie opened one eye for a moment, then groaned, and shive ing, closed it again.

"Or perhaps I'll be dead," he suggested.

On that cheery note, I made my way out into the dark compan-ionway, only to stumble over the prostrate form of Mr. Wil-loughby, curled up against the door of the cabin. He grunted in surprise, then, seeing that it was only me, rolled slowly onto all fours and crawled into the cabin, swaying with the rolling of the ship. Ignoring Fergus's exclamation of distate, he curled himself about the pedestal of the table, and fell promptly back asleep, an expression of beatific content on his small round face.

My own cabin was just across the companionway, but I paused for a moment, to breathe in the fresh air coming down from the deck above. There was an extraordinary variety of noises, from the creak and crack of timbers all around, to the snap of sails and the whine of rigging above, and the faint echo of a shout somewhere on deck.

Despite the racket and the cold air pouring in down the compan-ionway, Marsali was sound asleep, a humped black shape in one of the two berths. Just as well; at least I needn't try to make awkward conversation with her.

Despite myself, I felt a pang of sympathy for her; this was likely not what she had expected of her wedding night. It was too cold to undress; fully clothed, I crawled into my small box-berth and lay listening to the sounds of the ship around me. I could hear the hissing of the water passing the hull, only a foot or two beyond my head. It was an oddly comforting sound. To the accompaniment of the song of the wind and the faint sound of retching across the corridor, I fell peacefully asleep.

The *Artemis* was a tidy ship, as ships go, but when you cram thirty-two men—and two women—into a space eighty feet long and twenty-five wide, together with six tons of rough-cured hides, thirty-two barrels of sulfur, and enough sheets of copper and tin to sheathe the *Queen Mary,* basic hygiene is bound to suffer.

By the second day, I had already flushed a rat—a small rat, as Fergus pointed out—but still a rat—in the hold where I went to retrieve my large medicine box, packed away there by mistake during the loading. There was a soft shuffling noise in my cabin at night, which when the lantern was lit proved to be the footsteps of

several dozen middling-size cockroaches, all fleeing frantically f
the shelter of the shadows.

The heads, two small quarter-galleries on either side of the sh
toward the bow, were nothing more than a pair of boards—with
strategic slot between them—suspended over the bounding wav
eight feet below, so that the user was likely to get an unexpecte
dash of cold seawater at some highly inopportune moment. I su
pected that this, coupled with a diet of salt pork and hardtac
likely caused constipation to be epidemic among seamen.

Mr. Warren, the ship's master, proudly informed me that t
decks were swabbed regularly every morning, the brass polishe
and everything generally made shipshape, which seemed a desi
able state of affairs, given that we were in fact aboard a ship. Sti
all the holystoning in the world could not disguise the fact th
thirty-four human beings occupied this limited space, and on
one of us bathed.

Given such circumstances, I was more than startled when
opened the door of the galley on the second morning, in search
boiling water.

I had expected the same dim and grubby conditions that o
tained in the cabins and holds, and was dazzled by the glitter
sunlight through the overhead lattice on a rank of copper pans,
scrubbed that the metal of their bottoms shone pink. I blink
against the dazzle, my eyes adjusting, and saw that the walls of t
galley were solid with built-in racks and cupboards, so construct
as to be proof against the roughest seas.

Blue and green glass bottles of spice, each tenderly jacketed
felt against injury, vibrated softly in their rack above the po
Knives, cleavers, and skewers gleamed in deadly array, in a qua
tity sufficient to deal with a whale carcass, should one prese
itself. A rimmed double shelf hung from the bulkhead, thick wi
bulb glasses and shallow plates, on which a quantity of fresh-c
turnip tops were set to sprout for greens. An enormous pot bu
bled softly over the stove, emitting a fragrant steam. And in t
midst of all this spotless splendor stood the cook, surveying n
with baleful eye.

"Out," he said.

"Good morning," I said, as cordially as possible. "My name
Claire Fraser."

"Out," he repeated, in the same graveled tones.

"I am Mrs. Fraser, the wife of the supercargo, and ship's sur-on for this voyage," I said, giving him eyeball for eyeball. "I quire six gallons of boiling water, when convenient, for cleaning the head."

His small, bright blue eyes grew somewhat smaller and brighter, e black pupils of them training on me like gun barrels.

"I am Aloysius O'Shaughnessy Murphy," he said. "Ship's ook. And I require ye to take yer feet off my fresh-washed deck. I not allow women in my galley." He glowered at me under the ige of the black cotton kerchief that swathed his head. He was veral inches shorter than I, but made up for it by measuring out three feet more in circumference, with a wrestler's shoul-rs and a head like a cannonball, set upon them without apparent nefit of an intervening neck. A wooden leg completed the en-mble.

I took one step back, with dignity, and spoke to him from the lative safety of the passageway.

"In that case," I said, "you may send up the hot water by the essboy."

"I may," he agreed. "And then again, I may not." He turned s broad back on me in dismissal, busying himself with a chop-ng block, a cleaver, and a joint of mutton.

I stood in the passageway for a moment, thinking. The thud of e cleaver sounded regularly against the wood. Mr. Murphy iched up to his spice rack, grasped a bottle without looking, and rinkled a good quantity of the contents over the diced meat. The sty scent of sage filled the air, superseded at once by the pun-ncy of an onion, whacked in two with a casual swipe of the eaver and tossed into the mixture.

Evidently the crew of the *Artemis* did not subsist entirely upon it pork and hardtack, then. I began to understand the reasons for ptain Raines's rather pear-shaped physique. I poked my head ck through the door, taking care to stand outside.

"Cardamom," I said firmly. "Nutmeg, whole. Dried this year. esh extract of anise. Ginger root, two large ones, with no blem-es." I paused. Mr. Murphy had stopped chopping, cleaver ised motionless above the block.

"And," I added, "half a dozen whole vanilla beans. From ylon."

He turned slowly, wiping his hands upon his leather apron.

Unlike his surroundings, neither the apron nor his other appar
was spotless.

He had a broad, florid face, edged with stiff sandy whiskers li
a scrubbing brush, which quivered slightly as he looked at me, li
the antennae of some large insect. His tongue darted out to li
pursed lips.

"Saffron?" he asked hoarsely.

"Half an ounce," I said promptly, taking care to conceal a
trace of triumph in my manner.

He breathed in deeply, lust gleaming bright in his small bl
eyes.

"Ye'll find a mat just outside, ma'am, should ye care to wi
yer boots and come in."

One head sterilized within the limits of boiling water and F
gus's tolerance, I made my way back to my cabin to clean up
luncheon. Marsali was not there; she was undoubtedly attending
Fergus, whose labors at my insistence had been little short
heroic.

I rinsed my own hands with alcohol, brushed my hair, and th
went across the passage to see whether—by some wild chance
Jamie wanted anything to eat or drink. One glance disabused
of this notion.

Marsali and I had been given the larger cabin, which meant th
each of us had approximately six square feet of space, not inclu
ing the beds. These were box-berths, a sort of enclosed bed bu
into the wall, about five and a half feet long. Marsali fitted nea
into hers, but I was forced to adopt a slightly curled position, lik
caper on toast, which caused me to wake up with pins and need
in my feet.

Jamie and Fergus had similar berths. Jamie was lying on
side, wedged into one of these like a snail into its shell; one
which beasts he strongly resembled at the moment, being a p
and viscid gray in color, with streaks of green and yellow th
contrasted nastily with his red hair. He opened one eye when
heard me come in, regarded me dimly for a moment, and close
again.

"Not so good, hm?" I said sympathetically.

The eye opened again, and he seemed to be preparing to

nething. He opened his mouth, changed his mind, and closed it
in.

'No,'' he said, and shut the eye once more.

tentatively smoothed his hair, but he seemed too sunk in mis-
to notice.

'Captain Raines says it will likely be calmer by tomorrow,'' I
ered. The sea wasn't terribly rough as it was, but there was a
iceable rise and fall.

'It doesna matter,'' he said, not opening his eyes. ''I shall be
d by then—or at least I hope so.''

'Afraid not,'' I said, shaking my head. ''Nobody dies of sea-
kness; though I must say it seems a wonder that they don't,
king at you.''

'Not that.'' He opened his eyes, and struggled up on one el-
v, an effort that left him clammy with sweat and white to the
.

'Claire. Be careful. I should have told ye before—but I didna
nt to worry ye, and I thought—'' His face changed. Familiar as
as with expressions of bodily infirmity, I had the basin there
t in time.

'Oh, God.'' He lay limp and exhausted, pale as the sheet.

'What should you have told me?'' I asked, wrinkling my nose
put the basin on the floor near the door. ''Whatever it was, you
uld have told me before we sailed, but it's too late to think of
.''

'I didna think it would be so bad,'' he murmured.

'You never do,'' I said, rather tartly. ''What did you want to tell
, though?''

'Ask Fergus,'' he said. ''Say I said he must tell ye. And tell
Innes is all right.''

'What are you talking about?'' I was mildly alarmed; delirium
sn't a common effect of seasickness.

His eyes opened, and fixed on mine with great effort. Beads of
at stood out on his brow and upper lip.

'Innes,'' he said. ''He canna be the one. He doesna mean to
me.''

A small shiver ran up my spine.

'Are you quite all right, Jamie?'' I asked. I bent and wiped his
e, and he gave me the ghost of an exhausted smile. He had no
er, and his eyes were clear.

"Who?" I said carefully, with a sudden feeling that there we
eyes fixed on my back. "Who *does* mean to kill you?"

"I don't know." A passing spasm contorted his features, but
clamped his lips tight, and managed to subdue it.

"Ask Fergus," he whispered, when he could talk again. "
private. He'll tell ye."

I felt exceedingly helpless. I had no notion what he was talki
about, but if there was any danger, I wasn't about to leave hi
alone.

"I'll wait until he comes down," I said.

One hand was curled near his nose. It straightened slowly a
slid under the pillow, coming out with his dirk, which he clasp
to his chest.

"I shall be all right," he said. "Go on, then, Sassenach
shouldna think they'd try anything in daylight. If at all."

I didn't find this reassuring in the slightest, but there seem
nothing else to do. He lay quite still, the dirk held to his chest li
a stone tomb-figure.

"Go," he murmured again, his lips barely moving.

Just outside the cabin door, something stirred in the shadows
the end of the passage. Peering sharply, I made out the crouch
silk shape of Mr. Willoughby, chin resting on his knees. He spre
his knees apart, and bowed his head politely between them.

"Not worry, honorable First Wife," he assured me in a sibila
whisper. "I watch."

"Good," I said, "keep doing it." And went, in considera
distress of mind, to find Fergus.

Fergus, found with Marsali on the after deck, peering into
ship's wake at several large white birds, was somewhat more re
suring.

"We are not sure that anyone intends actually to kill milor
he explained. "The casks in the warehouse might have been
accident—I have seen such things happen more than once—a
likewise the fire in the shed, but—"

"Wait one minute, young Fergus," I said, gripping him by
sleeve. "*What* casks, and *what* fire?"

"Oh," he said, looking surprised. "Milord did not tell you

"Milord is sick as a dog, and incapable of telling me anything more than that I should ask you."

Fergus shook his head, clicking his tongue in a censorious French way.

"He never thinks he will be so ill," he said. "He always is, and yet every time he must set foot on a ship, he insists that it is only a matter of will; his mind will be master, and he will not allow his stomach to be dictating his actions. Then within ten feet of the dock, he has turned green."

"He never told me that," I said, amused at this description. "Stubborn little fool."

Marsali had been hanging back behind Fergus with an air of haughty reserve, pretending that I wasn't there. At this unexpected description of Jamie, though, she was surprised into a brief snort of laughter. She caught my eye and turned hastily away, cheeks flaming, to stare out to sea.

Fergus smiled and shrugged. "You know what he is like, milady," he said, with tolerant affection. "He could be dying, and he would never know."

"You'd know if you went down and looked at him now," I said tartly. At the same time, I was conscious of surprise, accompanied by a faint feeling of warmth in the pit of my stomach. Fergus had been with Jamie almost daily for twenty years, and still Jamie would not admit to him the weakness that he would readily let me see. Were he dying, *I* would know about it, all right.

"Men," I said, shaking my head.

"Milady?"

"Never mind," I said. "You were telling me about casks and wines."

"Oh, indeed, yes." Fergus brushed back his thick shock of black hair with his hook. "It was the day before I met you again, milady, at Madame Jeanne's."

The day I had returned to Edinburgh, no more than a few hours before I had found Jamie at the printshop. He had been at the Burntisland docks with Fergus and a gang of six men during the night, taking advantage of the late dawn of winter to retrieve several casks of unbonded Madeira, smuggled in among a shipment of innocent flour.

"Madeira does not soak through the wood so quickly as some other wines do," Fergus explained. "You cannot bring in brandy

under the noses of the Customs like that, for the dogs will smell
at once, even if their masters do not. But not Madeira, provided
has been freshly casked.''

"Dogs?''

"Some of the Customs inspectors have dogs, milady, trained t
smell out such contraband as tobacco and brandy.'' He wave
away the interruption, squinting his eyes against the brisk se
wind.

"We had removed the Madeira safely, and brought it to th
warehouse—one of those belonging apparently to Lord Dunda
but in fact it belongs jointly to milord and Madame Jeanne.''

"Indeed,'' I said, again with that minor dip of the stomach I ha
felt when Jamie opened the door of the brothel on Queen Stree
"Partners, are they?''

"Well, of a sort.'' Fergus sounded regretful. "Milord has only
five percent share, in return for his finding the place, and makin
the arrangements. Printing as an occupation is much less profi
able than keeping a *hôtel de joie*.'' Marsali didn't look round, but
thought her shoulders stiffened further.

"I daresay,'' I said. Edinburgh and Madame Jeanne were a lon
way behind us, after all. "Get on with the story. Someone may c
Jamie's throat before I find out why.''

"Of course, milady.'' Fergus bobbed his head apologetically.

The contraband had been safely hidden, awaiting disguise an
sale, and the smugglers had paused to refresh themselves with
drink in lieu of breakfast, before making their way home in th
brightening dawn. Two of the men had asked for their shares
once, needing the money to pay gaming debts and buy food fo
their families. Jamie agreeing to this, he had gone across to th
warehouse office, where some gold was kept.

As the men relaxed over their whisky in a corner of the ware
house, their joking and laughter was interrupted by a sudden v
bration that shook the floor beneath their feet.

"Come-down!'' shouted MacLeod, an experienced warehouse
man, and the men had dived for cover, even before they had see
the great rack of hogsheads near the office quiver and rumble, on
two-ton cask rolling down the stack with ponderous grace, t
smash in an aromatic lake of ale, followed within seconds by
cascade of its monstrous fellows.

"Milord was crossing in front of the rank,'' Fergus said, shak ng his head. "It was only by the grace of the Blessed Virgin herself that he was not crushed." A bounding cask had missed him by inches, in fact, and he had escaped another only by diving headfirst out of its way and under an empty wine rack that had deflected its course.

"As I say, such things happen often," Fergus said, shrugging. "A dozen men are killed each year in such accidents, in the warehouses near Edinburgh alone. But with the other things . . ."

The week before the incident of the casks, a small shed full of packing straw had burst into flames while Jamie was working in it. A lantern placed between him and the door had apparently fallen over, setting the straw alight and trapping Jamie in the windowless shed, behind a sudden wall of flame.

"The shed was fortunately of a most flimsy construction, and the boards half-rotted. It went up like matchwood, but milord was able to kick a hole in the back wall and crawl out, with no injury. We thought at first that the lantern had merely fallen of its own accord, and were most grateful for his escape. It was only later that milord told me he thought that he had heard a noise—perhaps a shot, perhaps only the cracking noises an old warehouse makes as its boards settle—and when he turned to see, found the flames shooting up before him."

Fergus sighed. He looked rather tired, and I wondered whether perhaps he had stayed awake to stand watch over Jamie during the night.

"So," he said, shrugging once more. "We do not know. Such incidents may have been no more than accident—they may not. But taking such occurrences together with what happened at Arroath—"

"You may have a traitor among the smugglers," I said.

"Just so, milady." Fergus scratched his head. "But what is more disturbing to milord is the man whom the Chinaman shot at Madame Jeanne's."

"Because you think he was a Customs agent, who'd tracked Jamie from the docks to the brothel? Jamie said he couldn't be, because he had no warrant."

"Not proof," Fergus noted. "But worse, the booklet he had in his pocket."

"The New Testament?" I saw no particular relevance to that and said so.

"Oh, but there is, milady—or might be, I should say," Fergus corrected himself. "You see, the booklet was one that milord himself had printed."

"I see," I said slowly, "or at least I'm beginning to."

Fergus nodded gravely. "To have the Customs trace brandy from the points of delivery to the brothel would be bad, of course but not fatal—another hiding place could be found; in fact, milord has arrangements with the owners of two taverns that . . . but that is of no matter." He waved it away. "But to have the agents of the Crown connect the notorious smuggler Jamie Roy with the respectable Mr. Malcolm of Carfax Close . . ." He spread his hands wide. "You see?"

I did. Were the Customs to get too close to his smuggling operations, Jamie could merely disperse his assistants, cease frequenting his smugglers' haunts, and disappear for a time, retreating into his guise as a printer until it seemed safe to resume his illegal activities. But to have his two identities both detected and merged was not only to deprive him of both his sources of income but to arouse such suspicion as might lead to discovery of his real name, his seditious activities, and thence to Lallybroch and his history as rebel and convicted traitor. They would have evidence to hang him a dozen times—and once was enough.

"I certainly do see. So Jamie wasn't only worried about Laoghaire and Hobart MacKenzie, when he told Ian he thought it would be as well for us to skip to France for a bit."

Paradoxically, I felt somewhat relieved by Fergus's revelations. At least I hadn't been single-handedly responsible for Jamie's exile. My reappearance might have precipitated the crisis with Laoghaire, but I had had nothing to do with any of this.

"Exactly, milady. And still, we do not know for certain that one of the men has betrayed us—or whether, even if there should be a traitor among them, he should wish to kill milord."

"That's a point." It was, but not a large one. If one of the smugglers had undertaken to betray Jamie for money, that was one thing. If it was for some motive of personal vengeance, though, the man might well feel compelled to take matters into his own hands now that we were—temporarily, at least—out of reach of the King's Customs.

"If so," Fergus was continuing, "it will be one of six men—the six milord sent me to collect, to sail with us. These six were present both when the casks fell, and when the shed caught fire; all have been to the brothel." He paused. "And all of them were present on the road at Arbroath, when we were ambushed, and found the exciseman hanged."

"Do they all know about the printshop?"

"Oh, no, milady! Milord has always been most careful to let none of the smuggling men know of that—but it is always possible that one of them shall have seen him on the streets in Edinburgh, followed him to Carfax Close, and so learned of A. Malcolm." He smiled wryly. "Milord is not the most inconspicuous of men, milady."

"Very true," I said, matching his tone. "But now all of them know Jamie's real name—Captain Raines calls him Fraser."

"Yes," he said, with a faint, grim smile. "That is why we must discover whether we do indeed sail with a traitor—and who it is."

I looked at him, and it occurred to me for the first time that Fergus was indeed a grown man now—and a dangerous one. I had known him as an eager, squirrel-toothed boy of ten, and to me, something of that boy would always remain in his face. But some time had passed since he had been a Paris street urchin.

Marsali had remained staring out to sea during most of this discussion, preferring to take no risk of having to converse with me. She had obviously been listening, though, and now I saw a shiver pass through her thin shoulders—whether of cold or apprehension, I couldn't tell. She likely hadn't planned on shipping with a potential murderer when she had agreed to elope with Fergus.

"You'd better take Marsali below," I said to Fergus. "She's going blue round the edges. Don't worry," I said to Marsali, in a cool voice, "I shan't be in the cabin for some time."

"Where are you going, milady?" Fergus was squinting at me, slightly suspicious. "Milord will not wish you to be—"

"I don't mean to," I assured him. "I'm going to the galley."

"The galley?" His fine black brows shot up.

"To see whether Aloysius O'Shaughnessy Murphy has anything to suggest for seasickness," I said. "If we don't get Jamie back on his feet, he isn't going to care whether anyone cuts his throat or not."

Murphy, sweetened by an ounce of dried orange peel and a bottle of Jared's best claret, was quite willing to oblige. In fact, he seemed to consider the problem of keeping food in Jamie's stomach something of a professional challenge, and spent hours in mystic contemplation of his spice rack and pantries—all to no avail.

We encountered no storms, but the winter winds drove a heavy swell before them, and the *Artemis* rose and fell ten feet at a time, laboring up and down the great glassy peaks of the waves. There were times, watching the hypnotic rise and lurch of the taffrail against the horizon, when I felt a few interior qualms of my own, and turned hastily away.

Jamie showed no signs of being about to fulfill Jared's heartening prophecy and spring to his feet, suddenly accustomed to the motion. He remained in his berth, the color of rancid custard, moving only to stagger to the head, and guarded in turns day and night by Mr. Willoughby and Fergus.

On the positive side of things, none of the six smugglers made any move that might be considered threatening. All expressed a sympathetic concern for Jamie's welfare, and—carefully watched —all had visited him briefly in his cabin, with no suspicious circumstances attending.

For my part, I spent the days in exploring the ship, attending to such small medical emergencies as arose from the daily business of sailing—a smashed finger, a cracked rib, bleeding gums and an abscessed tooth—and pounding herbs and making medicines in a corner of the galley, allowed to work there by Murphy's grace.

Marsali was absent from our shared cabin when I rose, already asleep when I returned to it, and silently hostile when the cramped confines of shipboard forced us to meet on deck or over meals. I assumed that the hostility was in part the result of her natural feelings for her mother, and in part the result of frustration over passing her night hours in my company, rather than Fergus's.

For that matter, if she remained untouched—and judging from her sullen demeanor, I was reasonably sure she did—it was owing entirely to Fergus's respect for Jamie's dictates. In terms of his role as guardian of his stepdaughter's virtue, Jamie himself was a negligible force at the moment.

"Wot, not the broth, too?" Murphy said. The cook's broad red face lowered menacingly. "Which I've had folk rise from their deathbeds after a sup of that broth!"

He took the pannikin of broth from Fergus, sniffed at it critically, and thrust it under my nose.

"Here, smell that, missus. Marrow bones, garlic, caraway seed, and a lump o' pork fat to flavor, all strained careful through muslin, same as some folks bein' poorly to their stomachs can't abide chunks, but chunks you'll not find there, not a one!"

The broth was in fact a clear golden brown, with an appetizing smell that made my own mouth water, despite the excellent breakfast I had made less than an hour before. Captain Raines had a delicate stomach, and in consequence had taken some pains both in the procurement of a cook and the provisioning of the galley, to the benefit of the officers' table.

Murphy, with a wooden leg and the general dimensions of a rum cask, looked the picture of a thoroughgoing pirate, but in fact had a reputation as the best sea-cook in Le Havre—as he had told me himself, without the least boastfulness. He considered cases of seasickness a challenge to his skill, and Jamie, still prostrate after four days, was a particular affront to him.

"I'm sure it's wonderful broth," I assured him. "It's just that he can't keep *anything* down."

Murphy grunted dubiously, but turned and carefully poured the remains of the broth into one of the numerous kettles that steamed day and night over the galley fire.

Scowling horribly and running one hand through the wisps of his scanty blond hair, he opened a cupboard and closed it, then went to rummage through a chest of provisions, muttering under his breath.

"A bit o' hardtack, maybe?" he muttered. "Dry, that's what's wanted. Maybe a whiff o' vinegar, though; tart pickle, say . . ."

I watched in fascination as the cook's huge, sausage-fingered hands flicked deftly through the stock of provisions, plucking dainties and assembling them swiftly on a tray.

" 'Ere, let's try this, then," he said, handing me the finished tray. "Let 'im suck on the pickled gherkins, but don't let 'im bite 'em yet. Then follow on with a bite of the plain hardtack—there isn't no weevils in it yet, I don't think—but see as he don't drink water with it. Then a bite of gherkin, well-chewed, to make the spittle flow, a bite of hardtack, and so to go on with. That much stayin' down, then, we can proceed to the custard, which it's fresh-made last evening for the Captain's supper. Then if tha' sticks . . ." His voice followed me out of the galley, continuing the catalogue of available nourishment. ". . . milk toast, which it's made with goat's milk, and fresh-milked, too . . .

". . . syllabub beat up well with whisky and a nice *egg* . . ." boomed down the passageway as I negotiated the narrow turn with the loaded tray, carefully stepping over Mr. Willoughby, who was as usual crouched in a corner of the passage by Jamie's door like a small blue lapdog.

One step inside the cabin, though, I could see that the exercise of Murphy's culinary skill was going to be once again in vain. In the usual fashion of a man feeling unwell, Jamie had managed to arrange his surroundings to be as depressing and uncomfortable as possible. The tiny cabin was dank and squalid, the cramped berth covered with a cloth so as to exclude both light and air, and half piled with a tangle of clammy blankets and unwashed clothes.

"Rise and shine," I said cheerfully. I set down the tray and pulled off the makeshift curtain, which appeared to be one of Fergus's shirts. What light there was came from a large prism embedded in the deck overhead. It struck the berth, illuminating a countenance of ghastly pallor and baleful mien.

He opened one eye an eighth of an inch.

"Go away," he said, and shut it again.

"I've brought you some breakfast," I said firmly.

The eye opened again, coldly blue and gelid.

"Dinna mention the word 'breakfast' to me," he said.

"Call it luncheon then," I said. "It's late enough." I pulled up a stool next to him, picked a gherkin from the tray, and held it invitingly under his nose. "You're supposed to suck on it," I told him.

Slowly, the other eye opened. He said nothing, but the pair of blue orbs swiveled around, resting on me with an expression of such ferocious eloquence that I hastily withdrew the pickle.

The eyelids drooped slowly shut once more.

I surveyed the wreckage, frowning. He lay on his back, his knees drawn up. While the built-in berth provided more stability for the sleeper than the crew's swinging hammocks, it was de-signed to accommodate the usual run of passengers, who—judg-

ıg from the size of the berth—were assumed to be no more than a
ıodest five feet three or so.

"You can't be at all comfortable in there," I said.

"I am not."

"Would you like to try a hammock instead? At least you could
retch—"

"I would not."

"The captain says he requires a list of the cargo from you—at
ɔur convenience."

He made a brief and unrepeatable suggestion as to what Captain
ɔines might do with his list, not bothering to open his eyes.

I sighed, and picked up his unresisting hand. It was cold and
ımp, and his pulse was fast.

"Well," I said after a pause. "Perhaps we could try something I
ed to do with surgical patients. It seemed to help sometimes."

He gave a low groan, but didn't object. I pulled up a stool and
ıt down, still holding his hand.

I had developed the habit of talking with the patients for a few
ınutes before they were taken to surgery. My presence seemed to
ıssure them, and I had found that if I could fix their attention on
ımething beyond the impending ordeal, they seemed to do better
-there was less bleeding, the postanesthetic nausea was less, and
ey seemed to heal better. I had seen it happen often enough to
ːlieve that it was not imagination; Jamie hadn't been altogether
ɾong when assuring Fergus that the power of mind over flesh was
ɔssible.

"Let's think of something pleasant," I said, pitching my voice
be as low and soothing as possible. "Think of Lallybroch, of
e hillside above the house. Think of the pine trees there—can
ıu smell the needles? Think of the smoke coming up from the
tchen chimney on a clear day, and an apple in your hand. Think
out how it feels in your hand, all hard and smooth, and then—"

"Sassenach?" Both Jamie's eyes were open, and fixed on me in
tense concentration. Sweat gleamed in the hollow of his temples.

"Yes?"

"Go away."

"What?"

"Go away," he repeated, very gently, "or I shall break your
ːck. Go away *now.*"

I rose with dignity and went out.

Mr. Willoughby was leaning against an upright in the passage peering thoughtfully into the cabin.

"Don't have those stone balls with you, do you?" I asked.

"Yes," he answered, looking surprised. "Wanting healthy ball for Tsei-mi?" He began to fumble in his sleeve, but I stopped him with a gesture.

"What I want to do is bash him on the head with them, but suppose Hippocrates would frown on that."

Mr. Willoughby smiled uncertainly and bobbed his head several times in an effort to express appreciation of whatever I thought meant.

"Never mind," I said. I glared back over my shoulder at the heap of reeking bedclothes. It stirred slightly, and a groping hand emerged, patting gingerly around the floor until it found the basin that stood there. Grasping this, the hand disappeared into the murky depths of the berth, from which presently emerged the sound of dry retching.

"Bloody man!" I said, exasperation mingled with pity—and slight feeling of alarm. The ten hours of a Channel crossing were one thing; what would his state be like after two months of this

"Head of pig," Mr. Willoughby agreed, with a lugubrious nod "He is rat, you think, or maybe dragon?"

"He smells like a whole zoo," I said. "Why dragon, though?

"One is born in Year of Dragon, Year of Rat, Year of Sheep Year of Horse," Mr. Willoughby explained. "Being different each year, different people. You are knowing is Tsei-mi rat, or dragon?"

"You mean which year was he born in?" I had vague memories of the menus in Chinese restaurants, decorated with the animals of the Chinese zodiac, with explanations of the supposed character traits of those born in each year. "It was 1721, but I don't know offhand which animal that was the year of."

"I am thinking rat," said Mr. Willoughby, looking thoughtful at the tangle of bedclothes, which were heaving in a mildly agitated manner. "Rat very clever, very lucky. But dragon, too, could be. He is most lusty in bed, Tsei-mi? Dragons most passionate people."

"Not so as you would notice lately," I said, watching the heap of bedclothes out of the corner of my eye. It heaved upward and fell back, as though the contents had turned over suddenly.

"I have Chinese medicine," Mr. Willoughby said, observing
〈th〉is phenomenon thoughtfully. "Good for vomit, stomach, head,
〈an〉d making most peaceful and serene."

I looked at him with interest. "Really? I'd like to see that. Have
〈yo〉u tried it on Jamie yet?"

The little Chinese shook his head regretfully.

"Not want," he replied. "Say damn-all, throwing overboard if I
〈ca〉n come near."

Mr. Willoughby and I looked at each other with a perfect under-
〈st〉anding.

"You know," I said, raising my voice a decibel or two, "pro-
〈lo〉nged dry retching is very bad for a person."

"Oh, most bad, yes." Mr. Willoughby had shaved the forward
〈pa〉rt of his skull that morning; the bald curve shone as he nodded
〈vi〉gorously.

"It erodes the stomach tissues, and irritates the esophagus."

"This is so?"

"Quite so. It raises the blood pressure and strains the abdominal
〈m〉uscles, too. Can even tear them, and cause a hernia."

"Ah."

"And," I continued, raising my voice just a trifle, "it can cause
〈th〉e testicles to become tangled round each other inside the scro-
〈tu〉m, and cuts off the circulation there."

"Ooh!" Mr. Willoughby's eyes went round.

"If *that* happens," I said ominously, "the only thing to do,
〈us〉ually, is to amputate before gangrene sets in."

Mr. Willoughby made a hissing sound indicative of understand-
〈in〉g and deep shock. The heap of bedclothes, which had been
〈to〉ssing to and fro in a restless manner during this conversation,
〈w〉as quite still.

I looked at Mr. Willoughby. He shrugged. I folded my arms and
〈w〉aited. After a minute, a long foot, elegantly bare, was extruded
〈fr〉om the bedclothes. A moment later, its fellow joined it, resting
〈on〉 the floor.

"Damn the pair of ye," said a deep Scottish voice, in tones of
〈ex〉treme malevolence. "Come in, then."

Fergus and Marsali were leaning over the aft rail, cozily shoulder to shoulder, Fergus's arm about the girl's waist, her long fair hair fluttering in the wind.

Hearing approaching footsteps, Fergus glanced back over his shoulder. Then he gasped, whirled round, and crossed himself, eyes bulging.

"Not . . . one . . . word, if ye please," Jamie said between clenched teeth.

Fergus opened his mouth, but nothing came out. Marsali, turning to look too, emitted a shrill scream.

"Da! What's happened to ye?"

The obvious fright and concern in her face stopped Jamie from whatever acerbic remark he had been about to make. His face relaxed slightly, making the slender gold needles that protruded from behind his ears twitch like ant's feelers.

"It's all right," he said gruffly. "It's only some rubbish of the Chinee's, to cure the puking."

Wide-eyed, Marsali came up to him, gingerly extending a finger to touch the needles embedded in the flesh of his wrist below the palm. Three more flashed from the inside of his leg, a few inches above the ankle.

"Does—does it work?" she asked. "How does it feel?"

Jamie's mouth twitched, his normal sense of humor beginning to reassert itself.

"I feel like a bloody ill-wish doll that someone's been poking full o' pins," he said. "But then I havena vomited in the last quarter-hour, so I suppose it must work." He shot a quick glare at me and Mr. Willoughby, standing side by side near the rail.

"Mind ye," he said, "I dinna feel like sucking on gherkins just yet, but I could maybe go so far as to relish a glass of ale, if ye mind where some might be found, Fergus."

"Oh. Oh, yes, milord. If you will come with me?" Unable to refrain from staring, Fergus reached out a tentative hand to take Jamie's arm, but thinking better of it, turned in the direction of the after gangway.

"Shall I tell Murphy to start cooking your luncheon?" I called after Jamie as he turned to follow Fergus. He gave me a long, level look over one shoulder. The golden needles sprouted through his hair in twin bunches, gleaming in the morning light like a pair of devil's horns.

"Dinna try me too high, Sassenach," he said. "I'm no going to forget, ye ken. Tangled testicles—pah!"

Mr. Willoughby had been ignoring this exchange, squatting on his heels in the shadow of the aft-deck scuttlebutt, a large barrel filled with water for refreshment of the deck watch. He was counting on his fingers, evidently absorbed in some kind of calculation. As Jamie stalked away, he looked up.

"Not rat," he said, shaking his head. "Not dragon, too. Tsei-mi born in Year of Ox."

"Really?" I said, looking after the broad shoulders and red head, lowered stubbornly against the wind. "How appropriate."

42

The Man in the Moon

s his title suggested, Jamie's job as supercargo was not onerous. Beyond checking the contents of the hold against the bills of lading to ensure that the *Artemis* was in fact carrying the requisite quantities of hides, tin, and sulfur, there was nothing for him to do while at sea. His duties would begin once we reached Jamaica, when the cargo must be unloaded, rechecked, and sold, with the requisite taxes paid, commissions deducted, and paperwork filed.

In the meantime, there was little for him—or me—to do. While Mr. Picard, the bosun, eyed Jamie's powerful frame covetously, it was obvious that he would never make a seaman. Quick and agile as any of the crew, his ignorance of ropes and sails made him useless for anything beyond the occasional situation where sheer strength was required. It was plain he was a soldier, not a sailor.

He did assist with enthusiasm at the gunnery practice that was held every other day, helping to run the four huge guns on their carriages in and out with a tremendous racket, and spending hours in rapt discussion of esoteric cannon lore with Tom Sturgis, the gunner. During these thunderous exercises, Marsali, Mr. Willoughby, and I sat safely out of the way under the care of Fergus, who was excluded from the fireworks because of his missing hand.

Somewhat to my surprise, I had been accepted as the ship's surgeon with little question from the crew. It was Fergus who explained that in small merchant ships, even barber-surgeons were uncommon. It was commonly the gunner's wife—if he had one— who dealt with the small injuries and illnesses of the crew.

I saw the normal run of crushed fingers, burnt hands, skin infections, abscessed teeth, and digestive ills, but in a crew of only thirty-two men, there was seldom enough work to keep me busy beyond the hour of sick call each morning.

In consequence, both Jamie and I had a great deal of free time. And, as the *Artemis* drew gradually south into the great gyre of the Atlantic, we began to spend most of this time with each other.

For the first time since my return to Edinburgh, there was time to talk; to relearn all the half-forgotten things we knew of each other, to find out the new facets that experience had polished, and simply to take pleasure in each other's presence, without the distractions of danger and daily life.

We strolled the deck constantly, up and down, marking off miles as we conversed of everything and nothing, pointing out to each other the phenomena of a sea voyage; the spectacular sunrises and sunsets, schools of strange green and silver fish, enormous islands of floating seaweed, harboring thousands of tiny crabs and jellyfish, the sleek dolphins that appeared for several days in a row, swimming parallel with the ship, leaping out of the water now and then, as though to get a look at the curious creatures above the water.

The moon rose huge and fast and golden, a great glowing disc that slid upward, out of the water and into the sky like a phoenix rising. The water was dark now, and the dolphins invisible, but I thought somehow that they were still there, keeping pace with the ship on her flight through the dark.

It was a scene breathtaking enough even for the sailors, who had seen it a thousand times, to stop and sigh with pleasure at the sight, as the huge orb rose to hang just over the edge of the world, seeming almost near enough to touch.

Jamie and I stood close together by the rail, admiring it. It seemed so close that we could make out with ease the dark spots and shadows on its surface.

"It seems so close ye could speak to the Man in the Moon," he said, smiling, and waved a hand in greeting to the dreaming golden face above.

" 'The weeping Pleiads wester / and the moon is under seas,' " I quoted. "And look, it is, down there, too." I pointed over the rail, to where the trail of moonlight deepened, glowing in the water as though a twin of the moon itself were sunken there.

"When I left," I said, "men were getting ready to fly to the moon. I wonder whether they'll make it."

"Do the flying machines go so high, then?" Jamie asked. He squinted at the moon. "I should say it's a great way, for all it looks so close just now. I read a book by an astronomer—he said it was perhaps three hundred leagues from the earth to the moon. Is he wrong, then, or is it only that the—airplanes, was it?—will fly so far?"

"It takes a special kind, called a rocket," I said. "Actually, it's a lot farther than that to the moon, and once you get far away from the earth, there's no air to breathe in space. They'll have to carry air with them on the voyage, like food and water. They put it in sort of canisters."

"Really?" He gazed up, face full of light and wonder. "What will it look like there, I wonder?"

"I know that," I said. "I've seen pictures. It's rocky, and barren, with no life at all—but very beautiful, with cliffs and mountains and craters—you can see the craters from here; the dark spots." I nodded toward the smiling moon, then smiled at Jamie myself. "It's not unlike Scotland—except that it isn't green."

He laughed, then evidently reminded by the word "pictures," reached into his coat and drew out the little packet of photographs. He was cautious about them, never taking them out where they might be seen by anyone, even Fergus, but we were alone back here, with little chance of interruption.

The moon was bright enough to see Brianna's face, glowing and mutable, as he thumbed slowly through the pictures. The edges were becoming frayed, I saw.

"Will she walk about on the moon, d'ye think?" he asked softly, pausing at a shot of Bree looking out a window, secretly dreaming, unaware of being photographed. He glanced up again at the orb above us, and I realized that for him, a voyage to the moon seemed very little more difficult or farfetched than the one in which we were engaged. The moon, after all, was only another distant, unknown place.

"I don't know," I said, smiling a bit.

He thumbed through the pictures slowly, absorbed as he always was by the sight of his daughter's face, so like his own. I watched

n quietly, sharing his silent joy at this promise of our immortal-
.

I thought briefly of that stone in Scotland, engraved with his
me, and took comfort from its distance. Whenever our parting
ght come, chances were it would not be soon. And even when
d where it did—Brianna would still be left of us.

More of Housman's lines drifted through my head—*Halt by the*
adstone naming / The heart no longer stirred, / And say the lad
it loved you / Was one that kept his word.

I drew close to him, feeling the heat of his body through coat
d shirt, and rested my head against his arm as he turned slowly
'ough the small stack of photographs.

"She is beautiful," he murmured, as he did every time he saw
: pictures. "And clever, too, did ye not say?"

"Just like her father," I told him, and felt him chuckle softly.

I felt him stiffen slightly as he turned one picture over, and
ted my head to see which one he was looking at. It was one
:en at the beach, when Brianna was about sixteen. It showed her
nding thigh-deep in the surf, hair in a sandy tangle, kicking
ter at her friend, a boy named Rodney, who was backing away,
ighing too, hands held up against the spray of water.

Jamie frowned slightly, lips pursed.

"That—" he began. "Do they—" He paused and cleared his
oat. "I wouldna venture to criticize, Claire," he said, very
'efully, "but do ye not think this is a wee bit . . . indecent?"

I suppressed an urge to laugh.

"No," I said, composedly. "That's really quite a modest bath-
; suit—for the time." While the suit in question *was* a bikini, it
s by no means skimpy, rising to at least an inch below Bree's
vel. "I chose this picture because I thought you'd want to, er
. see as much of her as possible."

He looked mildly scandalized at this thought, but his eyes re-
ned to the picture, drawn irresistibly. His face softened as he
•ked at her.

"Aye, well," he said. "Aye, she's verra lovely, and I'm glad to
ow it." He lifted the picture, studying it carefully. "No, it's no
thing she's wearing I meant; most women who bathe outside
it naked, and their skins are no shame to them. It's only—this
i. Surely she shouldna be standing almost naked before a man?"

scowled at the hapless Rodney, and I bit my lip at the thought

of the scrawny little boy, whom I knew very well, as a mascul
threat to maidenly purity.

"Well," I said, drawing a deep breath. We were on sligh
delicate ground here. "No. I mean, boys and girls do play toget
—like that. You know people dress differently then; I've told ye
No one's really covered up a great deal except when the weathe
cold."

"Mmphm," he said. "Aye, ye've told me." He managed
convey the distinct impression that on the basis of what I'd to
him, he was not impressed with the moral conditions under whi
his daughter was living.

He scowled at the picture again, and I thought it was fortun
that neither Bree nor Rodney was present. I had seen Jamie
lover, husband, brother, uncle, laird, and warrior, but never befo
in his guise as a ferocious Scottish father. He was quite formic
ble.

For the first time, I thought that perhaps it was not altogethe
bad thing that he wasn't able to oversee Bree's life personally;
would have frightened the living daylights out of any lad bo
enough to try to court her.

Jamie blinked at the picture once or twice, then took a de
breath, and I could feel him brace himself to ask.

"D'ye think she is—a virgin?" The halt in his voice was bar
perceptible, but I caught it.

"Of course she is," I said firmly. I thought it very likely,
fact, but this wasn't a situation in which to admit the possibility
doubt. There were things I could explain to Jamie about my o
time, but the idea of sexual freedom wasn't one of them.

"Oh." The relief in his voice was inexpressible, and I bit my
to keep from laughing. "Aye, well, I was sure of it, only I—t
is—" He stopped and swallowed.

"Bree's a very good girl," I said. I squeezed his arm light
"Frank and I may not have got on so well together, but we w
both good parents to her, if I do say so."

"Aye, I know ye were. I didna mean to say otherwise." He h
the grace to look abashed, and tucked the beach picture carefu
back into the packet. He put the pictures back into his pock
patting them to be sure they were safe.

He stood looking up at the moon, then his brows drew toget
in a slight frown. The sea wind lifted strands of his hair, tugg

em loose from the ribbon that bound it, and he brushed them
ck absentmindedly. Clearly there was still something on his
ind.

"Do ye think," he began slowly, not looking at me. "Do ye
ink that it was quite wise to come to me now, Claire? Not that I
nna want ye," he added hastily, feeling me stiffen beside him.
caught my hand, preventing my turning away.

"No, I didna mean that at all! Christ, I do want ye!" He drew
closer, pressing my hand in his against his heart. "I want ye so
dly that sometimes I think my heart will burst wi' the joy of
ving ye," he added more softly. "It's only—Brianna's alone
w. Frank is gone, and you. She has no husband to protect her, no
en of her family to see her safely wed. Will she not have need of
awhile yet? Should ye no have waited a bit, I mean?"

I paused before answering, trying to get my own feelings under
ntrol.

"I don't know," I said at last; my voice quivered, in spite of my
uggle to control it. "Look—things aren't the same then."

"I know that!"

"You don't!" I pulled my hand loose, and glared at him. "You
n't know, Jamie, and there isn't any way for me to tell you,
cause you won't believe me. But Bree's a grown woman; she'll
arry when and as she likes, not when someone arranges it for
r. She doesn't *need* to marry, for that matter. She's having a
od education; she can earn her own living—women do that. She
n't have to have a man to protect her—"

"And if there's no need for a man to protect a woman, and care
r her, then I think it will be a verra poor time!" He glared back
me.

I drew a deep breath, trying to be calm.

"I didn't say there's no need for it." I placed a hand on his
oulder, and spoke in a softer tone. "I said, she can choose. She
edn't take a man out of necessity; she can take one for love."

His face began to relax, just slightly.

"You took me from need," he said. "When we wed."

"And I came back for love," I said. "Do you think I needed
u any less, only because I could feed myself?"

The lines of his face eased, and the shoulder under my hand
axed a bit as he searched my face.

"No," he said softly. "I dinna think that."

He put his arm around me and drew me close. I put my arm
around his waist and held him, feeling the small flat patch
Brianna's pictures in his pocket under my cheek.

"I did worry about leaving her," I whispered, a little late
"She made me go; we were afraid that if I waited longer, I mig
not be able to find you. But I did worry."

"I know. I shouldna ha' said anything." He brushed my cur
away from his chin, smoothing them down.

"I left her a letter," I said. "It was all I could think to do
knowing I might . . . might not see her again." I pressed my li
tight together and swallowed hard.

His fingertips stroked my back, very softly.

"Aye? That was good, Sassenach. What did ye say to her?"
I laughed, a little shakily.

"Everything I could think of. Motherly advice and wisdom
what I had of it. All the practical things—where the deed to tl
house and the family papers were. And everything I knew or cou
think of, about how to live. I expect she'll ignore it all, and have
wonderful life—but at least she'll know I thought about her."

It had taken me nearly a week, going through the cupboards an
desk drawers of the house in Boston, finding all of the busine
papers, the bankbooks and mortgage papers and the family thing
There were a good many bits and pieces of Frank's family lyi
about; huge scrapbooks and dozens of genealogy charts, albun
of photographs, cartons of saved letters. My side of the family w
a good deal simpler to sum up.

I lifted down the box I kept on the shelf of my closet. It was
small box. Uncle Lambert was a saver, as all scholars are, b
there had been little to save. The essential documents of a sm
family—birth certificates, mine and my parents', their marria
lines, the registration for the car that had killed them—what iror
whim had prompted Uncle Lamb to save that? More likely he h
never opened the box, but only kept it, in a scholar's blind fa
that information must never be destroyed, for who knew what u
it might be, and to whom?

I had seen its contents before, of course. There had been
period in my teens when I opened it nightly to look at the fe
photos it contained. I remembered the bone-deep longing for t
mother I didn't remember, and the vain effort to imagine her,
bring her back to life from the small dim images in the box.

The best of them was a close-up photograph of her, face turned toward the camera, warm eyes and a delicate mouth, smiling under the brim of a felt cloche hat. The photograph had been hand-tinted; the cheeks and lips were an unnatural rose-pink, the eyes soft brown. Uncle Lamb said that that was wrong; her eyes had been gold, he said, like mine.

I thought perhaps that time of deep need had passed for Brianna, but was not sure. I had had a studio portrait made of myself the week before; I placed it carefully in the box and closed it, and put the box in the center of my desk, where she would find it. Then I sat down to write.

My dear Bree— I wrote, and stopped. I couldn't. Couldn't possibly be contemplating abandoning my child. To see those three black words stark on the page brought the whole mad idea into a cold clarity that struck me to the bone.

My hand shook, and the tip of the pen made small wavering circles in the air above the paper. I put it down, and clasped my hands between my thighs, eyes closed.

"Get a grip on yourself, Beauchamp," I muttered. "Write the bloody thing and have done. If she doesn't need it, it will do no harm, and if she does, it will be there." I picked up the pen and began again.

I don't know if you will ever read this, but perhaps it's as well to set it down. This is what I know of your grandparents (your real ones), your great-grandparents, and your medical history . . .

I wrote for some time, covering page after page. My mind grew calmer with the effort of recall, and the necessity of setting down the information clearly, and then I stopped, thinking.

What could I tell her, beyond those few bare bloodless facts? How to impart what sparse wisdom I had gained in forty-eight years of a fairly eventful life? My mouth twisted wryly in consideration of that. Did any daughter listen? Would I, had my mother been there to tell me?

It made no difference, though; I would just have to set it down, be of use if it could.

But what was true, that would last forever, in spite of changing times and ways, what would stand her in good stead? Most of all how could I tell her just how much I loved her?

The enormity of what I was about to do gaped before me, and my fingers clenched tight on the pen. I couldn't think—not and do this. I could only set the pen to the paper and hope.

Baby— I wrote, and stopped. Then swallowed hard, and started again.

> *You are my baby, and always will be. You won't know what that means until you have a child of your own, but I tell you now, anyway—you'll always be as much a part of me as when you shared my body and I felt you move inside. Always.*
>
> *I can look at you, asleep, and think of all the nights I tucked you in, coming in the dark to listen to your breathing, lay my hand on you and feel your chest rise and fall, knowing that no matter what happens, everything is right with the world because you are alive.*
>
> *All the names I've called you through the years—my chick, my pumpkin, precious dove, darling, sweetheart, dinky, smudge . . . I know why the Jews and Muslims have nine hundred names for God; one small word is not enough for love.*

I blinked hard to clear my vision, and went on writing, fast; didn't dare take time to choose my words, or I would never write them.

> *I remember everything about you, from the tiny line of golden down that zigged across your forehead when you were hours old to the bumpy toenail on the big toe you broke last year, when you had that fight with Jeremy and kicked the door of his pickup truck.*
>
> *God, it breaks my heart to think it will stop now—that watching you, seeing all the tiny changes—I won't know when you stop biting your nails, if you ever do—seeing you grow suddenly taller than I, and your face take its shape. I always will remember, Bree, I always will.*
>
> *There's probably no one else on earth, Bree, who knows*

what the back of your ears looked like when you were three years old. I used to sit beside you, reading "One Fish, Two Fish, Red Fish, Blue Fish," or "The Three Billy Goats Gruff," and see those ears turn pink with happiness. Your skin was so clear and fragile, I thought a touch would leave fingerprints on you.

You look like Jamie, I told you. You have something from me, too, though—look at the picture of my mother, in the box, and the little black-and-white one of her mother and grandmother. You have that broad clear brow they have; so do I. I've seen a good many of the Frasers, too—I think you'll age well, if you take care of your skin.

Take care of everything, Bree—oh, I wish—well, I have wished I could take care of you and protect you from everything all your life, but I can't, whether I stay or go. Take care of yourself, though—for me.

The tears were puckering the paper now; I had to stop to blot them, lest they smear the ink beyond reading. I wiped my face, and resumed, slower now.

You should know, Bree—I don't regret it. In spite of everything, I don't regret it. You'll know something now, of how lonely I was for so long, without Jamie. It doesn't matter. If the price of that separation was your life, neither Jamie nor I can regret it—I know he wouldn't mind my speaking for him.

Bree . . . you are my joy. You're perfect, and wonderful—and I hear you saying now, in that tone of exasperation, "But of course you think that—you're my mother!" Yes, that's how I know.

Bree, you are worth everything—and more. I've done a great many things in my life so far, but the most important of them all was to love your father and you.

I blew my nose and reached for another fresh sheet of paper. That was the most important thing; I could never say all I felt, but this was the best I could do. What might I add, to be of aid in living well, in growing up and growing old? What had I learned, that I might pass on to her?

Choose a man like your father, I wrote. *Either of them.* I shook my head over that—could there be two men more different? —but left it, thinking of Roger Wakefield. *Once you've chosen a man, don't try to change him,* I wrote, with more confidence. *It can't be done. More important—don't let him try to change you. He can't do it either, but men always try.*

I bit the end of the pen, tasting the bitter tang of India ink. And finally I put down the last and the best advice I knew, on growing older.

> *Stand up straight and try not to get fat.*
> *With All My Love Always,*
> *Mama*

Jamie's shoulders shook as he leaned against the rail, whether with laughter or some other emotion, I couldn't tell. His linen glowed white with moonlight, and his head was dark against the moon. At last he turned and pulled me to him.

"I think she will do verra well," he whispered. "For no matter what poor gowk has fathered her, no lass has ever had a better mother. Kiss me, Sassenach, for believe me—I wouldna change ye for the world."

43

Phantom Limbs

ergus, Mr. Willoughby, Jamie, and I had all kept careful watch upon the six Scottish smugglers since our departure from Scotland, but there was not the slightest hint of suspicious behavior from any of them, and after a time, I found myself relaxing my wariness around them. Still, I felt some reserve toward most of them, save Innes. I had finally realized why neither Fergus nor Jamie thought him a possible traitor; with but one arm, Innes was the only smuggler who could not have strung up the exciseman on the Arbroath road.

Innes was a quiet man. None of the Scots was what one might call garrulous, but even by their high standards of taciturnity, he was reserved. I was therefore not surprised to see him grimacing silently one morning, bent over behind a hatch cover, evidently engaged in some silent internal battle.

"Have you a pain, Innes?" I asked, stopping.

"Och!" He straightened, startled, but then fell back into his half-crouched position, his one arm locked across his belly. "Mmphm," he muttered, his thin face flushing at being so discovered.

"Come along with me," I said, taking him by the elbow. He looked frantically about for salvation, but I towed him, resisting but not audibly protesting, back to my cabin, where I forced him to sit upon the table and removed his shirt so that I could examine him.

I palpated his lean and hairy abdomen, feeling the firm, smooth mass of the liver on one side, and the mildly distended curve of the

stomach on the other. The intermittent way in which the pai
came on, causing him to writhe like a worm on a hook, the
passing off, gave me a good idea that what troubled him w
simple flatulence, but best to be thorough.

I probed for the gallbladder, just in case, wondering as I did
just what I would do, should it prove to be an acute attack
cholecystitis or an inflamed appendix. I could envision the cavi
of the belly in my mind, as though it lay open in fact before m
my fingers translating the soft, lumpy shapes beneath the skin in
vision—the intricate folds of the intestines, softly shielded by the
yellow quilting of fat-padded membrane, the slick, smooth lob
of the liver, deep purple-red, so much darker than the vivid scarl
of the heart's pericardium above. Opening that cavity was a ris
thing to do, even equipped with modern anesthetics and antibi
ics. Sooner or later, I knew, I would be faced with the necessity
doing it, but I sincerely hoped it would be later.

"Breathe in," I said, hands on his chest, and saw in my mi
the pink-flushed grainy surface of a healthy lung. "Breathe o
now," and felt the color fade to soft blue. No rales, no halting,
nice clear flow. I reached for one of the thick sheets of vellu
paper I used for stethoscopes.

"When did you last move your bowels?" I inquired, rolling t
paper into a tube. The Scot's thin face turned the color of fre
liver. Fixed with my gimlet eye, he mumbled something incohe
ent, in which the word "four" was just distinguishable.

"Four *days*?" I said, forestalling his attempts to escape
putting a hand on his chest and pinning him flat to the tab
"Hold still, I'll just have a listen here, to be sure."

The heart sounds were reassuringly normal; I could hear t
valves open and close with their soft, meaty clicks, all in the rig
places. I was quite sure of the diagnosis—had been virtually fro
the moment I had looked at him—but by now there was an aud
ence of heads peering curiously round the doorway; Innes's mate
watching. For effect, I moved the end of my tubular stethosco
down farther, listening for belly sounds.

Just as I thought, the rumble of trapped gas was clearly audib
in the upper curve of the large intestine. The lower sigmoid col
was blocked, though; no sound at all down there.

"You have belly gas," I said, "and constipation."

"Aye, I ken that fine," Innes muttered, looking frantically for is shirt.

I put my hand on the garment in question, preventing him from eaving while I catechized him about his diet of late. Not surprisngly, this consisted almost entirely of salt pork and hardtack.

"What about the dried peas and the oatmeal?" I asked, surrised. Having inquired as to the normal fare aboard ship, I had aken the precaution of stowing—along with my surgeon's cask of me juice and the collection of medicinal herbs—three hundred ounds of dried peas and a similar quantity of oatmeal, intending aat this should be used to supplement the seamen's normal diet.

Innes remained tongue-tied, but this inquiry unleashed a flood f revelation and grievance from the onlookers in the doorway.

Jamie, Fergus, Marsali, and I all dined daily with Captain aines, feasting on Murphy's ambrosia, so I was unaware of the eficiencies of the crew's mess. Evidently the difficulty was Murhy himself, who, while holding the highest culinary standards for ae captain's table, considered the crew's dinner to be a chore ather than a challenge. He had mastered the routine of producing ae crew's meals quickly and competently, and was highly resisant to any suggestions for an improved menu that might require arther time or trouble. He declined absolutely to trouble with uch nuisances as soaking peas or boiling oatmeal.

Compounding the difficulty was Murphy's ingrained prejudice gainst oatmeal, a crude Scottish mess that offended his aesthetic ense. I knew what he thought about that, having heard him mutering things about "dog's vomit" over the trays of breakfast that acluded the bowls of parritch to which Jamie, Marsali, and Fergus ere addicted.

"Mr. Murphy says as how salt pork and hardtack is good nough for every crew he's had to feed for thirty year—given ggy-dowdy or plum duff for pudding, and beef on Sundays, too -though if that's beef, I'm a Chinaman—and it's good enough or us," Gordon burst in.

Accustomed to polyglot crews of French, Italian, Spanish, and orwegian sailors, Murphy was also accustomed to having his aeals accepted and consumed with a voracious indifference that anscended nationalities. The Scots' stubborn insistence on atmeal roused all his own Irish intransigence, and the matter, at first a small, simmering disagreement, was now beginning to rise to a boil.

"We knew as there was meant to be parritch," MacLeod explained, "for Fergus did say so, when he asked us to come. But it's been nothing but the meat and biscuit since we left Scotland which is a wee bit griping to the belly if ye're not used to it."

"We didna like to trouble Jamie Roy ower such a thing," Raeburn put in. "Geordie's got his girdle, and we've been makin our own oatcake ower the lamps in the crew quarters. But we've run through what corn we brought in our bags, and Mr. Murphy's got the keys to the pantry store." He glanced shyly at me under his sandy blond lashes. "We didna like to ask, knowin' what he thought of us."

"Ye wouldna ken what's meant by the term 'spalpeens,' would ye, Mistress Fraser?" MacRae asked, raising one bushy brow.

While listening to this outpouring of woe, I had been selecting assorted herbs from my box—anise and angelica, two large pinches of horehound, and a few sprigs of peppermint. Tying these into a square of gauze, I closed the box and handed Innes his shirt, into which he burrowed at once, in search of refuge.

"I'll speak to Mr. Murphy," I promised the Scots. "Meanwhile," I said to Innes, handing him the gauze bundle, "brew yo a good pot of tea from that, and drink a cupful at every watc change. If we've had no results by tomorrow, we'll try stronger measures."

As if in answer to this, a high, squeaking fart emerged from under Innes, to an ironic cheer from his colleagues.

"Aye, that's right, Mistress Fraser; maybe ye can scare the sh out o' him," MacLeod said, a broad grin splitting his face.

Innes, scarlet as a ruptured artery, took the bundle, bobbed hi head in inarticulate thanks, and fled precipitously, followed i more leisurely fashion by the other smugglers.

A rather acrimonious debate with Murphy followed, terminat ing without bloodshed, but with the compromise that *I* would b responsible for the preparation of the Scots' morning parritch permitted to do so under provision that I confined myself to single pot and spoon, did not sing while cooking, and was caref not to make a mess in the precincts of the sacred galley.

It was only that night, tossing restlessly in the cramped an chilly confines of my berth, that it occurred to me how odd the morning's incident had been. Were this Lallybroch, and the Scots Jamie's tenants, not only would they have had no hesitation in approaching him about the matter, they would have had no need to. He would have known already what was wrong, and taken steps to remedy the situation. Accustomed as I had always been to the intimacy and unquestioning loyalty of Jamie's own men, I found his distance troubling.

Jamie was not at the captain's table next morning, having gone out in the small boat with two of the sailors to catch whitebait, but I met him on his return at noon, sunburned, cheerful, and covered with scales and fish blood.

"What have ye done to Innes, Sassenach?" he said, grinning. "He's hiding in the starboard head, and says ye told him he mustna come out at all until he'd shit."

"I didn't tell him *that,* exactly," I explained. "I just said if he hadn't moved his bowels by tonight, I'd give him an enema of slippery elm."

Jamie glanced over his shoulder in the direction of the head.

"Well, I suppose we will hope that Innes's bowels cooperate, or I doubt but he'll spend the rest of the voyage in the head, wi' a threat like that hangin' ower him."

"Well, I shouldn't worry; now that he and the others have their parritch back, their bowels ought to take care of themselves without undue interference from me."

Jamie glanced down at me, surprised.

"Got their parritch back? Whatever d'ye mean, Sassenach?"

I explained the genesis of the Oatmeal War, and its outcome, as he fetched a basin of water to clean his hands. A small frown drew his brows close together as he pushed his sleeves up his arms.

"They ought to have come to me about it," he said.

"I expect they would have, sooner or later," I said. "I only happened to find out by accident, when I found Innes grunting behind a hatch cover."

"Mmphm." He set about scouring the bloodstains off his fingers, rubbing the clinging scales free with a small pumice stone.

"These men aren't like your tenants at Lallybroch, are they?" I said, voicing the thought I had had.

"No," he said quietly. He dipped his fingers in the basin, leav-

ing tiny shimmering circles where the fish scales floated. "I'm no
their laird; only the man who pays them."

"They like you, though," I protested, then remembered Fergus's story and amended this rather weakly to, "or at least five of
them do."

I handed him the towel. He took it with a brief nod, and dried
his hands. Looking down at the strip of cloth, he shook his head.

"Aye, MacLeod and the rest like me well enough—or five of
them do," he repeated ironically. "And they'll stand by me if it's
needful—five of them. But they dinna ken me much, nor me them,
save Innes."

He tossed the dirty water over the side, and tucking the empty
basin under his arm, turned to go below, offering me his arm.

"There was more died at Culloden than the Stuart cause, Sassenach," he said. "You'll be coming for your dinner now?"

I did not find out why Innes was different, until the next week.
Perhaps emboldened by the success of the purgative I had given
him, Innes came voluntarily to call upon me in my cabin a week
later.

"I am wondering, mistress," he said politely, "whether there
might be a medicine for something as isna there."

"What?" I must have looked puzzled at this description, for he
lifted the empty sleeve of his shirt in illustration.

"My arm," he explained. "It's no there, as ye can plainly see.
And yet it pains me something terrible sometimes." He blushed
slightly.

"I did wonder for some years was I only a bit mad," he confided, in lowered tones. "But I spoke a bit wi' Mr. Murphy, and he
tells me it's the same with his leg that got lost, and Fergus says he
wakes sometimes, feeling his missing hand slide into someone's
pocket." He smiled briefly, teeth a flash under his drooping mustache. "So I thought maybe if it was a common thing, to feel a
limb that wasn't there, perhaps there was something that might be
done about it."

"I see." I rubbed my chin, pondering. "Yes, it is common; it's
called a phantom limb, when you still have feelings in a part that's
been lost. As for what to do about it. . . ." I frowned, trying to

think whether I had ever heard of anything therapeutic for such a situation. To gain time, I asked, "How did you happen to lose the arm?"

"Oh, 'twas the blood poison," he said, casually. "I tore a small hole in my hand wi' a nail one day, and it festered."

I stared at the sleeve, empty from the shoulder.

"I suppose it did," I said faintly.

"Oh, aye. It was a lucky thing, though; it was that stopped me bein' transported wi' the rest."

"The rest of whom?"

He looked at me, surprised. "Why, the other prisoners from Ardsmuir. Did Mac Dubh not tell ye about that? When they stopped the fortress from being a prison, they sent off all of the Scottish prisoners to be indenture men in the Colonies—all but Mac Dubh, for he was a great man, and they didna want him out o' their sight, and me, for I'd lost the arm, and was no good for hard labor. So Mac Dubh was taken somewhere else, and I was let go—pardoned and set free. So ye see, it was a most fortunate accident, save only for the pain that comes on sometimes at night." He grimaced, and made as though to rub the nonexistent arm, stopping and shrugging at me in illustration of the problem.

"I see. So you were with Jamie in prison. I didn't know that." I was turning through the contents of my medicine chest, wondering whether a general pain reliever like willow-bark tea or horehound with fennel would work on a phantom pain.

"Oh, aye." Innes was losing his shyness, and beginning to speak more freely. "I should have been dead of starvation by now, had Mac Dubh not come to find me, when he was released himself."

"He went looking for you?" Out of the corner of my eye, I spotted a flash of blue, and beckoned to Mr. Willoughby, who was passing by.

"Aye. When he was released from his parole, he came to inquire, to see whether he could trace any of the men who'd been taken to America—to see whether any might have returned." He shrugged, the missing arm exaggerating the gesture. "But there were none in Scotland, save me."

"I see. Mr. Willoughby, have you a notion what might be done about this?" Motioning to the Chinese to come and look, I explained the problem, and was pleased to hear that he did indeed have a notion. We stripped Innes of his shirt once again, and I watched, taking careful notes, as Mr. Willoughby pressed hard with his fingers at certain spots on the neck and torso, explaining as best he might what he was doing.

"Arm is in the ghost world," he explained. "Body not; here in upper world. Arm tries to come back, for it does not like to be away from body. This—*An-mo*—press-press—this stops pain. But also we tell arm not come back."

"And how d'ye do that?" Innes was becoming interested in the procedure. Most of the crew would not let Mr. Willoughby touch them, regarding him as heathen, unclean, and a pervert to boot, but Innes had known and worked with the Chinese for the last two years.

Mr. Willoughby shook his head, lacking words, and burrowed in my medicine box. He came up with the bottle of dried hot peppers, and shaking out a careful handful, put it into a small dish.

"Have fire?" he inquired. I had a flint and steel, and with these he succeeded in kindling a spark to ignite the dried herb. The pungent smell filled the cabin, and we all watched as a small plume of white rose up from the dish and formed a small, hovering cloud over the dish.

"Send smoke of *fan jiao* messenger to ghost world, speak arm," Mr. Willoughby explained. Inflating his lungs and puffing out his cheeks like a blowfish, he blew lustily at the cloud, dispersing it. Then, without pausing, he turned and spat copiously on Innes's stump.

"Why, ye heathen bugger!" Innes cried, eyes bulging with fury. "D'ye dare spit on me?"

"Spit on ghost," Mr. Willoughby explained, taking three quick steps backward, toward the door. "Ghost afraid spittle. Not come back now right away."

I laid a restraining hand on Innes's remaining arm.

"Does your missing arm hurt now?" I asked.

The rage began to fade from his face as he thought about it.

"Well . . . no," he admitted. Then he scowled at Mr. Willoughby. "But that doesna mean I'll have ye spit on me whenever the fancy takes ye, ye wee poutworm!"

"Oh, no," Mr. Willoughby said, quite cool. "I not spit. You spit now. Scare you own ghost."

Innes scratched his head, not sure whether to be angry or amused.

"Well, I will be damned," he said finally. He shook his head, and picking up his shirt, pulled it on. "Still," he said, "I think perhaps next time, I'll try your tea, Mistress Fraser."

44

Forces of Nature

"I," said Jamie, "am a fool." He spoke broodingly, watching Fergus and Marsali, who were absorbed in close conversation by the rail on the opposite side of the ship.

"What makes you think so?" I asked, though I had a reasonably good idea. The fact that all four of the married persons aboard were living in unwilling celibacy had given rise to a certain air of suppressed amusement among the members of the crew, whose celibacy was involuntary.

"I have spent twenty years longing to have ye in my bed," he said, verifying my assumption, "and within a month of having ye back again, I've arranged matters so that I canna even kiss ye without sneakin' behind a hatch cover, and even then, half the time I look round to find Fergus looking cross-eyed down his nose at me, the little bastard! And no one to blame for it but my own foolishness. What did I think I was doing?" he demanded rhetorically, glaring at the pair across the way, who were nuzzling each other with open affection.

"Well, Marsali *is* only fifteen," I said mildly. "I expect you thought you were being fatherly—or stepfatherly."

"Aye, I did." He looked down at me with a grudging smile. "The reward for my tender concern being that I canna even touch my own wife!"

"Oh, you can touch me," I said. I took one of his hands, caressing the palm gently with my thumb. "You just can't engage in acts of unbridled carnality."

We had had a few abortive attempts along those lines, all fru

rated by either the inopportune arrival of a crew member or the
sheer uncongeniality of any nook aboard the *Artemis* sufficiently
secluded as to be private. One late-night foray into the after hold
had ended abruptly when a large rat had leapt from a stack of
hides onto Jamie's bare shoulder, sending me into hysterics and
depriving Jamie abruptly of any desire to continue what he was
doing.

He glanced down at our linked hands, where my thumb continued to make secret love to his palm, and narrowed his eyes at me,
but let me continue. He closed his fingers gently round my hand,
his own thumb feather-light on my pulse. The simple fact was that
we couldn't keep our hands off each other—no more than Fergus
and Marsali could—despite the fact that we knew very well such
behavior would lead only to greater frustration.

"Aye, well, in my own defense, I meant well," he said ruefully,
smiling down into my eyes.

"Well, you know what they say about good intentions."

"What do they say?" His thumb was stroking gently up and
down my wrist, sending small fluttering sensations through the pit
of my stomach. I thought it must be true what Mr. Willoughby
said, about sensations on one part of the body affecting another.

"They pave the road to Hell." I gave his hand a squeeze, and
tried to take mine away, but he wouldn't let go.

"Mmphm." His eyes were on Fergus, who was teasing Marsali
with an albatross's feather, holding her by one arm and tickling
her beneath the chin as she struggled ineffectually to get away.

"Verra true," he said. "I meant to make sure the lass had a
chance to think what she was about before the matter was too late
for mending. The end result of my interference being that I lie
awake half the night trying not to think about you, and listening to
Fergus lust across the cabin, and come up in the morning to find
the crew all grinning in their beards whenever they see me." He
aimed a vicious glare at Maitland, who was passing by. The beardless cabin boy looked startled, and edged carefully away, glancing
nervously back over his shoulder.

"How do you hear someone lust?" I asked, fascinated.

He glanced down at me, looking mildly flustered.

"Oh! Well . . . it's only . . ."

He paused for a moment, then rubbed the bridge of his nose,
which was beginning to redden in the sharp breeze.

''Have ye any idea what men in a prison do, Sassenach, having
no women for a verra long time?''

''I could guess,'' I said, thinking that perhaps I didn't really
want to hear, firsthand. He hadn't spoken to me before about his
time in Ardsmuir.

''I imagine ye could,'' he said dryly. ''And ye'd be right, too.
There's the three choices; use each other, go a bit mad, or deal
with the matter by yourself, aye?''

He turned to look out to sea, and bent his head slightly to look
down at me, a slight smile visible on his lips. ''D'ye think me
mad, Sassenach?''

''Not most of the time,'' I replied honestly, turning round beside him. He laughed and shook his head ruefully.

''No, I dinna seem able to manage it. I now and then wished I
could go mad''—he said thoughtfully ''—it seemed a great deal
easier than having always to think what to do next—but it doesn't
seem to come natural to me. Nor does buggery,'' he added, with a
wry twist of his mouth.

''No, I shouldn't think so.'' Men who might in the ordinary way
recoil in horror from the thought of using another man could still
bring themselves to the act, out of desperate need. Not Jamie.
Knowing what I did of his experiences at the hands of Jack Randall, I suspected that he very likely *would* have gone mad before
seeking such resort himself.

He shrugged slightly, and stood silent, looking out to sea. Then
he glanced down at his hands, spread before him, clutching the
rail.

''I fought them—the soldiers who took me. I'd promised Jenny
I wouldn't—she thought they'd hurt me—but when the time
came, I couldna seem to help it.'' He shrugged again, and slowly
opened and closed his right hand. It was his crippled hand, the
third finger marked by a thick scar that ran the length of the first
two joints, the fourth finger's second joint fused into stiffness, so
that the finger stuck out awkwardly, even when he made a fist.

''I broke this again then, against a dragoon's jaw,'' he said
ruefully, waggling the finger slightly. ''That was the third time;
the second was at Culloden. I didna mind it much. But they put me
in chains, and I minded that a great deal.''

''I'd think you would.'' It was hard—not difficult, but surprisngly painful—to think of that lithe, powerful body subdued by metal, bound and humbled.

"There's nay privacy in prison," he said. "I minded that more than the fetters, I think. Day and night, always in sight of someone, wi' no guard for your thoughts but to feign sleep. As for the other . . ." He snorted briefly, and shoved the loose hair back behind his ear. "Well, ye wait for the light to go, for the only modesty there is, is darkness."

The cells were not large, and the men lay close together for warmth in the night. With no modesty save darkness, and no privacy save silence, it was impossible to remain unaware of the accommodation each man made to his own needs.

"I was in irons for more than a year, Sassenach," he said. He lifted his arms, spread them eighteen inches apart, and stopped abruptly, as though reaching some invisible limit. "I could move that far—and nay more," he said, staring at his immobile hands. "And I couldna move my hands at all without the chain makin' a sound."

Torn between shame and need, he would wait in the dark, breathing in the stale and brutish scent of the surrounding men, listening to the murmurous breath of his companions, until the stealthy sounds nearby told him that the telltale clinking of his irons would be ignored.

"If there's one thing I ken verra well, Sassenach," he said quietly, with a brief glance at Fergus, "it's the sound of a man makin' love to a woman who's not there."

He shrugged and jerked his hands suddenly, spreading them wide on the rail, bursting his invisible chains. He looked down at me then with a half-smile, and I saw the dark memories at the back of his eyes, under the mocking humor.

I saw too the terrible need there, the desire strong enough to have endured loneliness and degradation, squalor and separation.

We stood quite still, looking at each other, oblivious of the deck traffic passing by. He knew better than any man how to hide his thoughts, but he wasn't hiding them from me.

The hunger in him went bone-deep, and my own bones seemed to dissolve in recognition of it. His hand was an inch from mine, resting on the wooden rail, long-fingered and powerful. . . . If I touched him, I thought suddenly, he would turn and take me, here, on the deck boards.

As though hearing my thought, he took my hand suddenly, pressing it tight against the hard muscle of his thigh.

"How many times have we lain together, since ye came back to me?" he whispered. "Once, twice, in the brothel. Three times in the heather. And then at Lallybroch, again in Paris." His finger tapped lightly against my wrist, one after the other, in time with my pulse.

"Each time, I left your bed as hungry as ever I came to it. It takes no more to ready me now than the scent of your hair brushing past my face, or the feel of your thigh against mine when we sit to eat. And to see ye stand on deck, wi' the wind pressing your gown tight to your body . . ."

The corner of his mouth twitched slightly as he looked at me. I could see the pulse beat strong in the hollow of his throat, his skin flushed with wind and desire.

"There are moments, Sassenach, when for one copper penny I'd have ye on the spot, back against the mast and your skirt about your waist, and devil take the bloody crew!"

My fingers convulsed against his palm, and he tightened his grasp, nodding pleasantly in response to the greeting of the gunner, coming past on his way toward the quarter-gallery.

The bell for the Captain's dinner sounded beneath my feet, a sweet metallic vibration that traveled up through the soles of my feet and melted the marrow of my bones. Fergus and Marsali left their play and went below, and the crew began preparations for the changing of the watch, but we stayed standing by the rail, fixed in each other's eyes, burning.

"The Captain's compliments, Mr. Fraser, and will you be joining him for dinner?" It was Maitland, the cabin boy, keeping cautious distance as he relayed this message.

Jamie took a deep breath, and pulled his eyes away from mine.

"Aye, Mr. Maitland, we'll be there directly." He took another breath, settled his coat on his shoulders, and offered me his arm.

"Shall we go below, Sassenach?"

"Just a minute." I drew my hand out of my pocket, having found what I was looking for. I took his hand and pressed the object into his palm.

He stared down at the image of King George III in his hand, then up at me.

"On account," I said. "Let's go and eat."

The next day found us on deck again; though the air was still chilly, the cold was far preferable to the stuffiness of the cabins. We took our usual path, down one side of the ship and up the other, but then Jamie stopped, pausing to lean against the rail as he told me some anecdote about the printing business.

A few feet away, Mr. Willoughby sat cross-legged in the protection of the mainmast, a small cake of wet black ink by the toe of his slipper and a large sheet of white paper on the deck before him. The tip of his brush touched the paper lightly as a butterfly, leaving surprising strong shapes behind.

As I watched, fascinated, he began again at the top of the page. He worked rapidly, with a sureness of stroke that was like watching a dancer or a fencer, sure of his ground.

One of the deckhands passed dangerously close to the edge of the paper, almost—but not quite—placing a large dirty foot on the snowy white. A few moments later, another man did the same thing, though there was plenty of room to pass by. Then the first man came back, this time careless enough to kick over the small cake of black ink as he passed.

"Tck!" the seaman exclaimed in annoyance. He scuffed at the black splotch on the otherwise immaculate deck. "Filthy heathen! Look 'ere, wot he's done!"

The second man, returning from his brief errand, paused in interest. "On the clean deck? Captain Raines won't be pleased, will he?" He nodded at Mr. Willoughby, mock-jovial. "Best hurry and lick it up, little fella, before the Captain comes."

"Aye, that'll do; lick it up. Quick, now!" The first man moved a step nearer the seated figure, his shadow falling on the page like a blot. Mr. Willoughby's lips tightened just a shade, but he didn't look up. He completed the second column, righted the ink cake and dipped his brush without taking his eyes from the page, and began a third column, hand moving steadily.

"I *said*," began the first seaman, loudly, but stopped in surprise as a large white handkerchief fluttered down on the deck in front of him, covering the inkblot.

"Your pardon, gentlemen," said Jamie. "I seem to have dropped something." With a cordial nod to the seamen, he bent down and swept up the handkerchief, leaving nothing but a faint smear on the decking. The seamen glanced at each other, uncertain, then at Jamie. One man caught sight of the blue eyes over the blandly smiling mouth, and blanched visibly. He turned hastily away, tugging at his mate's arm.

"Norratall, sir," he mumbled. "C'mon, Joe, we're wanted aft."

Jamie didn't look either at the departing seamen or at Mr Willoughby, but came toward me, tucking his handkerchief back in his sleeve.

"A verra pleasant day, is it not, Sassenach?" he said. He threw back his head, inhaling deeply. "Refreshing air, aye?"

"More so for some than for others, I expect," I said, amused. The air at this particular spot on deck smelled rather strongly of the alum-tanned hides in the hold below.

"That was kind of you," I said as he leaned back against the rail next to me. "Do you think I should offer Mr. Willoughby the use of my cabin to write?"

Jamie snorted briefly. "No. I've told him he can use my cabin or the table in the mess between meals, but he'd rather be here—stubborn wee fool that he is."

"Well, I suppose the light's better," I said dubiously, eyeing the small hunched figure, crouched doggedly against the mast. As I watched, a gust of wind lifted the edge of the paper; Mr. Willoughby pinned it at once, holding it still with one hand while continuing his short, sure brushstrokes with the other. "It doesn't look comfortable, though."

"It's not." Jamie ran his fingers through his hair in mild exasperation. "He does it on purpose, to provoke the crew."

"Well, if that's what he's after, he's doing a good job," I observed. "What on earth for, though?"

Jamie leaned back against the rail beside me, and snorted once more.

"Aye, well, that's complicated. Ever met a Chinaman before, have ye?"

"A few, but I suspect they're a bit different in my time," I said dryly. "They tend not to wear pigtails and silk pajamas, for one thing, nor do they have obsessions about ladies' feet—or if they did, they didn't tell me about it," I added, to be fair.

Jamie laughed and moved a few inches closer, so that his hand on the rail brushed mine.

"Well, it's to do wi' the feet," he said. "Or that's the start of it, ʌyway. See, Josie, who's one of the whores at Madame Jeanne's, ld Gordon about it, and of course he's told everyone now."

"What on earth is it about the feet?" I demanded, curiosity ᵖcoming overwhelming. "What does he *do* to them?"

Jamie coughed, and a faint flush rose in his cheeks. "Well, it's a ʈ ... ."

"You couldn't possibly tell me anything that would shock me," ʌssured him. "I *have* seen quite a lot of things in my life, you ɪow—and a good many of them with you, come to that."

"I suppose ye have, at that," he said, grinning. "Aye, well, it's ⁕ so much what he does, but—well, in China, the highborn ladies ve their feet bound."

"I've heard of that," I said, wondering what all the fuss was out. "It's supposed to make their feet small and graceful."

Jamie snorted again. "Graceful, aye? D'ye know how it's ne?" And proceeded to tell me.

"They take a tiny lassie—nay more than a year old, aye?—and ɾn under the toes of her feet until they touch her heel, then tie ɪndages about the foot to hold it so."

"Ouch!" I said involuntarily.

"Yes, indeed," he said dryly. "Her nanny will take the ban-ges off now and then to clean the foot, but puts them back ʳectly. After some time, her wee toes rot and fall off. And by the ɪe she's grown, the poor lassie's little more at the end of her ɡs than a crumple of bones and skin, smaller than the size o' my ʈ." His closed fist knocked softly against the wood of the rail in ɪstration. "But she's considered verra beautiful then," he ded. "Graceful, as ye say."

"That's perfectly disgusting!" I said. "But what has that got to with—" I glanced at Mr. Willoughby, but he gave no sign of aring us; the wind was blowing from him toward us, carrying r words out to sea.

"Say this was a lassie's foot, Sassenach," he said, stretching ꜱ right hand out flat before him. "Curl the toes under to touch ᵗ heel, and what have ye in the middle?" He curled his fingers ᵓsely into a fist in illustration.

"What?" I said, bewildered. Jamie extended the middle finger his left hand, and thrust it abruptly through the center of his fist an unmistakably graphic gesture.

"A hole," he said succinctly.

"You're kidding! *That's* why they do it?"

His forehead furrowed slightly, then relaxed. "Oh, am I jesting By no means, Sassenach. He says"—he nodded delicately at M Willoughby—"that it's a most remarkable sensation. To a man.

"Why, that perverted little beast!"

Jamie laughed at my indignation.

"Aye, well, that's about what the crew thinks, too. Of course, l canna get quite the same effect wi' a European woman, but gather he . . . tries, now and then."

I began to understand the general feeling of hostility toward tl little Chinese. Even a short acquaintance with the crew of tl *Artemis* had taught me that seamen on the whole tended to l gallant creatures, with a strong romantic streak where wom were concerned—no doubt because they did without female con pany for a good part of the year.

"Hm," I said, with a glance of suspicion at Mr. Willoughb "Well, that explains them, all right, but what about him?"

"That's what's a wee bit complicated." Jamie's mouth curl upward in a wry smile. "See, to Mr. Yi Tien Cho, late of tl Heavenly Kingdom of China, *we're* the barbarians."

"Is that so?" I glanced up at Brodie Cooper, coming down tl ratlines above, the filthy, callused soles of his feet all that w visible from below. I rather thought both sides had a point. "Ev you?"

"Oh, aye. I'm a filthy, bad-smelling *gwao-fe*—that means foreign devil, ye ken—wi' the stink of a weasel—I think that what *huang-shu-lang* means—and a face like a gargoyle," finished cheerfully.

"He *told* you all that?" It seemed an odd recompense for sa ing someone's life. Jamie glanced down at me, cocking one ey brow.

"Have ye noticed, maybe, that verra small men will say an thing to ye, when they've drink taken?" he asked. "I think bran makes them forget their size; they think they're great hairy brut and swagger something fierce."

He nodded at Mr. Willoughby, industriously painting. "He's bit more circumspect when he's sober, but it doesna change wl he thinks. It fair galls him, aye? Especially knowing that if vasna for me, someone would likely knock him on the head or put im through the window into the sea some quiet night.''

He spoke with simple matter-of-factness, but I hadn't missed he sideways looks directed at us by the passing seamen, and had lready realized just why Jamie was passing time in idle conversaon by the rail with me. If anyone had been in doubt about Mr. Villoughby's being under Jamie's protection, they would be rapdly disabused of the notion.

''So you saved his life, gave him work, and keep him out of ouble, and he insults you and thinks you're an ignorant barbaran,'' I said dryly. ''Sweet little fellow.''

''Aye, well.'' The wind had shifted slightly, blowing a lock of amie's hair free across his face. He thumbed it back behind his ar and leaned farther toward me, our shoulders nearly touching. Let him say what he likes; I'm the only one who understands im.''

''Really?'' I laid a hand over Jamie's where it rested on the rail.

''Well, maybe not to say understand him,'' he admitted. He oked down at the deck between his feet. ''But I do remember,'' e said softly, ''what it's like to have nothing but your pride—and friend.''

I remembered what Innes had said, and wondered whether it as the one-armed man who had been his friend in time of need. I new what he meant; I had had Joe Abernathy, and knew what a ifference it made.

''Yes, I had a friend at the hospital . . .'' I began, but was terrupted by loud exclamations of disgust emanating from under y feet.

''Damn! Blazing Hades! That filth-eating son of a pig-fart!''

I looked down, startled, then realized, from the muffled Irish aths proceeding from below, that we were standing directly over e galley. The shouting was loud enough to attract attention from e hands forward, and a small group of sailors gathered with us, atching in fascination as the cook's black-kerchiefed head poked t of the hatchway, glaring ferociously at the crowd.

''Burry-arsed swabs!'' he shouted. ''What're ye lookin' at? vo of yer idle barsteds tumble arse down here and toss this muck ver the side! D'ye mean me to be climbin' ladders all day, and e with half a leg?'' The head disappeared abruptly, and with a good-natured shrug, Picard motioned to one of the younger sailors to come along below.

Shortly there was a confusion of voices and a bumping of some large object down below, and a terrible smell assaulted my nostrils.

"Jesus Christ on a piece of toast!" I snatched a handkerchief from my pocket and clapped it to my nose; this wasn't the first smell I had encountered afloat, and I usually kept a linen square soaked in wintergreen in my pocket, as a precaution. "What's that?"

"By the smell of it, dead horse. A verra old horse, at that, and a long time dead." Jamie's long, thin nose looked a trifle pinched around the nostrils, and all around, sailors were gagging, holding their noses, and generally commenting unfavorably on the smell.

Maitland and Grosman, faces averted from their burden, but slightly green nonetheless, manhandled a large cask through the hatchway and onto the deck. The top had been split, and I caught a brief glimpse of a yellowish-white mass in the opening, glistening faintly in the sun. It seemed to be moving. Maggots, in profusion.

"Eew!" The exclamation was jerked from me involuntarily. The two sailors said nothing, their lips being pressed tightly together, but both of them looked as though they agreed with me. Together, they manhandled the cask to the rail and heaved it up and over.

Such of the crew as were not otherwise employed gathered at the rail to watch the cask bobbing in the wake, and be entertained by Murphy's outspokenly blasphemous opinion of the ship's chandler who had sold it to him. Manzetti, a small Italian seaman with a thick russet pigtail, was standing by the rail, loading a musket.

"Shark," he explained with a gleam of teeth beneath his mustache, seeing me watching him. "Very good to eat."

"Ar," said Sturgis approvingly.

Such of the crew as were not presently occupied gathered at the stern, watching. There were sharks, I knew; Maitland had pointed out to me two dark, flexible shapes hovering in the shadow of the hull the evening before, keeping pace with the ship with no apparent effort save a small and steady oscillation of sickled tails.

"There!" A shout went up from several throats as the cask jerked suddenly in the water. A pause, and Manzetti fixed his aim carefully in the vicinity of the floating cask. Another jerk, as though something had bumped it violently, and another.

The water was a muddy gray, but clear enough for me to catch a glimpse of something moving under the surface, fast. Another jerk, the cask heeled to one side, and suddenly the sharp edge of a fin creased the surface of the water, and a gray back showed briefly, tiny waves purling off it.

The musket discharged next to me with a small roar and a cloud of black-powder smoke that left my eyes stinging. There was a universal shout from the observers, and when the watering of my eyes subsided, I could see a small brownish stain spreading round the cask.

"Did he hit the shark, or the horsemeat?" I asked Jamie, in a low-voiced aside.

"The cask," he said with a smile. "Still, it's fine shooting."

Several more shots went wild, while the cask began to dance an agitated jig, the frenzied sharks striking it repeatedly. Bits of white and brown flew from the broken cask, and a large circle of grease, rotten blood, and debris spread round the shark's feast. As though by magic, seabirds began to appear, one and two at a time, diving for tidbits.

"No good," said Manzetti at last, lowering the musket and wiping his face with his sleeve. "Too far." He was sweating and stained from neck to hairline with black powder; the wiping left a streak of white across his eyes, like a raccoon's mask.

"I could relish a slab of shark," said the Captain's voice near my ear. I turned to see him peering thoughtfully over the rail at the scene of carnage. "Perhaps we might lower a boat, Mr. Picard."

The bosun turned with an obliging roar, and the *Artemis* hauled her wind, coming round in a small circle to draw near the remains of the floating cask. A small boat was launched, containing Manzetti, with musket, and three seamen armed with gaffs and rope.

By the time they reached the spot, there was nothing left of the cask but a few shattered bits of wood. There was still plenty of activity, though; the water roiled with the sharks' thrashing beneath the surface, and the scene was nearly obscured by a raucous cloud of seabirds. As I watched, I saw a pointed snout rise suddenly from the water, mouth open, seize one of the birds and disappear beneath the waves, all in the flick of an eyelash.

"Did you see that?" I said, awed. I was aware, in a general wa⟩ that sharks were well-equipped with teeth, but this practical den onstration was more striking than any number of *National Gec graphic* photographs.

"Why, Grandmother dear, what big teeth ye have!" said Jami⟨ sounding suitably impressed.

"Oh, they do indeed," said a genial voice nearby. I glance⟨ aside to find Murphy grinning at my elbow, broad face shinin with a savage glee. "Little good it will do the buggers, with a ba blown clean through their fucking brains!" He pounded a hamlik fist on the rail, and shouted, "Get me one of them jagged bugger Manzetti! There's a bottle o' cookin' brandy waitin' if ye do!"

"Is it a personal matter to ye, Mr. Murphy?" Jamie aske⟨ politely. "Or professional concern?"

"Both, Mr. Fraser, both," the cook replied, watching the hu⟨ with a fierce attention. He kicked his wooden leg against the sid with a hollow clunk. "They've had a taste o' me," he said wi⟨ grim relish, "but I've tasted a good many more o' them!"

The boat was barely visible through the flapping screen of bird and their screams made it hard to hear anything other than Mu phy's war cries.

"Shark steak with mustard!" Murphy was bellowing, ey⟨ mere slits in an ecstasy of revenge. "Stewed liver wi' piccalill I'll make soup o' yer fins, and jelly yer eyeballs in sherry wine, y wicked barsted!"

I saw Manzetti, kneeling in the bows, take aim with his muske and the puff of black smoke as he fired. And then I saw M Willoughby.

I hadn't seen him jump from the rail; no one had, with all ey⟨ fixed on the hunt. But there he was, some distance away from th melee surrounding the boat, his shaven head glistening like fishing float as he wrestled in the water with an enormous bird, i wings churning the water like an eggbeater.

Alerted by my cry, Jamie tore his eyes from the hunt, goggle for an instant, and before I could move or speak, was perched ⟨ the rail himself.

My shout of horror coincided with a surprised roar from Mu phy, but Jamie was gone, too, lancing into the water near th Chinaman with barely a splash.

There were shouts and cries from the deck—and a shrill scree⟨

from Marsali—as everyone realized what had happened. Jamie's
wet red head emerged next to Mr. Willoughby, and in seconds, he
had an arm tight about the Chinaman's throat. Mr. Willoughby
clung tightly to the bird, and I wasn't sure, just for the moment,
whether Jamie intended rescue or throttling, but then he kicked
strongly, and began to tow the struggling mass of bird and man
back toward the ship.

Triumphant shouts from the boat, and a spreading circle of deep
red in the water. There was a tremendous thrashing as one shark
was gaffed and hauled behind the small boat by a rope about its
tail. Then everything was confusion, as the men in the boat noticed
what else was going on in the water nearby.

Lines were thrown over one side and then the other, and crewmen rushed back and forth in high excitement, undecided whether
to help with rescue or shark, but at last Jamie and his burdens were
hauled in to starboard, and dumped dripping on the deck, while
the captured shark—several large bites taken out of its body by its
hungry companions—was drawn in, still feebly snapping, to port.

"Je . . . sus . . . Christ," Jamie said, chest heaving. He lay
flat on the deck, gasping like a landed fish.

"Are you all right?" I knelt beside him, and wiped the water
off his face with the hem of my skirt. He gave me a lopsided smile
and nodded, still gasping.

"Jesus," he said at last, sitting up. He shook his head and
sneezed. "I thought I was eaten, sure. Those fools in the boat
started toward us, and there were sharks all round them, under the
water, bitin' at the gaffed one." He tenderly massaged his calves.
"It's nay doubt oversensitive of me, Sassenach, but I've always
dreaded the thought of losing a leg. It seems almost worse than
bein' killed outright."

"I'd as soon you didn't do either," I said dryly. He was beginning to shiver; I pulled off my shawl and wrapped it around his
shoulders, then looked about for Mr. Willoughby.

The little Chinese, still clinging stubbornly to his prize, a young
pelican nearly as big as he was, ignored both Jamie and the considerable abuse flung in his direction. He squelched below, dripping, protected from physical castigation by the clacking bill of
his captive, which discouraged anyone from getting too close to
him.

A nasty chunking sound and a crow of triumph from the other

side of the deck announced Murphy's use of an ax to dispatch hi
erstwhile nemesis. The seamen clustered round the corpse, knive
drawn, to get pieces of the skin. Further enthusiastic chopping
and Murphy came strolling past, beaming, a choice section of tai
under his arm, the huge yellow liver hanging from one hand in a
bag of netting, and the bloody ax slung over his shoulder.

"Not drowned, are ye?" he said, ruffling Jamie's damp hai
with his spare hand. "I can't see why ye'd bother wi' the littl
bugger, myself, but I'll say 'twas bravely done. I'll brew ye up a
fine broth from the tail, to keep off the chill," he promised, an
stumped off, planning menus aloud.

"Why did he do it?" I asked. "Mr. Willoughby, I mean."

Jamie shook his head and blew his nose on his shirttail.

"Damned if I know. He wanted the bird, I expect, but I couldn
say why. To eat, maybe?"

Murphy overheard this and swung round at the head of th
galley ladder, frowning.

"Ye can't eat pelicans," he said, shaking his head in disap
proval. "Fishy-tasting, no matter how ye cook 'em. And Go
knows what one's doing out here anyway; they're shorebirds, peli
cans. Blown out by a storm I suppose. Awkward buggers." Hi
bald head disappeared into his realm, murmuring happily of drie
parsley and cayenne.

Jamie laughed and stood up.

"Aye, well, perhaps it's only he wants the feathers to mak
quills of. Come along below, Sassenach. Ye can help me dry m
back."

He had spoken jokingly, but as soon as the words were out o
his mouth, his face went blank. He glanced quickly to port, wher
the crew was arguing and jostling over the remains of the shark
while Fergus and Marsali cautiously examined the severed head
lying gape-jawed on the deck. Then his eyes met mine, with
perfect understanding.

Thirty seconds later, we were below in his cabin. Cold drop
from his wet hair rained over my shoulders and slid down m
bosom, but his mouth was hot and urgent. The hard curves of hi
back glowed warm through the soaked fabric of the shirt that stuc
to them.

"*Ifrinn!*" he said breathlessly, breaking loose long enough

nk at his breeches. "Christ, they're stuck to me! I canna get
m off!"

Snorting with laughter, he jerked at the laces, but the water had
aked them into a hopeless knot.

"A knife!" I said. "Where's a knife?" Snorting myself at the
ht of him, struggling frantically to get his drenched shirttail out
his breeches, I began to rummage through the drawers of the
sk, tossing out bits of paper, bottle of ink, a snuffbox—every-
ng but a knife. The closest thing was an ivory letter opener,
de in the shape of a hand with a pointing finger.

I seized upon this and grasped him by the waistband, trying to
v at the tangled laces.

He yelped in alarm and backed away.

"Christ, be careful wi' that, Sassenach! It's no going to do ye
y good to get my breeks off, and ye geld me in the process!"

Half-crazed with lust as we were, that seemed funny enough to
uble us both up laughing.

"Here!" Rummaging in the chaos of his berth, he snatched up
dirk and brandished it triumphantly. An instant later, the laces
re severed and the sopping breeks lay puddled on the floor.

He seized me, picked me up bodily, and laid me on the desk,
edless of crumpled papers and scattered quills. Tossing my
rts up past my waist, he grabbed my hips and half-lay on me,
hard thighs forcing my legs apart.

It was like grasping a salamander; a blaze of heat in a chilly
oud. I gasped as the tail of his sopping shirt touched my bare
ly, then gasped again as I heard footsteps in the passage.

'Stop!" I hissed in his ear. "Someone's coming!"

'Too late," he said, with breathless certainty. "I must have ye,
die."

He took me, with one quick, ruthless thrust, and I bit his shoul-
hard, tasting salt and wet linen, but he made no sound. Two
kes, three, and I had my legs locked tight around his buttocks,
cry muffled in his shirt, not caring either who else might be
ning.

He had me, quickly and thoroughly, and thrust himself home,
home, and home again, with a deep sound of triumph in his
oat, shuddering and shaking in my arms.

Two minutes later, the cabin door swung open. Innes looked
wly round the wreckage of the room. His soft brown gaze

traveled from the ravaged desk to me, sitting damp and dishevel
but respectably clothed, upon the berth, and rested at last on
mie, who sat collapsed on a stool, still clad in his wet shirt, ch
heaving and the deep red color fading slowly from his face.

Innes's nostrils flared delicately, but he said nothing. He walk
into the cabin, nodding at me, and bent to reach under Fergu
berth, whence he pulled out a bottle of brandywine.

"For the Chinee," he said to me. "So as he mightn't tak
chill." He turned toward the door and paused, squinting thoug
fully at Jamie.

"Ye might should have Mr. Murphy make ye some broth on t
same account, Mac Dubh. They do say as 'tis dangerous to
chilled after hard work, aye? Ye dinna want to take the ague
There was a faint twinkle in the mournful brown depths.

Jamie brushed back the salty tangle of his hair, a slow sm
spreading across his face.

"Aye, well, and if it should come to that, Innes, at least I sh
die a happy man."

We found out the next day what Mr. Willoughby wanted
pelican for. I found him on the afterdeck, the bird perched o
sail-chest beside him, its wings bound tight to its body by me
of strips of cloth. It glared at me with round yellow eyes, a
clacked its bill in warning.

Mr. Willoughby was pulling in a line, on the end of which wa
small, wriggling purple squid. Detaching this, he held it up
front of the pelican and said something in Chinese. The bird
garded him with deep suspicion, but didn't move. Quickly,
seized the upper bill in his hand, pulled it up, and tossed the sq
into the bird's pouch. The pelican, looking surprised, gulped c
vulsively and swallowed it.

"*Hao-liao*," Mr. Willoughby said approvingly, stroking
bird's head. He saw me watching, and beckoned me to co
closer. Keeping a cautious eye on the wicked bill, I did so.

"Ping An," he said, indicating the pelican. "Peaceful on
The bird erected a small crest of white feathers, for all the worl
though it were pricking up its ears at its name, and I laughed

"Really? What are you going to do with him?"

"I teach him hunt for me," the little Chinese said matter-of-factly. "You watch."

I did. After several more squid and a couple of small fish had en caught and fed to the pelican, Mr. Willoughby removed an-er strip of soft cloth from the recesses of his costume, and apped this snugly round the bird's neck.

"Not want choke," he explained. "Not swallow fish." He then d a length of light line tightly to this collar, motioned to me to nd back, and with a swift jerk, released the bindings that held e bird's wings.

Surprised at the sudden freedom, the pelican waddled back and th on the locker, flapped its huge bony wings once or twice, and n shot into the sky in an explosion of feathers.

A pelican on the ground is a comical thing, all awkward angles, ayed feet, and gawky bill. A soaring pelican, circling over wa-, is a thing of wonder, graceful and primitive, startling as a rodactyl among the sleeker forms of gulls and petrels.

Ping An, the peaceful one, soared to the limit of his line, strug-d to go higher, then, as though resigned, began to circle. Mr. lloughby, eyes squinted nearly shut against the sun, spun slowly nd and round on the deck below, playing the pelican like a kite. the hands in the rigging and on deck nearby stopped what they re doing to watch in fascination.

Sudden as a bolt from a crossbow, the pelican folded its wings dived, cleaving the water with scarcely a splash. As it popped the surface, looking mildly surprised, Mr. Willoughby began to it in. Aboard once more, the pelican was persuaded with some ficulty to give up its catch, but at last suffered its captor to reach tiously into the leathery subgular pouch and extract a fine, fat bream.

Mr. Willoughby smiled pleasantly at a gawking Picard, took out mall knife, and slit the still-living fish down the back. Pinioning bird in one wiry arm, he loosened the collar with his other d, and offered it a flapping piece of bream, which Ping An erly snatched from his fingers and gulped.

"His," Mr. Willoughby explained, wiping blood and scales elessly on the leg of his trousers. "Mine," nodding toward the f-fish still sitting on the locker, now motionless.

Within a week, the pelican was entirely tame, able to fly free, ared, but without the tethering line, returning to his master to

regurgitate a pouchful of shining fish at his feet. When not fishi
Ping An either took up a position on the crosstrees, much to
displeasure of the crewmen responsible for swabbing the de
beneath, or followed Mr. Willoughby around the deck, waddl
absurdly from side to side, eight-foot wings half-spread for b
ance.

The crew, both impressed by the fishing and wary of Ping A
great snapping bill, steered clear of Mr. Willoughby, who ma
his words each day beside the mast, weather permitting, sec
under the benign yellow eye of his new friend.

I paused one day to watch Mr. Willoughby at his work, stay
out of sight behind the shelter of the mast. He sat for a momen
look of quiet satisfaction on his face, contemplating the finish
page. I couldn't read the characters, of course, but the shape of
whole thing was somehow very pleasing to look at.

Then he glanced quickly around, as though checking to see t
no one was coming, picked up the brush, and with great ca
added a final character, in the upper left corner of the page. Wi
out asking, I knew it was his signature.

He sighed then, and lifted his face to look out over the rail. N
inscrutable, by any means, his expression was filled with a drea
ing delight, and I knew that whatever he saw, it was neither
ship nor the heaving ocean beyond.

At last, he sighed again and shook his head, as though to hi
self. He laid hands on the paper, and quickly, gently, folded
once, and twice, and again. Then rising to his feet, he went to
rail, extended his hands over the water, and let the folded wh
shape fall.

It tumbled toward the water. Then the wind caught it a
whirled it upward, a bit of white receding in the distance, look
much like the gulls and terns who squawked behind the ship
.search of scraps.

Mr. Willoughby didn't stay to watch it, but turned away fr
the rail and went below, the dream still stamped on his sn
round face.

45

Mr. Willoughby's Tale

As we passed the center of the Atlantic gyre and headed south, the days and evenings became warm, and the off-duty crew began to congregate on the forecastle for a time after supper, to sing songs, dance to Brodie Cooper's fiddle, or listen to stories. With the same instinct that makes children camping in the wood tell ghost stories, the men seemed particularly fond of horrible tales of shipwreck and the perils of the sea.

As we passed farther south, and out the realm of Kraken and sea serpent, the mood for monsters passed, and the men began instead to tell stories of their homes.

It was after most of these had been exhausted that Maitland, the cabin boy, turned to Mr. Willoughby, crouched as usual against the foot of the mast, with his cup cradled to his chest.

"How was it that you came from China, Willoughby?" Maitland asked curiously. "I've not seen more than a handful of Chinese sailors, though folk do say as there's a great many people in China. Is it such a fine place that the inhabitants don't care to take leave of it, perhaps?"

At first demurring, the little Chinese seemed mildly flattered at the interest provoked by this question. With a bit more urging, he consented to tell of his departure from his homeland—requiring only that Jamie should translate for him, his own English being inadequate to the task. Jamie readily agreeing, he sat down beside Mr. Willoughby, and cocked his head to listen.

"I was a Mandarin," Mr. Willoughby began, in Jamie's voice, "a Mandarin of letters, one gifted in composition. I wore a silk

gown, embroidered in very many colors, and over this, th
scholar's blue silk gown, with the badge of my office embroidere
upon breast and back—the figure of a *feng-huang*—a bird of fire."

"I think he means a phoenix," Jamie added, turning to me for
moment before directing his attention back to the patiently waitin
Mr. Willoughby, who began speaking again at once.

"I was born in Pekin, the Imperial City of the Son
Heaven—"

"That is how they call their emperor," Fergus whispered to m
"Such presumption, to equate their king with the Lord Jesus!"

"Shh," hissed several people, turning indignant faces towar
Fergus. He made a rude gesture at Maxwell Gordon, but fell silen
turning back to the small figure sitting crouched against the mas

"I was found early to have some skill in composition, and whi
I was not at first adept in the use of brush and ink, I learned at la
with great effort to make the representations of my brush resemb
the ideas that danced like cranes within my mind. And so I cam
to the notice of Wu-Xien, a Mandarin of the Imperial Househol
who took me to live with him, and oversaw my training.

"I rose rapidly in merit and eminence, so that before m
twenty-sixth birthday, I had attained a globe of red coral upon m
hat. And then came an evil wind, that blew the seeds of misfortu
into my garden. It may be that I was cursed by an enemy,
perhaps that in my arrogance I had omitted to make proper sacr
fice—for surely I was not lacking in reverence to my ancestor
being careful always to visit my family's tomb each year, and
have joss sticks always burning in the Hall of Ancestors—"

"If his compositions were always so long-winded, no doubt th
Son of Heaven lost patience and tossed him in the river," Fergu
muttered cynically.

"—but whatever the cause," Jamie's voice continued, "n
poetry came before the eyes of Wan-Mei, the Emperor's Secor
Wife. Second Wife was a woman of great power, having borne r
less than four sons, and when she asked that I might become pa
of her own household, the request was granted at once."

"And what was wrong wi' that?" demanded Gordon, leanin
forward in interest. "A chance to get on in the world, surely?"

Mr. Willoughby evidently understood the question, for he no
ded in Gordon's direction as he continued, and Jamie's voice too
up the story.

"Oh, the honor was inestimable; I should have had a large ouse of my own within the walls of the palace, and a guard of oldiers to escort my palanquin, with a triple umbrella borne be- •re me in symbol of my office, and perhaps even a peacock ather for my hat. My name would have been inscribed in letters f gold in the Book of Merit."

The little Chinaman paused, scratching at his scalp. The hair ad begun to sprout from the shaved part, making him look rather ke a tennis ball.

"However, there is a condition of service within the Imperial ousehold; all the servants of the royal wives must be eunuchs."

A gasp of horror greeted this, followed by a babble of agitated omment, in which the remarks "Bloody heathen!" and "Yellow astards!" were heard to predominate.

"What is a eunuch?" Marsali asked, looking bewildered.

"Nothing you need ever concern yourself with, *chérie*," Fergus ssured her, slipping an arm about her shoulders. "So you ran, *on ami*?" he addressed Mr. Willoughby in tones of deepest ympathy. "I should do the same, without doubt!"

A deep murmur of heartfelt approbation reinforced this senti- ent. Mr. Willoughby seemed somewhat heartened by such evi- :nt approval; he bobbed his head once or twice at his listeners :fore resuming his story.

"It was most dishonorable of me to refuse the Emperor's gift. nd yet—it is a grievous weakness—I had fallen in love with a oman."

There was a sympathetic sigh at this, most sailors being wildly •mantic souls, but Mr. Willoughby stopped, jerking at Jamie's eeve and saying something to him.

"Oh, I'm wrong," Jamie corrected himself. "He says it was •t *'a woman'*—just 'Woman'—all women, or the idea of women general, he means. That's it?" he asked, looking down at Mr. illoughby.

The Chinaman nodded, satisfied, and sat back. The moon was ll up by now, three-quarters full, and bright enough to show the •le Mandarin's face as he talked.

"Yes," he said, through Jamie, "I thought much of women; eir grace and beauty, blooming like lotus flowers, floating like ilkweed on the wind. And the myriad sounds of them, some- nes like the chatter of ricebirds, or the song of nightingales;

sometimes the cawing of crows,'' he added with a smile tha
creased his eyes to slits and brought his hearers to laughter, "bu
even then I loved them.

"I wrote all my poems to Woman—sometimes they were ad
dressed to one lady or another, but most often to Woman alone. T
the taste of breasts like apricots, the warm scent of a woman'
navel when she wakens in the winter, the warmth of a mound tha
fills your hand like a peach, split with ripeness."

Fergus, scandalized, put his hands over Marsali's ears, but th
rest of his hearers were most receptive.

"No wonder the wee fellow was an esteemed poet," Raebur
said with approval. "It's verra heathen, but I like it!"

"Worth a red knob on your hat, any day," Maitland agreed.

"Almost worth learning a bit of Chinee for," the master's mat
chimed in, eyeing Mr. Willoughby with fresh interest. "Does h
have a lot of those poems?"

Jamie waved the audience—by now augmented by most of th
off-duty hands—to silence and said, "Go on, then," to Mr. Wi
loughby.

"I fled on the Night of Lanterns," the Chinaman said. "A grea
festival, and one when people would be thronging the streets; ther
would be no danger of being noticed by the watchmen. Just afte
dark, as the processions were assembling throughout the city, I pu
on the garments of a traveler—"

"That's like a pilgrim," Jamie interjected, "they go to vis
their ancestors' tombs far away, and wear white clothes—that'
for mourning, ye ken?"

"—and I left my house. I made my way through the crowd
without difficulty, carrying a small anonymous lantern I ha
bought—one without my name and place of residence painted o
it. The watchmen were hammering upon their bamboo drums, th
servants of the great households beating gongs, and from the roo
of the palace, fireworks were being set off in great profusion."

The small round face was marked by nostalgia, as he remem
bered.

"It was in a way a most appropriate farewell for a poet," h
said. "Fleeing nameless, to the sound of great applause. As
passed the soldiers' garrison at the city gate, I looked back, to se
the many roofs of the Palace outlined by bursting flowers of re

d gold. It looked like a magic garden—and a forbidden one, for
e.''

Yi Tien Cho had made his way without incident through the
ght, but had nearly been caught the next day.

''I had forgotten my fingernails,'' he said. He spread out a hand,
ıall and short-fingered, the nails bitten to the quicks. ''For a
ındarin has long nails, as symbol that he is not obliged to work
th his hands, and my own were the length of one of my finger
nts.''

A servant at the house where he had stopped for refreshment
xt day saw them, and ran to tell the guard. Yi Tien Cho ran, too,
d succeeded at last in eluding his pursuers by sliding into a wet
ch and lying hidden in the bushes.

''While lying there, I destroyed my nails, of course,'' he said.
: waggled the little finger of his right hand. ''I was obliged to
ır that nail out, for it had a golden *da zi* inlaid in it, which I
ıld not dislodge.''

He had stolen a peasant's clothes from a bush where they had
ın hung to dry, leaving the torn-out nail with its golden charac-
in exchange, and made his way slowly across country toward
: coast. At first he paid for his food with the small store of
ıney he had brought away, but outside Lulong he met with a
ıd of robbers, who took his money but left him his life.

''And after that,'' he said simply, ''I stole food when I could,
d starved when I could not. And at last the wind of fortune
ınged a little, and I met with a group of traveling apothecaries,
their way to the physicians' fair near the coast. In return for my
ıl at drawing banners for their booth and composing labels
olling the virtues of their medicines, they carried me along with
m.''

Once reaching the coast, he had made his way to the waterfront,
I tried there to pass himself off as a seaman, but failed utterly,
his fingers, so skillful with brush and ink, knew nothing of the
of knots and lines. There were several foreign ships in port; he
I chosen the one whose sailors looked the most barbarous as
ng likely to carry him farthest away, and seizing his chance,
I slipped past the deck guard and into the hold of the *Serafina,*
ınd for Edinburgh.

''You had always meant to leave the country altogether?'' Fer-
; asked, interested. ''It seems a desperate choice.''

"Emperor's reach very long," Mr. Willoughby said softly
English, not waiting for translation. "I am exile, or I am dead.

His listeners gave a collective sigh at the awesome contempl
tion of such bloodthirsty power, and there was a moment of s
lence, with only the whine of the rigging overhead, while M
Willoughby picked up his neglected cup and drained the last dro
of his grog.

He set it down, licking his lips, and laid his hand once more o
Jamie's arm.

"It is strange," Mr. Willoughby said, and the air of reflection
his voice was echoed exactly by Jamie's, "but it was my joy
women that Second Wife saw and loved in my words. Yet
desiring to possess me—and my poems—she would have forev
destroyed what she admired."

Mr. Willoughby uttered a small chuckle, whose irony was u
mistakable.

"Nor is that the end of the contradiction my life has becom
Because I could not bring myself to surrender my manhood, I ha
lost all else—honor, livelihood, country. By that, I mean not on
the land itself, with the slopes of noble fir trees where I spent n
summers in Tartary, and the great plains of the south, the flowi
of rivers filled with fish, but also the loss of myself. My parents a
dishonored, the tombs of my ancestors fall into ruin, and no jo
burns before their images.

"All order, all beauty is lost. I am come to a place where t
golden words of my poems are taken for the clucking of hens, a
my brushstrokes for their scratchings. I am taken as less than t
meanest beggar who swallows serpents for the entertainment
the crowds, allowing passersby to draw the serpent from n
mouth by its tail for the tiny payment that will let me live anoth
day."

Mr. Willoughby glared round at his hearers, making his paral
evident.

"I am come to a country of women coarse and rank as bears
The Chinaman's voice rose passionately, though Jamie kept to
even tone, reciting the words, but stripping them of feeling. "Th
are creatures of no grace, no learning, ignorant, bad-smelli
their bodies gross with sprouting hair, like dogs! And these
these! disdain me as a yellow worm, so that even the low
whores will not lie with me.

"For the love of Woman, I am come to a place where no woman worthy of love!" At this point, seeing the dark looks on the amen's faces, Jamie ceased translating, and instead tried to calm e Chinaman, laying a big hand on the blue-silk shoulder.

"Aye, man, I quite see. And I'm sure there's no a man present uld have done otherwise, given the choice. Is that not so, lads?" asked, glancing over his shoulder with eyebrows raised signifintly.

His moral force was sufficient to extort a grudging murmur of reement, but the crowd's sympathy with the tale of Mr. Wilghby's travails had been quite dissipated by his insulting consion. Pointed remarks were made about licentious, ungrateful athen, and a great many extravagantly admiring compliments d to Marsali and me, as the men dispersed aft.

Fergus and Marsali left then, too, Fergus pausing en route to orm Mr. Willoughby that any further remarks about European men would cause him, Fergus, to be obliged to wrap his, Wilghby's, queue about his neck and strangle him with it.

Mr. Willoughby ignored remarks and threats alike, merely star straight ahead, his black eyes shining with memory and grog. nie at last stood up, too, and held out a hand to help me down m my cask.

It was as we were turning to leave that the Chinaman reached wn between his legs. Completely without lewdness, he cupped testicles, so that the rounded mass pressed against the silk. He led them slowly in the palm of his hand, staring at the bulge in ep meditation.

"Sometime," he said, as though to himself, "I think not worth

46

We Meet a Porpois

I had been conscious for some time that Marsali was trying
get up the nerve to speak to me. I had thought she wou
sooner or later; whatever her feelings toward me, I was the on
other woman aboard. I did my best to help, smiling kindly a
saying "Good morning," but the first move would have to be he

She made it, finally, in the middle of the Atlantic Ocean,
month after we had left Scotland.

I was writing in our shared cabin, making surgical notes or
minor amputation—two smashed toes on one of the forede
hands. I had just completed a drawing of the surgical site, wher
shadow darkened the doorway of the cabin, and I looked up to s
Marsali standing there, chin thrust out pugnaciously.

"I need to know something," she said firmly. "I dinna like
and I reckon ye ken that, but Da says you're a wisewoman, an
think you're maybe an honest woman, even if ye are a whore,
you'll maybe tell me."

There were any number of possible responses to this remarkal
statement, but I refrained from making any of them.

"Maybe I will," I said, putting down the pen. "What is it y
need to know?"

Seeing that I wasn't angry, she slid into the cabin and sat do
on the stool, the only available spot.

"Weel, it's to do wi' bairns," she explained. "And how ye
them."

I raised one eyebrow. "Your mother didn't tell you where
bies come from?"

She snorted impatiently, her small blond brows knotted in fierce
orn. "O' course I ken where they come from! Any fool knows
at much. Ye let a man put his prick between your legs, and
ere's the devil to pay, nine months later. What I want to know is
w ye *don't* get them."

"I see." I regarded her with considerable interest. "You don't
ant a child? Er . . . once you're properly married, I mean?
ost young women seem to."

"Well," she said slowly, twisting a handful of her dress. "I
ink I maybe would like a babe sometime. For itself, I mean. If it
aybe had dark hair, like Fergus." A hint of dreaminess flitted
cross her face, but then her expression hardened once more.
"But I can't," she said.

"Why not?"

She pushed out her lips, thinking, then pulled them in again.
Well, because of Fergus. We havena lain together yet. We havena
en able to do more than kiss each other now and again behind
e hatch covers—thanks to Da and his bloody-minded notions,"
e added bitterly.

"Amen," I said, with some wryness.

"Eh?"

"Never mind." I waved a hand, dismissing it. "What has that
t to do with not wanting babies?"

"I want to like it," she said matter-of-factly. "When we get to
e prick part."

I bit the inside of my lower lip.

"I . . . er . . . imagine that has something to do with Fer-
s, but I'm afraid I don't quite see what it has to do with babies."

Marsali eyed me warily. Without hostility for once, more as
ough she was estimating me in some fashion.

"Fergus likes ye," she said.

"I'm fond of him, too," I answered cautiously, not sure where
e conversation was heading. "I've known him for quite a long
e, ever since he was a boy."

She relaxed suddenly, some of the tension going out of the
nder shoulders.

"Oh. You'll know about it, then—where he was born?"

Suddenly I understood her wariness.

"The brothel in Paris? Yes, I know about that. He told you,
n?"

She nodded. "Aye, he did. A long time ago, last Hogmanay.' Well, I supposed a year was a long time to a fifteen-year-old.

"That's when I told him I loved him," she went on. Her eye were fixed on her skirt, and a faint tinge of pink showed in he cheeks. "And he said he loved me, too, but my mother wasn going to ever agree to the match. And I said why not, there wa nothing so awful about bein' French, not everybody could b Scots, and I didna think his hand mattered a bit either—after al there was Mr. Murray wi' his wooden leg, and Mother liked *hi* well enough—but then he said, no, it was none of those thing and then he told me—about Paris, I mean, and being born in brothel and being a pickpocket until he met Da.''

She raised her eyes, a look of incredulity in the light blu depths. "I think he thought I'd *mind,*" she said, wondering! "He tried to go away, and said he wouldna see me anymor Well—'' she shrugged, tossing her fair hair out of the way, ' soon took care of that.'' She looked at me straight on then, han clasped in her lap.

"It's just I didna want to mention it, in case ye didn't kno already. But since ye do . . . well, it's no Fergus I'm worri about. He says he knows what to do, and I'll like it fine, on we're past the first time or two. But that's not what my mam to me.''

"What *did* she tell you?" I asked, fascinated.

A small line showed between the light brows. "Well . . Marsali said slowly, "it wasna so much she said it—though s did say, when I told her about Fergus and me, that he'd do terrib things to me because of living wi' whores and having one for mother—it was more she . . . she acted like it.''

Her face was a rosy pink now, and she kept her eyes in her la where her fingers twisted themselves in the folds of her skirt. T wind seemed to be picking up; small strands of blond hair ro gently from her head, wafted by the breeze from the window.

"When I started to bleed the first time, she told me what to and about how it was part o' the curse of Eve, and I must just up wi' it. And I said, what was the curse of Eve? And she read from the Bible all about how St. Paul said women were terrib filthy sinners because of what Eve did, but they could still saved by suffering and bearing children.''

"I never did think a lot of St. Paul," I observed, and she looked p, startled.

"But he's in the Bible!" she said, shocked.

"So are a lot of other things," I said dryly. "Heard that story out Gideon and his daughter, have you? Or the fellow who sent s lady out to be raped to death by a crowd of ruffians, so they ouldn't get *him*? God's chosen men, just like Paul. But go on, ."

She gaped at me for a minute, but then closed her mouth and odded, a little stunned.

"Aye, well. Mother said as how it meant I was nearly old nough to be wed, and when I did marry, I must be sure to member it was a woman's duty to do as her husband wanted, hether she liked it or no. And she looked so sad when she told e that . . . I thought whatever a woman's duty was, it must be vful, and from what St. Paul said about suffering and bearing ildren . . ."

She stopped and sighed. I sat quietly, waiting. When she re- med, it was haltingly, as though she had trouble choosing her ords.

"I canna remember my father. I was only three when the En- ish took him away. But I was old enough when my mother wed wed Jamie—to see how it was between them." She bit her lip; e wasn't used to calling Jamie by his name.

"Da—Jamie, I mean—he's kind, I think; he always was to Joan d me. But I'd see, when he'd lay his hand on my mother's waist d try to draw her close—she'd shrink away from him." She awed her lip some more, then continued.

"I could see she was afraid; she didna like him to touch her. t I couldna see that he ever did anything to be afraid *of*, not ere we could see—so I thought it must be something he did en they were in their bed, alone. Joan and I used to wonder at it could be; Mam never had marks on her face or her arms, d she didna limp when she walked—not like Magdalen Wallace, ose husband always beats her when he's drunk on market day— we didna think Da hit her."

Marsali licked her lips, dried by the warm salt air, and I pushed jug of water toward her. She nodded in thanks and poured a ful.

"So I thought," she said, eyes fixed on the stream of water, "that it must be because Mam had had children—had us—and sh knew it would be terrible again and so she didna want to go to be with—with Jamie for fear of it."

She took a drink, then set down the cup and looked at m directly, firming her chin in challenge.

"I saw ye with my da," she said. "Just that minute, before h saw me. I—I think ye liked what he was doing to you in the bed.

I opened my mouth, and closed it again.

"Well . . . yes," I said, a little weakly. "I did."

She grunted in satisfaction. "Mmphm. And ye like it when h touches ye; I've seen. Well, then. Ye havena got any children. An I'd heard there are ways not to have them, only nobody seems know just how, but you must, bein' a wisewoman and all."

She tilted her head to one side, studying me.

"I'd like a babe," she admitted, "but if it's got to be a babe liking Fergus, then it's Fergus. So it won't be a babe—if you'll te me how."

I brushed the curls back behind my ear, wondering where earth to start.

"Well," I said, drawing a deep breath, "to begin with, I ha had children."

Her eyes sprang wide and round at this.

"Ye do? Does Da—does Jamie know?"

"Well, of course he does," I replied testily. "They were his.

"I never heard Da had any bairns at all." The pale eyes na rowed with suspicion.

"I don't imagine he thought it was any of your business," said, perhaps a trifle more sharply than necessary. "And it's n either," I added, but she just raised her brows and went on looki suspicious.

"The first baby died," I said, capitulating. "In France. She buried there. My—our second daughter is grown now; she w born after Culloden."

"So he's never seen her? The grown one?" Marsali spo slowly, frowning.

I shook my head, unable to speak for a moment. There seem to be something stuck in my throat, and I reached for the wate Marsali pushed the jug absently in my direction, leaning agair the swing of the ship.

"That's verra sad," she said softly, to herself. Then she glanc ɪp at me, frowning once more in concentration as she tried to work it all out.

"So ye've had children, and it didna make a difference to you? Mmphm. But it's been a long while, then—did ye have other men whilst ye were away in France?" Her lower lip came up over the upper one, making her look very much like a small and stubborn bulldog.

"That," I said firmly, putting the cup down, "is definitely none of your business. As to whether childbirth makes a difference, possibly it does to some women, but not all of them. But whether it does or not, there are good reasons why you might not want to have a child right away."

She withdrew the pouting underlip and sat up straight, interested.

"So there is a way?"

"There are a lot of ways, and unfortunately most of them don't work," I told her, with a pang of regret for my prescription pad and the reliability of contraceptive pills. Still, I remembered well enough the advice of the *maîtresses sages-femmes,* the experienced midwives of the Hôpital des Anges, where I had worked in Paris twenty years before.

"Hand me the small box in the cupboard over there," I said, pointing to the doors above her head. "Yes, that one.

"Some of the French midwives make a tea of bayberry and valerian," I said, rummaging in my medicine box. "But it's rather dangerous, and not all that dependable, I don't think."

"D'ye miss her?" Marsali asked abruptly. I glanced up, started. "Your daughter?" Her face was abnormally expressionless, and I suspected the question had more to do with Laoghaire than with me.

"Yes," I said simply. "But she's grown; she has her own life." The lump in my throat was back, and I bent my head over the medicine box, hiding my face. The chances of Laoghaire ever seeing Marsali again were just about as good as the chances that I would ever see Brianna; it wasn't a thought I wanted to dwell on.

"Here," I said, pulling out a large chunk of cleaned sponge. I took one of the thin surgical knives from the fitted slots in the lid of the box and carefully sliced off several thin pieces, about three inches square. I searched through the box again and found the small bottle of tansy oil, with which I carefully saturated one square under Marsali's fascinated gaze.

"All right," I said. "That's about how much oil to use. If you haven't any oil, you can dip the sponge in vinegar—even wine will work, in a pinch. You put the bit of sponge well up inside you before you go to bed with a man—mind you do it even the first time; you can get with child from even once."

Marsali nodded, her eyes wide, and touched the sponge gently with a forefinger. "Aye? And—and after? Do I take it out again or—"

An urgent shout from above, coupled with a sudden heeling of the *Artemis* as she backed her mainsails, put an abrupt end to the conversation. Something was happening up above.

"I'll tell you later," I said, pushing the sponge and bottle toward her, and headed for the passage.

Jamie was standing with the Captain on the afterdeck, watching the approach of a large ship behind us. She was perhaps three times the size of the *Artemis,* three-masted, with a perfect forest of rigging and sail, through which small black figures hopped like fleas on a bedsheet. A puff of white smoke floated in her wake, token of a cannon recently fired.

"Is she firing on us?" I asked in amazement.

"No," Jamie said grimly. "A warning shot only. She means to board us."

"Can they?" I addressed the question to Captain Raines, who was looking even more glum than usual, the downturned corner of his mouth sunk in his beard.

"They can," he said. "We'll not outrun her in a stiff breeze like this, on the open sea."

"What is she?" Her ensign flew at the masthead, but seen against the sun at this distance, it looked completely black.

Jamie glanced down at me, expressionless. "A British man-o-war, Sassenach. Seventy-four guns. Perhaps ye'd best go below."

This was bad news. While Britain was no longer at war with France, relations between the two countries were by no means cordial. And while the *Artemis* was armed, she had only four twelve-pound guns; sufficient to deter small pirates, but no match for a man-of-war.

"What can they want of us?" Jamie asked the Captain. Raines shook his head, his soft, plump face set grimly.

"Likely pressing," he answered. "She's shorthanded; you can see by her rigging—and her foredeck all ahoo," he noted disapprovingly, eyes fixed on the man-of-war, now looming as she drew alongside. He glanced at Jamie. "They can press any of our hands who look to be British—which is something like half the crew. And yourself, Mr. Fraser—unless you wish to pass for French?"

"Damn," Jamie said softly. He glanced at me and frowned. "Did I not tell ye to get below?"

"You did," I said, not going. I drew closer to him, my eyes fixed on the man-of-war, where a small boat was now being lowered. One officer, in a gilded coat and laced hat, was climbing down the side.

"If they press the British hands," I asked Captain Raines, "what will happen to them?"

"They'll serve aboard the *Porpoise*—that's her," he nodded at the man-of-war, which sported a puff-lipped fish as the figurehead, "as members of the Royal Navy. She may release the pressed hands when she reaches port—or she may not."

"What? You mean they can just kidnap men and make them serve as sailors for as long as they please?" A thrill of fear shot through me, at the thought of Jamie's being abruptly taken away.

"They can," the Captain said shortly. "And if they do, we'll have a job of it to reach Jamaica ourselves, with half a crew." He turned abruptly and went forward, to greet the arriving boat.

Jamie gripped my elbow and squeezed.

"They'll not take Innes or Fergus," he said. "They'll help ye to hunt for Young Ian. If they take us"— I noted the "us" with a sharp pang —"you'll go on to Jared's place at Sugar Bay, and search from there." He looked down and gave me a brief smile. "I'll meet ye there," he said, and gave my elbow a reassuring squeeze. "I canna say how long it might be, but I'll come to ye there."

"But you could pass as a Frenchman!" I protested. "You know you could!"

He looked at me for a moment, and shook his head, smiling faintly.

"No," he said softly. "I canna let them take my men, and stay behind, hiding under a Frenchman's name."

"But—" I started to protest that the Scottish smugglers were *not* his men, had no claim on his loyalty, and then stopped, realizing that it was useless. The Scots might not be his tenants or his kin, and one of them might well be a traitor. But he had brought them here, and if they went, he would go with them.

"Dinna mind it, Sassenach," he said softly. "I shall be all right, one way or the other. But I think it is best if our name is Malcolm, for the moment."

He patted my hand, then released it and went forward, shoulders braced to meet whatever was coming. I followed, more slowly. As the gig pulled alongside, I saw Captain Raines's eyebrows rise in astonishment.

"God save us, what is this?" he murmured under his breath, as a head appeared above the *Artemis*'s rail.

It was a young man, evidently in his late twenties, but with his face drawn and shoulders slumping with fatigue. A uniform coat that was too big for him had been tugged on over a filthy shirt, and he staggered slightly as the deck of the *Artemis* rose beneath him.

"You are the captain of this ship?" The Englishman's eyes were red-rimmed from tiredness, but he picked Raines from the crowd of grim-faced hands at a glance. "I am acting captain Thomas Leonard, of His Majesty's ship *Porpoise*. For the love of God," he said, speaking hoarsely, "have you a surgeon aboard?"

Over a warily offered glass of port below, Captain Leonard explained that the *Porpoise* had suffered an outbreak of some infectious plague, beginning some four weeks before.

"Half the crew are down with it," he said, wiping a crimson drop from his stubbled chin. "We've lost thirty men so far, and look fair to lose a lot more."

"You lost your captain?" Raines asked.

Leonard's thin face flushed slightly. "The—the captain and the two senior lieutenants died last week, and the surgeon and the surgeon's mate, as well. I was third lieutenant." That explained both his surprising youth and his nervous state; to be landed suddenly in sole command of a large ship, a crew of six hundred men and a rampant infection aboard, was enough to rattle anyone.

"If you have anyone aboard with some medical expe-ence . . ." He looked hopefully from Captain Raines to Jamie, who stood by the desk, frowning slightly.

"I'm the *Artemis*'s surgeon, Captain Leonard," I said, from my place in the doorway. "What symptoms do your men have?"

"You?" The young captain's head swiveled to stare at me. His jaw hung slackly open, showing the furred tongue and stained teeth of a tobacco-chewer.

"My wife's a rare healer, Captain," Jamie said mildly. "If it's help ye came for, I'd advise ye to answer her questions, and do as she tells ye."

Leonard blinked once, but then took a deep breath and nodded. "Yes. Well, it seems to start with griping pains in the belly, and a terrible flux and vomiting. The afflicted men complain of headache, and they have considerable fever. They—"

"Do some of them have a rash on their bellies?" I interrupted.

He nodded eagerly. "They do. And some of them bleed from the arse as well. Oh, I beg pardon, ma'am," he said, suddenly flustered. "I meant no offense, only that—"

"I think I know what that might be," I interrupted his apologies. A feeling of excitement began to grow in me; the feeling of a diagnosis just under my hands, and the sure knowledge of how to proceed with it. The call of trumpets to a warhorse, I thought with wry amusement. "I'd need to look at them, to be sure, but—"

"My wife would be pleased to advise ye, Captain," Jamie said firmly. "But I'm afraid she canna go aboard your ship."

"Are you sure?" Captain Leonard looked from one to the other of us, eyes desperate with disappointment. "If she could only look at my crew . . ."

"No," Jamie said, at the same moment I replied, "Yes, of course!"

There was an awkward silence for a moment. Then Jamie rose to his feet, said politely, "You'll excuse us, Captain Leonard?" and dragged me bodily out of the cabin, down the passage to the afterhold.

"Are ye daft?" he scowled, still clutching me by one arm. "Ye canna be thinking of setting foot on a ship wi' the plague! Risk your life and the crew and Young Ian, all for the sake of a pack of Englishmen?"

"It isn't plague," I said, struggling to get free. "And I wouldn't be risking my life. Let go of my arm, you bloody Scot!"

He let go, but stood blocking the ladder, glowering at me.

"Listen," I said, striving for patience. "It isn't plague; I'm almost sure it's typhoid fever—the rash sounds like it. I can't catch that, I've been vaccinated for it."

Momentary doubt flitted across his face. Despite my explanations, he was still inclined to consider germs and vaccines in the same league with black magic.

"Aye?" he said skeptically. "Well, perhaps that's so, but still . . ."

"Look," I said, groping for words. "I'm a doctor. They're sick, and I can do something about it. I . . . it's . . . well, I have to, that's all!"

Judging from its effect, this statement appeared to lack something in eloquence. Jamie raised one eyebrow, inviting me to go on.

I took a deep breath. How should I explain it—the need to touch, the compulsion to heal? In his own way, Frank had understood. Surely there was a way to make it clear to Jamie.

"I took an oath," I said. "When I became a physician."

Both eyebrows went up. "An oath?" he echoed. "What sort of oath?"

I had said it aloud only the one time. Still, I had had a framed copy in my office; Frank had given it to me, a gift when I graduated from medical school. I swallowed a small thickening in my throat, closed my eyes, and read what I could remember from the scroll before my mind's eye.

"I swear by Apollo the physician, by Aesculapius, Hygeia, and Panacea, and I take to witness all the gods, all the goddesses, to keep according to my ability and my judgment the following Oath:

I will prescribe regimen for the good of my patients according to my ability and my judgment and never do harm to anyone. To please no one will I prescribe a deadly drug, nor give advice which may cause his death. But I will preserve the purity of my life and my art. In every house where I come I will enter only for the good of my patients, keeping myself far from all intentional ill-doing and all seduction, and especially from the pleasures of love with women or with men, be they free or slaves. All that may come to my knowledge in the exercise of my profession or outside of my profession or in daily commerce with men, which ought not to be spread abroad, I will keep secret and will never reveal. If I keep his oath faithfully, may I enjoy my life and practice my art, re-spected by all men and in all times; but if I swerve from it or violate it, may the reverse be my lot.''

I opened my eyes, to find him looking down at me thoughtfully. 'Er . . . parts of it are just for tradition,'' I explained.

The corner of his mouth twitched slightly. ''I see,'' he said. 'Well, the first part sounds a wee bit pagan, but I like the part about how ye willna seduce anyone.''

''I thought you'd like that one,'' I said dryly. ''Captain Leonard's virtue is safe with me.''

He gave a small snort and leaned back against the ladder, running one hand slowly through his hair.

''Is that how it's done, then, in the company of physicians?'' he asked. ''Ye hold yourself bound to help whoever calls for it, even an enemy?''

''It doesn't make a great difference, you know, if they're ill or hurt.'' I looked up, searching his face for understanding.

''Aye, well,'' he said slowly. ''I've taken an oath now and then, myself—and none of them lightly.'' He reached out and took my right hand, his fingers resting on my silver ring. ''Some weigh heavier than others, though,'' he said, watching my face in turn.

He was very close to me, the sun from the hatchway overhead striping the linen of his sleeve, the skin of his hand a deep ruddy bronze where it cradled my own white fingers, and the glinting silver of my wedding ring.

''It does,'' I said softly, speaking to his thought. ''You know it does.'' I laid my other hand against his chest, its gold ring glowing in a bar of sunlight. ''But where one vow can be kept, without damage to another . . . ?''

He sighed, deeply enough to move the hand on his chest, then bent and kissed me, very gently.

''Aye, well, I wouldna have ye be forsworn,'' he said, straightening up with a wry twist to his mouth. ''You're sure of this vaccination of yours? It does work?''

''It works,'' I assured him.

''Perhaps I should go with ye,'' he said, frowning slightly.

''You can't—you haven't been vaccinated, and typhoid's awfully contagious.''

"You're only thinking it's typhoid, from what Leonard says," he pointed out. "Ye dinna ken for sure that it's that."

"No," I admitted. "But there's only one way to find out."

I was assisted up onto the deck of the *Porpoise* by means of a bosun's chair, a terrorizing swing over empty air and frothing sea. I landed ignominiously in a sprawl on the deck. Once I regained my feet, I was astonished to find how solid the deck of the man-of-war felt, compared to the tiny, pitching quarterdeck of the *Artemis* far below. It was like standing on the Rock of Gibraltar.

My hair had blown loose during the trip between the ships; I twisted it up and repinned it as best I could, then reached to take the medicine box I had brought from the midshipman who held it.

"You'd best show me where they are," I said. The wind was brisk, and I was aware that it was taking a certain amount of work on the part of both crews to keep the two ships close together, even as both drifted leeward.

It was dark in the tween-decks, the confined space lit by small oil lamps that hung from the ceiling, swaying gently with the rise and fall of the ship, so that the ranks of hammocked men lay in deep shadow, blotched with dim patches of light from above. They looked like pods of whales, or sleeping sea beasts, lying humped and black, side by side, swaying with the movement of the sea beneath.

The stench was overpowering. What air there was came down through crude ventilator shafts that reached the upper deck, but that wasn't a lot. Worse than unwashed seamen was the reek of vomitus and the ripe, throat-clogging smell of blood-streaked diarrhea, which liberally spattered the decking beneath the hammocks where sufferers had been too ill to reach the few available chamber pots. My shoes stuck to the deck, coming away with a nasty sucking noise as I made my way cautiously into the area.

"Give me a better light," I said peremptorily to the apprehensive-looking young midshipman who had been told off to accompany me. He was holding a kerchief to his face and looked both scared and miserable, but he obeyed, holding up the lantern he carried so that I could peer into the nearest hammock.

The occupant groaned and turned away his face as the light struck him. He was flushed with fever, and his skin hot to the

ouch. I pulled his shirt up and felt his stomach; it too was hot, the
skin distended and hard. As I prodded gently here and there, the
man writhed like a worm on a hook, uttering piteous groans.

"It's all right," I said soothingly, urging him to flatten out
again. "Yes, I'll help you; it will feel better soon. Let me look into
your eyes, now. Yes, that's right."

I pulled back the eyelid; his pupil shrank in the light, leaving his
eyes brown and red-rimmed with suffering.

"Christ, take away the light!" he gasped, jerking his head away.
"It splits my head!" Fever, vomiting, abdominal cramps, headache.

"Do you have chills?" I asked, waving back the midshipman's
lantern.

The answer was more a moan than a word, but in the affirmative. Even in the shadows, I could see that many of the men in the
hammocks were wrapped in their blankets, though it was stifling
hot here below.

If not for the headache, it could be simple gastroenteritis—but
not with this many men stricken. Something very contagious indeed, and I was fairly sure what. Not malaria, coming *from* Europe
to the Caribbean. Typhus was a possibility; carried by the common
body louse, it was prone to rapid spread in close quarters like
these, and the symptoms were similar to those I saw around me—
with one distinctive difference.

That seaman didn't have the characteristic belly rash, nor the
next, but the third one did. The light red rosettes were plain on the
clammy white skin. I pressed firmly on one, and it disappeared,
sinking back into existence a moment later, as the blood returned
to the skin. I squeezed my way between the hammocks, the heavy,
sweating bodies pressing in on me from either side, and made my
way back to the companionway where Captain Leonard and two
more of his midshipmen waited for me.

"It's typhoid," I told the Captain. I was as sure as I could be,
lacking a microscope and blood culture.

"Oh?" His drawn face remained apprehensive. "Do you know
what to do for it, Mrs. Malcolm?"

"Yes, but it won't be easy. The sick men need to be taken
above, washed thoroughly, and laid where they can have fresh air
to breathe. Beyond that, it's a matter of nursing; they'll need to
have a liquid diet—and lots of water—*boiled* water, that's very

important!—and sponging to bring down the fever. The most im
portant thing is to avoid infecting any more of your crew, though
There are several things that need to be done—''

"Do them," he interrupted. "I shall give orders to have a
many of the healthy men as can be spared to attend you; orde
them as you will."

"Well," I said, with a dubious glance at the surroundings. ''
can make a start, and tell you how to be going on, but it's going t
be a big job. Captain Raines and my husband will be anxious to b
on our way."

"Mrs. Malcolm," the Captain said earnestly, "I shall be eter
nally grateful for any assistance you can render us. We are mos
urgently bound for Jamaica, and unless the remainder of my crev
can be saved from this wicked illness, we will never reach tha
island." He spoke with profound seriousness, and I felt a twing
of pity for him.

"All right," I said with a sigh. "Send me a dozen health
crewmen, for a start."

Climbing to the quarterdeck, I went to the rail and waved a
Jamie, who was standing by the *Artemis*'s wheel, looking upward
I could see his face clearly, despite the distance; it was worrie
but relaxed into a broad smile when he saw me.

"Are ye comin' down now?" he shouted, cupping his hands

"Not yet!" I shouted back. "I need two hours!" Holding u
two fingers to make my meaning clear in case he hadn't heard,
stepped back from the rail, but not before I saw the smile fad
from his face. He'd heard.

I saw the sick men removed to the afterdeck, and a crew c
hands set to strip them of their filthy clothes, and hose and spong
them with seawater from the pumps. I was in the galley, i
structing the cook and galley crew in food-handling precaution
when I felt the movement of the deck under my feet.

The cook to whom I was talking snaked out a hand and snappe
shut the latch of the cupboard behind him. With the utmost di
patch, he grabbed a loose pot that leapt off its shelf, thrust a larg
ham on a spit into the lower cupboard, and whirled to clap a lid o
the boiling pot hung over the galley fire.

I stared at him in astonishment. I had seen Murphy perform th
same odd ballet, whenever the *Artemis* cast off or changed cours
abruptly.

"What—" I said, but then abandoned the question, and headed or the quarterdeck, as fast as I could go. We were under way; big nd solid as the *Porpoise* was, I could feel the vibration that ran irough the keel as she took the wind.

I burst onto the deck to find a cloud of sails overhead, set and rawing, and the *Artemis* falling rapidly behind us. Captain Leon- rd was standing by the helmsman, looking back to the *Artemis,* as e master bawled commands to the men overhead.

"What are you doing?" I shouted. "You bloody little bastard, /hat's going on here?"

The Captain glanced at me, plainly embarrassed, but with his w set stubbornly.

"We must get to Jamaica with the utmost dispatch," he said. [is cheeks were chapped red with the rushing sea wind, or he ight have blushed. "I am sorry, Mrs. Malcolm—indeed I regret e necessity, but—"

"But nothing!" I said, furious. "Put about! Heave to! Drop the loody anchor! You can't take me away like this!"

"I regret the necessity," he said again, doggedly. "But I be- eve that we require your continuing services most urgently, Mrs. Ialcolm. Don't worry," he said, striving for a reassurance that he idn't achieve. He reached out as though to pat my shoulder, but ien thought better of it. His hand dropped to his side.

"I have promised your husband that the navy will provide you ccommodation in Jamaica until the *Artemis* arrives there."

He flinched backward at the look on my face, evidently afraid iat I might attack him—and not without reason.

"What do you *mean,* you promised my husband?" I said, irough gritted teeth. "Do you mean that J—that Mr. Malcolm *rmitted* you to abduct me?"

"Er . . . no. No, he didn't." The Captain appeared to be find- g the interview a strain. He dragged a filthy handkerchief from s pocket and wiped his brow and the back of his neck. "He was ost intransigent, I'm afraid."

"Intransigent, eh? Well, so am I!" I stamped my foot on the :ck, aiming for his toes, and missing only because he leapt ag- :ly backward. "If you expect me to help you, you bloody kid- ipper, just bloody think again!"

The Captain tucked his handkerchief away and set his jaw. Mrs. Malcolm. You compel me to tell you what I told your husband. The *Artemis* sails under a French flag, and with French papers, but more than half her crew are Englishmen or Scots. I could have pressed these men to service here—and I badly need them. Instead, I have agreed to leave them unmolested, in return for the gift of your medical knowledge.''

''So you've decided to press me instead. And my husband *agreed* to this . . . this *bargain*?''

''No, he didn't,'' the young man said, rather dryly. ''The captain of the *Artemis,* however, perceived the force of my argument.'' He blinked down at me, his eyes swollen from days without sleep, the too-big jacket flapping around his slender torso. Despite his youth and his slovenly appearance, he had considerable dignity.

''I must beg your pardon for what must seem the height of ungentlemanly behavior, Mrs. Malcolm—but the truth is that I am desperate,'' he said simply. ''You may be our only chance. I must take it.''

I opened my mouth to reply, but then closed it. Despite my fury —and my profound unease about what Jamie was going to say when I saw him again—I felt some sympathy for his position. It was quite true that he stood in danger of losing most of his crew without help. Even with my help, we would lose some—but that wasn't a prospect I cared to dwell on.

''All right,'' I said, through my teeth. ''All . . . *right*!'' I looked out over the rail, at the dwindling sails of the *Artemis.* I wasn't prone to seasickness, but I felt a distinct hollowing in the pit of my stomach as the ship—and Jamie—fell far behind. ''I wouldn't appear to have a lot of choice in the matter. If you can spare as many men as possible to scrub down the tween-decks— oh, and have you any alcohol on board?''

He looked mildly surprised. ''Alcohol? Well, there is the rum for the hands' grog, and possibly some wine from the gun room locker. Will that do?''

''If that's what you have, it will have to do.'' I tried to push aside my own emotions, long enough to deal with the situation. ''I suppose I must speak to the purser, then.''

''Yes, of course. Come with me.'' Leonard started toward the companionway that led belowdecks, then, flushing, stood back and gestured awkwardly to let me go first—lest my descent expose my lower limbs indelicately, I supposed. Biting my lip with a mixture of anger and amusement, I went.

I had just reached the bottom of the ladder when I heard a confusion of voices above.

"No, I tell 'ee, the Captain's not to be disturbed! Whatever you have to say will—"

"Leave go! I tell *you,* if you don't let me speak to him now, it will be too late!"

And then Leonard's voice, suddenly sharp as he turned to the interlopers. "Stevens? What is this? What's the matter?"

"No matter, sir," said the first voice, suddenly obsequious. "Only that Tompkins here is sure as he knows the cove what was on that ship—the big 'un, with the red hair. He says—"

"I haven't time," the Captain said shortly. "Tell the mate, Tompkins, and I shall attend to it later."

I was, naturally, halfway back up the ladder by the time these words were spoken, and listening for all I was worth.

The hatchway darkened as Leonard began the backward descent down the ladder. The young man glanced at me sharply, but I kept my face carefully blank, saying only, "Have you many food stores left, Captain? The sick men will need to be fed very carefully. I don't suppose there would be any milk aboard, but—"

"Oh, there's milk," he said, suddenly more cheerful. "We have six milch goats, in fact. The gunner's wife, Mrs. Johansen, does quite wonderfully with them. I'll send her to talk with you, after we've seen the purser."

Captain Leonard introduced me briefly to Mr. Overholt, the purser, and then left, with the injunction that I should be afforded very possible service. Mr. Overholt, a small, plump man with a bald and shining head, peered at me out of the deep collar of his coat like an undersized Humpty-Dumpty, murmuring unhappily about the scarcity of everything near the end of a cruise, and how unfortunate everything was, but I scarcely attended to him. I was much too agitated, thinking of what I had overheard.

Who was this Tompkins? The voice was entirely unfamiliar, and I was sure I had never heard the name before. More important, what did he know about Jamie? And what was Captain Leonard likely to do with the information? As it was, there was nothing I could do now, save contain my impatience, and with the half of my mind not busy with fruitless speculation, work out with Mr. Overholt what supplies were available for use in sickroom feeding.

Not a great deal, as it turned out.

"No, they certainly can't eat salt beef," I said firmly. "Nor yet hardtack, though if we soak the biscuit in boiled milk, perhaps we can manage that as they begin to recover. If you knock the weevils out first," I added, as an afterthought.

"Fish," Mr. Overholt suggested, in a hopeless sort of way. "We often encounter substantial schools of mackerel or even bonita, as we approach the Caribbean. Sometimes the crew will have luck with baited lines."

"Maybe that would do," I said, absently. "Boiled milk and water will be enough in the early stages, but as the men begin to recover, they should have something light and nourishing—soup, for instance. I suppose we could make a fish soup? Unless you have something else that might be suitable?"

"Well . . ." Mr. Overholt looked profoundly uneasy. "There *is* a small quantity of dried figs, ten pound of sugar, some coffee, a quantity of Naples biscuit, and a large cask of Madeira wine, but of course we cannot use that."

"Why not?" I stared at him, and he shuffled his feet uneasily.

"Why, those supplies are intended for the use of our passenger," he said.

"What sort of passenger?" I asked blankly.

Mr. Overholt looked surprised. "The Captain did not tell you? We are carrying the new governor for the island of Jamaica. That is the cause—well, *one* cause"—he corrected himself, dabbing nervously at his bald head with a handkerchief—"of our haste."

"If he's not sick, the Governor can eat salt beef," I said firmly. "Be good for him, I shouldn't wonder. Now, if you'll have the wine taken to the galley, I've work to do."

Aided by one of the remaining midshipmen, a short, stocky youth named Pound, I made a rapid tour of the ship, ruthlessly dragooning supplies and hands. Pound, trotting beside me like a small, ferocious bulldog, firmly informed surprised and resentful cooks, carpenters, sweepers, swabbers, sailmakers, and holdsmen that all my wishes—no matter how unreasonable—must be gratified instantly, by the Captain's orders.

Quarantine was the most important thing. As soon as the tween-decks had been scrubbed and aired, the patients would have to be carried down again, but the hammocks restrung with plenty of space between—the unaffected crew would have to sleep on deck —and provided with adequate toilet facilities. I had seen a pair of large kettles in the galley that I thought might do. I made a quick note on the mental list I was keeping, and hoped the chief cook was not as possessive of his receptacles as Murphy was.

I followed Pound's round head, covered with close-clipped brown curls, down toward the hold in search of worn sails that might be used for cloths. Only half my mind was on my list; with the other half, I was contemplating the possible source of the typhoid outbreak. Caused by a bacillus of the *Salmonella* genus, it was normally spread by ingestion of the bacillus, carried on hands contaminated by urine or feces.

Given the sanitary habits of seamen, any one of the crew could be the carrier of the disease. The most likely culprit was one of the food handlers, though, given the widespread and sudden nature of the outbreak—the cook or one of his two mates, or possibly one of the stewards. I would have to find out how many of these there were, which messes they served, and whether anyone had changed duties four weeks ago—no, five, I corrected myself. The outbreak had begun four weeks ago, but there was an incubation period for the disease to be considered, too.

"Mr. Pound," I called, and a round face peered up at me from the foot of the ladder.

"Yes, ma'am?"

"Mr. Pound—what's your first name, by the way?" I asked.

"Elias, ma'am," he said, looking mildly bewildered.

"Do you mind if I call you so?" I dropped off the foot of the ladder and smiled at him. He smiled hesitantly back.

"Er . . . no, ma'am. The Captain might mind, though," he added cautiously. " 'Tisn't really naval, you know."

Elias Pound couldn't be more than seventeen or eighteen; I doubted that Captain Leonard was more than five or six years older. Still, protocol was protocol.

"I'll be very naval in public," I assured him, suppressing a smile. "But if you're going to work with me, it will be easier to call you by name." I knew, as he didn't, what lay ahead—hours and days and possibly weeks of labor and exhaustion, when the

senses would blur, and only bodily habit and blind instinct—and
the leadership of a tireless chief—would keep those caring for the
sick on their feet.

I was far from tireless, but the illusion would have to be kept up.
This could be done with the help of two or three others, whom I
could train; substitutes for my own hands and eyes, who could
carry on when I must rest. Fate—and Captain Leonard—had designated Elias Pound as my new right hand; best to be on comfortable terms with him at once.

"How long have you been at sea, Elias?" I asked, stopping to
peer after him as he ducked under a low platform that held enormous loops of a huge, evil-smelling chain, each link more than
twice the size of my fist. The anchor chain? I wondered, touching
it curiously. It looked strong enough to moor the *Queen Elizabeth*,
which seemed a comforting thought.

"Since I was seven, ma'am," he said, working his way out
backward, dragging a large chest. He stood up puffing slightly
from the exertion, and wiped his round, ingenuous face. "My
uncle's commander in *Triton,* so he was able to get me a berth in
her. I come to join the *Porpoise* just this voyage, though, out of
Edinburgh." He flipped open the chest, revealing an assortment of
rust-smeared surgical implements—at least I hoped it was rust—
and a jumbled collection of stoppered bottles and jugs. One of the
jars had cracked, and a fine white dust like plaster of Paris lay over
everything in the chest.

"This is what Mr. Hunter, the surgeon, had with him, ma'am,"
he said. "Will you have use for it?"

"God knows," I said, peering into the chest. "But I'll have a
look. Have someone else fetch it up to the sickbay, though, Elias. I
need you to come and speak firmly to the cook."

As I oversaw the scrubbing of the tween-decks with boiling
seawater, my mind was occupied with several distinct trains of
thought.

First, I was mentally charting the necessary steps to take in
combating the disease. Two men, far gone from dehydration and
malaise, had died during the removal from the tween-decks, and
now lay at the far end of the afterdeck, where the sailmaker was
industriously stitching them into their hammocks for burial, a pair

f round shot sewn in at their feet. Four more weren't going to
ake it through the night. The remaining forty-five had chances
anging from excellent to slim; with luck and skill, I might save
ost of them. But how many new cases were brewing, undetected,
mong the remaining crew?

Huge quantities of water were boiling in the galley at my order;
ot seawater for cleansing, boiled fresh water for drinking. I made
another tick on my mental list; I must see Mrs. Johansen, she of
e milch goats, and arrange for the milk to be sterilized as well.

I must interview the galley hands about their duties; if a single
ource of infection could be found and isolated, it would do a lot
halt the spread of the disease. Tick.

All of the available alcohol on the ship was being gathered in
e sickbay, to the profound horror of Mr. Overholt. It could be
sed in its present form, but it would be better to have purified
cohol. Could a means be found of distilling it? Check with the
urser. Tick.

All the hammocks must be boiled and dried before the healthy
ands slept in them. That would have to be done quickly, before
e next watch went to its rest. Send Elias for a crew of swabbers
ad sweepers; laundry duty seemed most in their line. Tick.

Under the growing mental list of necessities were vague but
ontinuing thoughts of the mysterious Tompkins and his unknown
formation. Whatever it was, it had not resulted in our changing
ourse to return to the *Artemis*. Either Captain Leonard had not
ken it seriously, or he was simply too eager to get to Jamaica to
low anything to hinder his progress.

I had paused for a moment by the rail, to organize my thoughts.
ushed back the hair from my forehead, and lifted my face to the
eansing wind, letting it blow away the stench of sickness. Puffs
ill-smelling steam rose from the nearby hatchway, from the hot-
ater cleansing going on below. It would be better down there
en they had finished, but a long way from fresh air.

I looked out over the rail, hoping vainly for the glimpse of a sail,
t the *Porpoise* was alone, the *Artemis*—and Jamie—left far bend.

I pushed away the sudden rush of loneliness and panic. I must
eak soon with Captain Leonard. Answers to two, at least, of the
oblems that concerned me lay with him; the possible source of
e typhoid outbreak—and the role of the unknown Mr. Tompkins

in Jamie's affairs. But for the moment, there were more pressin
matters.

"Elias!" I called, knowing he would be somewhere withi
reach of my voice. "Take me to Mrs. Johansen and the goat
please."

Two days later, I had still not found time to speak to Captain Leonard. Twice, I had gone to his cabin, but found the young Captain gone or unavailable—taking position, I was ld, or consulting charts, or otherwise engaged in some bit of iling arcana.

Mr. Overholt had taken to avoiding me and my insatiable deands, locking himself in his cabin with a pomander of dried sage d hyssop tied round his neck to ward off plague. The able-died crewmen assigned to the work of cleaning and shifting had en lethargic and dubious at first, but I had chivvied and scolded, ared and shouted, stamped my foot and shrieked, and got them adually moving. I felt more like a sheepdog than a doctor—apping and growling at their heels, and hoarse now with the fort.

It was working, though; there was a new feeling of hope and rpose among the crew—I could feel it. Four new deaths today, d ten new cases reporting, but the sounds of groaning distress om the tween-decks were much less, and the faces of the still-althy showed the relief that comes of doing something—any-ing. I had so far failed to find the source of the contagion. If I uld do that, and prevent any fresh outbreaks, I might—just ssibly—halt the devastation within a week, while the *Porpoise* ll had hands enough to sail her.

A quick canvass of the surviving crew had turned up two men essed from a county jail where they had been imprisoned for ewing illicit liquor. I had seized on these gratefully and put them

to work building a still in which—to the horror of the crew—ha
the ship's store of rum was being distilled into pure alcohol fo
disinfection.

I had posted one of the surviving midshipmen by the entrance t
the sick bay and another by the galley, each armed with a basin o
pure alcohol and instructions to see that no one went in or cam
out without dipping their hands. Beside each midshipman stood
marine with his rifle, charged with the duty of seeing that no on
should drink the grimy contents of the barrel into which the use
alcohol was emptied when it became too filthy to be used an
longer.

In Mrs. Johansen, the gunner's wife, I had found an unexpecte
ally. An intelligent woman in her thirties, she had understood-
despite her having only a few words of broken English, and n
having no Swedish at all—what I wanted done, and had done i

If Elias was my right hand, Annekje Johansen was the left. Sh
had single-handedly taken over the responsibility of scalding th
goats' milk, patiently pounding hard biscuit—removing the we
vils as she did so—to be mixed with it, and feeding the resultin
mixture to those hands strong enough to digest it.

Her own husband, the chief gunner, was one of the victims o
the typhoid, but he fortunately seemed one of the lighter case
and I had every hope that he might recover—as much because o
his wife's devoted nursing as because of his own hardy constitu
tion.

"Ma'am, Ruthven says as somebody's been a-drinking of th
pure alcohol again." Elias Pound popped up at my elbow, hi
round pink face looking drawn and wan, substantially thinned b
the pressures of the last few days.

I said something extremely bad, and his brown eyes widene

"Sorry," I said. I wiped the back of a hand across my brov
trying to get my hair out of my eyes. "Don't mean to offend yo
tender ears, Elias."

"Oh, I've heard it before, ma'am," Elias assured me. "Just n
from a lady, like."

"I'm not a lady, Elias," I said tiredly. "I'm a doctor. Hav
someone go and search the ship for whoever it was; they'll like
be unconscious by now." He nodded and whirled on one foot.

"I'll look in the cable tier," he said. "That's where they usu
ally hide when they're drunk."

This was the fourth in the last three days. Despite all guards set
ver the still and the purified alcohol, the hands, living on half
heir usual daily ration of grog, were so desperate for drink that
hey contrived somehow to get at the pure grain alcohol meant for
terilization.

"Goodness, Mrs. Malcolm," the purser had said, shaking his
bald head when I complained about the problem. "Seamen will
drink *anything,* ma'am! Spoilt plum brandy, peaches mashed in-
ide a rubber boot and left to ferment—why, I've even known a
hand caught stealing the old bandages from the surgeon's quarters
nd soaking them, in hopes of getting a whiff of alcohol. No,
ma'am, telling them that drinking it will kill them certainly won't
top them."

Kill them it did. One of the four men who had drunk it had died;
wo more were in their own boarded-off section of the sick bay,
eeply comatose. If they survived, they were likely to be perma-
ently brain-damaged.

"Not that being on a bloody floating hellhole like this isn't
kely to brain-damage anyone," I remarked bitterly to a tern who
lighted on the rail nearby. "As if it isn't enough, trying to save
alf the miserable lot from typhoid, now the other half is trying to
ill themselves with my alcohol! Damn the bloody lot of them!"

The tern cocked its head, decided I was not edible, and flew
way. The ocean stretched empty all around—before us, where the
nknown West Indies concealed Young Ian's fate, and behind,
here Jamie and the *Artemis* had long since vanished. And me in
he middle, with six hundred drink-mad English sailors and a hold
ll of inflamed bowels.

I stood fuming for a moment, then turned with decision toward
he forward gangway. I didn't care if Captain Leonard was person-
ly pumping the bilges, he was going to talk to me.

I stopped just inside the door of the cabin. It was not yet noon,
ut the Captain was asleep, head pillowed on his forearms, on top
f an outspread book. The quill had fallen from his fingers, and
he glass inkstand, cleverly held in its anchored bracket, swayed
ently with the motion of the ship. His face was turned to the side,
heek pressed flat on his arm. Despite the heavy beard stubble, he
oked absurdly young.

I turned, meaning to come back later, but in moving, brushe
against the locker, where a stack of books was precariously ba
anced amid a rubble of papers, navigational instruments, and hal
rolled charts. The top volume fell with a thump to the deck.

The sound was scarcely audible above the general sounds o
creaking, flapping, whining rigging, and shouting that made up th
background of life on shipboard, but it brought him awake, blink
ing and looking startled.

"Mrs. Fra—Mrs. Malcolm!" he said. He rubbed a hand ove
his face, and shook his head quickly, trying to wake himsel
"What—that is—you required something?"

"I didn't mean to wake you," I said. "But I do need mor
alcohol—if necessary, I can use straight rum—and you real
must speak to the hands, to see if there is some way of stoppin
them trying to drink the distilled alcohol. We've had another that
poisoned himself today. And if there's any way of bringing mor
fresh air down to the sick bay . . ." I stopped, seeing that I wa
overwhelming him.

He blinked and scratched, slowly pulling his thoughts into o
der. The buttons on his sleeve had left two round red imprints o
his cheek, and his hair was flattened on that side.

"I see," he said, rather stupidly. Then, as he began to wake, h
expression cleared. "Yes. Of course. I will give orders to have
windsail rigged, to bring more air below. As for the alcohol—
must beg leave to consult the purser, as I do not myself know ou
present capacities in that regard." He turned and took a breath, a
though to shout, but then remembered that his steward was n
longer within earshot, being now below in the sick bay. Just the
the *ting* of the ship's bell came faintly from above.

"I beg your pardon, Mrs. Malcolm," he said, politeness reco
ered. "It is nearly noon; I must go and take our position. I wi
send the purser to you, should you care to remain here for
moment."

"Thank you." I sat down in the chair he had just vacated. H
turned to go, making an attempt to straighten the too-large braide
coat over his shoulders.

"Captain Leonard?" I said, moved by a sudden impulse. H
turned back, questioning.

"If you don't mind my asking—how old are you?"

He blinked and his face tightened, but he answered me.

"I am nineteen, ma'am. Your servant, ma'am." And with that, e vanished through the door. I could hear him in the companion-vay, calling out in a voice half-cracked with fatigue.

Nineteen! I sat quite still, paralyzed with shock. I had thought im very young, but not nearly that young. His face weathered rom exposure and lined with strain and sleeplessness, he had ooked to be at least in his mid-twenties. *My God!* I thought, ppalled. *He's no more than a baby!*

Nineteen. Just Brianna's age. And to be suddenly thrust into ommand not only of a ship—and not just a ship, but an English ian-of-war—and not merely a man-of-war, but one with a plague board that had deprived her suddenly of a quarter of her crew and irtually all her command—I felt the fright and fury that had ubbled inside me for the last few days begin to ebb, as I realized aat the high-handedness that had led him to kidnap me was in fact ot arrogance or ill-judgment, but the result of sheer desperation.

He had to have help, he had said. Well, he was right, and I was . I took a deep breath, visualizing the mess I had left behind in ae sick bay. That was mine, and mine alone, to do the best I could ith.

Captain Leonard had left the logbook open on the desk, his ntry half-complete. There was a small damp spot on the page; he ad drooled slightly in his sleep. In a spasm of irritated pity, I ipped over the page, wishing to hide this further evidence of his ulnerability.

My eye caught a word on the new page, and I stopped, a chill naking down from the nape of my neck as I remembered some-ing. When I had wakened him unexpectedly, the captain had arted up, seen me, and said, "Mrs. Fra—" before catching him-lf. And the name on the page before me, the word that had aught my attention, was "Fraser." He knew who I was—and ho Jamie was.

I rose quickly and shut the door, dropping the bolt. At least I ould have warning if anyone came. Then I sat down at the Cap-in's desk, pressed flat the pages, and began to read.

I flipped back to find the record of the meeting with the *Artemis,* aree days before. Captain Leonard's entries were distinct from aose of his predecessor, and mostly quite brief—not surprising, onsidering how much he had had to deal with of late. Most ntries contained only the usual navigational information, with a brief note of the names of those men who had died since the previous day. The meeting with the *Artemis* was noted, though and my own presence.

   3 February 1767. Met near eight bells with *Artemis,* a small two-masted brig under French colors. Hailed her and requested the assistance of her surgeon, C. Malcolm, who was taken on board and remains with us to assist with the sick.

C. Malcolm, eh? No mention of my being a woman; perhaps he thought it irrelevant, or wished to avoid any inquiries over the propriety of his actions. I went on to the next entry.

   4 February 1767. I have rec'd information this day from Harry Tompkins, able seaman, that the supercargo of the brig *Artemis* is known to him as a criminal by the name of James Fraser, known also by the names of Jamie Roy and of Alexandr Malcolm. This Fraser is a seditionist, and a notorious smuggler, for whose capture a substantial reward is offered by the King's Customs. Information was received from Tompkins after we had parted company with *Artemis;* I thought it not expeditious to pursue *Artemis,* as we are ordered with all possible dispatch for Jamaica, because of our passenger. However, as I have promised to return the *Artemis*'s surgeon to them there, Fraser may be arrested at that time.
   Two men dead of the plague—which the *Artemis*'s surgeon informs me is the Typhoide. Jno. Jaspers, able seaman, DD, Harty Kepple, cook's mate, DD.

That was all; the next day's entry was confined entirely to navigation and the recording of the death of six men, all with "DD" written beside their names. I wondered what it meant, but was too distracted to worry about it.

I heard steps coming down the passageway, and barely got the bolt lifted before the purser's knock sounded on the door. scarcely heard Mr. Overholt's apologies; my mind was too busy trying to make sense of this new revelation.

Who in blinking, bloody hell was this man Tompkins? No one

ad ever seen or heard about, I was sure, and yet he obviously
knew a dangerous amount about Jamie's activities. Which led to
two questions: How had an English seaman come by such information—and who else knew it?

". . . cut the grog rations further, to give you an additional
ask of rum," Mr. Overholt was saying dubiously. "The hands
won't like it, but we might manage; we're only two weeks out of
Jamaica now."

"Whether they like it or not, I need the alcohol more than they
need grog," I answered brusquely. "If they complain too much,
tell them if I don't have the rum, none of them may *make* it to
Jamaica."

Mr. Overholt sighed, and wiped small beads of sweat from his
shiny brow.

"I'll tell them, ma'am," he said, too beaten down to object.

"Fine. Oh, Mr. Overholt?" He turned back, questioning.
"What does the legend 'DD' mean? I saw the Captain write it in
his log."

A small flicker of humor lighted in the purser's deep-sunk eyes.

"It means 'Discharged, Dead,' ma'am," he replied. "The only
sure way for most of us, of leaving His Majesty's Navy."

As I oversaw the bathing of bodies and the constant infusions of
sweetened water and boiled milk, my mind continued to work on
the problem of the unknown Tompkins.

I knew nothing of the man, save his voice. He might be one of
the faceless horde overhead, the silhouettes that I saw in the rigging when I came up on deck for air, or one of the hurrying
anonymous bodies, hurtling up and down the decks in a vain effort
to do the work of three men.

I would meet him, of course, if he became infected; I knew the
names of each patient in the sick bay. But I could hardly allow the
matter to wait, in the rather ghoulish hope that Tompkins would
contract typhoid. At last I made up my mind to ask; the man
presumably knew who I was, anyway. Even if he found out that I
had been asking about him, it was unlikely to do any harm.

Elias was the natural place to begin. I waited until the end of the
day to ask, trusting to fatigue to dull his natural curiosity.

"Tompkins?" The boy's round face drew together in a brief

frown, then cleared. "Oh, yes, ma'am. One o' the forecastle hands."

"Where did he come aboard, do you know?" There was no good way of accounting for this sudden interest in a man I had never met, but luckily, Elias was much too tired to wonder about it.

"Oh," he said vaguely, "at Spithead, I think. Or—no! I remember now, 'twas Edinburgh." He rubbed his knuckles under his nose to stifle a yawn. "That's it, Edinburgh. I wouldn' remember, only he was a pressed man, and a unholy fuss he made about it, claimin' as how they couldn' press him, he was protected account of he worked for Sir Percival Turner, in the Customs." The yawn got the better of him and he gaped widely, then subsided. "But he didn' have no written protection from Sir Percival," he concluded, blinking, "so there wasn' nothing to be done."

"A Customs agent, was he?" *That* went quite some way toward explaining things, all right.

"Mm-hm. Yes, mum, I mean." Elias was trying manfully to stay awake, but his glazing eyes were fixed on the swaying lantern at the end of the sick bay, and he was swaying with it.

"You go on to bed, Elias," I said, taking pity on him. "I'll finish here."

He shook his head quickly, trying to shake off sleep.

"Oh, no, ma'am! I ain't sleepy, not a bit!" He reached clumsily for the cup and bottle I held. "You give me that, mum, and go to rest yourself." He would not be moved, but stubbornly insisted on helping to administer the last round of water before staggering off to his cot.

I was nearly as tired as Elias by the time we finished, but sleep would not come. I lay in the dead surgeon's cabin, staring up at the shadowy beam above my head, listening to the creak and rumble of the ship about me, wondering.

So Tompkins worked for Sir Percival. And Sir Percival surely knew that Jamie was a smuggler. But was there more to it than that? Tompkins knew Jamie by sight. How? And if Sir Percival had been willing to tolerate Jamie's clandestine activities in return for bribes, then—well, perhaps none of those bribes had made it to Tompkins's pockets. But in that case . . . and what

bout the ambush at Arbroath cove? Was there a traitor among the
mugglers? And if so . . .

My thoughts were losing coherence, spinning in circles like the
evolutions of a dying top. The powdered white face of Sir Perci-
al faded into the purple mask of the hanged Customs agent on the
Arbroath road, and the gold and red flames of an exploding lantern
it the crevices of my mind. I rolled onto my stomach, clutching
he pillow to my chest, the last thought in my mind that I must find
ompkins.

As it was, Tompkins found me. For more than two days, the
ituation in the sick bay was too pressing for me to leave for more
han the barest space of time. On the third day, though, matters
eemed easier, and I retired to the surgeon's cabin, intending to
vash myself and rest briefly before the midday drum beat for the
oon meal.

I was lying on the cot, a cool cloth over my tired eyes, when I
eard the sound of bumping and voices in the passage outside my
oor. A tentative knock sounded on my door, and an unfamiliar
oice said, "Mrs. Malcolm? There's been a h'accident, if you
lease, ma'am."

I swung open the door to find two seamen supporting a third,
vho stood storklike on one leg, his face white with shock and
ain.

It took no more than a single glance for me to know whom I was
ooking at. The man's face was ridged down one side with the
vid scars of a bad burn, and the twisted eyelid on that side
xposed the milky lens of a blind eye, had I needed any further
onfirmation that here stood the one-eyed seaman Young Ian had
ought he'd killed, lank brown hair grew back from a balding
row to a scrawny pigtail that drooped over one shoulder, expos-
g a pair of large, transparent ears.

"Mr. Tompkins," I said with certainty, and his remaining eye
idened in surprise. "Put him down over there, please."

The men deposited Tompkins on a stool by the wall, and went
ack to their work; the ship was too shorthanded to allow for
istraction. Heart beating heavily, I knelt down to examine the
ounded leg.

He knew who I was, all right; I had seen it in his face when I

opened the door. There was a great deal of tension in the leg under
my hand. The injury was gory, but not serious, given suitable care
a deep gash scored down the calf of the leg. It had bled substan
tially, but there were no deep arteries cut; it had been well
wrapped with a piece of someone's shirt, and the bleeding had
nearly stopped when I unwound the homemade bandage.

"How did you do this, Mr. Tompkins?" I asked, standing up
and reaching for the bottle of alcohol. He glanced up, his single
eye alert and wary.

"Splinter wound, ma'am," he answered, in the nasal tones
had heard once before. "A spar broke as I was a-standing on it."
The tip of his tongue stole out, furtively wetting his lower lip.

"I see." I turned and flipped open the lid of my empty medi
cine box, pretending to survey the available remedies. I studied
him out of the corner of one eye, while I tried to think how best to
approach him. He was on his guard; tricking him into revelation
or winning his trust was clearly out of the question.

My eyes flicked over the tabletop, seeking inspiration. And
found it. With a mental apology to the shade of Aesculapius the
physician, I picked up the late surgeon's bone-saw, a wicked thin
some eighteen inches long, of rust-flecked steel. I looked at this
thoughtfully, turned, and laid the toothed edge of the instrument
gently against the injured leg, just above the knee. I smiled charm
ingly into the seaman's terrified single eye.

"Mr. Tompkins," I said, "let us talk frankly."

An hour later, able-bodied seaman Tompkins had been restored
to his hammock, stitched and bandaged, shaking in every limb, but
able-bodied still. For my part, I felt a little shaky as well.

Tompkins was, as he had insisted to the press-gang in Edin
burgh, an agent of Sir Percival Turner. In that capacity, he wer
about the docks and warehouses of all the shipping ports in the
Firth of Forth, from Culross and Donibristle to Restalrig and Mus
selburgh, picking up gossip and keeping his beady eye sharp
peeled to catch any evidence of unlawful activity.

The attitude of Scots toward English tax laws being what it was
there was no lack of such activity to report. What was done with
such reports, though, varied. Small smugglers, caught red-handed
with a bottle or two of unbonded rum or whisky, might be sum

narily arrested, tried and convicted, and sentenced to anything from penal servitude to transportation, with forfeiture of all their property to the Crown.

The bigger fish, though, were reserved to Sir Percival's private judgment. In other words, allowed to pay substantial bribes for the privilege of continuing their operations under the blind eye (here Tompkins laughed sardonically, touching the ruined side of his face) of the King's agents.

"Sir Percival's got ambitions, see?" While not noticeably relaxed, Tompkins had at least unbent enough to lean forward, one eye narrowing as he gestured in explanation. "He's in with Dundas and all them. Everything goes right, and he might have a peerage, not just a knighthood, eh? But that'll take more than money."

One thing that could help was some spectacular demonstration of competence and service to the Crown.

"As in the sort of arrest that might make 'em sit up and take notice, eh? Ooh! That smarts, missus. You sure of what you're a-doing of, there?" Tompkins squinted dubiously downward, to where I was sponging the site of the injury with dilute alcohol.

"I'm sure," I said. "Go on, then. I suppose a simple smuggler wouldn't have been good enough, no matter how big?"

Evidently not. However, when word had reached Sir Percival that there might just possibly be a major political criminal within his grasp, the old gentleman had nearly blown a gasket with excitement.

"But sedition's a harder thing to prove than smuggling, eh? You catch one of the little fish with the goods, and they're saying not a thing will lead you further on. Idealists, them seditionists," Tompkins said, shaking his head with disgust. "Never rat on each other, they don't."

"So you didn't know who you were looking for?" I stood and took one of my cat-gut sutures from its jar, threading it through a needle. I caught Tompkins's apprehensive look, but did nothing to allay his anxiety. I wanted him anxious—and voluble.

"No, we didn't know who the big fish was—not until another of Sir Percival's agents had the luck to tumble to one of Fraser's associates, what gave 'em the tip he was Malcolm the printer, and told his real name. Then it all come clear, o' course."

My heart skipped a beat.

"Who was the associate?" I asked. The names and faces of the six smugglers darted through my mind—little fish. Not idealists, any of them. But to which of them was loyalty no bar?

"I don't know. No, it's true, missus, I swear! Ow!" he said frantically as I jabbed the needle under the skin.

"I'm not trying to hurt you," I assured him, in as false a voice as I could muster. "I have to stitch the wound, though."

"Oh! Ow! I don't know, to be sure I don't! I'd tell, if I did, as God's my witness!"

"I'm sure you would," I said, intent on my stitching.

"Oh! Please, missus! Stop! Just for a moment! All I know is it was an Englishman! That's all!"

I stopped, and stared up at him. "An Englishman?" I said blankly.

"Yes, missus. That's what Sir Percival said." He looked down at me, tears trembling on the lashes of both his eyes. I took the final stitch, as gently as I could, and tied the suture knot. Without speaking, I got up, poured a small tot of brandy from my private bottle, and handed it to him.

He gulped it gratefully, and seemed much restored in consequence. Whether out of gratitude, or sheer relief for the end of the ordeal, he told me the rest of the story. In search of evidence to support a charge of sedition, he had gone to the printshop in Carfax Close.

"I know what happened there," I assured him. I turned his face toward the light, examining the burn scars. "Is it still painful?"

"No, Missus, but it hurt precious bad for some time," he said. Being incapacitated by his injuries, Tompkins had taken no part in the ambush at Arbroath cove, but he had heard—"not direct-like, but I heard, you know," he said, with a shrewd nod of the head—what had happened.

Sir Percival had given Jamie warning of an ambush, to lessen the chances of Jamie's thinking him involved in the affair, and possibly revealing the details of their financial arrangements in quarters where such revelations would be detrimental to Sir Percival's interests.

At the same time, Sir Percival had learned—from the associate, the mysterious Englishman—of the fallback arrangement with the French delivery vessel, and had arranged the grave-ambush on the beach at Arbroath.

"But what about the Customs officer who was killed on the road?" I asked sharply. I couldn't repress a small shudder, at memory of that dreadful face. "Who did that? There were only five men among the smugglers who could possibly have done it, and none of them are Englishmen!"

Tompkins rubbed a hand over his mouth; he seemed to be debating the wisdom of telling me or not. I picked up the brandy bottle and set it by his elbow.

"Why, I'm much obliged, Missus Fraser! You're a true Christian, missus, and so I shall tell anyone who asks!"

"Skip the testimonials," I said dryly. "Just tell me what you know about the Customs officer."

He filled the cup and drained it, sipping slowly. Then, with a sigh of satisfaction, he set it down and licked his lips.

"It wasn't none of the smugglers done him in, missus. It was his own mate."

"What!" I jerked back, startled, but he nodded, blinking his good eye in token of sincerity.

"That's right, missus. There was two of 'em, wasn't there? Well, the one of them had his instructions, didn't he?"

The instructions had been to wait until whatever smugglers escaped the ambush on the beach had reached the road, whereupon the Customs officer was to drop a noose over his partner's head in the dark and strangle him swiftly, then string him up and leave him as evidence of the smugglers' murderous wrath.

"But why?" I said, bewildered and horrified. "What was the point of doing that?"

"Do you not see?" Tompkins looked surprised, as though the logic of the situation should be obvious. "We'd failed to get the evidence from the printshop that would have proved the case of sedition against Fraser, and with the shop burnt to the ground, no possibility of another chance. Nor had we ever caught Fraser red-handed with the goods himself, only some of the small fish who worked for him. One of the other agents thought he'd a clue where the stuff was kept, but something happened to him—perhaps Fraser caught him or bought him off, for he disappeared one day in November, and wasn't heard of again, nor the hiding place for the contraband, neither."

"I see." I swallowed, thinking of the man who had accosted me on the stairs of the brothel. What had become of that cask of crème de menthe? "But—"

"Well, I'm telling you, missus, just you wait." Tompkins raised a monitory hand. "So—here's Sir Percival, knowing as he's got a rare case, with a man's not only one of the biggest smugglers on the Firth, *and* the author of some of the most first-rate seditious material it's been my privilege to see, *but* is also a pardoned Jacobite traitor, whose name will make the trial a sensation from one end of the kingdom to the other. The only trouble being"—he shrugged—"as there's no evidence."

It began to make a hideous sort of sense, as Tompkins explained the plan. The murder of a Customs officer killed in pursuit of duty would not only make any smuggler arrested for the crime subject to a capital charge, but was the sort of heinous crime that would cause a major public outcry. The matter-of-fact acceptance that smugglers enjoyed from the populace would not protect them in a matter of such callous villainy.

"Your Sir Percival has got the makings of a really first-class son of a bitch," I observed. Tompkins nodded meditatively, blinking into his cup.

"Well, you've the right of it there, missus, I'll not say you're wrong."

"And the Customs officer who was killed—I suppose he was just a convenience?"

Tompkins sniggered, with a fine spray of brandy. His one eye seemed to be having some trouble focusing.

"Oh, very convenient, missus, more ways than one. Don't you grieve none on his account. There was a good many folk glad enough to see Tom Oakie swing—and not the least of 'em, Sir Percival."

"I see." I finished fastening the bandage about his calf. It was getting late; I would have to get back to the sick bay soon.

"I'd better call someone to take you to your hammock," I said, taking the nearly empty bottle from his unresisting hand. "You should rest your leg for at least three days; tell your officer I said you can't go aloft until I've taken out the stitches."

"I'll do that, missus, and I thank you for your kindness to a poor unfortunate sailor." Tompkins made an abortive attempt to stand, looking surprised when he failed. I got a hand under his

rmpit and heaved, getting him on his feet, and—he declining my
ffer to summon him assistance—helped him to the door.

"You needn't worry about Harry Tompkins, missus," he said,
veaving unsteadily into the corridor. He turned and gave me an
xaggerated wink. "Old Harry always ends up all right, no matter
vhat." I looked at him, with his long nose, pink-tipped from
iquor, his large, transparent ears, and his single sly brown eye. It
ame to me suddenly what he reminded me of.

"When were you born, Mr. Tompkins?" I asked.

He blinked for a moment, uncomprehending, but then said,
'The Year of Our Lord 1713, missus. Why?"

"No reason," I said, and waved him off, watching as he
aromed slowly down the corridor, dropping out of sight at the
idder like a bag of oats. I would have to check with Mr. Wil-
>ughby to be sure, but at the moment, I would have wagered my
hemise that 1713 had been a Year of the Rat.

48

Moment of Grace

Over the next few days, a routine set in, as it does in even the most desperate circumstances, provided that they continue long enough. The hours after a battle are urgent and chaotic, with men's lives hanging on a second's action. Here a doctor can be heroic, knowing for certain that the wound just stanched has saved a life, that the quick intervention will save a limb. But in an epidemic, there is none of that.

Then come the long days of constant watching and battles fought on the field of germs—and with no weapons suited to that field, it can be no more than a battle of delay, doing the small things that may not help but must be done, over and over and over again, fighting the invisible enemy of disease, in the tenuous hope that the body can be supported long enough to outlast its attacker.

To fight disease without medicine is to push against a shadow; a darkness that spreads as inexorably as night. I had been fighting for nine days, and forty-six more men were dead.

Still, I rose each day at dawn, splashed water into my grainy eyes, and went once more to the field of war, unarmed with anything save persistence—and a barrel of alcohol.

There were some victories, but even these left a bitter taste in my mouth. I found the likely source of infection—one of the messmates, a man named Howard. First serving on board as a member of one of the gun crews, Howard had been transferred to galley duty six weeks before, the result of an accident with a recoiling gun-carriage that had crushed several fingers.

Howard had served the gun room, and the first known case of

he disease—taken from the incomplete records of the dead surgeon, Mr. Hunter—was one of the marines who messed there.
'our more cases, all from the gun room, and then it had begun to
pread, as infected but still ambulatory men left the deadly con-
amination smeared in the ship's heads, to be picked up there and
passed to the crew at large.

Howard's admission that he had seen sickness like this before,
n other ships where he had served, was enough to clinch the
natter. However, the cook, shorthanded as everyone else aboard,
ad declined absolutely to part with a valuable hand, only because
f "a goddamned female's silly notion!"

Elias could not persuade him, and I had been obliged to sum-
non the Captain himself, who—misunderstanding the nature of
he disturbance, had arrived with several armed marines. There
vas a most unpleasant scene in the galley, and Howard was re-
noved to the brig—the only place of certain quarantine—pro-
esting in bewilderment, and demanding to know his crime.

As I came up from the galley, the sun was going down into the
cean in a blaze that paved the western sea with gold like the
treets of Heaven. I stopped for a moment, just a moment, trans-
xed by the sight.

It had happened many times before, but it always took me by
urprise. Always in the midst of great stress, wading waist-deep in
ouble and sorrow, as doctors do, I would glance out a window,
pen a door, look into a face, and there it would be, unexpected
nd unmistakable. A moment of peace.

The light spread from the sky to the ship, and the great horizon
vas no longer a blank threat of emptiness, but the habitation of
oy. For a moment, I lived in the center of the sun, warmed and
leansed, and the smell and sight of sickness fell away; the bitter-
ess lifted from my heart.

I never looked for it, gave it no name; yet I knew it always, when
he gift of peace came. I stood quite still for the moment that it
isted, thinking it strange and not strange that grace should find
ae here, too.

Then the light shifted slightly and the moment passed, leaving
ae as it always did, with the lasting echo of its presence. In a
eflex of acknowledgment, I crossed myself and went below, my
arnished armor faintly gleaming.

Elias Pound died of the typhoid four days later. It was a virulen infection; he came to the sick bay heavy-eyed with fever and wincing at the light; six hours later he was delirious and unable to rise. The next dawn he pressed his cropped round head against my bosom, called me "Mother," and died in my arms.

I did what had to be done throughout the day, and stood by Captain Leonard at sunset, when he read the burial service. The body of Midshipman Pound was consigned to the sea, wrapped in his hammock.

I declined the Captain's invitation to dinner, and went instead to sit in a remote corner of the afterdeck, next to one of the great guns, where I could look out over the water, showing my face to no one. The sun went down in gold and glory, succeeded by night of starred velvet, but there was no moment of grace, no peace in either sight for me.

As the darkness settled over the ship, all her movements began to slow. I leaned my head against the gun, the polished metal cool under my cheek. A seaman passed me at a fast walk, intent on his duties, and then I was alone.

I ached desperately; my head throbbed, my back was stiff and my feet swollen, but none of these was of any significance, compared to the deeper ache that knotted my heart.

Any doctor hates to lose a patient. Death is the enemy, and to lose someone in your care to the clutch of the dark angel is to be vanquished yourself, to feel the rage of betrayal and impotence beyond the common, human grief of loss and the horror of death' finality. I had lost twenty-three men between dawn and sunset of this day. Elias was only the first.

Several had died as I sponged their bodies or held their hands others, alone in their hammocks, had died uncomforted even by touch, because I could not reach them in time. I thought I had resigned myself to the realities of this time, but knowing—even as I held the twitching body of an eighteen-year-old seaman as his bowels dissolved in blood and water—that penicillin would have saved most of them, and I had none, was galling as an ulcer, eating at my soul.

The box of syringes and ampules had been left behind on the *Artemis,* in the pocket of my spare skirt. If I had had it, I could no

ave used it. If I had used it, I could have saved no more than one
r two. But even knowing that, I raged at the futility of it all,
lenching my teeth until my jaw ached as I went from man to man,
rmed with nothing but boiled milk and biscuit, and my two empty
ands.

My mind followed the same dizzying lines my feet had traveled
arlier, seeing faces—faces contorted in anguish or smoothing
lowly in the slackness of death, but all of them looking at me. At
e. I lifted my futile hand and slammed it hard against the rail. I
id it again, and again, scarcely feeling the sting of the blows, in a
renzy of furious rage and grief.

"Stop that!" a voice spoke behind me, and a hand seized my
rist, preventing me from slapping the rail yet again.

"Let go!" I struggled, but his grip was too strong.

"Stop," he said again, firmly. His other arm came around my
aist, and he pulled me back, away from the rail. "You mustn't do
at," he said. "You'll hurt yourself."

"I don't bloody care!" I wrenched against his grasp, but then
umped, defeated. What did it matter?

He let go of me then, and I turned to find myself facing a man I
ad never seen before. He wasn't a sailor; while his clothes were
rumpled and stale with long wear, they had originally been very
ne; the dove-gray coat and waistcoat had been tailored to flatter
is slender frame, and the wilted lace at his throat had come from
russels.

"Who the hell are you?" I said in astonishment. I brushed at
y wet cheeks, sniffed, and made an instinctive effort to smooth
own my hair. I hoped the shadows hid my face.

He smiled slightly, and handed me a handkerchief, crumpled,
ut clean.

"My name is Grey," he said, with a small, courtly bow. "I
xpect that you must be the famous Mrs. Malcolm, whose heroism
aptain Leonard has been so strongly praising." I grimaced at
at, and he paused.

"I am sorry," he said. "Have I said something amiss? My
ologies, Madame, I had no notion of offering you offense." He
oked anxious at the thought, and I shook my head.

"It is not heroic to watch men die," I said. My words were
ick, and I stopped to blow my nose. "I'm just here, that's all.
hank you for the handkerchief." I hesitated, not wanting to hand

the used handkerchief back to him, but not wanting simply t
pocket it, either. He solved the dilemma with a dismissive wave c
his hand.

"Might I do anything else for you?" He hesitated, irresolute
"A cup of water? Some brandy, perhaps?" He fumbled in hi
coat, drawing out a small silver pocket flask engraved with a coa
of arms, which he offered to me.

I took it, with a nod of thanks, and took a swallow deep enoug
to make me cough. It burned down the back of my throat, but
sipped again, more cautiously this time, and felt it warm me
easing and strengthening. I breathed deeply and drank again.
helped.

"Thank you," I said, a little hoarsely, handing back the flash
That seemed somewhat abrupt, and I added, "I'd forgotten tha
brandy is good to drink; I've been using it to wash people in th
sick bay." The statement brought back the events of the day to m
with crushing vividness, and I sagged back onto the powder bo
where I had been sitting.

"I take it the plague continues unabated?" he asked quietly. H
stood in front of me, the glow of a nearby lantern shining on h
dark blond hair.

"Not unabated, no." I closed my eyes, feeling unutterab
bleak. "There was only one new case today. There were four th
day before, and six the day before that."

"That sounds hopeful," he observed. "As though you are d
feating the disease."

I shook my head slowly. It felt dense and heavy as one of th
cannonballs piled in the shallow bins by the guns.

"No. All we're doing is to stop more men being infected. The
isn't a bloody thing I can do for the ones who already have it."

"Indeed." He stooped and picked up one of my hands. Su
prised, I let him have it. He ran a thumb lightly over the blist
where I had burned myself scalding milk, and touched my knuc
les, reddened and cracked from the constant immersion in alcoh

"You would appear to have been very active, Madame, f
someone who is doing nothing," he said dryly.

"Of course I'm doing something!" I snapped, yanking m
hand back. "It doesn't do any good!"

"I'm sure—" he began.

"It doesn't!" I slammed my fist on the gun, the noiseless blo eeming to symbolize the pain-filled futility of the day. "Do you now how many men I lost today? Twenty-three! I've been on my eet since dawn, elbow-deep in filth and vomit and my clothes tuck to me, and none of it's been any good! I couldn't help! Do ou hear me? I couldn't help!"

His face was turned away, in shadow, but his shoulders were tiff.

"I hear you," he said quietly. "You shame me, Madame. I had ept to my cabin at the Captain's orders, but I had no idea that the ircumstances were such as you describe, or I assure you that I hould have come to help, in spite of them."

"Why?" I said blankly. "It isn't your job."

"Is it yours?" He swung around to face me, and I saw that he as handsome, in his late thirties, perhaps, with sensitive, fine-cut eatures, and large blue eyes, open in astonishment.

"Yes," I said.

He studied my face for a moment, and his own expression hanged, fading from surprise to thoughtfulness.

"I see."

"No, you don't, but it doesn't matter." I pressed my fingertips ard against my brow, in the spot Mr. Willoughby had shown me, o relieve headache. "If the Captain means you to keep to your abin, then you likely should. There are enough hands to help in he sick bay; it's just that . . . nothing helps," I ended, dropping y hands.

He walked over to the rail, a few feet away from me, and stood ooking out over the expanse of dark water, sparked here and there s a random wave caught the starlight.

"I do see," he repeated, as though talking to the waves. "I had ought your distress due only to a woman's natural compassion, ut I see it is something quite different." He paused, hands gripping the rail, an indistinct figure in the starlight.

"I have been a soldier, an officer," he said. "I know what it is, o hold men's lives in your hand—and to lose them."

I was quiet, and so was he. The usual shipboard sounds went on the distance, muted by night and the lack of men to make them. t last he sighed and turned toward me again.

"What it comes to, I think, is the knowledge that you are not od." He paused, then added, softly, "And the very real regret aat you cannot be."

I sighed, feeling some of the tension drain out of me. The coo
wind lifted the weight of my hair from my neck, and the curlin
ends drifted across my face, gentle as a touch.

"Yes," I said.

He hesitated a moment, as though not knowing what to say nex
then bent, picked up my hand, and kissed it, very simply, withou
affectation.

"Good night, Mrs. Malcolm," he said, and turned away, th
sound of his footsteps loud on the deck.

He was no more than a few yards past me when a seama
hurrying by, spotted him and stopped with a cry. It was Jones, on
of the stewards.

"My Lord! You shouldn't ought to be out of your cabin, si
The night air's mortal, and the plague loose on board—and th
Captain's orders—whatever is your servant a-thinking of, sir, t
let you walk about like this?"

My acquaintance nodded apologetically.

"Yes, yes, I know. I shouldn't have come up; but I thought tha
if I stayed in the cabin a moment longer I should be stifled alto
gether."

"Better stifled than dead o' the bloody flux, sir, and you'
pardon of my saying so," Jones replied sternly. My acquaintanc
made no remonstrance to this, but merely murmured somethin
and disappeared in the shadows of the afterdeck.

I reached out a hand and grasped Jones by the sleeve as h
passed, causing him to start, with a wordless yelp of alarm.

"Oh! Mrs. Malcolm," he said, coming to earth, a bony han
splayed across his chest. "Christ, I did think you was a ghos
mum, begging your pardon."

"I beg yours," I said, politely. "I only wanted to ask—who wa
the man you were just talking to?"

"Oh, him?" Jones twisted about to look over his shoulder, b
the aptly named Mr. Grey had long since vanished. "Why, that
Lord John Grey, mum, him as is the new governor of Jamaica.
He frowned censoriously in the direction taken by my acquai
tance. "He ain't supposed to be up here; the Captain's give stri
orders he's to stay safe below, out o' harm's way. All we need's
come into port with a dead political aboard, and there'll be t
devil to pay, mum, savin' your presence."

He shook his head disapprovingly, then turned to me with a bob f the head.

"You'll be retiring, mum? Shall I bring you down a nice cup of a and maybe a bit o' biscuit?"

"No, thank you, Jones," I said. "I'll go and check the sick bay ;ain before I go to bed. I don't need anything."

"Well, you do, mum, and you just say. Anytime. Good night to)u, mum." He touched his forelock briefly and hurried off.

I stood at the rail alone for a moment before going below, rawing in deep breaths of the clean, fresh air. It would be a good any hours yet until dawn; the stars burned bright and clear over y head, and I realized, quite suddenly, that the moment of grace I id wordlessly prayed for had come, after all.

"You're right," I said at last, aloud, to the sea and sky. "A nset wouldn't have been enough. Thank you," I added, and ent below.

I t's true, what the sailors say. You can smell land, a long tim
before you see it.

Despite the long voyage, the goat pen in the hold was
surprisingly pleasant place. By now, the fresh straw had bee
exhausted, and the goats' hooves clicked restlessly to and fro o
bare boards. Still, the heaps of manure were swept up daily, an
neatly piled in baskets to be heaved overboard, and Annekje Jc
hansen brought dry armloads of hay to the manger each morning
There was a strong smell of goat, but it was a clean, animal scen
and quite pleasant by contrast with the stench of unwashed sailor;

"Komma, komma, komma, dyr get," she crooned, luring a year
ling within reach with a twiddled handful of hay. The anima
stretched out cautious lips, and was promptly seized by the nec
and pulled forward, its head secured under Annekje's brawny arn

"Ticks, is it?" I asked, coming forward to help. Annekj
looked up and gave me her broad, gap-toothed smile.

"Guten Morgen, Mrs. Claire," she said. *"Ja,* tick. Here." Sh
took the young goat's drooping ear in one hand and turned up th
silky edge to show me the blueberry bulge of a blood-gorged tich
burrowed deep in the tender skin.

She clutched the goat to hold it still, and dug into the ea
pinching the tick viciously between her nails. She pulled it fro
with a twist, and the goat blatted and kicked, a tiny spot of bloo
welling from its ear where the tick had been detached.

"Wait," I said, when she would have released the animal. Sh
glanced at me, curious, but kept her hold and nodded. I took th

ottle of alcohol I wore slung at my belt like a sidearm, and
oured a few drops on the ear. It was soft and tender, the tiny veins
learly visible beneath the satin skin. The goat's square-pupiled
yes bulged farther and its tongue stuck out in agitation as it
leated.

"No sore ear," I said, in explanation, and Annekje nodded in
pproval.

Then the goatling was free, and went plunging back into the
erd, to butt its head against its mother's side in a frantic search
or milky reassurance. Annekje looked about for the discarded tick
nd found it lying on the deck, tiny legs helpless to move its
wollen body. She smashed it casually under the heel of her shoe,
:aving a tiny dark blotch on the board.

"We come to land?" I asked, and she nodded, with a wide,
appy smile. She waved expansively upward, where sunlight fell
rough the grating overhead.

"*Ja*. Smell?" she said, sniffing vigorously in illustration. She
eamed. "Land, *ja*! Water, grass. Is goot, goot!"

"I need to go to land," I said, watching her carefully. "Go
uiet. Secret. Not tell."

"Ah?" Annekje's eyes widened, and she looked at me specula-
vely. "Not tell Captain, *ja*?"

"Not tell anyone," I said, nodding hard. "You can help?"

She was quiet for a moment, thinking. A big, placid woman, she
:minded me of her own goats, adapting cheerfully to the queer
fe of shipboard, enjoying the pleasures of hay and warm com-
any, thriving despite the lurching deck and stuffy shadows of the
old.

With that same air of capable adaptation, she looked up at me
nd nodded calmly.

"*Ja*, I help."

It was past midday when we anchored off what one of the
idshipmen told me was Watlings Island.

I looked over the rail with considerable curiosity. This flat is-
nd, with its wide white beaches and lines of low palms, had once
:en called San Salvador. Renamed for the present in honor of a
otorious buccaneer of the last century, this dot of land was pre-
:mably Christopher Columbus's first sight of the New World.

I had the substantial advantage over Columbus of having known
·r a fact that the land was here, but still I felt a faint echo of the

joy and relief that the sailors of those tiny wooden caravels had fel
at that first landfall.

Long enough on a rolling ship, and you forget what it is to wall
on land. Getting sea legs, they call it. It's a metamorphosis, thi
leg-getting, like the change from tadpole to frog, a painless shif
from one element to another. But the smell and sight of lan
makes you remember that you were born to the earth, and you
feet ache suddenly for the touch of solid ground.

The problem at the moment was actually getting my feet o
solid ground. Watlings Island was no more than a pause, to replen
ish our severely depleted water supply before the run through th
Windward Isles down to Jamaica. It would be at least anothe
week's sail, and the presence of so many invalids aboard requirin,
vast infusions of liquid had run the great water casks in the hol
nearly dry.

San Salvador was a small island, but I had learned from carefu
questioning of my patients that there was a fair amount of shippin,
traffic through its main port in Cockburn Town. It might not be th
ideal place to escape, but it looked as though there would be littl
other choice; I had no intention of enjoying the navy's ''hospita
ity'' on Jamaica, serving as the bait that would lure Jamie t
arrest.

Starved as the crew was for the sight and feel of land, no on
was allowed to go ashore save the watering party, now busy wit
their casks and sledges up Pigeon Creek, at whose foot we wer
anchored. One of the marines stood at the head of the gangway
blocking any attempt at leaving.

Such members of the crew as were not involved in watering c
on watch stood by the rail, talking and joking or merely gazing a
the island, the dream of hope fulfilled. Some way down the deck,
caught sight of a long, blond tail of hair, flying in the shore breeze
The Governor too had emerged from seclusion, pale face upturne
to the tropic sun.

I would have gone to speak to him, but there was no time
Annekje had already gone below for the goat. I wiped my hand
on my skirt, making my final estimations. It was no more than tw
hundred yards to the thick growth of palms and underbrush. If
could get down the gangway and into the jungle, I thought I had
good chance of getting away.

Anxious as he was to be on his way to Jamaica, Captain Leor

rd was unlikely to waste much time in trying to catch me. And if hey did catch me—well, the Captain could hardly punish me for rying to leave the ship; I was neither a seaman nor a formal aptive, after all.

The sun shone on Annekje's blond head as she made her way arefully up the ladder, a young goat cozily nestled against her ide bosom. A quick glance, to see that I was in place, and she eaded for the gangway.

Annekje spoke to the sentry in her queer mixture of English and wedish, pointing to the goat and then ashore, insisting that it nust have fresh grass. The marine appeared to understand her, but tood firm.

"No, ma'am," he said, respectfully enough, "no one is to go shore save the watering party; Captain's orders."

Standing just out of sight, I watched as she went on arguing, rusting her goatling urgently in his face, forcing him a step back, step to the side, maneuvering him artfully just far enough that I ould slip past behind him. No more than a moment, now; he was lmost in place. When she had drawn him away from the head of he gangplank, she would drop the goat and cause sufficient confu- ion in the catching of it that I would have a minute or two to make y escape.

I shifted nervously from foot to foot. My feet were bare; it ould be easier to run on the sandy beach. The sentry moved, his d-coated back fully turned to me. A foot more, I thought, just a ot more.

"Such a fine day, is it not, Mrs. Malcolm?"

I bit my tongue.

"Very fine, Captain Leonard," I said, with some difficulty. My eart seemed to have stopped dead when he spoke. It now resumed eating much faster than usual, to make up for lost time.

The Captain stepped up beside me and looked over the rail, his oung face shining with Columbus's joy. Despite my strong desire push him overboard, I felt myself smile grudgingly at the sight f him.

"This landfall is as much your victory as mine, Mrs. Mal- lm," he said. "Without you, I doubt we should ever have rought the *Porpoise* to land." He very shyly touched my hand, d I smiled again, a little less grudgingly.

"I'm sure you would have managed, Captain," I said. "You seem to be a most competent sailor."

He laughed, and blushed. He had shaved in honor of the land and his smooth cheeks glowed pink and raw.

"Well, it is mostly the hands, ma'am; I may say they have done nobly. And their efforts, of course, are due in turn to your skill as physician." He looked at me, brown eyes shining earnestly.

"Indeed, Mrs. Malcolm—I cannot say what your skill and kindness have meant to us. I—I mean to say so, too, to the Governor and to Sir Greville—you know, the King's Commissioner on Antigua. I shall write a letter, a most sincere testimonial to you and to your efforts on our behalf. Perhaps—perhaps it will help." He dropped his eyes.

"Help with what, Captain?" My heart was still beating fast.

Captain Leonard bit his lip, then looked up.

"I had not meant to say anything to you, ma'am. But I—really cannot in honor keep silence. Mrs. Fraser, I know your name, and I know what your husband is."

"Really?" I said, trying to keep control of my own emotions. "What is he?"

The boy looked surprised at that. "Why, ma'am, he is a criminal." He paled a little. "You mean—you did not know?"

"Yes, I knew that," I said dryly. "Why are you telling me, though?"

He licked his lips, but met my eyes bravely enough. "When I discovered your husband's identity, I wrote it in the ship's log. I regret that action now, but it is too late; the information is official. Once I reach Jamaica, I must report his name and destination to the authorities there, and likewise to the commander at the naval barracks on Antigua. He will be taken when the *Artemis* docks." He swallowed. "And if he is taken—"

"He'll be hanged," I said, finishing what he could not. The boy nodded, wordless. His mouth opened and closed, seeking words.

"I have seen men hanged," he said at last. "Mrs. Fraser, I just —I—" He stopped then, fighting for control, and found it. He drew himself up straight and looked at me straight on, the joy of his landing drowned in sudden misery.

"I am sorry," he said softly. "I cannot ask you to forgive me; I can only say that I am most terribly sorry."

He turned on his heel and walked away. Directly before him

tood Annekje Johansen and her goat, still in heated conversation
ith the sentry.

"What is this?" Captain Leonard demanded angrily. "Remove
his animal from the deck at once! Mr. Holford, what are you
inking of?"

Annekje's eyes flicked from the Captain to my face, instantly
ivining what had gone wrong. She stood still, head bowed to the
aptain's scolding, then marched away toward the hatchway to the
oats' hold, clutching her yearling. As she passed, one big blue
ye winked solemnly. We would try again. But how?

Racked by guilt and bedeviled by contrary winds, Captain
eonard avoided me, seeking refuge on his quarterdeck as we
ade our cautious way past Acklin Island and Samana Cay. The
eather aided him in this evasion; it stayed bright, but with odd,
ght breezes alternating with sudden gusts, so that constant ad-
stment of the sails was required—no easy task, in a ship so
orthanded.

It was four days later, as we shifted course to enter the Caicos
assage, that a sudden booming gust of wind struck the ship out of
owhere, catching her ill-rigged and unprepared.

I was on deck when the gust struck. There was a sudden *whoosh*
hat sent my skirts billowing and propelled me flying down the
eck, followed by a sharp, loud *crack!* somewhere overhead. I
rashed head-on into Ramsdell Hodges, one of the forecastle
ew, and we whirled together in a mad pirouette before falling
ntangled to the deck.

There was confusion all around, with hands running and orders
outed. I sat up, trying to collect my scattered wits.

"What is it?" I demanded of Hodges, who staggered to his feet
d reached down to lift me up. "What's happened?"

"The fucking mainmast's split," he said succinctly. "Saving
ur presence, ma'am, but it has. And now there'll be hell to
y."

The *Porpoise* limped slowly south, not daring to risk the banks
d shoals of the passage without a mainmast. Instead, Captain

Leonard put in for repairs at the nearest convenient anchorag
Bottle Creek, on the shore of North Caicos Island.

This time, we were allowed ashore, but no great good did it d
me. Tiny and dry, with few sources of fresh water, the Turks ar
Caicos provided little more than numerous tiny bays that mig
shelter passing ships caught in storms. And the idea of hiding on
foodless, waterless island, waiting for a convenient hurricane
blow me a ship, did not appeal.

To Annekje, though, our change of course suggested a ne
plan.

"I know these island," she said, nodding wisely. "We go rour
now, Grand Turk, Mouchoir. Not Caicos."

I looked askance, and she squatted, drawing with a blunt for•
finger in the yellow sand of the beach.

"See—Caicos Passage," she said, sketching a pair of lines. A
the top, between the lines, she sketched the small triangle of a sai
"Go through," she said, indicating the Caicos Passage, "but ma
is gone. Now—" She quickly drew several irregular circles, to th
right of the passage. "North Caicos, South Caicos, Caicos, Grar
Turk," she said, stabbing a finger at each circle in turn. Go rour
now—reefs. Mouchoir." And she drew another pair of lines, ind•
cating a passage to the southeast of Grand Turk Island.

"Mouchoir Passage?" I had heard the sailors mention it, b
had no idea how it applied to my potential escape from the *Po
poise.*

Annekje nodded, beaming, then drew a long, wavy line, son
way below her previous illustrations. She pointed at it proudl
"Hispaniola. St. Domingue. Big island, is there towns, lc
ships."

I raised my eyebrows, still baffled. She sighed, seeing that
didn't understand. She thought a moment, then stood up, dusti•
her heavy thighs. We had been gathering whelks from the rocks
a shallow pan. She seized this, dumped out the whelks, and filled
with seawater. Then, laying it on the sand, she motioned to me
watch.

She stirred the water carefully, in a circular motion, then lifte
her finger out, stained dark with the purple blood of the whelk
The water continued to move, swirling past the tin sides.

Annekje pulled a thread from the raveling hem of her skirt, b

f a short piece, and spat it into the water. It floated, following the
virl of the water in lazy circles round the pan.

"You," she said, pointing at it. "Vater move you." She pointed
ack to her drawing in the sand. A new triangle, in the Mouchoir
assage. A line, curving from the tiny sail down to the left, indi-
ting the ship's course. And now, the blue thread representing
e, rescued from its immersion. She placed it by the tiny sail
presenting the *Porpoise,* then dragged it off, down the Passage
ward the coast of Hispaniola.

"Jump," she said simply.

"You're crazy!" I said in horror.

She chuckled in deep satisfaction at my understanding. "*Ja,*"
e said. "But it vork. Vater move you." She pointed to the end of
e Mouchoir Passage, to the coast of Hispaniola, and stirred the
ater in the pan once more. We stood side by side, watching the
ples of her manufactured current die away.

Annekje glanced thoughtfully sideways at me. "You try not
own, *ja*?"

I took a deep breath and brushed the hair out of my eyes.

"*Ja,*" I said. "I'll try."

T he sea was remarkably warm, as seas go, and like a war
bath as compared to the icy surf off Scotland. On the oth
hand, it was extremely wet. After two or three hours
immersion, my feet were numb and my fingers chilled where th
gripped the ropes of my makeshift life preserver, made of t
empty casks.

The gunner's wife was as good as her word, though. The lon
dim shape I had glimpsed from the *Porpoise* grew steadily near
its low hills dark as black velvet against a silver sky. Hispaniola
Haiti.

I had no way of telling time, and yet two months on shipboa
with its constant bells and watch-changes, had given me a rou
feeling for the passage of the night hours. I thought it must ha
been near midnight when I left the *Porpoise;* now it was like
near 4:00 A.M., and still over a mile to the shore. Ocean curre
are strong, but they take their time.

Worn out from work and worry, I twisted the rope awkwar
about one wrist to prevent my slipping out of the harness, laid
forehead on one cask, and drifted off to sleep with the scent
rum strong in my nostrils.

The brush of something solid beneath my feet woke me to
opal dawn, the sea and sky both glowing with the colors for
inside a shell. With my feet planted in cold sand, I could feel
strength of the current flowing past me, tugging on the casks
disentangled myself from the rope harness and with considera
relief, let the unwieldy things go bobbing toward the shore.

There were deep red indentations on my shoulders. The wrist I
⹂d twisted through the wet rope was rubbed raw; I was chilled,
⹂hausted, and very thirsty, and my legs were rubbery as boiled
⹂uid.

On the other hand, the sea behind me was empty, the *Porpoise*
⹂where in sight. I had escaped.

Now, all that remained to be done was to get ashore, find water,
⹂d some means of quick transport to Jamaica, and find Jamie and
⹂e *Artemis,* preferably before the Royal Navy did. I thought I
⹂uld just about manage the first item on the agenda.

Such little as I knew of the Caribbean from postcards and tour-
⹂ brochures had led me to think in terms of white-sand beaches
⹂d crystal lagoons. In fact, prevailing conditions ran more toward
⹂lot of dense and ugly vegetation, embedded in extremely sticky
⹂rk-brown mud.

The thick bushlike plants must be mangroves. They stretched as
⹂r as I could see in either direction; there was no alternative but to
⹂amber through them. Their roots rose out of the mud in big loops
⹂e croquet wickets, which I tripped over regularly, and the pale,
⹂nooth gray twigs grew in bunches like finger bones, snatching at
⹂y hair as I passed.

Squads of tiny purple crabs ran off in profound agitation at my
⹂proach. My feet sank into the mud to the ankles, and I thought
⹂tter of putting on my shoes, wet as they were. I rolled them up in
⹂y wet skirt, kirtling it up above my knees and took out the fish
⹂ife Annekje had given me, just in case. I saw nothing threaten-
⹂g, but felt better with a weapon in my hand.

The rising sun on my shoulders at first was welcome, as it
⹂awed my chilled flesh and dried my clothes. Within an hour,
⹂ough, I wished that it would go behind a cloud. I was sweating
⹂avily as the sun rose higher, caked to the knees with drying
⹂d, and growing thirstier by the moment.

I tried to see how far the mangroves extended, but they rose
⹂ove my head, and tossing waves of narrow, gray-green leaves
⹂re all I could see.

"The whole bloody island can't be mangroves," I muttered,
⹂gging on. "There has to be solid land *someplace.*" And water,
⹂oped.

A noise like a small cannon going off nearby startled me so that
⹂ropped the fish knife. I groped frantically in the mud for it, then

dived forward onto my face as something large whizzed past ̷ head, missing me by inches.

There was a loud rattling of leaves, and then a sort of convers̷ tional-sounding *"Kwark?"*

"What?" I croaked. I sat up cautiously, knife in one hand, a̷ wiped the wet, muddy curls out of my face with the other. Six f̷ away, a large black bird was sitting on a mangrove, regarding ̷ with a critical eye.

He bent his head, delicately preening his sleek black feathers, though to contrast his immaculate appearance with my ov̷ dishevelment.

"Well, la-di-dah," I said sarcastically. "You've got win̷ mate."

The bird stopped preening and eyed me censoriously. Then̷ lifted his beak into the air, puffed his chest, and as though ̷ further establish his sartorial superiority, suddenly inflated a la̷ pouch of brilliant red skin that ran from the base of his ne̷ halfway down his body.

"Bwoom!" he said, repeating the cannon-like noise that h̷ startled me before. It startled me again, but not so much.

"Don't *do* that," I said irritably. Paying no attention, the b̷ slowly flapped its wings, settled back on its branch, and boom̷ again.

There was a sudden harsh cry from above, and with a lo̷ flapping of wings, two more large black birds plopped dov̷ landing in a mangrove a few feet away. Encouraged by the au̷ ence, the first bird went on booming at regular intervals, the s̷ of his pouch flaming with excitement. Within moments, thr̷ more black shapes had appeared overhead.

I was reasonably sure they weren't vultures, but I still was̷ inclined to stay. I had miles to go before I slept—or found Jam̷ The chances of finding him in time were something I preferred ̷ to dwell on.

A half-hour later, I had made so little progress that I could s̷ hear the intermittent booming of my fastidious acquaintance, n̷ joined by a number of similarly vocal friends. Panting with ex̷ tion, I picked a thickish root and sat down to rest.

My lips were cracked and dry, and the thought of water v̷ occupying my mind to the exclusion of virtually everything el̷ even Jamie. I had been struggling through the mangroves for w̷ eemed like forever, yet I could still hear the sound of the ocean. 1 fact, the tide must have been following me, for as I sat, a thin heet of foaming, dirty seawater came purling through the man- rove roots to touch my toes briefly before receding.

"Water, water everywhere," I said ruefully, watching it, "nor 1y drop to drink."

A small movement on the damp mud caught my eye. Bending own, I saw several small fishes, of a sort I had never seen before. o far from flopping about, gasping for breath, these fish were tting upright, propped on their pectoral fins, looking as though 1e fact that they were out of water was of no concern at all.

Fascinated, I bent closer to inspect them. One or two shifted on 1eir fins, but they seemed not to mind being looked at. They oggled solemnly back at me, eyes bulging. It was only as I looked oser that I realized that the goggling appearance was caused by 1e fact that each fish appeared to have four eyes, not two.

I stared at one for a long minute, feeling the sweat trickle down :tween my breasts.

"Either I'm hallucinating," I told it conversationally, "or *you* e."

The fish didn't answer, but hopped suddenly, landing on a anch several inches above the ground. Perhaps it sensed some- ing, for a moment later, another wave washed through, this one *lashing up to my ankles.

A sudden welcome coolness fell on me. The sun had obligingly one behind a cloud, and with its vanishing, the whole feel of the angrove forest changed.

The gray leaves rattled as a sudden wind came up, and all the 1y crabs and fish and sand fleas disappeared as though by magic. 1ey obviously knew something I didn't, and I found their going ther sinister.

I glanced up at the cloud where the sun had vanished, and sped. A huge purple mass of boiling cloud was coming up hind the hills, so fast that I could actually see the leading edge the mass, blazing white with shielded sunlight, moving forward ward me.

The next wave came through, two inches higher than the last, d taking longer to recede. I was neither a fish nor a crab, but by is time I had tumbled to the fact that a storm was on its way, and oving with amazing speed.

I glanced around, but saw nothing more than the seemingl‐
infinite stretch of mangroves before me. Nothing that could b‐
used for shelter. Still, being caught out in a rainstorm was hardl‐
the worst that could happen, under the circumstances. My tongu‐
felt dry and sticky, and I licked my lips at the thought of coo‐
sweet rain falling on my face.

The swish of another wave halfway up my shins brought me to‐
sudden awareness that I was in danger of more than getting wet. ‐
quick glance into the upper branches of the mangroves showed m‐
dried tufts of seaweed tangled in the twigs and crotches—hig‐
tide level—and well above my head.

I felt a moment's panic, and tried to calm myself. If I lost m‐
bearings in this place, I was done for. "Hold on, Beauchamp,"‐
muttered to myself. I remembered a bit of advice I'd learned as a‐
intern—"The first thing to do in a cardiac arrest is take your ow‐
pulse." I smiled at the memory, feeling panic ebb at once. As ‐
gesture, I did take my pulse; a little fast, but strong and steady.

All right, then, which way? Toward the mountain; it was th‐
only thing I could see above the sea of mangroves. I pushed m‐
way through the branches as fast as I could, ignoring the ripping ‐
my skirts and the increasing pull of each wave on my legs. Th‐
wind was coming from the sea behind me, pushing the wave‐
higher. It blew my hair constantly into my eyes and mouth, and ‐
wiped it back again and again, cursing out loud for the comfort ‐
hearing a voice, but my throat was soon so dry that it hurt to tal‐

I squelched on. My skirt kept pulling loose from my belt, an‐
somewhere I dropped my shoes, which disappeared at once in th‐
boiling foam that now washed well above my knees. It didn't see‐
to matter.

The tide was midthigh when the rain hit. With a roar tha‐
drowned the rattle of the leaves, it fell in drenching sheets tha‐
soaked me to the skin in moments. At first I wasted time vain‐
tilting my head back, trying to direct the rivulets that ran down m‐
face into my open mouth. Then sense reasserted itself; I took o‐
the kerchief tucked around my shoulders, let the rain soak it ar‐
wrung it out several times, to remove the vestiges of salt. The‐
let it soak in the rain once more, lifted the wadded fabric to m‐
mouth, and sucked the water from it. It tasted of sweat and se‐
weed and coarse cotton. It was delicious.

I had kept going, but was still in the clutches of the mangrove‐

he incoming tide was nearly waist-deep, and the walking getting
uch harder. Thirst slaked momentarily, I put my head down and
shed forward as fast as I could.

Lightning flashed over the mountains, and a moment later came
e growl of thunder. The wash of the tide was so strong now that I
uld move forward only as each wave came in, half-running as
e water shoved me along, then clinging to the nearest mangrove
em as the wash sucked back, dragging my trailing legs.

I was beginning to think that I had been over-hasty in aban-
oning Captain Leonard and the *Porpoise.* The wind was rising
ill further, dashing rain into my face so that I could barely see.
ailors say every seventh wave is higher. I found myself counting,
I slogged forward. It was the ninth wave, in fact, that struck me
etween the shoulder blades and knocked me flat before I could
asp a branch.

I floundered, helpless and choking in a blur of sand and water,
en found my feet and stood upright again. The wave had half-
owned me, but had also altered my direction. I was no longer
cing the mountain. I was, however, facing a large tree, no more
an twenty feet away.

Four more waves, four more surging rushes forward, four more
im clutchings as the tide-race sought to pull me back, and I was
the muddy bank of a small inlet, where a tiny stream ran
rough the mangroves and out to sea. I crawled up it, slipping and
aggering as I clambered into the welcoming embrace of the tree.

From a perch twelve feet up, I could see the stretch of the
angrove swamp behind me, and beyond that, the open sea. I
anged my mind once more about the wisdom of my leaving the
orpoise;* no matter how awful things were on land, they were a
od deal worse out there.

Lightning shattered over a surface of boiling water, as wind and
e-race fought for control of the waves. Farther out, in the
ouchoir Passage, the swell was so high, it looked like rolling
lls. The wind was high enough now to make a thin, whistling
ream as it passed by, chilling me to the skin in my wet clothes.
under cracked together with the lightning flashes now, as the
orm moved over me.

The *Artemis* was slower than the man-of-war; slow enough, I
ped, to be still safe, far out in the Atlantic.

I saw one clump of mangroves struck, a hundred feet away; the water hissed back, boiled away, and the dry land showed for moment, before the waves rolled back, drowning the black wire o the blasted stems. I wrapped my arms about the trunk of the tree pressed my face against the bark, and prayed. For Jamie, and th *Artemis.* For the *Porpoise,* Annekje Johansen and Tom Leonar and the Governor. And for me.

It was full daylight when I woke, my leg wedged between tw branches, and numb from the knee down. I half-climbed, half-fe from my perch, landing in the shallow water of the inlet. I scoope up a handful of the water, tasted it, and spat it out. Not salt, but to brackish to drink.

My clothes were damp, but I was parched. The storm was lon gone; everything around me was peaceful and normal, with th exception of the blackened mangroves. In the distance, I coul hear the booming of the big black birds.

Brackish water here promised fresher water farther up the inle I rubbed my leg, trying to work out the pins-and-needles, the limped up the bank.

The vegetation began to change from the gray-green mangrov to a lusher green, with a thick undergrowth of grass and moss plants that obliged me to walk in the water. Tired and thirsty as was, I could go only a short distance before having to sit down an rest. As I did so, several of the odd little fish hopped up onto th bank beside me, goggling as though in curiosity.

"Well, I think you look rather peculiar, too," I told one.

"Are you English?" said the fish incredulously. The impre sion of Alice in Wonderland was so pronounced that I mere blinked stupidly at it for a moment. Then my head snapped up, an I stared into the face of the man who had spoken.

His face was weathered and sunburned to the color of mahog any, but the black hair that curled back from his brow was thic and ungrizzled. He stepped out from behind the mangrove, mov ing cautiously, as though afraid to startle me.

He was a bit above middle height and burly, thick through th shoulder, with a broad, boldly carved face, whose natural friendly expression was tinged with wariness. He was dresse shabbily, with a heavy canvas bag slung across his shoulder—an a canteen made of goatskin hung from his belt.

"Vous êtes anglaise?" he asked, repeating his original question
 French. *"Comment ça va?"*

"Yes, I'm English," I said, croaking. "May I have some water,
 ease?"

His eyes popped wide open—they were a light hazel—but he
 dn't say anything, just took the skin bag from his belt and
 nded it to me.

I laid the fish knife on my knee, close within reach, and drank
 eply, scarcely able to gulp fast enough.

"Careful," he said. "It's dangerous to drink too fast."

"I know," I said, slightly breathless as I lowered the bag. "I'm
 doctor." I lifted the canteen and drank again, but forced myself
 swallow more slowly this time.

My rescuer was regarding me quizzically—and little wonder, I
 pposed. Sea-soaked and sun-dried, mud-caked and sweat-
 ained, with my hair straggling down over my face, I looked like a
 ggar, and probably a demented one at that.

"A doctor?" he said in English, showing that his thoughts had
 en traveling in the direction I suspected. He eyed me closely, in
 way strongly reminiscent of the big black bird I had met earlier.
 A doctor of *what,* if I might ask?"

"Medicine," I said, pausing briefly between gulps.

He had strongly drawn black brows. These rose nearly to his
 irline.

"Indeed," he said, after a noticeable pause.

"Indeed," I said in the same tone of voice, and he laughed.

He inclined his head toward me in a formal bow. "In that case,
 adame Physician, allow me to introduce myself. Lawrence
 ern, Doctor of Natural Philosophy, of the Gesellschaft von
 aturwissenschaft Philosophieren, Munich."

I blinked at him.

"A naturalist," he elaborated, gesturing at the canvas bag over
 s shoulder. "I was making my way toward those frigate birds in
 pes of observing their breeding display, when I happened to
 erhear you, er . . ."

"Talking to a fish," I finished. "Yes, well . . . have they
 ally got four eyes?" I asked, in hopes of changing the subject.

"Yes—or so it seems." He glanced down at the fish, who ap-
 ared to be following the conversation with rapt attention. "They
 em to employ their oddly shaped optics when submerged, so that

the upper pair of eyes observes events above the surface of th
water, and the lower pair similarly takes note of happenings belo
it."

He looked then at me, with a hint of a smile. "Might I perha
have the honor of knowing your name, Madame Physician?"

I hesitated, unsure what to tell him. I pondered the assortme
of available aliases and decided on the truth.

"Fraser," I said. "Claire Fraser. Mrs. James Fraser," I add
for good measure, feeling vaguely that marital status might mal
me seem slightly more respectable, appearances notwithstandin
I fingered back the curl hanging in my left eye.

"Your servant, Madame," he said with a gracious bow. H
rubbed the bridge of his nose thoughtfully, looking at me.

"You have been shipwrecked, perhaps?" he ventured.
seemed the most logical—if not the only—explanation of my pre
ence, and I nodded.

"I need to find a way to get to Jamaica," I said. "Do you thi
you can help me?"

He stared at me, frowning slightly, as though I were a specim
he couldn't quite decide how to classify, but then he nodded. H
had a broad mouth that looked made for smiling; one corn
turned up, and he extended a hand to help me up.

"Yes," he said. "I can help. But I think maybe first we find y
some food, and maybe clothes, eh? I have a friend, who lives n
so far away. I will take you there, shall I?"

What with parching thirst and the general press of events, I ha
paid little attention to the demands of my stomach. At the menti
of food, however, it came immediately and vociferously to life

"That," I said loudly, in hopes of drowning it out, "would
very nice indeed." I brushed back the tangle of my hair as well
I could, and ducking under a branch, followed my rescuer into t
trees.

＊

As we emerged from a palmetto grove, the ground opened c
into a meadow-like space, then rose up in a broad hill before
At the top of the hill, I could see a house—or at least a ruin.
yellow plaster walls were cracked and overrun by pink bougainv
laeas and straggling guavas, the tin roof sported several visil

ɔles, and the whole place gave off an air of mournful dilapida-
ɔn.

"Hacienda de la Fuente," my new acquaintance said, with a
ɪd toward it. "Can you stand the walk up the hill, or—" He
ɪsitated, eyeing me as though estimating my weight. "I could
ɪrry you, I suppose," he said, with a not altogether flattering tone
ɪ doubt in his voice.

"I can manage," I assured him. My feet were bruised and sore,
ɪd punctured by fallen palmetto fronds, but the path before us
ɔked relatively smooth.

The hillside leading up to the house was crisscrossed with the
ɪint lines of sheep trails. There were a number of these animals
ɪesent, peacefully grazing under the hot Hispaniola sun. As we
ɪpped out of the trees, one sheep spotted us and uttered a short
ɪeat of surprise. Like clockwork, every sheep on the hillside lifted
ɪ head in unison and stared at us.

Feeling rather self-conscious under this unblinking phalanx of
ɪspicious eyes, I picked up my muddy skirts and followed Dr.
ɪern toward the main path—trodden by more than sheep, to judge
ɔm its width—that led up and over the hill.

It was a fine, bright day, and flocks of orange and white butter-
ɪes flickered through the grass. They lighted on the scattered
ɔoms with here and there a brilliant yellow butterfly shining like
ɪtiny sun.

I breathed in deeply, a lovely smell of grass and flowers, with
ɪinor notes of sheep and sun-warmed dust. A brown speck lighted
ɪr a moment on my sleeve and clung, long enough for me to see
ɪ velvet scales on its wing, and the tiny curled hose of its pro-
ɪscis. The slender abdomen pulsed, breathing to its wing-beats,
ɪd then it was gone.

It might have been the promise of help, the water, the butter-
ɪes, or all three, but the burden of fear and fatigue under which I
ɪd labored for so long began to lift. True, I still had to face the
ɔblem of finding transport to Jamaica, but with thirst assuaged, a
ɪfriend at hand, and the possibility of lunch just ahead, that no
ɪger appeared the impossible task it had seemed in the man-
ɪoves.

"There he is!" Lawrence stopped, waiting for me to come up
ɔngside him on the path. He gestured upward, toward a slight,
ɪry figure, picking its way carefully down the hillside toward us.

I squinted at the figure as it wandered through the sheep, who too[k]
no apparent notice of his passage.

"Jesus!" I said. "It's St. Francis of Assisi."

Lawrence glanced at me in surprise.

"No, neither one. I told you he's English." He raised an ar[m]
and shouted, *"¡Hola!* Señor Fogden!"

The gray-robed figure paused suspiciously, one hand twine[d]
protectively in the wool of a passing ewe.

"¿Quien es?"

"Stern!" called Lawrence. "Lawrence Stern! Come along," h[e]
said, and extended a hand to pull me up the steep hillside onto th[e]
sheep path above.

The ewe was making determined efforts to escape her protecto[r,]
which distracted him from our approach. A slender man a bit tall[er]
than I, he had a lean face that might have been handsome if n[ot]
disfigured by a reddish beard that straggled dust-mop-like rou[nd]
the edges of his chin. His long and straying hair had gone to gr[ay]
in streaks and runnels, and fell forward into his eyes with so[me]
frequency. An orange butterfly took wing from his head as w[e]
reached him.

"Stern?" he said, brushing back the hair with his free hand a[nd]
blinking owlishly in the sunlight. "I don't know any . . . oh, it[']
you!" His thin face brightened. "Why didn't you say it was th[e]
shitworm man; I should have known you at once!"

Stern looked mildly embarrassed at this, and glanced at m[e]
apologetically. "I . . . ah . . . collected several interesting pa[r]
asites from the excrement of Mr. Fogden's sheep, upon the occ[a]
sion of my last visit," he explained.

"Horrible great worms!" Father Fogden said, shuddering vi[o]
lently in recollection. "A foot long, some of them, at least!"

"No more than eight inches," Stern corrected, smiling. [He]
glanced at the nearest sheep, his hand resting on his collecting b[ag]
as though in anticipation of further imminent contributions [to]
science. "Was the remedy I suggested effective?"

Father Fogden looked vaguely doubtful, as though trying [to]
remember quite what the remedy had been.

"The turpentine drench," the naturalist prompted.

"Oh, yes!" The sun broke out on the priest's lean countenan[ce]
and he beamed fondly upon us. "Of course, of course! Yes,

orked splendidly. A few of them died, but the rest were quite
ured. Capital, entirely capital!''

Suddenly it seemed to dawn on Father Fogden that he was being
ss than hospitable.

"But you must come in!" he said. "I was just about to partake
f the midday meal; I insist you must join me." The priest turned
me. "This will be Mrs. Stern, will it?"

Mention of eight-inch intestinal worms had momentarily sup-
essed my hunger pangs, but at the mention of food, they came
rgling back in full force.

"No, but we should be delighted to partake of your hospital-
y," Stern answered politely. "Pray allow me to introduce my
mpanion—a Mrs. Fraser, a countrywoman of yours."

Fogden's eyes grew quite round at this. A pale blue, with a
ndency to water in bright sun, they fixed wonderingly upon me.
"An Englishwoman?" he said, disbelieving. "Here?" The
und eyes took in the mud and salt stains on my crumpled dress,
d my general air of disarray. He blinked for a moment, then
epped forward, and with the utmost dignity, bowed low over my
nd.

"Your most obedient servant, Madame," he said. He rose and
stured grandly at the ruin on the hill. *"Mi casa es su casa."* He
histled sharply, and a small King Charles cavalier spaniel poked
face inquiringly out of the weeds.

"We have a guest, Ludo," the priest said, beaming. "Isn't that
ce?" Tucking my hand firmly under one elbow, he took the
eep by its topknot of wool and towed us both toward the Haci-
da de la Fuente, leaving Stern to follow.

The reason for the name became clear as we entered the dilapi-
ted courtyard; a tiny cloud of dragonflies hovered like blinking
hts over an algae-filled pool in one corner; it looked like a
tural spring that someone had curbed in when the house was
ilt. At least a dozen jungle fowl sprang up from the shattered
vement and flapped madly past our feet, leaving a small cloud of
st and feathers behind them. From other evidences left behind, I
duced that the trees overhanging the patio were their customary
ost, and had been for some time.

"And so I was fortunate enough to encounter Mrs. Fraser
ong the mangroves this morning," Stern concluded. "I thought

that perhaps you might . . . oh, look at that beauty! A magnifi cent *Odonata!''*

A tone of amazed delight accompanied this last statement, and he pushed unceremoniously past us to peer up into the shadows of the palm-thatched patio roof, where an enormous dragonfly, at least four inches across, was darting to and fro, blue body catching fire when it crossed one of the errant rays of sunshine poking through the tattered roof.

''Oh, do you want it? Be my guest.'' Our host waved a gracious hand at the dragonfly. ''Here, Becky, trot in there and I'll see your hoof in a bit.'' He shooed the ewe into the patio with a slap on the rump. It snorted and galloped off a few feet, then fell once to browsing on the scattered fruit of a huge guava that over hung the ancient wall.

In fact, the trees around the patio had grown up to such an extent that the branches at many points interlaced. The whole the courtyard seemed roofed with them, a sort of leafy tunnel leading down the length of the patio into the gaping cavern of the house's entrance.

Drifts of dust and the pink paper leaves of bougainvillaea lay heaped against the sill, but just beyond, the dark wood floor gleamed with polish, bare and immaculate. It was dark inside after the brilliance of the sunlight, but my eyes quickly adapted the surroundings, and I looked around curiously.

It was a very plain room, dark and cool, furnished with no more than a long table, a few stools and chairs, and a small sideboard over which hung a hideous painting in the Spanish style—an ema ciated Christ, goateed and pallid in the gloom, indicating with one skeletal hand the bleeding heart that throbbed in his chest.

This ghastly object so struck my eye that it was a moment before I realized there was someone else in the room. The shad ows in one corner of the room coalesced, and a small round face emerged, wearing an expression of remarkable malignity. I blinked and took a step back. The woman—for so she was—took a step forward, black eyes fixed on me, unblinking as the sheep.

She was no more than four feet tall, and so thick through the body as to seem like a solid block, without joint or indentation. Her head was a small round knob atop her body, with the small knob of a sparse gray bun scraped tightly back behind it. She was a light mahogany color—whether from the sun or naturally uldn't tell—and looked like nothing so much as a carved ooden doll. An ill-wish doll.

"Mamacita," said the priest, speaking Spanish to the graven age, "what good fortune! We have guests who will eat with us. u remember Señor Stern?" he added, gesturing at Lawrence.

"Sí, claro," said the image, through invisible wooden lips. The Christ-killer. And who is the *puta alba*?"

"And this is Señora Fraser," Father Fogden went on, beaming though she had not spoken. "The poor lady has had the misfor-ne to be shipwrecked; we must assist her as much as we can."

Mamacita looked me over slowly from top to toe. She said thing, but the wide nostrils flared with infinite contempt.

"Your food's ready," she said, and turned away.

"Splendid!" the priest said happily. "Mamacita welcomes you; e'll bring us some food. Won't you sit down?"

The table was already laid with a large cracked plate and a ooden spoon. The priest took two more plates and spoons from e sideboard, and distributed them haphazardly about the table, sturing hospitably at us to be seated.

A large brown coconut sat on the chair at the head of the table. gden tenderly picked this up and set it alongside his plate. The rous husk was darkened with age, and the hair was worn off it in tches, showing an almost polished appearance; I thought he st have had it for some time.

"Hallo there," he said, patting it affectionately. "And how are u keeping this fine day, Coco?"

I glanced at Stern, but he was studying the portrait of Christ, a all frown between his thick black brows. I supposed it was up to to open a conversation.

"You live alone here, Mr.—ah, Father Fogden?" I inquired of r host. "You, and—er, Mamacita?"

"Yes, I'm afraid so. That's why I'm so pleased to see you. I ven't any real company but Ludo and Coco, you know," he plained, patting the hairy nut once more.

"Coco?" I said politely, thinking that on the evidence to hand far, Coco wasn't the only nut among those present. I darted ther glance at Stern, who looked mildly amused, but not rmed.

"Spanish for bugbear—*coco*," the priest explained. "A bgoblin. See him there, wee button nose and his dark little

eyes?'' Fogden jabbed two long, slender fingers suddenly into t
depressions in the end of the coconut and jerked them back, cho
tling.

"Ah-ah!" he cried. "Mustn't stare, Coco, it's rude, y
know!"

The pale blue eyes darted a piercing glance at me, and wi
some difficulty, I removed my teeth from my lower lip.

"Such a pretty lady," he said, as though to himself. "Not lil
my Ermenegilda, but very pretty nonetheless—isn't she, Ludo?

The dog, thus addressed, ignored me, but bounded joyfully at
master, shoving its head under his hand and barking. He scratch
its ears affectionately, then turned his attention back to me.

"Would one of Ermenegilda's dresses fit you, I wonder?"

I didn't know whether to answer this or not. Instead, I mere
smiled politely, and hoped what I was thinking didn't show on n
face. Fortunately, at this point Mamacita came back, carrying
steaming clay pot wrapped in towels. She slapped a ladleful of t
contents on each plate, then went out, her feet—if she had any
moving invisibly beneath the shapeless skirt.

I stirred the mess on my plate, which appeared to be vegetal
in nature. I took a cautious bite, and found it surprisingly goo

"Fried plantain, mixed with manioc and red beans," Lawren
explained, seeing my hesitation. He took a large spoonful of t
steaming pulp himself and ate it without pausing for it to cool

I had expected something of an inquisition about my presen
identity, and prospects. Instead, Father Fogden was singing sof
under his breath, keeping time on the table with his spoon betwe
bites.

I darted a glance at Lawrence, eyebrows up. He merely smil
raised one shoulder in a slight shrug, and bent to his own foo

No real conversation occurred until the conclusion of the me
when Mamacita—"unsmiling" seemed an understatement of
expression—removed the plates, replacing them with a platter
fruit, three cups, and a gigantic clay pitcher.

"Have you ever drunk sangria, Mrs. Fraser?"

I opened my mouth to say "Yes," thought better of it, and sa
"No, what is it?" Sangria had been a popular drink in the 196
and I had had it many times at faculty parties and hospital soc
events. But for now, I was sure that it was unknown in Engla

nd Scotland; Mrs. Fraser of Edinburgh would never have heard of ;angria.

"A mixture of red wine and the juices of orange and lemon," Lawrence Stern was explaining. "Mulled with spices, and served 1ot or cold, depending upon the weather. A most comforting and 1ealthful beverage, is it not, Fogden?"

"Oh, yes. Oh, yes. Most comforting." Not waiting for me to ind out for myself, the priest drained his cup, and reached for the >itcher before I had taken the first sip.

It was the same; the same sweet, throat-rasping taste, and I uffered the momentary illusion that I was back at the party where had first tasted it, in company with a marijuana-smoking gradu- ite student and a professor of botany.

This illusion was fostered by Stern's conversation, which dealt vith his collections, and by Father Fogden's behavior. After sev- ral cups of sangria, he had risen, rummaged through the side- •oard, and emerged with a large clay pipe. This he packed full of a trong-smelling herb shaken out of a paper twist, and proceeded to moke.

"Hemp?" Stern asked, seeing this. "Tell me, do you find it ettling to the digestive processes? I have heard it is so, but the ierb is unobtainable in most European cities, and I have no first- 1and observations of its effect."

"Oh, it is most genial and comforting to the stomach," Father 'ogden assured him. He drew in a huge breath, held it, then ex- aled long and dreamily, blowing a stream of soft white smoke 1at floated in streamers of haze near the room's low ceiling. "I hall send a packet home with you, dear fellow. Do say, now, what o you mean doing, you and this shipwrecked lady you have escued?"

Stern explained his plan; after a night's rest, we intended to valk as far as the village of St. Luis du Nord, and from there see vhether a fishing boat might carry us to Cap-Haïtien, thirty miles istant. If not, we would have to make our way overland to Le Cap, 1e nearest port of any size.

The priest's sketchy brows drew close together, frowning gainst the smoke.

"Mm? Well, I suppose there isn't much choice, is there? Still, ou must go careful, particularly if you go overland to Le Cap. 1aroons, you know."

"Maroons?" I glanced quizzically at Stern, who nodded, frowning.

"That's true. I did meet with two or three small bands as I came north through the valley of the Artibonite. They didn't molest me, though—I daresay I looked little better off than they, poor wretches. The Maroons are escaped slaves," he explained to me. "Having fled the cruelty of their masters, they take refuge in the remote hills, where the jungle hides them."

"They might not trouble you," Father Fogden said. He sucked deeply on his pipe, with a low, slurping noise, held his breath for a long count and then let it out reluctantly. His eyes were becoming markedly bloodshot. He closed one of them and examined me rather blearily with the other. "She doesn't look worth robbing, really."

Stern smiled broadly, looking at me, then quickly erased the smile, as though feeling he had been less than tactful. He coughed and took another cup of sangria. The priest's eyes gleamed over the pipe, red as a ferret's.

"I believe I need a little fresh air," I said, pushing back my chair. "And perhaps a little water, to wash with?"

"Oh, of course, of course!" Father Fogden cried. He rose swaying unsteadily, and thumped the coals from his pipe carelessly out onto the sideboard. "Come with me."

The air in the patio seemed fresh and invigorating by comparison, despite its mugginess. I inhaled deeply, looking on with interest as Father Fogden fumbled with a bucket by the fountain in the corner.

"Where does the water come from?" I asked. "Is it a spring?" The stone trough was lined with soft tendrils of green algae, and I could see these moving lazily; evidently there was a current of some kind.

It was Stern who answered.

"Yes, there are hundreds of such springs. Some of them are said to have spirits living in them—but I do not suppose you subscribe to such superstition, sir?"

Father Fogden seemed to have to think about this. He set the half-filled bucket down on the coping and squinted into the water, trying to fix his gaze on one of the small silver fish that swam there.

"Ah?" he said vaguely. "Well, no. Spirits, no. Still—oh, yes,

ad forgotten. I had something to show you.'' Going to a cupboard
et into the wall, he pulled open the cracked wooden door and
emoved a small bundle of coarse unbleached muslin, which he
ut gingerly into Stern's hands.

"It came up in the spring one day last month," he said. "It died
vhen the noon sun struck it, and I took it out. I'm afraid the other
ish nibbled it a bit," he said apologetically, "but you can still
ee."

Lying in the center of the cloth was a small dried fish, much like
hose darting about in the spring, save that this one was pure
vhite. It was also blind. On either side of the blunt head, there was
small swelling where an eye should have been, but that was all.

"Do you think it is a ghost fish?" the priest inquired. "I
hought of it when you mentioned spirits. Still, I can't think what
ort of sin a fish might have committed, so as to be doomed to
oam about like that—eyeless, I mean. I mean"—he closed one
ye again in his favorite expression—"one doesn't think of fish as
aving souls, and yet, if they don't, how can they become
hosts?"

"I shouldn't think they do, myself," I assured him. I peered
nore closely at the fish, which Stern was examining with the rapt
oy of the born naturalist. The skin was very thin, and so transpar-
nt that the shadows of the internal organs and the knobbly line of
ne vertebrae were clearly visible, yet it did have scales, tiny and
anslucent, though dulled by dryness.

"It is a blind cave fish," Stern said, reverently stroking the tiny
lunt head. "I have seen one only once before, in a pool deep
side a cave, at a place called Abandawe. And that one escaped
efore I could examine it closely. My dear fellow—" He turned to
ne priest, eyes shining with excitement. "Might I have it?"

"Of course, of course." The priest fluttered his fingers in off-
and generosity. "No use to me. Too small to eat, you know, even
Mamacita would think of cooking it, which she wouldn't." He
lanced around the patio, kicking absently at a passing hen.
Where *is* Mamacita?"

"Here, *cabrón,* where else?" I hadn't seen her come out of the
ouse, but there she was, a dusty, sun-browned little figure stoop-
g to fill another bucket from the spring.

A faintly musty, unpleasant smell reached my nostrils, and they twitched uneasily. The priest must have noticed, for he said, ''Oh you mustn't mind, it's only poor Arabella.''

''Arabella?''

''Yes, in here.'' The priest held aside a ragged curtain of burlap that screened off a corner of the patio, and I glanced behind it.

A ledge jutted out of the stone wall at waist-height. On it were ranged a long row of sheep's skulls, pure white and polished.

''I can't bear to part with them, you see.'' Father Fogden gently stroked the heavy curve of a skull. ''This was Beatriz—so sweet and gentle. She died in lambing, poor thing.'' He indicated two much smaller skulls nearby, shaped and polished like the rest.

''Arabella is a—a sheep, too?'' I asked. The smell was much stronger here, and I thought I really didn't want to know where it was coming from at all.

''A member of my flock, yes, certainly.'' The priest turned his oddly bright blue eyes on me, looking quite fierce. ''She was murdered! Poor Arabella, such a gentle, trusting soul. How they can have had the wickedness to betray such innocence for the sake of carnal lusts!''

''Oh, dear,'' I said, rather inadequately. ''I'm terribly sorry to hear that. Ah—who murdered her?''

''The sailors, the wicked heathen! Killed her on the beach and roasted her poor body over a gridiron, just like St. Lawrence the Martyr.''

''Heavens,'' I said.

The priest sighed, and his spindly beard appeared to droop with mourning.

''Yes, I must not forget the hope of Heaven. For if Our Lord observes the fall of every sparrow, He can scarcely have failed to observe Arabella. She must have weighed near on ninety pounds at least, such a good grazer as she was, poor child.''

''Ah,'' I said, trying to infuse the remark with a suitable sympathy and horror. It then occurred to me what the priest had said.

''Sailors?'' I asked. ''When did you say this—this sad occurrence took place?'' It couldn't be the *Porpoise,* I thought. Surely Captain Leonard would not have thought me so important that he had risked bringing his ship in so close to the island, in order to pursue me? But my hands grew damp at the thought, and I wiped them unobtrusively on my robe.

''This morning,'' Father Fogden replied, setting back the

amb's skull he had picked up to fondle. "But," he added, his
manner brightening a bit, "I must say they're making wonderful
progress with her. It usually takes more than a week, and already
ou can quite see . . ."

He opened the cupboard again, revealing a large lump, covered
with several layers of damp burlap. The smell was markedly
stronger now, and a number of small brown beetles scuttled away
rom the light.

"Are those members of the Dermestidae you have there,
ogden?" Lawrence Stern, having tenderly committed the corpse
f his cave fish to a jar of alcoholic spirits, had come to join us. He
eered over my shoulder, sunburned features creased in interest.

Inside the cupboard, the white maggot larvae of dermestid bee-
es were hard at work, polishing the skull of Arabella the sheep.
hey had made a good start on the eyes. The manioc shifted
eavily in my stomach.

"Is that what they are? I suppose so; dear voracious little fel-
ows." The priest swayed alarmingly, catching himself on the
dge of the cupboard. As he did so, he finally noticed the old
woman, standing glaring at him, a bucket in either hand.

"Oh, I had quite forgotten! You will be needing a change of
lothing, will you not, Mrs. Fraser?"

I looked down at myself. The dress and shift I was wearing were
pped in so many places that they were barely decent, and so
aked and sodden with water and swamp-mud that I was scarcely
lerable, even in such undemanding company as that of Father
ogden and Lawrence Stern.

Father Fogden turned to the graven image. "Have we not some-
ing this unfortunate lady might wear, Mamacita?" he asked in
panish. He seemed to hesitate, swaying gently. "Perhaps, one of
e dresses in—"

The woman bared her teeth at me. "They are much too small
r such a cow," she said, also in Spanish. "Give her your old
be, if you must." She cast an eye of scorn on my tangled hair
d mud-streaked face. "Come," she said in English, turning her
ack on me. "You wash."

She led me to a smaller patio at the back of the house, where
e provided me with two buckets of cold, fresh water, a worn
en towel, and a small pot of soft soap, smelling strongly of lye.
dding a shabby gray robe with a rope belt, she bared her teeth at

me again and left, remarking genially in Spanish, "Wash away the blood on your hands, Christ-killing whore."

I shut the patio gate after her with a considerable feeling of relief, stripped off my sticky, filthy clothes with even more relief and made my toilet as well as might be managed with cold water and no comb.

Clad decently, if oddly, in Father Fogden's extra robe, I combed out my wet hair with my fingers, contemplating my peculiar host. wasn't sure whether the priest's excursions into oddness were some form of dementia, or only the side effects of long-term alcoholism and cannabis intoxication, but he seemed a gentle kindly soul, in spite of it. His servant—if that's what she was— was another question altogether.

Mamacita made me more than slightly nervous. Mr. Stern had announced his intention of going down to the seaside to bathe, and I was reluctant to go back into the house until he returned. There had been quite a lot of sangria left, and I suspected that Father Fogden—if he was still conscious—would be little protection by this time against that basilisk glare.

Still, I couldn't stay outside all afternoon; I was very tired, and wanted to sit down at least, though I would have preferred to find bed and sleep for a week. There was a door opening into the house from my small patio; I pushed it open and stepped into the dark interior.

I was in a small bedroom. I looked around, amazed; it didn't seem part of the same house as the Spartan main room and the shabby patios. The bed was made up with feather pillows and coverlet of soft red wool. Four huge patterned fans were spread like bright wings across the whitewashed walls, and wax candles in a branched brass candelabrum sat on the table.

The furniture was simply but carefully made, and polished with oil to a soft, deep gloss. A curtain of striped cotton hung across the end of the room. It was pushed partway back, and I could see row of dresses hung on hooks behind it, in a rainbow of silken color.

These must be Ermenegilda's dresses, the ones that Father Fogden had mentioned. I walked forward to look at them, my bare feet quiet on the floor. The room was dustless and clean, but very quiet, without the scent or vibration of human occupancy. No one lived in this room anymore.

The dresses were beautiful; all of silk and velvet, moiré and satin, mousseline and panne. Even hanging lifeless here from their hooks, they had the sheen and beauty of an animal's pelt, where some essence of life lingers in the fur.

I touched one bodice, purple velvet, heavy with embroidered silver pansies, centered with pearls. She had been small, this Ermenegilda, and slightly built—several of the dresses had ruffles and pads cleverly sewn inside the bodices, to add to the illusion of bust. The room was comfortable, though not luxurious; the dresses were splendid—things that might have been worn at Court in Madrid.

Ermenegilda was gone, but the room still seemed inhabited. I touched a sleeve of peacock blue in farewell and tiptoed away, leaving the dresses to their dreams.

I found Lawrence Stern on the veranda at the back of the house, overlooking a precipitous slope of aloe and guava. In the distance, a small humped island sat cradled in a sea of glimmering turquoise. He rose in courtesy, giving me a small bow and a look of surprise.

"Mrs. Fraser! You are in greatly improved looks, I must say. The Father's robe suits you somewhat more than it does him." He smiled at me, hazel eyes creasing in a flattering expression of admiration.

"I expect the absence of dirt has more to do with it," I said, sitting down in the chair he offered. "Is that something to drink?" There was a pitcher on the rickety wooden table between the chairs; moisture had condensed in a heavy dew on the sides and droplets ran enticingly down the sides. I had been thirsty so long that the sight of anything liquid automatically made my cheeks draw in with longing.

"More sangria," Stern said. He poured out a small cupful for each of us, and sipped his own, sighing with enjoyment. "I hope you will not think me intemperate, Mrs. Fraser, but after months of tramping country, drinking nothing but water and the slaves' rude rum—" He closed his eyes in bliss. "Ambrosia."

I was rather disposed to agree.

"Er . . . is Father Fogden . . . ?" I hesitated, looking for some tactful way of inquiring after our host's state. I needn't have bothered.

"Drunk," Stern said frankly. "Limp as a worm, laid out on the table in the *sala.* He nearly always is, by the time the sun's gon down," he added.

"I see." I settled back in the chair, sipping my own sangri "Have you known Father Fogden long?"

Stern rubbed a hand over his forehead, thinking. "Oh, for a fe years." He glanced at me. "I was wondering—do you by chanc know a James Fraser, from Edinburgh? I realize it is a commc name, but—oh, you do?"

I hadn't spoken, but my face had given me away, as it alway did, unless I was carefully prepared to lie.

"My husband's name is James Fraser," I said.

Stern's face lighted with interest. "Indeed!" he exclaime "And is he a very large fellow, with—"

"Red hair," I agreed. "Yes, that's Jamie." Something occurre to me. "He told me he'd met a natural philosopher in Edinburg and had a most interesting conversation about . . . variou things." What I was wondering was where Stern had learne Jamie's real name. Most people in Edinburgh would have know him only as "Jamie Roy," the smuggler, or as Alexander Ma colm, the respectable printer of Carfax Close. Surely Dr. Ster with his distinct German accent, couldn't be the "Englishman Tompkins had spoken of?

"Spiders," Stern said promptly. "Yes, I recall perfectly. Sp ders and caves. We met in a—a—" His face went blank for moment. Then he coughed, masterfully covering the lapse. "In um, drinking establishment. One of the—ah—female employee happened to encounter a large specimen of *Arachnida* hangir from the ceiling in her—that is, from the ceiling as she was er gaged in . . . ah, conversation with me. Being somewhat frigh ened in consequence, she burst into the passageway, shriekir incoherently." Stern took a large gulp of sangria as a restorativ evidently finding the memory stressful.

"I had just succeeded in capturing the animal and securing it a specimen jar when Mr. Fraser burst into the room, pointed species of firearm at me, and said—" Here Stern developed prolonged coughing fit, pounding himself vigorously on the ches

"Eheu! Do you not find this particular pitcher perhaps a trif strong, Mrs. Fraser? I suspect that the old woman has added tc many sliced lemons."

I suspected that Mamacita would have added cyanide, had she ny to hand, but in fact the sangria was excellent.

"I hadn't noticed," I said, sipping. "But do go on. Jamie came a with a pistol and said—?"

"Oh. Well, in fact, I cannot say I recall precisely what was said. here appeared to have been a slight misapprehension, owing to is impression that the lady's outcry was occasioned by some opportune motion or speech of my own, rather than by the arach- id. Fortunately, I was able to display the beast to him, whereupon e lady was induced to come so far as the door—we could not ersuade her to enter the room again—and identify it as the cause f her distress."

"I see," I said. I could envision the scene very well indeed, ve for one point of paramount interest. "Do you happen to recall hat he was wearing? Jamie?"

Lawrence Stern looked blank. "Wearing? Why . . . no. My npression is that he was clad for the street, rather than in disha- ille, but—"

"That's quite all right," I assured him. "I only wondered." Clad," after all, was the operative word. "So he introduced imself to you?"

Stern frowned, running a hand through his thick black curls. "I on't believe he did. As I recall, the lady referred to him as Mr. raser; sometime later in the conversation—we availed ourselves f suitable refreshment and remained conversing nearly until the awn, finding considerable interest in each other's company, you e. At some point, he invited me to address him by his given me." He raised one eyebrow sardonically. "I trust you do not ink it overfamiliar of me to have done so, upon such brief ac- uaintance?"

"No, no. Of course not." Wanting to change the subject, I ontinued, "You said you talked about spiders and caves? Why ves?"

"By way of Robert the Bruce and the story—which your hus- nd was inclined to think apocryphal—regarding his inspiration persevere in his quest for the throne of Scotland. Presumably, e Bruce was in hiding in a cave, pursued by his enemies, and—"

"Yes, I know the story," I interrupted.

"It was James's opinion that spiders do not frequent caves in hich humans dwell; an opinion with which I basically concurred, though pointing out that in the larger type of cave, such as occur on this island—''

''There are caves here?'' I was surprised, and then felt foolish ''But of course, there must be, if there are cave fish, like the one i the spring. I always thought Caribbean islands were made of coral though. I shouldn't have thought you'd find caves in coral.''

''Well, it is possible, though not highly likely,'' Stern said judi ciously. ''However, the island of Hispaniola is not a coral atoll bu is basically volcanic in origin—with the addition of crystallin schists, fossiliferous sedimentary deposits of a considerable antiq uity, and widespread deposits of limestone. The limestone is par ticularly karstic in spots.''

''You don't say.'' I poured a fresh cup of spiced wine.

''Oh, yes.'' Lawrence leaned over to pick up his bag from th floor of the veranda. Pulling out a notebook, he tore a sheet o paper from it and crumpled it in his fist.

''There,'' he said, holding out his hand. The paper slowly un folded itself, leaving a mazed topography of creases and crumple peaks. ''That is what this island is like—you remember wha Father Fogden was saying about the Maroons? The runaway slave who have taken refuge in these hills? It is not lack of pursuit on th part of their masters that allows them to vanish with such ease There are many parts of this island where no man—white or black I daresay—has yet set foot. And in the lost hills, there are cave still more lost, whose existence no one knows save perhaps th aboriginal inhabitants of this place—and they are long gone, Mrs Fraser.

''I have seen one such cave,'' he added reflectively ''Abandawe, the Maroons call it. They consider it a most siniste and sacred spot, though I do not know why.''

Encouraged by my close attention, he took another gulp c sangria and continued his natural history lecture.

''Now that small island''—he nodded at the floating islan visible in the sea beyond—''that is the Ile de la Tortue—Tortuga That one is in fact a coral atoll, its lagoon long since filled in b the actions of the coral animalculae. Did you know it was once th haunt of pirates?'' he asked, apparently feeling that he ought t infuse his lecture with something of more general interest tha karstic formations and crystalline schists.

"Real pirates? Buccaneers, you mean?" I viewed the little is-
and with more interest. "That's rather romantic."

Stern laughed, and I glanced at him in surprise.

"I am not laughing at you, Mrs. Fraser," he assured me. A
mile lingered on his lips as he gestured at the Ile de la Tortue. "It
; merely that I had occasion once to talk with an elderly resident
f Kingston, regarding the habits of the buccaneers who had at one
oint made their headquarters in the nearby village of Port
oyal."

He pursed his lips, decided to speak, decided otherwise, then,
ith a sideways glance at me, decided to risk it. "You will pardon
te indelicacy, Mrs. Fraser, but as you are a married woman, and
; I understand, have some familiarity with the practice of medi-
ne—" He paused, and might have stopped there, but he had
runk nearly two-thirds of the pitcher; the broad, pleasant face was
eeply flushed.

"You have perhaps heard of the abominable practices of sod-
my?" he asked, looking at me sideways.

"I have," I said. "Do you mean—"

"I assure you," he said, with a magisterial nod. "My informant
as most discursive upon the habits of the buccaneers. Sodomites
a man," he said, shaking his head.

"What?"

"It was a matter of public knowledge," he said. "My informant
ld me that when Port Royal fell into the sea some sixty years
3o, it was widely assumed to be an act of divine vengeance upon
ese wicked persons in retribution for their vile and unnatural
sages."

"Gracious," I said. I wondered what the voluptuous Tessa of
te *Impetuous Pirate* would have thought about this.

He nodded, solemn as an owl.

"They say you can hear the bells of the drowned churches of
ort Royal when a storm is coming, ringing for the souls of the
tmned pirates."

I thought of inquiring further into the precise nature of the vile
id unnatural usages, but at this point in the proceedings, Mama-
ta stumped out onto the veranda, said curtly, "Food," and disap-
eared again.

"I wonder which cave Father Fogden found *her* in," I said,
toving back my chair.

Stern glanced at me in surprise. "Found her? But I forgot," h
said, face clearing, "you don't know." He peered at the open doo
where the old woman had vanished, but the interior of the hous
was quiet and dark as a cave.

"He found her in Habana," he said, and told me the rest of th
story.

Father Fogden had been a priest for ten years, a missionary c
the order of St. Anselm, when he had come to Cuba fifteen year
before. Devoted to the needs of the poor, he had worked amon
the slums and stews of Habana for several years, thinking c
nothing more than the relief of suffering and the love of God—
until the day he met Ermenegilda Ruiz Alcantara y Meroz in th
marketplace.

"I don't suppose he knows, even now, how it happened," Ster
said. He wiped away a drop of wine that ran down the side of hi
cup, and drank again. "Perhaps she didn't know, either, or per
haps she planned it from the moment she saw him."

In any case, six months later the city of Habana was agog at th
news that the young wife of Don Armando Alcantara had ru
away—with a priest.

"And her mother," I said, under my breath, but he heard me
and smiled slightly.

"Ermenegilda would never leave Mamacita behind," he said
"Nor her dog Ludo."

They would never have succeeded in escaping—for the reach c
Don Armando was long and powerful—save for the fact that th
English conveniently chose the day of their elopement to invad
the island of Cuba, and Don Armando had many things mor
important to worry him than the whereabouts of his runawa
young wife.

The fugitives rode to Bayamo—much hampered b
Ermenegilda's dresses, with which she would not part—and ther
hired a fishing boat, which carried them to safety on Hispaniol.

"She died two years later," Stern said abruptly. He set dow
his cup, and refilled it from the sweating pitcher. "He buried he
himself, under the bougainvillaea."

"And here they've stayed since," I said. "The priest, and Lud
and Mamacita."

"Oh, yes." Stern closed his eyes, his profile dark against th setting sun. "Ermenegilda would not leave Mamacita, and Mamacita will never leave Ermenegilda."

He tossed back the rest of his cup of sangria.

"No one comes here," he said. "The villagers won't set foot on the hill. They're afraid of Ermenegilda's ghost. A damned sinner, buried by a reprobate priest in unhallowed ground—of course she will not lie quiet."

The sea breeze was cool on the back of my neck. Behind us, even the chickens in the patio had grown quiet with falling twilight. The Hacienda de la Fuente lay still.

"You come," I said, and he smiled. The scent of oranges rose up from the empty cup in my hands, sweet as bridal flowers.

"Ah, well," he said. "I am a scientist. I don't believe in ghosts." He extended a hand to me, somewhat unsteadily. "Shall we dine, Mrs. Fraser?"

After breakfast the next morning, Stern was ready to set off for St. Luis. Before leaving, though, I had a question or two about the ship the priest had mentioned; if it was the *Porpoise,* I wanted to steer clear of it.

"What sort of ship was it?" I asked, pouring a cup of goat's milk to go with the breakfast of fried plantain.

Father Fogden, apparently little the worse for his excesses of the day before, was stroking his coconut, humming dreamily to himself.

"Ah?" he said, startled out of his reverie by Stern's poking him in the ribs. I patiently repeated my query.

"Oh." He squinted in deep thought, then his face relaxed. "A wooden one."

Lawrence bent his broad face over his plate, hiding a smile. I took a breath and tried again.

"The sailors who killed Arabella—did you see them?"

His narrow brows rose.

"Well, of course I saw them. How else would I know they had done it?"

I seized on this evidence of logical thought.

"Naturally. And did you see what they were wearing? I mean"—I saw him opening his mouth to say "clothes," and hastily forestalled him —"did they seem to be wearing any sort of uniform?'' The crew of the *Porpoise* commonly wore ''slops'' when not performing any ceremonial duty, but even these rough clothes bore the semblance of a uniform, being mostly all of a dirty white and similar in cut.

Father Fogden laid down his cup, leaving a milky mustache across his upper lip. He brushed at this with the back of his hand, frowning and shaking his head.

''No, I think not. All I recall of them, though, is that the leader wore a hook—missing a hand, I mean.'' He waggled his own long fingers at me in illustration.

I dropped my cup, which exploded on the tabletop. Stern sprang up with an exclamation, but the priest sat still, watching in surprise as a thin white stream ran across the table and into his lap.

''Whatever did you do that for?'' he said reproachfully.

''I'm sorry,'' I said. My hands were trembling so that I couldn't even manage to pick up the shards of the shattered cup. I was afraid to ask the next question. ''Father—has the ship sailed away?''

''Why no,'' he said, looking up in surprise from his damp robe. ''How could it? It's on the beach.''

Father Fogden led the way, his skinny shanks a gleaming white as he kirtled his cassock about his thighs. I was obliged to do the same, for the hillside above the house was thick with grass and thorny shrubs that caught at the coarse wool skirts of my borrowed robe.

The hill was crisscrossed with sheep paths, but these were narrow and faint, losing themselves under the trees and disappearing abruptly in thick grass. The priest seemed confident about his destination, though, and scampered briskly through the vegetation, never looking back.

I was breathing hard by the time we reached the crest of the hill, even though Lawrence Stern had gallantly assisted me, pushing branches out of my way, and taking my arm to haul me up the steeper slopes.

''Do you think there really is a ship?'' I said to him, low voiced, as we approached the top of the hill. Given our host's behavior so far, I wasn't so sure he might not have imagined it just to be sociable.

Stern shrugged, wiping a trickle of sweat that ran down his bronzed cheek.

"I suppose there will be *something* there," he replied. "After all, there is a dead sheep."

A qualm ran over me in memory of the late departed Arabella. Someone *had* killed the sheep, and I walked as quietly as I could, as we approached the top of the hill. It couldn't be the *Porpoise;* none of her officers or men wore a hook. I tried to tell myself that it likely wasn't the *Artemis,* either, but my heart beat still faster as we came to a stand of giant agave on the crest of the hill.

I could see the Caribbean glowing blue through the succulents' branches, and a narrow strip of white beach. Father Fogden had come to a halt, beckoning us to his side.

"There they are, the wicked creatures," he muttered. His blue eyes glittered bright with fury, and his scanty hair fairly bristled, like a moth-eaten porcupine. "Butchers!" he said, hushed but vehement, as though talking to himself. "Cannibals!"

I gave him a startled look, but then Lawrence Stern grasped my arm, drawing me to a wider opening between two trees.

"Oy! There *is* a ship," he said.

There was. It was lying tilted on its side, drawn up on the beach, its masts unstepped, untidy piles of cargo, sails, rigging, and water casks scattered all about it. Men crawled over the beached carcass like ants. Shouts and hammer blows rang out like gunshots, and the smell of hot pitch was thick on the air. The unloaded cargo gleamed dully in the sun; copper and tin, slightly tarnished by the sea air. Tanned hides had been laid flat on the sand, brown stiff blotches drying in the sun.

"It *is* them! It's the *Artemis!*" The matter was settled by the appearance near the hull of a squat, one-legged figure, head shaded from the sun by a gaudy kerchief of yellow silk.

"Murphy!" I shouted. "Fergus! *Jamie!*" I broke from Stern's grasp and ran down the far side of the hill, his cry of caution disregarded in the excitement of seeing the *Artemis.*

Murphy whirled at my shout, but was unable to get out of my way. Carried by momentum and moving like a runaway freight, I crashed straight into him, knocking him flat.

"Murphy!" I said, and kissed him, caught up in the joy of the moment.

"Hoy!" he said, shocked. He wriggled madly, trying to get out from under me.

"Milady!" Fergus appeared at my side, crumpled and vivid, his beautiful smile dazzling in a sun-dark face. "Milady!" He helped me off the grunting Murphy, then grabbed me to him in a rib-cracking hug. Marsali appeared behind him, a broad smile on her face.

"Merci aux saints!" he said in my ear. "I was afraid we would never see you again!" He kissed me heartily himself, on both cheeks and the mouth, then released me at last.

I glanced at the *Artemis,* lying on her side on the beach like a stranded whale. "What on earth happened?"

Fergus and Marsali exchanged a glance. It was the sort of look in which questions are asked and answered, and it rather startled me to see the depths of intimacy between them. Fergus drew a deep breath and turned to me.

"Captain Raines is dead," he said.

The storm that had come upon me during my night in the mangrove swamp had also struck the *Artemis.* Carried far off her path by the howling wind, she had been forced over a reef, tearing a sizable hole in her bottom.

Still, she had remained afloat. The aft hold filling rapidly, she had limped toward the small inlet that opened so near, offering shelter.

"We were no more than three hundred yards from the shore when the accident happened," Fergus said, his face drawn by the memory. The ship had heeled suddenly over, as the contents of the aft hold had shifted, beginning to float. And just then, an enormous wave, coming from the sea, had struck the leaning ship, washing across the tilting quarterdeck, and carrying away Captain Raines, and four seamen with him.

"The shore was so near!" Marsali said, her face twisted with distress. "We were aground ten minutes later! If only—"

Fergus stopped her with a hand on her arm.

"We cannot guess God's ways," he said. "It would have been the same, if we had been a thousand miles at sea, save that we would not have been able to give them decent burial." He nodded toward the far edge of the beach, near the jungle, where five small mounds, topped with crude wooden crosses, marked the final resting places of the drowned men.

"I had some holy water that Da brought me from Notre Dame n Paris," Marsali said. Her lips were cracked, and she licked hem. "In a little bottle. I said a prayer, and sprinkled it on the graves. D'ye—d'ye think they would have l-liked that?"

I caught the quaver in her voice, and realized that for all her elf-possession, the last two days had been a terrifying ordeal for he girl. Her face was grimy, her hair coming down, and the harpness was gone from her eyes, softened by tears.

"I'm sure they would," I said gently, patting her arm. I glanced t the faces crowding around, searching for Jamie's great height nd fiery head, even as the realization dawned that he was not here.

"Where *is* Jamie?" I said. My face was flushed from the run own the hill. I felt the blood begin to drain from my cheeks, as a rickle of fear rose in my veins.

Fergus was staring at me, lean face mirroring mine.

"He is not with you?" he said.

"No. How could he be?" The sun was blinding, but my skin elt cold. I could feel the heat shimmer over me, but to no effect. My lips were so chilled, I could scarcely form the question.

"Where is he?"

Fergus shook his head slowly back and forth, like an ox stunned y the slaughterer's blow.

"I don't know."

51

In Which Jamie
Smells a Rat

Jamie Fraser lay in the shadows under the *Porpoise*'s jolly boat, chest heaving with effort. Getting aboard the man-of-war without being seen had been no small task; his right side was bruised from being slammed against the side of the ship as he hung from the boarding nets, struggling to pull himself up to the rail. His arms felt as though they had been jerked from the sockets and there was a large splinter in one hand. But he was here, and so far unseen.

He chewed delicately at his palm, groping for the end of the splinter with his teeth, as he got his bearings. Russo and Stone, *Artemis* hands who had served aboard men-of-war, had spent hours describing to him the structure of a large ship, the compartments and decks, and the probable location of the surgeon's quarters. Hearing something described and being able to find your way about in it were two different things, though. At least the miserable thing rocked less than the *Artemis*, though he could still feel the subtle, nauseating heave of the deck beneath him.

The end of the splinter worked free; nipping it between his teeth, he drew it slowly out and spat it on the deck. He sucked the tiny wound, tasting blood, and slid cautiously out from under the jolly boat, ears pricked to catch the sound of an approaching footstep.

The deck below this one, down the forward companionway. The officers' quarters would be there, and with luck, the surgeon's cabin as well. Not that she was likely to be in her quarters; not he

She'd cared enough to come tend the sick—she would be with them.

He had waited until dark to have Robbie MacRae row him out. Raines had told him that the *Porpoise* would likely weigh anchor with the evening tide, two hours from now. If he could find Claire and escape over the side before that—he could swim ashore with her, easily—the *Artemis* would be waiting for them, concealed in a small cove on the other side of Caicos Island. If he couldn't—well, he would deal with that when he came to it.

Fresh from the cramped small world of the *Artemis,* the below-decks of the *Porpoise* seemed huge and sprawling; a shadowed warren. He stood still, nostrils flaring as he deliberately drew the fetid air deep into his lungs. There were all the nasty stenches associated with a ship at sea for a long time, overlaid with the faint floating stink of feces and vomit.

He turned to the left and began to walk softly, long nose twitching. Where the smell of sickness was the strongest; that was where he would find her.

Four hours later, in mounting desperation, he made his way aft for the third time. He had covered the entire ship—keeping out of sight with some difficulty—and Claire was nowhere to be found.

"Bloody woman!" he said under his breath. "Where have ye gone, ye fashious wee hidee?"

A small worm of fear gnawed at the base of his heart. She had said her vaccine would protect her from the sickness, but what if she had been wrong? He could see for himself that the man-of-war's crew had been badly diminished by the deadly sickness—knee-deep in it, the germs might have attacked her too, vaccine or not.

He thought of germs as small blind things, about the size of maggots, but equipped with vicious razor teeth, like tiny sharks. He could all too easily imagine a swarm of the things fastening on to her, killing her, draining her flesh of life. It was just such a vision that had made him pursue the *Porpoise*—that, and a murderous rage toward the English bugger who had had the filthy-ating insolence to steal away his wife beneath his very nose, with a vague promise to return her, once they'd made use of her.

Leave her to the Sassenachs, unprotected?

"Not bloody likely," he muttered under his breath, dropping down into a dark cargo space. She wouldn't be in such a place, of course, but he must think a moment, what to do. Was this the cable tier, the aft cargo hatch, the forward stinking God knew what? Christ, he hated boats!

He drew in a deep breath and stopped, surprised. There were animals here; goats. He could smell them plainly. There was also a light, dimly visible around the edge of a bulkhead, and the murmur of voices. Was one of them a woman's voice?

He edged forward, listening. There were feet on the deck above, a patter and thump that he recognized; bodies dropping from the rigging. Had someone above seen him? Well, and if they had? It was no crime, so far as he knew, for a man to come seeking his wife.

The *Porpoise* was asail; he had felt the thrum of the sails passing through the wood all the way to the keel as she took the wind. They had long since missed the rendezvous with the *Artemis*.

That being so, there was likely nothing to lose by appearing boldly before the Captain and demanding to see Claire. But perhaps she was here—it *was* a woman's voice.

It was a woman's figure, too, silhouetted against the lantern's light, but the woman wasn't Claire. His heart leapt convulsively at the gleam of light on her hair, but then fell at once as he saw the thick, square shape of the woman by the goat pen. There was a man with her; as Jamie watched, the man bent and picked up a basket. He turned and came toward Jamie.

He stepped into the narrow aisle between the bulkheads, blocking the seaman's way.

"Here, what you mean—" the man began, and then, raising his eyes to Jamie's face, stopped, gasping. One eye was fixed on him in horrified recognition; the other showed only as a bluish white crescent beneath the withered lid.

"God preserve us!" the seaman said. "What are *you* doing here?" The seaman's face gleamed pale and jaundiced in the dim light.

"Ye ken me, do ye?" Jamie's heart was hammering against his ribs, but he kept his voice level and low. "I have not the honor to know your own name, I think?"

"I should prefer to leave that particular circumstance unchanged, your honor, if you've no objection." The one-eyed sea-man began to edge backward, but was forestalled as Jamie gripped his arm, hard enough to elicit a small yelp.

"Not quite so fast, if ye please. Where is Mrs. Malcolm, the surgeon?"

It would have been difficult for the seaman to look more alarmed, but at this question, he managed it.

"I don't know!" he said.

"You do," Jamie said sharply. "And ye'll tell me this minute, or I shall break your neck."

"Well, now, I can't be tellin' you anything if you break my neck, can I?" the seaman pointed out, beginning to recover his nerve. He lifted his chin pugnaciously over his basket of manure. "Now, you leave go of me, or I'll call—" The rest was lost in a squawk as a large hand fastened about his neck and began inexora-bly to squeeze. The basket fell to the deck, and balls of goat manure exploded out of it like shrapnel.

"Ak!" Harry Tompkins's legs thrashed wildly, scattering goat dung in every direction. His face turned the color of a beetroot as he clawed ineffectually at Jamie's arm. Judging the results clini-cally, Jamie let go as the man's eye began to bulge. He wiped his hand on his breeches, disliking the greasy feel of the man's sweat on his palm.

Tompkins lay on the deck in a sprawl of limbs, wheezing faintly.

"Ye're quite right," Jamie said. "On the other hand, if I break your arm, I expect you'll still be able to speak to me, aye?" He bent, grasped the man by one skinny arm and jerked him to his feet, twisting the arm roughly behind his back.

"I'll tell you, I'll tell you!" The seaman wriggled madly, pan-icked. "Damn you, you're as wicked cruel as she was!"

"Was? What do you mean, 'was'?" Jamie's heart squeezed tight in his chest, and he jerked the arm, more roughly than he had meant to do. Tompkins let out a screech of pain, and Jamie slack-ened the pressure slightly.

"Let go! I'll tell you, but for pity's sake, let go!" Jamie less-ened his grasp, but didn't let go.

"Tell me where my wife is!" he said, in a tone that had made stronger men than Harry Tompkins fall over their feet to obey.

"She's lost!" the man blurted. "Gone overboard!"

"What!" He was so stunned that he let go his hold. Overboard. Gone overboard. Lost.

"When?" he demanded. "How? Damn you, tell me what happened!" He advanced on the seaman, fists clenched.

The seaman was backing away, rubbing his arm and panting, a look of furtive satisfaction in his one eye.

"Don't worry, your honor," he said, a queer, jeering tone in his voice. "You won't be lonesome long. You'll join her in hell in a few days—dancing from the yardarm over Kingston Harbor!"

Too late, Jamie heard the footfall on the boards behind him. He had no time even to turn his head before the blow fell.

He had been struck in the head frequently enough to know that the sensible thing was to lie still until the giddiness and the lights that pulsed behind your eyelids with each heartbeat stopped. Sit up too soon and the pain made you vomit.

The deck was rising and falling, rising and falling under him, in the horrible way of ships. He kept his eyes tight closed, concentrating on the knotted ache at the base of his skull in order not to think of his stomach.

Ship. He should be on a ship. Yes, but the surface under his cheek was wrong—hard wood, not the linen of his berth's bedding. And the smell, the smell was wrong, it was—

He shot bolt upright, memory shooting through him with a vividness that made the pain in his head pale by comparison. The darkness moved queasily around him, blinking with colored lights, and his stomach heaved. He closed his eyes and swallowed hard, trying to gather his scattered wits about the single appalling thought that had lanced through his brain like a spit through mutton.

Claire. Lost. Drowned. Dead.

He leaned to the side and threw up. He retched and coughed, as though his body were trying forcibly to expel the thought. It didn't work; when he finally stopped, leaning against the bulkhead in exhaustion, it was still with him. It hurt to breathe, and he clenched his fists on his thighs, trembling.

There was the sound of a door opening, and bright light struck him in the eyes with the force of a blow. He winced, closing his eyes against the glare of the lantern.

"Mr. Fraser," a soft, well-bred voice said. "I am—truly sorry. I wish you to know that, at least."

Through a cracked eyelid, he saw the drawn, harried face of young Leonard—the man who had taken Claire. The man wore a look of regret. Regret! Regret, for killing her.

Fury pulled him up against the weakness, and sent him lunging across the slanted deck in an instant. There was an outcry as he hit Leonard and bore him backward into the passage, and a good, juicy *thunk!* as the bugger's head hit the boards. People were shouting, and shadows leapt crazily all round him as the lanterns swayed, but he paid no attention.

He smashed Leonard's jaw with one great blow, his nose with the next. The weakness mattered nothing. He would spend all his strength and die here glad, but let him batter and maim now, feel the bones crack and the blood hot and slick on his fists. Blessed Michael, let him avenge her first!

There were hands on him, snatching and jerking, but they didn't matter. They would kill him now, he thought dimly, and that didn't matter, either. The body under him jerked and twitched between his legs, and lay still.

When the next blow came, he went willingly into the dark.

The light touch of fingers on his face awakened him. He reached drowsily up to take her hand, and his palm touched . . .

"Aaaah!"

With an instinctive revulsion, he was on his feet, clawing at his face. The big spider, nearly as frightened as he was, made off toward the shrubbery at high speed, long hairy legs no more than a blur.

There was an outburst of giggling behind him. He turned round, his heart pounding like a drum, and found six children, roosting in the branches of a big green tree, all grinning down at him with tobacco-stained teeth.

He bowed to them, feeling dizzy and rubber-legged, the start of fright that had got him up now dying in his blood.

"Mesdemoiselles, messieurs," he said, croaking, and in the half-awake recesses of his brain wondered what had made him speak to them in French? Had he half-heard them speaking, as he lay asleep?

French they were, for they answered him in that language, strongly laced with a guttural sort of creole accent that he had never heard before.

"Vous êtes matelot?" the biggest boy asked, eyeing him with interest.

His knees gave way and he sat down on the ground, suddenly enough to make the children laugh again.

"Non," he replied, struggling to make his tongue work. *"Je suis guerrier."* His mouth was dry and his head ached like a fiend. Faint memories swam about in the parritch that filled his head, too vague to grasp.

"A soldier!" exclaimed one of the smaller children. His eyes were round and dark as sloes. "Where is your sword and *pistola,* eh?"

"Don't be silly," an older girl told him loftily. "How could he swim with a *pistola*? It would be ruined. Don't you know any better, guava-head?"

"Don't call me that!" the smaller boy shouted, face contorting in rage. "Shitface!"

"Frog-guts!"

"Caca-brains!"

The children were scrabbling through the branches like monkeys, screaming and chasing each other. Jamie rubbed a hand hard over his face, trying to think.

"Mademoiselle!" He caught the eye of the older girl and beckoned to her. She hesitated for a moment, then dropped from her branch like a ripe fruit, landing on the ground before him in a puff of yellow dust. She was barefoot, wearing nothing but a muslin shift and a colored kerchief round her dark, curly hair.

"Monsieur?"

"You seem a woman of some knowledge, Mademoiselle," he said. "Tell me, please, what is the name of this place?"

"Cap-Haïtien," she replied promptly. She eyed him with considerable curiosity. "You talk funny," she said.

"I am thirsty. Is there water nearby?" Cap-Haïtien. So he was on the island of Hispaniola. His mind was slowly beginning to function again; he had a vague memory of terrible effort, of swimming for his life in a frothing cauldron of heaving waves, and rain pelting his face so hard that it made little difference whether his head was above or below the surface. And what else?

"This way, this way!" The other children had dropped out of the tree, and a little girl was tugging his hand, urging him to follow.

He knelt by the little stream, splashing water over his head, gulping delicious cool handfuls, while the children scampered over the rocks, pelting each other with mud.

Now he remembered—the rat-faced seaman, and Leonard's surprised young face, the deep-red rage and the satisfying feel of flesh crushed against bone under his fist.

And Claire. The memory came back suddenly, with a sense of confused emotion—loss and terror, succeeded by relief. What had happened? He stopped what he was doing, not hearing the questions the children were flinging at him.

"Are you a deserter?" one of the boys asked again. "Have you been in a fight?" The boy's eyes rested curiously on his hands. His knuckles were cut and swollen, and his hands ached badly; the fourth finger felt as though he had cracked it again.

"Yes," he said absently, his mind occupied. Everything was coming back; the dark, stuffy confines of the brig where they had left him to wake, and the dreadful waking, to the thought that Claire was dead. He had huddled there on the bare boards, too shaken with grief to notice at first the increasing heave and roll of the ship, or the high-pitched whine of the rigging, loud enough to filter down even to his oubliette.

But after a time, the motion and noise were great enough to penetrate even the cloud of grief. He had heard the sounds of the growing storm, and the shouts and running overhead, and then was much too occupied to think of anything.

There was nothing in the small room with him, nothing to hold to. He had bounced from wall to wall like a dried pea in a wean's rattle, unable to tell up from down, right from left in the heaving dark, and not much caring, either, as waves of seasickness rolled through his body. He had thought then of nothing but death, and that with a fervor of longing.

He had been nearly unconscious, in fact, when the door to his prison had opened, and a strong smell of goat assailed his nostrils. He had no idea how the woman had got him up the ladder to the afterdeck, or why. He had only a confused memory of her babbling urgently to him in broken English as she pulled him along, half-supporting his weight as he stumbled and slid on the rain-wet decking.

He remembered the last thing she had said, though, as she pushed him toward the tilting taffrail.

"She is not dead," the woman had said. "She go there"—pointing at the rolling sea—"you go, too. Find her!" and then she had bent, got a hand in his crutch and a sturdy shoulder under his rump, and heaved him neatly over the rail and into the churning water.

"You are not an Englishman," the boy was saying. "It's an English ship, though, isn't it?"

He turned automatically, to look where the boy pointed, and saw the *Porpoise,* riding at anchor far out in the shallow bay. Other ships were scattered throughout the harbor, all clearly visible from this vantage point on a hill just outside the town.

"Yes," he said to the boy. "An English ship."

"One for me!" the boy exclaimed happily. He turned to shout to another lad. "Jacques! I was right! English! That's four for me, and only two for you this month!"

"Three!" Jacques corrected indignantly. "I get Spanish *and* Portuguese. *Bruja* was Portuguese, so I can count that, too!"

Jamie reached out and caught the older boy's arm.

"*Pardon,* Monsieur," he said. "Your friend said *Bruja*?"

"Yes, she was in last week," the boy answered. "Is *Bruja* a Portuguese name, though? We weren't sure whether to count it Spanish or Portuguese."

"Some of the sailors were in my *maman*'s taverna," one of the little girls chimed in. "They sounded like they were talking Spanish, but it wasn't like Uncle Geraldo talks."

"I think I should like to talk to your *maman, chérie,*" he said to the little girl. "Do any of you know, perhaps, where this *Bruja* was going when she left?"

"Bridgetown," the oldest girl put in promptly, trying to regain his attention. "I heard the clerk at the garrison say so."

"The garrison?"

"The barracks are next door to my *maman*'s taverna," the smaller girl chimed in, tugging at his sleeve. "The ship captain all go there with their papers, while the sailors get drunk. Come, come! *Maman* will feed you if I tell her to."

"I think your *maman* will throw me out the door," he told her rubbing a hand across the heavy stubble on his chin. "I look like a vagabond." He did. There were stains of blood and vomit on his clothes despite the swim, and he knew by the feel of his face that it was bruised and bloodshot.

"*Maman* has seen much worse than you," the little girl assured him. "Come on!"

He smiled and thanked her, and allowed them to lead him down the hill, staggering slightly, as his land legs had not yet returned. He found it odd but somehow comforting that the children should not be frightened of him, horrible as he no doubt looked.

Was this what the goat-woman had meant? That Claire had swum ashore on this island? He felt a welling of hope that was as refreshing to his heart as the water had been to his parched throat. Claire was stubborn, reckless, and had a great deal more courage than was safe for a woman, but she was by no means such a fool as to fall off a man-of-war by accident.

And the *Bruja*—and Ian—were nearby! He would find them both, then. The fact that he was barefoot, penniless, and a fugitive from the Royal Navy seemed of no consequence. He had his wits and his hands, and with dry land once more beneath his feet, all things seemed possible.

52

A Wedding Takes Place

There was nothing to be done, but to repair the *Artemis* as quickly as possible, and make sail for Jamaica. I did my best to put aside my fear for Jamie, but I scarcely ate for the next two days, my appetite impeded by the large ball of ice that had taken up residence in my stomach.

For distraction, I took Marsali up to the house on the hill, where she succeeded in charming Father Fogden by recalling—and mixing for him—a Scottish receipt for a sheep-dip guaranteed to destroy ticks.

Stern helpfully pitched in with the labor of repair, delegating to me the guardianship of his specimen bag, and charging me with the task of searching the nearby jungle for any curious specimens of *Arachnida* that might come to hand as I looked for medicinal plants. While thinking privately that I would prefer to meet any of the larger specimens of *Arachnida* with a good stout boot, rather than my bare hands, I accepted the charge, peering into the internal water-filled cups of bromeliads in search of the bright-colored frogs and spiders who inhabited these tiny worlds.

I returned from one of these expeditions on the afternoon of the third day, with several large lily-roots, some shelf fungus of a vivid orange, and an unusual moss, together with a live tarantula—carefully trapped in one of the sailor's stocking caps and held at arm's length—large and hairy enough to send Lawrence into paroxysms of delight.

When I emerged from the jungle's edge, I saw that we had reached a new stage of progress; the *Artemis* was no longer canted on her side, but was slowly regaining an upright position on the sand, assisted by ropes, wedges, and a great deal of shouting.

"It's nearly finished, then?" I asked Fergus, who was standing near the stern, doing a good bit of the shouting as he instructed his crew in the placement of wedges. He turned to me, grinning and wiping the sweat from his forehead.

"Yes, milady! The caulking is complete. Mr. Warren gives it as his opinion that we may launch the ship near evening, when the day is grown cool, so the tar is hardened."

"That's marvelous!" I craned my neck back, looking up at the naked mast that towered high above. "Have we got sails?"

"Oh, yes," he assured me. "In fact, we have everything except—"

A shout of alarm from MacLeod interrupted whatever he had been about to say. I whirled to look toward the distant road out of the palmettos, where the sun winked off the glint of metal.

"Soldiers!" Fergus reacted faster than anyone, leaping from the scaffolding to land in a thudding spray of sand beside me. "Quick, milady! To the wood! Marsali!" he shouted, looking wildly about for the girl.

He licked sweat from his upper lip, eyes darting from the jungle to the approaching soldiers. "Marsali!" he shouted, once more.

Marsali appeared round the edge of the hull, pale and startled. Fergus grasped her by the arm and shoved her toward me. "Go with milady! Run!"

I snatched Marsali's hand and ran for the forest, sand spurting beneath our feet. There were shouts from the road behind us, and a shot cracked overhead, followed by another.

Ten steps, five, and then we were in the shadow of the trees. I collapsed behind the shelter of a thorny bush, gasping for breath against the stabbing pain of a stitch in my side. Marsali knelt on the earth beside me, her cheeks streaked with tears.

"What?" she gasped, struggling for breath. "Who are they? What—will they—do? To Fergus. What?"

"I don't know." Still breathing heavily, I grasped a cedar sapling and pulled myself to my knees. Peering through the underbrush on all fours, I could see that the soldiers had reached the ship.

It was cool and damp under the trees, but the lining of my

mouth was dry as cotton. I bit the inside of my cheek, trying to encourage a little saliva to flow.

"I think it will be all right." I patted Marsali's shoulder, trying to be reassuring. "Look, there are only ten of them," I whispered, counting as the last soldier trotted out of the palmetto grove. "They're French; the *Artemis* has French papers. It may be all right."

And then again, it might not. I was well aware that a ship aground and abandoned was legal salvage. It was a deserted beach. And all that stood between these soldiers and a rich prize were the lives of the *Artemis*'s crew.

A few of the seamen had pistols to hand; most had knives. But the soldiers were armed to the teeth, each man with musket, sword, and pistols. If it came to a fight, it would be a bloody one, but the odds were heavily on the mounted soldiers.

The men near the ship were silent, grouped close together behind Fergus, who stood out, straight-backed and grim, as the spokesman. I saw him push back his shock of hair with his hook, and plant his feet solidly in the sand, ready for whatever might come. The creak and jingle of harness seemed muted in the damp, hot air, and the horses moved slowly, hooves muffled in the sand.

The soldiers came to a halt ten feet away from the little knot of seamen. A big man who seemed to be in command raised one hand in an order to stay, and swung down from his horse.

I was watching Fergus, rather than the soldiers. I saw his face change, then freeze, white under his tan. I glanced quickly at the soldier coming toward him across the sand, and my own blood froze.

"*Silence, mes amis,*" said the big man, in a voice of pleasant command. "*Silence, et restez, s'il vous plaît.*" Silence, my friends, and do not move, if you please.

I would have fallen, were I not already on my knees. I closed my eyes in a wordless prayer of thanksgiving.

Next to me, Marsali gasped. I opened my eyes and clapped a hand over her open mouth.

The commander took off his hat, and shook out a thick mass of sweat-soaked auburn hair. He grinned at Fergus, teeth white and wolfish in a short, curly red beard.

"You are in charge here?" Jamie said in French. "You, come with me. The rest"—he nodded at the crew, several of whom were goggling at him in open amazement—"you stay where you are. Don't talk," he added, offhandedly.

Marsali jerked at my arm, and I realized how tightly I had been holding her.

"Sorry," I whispered, letting go, but not taking my eyes from the beach.

"What is he doing?" Marsali hissed in my ear. Her face was pale with excitement, and the little freckles left by the sun stood out on her nose in contrast. "How did he get here?"

"I don't know! Be quiet, for God's sake!"

The crew of the *Artemis* exchanged glances, waggled their eyebrows, and nudged each other in the ribs, but fortunately also obeyed orders and didn't speak. I hoped to heaven that their obvious excitement would be construed merely as consternation over their impending fate.

Jamie and Fergus had walked over toward the shore, conferring in low voices. Now they separated, Fergus coming back toward the hull with an expression of grim determination, Jamie calling the soldiers to dismount and gather round him.

I couldn't tell what Jamie was saying to the soldiers, but Fergus was close enough for us to hear.

"These are soldiers from the garrison at Cap-Haïtien," he announced to the crew members. "Their commander—Captain Alessandro—" he said, lifting his eyebrows and grimacing hideously to emphasize the name, "says that they will assist us in launching the *Artemis.*" This announcement was greeted with faint cheers from some of the men, and looks of bewilderment from others.

"But how did Mr. Fraser—" began Royce, a rather slow-witted seaman, his heavy brows drawn together in a puzzled frown. Fergus allowed no time for questions, but plunged into the midst of the crew, putting an arm about Royce's shoulders and dragging him toward the scaffolding, talking loudly to drown out any untoward remarks.

"Yes, is it not a most fortunate accident?" he said loudly. I could see that he was twisting Royce's ear with his sound hand. "Most fortunate indeed! Captain Alessandro says that a *habitant* on his way from his plantation saw the ship aground, and reported it to the garrison. With so much help, we will have the *Artemis* aswim in no time at all.'' He let go of Royce and clapped his hand sharply against his thigh.

"Come, come, let us set to work at once! Manzetti—up you go! MacLeod, MacGregor, seize your hammers! Maitland—'' He spotted Maitland, standing on the sand gawking at Jamie. Fergus whirled and clapped the cabin boy on the back hard enough to make him stagger.

"Maitland, *mon enfant!* Give us a song to speed our efforts!'' Looking rather dazed, Maitland began a tentative rendition of "The Nut-Brown Maid.'' A few of the seamen began to climb back onto the scaffolding, glancing suspiciously over their shoulders.

"Sing!'' Fergus bellowed, glaring up at them. Murphy, who appeared to be finding something extremely funny, mopped his sweating red face and obligingly joined in the song, his wheezing bass reinforcing Maitland's pure tenor.

Fergus stalked up and down beside the hull, exhorting, directing, urging—and making such a spectacle of himself that few telltale glances went in Jamie's direction. The uncertain tap of hammers started up again.

Meanwhile, Jamie was giving careful directions to his soldiers. I saw more than one Frenchman glance at the *Artemis* as he talked, with a look of dimly concealed greed that suggested that a selfless desire to help their fellow beings was perhaps not the motive uppermost in the soldiers' minds, no matter what Fergus had announced.

Still, the soldiers went to work willingly enough, stripping off their leather jerkins and laying aside most of their arms. Three of the soldiers, I noticed, did not join the work party, but remained on guard, fully armed, eyes sharp on the sailors' every move. Jamie alone remained aloof, watching everything.

"Should we come out?'' Marsali murmured in my ear. "It seems safe, now.''

"No,'' I said. My eyes were fixed on Jamie. He stood in the shade of a tall palmetto, at ease, but erect. Behind the unfamiliar beard, his expression was unreadable, but I caught the faint movement at his side, as the two stiff fingers flickered once against his thigh.

"No,'' I said again. "It isn't over yet.''

The work went on through the afternoon. The stack of wooden ɔllers mounted, cut ends scenting the air with the tang of fresh ap. Fergus's voice was hoarse, and his shirt clung wetly to his :an torso. The horses, hobbled, wandered slowly under the edge f the forest, browsing. The sailors had given up singing now, and ad settled to work, with no more than an occasional glance ɔward the palmetto where Captain Alessandro stood in the shade, rms folded.

The sentry near the trees paced slowly up and down, musket arried at the ready, a wistful eye on the cool green shadows. He assed close enough on one circuit for me to see the dark, greasy urls dangling down his neck, and the pockmarks on his plump heeks. He creaked and jingled as he walked. The rowel was iissing from one of his spurs. He looked hot, and fairly cross.

It was a long wait, and the inquisitiveness of the forest midges 1ade it longer still. After what seemed forever, though, I saw imie give a nod to one of the guards, and come from the beach ɔward the trees. I signed to Marsali to wait, and ducking under ranches, ignoring the thick brush, I dodged madly toward the lace where he had disappeared.

I popped breathlessly out from behind a bush, just as he was ɔing up the laces of his flies. His head jerked up at the sound, his 'es widened, and he let out a yell that would have summoned rabella the sheep back from the dead, let alone the waiting sen-y.

I dodged back into hiding, as crashing boots and shouts of quiry headed in our direction.

"*C'est bien!*" Jamie shouted. He sounded a trifle shaken. "*Ce 'est qu'un serpent!*"

The sentry spoke an odd dialect of French, but appeared to be king rather nervously whether the serpent was dangerous.

"*Non, c'est innocent,*" Jamie answered. He waved at the sen-y, whose inquiring head I could just see, peering reluctantly over e bush. The sentry, who seemed unenthusiastic about snakes, ɔwever innocent, disappeared promptly back to his duty.

Without hesitation, Jamie plunged into the bush.

"Claire!" He crushed me tight against his chest. Then he abbed me by the shoulders and shook me, hard.

"Damn you!" he said, in a piercing whisper. "I thought y
were dead for sure! How dare ye do something harebrained lik
jump off a ship in the middle of the night! Have ye no sense a
all?"

"Let go!" I demanded. The shaking had made me bite my lip
"Let go, I say! What do you mean, how dare *I* do somethin
harebrained? You idiot, what possessed you to follow me?"

His face was darkened by the sun; now a deep red began t
darken it further, washing up from the edges of his new beard.

"What possessed me?" he repeated. "You're my wife, for th
Lord's sake! Of course I would follow ye; why did ye not wait fe
me? Christ, if I had time, I'd—" The mention of time evidentl
reminded him that we hadn't much, and with a noticeable effor
he choked back any further remarks, which was just as well, be
cause I had a number of things to say in that vein myself.
swallowed them, with some difficulty.

"What in bloody hell are you doing here?" I asked instead.

The deep flush subsided slightly, succeeded by the merest hir
of a smile amid the unfamiliar foliage.

"I'm the Captain," he said. "Did ye not notice?"

"Yes, I noticed! Captain Alessandro, my foot! What do yo
mean to do?"

Instead of answering, he gave me a final, gentle shake an
divided a glare between me and Marsali, who had poked an inqui
ing head out.

"Stay here, the both of ye, and dinna stir a foot or I swear I'
beat ye senseless."

Without pausing for a response, he whirled and strode bac
through the trees, toward the beach.

Marsali and I exchanged stares, which were interrupted a sec
ond later, when Jamie, breathless, hurtled back into the sma
clearing. He grabbed me by both arms, and kissed me briefly bi
thoroughly.

"I forgot. I love you," he said, giving me another shake fe
emphasis. "And I'm glad you're no dead. Dinna do that again!
Letting go, he crashed back into the brush and disappeared.

I felt breathless, myself, and more than a little rattled, but und
niably happy.

Marsali's eyes were round as saucers.

"What shall we do?" she asked. "What's Da going to do?"

"I don't know," I said. My cheeks were flushed, and I could till feel the touch of his mouth on mine, and the unfamiliar ngling left by the brush of beard and mustache. My tongue uched the small stinging place where I had bitten my lip. "I on't know what he's going to do," I repeated. "I suppose we'll ave to wait and see."

It was a long wait. I was dozing against the trunk of a huge tree, ear dusk, when Marsali's hand on my shoulder brought me wake.

"They're launching the ship!" she said in an excited whisper.

They were; under the eyes of the sentries, the remaining soldiers nd the crew of the *Artemis* were all manning the ropes and rollers at would move her down the beach into the waters of the inlet. ven Fergus, Innes, and Murphy joined in the labor, missing limbs otwithstanding.

The sun was going down; its disc shone huge and orange-gold, inding above a sea gone the purple of whelks. The men were no ore than black silhouettes against the light, anonymous as the aves of an Egyptian wall-painting, tethered by ropes to their assive burden.

The monotonous "Heave!" of the bosun's shout was succeeded a weak cheer as the hull slid the last few feet, drawn away from e shore by towropes from the *Artemis*'s jolly boat and cutter.

I saw the flash of red hair as Jamie moved up the side and vung aboard, then the gleam of metal as one of the soldiers llowed him. They stood guard together, red hair and black no ore than dots at the head of the rope ladder, as the crew of the *rtemis* entered the jolly boat, rowed out and came up the ladder, terspersed with the rest of the French soldiers.

The last man disappeared up the ladder. The men in the boats t on their oars, looking up, tense and alert. Nothing happened. Next to me, I heard Marsali exhale noisily, and realized I had en holding my own breath much too long.

"What are they *doing*?" she said, in exasperation.

As though in answer to this, there was one loud, angry shout om the *Artemis*. The men in the boats jerked up, ready to lunge oard. No other signal came, though. The *Artemis* floated se- nely on the rising waters of the inlet, perfect as an oil painting.

"I've had enough," I said suddenly to Marsali. "Whatever ose bloody men are doing, they've done it. Come on."

I drew in a fresh gulp of the cool evening air, and walked out of the trees, Marsali behind me. As we came down the beach, a slim black figure dropped over the ship's side and galloped through the shallows, gleaming gouts of green and purple seawater spouting from his footsteps.

"Mo chridhe chérie!" Fergus ran dripping toward us, face beaming, and seizing Marsali, swung her off her feet with exuberance and whirled her round.

"Done!" he crowed. "Done without a shot fired! Trussed like geese and packed like salted herrings in the hold!" He kissed Marsali heartily, then set her down on the sand, and turning to me bowed ceremoniously, with the elaborate flourish of an imaginary hat.

"Milady, the captain of the *Artemis* desires you will honor him with your company over supper."

The new captain of the *Artemis* was standing in the middle of his cabin, eyes closed and completely naked, blissfully scratching his testicles.

"Er," I said, confronted with this sight. His eyes popped open and his face lit with joy. The next moment, I was enfolded in his embrace, face pressed against the red-gold curls of his chest.

We didn't say anything for quite some time. I could hear the thrum of footsteps on the deck overhead, the shouts of the crew ringing with joy at the imminence of escape, and the creak and flap of sails being rigged. The *Artemis* was coming back to life around us.

My face was warm, tingling from the rasp of his beard. I felt suddenly strange and shy holding him, he naked as a jay and myself as bare under the remnants of Father Fogden's tattered robe.

The body that pressed against my own with mounting urgency was the same from the neck down, but the face was a stranger's, a Viking marauder's. Besides the beard that transformed his face, he smelled unfamiliar, his own sweat overlaid with rancid cooking oil, spilled beer, and the reek of harsh perfume and unfamiliar spices.

I let go, and took a step back.

"Shouldn't you dress?" I asked. "Not that I don't enjoy the

enery,'' I added, blushing despite myself. ''I—er . . . I think I
ke the beard. Maybe,'' I added doubtfully, scrutinizing him.

''I don't,'' he said frankly, scratching his jaw. ''I'm crawling
i' lice, and it itches like a fiend.''

''Eew!'' While I was entirely familiar with *Pediculus humanus,*
e common body louse, acquaintance had not endeared me. I
bbed a hand nervously through my own hair, already imagining
e prickle of feet on my scalp, as tiny sestets gamboled through
e thickets of my curls.

He grinned at me, white teeth startling in the auburn beard.

''Dinna fash yourself, Sassenach,'' he assured me. ''I've al-
ady sent for a razor and hot water.''

''Really? It seems rather a pity to shave it off right away.''
espite the lice, I leaned forward to peer at his hirsute adornment.
t's like your hair, all different colors. Rather pretty, really.''

I touched it, warily. The hairs were odd; thick and wiry, very
rly, in contrast to the soft thick smoothness of the hair on his
ad. They sprang exuberantly from his skin in a profusion of
lors; copper, gold, amber, cinnamon, a roan so deep as almost to
black. Most startling of all was a thick streak of silver that ran
om his lower lip to the line of his jaw.

''That's funny,'' I said, tracing it. ''You haven't any white hairs
your head, but you have right here.''

''I have?'' He put a hand to his jaw, looking startled, and I
ddenly realized that he likely had no idea what he looked like.
en he smiled wryly, and bent to pick up the pile of discarded
othes from the floor.

''Aye, well, little wonder if I have; I wonder I've not gone
ite-haired altogether from the things I've been through this
onth.'' He paused, eyeing me over the wadded white breeches.

''And speaking of that, Sassenach, as I was saying to ye in the
es—''

''Yes, speaking of that,'' I interrupted. ''What in the name of
d did you *do*?''

''Oh, the soldiers, ye mean?'' He scratched his chin medita-
ely. ''Well, it was simple enough. I told the soldiers that as soon
the ship was launched, we'd gather everyone on deck, and at my
nal, they were to fall on the crew and push them into the hold.''
broad grin blossomed through the foliage. ''Only Fergus had
entioned it to the crew, ye see; so when each soldier came

aboard, two of the crewmen snatched him by the arms while third gagged him, bound his arms, and took away his weapon Then we pushed all of *them* into the hold. That's all.'' H shrugged, modestly nonchalant.

''Right,'' I said, exhaling. ''And as for just how you happene to be here in the first place . . .''

At this juncture we were interrupted by a discreet knock on th cabin's door.

''Mr. Fraser? Er . . . Captain, I mean?'' Maitland's angul; young face peered round the jamb, cautious over a steaming bow ''Mr. Murphy's got the galley fire going, and here's your h water, with his compliments.''

''Mr. Fraser will do,'' Jamie assured him, taking the tray wi bowl and razor in one hand. ''A less seaworthy captain does bear thinking of.'' He paused, listening to the thump of feet abo our heads.

''Though since I *am* the captain,'' he said slowly, ''I suppo that means I shall say when we sail and when we stop?''

''Yes, sir, that's one thing a captain does,'' Maitland said. I added helpfully, ''The captain also says when the hands are have extra rations of food and grog.''

''I see.'' The upward curl of Jamie's mouth was still visibl beard notwithstanding. ''Tell me, Maitland—how much d'ye thi the hands can drink and still sail the ship?''

''Oh, quite a lot, sir,'' Maitland said earnestly. His brow wri kled in thought. ''Maybe—an extra double ration all round?''

Jamie lifted one eyebrow. ''Of brandy?''

''Oh, no, sir!'' Maitland looked shocked. ''Grog. If it was to brandy, only an extra half-ration, or they'd be rolling in t bilges.''

''Double grog, then.'' Jamie bowed ceremoniously to Maitlar unhampered by the fact that he was still completely uncl; ''Make it so, Mr. Maitland. And the ship will not lift anchor unti have finished my supper.''

''Yes, sir!'' Maitland bowed back; Jamie's manners were catc ing. ''And shall I desire the Chinee to attend you directly after anchor is weighed?''

''Somewhat before that, Mr. Maitland, thank ye kindly.''

Maitland was turning to leave, with a last admiring glance Jamie's scars, but I stopped him.

"One more thing, Maitland," I said.

"Oh, yes, mum?"

"Will you go down to the galley and ask Mr. Murphy to send p a bottle of his strongest vinegar? And then find where the men ave put some of my medicines, and fetch them as well?"

His narrow forehead creased in puzzlement, but he nodded bligingly. "Oh, yes, mum. This direct minute."

"Just what d'ye mean to do wi' the vinegar Sassenach?" Jamie bserved me narrowly, as Maitland vanished into the corridor.

"Souse you in it to kill the lice," I said. "I don't intend to sleep ith a seething nest of vermin."

"Oh," he said. He scratched the side of his neck meditatively. Ye mean to sleep with me, do you?" He glanced at the berth, an inviting hole in the wall.

"I don't know where, precisely, but yes, I do," I said firmly. And I wish you wouldn't shave your beard just yet," I added, as : bent to set down the tray he was holding.

"Why not?" He glanced curiously over his shoulder at me, and felt the heat rising in my cheeks.

"Er . . . well. It's a bit . . . different."

"Oh, aye?" He stood up and took a step toward me. In the amped confines of the cabin, he seemed even bigger—and a lot ore naked—than he ever had on deck.

The dark blue eyes had slanted into triangles of amusement. "How, different?" he asked.

"Well, it . . . um . . ." I brushed my fingers vaguely past my rning cheeks. "It feels different. When you kiss me. On my . . skin."

His eyes locked on mine. He hadn't moved, but he seemed uch closer.

"Ye have verra fine skin, Sassenach," he said softly. "Like arls and opals." He reached out a finger and very gently traced ε line of my jaw. And then my neck, and the wide flare of llarbone and back, and down, in a slow-moving serpentine that ushed the tops of my breasts, hidden in the deep cowl neck of : priest's robe. "Ye have a *lot* of verra fine skin, Sassenach," he ded. One eyebrow quirked up. "If that's what ye were think-?"

I swallowed and licked my lips, but didn't look away.

"That's more or less what I was thinking, yes."

He took his finger away and glanced at the bowl of steami̲
water.

"Aye, well. It seems a shame to waste the water. Shall I send
back to Murphy to make soup, or shall I drink it?"

I laughed, both tension and strangeness dissolving at once.

"You shall sit down," I said, "and wash with it. You smell li̲
a brothel."

"I expect I do," he said, scratching. "There's one upstairs
the tavern where the soldiers go to drink and gamble." He took ̲
the soap and dropped it in the hot water.

"Upstairs, eh?" I said.

"Well, the girls come down, betweentimes," he explained. "̲
wouldna be mannerly to stop them sitting on your lap, after all̲

"And your mother brought you up to have nice manners,̲
expect," I said, very dryly.

"Upon second thoughts, I think perhaps we shall anchor he̲
for the night," he said thoughtfully, looking at me.

"Shall we?"

"And sleep ashore, where there's room."

"Room for *what*?" I asked, regarding him with suspicion.

"Well, I have it planned, aye?" he said, sloshing water over ̲
face with both hands.

"You have *what* planned?" I asked. He snorted and shook t̲
excess water from his beard before replying.

"I have been thinking of this for months, now," he said, wi̲
keen anticipation. "Every night, folded up in that godforsak̲
nutshell of a berth, listening to Fergus grunt and fart across t̲
cabin. I thought it all out, just what I would do, did I have ye nak̲
and willing, no one in hearing, and room enough to serve̲
suitably." He lathered the cake of soap vigorously between ̲
palms, and applied it to his face.

"Well, I'm willing enough," I said, intrigued. "And ther̲
room, certainly. As for naked . . ."

"I'll see to that," he assured me. "That's part o' the plan, ay̲
I shall take ye to a private spot, spread out a quilt to lie on, a̲
commence by sitting down beside you."

"Well, that's a start, all right," I said. "What then?" I sat do̲
next to him on the berth. He leaned close and bit my earlobe ve̲
delicately.

"As for what next, then I shall take ye on my knee and kiss ye̲

e paused to illustrate, holding my arms so I couldn't move. He
t go a minute later, leaving my lips slightly swollen, tasting of
e, soap, and Jamie.

"So much for step one," I said, wiping soapsuds from my
outh. "What then?"

"Then I shall lay ye down upon the quilt, twist your hair up in
y hand and taste your face and throat and ears and bosom wi' my
s," he said. "I thought I would do that until ye start to make
ueaking noises."

"I don't make squeaking noises!"

"Aye, ye do," he said. "Here, hand me the towel, aye?"

"Then," he went on cheerfully, "I thought I would begin at the
her end. I shall lift up your skirt and—" His face disappeared
to the folds of the linen towel.

"And what?" I asked, thoroughly intrigued.

"And kiss the insides of your thighs, where the skin's so soft.
e beard might help there, aye?" He stroked his jaw, consider-
g.

"It might," I said, a little faintly. "What am I supposed to be
ing while you do this?"

"Well, ye might moan a bit, if ye like, to encourage me, but
herwise, ye just lie still."

He didn't sound as though he needed any encouragement what-
er. One of his hands was resting on my thigh as he used the
her to swab his chest with the damp towel. As he finished, the
nd slid behind me, and squeezed.

"My beloved's arm is under me," I quoted. "And his hand
hind my head. Comfort me with apples, and stay me with flag-
s, For I am sick of love."

There was a flash of white teeth in his beard.

"More like grapefruit," he said, one hand cupping my behind.
)r possibly gourds. Grapefruit are too small."

"Gourds?" I said indignantly.

"Well, wild gourds get that big sometimes," he said. "But aye,
t's next." He squeezed once more, then removed the hand in
ler to wash the armpit on that side. "I lie upon my back and
ve ye stretched at length upon me, so that I can get hold of your
ttocks and fondle them properly." He stopped washing to give
 a quick example of what he thought proper, and I let out an
oluntary gasp.

"Now," he went on, resuming his ablutions, "should ye wis
to kick your legs a bit, or make lewd motions wi' your hips an
pant in my ear at that point in the proceedings, I should have n
great objection."

"I do not pant!"

"Aye, ye do. Now, about your breasts—"

"Oh, I thought you'd forgotten those."

"Never in life," he assured me. "No," he went blithely or
"that's when I take off your gown, leaving ye in naught but you
shift."

"I'm not wearing a shift."

"Oh? Well, no matter," he said, dismissing this. "I meant t
suckle ye through the thin cotton, 'til your nipples stood up hard i
my mouth, and then take it off, but it's no great concern; I'
manage without. So, allowing for the absence of your shift, I sha
attend to your breasts until ye make that wee bleating noise—"

"I don't—"

"And then," he said, interrupting, "since ye will, according t
the plan, be naked, and—provided I've done it right so far—
possibly willing as well—"

"Oh, just possibly," I said. My lips were still tingling from ste
one.

"—then I shall spread open your thighs, take down my breek
and—" He paused, waiting.

"And?" I said, obligingly.

The grin widened substantially.

"And we'll see what sort of noise it is ye don't make the
Sassenach."

There was a slight cough in the doorway behind me.

"Oh, your pardon, Mr. Willoughby," Jamie said apologeticall
"I wasna expecting ye so soon. Perhaps ye'd care to go and have
bit of supper? And if ye would, take those things along and as
Murphy will he burn them in the galley fire." He tossed th
remains of his uniform to Mr. Willoughby, and bent to rumma
in a sealocker for fresh clothing.

"I never thought to meet Lawrence Stern again," he remarke
burrowing through the tangled linen. "How does he come to l
here?"

"Oh, he *is* the Jewish natural philosopher you told me about?

"He is. Though I shouldna think there are so many Jewish philosophers about as to cause great confusion."

I explained how I had come to meet Stern in the mangroves. . . . and then he brought me up to the priest's house," I said, d stopped, suddenly reminded. "Oh, I almost forgot! You owe e priest two pounds sterling, on account of Arabella."

"I do?" Jamie glanced at me, startled, a shirt in his hand.

"You do. Maybe you'd best ask Lawrence if he'll act as ambas-dor; the priest seems to get on with him."

"All right. What's happened to this Arabella, though? Has one f the crew debauched her?"

"I suppose you might say that." I drew breath to explain fur-er, but before I could speak, another knock sounded on the door.

"Can a man not dress in peace?" Jamie demanded irritably. Come, then!"

The door swung open, revealing Marsali, who blinked at the ght of her nude stepfather. Jamie hastily swathed his midsection the shirt he was holding, and nodded to her, sangfroid only ightly impaired.

"Marsali, lass. I'm glad to see ye unhurt. Did ye require some-ing?"

The girl edged into the room, taking up a position between the ble and a sea chest.

"Aye, I do," she said. She was sunburned, and her nose was eeling, but I thought she seemed pale nonetheless. Her fists were enched at her sides, and her chin lifted as for battle.

"I require ye to keep your promise," she said.

"Aye?" Jamie looked wary.

"Your promise to let me and Fergus be married, so soon as we me to the Indies." A small wrinkle appeared between her fair ebrows. "Hispaniola *is* in the Indies, no? The Jew said so."

Jamie scratched at his beard, looking reluctant.

"It is," he said. "And aye, I suppose if I . . . well, aye. I did omise. But—you're still sure of yourselves, the two of ye?" She ted her chin higher, jaw set firmly.

"We are."

Jamie lifted one eyebrow.

"Where's Fergus?"

"Helping stow the cargo. I kent we'd be under way soon, so I ought I'd best come and ask now."

"Aye. Well." Jamie frowned, then sighed with resignatior "Aye, I said. But I did say as ye must be blessed by a priest, did no? There's no priest closer than Bayamo, and that's three days ride. But perhaps in Jamaica . . ."

"Nay, you're forgetting!" Marsali said triumphantly. "We've priest right here. Father Fogden can marry us."

I felt my jaw drop, and hastily closed it. Jamie was scowling her.

"We sail first thing in the morning!"

"It won't take long," she said. "It's only a few words, after al We're already married, by law; it's only to be blessed by th Church, aye?" Her hand flattened on her abdomen where h marriage contract presumably resided beneath her stays.

"But your mother . . ." Jamie glanced helplessly at me f reinforcement. I shrugged, equally helpless. The task of tryir either to explain Father Fogden to Jamie or to dissuade Marsa was well beyond me.

"He likely won't do it, though." Jamie came up with th objection with a palpable air of relief. "The crew have been tr fling with one of his parishioners named Arabella. He willna wa anything to do wi' us, I'm afraid."

"Yes, he will! He'll do it for me—he likes me!" Marsali w almost dancing on her toes with eagerness.

Jamie looked at her for a long moment, eyes fixed on her reading her face. She was very young.

"You're sure, then, lassie?" he said at last, very gently. "Y want this?"

She took a deep breath, a glow spreading over her face.

"I am, Da. I truly am. I want Fergus! I love him!"

Jamie hesitated a moment, then rubbed a hand through his ha and nodded.

"Aye, then. Go and send Mr. Stern to me, then fetch Fergus a tell him to make ready."

"Oh, Da! Thank you, thank you!" Marsali flung herself at hi and kissed him. He held her with one arm, clutching the sh about his middle with the other. Then he kissed her on the for head and pushed her gently away.

"Take care," he said, smiling. "Ye dinna want to go to yo bridal covered wi' lice."

"Oh!" This seemed to remind her of something. She glanced

e and blushed, putting up a hand to her own pale locks, which
ere matted with sweat and straggling down her neck from a
areless knot.

"Mother Claire," she said shyly, "I wonder—would ye—could
₂ lend me a bit of the special soap ye make wi' the chamomile? I
-if there's time—" she added, with a hasty glance at Jamie, "I
ould like to wash my hair."

"Of course," I said, and smiled at her. "Come along and we'll
ake you pretty for your wedding." I looked her over apprais-
gly, from glowing round face to dirty bare feet. The crumpled
uslin of her sea-shrunk gown stretched tight over her bosom,
ight as it was, and the grubby hem hovered several inches above
ₑr sandy ankles.

A thought struck me, and I turned to Jamie. "She should have a
ₑce dress to be married in," I said.

"Sassenach," he said, with obviously waning patience, "we
avena—"

"No, but the priest does," I interrupted. "Tell Lawrence to ask
ather Fogden whether we might borrow one of his gowns;
ₑrmenegilda's, I mean. I think they're almost the right size."

Jamie's face went blank with surprise above his beard.

"Ermenegilda?" he said. "Arabella? Gowns?" He narrowed
ₛ eyes at me. "What sort of priest *is* this man, Sassenach?"

I paused in the doorway, Marsali hovering impatiently in the
assage beyond.

"Well," I said, "he drinks a bit. And he's rather fond of sheep.
ₐt he might remember the words to the wedding ceremony."

It was one of the more unusual weddings I had attended. The
ₙ had long since sunk into the sea by the time all arrangements
ₑre made. To the disgruntlement of Mr. Warren, the ship's mas-
ₑr, Jamie had declared that we would not leave until the next day,
 as to allow the newlyweds one night of privacy ashore.

"Damned if I'd care to consummate a marriage in one of those
ₒdforsaken pesthole berths," he told me privately. "If they got
ₒupled in there to start wi', we'd never pry them out. And the
ought of takin' a maidenhead in a hammock—"

"Quite," I said. I poured more vinegar on his head, smiling to
yself. "Very thoughtful of you."

Now Jamie stood by me on the beach, smelling rather strongl
of vinegar, but handsome and dignified in blue coat, clean stoc
and linen, and gray serge breeks, with his hair clubbed back an
ribboned. The wild red beard was a bit incongruous above h
otherwise sober garb, but it had been neatly trimmed and fine
combed with vinegar, and stocking feet notwithstanding, he mad
a fine picture as father of the bride.

Murphy, as one chief witness, and Maitland, as the other, wei
somewhat less prepossessing, though Murphy had washed h
hands and Maitland his face. Fergus would have preferred Law
rence Stern as a witness, and Marsali had asked for me, but bo
were dissuaded; first on grounds that Stern was not a Christian, l
alone a Catholic, and then, by consideration that while I wa
religiously qualified, that fact was unlikely to weigh heavily wi
Laoghaire, once she found out about it.

"I've told Marsali she must write to her mother to say she
wed," Jamie murmured to me as we watched the preparations c
the beach go forward. "But perhaps I shall suggest she doesna sa
much more about it than that."

I saw his point; Laoghaire was not going to be pleased at hea
ing that her eldest daughter had eloped with a one-handed e
pickpocket twice her age. Her maternal feelings were unlikely
be assuaged by hearing that the marriage had been performed
the middle of the night on a West Indian beach by a disgraced—
not actually defrocked—priest, witnessed by twenty-five seame
ten French horses, a small flock of sheep—all gaily beribboned
honor of the occasion—and a King Charles spaniel, who added
the generally festive feeling by attempting to copulate with Mu
phy's wooden leg at every opportunity. The only thing that cou
make things worse, in Laoghaire's view, would be to hear that
had participated in the ceremony.

Several torches were lit, bound to stakes pounded into the san
and the flames streamed seaward in tails of red and orange, brig
against the black velvet night. The brilliant stars of the Caribbe
shone overhead like the lights of heaven. While it was not
church, few brides had had a more beautiful setting for their nu
tials.

I didn't know what prodigies of persuasion had been requir
on Lawrence's part, but Father Fogden was there, frail and insu
stantial as a ghost, the blue sparks of his eyes the only real signs

fe. His skin was gray as his robe, and his hands trembled on the
orn leather of his prayer book.

Jamie glanced sharply at him, and appeared to be about to say
mething, but then merely muttered under his breath in Gaelic
d pressed his lips tightly together. The spicy scent of sangria
afted from Father Fogden's vicinity, but at least he had reached
e beach under his own power. He stood swaying between two
rches, laboriously trying to turn the pages of his book as the
ght offshore wind jerked them fluttering from his fingers.

At last he gave up, and dropped the book on the sand with a
tle *plop*!

"Um," he said, and belched. He looked about and gave us a
all, saintlike smile. "Dearly beloved of God."

It was several moments before the throng of shuffling, murmur-
g spectators realized that the ceremony had started, and began to
ke each other and straighten to attention.

"Wilt thou take this woman?" Father Fogden demanded, sud-
nly rounding ferociously on Murphy.

"No!" said the cook, startled. "I don't hold wi' women. Messy
ings."

"You don't?" Father Fogden closed one eye, the remaining orb
ght and accusing. He looked at Maitland.

"Do *you* take this woman?"

"Not me, sir, no. Not that anyone wouldn't be pleased," he
ded hastily. "Him, please." Maitland pointed at Fergus, who
od next to the cabin boy, glowering at the priest.

"Him? You're sure? He hasn't a hand," Father Fogden said
ubtfully. "Won't she mind?"

"I will not!" Marsali, imperious in one of Ermenegilda's
wns, blue silk encrusted with gold embroidery along the low,
uare neckline and puffed sleeves, stood beside Fergus. She
oked lovely, with her hair clean and bright as fresh straw,
ushed to a gloss and floating loose round her shoulders, as
came a maiden. She also looked angry.

"Go on!" She stamped her foot, which made no noise on the
id, but seemed to startle the priest.

"Oh, yes," he said nervously, taking one step back. "Well, I
n't suppose it's an impt—impeddy—impediment, after all. Not
though he'd lost his cock, I mean. He hasn't, has he?" the

priest inquired anxiously, as the possibility occurred to him. '
can't marry you if he has. It's not allowed.''

Marsali's face was already bathed in red by torchlight. Th
expression on it at this point reminded me strongly of how h
mother had looked upon finding me at Lallybroch. A visibl
tremor ran through Fergus's shoulders, whether of rage or laugh
ter, I couldn't tell.

Jamie quelled the incipient riot by striding firmly into the mid
dle of the wedding and placing a hand on the shoulders of Fergu
and Marsali.

"This man," he said, with a nod toward Fergus, "and th
woman," with another toward Marsali. "Marry them, Fathe
Now. Please," he added, as an obvious afterthought, and stoo
back a pace, restoring order among the audience by dint of dar
glances from side to side.

"Oh, quite. Quite," Father Fogden repeated, swaying gentl
"Quite, quite." A long pause followed, during which the prie
squinted at Marsali.

"Name," he said abruptly. "I have to have a name. Can't g
married without a name. Just like a cock. Can't get married wit
out a name; can't get married without a c—"

"Marsali Jane MacKimmie Joyce!" Marsali spoke up loudl
drowning him out.

"Yes, yes," he said hurriedly. "Of course it is. Marsali. Ma
sa-lee. Just so. Well, then, do you Mar-sa-lee take this man—ev
though he's missing a hand and possibly other parts not visible
to be your lawful husband? To have and to hold, from this d
forward, forsaking . . ." At this point he trailed off, his attenti
fixed on one of the sheep that had wandered into the light and w
chewing industriously on a discarded stocking of striped wool.

"I do!"

Father Fogden blinked, brought back to attention. He made
unsuccessful attempt to stifle another belch, and transferred h
bright blue gaze to Fergus.

"You have a name, too? *And* a cock?"

"Yes," said Fergus, wisely choosing not to be more specifi
"Fergus."

The priest frowned slightly at this. "Fergus?" he said. "Ferg
Fergus. Yes, Fergus, got that. That's all? No more name? Ne
more names, surely."

"Fergus," Fergus repeated, with a note of strain in his voice. Fergus was the only name he had ever had—bar his original French name of Claudel. Jamie had given him the name Fergus in Paris, when they had met, twenty years before. But naturally a brothel-born bastard would have no last name to give a wife.

"Fraser," said a deep, sure voice beside me. Fergus and Marsali both glanced back in surprise, and Jamie nodded. His eyes met Fergus's, and he smiled faintly.

"Fergus Claudel Fraser," he said, slowly and clearly. One eyebrow lifted as he looked at Fergus.

Fergus himself looked transfixed. His mouth hung open, eyes wide black pools in the dim light. Then he nodded slightly, and a glow rose in his face, as though he contained a candle that had just been lit.

"Fraser," he said to the priest. His voice was husky, and he cleared his throat. "Fergus Claudel Fraser."

Father Fogden had his head tilted back, watching the sky, where a crescent of light floated over the trees, holding the black orb of the moon in its cup. He lowered his head to face Fergus, looking dreamy.

"Well, that's good," he said. "Isn't it?"

A small poke in the ribs from Maitland brought him back to an awareness of his responsibilities.

"Oh! Um. Well. Man and wife. Yes, I pronounce you man—no, that's not right, you haven't said whether you'd take her. She has both hands," he added helpfully.

"I will," Fergus said. He had been holding Marsali's hand; now he let go and dug hastily in his pocket, coming out with a small gold ring. He must have bought it in Scotland, I realized, and kept ever since, not wanting to make the marriage official until it had been blessed. Not by a priest—by Jamie.

The beach was silent as he slid the ring on her finger, all eyes fixed on the small gold circle and the two heads bent close together over it, one bright, one dark.

So she had done it. One fifteen-year-old girl, with nothing but stubbornness as a weapon. "I want him," she had said. And kept saying it, through her mother's objections and Jamie's arguments, through Fergus's scruples and her own fears, through three thousand miles of homesickness, hardship, ocean storm, and shipwreck.

She raised her face, shining, and found her mirror in Fergus eyes. I saw them look at each other, and felt the tears prickl behind my lids.

"I want him." I had not said that to Jamie at our marriage; had not wanted him, then. But I had said it since, three times; two moments of choice at Craigh na Dun, and once again Lallybroch.

"I want him." I wanted him still, and nothing whatever cou stand between us.

He was looking down at me; I could feel the weight of his gaz dark blue and tender as the sea at dawn.

"What are ye thinking, *mo chridhe*?" he asked softly.

I blinked back the tears and smiled at him. His hands were larg and warm on mine.

"What I tell you three times is true," I said. And standing tiptoe, I kissed him as the sailors' cheer went up.

PART NINE

Worlds Unknown

53

Bat Guano

Bat guano is a slimy blackish green when fresh, a powdery light brown when dried. In both states, it emits an eye-watering reek of musk, ammonia, and decay.

"*How* much of this stuff did you say we're taking?" I asked, through the cloth I had wrapped about my lower face.

"Ten tons," Jamie replied, his words similarly muffled. We were standing on the upper deck, watching as the slaves trundled barrowloads of the reeking stuff down the gangplank and over to the open hatchway of the after hold.

Tiny particles of the dried guano blew from the barrows and filled the air around us with a deceptively beautiful cloud of gold, that sparked and glimmered in the late afternoon sun. The men's bodies were coated with the stuff as well; the runnels of sweat carved dark channels in the dust on their bare torsos, and the constant tears ran down their faces and chests, so that they were striped in black and gold like exotic zebras.

Jamie dabbed at his own streaming eyes as the wind veered slightly toward us. "D'ye ken how to keelhaul someone, Sassenach?"

"No, but if it's Fergus you have in mind as a candidate, I'm with you. How far is it to Jamaica?" It was Fergus, making inquiries in the marketplace on King's Street in Bridgetown, who had gained the *Artemis* her first commission as a trading and hauling vessel; the shipment of ten cubic tons of bat guano from Barbados to Jamaica, for use as fertilizer on the sugar plantation of one Mr. Grey, planter.

Fergus himself was rather self-consciously overseeing the loading of the huge quarried blocks of dried guano, which were tipped from their barrows and handed down one by one into the hold Marsali, never far from his side, had in this case moved as far as the forecastle, where she sat on a barrel filled with oranges, the lovely new shawl Fergus had bought her in the market wrapped over her face.

"We are meant to be traders, no?" Fergus had argued. "We have an empty hold to fill. Besides," he had added logically clinching the argument, "Monsieur Grey will pay us more than adequately."

"How far, Sassenach?" Jamie squinted at the horizon, a though hoping to see land rising from the sparkling waves. Mr Willoughby's magic needles rendered him seaworthy, but he submitted to the process with no real enthusiasm. "Three or four days' sail, Warren says," he admitted with a sigh, "and the weather holds fair."

"Maybe the smell will be better at sea," I said.

"Oh, yes, milady," Fergus assured me, overhearing as he passed. "The owner tells me that the stench dissipates itself significantly, once the dried material is removed from the cave where it accumulates." He leapt into the rigging and went up climbing like a monkey despite his hook. Reaching the top rigging, Fergus tied the red kerchief that was the signal to hands o shore to come aboard, and slid down again, pausing to say something rude to Ping An, who was perched on the lowest crosstrees keeping a bright yellow eye on the proceedings below.

"Fergus seems to be taking quite a proprietary interest in this cargo," I observed.

"Aye, well, he's a partner," Jamie said. "I told him if he'd wife to support, he must think of how to do it. And as it may b some time before we're in the printing business again, he mu turn his hand to what offers. He and Marsali have half the profit o this cargo—against the dowry I promised her," he added wryl and I laughed.

"You know," I said, "I really would like to read the lette Marsali's sending to her mother. First Fergus, I mean, then Fath Fogden and Mamacita, and now a dowry of ten tons of bat shit.

"I shall never be able to set foot in Scotland again, one

aoghaire reads it,'' said Jamie, but he smiled nonetheless. ''Have
: thought yet what to do wi' your new acquisition?''

''Don't remind me,'' I said, a little grimly. ''Where is he?''

''Somewhere below,'' Jamie said, his attention distracted by a
.an coming down the wharf toward us. ''Murphy's fed him, and
nes will find a place for him. Your pardon, Sassenach; I think
.is will be someone looking for me.'' He swung down from the
.il and went down the gangplank, neatly skipping around a slave
.ming up with a barrowload of guano.

I watched with interest as he greeted the man, a tall colonial in
.e dress of a prosperous planter, with a weathered red face that
.oke of long years in the islands. He extended a hand toward
.mie, who took it in a firm clasp. Jamie said something, and the
.an replied, his expression of wariness changing to an instant
.rdiality.

This must be the result of Jamie's visit to the Masonic lodge in
.idgetown, where he had gone immediately upon landing the day
.fore, mindful of Jared's suggestion. He had identified himself as
.member of the brotherhood, and spoken to the Master of the
.dge, describing Young Ian and asking for any news of either the
.y or the ship *Bruja*. The Master had promised to spread the
.rd among such Freemasons as might have occasion to frequent
.e slave market and the shipping docks. With luck, this was the
.iit of that promise.

I watched eagerly as the planter reached into his coat and with-
.ew a paper, which he unfolded and showed to Jamie, apparently
.plaining something. Jamie's face was intent, his ruddy brows
.awn together with concentration, but showed neither exultation
.r disappointment. Maybe it was not news of Ian at all. After our
.iit to the slave market the day before, I was half-inclined to hope
.t.

Lawrence, Fergus, Marsali, and I had gone to the slave market
.der the cranky chaperonage of Murphy, while Jamie called on
.e Masonic Master. The slave market was near the docks, down a
.sty road lined with sellers of fruit and coffee, dried fish and
.conuts, yams and red cochineal bugs, sold for dye in small,
.:ked glass bottles.

Murphy, with his passion for order and propriety, had insisted

that Marsali and I must each have a parasol, and had forced Fergu
to buy two from a roadside vendor.

"All the white women in Bridgetown carry parasols," he sai
firmly, trying to hand me one.

"I don't need a parasol," I said, impatient at talk of somethin
so inconsequential as my complexion, when we might be near t
finding Ian at last. "The sun isn't that hot. Let's go!"

Murphy glowered at me, scandalized.

"Ye don't want folk to think ye ain't respectable, that ye don
care enough to keep yer skin fine!"

"I wasn't planning to take up residence here," I said tartly. '
don't care *what* they think." Not pausing to argue further, I bega
walking down the road, toward a distant murmur of noise that
took to be the slave market.

"Yer face will . . . get . . . red!" Murphy said, huffing ir
dignantly alongside me, attempting to open the parasol as h
stumped along.

"Oh, a fate worse than death, I'm sure!" I snapped. My nerve
were strung tight, in anticipation of what we might find. "A
right, then, give me the bloody thing!" I snatched it from hir
snapped it open, and set it over my shoulder with an irritable twir

As it was, within minutes I was grateful for Murphy's intrans
gence. While the road was shaded by tall palms and cecropia tree
the slave market itself was held in a large, stone-paved spac
without the grace of any shade, save that provided by ramshack
open booths roofed with sheets of tin or palm fronds, in which th
slave-dealers and auctioneers sought occasional refuge from th
sun. The slaves themselves were mostly held in large pens at th
side of the square, open to the elements.

The sun *was* fierce in the open, and the light bouncing off th
pale stones was blinding after the green shade of the road.
blinked, eyes watering, and hastily adjusted my parasol over n
head.

So shaded, I could see a bewildering array of bodies, naked
nearly so, gleaming in every shade from pale café au lait to a dec
blue-black. Bouquets of color blossomed in front of the auctie
blocks, where the plantation owners and their servants gathered
inspect the wares, vivid amid the stark blacks and whites.

The stink of the place was staggering, even to one accustome
to the stenches of Edinburgh and the reeking tween-decks of th

orpoise. Heaps of wet human excrement lay in the corners of the lave pens, buzzing with flies, and a thick oily reek floated on the ir, but the major component of the smell was the unpleasantly timate scent of acres of hot bare flesh, baking in the sun.

"Jesu," Fergus muttered next to me. His dark eyes flicked right nd left in shocked disapproval. "It's worse than the slums in Iontmartre." Marsali didn't say a word, but drew closer to his de, her nostrils pinched.

Lawrence was more matter-of-fact; I supposed he must have en slave markets before during his explorations of the islands.

"The whites are at that end," he said, gesturing toward the far de of the square. "Come; we'll ask for news of any young men ld recently." He placed a large square hand in the center of my ack and urged me gently forward through the crowd.

Near the edge of the market, an old black woman squatted on e ground, feeding charcoal to a small brazier. As we drew near, a ttle group of people approached her: a planter, accompanied by vo black men dressed in rough cotton shirts and trousers, evi- ntly his servants. One of them was holding the arm of a newly urchased female slave; two other girls, naked but for small strips cloth wrapped about their middles, were led by ropes around eir necks.

The planter bent and handed the old woman a coin. She turned d drew several short brass rods from the ground behind her, lding them up for the man's inspection. He studied them for a oment, picked out two, and straightened up. He handed the anding irons to one of his servants, who thrust the ends into the d woman's brazier.

The other servant stepped behind the girl and pinioned her ms. The first man then pulled the irons from the fire and planted th together on the upper slope of her right breast. She shrieked, high steam-whistle sound loud enough to turn a few heads arby. The irons pulled away, leaving the letters HB in raw pink sh.

I had stopped dead at the sight of this. Not realizing that I was longer with them, the others had gone on. I turned round and und, looking vainly for any trace of Lawrence or Fergus. I never d any difficulty finding Jamie in crowds; his bright head was ways visible above everyone else's. But Fergus was a small man, urphy, no taller, and Lawrence, no more than middle height;

even Marsali's yellow parasol was lost among the many others in the square.

I turned away from the brazier with a shudder, hearing screams and whimpers behind me, but not wanting to look back. I hurried past several auction blocks, eyes averted, but then was slowed and finally stopped by a thickening of the crowd around me.

The men and women blocking my way were listening to an auctioneer who was touting the virtues of a one-armed slave who stood naked on the block for inspection. He was a short man, but broadly built, with massive thighs and a strong chest. The missing arm had been crudely amputated above the elbow; sweat dripped from the end of the stump.

"No good for field work, that's true," the auctioneer was admitting. "But a sound investment for breeding. Look at those legs!" He carried a long rattan cane, which he flicked against the slave's calves, then grinned fatly at the crowd.

"Will you give a guarantee of virility?" the man standing behind me said, with a distinct tone of skepticism. "I had a buck three year past, big as a mule, and not a foal dropped on his account; couldn't do a thing, the juba-girls said."

The crowd tittered at that, and the auctioneer pretended to be offended.

"Guarantee?" he said. He wiped a hand theatrically over his jowls, gathering oily sweat on the palm. "See for yourselves, O ye of little faith!" Bending slightly, he grasped the slave's penis and began to massage it vigorously.

The man grunted in surprise and tried to draw back, but was prevented by the auctioneer's assistant, who clutched him firmly by his single arm. There was an outburst of laughter from the crowd, and a few scattered cheers as the soft black flesh hardened and began to swell.

Some small thing inside me suddenly snapped; I heard it, distinctly. Outraged by the market, the branding, the nakedness, the crude talk and casual indignity, outraged most of all by my own presence here, I could not even think what I was doing, but began to do it, all the same. I felt very oddly detached, as though I stood outside myself, watching.

"Stop it!" I said, very loudly, hardly recognizing my own voice. The auctioneer looked up, startled, and smiled ingratiatingly at me. He looked directly into my eyes, with a knowing leer.

"Sound breeding stock, ma'am," he said. "Guaranteed, as you see."

I folded my parasol, lowered it, and stabbed the pointed end of it as hard as I could into his fat stomach. He jerked back, eyes bulging in surprise. I yanked the parasol back and smashed it on his head, then dropped it and kicked him, hard.

Somewhere deep inside, I knew it would make no difference, would not help in any way, would do nothing but harm. And yet I could not stand here, consenting by silence. It was not for the branded girls, the man on the block, not for any of them that I did it; it was for myself.

There was a good deal of noise around me, and hands snatched at me, pulling me off the auctioneer. This worthy, recovered sufficiently from his initial shock, grinned nastily at me, took aim, and slapped the slave hard across the face.

I looked around for reinforcements, and caught a quick glimpse of Fergus, face contorted in rage, lunging through the crowd toward the auctioneer. There was a shout, and several men turned in his direction. People began to push and shove. Someone tripped me and I sat down hard on the stones.

Through a haze of dust, I saw Murphy, six feet away. With a resigned expression on his broad red face, he bent, detached his wooden leg, straightened up, and hopping gracefully forward, brought it down with great force on the auctioneer's head. The man tottered and fell, as the crowd surged back, trying to get out of the way.

Fergus, baffled of his prey, skidded to a halt by the fallen man and glared ferociously round. Lawrence, dark, grim, and bulky, came striding through the crowd from the other direction, hand on the cane-knife at his belt.

I sat on the ground, shaken. I no longer felt detached. I felt sick, and terrified, realizing that I had just committed an act of folly that was likely to result in Fergus, Lawrence, and Murphy being badly beaten, if nothing worse.

And then Jamie was there.

"Stand up, Sassenach," he said quietly, stooping over me and giving me his hands. I managed it, knees shaking. I saw Raeburn's long mustache twitching at one side, MacLeod behind him, and realized that his Scots were with him. Then my knees gave way, but Jamie's arms held me up.

"Do something," I said in a choked voice into his ches
"Please. Do something."

He had. With his usual presence of mind, he had done the onl
thing that would quell the riot and prevent harm. He had boug
the one-armed man. And as the ironic result of my little outbur
of sensibilities, I was now the appalled owner of a genuine ma
Guinea slave, one-armed, but in glowing health and of guarantee
virility.

I sighed, trying not to think of the man, presumably now som
where under my feet, fed, and—I hoped—clad. The papers
ownership, which I had refused even to touch, said that he was
full-blooded Gold Coast Negro, a Yoruba, sold by a French plant
from Barbuda, one-armed, bearing a brand on the left shoulder
a fleur-de-lys and the initial "A," and known by the name Teme
aire. The Bold One. The papers did not suggest what in the nam
of God I was to do with him.

Jamie had finished looking at the papers his Masonic acquai
tance had brought—they were very like the ones I had received f
Temeraire, so far as I could see from the rail of the ship. F
handed them back with a bow of thanks, a slight frown on his fac
The men exchanged a few more words, and parted with anoth
handshake.

"Is everyone aboard?" Jamie asked, stepping off the gan
plank. There was a light breeze; it fluttered the dark blue ribb
that tied back the thick tail of his hair.

"Aye, sir," said Mr. Warren, with the casual jerk of the he
that passed for a salute in a merchant ship. "Shall we make sail?

"We shall, if ye please. Thank ye, Mr. Warren." With a sma
bow, Jamie passed him and came to stand beside me.

"No," he said quietly. His face was calm, but I could feel t
depths of his disappointment. Interviews the day before with t
two men who dealt in white indentured labor at the slave mark
had provided no useful information—the Masonic planter h
been a beacon of last-minute hope.

There wasn't anything helpful to be said. I put my hand over h
where it lay on the rail, and squeezed lightly. Jamie looked do
and gave me a faint smile. He took a deep breath and straighten
his shoulders, shrugging to settle his coat over them.

"Aye, well. I've learned something, at least. That was a Mr. 'illiers, who owns a large sugar plantation here. He bought six laves from the captain of the ship *Bruja,* three days ago—but one of them Ian."

"Three days?" I was startled. "But—the *Bruja* left Hispaniola nore than two weeks ago!"

He nodded, rubbing his cheek. He had shaved, a necessity be-ore making public inquiries, and his skin glowed fresh and ruddy bove the snowy linen of his stock.

"She did. And she arrived here on Wednesday—five days ago."

"So she'd been somewhere else, before coming to Barbados! o we know where?"

He shook his head.

"Villiers didna ken. He said he had spoken some time wi' the aptain of the *Bruja,* and the man seemed verra secretive about here he'd been and what he'd been doing. Villiers thought no eat thing of it, knowin' as the *Bruja* has a reputation as a crook iip—and seein' as how the captain was willing to sell the slaves r a good price."

"Still"—he brightened slightly—"Villiers did show me the apers for the slaves he'd bought. Ye'll have seen those for your ave?"

"I wish you wouldn't call him that," I said. "But yes. Were the es you saw the same?"

"Not quite. Three o' the papers gave no previous owner— ough Villiers says they were none of them fresh from Africa; all them have a few words of English, at least. One listed a previ-s owner, but the name had been scratched out; I couldna read it. ie other two gave a Mrs. Abernathy of Rose Hall, Jamaica, as the evious owner."

"Jamaica? How far—"

"I dinna ken," he interrupted. "But Mr. Warren will know. It ay be right. In any case, I think we must go to Jamaica next—if ly to dispose of our cargo before we all die o' disgust." He rinkled his long nose fastidiously and I laughed.

"You look like an anteater when you do that," I told him. The attempt to distract him was successful; the wide mouth rved upward slightly.

"Oh, aye? There's a beastie eats ants, is there?" He did his best respond to the teasing, turning his back on the Barbados docks.

He leaned against the rail and smiled down at me. "I shouldn' think they'd be verra filling."

"I suppose it must eat a lot of them. They can't be any wors than haggis, after all." I took a breath before going on, and let out quickly, coughing. "God, what's that?"

The *Artemis* had by now slid free of the loading wharf and o into the harbor. As we came about into the wind, a deep, punge smell struck the ship, a lower and more sinister note in the olfa tory dockside symphony of dead barnacles, wet wood, fish, rotte seaweed, and the constant warm breath of the tropical vegetatic on shore.

I pressed my handkerchief hard over my nose and mout "What is it?"

"We're passing the burning ground, mum, at the foot o' t slave market," Maitland explained, overhearing my question. I pointed toward the shore, where a plume of white smoke rose fro behind a screen of bayberry bushes. "They burn the bodies of t slaves who don't survive their passage from Africa," he e plained. "First they unload the living cargo, and then, as the sh is swabbed out, the bodies are removed and thrown onto the py here, to prevent sickness spreading into the town."

I looked at Jamie, and found the same fear in his face th showed in my own.

"How often do they burn bodies?" I asked. "Every day?"

"Don't know, mum, but I don't think so. Maybe once a week? Maitland shrugged and went on about his duties.

"We have to look," I said. My voice sounded strange to n own ears, calm and clear. I didn't feel that way.

Jamie had gone very pale. He had turned round again, and h eyes were fixed on the plume of smoke, rising thick and whi from behind the palm trees.

His lips pressed tight, then, and his jaw set hard.

"Aye," was all he said, and turned to tell Mr. Warren to p about.

The keeper of the flames, a wizened little creature of indisti guishable color and accent, was vociferously shocked at the noti that a lady should enter the burning ground, but Jamie elbow

m brusquely aside. He didn't try to prevent me following him, or
rn to see that I did; he knew I would not leave him alone here.

It was a small hollow, set behind a screen of trees, convenient to
small wharf that extended into the river. Black-smeared pitch
rrels and piles of dry wood stood in grim sticky clumps amid
e brilliant greens of tree-ferns and dwarf poinciana. To the right,
huge pyre had been built, with a platform of wood, onto which
e bodies had been thrown, dribbled with pitch.

This had been lit only a short time before; a good blaze had
rted at one side of the heap, but only small tongues of flame
ked up from the rest. It was smoke that obscured the bodies,
lling up over the heap in a wavering thick veil that gave the
tflung limbs a horrid illusion of movement.

Jamie had stopped, staring at the heap. Then he sprang onto the
atform, heedless of smoke and scorching, and began jerking
dies loose, grimly pawing through the grisly remains.

A smaller heap of gray ashes and shards of pure white friable
ne lay nearby. The curve of an occiput lay on top of the heap,
gile and perfect as an eggshell.

"Makee fine crop." The soot-smeared little creature who
ded the fire was at my elbow, offering information in evident
pes of reward. He—or she—pointed at the ashes. "Put on crop;
kee grow-grow."

"No, thank you," I said faintly. The smoke obscured Jamie's
ure for a moment, and I had the terrible feeling that he had
len, was burning in the pyre. The horrible, jolly smell of roast-
meat rose on the air, and I thought I would be sick.

"Jamie!" I called. *"Jamie!"*

He didn't answer, but I heard a deep, racking cough from the
rt of the fire. Several long minutes later, the veil of smoke
ted, and he staggered out, choking.

He made his way down the platform and stood bent over,
ghing his lungs out. He was covered with an oily soot, his
ds and clothes smeared with pitch. He was blind with the
oke; tears poured down his cheeks, making runnels in the soot.

threw several coins to the keeper of the pyre, and taking Jamie
the arm, led him, blind and choking, out of the valley of death.
der the palms, he sank to his knees and threw up.

'Don't touch me," he gasped, when I tried to help him. He

retched over and over again, but finally stopped, swaying on h knees. Then he slowly staggered to his feet.

"Don't touch me," he said again. His voice, roughened ! smoke and sickness, was that of a stranger.

He walked to the edge of the dock, removed his coat and shoe and dived into the water, fully clothed. I waited for a moment, th stooped and picked up the coat and shoes, holding them ginger at arm's length. I could see in the inner pocket the faint rectang lar bulge of Brianna's pictures.

I waited until he came back and hoisted himself out of t water, dripping. The pitch smears were still there, but most of t soot and the smell of the fire were gone. He sat on the wharf, he on his knees, breathing hard. A row of curious faces edged t *Artemis*'s rail above us.

Not knowing what else to do, I leaned down and laid a hand his shoulder. Without raising his head, he reached up a hand a grasped mine.

"He wasn't there," he said, in his muffled, rasping stranger voice.

The breeze was freshening; it stirred the tendrils of wet hair th lay across his shoulders. I looked back, to see that the plume smoke rising from the little valley had changed to black. It fl tened and began to drift out over the sea, the ashes of the de slaves fleeing on the wind, back toward Africa.

54

"The Impetuous Pirate"

"I can't own anyone, Jamie," I said, looking in dismay at the papers spread out in the lamplight before me. "I just *can't*. It isn't right."

"Well, I'm inclined to agree wi' ye, Sassenach. But what are we to do with the fellow?" Jamie sat on the berth next to me, close enough to see the ownership documents over my shoulder. He rubbed a hand through his hair, frowning.

"We could set him free—that would seem the right thing—and yet, if we do—what will happen to him then?" He hunched forward, squinting down his nose to read the papers. "He's no more than a bit of French and English; no skills to speak of. If we were to set him free, or even give him a bit of money—can he manage to live, on his own?"

I nibbled thoughtfully on one of Murphy's cheese rolls. It was good, but the smell of the burning oil in the lamp blended oddly with the aromatic cheese, underlaid—as everything was—with the insidious scent of bat guano that permeated the ship.

"I don't know," I said. "Lawrence told me there are a lot of free blacks on Hispaniola. Lots of Creoles and mixed-race people, and a good many who own their own businesses. Is it like that on Jamaica, too?"

He shook his head, and reached for a roll from the tray.

"I dinna think so. It's true, there are some free blacks who earn living for themselves, but those are the ones who have some skill —sempstresses and fishers and such. I spoke to this Temeraire a bit. He was a cane-cutter until he lost his arm, and doesna ken how to do anything else much.''

I laid the roll down, barely tasted, and frowned unhappily at the papers. The mere idea of owning a slave frightened and disgusted me, but it was beginning to dawn on me that it might not be so simple to divest myself of the responsibility.

The man had been taken from a barracoon on the Guinea coast five years before. My original impulse, to return him to his home, was clearly impossible; even had it been possible to find a ship headed for Africa that would agree to take him as a passenger, the overwhelming likelihood was that he would be immediately enslaved again, either by the ship that accepted him, or by another slaver in the West African ports.

Traveling alone, one-armed and ignorant, he would have no protection at all. And even if he should by some miracle reach Africa safely and keep himself out of the hands of both European and African slavers, there was virtually no chance of his ever finding his way back to his village. Should he do so, Lawrence had kindly explained, he would likely be killed or driven away, as his own people would regard him now as a ghost, and a danger to them.

''I dinna suppose ye would consider selling him?'' Jamie put the question delicately, raising one eyebrow. ''To someone we could be sure would treat him kindly?''

I rubbed two fingers between my brows, trying to soothe the growing headache.

''I can't see that that's any better than owning him ourselves,'' I protested. ''Worse, probably, because we couldn't be sure what the new owners would do with him.''

Jamie sighed. He had spent most of the day climbing through the dark, reeking cargo holds with Fergus, making up inventories against our arrival in Jamaica, and he was tired.

''Aye, I see that,'' he said. ''But it's no kindness to free him to starve, that I can see.''

''No.'' I fought back the uncharitable wish that I had never seen the one-armed slave. It would have been a great deal easier for me if I had not—but possibly not for him.

Jamie rose from the berth and stretched himself, leaning on the desk and flexing his shoulders to ease them. He bent and kissed me on the forehead, between the brows.

"Dinna fash, Sassenach. I'll speak to the manager at Jared's plantation. Perhaps he can find the man some employment, or else—"

A warning shout from above interrupted him.

"Ship ahoy! Look alive, below! Off the port bow, ahoy!" The lookout's cry was urgent, and there was a sudden rush and stir, as hands began to turn out. Then there was a lot more shouting, and a jerk and shudder as the *Artemis* backed her sails.

"What in the name of God—" Jamie began. A rending crash drowned his words, and he pitched sideways, eyes wide with alarm, as the cabin tilted. The stool I was on fell over, throwing me onto the floor. The oil lamp had shot from its bracket, luckily extinguishing itself before hitting the floor, and the place was in darkness.

"Sassenach! Are ye all right?" Jamie's voice came out of the murk close at hand, sharp with anxiety.

"Yes," I said, scrambling out from under the table. "Are you? What happened? Did someone hit us?"

Not pausing to answer any of these questions, Jamie had reached the door and opened it. A babel of shouts and thumps came down from the deck above, punctuated by the sudden popcorn-sound of small-arms fire.

"Pirates," he said briefly. "We've been boarded." My eyes were becoming accustomed to the dim light; I saw his shadow lunge for the desk, reaching for the pistol in the drawer. He paused to snatch the dirk from under the pillow of his berth, and made for the door, issuing instructions as he went.

"Take Marsali, Sassenach, and get below. Go aft as far as ye can get—the big hold where the guano blocks are. Get behind them, and stay there." Then he was gone.

I spent a moment feeling my way through the cupboard over my berth, in search of the morocco box Mother Hildegarde had given me when I saw her in Paris. A scalpel might be little use against pirates, but I would feel better with a weapon of some kind in my hand, no matter how small.

"Mother Claire?" Marsali's voice came from the door, high and scared.

"I'm here," I said. I caught the gleam of pale cotton as she moved, and pressed the ivory letter-opener into her hand. "Here, take this, just in case. Come on; we're to go below."

With a long-handled amputation blade in one hand, and a cluster of scalpels in the other, I led the way through the ship to the after hold. Feet thundered on the deck overhead, and curses and shouts rang through the night, overlaid with a dreadful groaning, scraping noise that I thought must be caused by the rubbing of the *Artemis*'s timbers against those of the unknown ship that had rammed us.

The hold was black as pitch and thick with dusty fumes. We made our way slowly, coughing, toward the back of the hold.

"Who are they?" Marsali asked. Her voice had a strangely muffled sound, the echoes of the hold deadened by the blocks of guano stacked around us. "Pirates, d'ye think?"

"I expect they must be." Lawrence had told us that the Caribbean was a rich hunting ground for pirate luggers and unscrupulous craft of all kinds, but we had expected no trouble, as our cargo was not particularly valuable. "I suppose they must not have much sense of smell."

"Eh?"

"Never mind," I said. "Come sit down; there's nothing we can do but wait."

I knew from experience that waiting while men fought was one of the most difficult things in life to do, but in this case, there wasn't any sensible alternative.

Down here, the sounds of the battle were muted to a distant thumping, though the constant rending groan of the scraping timbers echoed through the whole ship.

"Oh, God, Fergus," Marsali whispered, listening, her voice filled with agony. "Blessed Mary, save him!"

I silently echoed the prayer, thinking of Jamie somewhere in the chaos overhead. I crossed myself in the dark, touching the small spot between my brows that he had kissed a few minutes before, not wanting to think that it could so easily be the last touch of him I would ever know.

Suddenly, there was an explosion overhead, a roar that sent vibrations through the jutting timbers we were sitting on.

"They're blowing up the ship!" Marsali jumped to her feet, panicked. "They'll sink us! We must get out! We'll drown down here!"

"Wait!" I called. "It's only the guns!" but she had not waited to hear. I could hear her, blundering about in a blind panic, whimpering among the blocks of guano.

"Marsali! Come back!" There was no light at all in the hold; I took a few steps through the smothering atmosphere, trying to locate her by sound, but the deadening effect of the crumbling blocks hid her movements from me. There was another booming explosion overhead, and a third close on its heels. The air was filled with dust loosed from the vibrations, and I choked, eyes watering.

I wiped at my eyes with a sleeve, and blinked. I was not imagining it; there was a light in the hold, a dim glow that limned the edge of the nearest block.

"Marsali?" I called. "Where are you?"

The answer was a terrified shriek, from the direction of the light. I dashed around the edge of the block, dodged between two others, and emerged into the space by the ladder, to find Marsali in the clutches of a large, half-naked man.

He was hugely obese, the rolling layers of his fat decorated with a stipple of tattoos, a jangling necklace of coins and buttons hung round his neck. Marsali slapped at him, shrieking, and he jerked his face away, impatient.

Then he caught sight of me, and his eyes widened. He had a wide, flat face, and a tarred topknot of black hair. He grinned nastily at me, showing a marked lack of teeth, and said something that sounded like slurred Spanish.

"Let her go!" I said loudly. *"Basta, cabrón!"* That was as much Spanish as I could summon; he seemed to think it funny, for he grinned more widely, let go of Marsali, and turned toward me. I threw one of my scalpels at him.

It bounced off his head, startling him, and he ducked wildly. Marsali dodged past him, and sprang for the ladder.

The pirate waffled for a moment, torn between us, but then turned to the ladder, leaping up several rungs with an agility that belied his weight. He caught Marsali by the foot as she dived through the hatch, and she screamed.

Cursing incoherently under my breath, I ran to the bottom of the ladder, and reaching up, swung the long-handled amputation knife at his foot, as hard as I could. There was a high-pitched screech from the pirate. Something flew past my head, and a spray of blood spattered across my cheek, wet-hot on my skin.

Startled, I dropped back, looking down by reflex to see what had fallen. It was a small brown toe, callused and black-nailed, smudged with dirt.

The pirate hit the deck beside me with a thud that shivered the floorboards, and lunged. I ducked, but he caught a handful of my sleeve. I yanked away, ripping fabric, and jabbed at his face with the blade in my hand.

Jerking back in surprise, he slipped on his own blood and fell. I jumped for the ladder and climbed for my life, dropping the blade.

He was so close behind me that he succeeded in catching hold of the hem of my skirt, but I pulled it from his grasp and lunged upward, lungs burning from the dust of the choking hold. The man was shouting, a language I didn't know. Some dim recess of my brain, not occupied with immediate survival, speculated that it might be Portuguese.

I burst out of the hold onto the deck, into the midst of a surging chaos. The air was thick with black-powder smoke, and small knots of men were pushing and shoving, cursing and stumbling all over the deck.

I couldn't take time to look around; there was a hoarse bellow from the hatchway behind me, and I dived for the rail. I hesitated for a moment, balanced on the narrow wooden strip. The sea spun past in a dizzy churn of black below. I grasped the rigging and began to climb.

It was a mistake; I knew that almost at once. He was a sailor, was not. Neither was he hampered by wearing a dress. The ropes danced and jerked in my hands, vibrating under the impact of his weight as he hit the lines below me.

He was coming up the underside of the lines, climbing like a gibbon, even as I made my slower way across the upper slope of the rigging. He drew even with me, and spat in my face. I kept climbing, propelled by desperation; there was nothing else to do. He kept pace with me, easily, hissing words through an evil half-toothed grin. It didn't matter what language he was speaking; his meaning was perfectly clear. Hanging by one hand, he drew the cutlass from his sash, and swung it in a vicious cut that barely missed me.

I was too frightened even to scream. There was nowhere to go, nothing to do. I squeezed my eyes tight shut, and hoped it would be quick.

It was. There was a sort of thump, a sharp grunt, and a strong smell of fish.

I opened my eyes. The pirate was gone. Ping An was sitting on the crosstrees, three feet away, crest erect with irritation, wings half-spread to keep his balance.

"Gwa!" he said crossly. He turned a beady little yellow eye on me, and clacked his bill in warning. Ping An hated noise and commotion. Evidently, he didn't like Portuguese pirates, either.

There were spots before my eyes, and I felt light-headed. I clung tight to the rope, shaking, until I thought I could move again. The noise below had slackened now, and the tenor of the shouting had changed. Something had happened; I thought it was over.

There was a new noise, a sudden flap of sails, and a long, grinding sound, with a vibration that made the line I was holding sing in my hand. It *was* over; the pirate ship was moving away. On the far side of the *Artemis,* I saw the web of the pirate's mast and rigging begin to move, black against the silver Caribbean sky. Very, very slowly, I began the long trip back down.

The lanterns were still lit below. A haze of black-powder smoke lay over everything, and bodies lay here and there about the deck. My glance flickered over them as I lowered myself, searching for red hair. I found it, and my heart leapt.

Jamie was sitting on a cask near the wheel, with his head tilted back, eyes closed, a cloth pressed to his brow, and a cup of whisky in his hand. Mr. Willoughby was on his knees alongside, administering first aid—in the form of more whisky—to Willie MacLeod, who sat against the foremast, looking sick.

I was shaking all over from exertion and reaction. I felt giddy and slightly cold. Shock, I supposed, and no wonder. I could do with a bit of that whisky as well.

I grasped the smaller lines above the rail, and slid the rest of the way to the deck, not caring that my palms were skinned raw. I was sweating and cold at the same time, and the down-hairs on my face were prickling unpleasantly.

I landed clumsily, with a thump that made Jamie straighten up and open his eyes. The look of relief in them pulled me the few feet to him. I felt better, with the warm solid flesh of his shoulder under my hand.

"Are you all right?" I said, leaning over him to look.

"Aye, it's no more than a wee dunt," he said, smiling up at me.

There was a small gash at his hairline, where something like a pistol butt had caught him, but the blood had clotted already. There were stains of dark, drying blood on the front of his shirt, but the sleeve of his shirt was also bloody. In fact, it was nearly soaked, with fresh bright red.

"Jamie!" I clutched at his shoulder, my vision going white at the edges. "You aren't all right—look, you're bleeding!"

My hands and feet were numb, and I only half-felt his hands grasp my arms as he rose from the cask in sudden alarm. The last thing I saw, amid flashes of light, was his face, gone white beneath the tan.

"My God!" said his frightened voice, out of the whirling blackness. "It's no my blood, Sassenach, it's yours!"

"I am not going to die," I said crossly, "unless it's from heat exhaustion. Take some of this bloody stuff off me!"

Marsali, who had been tearfully pleading with me not to expire looked rather relieved at this outburst. She stopped crying and sniffed hopefully, but made no move to remove any of the cloaks, coats, blankets, and other impedimenta in which I was swaddled.

"Oh, I canna do that, Mother Claire!" she said. "Da says ye must be kept warm!"

"Warm? I'm being boiled alive!" I was in the captain's cabin and even with the stern windows wide open, the atmosphere below decks was stifling, hot with sun and acrid with the fumes of the cargo.

I tried to struggle out from under my wrappings, but got no more than a few inches before a bolt of lightning struck me in the right arm. The world went dark, with small bright flashes zigging through my vision.

"Lie still," said a stern Scots voice, through a wave of giddy sickness. An arm was under my shoulders, a large hand cradling my head. "Aye, that's right, lie back on my arm. All right now, Sassenach?"

"No," I said, looking at the colored pinwheels inside my eyelids. "I'm going to be sick."

I was, and a most unpleasant process it was, too, with fiery knives being jabbed into my right arm with each spasm.

"Jesus H. Roosevelt Christ," I said at last, gasping.

"Finished, are ye?" Jamie lowered me carefully and eased my head back onto the pillow.

"If you mean am I dead, the answer is unfortunately no." I cracked one eyelid open. He was kneeling by my berth, looking no end piratical himself, with a bloodstained strip of cloth bound round his head, and still wearing his blood-soaked shirt.

He stayed still, and so did the cabin, so I cautiously opened the other eye. He smiled faintly at me.

"No, you're no dead; Fergus will be glad to hear it."

As though this had been a signal, the Frenchman's head poked anxiously into the cabin. Seeing me awake, his face broke into a dazzling smile and disappeared. I could hear his voice overhead, loudly informing the crew of my survival. To my profound embarrassment, the news was greeted with a rousing cheer from the upper deck.

"What happened?" I asked.

"What *happened*?" Jamie, pouring water into a cup, stopped and stared over the rim at me. He knelt down again beside me, snorting, and raised my head for a sip of water.

"What happened, she says! Aye, what indeed? I tell ye to stay snug below wi' Marsali, and next thing I ken, ye've dropped out of the sky and landed at my feet, sopping wi' blood!"

He shoved his face into the berth and glared at me. Sufficiently impressive when clean-shaven and unhurt, he was considerably more ferocious when viewed, stubbled, bloodstained, and angry, at a distance of six inches. I promptly shut my eyes again.

"Look at me!" he said peremptorily, and I did, against my better judgment.

Blue eyes bored into mine, narrowed with fury.

"D'ye ken ye came damn close to dying?" he demanded. "Ye've a bone-deep slash down your arm from oxter to elbow, and had I not got a cloth round it in time, ye'd be feeding the sharks this minute!"

One big fist crashed down on the side of the berth next to me, making me start. The movement hurt my arm, but I didn't make a sound.

"Damn ye, woman! Will ye never do as you're told?"

"Probably not," I said meekly.

He turned a black scowl on me, but I could see the corner of his mouth twitching under the copper stubble.

"God," he said longingly. "What I wouldna give to have ye tied facedown over a gun, and me wi' a rope's end in my hand." He snorted again, and pulled his face out of the berth.

"Willoughby!" he bellowed. In short order, Mr. Willoughby trotted in, beaming, with a steaming pot of tea and a bottle of brandy on a tray.

"Tea!" I breathed, struggling to sit up. "Ambrosia." In spite of the stifling atmosphere of the cabin, the hot tea was just what I needed. The delightful, brandy-laced stuff slid down my throat and glowed peacefully in the pit of my quivering stomach.

"Nobody makes tea better than the English," I said, inhaling the aroma, "except the Chinese."

Mr. Willoughby beamed in gratification and bowed ceremoniously. Jamie snorted again, bringing his total up to three for the afternoon.

"Aye? Well, enjoy it while ye can."

This sounded more or less sinister, and I stared at him over the rim of the cup. "And just what do you mean by that?" I demanded.

"I'm going to doctor your arm when you're finished," he informed me. He picked up the pot and peered into it.

"How much blood did ye tell me a person has in his body?" he asked.

"About eight quarts," I said, bewildered. "Why?"

He lowered the pot and glared at me.

"Because," he said precisely, "judging from the amount ye left on the deck, you've maybe four of them left. Here, have some more." He refilled the cup, set down the pot, and stalked out.

"I'm afraid Jamie's rather annoyed with me," I observed ruefully to Mr. Willoughby.

"Not angry," he said comfortingly. "Tsei-mi scared very bad." The little Chinaman laid a hand on my right shoulder, delicate as a resting butterfly. "This hurts?"

I sighed. "To be perfectly honest," I said, "yes, it does."

Mr. Willoughby smiled and patted me gently. "I help," he said consolingly. "Later."

In spite of the throbbing in my arm, I was feeling sufficiently restored to inquire about the rest of the crew, whose injuries, as reported by Mr. Willoughby, were limited to cuts and bruises, plus one concussion and a minor arm fracture.

A clatter in the passage heralded Jamie's return, accompanied by Fergus, who carried my medicine box under one arm, and yet another bottle of brandy in his hand.

"All right," I said, resigned. "Let's have a look at it."

I was no stranger to horrible wounds, and this one—technically speaking—was not all that bad. On the other hand, it was my own personal flesh involved here, and I was not disposed to be technical.

"Ooh," I said rather faintly. While being a bit picturesque about the nature of the wound, Jamie had also been quite accurate. It was a long, clean-edged slash, running at a slight angle across the front of my biceps, from the shoulder to an inch or so above the elbow joint. And while I couldn't actually see the bone of my humerus, it was without doubt a very deep wound, gaping widely at the edges.

It was still bleeding, in spite of the cloth that had been wrapped tightly round it, but the seepage was slow; no major vessels seemed to have been severed.

Jamie had flipped open my medical box and was rootling meditatively through it with one large forefinger.

"You'll need sutures and a needle," I said, feeling a sudden jolt of alarm as it occurred to me that I was about to have thirty or forty stitches taken in my arm, with no anesthesia bar brandy.

"No laudanum?" Jamie asked, frowning into the box. Evidently, he had been thinking along the same lines.

"No. I used it all on the *Porpoise*." Controlling the shaking of my left hand, I poured a sizable tot of straight brandy into my empty teacup, and took a healthy mouthful.

"That was thoughtful of you, Fergus," I said, nodding at the fresh brandy bottle as I sipped, "but I don't think it's going to take two bottles." Given the potency of Jared's French brandy, it was unlikely to take more than a teacupful.

I was wondering whether it was more advisable to get dead drunk at once, or to stay at least half-sober in order to supervise operations; there wasn't a chance in hell that I could do the suturing myself, left-handed and shaking like a leaf. Neither could Fergus do it one-handed. True, Jamie's big hands could move with amazing lightness over some tasks, but . . .

Jamie interrupted my apprehensions, shaking his head and picking up the second bottle.

"This one's no for drinking, Sassenach, that's for washing out the wound."

"What!" In my state of shock, I had forgotten the necessity for disinfection. Lacking anything better, I normally washed out wounds with distilled grain alcohol, cut half and half with water, but I had used my supply of that as well, in our encounter with the man-of-war.

I felt my lips go slightly numb, and not just because the internal brandy was taking effect. Highlanders were among the most stoic and courageous of warriors, and seamen as a class weren't far behind. I had seen such men lie uncomplaining while I set broken bones, did minor surgery, sewed up terrible wounds, and put them through hell generally, but when it came to disinfection with alcohol, it was a different story—the screams could be heard for miles.

"Er . . . wait a minute," I said. "Maybe just a little boiled water. . . ."

Jamie was watching me, not without sympathy.

"It willna get easier wi' waiting, Sassenach," he said. "Fergus, take the bottle." And before I could protest, he had lifted me out of the berth and sat down with me on his lap, holding me tight about the body, pinning my left arm so I couldn't struggle, while he took my right wrist in a firm grip and held my wounded arm out to the side.

I believe it was bloody old Ernest Hemingway who said you're supposed to pass out from pain, but unfortunately you never do. All I can say in response to that is that either Ernest had a fine distinction for states of consciousness, or else no one ever poured brandy on several cubic inches of *his* raw flesh.

To be fair, I suppose I must not absolutely have lost consciousness myself, since when I began noticing things again, Fergus was saying, "Please, milady! You must not scream like that; it upsets the men."

Clearly it upset Fergus; his lean face was pale, and droplets of sweat ran down his jaw. He was right about the men, too—several faces were peering into the cabin from door and window, wearing expressions of horror and concern.

I summoned the presence of mind to nod weakly at them. Jamie's arm was still locked about my middle; I couldn't tell which of us was shaking; both, I thought.

I made it into the wide captain's chair, with considerable assis tance, and lay back palpitating, the fire in my arm still sizzling. Jamie was holding one of my curved suture needles and a length of sterilized cat-gut, looking as dubious over the prospects as I felt.

It was Mr. Willoughby who intervened, quietly taking the needle from Jamie's hands.

"I can do this," he said, in tones of authority. "A moment." And he disappeared aft, presumably to fetch something.

Jamie didn't protest, and neither did I. We heaved twin sighs of relief, in fact, which made me laugh.

"And to think," I said, "I once told Bree that big men were kind and gentle, and the short ones tended to be nasty."

"Well, I suppose there's always the exception that proves the rule, no?" He mopped my streaming face with a wet cloth, quite gently.

"I dinna want to know how ye did this," he said, with a sigh, "but for God's sake, Sassenach, don't do it again!"

"Well, I didn't *intend* to do anything . . ." I began crossly, when I was interrupted by the return of Mr. Willoughby. He was carrying the little roll of green silk I had seen when he cured Jamie's seasickness.

"Oh, ye've got the wee stabbers?" Jamie peered interestedly at the small gold needles, then smiled at me. "Dinna fash yourself, Sassenach, they don't hurt . . . or not much, anyway," he added.

Mr. Willoughby's fingers probed the palm of my right hand, prodding here and there. Then he grasped each of my fingers, wiggled it, and pulled it gently, so that I felt the joints pop slightly. Then he laid two fingers at the base of my wrist, pressing down in the space between the radius and the ulna.

"This is the Inner Gate," he said softly. "Here is quiet. Here is peace." I sincerely hoped he was right. Picking up one of the tiny gold needles, he placed the point over the spot he had marked, and with a dexterous twirl of thumb and forefinger, pierced the skin.

The prick made me jump, but he kept a tight, warm hold on my hand, and I relaxed again.

He placed three needles in each wrist, and a rakish, porcupine-like spray on the crest of my right shoulder. I was getting interested, despite my guinea pig status. Beyond an initial prick at placement, the needles caused no discomfort. Mr. Willoughby was humming, in a low, soothing sort of way, tapping and pressing places on my neck and shoulder.

I couldn't honestly tell whether my right arm was numbed, or whether I was simply distracted by the goings-on, but it did feel somewhat less agonized—at least until he picked up the suture needle and began.

Jamie was sitting on a stool by my left side, holding my left hand as he watched my face. After a moment, he said, rather gruffly, "Let your breath out, Sassenach; it's no going to get any worse than that."

I let go of the breath I hadn't realized I was holding, and realized as well what he was telling me. It was dread of being hurt that had me rigid as a board in the chair. The actual pain of the stitches was unpleasant, all right, but nothing I couldn't stand.

I let my breath out cautiously, and gave him a rough approximation of a smile. Mr. Willoughby was singing under his breath in Chinese. Jamie had translated the words for me a week earlier; it was a pillow-song, in which a young man catalogued the physical charms of his partner, one by one. I hoped he would finish the stitching before he got to her feet.

"That's a verra wicked slash," Jamie said, eyes on Mr. Willoughby's work. I preferred not to look myself. "A parang, was it, or a cutlass, I wonder."

"I think it was a cutlass," I said. "In fact, I know it was. He came after . . ."

"I wonder what led them to attack us," Jamie said, not paying any attention to me. His brows were drawn in speculation. "I canna ha' been the cargo, after all."

"I shouldn't think so," I said. "But maybe they didn't know what we were carrying?" This seemed grossly unlikely; any ship that came within a hundred yards of us would have known—the ammoniac reek of bat guano hovered round us like a miasma.

"Perhaps it's only they thought the ship small enough to take. The *Artemis* itself would bring a fair price, cargo or no."

I blinked as Mr. Willoughby paused in his song to tie a knot. I thought he was down to the navel by now, but wasn't paying close attention.

"Do we know the name of the pirate ship?" I asked. "Granted there's likely a lot of pirates in these waters, but we do know that the *Bruja* was in this area three days ago, and—"

"That's what I'm wondering," he said. "I couldna see a great deal in the darkness, but she was the right size, wi' that wide Spanish beam."

"Well, the pirate that was after me spoke—" I started, but the sound of voices in the corridor made me stop.

Fergus edged in, shy of interrupting, but obviously bursting with excitement. He held something shiny and jingling in one hand.

"Milord," he said, "Maitland has found a dead pirate on the forward deck."

Jamie's red brows went up, and he looked from Fergus to me. "Dead?"

"Very dead, milord," said Fergus, with a small shudder. Maitland was peeking over his shoulder, anxious to claim his share of the glory. "Oh, yes, sir," he assured Jamie earnestly. "Dead as a doornail; his poor head's bashed in something shocking!"

All three men turned and stared at me. I gave them a modest little smile.

Jamie rubbed a hand over his face. His eyes were bloodshot, and a trickle of blood had dried in front of his ear.

"Sassenach," he began, in measured tones.

"I tried to tell you," I said virtuously. With the shock, brandy, acupuncture, and the dawning realization of survival, I was beginning to feel quite pleasantly light-headed. I scarcely noticed Mr. Willoughby's final efforts.

"He was wearing this, milord." Fergus stepped forward and laid the pirate's necklace on the table in front of us. It had the silver buttons from a military uniform, polished *kona* nuts, several large shark's teeth, pieces of polished abalone shell and chunks of mother of pearl, and a large number of jingling coins, all pierced for stringing on a leather thong.

"I thought you should see this at once, milord," Fergus continued. He reached out a hand and lifted one of the shimmering coins. It was silver, untarnished, and through the gathering brandy haze, I could see on its face the twin heads of Alexander. A tetradrachm, of the fourth century B.C. Mint condition.

Thoroughly worn out by the events of the afternoon, I had fallen asleep at once, the pain in my arm dulled by brandy. Now it was full dark, and the brandy had worn off. My arm seemed to swell and throb with each beat of my heart, and any small movement sent tiny jabs of a sharper pain whipping through my arm, like warning flicks of a scorpion's tail.

The moon was three-quarters full, a huge lopsided shape like a golden teardrop, hanging just above the horizon. The ship heeled slightly, and the moon slid slowly out of sight, the Man in the Moon leering rather unpleasantly as he went. I was hot, and possibly a trifle feverish.

There was a jug of water in the cupboard on the far side of the cabin. I felt weak and giddy as I swung my feet over the edge of the berth, and my arm registered a strong protest against being disturbed. I must have made some sound, for the darkness on the floor of the cabin stirred suddenly, and Jamie's voice came drowsily from the region of my feet.

"Are ye hurting, Sassenach?"

"A little," I said, not wanting to be dramatic about it. I set my lips and rose unsteadily to my feet, cradling my right elbow in my left hand.

"That's good," he said.

"That's *good*?" I said, my voice rising indignantly.

There was a soft chuckle from the darkness, and he sat up, his head popping suddenly into sight as it rose above the shadows into the moonlight.

"Aye, it is," he said. "When a wound begins to hurt ye, it means it's healing. Ye didna feel it when it happened, did you?"

"No," I admitted. I certainly felt it now. The air was a good deal cooler out on the open sea, and the salt wind coming through the window felt good on my face. I was damp and sticky with sweat, and the thin chemise clung to my breasts.

"I could see ye didn't. That's what frightened me. Ye never feel a fatal wound, Sassenach," he said softly.

I laughed shortly, but cut it off as the movement jarred my arm.

"And how do you know that?" I asked, fumbling left-handed to pour water into a cup. "Not the sort of thing you'd learn firsthand, I mean."

"Murtagh told me."

The water seemed to purl soundlessly into the cup, the sound o

s pouring lost in the hiss of the bow-wave outside. I set down the
g and lifted the cup, the surface of the water black in the moon-
ght. Jamie had never mentioned Murtagh to me, in the months of
ir reunion. I had asked Fergus, who told me that the wiry little
:ot had died at Culloden, but he knew no more than the bare fact.

"At Culloden." Jamie's voice was barely loud enough to be
:ard above the creak of timber and the whirring of the wind that
•re us along. "Did ye ken they burnt the bodies there? I won-
•red, listening to them do it—what it would be like inside the fire
hen it came my turn." I could hear him swallow, above the
•eaking of the ship. "I found that out, this morning."

The moonlight robbed his face of depth and color; he looked
:e a skull, with the broad, clean planes of cheek and jawbone
hite and his eyes black empty pits.

"I went to Culloden meaning to die," he said, his voice
arcely more than a whisper. "Not the rest of them. I should have
en happy to stop a musket ball at once, and yet I cut my way
ross the field and halfway back, while men on either side o' me
•re blown to bloody bits." He stood up, then, looking down at
•.

"Why?" he said. "Why, Claire? Why am I alive, and they are
t?"

"I don't know," I said softly. "For your sister, and your family,
aybe? For me?"

"They had families," he said. "Wives, and sweethearts; chil-
:n to mourn them. And yet they are gone. And I am still here."

"I don't know, Jamie," I said at last. I touched his cheek,
eady roughened by newly sprouting beard, irrepressible evi-
nce of life. "You aren't ever going to know."

He sighed, his cheekbone pressed against my palm for a mo-
:nt.

"Aye, I ken that well enough. But I canna help the asking, when
iink of them—especially Murtagh." He turned restlessly away,
eyes empty shadows, and I knew he walked Drumossie Moor
ain, with the ghosts.

"We should have gone sooner; the men had been standing for
urs, starved and half-frozen. But they waited for His Highness
give the order to charge."

And Charles Stuart, perched safely on a rock, well behind the
e of battle, having seized personal command of his troops for

the first time, had dithered and delayed. And the English canno
had had time to bear squarely on the lines of ragged Highlande
and opened fire.

"It was a relief, I think," Jamie said softly. "Every man on th
field knew the cause was lost, and we were dead. And still w
stood there, watching the English guns come up, and the cann
mouths open black before us. No one spoke. I couldna hear an
thing but the wind, and the English soldiers shouting, on the oth
side of the field."

And then the guns had roared, and men had fallen, and tho
still standing, rallied by a late and ragged order, had seized th
swords and charged the enemy, the sound of their Gaelic shrieki
drowned by the guns, lost in the wind.

"The smoke was so thick, I couldna see more than a few f
before me. I kicked off my shoon and ran into it, shouting." T
bloodless line of his lips turned up slightly.

"I was happy," he said, sounding a bit surprised. "Not scair
all. I meant to die, after all; there was nothing to fear except tha
might be wounded and not die at once. But I would die, and the
would be all over, and I would find ye again, and it would be
right."

I moved closer to him, and his hand rose up from the shadows
take mine.

"Men fell to either side of me, and I could hear the grapes
and the musket balls hum past my head like bumblebees. Bu
wasna touched."

He had reached the British lines unscathed, one of very f
Highlanders to have completed the charge across Culloden Mo
An English gun crew looked up, startled, at the tall Highlan
who burst from the smoke like a demon, the blade of his bro
sword gleaming with rain and then dull with blood.

"There was a small part of my mind that asked why I should
killin' them," he said reflectively. "For surely I knew that
were lost; there was no gain to it. But there is a lust to killing
you'll know that?" His fingers tightened on mine, questioni
and I squeezed back in affirmation.

"I couldna stop—or I would not." His voice was quiet, with
bitterness or recrimination. "It's a verra old feeling, I think;
wish to take an enemy with ye to the grave. I could feel it ther

ot red thing in my chest and belly, and . . . I gave myself to it,"
ᵉ ended simply.

There were four men tending the cannon, none armed with
ore than a pistol and knife, none expecting attack at such close
ᵤarters. They stood helpless against the berserk strength of his
ᵉspair, and he killed them all.

"The ground shook under my feet," he said, "and I was near
ᵉafened by the noise. I couldna think. And then it came to me
at I was behind the English guns." A soft chuckle came from
ᵉlow. "A verra poor place to try to be killed, no?"

So he had started back across the moor, to join the Highland
ᵊad.

"He was sitting against a tussock near the middle of the field—
ᵤurtagh. He'd been struck a dozen times at least, and there was a
ᵊeadful wound in his head—I knew he was dead."

He hadn't been, though; when Jamie had fallen to his knees
ᵊside his godfather and taken the small body in his arms, Mur-
ᵍh's eyes had opened.

"He saw me. And he smiled." And then the older man's hand
ᵈd touched his cheek briefly. "Dinna be afraid, *a bhalaich*,"
ᵘurtagh had said, using the endearment for a small, beloved boy.
ᵗt doesna hurt a bit to die."

I stood quietly for a long time, holding Jamie's hand. Then he
ᵍhed, and his other hand closed very, very gently about my
ᵒunded arm.

"Too many folk have died, Sassenach, because they knew me—
 suffered for the knowing. I would give my own body to save ye
ᵐoment's pain—and yet I could wish to close my hand just now,
at I might hear ye cry out and know for sure that I havena killed
ᵤu, too."

I leaned forward, pressing a kiss on the skin of his chest. He
ᵉpt naked in the heat.

"You haven't killed me. You didn't kill Murtagh. And we'll find
ᵃ. Take me back to bed, Jamie."

Sometime later, as I drowsed on the edge of sleep, he spoke
ᵒm the floor beside my bed.

"Ye know, I seldom wanted to go home to Laoghaire," he said
ᵑtemplatively. "And yet, at least when I did, I'd find her where
ᵗ left her."

ᴵ turned my head to the side, where his soft breathing came

from the darkened floor. "Oh? And is that the kind of wife yo
want? The sort who stays put?"

He made a small sound between a chuckle and a cough, b
didn't answer, and after a few moments, the sound of his breathin
changed to a soft, rhythmic snore.

55

Ishmael

slept restlessly, and woke up late and feverish, with a throbbing headache just behind my eyes. I felt ill enough not to protest when Marsali insisted on bathing my forehead, but relaxed gratefully, eyes closed, enjoying the cool touch of the vinegar-soaked cloth on my pounding temples.

It was so soothing, in fact, that I drifted off to sleep again after she left. I was dreaming uneasily of dark mine shafts and the chalk of charred bones, when I was suddenly roused by a crash that brought me bolt upright and sent a shaft of pure white pain ripping through my head.

"What?" I exclaimed, clutching my head in both hands, as though this might prevent it falling off. "What is it?" The window had been covered to keep the light from disturbing me, and it took a moment for my stunned vision to adapt to the dimness.

On the opposite side of the cabin, a large figure was mimicking me, clutching its own head in apparent agony. Then it spoke, releasing a volley of very bad language, in a mixture of Chinese, French, and Gaelic.

"Damn!" it said, the exclamations tapering off into milder English. "Goddamn it to hell!" Jamie staggered to the window, still rubbing the head he had smashed on the edge of my cupboard. He shoved aside the covering and pushed the window open, bringing a welcome draft of fresh air in along with a dazzle of light.

"What in the name of bloody hell do you think you're doing?" I demanded, with considerable asperity. The light jabbed my

tender eyeballs like needles, and the movement involved in clutch
ing my head had done the stitches in my arm no good at all.

"I was looking for your medicine box," he replied, wincing a
he felt the crown of his head. "Damn, I've caved in my skull
Look at that!" He thrust two fingers, slightly smeared with blood
under my nose. I dropped the vinegar-soaked cloth over the finger
and collapsed back on my pillow.

"Why do you need the medicine box, and why didn't you ask
me in the first place, instead of bumping around like a bee in
bottle?" I said irritably.

"I didna want to wake ye from your sleep," he said, sheepishl
enough that I laughed, despite the various throbbings going on in
my anatomy.

"That's all right; I wasn't enjoying it," I assured him. "Why do
you need the box? Is someone hurt?"

"Aye. I am," he said, dabbing gingerly at the top of his head
with the cloth and scowling at the result. "Ye dinna want to look a
my head?"

The answer to this was "Not especially," but I obligingly mo
tioned to him to bend over, presenting the top of his head fo
inspection. There was a reasonably impressive lump under th
thick hair, with a small cut from the edge of the shelf, but th
damage seemed a bit short of concussion.

"It's not fractured," I assured him. "You have the thicke
skull I've ever seen." Moved by an instinct as old as motherhood
I leaned forward and kissed the bump gently. He lifted his hea
eyes wide with surprise.

"That's supposed to make it feel better," I explained. A smil
tugged at the corner of his mouth.

"Oh. Well, then." He bent down and gently kissed the bandag
on my wounded arm.

"Better?" he inquired, straightening up.

"Lots."

He laughed, and reaching for the decanter, poured out a tot o
whisky, which he handed to me.

"I wanted that stuff ye use to wash out scrapes and such," h
explained, pouring another for himself.

"Hawthorn lotion. I haven't got any ready-made, because
doesn't keep," I said, pushing myself upright. "If it's urgen
though, I can brew some; it doesn't take long." The thought o

getting up and walking to the galley was daunting, but perhaps I'd feel better once I was moving.

"Not urgent," he assured me. "It's only there's a prisoner in the hold who's a bit bashed about."

I lowered my cup, blinking at him.

"A prisoner? Where did we get a prisoner?"

"From the pirate ship." He frowned at his whisky. "Though I dinna think he's a pirate."

"What is he?"

He tossed off the whisky neatly, in one gulp, and shook his head.

"Damned if I know. From the scars on his back, likely a runaway slave, but in that case, I canna think why he did what he did."

"What did he do?"

"Dived off the *Bruja* into the sea. MacGregor saw him go, and then after the *Bruja* made sail, he saw the man bobbing about in the waves and threw him a rope."

"Well, that is funny; why should he do that?" I asked. I was becoming interested, and the throbbing in my head seemed to be lessening as I sipped my whisky.

Jamie ran his fingers through his hair, and stopped, wincing.

"I dinna ken, Sassenach," he said, gingerly smoothing the hair on his crown flat. "It wouldna be likely for a crew like ours to try to board the pirate—any merchant would just fight them off; there's no reason to try to take them. But if he didna mean to escape from us—perhaps he meant to escape from them, aye?"

The last golden drops of the whisky ran down my throat. It was Jared's special blend, the next-to-last bottle, and thoroughly justified the name he had given it—*Ceò Gheasacach.* "Magic Mist." Feeling somewhat restored, I pushed myself upright.

"If he's hurt, perhaps I should take a look at him," I suggested, swinging my feet out of the berth.

Given Jamie's behavior of the day before, I fully expected him to press me flat and call for Marsali to come and sit on my chest. Instead, he looked at me thoughtfully, and nodded.

"Aye, well. If ye're sure ye can stand, Sassenach?"

I wasn't all that sure, but gave it a try. The room tilted when I stood up, and black and yellow spots danced before my eyes, but I stayed upright, clinging to Jamie's arm. After a moment, a small

amount of blood reluctantly consented to reenter my head, and the
spots went away, showing Jamie's face looking anxiously down at
me.

"All right," I said, taking a deep breath. "Carry on."

The prisoner was below in what the crew called the orlop, a
lower-deck space full of miscellaneous cargo. There was a small
timbered area, walled off at the bow of the ship, that sometimes
housed drunk or unruly seamen, and here he had been secured.

It was dark and airless down in the bowels of the ship, and I felt
myself becoming dizzy again as I made my way slowly along the
companionway behind Jamie and the glow of his lantern.

When he unlocked the door, at first I saw nothing at all in the
makeshift brig. Then, as Jamie stooped to enter with his lantern,
the shine of the man's eyes betrayed his presence. "Black as the
ace of spades" was the first thought that popped into my slightly
addled mind, as the edges of face and form took shape against the
darkness of the timbers.

No wonder Jamie had thought him a runaway slave. The man
looked African, not island-born. Besides the deep red-black of his
skin, his demeanor wasn't that of a man raised as a slave. He was
sitting on a cask, hands bound behind his back and feet tied together, but I saw his head rise and his shoulders straighten as
Jamie ducked under the lintel of the tiny space. He was very thin
but very muscular, clad in nothing but a ragged pair of trousers.
The lines of his body were clear; he was tensed for attack or
defense, but not submission.

Jamie saw it, too, and motioned me to stay well back against the
wall. He placed the lantern on a cask, and squatted down before
the captive, at eye-level.

"*Amiki*," he said, spreading out his empty hands, palm up.
"*Amiki. Bene-bene.*" Friend. Is good. It was taki-taki, the all-
purpose pidgin polyglot that the traders from Barbados to Trinidad
spoke in the ports.

The man stared impassively at Jamie for a moment, eyes still as
tide pools. Then one eyebrow flicked up and he extended his
bound feet before him.

"*Bene-bene, amiki?*" he said, with an ironic intonation that
couldn't be missed, whatever the language. Is good, friend?

Jamie snorted briefly, amused, and rubbed a finger under his
nose.

"It's a point," he said in English.

"Does he speak English, or French?" I moved a little closer. The captive's eyes rested on me for a moment, then passed away, indifferent.

"If he does, he'll no admit it. Picard and Fergus tried talking to him last night. He willna say a word, just stares at them. What he just said is the first he's spoken since he came aboard. *¿Habla Español?*" he said suddenly to the prisoner. There was no response. The man didn't even look at Jamie; just went on staring impassively at the square of open doorway behind me.

"Er, *sprechen Sie Deutsch*?" I said tentatively. He didn't answer, which was just as well, as the question had exhausted my own supply of German. "*Nicht* Hollander, either, I don't suppose."

Jamie shot me a sardonic look. "I canna tell much about him, Sassenach, but I'm fairly sure he's no a Dutchman."

"They have slaves on Eleuthera, don't they? That's a Dutch island," I said irritably. "Or St. Croix—that's Danish, isn't it?" Slowly as my mind was working this morning, it hadn't escaped me that the captive was our only clue to the pirates' whereabouts —and the only frail link to Ian. "Do you know enough taki-taki to ask him about Ian?"

Jamie shook his head, eyes intent on the prisoner. "No. Besides what I said to him already, I ken how to say '*not* good,' 'how much?' 'give it to me,' and 'drop that, ye bastard,' none of which seems a great deal to the point at present."

Stymied for the moment, we stared at the prisoner, who stared impassively back.

"To hell with it," Jamie said suddenly. He drew the dirk from his belt, went behind the cask, and sawed through the thongs round the prisoner's wrists.

He cut the ankle bindings as well, then sat back on his heels, the knife laid across his thigh.

"Friend," he said firmly in taki-taki. "Is good?"

The prisoner didn't say anything, but after a moment, he nodded slightly, his expression warily quizzical.

"There's a chamber pot in the corner," Jamie said in English, rising and sheathing his dirk. "Use it, and then my wife will tend your wounds."

A very faint flicker of amusement crossed the man's face. He

nodded once more, this time in acceptance of defeat. He ros
slowly from the cask and turned, stiff hands fumbling at his trou
sers. I looked askance at Jamie.

"It's one of the worst things about being bound that way," h
explained matter-of-factly. "Ye canna take a piss by yourself."

"I see," I said, not wanting to think about how he knew that

"That, and the pain in your shoulders," he said. "Be carefu
touching him, Sassenach." The note of warning in his voice wa
clear, and I nodded. It wasn't the man's shoulders he was con
cerned about.

I still felt light-headed, and the stuffiness of the surrounding
had made my headache throb again, but I was less battered tha
the prisoner, who had indeed been "bashed about" at some stag
of the proceedings.

Bashed though he was, his injuries seemed largely superficia
A swollen knot rose on the man's forehead, and a deep scrape ha
left a crusted reddish patch on one shoulder. He was undoubted
bruised in a number of places, but given the remarkably dee
shade of his skin and the darkness of the surroundings, I couldn
tell where.

There were deep bands of rawness on ankles and wrists, whe
he had pulled against the thongs. I hadn't made any of the haw
thorn lotion, but I had brought the jar of gentian salve. I ease
myself down on the deck next to him, but he took no more notic
of me than of the deck beneath his feet, even when I began
spread the cool blue cream on his wounds.

What was more interesting than the fresh injuries, though, we
the healed ones. At close range, I could see the faint white lines
three parallel slashes, running across the slope of each cheekbon
and a series of three short vertical lines on the high, narrow for
head, just between his brows. Tribal scars. African-born for sur
then; such scars were made during manhood rituals, or so Murph
had told me.

His flesh was warm and smooth under my fingers, slicked wi
sweat. I felt warm, too; sweaty and unwell. The deck rose gent
beneath me, and I put my hand on his back to keep my balanc
The thin, tough lines of healed whipstrokes webbed his shoulder
like the furrows of tiny worms beneath his skin. The feel of the
was unexpected; so much like the feel of the marks on Jamie

own back. I swallowed, feeling queasy, but went on with my doctoring.

The man ignored me completely, even when I touched spots I knew must be painful. His eyes were fixed on Jamie, who was watching the prisoner with equal intentness.

The problem was plain. The man was almost certainly a runaway slave. He hadn't wanted to speak to us, for fear that his speech would give away his owner's island, and that we would then find out his original owner and return him to captivity.

Now we knew that he spoke—or at least understood—English, it was bound to increase his wariness. Even if we assured him that it was not our intention either to return him to an owner or to enslave him ourselves, he was unlikely to trust us. I couldn't say that I blamed him, under the circumstances.

On the other hand, this man was our best—and possibly the only—chance of finding out what had happened to Ian Murray aboard the *Bruja*.

When at length I had bandaged the man's wrists and ankles, Jamie gave me a hand to rise, then spoke to the prisoner.

"You'll be hungry, I expect," he said. "Come along to the cabin, and we'll eat." Not waiting for a response, he took my good arm and turned to the door. There was silence behind us as we moved into the corridor, but when I looked back, the slave was there, following a few feet behind.

Jamie led us to my cabin, disregarding the curious glances of the sailors we passed, only stopping by Fergus long enough to order food to be sent from the galley.

"Back to bed with ye, Sassenach," he said firmly, when we reached the cabin. I didn't argue. My arm hurt, my head hurt, and I could feel little waves of heat flickering behind my eyes. It looked as though I would have to break down and use a little of the precious penicillin on myself, after all. There was still a chance that my body could throw off the infection, but I couldn't afford to wait too long.

Jamie had poured out a glass of whisky for me, and another for our guest. Still wary, the man accepted it, and took a sip, eyes widening in surprise. I supposed Scotch whisky must be a novelty to him.

Jamie took a glass for himself and sat down, motioning the slave to the other seat, across the small table.

"My name is Fraser," he said. "I am captain here. My wife,'
he added, with a nod toward my berth.

The prisoner hesitated, but then set down his glass with an air o
decision.

"They be callin' me Ishmael," he said, in a voice like hone
poured over coal. "I ain't no pirate. I be a cook."

"Murphy's going to like that," I remarked, but Jamie ignore
me. There was a faint line between the ruddy brows, as he felt hi
way into the conversation.

"A ship's cook?" he asked, taking care to make his voic
sound casual. Only the tap of his two stiff fingers against his thigl
betrayed him—and that, only to me.

"No, mon, I don't got nothin' to do with that ship!" Ishmae
was vehement. "They taken me off the shore, say they kill me,
don' go long by them, be easy. I ain't no pirate!" he repeated, an
it dawned on me belatedly that of course he wouldn't wish to b
taken for a pirate—whether he was one or not. Piracy was punish
able by hanging, and he could have no way of knowing that w
were as eager as he to stay clear of the Royal Navy.

"Aye, I see." Jamie hit the right balance, between soothing an
skeptical. He leaned back slightly in the big wheel-backed chai
"And how did the *Bruja* come to take ye prisoner, then? No
where," he added quickly, as a look of alarm flitted across th
prisoner's face.

"Ye needna tell me where ye came from; that's of no concern t
me. Only I should care to know how ye came to fall into thei
hands, and how long ye've been with them. Since, as ye say, y
werena one of them." The hint was broad enough to spread butte
on. We didn't mean to return him to his owner; however, if h
didn't oblige with information, we might just turn him over to th
Crown as a pirate.

The prisoner's eyes darkened; no fool, he had grasped the poir
at once. His head twitched briefly sideways, and his eyes na
rowed.

"I be catchin' fish by the river," he said. "Big ship, he com
sailin' up the river slow, little boats be pullin' him. Men in th
little boat, they see me, holler out. I drop the fish, be runnin', b
they close by. They men jump out, kotch me by the cane fiel
figure they take me to sell. Tha's all, mon." He shrugged, signa
ing the conclusion of his story.

"Aye, I see." Jamie's eyes were intent on the prisoner. He esitated, wanting to ask where the river was, but not quite daring , for fear the man would clam up again. "While ye were on the iip—did ye see any boys among the crew, or as prisoners, too? oys, young men?"

The man's eyes widened slightly; he hadn't been expecting that. e paused warily, but then nodded, with a faintly derisive glint in s eye.

"Yes, mon, they have boys. Why? You be wantin' one?" His ance flicked to me and then back to Jamie, one eyebrow raised. Jamie's head jerked, and a slight flush rose on his cheekbones at e implication.

"I do," he said levelly. "I am looking for a young kinsman ho was taken by pirates. I should feel myself greatly obliged to yone who might assist me in finding him." He lifted one eye- ow significantly.

The prisoner grunted slightly, his nostrils flaring.

"That so? What you be doin' for me, I be helpin' you fin' this y?"

"I should set you ashore at any port of your choosing, with a ir sum in gold," Jamie replied. "But of course I should require oof that ye did have knowledge of my nephew's whereabouts, e?"

"Huh." The prisoner was still wary, but beginning to relax. You tell me, mon—what this boy be like?"

Jamie hesitated for a moment, studying the prisoner, but then ook his head.

"No," he said thoughtfully. "I dinna think that will work. *You* scribe to *me* such lads as ye saw on the pirate vessel."

The prisoner eyed Jamie for a moment, then broke out in a low, h laugh.

"You no particular fool, mon," he said. "You know that?"

"I know that," Jamie said dryly. "So long as ye know it as ll. Tell me, then."

Ishmael snorted briefly, but complied, pausing only to refresh mself from the tray of food Fergus had brought. Fergus himself unged against the door, watching the prisoner through half-lid- d eyes.

"They be twelve boys talkin' strange, like you."

Jamie's eyebrows shot up, and he exchanged a glance of astonishment with me. Twelve?

"Like me?" He said. "White boys, English? Or Scots, d'y mean?"

Ishmael shook his head in incomprehension; "Scot" was not i his vocabulary.

"Talkin' like dogs fightin'," he explained. "Grrrr! Wuff!" H growled, shaking his head in illustration like a dog worrying a ra and I saw Fergus's shoulders shake in suppressed hilarity.

"Scots for sure," I said, trying not to laugh. Jamie shot me brief dirty look, then returned his attention to Ishmael.

"Verra well, then," he said, exaggerating his natural soft bur "Twelve Scottish lads. What did they look like?"

Ishmael squinted dubiously, chewing a piece of mango from th tray. He wiped the juice from the corner of his mouth and shoo his head.

"I only see them once, mon. Tell you all I see, though." H closed his eyes and frowned, the vertical lines on his forehea drawing close together.

"Four boys be yellow-haired, six brown, two with black hai Two shorter than me, one maybe the size that *griffon* there"—h nodded toward Fergus, who stiffened in outrage at the insult— "one big, not so big as you . . ."

"Aye, and how will they have been dressed?" Slowly, car fully, Jamie drew him through the descriptions, asking for detail demanding comparisons—how tall? how fat? what color eyes?— carefully concealing the direction of his interest as he drew th man further into conversation.

My head had stopped spinning, but the fatigue was still ther weighting my senses. I let my eyes close, obscurely soothed by th deep, murmuring voices. Jamie *did* sound rather like a big, fier dog, I thought, with his soft growling burr and the abrupt, clippe sound of his consonants.

"Wuff," I murmured under my breath, and my belly muscl quivered slightly under my folded hands.

Ishmael's voice was just as deep, but smooth and low, rich hot chocolate made with cream. I began to drift, lulled by th sound of it.

He sounded like Joe Abernathy, I thought drowsily, dictating a

utopsy report—unvarnished and unappetizing physical details,
elated in a voice like a deep golden lullaby.

I could see Joe's hands in memory, dark on the pale skin of an
accident victim, moving swiftly as he made his verbal notes to the
ape recorder.

"Deceased is a tall man, approximately six feet in height, and
slender in build. . . ."

A tall man, slender.

"—that one, he bein' tall, bein' thin . . ."

I came awake suddenly, heart pounding, hearing the echo of
oe's voice coming from the table a few feet away.

"No!" I said, quite suddenly, and all three men stopped and
ooked at me in surprise. I pushed back the weight of my damp
hair and waved weakly at them.

"Don't mind me; I was dreaming, I think."

They returned to their conversation, and I lay still, eyes half-
losed, but no longer sleepy.

There was no physical resemblance. Joe was stocky and bear-
ike; this Ishmael slender and lean, though the swell of muscle
ver the curve of his shoulder suggested considerable strength.

Joe's face was broad and amiable; this man's narrow and wary-
yed, with a high forehead that made his tribal scars the more
triking. Joe's skin was the color of fresh coffee, Ishmael's the
eep red-black of a burning ember, which Stern had told me was
haracteristic of slaves from the Guinea coast—not so highly
rized as the blue-black Senegalese, but more valuable than the
ellow-brown Yaga and Congolese.

But if I closed my eyes entirely, I could hear Joe's voice speak-
ng, even allowing for the faint Caribbean lilt of slave-English. I
racked my eyelids and looked carefully, searching for any signs
f resemblance. There were none, but I did see what I had seen
efore, and not noticed, among the other scars and marks on the
man's battered torso. What I had thought merely a scrape was in
act a deep abrasion that overlay a wide, flat scar, cut in the form
f a rough square just below the point of the shoulder. The mark
as raw and pink, newly healed. I should have seen it at once, if
ot for the darkness of the orlop, and the scrape that obscured it.

I lay quite still, trying to remember. "No *slave* name," Joe had
aid derisively, referring to his son's self-christening. Clearly, Ishmael had cut away an owner's brand, to prevent identification,

should he be recaptured. But whose? And surely the name Ishmael was no more than coincidence.

Maybe not so farfetched a one, though; "Ishmael" almost certainly wasn't the man's real name. "They be *callin'* me Ishmael," he had said. That, too, was a slave name, given him by one owner or another. And if young Lenny had been climbing his family tree, as it seemed, what more likely than that he should have chosen one of his ancestors' given names in symbol? If. But if he was . . .

I lay looking up at the claustrophobic ceiling of the berth, suppositions spinning through my head. Whether this man had any link with Joe or not, the possibility had reminded me of something.

Jamie was catechizing the man about the personnel and structure of the *Bruja*—for so the ship that had attacked us had been—but I was paying no attention. I sat up, cautiously, so as not to make the dizziness worse, and signaled to Fergus.

"I need air," I said. "Help me up on deck, will you?" Jamie glanced at me with a hint of worry, but I smiled reassuringly at him, and took Fergus's arm.

"Where are the papers for that slave we bought on Barbados?" I demanded, as soon as we were out of earshot of the cabin. "And where's the slave, for that matter?"

Fergus looked at me curiously, but obligingly rummaged in his coat.

"I have the papers here, milady," he said, handing them to me. "As for the slave, I believe he is in the crew's quarters. Why?" he added, unable to restrain his curiosity.

I ignored the question, fumbling through the grubby, repellent bits of paper.

"There it is," I said, finding the bit I remembered Jamie reading to me. "Abernathy! It *was* Abernathy! Branded on the left shoulder with a fleur-de-lys. Did you notice that mark, Fergus?"

He shook his head, looking mildly bewildered.

"No, milady."

"Then come with me," I said, turning toward the crew's quarters. "I want to see how big it is."

The mark was about three inches long and three wide; a flower surmounting the initial "A," burned into the skin a few inches below the point of the shoulder. It was the right size, and in the right place, to match the scar on the man Ishmael. It wasn' however, a fleur-de-lys; that had been the mistake of a careless transcriber. It was a sixteen-petaled rose—the Jacobite emblem of Charles Stuart. I blinked at it in amazement; what patriotic exile had chosen this bizarre method of maintaining allegiance to the vanquished Stuarts?

"Milady, I think you should return to your bed," Fergus said. He was frowning at me as I stooped over Temeraire, who bore this inspection as stolidly as everything else. "You are the color of goose turds, and milord will not like it at all if I allow you to fall down on the deck."

"I won't fall down," I assured him. "And I don't care what color I am. I think we've just had a stroke of luck. Listen, Fergus, I want you to do something for me."

"Anything, milady," he said, grabbing me by the elbow as a shift in the wind sent me staggering across the suddenly tilting deck. "But not," he added firmly, "until you are safely back in your bed."

I allowed him to lead me back to the cabin, for I really didn't feel at all well, but not before giving him my instructions. As we entered the cabin, Jamie stood up from the table to greet us.

"There ye are, Sassenach! Are ye all right?" he asked, frowning down at me. "Ye've gone a nasty color, like a spoilt custard."

"I am perfectly fine," I said, through my teeth, easing myself down on the bunk to avoid jarring my arm. "Have you and Mr. Ishmael finished your conversation?"

Jamie glanced at the prisoner, and I saw the flat black gaze that locked with his. The atmosphere between them was not hostile, but it was charged in some way. Jamie nodded in dismissal.

"We've finished—for the moment," he said. He turned to Fergus. "See our guest below, will ye, Fergus, and see to it that he's fed and clothed?" He remained standing until Ishmael had left under Fergus's wing. Then he sat down beside my berth and squinted into the darkness at me.

"Ye look awful," he said. "Had I best fetch your kit and be feeding ye a wee tonic or somesuch?"

"No," I said. "Jamie, listen—I think I know where our friend Ishmael came from."

He lifted one brow.

"You do?"

I explained about the scar on Ishmael, and the almost matching brand on the slave Temeraire, without mentioning what had given me the idea in the first place.

"Five will get you ten that they came from the same place—from this Mrs. Abernathy's, on Jamaica." I said.

"Five will . . . ? Och," he said, waving away my confusing reference in the interests of continuing the discussion. "Well, ye could be right, Sassenach, and I hope so. The wily black bastard wouldna say where he was from. Not that I can blame him," he added fairly. "God, if I'd got away from such a life, there's no power on earth would take me back!" He spoke with a surprising vehemence.

"No, I wouldn't blame him either," I said. "But what did he tell you, about the boys? Has he seen Young Ian?"

The frowning lines of his face relaxed.

"Aye, I'm almost sure he has." One fist curled on his knee in anticipation. "Two of the lads he described could be Ian. And knowin' it was the *Bruja,* I canna think otherwise. And if you're right about where he's come from, Sassenach, we might have him —we may find him at last!" Ishmael, while refusing to give any clue as to where the *Bruja* had picked him up, had gone so far as to say that the twelve boys—all prisoners—had been taken off the ship together, soon after his own capture.

"Twelve lads," Jamie repeated, his momentary look of excitement fading back into a frown. "What in the name of God would someone be wanting, to kidnap twelve lads from Scotland?"

"Perhaps he's a collector," I said, feeling more light-headed by the moment. "Coins, and gems, and Scottish boys."

"Ye think whoever's got Ian has the treasure as well?" He glanced curiously at me.

"I don't know," I said, feeling suddenly very tired. I yawned rackingly. "We may know for sure about Ishmael, though. I told Fergus to see that Temeraire gets a look at him. If they are from the same place . . ." I yawned again, my body seeking the oxygen that loss of blood had deprived me of.

"That's verra sensible of ye, Sassenach," Jamie said, sounding faintly surprised that I was capable of sense. For that matter, I was a little surprised myself; my thoughts were becoming more fragmented by the moment, and it was an effort to keep talking logically.

Jamie saw it; he patted my hand and stood up.

"Ye dinna trouble yourself about it now, Sassenach. Rest, and I'll send Marsali down wi' some tea."

"Whisky," I said, and he laughed.

"All right, then, whisky," he agreed. He smoothed my hair back, and leaning into the berth, kissed my hot forehead.

"Better?" he asked, smiling.

"Lots." I smiled back and closed my eyes.

56

Turtle Soup

hen I woke again, in the late afternoon, I ached all over. I had thrown off the covers in my sleep, and lay sprawled in my shift, my skin hot and dry in the soft air. My arm ached abominably, and I could feel each of Mr. Willoughby's forty-three elegant stitches like red-hot safety pins stuck through my flesh.

No help for it; I was going to have to use the penicillin. I might be proof against smallpox, typhoid, and the common cold in its eighteenth-century incarnation, but I wasn't immortal, and God only knew what insanitary substances the Portuguese had been employing his cutlass on before applying it to me.

The short trip across the room to the cupboard where my clothes hung left me sweating and shivering, and I had to sit down quite suddenly, the skirt clutched to my bosom, in order to avoid falling.

"Sassenach! Are ye all right?" Jamie poked his head through the low doorway, looking worried.

"No," I said. "Come here a minute, will you? I need you to do something."

"Wine? A biscuit? Murphy's made a wee broth for ye, special." He was beside me in a moment, the back of his hand cool against my flushed cheek. "God, you're burning!"

"Yes, I know," I said. "Don't worry, though; I have medicine for it."

I fumbled one-handed in the pocket of the skirt, and pulled out

he case containing the syringes and ampules. My right arm was
ore enough that any movement made me clench my teeth.

"Your turn," I said wryly, shoving the case across the table
oward Jamie. "Here's your chance for revenge, if you want it."

He looked blankly at the case, then at me.

"What?" he said. "Ye want me to stab ye with one of these
pikes?"

"I wish you wouldn't put it quite that way, but yes," I said.

"In the bum?" His lips twitched.

"Yes, damn you!"

He looked at me for a moment, one corner of his mouth curling
lightly upward. Then he bowed his head over the case, red hair
lowing in the shaft of sun from the window.

"Tell me what to do, then," he said.

I directed him carefully, guiding him through the preparation
nd filling of the syringe, and then took it myself, checking for air
ubbles, clumsily left-handed. By the time I had given it back to
im and arranged myself on the berth, he had ceased to find
nything faintly funny about the situation.

"Are ye sure ye want me to do it?" he said doubtfully. "I'm no
erra good with my hands."

That made me laugh, in spite of my throbbing arm. I had seen
im do everything with those hands, from delivering foals and
uilding walls, to skinning deer and setting type, all with the same
ght and dextrous touch.

"Well, aye," he said, when I said as much. "But it's no quite
e same, is it? The closest thing I've done to this is to dirk a man
the wame, and it feels a bit strange to think of doin' such a thing
you, Sassenach."

I glanced back over my shoulder, to find him gnawing dubiously
n his lower lip, the brandy-soaked pad in one hand, the syringe
eld gingerly in the other.

"Look," I said. "I did it to you; you *know* what it feels like. It
asn't that bad, was it?" He was beginning to make me rather
ervous.

"Mmphm." Pressing his lips together, he knelt down by the
ed and gently wiped a spot on my backside with the cool, wet
ad. "Is this all right?"

"That's fine. Press the point in at a bit of an angle, not straight
—you see how the point of the needle's cut at an angle? Push it

in about a quarter-inch—don't be afraid to jab a bit, skin's toughe than you think to get through—and then push down the plunge very slowly, you don't want to do it too fast."

I closed my eyes and waited. After a moment, I opened them and looked back. He was pale, and a faint sheen of sweat glim mered over his cheekbones.

"Never mind." I heaved myself upright, bracing against th wave of dizziness. "Here, give me that." I snatched the pad from his hand and swiped a patch across the top of my thigh. My han trembled slightly from the fever.

"But—"

"Shut up!" I took the syringe and aimed it as well as I could left-handed, then plunged it into the muscle. It hurt. It hurt mor when I pressed down on the plunger, and my thumb slipped off

Then Jamie's hands were there, one steadying my leg, the othe on the needle, slowly pressing down until the last of the whit liquid had vanished from the tube. I took one quick, deep breat when he pulled it out.

"Thanks," I said, after a moment.

"I'm sorry," he said softly, a minute later. His hand cam behind my back, easing me down.

"It's all right." My eyes were closed, and there were littl colored patterns on the inside of my eyelids. They reminded me c the lining of a doll's suitcase I had had as a child; tiny pink an silver stars on a dark background. "I'd forgotten; it's hard to do the first few times. I suppose sticking a dirk in someone *is* easier, I added. "You aren't worried about hurting them, after all."

He didn't say anything, but exhaled rather strongly through h nose. I could hear him moving about the room, putting the case c syringes away and hanging up my skirt. The site of the injectio felt like a knot under my skin.

"I'm sorry," I said. "I didn't mean it that way."

"Well, ye should," he said evenly. "It *is* easier to kill someon to save your own life than it is to hurt someone to save their Ye're a deal braver than I am, and I dinna mind your saying so."

I opened my eyes and looked at him.

"The hell you don't."

He stared down at me, blue eyes narrowed. The corner of h mouth turned up.

"The hell I don't," he agreed.

I laughed, but it hurt my arm.

"I'm not, and you aren't, and I didn't mean it that way, anyway," I said, and closed my eyes again.

"Mmphm."

I could hear the thump of feet on the deck above, and Mr. Warren's voice, raised in organized impatience. We had passed Great Abaco and Eleuthera in the night, and were now headed south toward Jamaica, with the wind behind us.

"*I* wouldn't risk being shot and hacked at, and arrested and hanged, if there were any choice about it," I said.

"Neither would I," he said dryly.

"But you—" I began, and then stopped. I looked at him curiously. "You really think that," I said slowly. "That you don't have a choice about it. Don't you?"

He was turned slightly away from me, eyes fixed on the port. The sun shone on the bridge of his long, straight nose and he rubbed a finger slowly up and down it. The broad shoulders rose slightly, and fell.

"I'm a man, Sassenach," he said, very softly. "If I thought there was a choice . . . then I maybe couldna do it. Ye dinna need to be so brave about things if ye ken ye canna help it, aye?" He looked at me then, with a faint smile. "Like a woman in childbirth, aye? Ye must do it, and it makes no difference if you're afraid—ye'll do it. It's only when ye ken ye can say no that it takes courage."

I lay quiet for a bit, watching him. He had closed his eyes and leaned back in the chair, auburn lashes long and absurdly childish against his cheeks. They contrasted strangely with the smudges beneath his eyes and the deeper lines at the corners. He was tired; he'd barely slept since the sighting of the pirate vessel.

"I haven't told you about Graham Menzies, have I?" I said at last. The blue eyes opened at once.

"No. Who was he?"

"A patient. At the hospital in Boston."

Graham had been in his late sixties when I knew him; a Scottish immigrant who hadn't lost his burr, despite nearly forty years in Boston. He was a fisherman, or had been; when I knew him he owned several lobster boats, and let others do the fishing for him. He was a lot like the Scottish soldiers I had known at Preston-

pans and Falkirk; stoic and humorous at once, willing to jok‹
about anything that was too painful to suffer in silence.

"You'll be careful, now, lassie," was the last thing he said t‹
me as I watched the anesthetist set up the intravenous drip tha‹
would maintain him while I amputated his cancerous left leg. "B‹
sure ye're takin' off the right one, now."

"Don't worry," I assured him, patting the weathered hand tha‹
lay on the sheet. "I'll get the right one."

"Ye will?" His eyes widened in simulated horror. "I though‹
'twas the *left* one was bad!" He was still chuckling asthmaticall‹
as the gas mask came down over his face.

The amputation had gone well, and Graham had recovered an‹
gone home, but I was not really surprised to see him back agai‹
six months later. The lab report on the original tumor had bee‹
dubious, and the doubts were now substantiated; metastasis to th‹
lymph nodes in the groin.

I removed the cancerous nodes. Radiation treatment was ap‹
plied. Cobalt. I removed the spleen, to which the disease ha‹
spread, knowing that the surgery was entirely in vain, but n‹
willing to give up.

"It's a lot easier not to give up, when it isn't you that's sick,"‹
said, staring up at the timbers overhead.

"Did he give up, then?" Jamie asked.

"I don't think I'd call it that, exactly."

*"I have been thinking," Graham announced. The sound of
his voice echoed tinnily through the earpieces of my stethoscope.*

*"Have you?" I said. "Well, don't do it out loud 'til I've
finished here, that's a good lad."*

*He gave a brief snort of laughter, but lay quietly as I
auscultated his chest, moving the disc of the stethoscope
swiftly from ribs to sternum.*

*"All right," I said at last, slipping the tubes out of my ears
and letting them fall over my shoulders. "What have you
been thinking about?"*

"Killing myself."

*His eyes met mine straight on, with just a hint of challenge.
I glanced behind me, to be sure that the nurse had left, then*

pulled up the blue plastic visitor's chair and sat down next to him.

"Pain getting bad?" I asked. "There are things we can do, you know. You only need to ask." I hesitated before adding the last; he never had asked. Even when it was obvious that he needed medication, he never mentioned his discomfort. To mention it myself seemed an invasion of his privacy; I saw the small tightening at the corners of his mouth.

"I've a daughter," he said. "And two grandsons; bonny lads. But I'm forgetting; you'll have seen them last week, aye?"

I had. They came at least twice a week to see him, bringing scribbled school papers and autographed baseballs to show their grandpa.

"And there's my mother, living up to the rest home on Canterbury," he said thoughtfully. "It costs dearly, that place, but it's clean, and the food's good enough she enjoys complainin' about it while she eats."

He glanced dispassionately at the flat bedsheet, and lifted his stump.

"A month, d'ye think? Four? Three?"

"Maybe three," I said. "With luck," I added idiotically.

He snorted at me, and jerked his head at the IV drip above him.

"Tcha! And worse luck I wouldna wish on a beggar." He looked around at all the paraphernalia; the automatic respirator, the blinking cardiac monitor, the litter of medical technology. "Nearly a hundred dollars a day it's costing, to keep me here," he said. "Three months, that would be—great heavens, ten thousand dollars!" He shook his head, frowning.

"A bad bargain, I call that. Not worth it." His pale gray eyes twinkled suddenly up at me. "I'm Scots, ye know. Born thrifty, and not likely to get over it now."

"So I did it for him," I said, still staring upward. "Or rather, ⁞ did it together. He was prescribed morphia for the pain—that's ⁞ laudanum, only much stronger. I drew off half of each ampule ⁞ replaced the missing bit with water. It meant he didn't get the

relief of a full dose for nearly twenty-four hours, but that was th
safest way to get a big dose with no risk of being found out.

"We talked about using one of the botanical medicines I wa
studying; I knew enough to make up something fatal, but I wasn'
sure of it being painless, and he didn't want to risk me bein
accused, if anyone got suspicious and did a forensic examina
tion." I saw Jamie's eyebrow lift, and flapped a hand. "It doesn
matter; it's a way of finding out how someone died."

"Ah. Like a coroner's court?"

"A bit. Anyway, he'd be supposed to have morphia in hi
blood; that wouldn't prove anything. So that's what we did."

I drew a deep breath.

"There would have been no trouble, if I'd given him the injec
tion, and left. That's what he'd asked me to do."

Jamie was quiet, eyes fixed intently on me.

"I couldn't do it, though." I looked at my left hand, seeing n
my own smooth flesh, but the big, swollen knuckles of a commer
cial fisherman, and the fat green veins that crossed his wrist.

"I got the needle in," I said. I rubbed a finger over the spot c
the wrist, where a large vein crosses the distal head of the radiu
"But I couldn't press down the plunger."

In memory, I saw Graham Menzies's other hand rise from h
side, trailing tubes, and close over my own. He hadn't muc
strength, then, but enough.

"I sat there until he was gone, holding his hand." I felt it stil
the steady beat of the wrist-pulse under my thumb, growin
slower, and slower still, as I held his hand, and then waiting for
beat that did not come.

I looked up at Jamie, shaking off the memory.

"And then a nurse came in." It had been one of the young
nurses—an excitable girl, with no discretion. She wasn't ver
experienced, but knew enough to tell a dead man when she sa
one. And me just sitting there, doing nothing—most undoctorlil
conduct. And the empty morphia syringe, lying on the table besi
me.

"She talked, of course," I said.

"I expect she would."

"I had the presence of mind to drop the syringe into the incine
ator chute after she left, though. It was her word against mine, ar
the whole matter was just dismissed."

My mouth twisted wryly. "Except that the next week, they offered me a job as head of the whole department. Very important. A lovely office on the sixth floor of the hospital—safely away from the patients, where I couldn't murder anyone else."

My finger was still rubbing absently across my wrist. Jamie reached out and stopped it by laying his own hand over mine.

"When was this, Sassenach?" he asked, his voice very gentle.

"Just before I took Bree and went to Scotland. That's why I went, in fact; they gave me an extended leave—said I'd been working too hard, and deserved a nice vacation." I didn't try to keep the irony out of my voice.

"I see." His hand was warm on mine, despite the heat of my fever. "If it hadna been for that, for losing your work—would ye have come, Sassenach? Not just to Scotland. To me?"

I looked up at him and squeezed his hand, taking a deep breath.

"I don't know," I said. "I really don't. If I hadn't come to Scotland, met Roger Wakefield, found out that you—" I stopped and swallowed, overwhelmed. "It was Graham who sent me to Scotland," I said at last, feeling slightly choked. "He asked me to go someday—and say hello to Aberdeen for him." I glanced up at Jamie suddenly.

"I didn't! I never did go to Aberdeen."

"Dinna trouble yourself, Sassenach." Jamie squeezed my hand. "I'll take ye there myself—when we go back. Not," he added practically, "that there's anything to see there."

It was growing stuffy in the cabin. He rose and went to open one of the stern windows.

"Jamie," I said, watching his back, "what do you want?"

He glanced around, frowning slightly in thought.

"Oh—an orange would be good," he said. "There's some in the desk, aye?" Without waiting for a reply, he rolled back the lid of the desk, revealing a small bowl of oranges, bright among the clutter of quills and papers. "D'ye want one, too?"

"All right," I said, smiling. "That wasn't really what I meant, though. I meant—what do you want to do, once we've found in?"

"Oh." He sat down by the berth, an orange in his hands, and stared at it for a moment.

"D'ye know," he said at last, "I dinna think anyone has eve
asked me that—what it was I wanted to do." He sounded mildly
surprised.

"Not as though you very often had a choice about it, is it?"
said dryly. "Now you do, though."

"Aye, that's true." He rolled the orange between his palms
head bent over the dimpled sphere. "I suppose it's come to ye tha
we likely canna go back to Scotland—at least for a time?" he said
I had told him of Tompkins's revelations about Sir Percival and hi
machinations, of course, but we had had little time to discuss th
matter—or its implications.

"It has," I said. "That's why I asked."

I was quiet then, letting him come to terms with it. He had live
as an outlaw for a good many years, hiding first physically, an
then by means of secrecy and aliases, eluding the law by slipping
from one identity to another. But now all these were known; ther
was no way for him to resume any of his former activities—o
even to appear in public in Scotland.

His final refuge had always been Lallybroch. But even tha
avenue of retreat was lost to him now. Lallybroch would always b
his home, but it was no longer his; there was a new laird now.
knew he would not begrudge the fact that Jenny's family pos
sessed the estate—but he must, if he was human, regret the loss o
his heritage.

I could hear his faint snort, and thought he had probabl
reached the same point in his thinking that I had in mine.

"Not Jamaica or the English-owned islands, either," he ob
served ruefully. "Tom Leonard and the Royal Navy may think u
both dead for the moment, but they'll be quick enough to notic
otherwise if we stay for any length of time."

"Have you thought of America?" I asked this delicately. "Th
Colonies, I mean."

He rubbed his nose doubtfully.

"Well, no. I hadna really thought of it. It's true we'd likely b
safe from the Crown there, but . . ." He trailed off, frowning. H
picked up his dirk and scored the orange, quickly and neatly, the
began to peel it.

"No one would be hunting you there," I pointed out. "S
Percival hasn't got any interest in you, unless you're in Scotlan
where arresting you would do him some good. The British Nav

an't very well follow you ashore, and the West Indian governors haven't anything to say about what goes on in the Colonies, either."

"That's true," he said slowly. "But the Colonies . . ." He took the peeled orange in one hand, and began to toss it lightly, a few inches in the air. "It's verra primitive, Sassenach," he said. "A wilderness, aye? I shouldna like to take ye into danger."

That made me laugh, and he glanced sharply at me, then, catching my thought, relaxed into a half-rueful smile.

"Aye, well, I suppose draggin' ye off to sea and letting ye be kidnapped and locked up in a plague ship is dangerous enough. But at least I havena let ye be eaten by cannibals, yet."

I wanted to laugh again, but there was a bitter note to his voice that made me bite my lip instead.

"There aren't any cannibals in America," I said.

"There are!" he said heatedly. "I printed a book for a society of Catholic missionaries, that told all about the heathen Iroquois in the north. They tie up their captives and chop bits off of them, and then rip out their hearts and eat them before their eyes!"

"Eat the hearts first and then the eyes, do they?" I said, laughing in spite of myself. "All right," I said, seeing his scowl, "I'm sorry. But for one thing, you can't believe everything you read, and for another—"

I didn't get to finish. He leaned forward and grasped my good arm, tight enough to make me squeak with surprise.

"Damn you, listen to me!" he said. "It's no light matter!"

"Well . . . no, I suppose not," I said, tentatively. "I didn't mean to make fun of you—but, Jamie, I *did* live in Boston for nearly twenty years. You've never set foot in America!"

"That's true," he said evenly. "And d'ye think the place ye lived in is anything like what it's like now, Sassenach?"

"Well—" I began, then paused. While I had seen any number of historic buildings near Boston Common, sporting little brass plaques attesting to their antiquity, the majority of them had been built later than 1770; many a lot later. And beyond a few buildings . . .

"Well, no," I admitted. "It's not; I know it's not. But I don't think it's a complete wilderness. There *are* cities and towns now; I know that much."

He let go of my arm and sat back. He still held the orange in his other hand.

"I suppose that's so," he said slowly. "Ye dinna hear so much of the towns—only that it's such a wild savage place, though verra beautiful. But I'm no a fool, Sassenach." His voice sharpened slightly, and he dug his thumb savagely into the orange, splitting it in half.

"I dinna believe something only because someone's set words down in a book—for God's sake, I print the damn things! I ken verra well just what charlatans and fools some writers are—I see them! And surely I ken the difference between a romance and a fact set down in cold blood!"

"All right," I said. "Though I'm not sure it's all that easy to tell the difference between romance and fact in print. But even if it's dead true about the Iroquois, the whole continent isn't swarming with bloodthirsty savages. I *do* know that much. It's a very big place, you know," I added, gently.

"Mmphm," he said, plainly unconvinced. Still, he bent his attention to the orange, and began to divide it into segments.

"This is very funny," I said ruefully. "When I made up my mind to come back, I read everything I could find about England and Scotland and France about this time, so I'd know as much as I could about what to expect. And here we end up in a place I know nothing about, because it never dawned on me we'd cross the ocean, with you being so seasick."

That made him laugh, a little grudgingly.

"Aye, well, ye never ken what ye can do 'til ye have to. Believe me, Sassenach, once I've got Ian safely back, I shall never set foot on a filthy, godforsaken floating plank in my life again—except to go home to Scotland, when it's safe," he added, as an afterthought. He offered me an orange segment and I took it, token of peace offering.

"Speaking of Scotland, you still have your printing press there, safe in Edinburgh," I said. "We could have it sent over, maybe—if we settled in one of the larger American cities."

He looked up at that, startled.

"D'ye think it would be possible to earn a living, printing? There are that many people? It takes a fair-sized city, ye ken, to need a printer or bookseller."

"I'm sure you could. Boston, Philadelphia . . . not New York yet, I don't think. Williamsburg, maybe? I don't know which ones, but there are several places big enough to need printing—the shipping ports, certainly.'' I remembered the flapping posters, advertising dates of embarkation and arrival, sales of goods and recruitment of seamen, that decorated the walls of every seaside tavern in Le Havre.

"Mmphm." This one was a thoughtful noise. "Aye, well, if we might do that . . ."

He poked a piece of fruit into his mouth and ate it slowly.

"What about you?" he said abruptly.

I glanced at him, startled.

"What about me?"

His eyes were fixed intently on me, reading my face.

"Would it suit ye to go to such a place?" He looked down then, carefully separating the other half of the fruit. "I mean—you've your work to do as well, aye?" He looked up and smiled, wryly. "I learned in Paris that I couldna stop ye doing it. And ye said yourself, ye might not have come, had Menzies's death not topped you, where ye were. Can ye be a healer in the Colonies, 'ye think?"

"I expect I can," I said slowly. "There are people sick and injured, almost anywhere you go, after all." I looked at him, curious.

"You're a very odd man, Jamie Fraser."

He laughed at that, and swallowed the rest of his orange.

"Oh, I am, aye? And what d'ye mean by that?"

"Frank loved me," I said slowly. "But there were . . . pieces of me, that he didn't know what to do with. Things about me that he didn't understand, or maybe that frightened him." I glanced at Jamie. "Not you."

His head was bent over a second orange, hands moving swiftly as he scored it with his dirk, but I could see the faint smile in the corner of his mouth.

"No, Sassenach, ye dinna frighten me. Or rather ye do, but only when I think ye may kill yourself from carelessness."

I snorted briefly.

"You scare me, for the same reason, but I don't suppose there's anything I can do about it."

His chuckle was deep and easy.

"And ye think I canna do anything about it, either, so shouldna be worrit?"

"I didn't say you shouldn't worry—do you think I don't worry But no, you probably can't do anything about me."

I saw him opening his mouth to disagree. Then he changed hi mind, and laughed again. He reached out and popped an orang segment into my mouth.

"Well, maybe no, Sassenach, and maybe so. But I've lived long enough time now to think it maybe doesna matter so much— so long as I can love you."

Speechless with orange juice, I stared at him in surprise.

"And I do," he said softly. He leaned into the berth and kisse me, his mouth warm and sweet. Then he drew back, and gentl touched my cheek.

"Rest now," he said firmly. "I'll bring ye some broth, in bit."

I slept for several hours, and woke up still feverish, but hungr Jamie brought me some of Murphy's broth—a rich green concoc tion, swimming in butter and reeking with sherry—and insiste despite my protests, on feeding it to me with a spoon.

"I have a perfectly good hand," I said crossly.

"Aye, and I've seen ye use it, too," he replied, deftly gaggin me with the spoon. "If ye're clumsy with a spoon as wi' th needle, you'll have this all spilt down your bosom and wasted, an Murphy will brain me wi' the ladle. Here, open up."

I did, my resentment gradually melting into a sort of warm an glowing stupor as I ate. I hadn't taken anything for the pain in m arm, but as my empty stomach expanded in grateful relief, I mo or less quit noticing it.

"Will ye have another bowl?" Jamie asked, as I swallowed th last spoonful. "Ye'll need your strength kept up." Not waiting f an answer, he uncovered the small tureen Murphy had sent, a refilled the bowl.

"Where's Ishmael?" I asked, during the brief hiatus.

"On the after deck. He didna seem comfortable belowdecks— and I canna say I blame him, having seen the slavers at Bridg town. I had Maitland sling him a hammock."

"Do you think it's safe to leave him loose like that? What ki

soup is this?'' The last spoonful had left a delightful, lingering
⸴te on my tongue; the next revived the full flavor.

''Turtle; Stern took a big hawksbill last night. He sent word he's
⸝ving ye the shell to make combs of, for your hair.'' Jamie
⸝wned slightly, whether at the thought of Lawrence Stern's gal-
⸝try or Ishmael's presence, I couldn't tell. ''As for the black,
's not loose—Fergus is watching him.''

''Fergus is on his honeymoon,'' I protested. ''You shouldn't
⸝ke him do it. Is this really turtle soup? I've never had it before.
s marvelous.''

Jamie was unmoved by contemplation of Fergus's tender state.
''Aye, well, he'll be wed a long time,'' he said callously. ''Do
⸝ no harm to keep his breeches on for one night. And they do
⸝ that abstinence makes the heart grow firmer, no?''

''Absence,'' I said, dodging the spoon for a moment. ''And
⸝der. If anything's growing firmer from abstinence, it wouldn't
his heart.''

''That's verra bawdy talk for a respectable marrit woman,''
⸝nie said reprovingly, sticking the spoon in my mouth. ''And
⸝nsiderate, forbye.''

⸤ swallowed. ''Inconsiderate?''

''I'm a wee bit firm myself at the moment,'' he replied evenly,
⸝pping and spooning. ''What wi' you sitting there wi' your hair
⸝se and your nipples starin' me in the eye, the size of cherries.''

⸤ glanced down involuntarily, and the next spoonful bumped my
⸝se. Jamie clicked his tongue, and picking up a cloth, briskly
⸝tted my bosom with it. It was quite true that my shift was made
thin cotton, and even when dry, reasonably easy to see through.

'It's not as though you haven't seen them before,'' I said,
used.

He laid down the cloth and raised his brows.

'I have drunk water every day since I was weaned,'' he pointed
‥ ''It doesna mean I canna be thirsty, still.'' He picked up the
⸝on. ''You'll have a wee bit more?''

'No, thanks,'' I said, dodging the oncoming spoon. ''I want to
⸝r more about this firmness of yours.''

'No, ye don't; you're ill.''

'I feel much better,'' I assured him. ''Shall I have a look at
' He was wearing the loose petticoat breeches the sailors wore,

in which he could easily have concealed three or four dead mull
let alone a fugitive firmness.

"You shall not," he said, looking slightly shocked. "Someo
might come in. And I canna think your looking at it would hel|
bit."

"Well, you can't tell that until I *have* looked at it, can you?"
said. "Besides, you can bolt the door."

"Bolt the door? What d'ye think I'm going to do? Do I look |
sort of man would take advantage of a woman who's not o|
wounded and boiling wi' fever, but drunk as well?" he demand|
He stood up, nonetheless.

"I am not drunk," I said indignantly. "You can't get drunk
turtle soup!" Nonetheless, I was conscious that the glowi
warmth in my stomach seemed to have migrated somewhat low
taking up residence between my thighs, and there was undenia|
a slight lightness of head not strictly attributable to fever.

"You can if ye've been drinking turtle soup as made by Al|
sius O'Shaughnessy Murphy," he said. "By the smell of it, h|
put at least a full bottle o' the sherry in it. A verra intempe|
race, the Irish."

"Well, I'm still not drunk." I straightened up against the |
lows as best I could. "You told me once that if you could s
stand up, you weren't drunk."

"You aren't standing up," he pointed out.

"You are. And I could if I wanted to. Stop trying to change
subject. We were talking about your firmness."

"Well, ye can just stop talking about it, because—" He br|
off with a small yelp, as I made a fortunate grab with my left ha|

"Clumsy, am I?" I said, with considerable satisfaction. "|
my. Heavens, you *do* have a problem, don't you?"

"Will ye leave go of me?" he asked, looking frantically c
his shoulder at the door. "Someone could come in any momen|

"I told you you should have bolted the door," I said, not lett|
go. Far from being a dead mullet, the object in my hand |
exhibiting considerable liveliness.

He eyed me narrowly, breathing through his nose.

"I wouldna use force on a sick woman," he said through |
teeth, "but you've a damn healthy grip for someone with a fe|
Sassenach. If you—"

"I told you I felt better," I interrupted, "but I'll make yo|

rgain; you bolt the door and I'll prove I'm not drunk." I rather
gretfully let go, to indicate good faith. He stood staring at me for
moment, absentmindedly rubbing the site of my recent assault
his virtue. Then he lifted one ruddy eyebrow, turned, and went
bolt the door.

By the time he turned back, I had made it out of the berth and
s standing—a trifle shakily, but still upright—against the frame.
eyed me critically.

"It's no going to work, Sassenach," he said, shaking his head.
looked rather regretful, himself. "We'll never stay upright, wi'
swell like there is underfoot tonight, and ye know I'll not fit in
at berth by myself, let alone wi' you."

There was a considerable swell; the lantern on its swivel-bracket
ng steady and level, but the shelf above it tilted visibly back and
rth as the *Artemis* rode the waves. I could feel the faint shudder
the boards under my bare feet, and knew Jamie was right. At
st he was too absorbed in the discussion to be seasick.

"There's always the floor," I suggested hopefully. He glanced
wn at the limited floor space and frowned. "Aye, well. There is,
t we'd have to do it like snakes, Sassenach, all twined round
ch other amongst the table legs."

"I don't mind."

"No," he said, shaking his head, "it would hurt your arm." He
bbed a knuckle across his lower lip, thinking. His eyes passed
sently across my body at about hip level, returned, fixed, and
t their focus. I thought the bloody shift must be more transpar-
t than I realized.

Deciding to take matters into my own hands, I let go my hold on
frame of the berth and lurched the two paces necessary to
ch him. The roll of the ship threw me into his arms, and he
rely managed to keep his own balance, clutching me tightly
nd the waist.

"Jesus!" he said, staggered, and then, as much from reflex as
m desire, bent his head and kissed me.

It was startling. I was accustomed to be surrounded by the
rmth of his embrace; now it was I who was hot to the touch and
who was cool. From his reaction, he was enjoying the novelty
much as I was.

Light-headed, and reckless with it, I nipped the side of his neck

with my teeth, feeling the waves of heat from my face pulsa
against the column of his throat. He felt it, too.

"God, you're like holding a hot coal!" His hands dropp
lower and pressed me hard against him.

"Firm is it? Ha," I said, getting my mouth free for a momer
"Take those baggy things off." I slid down his length and onto n
knees in front of him, fumbling mazily at his flies. He freed t
laces with a quick jerk, and the petticoat breeches ballooned to t
floor with a whiff of wind.

I didn't wait for him to remove his shirt; just lifted it and to
him. He made a strangled sound and his hands came down on n
head as though he wanted to restrain me, but hadn't the streng

"Oh, Lord!" he said. His hands tightened in my hair, but
wasn't trying to push me away. "This must be what it's like
make love in Hell," he whispered. "With a burning she-devil.

I laughed, which was extremely difficult under the circu
stances. I choked, and pulled back a moment, breathless.

"Is this what a succubus does, do you think?"

"I wouldna doubt it for a moment," he assured me. His han
were still in my hair, urging me back.

A knock sounded on the door, and he froze. Confident that
door was indeed bolted, I didn't.

"Aye? What is it?" he said, with a calmness rather remarka
for a man in his position.

"Fraser?" Lawrence Stern's voice came through the do
"The Frenchman says the black is asleep, and may he lea
to go to bed now?"

"No," said Jamie shortly. "Tell him to stay where he is;
come along and relieve him in a bit."

"Oh." Stern's voice sounded a little hesitant. "Surely.
. . . um, his wife seems . . . eager for him to come now."

Jamie inhaled sharply.

"Tell her," he said, a small note of strain becoming evident
his voice, "that he'll be there . . . presently."

"I will say so." Stern sounded dubious about Marsali's rec
tion of this news, but then his voice brightened. "Ah . . . is M
Fraser feeling somewhat improved?"

"Verra much," said Jamie, with feeling.

"She enjoyed the turtle soup?"

"Greatly. I thank ye." His hands on my head were trembli

"Did you tell her that I've put aside the shell for her? It was a ᵣe hawksbill turtle; a most elegant beast."

"Aye. Aye, I did." With an audible gasp, Jamie pulled away and aching down, lifted me to my feet.

"Good night, Mr. Stern!" he called. He pulled me toward the ᵣrth; we struggled four-legged to keep from crashing into tables ᵣd chairs as the floor rose and fell beneath us.

"Oh." Lawrence sounded faintly disappointed. "I suppose ᵣrs. Fraser is asleep, then?"

"Laugh, and I'll throttle ye," Jamie whispered fiercely in my ᵣr. "She is, Mr. Stern," he called through the door. "I shall give ᵣr your respects in the morning, aye?"

"I trust she will rest well. There seems to be a certain rough- ᵣss to the sea this evening."

"I . . . have noticed, Mr. Stern." Pushing me to my knees in ᵣnt of the berth, he knelt behind me, groping for the hem of my ᵣift. A cool breeze from the open stern window blew over my ᵣked buttocks, and a shiver ran down the backs of my thighs.

"Should you or Mrs. Fraser find yourselves discommoded by ᵣe motion, I have a most capital remedy to hand—a compound of ᵣgwort, bat dung, and the fruit of the mangrove. You have only ᵣ ask, you know."

Jamie didn't answer for a moment.

"Oh, Christ!" he whispered. I took a sizable bite of the bed- ᵣothes.

"Mr. Fraser?"

"I said, 'Thank you'!" Jamie replied, raising his voice.

"Well, I shall bid you a good evening, then."

Jamie let out his breath in a long shudder that was not quite a ᵣan.

"Mr. Fraser?"

"Good evening, Mr. Stern!" Jamie bellowed.

"Oh! Er . . . good evening."

Stern's footsteps receded down the companionway, lost in the ᵣnd of the waves that were now crashing loudly against the hull. ᵣpit out the mouthful of quilt.

"Oh . . . my . . . God!"

His hands were large and hard and cool on my heated flesh.

"You've the roundest arse I've ever seen!"

A lurch by the *Artemis* here aiding his efforts to an untowar
degree, I uttered a loud shriek.

"Shh!" He clasped a hand over my mouth, bending over me s
that he lay over my back, the billowing linen of his shirt fallin
around me and the weight of him pressing me to the bed. My ski
crazed with fever, was sensitive to the slightest touch, and I shoo
in his arms, the heat inside me rushing outward as he move
within me.

His hands were under me then, clutching my breasts, the onl
anchor as I lost my boundaries and dissolved, conscious thought
displaced element in the chaos of sensations—the warm damp
tangled quilts beneath me, the cold sea wind and misty spray tha
wafted over us from the rough sea outside, the gasp and brush
Jamie's warm breath on the back of my neck, and the sudde
prickle and flood of cold and heat, as my fever broke in a dew
satisfied desire.

Jamie's weight rested on my back, his thighs behind mine.
was warm, and comforting. After a long time, his breathing ease
and he rose off me. The thin cotton of my shift was damp, and th
wind plucked it away from my skin, making me shiver.

Jamie closed the window with a snap, then bent and picked n
up like a rag doll. He lowered me into the berth, and pulled th
quilt up over me.

"How is your arm?" he said.

"What arm?" I murmured drowsily. I felt as though I had be
melted and poured into a mold to set.

"Good," he said, a smile in his voice. "Can ye stand up?"

"Not for all the tea in China."

"I'll tell Murphy ye liked the soup." His hand rested for
moment on my cool forehead, passed down the curve of my che
in a light caress, and then was gone. I didn't hear him leave.

57

Promised Land

It's persecution!'' Jamie said indignantly. He stood behind me, looking over the rail of the *Artemis*. Kingston Harbor stretched to our left, glowing like liquid sapphires in the orning light, the town above half-sunk in jungle green, cubes of llowed ivory and pink rose-quartz in a lush setting of emerald d malachite. And on the cerulean bosom of the water below ated the majestic sight of a great three-masted ship, furled can- s white as gull wings, gun decks proud and brass gleaming in e sun. His Majesty's man-of-war *Porpoise*.

"The filthy boat's pursuing me,'' he said, glaring at it as we led past at a discreet distance, well outside the harbor mouth. Everywhere I go, there it is again!''

I laughed, though in truth, the sight of the *Porpoise* made me ghtly nervous, too.

"I don't suppose it's personal,'' I told him. "Captain Leonard d say they were bound for Jamaica.''

"Aye, but why would they no head straight to Antigua, where e naval barracks and the navy shipyards are, and them in such aits as ye left them?'' He shaded his eyes, peering at the *Por- ise*. Even at this distance, small figures were visible in the ging, making repairs.

"They had to come here first,'' I explained. "They were carry- g a new governor for the colony.'' I felt an absurd urge to duck low the rail, though I knew that even Jamie's red hair would be distinguishable at this distance.

"Aye? I wonder who's that?'' Jamie spoke absently; we were

no more than an hour away from arrival at Jared's plantation o
Sugar Bay, and I knew his mind was busy with plans for findin
Young Ian.

"A chap named Grey," I said, turning away from the rai
"Nice man; I met him on the ship, just briefly."

"Grey?" Startled, Jamie looked down at me. "Not Lord Joh
Grey, by chance?"

"Yes, that was his name? Why?" I glanced up at him, curiou
He was staring at the *Porpoise* with renewed interest.

"Why?" He heard me when I repeated the question a secon
time, and glanced down at me, smiling. "Oh. It's only that I ke
Lord John; he's a friend of mine."

"Really?" I was no more than mildly surprised. Jamie's frien
had once included the French minister of finance and Charle
Stuart, as well as Scottish beggars and French pickpockets. I sup
posed it was not remarkable that he should now count Englis
aristocrats among his acquaintance, as well as Highland smuggle
and Irish seacooks.

"Well, that's luck," I said. "Or at least I suppose it is. Whe
do you know Lord John from?"

"He was the Governor of Ardsmuir prison," he replied, su
prising me after all. His eyes were still fixed on the *Porpoise*
narrowed in speculation.

"And he's a *friend* of yours?" I shook my head. "I'll nev
understand men."

He turned and smiled at me, taking his attention at last from t
English ship.

"Well, friends are where ye find them, Sassenach," he said. F
squinted toward the shore, shading his eyes with his hand. "Let
hope this Mrs. Abernathy proves to be one."

As we rounded the tip of the headland, a lithe black figu
materialized next to the rail. Now clothed in spare seaman
clothes, with his scars hidden, Ishmael looked less like a slave a
a good deal more like a pirate. Not for the first time, I wonder
just how much of what he had told us was the truth.

"I be leavin' now," he announced abruptly.

Jamie lifted one eyebrow and glanced over the rail, into the s
blue depths.

"Dinna let me prevent ye," he said politely. "But would ye not ther have a boat?"

Something that might have been humor flickered briefly in the ack man's eyes, but didn't disturb the severe outlines of his face.

"You say you put me ashore where I want, I be tellin' you 'bout ose boys," he said. He nodded toward the island, where a riotous owth of jungle spilled down the slope of a hill to meet its own een shadow in the shallow water. "That be where I want."

Jamie looked thoughtfully from the uninhabited shore to Ish-ael, and then nodded.

"I'll have a boat lowered." He turned to go to the cabin. "I omised ye gold as well, no?"

"Don't be wantin' gold, mon." Ishmael's tone, as well as his ords, stopped Jamie in his tracks. He looked at the black man th interest, mingled with a certain reserve.

"Ye'll have something else in mind?"

Ishmael jerked his head in a short nod. He didn't seem out-rdly nervous, but I noticed the faint gleam of sweat on his mples, despite the mild noon breeze.

"I be wantin' that one-arm nigger." He stared boldly at Jamie he spoke, but there was a diffidence under the confident facade.

"Temeraire?" I blurted out in astonishment. "Why?"

Ishmael flicked a glance at me, but addressed his words to nie, half-bold, half-cajoling.

"He ain't no good to you, mon; can't be doin' field work or p work neither, ain't got but one arm."

Jamie didn't reply directly, but stared at Ishmael for a moment. en he turned and called for Fergus to bring up the one-armed ve.

Temeraire, brought up on deck, stood expressionless as a block wood, barely blinking in the sun. He too had been provided with man's clothes, but he lacked Ishmael's raffish elegance in m. He looked like a stump upon which someone had spread out shing to dry.

"This man wants you to go with him, to the island there," nie said to Temeraire, in slow, careful French. "Do you want to this thing?"

Temeraire did blink at that, and a brief look of startlement ened his eyes. I supposed that no one had asked him what he

wanted in many years—if ever. He glanced warily from Jamie
Ishmael and back again, but didn't say anything.

Jamie tried again.

"You do not have to go with this man," he assured the slav
"You may come with us, and we will take care of you. No one w
hurt you. But you can go with him, if you like."

Still the slave hesitated, eyes flicking right and left, clear
startled and disturbed by the unexpected choice. It was Ishma
who decided the matter. He said something, in a strange tong
full of liquid vowels and syllables that repeated like a drumbea

Temeraire let out a gasp, fell to his knees, and pressed h
forehead to the deck at Ishmael's feet. Everyone on deck stared
him, then looked at Ishmael, who stood with arms folded with
sort of wary defiance.

"He be goin' with me," he said.

And so it was. Picard rowed the two blacks ashore in the dingh
and left them on the rocks at the edge of the jungle, supplied wi
a small bag of provisions, each equipped with a knife.

"Why there?" I wondered aloud, watching the two small fi
ures make their way slowly up the wooded slope. "There are
any towns nearby, are there? Or any plantations?" To the eye, t
shore presented an unbroken expanse of jungle.

"Oh, there are plantations," Lawrence assured me. "Far up
the hills; that's where they grow the coffee and indigo—the suga
cane grows better near the coast." He squinted toward the sho
where the two dark figures had disappeared. "It is more likely tl
they have gone to join a band of Maroons, though," he said.

"There are Maroons on Jamaica as well as on Hispaniola'
Fergus asked, interested.

Lawrence smiled, a little grimly.

"There are Maroons wherever there are slaves, my friend,"
said. "There are always men who prefer to take the chance
dying like animals, rather than live as captives."

Jamie turned his head sharply to look at Lawrence, but sa
nothing.

Jared's plantation at Sugar Bay was called Blue Mounta
House, presumably for the sake of the low, hazy peak that r
inland a mile behind it, blue with pines and distance. The how

elf was set near the shore, in the shallow curve of the bay. In
ct, the veranda that ran along one side of the house overhung a
nall lagoon, the building set on sturdy silvered-wood pilings that
se from the water, crusted with a spongy growth of tunicates and
ussels and the fine green seaweed called mermaid's hair.

We were expected; Jared had sent a letter by a ship that left Le
avre a week before the *Artemis*. Owing to our delay on Hispan-
la, the letter had arrived nearly a month in advance of ourselves,
d the overseer and his wife—a portly, comfortable Scottish cou-
e named MacIvers—were relieved to see us.

"I thought surely the winter storms had got ye," Kenneth Mac-
er said for the fourth time, shaking his head. He was bald, the
o of his head scaly and freckled from long years' exposure to the
pic sun. His wife was a plump, genial, grandmotherly soul—
no, I realized to my shock, was roughly five years younger than
self. She herded Marsali and me off for a quick wash, brush,
d nap before supper, while Fergus and Jamie went with Mr.
acIver to direct the partial unloading of the *Artemis*'s cargo and
disposition of her crew.

I was more than willing to go; while my arm had healed suffi-
ntly to need no more than a light bandage, it had prevented me
m bathing in the sea as was my usual habit. After a week aboard
Artemis, unbathed, I looked forward to fresh water and clean
eets with a longing that was almost hunger.

I had no landlegs yet; the worn wooden floorboards of the
ntation house gave the disconcerting illusion of seeming to rise
d fall beneath my feet, and I staggered down the hallway after
s. MacIver, bumping into walls.

The house had an actual bathtub in a small porch; wooden, but
ed—*mirabile dictu!*—with hot water, by the good offices of two
ck slave women who heated kettles over a fire in the yard and
ried them in. I should have felt much too guilty at this exploita-
n to enjoy my bath, but I didn't. I wallowed luxuriously, scrub-
g the salt and grime from my skin with a loofah sponge and
hering my hair with a shampoo made from chamomile, gera-
m oil, fat-soap shavings, and the yolk of an egg, graciously
plied by Mrs. MacIver.

Smelling sweet, shiny-haired, and languid with warmth, I col-
sed gratefully into the bed I was given. I had time only to think

how delightful it was to stretch out at full length, before I f
asleep.

When I woke, the shadows of dusk were gathering on the v
randa outside the open French doors of my bedroom, and Jam
lay naked beside me, hands folded on his belly, breathing deep a
slow.

He felt me stir, and opened his eyes. He smiled sleepily a
reaching up a hand, pulled me down to his mouth. He had had
bath, too; he smelled of soap and cedar needles. I kissed him
length, slowly and thoroughly, running my tongue across the w
curve of his lip, finding his tongue with mine in a soft, dark jo
of greeting and invitation.

I broke loose, finally, and came up for air. The room was fill
with a wavering green light, reflections from the lagoon outside,
though the room itself were underwater. The air was at once wa
and fresh, smelling of sea and rain, with tiny currents of bree
that caressed the skin.

"Ye smell sweet, Sassenach," he murmured, voice husky w
sleep. He smiled, reaching up to twine his fingers into my ha
"Come here to me, curly-wig."

Freed from pins and freshly washed, my hair was clouding o
my shoulders in a perfect explosion of Medusa-like curls
reached up to smooth it back, but he tugged gently, bending n
forward so the veil of brown and gold and silver fell loose over
face.

I kissed him, half-smothered in clouds of hair, and lowe
myself to lie on top of him, letting the fullness of my brea
squash gently against his chest. He moved slightly, rubbing, a
sighed with pleasure.

His hands cupped my buttocks, trying to move me upwa
enough to enter me.

"Not bloody yet," I whispered. I pressed my hips down, roll
them, enjoying the feel of the silky stiffness trapped beneath
belly. He made a small breathless sound.

"We haven't had room or time to make love properly
months," I told him. "So we're taking our time about it no
right?"

"Ye take me at something of a disadvantage, Sassenach,"
murmured into my hair. He squirmed under me, pressing upwa
urgently. "Ye dinna think we could take our time next time?"

"No, we couldn't," I said firmly. "Now. Slow. Don't move."

He made a sort of rumbling noise in his throat, but sighed and laxed, letting his hands fall away to the sides. I squirmed lower his body, making him inhale sharply, and set my mouth on his pple.

I ran my tongue delicately round the tiny nub, making it stand stiff, enjoying the coarse feel of the curly auburn hairs that rrounded it. I felt him tense under me, and put my hands on his per arms to hold him still while I went on with it, biting gently, cking and flicking with my tongue.

A few minutes later, I raised my head, brushed my hair back ith one hand, and asked, "What's that you're saying?"

He opened one eye.

"The rosary," he informed me. "It's the only way I'm going to nd it." He closed his eyes and resumed murmuring in Latin. *1ve Maria, gratia plena . . . "*

I snorted and went to work on the other one.

"You're losing your place," I said, next time I came up for air. ou've said the Lord's Prayer three times in a row."

"I'm surprised to hear I'm still makin' any sense at all." His es were closed, and a dew of moisture gleamed on his cheek-nes. He moved his hips with increasing restiveness. "Now?"

"Not yet." I dipped my head lower and seized by impulse, went *ft!* into his navel. He convulsed, and taken by surprise, emitted noise that could only be described as a giggle.

"Don't do that!" he said.

"Will if I want to," I said, and did it again. "You sound just e Bree," I told him. "I used to do that to her when she was a by; she loved it."

"Well, I'm no a wee bairn, if ye hadna noticed the difference," said a little testily. "If ye must do that, at least try it a bit lower, ?"

I did.

"You don't have any hair at all at the tops of your thighs," I d, admiring the smooth white skin there. "Why is that, do you nk?"

'The cow licked it all off last time she milked me," he said ween his teeth. "For God's sake, Sassenach!"

I laughed, and returned to my work. At last I stopped and raised self on my elbows.

"I think you've had enough," I said, brushing hair out of m
eyes. "You haven't said anything but 'Jesus Christ' over and ov
again for the last few minutes."

Given the cue, he surged upward, and flipped me onto my bac
pinning me with the solid weight of his body.

"You're going to live to regret this, Sassenach," he said with
grim satisfaction.

I grinned at him, unrepentant.

"Am I?"

He looked down at me, eyes narrowed. "Take my time, was
You'll beg for it, before I've done wi' ye."

I tugged experimentally at my wrists, held tight in his grasp, a
wriggled slightly under him with anticipation.

"Ooh, mercy," I said. "You beast."

He snorted briefly, and bent his head to the curve of my brea
white as pearl in the dim green water-light.

I closed my eyes and lay back against the pillows.

"Pater noster, qui es in coelis . . ." I whispered.

We were very late to supper.

Jamie lost no time over supper in asking about Mrs. Aberna
of Rose Hall.

"Abernathy?" MacIver frowned, tapping his knife on the tal
to assist thought. "Aye, seems I've heard the name, though
canna just charge my memory."

"Och, ye ken Abernathy's fine," his wife interrupted, pausi
in her instructions to a servant for the preparation of the
pudding. "It's that place up the Yallahs River, in the mountai
Cane, mostly, but a wee bit of coffee, too."

"Oh, aye, to be sure!" her husband exclaimed. "What a me
ory ye've got, Rosie!" He beamed fondly at his wife.

"Well, I might not ha' brought it to mind mysel'," she s
modestly, "only as how that minister over to New Grace kirk l
week was askin' after Mrs. Abernathy, too."

"What minister is this, ma'am?" Jamie asked, taking a sp
roast chicken from the huge platter presented to him by a bla
servant.

"Such a fine braw appetite as ye have, Mr. Fraser!" Mrs. M

er exclaimed admiringly, seeing his loaded plate. "It's the is-
nd air does it, I expect."

The tips of Jamie's ears turned pink.

"I expect it is," he said, carefully not looking at me. "This
inister . . . ?"

"Och, aye. Campbell, his name was, Archie Campbell." I
arted, and she glanced quizzically at me. "You'll know him?"

I shook my head, swallowing a pickled mushroom. "I've met
m once, in Edinburgh."

"Oh. Well, he's come to be a missionary, and bring the heathen
acks to the salvation of Our Lord Jesus." She spoke with admi-
tion, and glared at her husband when he snorted. "Now, ye'll no
makin' your Papist remarks, Kenny! The Reverend Campbell's
fine holy man, and a great scholar, forbye. I'm Free Church
yself," she said, leaning toward me confidingly. "My parents
sowned me when I wed Kenny, but I told them I was sure he'd
me to see the light sooner or later."

"A lot later," her husband remarked, spooning jam onto his
ate. He grinned at his wife, who sniffed and returned to her
ry.

"So, 'twas on account of the Reverend's bein' a great scholar
it Mrs. Abernathy had written him, whilst he was still in Edin-
rgh, to ask him questions. And now that he's come here, he had
n mind to go and see her. Though after all Myra Dalrymple and
: Reverend Davis telt him, I should be surprised he'd set foot on
r place," she added primly.

Kenny MacIver grunted, motioning to a servant in the doorway
th another huge platter.

"I wouldna put a great deal of stock in anything the Reverend
vis says, myself," he said. "The man's too godly to shit. But
vra Dalrymple's a sensible woman. Ouch!" He snatched back
: fingers his wife had just cracked with a spoon, and sucked
m.

"What did Miss Dalrymple have to say of Mrs. Abernathy?"
nie inquired, hastily intervening before full-scale marital war-
e could break out.

Mrs. MacIver's color was high, but she smoothed the frown
m her brow as she turned to answer him.

"Well, a great deal of it was no more than ill-natured gossip,"
: admitted. "The sorts of things folk will always say about a

woman as lives alone. That she's owerfond of the company of he men-slaves, aye?''

''But there was the talk when her husband died,'' Kenny inte rupted. He slid several small, rainbow-striped fish off the platt the stooping servant held for him. ''I mind it well, now I come think on the name.''

Barnabas Abernathy had come from Scotland, and had pu chased Rose Hall five years before. He had run the place decentl turning a small profit in sugar and coffee, causing no comme among his neighbors. Then, two years ago, he had married woman no one knew, bringing her home from a trip to Guad loupe.

''And six months later, he was dead,'' Mrs. MacIver conclude with grim relish.

''And the talk is that Mrs. Abernathy had something to do wi it?'' Having some idea of the plethora of tropical parasites a diseases that attacked Europeans in the West Indies, I was inclin to doubt it, myself. Barnabas Abernathy could easily have died anything from malaria to elephantiasis, but Rosie MacIver w right—folk were partial to ill-natured gossip.

''Poison,'' Rosie said, low-voiced, with a quick glance at t door to the kitchen. ''The doctor who saw him said so. Mind, could ha' been the slave-women. There was talk about Barnab and his female slaves, and it's more common than folk like to s for a plantation cook-girl to be slipping something into the ste but—'' She broke off as another servant came in, carrying a c glass relish pot. Everyone was silent as the woman placed it on t table and left, curtsying to her mistress.

''You needn't worry,'' Mrs. MacIver said reassuringly, seei me look after the woman. ''We've a boy who tastes everythir before it's served. It's all quite safe.''

I swallowed the mouthful of fish I had taken, with some di culty.

''Did the Reverend Campbell go to see Mrs. Abernathy, then Jamie put in.

Rosie took the distraction gratefully. She shook her head, a tating the lace ruffles on her cap.

''No, I'm sure not, for 'twas the very next day there was stramash about his sister.''

In the excitement of tracking Ian and the *Bruja,* I had nearly forgotten Margaret Jane Campbell.

"What happened to his sister?" I asked, curious.

"Why, she's disappeared!" Mrs. MacIver's blue eyes went wide with importance. Blue Mountain House was remote, some ten miles out of Kingston by land, and our presence provided an unparalleled opportunity for gossip.

"What?" Fergus had been addressing himself to his plate with single-minded devotion, but now looked up, blinking. "Disappeared? Where?"

"The whole island's talking of it," Kenny put in, snatching the conversational ball from his wife. "Seems the Reverend had a woman engaged as abigail to his sister, but the woman died of a fever on the voyage."

"Oh, that's too bad!" I felt a real pang for Nellie Cowden, with her broad, pleasant face.

"Aye." Kenny nodded offhandedly. "Well, and so the Reverend found a place for his sister to lodge. Feebleminded, I understand?" He lifted a brow at me.

"Something like that."

"Aye, well, the lass seemed quiet and biddable, and Mrs. Forrest, who had the house where she lodged, would take her to sit on the veranda in the cool part of the day. So Tuesday last, a boy comes to say as Mrs. Forrest is wanted quicklike to come to her sister, who's having a child. And Mrs. Forrest got flustered and went straight off, forgetting Miss Campbell on the veranda. And when she thought of it, and sent someone back to see—why Miss Campbell was gone. And not a smell of her since, in spite of the Reverend raising heaven and earth, ye might say." MacIver rocked back on his chair, puffing out his sun-mottled cheeks.

Mrs. MacIver wagged her head, *tsk*ing mournfully.

"Myra Dalrymple told the Reverend as how he should go to the Governor for help to find her," she said. "But the Governor's scarce settled, and not yet ready to receive anyone. He's having a great reception this coming Thursday, for to meet all the important folk o' the island. Myra said as the Reverend must go, and speak to the Governor there, but he's no of a mind to do that, it bein' such a worldly occasion, aye?"

"A reception?" Jamie set down his spoon, looking at Mrs. MacIver with interest. "Is it by invitation, d'ye know?"

"Oh, no," she said, shaking her head. "Anyone may come as likes to, or so I've heard."

"Is that so?" Jamie glanced at me, smiling. "What d'ye think, Sassenach—would ye care to step out wi' me at the Governor's Residence?"

I stared at him in astonishment. I should have thought that the last thing he would wish to do was show himself in public. I was also surprised that he would let anything at all stop his visiting Rose Hall at the earliest opportunity.

"It's a good opportunity to ask about Ian, no?" he explained. "After all, he might not be at Rose Hall, but someplace else on the island."

"Well, aside from the fact that I've nothing to wear . . ." I temporized, trying to figure out what he was really up to.

"Och, that's no trouble," Rosie MacIver assured me. "I've one of the cleverest sempstresses on the island; she'll have ye tricked out in no time."

Jamie was nodding thoughtfully. He smiled, eyes slanting as he looked at me over the candle flame.

"Violet silk, I think," he said. He plucked the bones delicately from his fish and set them aside. "And as for the other—dinna fash, Sassenach. I've something in mind. You'll see."

58

Masque of the Red Death

"Oh who is that young sinner with the handcuffs on his wrists?
And what has be been after that they groan and shake their
*   fists?*
And wherefore is he wearing such a conscience-stricken air?
Oh they're taking him to prison for the colour of his hair."

Jamie put down the wig in his hand and raised one eyebrow at
me in the mirror. I grinned at him and went on, declaiming with
gestures:

" 'Tis a shame to human nature, such a head of hair as his;
In the good old time 'twas hanging for the colour that it is;
Though hanging isn't bad enough and flaying would be fair
For the nameless and abominable colour of his hair!"

"Did ye not tell me ye'd studied for a doctor, Sassenach?" he
inquired. "Or was it a poet, after all?"

"Not me," I assured him, coming to straighten his stock.
"Those sentiments are by one A. E. Housman."

"Surely one of him is sufficient," Jamie said dryly. "Given the
quality of his opinions." He picked up the wig and fitted it carefully on his head, raising little puffs of scented powder as he poked
it here and there. "Is Mr. Housman an acquaintance of yours,
then?"

"You might say so." I sat down on the bed to watch. "It's only
that the doctors' lounge at the hospital I worked at had a copy of

Housman's collected works that someone had left there. There isn't time between calls to read most novels, but poems are ideal. I expect I know most of Housman by heart, now.''

He looked warily at me, as though expecting another outburst of poetry, but I merely smiled at him, and he returned to his work. I watched the transformation in fascination.

Red-heeled shoes and silk stockings clocked in black. Gray satin breeches with silver knee buckles. Snowy linen, with Brussels lace six inches deep at cuff and jabot. The coat, a masterpiece in heavy gray with blue satin cuffs and crested silver buttons, hung behind the door, awaiting its turn.

He finished the careful powdering of his face, and licking the end of one finger, picked up a false beauty mark, dabbed it in gum arabic, and affixed it neatly near the corner of his mouth.

''There,'' he said, swinging about on the dressing stool to face me. ''Do I look like a red-heided Scottish smuggler?''

I inspected him carefully, from full-bottomed wig to morocco-heeled shoes.

''You look like a gargoyle,'' I said. His face flowered in a wide grin. Outlined in white powder, his lips seemed abnormally red, his mouth even wider and more expressive than it usually was.

''*Non!*'' said Fergus indignantly, coming in in time to hear this. ''He looks like a Frenchman.''

''Much the same thing,'' Jamie said, and sneezed. Wiping his nose on a handkerchief, he assured the young man, ''Begging your pardon, Fergus.''

He stood up and reached for the coat, shrugging it over his shoulders and settling the edges. In three-inch heels, he towered to a height of six feet seven; his head nearly brushed the plastered ceiling.

''I don't know,'' I said, looking up at him dubiously. ''I've never seen a Frenchman that size.''

Jamie shrugged, his coat rustling like autumn leaves. ''Aye, well, there's no hiding my height. But so long as my hair is hidden, I think it will be all right. Besides,'' he added, gazing with approval at me, ''folk willna be looking at me. Stand up and let me see, aye?''

I obliged, rotating slowly to show off the deep flare of the violet silk skirt. Cut low in the front, the décolletage was filled with a froth of lace that rippled down the front of the bodice in a series of

V's. Matching lace cascaded from the elbow-length sleeves in graceful white falls that left my wrists bare.

"Rather a pity I don't have your mother's pearls," I remarked. I didn't regret their lack; I had left them for Brianna, in the box with the photographs and family documents. Still, with the deep décolletage and my hair twisted up in a knot, the mirror showed a long expanse of bare neck and bosom, rising whitely out of the violet silk.

"I thought of that." With the air of a conjuror, Jamie produced a small box from his inside pocket and presented it to me, making a leg in his best Versailles fashion.

Inside was a small, gleaming fish, carved in a dense black material, the edges of its scales touched with gold.

"It's a pin," he explained. "Ye could maybe wear it fastened to a white ribbon round your neck?"

"It's beautiful!" I said, delighted. "What's it made of? Ebony?"

"Black coral," he said. "I got it yesterday, when Fergus and I were in Montego Bay." He and Fergus had taken the *Artemis* round the island, disposing at last of the cargo of bat guano, delivered to its purchaser.

I found a length of white satin ribbon, and Jamie obligingly tied it about my neck, bending to peer over my shoulder at the reflection in the mirror.

"No, they won't be looking at me," he said. "Half o' them will be lookin' at you, Sassenach, and the other half at Mr. Willoughby."

"Mr. Willoughby? Is that safe? I mean—" I stole a look at the little Chinese, sitting patiently cross-legged on a stool, gleaming in clean blue silk, and lowered my voice. "I mean, they'll have wine, won't they?"

Jamie nodded. "And whisky, and cambric, and claret cup, and port, and champagne punch—and a wee cask of the finest French brandy—contributed by the courtesy of Monsieur Etienne Marcel de Provac Alexandre." He put a hand on his chest and bowed again, in an exaggerated pantomime that made me laugh. "Nay worry," he said, straightening up. "He'll behave, or I'll have his oral globe back—will I no, ye wee heathen?" he added with a grin to Mr. Willoughby.

The Chinese scholar nodded with considerable dignity. The

embroidered black silk of his round cap was decorated with a small carved knob of red coral—the badge of his calling, restored to him by the chance encounter with a coral trader on the docks at Montego, and Jamie's good nature.

"You're quite sure we have to go?" The palpitations I was experiencing were due in part to the tightness of the stays I was wearing, but in greater degree to recurring visions of Jamie's wig falling off and the reception coming to a complete stop as the entire assemblage paused to stare at his hair before calling en masse for the Royal Navy.

"Aye, we do." He smiled at me reassuringly. "Dinna worry, Sassenach; if anyone's there from the *Porpoise,* it's not likely they'll recognize me—not like this."

"I hope not. Do you think anyone from the ship *will* be there tonight?"

"I doubt it." He scratched viciously at the wig above his left ear. "Where did ye get this thing, Fergus? I believe it's got lice."

"Oh, no, milord," Fergus assured him. "The wigmaker from whom I rented it assured me that it had been well dusted with hyssop and horse nettle to prevent any such infestations." Fergus himself was wearing his own hair, thickly powdered, and was handsome—if less startling than Jamie—in a new suit of dark blue velvet.

There was a tentative knock at the door, and Marsali stepped in. She too had had her wardrobe refurbished, and glowed in a dress of soft pink, with a deep rose sash.

She glowed somewhat more than I thought the dress accounted for, in fact, and as we made our way down the narrow corridor to the carriage, pulling in our skirts to keep them from brushing the walls, I managed to lean forward and murmur in her ear.

"Are you using the tansy oil?"

"Mm?" she said absently, her eyes on Fergus as he bowed and held open the carriage door for her. "What did ye say?"

"Never mind," I said, resigned. That was the least of our worries at the moment.

The Governor's mansion was ablaze with lights. Lanterns were perched along the low wall of the veranda, and hung from the trees along the paths of the ornamental garden. Gaily dressed people were emerging from their carriages on the crushed-shell drive, passing into the house through a pair of huge French doors.

We dismissed our own—or, rather, Jared's—carriage, but stood for a moment on the drive, waiting for a brief lull in the arrivals. Jamie seemed mildly nervous—for him; his fingers twitched now and then against the gray satin, but his manner was outwardly as calm as ever.

There was a short reception line in the foyer; several of the minor dignitaries of the island had been invited to assist the new governor in welcoming his guests. I passed ahead of Jamie down the line, smiling and nodding to the Mayor of Kingston and his wife. I quailed a bit at the sight of a fully decorated admiral next in line, resplendent in gilded coat and epaulettes, but no sign of anything beyond a mild amazement crossed his features as he shook hands with the gigantic Frenchman and the tiny Chinese who accompanied me.

There was my acquaintance from the *Porpoise;* Lord John's blond hair was hidden under a formal wig tonight, but I recognized the fine, clear features and slight, muscular body at once. He stood a little apart from the other dignitaries, alone. Rumor had it that his wife had refused to leave England to accompany him to this posting.

He turned to greet me, his face fixed in an expression of formal politeness. He looked, blinked, and then broke into a smile of extraordinary warmth and pleasure.

"Mrs. Malcolm!" he exclaimed, seizing my hands. "I am vastly pleased to see you!"

"The feeling is entirely mutual," I said, smiling back at him. "I didn't know you were the Governor, last time we met. I'm afraid I was a bit informal."

He laughed, his face glowing with the light of the candles in the wall sconces. Seen clearly in the light for the first time, I realized what a remarkably handsome man he was.

"You might be thought to have had an excellent excuse," he said. He looked me over carefully. "May I say that you are in remarkable fine looks this evening? Clearly the island air must agree with you somewhat more than the miasmas of shipboard. I had hoped to meet you again before leaving the *Porpoise,* but when I inquired for you, I was told by Mr. Leonard that you were unwell. I trust you are entirely recovered?"

"Oh, entirely," I told him, amused. Unwell, eh? Evidently Tom Leonard was not about to admit to losing me overboard. I wondered whether he had put my disappearance in the log.

"May I introduce my husband?" I turned to wave at Jamie, who had been detained in animated conversation with the admiral, but who was now advancing toward us, accompanied by Mr. Willoughby.

I turned back to find the Governor gone green as a gooseberry. He stared from Jamie to me, and back again, pale as though confronted by twin specters.

Jamie came to a stop beside me, and inclined his head graciously toward the Governor.

"John," he said softly. "It's good to see ye, man."

The Governor's mouth opened and shut without making a sound.

"Let us make an opportunity to speak, a bit later," Jamie murmured. "But for now—my name is Etienne Alexandre." He took my arm, and bowed formally. "And may I have the pleasure to present to you my wife, Claire?" he said aloud, shifting effortlessly into French.

"Claire?" The Governor looked wildly at me. *"Claire?"*

"Er, yes," I said, hoping he wasn't going to faint. He looked very much as though he might, though I had no idea why the revelation of my Christian name ought to affect him so strongly.

The next arrivals were waiting impatiently for us to move out of the way. I bowed, fluttering my fan, and we walked into the main salon of the Residence. I glanced back over my shoulder to see the Governor shaking hands mechanically with the new arrival, staring after us with a face like white paper.

The salon was a huge room, low-ceilinged and filled with people, noisy and bright as a cageful of parrots. I felt some relief at the sight. Among this crowd, Jamie wouldn't be terribly conspicuous, despite his size.

A small orchestra played at one side of the room, near a pair of doors thrown open to the terrace outside. I saw a number of people strolling there, evidently seeking either a breath of air or sufficient quiet to hold a private conversation. At the other side of the room, yet another pair of doors opened into a short hallway, where the retiring rooms were.

We knew no one, and had no social sponsor to make introducions. However, due to Jamie's foresight, we had no need of one. Within moments of our arrival, women had begun to cluster round us, fascinated by Mr. Willoughby.

"My acquaintance, Mr. Yi Tien Cho," Jamie introduced him to stout young woman in tight yellow satin. "Late of the Celestial Kingdom of China, Madame."

"Ooh!" The young lady fluttered her fan before her face, impressed. "Really from China? But what an unthinkable distance you must have come! Do let me welcome you to our small island, Mr.—Mr. Cho?" She extended a hand to him, clearly expecting it to be kissed.

Mr. Willoughby bowed deeply, hands in his sleeves, and obligingly said something in Chinese. The young woman looked thrilled. Jamie looked momentarily startled, and then the mask of urbanity dropped back over his face. I saw Mr. Willoughby's shining black eyes fix on the tips of the lady's shoes, protruding from under the hem of her dress, and wondered just what he had said to her.

Jamie seized the opportunity—and the lady's hand—bowing over it with extreme politeness.

"Your servant, Madame," he said in thickly accented English. "Etienne Alexandre. And might I present to you my wife, Claire?"

"Oh, yes, so pleased to meet you!" The young woman, flushed with excitement, took my hand and squeezed it. "I'm Marcelline Williams; perhaps you'll be acquainted with my brother, Judah? He owns Twelvetrees—you know, the large coffee plantation? I've come to stay with him for the season, and I'm having ever so marvelous a time!"

"No, I'm afraid we don't know anyone here," I said apologetically. "We've only just arrived ourselves—from Martinique, where my husband's sugar business is."

"Oh," Miss Williams cried, her eyes flying wide open. "But you must allow me to make you acquainted with my particular friends, the Stephenses! I believe they once visited Martinique, and Georgina Stephens is such a charming person—you will like her at once, I promise!"

And that was all there was to it. Within an hour, I had been introduced to dozens of people, and was being carried slowly round the room, eddying from one group to the next, passed hand to hand by the current of introductions launched by Miss Williams.

Across the room, I could see Jamie, standing head and shoulders above his companions, the picture of aristocratic dignity. He was conversing cordially with a group of men, all eager to make the acquaintance of a prosperous businessman who might offer useful contacts with the French sugar trade. I caught his eye once in passing, and he gave me a brilliant smile and a gallant French bow. I still wondered what in the name of God he thought he was up to, but shrugged mentally. He would tell me when he was ready.

Fergus and Marsali, as usual needing no one's company but each other's, were dancing at one end of the floor, her glowing pink face smiling into his. For the sake of the occasion, Fergus had forgone his useful hook, replacing it with a black leather glove filled with bran, pinned to the sleeve of his coat. This rested against the back of Marsali's gown, a trifle stiff-looking, but not so unnatural as to provoke comment.

I danced past them, revolving sedately in the arms of a short tubby English planter named Carstairs, who wheezed pleasantries into my bosom, red face streaming sweat.

As for Mr. Willoughby, he was enjoying an unparalleled social triumph, the center of attention of a cluster of ladies who vied with each other in pressing dainties and refreshments on him. His eyes were bright, and a faint flush shone on his sallow cheeks.

Mr. Carstairs deposited me among a group of ladies at the end of the dance, and gallantly went to fetch a cup of claret. I at once returned to the business of the evening, asking the ladies whether they might be familiar with people to whose acquaintance I had been recommended, named Abernathy.

"Abernathy?" Mrs. Hall, a youngish matron, fluttered her fan and looked blank. "No, I cannot say I am acquainted with them. Do they take a great part in society, do you know?"

"Oh, no, Joan!" Her friend, Mrs. Yoakum, looked shocked, with the particular kind of enjoyable shock that precedes some juicy revelation. "You've heard of the Abernathys! You remember, the man who bought Rose Hall, up on the Yallahs River?"

"Oh, yes!" Mrs. Hall's blue eyes widened. "The one who died so soon after buying it?"

"Yes, that's the one," another lady chimed in, overhearing

"Malaria, they *said* it was, but *I* spoke to the doctor who attended him—he had come to dress Mama's bad leg, you know she is such a martyr to the dropsy—and *he* told me—in strictest confidence, of course . . ."

The tongues wagged merrily. Rosie MacIver had been a faithful reporter; all the stories she had conveyed were here, and more. I caught hold of the conversational thread and gave it a jerk in the desired direction.

"Does Mrs. Abernathy have indentured labor, as well as slaves?"

Here opinion was more confused. Some thought that she had several indentured servants, some thought only one or two—no one present had actually set foot in Rose Hall, but of course people *said* . . .

A few minutes later, the gossip had turned to fresh meat, and the *incredible* behavior of the new curate, Mr. Jones, with the widowed Mrs. Mina Alcott, but then, what could be expected of a woman with *her* reputation, and surely it was not entirely the young man's fault, and she so much older, though of course, one in Holy Orders might be expected to be held to a higher standard . . I made an excuse and slipped away to the ladies' retiring room, my ears ringing.

I saw Jamie as I went, standing near the refreshment table. He was talking to a tall, red-haired girl in embroidered cotton, a trace of unguarded tenderness lingering in his eyes as he looked at her. She was smiling eagerly up at him, flattered by his attention. I smiled at the sight, wondering what the young lady would think, did she realize that he was not really looking at her at all, but imagining her as the daughter he had never seen.

I stood in front of the looking glass in the outer retiring room, tucking in stray curls loosened by the exertion of dancing, and took pleasure in the temporary silence. The retiring room was luxuriously appointed, being in fact three separate chambers, with the privy facilities and a room for the storage of hats, shawls, and extraneous clothing opening off the main room, where I stood. This had not only a long pier-glass and a fully appointed dressing table, but also a chaise longue, covered in red velvet. I eyed it with some wistfulness—the slippers I was wearing were pinching my feet badly—but duty called.

So far, I had learned nothing beyond what we already knew

about the Abernathy plantation, though I had compiled a useful list of several other plantations near Kingston that employed indentured labor. I wondered whether Jamie intended to call upon his friend the Governor to help in the search for Ian—that might possibly justify risking an appearance here tonight.

But Lord John's response to the revelation of my identity was both puzzling and disturbing; you would think the man had seen a ghost. I squinted at my violet reflection, admiring the glitter of the black-and-gold fish at my throat, but failed to see anything unsettling in my appearance. My hair was tucked up with pins decorated with seed pearls and brilliants, and discreet use of Mrs MacIver's cosmetics had darkened my lids and blushed my cheeks quite becomingly, if I did say so myself.

I shrugged, fluttered my lashes seductively at my image, then patted my hair and returned to the salon.

I made my way toward the long tables of refreshments, where a huge array of cakes, pastries, savories, fruits, candies, stuffed rolls, and a number of objects I couldn't put a name to but presumed edible were displayed. As I turned absentmindedly from the refreshment table with a plate of fruit, I collided headlong with a dark-hued waistcoat. Apologizing to its owner in confusion, found myself looking up into the dour face of the Reverend Archibald Campbell.

"Mrs. Malcolm!" he exclaimed in astonishment.

"Er . . . Reverend Campbell," I replied, rather weakly. "What a surprise." I dabbed tentatively at a smear of mango on his abdomen, but he took a marked step backward, and I desisted.

He looked rather coldly at my décolletage.

"I trust I find you well, Mrs. Malcolm?" he said.

"Yes, thank you," I said. I wished he would stop calling me Mrs. Malcolm before someone to whom I had been introduced as Madame Alexandre heard him.

"I was so sorry to hear about your sister," I said, hoping to distract him. "Have you any word of her yet?"

He bent his head stiffly, accepting my sympathy.

"No. My own attempts at instigating a search have of course been limited," he said. "It was at the suggestion of one of my parishioners that I accompanied him and his wife here tonight with the intention of putting my case before the Governor, and begging his assistance in locating my sister. I assure you, Mrs

Malcolm, no less weighty a consideration would have impelled my attendance at a function such as this.''

He cast a glance of profound dislike at a laughing group nearby, where three young men were competing with each other in the composition of witty toasts to a group of young ladies, who received these attentions with much giggling and energetic fan-fluttering.

''I'm truly sorry for your misfortune, Reverend,'' I said, edging aside. ''Miss Cowden told me a bit about your sister's tragedy. If I should be able to be of help . . .''

''No one can help,'' he interrupted. His eyes were bleak. ''It was the fault of the Papist Stuarts, with their wicked attempt upon the throne, and the licentious Highlanders who followed them. No, no one can help, save God. He has destroyed the house of Stuart; he will destroy the man Fraser as well, and on that day, my sister will be healed.''

''Fraser?'' The trend of the conversation was making me distinctly uneasy. I glanced quickly across the room, but luckily Jamie was nowhere in sight.

''That is the name of the man who seduced Margaret from her family and her proper loyalties. His may not have been the hand that struck her down, but it was on his account that she had left her home and safety, and placed herself in danger. Aye, God will requite James Fraser fairly,'' he said with a sort of grim satisfaction at the thought.

''Yes, I'm sure he will,'' I murmured. ''If you will excuse me, I believe I see a friend . . .'' I tried to escape, but a passing procession of footmen bearing dishes of meat blocked my way.

''God will not suffer lewdness to endure forever,'' the Reverend went on, evidently feeling that the Almighty's opinions coincided largely with his own. His small gray eyes rested with icy disapproval on a group nearby, where several ladies fluttered around Mr. Willoughby like bright moths about a Chinese lantern.

Mr. Willoughby was brightly lit, too, in more than one sense of the word. His high-pitched giggle rose above the laughter of the ladies, and I saw him lurch heavily against a passing servant, nearly upsetting a tray of sorbet cups.

''Let the women learn with all sobriety,'' the Reverend was intoning, ''avoiding all gaudiness of clothing and broided hair.'' He seemed to be hitting his stride; no doubt Sodom and Gomorrah would be up next. "A woman who has no husband should devote herself to the service of the Lord, not be disporting herself with abandon in public places. Do you see Mrs. Alcott? And she a widow, who should be engaged in pious works!"

I followed the direction of his frown and saw that he was looking at a chubby, jolly-looking woman in her thirties, with light brown hair done in gathered ringlets, who was giggling at Mr. Willoughby. I looked at her with interest. So this was the infamous merry widow of Kingston!

The little Chinese had now got down upon his hands and knees and was crawling around on the floor, pretending to look for a lost earring, while Mrs. Alcott squeaked in mock alarm at his forays toward her feet. I thought perhaps I had better find Fergus without delay, and have him detach Mr. Willoughby from his new acquaintance before matters went too far.

Evidently offended beyond bearing by the sight, the Reverend abruptly put down the cup of lemon squash he had been holding turned and made his way through the crowd toward the terrace vigorously elbowing people out of his way.

I breathed a sigh of relief; conversation with the Reverend Campbell was a lot like exchanging frivolities with the public hangman—though, in fact, the only hangman with whom I had been personally acquainted was much better company than the Reverend.

Suddenly I saw Jamie's tall figure, heading for a door on the far side of the room, where I assumed the Governor's private quarter to be. He must be going to talk to Lord John now. Moved by curiosity, I decided to join him.

The floor was by now so crowded that it was difficult to make my way across it. By the time I reached the door through which Jamie had gone, he had long since disappeared, but I pushed my way through.

I was in a long hallway, dimly lighted by candles in sconces and pierced at intervals by long casement windows, through which red light from the torches on the terrace outside flickered, picking up the gleam of metal from the decorations on the walls. These were largely military, consisting of ornamental sprays of pistols knives, shields and swords. Lord John's personal souvenirs? wondered, or had they come with the house?

Away from the clamor of the salon, it was remarkably quiet.

walked down the hallway, my steps muffled by the long Turkey carpet that covered the parquet.

There was an indistinguishable murmur of male voices ahead. I turned a corner into a shorter corridor and saw a door ahead from which light spilled—that must be the Governor's private office. Inside, I heard Jamie's voice.

"Oh, God, John!" he said.

I stopped dead, halted much more by the tone of that voice than by the words—it was broken with an emotion I had seldom heard from him.

Walking very quietly, I drew closer. Framed in the half-open door was Jamie, head bowed as he pressed Lord John Grey tight in a fervent embrace.

I stood still, completely incapable of movement or speech. As I watched, they broke apart. Jamie's back was turned to me, but Lord John faced the hallway; he could have seen me easily, had he looked. He wasn't looking toward the hallway, though. He was staring at Jamie, and on his face was a look of such naked hunger that the blood rushed to my own cheeks when I saw it.

I dropped my fan. I saw the Governor's head turn, startled at the sound. Then I was running down the hall, back toward the salon, my heartbeat drumming in my ears.

I shot through the door into the salon and came to a halt behind a potted palm, heart pounding. The wrought-iron chandeliers were thick with beeswax candles, and pine torches burned brightly on the walls, but even so, the corners of the room were dark. I stood in the shadows, trembling.

My hands were cold, and I felt slightly sick. What in the name of God was going on?

The Governor's shock at learning that I was Jamie's wife was now at least partially explained; that one glimpse of unguarded, painful yearning had told me exactly how matters stood on his side. Jamie was another question altogether.

He was the Governor of Ardsmuir prison, he had said, casually. And less casually, on another occasion, *D'ye ken what men in prison do?*

I did know, but I would have sworn on Brianna's head that Jamie didn't; hadn't, couldn't, under any circumstances whatever. At least I would have sworn that before tonight. I closed my eyes, chest heaving, and tried not to think of what I had seen.

I couldn't, of course. And yet, the more I thought of it, the more impossible it seemed. The memories of Jack Randall might have faded with the physical scars he had left, but I could not believe that they would ever fade sufficiently for Jamie to tolerate the physical attentions of another man, let alone to welcome them.

But if he knew Grey so intimately as to make what I had witnessed plausible in the name of friendship alone, then why had he not told me of him before? Why go to such lengths to see the man, as soon as he learned that Grey was in Jamaica? My stomach dropped once more, and the feeling of sickness returned. I wanted badly to sit down.

As I leaned against the wall, trembling in the shadows, the door to the Governor's quarters opened, and the Governor came out, returning to his party. His face was flushed and his eyes shone. I could at that moment easily have murdered him, had I anything more lethal than a hairpin to hand.

The door opened again a few minutes later, and Jamie emerged no more than six feet away. His mask of cool reserve was in place, but I knew him well enough to see the marks of a strong emotion under it. But while I could see it, I couldn't interpret it. Excitement? Apprehension? Fear and joy mingled? Something else? I had simply never seen him look that way before.

He didn't seek conversation or refreshments, but instead began to stroll about the room, obviously looking for someone. For me.

I swallowed heavily. I couldn't face him—not in front of a crowd. I stayed where I was, watching him, until he finally went out onto the terrace. Then I left my hiding place, and crossed the room as quickly as I could, heading for the refuge of the retiring room. At least there I would be able to sit down for a moment.

I pushed open the heavy door and stepped inside, relaxing at once as the warm, comforting scents of women's perfume and powder surrounded me. Then the other smell struck me. It too was a familiar scent—one of the smells of my profession. But not expected here.

The retiring room was still quiet; the loud rumble from the salon had dropped abruptly to a faint murmur, like a far-off thunderstorm. It was, however, no longer a place of refuge.

Mina Alcott lay sprawled across the red velvet chaise, her head hanging backward over the edge, her skirts in disarray about her neck. Her eyes were open, fixed in upside-down surprise. Th

lood from her severed throat had turned the velvet black beneath
er, and dripped down into a large pool beneath her head. Her
ght brown hair had come loose from its dressing, the matted ends
f her ringlets dangling in the puddle.

I stood frozen, too paralyzed even to call for help. Then I heard
he sound of gay voices in the hallway outside, and the door
ushed open. There was a moment's silence as the women behind
he saw it too.

Light from the corridor spilled through the door and across the
oor, and in the moment before the screaming began, I saw the
otprints leading toward the window—the small neat prints of a
lt-soled foot, outlined in blood.

In Which Much Is Reveale

They had taken Jamie somewhere. I, shaking and incohe
ent, had been put—with a certain amount of irony—in t
Governor's private office with Marsali, who insisted
trying to bathe my face with a damp towel, in spite of my res
tance.

"They canna think Da had anything to do with it!" she said, f
the fifth time.

"They don't." I finally pulled myself together enough to talk
her. "But they think Mr. Willoughby did—and Jamie brought h
here."

She stared at me, wide-eyed with horror.

"Mr. Willoughby? But he couldn't!"

"I wouldn't have thought so." I felt as though someone h
been beating me with a club; everything ached. I sat slumped o
small velvet love seat, aimlessly twirling a glass of brandy b
tween my hands, unable to drink it.

I couldn't even decide what I *ought* to feel, let alone sort out
conflicting events and emotions of the evening. My mind k
jumping between the grisly scene in the retiring room, and
tableau I had seen a half-hour earlier, in this very room.

I sat looking at the Governor's big desk. I could still see the t
of them, Jamie and Lord John, as though they had been painted
the wall before me.

"I just don't believe it," I said out loud, and felt slightly bet
for the saying.

"Neither do I," said Marsali. She was pacing the floor,

ootsteps changing from the click of heels on parquet to a muffled ump as she hit the flowered carpet. "He can't have! I ken he's a eathen, but we've lived wi' the man! We *know* him!"

Did we? Did I know Jamie? I would have sworn I did, and yet . . I kept remembering what he had said to me at the brothel, uring our first night together. *Will ye take me, and risk the man* at I am, for the sake of the man ye knew? I had thought then— nd since—that there was not so much difference between them. ut if I were wrong?

"I'm not wrong!" I muttered, clutching my glass fiercely. "I'm ot!" If Jamie could take Lord John Grey as a lover, and hide it om me, he wasn't remotely the man I thought he was. There had be some other explanation.

He didn't tell you about Laoghaire, said an insidious little voice side my head.

"That's different," I said to it stoutly.

"What's different?" Marsali was looking at me in surprise.

"I don't know; don't mind me." I brushed a hand across my ace, trying to wipe away confusion and weariness. "It's taking em a long time."

The walnut case-clock had struck two o'clock in the morning efore the door of the office opened and Fergus came in, accompaed by a grim-looking militiaman.

Fergus was somewhat the worse for wear; most of the powder d gone from his hair, shaken onto the shoulders of his dark blue oat like dandruff. What was left gave his hair a grayish cast, as ough he had aged twenty years overnight. No surprise; I felt as ough I had.

"We can go now, *chérie,*" he said quietly to Marsali. He turned me. "Will you come with us, milady, or wait for milord?"

"I'll wait," I said. I wasn't going to bed until I had seen Jamie, matter how long it took.

"I will have the carriage return for you, then," he said, and put hand on Marsali's back to usher her out.

The militiaman said something under his breath as they passed m. I didn't catch it, but evidently Fergus did. He stiffened, eyes arrowing, and turned back toward the man. The militiaman cked up onto the balls of his feet, smiling evilly and looking pectant. Clearly he would like nothing better than an excuse to t Fergus.

To his surprise, Fergus smiled charmingly at him, square whi teeth gleaming.

"My thanks, *mon ami*," he said, "for your assistance in th most trying situation." He thrust out a black-gloved hand, whi the militiaman accepted in surprise.

Then Fergus jerked his arm suddenly backward. There was brief rip, and a pattering sound, as a small stream of bran stru the parquet floor.

"Keep it," he told the militiaman graciously. "A small tok of my appreciation." And then they were gone, leaving the ma slack-jawed, staring down in horror at the apparently severed ha in his grasp.

It was another hour before the door opened again, this time admit the Governor. He was still handsome and neat as a whi camellia, but definitely beginning to turn brown round the edges set the untouched glass of brandy down and got to my feet to fa him.

"Where is Jamie?"

"Still being questioned by Captain Jacobs, the militia co mander." He sank into his chair, looking bemused. "I had notion he spoke French so remarkably well."

"I don't suppose you know him all that well," I said, delib ately baiting. What I wanted badly to know was just how well did know Jamie. He didn't rise to it, though; merely took off formal wig and laid it aside, running a hand through his dar blond hair with relief.

"Can he keep up such an impersonation, do you think?" asked, frowning, and I realized that he was so occupied w thoughts of the murder and of Jamie that he was paying little, any, attention to me.

"Yes," I said shortly. "Where do they have him?" I got heading for the door.

"In the formal parlor," he said. "But I don't think y should—"

Not pausing to listen, I yanked open the door and poked head into the hall, then hastily drew it back and slammed the do

Coming down the hall was the Admiral I had met in the rece ing line, face set in lines of gravity suitable to the situation. Adm

als I could deal with. However, he was accompanied by a flotilla
of junior officers, and among the entourage I had spotted a face I
new, though he was now wearing the uniform of a first lieutenant,
instead of an oversized captain's coat.

He was shaved and rested, but his face was puffy and discol-
red; someone had beaten him up in the not too distant past.
Despite the differences in his appearance, I had not the slightest
ifficulty in recognizing Thomas Leonard. I had the distinct feel-
ng that he wouldn't have any trouble recognizing me, either,
iolet silk notwithstanding.

I looked frantically about the office for someplace to hide, but
hort of crawling into the kneehole of the desk, there was no place
t all. The Governor was watching me, fair brows raised in aston-
shment.

"What—" he began, but I rounded on him, finger to my lips.

"Don't give me away, if you value Jamie's life!" I whispered
nelodramatically, and so saying, flung myself onto the velvet love
eat, snatched up the damp towel and dropped it on my face, and
—with a superhuman effort of will—forced all my limbs to go
imp.

I heard the door open, and the Admiral's high, querulous voice.

"Lord John—" he began, and then evidently noticed my supine
orm, for he broke off and resumed in a slightly lower voice, "Oh!
collect you are engaged?"

"Not precisely engaged, Admiral, no." Grey had fast reflexes, I
ould say that for him; he sounded perfectly self-possessed, as
ough he were quite used to being found in custody of uncon-
ious females. "The lady was overcome by the shock of discover-
g the body."

"Oh!" said the Admiral again, this time dripping with sympa-
y. "I quite see that. Beastly shock for a lady, to be sure." He
esitated, then dropping his voice to a sort of hoarse whisper, said,
D'you think she's asleep?"

"I should think so," the Governor assured him. "She's had
ough brandy to fell a horse." My fingers twitched, but I man-
;ed to lie still.

"Oh, quite. Best thing for shock, brandy." The Admiral went
a whispering, sounding like a rusted hinge. "Meant to tell you I
ave sent to Antigua for additional troops—quite at your disposal

—guards, search the town—if the militia don't find the fellov first," he added.

"I hope they may not," said a viciously determined voic among the officers. "I'd like to catch the yellow bugger mysel. There wouldn't be enough of him left to hang, believe me!"

A deep murmur of approval at this sentiment went through th men, to be sternly quelled by the Admiral.

"Your sentiments do you credit, gentlemen," he said, "but th law will be observed in all respects. You will make that clear to th troops in your command; when the miscreant is taken, he is to b brought to the Governor, and justice will be properly executed, assure you." I didn't like the way he emphasized the word "exe cuted," but he got a grudging chorus of assent from his officer:

The Admiral, having delivered this order in his ordinary voic dropped back into a whisper to take his leave.

"I shall be staying in the town, at MacAdams Hotel," h croaked. "Do not hesitate to send to me for any assistance, You Excellency."

There was a general shuffle and murmur as the naval office: took their leave, observing discretion for the sake of my slumber Then came the sound of a single pair of footsteps, and then th *whoosh* and creak of someone settling heavily into a chair. Ther was silence for a moment.

Then Lord John said "You can get up now, if you wish. I ar supposing that you are not in fact prostrate with shock," he adde ironically. "Somehow I suspect that a mere murder would not b sufficient to discompose a woman who could deal single-handed with a typhoid epidemic."

I removed the towel from my face and swung my feet off th chaise, sitting up to face him. He was leaning on his desk, chin his hands, staring at me.

"There are shocks," I said precisely, smoothing back my dam curls and giving him an eyeball, "and then there are shocks. If yc know what I mean."

He looked surprised; then a flicker of understanding came in his expression. He reached into the drawer of his desk, and pull out my fan, white silk embroidered with violets.

"This is yours, I suppose? I found it in the corridor." H mouth twisted wryly as he looked at me. "I see. I suppose, the you will have some notion of how your appearance earlier this evening affected *me*."

"I doubt it very much," I said. My fingers were still icy, and I felt as though I had swallowed some large, cold object that pressed uncomfortably under my breastbone. I breathed deeply, trying to force it down, to no avail. "You didn't know that Jamie was married?"

He blinked, but not in time to keep me from seeing a small grimace of pain, as though someone had struck him suddenly across the face.

"I knew he *had* been married," he corrected. He dropped his hands, fiddling aimlessly with the small objects that littered his desk. "He told me—or gave me to understand, at least—that you were dead."

Grey picked up a small silver paperweight, and turned it over and over in his hands, eyes fixed on the gleaming surface. A large sapphire was set in it, winking blue in the candlelight.

"Has he never mentioned me?" he asked softly. I wasn't sure whether the undertone in his voice was pain or anger. Despite myself, I felt some small sense of pity for him.

"Yes, he did," I said. "He said you were his friend." He glanced up, the fine-cut face lightening a bit.

"Did he?"

"You have to understand," I said. "He—I—we were separated by the war, the Rising. Each of us thought the other was dead. I found him again only—my God, was it only four months ago?" I felt staggered, and not only by the events of the evening. I felt as though I had lived several lifetimes since the day I had opened the door of the printshop in Edinburgh, to find A. Malcolm bending over his press.

The lines of stress in Grey's face eased a little.

"I see," he said slowly. "So—you have not seen him since—my God, that's twenty years!" He stared at me, dumbfounded. "And four months? Why—how—" He shook his head, brushing away the questions.

"Well, that's of no consequence just now. But he did not tell you—that is—has he not told you about Willie?"

I stared at him blankly.

"Who's Willie?"

Instead of explaining, he bent and opened the drawer of his

desk. He pulled out a small object and laid it on the desk, motioning me to come closer.

It was a portrait, an oval miniature, set in a carved frame of some fine-grained dark wood. I looked at the face, and sat down abruptly, my knees gone to water. I was only dimly aware of Grey's face, floating above the desk like a cloud on the horizon, as I picked up the miniature to look at it more closely.

He might have been Bree's brother, was my first thought. The second, coming with the force of a blow to the solar plexus, was "My God in heaven, he *is* Bree's brother!"

There couldn't be much doubt about it. The boy in the portrait was perhaps nine or ten, with a childish tenderness still lingering about his face, and his hair was a soft chestnut brown, not red. But the slanted blue eyes looked out boldly over a straight nose a fraction of an inch too long, and the high Viking cheekbones pressed tight against smooth skin. The tilt of the head held the same confident carriage as that of the man who had given him that face.

My hands trembled so violently that I nearly dropped it. I set it back on the desk, but kept my hand over it, as though it might leap up and bite me. Grey was watching me, not without sympathy.

"You didn't know?" he said.

"Who—" My voice was hoarse with shock, and I had to stop and clear my throat. "Who is his mother?"

Grey hesitated, eyeing me closely, then shrugged slightly.

"Was. She's dead."

"Who was she?" The ripples of shock were still spreading from an epicenter in my stomach, making the crown of my head tingle and my toes go numb, but at least my vocal cords were coming back under my control. I could hear Jenny saying, *He's no the sort of man should sleep alone, aye?* Evidently he wasn't.

"Her name was Geneva Dunsany," Grey said. "My wife' sister."

My mind was reeling, in an effort to make sense of all this, and I suppose I was less than tactful.

"Your *wife*?" I said, goggling at him. He flushed deeply and looked away. If I had been in any doubt about the nature of th look I had seen him give Jamie, I wasn't any longer.

"I think you had better bloody well explain to me just what yo ave to do with Jamie, and this Geneva, and this boy," I said, icking up the portrait once more.

He raised one brow, cool and reserved; he had been shocked, oo, but the shock was wearing off.

"I cannot see that I am under any particular obligation to do o," he said.

I fought back the urge to rake my nails down his face, but the mpulse must have shown on my face, for he pushed back his chair and got his feet under him, ready to move quickly. He eyed me varily across the expanse of dark wood.

I took several deep breaths, unclenched my fists, and spoke as almly as I could.

"Right. You're not. But I would appreciate it very much if you lid. And why did you show me the picture if you didn't mean me o know?" I added. "Since I know that much, I'll certainly find ut the rest from Jamie. You might as well tell me your side of it ow." I glanced at the window; the slice of sky that showed etween the half-open shutters was still a velvet black, with no ign of dawn. "There's time."

He breathed deeply, and laid down the paperweight. "I suppose here is." He jerked his head abruptly at the decanter. "Will you ave brandy?"

"I will," I said promptly, "and I strongly suggest you have ome, too. I expect you need it as much as I do."

A slight smile showed briefly at the corner of his mouth.

"Is that a medical opinion, Mrs. Malcolm?" he asked dryly.

"Absolutely," I said.

This small truce established, he sat back, rolling his beaker of randy slowly between his hands.

"You said Jamie mentioned me to you," he said. I must have inched slightly at his use of Jamie's name, for he frowned at me. Would you prefer that I referred to him by his surname?" he aid, coldly. "I should scarcely know which to use, under the ircumstances."

"No." I waved it away, and took a sip of brandy. "Yes, he entioned you. He said you had been the Governor of the prison t Ardsmuir, and that you were a friend—and that he could trust ou," I added reluctantly. Possibly Jamie felt he could trust Lord ohn Grey, but I was not so sanguine.

The smile this time was not quite so brief.

"I am glad to hear that," Grey said softly. He looked down into the amber liquid in his cup, swirling it gently to release its heady bouquet. He took a sip, then set the cup down with decision.

"I met him at Ardsmuir, as he said," he began. "And when the prison was shut down and the other prisoners sold to indenture in America, I arranged that Jamie should be paroled instead to a place in England, called Helwater, owned by friends of my family." He looked at me, hesitating, then added simply, "I could not bear the thought of never seeing him again, you see."

In a few brief words, he acquainted me with the bare facts of Geneva's death and Willie's birth.

"Was he in love with her?" I asked. The brandy was doing its bit to warm my hands and feet, but it didn't touch the large cold object in my stomach.

"He has never spoken to me of Geneva," Grey said. He gulped the last of his brandy, coughed, and reached to pour another cup. It was only when he finished this operation that he looked at me again, and added, "But I doubt it, having known her." His mouth twisted wryly.

"He never told me about Willie, either, but there was a certain amount of gossip about Geneva and old Lord Ellesmere, and by the time the boy was four or five, the resemblance made it quite clear who his father was—to anyone who cared to look." He took another deep swallow of brandy. "I suspect that my mother-in-law knows, but of course she would never breathe a word."

"She wouldn't?"

He stared at me over the rim of his cup.

"No, would you? If it were a choice of your only grandchild being either the ninth Earl of Ellesmere, and heir to one of the wealthiest estates in England, or the penniless bastard of a Scottish criminal?"

"I see." I drank some more of my own brandy, trying to imagine Jamie with a young English girl named Geneva—and succeeding all too well.

"Quite," Grey said dryly. "Jamie saw, too. And very wisely arranged to leave Helwater before it became obvious to everyone."

"And that's where you come back into the story, is it?" I asked.

He nodded, eyes closed. The Residence was quiet, though there was a certain distant stir that made me aware that people were still about.

"That's right," he said. "Jamie gave the boy to me."

The stable at Ellesmere was well-built; cozy in the winter, it was a cool haven in summer. The big bay stallion flicked its ears lazily at a passing fly, but stood stolidly content, enjoying the attentions of his groom.

"Isobel is most displeased with you," Grey said.

"Is she?" Jamie's voice was indifferent. There was no need any longer to worry about displeasing any of the Dunsanys.

"She said you had told Willie you were leaving, which upset him dreadfully. He's been howling all day."

Jamie's face was turned away, but Grey saw the faint tightening at the side of his throat. He rocked backward, leaning against the stable wall as he watched the curry comb come down and down and down in hard, even strokes that left dark trails across the shimmering coat.

"Surely it would have been easier to say nothing to the boy?" Grey said quietly.

"I suppose it would—for Lady Isobel." Fraser turned to put up the curry comb, and slapped a hand on the stallion's rump in dismissal. Grey thought there was an air of finality in the gesture; tomorrow Jamie would be gone. He felt a slight thickening in his own throat, but swallowed it. He rose and followed Fraser toward the door of the stall.

"Jamie—" he said, putting his hand on Fraser's shoulder. The Scot swung round, his features hastily readjusting themselves, but not fast enough to hide the misery in his eyes. He stood still, looking down at the Englishman.

"You're right to go," Grey said. Alarm flared in Fraser's eyes, quickly supplanted by wariness.

"Am I?" he said.

"Anyone with half an eye could see it," Grey said dryly. "If anyone ever actually looked at a groom, someone would have noticed long before now." He glanced back at the bay stallion, and cocked one brow. "Some sires stamp their get. I have the distinct impression that any offspring of yours would be unmistakable."

Jamie said nothing, but Grey fancied that he had grown a shade paler than usual.

"Surely you can see—well, no, perhaps not," he corrected himself, "I don't suppose you have a looking glass, have you?"

Jamie shook his head mechanically. "No," he said absently. "I shave in the reflection from the trough." He drew in a deep breath, and let it out slowly.

"Aye, well," he said. He glanced toward the house, where the French doors were standing open onto the lawn. Willie was accustomed to play there after lunch on fine days.

Fraser turned to him with sudden decision. "Will ye walk with me?" he said.

Not pausing for an answer, he set off past the stable, turning down the lane that led from the paddock to the lower pasture. It was nearly a quarter-mile before he came to a halt, in a sunny clearing by a clump of willows, near the edge of the mere.

Grey found himself puffing slightly from the quick pace—too much soft living in London, he chided himself. Fraser, of course, was not even sweating, despite the warmth of the day.

Without preamble, turning to face Grey, he said, "I wish to ask a favor of ye." The slanted blue eyes were direct as the man himself.

"If you think I would tell anyone . . ." Grey began, then shook his head. "Surely you don't think I could do such a thing. After all, I have known—or at least suspected—for some time."

"No." A faint smile lifted Jamie's mouth. "No, I dinna think ye would. But I would ask ye . . ."

"Yes," Grey said promptly. The corner of Jamie's mouth twitched.

"Ye dinna wish to know what it is first?"

"I should imagine that I know; you wish me to look out for Willie; perhaps to send you word of his welfare."

Jamie nodded.

"Aye, that's it." He glanced up the slope, to where the house lay half-hidden in its nest of fiery maples. "It's an imposition, maybe, to ask ye to come all the way from London to see him now and then."

"Not at all," Grey interrupted. "I came this afternoon to give you some news of my own; I am to be married."

"Married?" The shock was plain on Fraser's face. "To a woman?"

"I think there are not many alternatives," Grey replied dryly. "But yes, since you ask, to a woman. To the Lady Isobel."

"Christ, man! Ye canna do that!"

"I can," Grey assured him. He grimaced. "I made trial of my capacity in London; be assured that I shall make her an adequate husband. You needn't necessarily enjoy the act in order to perform it—or perhaps you were aware of that?"

There was a small reflexive twitch at the corner of Jamie's eye; not quite a flinch, but enough for Grey to notice. Jamie opened his mouth, then closed it again and shook his head, obviously thinking better of what he had been about to say.

"Dunsany is growing too old to take a hand in the running of the estate," Grey pointed out. "Gordon is dead, and Isobel and her mother cannot manage the place alone. Our families have known each other for decades. It is an entirely suitable match."

"Is it, then?" The sardonic skepticism in Jamie's voice was clear. Grey turned to him, fair skin flushing as he answered sharply.

"It is. There is more to a marriage than carnal love. A great deal more."

Fraser swung sharply away. He strode to the edge of the mere, and stood, boots sunk in the reedy mud, looking over the ruffled waves for some time. Grey waited patiently, taking the time to unribbon his hair and reorder the thick blond mass.

At long last, Fraser came back, walking slowly, head down as though still thinking. Face-to-face with Grey he looked up again.

"You are right," he said quietly. "I have no right to think ill of you, if ye mean no dishonor to the lady."

"Certainly not," Grey said. "Besides," he added more cheerfully, "it means I will be here permanently, to see to Willie."

"You mean to resign your commission, then?" One copper eyebrow flicked upward.

"Yes," Grey said. He smiled, a little ruefully. "It will be a relief, in a way. I was not meant for army life, I think."

Fraser seemed to be thinking. "I should be . . . grateful, then," he said, "if you would stand as stepfather to—to my son." He had likely never spoken the word aloud before, and the sound of it seemed to shock him. "I . . . would be obliged to you." Jamie sounded as though his collar were too tight, though in fact his shirt was open at the throat. Grey looked curiously at him, and saw that his countenance was slowly turning a dark and painful red.

"In return . . . If you want . . . I mean, I would be willing to . . . that is . . ."

Grey suppressed the sudden desire to laugh. He laid a light hand on the big Scot's arm, and saw Jamie brace himself not to flinch at the touch.

"My dear Jamie," he said, torn between laughter and exasperation. "Are you actually offering me your body in payment for my promise to look after Willie?"

Fraser's face was red to the roots of his hair.

"Aye, I am," he snapped, tight-lipped. "D'ye want it, or no?"

At this, Grey did laugh, in long gasping whoops, finally having to sit down on the grassy bank in order to recover himself.

"Oh, dear God," he said at last, wiping his eyes. "That I should live to hear an offer like that!"

Fraser stood above him, looking down, the morning light silhouetting him, lighting his hair in flames against the pale blue sky. Grey thought he could see a slight twitch of the wide mouth in the darkened face—humor, tempered with a profound relief.

"Ye dinna want me, then?"

Grey got to his feet, dusting the seat of his breeches. "I shall probably want you to the day I die," he said matter-of-factly. "But tempted as I am—" He shook his head, brushing wet grass from his hands.

"Do you really think that I would demand—or accept—any payment for such a service?" he asked. "Really, I should

*feel my honor most grossly insulted by that offer, save that I
know the depth of feeling which prompted it.''*

"Aye, well,'' Jamie muttered. *"I didna mean to insult ye.''*

*Grey was not sure at this point whether to laugh or cry.
Instead, he reached a hand up and gently touched Jamie's
cheek, fading now to its normal pale bronze. More quietly, he
said, "Besides, you cannot give me what you do not have.''*

*Grey felt, rather than saw, the slight relaxation of tension
in the tall body facing him.*

"You shall have my friendship,'' Jamie said softly, *"if that
has any value to ye.''*

"A very great value indeed.'' The two men stood silent
together for a moment, then Grey sighed and turned to look
up at the sun. *"It's getting late. I suppose you will have a
great many things to do today?''*

*Jamie cleared his throat. "Aye, I have. I suppose I should
be about my business.''*

"Yes, I suppose so.''

*Grey tugged down the points of his waistcoat, ready to go.
But Jamie lingered awkwardly a moment, and then, as though
suddenly making up his mind to it, stepped forward and bending
down, cupped Grey's face between his hands.*

*Grey felt the big hands warm on the skin of his face, light
and strong as the brush of an eagle's feather, and then Jamie
Fraser's soft wide mouth touched his own. There was a fleeting
impression of tenderness and strength held in check, the
faint taste of ale and fresh-baked bread. Then it was gone,
and John Grey stood blinking in the brilliant sun.*

"Oh,'' he said.

Jamie gave him a shy, crooked smile.

"Aye, well,'' he said. *"I suppose I'm maybe not
poisoned.''* He turned then, and disappeared into the screen
of willows, leaving Lord John Grey alone by the mere.

The Governor was quiet for a moment. Then he looked up with
bleak smile.

"That was the first time that he ever touched me willingly," he
aid quietly. "And the last—until this evening, when I gave him
he other copy of that miniature."

I sat completely motionless, the brandy glass unregarded in my hands. I wasn't sure *what* I felt; shock, fury, horror, jealousy, and pity all washed through me in successive waves, mingling in eddies of confused emotion.

A woman had been violently done to death nearby, within the last few hours. And yet the scene in the retiring room seemed unreal by comparison with that miniature; a small and unimportant picture, painted in tones of red. For the moment, neither Lord John nor I was concerned with crime or justice—or with anything beyond what lay between us.

The Governor was examining my face, with considerable absorption.

"I suppose I should have recognized you on the ship," he said. "But of course, at the time, I had thought you long dead."

"Well, it was dark," I said, rather stupidly. I shoved a hand through my curls, feeling dizzy from brandy and sleeplessness. Then I realized what he had said.

"Recognized me? But you'd never met me!"

He hesitated, then nodded.

"Do you recall a dark wood, near Carryarrick in the Scottish Highlands, twenty years ago? And a young boy with a broken arm? You set it for me." He lifted one arm in demonstration.

"Jesus H. Roosevelt Christ." I picked up the brandy and took a swallow that made me cough and gasp. I blinked at him, eyes watering. Knowing now who he was, I could make out the fine light bones and see the slighter, softer outline of the boy he had been.

"Yours were the first woman's breasts I had ever seen," he said wryly. "It was a considerable shock."

"From which you appear to have recovered," I said, rather coldly. "You seem to have forgiven Jamie for breaking your arm and threatening to shoot you, at least."

He flushed slightly, and set down his beaker.

"I—well—yes," he said, abruptly.

We sat there for quite some time, neither of us having any idea what to say. He took a breath once or twice, as though about to say something, but then abandoned it. At last, he closed his eyes as though commending his soul to God, opened them and looked at me.

"Do you know—" he began, then stopped. He looked down at

is clenched hands, then, not at me. A blue stone winked on one knuckle, bright as a teardrop.

"Do you know," he said again, softly, addressing his hands, "what it is to love someone, and never—never!—be able to give them peace, or joy, or happiness?"

He looked up then, eyes filled with pain. "To know that you cannot give them happiness, not through any fault of yours or theirs, but only because you were not born the right person for them?"

I sat quiet, seeing not his, but another handsome face; dark, not fair. Not feeling the warm breath of the tropical night, but the icy hand of a Boston winter. Seeing the pulse of light like heart's blood, spilling across the cold snow of hospital linens.

. . . only because you were not born the right person for them.

"I know," I whispered, hands clenched in my lap. I had told Frank—Leave me. But he could not, no more than I could love him rightly, having found my match elsewhere.

Oh, Frank, I said, silently. Forgive me.

"I suppose I am asking whether you believe in fate," Lord John went on. The ghost of a smile wavered on his face. "You, of all people, would seem best suited to say."

"You'd think so, wouldn't you?" I said bleakly. "But I don't know, any more than you."

He shook his head, then reached out and picked up the minia-ture.

"I have been more fortunate than most, I suppose," he said quietly. "There was the one thing he would take from me." His expression softened as he looked down into the face of the boy in the palm of his hand. "And he has given me something most precious in return."

Without thinking, I let my hand spread out across my belly. Jamie had given me that same precious gift—and at the same great cost to himself.

The sound of footsteps came down the hall, muffled by the carpet. There was a sharp rap at the door, and a militiaman stuck his head into the office.

"Is the lady recovered yet?" he asked. "Captain Jacobs has finished his questions, and Monsieur Alexandre's carriage has returned."

I got hastily to my feet.

"Yes, I'm fine." I turned to the Governor, not knowing what to say to him. "I—thank you for—that is—"

He bowed formally to me, coming around the desk to see me out.

"I regret extremely that you should have been subjected to such a shocking experience, ma'am," he said, with no trace of anything but diplomatic regret in his voice. He had resumed his official manner, smooth and polished as his parquet floors.

I followed the militiaman, but at the door I turned impulsively.

"When we met, that night aboard the *Porpoise*—I'm glad you didn't know who I was. I . . . liked you. Then."

He stood for a second, polite, remote. Then the mask dropped away.

"I liked you, too," he said quietly. "Then."

I felt as though I were riding next to a stranger. The light was beginning to gray toward dawn, and even in the dimness of the coach, I could see Jamie sitting opposite me, his face drawn with weariness. He had taken off the ridiculous wig as soon as we drove away from Government House, discarding the facade of the polished Frenchman to let the disheveled Scot beneath show through. His unbound hair lay in waves over his shoulders, dark in the predawn light that robs everything of color.

"Do you think he did it?" I asked at last, only for something to say.

His eyes were closed. At this, they opened and he shrugged slightly.

"I don't know," he said. He sounded exhausted. "I have asked myself that a thousand times tonight—and been asked it even more." He rubbed his knuckles hard over his forehead.

"I canna imagine a man I know to do such a thing. And yet . . . well, ye ken he'll do anything when he's drink taken. An' he's killed before, drunk—you'll mind the Customs man at the brothel?" I nodded, and he leaned forward, elbows on his knees, sinking his head into his hands.

"This is different, though," he said. "I canna think—but maybe so. Ye ken what he said about women on the ship. And if this Mrs. Alcott was to have toyed wi' him—"

"She did," I said. "I saw her."

He nodded without looking up. "So did any number of other people. But if she led him to think she meant more than she maybe did, and then perhaps she put him off, maybe laughed at him . . . and him fu' as a puggie wi' drink, and knives to hand on every wall of the place . . ." He sighed and sat up.

"God knows," he said bleakly. "I don't." He ran a hand backward through his hair, smoothing it.

"There's something else about it. I had to tell them that I scarcely knew Willoughby—that we'd met him on the packet boat from Martinique, and thought it kindly to introduce him about, but didna ken a thing of where he came from, or the sort of fellow he truly was."

"Did they believe it?"

He glanced at me wryly.

"So far. But the packet boat comes in again in six days—at which point, they'll question the captain and discover that he's never laid eyes on Monsieur Etienne Alexandre and his wife, let alone a wee yellow murdering fiend."

"That might be a trifle awkward," I observed, thinking of Fergus and the militiaman. "We're already rather unpopular on Mr. Willoughby's account."

"Nothing to what we will be, if six days pass and they havena found him," he assured me. "Six days is also maybe as long as it will take for gossip to spread from Blue Mountain House to Kingston about the MacIvers' visitors—for ye ken the servants here all know who we are."

"Damn."

He smiled briefly at that, and my heart turned over to see it.

"You've a nice way wi' words, Sassenach. Aye, well, all it means is that we must find Ian within six days. I shall go to Rose Hall at once, but I think I must just have a wee rest before setting out." He yawned widely behind his hand and shook his head, blinking.

We didn't speak again until after we had arrived at Blue Mountain House and made our way on tiptoe through the slumbering house to our room.

I changed in the dressing room, dropping the heavy stays on the floor with relief, and taking out the pins to let my hair fall free. Wearing only a silk chemise, I came into the bedroom, to see

Jamie standing by the French door in his shirt, looking out over the lagoon.

He turned when he heard me, and beckoned, putting a finger to his lips.

"Come see," he whispered.

There was a small herd of manatees in the lagoon, big gray bodies gliding under the dark crystal water, rising gleaming like smooth, wet rocks. Birds were beginning to call in the trees near the house; besides this, the only sound was the frequent *whoosh* of the manatees' breath as they rose for air, and now and then an eerie sound like a hollow, distant wail, as they called to each other.

We watched them in silence, side by side. The lagoon began to turn green as the first rays of sun touched its surface. In that state of extreme fatigue where every sense is preternaturally heightened, I was as aware of Jamie as though I were touching him.

John Grey's revelations had relieved me of most of my fears and doubts—and yet there remained the fact that Jamie had not told me about his son. Of course he had reasons—and good ones —for his secrecy, but did he not think he could trust me to keep his secret? It occurred to me suddenly that perhaps he had kept quiet because of the boy's mother. Perhaps he had loved her, in spite of Grey's impressions.

She was dead; could it matter if he had? The answer was that it did. I had thought Jamie dead for twenty years, and it had made no difference at all in what I felt for him. What if he had loved this young English girl in such a way? I swallowed a small lump in my throat, trying to find the courage to ask him.

His face was abstracted, a small frown creasing his forehead despite the dawning beauty of the lagoon.

"What are you thinking?" I asked at last, unable to ask for reassurance, fearing to ask for the truth.

"It's only that I had a thought," he answered, still staring out at the manatees. "About Willoughby, aye?"

The events of the night seemed far away and unimportant. Yet murder had been done.

"What was that?"

"Well, I couldna think at first that Willoughby could do such thing—how could any man?" He paused, drawing a finger through the light mist of condensation that formed on the window panes as the sun rose. "And yet . . ." He turned to face me.

"Perhaps I can see." His face was troubled. "He was alone—erra much alone."

"A stranger, in a strange land," I said quietly, remembering the poems, painted in the open secrecy of bold black ink, sent flying toward a long-lost home, committed to the sea on wings of white paper.

"Aye, that's it." He stopped to think, rubbing a hand slowly through his hair, gleaming copper in the new daylight. "And when a man is alone that way—well, it's maybe no decent to say it, but making love to a woman is maybe the only thing will make him forget it for a time."

He looked down, turning his hands over, stroking the length of his scarred middle finger with the index finger of his left hand.

"That's what made me wed Laoghaire," he said quietly. "Not Jenny's nagging. Not pity for her or the wee lassies. Not even a pair of aching balls." His mouth turned up briefly at one corner, then relaxed. "Only needing to forget I was alone," he finished softly.

He turned restlessly, back to the window.

"So I am thinking that if the Chinee came to her, wanting that —needing that—and she wouldna take him . . ." He shrugged, staring out across the cool green of the lagoon. "Aye, maybe he could have done it," he said.

I stood beside him. Out in the center of the lagoon, a single manatee drifted lazily to the surface, turning on her back to hold the infant on her chest toward the sunlight.

He was silent for several minutes, and I was as well, not knowing how to take the conversation back to what I had seen and heard at Government House.

I felt rather than saw him swallow, and he turned from the window to face me. There were lines of tiredness in his face, but his expression was filled with a sort of determination—the sort of look he wore facing battle.

"Claire," he said, and at once I stiffened. He called me by my name only when he was most serious. "Claire, I must tell ye something."

"What?" I had been trying to think how to ask, but suddenly I didn't want to hear. I took half a step back, away from him, but he grabbed my arm.

He had something hidden in his fist. He took my unresisting

hand and put the object into it. Without looking, I knew what ┊ was; I could feel the carving of the delicate oval frame and th┊ slight roughness of the painted surface.

"Claire." I could see the slight tremor at the side of his thro┊ as he swallowed. "Claire—I must tell ye. I have a son."

I didn't say anything, but opened my hand. There it was; th┊ same face I had seen in Grey's office, a childish, cocky version ┊ the man before me.

"I should ha' told ye before." He was searching my face fo┊ some clue to my feelings, but for once, my giveaway countenanc┊ must have been perfectly blank. "I would have—only—" He too┊ a deep breath for strength to go on.

"I havena ever told anyone about him," he said. "Not eve┊ Jenny."

That startled me enough to speak.

"Jenny doesn't know?"

He shook his head, and turned away to watch the manatee┊ Alarmed by our voices, they had retreated a short distance, b┊ then had settled down again, feeding on the water weed at the edg┊ of the lagoon.

"It was in England. It's—he's—I couldna say he was min┊ He's a bastard, aye?" It might have been the rising sun th┊ flushed his cheeks. He bit his lip and went on.

"I havena seen him since he was a wee lad. I never will see hi┊ again—except it might be in a wee painting like this." He took t┊ small picture from me, cradling it in the palm of his hand like ┊ baby's head. He blinked, head bent over it.

"I was afraid to tell ye," he said, low-voiced. "For fear ┊ would think that perhaps I'd gone about spawning a dozen ba┊ tards . . . for fear ye'd think that I wouldna care for Brianna ┊ much, if ye kent I had another child. But I do care, Claire—a gre┊ deal more than I can tell ye." He lifted his head and look┊ directly at me.

"Will ye forgive me?"

"Did you—" The words almost choked me, but I had to s┊ them. "Did you love her?"

An extraordinary expression of sadness crossed his face, but ┊ didn't look away.

"No," he said softly. "She . . . wanted me. I should ha┊ found a way—should have stopped her, but I could not. S┊

vished me to lie wi' her. And I did, and . . . she died of it.'' He
did look down then, long lashes hiding his eyes. ''I am guilty of
er death, before God; perhaps the more guilty—because I did not
ove her.''

I didn't say anything, but put up a hand to touch his cheek. He
ressed his own hand over it, hard, and closed his eyes. There was
gecko on the wall beside us, nearly the same color as the yellow
laster behind it, beginning to glow in the gathering daylight.

''What is he like?'' I asked softly. ''Your son?''

He smiled slightly, without opening his eyes.

''He's spoilt and stubborn,'' he said softly. ''Ill-mannered.
oud. Wi' a wicked temper.'' He swallowed. ''And braw and
onny and canty and strong,'' he said, so softly I could barely hear
im.

''And yours,'' I said. His hand tightened on mine, holding it
gainst the soft stubble of his cheek.

''And mine,'' he said. He took a deep breath, and I could see
he glitter of tears under his closed lids.

''You should have trusted me,'' I said at last. He nodded,
lowly, then opened his eyes, still holding my hand.

''Perhaps I should,'' he said quietly. ''And yet I kept thinking
—how should I tell ye everything, about Geneva, and Willie, and
ohn—will ye know about John?'' He frowned slightly, then re-
axed as I nodded.

''He told me. About everything.'' His brows rose, but he went
n.

''Especially after ye found out about Laoghaire. How could I
ell ye, and expect ye to know the difference?''

''What difference?''

''Geneva—Willie's mother—she wanted my body,'' he said
oftly, watching the gecko's pulsing sides. ''Laoghaire needed my
ame, and the work of my hands to keep her and her bairns.'' He
urned his head then, dark blue eyes fixed on mine. ''John—well.''
Ie lifted his shoulders and let them drop. ''I couldna give him
hat he wanted—and he is friend enough not to ask it.

''But how shall I tell ye all these things,'' he said, the line of his
nouth twisting. ''And then say to you—it is only you I have ever
oved? How should you believe me?''

The question hung in the air between us, shimmering like the
eflection from the water below.

"If you say it," I said, "I'll believe you."

"You will?" He sounded faintly astonished. "Why?"

"Because you're an honest man, Jamie Fraser," I said, smilin
so that I wouldn't cry. "And may the Lord have mercy on you fe
it."

"Only you," he said, so softly I could barely hear him. "T
worship ye with my body, give ye all the service of my hands. T
give ye my name, and all my heart and soul with it. Only yo
Because ye will not let me lie—and yet ye love me."

I did touch him then.

"Jamie," I said softly, and laid my hand on his arm. "Yo
aren't alone anymore."

He turned then and took me by the arms, searching my face.

"I swore to you," I said. "When we married. I didn't mean
then, but I swore—and now I mean it." I turned his hand over i
both mine, feeling the thin, smooth skin at the base of his wris
where the pulse beat under my fingers, where the blade of his di
had cut his flesh once, and spilled his blood to mingle with mir
forever.

I pressed my own wrist against his, pulse to pulse, heartbeat i
heartbeat.

"Blood of my blood . . ." I whispered.

"Bone of my bone." His whisper was deep and husky. He kne
quite suddenly before me, and put his folded hands in mine; t
gesture a Highlander makes when swearing loyalty to his chie
tain.

"I give ye my spirit," he said, head bent over our hands.

" 'Til our life shall be done," I said softly. "But it isn't dor
yet, Jamie, is it?"

Then he rose and took the shift from me, and I lay back on t
narrow bed naked, pulled him down to me through the soft yello
light, and took him home, and home, and home again, and v
were neither one of us alone.

60

The Scent of Gemstones

Rose Hall was ten miles out of Kingston, up a steep and winding road of reddish dust that led into blue mountains. The road was overgrown, so narrow that we must ride in single file most of the way. I followed Jamie through the dark, sweet-scented caverns of cedar boughs, under trees nearly a hundred feet high. Huge ferns grew in the shade below, the fiddle-heads nearly the size of real violin necks.

Everything was quiet, save for the calling of birds in the shrubbery—and even that fell silent as we passed. Jamie's horse stopped dead, once, and backed up, snorting; we waited as a tiny green snake wriggled across the path and into the undergrowth. I looked after it, but could see no farther than ten feet from the edge of the road; everything beyond was cool green shadow. I half-hoped that Mr. Willoughby had come this way—no one would ever find him, in a place like this.

The Chinaman had not been found in spite of an intensive search of the town by the island militia. The special detachment of marines from the barracks on Antigua was expected to arrive tomorrow. In the meantime, every house in Kingston was shut up like a bank vault, the owners armed to the teeth.

The mood of the town was thoroughly dangerous. Like the naval officers; it was the militia colonel's opinion that if the Chinaman were found, he would be lucky to survive long enough to be hanged.

"Be torn to pieces, I expect," Colonel Jacobs had said as he escorted us from the Residence on the night of the murder. "Have his balls ripped off and thrust down his stinking throat, I daresay," he added, with obvious grim satisfaction at the thought.

"I daresay," Jamie had murmured in French, assisting me in the carriage. I knew that the question of Mr. Willoughby was still troubling him; he had been quiet and thoughtful on the ride through the mountains. And yet there was nothing we could do. the little Chinese was innocent, we could not save him; if he was guilty, we could not give him up. The best we might hope for was that he would not be found.

And in the meantime, we had five days to find Young Ian. If he was indeed at Rose Hall, all might be well. If he was not . . .

A fence and small gate marked the division of the plantation from the surrounding forest. Inside, the ground had been cleared and planted in sugarcane and coffee. Some distance from the house, on a separate rise, a large, plain, mud-daub building stood roofed with palm thatch. Dark-skinned people were going in and out, and the faint, cloying scent of burnt sugar hung over the place

Below the refinery—or so I assumed the building to be—stood a large sugar press. A primitive-looking affair, this consisted of pair of huge timbers crossed in the shape of an X, set on an enormous spindle, surmounting the boxlike body of the press. Two or three men were clambering over the press, but it was not working at present; the oxen who drove it were hobbled some distance away, grazing.

"How do they ever get the sugar down from here?" I asked curious, thinking of the narrow trail we had come up. "O mules?" I brushed cedar needles off the shoulders of my coat making myself presentable.

"No," Jamie answered absently. "They send it down the river on barges. The river's just over there, down the wee pass ye can see beyond the house." He pointed with his chin, reining up with one hand, and using the other to beat the dust of travel from the skirts of his coat.

"Ready, Sassenach?"

"As I'll ever be."

Rose Hall was a two-storied house; long and graciously proportioned, with a roof laid in expensive slates, rather than in the sheets of tin that covered most of the planters' residences. A long veranda ran all along one side of the house, with long windows and French doors opening onto it.

A great yellow rosebush grew by the front door, climbing on a trellis and spilling over the edge of the roof. The scent of its perfume was so heady that it made breathing difficult; or perhaps it was only excitement that made my breath come short and stick in my throat. I glanced around as we waited for the door to be answered, trying to catch a glimpse of any white-skinned figure near the sugar refinery above.

"Yes, sah?" A middle-aged slave woman opened the door, looking out curiously at us. She was wide-bodied, dressed in a white cotton smock, with a red turban wrapped round her head, and her skin was the deep, rich gold in the heart of the flowers on the trellis.

"Mr. and Mrs. Malcolm, to call upon Mrs. Abernathy, if ye please," Jamie said politely. The woman looked rather taken back, as though callers were not a common occurrence, but after a moment's indecision, she nodded and stepped back, swinging the door wide.

"You be waitin' in the salon, please, sah," she said, in a soft lilt that made it "*sall*ong." "I be askin' the mistress will she see you."

It was a large room, long and graciously proportioned, lit by huge casement windows all down one side. At the far end of the room was the fireplace, an enormous structure with a stone overmantel and a hearth of polished slates that occupied nearly the whole wall. You could have roasted an ox in it without the slightest difficulty, and the presence of a large spit suggested that the owner of the house did so on occasion.

The slave had shown us to a wicker sofa and invited us to be seated. I sat, looking about, but Jamie strolled restlessly about the room, peering through the windows that gave a view of the cane fields below the house.

It was an odd room; comfortably furnished with wicker and rattan furniture, well-equipped with fat, soft cushions, but ornamented with small, uncommon curios. On one window ledge sat a row of silver handbells, graduated from small to large. Several squat figures of stone and terra-cotta sat together on the table by my elbow; some sort of primitive fetishes or idols.

All of them were in the shape of women, hugely pregnant, or

with enormous, rounded breasts and exaggerated hips, and all with a vivid and mildly disturbing sexuality about them. It was not a prudish age, by any means, but I wouldn't have expected to find such objects in a drawing room in any age.

Somewhat more orthodox were the Jacobite relics. A silver snuffbox, a glass flagon, a decorated fan, a large serving platter— even the large woven rug on the floor; all decorated with the square white rose of the Stuarts. That wasn't so odd—a great many Jacobites who had fled Scotland after Culloden had come to the West Indies to seek the repair of their fortunes. I found the sight encouraging. A householder with Jacobite sympathies might be welcoming to a fellow Scot, and willing to oblige in the matter of Ian. *If he's here,* a small voice in my head warned.

Steps sounded in the inner part of the house, and there was a flutter at the door by the hearth. Jamie made a small grunting sound, as though someone had hit him, and I looked up, to see the mistress of the house step into the room.

I rose to my feet, and the small silver cup I had picked up fell to the floor with a clank.

"Kept your girlish figure, I see, Claire." Her head was tilted to one side, green eyes gleaming with amusement.

I was too paralyzed with surprise to respond aloud, but the thought drifted through my stunned mind that I couldn't say the same for her.

Geillis Duncan had always had a voluptuous abundance of creamy bosom and a generous swell of rounded hip. While still creamy-skinned, she was considerably more abundant and generous, in every dimension visible. She wore a loose muslin gown under which the soft, thick flesh wobbled and swayed as she moved. The delicate bones of her face had long since been submerged in swelling plumpness, but the brilliant green eyes were the same, filled with malice and humor.

I took a deep breath, and got my voice back.

"I trust you won't take this the wrong way," I said, sinking slowly back onto the wicker sofa, "but why aren't you dead?"

She laughed, the silver in her voice as clear as a young girl's.

"Think I should have been, do you? Well, you're no the first— and I daresay you'll no be the last to think so, either."

Eyes creased to bright green triangles by amusement, she sank into her own chair, nodded casually to Jamie, and clapped her

ands sharply to summon a servant. "Shall we have a dish of
ea?" she asked me. "Do, and I'll read the leaves in your cup for
e, after. I've a reputation as a reader, after all; a fine teller o' the
uture, to be sure—and why not?" She laughed again, plump
heeks pinkening with mirth. If she had been as shocked by my
ppearance as I was at hers, she disguised it masterfully.

"Tea," she said, to the black maidservant who appeared in
esponse to the summons. "The special kind in the blue tin, aye?
nd the bittie cakes wi' the nuts in, too."

"You'll take a bite?" she asked, turning back to me. " 'Tis
omething of an occasion, after all. I did wonder," she said, tilting
er head to one side, like a gull judging the chances of snatching a
sh, "whether our paths might cross again, after that day at
ranesmuir."

My heart was beginning to slow, the shock overcome in a great
ave of curiosity. I could feel the questions bubbling up by the
ozens, and picked one off the top at random.

"Did you know me?" I asked. "When you met me in Cranes-
uir?"

She shook her head, the strands of cream-white hair coming
ose from their pins and sliding down her neck. She poked hap-
azardly at her knot, still surveying me with interest.

"Not at the first, no. Though sure and I thought there was a
reat strangeness about ye—not that I was the only one to think
at. Ye didna come through the stones prepared, did ye? Not on
urpose, I mean?"

I bit back the words, "Not that time," and said instead, "No, it
as an accident. You came on purpose, though—from 1967?"

She nodded, studying me intently. The thickened flesh between
er brows was creased, and the crease deepened slightly as she
oked at me.

"Aye—to help Prince *Tearlach.*" Her mouth twisted to one
de, as though she tasted something bad, and quite suddenly, she
rned her head and spat. The globule of saliva hit the polished
ooden floor with an audible *plop.*

"An gealtaire salach Atailteach!" she said. "Filthy Italian
oward!" Her eyes darkened and shone with no pleasant light.
Had I known, I should have made my way to Rome and killed
im, while there was time. His brother Henry might ha' been no
etter, though—a ballock-less, sniveling priest, that one. Not that

it made a difference. After Culloden, any Stuart would be as use
less as another.''

She sighed, and shifted her bulk, the rattan of the chair creakin
beneath her. She waved a hand impatiently, dismissing the Stuart

''Still, that's done with for now. Ye came by accident—walke
through the stones near the date of a Fire Feast, did ye? That's ho
it usually happens.''

''Yes,'' I said, startled. ''I came through on Beltane. But wha
do you mean, 'usually happens'? Have you met a great man
others—like . . . us?'' I ended hesitantly.

She shook her head rather absently. ''Not many.'' She seeme
to be pondering something, though perhaps it was only the al
sence of her refreshments; she picked up the silver bell and rang
violently.

''Damn that Clotilda! Like us?'' she said, returning to the que
tion at hand. ''No, I haven't. Only one besides you, that I ken. Y
could ha' knocked me over wi' a feather, when I saw the wee sca
on your arm, and kent ye for one like myself.'' She touched th
great swell of her own upper arm, where the small vaccination sca
lay hidden beneath the puff of white muslin. She tilted her head i
that bird-like way again, surveying me with one bright green ey

''No, when I said that's how it usually happens, I meant, judg
ing from the stories. Folk who disappear in fairy rings and th
stone circles, I mean. They usually walk through near Beltane
Samhain; a few near the Sun Feasts—Midsummer's Day or th
winter solstice.''

''That's what the list was!'' I said suddenly, reminded of th
gray notebook I had left with Roger Wakefield. ''You had a list
dates and initials—nearly two hundred of them. I didn't kno
what they were, but I saw that the dates were mostly in late Apr
or early May, or near the end of October.''

''Aye, that's right.'' She nodded, eyes still fixed on me in spe
ulation. ''So ye found my wee book? Is that how ye knew to com
and look for me on Craigh na Dun? It *was* you, no? That shoute
my name, just before I stepped through the stones?''

''Gillian,'' I said, and saw her pupils widen at the name that ha
once been hers, though her face stayed smooth. ''Gillian Edgar
Yes, it was me. I didn't know if you saw me in the dark.'' I cou
see in memory the night-black circle of stones—and in the cente

he blazing bonfire, and the figure of a slim girl standing by it, pale
air flying in the heat of the fire.

"I didn't see ye," she said. " 'Twas only later, when I heard ye
all out at the witch trial and thought I'd heard your voice before.
nd then, when I saw the mark on your arm . . ." She shrugged
assively, the muslin tight across her shoulders as she settled
ack. "Who was with ye, that night?" she asked curiously.
There were two I saw—a bonnie dark lad, and a girl."

She closed her eyes, concentrating, then opened them again to
tare at me. "Later on, I thought I kent her—but I couldna put a
ame to her, though I could swear I'd seen the face. Who was
he?"

"Mistress Duncan? Or is it Mistress Abernathy, now?" Jamie
nterrupted, stepping forward and bowing to her formally. The
rst shock of her appearance was fading, but he was still pale, his
heekbones prominent under the stretched skin of his face.

She glanced at him, then looked again, as though noticing him
or the first time.

"Well, and if it's no the wee fox cub!" she said, looking
mused. She looked him carefully up and down, noting every
etail of his appearance with interest.

"Grown to a bonny man, have ye no?" she said. She leaned
ack in the chair, which creaked loudly under her weight, and
quinted appraisingly at him. "You've the look of the MacKenzies
out ye, laddie. Ye always did, but now you're older, you've the
ok of both your uncles in your face."

"I am sure both Dougal and Colum would be pleased ye'd
member them so well." Jamie's eyes were fixed on her as in-
ntly as hers on him. He had never liked her—and was unlikely to
hange his opinion now—but he could not afford to antagonize
er; not if she had Ian here somewhere.

The arrival of the tea interrupted whatever reply she might have
ade. Jamie moved to my side, and sat with me on the sofa, while
eilie carefully poured the tea and handed us each a cup, behaving
xactly like a conventional hostess at a tea party. As though wish-
g to preserve this illusion, she offered the sugar bowl and milk
g, and sat back to make light conversation.

"If ye dinna mind my asking, Mrs. Abernathy," Jamie said,
how did ye come to this place?" Politely left unspoken was the
rger question—*How did you escape being burned as a witch?*

She laughed, lowering her long lashes coquettishly over h
eyes.

"Well, and ye'll maybe recall I was wi' child, back at Crane
muir?"

"I seem to recall something of the sort." Jamie took a sip of h
tea, the tips of his ears turning slightly pink. He had cause
remember that, all right; she had torn off her clothes in the mid
of the witch trial, disclosing the secret bulge that would save h
life—at least temporarily.

A small pink tongue poked out and delicately skimmed the t
droplets from her upper lip.

"Have ye had children yourself?" she asked, cocking an ey
brow at me.

"I have."

"Terrible chore, isn't it? Dragging about like a mud-caked so
and then being ripped apart for the sake of something looks like
drowned rat." She shook her head, making a low noise of disgu
in her throat. "The beauty o' motherhood, is it? Still, I should n
complain, I suppose—the wee ratling saved my life for me. A
wretched as childbirth is, it's better than being burnt at the stake

"I'd suppose so," I said, "though not having tried the latter
couldn't say for sure."

Geillis choked in her tea, spraying brown droplets over the fro
of her dress. She mopped at them carelessly, eyeing me wi
amusement.

"Well, I've not done it either, but I've seen them burn, popp
And I think perhaps even lyin' in a muddy hole watching yo
belly grow is better than that."

"They kept you in the thieves' hole all the time?" The silv
spoon was cool in my hand, but my palm grew sweaty at t
memory of the thieves' hole in Cranesmuir. I had spent three da
there with Geillis Duncan, accused as a witch. How long had s
stayed there?

"Three months," she said, staring meditatively into her te
"Three mortal months of frozen feet and crawling vermin, stin
ing scraps of food and the grave-smell clinging to my skin day a
night."

She looked up then, mouth twisting in bitter amusement. "Bu
bore the child in style, at the end. When my pains began, they to

e from the hole—little chance I'd run then, aye?—and the babe
is born in my own old bedroom; in the fiscal's house.''

Her eyes were slightly clouded, and I wondered whether the
uid in her glass was entirely tea.

''I had diamond-paned windows, do ye recall? All in shades of
rple and green and white—the finest house in the village.'' She
iled reminiscently. ''They gave me the bairn to hold, and the
een light fell over his face. He looked as though he was drowned
deed. I thought he should be cold to the touch, like a corpse, but
wasn't; he was warm. Warm as his father's balls.'' She laughed
ddenly, an ugly sound.

''Why are men such fools? Ye can lead them anywhere by the
ck—for a while. Then give them a son and ye have them by the
lls again. But it's all ye are to them, whether they're coming in
going out—a cunt.''

She was leaning back in her chair. At this, she spread her thighs
de, and hoisted her glass in ironic toast above her pubic bone,
uinting down across the swelling bulge of belly.

''Well, here's to it, I say! Most powerful thing in the world. The
ggers know that, at least.'' She took a deep, careless swig of her
ink. ''They carve wee idols, all belly and cunt and breasts. Same
men do where we came from—you and I.'' She squinted at me,
eth bared in amusement. ''Seen the dirty mags men buy under
e counters then, aye?''

The bloodshot green eyes swiveled to Jamie. ''And you'll know
e pictures and the books the men pass about among themselves
Paris now, won't ye, fox? It's all the same.'' She waved a hand
d drank again, deeply. ''The only difference is the niggers have
e decency to worship it.''

''Verra perceptive of them,'' Jamie said calmly. He was sitting
ck in his chair, long legs stretched out in apparent relaxation,
t I could see the tension in the fingers of the hand that gripped
s own cup. ''And how d'ye ken the pictures men look at in Paris,
istress—Abernathy, is it now?''

She might be tipsy, but was by no means fuddled. She looked
sharply at the tone of his voice, and gave him a twisted smile.

''Oh, Mistress Abernathy will do well enough. When I lived in
ris, I had another name—Madame Melisande Robicheaux. Like
at one? I thought it a bit grand, but your uncle Dougal gave it
e, so I kept it—out of sentiment.''

My free hand curled into a fist, out of sight in the folds of skirt. I had heard of Madame Melisande, when we lived in Pa Not a part of society, she had had some fame as a seer of future; ladies of the court consulted her in deepest secrecy, advice on their love lives, their investments, and their pregnanc

"I imagine you could have told the ladies some interest things," I said dryly.

Her laugh this time was truly amused. "Oh, I could, inde Seldom did, though. Folk don't usually pay for the truth, ye kn Sometimes, though—did ye ken that Jean-Paul Marat's mot meant to name her bairn Rudolphe? I told her I thought Rudol was ill-omened. I wondered now and then about that—would grow up a revolutionary with a name like Rudolphe, or would take it all out in writing poems, instead? Ever think that, fox— a name might make a difference?" Her eyes were fixed on Jan green glass.

"Often," he said, and set down his cup. "It was Dougal go away from Cranesmuir, then?"

She nodded, stifling a small belch. "Aye. He came to take babe—alone, for fear someone would find out he was the fat aye? I wouldna let it go, though. And when he came near to w it from me—why, I snatched the dirk from his belt and presse to the child's throat." A small smile of satisfaction at the mem curved her lovely lips.

"Told him I'd kill it, sure, unless he swore on his brother's and his own soul to get me safe away."

"And he believed you?" I felt mildly ill at the thought of mother holding a knife to the throat of her newborn child, eve pretense.

Her gaze swiveled back to me. "Oh, yes," she said softly, the smile widened. "He knew me, did Dougal."

Sweating, even in the chill of December, and unable to take eyes off the tiny face of his sleeping son, Dougal had agreed.

"When he leaned over me to take the child, I thought of plu ing the dirk into his own throat instead," she said, reminiscen "But it would have been a good deal harder to get away by mys so I didn't."

Jamie's expression didn't change, but he picked up his tea took a deep swallow.

Dougal had summoned the locksman, John MacRae, and

urch sexton, and by means of discreet bribery, ensured that the
ooded figure dragged on a hurdle to the pitch barrel next morning
ould not be that of Geillis Duncan.

"I thought they'd use straw, maybe," she said, "but he was a
everer man than that. Auld Grannie Joan MacKenzie had died
ree days before, and was meant to be burying that same after-
oon. A few rocks in the coffin and the lid nailed down tight, and
ob's your uncle, eh? A real body, fine for burning." She
ughed, and gulped the last swallow of her drink.

"Not everyone's seen their own funeral; fewer still ha' seen
eir own execution, aye?"

It had been the dead of winter, and the small grove of rowan
es outside the village stood bare, drifted with their own dead
aves, the dried red berries showing here and there on the ground
ke spots of blood.

It was a cloudy day, with the promise of sleet or snow, but the
hole village turned out nonetheless; a witch-burning was not an
ent to be missed. The village priest, Father Bain, had died him-
lf three months before, of fever brought on by a festering sore,
it a new priest had been imported for the occasion from a village
arby. Perfuming his way with a censer held before him, the
iest had come down the path to the grove, chanting the service
r the dead. Behind him came the locksman and his two assis-
nts, dragging the hurdle and its black-robed burden.

"I expect Grannie Joan would have been pleased," Geilie said,
hite teeth gleaming at the vision. "She couldna have expected
ore nor four or five people to her burying—as it was, she had the
hole village, and the incense and special prayers to boot!"

MacRae had untied the body and carried it, lolling, to the barrel
pitch ready waiting.

"The court granted me the mercy to be weirrit before the burn-
g," Geillis explained ironically. "So they expected the body to
dead—no difficulty there, if I was strangled already. The only
ing anyone might ha' seen was that Grannie Joan weighed half
hat I did, newly delivered as I was, but no one seemed to notice
e was light in MacRae's arms."

"You were *there*?" I said.

She nodded smugly. "Oh, aye. Well muffled in a cloak—every-
e was, because o' the weather—but I wouldna have missed it."

As the priest finished his last prayer against the evils of enchant-

ment, MacRae had taken the pine torch from his assistant a⁣
stepped forward.

"God, omit not this woman from Thy covenant, and the ma⁣
evils that she in the body committed," he had said, and flung t⁣
fire into the pitch.

"It was faster than I thought it would be," Geillis said, soun⁣
ing mildly surprised. "A great *whoosh!* of fire—there was a bl⁣
of hot air and a cheer from the crowd, and naught to be seen b⁣
the flames, shooting up high enough to singe the rowan branch⁣
overhead."

The fire had subsided within a minute, though, and the da⁣
figure within was clear enough to be seen through the pale da⁣
light flames. The hood and the hair had burned away with the fi⁣
scorching rush, and the face itself was burned beyond recognitio⁣
A few moments more, and the clean dark shapes of the bon⁣
emerged from the melted flesh, an airy superstructure rising abo⁣
the charring barrel.

"Only great empty holes where her eyes had been," she sa⁣
The moss-green eyes turned toward me, clouded by memory.
thought perhaps she was looking at me. But then the skull e⁣
ploded, and it was all over, and folk began to come away—⁣
except a few who stayed in hopes of picking up a bit of bone a⁣
keepsake."

She rose and went unsteadily to the small table near the w⁣
dow. She picked up the silver bell and rang it, hard.

"Aye," she said, her back turned to us. "Childbirth is may⁣
easier."

"So Dougal got ye away to France," Jamie said. The fingers⁣
his right hand twitched slightly. "How came ye here to the W⁣
Indies?"

"Oh, that was later," she said carelessly. "After Culloden⁣
She turned then, and smiled from Jamie to me.

"And what might bring the two of ye here to this place? Sur⁣
not the pleasure of my company?"

I glanced at Jamie, seeing the slight tensing of his back as he⁣
up straighter. His face stayed calm, though, only his eyes bri⁣
with wariness.

"We've come to seek a young kinsman of mine," he said. "M⁣
nephew, Ian Murray. We've some reason to think he is indentur⁣
here."

Geilie's pale brows rose high, making soft ridges in her fore-
ad.

"Ian Murray?" she said, and shook her head in puzzlement.
've no indentured whites at all, here. No whites, come to that.
e only free man on the place is the overseer, and he's what they
ll a *griffon;* one-quarter black."

Unlike me, Geillis Duncan was a very good liar. Impossible to
ll, from her expression of mild interest, whether she had ever
ard the name Ian Murray before. But lying she was, and I knew

Jamie knew it, too; the expression that flashed through his eyes
as not disappointment, but fury, quickly suppressed.

"Indeed?" he said politely. "And are ye not fearful, then, alone
' your slaves here, so far from town?"

"Oh, no. Not at all."

She smiled broadly at him, then lifted her double chin and
iggled it gently in the direction of the terrace behind him. I
rned my head, and saw that the French door was filled from jamb
doorpost with an immense black man, several inches taller than
mie, from whose rolled-up shirt sleeves protruded arms like tree
inks, knotted with muscle.

"Meet Hercules," Geilie said, with a tiny laugh. "He has a
in brother, too."

"Named Atlas, by chance?" I asked, with an edge to my voice.

"You guessed! Is she no the clever one, eh, fox?" She winked
nspiratorially at Jamie, the rounded flesh of her cheek wobbling
th the movement. The light caught her from the side as she
rned her head, and I saw the red spiderwebs of tiny broken
pillaries that netted her jowls.

Hercule took no note of this, or of anything else. His broad face
as slack and dull, and there was no life in the deep-sunk eyes
neath the bony brow ridge. It gave me a very uneasy feeling to
ok at him, and not only because of his threatening size; looking
him was like passing by a haunted house, where something
rks behind blind windows.

"That will do, Hercule; ye can go back to work now." Geilie
cked up the silver bell and tinkled it gently, once. Without a
ord, the giant turned and lumbered off the veranda. "I have no
ar o' the slaves," she explained. "They're afraid o' me, for they

think I'm a witch. Verra funny, considering, is it not?'' Her ey⟨
twinkled behind little pouches of fat.

''Geilie—that man.'' I hesitated, feeling ridiculous in aski⟨
such a question. ''He's not a—a zombie?''

She laughed delightedly at that, clapping her hands together.

''Christ, a zombie? Jesus, Claire!'' She chortled with glee,
bright pink rising from throat to hair roots.

''Well, I'll tell ye, he's no verra bright,'' she said at last, st⟨
gasping and wheezing. ''But he's no dead, either!'' and went ⟨
into further gales of laughter.

Jamie stared at me, puzzled.

''Zombie?''

''Never mind,'' I said, my face nearly as pink as Geilie⟨
''How many slaves have you got here?'' I asked, wanting ⟨
change the subject.

''Hee hee,'' she said, winding down into giggles. ''Oh, a hu⟨
dred or so. It's no such a big place. Only three hundred acres ⟨
cane, and a wee bit of coffee on the upper slopes.''

She pulled a lace-trimmed handkerchief from her pocket a⟨
patted her damp face, sniffing a bit as she regained her composu⟨
I could feel, rather than see, Jamie's tension. I was sure he was
convinced as I that Geilie knew something about Ian Murray—
nothing else, she had betrayed no surprise whatever at our appea⟨
ance. Someone had told her about us, and that someone could on⟨
be Ian.

The thought of threatening a woman to extract informati⟨
wasn't one that would come naturally to Jamie, but it would to m⟨
Unfortunately, the presence of the twin pillars of Hercules had p⟨
a stop to that line of thought. The next best idea seemed to be ⟨
search the house and grounds for any trace of the boy. Thr⟨
hundred acres was a fair piece of ground, but if he was on t⟨
property, he would likely be in or near the buildings—the hous⟨
the sugar refinery, or the slave quarters.

I came out of my thoughts to realize that Geilie had asked me ⟨
question.

''What's that?''

''I said,'' she repeated patiently, ''that ye had a great deal ⟨
talent for the healing when I knew ye in Scotland; you'll may⟨
know more now?''

''I expect I might.'' I looked her over cautiously. Did she wa⟨

y skill for herself? She wasn't healthy; a glance at her mottled
mplexion and the dark circles beneath her eyes was enough to
ow that. But was she actively ill?

"Not for me," she said, seeing my look. "Not just now, any-
ay. I've two slaves gone sick. Maybe ye'd be so kind as to look at
em?"

I glanced at Jamie, who gave me the shadow of a nod. It was a
ance to get into the slave quarters and look for Ian.

"I saw when we came in as ye had a bit of trouble wi' your
gar press," he said, rising abruptly. He gave Geilie a cool nod.
'erhaps I shall have a look at it, whilst you and my wife tend the
:k." Without waiting for an answer, he took off his coat and
ng it on the peg by the door. He went out by the veranda, rolling
the sleeves of his shirt, sunlight glinting on his hair.

"A handy sort, is he?" Geilie looked after him, amused. "My
sband Barnabas was that sort—couldna keep his hands off any
d of machine. Or off the slave girls, either," she added. "Come
ng, the sick ones are back o' the kitchen."

The kitchen was in a separate small building of its own, con-
cted to the house by a breezeway covered with blooming jas-
ine. Walking through it was like floating through a cloud of
rfume, surrounded by a hum of bees loud enough to be felt on
e skin, like the low drone of a bagpipe.

"Ever been stung?" Geillis swiped casually at a low-flying
rry body, batting it out of the air.

"Now and then."

"So have I," she said. "Any number of times, and nothing
rse than a red welt on my skin to show for it. One of these wee
ggers stung one o' the kitchen slaves last spring, though, and
e wench swelled up like a toad and died, right before my eyes!"
e glanced at me, eyes wide and mocking. "Did wonders for my
utation, I can tell ye. The rest o' the slaves put it about I'd
tched the lass; put a spell on her to kill her for burning the
onge cake. I havena had so much as a scorched pot, since."
aking her head, she waved away another bee.

While appalled at her callousness, I was somewhat relieved by
e story. Perhaps the other gossip I had heard at the Governor's
l had as little foundation in fact.

I paused, looking out through the jasmine's lacy leaves at the
ne fields below. Jamie was in the clearing by the sugar press,

looking up at the gigantic crossbars of the machine while a man assumed to be the overseer pointed and explained. As I watched he said something, gesturing, and the overseer nodded emphatically, waving his hands in voluble reply. If I didn't find any trace of Ian in the kitchen quarters, perhaps Jamie would learn something from the overseer. Despite Geilie's denials, every instinct had insisted that the boy was here—somewhere.

There was no sign of him in the kitchen itself; only three or four women, kneading bread and snapping peas, who looked up curiously as we came through. I caught the eye of one young woman and nodded and smiled at her; perhaps I would have a chance to come back and talk, later. Her eyes widened in surprise, and she bent her head at once, eyes on the bowl of peapods in her lap. I saw her steal a quick glance at me as we crossed the long room, and noticed that she balanced the bowl in front of the small bulge of an early pregnancy.

The first sick slave was in a small pantry off the kitchen itself, lying on a pallet laid under shelves stacked high with gauze-wrapped cheeses. The patient, a young man in his twenties, sat up blinking at the sudden ray of light when I opened the door.

"What's the trouble with him?" I knelt down beside the man and touched his skin. Warm, damp, no apparent fever. He didn't seem in any particular distress, merely blinking sleepily as I examined him.

"He has a worm."

I glanced at Geilie in surprise. From what I had seen and heard so far in the islands, I thought it likely that at least three-quarters of the black population—and not a few of the whites—suffered from internal parasites. Nasty and debilitating as these could be, though, most were actively threatening only to the very young and the very old.

"Probably a lot more than one," I said. I pushed the slave gently onto his back and began to palpate his stomach. The spleen was tender and slightly enlarged—also a common finding here—but I felt no suspicious masses in the abdomen that might indicate a major intestinal infestation. "He seems moderately healthy; why have you got him in here in the dark?"

As though in answer to my question, the slave suddenly wrenched himself away from my hand, let out a piercing scream, and rolled up into a ball. Rolling and unrolling himself like

-yo, he reached the wall and began to bang his head against it, ll screaming. Then, as suddenly as the fit had come on, it passed f, and the young man sank back onto the pallet, panting heavily d soaked with sweat.

"Jesus H. Roosevelt Christ," I said. "What was *that*?"

"A *loa-loa* worm," Geilie said, looking amused at my reaction. They live in the eyeballs, just under the lining. They cross back d forth, from one eye to the other, and when they go across the idge o' the nose, I'm told it's rather painful." She nodded at the ave, still quivering slightly on his pallet.

"The dark keeps them from moving so much," she explained. The fellow from Andros who told me about them says ye must tch them when they've just come in one eye, for they're right ar the surface, and ye can lift them out with a big darning edle. If ye wait, they go deeper, and ye canna get them." She rned back to the kitchen and shouted for a light.

"Here, I brought the needle, just in case." She groped in the g at her waist and drew out a square of felt, with a three-inch el needle thrust through it, which she extended helpfully to me.

"Are you out of your mind?" I stared at her, appalled.

"No. Did ye not say ye were a good healer?" she asked reason- ly.

"I am, but—" I glanced at the slave, hesitated, then took the ndle one of the kitchenmaids was holding out to me.

"Bring me some brandy, and a small sharp knife," I said. "Dip e knife—and the needle—in the brandy, then hold the tip in a me for a moment. Let it cool, but don't touch it." As I spoke, I is gently pulling up one eyelid. The man's eye looked up at me, oddly irregular, blotched brown iris in a bloodshot sclera the llow of heavy cream. I searched carefully, bringing the candle me close enough to shrink the pupil, then drawing it away, but w nothing there.

I tried the other eye, and nearly dropped the candle. Sure ough, there was a small, transparent filament, *moving* under the njunctiva. I gagged slightly at the sight, but controlled myself, d reached for the freshly sterilized knife, still holding back the elid.

"Take him by the shoulders," I said to Geilie. "Don't let him ove, or I may blind him."

The surgery itself was horrifying to contemplate, but surpris-

ingly simple to perform. I made one quick, small incision alo
the inside corner of the conjunctiva, lifted it slightly with the tip
the needle, and as the worm undulated lazily across the open fie
I slipped the tip of the needle under the body and drew it out, n
as a loop of yarn.

Repressing a shudder of distaste, I flicked the worm away. It
the wall with a tiny wet splat! and vanished in the shadows und
the cheese.

There was no blood; after a brief debate with myself, I decid
to leave it to the man's own tear ducts to irrigate the incision. Th
would have to be left to heal by itself; I had no fine sutures, and t
wound was small enough not to need more than a stitch or two
any case.

I tied a clean pad of cloth over the closed eye with a banda
round the head, and sat back, reasonably pleased with my fi
foray into tropical medicine.

"Fine," I said, pushing back my hair. "Where's the oth
one?"

The next patient was in a shed outside the kitchen, dead
squatted next to the body, that of a middle-aged man with grizzl
hair, feeling both pity and outrage.

The cause of death was more than obvious: a strangulated he
nia. The loop of twisted, gangrenous bowel protruded from o
side of the belly, the stretched skin over it already tinged w
green, though the body itself was still nearly as warm as life. A
expression of agony was fixed on the broad features, and the lim
were still contorted, giving an unfortunately accurate witness
just what sort of death it had been.

"Why did you wait?" I stood up, glaring at Geilie. "For Go
sake, you kept me drinking tea and chatting, while *this* was goi
on? He's been dead less than an hour, but he must have been
trouble a long time since—days! Why didn't you bring me c
here at once?"

"He seemed pretty far gone this morning," she said, not at
disturbed by my agitation. She shrugged. "I've seen them
before; I didna think you could do anything much. It didna see
worth hurrying."

I choked back further recrimination. She was right; I could ha
operated, had I come sooner, but the chances of it doing any go
were slim to nonexistent. The hernia repair was something I mig

ve managed, even with such difficult conditions; after all, that
as nothing more than pushing back the bowel protrusion and
lling the ruptured layers of abdominal muscle back together
th sutures; infection was the only real danger. But once the loop
escaped intestine had twisted, so that the blood supply was cut
f and the contents began to putrefy, the man was doomed.

But to allow the man to die here in this stuffy shed, alone . . .
ll, perhaps he would not have found the presence of one white
oman more or less a comfort, in any case. Still, I felt an obscure
nse of failure; the same I always felt in the presence of death. I
ped my hands slowly on a brandy-soaked cloth, mastering my
elings.

One to the good, one to the bad—and Ian still to be found.

"Since I'm here now, perhaps I'd best have a look at the rest of
ur slaves," I suggested. "An ounce of prevention, you know."

"Oh, they're well enough." Geilie waved a careless hand.
Still, if ye want to take the time, you're welcome. Later, though;
ve a visitor coming this afternoon, and I want to talk more with
, first. Come back to the house, now—someone will take care o'
is." A brief nod disposed of "this," the slave's contorted body.
e linked her arm in mine, urging me out of the shed and back
ward the kitchen with soft thrustings of her weight.

In the kitchen, I detached myself, motioning toward the preg-
nt slave, now on her hands and knees, scrubbing the hearth-
ones.

"You go along; I want to have a quick look at this girl. She
oks a bit toxic to me—you don't want her to miscarry."

Geilie gave me a curious glance, but then shrugged.

"She's foaled twice with no trouble, but you're the doctor. Aye,
that's your notion of fun, go ahead. Don't take too long, though;
at parson said he'd come at four o'clock."

I made some pretense of examining the bewildered woman,
til Geilie's draperies had disappeared into the breezeway.

"Look," I said. "I'm looking for a young white boy named
n; I'm his aunt. Do you know where he might be?"

The girl—she couldn't be more than seventeen or eighteen—
oked startled. She blinked, and darted a glance at one of the
der women, who had quit her own work and come across the
om to see what was going on.

''No, ma'am,'' the older woman said, shaking her head. ''N
white boys here. None at all.''

''No, ma'am,'' the girl obediently echoed. ''We don' kno
nothin' 'bout your boy.'' But she hadn't said that at first, and h
eyes wouldn't meet mine.

The older woman had been joined now by the other two kitc
enmaids, coming to buttress her. I was surrounded by an imper
trable wall of bland ignorance, and no way to break through it.
the same time, I was aware of a current running among the wom
—a feeling of common warning; of wariness and secrecy. It mig
be only the natural reaction to the sudden appearance of a wh
stranger in their domain—or it might be something more.

I couldn't take longer; Geilie would be coming back to look f
me. I fumbled quickly in my pocket, and pulled out a silver flori
which I pressed into the girl's hand.

''If you should see Ian, tell him that his uncle is here to fi
him.'' Not waiting for an answer, I turned and hurried out of t
kitchen.

I glanced down toward the sugar mill as I passed through t
breezeway. The sugar press stood abandoned, the oxen grazi
placidly in the long grass at the edge of the clearing. There was
sign of Jamie or the overseer; had he come back to the house?

I came through the French windows into the salon, and stopp
short. Geilie sat in her wicker chair, Jamie's coat across the ar
and the photographs of Brianna spread over her lap. She heard n
step and looked up, one pale brow arched over an acid smile.

''What a pretty lassie, to be sure. What's her name?''

''Brianna.'' My lips felt stiff. I walked slowly toward her, figh
ing the urge to snatch the pictures from her hands and run.

''Looks a great deal like her father, doesn't she? I thought s
seemed familiar, that tall red-haired lass I saw that night on Crai
na Dun. He *is* her father, no?'' She inclined her head toward t
door where Jamie had vanished.

''Yes. Give them to me.'' It made no difference; she had se
the pictures already. Still, I couldn't stand to see her thick whi
fingers cupping Brianna's face.

Her mouth twitched as though she meant to refuse, but sl
tapped them neatly into a square and handed them to me witho
demur. I held them against my chest for a moment, not knowi

hat to do with them, then thrust them back into the pocket of my irt.

"Sit ye down, Claire. The coffee's come." She nodded toward e small table, and the chair alongside. Her eyes followed me as I oved to it, alive with calculation.

She gestured for me to pour the coffee for both of us, and took r own cup without words. We sipped silently for a few moments. e cup trembled in my hands, spilling hot liquid across my wrist. ut it down, wiping my hand on my skirt, wondering in some dim cess of my mind why I should be afraid.

"Twice," she said suddenly. She looked at me with something in to awe. "Sweet Christ Jesus, ye went through *twice*! Or no— *ree* times, it must have been, for here ye are now." She shook r head, marveling, never taking her bright green eyes from my ce.

"How?" she asked. "How could ye do it so many times, and e?"

"I don't know." I saw the look of hard skepticism flash across r face, and answered it, defensively. "I don't! I just—went."

"Was it not the same for you?" The green eyes had narrowed o slits of concentration. "What was it like, there between? Did not feel the terror? And the noise, fit to split your skull and spill ur brains?"

"Yes, it was like that." I didn't want to talk to about it; didn't en like to think of the time-passage. I had blocked it deliberately om my mind, the roar of death and dissolution and the voices of aos that urged me to join them.

"Did ye have blood to protect you, or stones? I wouldna think 'd the nerve for blood—but maybe I'm wrong. For surely ye're onger than I thought, to have done it three times, and lived rough it."

"Blood?" I shook my head, confused. "No. Nothing. I told you I . . . went. That's all." Then I remembered the night she had ne through the stones in 1968; the blaze of fire on Craigh na un, and the twisted, blackened shape in the center of that fire. 3reg Edgars," I said. The name of her first husband. "You dn't just kill him because he found you and tried to stop you, did u? He was—"

"The blood, aye." She was watching me, intent. "I didna think could be done at all, the crossing—not without the blood." She sounded faintly amazed. "The auld ones—they always used t‌ blood. That and the fire. They built great wicker cages, filled w‌ their captives, and set them alight in the circles. I thought that w‌ how they opened the passage."

My hands and my lips felt cold, and I picked up the cup to wa‌ them. Where in the name of God was Jamie?

"And ye didna use stones, either?"

I shook my head. "What stones?"

She looked at me for a moment, debating whether to tell m‌ Her little pink tongue flicked over her lip, and then she nodd‌ deciding. With a small grunt, she heaved herself up from the ch‌ and went toward the great hearth at the far end of the roo‌ beckoning me to follow.

She knelt, with surprising grace for one of her figure, a‌ pressed a greenish stone set into the mantelpiece, a foot or above the hearth. It moved slightly, and there was a soft *click!* one of the hearth slates rose smoothly out of its mortared setti‌

"Spring mechanism," Geilie explained, lifting the slate ca‌ fully and setting it aside. "A Danish fellow named Leiven from Croix made it for me."

She reached into the cavity beneath and drew out a wooden b‌ about a foot long. There were pale brown stains on the smo‌ wood, and it looked swollen and split, as though it had be‌ immersed in seawater at some time. I bit my lip hard at its appe‌ ance, and hoped my face didn't give anything away. If I had h‌ any doubts about Ian being here, they had vanished—for he‌ unless I was very much mistaken, was the silkies' treasure. For‌ nately, Geilie wasn't looking at me, but at the box.

"I learned about the stones from an Indian—not a red Indian‌ Hindoo from Calcutta," she explained. "He came to me, looki‌ for thornapple, and he told me about how to make medicines fr‌ the gemstones."

I looked over my shoulder for Jamie, but there was no sign‌ him. Where the hell was he? Had he found Ian, somewhere on ‌ plantation?

"Ye can get the powdered stones from a London apothecar‌ she was saying, frowning slightly as she pushed at the sliding ‌ "But they're mostly poor quality, and the *bhasmas* doesn't w‌ so well. Best to have a stone at least of the second quality—w‌ they call a *nagina* stone. That's a goodish-sized stone that's b‌

lished. A stone of the first quality is faceted, and unflawed for eference, but most folk canna afford to burn those to ash. The hes of the stone are the *bhasmas,*'' she explained, turning to ok up at me. "That's what ye use in the medicines. Here, can ye y this damn thing loose? It's been spoilt in seawater, and the cking bit swells whenever the weather's damp—which it is all e time, this season of the year," she added, making a face over r shoulder at the clouds rolling in over the bay, far below.

She thrust the box into my hands and rose heavily to her feet, unting with the effort.

It was a Chinese puzzle-box, I saw; a fairly simple one, with a hall sliding panel that unlocked the main lid. The problem was at the smaller panel had swollen, sticking in its slot.

"It's bad luck to break one," Geilie observed, watching my tempts. "Else I'd just smash the thing and be done with it. Here, aybe this will help." She produced a small mother-of-pearl pen-ife from the recesses of her gown and handed it to me, then ant to the window ledge and rang another of her silver bells.

I pried gently upward with the blade of the knife. I felt it catch the wood, and wiggled it gingerly. Little by little, the small ctangle of wood edged out of its place, until I could get hold of it tween thumb and forefinger and pull it all the way loose.

"There you go," I said, handing her back the box with some luctance. It felt heavy, and there was an unmistakable metallic inking as I tilted it.

"Thanks." As she took it, the black servingmaid came in rough the far door. Geilie turned to order the girl to bring a tray fresh tarts, and I saw that she had slipped the box between the lds of her skirts, hiding it.

"Nosy creatures," she said, frowning toward the departing aid's back as the girl passed through the door. "One of the fficulties wi' slaves; it's hard to have secrets." She put the box the table, and pushed at the top; with a small, sharp *skreek!* of otest, the lid slid back.

She reached into the box and drew out her closed hand. She miled mischievously at me, saying, "Little Jackie Horner sat in e corner, eating her Christmas pie. She put in her thumb, and lled out a plum"—she opened her hand with a flourish—"and id 'What a good girl am I!' ''

I had been expecting them, of course, but had no difficulty in

looking impressed anyway. The reality of a gem is both mo
immediate and more startling than its description. Six or seven
them flashed and glimmered in her palm, flaming fire and froz
ice, the gleam of blue water in the sun, and a great gold stone li
the eye of a lurking tiger.

Without meaning to, I drew near enough to look down into th
well of her hand, staring with fascination. "Big enough," Jam
had described them as being, with a characteristic Scottish tale
for understatement. Well, smaller than a breadbox, I supposed.

"I got them for the money, to start," Geilie was saying, pro
ding the stones with satisfaction. "Because they were easier
carry than a great weight of gold or silver, I mean; I didna thi
then what other use they might have."

"What, as *bhasmas*?" The idea of burning any of those glov
ing things to ash seemed a sacrilege.

"Oh, no, not these." Her hand closed on the stones, dipped in
her pocket, and back into the box for more. A small shower
liquid fire dropped into her pocket, and she patted it affectionate
"No, I've a lot o' the smaller stones for that. These are for som
thing else."

She eyed me speculatively, then jerked her head toward the do
at the end of the room.

"Come along up to my workroom," she said. "I've a fe
things there you'll maybe be interested to see."

"Interested" was putting it mildly, I thought.

It was a long, light-filled room, with a counter down one sic
Bunches of drying herbs hung from hooks overhead and lay «
gauze-covered drying racks along the inner wall. Drawered cat
nets and cupboards covered the rest of the wall space, and the
was a small glass-fronted bookcase at the end of the room.

The room gave me a mild sense of déjà-vu; after a moment
realized that it was because it strongly resembled Geilie's wor
room in the village of Cranesmuir, in the house of her first hu
band—no, second, I corrected myself, remember the flaming bo
of Greg Edgars.

"How many times have you been married?" I asked curious
She had begun building her fortune with her second husbar
procurator fiscal of the district where they lived, forging his sign
ture in order to divert money to her own use, and then murderi

im. Successful with this modus operandi, I imagined she had
ried it again; she was a creature of habit, was Geilie Duncan.

She paused a moment to count up. "Oh, five, I think. Since I
ame here," she added casually.

"Five?" I said, a little faintly. Not just a habit, it seemed; a
ositive addiction.

"A verra unhealthy atmosphere for Englishmen it is in the
ropics," she said, and smiled slyly at me. "Fevers, ulcers, fester-
ng stomachs; any little thing will carry them off." She had evi-
ently been mindful of her oral hygiene; her teeth were still very
ood.

She reached out and lightly caressed a small bottle that stood on
ne lowest shelf. It wasn't labeled, but I had seen crude white
rsenic before. On the whole, I was glad I hadn't taken any food.

"Oh, you'll be interested in this," she said, spying a jar on an
pper shelf. Grunting slightly as she stood on tiptoe, she reached it
own and handed it to me.

It contained a very coarse powder, evidently a mixture of sev-
ral substances, brown, yellow, and black, flecked with shreds of a
emitranslucent material.

"What's this?"

"Zombie poison," she said, and laughed. "I thought ye'd like
 see."

"Oh?" I said coldly. "I thought you told me there was no such
ing."

"No," she corrected, still smiling. "I told ye Hercule wasn't
ead; and he's not." She took the jar from me and replaced it on
ne shelf. "But there's no denying that he's a good bit more
anageable if he's had a dose of this stuff once a week, mixed
ith his grain."

"What the hell is it?"

She shrugged, offhanded. "A bit of this and a bit of that. The
ain thing seems to be a kind of fish—a little square thing wi'
ots; verra funny-looking. Ye take the skin and dry it, and the
ver as well. But there are a few other things ye put in with it—I
ish I kent what," she added.

"You don't know what's in it?" I stared at her. "Didn't you
ake it?"

"No. I had a cook," Geilie said, "or at least they sold him to
e as a cook, but damned if I'd feel safe eating a thing he turned

out of the kitchen, the sly black devil. He was a *houngan* though.''

''A what?''

''*Houngan* is what the blacks call one of their medicine-priests though to be quite right about it, I believe Ishmael said his sort o black called him an *oniseegun,* or somesuch.''

''Ishmael, hm?'' I licked my dry lips. ''Did he come with tha name?''

''Oh, no. He had some heathen name wi' six syllables, and the man who sold him called him 'Jimmy'—the auctioneers call al the bucks Jimmy. I named him Ishmael, because of the story the seller told me about him.''

Ishmael had been taken from a barracoon on the Gold Coast o Africa, one of a shipment of six hundred slaves from the village of Nigeria and Ghana, stowed between decks of the slave shi *Persephone,* bound for Antigua. Coming through the Caicos Pas sage, the *Persephone* had run into a sudden squall, and been ru aground on Hogsty Reef, off the island of Great Inagua. The shi had broken up, with barely time for the crew to escape in the ship's boats.

The slaves, chained and helpless between decks, had al drowned. All but one man who had earlier been taken from the hold to assist as a galley mate, both messboys having died of the pox en route from Africa. This man, left behind by the ship' crew, had nonetheless survived the wreck by clinging to a cask o spirits, which floated ashore on Great Inagua two days later.

The fishermen who discovered the castaway were more inter ested in his means of salvation than in the slave himself. Breakin open the cask, however, they were shocked and appalled to fin inside the body of a man, somewhat imperfectly preserved by th spirits in which he had been soaking.

''I wonder if they drank the crème de menthe anyway,'' I mur mured, having observed for myself that Mr. Overholt's assessmen of the alcoholic affinities of sailors was largely correct.

''I daresay,'' said Geilie, mildly annoyed at having her stor interrupted. ''In any case, when I heard of it, I named him Ishmae straight off. Because of the floating coffin, aye?''

''Very clever,'' I congratulated her. ''Er . . . did they find ou who the man in the cask was?''

''I don't think so.'' She shrugged carelessly. ''They gave him t

e Governor of Jamaica, who had him put in a glass case, wi'
esh spirits, as a curiosity.''

"What?" I said incredulously.

"Well, not so much the man himself, but some odd fungi that
ere growing on him," Geilie explained. "The Governor's got a
assion for such things. The old Governor, I mean; I hear there's a
ew one, now."

"Quite," I said, feeling a bit queasy. I thought the ex-governor
as more likely to qualify as a curiosity than the dead man, on the
hole.

Her back was turned, as she pulled out drawers and rummaged
rough them. I took a deep breath, hoping to keep my voice
sual.

"This Ishmael sounds an interesting sort; do you still have
m?"

"No," she said indifferently. "The black bastard ran off. He's
e one who made the zombie poison for me, though. Wouldn't
ll me how, no matter what I did to him," she added, with a short,
imorless laugh, and I had a sudden vivid memory of the weals
ross Ishmael's back. "He said it wasn't proper for women to
ake medicine, only men could do it. Or the verra auld women,
ice they'd quit bleeding. Hmph!''

She snorted, and reached into her pocket, pulling out a handful
stones.

"Anyway, that's not what I brought ye up to show ye.''

Carefully, she laid five of the stones in a rough circle on the
untertop. Then she took down from a shelf a thick book, bound
worn leather.

"Can ye read German?" she asked, opening it carefully.

"Not much, no," I said. I moved closer, to look over her shoul-
r. *Hexenhammer,* it said, in a fine, handwritten script.

"Witches' Hammer?" I asked. I raised one eyebrow. "Spells?
agic?"

The skepticism in my voice must have been obvious, for she
ared at me over one shoulder.

"Look, fool," she said. "Who are ye? Or what, rather?"

"What am I?" I said, startled.

"That's right." She turned and leaned against the counter,
udying me through narrowed eyes. "What are ye? Or me, come
that? What are we?"

I opened my mouth to reply, then closed it again.

"That's right," she said softly, watching. "It's not everyone can go through the stones, is it? Why us?"

"I don't know," I said. "And neither do you, I'll be bound. It doesn't mean we're witches, surely!"

"Doesn't it?" She lifted one brow, and turned several pages of the book.

"Some people can leave their bodies and travel miles away," she said, staring meditatively at the page. "Other people see them out wandering, and recognize them, and ye can bloody *prove* they were really tucked up safe in bed at the time. I've seen the records; all the eyewitness testimony. Some people have stigmata ye can see and touch—I've seen one. But not everybody. Only certain people."

She turned another page. "If everyone can do it, it's science. If only a few can, then it's witchcraft, or superstition, or whatever you like to call it," she said. "But it's real." She looked up at me, green eyes bright as a snake's over the crumbling book. "*We're* real, Claire—you and me. And special. Have ye never asked yourself why?"

I had. Any number of times. I had never gotten a reasonable answer to the question, though. Evidently, Geilie thought she had one.

She turned back to the stones she had laid on the counter, and pointed at them each in turn. "Stones of protection; amethyst, emerald, turquoise, lapis lazuli, and a male ruby."

"A *male* ruby?"

"Pliny says rubies have a sex to them; who am I to argue?" she said impatiently. "The male stones are what ye use, though; the female ones don't work."

I suppressed the urge to ask precisely how one distinguished the sex of rubies, in favor of asking, "Work for *what*?"

"For the travel," she said, glancing curiously at me. "Through the stones. They protect ye from the . . . whatever it is, out there." Her eyes grew slightly shadowed at the thought of the time-passage, and I realized that she was deathly afraid of it. Little wonder; so was I.

"When did ye come? The first time?" Her eyes were intent on mine.

"From 1945," I said slowly. "I came to 1743, if that's wha

ou mean." I was reluctant to tell her too much; still, my own
uriosity was overwhelming. She was right about one thing; she
nd I were different. I might never again have the chance to talk to
nother person who knew what she did. For that matter, the longer
could keep her talking, the longer Jamie would have to look for
n.

"Hm." She grunted in a satisfied manner. "Near enough. It's
wo hundred year, in the Highland tales—when folk fall asleep on
airy duns and end up dancing all night wi' the Auld Folk; it's
sually two hundred year later when they come back to their own
ace."

"You didn't, though. You came from 1968, but you'd been in
ranesmuir several years before I came there.".

"Five years, aye." She nodded, abstracted. "Aye, well, that was
e blood."

"Blood?"

"The sacrifice," she said, suddenly impatient. "It gives ye a
eater range. And at least a bit of control, so ye have some notion
w far ye're going. How did ye get to and fro three times, with-
t blood?" she demanded.

"I . . . just came." The need to find out as much as I could
ade me add the little else I knew. "I think—I think it has some-
ing to do with being able to fix your mind on a certain person
ho's in the time you go to."

Her eyes were nearly round with interest.

"Really," she said softly. "Think o' that, now." She shook her
ad slowly, thinking. "Hm. That might be so. Still, the stones
ould work as well; there's patterns ye make, wi' the different
ms, ye ken."

She pulled another fistful of shining stones from her pocket and
read them on the wooden surface, pawing through them.

"The protection stones are the points of the pentacle," she
plained, intent on her rummaging, "but inside that, ye lay the
ttern wi' different stones, depending which way ye mean to go,
d how far. And ye lay a line of quicksilver between them, and
e it when ye speak the spells. And of course ye draw the penta-
e wi' diamond dust."

"Of course," I murmured, fascinated.

"Smell it?" she asked, looking up for a moment and sniffing.

"Ye wouldna think stones had a scent, aye? But they do, when ye grind them to powder."

I inhaled deeply, and did seem to find a faint, unfamiliar scent among the smell of dried herbs. It was a dry scent, pleasant but indescribable—the scent of gemstones.

She held up one stone with a small cry of triumph.

"This one! This is the one I needed; couldna find one anywhere in the islands, and finally I thought o' the box I'd left in Scotland." The stone she held was a black crystal of some kind; the light from the window passed through it, and yet it glittered like piece of jet between her white fingers.

"What is it?"

"An adamant; a black diamond. The auld alchemists used them. The books say that to wear an adamant brings ye the knowledge of the joy in all things." She laughed, a short, sharp sound devoid of her usual girlish charm. "If anything can bring knowledge o' joy in that passage through the stones, I want one!"

Something was beginning to dawn on me, rather belatedly. In defense of my slowness, I can only argue that I was simultaneously listening to Geilie and keeping an ear out for any sign of Jamie returning below.

"You mean to go back, then?" I asked, as casually as I could.

"I might." A small smile played around the corners of her mouth. "Now that I've got the things I need. I tell ye, Claire, wouldna risk it, without." She stared at me, shaking her head. "Three times, wi' no blood," she murmured. "So it can be done."

"Well, best we go down now," she said, suddenly brisk, sweeping the stones up and dumping them back into her pocket. "The fox will be back—Fraser is his name, is it no? I thought Clotilda said something else, but the stupid bitch likely got it wrong."

As we made our way down the long workroom, something small and brown darted across the floor in front of me. Geilie was quick despite her size; her small foot stamped on the centipede before could react.

She watched the half-crushed beast wriggling on the floor for moment, then stooped and slid a sheet of paper under it. Scooping it up, she decanted the thing thriftily into a glass jar.

"Ye dinna want to believe in witches and zombies and things that go bump in the night?" she said, with a small, sly smile at me. She nodded at the centipede, struggling round and round in fresh ied, lopsided circles. "Well, legends are many-legged beasties, ye? But they generally have at least one foot on the truth."

She took down a clear brown-glass jug and poured the liquid into the centipede's bottle. The pungent scent of alcohol rose in the air. The centipede, washed up by the wave, kicked frantically for a moment, then sank to the bottom of the bottle, legs moving spasmodically. She corked the bottle neatly, and turned to go.

"You asked me why I thought we can pass through the stones," I said to her back. "Do you know why, Geilie?" She glanced over her shoulder at me.

"Why, to change things," she said, sounding surprised. "Why else? Come along; I hear your man down there."

Whatever Jamie had been doing, it had been hard work; his shirt was dampened with sweat, and clung to his shoulders. He swung round as we entered the room, and I saw that he had been looking at the wooden puzzle-box that Geilie had left on the table. It was obvious from his expression that I had been correct in my surmise—it was the box he had found on the silkies' isle.

"I believe I have succeeded in mending your sugar press, mistress," he said, bowing politely to Geilie. "A matter of a cracked cylinder, which your overseer and I contrived to stuff with wedges. Still, I fear ye may be needing another soon."

Geilie quirked her eyebrows, amused.

"Well, and I'm obliged to ye, Mr. Fraser. Can I not offer ye some refreshment after your labor?" Her hand hovered over the row of bells, but Jamie shook his head, picking up his coat from the sofa.

"I thank ye, mistress, but I fear we must take our leave. It's quite some way back to Kingston, and we must be on our way, if we mean to reach it before dark." His face went suddenly blank, and I knew he must have felt the pocket of his coat and realized that the photographs were missing.

He glanced quickly at me, and I gave him a brief nod, touching the side of my skirt where they lay.

"Thank you for your hospitality," I said, snatching up my hat, and moving toward the door with alacrity. Now that Jamie was back, I wanted nothing so much as to get quickly away from Rose Hall and its owner. Jamie hung back a moment, though.

"I wondered, Mistress Abernathy—since ye mentioned havin' lived in Paris for a time—whether ye might have been acquainte there wi' a gentleman of my own acquaintance. Did ye by chanc ken the Duke of Sandringham?"

She cocked her cream-blond head at him inquisitively, but as h said no more, she nodded.

"Aye, I kent him. Why?"

Jamie gave her his most charming smile. "No particular reason mistress; only a curiosity, ye might say."

The sky was completely overcast by the time we passed th gate, and it was clear that we weren't going to make it back t Kingston without getting soaked. Under the circumstances, didn't care.

"Ye've got Brianna's pictures?" was the first thing Jami asked, reining up for a moment.

"Right here." I patted my pocket. "Did you find any sign o Ian?"

He glanced back over his shoulder, as though fearing we migh be pursued.

"I couldna get anything out of the overseer or any o' the slave —they're bone-scairt of that woman, and I canna say I blame the a bit. But I know where he is." He spoke with considerable satis faction.

"Where? Can we sneak back and get him?" I rose slightly i my saddle, looking back; the slates of Rose Hall were all that wa visible through the treetops. I would have been most reluctant t set foot on the place again for any reason—except for Ian.

"Not now." Jamie caught at my bridle, turning the horse's hea back to the trail. "I'll need help."

Under the pretext of finding material to repair the damage sugar press, Jamie had managed to see most of the plantatio within a quarter-mile of the house, including a cluster of slav huts, the stables, a disued drying shed for tobacco, and the buil ing that housed the sugar refinery. Everyplace he went, he suffere no interference beyond curious or hostile glances—except near th refinery.

"That big black bugger who came up onto the porch was sittin on the ground outside," he said. "When I got too close to him, made the overseer verra nervous indeed; he kept calling me awa warning me not to get too close to the fellow."

"That sounds like a really excellent idea," I said, shuddering
ghtly. "Not getting close to him, I mean. But you think he has
mething to do with Ian?"

"He was sitting in front of a wee door fixed into the ground,
ssenach." Jamie guided his horse adroitly around a fallen log in
e path. "It must lead to a cellar beneath the refinery." The man
d not moved an inch, in all the time that Jamie contrived to
end around the refinery. "If Ian's there, that's where he is."

"I'm fairly sure he's there, all right." I told him quickly the
tails of my visit, including my brief conversation with the kitch-
maids. "But what are we going to do?" I concluded. "We can't
st leave him there! After all, we don't know what Geillis wants
th him, but it can't be innocent, if she wouldn't admit he was
ere, can it?"

"Not innocent at all," he agreed, grim-faced. "The overseer
uldna speak to me of Ian, but he told me other things that would
rl your hair, if it wasna already curled up like sheep's wool."
e glanced at me, and a half-smile lit his face, in spite of his
vious perturbation.

"Judging by the state of your hair, Sassenach, I should say that
s going to rain verra soon now."

"How observant of you," I said sarcastically, vainly trying to
ck in the curls and tendrils that were escaping from under my
t. "The fact that the sky's black as pitch and the air smells like
htning wouldn't have a thing to do with your conclusions, of
urse."

The leaves of the trees all round us were fluttering like tethered
tterflies, as the edge of the storm rose toward us up the slope of
 mountain. From the small rise where we stood, I could see the
rm clouds sweep in across the bay below, with a dark curtain of
n hanging beneath it like a veil.

Jamie rose in his saddle, looking over the terrain. To my unprac-
ed eye, our surroundings looked like solid, impenetrable jungle,
t other possibilities were visible to a man who had lived in the
ather for seven years.

"We'd best find a bit of shelter while we can, Sassenach," he
id. "Follow me."

On foot, leading the horses, we left the narrow path and pressed
o the forest, following what Jamie said was a wild pigs' trail.
ithin a few moments, he had found what he was looking for; a

small stream that cut deep through the forest floor, with a steep
bank, overgrown with ferns and dark, glossy bushes, interspersed
with stands of slender saplings.

He set me to gathering ferns, each frond the length of my arm,
and by the time I had returned with as many as I could carry, he
had the framework of a tidy snug, formed by the arch of the bent
saplings, tied to a fallen log, and covered over with branches cut
from the nearby bushes. Hastily roofed with the spread ferns, it
was not quite waterproof, but a great deal better than being caught
in the open. Ten minutes later, we were safe inside.

There was a moment of absolute quiet as the wind on the edge
of the storm passed by us. No birds chattered, no insects sang;
they were as well equipped as we were to predict the rain. A few
large drops fell, splattering on the foliage with an explosive sound
like snapping twigs. Then the storm broke.

Caribbean rainstorms are abrupt and vigorous. None of the
misty mousing about of an Edinburgh drizzle. The heavens
blacken and split, dropping gallons of water within a minute. For
as long as the rain lasts, speech is impossible, and a light fog rises
from the ground like steam, vapor raised by the force of the
raindrops striking the ground.

The rain pelted the ferns above us, and a faint mist filled the
green shadows of our shelter. Between the clatter of the rain and
the constant thunder that boomed among the hills, it was impossible to talk.

It wasn't cold, but there was a leak overhead, which dripped
steadily on my neck. There was no room to move away; Jamie took
off his coat and wrapped it around me, then put his arm around me
to wait out the storm. In spite of the terrible racket outside, I felt
suddenly safe, and peaceful, relieved of the strain of the last few
hours, the last few days. Ian was as good as found, and nothing
could touch us, here.

I squeezed his free hand; he smiled at me, then bent and kissed
me gently. He smelled fresh and earthy, scented with the sap of
the branches he had cut and the smell of his own healthy sweat.

It was nearly over, I thought. We had found Ian, and God willing, would get him back safely, very soon. And then what? We
would have to leave Jamaica, but there were other places, and the
world was wide. There were the French colonies of Martinique
and Grenada, the Dutch-held island of Eleuthera; perhaps we

ould even venture as far as the continent—cannibals notwith-
anding. So long as I had Jamie, I was not afraid of anything.

The rain ceased as abruptly as it had started. Drops fell singly
om the shrubs and trees, with a pit-a-pat drip that echoed the
inging left in my ears by the storm's roar. A soft, fresh breeze
me up the stream bed, carrying away humidity, lifting the damp
rls from my neck with delicious coolness. The birds and the
sects began again, quietly, and then in full voice, and the air
elf seemed to dance with green life.

I stirred and sighed, pushing myself upright and shrugging off
mie's coat.

"You know, Geilie showed me a special stone, a black diamond
lled an adamant," I said. "She said it's a stone the alchemists
ed; it gives a knowledge of the joy in all things. I think there
ght be one under this spot."

Jamie smiled at me.

"I shouldna be surprised at all, Sassenach," he said. "Here,
've water all down your face."

He reached into his coat for a handkerchief, then stopped.

"Brianna's pictures," he said suddenly.

"Oh, I forgot." I dug in my pocket, and handed him back the
tures. He took them and thumbed rapidly through them,
pped, then went through them again, more slowly.

"What's wrong?" I asked, suddenly alarmed.

"One of them's gone," he said quietly. I felt an inexpressible
ling of dread begin to grow in the pit of my stomach, and the
r of a moment before began to ebb away.

"Are you sure?"

"I know them as well as I know your face, Sassenach," he said.
ye, I'm sure. It's the one of her by the fire."

I remembered the picture in question well; it showed Brianna as
adult, sitting on a rock, outdoors by a campfire. Her knees were
wn up, her elbows resting on them, and she was looking di-
tly into the camera, but with no knowledge of its presence, her
e filled with firelit dreams, her hair blown back away from her
e.

"Geilie must have taken it. She found the pictures in your coat
ile I was in the kitchen, and I took them away from her. She
st have stolen it then."

"Damn the woman!" Jamie turned sharply to look toward the

road, eyes dark with anger. His hand was tight on the remainin
photographs. "What does she want with it?"

"Perhaps it's only curiosity," I said, but the feeling of drea
would not go away. "What *could* she do with it, after all? She isn
likely to show it to anyone—who would come here?"

As though in answer to this question, Jamie's head lifted sud
denly, and he grasped my arm in adjuration to be still. Som
distance below, a loop of the road was visible through the ove
growth, a thin ribbon of yellowish mud. Along this ribbon came
plodding figure on horseback, a man dressed in black, small an
dark as an ant at this distance.

Then I remembered what Geilie had said. *I'm expecting a vis
tor.* And later, *That parson said he'd come at four o'clock.*

"It's a parson, a minister of some kind," I said. "She said sh
was expecting him."

"It's Archie Campbell, is who it is," Jamie said, with som
grimness. "What the devil—or perhaps I shouldna use that parti
ular expression, wi' respect to Mistress Duncan."

"Perhaps he's come to exorcise her," I suggested, with a ne
vous laugh.

"He's his work cut out for him, if so." The angular figu
disappeared into the trees, but it was several minutes before Jam
deemed him safely past us.

"What do you plan to do about Ian?" I asked, once we ha
made our way back to the path.

"I'll need help," he answered briskly. "I mean to come up th
river with Innes and MacLeod and the rest. There's a landi
there, no great distance from the refinery. We'll leave the bo
there, go ashore and deal wi' Hercules—and Atlas, too, if he's
mind to be troublesome—break open the cellar, snatch Ian, an
make off again. The dark o' the moon's in two days—I wish
could be sooner, but it will likely take that long to get a suitab
boat and what arms we'll need."

"Using what for money?" I inquired bluntly. The expenditu
for new clothes and shoes had taken a substantial portion of J
mie's share of profit from the bat guano. What was left would fe
us for several weeks, and possibly be sufficient to rent a boat fo
day or two, but it wouldn't stretch to buying large quantities
weapons.

Neither pistols nor swords were manufactured on the island;

weapons were imported from Europe and were in consequence expensive. Jamie himself had Captain Raines's two pistols; the scots had nothing but their fish knives and the odd cutlass—insufficient for an armed raid.

He grimaced slightly, then glanced at me sidelong.

"I must ask John for help," he said simply. "Must I not?"

I rode silently for a moment, then nodded in acquiescence.

"I suppose you'll have to." I didn't like it, but it wasn't a question of my liking; it was Ian's life. "One thing, though, Jamie—"

"Aye, I know," he said, resigned. "Ye mean to come with me, so?"

"Yes," I said, smiling. "After all, what if Ian's hurt, or sick, or—"

"Aye, ye can come!" he said, rather testily. "Only do me the one wee favor, Sassenach. Try verra hard not to be killed or cut to pieces, aye? It's hard on a man's sensibilities."

"I'll try," I said, circumspectly. And nudging my horse closer to his, rode side by side down toward Kingston, through the dripping trees.

There was a surprising amount of traffic on the river at night. Lawrence Stern, who had insisted on accompanying the expedition, told me that most of the plantations up in the hills used the river as their main linkage with Kingston and the harbor; roads were either atrocious or nonexistent, swallowed by lush growth with each new rainy season.

I had expected the river to be deserted, but we passed two small craft and a barge headed downstream as we tacked laboriously up the broad waterway, under sail. The barge, an immense dark shape stacked high with casks and bales, passed us like a black iceberg, huge, humped, and threatening. The low voices of the slaves poling it carried across the water, talking softly in a foreign tongue.

"It was kind of ye to come, Lawrence," Jamie said. We had a small, single-masted open boat, which barely held Jamie, myself, the six Scottish smugglers, and Stern. Despite the crowded quarters, I too was grateful for Stern's company; he had a stolid, phlegmatic quality about him that was very comforting under the circumstances.

"Well, I confess to some curiosity," Stern said, flapping the front of his shirt to cool his sweating body. In the dark, all I could see of him was a moving blotch of white. "I have met the lady before, you see."

"Mrs. Abernathy?" I paused, then asked delicately, "Er . . . what did you think of her?"

"Oh . . . she was a very pleasant lady; most . . . gracious." Dark as it was, I couldn't see his face, but his voice held an odd

ote, half-pleased, half-embarrassed, that told me he had found
ie widow Abernathy quite attractive indeed. From which I con-
luded that Geilie had wanted something from the naturalist; I had
ever known her treat a man with any regard, save for her own
nds.

"Where did you meet her? At her own house?" According to
ie attendees at the Governor's ball, Mrs. Abernathy seldom or
ever left her plantation.

"Yes, at Rose Hall. I had stopped to ask permission to collect a
are type of beetle—one of the Cucurlionidae—that I had found
ear a spring on the plantation. She invited me in, and . . . made
ie most welcome." This time there was a definite note of self-
atisfaction in his voice. Jamie, handling the tiller next to me,
eard it and snorted briefly.

"What did she want of ye?" he asked, no doubt having formed
onclusions similar to mine about Geilie's motives and behavior.

"Oh, she was most gratifyingly interested in the specimens of
ora and fauna I had collected on the island; she asked me about
ie locations and virtues of several different herbs. Ah, and about
ie other places I had been. She was particularly interested in my
ories of Hispaniola." He sighed, momentarily regretful. "It is
ifficult to believe that such a lovely woman might engage in such
eprehensible behavior as you describe, James."

"Lovely, aye?" Jamie's voice was dryly amused. "A bit smit-
n, were ye, Lawrence?"

Lawrence's voice echoed Jamie's smile. "There is a sort of
arnivorous fly I have observed, friend James. The male fly,
hoosing a female to court, takes pains to bring her a bit of meat
r other prey, tidily wrapped in a small silk package. While the
emale is engaged in unwrapping her tidbit, he leaps upon her,
erforms his copulatory duties, and hastens away. For if she
hould finish her meal before he has finished his own activities, or
hould he be so careless as not to bring her a tasty present—she
ats him." There was a soft laugh in the darkness. "No, it was an
nteresting experience, but I think I shall not call upon Mrs. Aber-
athy again."

"Not if we're lucky about it, no," Jamie agreed.

The men left me by the riverbank to mind the boat, and melted into the darkness, with instructions from Jamie to stay put. I had primed pistol, given to me with the stern injunction not to shoot myself in the foot. The weight of it was comforting, but as the minutes dragged by in black silence, I found the dark and the solitude more and more oppressive.

From where I stood, I could see the house, a dark oblong with only the lower three windows lighted; that would be the salon, thought, and wondered why there was no sign of any activity by the slaves. As I watched, though, I saw a shadow cross one of the lighted windows, and my heart jumped into my throat.

It wasn't Geilie's shadow, by any conceivable stretch of the imagination. It was tall, thin, and gawkily angular.

I looked wildly around, wanting to call out; but it was too late. The men were all out of earshot, headed for the refinery. I hesitated for a moment, but there was really nothing else to do. I kilted up my skirts and stepped into the dark.

By the time I stepped onto the veranda, I was damp with perspiration, and my heart was beating loudly enough to drown out all other sounds. I edged silently next to the nearest window, trying to peer in without being seen from within.

Everything was quiet and orderly within. There was a small fire on the hearth, and the glow of the flames gleamed on the polished floor. Geilie's rosewood secretary was unfolded, the desk shelf covered with piles of handwritten papers and what looked like very old books. I couldn't see anyone inside, but I couldn't see the whole room, either.

My skin prickled with imagination, thinking of the dead-eyed Hercules, silently stalking me in the dark. I edged farther down the veranda, looking over my shoulder with every other step.

There was an odd sense of desertion about the place this evening. There were none of the subdued voices of slaves that had attended my earlier visit, muttering to one another as they went about their tasks. But that might mean nothing, I told myself. Most of the slaves would stop work and go to their own quarters at sundown. Still, ought there not to be house servants, to tend the fire and fetch food from the kitchen?

The front door stood open. Spilled petals from the yellow rose lay across the doorstep, glowing like ancient gold coins in the faint light from the entryway.

I paused, listening. I thought I heard a faint rustle from inside the salon, as of someone turning the pages of a book, but I couldn't be sure. Taking my courage in both hands, I stepped across the threshold.

The feeling of desertion was more pronounced in here. There were unmistakable signs of neglect visible; a vase of wilted flowers on the polished surface of a chest, a teacup and saucer left to sit on an occasional table, the dregs dried to a brown stain in the bottom of the cup. Where the hell was everybody?

I stopped at the door into the salon and listened again. I heard the quiet crackle of the fire, and again, that soft rustle, as of turning pages. By poking my head around the jamb, I could just see that there was someone seated in front of the secretary now. Someone undeniably male, tall and thin-shouldered, dark head bent over something before him.

"Ian!" I shouted, as loudly as I dared. "Ian!"

The figure started, pushed back the chair, and stood up quickly, sinking toward the shadows.

"Jesus!" I said.

"Mrs. Malcolm?" said the Reverend Archibald Campbell, astonished.

I swallowed, trying to force my heart down out of my throat. The Reverend looked nearly as startled as I, but it lasted only a moment. Then his features hardened, and he took a step toward the door.

"What are you doing here?" he demanded.

"I'm looking for my husband's nephew," I said; there was no point in lying, and perhaps he knew where Ian was. I glanced quickly round the room, but it was empty, save for the Reverend, and the one small lighted lamp he had been using. "Where's Mrs. Abernathy?"

"I have no idea," he said, frowning. "She appears to have left. What do you mean, your husband's nephew?"

"Left?" I blinked at him. "Where has she gone?"

"I don't know." He scowled, his pointed upper lip clamped beaklike over the lower one. "She was gone when I rose this morning—and all of the servants with her, apparently. A fine way to treat an invited guest!"

I relaxed slightly, despite my alarm. At least I was in no danger

of running into Geilie. I thought I could deal with the Reveren
Campbell.

"Oh," I said. "Well, that does seem a bit inhospitable, I admi
I suppose you haven't seen a boy of about fifteen, very tall an
thin, with thick dark brown hair? No, I didn't think you had. I
that case, I expect I should be go—"

"Stop!" He grabbed me by the upper arm, and I stoppe
surprised and unsettled by the strength of his grip.

"What is your husband's true name?" he demanded.

"Why—Alexander Malcolm," I said, tugging at my captiv
arm. "You know that."

"Indeed. And how is it, then, that when I described you an
your husband to Mrs. Abernathy, she told me that your famil
name is Fraser—that your husband in fact is James Fraser?"

"Oh." I took a deep breath, trying to think of something plaus
ble, but failed. I never had been good at lying on short notice.

"Where is your husband, woman?" he demanded.

"Look," I said, trying to extract myself from his grasp
"you're quite wrong about Jamie. He had nothing to do with you
sister, he told me. He—"

"You've spoken to him about Margaret?" His grip tightened.
gave a small grunt of discomfort and yanked a bit harder.

"Yes. He says that it wasn't him—he wasn't the man she wer
to Culloden to see. It was a friend of his, Ewan Cameron."

"Ye're lying," he said flatly. "Or he is. It makes little differ
ence. Where is he?" He gave me a small shake, and I jerked har
managing to detach my arm from his grip.

"I tell you, he had nothing to do with what happened to you
sister!" I was backing away, wondering how to get away from hir
without setting him loose to blunder about the grounds in searc
of Jamie, making noise and drawing unwelcome attention to th
rescue effort. Eight men were enough to overcome the pillars
Hercules, but not enough to withstand a hundred roused slaves.

"Where?" The Reverend was advancing on me, eyes borir
into mine.

"He's in Kingston!" I said. I glanced to one side; I was near
pair of French doors opening onto the veranda. I thought I coul
get out without his catching me, but then what? Having him cha:
me through the grounds would be worse than keeping him talkir
in here.

I looked back at the Reverend, who was scowling at me in isbelief, and then what I had seen on the terrace registered in my iind's eye, and I jerked my head back around, staring.

I *had* seen it. There was a large white pelican perched on the eranda railing, head turned back, beak buried comfortably in its athers. Ping An's plumage glinted silver against the night in the im light from the doorway.

"What is it?" Reverend Campbell demanded. "Who is it? Who's out there?"

"Just a bird," I said, turning back to him. My heart was beating a jerky rhythm. Mr. Willoughby must surely be nearby. Pelicans ere common, near the mouths of rivers, near the shore, but I had ever seen one so far inland. But if Mr. Willoughby was in fact arking nearby, what ought I to do about it?

"I doubt very much that your husband is in Kingston," the everend was saying, narrowed eyes fixed on me with suspicion. However, if he is, he will presumably be coming here, to retrieve ou."

"Oh, no!" I said.

"No," I repeated, with as much assurance as I could manage. Jamie isn't coming here. I came by myself, to visit Geillis—Mrs. bernathy. My husband isn't expecting me back until next onth."

He didn't believe me, but there was nothing he could do about , either. His mouth pursed up in a tiny rosette, then unpuckered nough to ask, "So you are staying here?"

"Yes," I said, pleased that I knew enough about the geography f the place to pretend to be a guest. If the servants were gone, ere was no one to say I wasn't, after all.

He stood still, regarding me narrowly for a long moment. Then is jaw tightened and he nodded grudgingly.

"Indeed. Then I suppose ye'll have some notion as to where our ostess has taken herself, and when she proposes to return?"

I was beginning to have a rather unsettling notion of where—if ot exactly *when*—Geillis Abernathy might have gone, but the everend Campbell didn't seem the proper person with whom to hare it.

"No, I'm afraid not," I said. "I . . . ah, I've been out visiting nce yesterday, at the neighboring plantation. Just came back this inute."

The Reverend eyed me closely, but I was in fact wearing
riding habit—because it was the only decent set of clothes
owned, besides the violet ball dress and two wash-muslin gowns—
and my story passed unchallenged.

"I see," he said. "Mmphm. Well, then." He fidgeted restlessly
his big bony hands clenching and unclenching themselves, a
though he were not certain what to do with them.

"Don't let me disturb you," I said, with a charming smile and
nod at the desk. "I'm sure you must have important work to do."

He pursed his lips again, in that objectionable way that mad
him look like an owl contemplating a juicy mouse. "The work ha
been completed. I was only preparing copies of some document
that Mrs. Abernathy had requested."

"How interesting," I said automatically, thinking that wit
luck, after a few moments' small talk, I could escape under th
pretext of retiring to my theoretical room—all the first-floor room
opened onto the veranda, and it would be a simple matter to sli
off into the night to meet Jamie.

"Perhaps you share our hostess's—and my own—interest i
Scottish history and scholarship?" His gaze had sharpened, an
with a sinking heart I recognized the fanatical gleam of the pas
sionate researcher in his eyes. I knew it well.

"Well, it's very interesting, I'm sure," I said, edging toward th
door, "but I must say, I really don't know very much about—"
caught sight of the top sheet on his pile of documents, and stoppe
dead.

It was a genealogy chart. I had seen plenty of those, living wit
Frank, but I recognized this particular one. It was a chart of th
Fraser family—the bloody thing was even *headed* "Fraser o
Lovat"—beginning somewhere around the 1400s, so far as I coul
see, and running down to the present. I could see Simon, the lat
—and not so lamented, in some quarters—Jacobite lord, who ha
been executed for his part in Charles Stuart's Rising, and hi
descendants, whose names I recognized. And down in one corne
with the sort of notation indicating illegitimacy, was Brian Frase
—Jamie's father. And beneath him, written in a precise blac
hand, *James A. Fraser*.

I felt a chill ripple up my back. The Reverend had noticed m
reaction, and was watching with a sort of dry amusement.

"Yes, it is interesting that it should be the Frasers, isn't it?"

"That . . . *what* should be the Frasers?" I said. Despite myself, I moved slowly toward the desk.

"The subject of the prophecy, of course," he said, looking faintly surprised. "Do ye not know of it? But perhaps, your husband being an illegitimate descendant . . ."

"I don't know of it, no."

"Ah." The Reverend was beginning to enjoy himself, seizing the opportunity to inform me. "I thought perhaps Mrs. Abernathy had spoken of it to you; she being so interested as to have written to me in Edinburgh regarding the matter." He thumbed through the stack, extracting one paper that appeared to be written in Gaelic.

"This is the original language of the prophecy," he said, shoving Exhibit A under my nose. "By the Brahan Seer; you'll have heard of the Brahan Seer, surely?" His tone held out little hope, but in fact, I had heard of the Brahan Seer, a sixteenth-century prophet along the lines of a Scottish Nostradamus.

"I have. It's a prophecy concerning the Frasers?"

"The Frasers of Lovat, aye. The language is poetic, as I pointed out to Mistress Abernathy, but the meaning is clear enough." He was gathering enthusiasm as he went along, notwithstanding his suspicions of me. "The prophecy states that a new ruler of Scotland will spring from Lovat's lineage. This is to come to pass following the eclipse of 'the kings of the white rose'—a clear reference to the Papist Stuarts, of course." He nodded at the white roses woven into the carpet. "There are somewhat more cryptic references included in the prophecy, of course; the time in which this ruler will appear, and whether it is to be a king or a queen—there is some difficulty in interpretation, owing to mishandling of the original . . ."

He went on, but I wasn't listening. If I had had any doubt about where Geilie had gone, it was fast disappearing. Obsessed with the rulers of Scotland, she had spent the better part of ten years in working for the restoration of a Stuart Throne. That attempt had failed most definitively at Culloden, and she had then expressed nothing but contempt for all extant Stuarts. And little wonder, if she thought she knew what was coming next.

But where would she go? Back to Scotland, perhaps, to involve herself with Lovat's heir? No, she was thinking of making the leap through time again; that much was clear from her conversation with me. She was preparing herself, gathering her resources—retrieving the treasure from the silkies' isle—and completing her researches.

I stared at the paper in a kind of fascinated horror. The genealogy, of course, was only recorded to the present. Did Geilie know who Lovat's descendants would be, in the future?

I looked up to ask the Reverend Campbell a question, but the words froze on my lips. Standing in the door to the veranda was Mr. Willoughby.

The little Chinese had evidently been having a rough time; his silk pajamas were torn and stained, and his round face was beginning to show the hollows of hunger and fatigue. His eyes passed over me with only a remote flicker of acknowledgment; all his attention was for the Reverend Campbell.

"Most holy fella," he said, and his voice held a tone I had never heard in him before; an ugly taunting note.

The Reverend whirled, so quickly that his elbow knocked against a vase; water and yellow roses cascaded over the rosewood desk, soaking the papers. The Reverend gave a cry of rage, and snatched the papers from the flood, shaking them frantically to remove the water before the ink should run.

"See what ye've done, ye wicked, murdering heathen!"

Mr. Willoughby laughed. Not his usual high giggle, but a low chuckle. It didn't sound at all amused.

"I murdering?" He shook his head slowly back and forth, eyes fixed on the Reverend. "Not me, holy fella. Is you, murderer."

"Begone, fellow," Campbell said coldly. "You should know better than to enter a lady's house."

"I know you." The Chinaman's voice was low and even, his gaze unwavering. "I see you. See you in red room, with the woman who laughs. See you too with stinking whores, in Scotland." Very slowly, he lifted his hand to his throat and drew it across, precise as a blade. "You kill pretty often, holy fella, I think."

The Reverend Campbell had gone pale, whether from shock or rage, I couldn't tell. I was pale, too—from fear. I wet my dry lips and forced myself to speak.

"Mr. Willoughby—"

"Not Willoughby." He didn't look at me; the correction was almost indifferent. "I am Yi Tien Cho."

Seeking escape from the present situation, my mind wondered absurdly whether the proper form of address would be Mr. Yi, or Mr. Cho?

"Get out at once!" The Reverend's paleness came from rage. He advanced on the little Chinese, massive fists clenched. Mr. Willoughby didn't move, seemingly indifferent to the looming minister.

"Better you leave, First Wife," he said, softly. "Holy fella king women—not with cock. With knife."

I wasn't wearing a corset, but felt as though I were. I couldn't get enough breath to form words.

"Nonsense!" the Reverend said sharply. "I tell you again—get out! Or I shall—"

"Just stand still, please, Reverend Campbell," I said. Hands shaking, I drew the pistol Jamie had given me out of the pocket of my habit and pointed it at him. Rather to my surprise, he did stand still, staring at me as though I had just grown two heads.

I had never held anyone at gunpoint before; the sensation was quite oddly intoxicating, in spite of the way the pistol's barrel wavered. At the same time, I had no real idea what to do.

"Mr.—" I gave up, and used all his names. "Yi Tien Cho. Did you see the Reverend at the Governor's ball with Mrs. Alcott?"

"I see him kill her," Yi Tien Cho said flatly. "Better shoot, First Wife."

"Don't be ridiculous! My dear Mrs. Fraser, surely you cannot believe the word of a savage, who is himself—" The Reverend turned toward me, trying for a superior expression, which was rather impaired by the small beads of sweat that had formed at the edge of his receding hairline.

"But I think I do," I said. "You were there. I saw you. And you were in Edinburgh when the last prostitute was killed there. Nellie Cowden said you'd lived in Edinburgh for two years; that's how long the Fiend was killing girls there." The trigger was slippery under my forefinger.

"That's how long *he* had lived there, too!" The Reverend's face was losing its paleness, becoming more flushed by the moment. He jerked his head toward the Chinese.

"Will you take the word of the man who betrayed your husband?"

"Who?"

"Him!" The Reverend's exasperation roughened his voice. "It is this wicked creature who betrayed Fraser to Sir Percival Turner. Sir Percival told me!"

I nearly dropped the gun. Things were happening a lot too fast for me. I hoped desperately that Jamie and his men had found Ian and returned to the river—surely they would come to the house, if I was not at the rendezvous.

I lifted the pistol a little, meaning to tell the Reverend to go down the breezeway to the kitchen; locking him in one of the storage pantries was the best thing I could think of to do.

"I think you'd better—" I began, and then he lunged at me.

My finger squeezed the trigger in reflex. Simultaneously, there was a loud report, the weapon kicked in my hand, and a small cloud of black-powder smoke rolled past my face, making my eyes water.

I hadn't hit him. The explosion had startled him, but now his face settled into new lines of satisfaction. Without speaking, he reached into his coat and drew out a chased-metal case, six inches long. From one end of this protruded a handle of white staghorn.

With the horrible clarity that attends crisis of all kinds, I noted everything, from the nick in the edge of the blade as he drew it from the case, to the scent of the rose he crushed beneath one foot as he came toward me.

There was nowhere to run. I braced myself to fight, knowing fight was useless. The fresh scar of the cutlass slash burned on my arm, a portent of what was coming that made my flesh shrink. There was a flash of blue in the corner of my vision, and a juicy *thunk!* as though someone had dropped a melon from some height. The Reverend turned very slowly on one shoe, eyes wide open and quite, quite blank. For that one moment, he looked like Margaret. Then he fell.

He fell all of a piece, not putting out a hand to save himself. One of the satinwood tables went flying, scattering potpourri and polished stones. The Reverend's head hit the floor at my feet, bounced slightly and lay still. I took one convulsive step back and stood trapped, back against the wall.

There was a dreadful contused depression in his temple. As I watched, his face changed color, fading before my eyes from the red of choler to a pasty white. His chest rose, fell, paused, rose again. His eyes were open; so was his mouth.

"Tsei-mi is here, First Wife?" The Chinese was putting the bag that held the stone balls back into his sleeve.

"Yes, he's here—out there." I waved vaguely toward the veranda. "What—he—did you really—?" I felt the waves of shock creeping over me and fought them back, closing my eyes and drawing in a breath as deep as I could manage.

"Was it you?" I said, my eyes still closed. If he was going to cave in my head as well, I didn't want to watch. "Did he tell the truth? Was it you who gave away the meeting place at Arbroath to Sir Percival? Who told him about Malcolm, and the printshop?"

There was neither answer nor movement, and after a moment, I opened my eyes. He was standing there, watching the Reverend Campbell.

Archibald Campbell lay still as death, but was not yet dead. The dark angel was coming, though; his skin had taken on the faint green tinge I had seen before in dying men. Still, his lungs moved, taking air with a high wheezing sound.

"It wasn't an Englishman, then," I said. My hands were wet, and I wiped them on my skirt. "An English *name*. Willoughby."

"Not Willoughby," he said sharply. "I am Yi Tien Cho!"

"Why!" I said, almost shouting. "Look at me, damn you! *Why*?"

He did look at me then. His eyes were black and round as marbles, but they had lost their shine.

"In China," he said, "there are . . . stories. Prophecy. That one day the ghosts will come. Everyone fear ghost." He nodded once, twice, then glanced again at the figure on the floor.

"I leave China to save my life. Waking up long time—I see ghosts. All round me, ghosts," he said softly.

"A big ghost comes—horrible white face, most horrible, hair on fire. I think he will eat my soul." His eyes had been fixed on the Reverend; now they rose to my face, remote and still as standing water.

"I am right," he said simply, and nodded again. He had not shaved his head recently, but the scalp beneath the black fuzz gleamed in the light from the window.

"He eat my soul, Tsei-mi. I am no more Yi Tien Cho."

"He saved your life," I said. He nodded once more.

"I know. Better I die. Better die than be Willoughby. Willoughby! Ptah!'' He turned his head and spat. His face contorted, suddenly angry.

"He talks my words, Tsei-mi! He eats my soul!'' The fit of anger seemed to pass as quickly as it had come on. He was sweating, though the room was not terribly warm. He passed a trembling hand over his face, wiping away the moisture.

"There is a man I see in tavern. Ask for Mac-Doo. I am drunk,'' he said dispassionately. "Wanting woman, no woman come with me—laugh, saying yellow worm, point . . .'' He waved a hand vaguely toward the front of his trousers. He shook his head, his queue rustling softly against the silk.

"No matter what *gwao-fei* do; all same to me. I am drunk,'' he said again. "Ghost-man wants Mac-Doo, ask I am knowing. Say yes, I know Mac-Doo.'' He shrugged. "It is not important what I say.''

He was staring at the minister again. I saw the narrow black chest rise slowly, fall . . . rise once more, fall . . . and remain still. There was no sound in the room; the wheezing had stopped.

"It is a debt,'' Yi Tien Cho said. He nodded toward the still body. "I am dishonored. I am stranger. But I pay. Your life for mine, First Wife. You tell Tsei-mi.''

He nodded once more, and turned toward the door. There was a faint rustling of feathers from the dark veranda. On the threshold he turned back.

"When I wake on dock, I am thinking ghosts have come, are all around me,'' Yi Tien Cho said softly. His eyes were dark and flat with no depth to them. "But I am wrong. It is me; I am the ghost.''

There was a stir of breeze at the French windows, and he was gone. The quick soft sound of felt-shod feet passed down the veranda, followed by the rustle of spread wings, and a soft, plaintive *Gwaaa!* that faded into the night-sounds of the plantation.

I made it to the sofa before my knees gave way. I bent down and laid my head on my knees, praying that I would not faint. The blood hammered in my ears. I thought I heard a wheezing breath and jerked up my head in panic, but the Reverend Campbell lay quite still.

I could not stay in the same room with him. I got up, circling as far around the body as I could get, but before I reached the ve

anda door, I had changed my mind. All the events of the evening
were colliding in my head like the bits of glass in a kaleidoscope.

I could not stop now to think, to make sense of it all. But I
remembered the Reverend's words, before Yi Tien Cho had come.
If there was any clue here to where Geillis Abernathy had gone, it
would be upstairs. I took a candle from the table, lighted it, and
made my way through the dark house to the staircase, resisting the
urge to look behind me. I felt very cold.

The workroom was dark, but a faint, eerie violet glow hovered
over the far end of the counter. There was an odd burnt smell in
the room, that stung the back of my nose and made me sneeze.
The faint metallic aftertaste in the back of my throat reminded me
of a long-ago chemistry class.

Quicksilver. Burning mercury. The vapor it gave off was not
only eerily beautiful, but highly toxic as well. I snatched out a
handkerchief and plastered it over my nose and mouth as I went
toward the site of the violet glow.

The lines of the pentacle had been charred into the wood of the
counter. If she had used stones to mark a pattern, she had taken
them with her, but she had left something else behind.

The photograph was heavily singed at the edges, but the center
was untouched. My heart gave a thump of shock. I seized the
picture, clutching Brianna's face to my chest with a mingled feeling of fury and panic.

What did she mean by this—this desecration? It couldn't have
been meant as a gesture toward me or Jamie, for she could not
have expected either of us ever to have seen it.

It must be magic—or Geilie's version of it. I tried frantically to
recall our conversation in this room; what had she said? She had
been curious about how I had traveled through the stones—that
was the main thing. And what had I said? Only something vague,
about fixing my attention on a person—yes, that was it—I said I
had fixed my attention on a specific person inhabiting the time to
which I was drawn.

I drew a deep breath, and discovered that I was trembling, both
with delayed reaction from the scene in the salon, and from a
dreadful, growing apprehension. It might be only that Geilie had
decided to try my technique—if one could dignify it with such a

word—as well as her own, and use the image of Brianna as a point of fixation for her travel. Or—I thought of the Reverend's piles of neat, handwritten papers, the carefully drawn genealogies, and thought I might just faint.

"One of the Brahan Seer's prophecies," he had said. "Concerning the Frasers of Lovat. Scotland's ruler will come from that lineage." But thanks to Roger Wakefield's researches, I knew— what Geilie almost certainly knew as well, obsessed as she was with Scottish history—that Lovat's direct line had failed in the 1800s. To all visible intents and purposes, that is. There was in fact one survivor of that line living in 1968—Brianna.

It took a moment for me to realize that the low, growling sound I heard was coming from my own throat, and a moment more of conscious effort to unclench my jaws.

I stuffed the mutilated photograph into the pocket of my skirt and whirled, running for the door as though the workroom were inhabited by demons. I had to find Jamie—now.

They were not there. The boat floated silently, empty in the shadows of the big cecropia where we had left it, but of Jamie and the rest, there was no sign at all.

One of the cane fields lay a short distance to my right, between me and the looming rectangle of the refinery beyond. The faint caramel smell of burnt sugar lingered over the field. Then the wind changed, and I smelled the clean, damp scent of moss and wet rocks from the stream, with all the tiny pungencies of the water plants intermingled.

The stream bank rose sharply here, going up in a mounded ridge that ended at the edge of the cane field. I scrambled up the slope, my palm slipping in soft sticky mud. I shook it off with a muffled exclamation of disgust and wiped my hand on my skirt. A thrill of anxiety ran through me. Bloody *hell,* where was Jamie? He should have been back long since.

Two torches burned by the front gate of Rose Hall, small dots of flickering light at this distance. There was a closer light as well; a glow from the left of the refinery. Had Jamie and his men met trouble there? I could hear a faint singing from that direction, and see a deeper glow that bespoke a large open fire. It seemed peace-

ful, but something about the night—or the place—made me very
uneasy.

Suddenly I became aware of another scent, above the tang of
watercress and burnt sugar—a strong putrid-sweet smell that I
recognized at once as the smell of rotten meat. I took a cautious
step, and all hell promptly broke loose underfoot.

It was as though a piece of the night had suddenly detached
itself from the rest and sprung into action at about the level of my
knees. A very large object exploded into movement close to me,
and there was a stunning blow across my lower legs that knocked
me off my feet.

My involuntary shriek coincided with a truly awful sound—a
sort of loud, grunting hiss that confirmed my impression that I was
in close juxtaposition to something large, alive, and reeking of
carrion. I didn't know what it was, but I wanted no part of it.

I had landed very hard on my bottom. I didn't pause to see what
was happening, but flipped over and made off through the mud
and leaves on all fours, followed by a repetition of the grunting
hiss, only louder, and a scrabbling, sliding sort of rush. Something
hit my foot a glancing blow, and I stumbled to my feet, running.

I was so panicked that I didn't realize that I suddenly could see,
until the man loomed up before me. I crashed into him, and the
torch he was carrying dropped to the ground, hissing as it struck
the wet leaves.

Hands grabbed my shoulders, and there were shouts behind me.
My face was pressed against a hairless chest with a strong musky
smell about it. I regained my balance, gasping, and leaned back to
look into the face of a tall black slave, who was gaping down at me
in perplexed dismay.

"Missus, what you be doin' here?" he said. Before I could
answer, though, his attention was distracted from me to what was
going on behind me. His grip on my shoulders relaxed, and I
turned to see.

Six men surrounded the beast. Two carried torches, which they
held aloft to light the other four, dressed only in loin cloths, who
cautiously circled, holding sharpened wooden poles at the ready.

My legs were still stinging and wobbly from the blow they had
taken; when I saw what had struck me, they nearly gave way again.
The thing was nearly twelve feet long, with an armored body the
size of a rum cask. The great tail whipped suddenly to one side;

the man nearest leapt aside, shouting in alarm, and the saurian's head turned, jaws opening slightly to emit another hiss.

The jaws clicked shut with an audible snap, and I saw the telltale carnassial tooth, jutting up from the lower jaw in an expression of grim and spurious pleasantry.

"Never smile at a crocodile," I said stupidly.

"No, ma'am, I surely won't," the slave said, leaving me and edging cautiously toward the scene of action.

The men with the poles were poking at the beast, evidently trying to irritate it. In this endeavor, they appeared to be succeeding. The fat, splayed limbs dug hard into the ground, and the crocodile charged, roaring. It lunged with astonishing speed; the man before it yelped and jumped back, lost his footing on the slippery mud and fell.

The man who had collided with me launched himself through the air and landed on the crocodile's back. The men with the torches danced back and forth, yelling encouragement, and one of the pole men, bolder than the others, dashed forward and whacked his pole across the broad, plated head to distract it, while the fallen slave scrabbled backward, bare heels scooping trenches in the black mud.

The man on the crocodile's back was groping—with what seemed to me suicidal mania—for the beast's mouth. Getting a hold with one arm about the thick neck, he managed to grab the end of the snout with one hand, and holding the mouth shut, screamed something to his companions.

Suddenly a figure I hadn't noticed before stepped out of the shadow of the cane. It went down on one knee before the struggling pair, and without hesitation, slipped a rope noose around the crocodile's jaws. The shouting rose in a yell of triumph, cut off by a sharp word from the kneeling figure.

He rose and motioned violently, shouting commands. He wasn't speaking English, but his concern was obvious; the great tail was still free, lashing from side to side with a force that would have felled any man who came within range of it. Seeing the power of that stroke, I could only marvel that my own legs were merely bruised, and not broken.

The pole men dashed in closer, in response to the commands of their leader. I could feel the half-pleasant numbness of shock stealing over me, and in that state of unreality, it somehow seemed no surprise to see that the leader was the man called Ishmael.

"*Huwe!*" he said, making violent upward gestures with his palms that made his meaning obvious. Two of the pole men had gotten their poles shoved under the belly; a third now managed a lucky strike past the tossing head, and lodged his pole under the chest.

"*Huwe!*" Ishmael said again, and all three threw themselves hard upon their poles. With a sucking *splat!* the reptile flipped over and landed thrashing on its back, its underside a sudden gleaming white in the torchlight.

The torchbearers were shouting again; the noise rang in my ears. Then Ishmael stopped them with a word, his hand thrown out in demand, palm up. I couldn't tell what the word was, but it could as easily have been "Scalpel!" The intonation—and the result—were the same.

One of the torchbearers hastily tugged the cane-knife from his loincloth, and slapped it into his leader's hand. Ishmael turned on his heel and in the same movement, drove the point of the knife deep into the crocodile's throat, just where the scales of the jaw joined those of the neck.

The blood welled black in the torchlight. All the men stepped back then, and stood at a safe distance, watching the dying frenzy of the great reptile with a respect mingled with deep satisfaction. Ishmael straightened, shirt a pale blur against the dark canes; unlike the other men, he was fully dressed, save for bare feet, and a number of small leather bags swung at his belt.

Owing to some freak of the nervous system, I had kept standing all this time. The increasingly urgent messages from my legs made it through to my brain at this point, and I sat down quite suddenly, my skirts billowing on the muddy ground.

The movement attracted Ishmael's notice; the narrow head turned in my direction, and his eyes widened. The other men, seeing him, turned also, and a certain amount of incredulous comment in several languages followed.

I wasn't paying much attention. The crocodile was still breathing, in stertorous, bubbling gasps. So was I. My eyes were fixed on the long scaled head, its eye with a slit pupil glowing the greenish gold of tourmaline, its oddly indifferent gaze seeming fixed in turn on me. The crocodile's grin was upside down, but still in place.

The mud was cool and smooth beneath my cheek, black as the thick stream that flowed between the reptile's scales. The tone of the questions and comments had changed to concern, but I was no longer listening.

I hadn't actually lost consciousness; I had a vague impression of jostling bodies and flickering light, and then I was lifted into the air, clutched tight in someone's arms. They were talking excitedly, but I caught only a word now and then. I dimly thought I should tell them to lay me down and cover me with something, but my tongue wasn't working.

Leaves brushed my face as my escort ruthlessly shouldered the canes aside; it was like pushing through a cornfield that had no ears, all stalks and rustling leaves. There was no conversation among the men now; the susurrus of our passage drowned even the sound of footsteps.

By the time we entered the clearing by the slave huts, both sight and wits had returned to me. Bar scrapes and bruises, I wasn't hurt, but I saw no point in advertising the fact. I kept my eyes closed and stayed limp as I was carried into one of the huts, fighting back panic, and hoping to come up with some sensible plan before I was obliged to wake up officially.

Where in bloody hell were Jamie and the others? If all went well —or worse, if it didn't—what were they going to do when they arrived at the landing place and found me gone, with traces— traces? the place was a bloody wallow!—of a struggle where I had been?

And what about friend Ishmael? What in the name of all merciful God was *he* doing here? I knew one thing—he wasn't bloody well cooking.

There was a good deal of festive noise outside the open door of the hut, and the scent of something alcoholic—not rum, something raw and pungent—floated in, a high note in the fuggy air of the hut, redolent of sweat and boiled yams. I cracked an eye and saw the reflected glimmer of firelight on the beaten earth. Shadows moved back and forth in front of the open door; I couldn't leave without being seen.

There was a general shout of triumph, and all the figures disappeared abruptly, in what I assumed was the direction of the fire, esumably they were doing something to the crocodile, who had rived when I did, swinging upside-down from the hunters' poles.

I rolled cautiously up onto my knees. Could I steal away while ey were occupied with whatever they were doing? If I could ake it to the nearest cane field, I was fairly sure they couldn't id me, but I was by no means so sure that I could find the river ;ain, alone in the pitch-dark.

Ought I to make for the main house, instead, in hopes of run-ng into Jamie and his rescue party? I shuddered slightly at the ought of the house, and the long, silent black form on the floor the salon. But if I didn't go to either house or boat, how was I to id them, on a moonless night black as the Devil's armpit?

My planning was interrupted by a shadow in the doorway that omentarily blocked the light. I risked a peek, then sat bolt up-ght and screamed.

The figure came swiftly in and knelt by my pallet.

"Don' you be makin' that noise, woman," Ishmael said. "It n't but me."

"Right," I said. Cold sweat prickled on my jaws and I could el my heart pounding like a triphammer. "Knew it all the time."

They had cut off the crocodile's head and sliced out the tongue id the floor of the mouth. He wore the huge, cold-eyed thing like hat, his eyes no more than a gleam in the depths beneath the ortcullised teeth. The empty lower jaw sagged, fat-jowled and imly jovial, hiding the lower half of his face.

"The *egungun,* he didn't hurt you none?" he asked.

"No," I said. "Thanks to the men. Er . . . you wouldn't con-der taking that off, would you?"

He ignored the request and sat back on his heels, evidently onsidering me. I couldn't see his face, but every line of his body pressed the most profound indecision.

"Why you bein' here?" he asked at last.

For lack of any better idea, I told him. He didn't mean to bash e on the head, or he would have done it already, when I col-psed below the cane field.

"Ah," he said, when I had finished. The reptile's snout dipped ightly toward me as he thought. A drop of moisture fell from the lved nostril onto my bare hand, and I wiped it quickly on my irt, shuddering.

"The missus not here tonight," he said, at last, as though wondering whether it was safe to trust me with the information.

"Yes, I know," I said. I gathered my feet under me, preparing to rise. "Can you—or one of the men—take me back to the big tree by the river? My husband will be looking for me," I added pointedly.

"Likely she be takin' the boy with her," Ishmael went on ignoring me.

My heart had lifted when he had verified that Geilie was gone; now it fell, with a distinct thud in my chest.

"She's taken Ian? Why?"

I couldn't see his face, but the eyes inside the crocodile mask shone with a gleam of something that was partly amusement—but only partly.

"Missus likes boys," he said, the malicious tone making his meaning quite clear.

"Does she," I said flatly. "Do you know when she'll be coming back?"

The long, toothy snout turned suddenly up, but before he could reply, I sensed someone standing behind me, and swung around on the pallet.

"I know you," she said, a small frown puckering the wide, smooth forehead as she looked down at me. "Do I not?"

"We've met," I said, trying to swallow the heart that had leapt into my mouth in startlement. "How—how do you do, Miss Campbell?"

Better than when last seen, evidently, in spite of the fact that her neat wool challis gown had been replaced with a loose smock of coarse white cotton, sashed with a broad, raggedly torn strip of the same, stained dark blue with indigo. Both face and figure had grown more slender, though, and she had lost the pasty, sagging look of too many months spent indoors.

"I am well, I thank ye, ma'am," she said politely. The pale blue eyes had still that distant, unfocused look to them, and despite the new sun-glow on her skin, it was clear that Miss Margaret Campbell was still not altogether in the here and now.

This impression was borne out by the fact that she appeared not to have noticed Ishmael's unconventional attire. Or to have noticed Ishmael himself, for that matter. She went on looking at me, vague interest passing across her snub features.

"It is most civil in ye to call upon me, ma'am," she said. "Might I offer ye refreshment of some kind? A dish of tea, per-ps? We keep no claret, for my brother holds that strong spirits a temptation to the lusts of the flesh."

"I daresay they are," I said, feeling that I could do with a brisk ot of temptation at the moment.

Ishmael had risen, and now bowed deeply to Miss Campbell, great head slipping precariously.

"You ready, *bébé*?" he asked softly. "The fire is waiting."

"Fire," she said. "Yes, of course," and turned to me.

"Will ye not join me, Mrs. Malcolm?" she asked graciously. Tea will be served shortly. I do so enjoy looking into a nice e," she confided, taking my arm as I rose. "Do you not find urself sometimes imagining that you see things in the flames?"

"Now and again," I said. I glanced at Ishmael, who was stand-g in the doorway. His indecision was apparent in his stance, but Miss Campbell moved inexorably toward him, towing me after r, he shrugged very slightly, and stepped aside.

Outside, a small bonfire burned brightly in the center of the earing before the row of huts. The crocodile had already been inned; the raw hide was stretched on a frame near one of the ts, throwing a headless shadow on the wooden wall. Several arpened sticks were thrust into the ground around the fire, each ung with chunks of meat, sizzling with an appetizing smell that netheless made my stomach clench.

Perhaps three dozen people, men, women and children, were thered near the fire, laughing and talking. One man was still ging softly, curled over a battered guitar.

As we appeared, one man caught sight of us, and turned arply, saying something that sounded like "Hau!" At once, the k and laughter stopped, and a respectful silence fell upon the owd.

Ishmael walked slowly toward them, the crocodile's head grin-ng in apparent delight. The firelight shone off faces and bodies e polished jet and melted caramel, all with deep black eyes that atched us come.

There was a small bench near the fire, set on a sort of dais made ' stacked planks. This was evidently the seat of honor, for Miss ampbell made for it directly, and gestured politely for me to sit wn next to her.

I could feel the weight of eyes upon me, with expressions ranging from hostility to guarded curiosity, but most of the attentio
was for Miss Campbell. Glancing covertly around the circle o
faces, I was struck by their strangeness. These were the faces o
Africa, and alien to me; not faces like Joe's, that bore only th
faint stamp of his ancestors, diluted by centuries of Europea
blood. Black or not, Joe Abernathy was a great deal more like m
than like these people—different to the marrow of their bones.

The man with the guitar had put it aside, and drawn out a sma
drum that he set between his knees. The sides were covered wi
the hide of some spotted animal; goat, perhaps. He began to tap
softly with the palms of his hands, in a half-halting rhythm like th
beating of a heart.

I glanced at Miss Campbell, sitting tranquil beside me, han
carefully folded in her lap. She was gazing straight ahead, into th
leaping flames, with a small, dreaming smile on her lips.

The swaying crowd of slaves parted, and two little girls cam
out, carrying a large basket between them. The handle of th
basket was twined with white roses, and the lid jerked up an
down, agitated by the movements of something inside.

The girls set the basket at Ishmael's feet, casting awed glanc
up at his grotesque headdress. He rested a hand on each of the
heads, murmured a few words, and then dismissed them, his u
raised palms a startling flash of yellow-pink, like butterflies risin
from the girls' knotted hair.

The attitude of the spectators had so far been quiet and respec
ful. It continued so, but now they crowded closer, necks craning
see what would happen next, and the drum began to beat faste
still softly. One of the women was holding a stone bottle, she too
one step forward, handed it to Ishmael, and melted back into th
crowd.

Ishmael took up the bottle of liquor and poured a small amou
on the ground, moving carefully in a circle around the basket. T
basket, momentarily quiescent, heaved to and fro, evidently di
turbed by the movement or the pungent scent of alcohol.

A man holding a stick wrapped in rags stepped forward, an
held the stick in the bonfire until the rags blazed up, bright red.
a word from Ishmael, he dipped his torch to the ground where t
liquor had been poured. There was a collective "Ah!" from th
watchers as a ring of flame sprang up, burned blue and died aw

once, as quickly as it came. From the basket came a loud
'ock-a-doodle-dooo!''

Miss Campbell stirred beside me, eyeing the basket with suspi-
n.

As though the crowing had been a signal—perhaps it was—a
te began to play, and the humming of the crowd rose to a higher
ch.

Ishmael came toward the makeshift dais where we sat, holding a
l headrag between his hands. This he tied about Margaret's
ist, placing her hand gently back in her lap when he had fin-
ed.

''Oh, there is my handkerchief!'' she exclaimed, and quite un-
fconsciously raised her wrist and wiped her nose.

No one but me seemed to notice. The attention was on Ishmael,
o was standing before the crowd, speaking in a language I
In't recognize. The cock in the basket crowed again, and the
ite roses on the handle quivered violently with its struggles.

''I do wish it wouldn't do that,'' said Margaret Campbell, rather
ulantly. ''If it does again, it will be three times, and that's bad
k, isn't it?''

''Is it?'' Ishmael was now pouring the rest of the liquor in a
cle round the dais. I hoped the flame wouldn't startle her.

''Oh, yes, Archie says so. 'Before the cock crows thrice, thou
It betray me.' Archie says women are always betrayers. Is that
do you think?''

''Depends on your point of view, I suppose,'' I murmured,
tching the proceedings. Miss Campbell seemed oblivious to the
aying, humming slaves, the music, the twitching basket, and
mael, who was collecting small objects handed to him out of
crowd.

''I'm hungry,'' she said. ''I do hope the tea will be ready
on.''

Ishmael heard this. To my amazement, he reached into one of
bags at his waist and unwrapped a small bundle, which proved
hold a cup of chipped and battered porcelain, the remnants of
ld leaf still visible on the rim. This he placed ceremoniously on
r lap.

''Oh, goody,'' Margaret said happily, clapping her hands to-
ther. ''Perhaps there'll be biscuits.''

I rather thought not. Ishmael had placed the objects given him

by the crowd along the edge of the dais. A few small bones, w
lines carved across them, a spray of jasmine, and two or thr
crude little figures made of wood, each one wrapped in a scrap
cloth, with little shocks of hair glued to the head-nubbins w
clay.

Ishmael spoke again, the torch dipped, and a sudden whiff
blue flame shot up around the dais. As it died away, leaving
scent of scorched earth and burnt brandy heavy in the cool ni
air, he opened the basket and brought out the cock.

It was a large, healthy bird, black feathers glistening in
torchlight. It struggled madly, uttering piercing squawks, but
was firmly trussed, its feet wrapped in cloth to prevent scratchi
Ishmael bowed low, saying something, and handed the bird
Margaret.

"Oh, thank you," she said graciously.

The cock stretched out its neck, wattles bright red with agi
tion, and crowed piercingly. Margaret shook it.

"Naughty bird!" she said crossly, and raising it to her mou
bit it just behind the head.

I heard the soft crack of the neck bones and the little grunt
effort as she flung her head up, wrenching off the head of
hapless cock.

She clutched the gurgling, struggling trussed carcass ti
against her bosom, crooning, "Now, then, now, then, it's all rig
darling," as the blood spurted and sprayed into the teacup and
over her dress.

The crowd had cried out at first, but now was quite still, wat
ing. The flute, too, had fallen silent, but the drum beat on, sou
ing much louder than before.

Margaret dropped the drained carcass carelessly to one si
where a boy darted out of the crowd to retrieve it. She brus
absently at the blood on her skirt, picking up the teacup with
red-swathed hand.

"Guests first," she said politely. "Will you have one lum
Mrs. Malcolm, or two?"

I was fortunately saved from answering by Ishmael, who thr
a crude horn cup into my hands, indicating that I should dr
from it. Considering the alternative, I raised it to my mouth wi
out hesitation.

It was fresh-distilled rum, sharp and raw enough to strip

oat, and I choked, wheezing. The tang of some herb rose up the
ck of my throat and into my nose; something had been mixed
th the liquor, or soaked in it. It was faintly tart, but not unpleas-
t.

Other cups like mine were making their way from hand to hand
ough the crowd. Ishmael made a sharp gesture, indicating that I
ould drink more. I obediently raised the cup to my lips, but let
e fiery liquid lap against my mouth without swallowing. What-
er was happening here, I thought I might need such wits as I
d.

Beside me, Miss Campbell was drinking from her teetotal cup
th genteel sips. The feeling of expectancy among the crowd was
ing; they were swaying now, and a woman had begun to sing,
w and husky, her voice an offbeat counterpoint to the thump of
drum.

The shadow of Ishmael's headdress fell across my face, and I
oked up. He too was swaying slowly, back and forth. The collar-
s white shirt he wore was speckled over the shoulders with
ck dots of blood, and stuck to his breast with sweat. I thought
ddenly that the raw crocodile's head must weigh thirty pounds
least, a terrible weight to support; the muscles of his neck and
oulders were taut with effort.

He raised his hands and began to sing as well. I felt a shiver run
wn my back and coil at the base of my spine, where my tail
uld have been. With his face masked, the voice could have been
e's; deep and honeyed, with a power that commanded attention.
I closed my eyes, it *was* Joe, with the light glinting off his
ectacles, and catching the gold tooth far back as he smiled.

Then I opened my eyes again, half-shocked to see instead the
ocodile's sinister yawn, and the fire gold-green in the cold, cruel
es. My mouth was dry and there was a faint buzzing in my ears,
aving around the strong, sweet words.

He was getting attention, all right; the night by the fire was full
eyes, black-wide and shiny, and small moans and shouts
rked the pauses in the song.

I closed my eyes and shook my head hard. I grabbed the edge of
wooden bench, clinging to its rough reality. I wasn't drunk, I
ew; whatever herb had been mixed with the rum was potent. I
uld feel it creeping snakelike through my blood, and kept my
es tight closed, fighting its progress.

I couldn't block my ears, though, or the sound of that voi[ce] rising and falling.

I didn't know how much time had passed. I came back to mys[elf] with a start, suddenly aware that the drum and the singing h[ad] stopped.

There was an absolute silence around the fire. I could hear [the] small rush of flame, and the rustle of cane leaves in the nig[ht] wind; the quick darting scuttle of a rat in the palm-frond roof [of] the hut behind me.

The drug was still in my bloodstream, but the effects we[re] dying; I could feel clarity coming back to my thoughts. Not so [for] the crowd; the eyes were fixed in a single, unblinking stare, lik[e a] wall of mirrors, and I thought suddenly of the voodoo legends [of] my time—of zombies and the *houngans* who made them. W[hat] had Geilie said? *Every legend has one foot on the truth.*

Ishmael spoke. He had taken off the crocodile's head. It lay [on] the ground at our feet, eyes gone dark in the shadow.

"Ils sont arrivés," Ishmael said quietly. *They have come.* [He] lifted his wet face, lined with exhaustion, and turned to the crow[d.]

"Who asks?"

As though in response, a young woman in a turban moved o[ut] of the crowd, still swaying, half-dazed, and sank down on [the] ground before the dais. She put her hand on one of the carv[ed] images, a crude wooden icon in the shape of a pregnant wom[an.]

Her eyes looked up with hope, and while I didn't recognize [the] words she spoke, it was clear what she asked.

"Aya, gado." The voice spoke from beside me, but it was [not] Margaret Campbell's. It was the voice of an old woman, crack[ed] and high, but confident, answering in the affirmative.

The young woman gasped with joy, and prostrated herself [on] the ground. Ishmael nudged her gently with a foot; she got [up] quickly and backed into the crowd, clutching the small image a[nd] bobbing her head, murmuring *"Mana, mana,"* over and over.

Next was a young man, by his face the brother of the first you[ng] woman, who squatted respectfully upon his haunches, touching [his] head before he spoke.

"Grandmère," he began, in high, nasal French. Grandmother[, I] thought.

He asked his question looking shyly down at the ground. "D[o]

woman I love return my love?'' His was the jasmine spray; he
d it so that it brushed the top of a bare, dusty foot.

The woman beside me laughed, her ancient voice ironic but not
kind. *"Certainement,"* she answered. "She returns it; and that
three other men, besides. Find another; less generous, but more
rthy."

The young man retired, crestfallen, to be replaced by an older
n. This one spoke in an African language I did not know, a tone
bitterness in his voice as he touched one of the clay figures.

"Setato hoye," said—who? The voice had changed. The voice
a man this time, full-grown but not elderly, answering in the
ne language with an angry tone.

I stole a look to the side, and despite the heat of the fire, felt the
ll ripple up my forearms. It was Margaret's face no longer. The
lines were the same, but the eyes were bright, alert and focused
the petitioner, the mouth set in grim command, and the pale
oat swelled like a frog's with the effort of strong speech as
oever-it-was argued with the man.

'They are here,'' Ishmael had said. "They," indeed. He stood
one side, silent but watchful, and I saw his eyes rest on me for a
ond before coming back to Margaret. Or whatever had been
rgaret.

'They.'' One by one the people came forward, to kneel and
. Some spoke in English, some French, or the slave patois,
ne in the African speech of their vanished homes. I couldn't
lerstand all that was said, but when the questions were in
nch or English, they were often prefaced by a respectful
randfather,'' or "Grandmother," once by "Aunt."

Both the face and the voice of the oracle beside me changed, as
ey'' came to answer their call; male and female, mostly mid-
-aged or old, their shadows dancing on her face with the flicker
the fire.

Do you not sometimes imagine that you see things in the fire?
e echo of her own small voice came back to me, thin and
ldish.

Listening, I felt the hair rise on the back of my neck, and
lerstood for the first time what had brought Ishmael back to this
ce, risking recapture and renewed slavery. Not friendship, not
e, nor any loyalty to his fellow slaves, but power.

What price is there for the power to tell the future? Any price,

was the answer I saw, looking out at the rapt faces of the congr
gation. He had come back for Margaret.

It went on for some time. I didn't know how long the dr
would last, but I saw people here and there sink down to th
ground, and nod to sleep; others melted silently back to the dar
ness of the huts, and after a time, we were almost alone. Only
few remained around the fire, all men.

They were all husky and confident, and from their attitud
accustomed to command some respect, among slaves at lea
They had hung back, together as a group, watching the procee
ings, until at last one, clearly the leader, stepped forward.

"They be done, mon," he said to Ishmael, with a jerk of h
head toward the sleeping forms around the fire. "Now you ask

Ishmael's face showed nothing but a slight smile, yet he seem
suddenly nervous. Perhaps it was the closing in of the other me
There was nothing overtly menacing about them, but they seem
both serious and intent—not upon Margaret, for a change, b
upon Ishmael.

At last he nodded, and turned to face Margaret. During t
hiatus, her face had gone blank; no one at home.

"Bouassa," he said to her. "Come you, Bouassa."

I shrank involuntarily away, as far as I could get on the ben
without falling into the fire. Whoever Bouassa was, he had co
promptly.

"I be hearin'." It was a voice as deep as Ishmael's, and shou
have been as pleasant. It wasn't. One of the men took an invol
tary step backward.

Ishmael stood alone; the other men seemed to shrink away fro
him, as though he suffered some contamination.

"Tell me what I want to know, you Bouassa," he said.

Margaret's head tilted slightly, a light of amusement in the pa
blue eyes.

"What you want to know?" the deep voice said, with m
scorn. "For why, mon? You be goin', I tell you anything or no

The small smile on Ishmael's face echoed that on Bouassa'

"You say true," he said softly. "But these—" He jerked
head toward his companions, not taking his eyes from the fa
"They be goin' with me?"

"Might as well," the deep voice said. It chuckled, rather
pleasantly. "The Maggot dies in three days. Won't be nothin'

m here. That all you be wantin' with me?'' Not waiting for an
swer, Bouassa yawned widely, and a loud belch erupted from
rgaret's dainty mouth.

Her mouth closed, and her eyes resumed their vacant stare, but
: men weren't noticing. An excited chatter erupted from them,
be hushed by Ishmael, with a significant glance at me. Abruptly
et, they moved away, still muttering, glancing at me as they
nt.

Ishmael closed his eyes as the last man left the clearing, and his
oulders sagged. I felt a trifle drained myself.

''What—'' I began, and then stopped. Across the fire, a man
l stepped from the shelter of the sugarcane. Jamie, tall as the
ae itself, with the dying fire staining shirt and face as red as his
r.

He raised a finger to his lips, and I nodded. I gathered my feet
utiously beneath me, picking up my stained skirt in one hand. I
ald be up, past the fire, and into the cane with him before
mael could reach me. But Margaret?

hesitated, turned to look at her, and saw that her face had
ae alive once again. It was lifted, eager, lips parted and shining
s narrowed so that they seemed slightly slanted, as she stared
oss the fire.

'Daddy?'' said Brianna's voice beside me.

The hairs rippled softly erect on my forearms. It was Brianna's
ce, Brianna's face, blue eyes dark and slanting with eagerness.

'Bree?'' I whispered, and the face turned to me.

'Mama,'' said my daughter's voice, from the throat of the
cle.

'Brianna,'' said Jamie, and she turned her head sharply to look
im.

'Daddy,'' she said, with great certainty. ''I knew it was you.
: been dreaming about you.''

amie's face was white with shock. I saw his lips form the word
sus,'' without sound, and his hand moved instinctively to cross
self.

'Don't let Mama go alone,'' said the voice with great certainty.
u go with her. I'll keep you safe.''

here was no sound save the crackling of the fire. Ishmael stood

transfixed, staring at the woman beside me. Then she spoke agai
in Brianna's soft, husky tones.

"I love you, Daddy. You too, Mama." She leaned toward m
and I smelled the fresh blood. Then her lips touched mine, an
screamed.

I was not conscious of leaping to my feet, or of crossing t
clearing. All I knew was that I was clinging to Jamie, my fa
buried in the cloth of his coat, shaking.

His heart was pounding under my cheek, and I thought that
was shaking, too. I felt his hand trace the sign of the cross up
my back, and his arm lock tight about my shoulders.

"It's all right," he said, and I could feel his ribs swell and bra
with the effort of keeping his voice steady. "She's gone."

I didn't want to look, but forced myself to turn my head towa
the fire.

It was a peaceful scene. Margaret Campbell sat quietly on h
bench, humming to herself, twiddling a long black tailfeath
upon her knee. Ishmael stood behind her, one hand smoothing h
hair in what looked like tenderness. He murmured something
her in a low, liquid tongue—a question—and she smiled placid

"Oh, I'm not a scrap tired!" she assured him, turning to lo
fondly up into the scarred face that hovered in the darkness abo
her. "Such a nice party, wasn't it?"

"Yes, *bébé*," he said gently. "But you rest now, eh?"
turned and clicked his tongue loudly. Suddenly two of the tu
baned women materialized out of the night; they must have be
waiting, just within call. Ishmael said something to them, and th
came at once to tend Margaret, lifting her to her feet and leadi
her away between them, murmuring soft endearments in Afric
and French.

Ishmael remained, watching us across the fire. He was still
one of Geilie's idols, carved out of night.

"I did not come alone," Jamie said. He gestured casually ov
his shoulder toward the cane field behind him, implying arm
regiments.

"Oh, you be alone, mon," Ishmael said, with a slight smi
"No matter. The *loa* speak to you; you be safe from me."
glanced back and forth between us, appraising.

"Huh," he said, in a tone of interest. "Never did hear a *l*
speak to *buckra*." He shook his head then, dismissing the matt

"You be going now," he said, quietly but with considerable
thority.

"Not yet." Jamie's arm dropped from my shoulder, and he
aightened up beside me. "I have come for the boy Ian; I will not
without him."

Ishmael's brows went up, compressing the three vertical scars
tween them.

"Huh," he said again. "You forget that boy; he be gone."

"Gone where?" Jamie asked sharply.

The narrow head tilted to one side, as Ishmael looked him over
refully.

"Gone with the Maggot, mon," he said. "And where she go,
u don' be going. That boy gone, mon," he said again, with
ality. "You leave too, you a wise man." He paused, listening. A
um was talking, somewhere far away, the pulse of it little more
an a disturbance of the night air.

"The rest be comin' soon," he remarked. "You safe from me,
on, not from them."

"Who are the rest?" I asked. The terror of the encounter with
loa was ebbing, and I was able to talk once more, though my
ine still rippled with fear of the dark cane field at my back.

"Maroons, I expect," Jamie said. He raised a brow at Ishmael.
Or ye will be?"

The priest nodded, one formal bob of the head.

"That be true," he said. "You hear Bouassa speak? His *loa*
ess us, we go." He gestured toward the huts and the dark hills
hind them. "The drum callin' them down from the hills, those
ong enough to go."

He turned away, the conversation obviously at an end.

"Wait!" Jamie said. "Tell us where she has gone—Mrs. Aber-
thy and the boy!"

Ishmael turned back, shoulders mantled in the crocodile's
ood.

"To Abandawe," he said.

"And where's that?" Jamie demanded impatiently. I put a hand
his arm.

"I know where it is," I said, and Ishmael's eyes widened in
tonishment. "At least—I know it's on Hispaniola. Lawrence
ld me. That was what Geilie wanted from him—to find out
ere it was."

"*What* is it? A town, a village? Where?" I could feel Jamie
arm tense under my hand, vibrating with the urgency to be gor

"It's a cave," I said, feeling cold in spite of the balmy air a
the nearness of the fire. "An old cave."

"Abandawe a magic place," Ishmael put in, deep voice soft,
though he feared to speak of it out loud. He looked at me ha
reassessing. "Clotilda say the Maggot take you to the room u
stairs. You maybe be knowin' what she do there?"

"A little." My mouth felt dry. I remembered Geilie's han
soft and plump and white, laying out the gems in their patter
talking lightly of blood.

As though he caught the echo of this thought, Ishmael took
sudden step toward me.

"I ask you, woman—you still bleed?"

Jamie jerked under my hand, but I squeezed his arm to be sti

"Yes," I said. "Why? What has that to do with it?"

The *oniseegun* was plainly uneasy; he glanced from me ba
toward the huts. A stir was perceptible in the dark behind hi
many bodies were moving to and fro, with a mutter of voices li
the whisper of the cane fields. They were getting ready to go.

"A woman bleeds, she kill magic. You bleed, got your woma
power, the magic don't work for you. The old women do mag
witch someone, call the *loas,* make sick, make well." He gave
a long, appraising look, and shook his head.

"You ain' gone do the magic, what the Maggot do. That ma
kill her, sure, but it kill you, too." He gestured behind him, towa
the empty bench. "You hear Bouassa speak? He say the Mag
die, three days. She taken the boy, he die. You go follow the
mon, you die, too, sure."

He stared at Jamie, and raised his hands in front of him, wri
crossed as though bound together. "I tell you, *amiki,*" he said.
let his hands fall, jerking them apart, breaking the invisible bo
He turned abruptly, and vanished into the darkness, where
shuffle of feet was growing louder, punctuated with bumps
heavy objects were shifted.

"Holy Michael defend us," muttered Jamie. He ran a hand ha
through his hair, making fiery wisps stand out in the flickeri
light. The fire was dying fast, with no one left to tend it.

"D'ye ken this place, Sassenach? Where Geillis has gone v
Ian?"

'No, all I know is that it's somewhere up in the far hills on paniola, and that a stream runs through it.''

'Then we must take Stern,'' he said with decision. "Come on; lads are by the river wi' the boat.''

I turned to follow him, but paused on the edge of the cane field look back.

'Jamie! Look!'' Behind us lay the embers of the *egungun*'s , and the shadowy ring of slave huts. Farther away, the bulk of se Hall made a light patch against the hillside. But farther still, yond the shoulder of the hill, the sky glowed faintly red.

'That will be Howe's place, burning,'' he said. He sounded dly calm, without emotion. He pointed to the left, toward the nk of the mountain, where a small orange dot glowed, no more his distance than a pinprick of light. "And that will be Twelve-es, I expect.''

The drum-voice whispered through the night, up and down the er. What had Ishmael said? *The drum callin' them down from hills—those strong enough to go.*

A small line of slaves was coming down from the huts, women rying babies and bundles, cooking pots slung over their shoul-s, heads turbaned in white. Next to one young woman, who d her arm with careful respect, walked Margaret Campbell, ewise turbaned.

Jamie saw her, and stepped forward.

'Miss Campbell!'' he said sharply. "Margaret!''

Margaret and her attendant stopped; the young woman moved though to step between her charge and Jamie, but he held up th hands as he came, to show he meant no harm, and she uctantly stepped back.

'Margaret,'' he said. "Margaret, do ye not know me?''

She stared vacantly at him. Very slowly, he touched her, holding r face between his hands.

'Margaret,'' he said to her, low-voiced, urgent. "Margaret, ar me! D'ye ken me, Margaret?''

She blinked once, then twice, and the smooth round face melted d thawed into life. It was not like the sudden possession of the us; this was a slow, tentative coming, of something shy and rful.

'Aye, I ken ye, Jamie,'' she said at last. Her voice was rich and

pure, a young girl's voice. Her lips curled up, and her eyes ca
alive once more, her face still held in the hollow of his hands

"It's been lang since I saw ye, Jamie," she said, looking up i
his eyes. "Will ye have word of Ewan, then? Is he well?"

He stood very still for a minute, his face that careful blank m
that hid strong feeling.

"He is well," he whispered at last. "Verra well, Margaret.
gave me this, to keep until I saw ye." He bent his head and kis
her gently.

Several of the women had stopped, standing silently by
watch. At this, they moved and began to murmur, glancing une
ily at each other. When he released Margaret Campbell a
stepped back, they closed in around her, protective and wa
nodding him back.

Margaret seemed oblivious; her eyes were still on Jamie's fa
the smile on her lips.

"I thank ye, Jamie!" she called, as her attendant took her a
and began to urge her away. "Tell Ewan I'll be with him soo
The little band of white-clothed women moved away, disappear
like ghosts into the darkness by the cane field.

Jamie made an impulsive move in their direction, but I stopp
him with a hand on his arm.

"Let her go," I whispered, mindful of what lay on the floor
the salon of the plantation house. "Jamie, let her go. You ca
stop her; she's better with them."

He closed his eyes briefly, then nodded.

"Aye, you're right." He turned, then stopped suddenly, an
whirled about to see what he had seen. There were lights in R
Hall now. Torchlight, flickering behind the windows, upstairs a
down. As we watched, a surly glow began to swell in the windo
of the secret workroom on the second floor.

"It's past time to go," Jamie said. He seized my hand and
went quickly, diving into the dark rustle of the canes, fleei
through air suddenly thick with the smell of burning sugar.

62

Abandawe

You can take the Governor's pinnace; that's small, but it's seaworthy." Grey fumbled through the drawer of his desk. "I'll write an order for the dockers to hand it over you."

"Aye, we'll need the boat—I canna risk the *Artemis;* as she's red's—but I think we'd best steal it, John." Jamie's brows were awn together in a frown. "I wouldna have ye be involved wi' me any visible way, aye? You'll be having trouble enough with ings, without that."

Grey smiled unhappily. "Trouble? Yes, you might call it trou-e, with four plantation houses burnt, and over two hundred aves gone—God knows where! But I vastly doubt that anyone ill take notice of my social acquaintance, under the circum-ances. Between fear of the Maroons and fear of the Chinaman, e whole island is in such a panic that a mere smuggler is the ost negligible of trivialities."

"It's a great relief to me to be thought trivial," Jamie said, very yly. "Still, we'll steal the boat. And if we're taken, ye've never ard my name or seen my face, aye?"

Grey stared at him, a welter of emotions fighting for mastery of s features, amusement, fear, and anger among them.

"Is that right?" he said at last. "Let you be taken, watch them ng you, and keep quiet about it—for fear of smirching my putation? For God's sake, Jamie, what do you take me for?"

Jamie's mouth twitched slightly.

"For a friend, John," he said. "And if I'll take your friendship

—and your damned boat!—then you'll take mine, and keep qui‹
Aye?''

The Governor glared at him for a moment, lips pressed tigʰ
but then his shoulders sagged in defeat.

''I will,'' he said shortly. ''But I should regard it as a grе
personal favor if you would endeavor not to be captured.''

Jamie rubbed a knuckle across his mouth, hiding a smile.

''I'll try verra hard, John.''

The Governor sat down, wearily. There were deep circles undе
his eyes, and his impeccable linen was wilted; obviously he hα
not changed his clothes from the day before.

''All right. I don't know where you're going, and it's likе
better I don't. But if you can, keep out of the sea-lanes north
Antigua. I sent a boat this morning, to ask for as many men as tʰ
barracks there can supply, marines and sailors both. They'll ⸱
heading this way by the day after tomorrow at the latest, to guα
the town and harbor against the escaped Maroons in case of ⸱
outright rebellion.''

I caught Jamie's eye, and raised one brow in question, but ⱶ
shook his head, almost imperceptibly. We had told the Governᵐ
of the uprising on the Yallahs River, and the escape of the slaves—
something he had heard about from other sources, anyway. Ⱳ
had not told him what we had seen later that night, lying to undе
cover of a tiny cove, sails taken down to hide their whiteness.

The river was dark as onyx, but with a fugitive gleam from tʰ
broad expanse of water. We had heard them coming, and had tiⅿ
to hide before the ship came down upon us; the beating of druⅿ
and a savage exultation of many voices echoing through the rivᵉ
valley as the *Bruja* sailed past us, carried by the downward cu‹
rent. The bodies of the pirates no doubt lay somewhere upriveᵉ
left to rot peacefully among the frangipani and cedar.

The escaped slaves of the Yallahs River had not gone into tʰ
mountains of Jamaica, but out to sea, presumably to jo⸱
Bouassa's followers on Hispaniola. The townsfolk of Kingstᵒ
had nothing to fear from the escaped slaves—but it was a goᵒ
deal better that the Royal Navy should concentrate their attentiᵒ
here than on Hispaniola, where we were bound.

Jamie rose to take our leave, but Grey stopped him.

''Wait. Will you not require a safe place for your—for Mrⱽ
Fraser?'' He didn't look at me, but at Jamie, eyes steady. ''

ould be honored if you would entrust her to my protection. She
uld stay here, in the Residence, until you return. No one would
ouble her—or even need to know she was here.''

Jamie hesitated, but there was no gentle way to phrase it.

''She must go with me, John,'' he said. ''There is no choice
out it; she must.''

Grey's glance flickered to me, then away, but not before I had
en the look of jealousy in his eyes. I felt sorry for him, but there
as nothing I could say; no way to tell him the truth.

''Yes,'' he said, and swallowed noticeably. ''I see. Quite.''

Jamie held out a hand to him. He hesitated for a moment, but
en took it.

''Good luck, Jamie,'' he said, voice a little husky. ''God go
ith you.''

Fergus had been somewhat more difficult to deal with. He had
sisted absolutely on accompanying us, offering argument after
gument, and arguing the more vehemently when he found that
e Scottish smugglers would sail with us.

''You take them, but you will go without *me*?'' Fergus's face
as alive with indignation.

''I will,'' Jamie said firmly. ''The smugglers are widowers or
chelors, all, but you're a marrit man.'' He glanced pointedly at
arsali, who stood watching the discussion, her face drawn with
xiety. ''I thought she was oweryoung to be wed, and I was
ong; but I *know* she's oweryoung to be widowed. You'll stay.''
d he turned aside, the matter settled.

It was full dark when we set sail in Grey's pinnace, a thirty-foot,
igle-decked sloop, leaving two docksmen bound and gagged in
e boathouse behind us. It was a small, single-masted ship, bigger
an the fishing boat in which we had traveled up the Yallahs
ver, but barely large enough to qualify for the designation
hip.''

Nonetheless, she seemed seaworthy enough, and we were soon
t of Kingston Harbor, heeling over in a brisk evening breeze, on
r way toward Hispaniola.

The smugglers handled the sailing among them, leaving Jamie,

Lawrence, and me to sit on one of the long benches along the ra
We chatted desultorily of this and that, but after a time, fell siler
absorbed in our own thoughts.

Jamie yawned repeatedly, and finally, at my urging, consente
to lie down upon the bench, his head resting in my lap. I wa
myself strung too tightly to want to sleep.

Lawrence too was wakeful, staring upward into the sky, hand
folded behind his head.

"There is moisture in the air tonight," he said, nodding upwar
toward the silver sliver of the crescent moon. "See the haze abo
the moon? It may rain before dawn; unusual for this time of year.

Talk about the weather seemed sufficiently boring to soothe n
jangled nerves. I stroked Jamie's hair, thick and soft under n
hand.

"Is that so?" I said. "You and Jamie both seem able to read th
weather from the sky. All I know is the old bit about 'Red sky
night, sailor's delight; red sky at morning, sailor take warning.'
didn't notice what color the sky was tonight, did you?"

Lawrence laughed comfortably. "Rather a light purple," I
said. "I cannot say whether it will be red in the morning, but it
surprising how frequently such signs are reliable. But of cour
there is a scientific principle involved—the refraction of light fro
the moisture in the air, just as I observed presently of the moon

I lifted my chin, enjoying the breeze that lifted the heavy ha
that fell on my neck.

"But what about odd phenomena? Supernatural things?"
asked him. "What about things where the rules of science see
not to apply?" *I am a scientist,* I heard him say in memory, l
slight accent seeming only to reinforce his matter-of-factness
don't believe in ghosts.

"Such as what, these phenomena?"

"Well—" I groped for a moment, then fell back on Geilie
own examples. "People who have bleeding stigmata, for exampl
Astral travel? Visions, supernatural manifestations . . . o
things, that can't be explained rationally."

Lawrence grunted, and settled his bulk more comfortably on t
bench beside me.

"Well, I say it is the place of science only to observe," he sa
"To seek cause where it may be found, but to realize that there a
many things in the world for which no cause shall *be* found; n

ecause it does not exist, but because we know too little to find it.
is not the place of science to insist on explanation—but only to
bserve, in hopes that the explanation will manifest itself.''

"That may be science, but it isn't human nature,'' I objected.
People go on wanting explanations.''

"They do.'' He was becoming interested in the discussion; he
aned back, folding his hands across his slight paunch, in a lec-
rer's attitude. "It is for this reason that a scientist constructs
ypotheses—suggestions for the cause of an observation. But a
ypothesis must never be confused with an explanation—with
roof.

"I have seen a great many things which might be described as
eculiar. Fish-falls, for instance, where a great many fish—all of
e same species, mind you, all the same size—fall suddenly from
clear sky, over dry land. There would appear to be no rational
use for this—and yet, is it therefore suitable to attribute the
henomenon to supernatural interference? On the face of it, does
seem more likely that some celestial intelligence should amuse
self by flinging shoals of fish at us from the sky, or that there is
me meteorological phenomenon—a waterspout, a tornado,
mething of the kind?—that while not visible to us, is still in
peration? And yet''—his voice became more pensive—"why—
d how!—might a natural phenomenon such as a waterspout
move the heads—and only the heads—of all the fish?''

"Have you seen such a thing yourself?'' I asked, interested, and
e laughed.

"There speaks a scientific mind!'' he said, chuckling. "The
rst thing a scientist asks—how do you know? Who has seen it?
an I see it myself? Yes, I have seen such a thing—three times, in
ct, though in one case the precipitation was of frogs, rather than
sh.

"Were you near a seashore or a lake?''

"Once near a shore, once near a lake—that was the frogs—but
e third time, it took place far inland; some twenty miles from the
earest body of water. And yet the fish were of a kind I have seen
nly in the deep ocean. In none of the cases did I see any sort of
sturbance of the upper air—no clouds, no great wind, none of
e fabled spouts of water that rise from the sea into the sky,
ssuredly. And yet the fish fell; so much is a fact, for I have seen
em.''

"And it isn't a fact if you haven't seen it?" I asked dryly.

He laughed in delight, and Jamie stirred, murmuring against my thigh. I smoothed his hair, and he relaxed into sleep again.

"It may be so; it may not. But a scientist could not say, could he? What is it the Christian Bible says—'Blest are they who have not seen, but have believed'?"

"That's what it says, yes."

"Some things must be accepted as fact without provable cause." He laughed again, this time without much humor. "As a scientist who is also a Jew, I have perhaps a different perspective on such phenomena as stigmata—and the idea of resurrection of the dead, which a very great proportion of the civilized world accepts as fact beyond question. And yet, this skeptical view is not one I could even breathe, to anyone save yourself, without grave danger of personal harm."

"Doubting Thomas was a Jew, after all," I said, smiling. "To begin with."

"Yes; and only when he ceased to doubt, did he become a Christian—and a martyr. One could argue that it was surety that killed him, no?" His voice was heavy with irony. "There is a great difference between those phenomena which are accepted on faith, and those which are proved by objective determination—though the cause of both may be equally 'rational' once known. And the chief difference is this: that people will treat with disdain such phenomena as are proved by the evidence of the senses, and commonly experienced—while they will defend to the death the reality of a phenomenon which they have neither seen nor experienced.

"Faith is as powerful a force as science," he concluded, voice soft in the darkness, "—but far more dangerous."

We sat quietly for a time, looking over the bow of the tiny ship, toward the thin slice of darkness that divided the night, darker than the purple glow of the sky, or the silver-gray sea. The black island of Hispaniola, drawing inexorably closer.

"Where did you see the headless fish?" I asked suddenly, and was not surprised to see the faint inclination of his head toward the bow.

"There," he said. "I have seen a good many odd things among these islands—but perhaps more there than anywhere else. Some places are like that."

I didn't speak for several minutes, pondering what might lie
.ead—and hoping that Ishmael had been right in saying that it
.as Ian whom Geillis had taken with her to Abandawe. A thought
.curred to me—one that had been lost or pushed aside during the
.ents of the last twenty-four hours.

"Lawrence—the other Scottish boys. Ishmael told us he saw
.elve of them, including Ian. When you were searching the plan-
.tion . . . did you find any trace of the others?"

He drew in his breath sharply, but did not answer at once. I
.uld feel him, turning over words in his mind, trying to decide
.w to say what the chill in my bones had already told me.

The answer, when it came, was not from Lawrence, but from
.mie.

"We found them," he said softly, from the darkness. His hand
.sted on my knee, and squeezed gently. "Dinna ask more, Sasse-
.ch—for I willna tell ye."

I understood. Ishmael had to have been right; it must be Ian
.ith Geilie, for Jamie could bear no other possibility. I laid a hand
. his head, and he stirred slightly, turning so that his breath
.uched my hand.

"Blest are they who have not seen," I whispered under my
.eath, *"but have believed."*

We dropped anchor near dawn, in a small, nameless bay on the
.rthern coast of Hispaniola. There was a narrow beach, faced
.ith cliffs, and through a split in the rock, a narrow, sandy trail
.as visible, leading into the interior of the island.

Jamie carried me the few steps to shore, set me down, and then
.rned to Innes, who had splashed ashore with one of the parcels
. food.

"I thank ye, *a charaid*," he said formally. "We shall part here;
.ith the Virgin's blessing, we will meet here again in four days'
.ne."

Innes's narrow face contracted in surprised disappointment;
.en resignation settled on his features.

"Aye," he said. "I'll mind the boatie then, 'til ye all come
.ck."

Jamie saw the expression, and shook his head, smiling.

"Not just you, man; did I need a strong arm, it would be yours I

should call on first. No, all of ye shall stay, save my wife and th
Jew.''

Resignation was replaced by sheer surprise.

''Stay here? All of us? But will ye not have need of us, Ma
Dubh?'' He squinted anxiously at the cliffs, with their burden o
flowering vines. ''It looks a fearsome place to venture into, with
out friends.''

''I shall count it the act of greatest friendship for ye to wa
here, as I say, Duncan,'' Jamie said, and I realized with a sligl
shock that I had never known Innes's given name.

Innes glanced again at the cliffs, his lean face troubled, the
bent his head in acquiescence.

''Well, it's you as shall say, Mac Dubh. But ye ken we ar
willing—all of us.''

Jamie nodded, his face turned away.

''Aye, I ken that fine, Duncan,'' he said softly. Then he turne
back, held out an arm, and Innes embraced him, his one arr
awkwardly thumping Jamie's back.

''If a ship should come,'' Jamie said, letting go, ''then I wish y
to take heed for yourselves. The Royal Navy will be looking fo
that pinnace, aye? I doubt they shall come here, looking, but
they should—or if anything else at all should threaten ye—the
leave. Sail away at once.''

''And leave ye here? Nay, ye can order me to do a great man
things, Mac Dubh, and do them I shall—but not that.''

Jamie frowned and shook his head; the rising sun struck spark
from his hair and the stubble of his beard, wreathing his head i
fire.

''It will do me and my wife no good to have ye killed, Duncar
Mind what I say. If a ship comes—go.'' He turned aside then, ar
went to take leave of the other Scots.

Innes sighed deeply, his face etched with disapproval, but h
made no further protest.

It was hot and damp in the jungle, and there was little tal
among the three of us as we made our way inland. There wa
nothing to say, after all; Jamie and I could not speak of Briann
before Lawrence, and there were no plans to be made until w
reached Abandawe, and saw what was there. I dozed fitfully a

ght, waking several times to see Jamie, back against a tree near
e, eyes fixed sightless on the fire.

At noon of the second day, we reached the place. A steep and
cky hillside of gray limestone rose before us, sprouted over with
iky aloes and a ruffle of coarse grass. And on the crest of the
ll, I could see them. Great standing stones, megaliths, in a rough
rcle about the crown of the hill.

"You didn't say there was a stone circle," I said. I felt faint, and
t only from the heat and damp.

"Are you quite well, Mrs. Fraser?" Lawrence peered at me in
me alarm, his genial face flushed beneath its tan.

"Yes," I said, but my face must as usual have given me away,
r Jamie was there in a moment, taking my arm and steadying me
ith a hand about my waist.

"For God's sake, be careful, Sassenach!" he muttered. "Dinna
 near those things!"

"We have to know if Geilie's there, with Ian," I said. "Come
." I forced my reluctant feet into motion, and he came with me,
ill muttering under his breath in Gaelic—I thought it was a
ayer.

"They were put up a very long time ago," Lawrence said, as we
me up onto the crest of the hill, within a few feet of the stones.
Not by slaves—by the aboriginal inhabitants of the islands."

The circle was empty, and innocent-looking. No more than a
aggered circle of large stones, set on end, motionless under the
n. Jamie was watching my face anxiously.

"Can ye hear them, Claire?" he said. Lawrence looked startled,
ut said nothing as I advanced carefully toward the nearest stone.

"I don't know," I said. "It isn't one of the proper days—not a
un Feast, or a Fire Feast, I mean. It may not be open now; I don't
ow."

Holding tightly to Jamie's hand, I edged forward, listening.
here seemed a faint hum in the air, but it might be no more than
e usual sound of the jungle insects. Very gently, I laid the palm
f my hand against the nearest stone.

I was dimly conscious of Jamie calling my name. Somewhere,
y mind was struggling on a physical level, making the conscious
fort to lift and lower my diaphragm, to squeeze and release the
ambers of my heart. My ears were filled with a pulsating hum, a
ibration too deep for sound, that throbbed in the marrow of my

bones. And in some small, still place in the center of the chaos wa
Geilie Duncan, green eyes smiling into mine.

"Claire!"

I was lying on the ground, Jamie and Lawrence bending ove
me, faces dark and anxious against the sky. There was dampnes
on my cheeks, and a trickle of water ran down my neck. I blinke
cautiously moving my extremities, to be sure I still possesse
them.

Jamie put down the handkerchief with which he had been bath
ing my face, and lifted me to a sitting position.

"Are ye all right, Sassenach?"

"Yes," I said, still mildly confused. "Jamie—she's here!"

"Who? Mrs. Abernathy?" Lawrence's heavy eyebrows shot up
and he glanced hastily behind him, as though expecting her t
materialize on the spot.

"I heard her—saw her—whatever." My wits were comin
slowly back. "She's here. Not in the circle; close by."

"Can ye tell where?" Jamie's hand was resting on his dirk, a
he darted quick glances all around us.

I shook my head, and closed my eyes, trying—reluctantly—t
recapture that moment of seeing. There was an impression o
darkness, of damp coolness, and the flicker of red torchlight.

"I think she's in a cave," I said, amazed. "Is it close by
Lawrence?"

"It is," he said, watching my face with intense curiosity. "Th
entrance is not far from here."

"Take us there." Jamie was on his feet, lifting me to mine.

"Jamie." I stopped him with a hand on his arm.

"Aye?"

"Jamie—she knows I'm here, too."

That stopped him, all right. He paused, and I saw him swallov
Then his jaw tightened, and he nodded.

"A Mhìcheal bheannaichte, dìon sinn bho dheamhainnean," h
said softly, and turned toward the edge of the hill. Blessed M
chael, defend us from demons.

The blackness was absolute. I brought my hand to my face; fe
my palm brush my nose, but saw nothing. It wasn't an empt
blackness, though. The floor of the passage was uneven, wit

all sharp particles that crunched underfoot, and the walls in
me places grew so close together that I wondered how Geilie
d ever managed to squeeze through.

Even in the places where the passage grew wider, and the stone
alls were too far away for my outstretched hands to brush
ainst, I could feel them. It was like being in a dark room with
other person—someone who kept quite silent, but whose pres-
ce I could feel, never more than an arm's length away.

Jamie's hand was tight on my shoulder, and I could feel his
esence behind me, a warm disturbance in the cool void of the
ve.

"Are we headed right?" he asked, when I stopped for a mo-
ent to catch my breath. "There are passages to the sides; I feel
em as we pass. How can ye tell where we're going?"

"I can hear. Hear them. It. Don't you hear?" It was a struggle
speak, to form coherent thoughts. The call here was different;
t the beehive sound of Craigh na Dun, but a hum like the
bration of the air following the striking of a great bell. I could
el it ringing in the long bones of my arms, echoing through
ctoral girdle and spine.

Jamie gripped my arm hard.

"Stay with me!" he said. "Sassenach—don't let it take ye;
ay!"

I reached blindly out and he caught me tight against his chest.
he thump of his heart against my temple was louder than the
m.

"Jamie. Jamie, hold on to me." I had never been more fright-
ed. "Don't let me go. If it takes me—Jamie, I can't come back
ain. It's worse every time. It will kill me, Jamie!"

His arms tightened round me 'til I felt my ribs crack, and
sped for breath. After a moment, he let go, and putting me
ntly aside, moved past me into the passage, taking care to keep
s hand always on me.

"I'll go first," he said. "Put your hand in my belt, and dinna let
for anything."

Linked together, we moved slowly down, farther into the dark.
awrence had wanted to come, but Jamie would not let him. We
d left him at the mouth of the cave, waiting. If we should not
turn, he was to go back to the beach, to keep the rendezvous
th Innes and the other Scots.

If we should not return . . .

He must have felt my grip tighten, for he stopped, and drew m
alongside him.

"Claire," he said softly. "I must say something."

I knew already, and groped for his mouth to stop him, but m
hand brushed by his face in the dark. He gripped my wrist, an
held tight.

"If it will be a choice between her and one of us—then it mu
be me. Ye know that, aye?"

I knew that. If Geilie should be there, still, and one of us migh
be killed in stopping her, it must be Jamie to take the risk. For wit
Jamie dead, I would be left—and I could follow her through th
stone, which he could not.

"I know," I whispered at last. I knew also what he did not say
and what he knew as well; that should Geilie have gone throug
already, then I must go as well.

"Then kiss me, Claire," he whispered. "And know that you ar
more to me than life, and I have no regret."

I couldn't answer, but kissed him, first his hand, its crooke
fingers warm and firm, and the brawny wrist of a sword-wielde
and then his mouth, haven and promise and anguish all mingle
and the salt of tears in the taste of him.

Then I let go, and turned toward the left-hand tunnel.

"This way," I said. Within ten paces, I saw the light.

It was no more than a faint glow on the rocks of the passage, bu
it was enough to restore the gift of sight. Suddenly, I could see m
hands and feet, though dimly. My breath came out in somethin
like a sob, of relief and fear. I felt like a ghost taking shape as
walked toward the light and the soft bell-hum before me.

The light was stronger, now, then dimmed again as Jamie slid i
front of me, and his back blocked my view. Then he bent an
stepped through a low archway. I followed, and stood up in ligh

It was a good-sized chamber, the walls farthest from the torc
still cold and black with the slumber of the cave. The wall befor
us had wakened, though. It flickered and gleamed, particles (
embedded mineral reflecting the flames of a pine torch, fixed in
crevice.

"So ye came, did you?" Geillis was on her knees, eyes fixed o
a glittering stream of white powder that fell from her folded fis
drawing a line on the dark floor.

I heard a small sound from Jamie, half relief, half horror, as he w Ian. The boy lay in the middle of the pentacle on his side, nds bound behind him, gagged with a strip of white cloth. Next him lay an ax. It was made of a shiny dark stone, like obsidian, ith a sharp, chipped edge. The handle was covered with gaudy adwork, in an African pattern of stripes and zigzags.

"Don't come any closer, fox." Geilie sat back on her heels, owing her teeth to Jamie in an expression that was not a smile. ne held a pistol in one hand; its fellow, charged and cocked, was rust through the leather belt she wore about her waist.

Eyes fixed on Jamie, she reached into the pouch suspended om the belt and withdrew another handful of diamond dust. I uld see beads of sweat standing on her broad white brow; the ll-hum from the time-passage must be reaching her as it reached e. I felt sick, and the sweat ran down my body in trickles under y clothes.

The pattern was almost finished. With the pistol carefully ained, she dribbled out the thin, shining stream until she had mpleted the pentagram. The stones were already laid inside it— ey glinted from the floor in sparks of color, connected by a eaming line of poured quicksilver.

"There, then." She sat back on her heels with a sigh of relief, d wiped the thick, creamy hair back with one hand. "Safe. The amond dust keeps out the noise," she explained to me. "Nasty, n't it?"

She patted Ian, who lay bound and gagged on the ground in ont of her, his eyes wide with fear above the white cloth of the g. "There, there, *mo chridhe.* Dinna fret, it will be soon over."

"Take your hand off him, ye wicked bitch!" Jamie took an npulsive step forward, hand on his dirk, then stopped, as she fted the barrel of the pistol an inch.

"Ye mind me o' your uncle Dougal, *a sionnach,*" she said, ting her head to one side coquettishly. "He was older when I et him than you are now, but you've the look of him about ye, e? Like ye'd take what ye pleased and damn anyone who stands your way."

Jamie looked at Ian, curled on the floor, then up at Geilie.

"I'll take what's mine," he said softly.

"But ye can't, now, can ye?" she said, pleasantly. "One more ep, and I kill ye dead. I spare ye now, only because Claire seems fond of ye.'' Her eyes shifted to me, standing in the shadow behind Jamie. She nodded to me.

''A life for a life, sweet Claire. Ye tried to save me once, c Craigh na Dun; I saved you from the witch-trial at Cranesmui We're quits now, aye?''

Geilie picked up a small bottle, uncorked it, and poured th contents carefully over Ian's clothes. The smell of brandy rose u strong and heady, and the torch flared brighter as the fumes c alcohol reached it. Ian bucked and kicked, making a strained noi of protest, and she kicked him sharply in the ribs.

''Be still!'' she said.

''Don't do it, Geilie,'' I said, knowing that words would do r good.

''I have to,'' she said calmly. ''I'm meant to. I'm sorry I sha have to take the girl, but I'll leave ye the man.''

''What girl?'' Jamie's, fists were clenched tight at his sid knuckles white even in the dim torchlight.

''Brianna? That's the name, isn't it?'' She shook back he heavy hair, smoothing it out of her face. ''The last of Lovat line.'' She smiled at me. ''What luck ye should have come to se me, aye? I'd never ha' kent it, otherwise. I thought they'd all die out before 1900.''

A thrill of horror shot through me. I could feel the same trem run through Jamie as his muscles tightened.

It must have shown on his face. Geilie cried out sharply an leapt back. She fired as he lunged at her. His head snapped bac and his body twisted, hands still reaching for her throat. Then h fell, his body limp across the edge of the glittering pentagran There was a strangled moan from Ian.

I felt rather than heard a sound rise in my throat. I didn't kno what I had said, but Geilie turned her face in my direction, sta tled.

When Brianna was two, a car had carelessly sideswiped min hitting the back door next to where she was sitting. I slowed to stop, checked briefly to see that she was unhurt, and then bounde out, headed for the other car, which had pulled over a little wa ahead.

The other driver was a man in his thirties, quite large, an probably entirely self-assured in his dealings with the world. H

▸ked over his shoulder, saw me coming, and hastily rolled up his
▸ndow, shrinking back in his seat.

▸ had no consciousness of rage or any other emotion; I simply
▸w, with no shadow of doubt, that I could—and would—shatter
▸ window with my hand, and drag the man out through it. He
▸w it, too.

▸ thought no further than that, and didn't have to; the arrival of a
▸lice car had recalled me to my normal state of mind, and then I
▸rted to shake. But the memory of the look on that man's face
yed with me.

▸Fire is a poor illuminator, but it would have taken total darkness
conceal that look on Geilie's face; the sudden realization of
▸at was coming toward her.

▸She jerked the other pistol from her belt and swung it to bear on
▸; I saw the round hole of the muzzle clearly—and didn't care.
▸e roar of the discharge caromed through the cave, the echoes
▸ding down showers of rocks and dirt, but by then I had seized
▸ ax from the floor.

▸ noted quite clearly the leather binding, ornamented with a
▸ded pattern. It was red, with yellow zigzags and black dots.
▸e dots echoed the shiny obsidian of the blade, and the red and
▸low picked up the hues of the flaming torch behind her.

▸ heard a noise behind me, but didn't turn. Reflections of the fire
▸rned red in the pupils of her eyes. *The red thing,* Jamie had
▸led it. *I gave myself to it,* he had said.

▸ didn't need to give myself; it had taken me.

There was no fear, no rage, no doubt. Only the stroke of the
▸inging ax.

The shock of it echoed up my arm, and I let go, my fingers
▸mbed. I stood quite still, not even moving when she staggered
▸ward me.

▸Blood in firelight is black, not red.

▸She took one blind step forward and fell, all her muscles gone
▸p, making no attempt to save herself. The last I saw of her face
▸s her eyes; set wide, beautiful as gemstones, a green water-clear
▸d faceted with the knowledge of death.

▸Someone was speaking, but the words made no sense. The cleft
▸ the rock buzzed loudly, filling my ears. The torch flickered,
▸ring sudden yellow in a draft; the beating of the dark angel's
▸ngs, I thought.

The sound came again, behind me.

I turned and saw Jamie. He had risen to his knees, swayir
Blood was pouring from his scalp, dyeing one side of his face re
black. The other side was white as a harlequin's mask.

Stop the bleeding, said some remnant of instinct in my bra
and I fumbled for a handkerchief. But by then he had crawled
where Ian lay, and was groping at the boy's bonds, jerking loo
the leather straps, drops of his blood pattering on the lad's shi
Ian squirmed to his feet, his face ghastly pale, and put out a ha
to help his uncle.

Then Jamie's hand was on my arm. I looked up, numbly offe
ing the cloth. He took it and wiped it roughly over his face, th
jerked at my arm, pulling me toward the tunnel mouth. I stumbl
and nearly fell, caught myself, and came back to the present.

"Come!" he was saying. "Can ye not hear the wind? There i
storm coming, above."

Wind? I thought. In a cave? But he was right; the draft had n
been my imagination; the faint exhalation from the crack near t
entrance had changed to a steady, whining wind, almost a keenir
that rang in the narrow passage.

I turned to look over my shoulder, but Jamie grasped my ar
hard and pushed me forward. My last sight of the cave was
blurred impression of jet and rubies, with a still white shape in t
middle of the floor. Then the draft came in with a roar, and t
torch went out.

"Jesus!" It was Young Ian's voice, filled with terror, som
where close by. "Uncle Jamie!"

"Here." Jamie's voice came out of the darkness just in front
me, surprisingly calm, raised to be heard above the noise. "He
lad. Come here to me, Ian. Dinna be afraid; it's only the ca
breathing."

It was the wrong thing to say. When he said it, I could *feel* t
cold breath of the rock touch my neck, and the hairs there rose
prickling. The image of the cave as a living thing, breathing a
around us, blind and malevolent, struck me cold with horror.

Apparently the notion was as terrifying to Ian as it was to m
for I heard a faint gasp, and then his groping hand struck me ar
clung for dear life to my arm.

I clutched his hand with one of mine and probed the dark ahea

ith the other, finding Jamie's reassuringly large shape almost at
nce.

"I've got Ian," I said. "For God's sake, let's get out of here!"

He gripped my hand in answer, and linked together, we began to
ake our way back down the winding tunnel, stumbling through
ie pitch dark and stepping on each other's heels. And all the time,
at ghostly wind whined at our backs.

I could see nothing; no hint of Jamie's shirt in front of my face,
nowy white as I knew it to be, not even a flicker of the movement
f my own light-colored skirts, though I heard them swish about
iy feet as I walked, the sound blending with that of the wind.

The thin rush of air rose and fell in pitch, whispering and
vailing. I tried to force my mind away from the memory of what
iy behind us, away from the morbid fancy that the wind held
ghing voices, whispering secrets just past hearing.

"I can hear her," Ian said suddenly behind me. His voice rose,
racking with panic. "I can hear her! God, oh God, she's com-
ig!"

I froze in my tracks, a scream wedged in my throat. The cool
bserver in my head knew quite well it was not so—only the wind
nd Ian's fright—but that made no difference to the spurt of sheer
:rror that rose from the pit of my stomach and turned my bowels
› water. I knew she was coming, too, and screamed out loud.

Then Jamie had me, and Ian too, gripped tight against him, one
i each arm, our ears muffled against his chest. He smelled of pine
moke and sweat and brandy, and I nearly sobbed in relief at the
loseness of him.

"Hush!" he said fiercely. "Hush, the both of ye! I willna let
er touch ye. Never!" He pressed us to him, hard; I felt his heart
eating fast beneath my cheek and Ian's bony shoulder, squeezed
gainst mine, and then the pressure relaxed.

"Come along now," Jamie said, more quietly. "It's but wind.
'aves blow through their cracks when the weather changes above-
round. I've heard it before. There is a storm coming, outside.
'ome, now."

The storm was a brief one. By the time we had stumbled to the
urface, blinking against the shock of sunlight, the rain had
assed, leaving the world reborn in its wake.

Lawrence was sheltering under a dripping palm near the cave's entrance. When he saw us, he sprang to his feet, a look of relief relaxing the creases of his face.

"It is all right?" he said, looking from me to a blood-stained Jamie.

Jamie gave him half a smile, nodding.

"It is all right," he said. He turned and motioned to Ian. "May I present my nephew, Ian Murray? Ian, this is Dr. Stern, who's been of great assistance to us in looking for ye."

"I'm much obliged to ye, Doctor," Ian said, with a bob of his head. He wiped a sleeve across his streaked face, and glanced at Jamie.

"I knew ye'd come, Uncle Jamie," he said, with a tremulous smile, "but ye left it a bit late, aye?" The smile widened, then broke, and he began to tremble. He blinked hard, fighting back tears.

"I did then, and I'm sorry, Ian. Come here, *a bhalaich.*" Jamie reached out and took him in a close embrace, patting his back and murmuring to him in Gaelic.

I watched for a moment, before I realized that Lawrence was speaking to me.

"Are you quite well, Mrs. Fraser?" he was asking. Without waiting for an answer, he took my arm.

"I don't quite know." I felt completely empty. Exhausted as though by childbirth, but without the exultation of spirit. Nothing seemed quite real; Jamie, Ian, Lawrence, all seemed like toy figures that moved and talked at a distance, making noises that I had to strain to understand.

"I think perhaps we should leave this place," Lawrence said, with a glance at the cave mouth from which we had just emerged. He looked slightly uneasy. He didn't ask about Mrs. Abernathy.

"I think you are right." The picture of the cave we had left was vivid in my mind—but just as unreal as the vivid green jungle and gray stones around us. Not waiting for the men to follow, I turned and walked away.

The feeling of remoteness increased as we walked. I felt like an automaton, built around an iron core, walking by clockwork. I followed Jamie's broad back through branches and clearings, shadow and sun, not noticing where we were going. Sweat ran down my sides and into my eyes, but I barely stirred to wipe it

ay. At length, toward sunset, we stopped in a small clearing
r a stream, and made our primitive camp.

I had already discovered that Lawrence was a most useful per-
a to have along on a camping trip. He was not only as good at
ding or building shelter as was Jamie, but was sufficiently fa-
liar with the flora and fauna of the area to be able to plunge into
: jungle and return within half an hour bearing handfuls of
ble roots, fungi, and fruit with which to augment the Spartan
ions in our packs.

Ian was set to gather firewood while Lawrence foraged, and I sat
nie down with a pan of water, to tend the damage to his head. I
shed away the blood from face and hair, to find to my surprise
t the ball had in fact not plowed a furrow through his scalp as I
d thought. Instead, it had pierced the skin just above his hairline
d—evidently—vanished into his head. There was no sign of an
t wound. Unnerved by this, I prodded his scalp with increasing
itation, until a sudden cry from the patient announced that I had
covered the bullet.

There was a large, tender lump on the back of his head. The
tol ball had traveled under the skin, skimming the curve of his
ull, and come to rest just over his occiput.

"Jesus H. Christ!" I exclaimed. I felt it again, unbelieving, but
re it was. "You always said your head was solid bone, and I'll
damned if you weren't right. She shot you point-blank, and the
ody ball bounced off your skull!"

Jamie, supporting his head in his hands as I examined him,
de a sound somewhere between a snort and a groan.

"Aye, well," he said, his voice somewhat muffled in his hands,
'll no say I'm not thick-heided, but if Mistress Abernathy had
ed a full charge of powder, it wouldna have been nearly thick
ough."

"Does it hurt a lot?"

"Not the wound, no, though it's sore. I've a terrible headache,
ough."

"I shouldn't wonder. Hold on a bit; I'm going to take the ball
t."

Not knowing in what condition we might find Ian, I had brought
e smallest of my medical boxes, which fortunately contained a
ttle of alcohol and a small scalpel. I shaved away a little of
mie's abundant mane, just below the swelling, and soused the

area with alcohol for disinfection. My fingers were chilled fr[c]
the alcohol, but his head was warm and comfortingly live to t
touch.

"Three deep breaths and hold on tight," I murmured. "I
going to cut you, but it will be fast."

"All right." The back of his neck looked a little pale, but t
pulse was steady. He obligingly drew in his breath deeply, a
exhaled, sighing. I held the area of scalp taut between the ind
and third fingers of my left hand. On the third breath, I sa
"Right now," and drew the blade hard and quick across the sca[l]
He grunted slightly, but didn't cry out. I pressed gently with r
right thumb against the swelling, slightly harder—and the b[.]
popped out of the incision I had made, falling into my left ha[n]
like a grape.

"Got it," I said, and only then realized that I had been holdi[n]
my breath. I dropped the little pellet—somewhat flattened by
contact with his skull—into his hand, and smiled, a little shaki[.]
"Souvenir," I said. I pressed a pad of cloth against the sm[.]
wound, wound a strip of cloth round his head to hold it, and th[.]
quite suddenly, with no warning whatever, began to cry.

I could feel the tears rolling down my face, and my shoulde[r]
shaking, but I felt still detached; somehow outside my body. I w[.]
conscious mostly of a mild amazement.

"Sassenach? Are ye all right?" Jamie was peering up at m[.]
eyes worried under the rakish bandage.

"Yes," I said, stuttering from the force of my crying. [.]
d-don't k-know why I'm c-crying. I d-don't know!"

"Come here." He took my hand and drew me down onto h[.]
knee. He wrapped his arms around me and held me tight, resti[.]
his cheek on the top of my head.

"It will be all right," he whispered. "It's fine now, *mo chridh[.]*
it's fine." He rocked me gently, one hand stroking my hair a[.]
neck, and murmured small unimportant things in my ear. Just [.]
suddenly as I had been detached, I was back inside my bod[.]
warm and shaking, feeling the iron core dissolve in my tears.

Gradually I stopped weeping, and lay still against his che[.]
hiccuping now and then, feeling nothing but peace and the co[.]
fort of his presence.

I was dimly aware that Lawrence and Ian had returned, but pa[.]
no attention to them. At one point, I heard Ian say, with mo[.]

riosity than alarm, "You're bleeding all down the back of your
ck, Uncle Jamie."

"Perhaps you'll fix me a new bandage, then, Ian," Jamie said.
s voice was soft and unconcerned. "I must just hold your auntie
w." And sometime later I went to sleep, still held tight in the
cle of his arms.

I woke up later, curled on a blanket next to Jamie. He was
ning against a tree, one hand resting on my shoulder. He felt me
ke, and squeezed gently. It was dark, and I could hear a rhyth-
c snoring somewhere close at hand. It must be Lawrence, I
ught drowsily, for I could hear Young Ian's voice, on the other
e of Jamie.

"No," he was saying slowly, "it wasna really so bad, on the
p. We were all kept together, so there was company from the
er lads, and they fed us decently, and let us out two at a time to
lk about the deck. Of course, we were all scairt, for we'd no
tion why we'd been taken—and none of the sailors would tell us
ything—but we were not mistreated."

The *Bruja* had sailed up the Yallahs River, and delivered her
man cargo directly to Rose Hall. Here the bewildered boys had
en warmly welcomed by Mrs. Abernathy, and promptly popped
o a new prison.

The basement beneath the sugar mill had been fitted up com-
tably enough, with beds and chamber pots, and aside from the
ise of the sugar-making above during the days, it was comfort-
le enough. Still, none of the boys could think why they were
re, though any number of suggestions were made, each more
probable than the last.

"And every now and then, a great black fellow would come
wn into the place with Mrs. Abernathy. We always begged to
ow what it was we were there for, and would she not be letting
go, for mercy's sake? but she only smiled and patted us and
d we would see, in good time. Then she would choose a lad, and
: black fellow would clamp on to the lad's arm and take him
a' wi' them." Ian's voice sounded distressed, and little wonder.

"Did the lads come back again?" Jamie asked. His hand patted
: softly, and I reached up and pressed it.

"No—or not usually. And that scairt us all something drea~~dful~~ ful."

Ian's turn had come eight weeks after his arrival. Three lads ha~~d~~ gone and not returned by then, and when Mistress Abernathy~~'s~~ bright green eyes rested on him, he was not disposed to coopera~~te~~

"I kicked the black fellow, and hit him—I even bit his hand. Ian said ruefully, "and verra nasty he tasted, too—all over som~~e~~ kind of grease, he was. But it made nay difference; he only clout~~ed~~ me over the head, hard enough to make my ears ring, then pick~~ed~~ me up and carried me off in his arms, as though I was no mo~~re~~ than a wee bairn."

Ian had been taken into the kitchen, where he was stripp~~ed~~ bathed, dressed in a clean shirt—but nothing else—and taken ~~to~~ the main house.

"It was just at night," he said wistfully, "and all the windo~~ws~~ lighted. It looked verra much like Lallybroch, when ye come do~~wn~~ from the hills just at dark, and Mam's just lit the lamps—it alm~~ost~~ broke my heart to see it, and think of home."

He had had little opportunity to feel homesick, though. Herc~~u~~les—or Atlas—had marched him up the stairs into what was ob~~vi~~ously Mistress Abernathy's bedroom. Mrs. Abernathy was waiti~~ng~~ for him, dressed in a soft, loose sort of gown with odd-looki~~ng~~ figures embroidered round the hem of it in red and silver threa~~d~~

She had been cordial and welcoming, and had offered him ~~a~~ drink. It smelled strange, but not nasty, and as he had little choi~~ce~~ in the matter, he had drunk it.

There were two comfortable chairs in the room, on either side ~~of~~ a long, low table, and a great bed at one side, swagged and can~~o~~pied like a king's. He had sat in one chair, Mrs. Abernathy in ~~the~~ other, and she had asked him questions.

"What sorts of questions?" Jamie asked, prompting as I~~an~~ seemed hesitant.

"Well, all about my home, and my family—she asked t~~he~~ names of all my sisters and brothers, and my aunts and uncles"~~—~~ I jerked a bit. So that *was* why Geilie had betrayed no surprise ~~at~~ our appearance! —"and all sorts of things, Uncle. Then she—s~~he~~ asked me had I—had I ever lain wi' a lassie. Just as though s~~he~~ were asking did I have parritch to my breakfast!" Ian sound~~ed~~ shocked at the memory.

"I didna want to answer her, but I couldna seem to help myse~~lf~~

elt verra warm, like I was fevered, and I couldna seem to move
sy. But I answered all her questions, and her just sitting there,
easant as might be, watching me close wi' those big green
es.''

"So ye told her the truth?"

"Aye. Aye, I did." Ian spoke slowly, reliving the scene. "I said
ad, and I told her about—about Edinburgh, and the printshop,
d the seaman, and the brothel, and Mary, and—everything.''

For the first time, Geilie had seemed displeased with one of his
swers. Her face had grown hard and her eyes narrowed, and for
moment, Ian was seriously afraid. He would have run, then, but
r the heaviness in his limbs, and the presence of the giant who
od against the door, unmoving.

"She got up and stamped about a bit, and said I was ruined,
en, as I wasna a virgin, and what business did a bittie wee lad
e me have, to be goin' wi' the lassies and spoiling myself?''
Then she had stopped her ranting, poured a glass of wine and
ank it off, and her temper had seemed to cool.

"She laughed then, and looked at me careful, and said as how I
ight not be such a loss, after all. If I was no good for what she
d in mind, perhaps I might have other uses." Ian's voice
unded faintly constricted, as though his collar were too tight.
mie made a soothing interrogatory sound, though, and he took a
ep breath, determined to go on.

"Well, she—she took my hand and made me stand up. Then she
ok off the shirt I was wearing, and she—I swear it's true, Uncle!
she knelt on the floor in front of me, and took my cock into her
outh!''

Jamie's hand tightened on my shoulder, but his voice betrayed
more than a mild interest.

"Aye, I believe ye, Ian. She made love to ye, then?''

"Love?" Ian sounded dazed. "No—I mean, I dinna ken. It—
e—well, she got my cock to stand up, and then she made me
me to the bed and lie down and she did things. But it wasna at
like it was with wee Mary!''

"No, I shouldna suppose it was," his uncle said dryly.

"God, it felt queer!" I could sense Ian's shudder from the tone
his voice. "I looked up in the middle, and there was the black
an, standing right by the bed, holding a candlestick. She told him
lift it higher, so that she could see better." He paused, and I

heard a small glugging noise as he drank from one of the bottle He let out a long, quivering breath.

"Uncle. Have ye ever—lain wi' a woman, when ye didna wa to do it?"

Jamie hesitated a moment, his hand tight on my shoulder, b then he said quietly, "Aye, Ian. I have."

"Oh." The boy was quiet, and I heard him scratch his hea "D'ye ken how it can be, Uncle? How ye can do it, and not wa to a bit, and hate doing it, and—and still it—it feels good?"

Jamie gave a small, dry laugh.

"Well, what it comes to, Ian, is that your cock hasna got conscience, and you have." His hand left my shoulder as l turned toward his nephew. "Dinna trouble yourself, Ian," he sai "Ye couldna help it, and it's likely that it saved your life for y The other lads—the ones who didna come back to the cellar— d'ye ken if they were virgins?"

"Well—a few I know were for sure—for we had a great deal time to talk, aye? and after a time we kent a lot about one anothe Some o' the lads boasted of havin' gone wi' a lassie, but I thoug —from what they said about it, ye ken—that they hadna done really." He paused for a moment, as though reluctant to ask wh he knew he must.

"Uncle—d'ye ken what happened to them? The rest of the la with me?"

"No, Ian," Jamie said, evenly. "I've no notion." He lean back against the tree, sighing deeply. "D'ye think ye can slee wee Ian? If ye can, ye should, for it will be a weary walk to t shore tomorrow."

"Oh, I can sleep, Uncle," Ian assured him. "But should I n keep watch? It's you should be resting, after bein' shot and a that." He paused and then added, rather shyly, "I didna say tha ye, Uncle Jamie."

Jamie laughed, freely this time.

"You're verra welcome, Ian," he said, the smile still in h voice. "Lay your head and sleep, laddie. I'll wake ye if there need."

Ian obligingly curled up and within moments, was breathi heavily. Jamie sighed and leaned back against the tree.

"Do you want to sleep too, Jamie?" I pushed myself up to beside him. "I'm awake; I can keep an eye out."

His eyes were closed, the dying firelight dancing on the lids. He
smiled without opening them and groped for my hand.

"No. If ye dinna mind sitting with me for a bit, though, you can
watch. The headache's better if I close my eyes."

We sat in contented silence for some time, hand in hand. An
occasional odd noise or far-off scream from some jungle animal
came from the dark, but nothing seemed threatening now.

"Will we go back to Jamaica?" I asked at last. "For Fergus and
Marsali?"

Jamie started to shake his head, then stopped, with a stifled
moan.

"No," he said, "I think we shall sail for Eleuthera. That's
Dutch-owned, and neutral. We can send Innes back wi' John's
Jatie, and he can take a message to Fergus to come and join us. I
would as soon not set foot on Jamaica again, all things considered."

"No, I suppose not." I was quiet for a moment, then said, "I
wonder how Mr. Willoughby—Yi Tien Cho, I mean—will manage. I don't suppose anyone will find him, if he stays in the
mountains, but—"

"Oh, he may manage brawly," Jamie interrupted. "He's the
pelican to fish for him, after all." One side of his mouth turned up
in a smile. "For that matter, if he's canny, he'll find a way south,
to Martinique. There's a small colony there of Chinese traders. I'd
told him of it; said I'd take him there, once our business on
Jamaica was finished."

"You aren't angry at him now?" I looked at him curiously, but
his face was smooth and peaceful, almost unlined in the firelight.
This time he was careful not to move his head, but lifted one
shoulder in a shrug, and grimaced.

"Och, no." He sighed and settled himself more comfortably.
"I dinna suppose he had much thought for what he did, or understood at all what might be the end of it. And it would be foolish to
hate a man for not giving ye something he hasna got in the first
place." He opened his eyes then, with a faint smile, and I knew he
was thinking of John Grey.

Ian twitched in his sleep, snorted loudly, and rolled over onto
his back, arms flung wide. Jamie glanced at his nephew, and the
smile grew wider.

"Thank God," he said. "*He* goes back to his mother by the fir ship headed for Scotland."

"I don't know," I said, smiling. "He might not want to go bac to Lallybroch, after all this adventure."

"I dinna care whether he wants to or not," Jamie said firml "He's going, if I must pack him up in a crate. Are ye looking fc something, Sassenach?" he added, seeing me groping in the dar

"I've got it," I said, pulling the flat hypodermic case out of m pocket. I flipped it open to check the contents, squinting to see b the waning light. "Oh, good; there's enough left for one whoppin dose."

Jamie sat up a little straighter.

"I'm not fevered a bit," he said, eyeing me warily. "And if y have it in mind to shove that filthy spike into my head, ye can ju think again, Sassenach!"

"Not you," I said. "Ian. Unless you mean to send him home t Jenny riddled with syphilis and other interesting forms of th clap."

Jamie's eyebrows rose toward his hairline, and he winced at th resultant sensation.

"Ow. Syphilis? Ye think so?"

"I shouldn't be a bit surprised. Pronounced dementia is one c the symptoms of the advanced disease—though I must say : would be hard to tell in her case. Still, better safe than sorry, hm?"

Jamie snorted briefly with amusement.

"Well, that may teach Young Ian the price o' dalliance. I'd be: distract Stern while ye take the lad behind a bush for his penance though; Lawrence is a bonny man for a Jew, but he's curious. dinna want ye burnt at the stake in Kingston, after all."

"I expect that would be awkward for the Governor," I sai dryly. "Much as he might enjoy it, personally."

"I shouldna think he would, Sassenach." His dryness matchec my own. "Is my coat within reach?"

"Yes." I found the garment folded on the ground near me, an handed it to him. "Are you cold?"

"No." He leaned back, the coat laid across his knees. "It' only that I wanted to feel the bairns all close to me while I sleep." He smiled at me, folded his hands gently atop the coat and it pictures, and closed his eyes again. "Good night, Sassenach."

63

Out of the Depths

n the morning, buoyed by rest and a breakfast of biscuit and
plantain, we pressed on toward the shore in good heart—even
Ian, who ceased to limp ostentatiously after the first quarter-
e. As we came down the defile that led onto the beach, though,
emarkable sight met our eyes.

'Jesus God, it's them!'' Ian blurted. ''The pirates!'' He turned,
dy to flee back into the hills, but Jamie grasped him by the arm.
'Not pirates,'' he said. ''It's the slaves. Look!''

Unskilled in the seamanship of large vessels, the escaped slaves
the Yallahs River plantations had evidently made a slow and
ndering passage toward Hispaniola, and having somehow ared at that island, had promptly run the ship aground. The *Bruja*
canted on her side in the shallows, her keel sunk deep in the
dy mud. A very agitated group of slaves surrounded her, some
hing up and down the beach shouting, others dashing off
ard the refuge of the jungle, a few remaining to help the last of
ir number off the beached hulk.

A quick glance out to sea showed the cause of their agitation. A
ch of white showed on the horizon, growing in size even as we
ched.

'A man-of-war,'' Lawrence said, sounding interested.

amie said something under his breath in Gaelic, and Ian
nced at him, shocked.

'Out of here,'' Jamie said tersely. He pulled Ian about and gave
a shove up the defile, then grabbed my hand.

"Wait!" said Lawrence, shading his eyes. "There's anotḥ ship coming. A little one."

The Governor of Jamaica's private pinnace, to be exact, leaniṇ at a perilous angle as she shot round the curve of the bay, ḥ canvas bellied by the wind on her quarter.

Jamie stood for a split second, weighing the possibilities, thẹ grabbed my hand again.

"Let's go!" he said.

By the time we reached the edge of the beach, the pinnacẹ small boat was plowing through the shallows, Raeburn and MaͅC Leod pulling hard at the oars. I was wheezing and gulping air, ṃ knees rubbery from the run. Jamie snatched me up bodily into ḥ arms and ran into the surf, followed by Lawrence and Ian, gaspịn like whales.

I saw Gordon, a hundred yards out in the pinnace's bow, aiṃ gun at the shore, and knew we were followed. The musket dͅ charged with a puff of smoke, and Meldrum, behind hịm promptly raised his own weapon and fired. Taking it in turns, ṭ two of them covered our splashing advance, until friendly hanͅd could pull us over the side and raise the boat.

"Come about!" Innes, manning the wheel, barked the ordͅe and the boom swung across, the sails filling at once. Jamie hauͅl me to my feet and deposited me on a bench, then flung himsͅe down beside me, panting.

"Holy God," he wheezed. "Did I no—tell ye to—stay awayͅ Duncan?"

"Save your breath, Mac Dubh," Innes said, a wide grin spreaͅ ing under his mustache. "Ye havena enough to be wasting it." Ḥ shouted something to MacLeod, who nodded and did something the lines. The pinnace heeled over, changed her course, and caṃ about, headed straight out of the tiny cove—and straight towaͅ the man-of-war, now close enough for me to see the fat-lippͅe porpoise grinning beneath its bowsprit.

MacLeod bellowed something in Gaelic, accompanied by a geͅs ture that left the meaning of what he had said in no doubt. Tͅo triumphant yodel from Innes, we shot past the *Porpoise,* direcͅt under her bow and close enough to see surprised-looking heaͅd poking out from the rail above.

I looked back as we left the cove, to see the *Porpoise* stͅi heading in, massive under her three great masts. The pinnaͅ

uld never outrace her on the open sea, but in close quarters, the
tle sloop was light and maneuverable as a feather by comparison
the leviathan man-of-war.

"It's the slave ship they'll be after," Meldrum said, turning to
ok alongside me. "We saw the man-o'-war pick her up, three
iles off the island. We thought whilst they were otherwise occu-
ed, we might as well nip in and pick ye all off the beach."

"Good enough," Jamie said with a smile. His chest was still
aving, but he had recovered his breath. "I hope the *Porpoise*
ll be sufficiently occupied for the time being."

A warning shout from Raeburn indicated that this was not to be,
wever. Looking back, I could see the gleam of brass on the
rpoise's deck as the pair of long guns called stern chasers were
covered and began their process of aiming.

Now it was us at gunpoint, and I found the sensation very
jectionable. Still, we were moving, and fast, at that. Innes put
e wheel hard over, then hard again, tacking a zigzag path past
e headland.

The stern chasers boomed together. There was a splash off the
rt bow, twenty yards away, but a good deal too close for com-
rt, given the fact that a twenty-four-pound ball through the floor
the pinnace would sink us like a rock.

Innes cursed and hunched his shoulders over the wheel, his
issing arm giving him an odd, lopsided appearance. Our course
came still more erratic, and the next three tries came nowhere
ar. Then came a louder boom, and I looked back to see the side
the canted *Bruja* erupt in splinters, as the *Porpoise* came in
nge and trained her forward guns on the grounded ship.

A rain of grapeshot hit the beach, striking dead in the center of
group of fleeing slaves. Bodies—and parts of bodies—flew into
e air like black stick-figures and fell to the sand, staining it with
d blotches. Severed limbs were scattered over the beach like
iftwood.

"Holy Mary, Mother of God." Ian, white to the lips, crossed
mself, staring in horror at the beach as the shelling went on. Two
ore shots struck the *Bruja,* opening up a great hole in her side.
veral landed harmlessly in the sand, and two more found their
ark among the fleeing people. Then we were round the edge of
e headland, and heading into the open sea, the beach and its
rnage lost to view.

"Pray for us sinners, now and at the hour of our death." I finished his prayer in a whisper, and crossed himself again.

There was little conversation in the boat, beyond Jamie's givi Innes instructions for Eleuthera, and a conference between Inn and MacLeod as to the proper heading. The rest of us were t appalled by what we had just seen—and too relieved at our o escape—to want to talk.

The weather was fair, with a bright, brisk breeze, and we ma good way. By sundown, the island of Hispaniola had dropp below the horizon, and Grand Turk Island was rising to the le

I ate my small share of the available biscuit, drank a cup water, and curled myself in the bottom of the boat, lying do between Ian and Jamie to sleep. Innes, yawning, took his own r in the bow, while MacLeod and Meldrum took it in turns to m the helm through the night.

A shout woke me in the morning. I rose on one elbow, blinki with sleep and stiff from a night spent on bare, damp boar Jamie was standing by me, his hair blowing back in the morni breeze.

"What?" I asked Jamie. "What is it?"

"I dinna believe it," he said, staring aft over the rail. "It's t bloody boat again!"

I scrambled to my feet, to find that it was true; far astern w tiny white sails.

"Are you sure?" I said, squinting. "Can you tell at this d tance?"

"I can't, no," Jamie said frankly, "but Innes and MacLe can, and they say it's the bloodsucking English, right enou They'll have guessed our heading, maybe, and come after us, soon as they'd dealt with those poor black buggers on Hisp iola." He turned away from the rail, shrugging.

"Damned little to be done about it, save to hope we stay ahe of them. Innes says there's a hope of giving them the slip off Island, if we reach there by dark."

As the day wore on, we kept just out of firing distance, but In looked more and more worried.

The sea between Cat Island and Eleuthera was shallow, a filled with coral heads. A man-of-war could never follow us

e maze—but neither could we move swiftly enough through it to
oid being sunk by the *Porpoise*'s long guns. Once in those
eacherous shoals and channels, we would be sitting ducks.

At last, reluctantly, the decision was made to head east, out to
a; we could not risk slowing, and there was a slight chance of
ving the man-of-war the slip in the dark.

When dawn came, all sight of land had disappeared. The *Por-
ise,* unfortunately, had not. She was no closer, but as the wind
se along with the sun, she shook out more sail, and began to
in. With every scrap of sail already hoisted, and nowhere to
de, there was nothing we could do but run—and wait.

All through the long hours of the morning, the *Porpoise* grew
eadily larger astern. The sky had begun to cloud over, and the
ind had risen considerably, but this helped the *Porpoise,* with her
ge spread of canvas, a great deal more than it did us.

By ten o'clock, she was close enough to risk a shot. It fell far
tern, but was frightening, nonetheless. Innes squinted back over
s shoulder, judging the distance, then shook his head and settled
imly to his course. There was nothing to be gained by tacking
w; we must head straight on, as long as we could, taking evasive
tion only when it was too late for anything else.

By eleven, the *Porpoise* had drawn within a quarter-mile, and
e monotonous boom of her forward guns had begun to sound
ery ten minutes, as her gunner tried the range. If I closed my
es, I could imagine Erik Johansen, bent sweating and powder-
ained over his gun, the smoking slow-match in his hand. I hoped
at Annekje had been left on Antigua with her goats.

By eleven-thirty, it had begun to rain, and a heavy sea was
nning. A sudden gust of wind struck us sideways, and the boat
eled over far enough to bring the port rail within a foot of the
ater. Dumped onto the deck by the motion, we disentangled
irselves as Innes and MacLeod skillfully righted the pinnace. I
anced back, as I did every few minutes, despite myself, and saw
e seamen scampering aloft in the *Porpoise,* reefing the topsails.

"That's luck!" MacGregor shouted in my ear, nodding where I
as looking. "That'll slow them."

By twelve-thirty, the sky had gone a peculiar purple-green, and
e wind had risen to an eerie whine. The *Porpoise* had taken in
t more canvas, and in spite of the action, had had a staysail
rried away, the scrap of canvas jerked from the mast and

whipped away, flapping like an albatross. She had long sin
stopped firing on us, unable to aim at such a small target in t
heavy swell.

With the sun gone from sight, I could no longer estimate tim
The storm caught us squarely, perhaps an hour later. There was
possibility of hearing anything; by sign language and grimace
Innes made the men lower the sails; to keep canvas flying, or ev
reefed, was to risk having the mast ripped from the floorboards

I clung tight to the rail with one hand, to Ian's hand with t
other. Jamie crouched behind us, arms spread to give us the shelt
of his back. The rain lashed past, hard enough to sting the ski
driven almost horizontal by the wind, and so thick that I bare
saw the faint shape on the horizon that I thought was Eleuther

The sea had risen to terrifying heights, with swells rolling for
feet high. The pinnace rode them lightly, carried up and up and
to dizzy heights, then dropped abruptly into a trough. Jamie's fa
was dead white in the storm-light, his sodden hair pasted again
his scalp.

It was near dark that it happened. The sky was nearly black, b
there was an eerie green glow all across the horizon that silho
etted the skeletal shape of the *Porpoise* behind us. Another of t
rain squalls slammed us sideways, lurching and swaying atop
huge wave.

As we picked ourselves up from yet another bruising spi
Jamie grabbed my arm, and pointed behind us. The *Porpoise*
foremast was oddly bent, the top of it leaning far to one sid
Before I had time to realize what was happening, the top fifte
feet of the mast had split off and pitched into the sea, carryir
with it rigging and spars.

The man-of-war swung heavily round this impromptu ancho
and came sliding sideways down the face of a wave. The wall
water towered over the ship, and came crashing down, catching h
broadside. The *Porpoise* heeled, spun around once. The next wav
rose, and took her stern first, pulling the high aft deck below t
water, whipping the masts through the air like snapping twigs.

It took three more waves to sink her; no time for escape for h
hapless crew, but plenty for those of us watching to share the
terror. There was a great bubbling flurry in the trough of a wav
and the man-of-war was gone.

Jamie's arm was rigid as iron beneath my hand. All the me

tared back, faces gone empty with horror. All save Innes, who
rouched doggedly over the wheel, meeting each wave as it came.

A new wave rose up beside the rail and seemed to hover there,
ooming above me. The great wall of water was glassy clear; I
ould see suspended in it the debris and the men of the wrecked
Porpoise, limbs outflung in grotesque ballet. The body of Thomas
Leonard hung no more than ten feet from me, drowned mouth
ipen in surprise, his long soft hair aswirl above the gilded collar of
iis coat.

Then the wave struck. I was snatched off the deck, and at once
ngulfed in chaos. Blind and deaf, unable to breathe, I was tum-
iled through space, my arms and legs wrenched awry by the force
if the water.

Everything was dark; there was nothing but sensation, and all of
hat intense but indistinguishable. Pressure and noise and over-
vhelming cold. I couldn't feel the pull of my clothing, or the jerk
if the rope—if it was still there—around my waist. A sudden faint
varmth swathed my legs, distinct in the surrounding cold as a
loud in a clear sky. Urine, I thought, but didn't know whether it
vas my own, or the last touch of another human body, swallowed
s I was in the belly of the wave.

My head hit something with a sickening crack, and suddenly I
vas coughing my lungs out on the deck of the pinnace, still mirac-
ilously afloat. I sat up slowly, choking and wheezing. My rope
vas still in place, yanked so tight about my waist that I was sure
ny lower ribs were broken. I jerked feebly at it, trying to breathe,
nd then Jamie was there, one arm around me, the other groping at
iis belt for a knife.

"Are ye all right?" he bellowed, his voice barely audible above
he shrieking wind.

"No!" I tried to shout back, but it came out as no more than a
vheeze. I shook my head, fumbling at my waist.

The sky was a queer purple-green, a color I had never seen
iefore. Jamie sawed at the rope, his bent head spray-soaked and
he color of mahogany, hair whipped across his face by the fury of
he wind.

The rope popped and I gulped in air, ignoring a stabbing pain in
ny side and the stinging of raw skin about my waist. The ship was
iitching wildly, the deck swinging up and down like a lawn glider.
amie fell down on the deck, pulling me with him, and began to

work his way on hands and knees toward the mast, some six feet away, dragging me.

My garments had been drenched through, plastered to me from my immersion in the wave. Now the blast of the wind was so great that it plucked my skirts away from my legs and flung them up, half-dried, to beat about my face like goose wings.

Jamie's arm was tight as an iron bar across my chest. I clung to him, trying to aid our progress by shoving with my feet on the slippery deckboards. Smaller waves washed over the rail, sousing us intermittently, but no more huge monsters followed them.

Reaching hands grasped us and hauled us the last few feet, into the nominal shelter of the mast. Innes had tied the wheel over long since; as I looked forward, I saw lightning strike the sea ahead, making the spokes of the wheel spring out black, leaving an image like a spider's web printed on my retina.

Speech was impossible—and unnecessary. Raeburn, Ian, Meldrum, and Lawrence were huddled against the mast, all tied. frightful. as it was on deck, no one wanted to go below, to be tossed to and fro in bruising darkness, with no notion of what was happening overhead.

I was sitting on the deck, legs splayed, with the mast at my back and the line passed across my chest. The sky had gone lead-gray on one side, a deep, lucent green on the other, and lightning was striking at random over the surface of the sea, bright jags of brilliance across the dark. The wind was so loud that even the thunderclaps reached us only now and then, as muffled booms, like ships' guns firing at a distance.

Then a bolt crashed down beside the ship, lightning and thunder together, close enough to hear the hiss of boiling water in the ringing aftermath of the thunderclap. The sharp reek of ozone flooded the air. Innes turned from the light, his tall, thin figure so sharply cut against the flash that he looked momentarily like a skeleton, black bones against the sky.

The momentary dazzle and his movement made it seem for an instant that he stood whole once more, two arms swinging, as though his missing limb had emerged from the ghost world to join him, here on the brink of eternity.

Oh, de headbone connected to de . . . neckbone. Joe Abernathy's voice sang softly in memory. *And de neckbone connected to de . . . backbone . . .* I had a sudden hideous vision of the

cattered limbs I had seen on the beach by the corpse of the *Bruja*,
nimated by the lightning, squirming and wriggling to reunite.

> *Dem bones, dem bones, are gonna walk around.*
> *Now, hear de word of de Lawd!*

Another clap of thunder and I screamed, not at the sound, but at
he lightning bolt of memory. A skull in my hands, with empty
yes that had once been the green of the hurricane sky.

Jamie shouted something in my ear, but I couldn't hear him. I
ould only shake my head in speechless shock, my skin rippling
/ith horror.

My hair, like my skirts, was drying in the wind; the strands of it
anced on my head, pulling at the roots. As it dried, I felt the
rackle of static electricity where my hair brushed my cheek.
here was a sudden movement among the sailors around me and I
oked up, to see the spars and rigging above coated in the blue
hosphorescence of St. Elmo's fire.

A fireball dropped to the deck and rolled toward us, streaming
hosphorescence. Jamie struck at it and it hopped delicately into
e air and rolled away along the rail, leaving a scent of burning in
s wake.

I looked up at Jamie to see if he was all right, and saw the loose
nds of his hair standing out from his head, coated with fire and
reaming backward like a demon's. Streaks of vivid blue outlined
e fingers of his hand when he brushed the hair from his face.
hen he looked down, saw me, and grasped my hand. A jolt of
lectricity shot through us both with the touch, but he didn't let
o.

I couldn't say how long it lasted; hours or days. Our mouths
ried from the wind, and grew sticky with thirst. The sky went
om gray to black, but there was no telling whether it was night,
r only the coming of rain.

The rain, when it did come, was welcome. It came with the
renching roar of a tropical shower, a drumming audible even
oove the wind. Better yet, it was hail, not rain; the hailstones hit
y skull like pebbles, but I didn't care. I gathered the icy globules
both hands, and swallowed them half-melted, a cool benison to
y tortured throat.

Meldrum and MacLeod crawled about the deck on hands and

knees, scooping the hailstones into buckets and pots, anything that would hold water.

I slept intermittently, head lolling on Jamie's shoulder, and woke to find the wind still screaming. Numb to terror now, I only waited. Whether we lived or died seemed of little consequence, if only the dreadful noise would stop.

There was no telling day from night, no way to keep time, while the sun hid its face. The darkness seemed a little lighter now and then, but whether it was by virtue of daylight or moonlight, I couldn't tell. I slept, and woke, and slept again.

Then I woke, to find the wind a little quieter. The seas still heaved, and the tiny boat pitched like a cockleshell, throwing us up and dropping us with stomach-churning regularity. But the noise was less; I could hear, when MacGregor shouted to Ian to pass a cup of water. The men's faces were chapped and raw, their lips cracked to bleeding by the whistling wind, but they were smiling.

"It's gone by." Jamie's voice was low and husky in my ear, rusted by weather. "The storm's past."

It was; there were breaks in the lead-gray sky, and small flashes of a pale, fresh blue. I thought it must be early morning, sometime just past dawn, but couldn't tell for sure.

While the hurricane had ceased to blow, there was still a strong wind, and the storm surge carried us at an amazing speed. Meldrum took the wheel from Innes, and bending to check the compass, gave a cry of surprise. The fireball that had come aboard during the storm had harmed no one, but the compass was now a melted mass of silver metal, the wooden casing around it untouched.

"Amazing!" said Lawrence, touching it reverently with one finger.

"Aye, and inconvenient, forbye," said Innes dryly. He looked upward, toward the ragged remnants of the dashing clouds. "Much of a hand at celestial navigation, are ye, Mr. Stern?"

After much squinting at the rising sun and the remnants of the morning stars, Jamie, Innes, and Stern determined that our heading was roughly northeast.

"We must turn to the west," Stern said, leaning over the crude chart with Jamie and Innes. "We do not know where we are, but any land must surely be to the west."

Innes nodded, peering soberly at the chart, which showed a sprinkle of islands like coarse-ground pepper, floating on the waters of the Caribbean.

"Aye, that's so," he said. "We've been headed out to sea for God knows how long. The hull's in one piece, but that's all I'd say for it. As for the mast and sails—well, they'll maybe hold for a time." He sounded dubious in the extreme. "God knows where we may fetch up, though."

Jamie grinned at him, dabbing at a trickle of blood from his cracked lip.

"So long as it's land, Duncan, I'm no verra choosy about where."

Innes quirked an eyebrow at him, a slight smile on his lips.

"Aye? And here I thought ye'd settled for sure on a sailor's life, Mac Dubh; ye're sae canty on deck. Why, ye havena puked once in the last twa days!"

"That's because I havena eaten anything in the last twa days," Jamie said wryly. "I dinna much care if the island we find first is English, French, Spanish, or Dutch, but I should be obliged if ye'd find one with food, Duncan."

Innes wiped a hand across his mouth and swallowed painfully; the mention of food made everyone salivate, despite dry mouths.

"I'll do my best, Mac Dubh," he promised.

"Land! It's land!" The call came at last, five days later, in a voice rendered so hoarse by wind and thirst that it was no more than a faint croak, but full of joy, nonetheless. I dashed up on deck to see, my feet slipping on the ladder rungs. Everyone was hanging over the rail, looking at the humped black shape on the horizon. It was far off, but undeniably land, solid and distinct.

"Where do you think we are?" I tried to say, but my voice was so hoarse, the words came out in a tiny whisper, and no one heard. It didn't matter; if we were headed straight for the naval barracks at Antigua, I didn't care.

The waves were running in huge, smooth swells, like the backs of whales. The wind was gusting now, and Innes called for the helmsman to bring the bow another point nearer the wind.

I could see a line of large birds flying, a stately procession skimming down the distant shoreline. Pelicans, searching the shallows for fish, with the sun gleaming on their wings.

I tugged at Jamie's sleeve and pointed at them.

"Look—" I began, but got no further. There was a sharp *crack!* and the world exploded in black and fire. I came to in the water. Dazed and half-choked, I floundered and fought in a world of dark green. Something was wrapped about my legs, dragging me down.

I flailed wildly, kicking to free my leg of the deadly grip. Something floated past my head, and I grabbed for it. Wood, blessed wood, something to hold on to in the surging waves.

A dark shape sleeked by like a seal beneath the water, and a red head bobbed up six feet away, gasping.

"Hold on!" Jamie said. He reached me with two strokes, and ducking under the piece of wood I held, dived down. I felt a tugging at my leg, a sharp pain, and then the dragging tension eased. Jamie's head popped up again, across the spar. He grasped my wrists and hung there, gulping air, as the rolling swell carried us, up and down.

I couldn't see the ship anywhere; had it sunk? A wave broke over my head, and Jamie disappeared temporarily. I shook my head, blinking, and he was there again. He smiled at me, a savage grin of effort, and his grip on my wrists tightened harder.

"Hold on!" he rasped again, and I did. The wood was harsh and splintery under my hands, but I clung for all I was worth. We drifted, half-blinded by spray, spinning like a bit of flotsam, so that sometimes I saw the distant shore, sometimes nothing but the open sea from which we had come. And when the waves washed over us, I saw nothing but water.

There was something wrong with my leg; a strange numbness, punctuated with flashes of sharp pain. The vision of Murphy's peg and the razor-grin of an openmouthed shark drifted through my mind; had my leg been taken by some toothy beast? I thought of my tiny hoard of warm blood, streaming from the stump of a bitten limb, draining away into the cold vastness of the sea, and I panicked, trying to snatch my hand from Jamie's grasp in order to reach down and see for myself.

He snarled something unintelligible at me and held on to my wrists like grim death. After a moment of frenzied thrashing, reason returned, and I calmed myself, thinking that if my leg were indeed gone, I would have lost consciousness by now.

At that, I *was* beginning to lose consciousness. My vision was growing gray at the edges, and floating bright spots covered Jamie's face. Was I really bleeding to death, or was it only cold and shock? It hardly seemed to matter, I thought muzzily; the effect was the same.

A sense of lassitude and utter peace stole gradually over me. I couldn't feel my feet or legs, and only Jamie's crushing grip on my hands reminded me of their existence. My head went under water, and I had to remind myself to hold my breath.

The wave subsided and the wood rose slightly, bringing my nose above water. I breathed, and my vision cleared slightly. A foot away was the face of Jamie Fraser, hair plastered to his head, yet features contorted against the spray.

"Hold on!" he roared. "Hold on, God damn you!"

I smiled gently, barely hearing him. The sense of great peace was lifting me, carrying me beyond the noise and chaos. There was no more pain. Nothing mattered. Another wave washed over me, and this time I forgot to hold my breath.

The choking sensation roused me briefly, long enough to see the flash of terror in Jamie's eyes. Then my vision went dark again.

"Damn you, Sassenach!" his voice said, from a very great distance. His voice was choked with passion. "Damn you! I swear if ye die on me, I'll *kill* you!"

I was dead. Everything around me was a blinding white, and there was a soft, rushing noise like the wings of angels. I felt peaceful and bodiless, free of terror, free of rage, filled with quiet happiness. Then I coughed.

I wasn't bodiless, after all. My leg hurt. It hurt a lot. I became gradually aware that a good many other things hurt, too, but my left shin took precedence in no uncertain terms. I had the distinct impression that the bone had been removed and replaced with a red-hot poker.

At least the leg was demonstrably there. When I cracked my eyes open to look, the haze of pain that floated over my leg seemed almost visible, though perhaps that was only a product of the general fuzziness in my head. Whether mental or physical in origin, the general effect was of a sort of whirling whiteness, shot

with flickers of a brighter light. Watching it hurt my eyes, so I shu
them again.

"Thank God, you're awake!" said a relieved-sounding Scottis
voice near my ear.

"No I'm not," I said. My own voice emerged as a salt-cruste
croak, rusty with swallowed seawater. I could feel seawater in m
sinuses, too, which gave my head an unpleasant gurgling feel.
coughed again, and my nose began to run profusely. Then
sneezed.

"Eugh!" I said, in complete revulsion at the resultant cascad
of slime over my upper lip. My hand seemed far off and insubstan
tial, but I made the effort to raise it, swiping clumsily at my face

"Be still, Sassenach; I'll take care of ye." There was a definit
note of amusement in the voice, which irritated me enough t
open my eyes again. I caught a brief glimpse of Jamie's face
intent on mine, before vision vanished once again in the folds o
an immense white handkerchief.

He wiped my face thoroughly, ignoring my strangled noises o
protest and impending suffocation, then held the cloth to my nose

"Blow," he said.

I did as he said. Rather to my surprise, it helped quite a lot.
could think more or less coherently, now that my head was ur
clogged.

Jamie smiled down at me. His hair was rumpled and stiff wit
dried salt, and there was a wide abrasion on his temple, an angr
dark red against the bronzed skin. He seemed not to be wearing
shirt, but had a blanket of some kind draped about his shoulder

"Do ye feel verra bad?" he asked.

"Horrible," I croaked in reply. I was also beginning to b
annoyed at being alive, after all, and being required to take notic
of things again. Hearing the rasp in my voice, Jamie reached for
jug of water on the table by my bed.

I blinked in confusion, but it really was a bed, not a berth or
hammock. The linen sheets contributed to the overwhelming in
pression of whiteness that had first engulfed me. This was rein
forced by the whitewashed walls and ceiling, and the long whi
muslin draperies that bellied in like sails, rustling in the bree
from the open windows.

The flickering light came from reflections that shimmered ov
the ceiling; apparently there was water close by outside, and su

shining on it. It seemed altogether cozier than Davy Jones's locker. Still, I felt a brief moment of intense regret for the sense of infinite peace I had experienced in the heart of the wave—a regret made more keen by the slight movement that sent a bolt of white agony up my leg.

"I think your leg is broken, Sassenach," Jamie told me unnecessarily. "Ye likely shouldna move it much."

"Thanks for the advice," I said, through gritted teeth. "Where in bloody hell are we?"

He shrugged briefly. "I dinna ken. It's a fair-sized house, is all I could say. I wasna taking much note when they brought us in. One man said the place is called Les Perles." He held the cup to my lips and I swallowed gratefully.

"What happened?" So long as I was careful not to move, the pain in my leg was bearable. Automatically, I placed my fingers under the angle of my jaw to check my pulse; reassuringly strong. I wasn't in shock; my leg couldn't be badly fractured, much as it hurt.

Jamie rubbed a hand over his face. He looked very tired, and I noticed that his hand trembled with fatigue. There was a large bruise on his cheek, and a line of dried blood where something had scratched the side of his neck.

"The topmast snapped, I think. One of the spars fell and knocked ye overboard. When ye hit the water, ye sank like a stone, and I dived in after you. I got hold of you—and the spar, too, thank God. Ye had a bit of rigging tangled round your leg, dragging ye down, but I managed to get that off." He heaved a deep sigh, and rubbed his head.

"I just held to ye; and after a time, I felt sand under my feet. I carried ye ashore, and a bit later, some men found us and brought us here. That's all." He shrugged.

I felt cold, despite the warm breeze coming in through the windows.

"What happened to the ship? And the men? Ian? Lawrence?"

"Safe, I think. They couldna reach us, with the mast broken—by the time they'd rigged a makeshift sail, we were long gone." He coughed roughly, and rubbed the back of his hand across his mouth. "But they're safe; the men who found us said they'd seen a small ketch go aground on a mud flat a quarter-mile south of here; they've gone down to salvage and bring back the men."

He took a swallow of water, swished it about his mouth, and going to the window, spat it out.

"I've sand in my teeth," he said, grimacing, as he returned. "And my ears. And my nose, and the crack of my arse, too, I shouldna wonder."

I reached out and took his hand again. His palm was heavily callused, but still showed the tender swelling of rising blisters, with shreds of ragged skin and raw flesh, where earlier blisters had burst and bled.

"How long were we in the water?" I asked, gently tracing the lines of his swollen palm. The tiny "C" at the base of his thumb was faded almost to invisibility, but I could still feel it under my finger. "Just how long did you hold on?"

"Long enough," he said simply.

He smiled a little, and held my hand more tightly, despite the soreness of his own. It dawned on me suddenly that I wasn't wearing anything; the linen sheets were smooth and cool on my bare skin, and I could see the swell of my nipples, rising under the thin fabric.

"What happened to my clothes?"

"I couldna hold ye up against the drag of your skirts, so I ripped them off," he explained. "What was left didna seem worth saving."

"I don't suppose so," I said slowly, "but Jamie—what about you? Where's your coat?"

He shrugged, then let his shoulders drop, and smiled ruefully.

"At the bottom of the sea with my shoon, I expect," he said. And the pictures of Willie and Brianna there, too.

"Oh, Jamie. I'm so sorry." I reached for his hand and held it tightly. He looked away, and blinked once or twice.

"Aye, well," he said softly. "I expect I will remember them." He shrugged again, with a lopsided smile. "And if not, I can look in the glass, no?" I gave a laugh that was half a sob; he swallowed painfully, but went on smiling.

He glanced down at his tattered breeches then, and seeming to think of something, leaned back and worked a hand into the pocket.

"I didna come away completely empty-handed," he said, pulling a wry face. "Though I would as soon it had been the pictures I kept, and lost these."

He opened his hand, and I saw the gleam and glitter in his ruined palm. Stones of the first quality, cut and faceted, suitable for magic. An emerald, a ruby—male, I supposed—a great fiery opal, a turquoise blue as the sky I could see out the window, a golden stone like sun trapped in honey, and the strange crystal purity of Geilie's black diamond.

"You have the adamant," I said, touching it gently. It was still cool to the touch, in spite of being worn so close to his body.

"I have," he said, but he was looking at me, not at the stone, a slight smile on his face. "What is it an adamant gives ye? The knowledge of joy in all things?"

"So I was told." I lifted my hand to his face and stroked it lightly, feeling hard bone and lively flesh, warm to the touch, and joyful to behold above all things.

"We have Ian," I said softly. "And each other."

"Aye, that's true." The smile reached his eyes then. He dropped the stones in a glittering heap on the table and leaned back in his chair, cradling my hand between his.

I relaxed, feeling a warm peace begin to steal over me, in spite of the aches and scrapes and the pain in my leg. We were alive, safe and together, and very little else mattered; surely not clothes, nor a fractured tibia. Everything would be managed in time—but not now. For now, it was enough only to breathe, and look at Jamie.

We sat in a peaceful silence for some time, watching the sunlit curtains and the open sky. It might have been ten minutes later, or as much as an hour, when I heard the sound of light footsteps outside, and a delicate rap at the door.

"Come in," Jamie said. He sat up straighter, but didn't let go of my hand.

The door opened, and a woman stepped in, her pleasant face lit by welcome, tinged with curiosity.

"Good morning," she said, a little shyly. "I must beg your pardon, not to have waited upon you before; I was in the town, and learned of your—arrival"—she smiled at the word —"only when returned, just now."

"We must thank ye, Madame, most sincerely, for the kind treatment afforded to us," Jamie said. He rose and bowed formally to her, but kept hold of my hand. "Your servant, ma'am. Have ye word of our companions?"

She blushed slightly, and bobbed a curtsy in reply to his bow. She was young, only in her twenties, and seemed unsure quite how to conduct herself under the circumstances. She had light brown hair, pulled back in a knot, fair pink skin, and what I thought was a faint West Country accent.

"Oh, yes," she said. "My servants brought them back from the ship; they're in the kitchen now, being fed."

"Thank you," I said, meaning it. "That's terribly kind of you."

She blushed rosily with embarrassment.

"Not at all," she murmured, then glanced shyly at me. "I must beg your pardon for my lack of manners, ma'am," she said. "I am remiss in not introducing myself. I am Patsy Olivier—Mrs. Joseph Olivier, that is." She looked expectantly from me to Jamie, clearly expecting reciprocation.

Jamie and I exchanged a glance. Where, exactly, were we? Mrs. Olivier was English, that was clear enough. Her husband's name was French. The bay outside gave no clue; this could be any of the Windward Isles—Barbados, the Bahamas, the Exumas, Andros— even the Virgin Islands. Or—the thought struck me—we might have been blown south by the hurricane, and not north; in which case, this might even be Antigua—in the lap of the British Navy! —or Martinique, or the Grenadines . . . I looked at Jamie and shrugged.

Our hostess was still waiting, glancing expectantly from one to the other of us. Jamie tightened his hold on my hand and drew a deep breath.

"I trust ye willna think this an odd question, Mistress Olivier— but could ye tell me where we are?"

Mrs. Olivier's brows rose to the edge of her widow's peak, and she blinked in astonishment.

"Well . . . yes," she said. "We call it Les Perles."

"Thank you," I put in, seeing Jamie taking breath to try again, "but what we mean is—what island is this?"

A broad smile of understanding broke out on her round pink face.

"Oh, I see!" she said. "Of course, you were cast away by the storm. My husband was saying last night that he'd never seen such a dreadful blow at this time of year. What a mercy it is that you were saved! But you came from the islands to the south, then?"

The south. This couldn't be Cuba. Might we have come as far as

St. Thomas, or even Florida? We exchanged a quick glance, and I squeezed Jamie's hand. I could feel the pulse beating in his wrist.

Mrs. Olivier smiled indulgently. "You are not on an island at all. You are on the mainland; in the Colony of Georgia."

"Georgia," Jamie said. "America?" He sounded slightly stunned, and no wonder. We had been blown at least six hundred miles by the storm.

"America," I said softly. "The New World." The pulse beneath my fingers had quickened, echoing my own. A new world. Refuge. Freedom.

"Yes," said Mrs. Olivier, plainly having no idea what the news meant to us, but still smiling kindly from one to the other. "It is America."

Jamie straightened his shoulders and smiled back at her. The clean bright air stirred his hair like kindling flames.

"In that case, ma'am," he said, "my name is Jamie Fraser." He looked then at me, eyes blue and brilliant as the sky behind him, and his heart beat strong in the palm of my hand.

"And this is Claire," he said. "My wife."

If you loved VOYAGER,
then be sure to read the next
book in the acclaimed
OUTLANDER series . . .

DIANA GABALDON'S

DRUMS OF
AUTUMN

Available now
from Dell Books!

Read on for a preview. . . .

DRUMS OF AUTUMN
On Sale Now

Charleston, June 1767

heard the drums long before they came in sight. The beating echoed in the pit of my stomach, as though I too were hollow. The sound traveled through the crowd, a harsh military rhythm eant to be heard over speech or gunfire. I saw heads turn as the ople fell silent, looking up the stretch of East Bay Street, where ran from the half-built skeleton of the new Customs House ward White Point Gardens.

It was a hot day, even for Charleston in June. The best places ere on the seawall, where the air moved; here below, it was like ing roasted alive. My shift was soaked through, and the cotton dice clung between my breasts. I wiped my face for the tenth ne in as many minutes and lifted the heavy coil of my hair, ping vainly for a cooling breeze upon my neck.

I was morbidly aware of necks at the moment. Unobtrusively, I t my hand up to the base of my throat, letting my fingers circle I could feel the pulse beat in my carotid arteries, along with the ums, and when I breathed, the hot wet air clogged my throat as ough I were choking.

I quickly took my hand down, and drew in a breath as deep as I uld manage. That was a mistake. The man in front of me hadn't thed in a month or more; the edge of the stock about his thick ck was dark with grime and his clothes smelled sour and musty, ngent even amid the sweaty reek of the crowd. The smell of hot ead and frying pig fat from the food vendors' stalls lay heavy er a musk of rotting seagrass from the marsh, only slightly lieved by a whiff of salt-breeze from the harbor.

There were several children in front of me, craning and gawk- g, running out from under the oaks and palmettos to look up the reet, being called back by anxious parents. The girl nearest me d a neck like the white part of a grass stalk, slender and succu- nt.

There was a ripple of excitement through the crowd; the gallows procession was in sight at the far end of the street. The drums grew louder.

"Where is he?" Fergus muttered beside me, craning his own neck to see. "I knew I should have gone with him!"

"He'll be here." I wanted to stand on tiptoe, but didn't, feeling that this would be undignified. I did glance around, though searching. I could always spot Jamie in a crowd; he stood head and shoulders above most men, and his hair caught the light in blaze of reddish gold. There was no sign of him yet, only a bobbing sea of bonnets and tricornes, sheltering from the heat those citizens come too late to find a place in the shade.

The flags came first, fluttering above the heads of the excited crowd, the banners of Great Britain and of the Royal Colony of South Carolina. And another, bearing the family arms of the Lord Governor of the colony.

Then came the drummers, walking two by two in step, the sticks an alternate beat and blur. It was a slow march, grim inexorable. A dead march, I thought they called that particular cadence; very suitable under the circumstances. All other noise were drowned by the rattle of the drums.

Then came the platoon of red-coated soldiers and in their midst the prisoners.

There were three of them, hands bound before them, linked together by a chain that ran through rings on the iron collars above their necks. The first man was small and elderly, ragged and disreputable, a shambling wreck who lurched and staggered so that the dark-suited clergyman who walked beside the prisoners was obliged to grasp his arm to keep him from falling.

"Is that Gavin Hayes? He looks sick," I murmured to Fergus.

"He's drunk." The soft voice came from behind me, and whirled, to find Jamie standing at my shoulder, eyes fixed on the pitiful procession.

The small man's disequilibrium was disrupting the progress of the parade, as his stumbling forced the two men chained to him to zig and zag abruptly in order to keep their feet. The general impression was of three inebriates rolling home from the local tavern; grossly at odds with the solemnity of the occasion. I could hear the rustle of laughter over the drums, and shouts and jeers from the crowds on the wrought-iron balconies of the houses of East Bay Street.

"Your doing?" I spoke quietly, so as not to attract notice, but ld have shouted and waved my arms; no one had eyes for thing but the scene before us.

felt rather than saw Jamie's shrug, as he moved forward to d beside me.

"It was what he asked of me," he said. "And the best I could nage for him."

"Brandy or whisky?" asked Fergus, evaluating Hayes' appear- e with a practiced eye.

"The man's a Scot, wee Fergus." Jamie's voice was as calm as face, but I heard the small note of strain in it. "Whisky's what wanted."

"A wise choice. With luck, he won't even notice when they g him," Fergus muttered. The small man had slipped from the acher's grasp and fallen flat on his face in the sandy road, ing one of his companions to his knees; the last prisoner, a tall ng man, stayed on his feet but swayed wildly from side to side, ing desperately to keep his balance. The crowd on the point red with glee.

he captain of the guard glowed crimson between the white of wig and the metal of his gorget, flushed with fury as much as h sun. He barked an order as the drums continued their somber , and a soldier scrambled hastily to remove the chain that nd the prisoners together. Hayes was jerked unceremoniously his feet, a soldier grasping each arm, and the procession re- ned, in better order.

here was no laughter by the time they reached the gallows—a le-drawn cart placed beneath the limbs of a huge live oak. I ld feel the drums beating through the soles of my feet. I felt htly sick from the sun and the smells. The drums stopped uptly, and my ears rang in the silence.

"Ye dinna need to watch it, Sassenach," Jamie whispered to . "Go back to the wagon." His own eyes were fixed unblink- ly on Hayes, who swayed and mumbled in the soldiers' grasp, king blearily around.

he last thing I wanted was to watch. But neither could I leave nie to see it through alone. He had come for Gavin Hayes; I l come for him. I touched his hand.

"I'll stay."

amie drew himself straighter, squaring his shoulders. He ved a pace forward, making sure that he was visible in the wd. If Hayes was still sober enough to see anything, the last ng he saw on earth would be the face of a friend.

He could see; Hayes glared to and fro as they lifted him into cart, twisting his neck, desperately looking.

"Gabhainn! A charaid!" Jamie shouted suddenly. Hayes' e found him at once, and he ceased struggling.

The little man stood swaying slightly as the charge was re theft in the amount of six pounds, ten shillings. He was covered reddish dust, and pearls of sweat clung trembling to the g stubble of his beard. The preacher was leaning close, murmur urgently in his ear.

Then the drums began again, in a steady roll. The hangm guided the noose over the balding head and fixed it tight, k positioned precisely, just under the ear. The captain of the gu stood poised, saber raised.

Suddenly, the condemned man drew himself up straight. E on Jamie, he opened his mouth, as though to speak.

The saber flashed in the morning sun, and the drums stopp with a final *thunk*!

I looked at Jamie; he was white to the lips, eyes fixed wi From the corner of my eye, I could see the twitching rope, and faint, reflexive jerk of the dangling sack of clothes. A sharp st of urine and feces struck through the thick air.

On my other side, Fergus watched dispassionately.

"I suppose he noticed, after all," he murmured, with regret.

The body swung slightly, a dead weight oscillating like plumb-bob on its string. There was a sigh from the crowd, of a and release. Terns squawked from the burning sky, and the harb sounds came faint and smothered through the heavy air, but point was wrapped in silence. From where I stood, I could h the small *plit . . . plat . . . plit* of the drops that fell from toe of the corpse's dangling shoe.

I hadn't known Gavin Hayes, and felt no personal grief for death, but I was glad it had been quick. I stole a glance at hi with an odd feeling of intrusion. It was a most public way accomplishing a most private act, and I felt vaguely embarrass to be looking.

The hangman had known his business; there had been no u dignified struggle, no staring eyes, no protruding tongue; Gavi small round head tilted sharply to the side, neck grotesqu stretched but cleanly broken.

It was a clean break in more ways than one. The captain of

rd, satisfied that Hayes was dead, motioned with his saber for
next man to be brought to the gibbet. I saw his eyes travel
vn the red-clad file, and then widen in outrage.

t the same moment, there was a cry from the crowd, and a
le of excitement that quickly spread. Heads turned and people
hed each against his neighbor, striving to see where there was
hing to be seen.

He's gone!"

There he goes!"

Stop him!"

t was the third prisoner, the tall young man, who had seized
moment of Gavin's death to run for his life, sliding past the
rd who should have been watching him, but who had been
ble to resist the gallows' fascination.

saw a flicker of movement behind a vendor's stall, a flash of
y blond hair. Some of the soldiers saw it, too, and ran in that
ction, but many more were rushing in other directions, and
ong the collisions and confusion, nothing was accomplished.

he captain of the guard was shouting, face purple, his voice
ely audible over the uproar. The remaining prisoner, looking
ned, was seized and hustled back in the direction of the Court
Guard as the redcoats began hastily to sort themselves back
order under the lash of their captain's voice.

amie snaked an arm around my waist and dragged me out of
way of an oncoming wave of humanity. The crowd fell back
ore the advance of squads of soldiers, who formed up and
ched briskly off to quarter the area, under the grim and furi-
direction of their sergeant.

We'd best find Ian," Jamie said, fending off a group of ex-
d apprentices. He glanced at Fergus, and jerked his head
ard the gibbet and its melancholy burden. "Claim the body,
? We'll meet at the Willow Tree later."

Do you think they'll catch him?" I asked, as we pushed
ugh the ebbing crowd, threading our way down a cobbled lane
ard the merchants' wharves.

I expect so. Where can he go?" He spoke abstractedly, a nar-
line visible between his brows. Plainly the dead man was still
his mind, and he had little attention to spare for the living.

Did Hayes have any family?" I asked. He shook his head.

I asked him that, when I brought him the whisky. He thought
might have a brother left alive, but no notion where. The

brother was transported soon after the Rising—to Virginia, Ha[...] thought, but he'd heard nothing since."

Not surprising if he hadn't; an indentured laborer would h[...] had no facilities for communicating with kin left behind in Sc[...] land, unless the bondsman's employer was kind enough to sen[...] letter on his behalf. And kind or not, it was unlikely that a le[...] would have found Gavin Hayes, who had spent ten years in Ar[...] muir prison before being transported in his turn.

"Duncan!" Jamie called out, and a tall, thin man turned a[...] raised a hand in acknowledgment. He made his way through [...] crowd in a corkscrew fashion, his single arm swinging in a w[...] arc that fended off the passersby.

"Mac Dubh," he said, bobbing his head in greeting to Jam[...] "Mrs. Claire." His long, narrow face was furrowed with sadne[...] He too had once been a prisoner at Ardsmuir, with Hayes a[...] with Jamie. Only the loss of his arm to a blood infection [...] prevented his being transported with the others. Unfit to be s[...] for labor, he had instead been pardoned and set free to starve[...] until Jamie had found him.

"God rest poor Gavin," Duncan said, shaking his head do[...] ously.

Jamie muttered something in response in Gaelic, and cross[...] himself. Then he straightened, casting off the oppression of [...] day with a visible effort.

"Aye, well. I must go to the docks and arrange about Ia[...] passage, and then we'll think of burying Gavin. But I must h[...] the lad settled first."

We struggled through the crowd toward the docks, squeez[...] our way between knots of excited gossipers, eluding the drays a[...] barrows that came and went through the press with the ponder[...] indifference of trade.

A file of red-coated soldiers came at the quick-march from [...] other end of the quay, splitting the crowd like vinegar dropped [...] mayonnaise. The sun glittered hot on the line of bayonet po[...] and the rhythm of their tramping beat through the noise of [...] crowd like a muffled drum. Even the rumbling sledges and ha[...] carts stopped abruptly to let them pass by.

"Mind your pocket, Sassenach," Jamie murmured in my [...] ushering me through a narrow space between a turban-clad sla[...] clutching two small children and a street preacher perched o[...] box. He was shouting sin and repentance, but with only one w[...] in three audible through the noise.

'I sewed it shut," I assured him, nonetheless reaching to touch
   small weight that swung against my thigh. "What about
 rs?"

 Ie grinned and tilted his hat forward, dark blue eyes narrowing
 inst the bright sunlight.

 'It's where my sporran would be, did I have one. So long as I
 na meet with a quick-fingered harlot, I'm safe."

   glanced at the slightly bulging front of his breeches, and then
  at him. Broad-shouldered and tall, with bold, clean features
 1 a Highlander's proud carriage, he drew the glance of every
 man he passed, even with his bright hair covered by a sober
  e tricorne. The breeches, which were borrowed, were substan-
 ly too tight, and did nothing whatever to detract from the gen-
 l effect—an effect enhanced by the fact that he himself was
 lly ignorant of it.

 'You're a walking inducement to harlots," I said. "Stick by
 ; I'll protect you."

 Ie laughed and took my arm as we emerged into a small clear
 ce.

 'Ian!" he shouted, catching sight of his nephew over the heads
  the crowd. A moment later, a tall, stringy gawk of a boy
)ped out of the crowd, pushing a thatch of brown hair out of his
 s and grinning widely.

 'I thought I should never find ye, Uncle!" he exclaimed.
 hrist, there are more folk here than at the Lawnmarket in Edin-
 gh!" He wiped a coat sleeve across his long, half-homely face,
 ving a streak of grime down one cheek.

 amie eyed his nephew askance.

 'Ye're lookin' indecently cheerful, Ian, for having just seen a
 n go to his death."

 an hastily altered his expression into an attempt at decent so-
 nity.

 'Oh, no, Uncle Jamie," he said. "I didna see the hanging."
 ncan raised one brow and Ian blushed slightly. "I—I wasna
 aid to see; it was only I had . . . something else I wanted to
 '

 amie smiled slightly and patted his nephew on the back.

 'Don't trouble yourself, Ian; I'd as soon not have seen it my-
 f, only that Gavin was a friend."

 'I know, Uncle. I'm sorry for it." A flash of sympathy showed
 he boy's large brown eyes, the only feature of his face with any
 im to beauty. He glanced at me. "Was it awful, Auntie?"

"Yes," I said. "It's over, though." I pulled the damp handk‍‍‍chief out of my bosom and stood on tiptoe to rub away ‍smudge on his cheek.

Duncan Innes shook his head sorrowfully. "Aye, poor Ga‍‍Still, it's a quicker death than starving, and there was little left ‍him but that."

"Let's go," Jamie interrupted, unwilling to spend time in u‍less lamenting. "The *Bonnie Mary* should be near the far end ‍the quay." I saw Ian glance at Jamie and draw himself up ‍though about to speak, but Jamie had already turned toward ‍harbor and was shoving his way through the crowd. Ian glance‍me, shrugged, and offered me an arm.

We followed Jamie behind the warehouses that lined the doc‍sidestepping sailors, loaders, slaves, passengers, customers ‍merchants of all sorts. Charleston was a major shipping port, ‍business was booming, with as many as a hundred ships a mo‍coming and going from Europe in the season.

The *Bonnie Mary* belonged to a friend of Jamie's cousin Ja‍Fraser, who had gone to France to make his fortune in the w‍business and succeeded brilliantly. With luck, the *Bonnie Ma‍captain might be persuaded for Jared's sake to take Ian with ‍back to Edinburgh, allowing the boy to work his passage ‍cabin lad.

Ian was not enthused at the prospect, but Jamie was determi‍to ship his errant nephew back to Scotland at the earliest oppo‍nity. It was—among other concerns—news of the *Bonnie Ma‍presence in Charleston that had brought us here from Geor‍where we had first set foot in America—by accident—two mo‍before.

As we passed a tavern, a slatternly barmaid came out wi‍bowl of slops. She caught sight of Jamie and stood, bowl bra‍against her hip, giving him a slanted brow and a pouting sm‍He passed without a glance, intent on his goal. She tossed ‍head, flung the slops to the pig who slept by the step, ‍flounced back inside.

He paused, shading his eyes to look down the row of towe‍ships' masts, and I came up beside him. He twitched un‍sciously at the front of his breeches, easing the fit, and I took‍arm.

"Family jewels still safe, are they?" I murmured.

"Uncomfortable, but safe," he assured me. He plucked at

:ing of his flies, grimacing. "I would ha' done better to hide
:m up my bum, I think."

"Better you than me, mate," I said, smiling. "I'd rather risk
obery, myself."

The family jewels were just that. We had been driven ashore on
e coast of Georgia by a hurricane, arriving soaked, ragged, and
stitute—save for a handful of large and valuable gemstones.

I hoped the captain of the *Bonnie Mary* thought highly enough
Jared Fraser to accept Ian as a cabin boy, because if not, we
re going to have a spot of difficulty about the passage.

In theory, Jamie's pouch and my pocket contained a sizable
rtune. In practice, the stones might have been beach pebbles so
· as the good they were to us. While gems were an easy, com-
ct way of transporting wealth, the problem was changing them
ck into money.

Most trade in the southern colonies was conducted by means of
rter—what wasn't, was handled by the exchange of scrip or
ls written on a wealthy merchant or banker. And wealthy bank-
s were thin on the ground in Georgia; those willing to tie up
ir available capital in gemstones rarer still. The prosperous rice
·mer with whom we had stayed in Savannah had assured us that
himself could scarcely lay his hand on two pounds sterling in
sh—indeed, there was likely not ten pounds in gold and silver
be had in the whole colony.

Nor was there any chance of selling one of the stones in the
dless stretches of salt marsh and pine forest through which we
d passed on our journey north. Charleston was the first city we
d reached of sufficient size to harbor merchants and bankers
o might help to liquidate a portion of our frozen assets.

Not that anything was likely to stay frozen long in Charleston in
mmer, I reflected. Rivulets of sweat were running down my
ck and the linen shift under my bodice was soaked and crum-
d against my skin. Even so close to the harbor, there was no
nd at this time of day, and the smells of hot tar, dead fish, and
eating laborers were nearly overwhelming.

Despite their protestations, Jamie had insisted on giving one of
r gemstones to Mr. and Mrs. Olivier, the kindly people who had
:en us in when we were shipwrecked virtually on their doorstep,
some token of thanks for their hospitality. In return, they had
ovided us with a wagon, two horses, fresh clothes for traveling,
od for the journey north, and a small amount of money.

Of this, six shillings and threepence remained in my pocke constituting the entirety of our disposable fortune.

"This way, Uncle Jamie," Ian said, turning and beckoning h uncle eagerly. "I've got something to show ye."

"What is it?" Jamie asked, threading his way through a thron of sweating slaves, who were loading dusty bricks of dried indig into an anchored cargo ship. "And how did ye get whatever it i Ye havena got any money, have you?"

"No, I won it, dicing." Ian's voice floated back, his body invi ible as he skipped around a cartload of corn.

"Dicing! Ian, for God's sake, ye canna be gambling whe ye've not a penny to bless yourself with!" Holding my arm, J mie shoved a way through the crowd to catch up to his nephew.

"You do it all the time, Uncle Jamie," the boy pointed ou pausing to wait for us. "Ye've been doing it in every tavern an inn where we've stayed."

"My God, Ian, that's cards, not dice! And I know what I' doing!"

"So do I," said Ian, looking smug. "I won, no?"

Jamie rolled his eyes toward heaven, imploring patience.

"Jesus, Ian, but I'm glad you're going home before ye get yo head beaten in. Promise me ye willna be gambling wi' the sailor aye? Ye canna get away from them on a ship."

Ian was paying no attention; he had come to a half-crumble piling, around which was tied a stout rope. Here he stopped an turned to face us, gesturing at an object by his feet.

"See? It's a dog," Ian said proudly.

I took a quick half-step behind Jamie, grabbing his arm.

"Ian," I said, "that is not a dog. It's a wolf. It's a bloody b wolf, and I think you ought to get away from it before it takes bite out of your arse."

The wolf twitched one ear negligently in my direction, di missed me, and twitched it back. It continued to sit, panting wi the heat, its big yellow eyes fixed on Ian with an intensity th might have been taken for devotion by someone who hadn't met wolf before. I had.

"Those things are dangerous," I said. "They'd bite you soon as look at you."

Disregarding this, Jamie stooped to inspect the beast.

"It's not quite a wolf, is it?" Sounding interested, he held out loose fist to the so-called dog, inviting it to smell his knuckles. closed my eyes, expecting the imminent amputation of his han

aring no shrieks, I opened them again to find him squatting on
 ground, peering up the animal's nostrils.

He's a handsome creature, Ian," he said, scratching the thing
 iliarly under the chin. The yellow eyes narrowed slightly, ei-
 r in pleasure at the attention or—more likely, I thought—in
 icipation of biting off Jamie's nose. "Bigger than a wolf,
 ugh; it's broader through the head and chest, and a deal longer
 he leg."

His mother was an Irish wolfhound." Ian was hunkered down
 Jamie, eagerly explaining as he stroked the enormous gray-
 wn back. "She got out in heat, into the woods, and when she
 e back in whelp—"

Oh, aye, I see." Now Jamie was crooning in Gaelic to the
 nster while he picked up its huge foot and fondled its hairy
 s. The curved black claws were a good two inches long. The
 ig half closed its eyes, the faint breeze ruffling the thick fur at
 neck.

 glanced at Duncan, who arched his eyebrows at me, shrugged
 htly, and sighed. Duncan didn't care for dogs.

Jamie—" I said.

Balach Boidheach," Jamie said to the wolf. "Are ye no the
 ny laddie, then?"

What would he eat?" I asked, somewhat more loudly than
 essary.

amie stopped caressing the beast.

Oh," he said. He looked at the yellow-eyed thing with some
 ret. "Well." He rose to his feet, shaking his head reluctantly.
 I'm afraid your auntie's right, Ian. How are we to feed him?"
 Oh, that's no trouble, Uncle Jamie," Ian assured him. "He
 ts for himself."

Here?" I glanced around at the warehouses, and the stuccoed
 of shops beyond. "What does he hunt, small children?"
 an looked mildly hurt.

Of course not, Auntie. Fish."

.eeing three skeptical faces surrounding him, Ian dropped to
 knees and grabbed the beast's muzzle in both hands, prying
 mouth open.

He does! I swear, Uncle Jamie! Here, just smell his breath!"
 amie cast a dubious glance at the double row of impressively
 aming fangs on display, and rubbed his chin.

I—ah, I shall take your word for it, Ian. But even so—for
 ist's sake, be careful of your fingers, lad!" Ian's grip had

loosened, and the massive jaws clashed shut, spraying droplets
saliva over the stone quay.

"I'm all right, Uncle," Ian said cheerfully, wiping his hand
his breeks. "He wouldn't bite me, I'm sure. His name is Rollo."

Jamie rubbed his knuckles across his upper lip.

"Mmphm. Well, whatever his name is, and whatever he eat
dinna think the captain of the *Bonnie Mary* will take kindly to
presence in the crew's quarters."

Ian didn't say anything, but the look of happiness on his f
didn't diminish. In fact, it grew. Jamie glanced at him, caught si
of his glowing face, and stiffened.

"No," he said, in horror. "Oh, no."

"Yes," said Ian. A wide smile of delight split his b
face. "She sailed three days ago, Uncle. We're too late."

Jamie said something in Gaelic that I didn't understa
Duncan looked scandalized.

"Damn!" Jamie said, reverting to English. "Bloody dam
Jamie took off his hat and rubbed a hand over his face, hard.
looked hot, disheveled, and thoroughly disgruntled. He ope
his mouth, thought better of whatever he had been going to
closed it, and ran his fingers roughly through his hair, jerk
loose the ribbon that tied it back.

Ian looked abashed.

"I'm sorry, Uncle. I'll try not to be a worry to ye, truly I w
And I can work; I'll earn enough for my food."

Jamie's face softened as he looked at his nephew. He sig
deeply, and patted Ian's shoulder.

"It's not that I dinna want ye, Ian. You know I should
nothing better than to keep ye with me. But what in hell will y
mother say?"

The glow returned to Ian's face.

"I dinna ken, Uncle," he said, "but she'll be saying it in S
land, won't she? And we're here." He put his arms around R
and hugged him. The wolf seemed mildly taken aback by
gesture, but after a moment, put out a long pink tongue and d
tily licked Ian's ear. Testing him for flavor, I thought cynically

"Besides," the boy added, "she kens well enough that
safe; you wrote from Georgia to say I was with you."

Jamie summoned a wry smile.

"I canna say that that particular bit of knowledge will be o
comforting to her, Ian. She's known me a long time, aye?"

le sighed and clapped the hat back on his head, and turned to

I badly need a drink, Sassenach," he said. "Let's find that
ern."

The Willow Tree was dark, and might have been cool, had there
n fewer people in it. As it was, the benches and tables were
wded with sightseers from the hanging and sailors from the
ks, and the atmosphere was like a sweatbath. I inhaled as I
ped into the taproom, then let my breath out, fast. It was like
athing through a wad of soiled laundry, soaked in beer.

ollo at once proved his worth, parting the crowd like the Red
as he stalked through the taproom, lips drawn back from his
h in a constant, inaudible growl. He was evidently no stranger
averns. Having satisfactorily cleared out a corner bench, he
ed up under the table and appeared to go to sleep.

ut of the sun, with a large pewter mug of dark ale foaming
ly in front of him, Jamie quickly regained his normal self-
session.

We've the two choices," he said, brushing back the sweated hair from his temples. "We can stay in Charleston long
ugh to maybe find a buyer for one of the stones, and perhaps
k passage for Ian to Scotland on another ship. Or we can make
way north to Cape Fear, and maybe find a ship for him out of
mington or New Bern."

say north," Duncan said, without hesitation. "Ye've kin in
e Fear, no? I mislike the thought of staying ower-long among
agers. And your kinsman would see we were not cheated nor
ed. Here—" He lifted one shoulder in eloquent indication of
un-Scottish—and thus patently dishonest—persons surround-
1s.

Oh, do let's go north, Uncle!" Ian said quickly, before Jamie
d reply to this. He wiped away a small mustache of ale foam
his sleeve. "The journey might be dangerous; you'll need an
a man along for protection, aye?"

mie buried his expression in his own cup, but I was seated
e enough to feel a subterranean quiver go through him. Jamie
indeed very fond of his nephew. The fact remained that Ian
the sort of person to whom things happened. Usually through
ault of his own, but still, they happened.

ae boy had been kidnapped by pirates the year before, and it was the necessity of rescuing him that had brought us by cir[c]itous and often dangerous means to America. Nothing h[ad] happened recently, but I knew Jamie was anxious to get [his] fifteen-year-old nephew back to Scotland and his mother bef[ore] something did.

"Ah . . . to be sure, Ian," Jamie said, lowering his cup. [He] carefully avoided meeting my gaze, but I could see the corner [of] his mouth twitching. "Ye'd be a great help, I'm sure, but . . ."

"We might meet with Red Indians!" Ian said, eyes wide. [His] face, already a rosy brown from the sun, glowed with a flush [of] pleasurable anticipation. "Or wild beasts! Dr. Stern told me t[hat] the wilderness of Carolina is alive wi' fierce creatures—bears a[nd] wildcats and wicked panthers—and a great foul thing the India[ns] call a skunk!"

I choked on my ale.

"Are ye all right, Auntie?" Ian leaned anxiously across [the] table.

"Fine," I wheezed, wiping my streaming face with [a] kerchief. I blotted the drops of spilled ale off my bosom, pull[ing] the fabric of my bodice discreetly away from my flesh in hopes [of] admitting a little air.

Then I caught a glimpse of Jamie's face, on which the expr[es]sion of suppressed amusement had given way to a small frown [of] concern.

"Skunks aren't dangerous," I murmured, laying a hand on [his] knee. A skilled and fearless hunter in his native Highlands, Ja[mie] was inclined to regard the unfamiliar fauna of the New Wo[rld] with caution.

"Mmphm." The frown eased, but a narrow line remained [be]tween his brows. "Maybe so, but what of the other things [I] canna say I wish to be meeting a bear or a pack o' savages, [with] only this to hand." He touched the large sheathed knife that hu[ng] from his belt.

Our lack of weapons had worried Jamie considerably on the t[rip] from Georgia, and Ian's remarks about Indians and wild anim[als] had brought the concern to the forefront of his mind once mo[re.] Besides Jamie's knife, Fergus bore a smaller blade, suitable [for] cutting rope and trimming twigs for kindling. That was the [full] extent of our armory—the Oliviers had had neither guns [nor] swords to spare.

On the journey from Georgia to Charleston, we had had [the] company of a group of rice and indigo farmers—all bristling w[ith]

ves, pistols, and muskets—bringing their produce to the port to
shipped north to Pennsylvania and New York. If we left for
e Fear now, we would be alone, unarmed, and essentially
enseless against anything that might emerge from the thick
ests.

t the same time, there were pressing reasons to travel north,
lack of available capital being one. Cape Fear was the largest
lement of Scottish Highlanders in the American Colonies,
sting several towns whose inhabitants had emigrated from
tland during the last twenty years, following the upheaval after
lloden. And among these emigrants were Jamie's kin, who I
w would willingly offer us refuge: a roof, a bed, and time to
blish ourselves in this new world.

amie took another drink and nodded at Duncan.

I must say I'm of your mind, Duncan." He leaned back
inst the wall of the tavern, glancing casually around the
wded room. "D'ye no feel the eyes on your back?"

chill ran down my own back, despite the trickle of sweat
ng likewise. Duncan's eyes widened fractionally, then nar-
ed, but he didn't turn around.

Ah," he said.

Whose eyes?" I asked, looking rather nervously around. I
n't see anyone taking particular notice of us, though anyone
ght be watching surreptitiously; the tavern was seething with
ohol-soaked humanity, and the babble of voices was loud
ugh to drown out all but the closest conversation.

Anyone's, Sassenach," Jamie answered. He glanced sideways
ne, and smiled. "Dinna look so scairt about it, aye? We're in
danger. Not here."

Not yet," Innes said. He leaned forward to pour another cup
le. "*Mac Dubh* called out to Gavin on the gallows, d'ye see?
ere will be those who took notice—*Mac Dubh* bein' the bittie
fellow he is," he added dryly.

And the farmers who came with us from Georgia will have
d their stores by now, and be takin' their ease in places like
," Jamie said, evidently absorbed in studying the pattern of his
. "All of them are honest men—but they'll talk, Sasse-
h. It makes a good story, no? The folk cast away by the hurri-
e? And what are the chances that at least one of them kens a
about what we carry?"

I see," I murmured, and did. We had attracted public interest
our association with a criminal, and could no longer pass as

inconspicuous travelers. If finding a buyer took some time, as ⟶
likely, we risked inviting robbery from unscrupulous persons.
scrutiny from the English authorities. Neither prospect was
pealing.

Jamie lifted his cup and drank deeply, then set it down wit
sigh.

"No. I think it's perhaps not wise to linger in the city. W
see Gavin buried decently, and then we'll find a safe spot in
woods outside the town to sleep. Tomorrow we can dec
whether to stay or go."

The thought of spending several more nights in the wood
with or without skunks—was not appealing. I hadn't taken
dress off in eight days, merely rinsing the outlying portions of
anatomy whenever we paused in the vicinity of a stream.

I had been looking forward to a real bed, even if flea-infes
and a chance to scrub off the grime of the last week's travel. S
he had a point. I sighed, ruefully eyeing the hem of my slee
gray and grubby with wear.

The tavern door flung suddenly open at this point, distract
me from my contemplation, and four red-coated soldiers sho
their way into the crowded room. They wore full uniform, h
muskets with bayonets fixed, and were obviously not in pursui
ale or dice.

Two of the soldiers made a rapid circuit of the room, glanc
under tables, while another disappeared into the kitchen beyo
The fourth remained on watch by the door, pale eyes flicking o
the crowd. His gaze lighted on our table, and rested on us fo
moment, full of speculation, but then passed on, restlessly se
ing.

Jamie was outwardly tranquil, sipping his ale in apparent ob
iousness, but I saw the hand in his lap clench slowly into a ⟶
Duncan, less able to control his feelings, bent his head to hide
expression. Neither man would ever feel at ease in the presenc
a red coat, and for good reason.

No one else appeared much perturbed by the soldiers' preser
The little knot of singers in the chimney corner went on with
interminable version of "Fill Every Glass," and a loud argum
broke out between the barmaid and a pair of apprentices.

The soldier returned from the kitchen, having evidently fou
nothing. Stepping rudely through a dice game on the hearth,
rejoined his fellows by the door. As the soldiers shoved their ⟶

ut of the tavern, Fergus's slight figure squeezed in, pressing against the doorjamb to avoid swinging elbows and musket butts.

I saw one soldier's eyes catch the glint of metal and fasten with interest on the hook Fergus wore in replacement of his missing left hand. He glanced sharply at Fergus, but then shouldered his musket and hurried after his companions.

Fergus shoved through the crowd and plopped down on the bench beside Ian. He looked hot and irritated.

"Blood-sucking *salaud*," he said, without preamble.

Jamie's brows went up.

"The priest," Fergus elaborated. He took the mug Ian pushed in his direction and drained it, lean throat glugging until the cup was empty. He lowered it, exhaled heavily, and sat blinking, looking noticeably happier. He sighed and wiped his mouth.

"He wants ten shillings to bury the man in the churchyard," he said. "An Anglican church, of course; there are no Catholic churches here. Wretched usurer! He knows we have no choice about it. The body will scarcely keep till sunset, as it is." He ran a finger inside his stock, pulling the sweat-wilted cotton away from his neck, then banged his fist several times on the table to attract the attention of the servingmaid, who was being run off her feet by the press of patrons.

"I told the super-fatted son of a pig that you would decide whether to pay or not. We could just bury him in the wood, after all. Though we should have to purchase a shovel," he added, frowning. "These grasping townsfolk know we are strangers; they'll take our last coin if they can."

Last coin was perilously close to the truth. I had enough to pay for a decent meal here and to buy food for the journey north; perhaps enough to pay for a couple of nights' lodging. That was all. I saw Jamie's eyes flick round the room, assessing the possibilities of picking up a little money at hazard or loo.

Soldiers and sailors were the best prospects for gambling, but there were few of either in the taproom—likely most of the garrison was still searching the town for the fugitive. In one corner, a small group of men was being loudly convivial over several pitchers of brandywine; two of them were singing, or trying to, their attempts causing great hilarity among their comrades. Jamie gave an almost imperceptible nod at sight of them, and turned back to Fergus.

"What have ye done with Gavin for the time being?" Jamie asked. Fergus hunched one shoulder.

"Put him in the wagon. I traded the clothes he was wearing to ragwoman for a shroud, and she agreed to wash the body as pa of the bargain." He gave Jamie a faint smile. "Don't worr milord; he's seemly. For now," he added, lifting the fresh mug ale to his lips.

"Poor Gavin." Duncan Innes lifted his own mug in a ha salute to his fallen comrade.

"*Slàinte*," Jamie replied, and lifted his own mug in reply. H set it down and sighed.

"He wouldna like being buried in the wood," he said.

"Why not?" I asked, curious. "I shouldn't think it would ma ter to him one way or the other."

"Oh, no, we couldna do that, Mrs. Claire." Duncan was shal ing his head emphatically. Duncan was normally a most reserve man, and I was surprised at so much apparent feeling.

"He was afraid of the dark," Jamie said softly. I turned to sta at him, and he gave me a lopsided smile. "I lived wi' Gavi Hayes nearly as long as I've lived with you, Sassenach—and i much closer quarters. I kent him well."

"Aye, he was afraid of being alone in the dark," Dunca chimed in. "He was most mortally scairt of *tannagach*—of spirit aye?"

His long, mournful face bore an inward look, and I knew h was seeing in memory the prison cell that he and Jamie ha shared with Gavin Hayes—and with forty other men—for thre long years. "D'ye recall, *Mac Dubh*, how he told us one night the *tannasq* he met?"

"I do, Duncan, and could wish I did not." Jamie shuddere despite the heat. "I kept awake myself half the night after he tol us that one."

"What was it, Uncle?" Ian was leaning over his cup of al round-eyed. His cheeks were flushed and streaming, and his stoc crumpled with sweat.

Jamie rubbed a hand across his mouth, thinking.

"Ah. Well, it was a time in the late, cold autumn in the Higl lands, just when the season turns, and the feel of the air tells y the ground will be shivered wi' frost come dawn," he said. H settled himself in his seat and sat back, alecup in hand. He smile wryly, plucking at his own throat. "Not like now, aye?

"Well, Gavin's son brought back the kine that night, but the was one beast missing—the lad had hunted up the hills and dow

ie corries, but couldna find it anywhere. So Gavin set the lad to
ilk the two others, and set out himself to look for the lost cow."

He rolled the pewter cup slowly between his hands, staring
own into the dark ale as though seeing in it the bulk of the night-
lack Scottish peaks and the mist that floats in the autumn glens.

"He went some distance, and the cot behind him disappeared.
Vhen he looked back, he couldna see the light from the window
nymore, and there was no sound but the keening of the wind. It
as cold, but he went on, tramping through the mud and the
eather, hearing the crackle of ice under his boots.

"He saw a small grove through the mist, and thinking the cow
ight have taken shelter beneath the trees, he went toward it. He
aid the trees were birches, standing there all leafless, but with
eir branches grown together so he must bend his head to
queeze beneath the boughs.

"He came into the grove and saw it was not a grove at all, but a
ircle of trees. There were great tall trees, spaced verra evenly, all
round him, and smaller ones, saplings, grown up between to
ake a wall of branches. And in the center of the circle stood a
airn."

Hot as it was in the tavern, I felt as though a sliver of ice had
lid melting down my spine. I had seen ancient cairns in the
fighlands myself, and found them eerie enough in the broad light
f day.

Jamie took a sip of ale, and wiped away a trickle of sweat that
an down his temple.

"He felt quite queer, did Gavin. For he kent the place—every-
ne did, and kept well away from it. It was a strange place. And it
eemed even worse in the dark and the cold, from what it did in
ie light of day. It was an auld cairn, the kind laid wi' slabs of
ock, all heaped round with stones, and he could see before him
ie black opening of the tomb.

"He knew it was a place no man should come, and he without a
owerful charm. Gavin had naught but a wooden cross about his
eck. So he crossed himself with it and turned to go."

Jamie paused to sip his ale.

"But as Gavin went from the grove," he said softly, "he heard
ootsteps behind him."

I saw the Adam's apple bob in Ian's throat as he swallowed. He
eached mechanically for his own cup, eyes fixed on his uncle.

"He didna turn to see," Jamie went on, "but kept walking.
nd the steps kept pace wi' him, step by step, always following.

And he came through the peat where the water seeps up, and i
was crusted with ice, the weather bein' so cold. He could hear th
peat crackle under his feet, and behind him the crack! crack! o
breaking ice.

"He walked and he walked, through the cold, dark night
watching ahead for the light of his own window, where his wife
had set the candle. But the light never showed, and he began t
fear he had lost his way among the heather and the dark hills. An
all the time, the steps kept pace with him, loud in his ears.

"At last he could bear it no more, and seizing hold of th
crucifix he wore round his neck, he swung about wi' a great cry t
face whatever followed."

"What did he see?" Ian's pupils were dilated, dark with drink
and wonder. Jamie glanced at the boy, and then at Duncan, nod
ding at him to take up the story.

"He said it was a figure like a man, but with no body," Duncan
said quietly. "All white, like as it might have been made of th
mist. But wi' great holes where its eyes should be, and empt
black, fit to draw the soul from his body with dread."

"But Gavin held up his cross before his face, and he praye
aloud to the Blessed Virgin." Jamie took up the story, leaning
forward intently, the dim firelight outlining his profile in gold
"And the thing came no nearer, but stayed there, watching him.

"And so he began to walk backward, not daring to face roun
again. He walked backward, stumbling and slipping, fearing ever
moment as he might tumble into a burn or down a cliff and brea
his neck, but fearing worse to turn his back on the cold thing.

"He couldna tell how long he'd walked, only that his legs wer
trembling wi' weariness, when at last he caught a glimpse of ligh
through the mist, and there was his own cottage, wi' the candle i
the window. He cried out in joy, and turned to his door, but th
cold thing was quick, and slippit past him, to stand betwixt hin
and the door.

"His wife had been watching out for him, and when she hear
him cry out, she came at once to the door. Gavin shouted to he
not to come out, but for God's sake to fetch a charm to drive awa
the *tannasq*. Quick as thought, she snatched the pot from beneat
her bed, and a twig of myrtle bound wi' red thread and black, tha
she'd made to bless the cows. She dashed the water against th
doorposts, and the cold thing leapt upward, astride the lintel
Gavin rushed in beneath and barred the door, and stayed inside i
his wife's arms until the dawn. They let the candle burn all th

ight, and Gavin Hayes never again left his house past sunset—until he went to fight for Prince *Tearlach*."

Even Duncan, who knew the tale, sighed as Jamie finished speaking. Ian crossed himself, then looked about self-consciously, but no one seemed to have noticed.

"So, now Gavin has gone into the dark," Jamie said softly. "But we willna let him lie in unconsecrated ground."

"Did they find the cow?" Fergus asked, with his usual practicality. Jamie quirked one eyebrow at Duncan, who answered.

"Oh, aye, they did. The next morning they found the poor beast, wi' her hooves all clogged wi' mud and stones, staring mad and lathered about the muzzle, and her sides heavin' fit to burst." He glanced from me to Ian and back to Fergus. "Gavin did say," he said precisely, "that she looked as though she'd been ridden to Hell and back."

"Jesus." Ian took a deep gulp of his ale, and I did the same. In the corner, the drinking society was making attempts on a round of "Captain Thunder," breaking down each time in helpless laughter.

Ian put down his cup on the table.

"What happened to them?" he asked, his face troubled. "To Gavin's wife, and his son?"

Jamie's eyes met mine, and his hand touched my thigh. I knew, without being told, what had happened to the Hayes family. Without Jamie's own courage and intransigence, the same thing would likely have happened to me and to our daughter Brianna.

"Gavin never knew," Jamie said quietly. "He never heard aught of his wife—she will have been starved, maybe, or driven out to die of the cold. His son took the field beside him at Culloden. Whenever a man who had fought there came into our cell, Gavin would ask—'Have ye maybe seen a bold lad named Archie Hayes, about so tall?'" He measured automatically, five feet from the floor, capturing Hayes' gesture. "'A lad about fourteen,' he'd say, 'wi' a green plaidie and a small gilt brooch.' But no one ever came who had seen him for sure—either seen him fall or seen him run away safe."

Jamie took a sip of the ale, his eyes fixed on a pair of British officers who had come in and settled in the corner. It had grown dark outside, and they were plainly off duty. Their leather stocks were unfastened on account of the heat, and they wore only sidearms, glinting under their coats; nearly black in the dim light save where the firelight touched them with red.

"Sometimes he hoped the lad might have been captured and transported," he said. "Like his brother."

"Surely that would be somewhere in the records?" I said. "Did they—do they—keep lists?"

"They did," Jamie said, still watching the soldiers. A small, bitter smile touched the corner of his mouth. "It was such a list that saved me, after Culloden, when they asked my name before shooting me, so as to add it to their roll. But a man like Gavin would have no way to see the English dead-lists. And if he could have found out, I think he would not." He glanced at me. "Would you choose to know for sure, and it was your child?"

I shook my head, and he gave me a faint smile and squeezed my hand. Our child was safe, after all. He picked up his cup and drained it, then beckoned to the serving maid.

The girl brought the food, skirting the table widely in order to avoid Rollo. The beast lay motionless under the table, his head protruding into the room and his great hairy tail lying heavily across my feet, but his yellow eyes were wide open, watching everything. They followed the girl intently, and she backed nervously away, keeping an eye on him until she was safely out of biting distance.

Seeing this, Jamie cast a dubious look at the so-called dog.

"Is he hungry? Must I ask for a fish for him?"

"Oh, no, Uncle," Ian reassured him. "Rollo catches his own fish."

Jamie's eyebrows shot up, but he only nodded, and with a wary glance at Rollo, took a platter of roasted oysters from the tray.

"Ah, the pity of it." Duncan Innes was quite drunk by now. He sat slumped against the wall, his armless shoulder riding higher than the other, giving him a strange, hunchbacked appearance. "That a dear man like Gavin should come to such an end!" He shook his head lugubriously, swinging it back and forth over his alecup like the clapper of a funeral bell.

"No family left to mourn him, cast alone into a savage land— hanged as a felon, and to be buried in an unconsecrated grave. Not even a proper lament to be sung for him!" He picked up the cup, and with some difficulty, found his mouth with it. He drank deep and set it down with a muffled clang.

"Well, he *shall* have a *caithris*!" He glared belligerently from Jamie to Fergus to Ian. "Why not?"

Jamie wasn't drunk, but he wasn't completely sober either. He grinned at Duncan and lifted his own cup in salute.

"Why not, indeed?" he said. "Only it will have to be you
gin' it, Duncan. None of the rest knew Gavin, and I'm no
ger. I'll shout along wi' ye, though."

Duncan nodded magisterially, bloodshot eyes surveying us.
thout warning, he flung back his head and emitted a terrible
wl. I jumped in my seat, spilling half a cup of ale into my lap.
and Fergus, who had evidently heard Gaelic laments before,
ln't turn a hair.

All over the room, benches were shoved back, as men leapt to
ir feet in alarm, reaching for their pistols. The barmaid leaned
of the serving hatch, eyes big. Rollo came awake with an
losive *"Woof!"* and glared round wildly, teeth bared.

"Tha sinn cruinn a chaoidh ar caraid, Gabhainn Hayes,"
ncan thundered, in a ragged baritone. I had just about enough
elic to translate this as "We are met to weep and cry out to
ven for the loss of our friend, Gavin Hayes!"

'Èisd ris!' Jamie chimed in.

*'Rugadh e do Sheumas Immanuel Hayes agus Louisa N'ic a
llainn an am baile Chill-Mhartainn, ann an sgire Dhun
mhnuill, anns a bhliadhnaseachd ceud deug agus a haon!'* He
s born of Seaumais Emmanuel Hayes and of Louisa Maclellan,
he village of Kilmartin in the parish of Dodanil, in the year of
Lord seventeen hundred and one!

'Èisd ris!' This time Fergus and Ian joined in on the chorus,
ich I translated roughly as "Hear him!"

Rollo appeared not to care for either verse or refrain; his ears
flat against his skull, and his yellow eyes narrowed to slits. Ian
atched his head in reassurance, and he lay down again, mutter-
wolf curses under his breath.

he audience, having caught on to it that no actual violence
eatened, and no doubt bored with the inferior vocal efforts of
drinking society in the corner, settled down to enjoy the show.
the time Duncan had worked his way into an accounting of the
es of the sheep Gavin Hayes had owned before leaving his
ft to follow his laird to Culloden, many of those at the sur-
nding tables were joining enthusiastically in the chorus, shout-
"Èisd ris!" and banging their mugs on the tables, in perfect
rance of what was being said, and a good thing too.

uncan, drunker than ever, fixed the soldiers at the next table
1 a baleful glare, sweat pouring down his face.

*A Shasunnaich na galladh, 's olc a thig e dhuibh fanaid air
gasgaich. Gun toireadh an diabhul fhein leis anns a bhàs*

. *sibh, direach do Fhirinn!!"* Wicked Sassenach dogs, eaters
dead flesh! Ill does it become you to laugh and rejoice at the dea
of a gallant man! May the devil himself seize upon you in tl
hour of your death and take you straight to hell!

Ian blanched slightly at this, and Jamie cast Duncan a narro
look, but they stoutly shouted *"Èisd ris!"* along with the rest
the crowd.

Fergus, seized by inspiration, got up and passed his hat amol
the crowd, who, carried away by ale and excitement, happily flul
coppers into it for the privilege of joining in their own denunci
tion.

I had as good a head for drink as most men, but a much small
bladder. Head spinning from the noise and fumes as much
from alcohol, I got up and edged my way out from behind t
table, through the mob, and into the fresh air of the early evenir

It was still hot and sultry, though the sun was long since dow
Still, there was a lot more air out here, and a lot fewer peo
sharing it.

Having relieved the internal pressure, I sat down on the taver
chopping block with my pewter mug, breathing deeply. The nig
was clear, with a bright half-moon peeping silver over the ha
bor's edge. Our wagon stood nearby, no more than its outli
visible in the light from the tavern windows. Presumably, Ga
Hayes' decently shrouded body lay within. I trusted he had
joyed his *caithris.*

Inside, Duncan's chanting had come to an end. A clear te
voice, wobbly with drink, but sweet nonetheless, was singin
familiar tune, audible over the babble of talk.

> *"To Anacreon in heav'n, where he sat in full glee,*
> *A few sons of harmony sent a petition,*
> *That he their inspirer and patron would be!*
> *When this answer arrived from the jolly old Grecian:*
> *'Voice, fiddle, and flute,*
> *No longer be mute!*
> *I'll lend you my name and inspire you to boot.'"*

The singer's voice cracked painfully on "voice, fiddle, and flu
but he sang stoutly on, despite the laughter from his audienc
smiled wryly to myself as he hit the final couplet,

> "'And, besides, I'll instruct you like me to entwine,
> The Myrtle of Venus with Bacchus's vine!'"

I lifted my cup in salute to the wheeled coffin, softly echoing
the melody of the singer's last lines.

> "Oh, say, does that star-spangled banner yet wave
> O'er the land of the free and the home of the brave?"

I drained my cup and sat still, waiting for the men to come out.

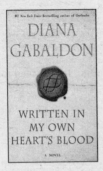

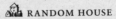

Also by Diana Gabaldon

THE COMPANION VOLUME

THE OUTLANDER GRAPHIC NOVEL

THE LORD JOHN SERIES

LORD JOHN AND THE PRIVATE MATTER
LORD JOHN AND THE BROTHERHOOD OF THE BLADE
LORD JOHN AND THE HAND OF DEVILS
THE SCOTTISH PRISONER

—————

Continue the saga with eNovellas,
three engrossing tales to complement the Outlander series.

A PLAGUE OF ZOMBIES
THE CUSTOM OF THE ARMY
A LEAF ON THE WIND OF ALL HOLLOWS

🏠 RANDOM HOUSE

www.DianaGabaldon.com

f Facebook.com/AuthorDianaGabaldon